·Major American Short Stories·

·Major·
American
·Short Stories·

edited by

·A. Walton Litz·
Princeton University

New York
· *Oxford University Press* ·
London 1975 Toronto

Selections from works by the following authors and publications were made possible by the kind permission of their respective publishers and representatives:

Sherwood Anderson: "I Want To Know Why" from *The Triumph of the Egg*. Copyright 1921 by B. W. Huebsch; renewed 1948 by Eleanor C. Anderson. Reprinted by permission of Harold Ober Associates Inc.

John Barth: "Lost in the Funhouse" from *Lost in the Funhouse*. Copyright © 1967 by The Atlantic Monthly Company. Reprinted by permission of Doubleday & Company, Inc., and the author's agent, Lurton Blassingame.

Donald Barthelme: "The Indian Uprising" from *Unspeakable Practices, Unnatural Acts*. Copyright © 1965, 1968, by Donald Barthelme. Reprinted by permission of Farrar, Straus & Giroux, Inc., and International Famous Agency. The story originally appeared in *The New Yorker*.

Saul Bellow: "Looking for Mr. Green" from *Mosby's Memoirs and Other Stories*. Copyright 1951 by Saul Bellow. Reprinted by permission of The Viking Press, Inc., and Weidenfeld & Nicolson.

John Cheever: "The World of Apples" from *The World of Apples*. Copyright © 1966, 1973, by John Cheever. Reprinted by permission of Alfred A. Knopf, Inc., and Candida Donadio & Associates, Inc.

Robert Coover: "The Magic Poker" from *Pricksongs & Descants*. Copyright © 1969 by Robert Coover. Reprinted by permission of E. P. Dutton & Co., Inc., and Jonathan Cape Ltd.

William Faulkner: "That Evening Sun" from *Collected Stories of William Faulkner*. Copyright 1931; renewed 1959 by William Faulkner. "Red Leaves" from *Selected Short Stories of William Faulkner*. Copyright 1930; renewed 1958 by The Curtis Publishing Co. Both reprinted by permission of Random House, Inc., and Curtis Brown Ltd.

F. Scott Fitzgerald: "Babylon Revisited." Copyright 1931 by The Curtis Publishing Company. Reprinted from *Taps at Reveille* by permission of Charles Scribner's Sons, and from *The Bodley Head Scott Fitzgerald, Volume 6*, by permission of The Bodley Head.

Ernest Hemingway: "Big Two-Hearted River." Copyright 1925 by Charles Scribner's Sons. Reprinted from *In Our Time* by permission of Charles Scribner's Sons, and from *The First Forty-Nine Stories* by permission of Jonathan Cape Ltd.

Bernard Malamud: "The Magic Barrel" from *The Magic Barrel*. Copyright © 1954, 1958, by Bernard Malamud. Reprinted by permission of Farrar, Straus & Giroux, Inc., and Eyre and Spottiswoode.

Flannery O'Connor: "A Good Man Is Hard To Find" from *A Good Man Is Hard To Find and Other Stories*. Copyright 1953 by Flannery O'Connor. Reprinted by permission of Harcourt Brace Jovanovich, Inc., and A. M. Heath & Company Ltd.

Joyce Carol Oates: "Upon the Sweeping Flood" from *Upon the Sweeping Flood and Other Stories*. Copyright 1963, 1966, by Joyce Carol Oates. Reprinted by permission of The Vanguard Press, Inc., and Victor Gollancz Ltd.

Peter Taylor: "Venus, Cupid, Folly and Time" from *Happy Families Are All Alike*. Reprinted by permission of Astor-Honor, Inc.

John Updike: "A & P" from *Pigeon Feathers and Other Stories*. Copyright © 1962 by John Updike. Reprinted by permission of Alfred A. Knopf, Inc., and Andre Deutsch Limited Publishers.

Robert Penn Warren: "Blackberry Winter" from *The Circus in the Attic and Other Stories*. Copyright 1947 by Robert Penn Warren. Reprinted by permission of Harcourt Brace Jovanovich, Inc.

Eudora Welty: "Petrified Man" from *A Curtain of Green and Other Stories*. Copyright 1941, 1969, by Eudora Welty. Reprinted by permission of Harcourt Brace Jovanovich, Inc., and A. M. Heath & Company Ltd.

Edith Wharton: "Roman Fever" from *The Collected Short Stories of Edith Wharton*. Copyright 1934 by Liberty Magazine; renewed 1962 by William R. Tyler. Reprinted by permission of Charles Scribner's Sons, and A. Watkins, Inc.

Richard Wright: "The Man Who Was Almost A Man" from *Eight Men*. Copyright © 1961, 1940, by Richard Wright. Reprinted by permission of The World Publishing Company, and Paul R. Reynolds, Inc.

·*Preface*·

Frank O'Connor, an Irishman with an acute sense of national values, once called the American short story "a national art form." This does not mean that the greatest short stories have been written by Americans, although our literature can claim more than its fair share, but that the history of the American short story is a faithful record of our literary and cultural development. No important American writer of fiction has neglected the short form, and in the case of many writers—from Hawthorne and Poe to Hemingway and Faulkner—the short story represented their greatest achievement.

This anthology indicates the range and variety of American short fiction. I have included as many subjects and forms as possible, while at the same time emphasizing the work of our major writers. The term "short story" has been taken in its broadest sense, and the needs of diverse courses in American literature and American fiction have been kept in mind. The stories range in time from 1819 to 1973, and in length from the brief sketch to the fully developed *nouvelle*. I have tried especially to do justice to our greatest writers of short fiction, and I regret that publishers' restrictions limited the selections from Fitzgerald and Hemingway to one story each. A similar policy prevented the publication of Faulkner's "The Bear." If these restrictions had not existed I would have given Fitzgerald and Hemingway and Faulkner the same space as was allotted to Hawthorne and Poe and James.

The explanatory notes for the stories, as well as the biographical and bibliographical notes for each author, are designed to provide the facts needed for critical interpretation. In the Introductions I have taken a more speculative approach to individual works, and to the development of the genre.

I should like to express my gratitude to John Wright of Oxford University Press, whose advice made this a better book, and to John Savarese of Princeton University, whose knowledge of the American short story facilitated the gathering of background material.

A. W. L.

Princeton
October 1974

·Contents·

·Contents·

·THE SEARCH FOR FORM·
Irving, Hawthorne, Poe, Melville, and James

Writers have always delighted in the making and recording of short fictions. Some of the earliest literary documents are Egyptian papyri dating from 4000—3000 B.C., which contain "Tales of the Magicians"; and the great stories of the Old Testament are only the most familiar of many short narratives that have survived from the ancient cultures of India, Greece, and the Near East. In the Middle Ages the short fiction retained its popularity as fabliau, exemplum, or romantic tale. The stories of the Arabian *Thousand Nights and a Night* were collected before the end of the thirteenth century, as were the Latin tales and anecdotes of the *Gesta Romanorum;* and in the middle of the fourteenth century Boccaccio brought together the one hundred stories of *The Decameron.* The penchant for story-telling revealed in *The Decameron* and Chaucer's *Canterbury Tales* continued unabated through the Renaissance and into the eighteenth century, with short fictions taking on an even greater variety of forms. Throughout this long and complex history, however, one factor remained constant: the vital relation between the written story and the oral tradition. This is a crucial fact to keep in mind when considering the development of the modern short story, since even the most sophisticated short fictions cannot succeed unless they conform in some way to the traditional rhythms of the story-teller's art.

The short fiction, therefore, is among the most ancient and enduring of literary forms, but the "short story" as a self-conscious genre did not appear until the beginning of the nineteenth century, and like the "novel" of the previous century it was the product of a special confluence of literary and cultural forces. These forces came together with particular urgency in early nineteenth-century America, so that the modern short story has some claim to be called an "American" art form; the genre may have reached its finest expression in such European writers as Flaubert and Chekhov and Joyce, but it can best be understood through an examination of its American "inventors," Irving, Hawthorne, and Poe. They were led to the short story in part by what Henry James would have called the "thinness" of American life, its lack of a rich and complex social texture: the brief poetic tale, rather than the sprawling novel of manners, seemed the natural form for their intense but isolated experiences. At the same time they were acutely responsive to the developments of English and European Romanticism. This collision of local and fragmented social experience with a cosmopolitan artistic vision proved ideal for the growth of the short story.

The present-day student looking for a definition of the short story will find that the standard textbook definitions have little relevance to his own reading experience. Certainly the following definition, culled from a recent handbook of literary terms, describes a rigid ideal seldom attained by the stories in this anthology.

A relatively short narrative (under 10,000 words) which is designed to produce a single dominant effect and which contains the elements of drama. A short story concentrates on a single character in a single situation at a single moment. Even if these conditions are not met, a short story still exhibits unity as its guiding principle. An effective short story consists of a character (or group of characters) presented against a background, or setting, involved, through mental or physical action, in a situation. Dramatic conflict—the collision of opposing forces—is at the heart of the story.

This textbook formula is the final residue of many earnest attempts to define the short story which flourished around the turn of the century. Beginning with Brander Matthews's "The Philosophy of the Short-Story" (1885), these critical and scholarly studies attempted to codify the structure of the popular genre, mainly through a refinement and dogmatic restatement of Poe's theoretical pronouncements. At their best these studies provided useful descriptions of one kind of short fiction, the well-made "Short-story" (Matthews preferred the hyphenated term); at their worst they degenerated into "How To" handbooks, where elaborate and often irrelevant descriptive categories are turned into formulas for the writing of "model" short stories. In J. Berg Esenwein's *Writing the Short-Story: A Practical Handbook on the Rise, Structure, Writing, and Sale of the Modern Short Story* (1909), an involved discussion of "What a Short-Story Is Not" leads to a classification of fourteen "Kinds of Tales," and this to a dogmatic seven-point definition of

"What a Short-Story Is." Esenwein's handbook is a travesty of an outdated critical method, but all purely theoretical discussions tend in that direction. The best way to gain a sense of the American short story, its essential qualities and its complex potentialities, is to explore its origins and subsequent development.

WASHINGTON IRVING

The earliest representatives of the short story genre emerged from a curious amalgamation of sources and influences: the eighteenth-century essay, the traditional ballad and tale, the new emphasis in painting and drawing on the concentrated "sketch," the Romantic insistence on unity of effect and atmosphere. And Washington Irving, by temperament and circumstance, was the ideal conductor for all these diverse energies. His position as a "colonial" writer made him especially conscious of recent trends in English literature; like his contemporary Walter Scott, Irving admired the eighteenth-century periodical essay, with its qualities of brevity and the fictitious narrator, and like Scott he was profoundly influenced by the new interest in the ballad and narrative folk-poetry (one of the most fruitful tensions in the development of the short story comes from the competition between the lyric impulse, with its stress on unity of emotion, and the ballad impulse, with its emphasis on a controlled unity of action). He was also closely familiar with the Gothic tale, which gave predominance to an emotional atmosphere and the poetic use of setting. All these elements are to be found, only partly assimilated, in Irving's *Tales of a Traveller* (1824), where "The Adventure of the German Student" looks forward to Hawthorne and Poe in its consistency of atmosphere and setting (although the emotional power of the story is vitiated at the end by Irving's strategic retreat to his favorite narrative viewpoint, that of the detached observer).

The key to Irving's success as a writer of short fictions is implicit in the title and epigraph of his first collection (1819–20):

The Sketch-Book of Geoffrey Crayon, Gent.

"I have no wife nor children, good or bad, to provide for. A mere spectator of other men's fortunes and adventures, and how they play their parts; which, methinks, are diversely presented unto me, as from a common theatre or scene."—Burton

This quotation from the seventeenth-century English author Robert Burton, with its implication that the artist must be a "mere spectator," suggests that the form of the typical Irving story does not depend upon a tightly-organized plot, but rather upon a detached point-of-view which, like the prospect from a mountain-top, endows

the whole scene with a quiet emotional unity. Irving acknowledged
as much in his well-known letter to Henry Brevoort, where he declared himself less interested in "the story" than in "the way in
which it is told."

> For my part I consider a story merely as a frame on which to stretch my
> materials. It is the play of thought, and sentiment and language; the
> weaving in of characters, lightly yet expressively delineated; the famil-
> iar and faithful exhibition of scenes in common life; and the half con-
> cealed vein of humour that is often playing through the whole—these
> are among what I aim at, and upon which I felicitate myself in propor-
> tion as I think I succeed. I have preferred adopting a mode of sketches
> & short tales rather than long works, because I chose to take a line of
> writing peculiar to myself; rather than fall into the manner or school of
> any other writer: and there is a constant activity of thought and a nicety
> of execution required in writings of the kind, more than the world ap-
> pears to imagine. It is comparatively easy to swell a story to any size
> when you have once the scheme & the characters in your mind; the
> mere interest of the story too carries the reader on through pages &
> pages of careless writing and the author may often be dull for half a
> volume at a time, if he has some striking scene at the end of it, but in
> these shorter writings every page must have its merit.

The language here is that of the late eighteenth-century artist
("Geoffrey Crayon"), with an eye for picturesque effects and unity
of composition. The painter's sketch, once a preliminary and semi-
private record of the artist's dominant impressions, had become by
Irving's lifetime a new art-form, and the term "picturesque" had
taken on psychological overtones in addition to its standard meaning (composed or designed as "in a picture"). As William L. Hedges
has demonstrated in his fine study of Irving's art, the "sketch" as an
art-form is "fundamentally the expression of a Crayon-like narrator," an ambivalent "spectator," who wishes to present a compact
and distanced subject, as in a sketch-book of the picturesque, but
also desires to infuse that subject with his own feelings and associations. "The convenience for Irving of the sketch, its intimate connection with his personality," depends in Hedges's view on the nature of the picturesque, "which is based less on belief in the
objective reality of an observed scene than on the associations read
into it by a spectator. Although it is visual, exploiting what can be
seen and taking as its point of departure a physical setting, the
sketch makes no attempt to distinguish sharply between nature or
the landscape as a thing in itself and nature as experience molded
by the observer's imagination. . . . But for all its dependence on
the narrator's presence in the scene, sketching tends to keep him at
a distance from his subject."

So Irving's great contribution to the short form was his notion of the "sketch," which combines in economic fashion unity of scene and unity of feeling. In "Rural Life in England" the intensely interested spectator finds "a picture" in every farmhouse and cottage, but then declares that the great charm of English landscape "is the moral feeling that seems to pervade it. It is associated in the mind with ideas of order, of quiet, of sober well-established principles, of hoary usage and reverend custom. Every thing seems to be the growth of ages of regular and peaceful existence." These sentiments, so typical of Irving, define the strengths and weaknesses of his stories. So long as he can deal with the rich tradition of England or Europe, or with the accumulated associations of the American past, Irving can produce his spendid sketches; but he lacks the ability to deal economically with the contemporary American scene. His art depends too much upon the external richness and associations of his subjects, and lacks the techniques necessary for controlled psychological exploration.

A number of recent studies have probed with some success the mythic and psychological dimensions of "Rip Van Winkle": his sleep has been interpreted as a return to the womb (Rip sleeps through the American Revolution), and his awakening has been analyzed as a rebirth fantasy. With a little help from Irving's German sources, critics have discerned both an Oedipal situation and a castration complex in the tale (Rip's rusty fowling piece). Many of these readings are less bizarre in fact than they appear to be in summary, and one can reasonably claim that "Rip Van Winkle" dramatizes certain permanent and regressive features of the American imagination. But these deeper meanings are never directly confronted by Irving; they are obscured by an overlay of fantasy and whimsy, and it seems unlikely that Irving was fully aware of his darker meanings. In "The Adventure of the German Student," for example, Irving presents a complex psychological drama but vitiates it with a "trick" ending. For a deeper *conscious* sense of the short story's possibilities, its ability to express what Hawthorne called the "moral picturesque," we must turn to Irving's successors.

NATHANIEL HAWTHORNE

In "The Old Apple Dealer," one of Hawthorne's slighter sketches in *Mosses from an Old Manse* (1846), the author refers to himself as a "lover of the moral picturesque" who must somehow strike beyond "word painting" to seize the essential, negative quality of his subject, a "faded and featureless" old man "who carries on a little trade of gingerbread and apples at the depot of one of our railroads." Hawthorne declares that he has "studied the old apple dealer until he has become a naturalized citizen of my inner

Nathaniel Hawthorne   (The Bettmann Archive)

world," and then, over several pages of apparently aimless description, Hawthorne gradually converts the old man into a symbol of "moral frost" and the "torpid melancholy" of old age. At the end of the sketch the old man stands in "picturesque" relation to the bustling world of the railway travelers: the final scene is a symbolic tableau, in which frenzied progress and the melancholy stasis of the past are "each other's antipodes."

> The travellers swarm forth from the cars. All are full of the momentum which they have caught from their mode of conveyance. It seems as if the whole world, both morally and physically, were detached from its old standfasts and set in rapid motion. And, in the midst of this terrible activity, there sits the old man of gingerbread. . . . See! he folds his lean arms around his lean figure with that quiet sigh and that scarcely

perceptible shiver which are the tokens of his inward state. I have him now.

"I have him now." Through a skillful process of description and suggestion, Hawthorne has possessed the "spiritual essence" of his solitary figure, so that the inner meaning of the sketch can be suddenly revealed, as in one of James Joyce's "epiphanies." In fact, the passage from Joyce's early *Stephen Hero* in which his fictional self, Stephen Dedalus, describes the artistic epiphany might be applied to many of Hawthorne's stories.

> By an epiphany he meant a sudden spiritual manifestation, whether in the vulgarity of speech or of gesture or in a memorable phase of the mind itself. He believed it was for the man of letters to record these epiphanies with extreme care, seeing that they themselves are the most delicate and evanescent of moments.

It is this command of the revelatory moment which separates the dark inner world of Hawthorne's stories from the more external world of Irving's tales and sketches.

Although most of Hawthorne's stories have the surface form of allegory or parable, suggesting a schematic interplay of ideas or moral concepts, this mechanical quality (which so troubled Henry James) is softened and complicated by his attention to the ambiguities of human psychology. Thus the character names and the plot of "Young Goodman Brown" belong to a world of simplified allegory ("Goodman," "Faith," the journey from home to forest); but the changes wrought within the mind of Goodman Brown are subtle and problematic, leading the reader to a divided view of the Puritan inheritance. When at the end of the story Goodman Brown looks "sternly and sadly" into the face of his wife, Faith, and then passes on "without a greeting," we have moved far beyond the schematic judgments of parable or allegory into the realm of the complex symbol. It is this psychological complexity that gives Hawthorne's best stories their lasting power, and enables us to see them as prophecies of the future as well as commentaries on the American past. In "My Kinsman, Major Molineux," for example, the surface historical allegory (New World against Old) is paralleled by a more ambiguous narrative of initiation into adult experience which has led some critics to describe the tale as a forerunner of Sherwood Anderson's "I Want to Know Why" or Hemingway's Nick Adams stories.

In his famous review-article "Hawthorne and His Mosses" (discussed later in this introduction), Herman Melville isolated the "power of blackness" as the key to Hawthorne's imagination, contending that it "derives its force from its appeals to that Calvinistic sense of Innate Depravity and Original Sin, from whose visitations, in some shape or other, no deeply thinking mind is always and wholly free." As Melville was the first to point out, it is Hawthorne's great themes of moral guilt and the anxious weight of the past that give him a central place in the American literary tradition. The exposure of superficial optimism and rationality in Melville's own "Benito Cereno," the explorations of guilt and anxiety in Henry James's ghostly tales, the parable of a "fall from grace" in Southern history underlying William Faulkner's most profound works—all these belong to an American moral drama of which Hawthorne was the first master. From the Unpardonable Sin of pride and self-centeredness that blights so many of Hawthorne's characters to the pride that destroys Sutpen's grand design in Faulkner's *Absalom, Absalom!* there runs the strong countercurrent of the Puritan sensibility, which has defined and criticized the more complacent assumptions of our culture and our literature. In his tortured and problematic treatments of the theme of guilt and expiation, Hawthorne set a compelling pattern for many of his successors. And it was in response to this dark strain in his fiction that Poe, Melville, and James produced some of their most revealing comments on the short tale and its artistic possibilities.

EDGAR ALLAN POE

Edgar Allan Poe's review of Hawthorne's *Twice-Told Tales* (1842) is the central document in the history of the short story as a special genre, and it deserves quotation at some length. Poe begins by dividing *Twice-Told Tales* into "essays" (sketches) and imaginative tales. He notes the affinities between Hawthorne's sketches and those of Irving: Hawthorne's brief sketches, like Irving's, combine the effects of the eighteenth-century periodical essay with the painterly quality of effortless containment, what Poe calls "repose." But they exceed the works of Irving in their imaginative power. In Irving the "repose is attained rather by the absence of novel combination, or of originality, than otherwise, and consists chiefly in the calm, quiet, unostentatious expression of commonplace thoughts . . . by strong effort, we are made to conceive the absence of all." In Hawthorne's sketches, on the other hand, "the absence of effort is too obvious to be mistaken, and a strong undercurrent of *suggestion* runs continuously beneath the upper stream of the tranquil thesis." This power of "suggestion" stems from a "truly imaginative intellect" that is restrained or repressed in the sketches but given free and original play in the longer stories. And it is these stories that give Poe the occasion to develop his aesthetic of the "tale."

> The tale proper, in our opinion, affords unquestionably the fairest field for the exercise of the loftiest talent, which can be afforded by the wide domains of mere prose. Were we bidden to say how the highest genius

Edgar Allan Poe   (The Granger Collection)

could be most advantageously employed for the best display of its own
powers, we should answer, without hesitation—in the composition of a
rhymed poem, not to exceed in length what might be perused in an
hour. Within this limit alone can the highest order of true poetry exist.
We need only here say, upon this topic, that, in almost all classes of
composition, the unity of effect or impression is a point of the greatest
importance. It is clear, moreover, that this unity cannot be thoroughly
preserved in productions whose perusal cannot be completed at one
sitting. We may continue the reading of a prose composition, from the
very nature of prose itself, much longer than we can persevere, to any
good purpose,in the perusal of a poem. This latter, if truly fulfilling the

demands of the poetic sentiment, induces an exaltation of the soul which cannot be long sustained. All high excitements are necessarily transient. Thus a long poem is a paradox. And, without unity of impression, the deepest effects cannot be brought about. Epics were the offspring of an imperfect sense of Art, and their reign is no more. A poem *too* brief may produce a vivid, but never an intense or enduring impression. Without a certain continuity of effort—without a certain duration or repetition of purpose—the soul is never deeply moved. . . .

Were we called upon, however, to designate that class of composition which, next to such a poem as we have suggested, should best fulfil the demands of high genius—should offer it the most advantageous field of exertion—we should unhesitatingly speak of the prose tale, as Mr. Hawthorne has here exemplified it. We allude to the short prose narrative, requiring from a half-hour to one or two hours in its perusal. The ordinary novel is objectionable, from its length, for reasons already stated in substance. As it cannot be read at one sitting, it deprives itself, of course, of the immense force derivable from *totality*. Worldly interests intervening during the pauses of perusal, modify, annul, or counteract, in a greater or less degree, the impressions of the book. But simple cessation in reading would, of itself, be sufficient to destroy the true unity. In the brief tale, however, the author is enabled to carry out the fulness of his intention, be it what it may. During the hour of perusal the soul of the reader is at the writer's control. There are no external or extrinsic influences—resulting from weariness or interruption.

A skilful literary artist has constructed a tale. If wise, he has not fashioned his thoughts to accommodate his incidents; but having conceived, with deliberate care, a certain unique or single *effect* to be wrought out, he then invents such incidents—he then combines such events as may best aid him in establishing this preconceived effect. If his very initial sentence tend not to the outbringing of this effect, then he has failed in his first step. In the whole composition there should be no word written, of which the tendency, direct or indirect, is not to the one pre-established design. And by such means, with such care and skill, a picture is at length painted which leaves in the mind of him who contemplates it with a kindred art, a sense of the fullest satisfaction. The idea of the tale has been presented unblemished, because undisturbed: and this is an end unattainable by the novel. Undue brevity is just as exceptionable here as in the poem; but undue length is yet more to be avoided.

We have said that the tale has a point of superiority even over the poem. In fact, while the *rhythm* of this latter is an essential aid in the development of the poem's highest idea—the idea of the Beautiful—the artificialities of this rhythm are an inseparable bar to the development of all points of thought or expression which have their basis in *Truth*. But Truth is often, and in very great degree, the aim of the tale. Some of the finest tales are tales of ratiocination. Thus the field of this species of composition, if not in so elevated a region on the mountain of Mind, is a table-land of far vaster extent than the domain of the mere poem. Its products are never so rich, but infinitely more numerous, and more appreciable by the mass of mankind. The writer of the prose tale, in short, may bring to his theme a vast variety of modes or inflections of thought and expression—(the ratiocinative, for example, the sarcastic, or the humorous) which are not only antagonistical to the nature of the poem, but absolutely forbidden by one of its peculiar and indispensable adjuncts; we allude, of course, to rhythm.

Here an extreme Romantic aesthetic is adapted to the composition of short fictions. We may suspect that Poe in this review, as in his notorious "Philosophy of Composition," is rationalizing his own achievements, using the systematic methods of his fictional detective M. Dupin to uncover the logical premises beneath his instinctive performances; but he is also making a theoretical pronouncement of major importance, which was to have a lasting impact on the development of the genre. In brief, he has accepted the Romantic emphasis on unity of effect or "impression" and fashioned a psychological defense for the short story. Poe's "tale" differs from the sketch or tale of earlier writers in many ways, and these differences are defined through its effect upon the reader. Psychological unity has superseded the traditional unity of action; a concept of organic totality links the reader's response with the structure of the story. In his stress upon the appropriate length for the tale, Poe is reaffirming the storyteller's primary concern with the attention span of his audience, but doing so in the context of a sophisticated Romantic aesthetic that cherishes the "lyric moment." The ideal short story that Poe never achieved, the economical story of Flaubert or Joyce in which every detail of setting and dialogue contributes to a single unifying design, is anticipated and justified in this marvelously suggestive review.

In our fascination with the more theoretical elements in Poe's defense of the "tale" we often overlook his major point—that the short story provides the greatest range of possibilities to the modern artist, enabling him to use "a vast variety of modes or inflections of thought and expression." Writing at a time when traditional distinctions between styles and genres were crumbling, Poe believed that the short story could stand at the juncture of prose and poetry, uniting the best qualities of each and reconciling Truth (Reason) with Beauty (Rhythm). Comic, grotesque, tragic, and logical effects can exist together in the same story, so long as they are united by some total effect on the reader.

It is conventional to divide Poe's career as a writer of short stories into three periods: the early grotesques of the 1830s; the "arabesque" tales of 1838–44 (such as "Ligeia" and "The Fall of the

House of Usher"); and the detective or "ratiocinative" fictions of the 1840s (such as "The Purloined Letter"). But these sharp divisions make little sense in a world where M. Dupin, like William Wilson, has *his* double (the Minister), and where the rational explanation of a "simple" problem can take on arabesque qualities. The detective fictions, like the earlier *Tales of the Grotesque and Arabesque*, combine intricacy with simplicity, and this combination is the essence of Poe's art.

In the Preface to his 1840 *Tales* Poe wrote that the "epithets 'Grotesque' and 'Arabesque' will be found to indicate with sufficient precision the prevalent tenor" of the stories in the volume; they also suggest the "prevalent tenor" of his entire fictional achievement. Poe must have savored the term "grotesque" because of its popular associations with "grottos" and the underworld, which hint that the macabre fantasies of his stories have their origins in the truth of the dreaming mind. "Arabesque," which literally means "Arabian," recalls the splendid world of the *Thousand Nights and a Night* and the ancient authority of the storyteller. Its more immediate suggestion, however, is of arabesque ornament, where the viewer is lost in the intricacies of the design unless he, like Dupin, can see the fundamental simplicity. We may take the epithet "arabesque" as a powerful metaphor for Edgar Allan Poe's contribution to the development of the short story: his demonstration, in theory and in practice, that within the narrow scope of the traditional tale an amazing number of diverse elements can be fused into a psychological and structural unity through poetic suggestion.

HERMAN MELVILLE

Melville's response to Hawthorne was as profound as that of Poe, but on a very different level. Where Poe had been fascinated by technique, Melville was grasped by Hawthorne's tragic vision. He read Hawthorne's *Mosses from an Old Manse* in the summer of 1850, while at work on *Moby-Dick*, and found in Hawthorne's allegorical treatments of guilt and anxiety the perfect correlative for the deepening "blackness" of his own artistic world. To Melville, Hawthorne was a symbol for the potentialities of American fiction, and wherever he looked in *Mosses from an Old Manse*—whether at a brief sketch like "The Old Apple Dealer" or a tale like "Young Goodman Brown"—he found a tragic tone that shamed the superficial optimism of American life and art.

> For spite of all the Indian-summer sunlight on the hither side of Hawthorne's soul, the other side—like the dark half of the physical sphere—is shrouded in a blackness, ten times black. But this darkness

Herman Melville   (The Granger Collection)

but gives more effect to the ever-moving dawn, that for ever advances
through it, and circumnavigates his world. Whether Hawthorne has
simply availed himself of this mystical blackness as a means to the
wondrous effects he makes it to produce in his lights and shades; or
whether there really lurks in him, perhaps unknown to himself, a touch
of Puritanic gloom,—this, I cannot altogether tell. Certain it is, however, that this great power of blackness in him derives its force from its
appeals to that Calvinistic sense of Innate Depravity and Original Sin,
from whose visitations, in some shape or other, no deeply thinking
mind is always and wholly free. For, in certain moods, no man can

weigh this world without throwing in something, somehow like Original Sin, to strike the uneven balance. At all events, perhaps no writer has ever wielded this terrific thought with greater terror than this same harmless Hawthorne. Still more: this black conceit pervades him through and through. You may be witched by his sunlight,— transported by the bright gildings in the skies he builds over you; but there is the blackness of darkness beyond; and even his bright gildings but fringe and play upon the edges of thunderclouds. . . .

Now, it is that blackness in Hawthorne, of which I have spoken, that so fixes and fascinates me. It may be, nevertheless, that it is too largely developed in him. Perhaps he does not give us a ray of his light for every shade of his dark. But however this may be, this blackness it is that furnishes the infinite obscure of his back-ground,—that background against which Shakespeare plays his grandest conceits, the things that have made for Shakespeare his loftiest but most circumscribed renown, as the profoundest of thinkers.

("Hawthorne and His Mosses," August 1850)

The "power of blackness" which attracted Melville to Hawthorne runs through all of Melville's major works; and in "Benito Cereno" and "Bartleby the Scrivener" we find the same themes that dominate *Moby-Dick* and *Pierre*. We find also the same ambiguity of treatment, and it is this quality that separates Melville from Hawthorne. Although Hawthorne's moral vision is often complex or ambivalent, we feel at all times a sense of control: the allegorical tradition gave Hawthorne a frame of reference, one explicitly humanistic and Christian. In Melville's fictional world, however, we often feel that nothing lies beyond the ambiguous problems of perception and moral choice, that we are adrift in an unstable universe where even the sense of evil may be an illusion. It is this quality that makes Melville's stories so "modern," and has given them such a vogue in the age of Kafka and Existentialism.

Readers may differ in their interpretation of Hawthorne's "Young Goodman Brown," for example, but most would agree on a moral frame of reference within which any interpretation must be validated. With "Bartleby the Scrivener," however, the process of interpretation is much more creative, reflecting the open-ended structure of the work itself. "Bartleby" has been variously interpreted as a parable of Melville's own artistic career, a drama of the impact of capitalist society on the individual, a symbolic tale of anonymous urban life, a psychological study of schizophrenia, or simply a presentation of the essential "absurdity" of the modern world. All these readings are related at some general level of interpretation, but their variety suggests that Melville is more interested in *how* we see than in *what* we see. Similarly, the complicated symbolism of black-and-white in "Benito Cereno," although derived from the traditional light-and-dark of moral allegory, is deeply ambiguous:

the reader is so limited by Captain Delano's partial mind and the extracts from the legal deposition that he can never be entirely sure whether Melville is inverting or affirming traditional values. This indeterminate quality is intensified in "Bartleby," where the story is as much the lawyer's as Bartleby's, and the limited narrator becomes a psychological double for the reader. It is this epistemological emphasis on the difficulties of knowing and perceiving that gives Melville's long tales their special fascination.

In "Hawthorne and His Mosses" Melville uses the language of landscape painting to describe Hawthorne's metaphysical world, thereby paying tribute to Hawthorne's sense of composition, his mastery of the "moral picturesque." Melville himself had a strong sense for the unified composition—the story framed like a picturesque sketch—and in 1854 he published a series of ten sketches called *The Encantadas, or Enchanted Isles*. Based on his early visit to the Galapagos islands, these sketches often recall the art of Irving in their scrupulous yet suggestive rendering of an "enchanted" landscape. Yet even in the most restrained of these sketches Melville's thirst for symbolism, for "black conceits," is apparent, and his desire for a larger canvas is revealed in the over-all pattern uniting the sketches.

Ultimately Melville could not be satisfied within the time span prescribed by Poe, and in "Bartleby" and "Benito Cereno" the architectural designs of the novelist are clearly evident. Both stories, however, remain within the broad limits of the shorter form, exhibiting a unity of scene and symbol—a powerful psychological totality—that would be broken by the more diverse rhythms of the novel. The general outline of Poe's theory will still hold in an examination of Melville's short fictions. In the case of Henry James, however, new definitions and discriminations are required.

HENRY JAMES

James's immense debt to Hawthorne is acknowledged explicitly in his critical biography of 1879, and implicitly throughout his hallucinatory tales. It was Hawthorne's poetic command of the inner world which fascinated James; yet—unlike Melville—James had too strong a sense of social realism to accept the extreme reaches of Hawthorne's poetic vision, where symbolism shades into allegory. After praising the scaffold scene in *The Scarlet Letter* as "imaginative, impressive, poetic," James deplores the more overt symbolism of the letter "A" beheld in the sky. The insistent allegory of the letter "A" weakens the novel: the "suggestion should have been just made and dropped; to insist upon it and return to it is to exaggerate the weak side of the subject."

Henry James   (The Bettmann Archive)

Time and again in his *Hawthorne* James invokes the "picturesque" as a term to define the sensible limits of Hawthorne's art.
"Hawthorne is perpetually looking for images which shall place
themselves in picturesque correspondence with the spiritual facts
with which he is concerned, and of course the search is of the very
essence of poetry. But in such a process discretion is everything,
and when the image becomes importunate it is in danger of seeming to stand for nothing more serious than itself." This comment
shows James shying away from the full implications of the "moral
picturesque," as Hawthorne would have used the term, toward a

more sociable world in which the standards of realistic behavior must control the poetic impulse. The same tendency is evident in James's curious remarks on Hawthorne's "blackness":

> When he was lightest at heart, he was most creative, and when he was most creative, the moral picturesqueness of the old secret of mankind in general and of the Puritans in particular most appealed to him—the secret that we are really not by any means so good as a well-regulated society requires us to appear.

This comment would seem to reduce Hawthorne's sense of primal guilt to a problem of social behavior, as would James's equally curious observation that "Young Goodman Brown" is "not a parable, but a picture," which "evidently means nothing as regards Hawthorne's own state of mind, his conviction of human depravity and his consequent melancholy; for the simple reason that if it meant anything, it would mean too much."

The explanation for James's attitude is actually quite simple, however, and it tells us a great deal about the forms his short fictions were to take. James is intent upon reducing "Young Goodman Brown" to a picture, not a parable, because he wishes to preserve decorum in fiction: disturbing psychological states can be dramatized in ghostly tales, where there is a traditional license, but in stories of contemporary or historical life the standards of dramatic realism should be observed. "Young Goodman Brown" must be seen as a picturesque sketch because James, in 1879, is unwilling to accept the parable as a fictional art-form; it is only later, in stories such as "The Jolly Corner," that he can combine the demands of parable and realistic drama by using the theories of a new psychology (note the use of *alter ego*, which is employed not in its traditional sense but as a psychoanalytical term).

James's sense of decorum, his search for the "right" form to match each subject, is reflected in three titles of 1878–81: *The Europeans, A Sketch; Daisy Miller, A Study;* and *The Portrait of a Lady.* The terms "sketch," "study," "portrait" might suggest a progression from the short tale to the full-length novel, but in fact *The Europeans* is a work of over two hundred pages, much longer than "Daisy Miller." The differences between the works involve, rather, distinctions in characterization and point of view. The personages in *The Europeans* are comic and "flat," the objects of social irony; Daisy Miller's character is more rounded, but it lacks subtlety, and James's rendering is essentially a "study" of a type; in Isabel Archer, however, James evolves a dynamic heroine whose progress toward self-recognition requires the full apparatus of fictional "portraiture." These distinctions and discriminations suggest that James's "short" fiction really falls into two broad categories: the

nouvelle or novelette, in which the elements of the conventional
novel are simply foreshortened; and the more concentrated story,
where James is observing within broad limits Poe's theory of the
poetic tale, and the aim is an intense psychological unity. The division between the two "kinds" is only roughly dependent on length,
since James rejected Poe's doctrinaire emphasis on an ideal time
span, preferring to let each subject or *donnée* develop to its full potential. This sense of elasticity is clear in James's lyric praise of the
nouvelle, which he identifies as a Continental form allied to the
novel of manners. The occasion for this praise, in the Preface to
Volume XV of the New York Edition, is James's fond memory of the
time when he was liberated from those hard-and-fast rules of magazine publication which did so much in the late nineteenth century
to turn Poe's aesthetic rationale into a meaningless formula.

> For any idea I might wish to express I might have space, in other
> words, elegantly to express it—and offered licence that, on the spot,
> opened up the millenium to the "short story." One had so often known
> this product to struggle, in one's hands, under the rude prescription of
> brevity at any cost, with the opposition so offered to its really becom-
> ing a story, that my friend's emphasized indifference to the arbitrary
> limit of length struck me, I remember, as the fruit of the finest artistic
> intelligence. We had been at one—that we already knew—on the truth
> that the forms of wrought things, in this order, *were,* all exquisitely and
> effectively, the things; so that, for the delight of mankind, form might
> compete with form and might correspond to fitness; might, that is, in
> the given case, have an inevitability, a marked felicity. Among forms,
> moreover, we had had, on the dimensional ground—for length and
> breadth—our ideal, the beautiful and blest *nouvelle;* the generous, the
> enlightened hour for which appeared thus at last to shine. It was under
> the star of the *nouvelle* that, in other languages, a hundred interesting
> and charming results, such studies on the minor scale as the best of
> Turgenieff's, of Balzac's, of Maupassant's, of Bourget's, and just lately,
> in our own tongue, of Kipling's, had been, all economically, arrived
> at—thanks to their authors', as "contributors," having been able to
> count, right and left, on a wise and liberal support. It had taken the
> blank misery of our Anglo-Saxon sense of such matters to organise, as
> might be said, the general indifference to this fine type of composition.
> In that dull view a "short story" was a "short story," and that was the
> end of it. Shades and differences, varieties and styles, the value above
> all of the idea happily *developed,* languished, to extinction, under the
> hard-and-fast rule of the "from six to eight thousand words"—when for
> one's benefit, the rigour was a little relaxed. For myself, I delighted in
> the shapely *nouvelle*—as, for that matter, I had from time to time and
> here and there been almost encouraged to show.

On the other hand, James clearly knew that a story such as "The
Jolly Corner," which depends on singleness of effect, belongs to

a different literary kind. As an "adventure-story" of the mind, a brief drama of consciousness, it substitutes our modern understanding of the mind's subconscious powers for Poe's Gothic imagination, but the sense of psychological "doubleness" is much the same. And, like Poe, James knew that the unity and force of such a psychological tale lies in the reader's mind, where the extraordinary events of the story find their dark but familiar counterparts.

The moving accident, the rare conjunction, whatever it be, doesn't make the story—in the sense that the story is our excitement, our amusement, our thrill and our suspense; the human emotion and the human attestation, the clustering human conditions we expect presented, only make it. The extraordinary is most extraordinary in that it happens to you and me, and it's of value (of value for others) but so far as visibly brought home to us. At any rate, odd though it may sound to pretend that one feels on safer ground in tracing such an adventure as that of the hero of "The Jolly Corner" than in pursuing a bright career among pirates or detectives, I allow that composition to pass as the measure or limit, on my own part, of any achievable comfort in the "adventure-story"; and this not because I may "render"—well, what my poor gentleman attempted and suffered in the New York house—better than I may render detectives or pirates or other splendid desperadoes, though even here too there would be something to say; but because the spirit engaged with the forces of violence interests me most when I can think of it as engaged most deeply, most finely and most "subtly" (precious term!). For then it is that, as with the longest and firmest prongs of consciousness, I grasp and hold the throbbing subject; *there* it is above all that I find the steady light of the picture.

·Washington Irving·

RIP VAN WINKLE

A Posthumous Writing of Diedrich Knickerbocker [1]

By Woden,[2] God of Saxons,
From whence comes Wensday, that is Wodensday.
Truth is a thing that ever I will keep
Unto thylke day in which I creep into
My sepulchre —Cartwright [3]

[The following Tale was found among the papers of the late Diedrich Knickerbocker, an old gentleman of New York, who was very curious in the Dutch history of the province, and the manners of the descendants from its primitive settlers. His historical researches, however, did not lie so much among books as among men; for the former are lamentably scanty on his favorite topics; whereas he found the old burghers, and still more their wives, rich in that legendary lore, so invaluable to true history. Whenever, therefore, he happened upon a genuine Dutch family, snugly shut up in its low-roofed farmhouse, under a spreading sycamore, he looked upon it

1. Diedrich Knickerbocker, like Geoffrey Crayon, is one of Irving's pen names. He first appeared as the supposed chronicler of Irving's burlesque *History of New York* (1809).
2. In Germanic and Norse mythology, Wodin or Woden (also Odin) was the chief deity, the god of storms ("The Thunderer") and of war.
3. William Cartwright (1611–43), English poet and dramatist, a follower of Ben Jonson. The lines are spoken by Moth, the antiquarian, in Cartwright's play *The Ordinary* (III.i.1050–54).

as a little clasped volume of black-letter,[4] and studied it with the zeal of a book-worm.

The result of all these researches was a history of the province during the reign of the Dutch governors, which he published some years since. There have been various opinions as to the literary character of his work, and to tell the truth, it is not a whit better than it should be. Its chief merit is its scrupulous accuracy, which indeed was a little questioned on its first appearance, but has since been completely established; and it is now admitted into all historical collections, as a book of unquestionable authority.

The old gentleman died shortly after the publication of his work, and now that he is dead and gone, it cannot do much harm to his memory to say that his time might have been much better employed in weightier labors. He, however, was apt to ride his hobby his own way; and though it did now and then kick up the dust a little in the eyes of his neighbors, and grieve the spirit of some friends, for whom he felt the truest deference and affection; yet his errors and follies are remembered "more in sorrow than in anger," [5] and it begins to be suspected, that he never intended to injure or offend. But however his memory may be appreciated by critics, it is still held dear by many folk, whose good opinion is well worth having; particularly by certain biscuit-bakers, who have gone so far as to imprint his likeness on their new-year cakes; and have thus given him a chance for immortality, almost equal to the being stamped on a Waterloo Medal, or a Queen Anne's Farthing.[6]]

Whoever has made a voyage up the Hudson must remember the Kaatskill mountains. They are a dismembered branch of the great Appalachian family, and are seen away to the west of the river, swelling up to a noble height, and lording it over the surrounding country. Every change of season, every change of weather, indeed, every hour of the day, produces some change in the magical hues and shapes of these mountains, and they are regarded by all the good wives, far and near, as perfect barometers. When the weather is fair and settled, they are clothed in blue and purple, and print their bold outlines on the clear evening sky; but, sometimes, when the rest of the landscape is cloudless, they will gather a hood of gray vapors about their summits, which, in the last rays of the setting sun, will glow and light up like a crown of glory.

4. Black-letter is a heavy-faced type (often called "Gothic") used by the early printers. It was supplanted in England by the more familiar Roman type, but the German printers continued to use it.
5. *Hamlet* I.ii.232.
6. The Waterloo Medal, commemorating the defeat of Napoleon, was given to all veterans of the Battle of Waterloo (June 18, 1815); Queen Anne's Farthing was a small coin of little value (one-fourth of a penny), minted during the reign of Queen Anne (1702–14). Irving is drawing an ironic contrast.

At the foot of these fairy mountains, the voyager may have descried the light smoke curling up from a village, whose shingle-roofs gleam among the trees, just where the blue tints of the upland melt away into the fresh green of the nearer landscape. It is a little village, of great antiquity, having been founded by some of the Dutch colonists, in the early times of the province, just about the beginning of the government of the good Peter Stuyvesant (may he rest in peace!) and there were some of the houses of the original settlers standing within a few years, built of small yellow bricks brought from Holland, having latticed windows and gabled fronts, surmounted with weather-cocks.

In that same village, and in one of these very houses (which, to tell the precise truth, was sadly time-worn and weather-beaten), there lived many years since, while the country was yet a province of Great Britain, a simple good-natured fellow, of the name of Rip Van Winkle. He was a descendant of the Van Winkles who figured so gallantly in the chivalrous days of Peter Stuyvesant, and accompanied him to the siege of Fort Christina.[7] He inherited, however, but little of the martial character of his ancestors. I have observed that he was a simple good-natured man; he was, moreover, a kind neighbor, and an obedient hen-pecked husband. Indeed, to the latter circumstance might be owing that meekness of spirit which gained him such universal popularity; for those men are most apt to be obsequious and conciliating abroad, who are under the discipline of shrews at home. Their tempers, doubtless, are rendered pliant and malleable in the fiery furnace of domestic tribulation; and a curtain lecture is worth all the sermons in the world for teaching the virtues of patience and long-suffering. A termagant wife may, therefore, in some respects, be considered a tolerable blessing; and if so, Rip Van Winkle was thrice blessed.

Certain it is, that he was a great favorite among all the good wives of the village, who, as usual, with the amiable sex, took his part in all family squabbles; and never failed, whenever they talked those matters over in their evening gossipings, to lay all the blame on Dame Van Winkle. The children of the village, too, would shout with joy whenever he approached. He assisted at their sports, made their playthings, taught them to fly kites and shoot marbles, and told them long stories of ghosts, witches, and Indians. Whenever he went dodging about the village, he was surrounded by a troop of them, hanging on his skirts, clambering on his back, and playing a thousand tricks on him with impunity; and not a dog would bark at him throughout the neighborhood.

The great error in Rip's composition was an insuperable aversion

7. Fort Christina (present-day Wilmington, Delaware), founded by the Swedes, was besieged and captured by the Dutch in 1654.

to all kinds of profitable labor. It could not be from the want of assi-
duity or perseverance, for he would sit on a wet rock, with a rod as
long and heavy as a Tartar's lance, and fish all day without a murmur, even though he should not be encouraged by a single nibble.
He would carry a fowling-piece on his shoulder for hours together,
trudging through woods and swamps, and up and down dale, to
shoot a few squirrels or wild pigeons. He would never refuse to assist a neighbor even in the roughest toil, and was a foremost man at
all country frolics for husking Indian corn, or building stone-fences;
the women of the village, too, used to employ him to run their errands, and to do such little odd jobs as their less obliging husbands
would not do for them. In a word Rip was ready to attend to anybody's business but his own; but as to doing family duty, and keeping his farm in order, he found it impossible.

In fact, he declared it was of no use to work on his farm; it was
the most pestilent little piece of ground in the whole country; every
thing about it went wrong, and would go wrong, in spite of him. His
fences were continually falling to pieces; his cow would either go
astray, or get among the cabbages; weeds were sure to grow quicker
in his fields than anywhere else; the rain always made a point of
setting in just as he had some out-door work to do; so that though
his patrimonial estate had dwindled away under his management,
acre by acre, until there was little more left than a mere patch of Indian corn and potatoes, yet it was the worst conditioned farm in the
neighborhood.

His children, too, were as ragged and wild as if they belonged to
nobody. His son Rip, an urchin begotten in his own likeness, promised to inherit the habits, with the old clothes of his father. He was
generally seen trooping like a colt at his mother's heels, equipped
in a pair of his father's cast-off galligaskins,[8] which he had much
ado to hold up with one hand, as a fine lady does her train in bad
weather.

Rip Van Winkle, however, was one of those happy mortals, of
foolish, well-oiled dispositions, who take the world easy, eat white
bread or brown, whichever can be got with least thought and
trouble, and would rather starve on a penny than work for a pound.
If left to himself, he would have whistled life away in perfect contentment; but his wife kept continually dinning in his ears about
his idleness, his carelessness, and the ruin he was bringing on his
family. Morning, noon, and night, her tongue was incessantly going,
and every thing he said or did was sure to produce a torrent of
household eloquence. Rip had but one way of replying to all lectures of the kind, and that, by frequent use, had grown into a habit.

8. A humorous term for loose or ill-fitting breeches.

He shrugged his shoulders, shook his head, cast up his eyes, but said nothing. This, however, always provoked a fresh volley from his wife; so that he was fain to draw off his forces, and take to the outside of the house—the only side which, in truth, belongs to a hen-pecked husband.

Rip's sole domestic adherent was his dog Wolf, who was as much hen-pecked as his master; for Dame Van Winkle regarded them as companions in idleness, and even looked upon Wolf with an evil eye, as the cause of his master's going so often astray. True it is, in all points of spirit befitting an honorable dog, he was as courageous an animal as ever scoured the woods—but what courage can withstand the ever-during and all-besetting terrors of a woman's tongue? The moment Wolf entered the house his crest fell, his tail drooped to the ground, or curled between his legs, he sneaked about with a gallows air, casting many a sidelong glance at Dame Van Winkle, and at the least flourish of a broomstick or ladle, he would fly to the door with yelping precipitation.

Times grew worse and worse with Rip Van Winkle as years of matrimony rolled on; a tart temper never mellows with age, and a sharp tongue is the only edged tool that grows keener with constant use. For a long time he used to console himself, when driven from home, by frequenting a kind of perpetual club of the sages, philosophers, and other idle personages of the village; which held its sessions on a bench before a small inn, designated by a rubicund portrait of His Majesty George the Third. Here they used to sit in the shade through a long lazy summer's day, talking listlessly over village gossip, or telling endless sleepy stories about nothing. But it would have been worth any statesman's money to have heard the profound discussions that sometimes took place, when by chance an old newspaper fell into their hands from some passing traveller. How solemnly they would listen to the contents, as drawled out by Derrick Van Bummel, the schoolmaster, a dapper learned little man, who was not to be daunted by the most gigantic word in the dictionary; and how sagely they would deliberate upon public events some months after they had taken place.

The opinions of this junto were completely controlled by Nicholas Vedder, a patriarch of the village, and a landlord of the inn, at the door of which he took his seat from morning till night, just moving sufficiently to avoid the sun and keep in the shade of a large tree; so that the neighbors could tell the hour by his movements as accurately as by a sun-dial. It is true he was rarely heard to speak, but smoked his pipe incessantly. His adherents, however (for every great man has his adherents), perfectly understood him, and knew how to gather his opinions. When any thing that was read or related displeased him, he was observed to smoke his pipe vehemently, and to send forth short, frequent and angry puffs; but when pleased, he would inhale the smoke slowly and tranquilly, and emit it in light and placid clouds; and sometimes, taking the pipe from his mouth, and letting the fragrant vapor curl about his nose, would gravely nod his head in token of perfect approbation.

From even this stronghold the unlucky Rip was at length routed by his termagant wife, who would suddenly break in upon the tranquillity of the assemblage and call the members all to naught; nor was that august personage, Nicholas Vedder himself, sacred from the daring tongue of this terrible virago, who charged him outright with encouraging her husband in habits of idleness.

Poor Rip was at last reduced almost to despair; and his only alternative, to escape from the labor of the farm and clamor of his wife, was to take gun in hand and stroll away into the woods. Here he would sometimes seat himself at the foot of a tree, and share the contents of his wallet with Wolf, with whom he sympathized as a fellow-sufferer in persecution. "Poor Wolf," he would say, "thy mistress leads thee a dog's life of it; but never mind, my lad, whilst I live thou shalt never want a friend to stand by thee!" Wolf would wag his tail, look wistfully in his master's face, and if dogs can feel pity I verily believe he reciprocated the sentiment with all his heart.

In a long ramble of the kind on a fine autumnal day, Rip had unconsciously scrambled to one of the highest parts of the Kaatskill mountains. He was after his favorite sport of squirrel shooting, and the still solitudes had echoed and re-echoed with the reports of his gun. Panting and fatigued, he threw himself, late in the afternoon, on a green knoll, covered with mountain herbage, that crowned the brow of a precipice. From an opening between the trees he could overlook all the lower country for many a mile of rich woodland. He saw at a distance the lordly Hudson, far, far below him, moving on its silent but majestic course, with the reflection of a purple cloud, or the sail of a lagging bark, here and there sleeping on its glassy bosom, and at last losing itself in the blue highlands.

On the other side he looked down into a deep mountain glen, wild, lonely, and shagged, the bottom filled with fragments from the impending cliffs, and scarcely lighted by the reflected rays of the setting sun. For some time Rip lay musing on this scene; evening was gradually advancing; the mountains began to throw their long blue shadows over the valleys; he saw that it would be dark long before he could reach the village, and he heaved a heavy sigh when he thought of encountering the terrors of Dame Van Winkle!

As he was about to descend, he heard a voice from a distance, hallooing, "Rip Van Winkle! Rip Van Winkle!" He looked round, but could see nothing but a crow winging its solitary flight across the mountain. He thought his fancy must have deceived him, and turned again to descend, when he heard the same cry ring through the still evening air; "Rip Van Winkle! Rip Van Winkle!"—at the same time Wolf bristled up his back, and giving a low growl, skulked to his master's side, looking fearfully down into the glen. Rip now felt a vague apprehension stealing over him; he looked anxiously in the same direction, and perceived a strange figure slowly toiling up the rocks, and bending under the weight of something he carried on his back. He was surprised to see any human being in this lonely and unfrequented place, but supposing it to be some one of the neighborhood in need of his assistance, he hastened down to yield it.

On nearer approach he was still more surprised at the singularity of the stranger's appearance. He was a short square-built old fellow, with thick bushy hair, and a grizzled beard. His dress was of the antique Dutch fashion—a cloth jerkin strapped round the waist—several pair of breeches, the outer one of ample volume, decorated with rows of buttons down the sides, and bunches at the knees. He bore on his shoulder a stout keg, that seemed full of liquor, and made signs for Rip to approach and assist him with the load. Though rather shy and distrustful of this new acquaintance, Rip complied with his usual alacrity; and mutually relieving one another, they clambered up a narrow gully, apparently the dry bed of a mountain torrent. As they ascended, Rip every now and then heard long rolling peals, like distant thunder, that seemed to issue out of a deep ravine, or rather cleft, between lofty rocks toward which their rugged path conducted. He paused for an instant, but supposing it to be the muttering of one of those transient thunder-showers which often take place in mountain heights, he proceeded. Passing through the ravine, they came to a hollow, like a small amphitheatre, surrounded by perpendicular precipices, over the brinks of which impending trees shot their branches, so that you only caught glimpses of the azure sky and the bright evening-cloud. During the whole time Rip and his companion had labored on in silence; for though the former marvelled greatly what could be the object of carrying a keg of liquor up this wild mountain, yet there was something strange and incomprehensible about the unknown, that inspired awe and checked familiarity.

On entering the amphitheatre, new objects of wonder presented themselves. On a level spot in the centre was a company of odd-looking personages playing at nine-pins. They were dressed in a quaint outlandish fashion; some wore short doublets, others jerkins, with long knives in their belts, and most of them had enormous breeches, of similar style with that of the guide's. Their visages, too, were peculiar: one had a large beard, broad face, and small piggish eyes: the face of another seemed to consist entirely of nose, and was surmounted by a white sugar-loaf hat, set off with a little red cock's tail. They all had beards, of various shapes and colors. There was one who seemed to be the commander. He was a stout old gentleman, with a weather-beaten countenance; he wore a laced doublet, broad belt and hanger,[9] high crowned hat and feather, red stockings, and high-heeled shoes, with roses [10] in them. The whole group reminded Rip of the figures in an old Flemish painting, in the parlor of Dominie Van Schaick, the village parson, and which had been brought over from Holland at the time of the settlement.

What seemed particularly odd to Rip was, that though these folks were evidently amusing themselves, yet they maintained the gravest faces, the most mysterious silence, and were, withal, the most melancholy party of pleasure he had ever witnessed. Nothing interrupted the stillness of the scene but the noise of the balls, which, whenever they were rolled, echoed along the mountains like rumbling peals of thunder.

As Rip and his companion approached them, they suddenly desisted from their play, and stared at him with such fixed statue-like gaze, and such strange, uncouth, lack-lustre countenances, that his heart turned within him, and his knees smote together. His companion now emptied the contents of the keg into large flagons, and made signs to him to wait upon the company. He obeyed with fear and trembling; they quaffed the liquor in profound silence, and then returned to their game.

By degrees Rip's awe and apprehension subsided. He even ventured, when no eye was fixed upon him, to taste the beverage, which he found had much of the flavor of excellent Hollands.[11] He was naturally a thirsty soul, and was soon tempted to repeat the draught. One taste provoked another; and he reiterated his visits to the flagon so often that at length his senses were overpowered, his eyes swam in his head, his head gradually declined, and he fell into a deep sleep.

On waking, he found himself on the green knoll whence he had first seen the old man of the glen. He rubbed his eyes—it was a bright sunny morning. The birds were hopping and twittering among the bushes, and the eagle was wheeling aloft, and breasting the pure mountain breeze. "Surely," thought Rip, "I have not slept here all night." He recalled the occurrences before he fell asleep. The strange man with a keg of liquor—the mountain ravine—the wild retreat among the rocks—the wobegone party at nine-pins—

9. A short sword hung from the belt.
10. Rosettes.
11. Dutch gin.

the flagon—"Oh! that flagon! that wicked flagon!" thought Rip—"what excuse shall I make to Dame Van Winkle!"

He looked round for his gun, but in place of the clean well-oiled fowling-piece, he found an old firelock lying by him, the barrel incrusted with rust, the lock falling off, and the stock worm-eaten. He now suspected that the grave roysters of the mountain had put a trick upon him, and, having dosed him with liquor had robbed him of his gun. Wolf, too, had disappeared, but he might have strayed away after a squirrel or partridge. He whistled after him and shouted his name, but all in vain; the echoes repeated his whistle and shout, but no dog was to be seen.

He determined to revisit the scene of the last evening's gambol, and if he met with any of the party, to demand his dog and gun. As he rose to walk, he found himself stiff in the joints, and wanting in his usual activity. "These mountain beds do not agree with me," thought Rip, "and if this frolic should lay me up with a fit of the rheumatism, I shall have a blessed time with Dame Van Winkle." With some difficulty he got down into the glen: he found the gully up which he and his companion had ascended the preceding evening; but to his astonishment a mountain stream was now foaming down it, leaping from rock to rock, and filling the glen with babbling murmurs. He, however, made shift to scramble up its sides, working his toilsome way through thickets of birch, sassafras, and witch-hazel, and sometimes tripped up or entangled by the wild grapevines that twisted their coils or tendrils from tree to tree, and spread a kind of network in his path.

At length he reached to where the ravine had opened through the cliffs to the amphitheatre; but no traces of such opening remained. The rocks presented a high impenetrable wall over which the torrent came tumbling in a sheet of feathery foam, and fell into a broad deep basin, black from the shadows of the surrounding forest. Here, then, poor Rip was brought to a stand. He again called and whistled after his dog; he was only answered by the cawing of a flock of idle crows, sporting high in air about a dry tree that overhung a sunny precipice; and who, secure in their elevation, seemed to look down and scoff at the poor man's perplexities. What was to be done? The morning was passing away, and Rip felt famished for want of his breakfast. He grieved to give up his dog and gun; he dreaded to meet his wife; but it would not do to starve among the mountains. He shook his head, shouldered the rusty firelock, and, with a heart full of trouble and anxiety, turned his steps homeward.

As he approached the village he met a number of people, but none whom he knew, which somewhat surprised him, for he had thought himself acquainted with every one in the country round. Their dress, too, was of a different fashion from that to which he was accustomed. They all stared at him with equal marks of surprise, and whenever they cast their eyes upon him, invariably stroked their chins. The constant recurrence of this gesture induced Rip, involuntarily, to do the same, when, to his astonishment, he found his beard had grown a foot long!

He had now entered the skirts of the village. A troop of strange children ran at his heels, hooting after him, and pointing at his gray beard. The dogs, too, not one of which he recognized for an old acquaintance, barked at him as he passed. The very village was altered; it was larger and more populous. There were rows of houses which he had never seen before, and those which had been his familiar haunts had disappeared. Strange names were over the doors—strange faces at the windows—every thing was strange. His mind now misgave him; he began to doubt whether both he and the world around him were not bewitched. Surely this was his native village, which he had left but the day before. There stood the Kaatskill mountains—there ran the silvery Hudson at a distance—there was every hill and dale precisely as it had always been—Rip was sorely perplexed—"That flagon last night," thought he, "has addled my poor head sadly."

It was with some difficulty that he found the way to his own house, which he approached with silent awe, expecting every moment to hear the shrill voice of Dame Van Winkle. He found the house gone to decay—the roof fallen in, the windows shattered, and the doors off the hinges. A half-starved dog that looked like Wolf was skulking about it. Rip called him by name, but the cur snarled, showed his teeth, and passed on. This was an unkind cut indeed—"My very dog," sighed poor Rip, "has forgotten me!"

He entered the house, which, to tell the truth, Dame Van Winkle had always kept in neat order. It was empty, forlorn, and apparently abandoned. This desolateness overcame all his connubial fears—he called loudly for his wife and children—the lonely chambers rang for a moment with his voice, and then all again was silence.

He now hurried forth, and hastened to his old resort, the village inn—but it too was gone. A large rickety wooden building stood in its place, with great gaping windows, some of them broken and mended with old hats and petticoats, and over the door was painted, "The Union Hotel, by Jonathan Doolittle." Instead of the great tree that used to shelter the quiet little Dutch inn of yore, there was now reared a tall naked pole, with something on the top that looked like a red night-cap,[12] and from it was fluttering a flag, on which was a singular assemblage of stars and stripes—all this

12. The "liberty cap," a symbol of freedom modeled after the conical caps given to freed slaves in ancient Rome. It was widely displayed at the time of the American and French revolutions.

was strange and incomprehensible. He recognized on the sign, however, the ruby face of King George, under which he had smoked so many a peaceful pipe; but even this was singularly metamorphosed. The red coat was changed for one of blue and buff, a sword was held in the hand instead of a sceptre, the head was decorated with a cocked hat, and underneath was painted in large characters, GENERAL WASHINGTON.

There was, as usual, a crowd of folk about the door, but none that Rip recollected. The very character of the people seemed changed. There was a busy, bustling, disputatious tone about it, instead of the accustomed phlegm and drowsy tranquillity. He looked in vain for the sage Nicholas Vedder, with his broad face, double chin, and fair long pipe, uttering clouds of tobacco-smoke instead of idle speeches; or Van Bummel, the schoolmaster, doling forth the contents of an ancient newspaper. In place of these, a lean, bilious-looking fellow, with his pockets full of handbills, was haranguing vehemently about rights of citizens—elections—members of congress—liberty—Bunker's Hill—heroes of seventy-six—and other words, which were a perfect Babylonish jargon [13] to the bewildered Van Winkle.

The appearance of Rip, with his long grizzled beard, his rusty fowling-piece, his uncouth dress, and an army of women and children at his heels, soon attracted the attention of the tavern politicians. They crowded round him, eyeing him from head to foot with great curiosity. The orator bustled up to him, and, drawing him partly aside, inquired "on which side he voted?" Rip stared in vacant stupidity. Another short but busy little fellow pulled him by the arm, and, rising on tiptoe, inquired in his ear, "Whether he was Federal or Democrat?" [14] Rip was equally at a loss to comprehend the question; when a knowing, self-important old gentleman, in a sharp cocked hat, made his way through the crowd, putting them to the right and left with his elbows as he passed, and planting himself before Van Winkle, with one arm akimbo, the other resting on his cane, his keen eyes and sharp hat penetrating, as it were, into his very soul, demanded in an austere tone, "what brought him to the election with a gun on his shoulder, and a mob at his heels, and whether he meant to breed a riot in the village?"—"Alas! gentlemen," cried Rip, somewhat dismayed, "I am a poor quiet man, a native of the place, and a loyal subject of the king, God bless him!"

Here a general shout burst from the by-standers—"A tory! a tory! a spy! a refugee! hustle him! away with him!" It was with great difficulty that the self-important man in the cocked hat restored order;

13. Confused speech; a reference to the Tower of Babel.
14. America's earliest political parties. The Federalists believed in strong central government, while the Democrats were Jeffersonian Republicans.

and, having assumed a tenfold austerity of brow, demanded again of the unknown culprit, what he came there for, and whom he was seeking? The poor man humbly assured him that he meant no harm, but merely came there in search of some of his neighbors, who used to keep about the tavern.

"Well—who are they?—name them."

Rip bethought himself a moment, and inquired, "Where's Nicholas Vedder?"

There was a silence for a little while, when an old man replied, in a thin piping voice, "Nicholas Vedder! why, he is dead and gone these eighteen years! There was a wooden tombstone in the church-yard that used to tell all about him, but that's rotten and gone too."

"Where's Brom Dutcher?"

"Oh, he went off to the army in the beginning of the war; some say he was killed at the storming of Stony Point—others say he was drowned in a squall at the foot of Anthony's Nose.[15] I don't know— he never came back again."

"Where's Van Bummel, the schoolmaster?"

"He went off to the wars too, was a great militia general, and is now in congress."

Rip's heart died away at hearing of these sad changes in his home and friends, and finding himself thus alone in the world. Every answer puzzled him, too, by treating of such enormous lapses of time, and of matters which he could not understand: war—congress— Stony Point;—he had no courage to ask after any more friends, but cried out in despair, "Does nobody here know Rip Van Winkle?"

"Oh, Rip Van Winkle!" exclaimed two or three, "Oh, to be sure! that's Rip Van Winkle yonder, leaning against the tree."

Rip looked, and beheld a precise counterpart of himself, as he went up the mountain: apparently as lazy, and certainly as ragged. The poor fellow was now completely confounded. He doubted his own identity, and whether he was himself or another man. In the midst of his bewilderment, the man in the cocked hat demanded who he was, and what was his name?

"God knows," exclaimed he, at his wit's end; "I'm not myself— I'm somebody else—that's me yonder—no—that's somebody else got into my shoes—I was myself last night, but I fell asleep on the mountain, and they've changed my gun, and every thing's changed, and I'm changed, and I can't tell what's my name, or who I am."

The by-standers began now to look at each other, nod, wink significantly, and tap their fingers against their foreheads. There was a

15. Stony Point and Anthony's Nose, prominent landmarks on the Hudson, were the scenes of bloody fighting during the Revolutionary War. Stony Point was stormed by "Mad Anthony" Wayne and the American Light Infantry on July 16, 1779.

whisper, also, about securing the gun, and keeping the old fellow from doing mischief, at the very suggestion of which the self-important man in the cocked hat retired with some precipitation. At this critical moment a fresh comely woman pressed through the throng to get a peep at the gray-bearded man. She had a chubby child in her arms, which, frightened at his looks, began to cry. "Hush, Rip," cried she, "hush, you little fool; the old man won't hurt you." The name of the child, the air of the mother, the tone of her voice, all awakened a train of recollections in his mind. "What is your name, my good woman?" asked he.

"Judith Gardenier."

"And your father's name?"

"Ah, poor man, Rip Van Winkle was his name, but it's twenty years since he went away from home with his gun, and never has been heard of since—his dog came home without him; but whether he shot himself, or was carried away by the Indians, nobody can tell. I was then but a little girl."

Rip had but one more question to ask; but he put it with a faltering voice:

"Where's your mother?"

"Oh, she too had died but a short time since; she broke a blood-vessel in a fit of passion at a New-England peddler."

There was a drop of comfort, at least, in this intelligence. The honest man could contain himself no longer. He caught his daughter and her child in his arms. "I am your father!" cried he—"Young Rip Van Winkle once—old Rip Van Winkle now!—Does nobody know poor Rip Van Winkle?"

All stood amazed, until an old woman, tottering out from among the crowd, put her hand to her brow, and peering under it in his face for a moment, exclaimed, "Sure enough! it is Rip Van Winkle—it is himself!—Welcome home again, old neighbor—Why, where have you been these twenty long years?"

Rip's story was soon told, for the whole twenty years had been to him but as one night. The neighbors stared when they heard it; some were seen to wink at each other, and put their tongues in their cheeks: and the self-important man in the cocked hat, who, when the alarm was over, had returned to the field, screwed down the corners of his mouth, and shook his head—upon which there was a general shaking of the head throughout the assemblage.

It was determined, however, to take the opinion of old Peter Vanderdonk, who was seen slowly advancing up the road. He was a descendant of the historian of that name, who wrote one of the earliest accounts of the province. Peter was the most ancient inhabitant of the village, and well versed in all the wonderful events and traditions of the neighborhood. He recollected Rip at once, and corroborated his story in the most satisfactory manner. He assured the company that it was a fact, handed down from his ancestor the historian,[16] that the Kaatskill mountains had always been haunted by strange beings. That it was affirmed that the great Hendrick Hudson, the first discoverer of the river and country, kept a kind of vigil there every twenty years, with his crew of the Half-moon; being permitted in this way to revisit the scenes of his enterprise, and keep a guardian eye upon the river, and the great city called by his name. That his father had once seen them in their old Dutch dresses playing at nine-pins in a hollow of the mountain; and that he himself had heard, one summer afternoon, the sound of their balls, like distant peals of thunder.

To make a long story short, the company broke up, and returned to the more important concerns of the election. Rip's daughter took him home to live with her; she had a snug, well-furnished house, and a stout cheery farmer for a husband, whom Rip recollected for one of the urchins that used to climb upon his back. As to Rip's son and heir, who was the ditto of himself, seen leaning against the tree, he was employed to work on the farm; but evinced an hereditary disposition to attend to any thing else but his business.

Rip now resumed his old walks and habits; he soon found many of his former cronies, though all rather the worse for the wear and tear of time; and preferred making friends among the rising generation, with whom he soon grew into great favor.

Having nothing to do at home, and being arrived at that happy age when a man can be idle with impunity, he took his place once more on the bench at the inn door, and was reverenced as one of the patriarchs of the village, and a chronicle of the old times "before the war." It was some time before he could get into the regular track of gossip, or could be made to comprehend the strange events that had taken place during his torpor. How that there had been a revolutionary war—that the country had thrown off the yoke of old England —and that, instead of being a subject of his Majesty George the Third, he was now a free citizen of the United States. Rip, in fact, was no politician; the changes of states and empires made but little impression on him; but there was one species of despotism under which he had long groaned, and that was—petticoat government. Happily that was at an end; he had got his neck out of the yoke of matrimony, and could go in and out whenever he pleased, without dreading the tyranny of Dame Van Winkle. Whenever her name was mentioned, however, he shook his head, shrugged his shoulders, and cast up his eyes; which might pass either for an expression of resignation to his fate, or joy at his deliverance.

16. Adriaen Van Der Donck (1620–55), who wrote a history of New Netherland.

He used to tell his story to every stranger that arrived at Mr. Doolittle's hotel. He was observed, at first, to vary on some points every time he told it, which was, doubtless, owing to his having so recently awaked. It at last settled down precisely to the tale I have related, and not a man, woman, or child in the neighborhood, but knew it by heart. Some always pretended to doubt the reality of it, and insisted that Rip had been out of his head, and that this was one point on which he always remained flighty. The old Dutch inhabitants, however, almost universally gave it full credit. Even to this day they never hear a thunderstorm of a summer afternoon about the Kaatskill, but they say Hendrick Hudson and his crew are at their game of nine-pins; and it is a common wish of all henpecked husbands in the neighborhood, when life hangs heavy on their hands, that they might have a quieting draught out of Rip Van Winkle's flagon.

NOTE

The foregoing Tale, one would suspect, had been suggested to Mr. Knickerbocker by a little German superstition about the Emperor Frederick *der Rothbart*,[17] and the Kypphauser mountain: the subjoined note, however, which he had appended to the tale, shows that it is an absolute fact, narrated with his usual fidelity:

"The story of Rip Van Winkle may seem incredible to many, but nevertheless I give it my full belief, for I know the vicinity of our old Dutch settlements to have been very subject to marvellous events and appearances. Indeed, I have heard many stranger stories than this, in the villages along the Hudson; all of which were too well authenticated to admit of a doubt. I have even talked with Rip Van Winkle myself, who, when last I saw him, was a very venerable old man, and so perfectly rational and consistent on every other point, that I think no conscientious person could refuse to take this into the bargain; nay, I have seen a certificate on the subject taken before a country justice and signed with a cross, in the justice's own handwriting. The story, therefore, is beyond the possibility of doubt.

D.K." [18]

POSTSCRIPT [19]

The following are travelling notes from a memorandum-book of Mr. Knickerbocker:

17. Frederick "the Red Beard" (Barbarossa), Emperor of the Holy Roman Empire (1155–90).
18. In this note Irving hints at the German sources of his tale. See Henry A. Pochmann, "Irving's German Sources in *The Sketch Book*," *Studies in Philology* 27 (1930): 489–98.
19. This "Postscript" was added by Irving after the original publication.

The Kaatsberg, or Catskill Mountains, have always been a region full of fable. The Indians considered them the abode of spirits, who influenced the weather, spreading sunshine or clouds over the landscape, and sending good or bad hunting seasons. They were ruled by an old squaw spirit, said to be their mother. She dwelt on the highest peak of the Catskills, and had charge of the doors of day and night to open and shut them at the proper hour. She hung up the new moons in the skies, and cut up the old ones into stars. In times of drought, if properly propitiated, she would spin light summer clouds out of cobwebs and morning dew, and send them off from the crest of the mountain, flake after flake, like flakes of carded cotton, to float in the air; until, dissolved by the heat of the sun, they would fall in gentle showers, causing the grass to spring, the fruits to ripen, and the corn to grow an inch an hour. If displeased, however, she would brew up clouds black as ink, sitting in the midst of them like a bottle-bellied spider in the midst of its web; and when these clouds broke, wo betide the valleys!

In old times, say the Indian traditions, there was a kind of Manitou or Spirit, who kept about the wildest recesses of the Catskill Mountains, and took a mischievous pleasure in wreaking all kinds of evils and vexations upon the real men. Sometimes he would assume the form of a bear, a panther, or a deer, lead the bewildered hunter a weary chase through tangled forests and among ragged rocks; and then spring off with a loud ho! ho! leaving him aghast on the brink of a beetling precipice or raging torrent.

The favorite abode of this Manitou is still shown. It is a great rock or cliff on the loneliest part of the mountains, and, from the flowering vines which clamber about it, and the wild flowers which abound in its neighborhhod, is known by the name of the Garden Rock. Near the foot of it is a small lake, the haunt of the solitary bittern, with water-snakes basking in the sun on the leaves of the pond-lilies which lie on the surface. This place was held in great awe by the Indians, insomuch that the boldest hunter would not pursue his game within its precincts. Once upon a time, however, a hunter who had lost his way, penetrated to the garden rock, where he beheld a number of gourds placed in the crotches of trees. One of these he seized and made off with it, but in the hurry of his retreat he let it fall among the rocks, when a great stream gushed forth, which washed him away and swept him down precipices, where he was dashed to pieces, and the stream made its way to the Hudson, and continues to flow to the present day; being the identical stream known by the name of the Kaaterskill.

From *The Sketch-Book of Geoffrey Crayon, Gent.* (1819–20)

THE ADVENTURE OF
THE GERMAN STUDENT

In a stormy night, in the tempestuous times of the French revolution, a young German was returning to his lodgings, at a late hour, across the old part of Paris. The lightning gleamed, and the loud claps of thunder rattled through the lofty narrow streets—but I should first tell you something about this young German.

Gottfried Wolfgang was a young man of good family. He had studied for some time at Göttingen,[1] but being of a visionary and enthusiastic character, he had wandered into those wild and speculative doctrines which have so often bewildered German students. His secluded life, his intense application, and the singular nature of his studies, had an effect on both mind and body. His health was impaired; his imagination diseased. He had been indulging in fanciful speculations on spiritual essences, until, like Swedenborg, he had an ideal world of his own around him.[2] He took up a notion, I do not know from what cause, that there was an evil influence hanging over him; an evil genius or spirit seeking to ensnare him and ensure his perdition. Such an idea working on his melancholy temperament, produced the most gloomy effects. He became haggard and desponding. His friends discovered the mental malady preying upon him, and determined that the best cure was a change of scene; he was sent, therefore, to finish his studies amid the splendors and gayeties of Paris.

Wolfgang arrived at Paris at the breaking out of the revolution. The popular delirium at first caught his enthusiastic mind, and he was captivated by the political and philosophical theories of the day: but the scenes of blood which followed shocked his sensitive nature, disgusted him with society and the world, and made him more than ever a recluse. He shut himself up in a solitary apartment in the *Pays Latin*, the quarter of students.[3] There, in a gloomy street not far from the monastic walls of the Sorbonne, he pursued his favorite speculations. Sometimes he spent hours together in the great libraries of Paris, those catacombs of departed authors, rummaging among their hoards of dusty and obsolete works in quest of food for his unhealthy appetite. He was, in a manner, a literary ghoul, feeding in the charnel-house of decayed literature.

Wolfgang, though solitary and recluse, was of an ardent temperament, but for a time it operated merely upon his imagination. He

1. A university town in Germany.
2. Emanuel Swedenborg (1688–1772), Swedish scientist, philosopher, and mystic. Swedenborg devoted the latter part of his life to psychical and spiritual inquiry.
3. The Latin Quarter, on the left (south) bank of the Seine, is adjacent to the Sorbonne, France's most famous university.

was too shy and ignorant of the world to make any advances to the fair, but he was a passionate admirer of female beauty, and in his lonely chamber would often lose himself in reveries on forms and faces which he had seen, and his fancy would deck out images of loveliness far surpassing the reality.

While his mind was in this excited and sublimated state, a dream produced an extraordinary effect upon him. It was of a female face of transcendent beauty. So strong was the impression made, that he dreamt of it again and again. It haunted his thoughts by day, his slumbers by night; in fine, he became passionately enamoured of this shadow of a dream. This lasted so long that it became one of those fixed ideas which haunt the minds of melancholy men, and are at times mistaken for madness.

Such was Gottfried Wolfgang, and such his situation at the time I mentioned. He was returning home late one stormy night, through some of the old and gloomy streets of the *Marais*, the ancient part of Paris.[4] The loud claps of thunder rattled among the high houses of the narrow streets. He came to the Place de Grève, the square where public executions are performed. The lightning quivered about the pinnacles of the ancient Hôtel de Ville,[5] and shed flickering gleams over the open space in front. As Wolfgang was crossing the square, he shrank back with horror at finding himself close by the guillotine. It was the height of the reign of terror, when this dreadful instrument of death stood ever ready, and its scaffold was continually running with the blood of the virtuous and the brave. It had that very day been actively employed in the work of carnage, and there it stood in grim array, amidst a silent and sleeping city, waiting for fresh victims.

Wolfgang's heart sickened within him, and he was turning shuddering from the horrible engine, when he beheld a shadowy form, cowering as it were at the foot of the steps which led up to the scaffold. A succession of vivid flashes of lightning revealed it more distinctly. It was a female figure, dressed in black. She was seated on one of the lower steps of the scaffold, leaning forward, her face hid in her lap; and her long dishevelled tresses hanging to the ground, streaming with the rain which fell in torrents. Wolfgang paused. There was something awful in this solitary monument of woe. The female had the appearance of being above the common order. He knew the times to be full of vicissitude, and that many a fair head, which had once been pillowed on down, now wandered houseless.

4. The *Marais*, a district of old streets and ancient houses, lies to the north of the Seine. The rue des Marais was the home of the famous public executioner, Sanson, and his descendants.
5. The Hôtel de Ville (town hall) faces the Place de l'Hôtel de Ville, formerly the Place de Grève.

Perhaps this was some poor mourner whom the dreadful axe had rendered desolate, and who sat here heart-broken on the strand of existence, from which all that was dear to her had been launched into eternity.

He approached, and addressed her in the accents of sympathy. She raised her head and gazed wildly at him. What was his astonishment at beholding, by the bright glare of the lightning, the very face which had haunted him in his dreams. It was pale and disconsolate, but ravishingly beautiful.

Trembling with violent and conflicting emotions, Wolfgang again accosted her. He spoke something of her being exposed at such an hour of the night, and to the fury of such a storm, and offered to conduct her to her friends. She pointed to the guillotine with a gesture of dreadful signification.

"I have no friend on earth!" said she.

"But you have a home," said Wolfgang.

"Yes—in the grave!"

The heart of the student melted at the words.

"If a stranger dare make an offer," said he, "without danger of being misunderstood, I would offer my humble dwelling as a shelter; myself as a devoted friend. I am friendless myself in Paris, and a stranger in the land; but if my life could be of service, it is at your disposal, and should be sacrificed before harm or indignity should come to you."

There was an honest earnestness in the young man's manner that had its effect. His foreign accent, too, was in his favor; it showed him not to be a hackneyed inhabitant of Paris. Indeed, there is an eloquence in true enthusiasm that is not to be doubted. The homeless stranger confided herself implicitly to the protection of the student.

He supported her faltering steps across the Pont Neuf,[6] and by the place where the statue of Henry the Fourth had been overthrown by the populace. The storm had abated, and the thunder rumbled at a distance. All Paris was quiet; that great volcano of human passion slumbered for a while, to gather fresh strength for the next day's eruption. The student conducted his charge through the ancient streets of the *Pays Latin,* and by the dusky walls of the Sorbonne, to the great dingy hotel which he inhabited. The old portress who admitted them stared with surprise at the unusual sight of the melancholy Wolfgang with a female companion.

On entering his apartment, the student, for the first time, blushed at the scantiness and indifference of his dwelling. He had but one

6. The Pont Neuf (New Bridge), now the oldest bridge in Paris, links the Latin Quarter with the right bank of the Seine.

chamber—an old-fashioned saloon—heavily carved, and fantastically furnished with the remains of former magnificence, for it was one of those hotels in the quarter of the Luxembourg palace, which had once belonged to nobility. It was lumbered with books and papers, and all the usual apparatus of a student, and his bed stood in a recess at one end.

When lights were brought, and Wolfgang had a better opportunity of contemplating the stranger, he was more than ever intoxicated by her beauty. Her face was pale, but of a dazzling fairness, set off by a profusion of raven hair that hung clustering about it. Her eyes were large and brilliant, with a singular expression approaching almost to wildness. As far as her black dress permitted her shape to be seen, it was of perfect symmetry. Her whole appearance was highly striking, though she was dressed in the simplest style. The only thing approaching to an ornament which she wore, was a broad black band round her neck, clasped by diamonds.

The perplexity now commenced with the student how to dispose of the helpless being thus thrown upon his protection. He thought of abandoning his chamber to her, and seeking shelter for himself elsewhere. Still, he was so fascinated by her charms, there seemed to be such a spell upon his thoughts and senses, that he could not tear himself from her presence. Her manner, too, was singular and unaccountable. She spoke no more of the guillotine. Her grief had abated. The attentions of the student had first won her confidence, and then, apparently, her heart. She was evidently an enthusiast like himself, and enthusiasts soon understand each other.

In the infatuation of the moment, Wolfgang avowed his passion for her. He told her the story of his mysterious dream, and how she had possessed his heart before he had even seen her. She was strangely affected by his recital, and acknowledged to have felt an impulse towards him equally unaccountable. It was the time for wild theory and wild actions. Old prejudices and superstitions were done away; everything was under the sway of the "Goddess of Reason." Among other rubbish of the old times, the forms and ceremonies of marriage began to be considered superfluous bonds for honorable minds. Social compacts were the vogue. Wolfgang was too much of a theorist not to be tainted by the liberal doctrines of the day.

"Why should we separate?" said he: "our hearts are united; in the eye of reason and honor we are as one. What need is there of sordid forms to bind high souls together?"

The stranger listened with emotion: she had evidently received illumination at the same school.

"You have no home nor family," continued he: "let me be everything to you, or rather let us be everything to one another. If form is necessary, form shall be observed—there is my hand. I pledge myself to you forever."

"Forever?" said the stranger, solemnly.

"Forever!" replied Wolfgang.

The stranger clasped the hand extended to her: "Then I am yours," murmured she, and sank upon his bosom.

The next morning the student left his bride sleeping, and sallied forth at an early hour to seek more spacious apartments suitable to the change in his situation. When he returned, he found the stranger lying with her head hanging over the bed, and one arm thrown over it. He spoke to her, but received no reply. He advanced to awaken her from her uneasy posture. On taking her hand, it was cold—there was no pulsation—her face was pallid and ghastly. In a word, she was a corpse.

Horrified and frantic, he alarmed the house. A scene of confusion ensued. The police was summoned. As the officer of police entered the room, he started back on beholding the corpse.

"Great heaven!" cried he, "how did this woman come here?"

"Do you know anything about her?" said Wolfgang eagerly.

"Do I?" exclaimed the officer: "she was guillotined yesterday."

He stepped forward; undid the black collar round the neck of the corpse, and the head rolled on the floor!

The student burst into a frenzy. "The fiend! the fiend has gained possession of me!" shrieked he: "I am lost forever."

They tried to soothe him, but in vain. He was possessed with the frightful belief that an evil spirit had reanimated the dead body to ensnare him. He went distracted, and died in a mad-house.

Here the old gentleman with the haunted head finished his narrative.

"And is this really a fact?" said the inquisitive gentleman.

"A fact not to be doubted," replied the other. "I had it from the best authority. The student told it me himself. I saw him in a mad-house in Paris."

From *Tales of a Traveller* (1824)

·Nathaniel Hawthorne·

MY KINSMAN, MAJOR MOLINEUX

After the kings of Great Britain had assumed the right of appointing the colonial governors, the measures of the latter seldom met with the ready and generous approbation which had been paid to those of their predecessors, under the original charters. The people looked with most jealous scrutiny to the exercise of power which did not emanate from themselves, and they usually rewarded their rulers with slender gratitude for the compliances by which, in softening their instructions from beyond the sea, they had incurred the reprehension of those who gave them. The annals of Massachusetts Bay will inform us, that of six governors in the space of about forty years from the surrender of the old charter, under James II, two were imprisoned by a popular insurrection; a third, as Hutchinson [1] inclines to believe, was driven from the province by the whizzing of a musket-ball; a fourth, in the opinion of the same historian, was hastened to his grave by continual bickerings with the House of Representatives; and the remaining two, as well as their successors, till the Revolution, were favored with few and brief intervals of peaceful sway. The inferior members of the court party, in times of high political excitement, led scarcely a more desirable life. These remarks may serve as a preface to the following adventures, which chanced upon a summer night, not far from a hundred years ago.[2]

1. Thomas Hutchinson, *History of the Colony and Province of Massachusetts Bay* (1764–1828). The "old charter," which guaranteed the colonists a considerable measure of independence, was annulled by the Crown in 1684.
2. The story was written in 1828–29.

The reader, in order to avoid a long and dry detail of colonial affairs, is requested to dispense with an account of the train of circumstances that had caused much temporary inflammation of the popular mind.

It was near nine o'clock of a moonlight evening, when a boat crossed the ferry with a single passenger, who had obtained his conveyance at that unusual hour by the promise of an extra fare. While he stood on the landing-place, searching in either pocket for the means of fulfilling his agreement, the ferryman lifted a lantern, by the aid of which, and the newly risen moon, he took a very accurate survey of the stranger's figure. He was a youth of barely eighteen years, evidently country-bred, and now, as it should seem, upon his first visit to town. He was clad in a coarse gray coat, well worn, but in excellent repair; his under garments were durably constructed of leather, and fitted tight to a pair of serviceable and well-shaped limbs; his stockings of blue yarn were the incontrovertible work of a mother or a sister; and on his head was a three-cornered hat, which in its better days had perhaps sheltered the graver brow of the lad's father. Under his left arm was a heavy cudgel formed of an oak sapling, and retaining a part of the hardened root; and his equipment was completed by a wallet, not so abundantly stocked as to incommode the vigorous shoulders on which it hung. Brown, curly hair, well-shaped features, and bright, cheerful eyes were nature's gifts, and worth all that art could have done for his adornment.

The youth, one of whose names was Robin, finally drew from his pocket the half of a little province bill of five shillings, which, in the depreciation in that sort of currency, did but satisfy the ferryman's demand, with the surplus of a sexangular piece of parchment, valued at three pence. He then walked forward into the town, with as light a step as if his day's journey had not already exceeded thirty miles, and with as eager an eye as if he were entering London city, instead of the little metropolis of a New England colony. Before Robin had proceeded far, however, it occurred to him that he knew not whither to direct his steps; so he paused, and looked up and down the narrow street, scrutinizing the small and mean wooden buildings that were scattered on either side.

"This low hovel cannot be my kinsman's dwelling," thought he, "nor yonder old house, where the moonlight enters at the broken casement; and truly I see none hereabouts that might be worthy of him. It would have been wise to inquire my way of the ferryman, and doubtless he would have gone with me, and earned a shilling from the Major for his pains. But the next man I meet will do as well."

He resumed his walk, and was glad to perceive that the street now became wider, and the houses more respectable in their appearance. He soon discerned a figure moving on moderately in advance, and hastened his steps to overtake it. As Robin drew nigh, he saw that the passenger was a man in years, with a full periwig of gray hair, a wide-skirted coat of dark cloth, and silk stockings rolled above his knees. He carried a long and polished cane, which he struck down perpendicularly before him at every step; and at regular intervals he uttered two successive hems, of a peculiarly solemn and sepulchral intonation. Having made these observations, Robin laid hold of the skirt of the old man's coat, just when the light from the open door and windows of a barber's shop fell upon both their figures.

"Good evening to you, honored sir," said he, making a low bow, and still retaining his hold of the skirt. "I pray you tell me whereabouts is the dwelling of my kinsman, Major Molineux."

The youth's question was uttered very loudly; and one of the barbers, whose razor was descending on a well-soaped chin, and another who was dressing a Ramillies wig,[3] left their occupations, and came to the door. The citizen, in the mean time, turned a long-favored countenance upon Robin, and answered him in a tone of excessive anger and annoyance. His two sepulchral hems, however, broke into the very centre of his rebuke, with most singular effect, like a thought of the cold grave obtruding among wrathful passions.

"Let go my garment, fellow! I tell you, I know not the man you speak of. What! I have authority, I have—hem, hem—authority; and if this be the respect you show for your betters, your feet shall be brought acquainted with the stocks by daylight, tomorrow morning!"

Robin released the old man's skirt, and hastened away, pursued by an ill-mannered roar of laughter from the barber's shop. He was at first considerably surprised by the result of his question, but, being a shrewd youth, soon thought himself able to account for the mystery.

"This is some country representative," was his conclusion, "who has never seen the inside of my kinsman's door, and lacks the breeding to answer a stranger civilly. The man is old, or verily—I might be tempted to turn back and smite him on the nose. Ah, Robin, Robin! even the barber's boys laugh at you for choosing such a guide! You will be wiser in time, friend Robin."

He now became entangled in a succession of crooked and narrow streets, which crossed each other, and meandered at no great distance from the water-side. The smell of tar was obvious to his nostrils, the masts of vessels pierced the moonlight above the tops of

3. A wig having a long plait tied with a bow at both bottom and top. It was named for the town of Ramillies in Belgium, where the British defeated the French in 1706.

the buildings, and the numerous signs, which Robin paused to read, informed him that he was near the centre of business. But the streets were empty, the shops were closed, and lights were visible only in the second stories of a few dwelling-houses. At length, on the corner of a narrow lane, through which he was passing, he beheld the broad countenance of a British hero swinging before the door of an inn,[4] whence proceeded the voices of many guests. The casement of one of the lower windows was thrown back, and a very thin curtain permitted Robin to distinguish a party at supper, round a well-furnished table. The fragrance of the good cheer steamed forth into the outer air, and the youth could not fail to recollect that the last remnant of his travelling stock of provision had yielded to his morning appetite, and that noon had found and left him din-nerless.

"Oh, that a parchment three-penny might give me a right to sit down at yonder table!" said Robin, with a sigh. "But the Major will make me welcome to the best of his victuals; so I will even step boldly in, and inquire my way to his dwelling."

He entered the tavern, and was guided by the murmur of voices and the fumes of tobacco to the public-room. It was a long and low apartment, with oaken walls, grown dark in the continual smoke, and a floor which was thickly sanded, but of no immaculate purity. A number of persons—the larger part of whom appeared to be mariners, or in some way connected with the sea—occupied the wooden benches, or leather-bottomed chairs, conversing on various matters, and occasionally lending their attention to some topic of general interest. Three or four little groups were draining as many bowls of punch, which the West India trade had long since made a familiar drink in the colony. Others, who had the appearance of men who lived by regular and laborious handicraft, preferred the insulated bliss of an unshared potation, and became more taciturn under its influence. Nearly all, in short, evinced a predilection for the Good Creature [5] in some of its various shapes, for this is a vice to which, as Fast Day sermons [6] of a hundred years ago will testify, we have a long hereditary claim. The only guests to whom Robin's sympathies inclined him were two or three sheepish countrymen, who were using the inn somewhat after the fashion of a Turkish caravansary; [7] they had gotten themselves into the darkest corner of the room, and

---

4. The signboard of the inn would carry the picture of the British hero for which it was named (probably the Duke of Marlborough, hero of the Battle of Ramillies).

5. Liquor; see 1 Tim. 4:4—"For every creature of God *is* good, and nothing to be refused, if it be received with thanksgiving."

6. The Fast Day was the day appointed every spring by the governor for fasting and penance.

7. An inn in Eastern countries where caravans stay and prepare the food they have brought with them.

heedless of the Nicotian [8] atmosphere, were supping on the bread of their own ovens, and the bacon cured in their own chimney-smoke. But though Robin felt a sort of brotherhood with these strangers, his eyes were attracted from them to a person who stood near the door, holding whispered conversation with a group of ill-dressed associates. His features were separately striking almost to grotesqueness, and the whole face left a deep impression on the memory. The forehead bulged out into a double prominence, with a vale between; the nose came boldly forth in an irregular curve, and its bridge was of more than a finger's breadth; the eyebrows were deep and shaggy, and the eyes glowed beneath them like fire in a cave.

While Robin deliberated of whom to inquire respecting his kinsman's dwelling, he was accosted by the innkeeper, a little man in a stained white apron, who had come to pay his professional welcome to the stranger. Being in the second generation from a French Protestant,[9] he seemed to have inherited the courtesy of his parent nation; but no variety of circumstances was every known to change his voice from the one shrill note in which he now addressed Robin.

"From the country, I presume, sir?" said he, with a profound bow. "Beg leave to congratulate you on your arrival, and trust you intend a long stay with us. Fine town here, sir, beautiful buildings, and much that may interest a stranger. May I hope for the honor of your commands in respect to supper?"

"The man sees a family likeness! the rogue has guessed that I am related to the Major!" thought Robin, who had hitherto experienced little superfluous civility.

All eyes were now turned on the country lad, standing at the door, in his worn three-cornered hat, gray coat, leather breeches, and blue yarn stockings, leaning on an oaken cudgel, and bearing a wallet on his back.

Robin replied to the courteous innkeeper, with such an assumption of confidence as befitted the Major's relative. "My honest friend," he said, "I shall make it a point to patronize your house on some occasion, when"—here he could not help lowering his voice—"when I may have more than a parchment three-pence in my pocket. My present business," continued he, speaking with lofty confidence, "is merely to inquire my way to the dwelling of my kinsman, Major Molineux."

There was a sudden and general movement in the room, which Robin interpreted as expressing the eagerness of each individual to

8. Filled with tobacco smoke (Jacques Nicot introduced tobacco into France in 1560).
9. Descendant of a Huguenot refugee (some of the seventeenth-century French Protestants emigrated to New England).

become his guide. But the innkeeper turned his eyes to a written paper on the wall, which he read, or seemed to read, with occasional recurrences to the young man's figure.

"What have we here?" said he, breaking his speech into little dry fragments, " 'Left the house of the subscriber, bounden servant,[10] Hezekiah Mudge,—had on, when he went away, gray coat, leather breeches, master's third-best hat. One pound currency reward to whosoever shall lodge him in any jail of the providence.' Better trudge, boy; better trudge!"

Robin had begun to draw his hand towards the lighter end of the oak cudgel, but a strange hostility in every countenance induced him to relinquish his purpose of breaking the courteous innkeeper's head. As he turned to leave the room, he encountered a sneering glance from the bold-featured personage whom he had before noticed; and no sooner was he beyond the door, than he heard a general laugh, in which the innkeeper's voice might be distinguished, like the dropping of small stones into a kettle.

"Now, is it not strange," thought Robin, with his usual shrewdness,—"is it not strange that the confession of an empty pocket should outweigh the name of my kinsman, Major Molineux? Oh, if I had one of those grinning rascals in the woods, where I and my oak sapling grew up together, I would teach him that my arm is heavy though my purse be light!"

On turning the corner of the narrow lane, Robin found himself in a spacious street, with an unbroken line of lofty houses on each side, and a steepled building at the upper end, whence the ringing of a bell announced the hour of nine. The light of the moon, and the lamps from the numerous shop-windows, discovered people promenading on the pavement, and amongst them Robin had hoped to recognize his hitherto inscrutable relative. The result of his former inquiries made him unwilling to hazard another, in a scene of such publicity, and he determined to walk slowly and silently up the street, thrusting his face close to that of every elderly gentleman, in search of the Major's lineaments. In his progress, Robin encountered many gay and gallant figures. Embroidered garments of showy colors, enormous periwigs, gold-laced hats, and silver-hilted swords glided past him and dazzled his optics. Travelled youths, imitators of the European fine gentlemen of the period, trod jauntily along, half dancing to the fashionable tunes which they hummed, and making poor Robin ashamed of his quiet and natural gait. At length, after many pauses to examine the gorgeous display of goods in the shop-windows, and after suffering some rebukes for the impertinence of his scrutiny into people's faces, the Major's

10. An indentured servant, bound to serve his master for seven years before receiving his freedom.

kinsman found himself near the steepled building, still unsuccessful in his search. As yet, however, he had seen only one side of the thronged street; so Robin crossed, and continued the same sort of inquisition down the opposite pavement, with stronger hopes than the philosopher seeking an honest man, but with no better fortune. He had arrived about midway towards the lower end, from which his course began, when he overheard the approach of some one who struck down a cane on the flag-stones at every step, uttering at regular intervals, two sepulchral hems.

"Mercy on us!" quoth Robin, recognizing the sound.

Turning a corner, which chanced to be close at his right hand, he hastened to pursue his researches in some other part of the town. His patience now was wearing low, and he seemed to feel more fatigue from his rambles since he crossed the ferry, than from his journey of several days on the other side. Hunger also pleaded loudly within him, and Robin began to balance the propriety of demanding, violently, and with lifted cudgel, the necessary guidance from the first solitary passenger whom he should meet. While a resolution to this effect was gaining strength, he entered a street of mean appearance, on either side of which a row of ill-built houses was straggling towards the harbor. The moonlight fell upon no passenger along the whole extent, but in the third domicile which Robin passed there was a half-opened door, and his keen glance detected a woman's garment within.

"My luck may be better here," said he to himself.

Accordingly, he approached the door, and beheld it shut closer as he did so; yet an open space remained, sufficing for the fair occupant to observe the stranger, without a corresponding display on her part. All that Robin could discern was a strip of scarlet petticoat, and the occasional sparkle of an eye, as if the moonbeams were trembling on some bright thing.

"Pretty mistress," for I may call her so with a good conscience, thought the shrewd youth, since I know nothing to the contrary,— "my sweet pretty mistress, will you be kind enough to tell me whereabouts I must seek the dwelling of my kinsman, Major Molineux?"

Robin's voice was plaintive and winning, and the female, seeing nothing to be shunned in the handsome country youth, thrust open the door, and came forth into the moonlight. She was a dainty little figure, with a white neck, round arms, and a slender waist, at the extremity of which her scarlet petticoat jutted out over a hoop, as if she were standing in a balloon. Moreover, her face was oval and pretty, her hair dark beneath the little cap, and her bright eyes possessed a sly freedom, which triumphed over those of Robin.

"Major Molineux dwells here," said this fair woman.

Now, her voice was the sweetest Robin had heard that night, yet he could not help doubting whether that sweet voice spoke Gospel truth. He looked up and down the mean street, and then surveyed the house before which they stood. It was a small, dark edifice of two stories, the second of which projected over the lower floor, and the front apartment had the aspect of a shop for petty commodities.

"Now, truly, I am in luck," replied Robin, cunningly, "and so indeed is my kinsman, the Major, in having so pretty a house-keeper. But I prithee trouble him to step to the door; I will deliver him a message from his friends in the country, and then go back to my lodgings at the inn."

"Nay, the Major has been abed this hour or more," said the lady of the scarlet petticoat; "and it would be to little purpose to disturb him to-night, seeing his evening draught was of the strongest. But he is a kind-hearted man, and it would be as much as my life's worth to let a kinsman of his turn away from the door. You are the good old gentleman's very picture, and I could swear that was his rainy-weather hat. Also he has garments very much resembling those leather small-clothes. But come in, I pray, for I bid you hearty welcome in his name."

So saying, the fair and hospitable dame took our hero by the hand; and the touch was light, and the force was gentleness, and though Robin read in her eyes what he did not hear in her words, yet the slender-waisted woman in the scarlet petticoat proved stronger than the athletic country youth. She had drawn his half-willing footsteps nearly to the threshold, when the opening of a door in the neighborhood startled the Major's housekeeper, and, leaving the Major's kinsman, she vanished speedily into her own domicile. A heavy yawn preceded the appearance of a man, who, like the Moonshine of Pyramus and Thisbe,[11] carried a lantern, needlessly aiding his sister luminary in the heavens. As he walked sleepily up the street, he turned his broad, dull face on Robin, and displayed a long staff, spiked at the end.

"Home, vagabond, home!" said the watchman, in accents that seemed to fall asleep as soon as they were uttered. "Home, or we'll set you in the stocks by peep of day!"

"This is the second hint of the kind," thought Robin. "I wish they would end my difficulties, by setting me there to-night."

Nevertheless, the youth felt an instinctive antipathy towards the guardian of midnight order, which at first prevented him from asking his usual question. But just when the man was about to vanish

11. In the comic play of Pyramus and Thisbe which climaxes the subplot of Shakespeare's *A Midsummer Night's Dream*, Moonshine is represented by an actor with a lantern.

behind the corner, Robin resolved not to lose the opportunity, and shouted lustily after him,—

"I say, friend! will you guide me to the house of my kinsman, Major Molineux?"

The watchman made no reply, but turned the corner and was gone; yet Robin seemed to hear the sound of drowsy laughter stealing along the solitary street. At that moment, also, a pleasant titter saluted him from the open window above his head; he looked up, and caught the sparkle of a saucy eye; a round arm beckoned to him, and next he heard light footsteps descending the staircase within. But Robin, being of the household of a New England clergyman, was a good youth, as well as a shrewd one; so he resisted temptation, and fled away.

He now roamed desperately, and at random, through the town, almost ready to believe that a spell was on him, like that by which a wizard of his country had once kept three pursuers wandering, a whole winter night, within twenty paces of the cottage which they sought. The streets lay before him, strange and desolate, and the lights were extinguished in almost every house. Twice, however, little parties of men, among whom Robin distinguished individuals in outlandish attire, came hurrying along; but, though on both occasions, they paused to address him, such intercourse did not at all enlighten his perplexity. They did but utter a few words in some language of which Robin knew nothing, and perceiving his inability to answer, bestowed a curse upon him in plain English and hastened away. Finally, the lad determined to knock at the door of every mansion that might appear worthy to be occupied by his kinsman, trusting that perseverance would overcome the fatality that had hitherto thwarted him. Firm in this resolve, he was passing beneath the walls of a church, which formed the corner of two streets, when, as he turned into the shade of its steeple, he encountered a bulky stranger, muffled in a cloak. The man was proceeding with the speed of earnest business, but Robin planted himself full before him, holding the oak cudgel with both hands across his body as a bar to further passage.

"Halt, honest man, and answer me a question," said he, very resolutely. "Tell me, this instant, whereabouts is the dwelling of my kinsman, Major Molineux!"

"Keep your tongue between your teeth, fool, and let me pass!" said a deep, gruff voice, which Robin partly remembered. "Let me pass, or I'll strike you to the earth!"

"No, no, neighbor!" cried Robin, flourishing his cudgel, and then thrusting its larger end close to the man's muffled face. "No, no, I'm not the fool you take me for, nor do you pass till I have an answer to my question. Whereabouts is the dwelling of my kinsman, Major Molineux?"

The stranger, instead of attempting to force his passage, stepped back into the moonlight, unmuffled his face, and stared full into that of Robin.

"Watch here an hour, and Major Molineux will pass by," said he.

Robin gazed with dismay and astonishment on the unprecedented physiognomy of the speaker. The forehead with its double prominence, the broad hooked nose, the shaggy eyebrows, and fiery eyes were those which he had noticed at the inn, but the man's complexion had undergone a singular, or, more properly, a twofold change. One side of the face blazed an intense red, while the other was black as midnight, the division line being in the broad bridge of the nose; and a mouth which seemed to extend from ear to ear was black or red, in contrast to the color of the cheek. The effect was as if two individual devils, a fiend of fire and a fiend of darkness, had united themselves to form this infernal visage. The stranger grinned in Robin's face, muffled his party-colored features, and was out of sight in a moment.

"Strange things we travellers see!" ejaculated Robin.

He seated himself, however, upon the steps of the church-door, resolving to wait the appointed time for his kinsman. A few moments were consumed in philosophical speculations upon the species of man who had just left him; but having settled this point shrewdly, rationally, and satisfactorily, he was compelled to look elsewhere for his amusement. And first he threw his eyes along the street. It was of more respectable appearance than most of those into which he had wandered; and the moon, creating, like the imaginative power, a beautiful strangeness in familiar objects, gave something of romance to a scene that might not have possessed it in the light of day. The irregular and often quaint architecture of the houses, some of whose roofs were broken into numerous little peaks, while others ascended, steep and narrow, into a single point, and others again were square; the pure snow-white of some of their complexions, the aged darkness of others, and the thousand sparklings, reflected from bright substances in the walls of many; these matters engaged Robin's attention for a while, and then began to grow wearisome. Next he endeavored to define the forms of distant objects, starting away, with almost ghostly indistinctness, just as his eye appeared to grasp them; and finally he took a minute survey of an edifice which stood on the opposite side of the street, directly in front of the church-door, where he was stationed. It was a large, square mansion, distinguished from its neighbors by a balcony, which rested on tall pillars, and by an elaborate Gothic window, communicating therewith.

"Perhaps this is the very house I have been seeking," thought
Robin.

Then he strove to speed away the time, by listening to a murmur
which swept continually along the street, yet was scarcely audible,
except to an unaccustomed ear like his; it was a low, dull, dreamy
sound, compounded of many noises, each of which was at too great
a distance to be separately heard. Robin marvelled at this snore of a
sleeping town, and marvelled more whenever its continuity was
broken by now and then a distant shout, apparently loud where it
originated. But altogether it was a sleep-inspiring sound, and, to
shake off its drowsy influence, Robin arose, and climbed a window-
frame, that he might view the interior of the church. There the
moonbeams came trembling in, and fell down upon the deserted
pews, and extended along the quiet aisles. A fainter yet more awful
radiance was hovering around the pulpit, and one solitary ray had
dared to rest upon the open page of the great Bible. Had nature, in
that deep hour, become a worshipper in the house which man had
builded? Or was that heavenly light the visible sanctity of the
place,—visible because no earthly and impure feet were within the
walls? The scene made Robin's heart shiver with a sensation of
loneliness stronger than he had ever felt in the remotest depths of
his native woods; so he turned away and sat down again before the
door. There were graves around the church, and now an uneasy
thought obtruded into Robin's breast. What if the object of his
search, which had been so often and so strangely thwarted, were all
the time mouldering in his shroud? What if his kinsman should
glide through yonder gate, and nod and smile to him in dimly passing by?

"Oh that any breathing thing were here with me!" said Robin.

Recalling his thoughts from this uncomfortable track, he sent
them over forest, hill, and stream, and attempted to imagine how
that evening of ambiguity and weariness had been spent by his father's household. He pictured them assembled at the door, beneath
the tree, the great old tree, which had been spared for its huge
twisted trunk and venerable shade, when a thousand leafy brethren
fell. There, at the going down of the summer sun, it was his father's
custom to perform domestic worship, that the neighbors might
come and join with him like brothers of the family, and that the
wayfaring man might pause to drink at that fountain, and keep his
heart pure by freshening the memory of home. Robin distinguished
the seat of every individual of the little audience; he saw the good
man in the midst, holding the Scriptures in the golden light that fell
from the western clouds; he beheld him close the book and all rise
up to pray. He heard the old thanksgivings for daily mercies, the
old supplications for their continuance, to which he had so often lis-

tened in weariness, but which were now among his dear remembrances. He preceived the slight inequality of his father's voice when he came to speak of the absent one; he noted how his mother turned her face to the broad and knotted trunk; how his elder brother scorned, because the beard was rough upon his upper lip, to permit his features to be moved; how the younger sister drew down a low hanging branch before her eyes; and how the little one of all, whose sports had hitherto broken the decorum of the scene, understood the prayer for her playmate, and burst into clamorous grief. Then he saw them go in at the door; and when Robin would have entered also, the latch tinkled into its place, and he was excluded from his home.

"Am I here, or there?" cried Robin, starting; for all at once, when his thoughts had become visible and audible in a dream, the long, wide, solitary street shone out before him.

He aroused himself, and endeavored to fix his attention steadily upon the large edifice which he had surveyed before. But still his mind kept vibrating between fancy and reality; by turns, the pillars of the balcony lengthened into the tall, bare stems of pines, dwindled down to human figures, settled again into their true shape and size, and then commenced a new succession of changes. For a single moment, when he deemed himself awake, he could have sworn that a visage—one which he seemed to remember, yet could not absolutely name as his kinsman's—was looking towards him from the Gothic window. A deeper sleep wrestled with and nearly overcame him, but fled at the sound of footsteps along the opposite pavement. Robin rubbed his eyes, discerned a man passing at the foot of the balcony, and addressed him in a loud, peevish, and lamentable cry.

"Hallo, friend! must I wait here all night for my kinsman, Major Molineux?"

The sleeping echoes awoke, and answered the voice; and the passenger, barely able to discern a figure sitting in the oblique shade of the steeple, traversed the street to obtain a nearer view. He was himself a gentleman in his prime, of open, intelligent, cheerful, and altogether prepossessing countenance. Perceiving a country youth, apparently homeless and without friends, he accosted him in a tone of real kindness, which had become strange to Robin's ears.

"Well, my good lad, why are you sitting here?" inquired he. "Can I be of service to you in any way?"

"I am afraid not, sir," replied Robin, despondingly; "yet I shall take it kindly, if you'll answer me a single question. I've been searching, half the night, for one Major Molineux; now, sir, is there really such a person in these parts, or am I dreaming?"

"Major Molineux! The name is not altogether strange to me," said the gentleman, smiling. "Have you any objection to telling me the nature of your business with him?"

Then Robin briefly related that his father was a clergyman, settled on a small salary, at a long distance back in the country, and that he and Major Molineux were brothers' children. The Major, having inherited riches, and acquired civil and military rank, had visited his cousin, in great pomp, a year or two before; had manifested much interest in Robin and an elder brother, and, being childless himself, had thrown out hints respecting the future establishment of one of them in life. The elder brother was destined to succeed to the farm which his father cultivated in the interval of sacred duties; it was therefore determined that Robin should profit by his kinsman's generous intentions, especially as he seemed to be rather the favorite, and was thought to possess other necessary endowments.

"For I have the name of being a shrewd youth," observed Robin, in this part of his story.

"I doubt not you deserve it," replied his new friend, good-naturedly; "but pray proceed."

"Well, sir, being nearly eighteen years old, and well grown, as you see," continued Robin, drawing himself up to his full height, "I thought it high time to begin in the world. So my mother and sister put me in handsome trim, and my father gave me half the remnant of his last year's salary, and five days ago I started for this place, to pay the Major a visit. But, would you believe it, sir! I crossed the ferry a little after dark, and have yet found nobody that would show me the way to his dwelling; only, an hour or two since, I was told to wait here, and Major Molineux would pass by."

"Can you describe the man who told you this?" inquired the gentleman.

"Oh, he was a very ill-favored fellow, sir," replied Robin, "with two great bumps on his forehead, a hook nose, fiery eyes; and, what struck me as the strangest, his face was of two different colors. Do you happen to know such a man, sir?"

"Not intimately," answered the stranger, "but I chanced to meet him a little time previous to your stopping me. I believe you may trust his word, and that the Major will very shortly pass through this street. In the mean time, as I have a singular curiosity to witness your meeting, I will sit down here upon the steps and bear you company."

He seated himself accordingly, and soon engaged his companion in animated discourse. It was but a brief continuance, however, for a noise of shouting, which had long been remotely audible, drew so much nearer that Robin inquired its cause.

"What may be the meaning of this uproar?" asked he. "Truly, if your town be always as noisy, I shall find little sleep while I am an inhabitant."

"Why, indeed, friend Robin, there do appear to be three or four riotous fellows abroad to-night," replied the gentleman. "You must not expect all the stillness of your native woods here in our streets. But the watch will shortly be at the heels of these lads and"—

"Ay, and set them in the stocks by peep of day," interrupted Robin, recollecting his own encounter with the drowsy lantern-bearer. "But, dear sir, if I may trust my ears, an army of watchmen would never make head against such a multitude of rioters. There were at least a thousand voices went up to make that one shout."

"May not a man have several voices, Robin, as well as two complexions?" said his friend.

"Perhaps a man may; but Heaven forbid that a woman should!" responded the shrewd youth, thinking of the seductive tones of the Major's housekeeper.

The sounds of a trumpet in some neighboring street now became so evident and continual, that Robin's curiosity was strongly excited. In addition to the shouts, he heard frequent bursts from many instruments of discord, and a wild and confused laughter filled up the intervals. Robin rose from the steps, and looked wistfully towards a point whither people seemed to be hastening.

"Surely some prodigious merry-making is going on," exclaimed he. "I have laughed very little since I left home, sir, and should be sorry to lose an opportunity. Shall we step round the corner by that darkish house, and take our share of the fun?"

"Sit down again, sit down, good Robin," replied the gentleman, laying his hand on the skirt of the gray coat. "You forget that we must wait here for your kinsman; and there is reason to believe that he will pass by, in the course of a very few moments."

The near approach of the uproar had now disturbed the neighborhood; windows flew open on all sides; and many heads, in the attire of the pillow, and confused by sleep suddenly broken, were protruded to the gaze of whoever had leisure to observe them. Eager voices hailed each other from house to house, all demanding the explanation, which not a soul could give. Half-dressed men hurried towards the unknown commotion, stumbling as they went over the stone steps that thrust themselves into the narrow foot-walk. The shouts, the laughter, and the tuneless bray, the antipodes of music, came onwards with increasing din, till scattered individuals, and then denser bodies, began to appear round a corner at the distance of a hundred yards.

"Will you recognize your kinsman, if he passes in this crowd?" inquired the gentleman.

"Indeed, I can't warrant it, sir; but I'll take my stand here, and keep a bright lookout," answered Robin, descending to the outer edge of the pavement.

A mighty stream of people now emptied into the street, and came rolling slowly towards the church. A single horseman wheeled the corner in the midst of them, and close behind him came a band of fearful wind-instruments, sending forth a fresher discord now that no intervening buildings kept it from the ear. Then a redder light disturbed the moonbeams, and a dense multitude of torches shone along the street, concealing, by their glare, whatever object they illuminated. The single horseman, clad in a military dress, and bearing a drawn sword, rode onward as the leader, and, by his fierce and variegated countenance, appeared like war personified; the red of one cheek was an emblem of fire and sword; the blackness of the other betokened the mourning that attends them. In his train were wild figures in the Indian dress, and many fantastic shapes without a model, giving the whole march a visionary air, as if a dream had broken forth from some feverish brain, and were sweeping visibly through the midnight streets. A mass of people, inactive, except as applauding spectators, hemmed the procession in; and several women ran along the sidewalk, piercing the confusion of heavier sounds with their shrill voices of mirth or terror.

"The double-faced fellow has his eye upon me," muttered Robin, with an indefinite but an uncomfortable idea that he was himself to bear a part in the pageantry.

The leader turned himself in the saddle, and fixed his glance full upon the country youth, as the steed went slowly by. When Robin had freed his eyes from those fiery ones, the musicians were passing before him, and the torches were close at hand; but the unsteady brightness of the latter formed a veil which he could not penetrate. The rattling of wheels over the stones sometimes found its way to his ear, and confused traces of a human form appeared at intervals, and then melted into the vivid light. A moment more, and the leader thundered a command to halt: the trumpets vomited a horrid breath, and then held their peace; the shouts and laughter of the people died away, and there remained only a universal hum, allied to silence. Right before Robin's eyes was an uncovered cart. There the torches blazed the brightest, there the moon shone out like day, and there, in tar-and-feathery dignity, sat his kinsman, Major Molineux!

He was an elderly man, of large and majestic person, and strong, square features, betokening a steady soul; but steady as it was, his enemies had found means to shake it. His face was pale as death, and far more ghastly; the broad forehead was contracted in his agony, so that his eyebrows formed one grizzled line; his eyes were red and wild, and the foam hung white upon his quivering lip. His whole frame was agitated by a quick and continual tremor, which his pride strove to quell, even in those circumstances of overwhelming humiliation. But perhaps the bitterest pang of all was when his eyes met those of Robin; for he evidently knew him on the instant, as the youth stood witnessing the foul disgrace of a head grown gray in honor. They stared at each other in silence, and Robin's knees shook, and his hair bristled, with a mixture of pity and terror. Soon, however, a bewildering excitement began to seize upon his mind; the preceding adventures of the night, the unexpected appearance of the crowd, the torches, the confused din and the hush that followed, the spectre of his kinsman reviled by that great multitude,—all this, and, more than all, a perception of tremendous ridicule in the whole scene, affected him with a sort of mental inebriety. At that moment a voice of sluggish merriment saluted Robin's ears; he turned instinctively, and just behind the corner of the church stood the lantern-bearer, rubbing his eyes, and drowsily enjoying the lad's amazement. Then he heard a peal of laughter like the ringing of silvery bells; a woman twitched his arm, a saucy eye met his, and he saw the lady of the scarlet petticoat. A sharp, dry cachinnation appealed to his memory, and, standing on tiptoe in the crowd, with his white apron over his head, he beheld the courteous little innkeeper. And lastly, there sailed over the heads of the multitude a great, broad laugh, broken in the midst by two sepulchral hems; thus, "Haw, haw, haw,—hem, hem,—haw, haw, haw, haw!"

The sound proceeded from the balcony of the opposite edifice, and thither Robin turned his eyes. In front of the Gothic window stood the old citizen, wrapped in a wide gown, his gray periwig exchanged for a nightcap, which was thrust back from his forehead, and his silk stockings hanging about his legs. He supported himself on his polished cane in a fit of convulsive merriment, which manifested itself on his solemn old features like a funny inscription on a tombstone. Then Robin seemed to hear the voices of the barbers, of the guests of the inn, and of all who had made sport of him that night. The contagion was spreading among the multitude, when all at once, it seized upon Robin, and he sent forth a shout of laughter that echoed through the street,—every man shook his sides, every man emptied his lungs, but Robin's shout was the loudest there. The cloud-spirits peeped from their silvery islands, as the congregated mirth went roaring up the sky! The Man in the Moon heard the far bellow. "Oho," quoth he, "the old earth is frolicsome to-night!"

When there was a momentary calm in that tempestuous sea of sound, the leader gave the sign, the procession resumed its march. On they went, like fiends that throng in mockery around some dead

potentate, mighty no more, but majestic still in his agony. On they
went, in counterfeited pomp, in senseless uproar, in frenzied merriment, trampling all on an old man's heart. On swept the tumult, and
left a silent street behind.

"Well, Robin, are you dreaming?" inquired the gentleman, laying
his hand on the youth's shoulder.

Robin started, and withdrew his arm from the stone post to which
he had instinctively clung, as the living stream rolled by him. His
cheek was somewhat pale, and his eye not quite as lively as in the
earlier part of the evening.

"Will you be kind enough to show me the way to the ferry?" said
he, after a moment's pause.

"You have, then, adopted a new subject of inquiry?" observed his
companion, with a smile.

"Why, yes, sir," replied Robin, rather dryly. "Thanks to you, and
to my other friends, I have at last met my kinsman, and he will
scarce desire to see my face again. I begin to grow weary of a town
life, sir. Will you show me the way to the ferry?"

"No, my good friend Robin,—not to-night, at least," said the gentleman. "Some few days hence, if you wish it, I will speed you on
your journey. Or, if you prefer to remain with us, perhaps, as you
are a shrewd youth, you may rise in the world without the help of
your kinsman, Major Molineux."

From *The Snow-Image* (1852; first published in 1832)

YOUNG GOODMAN BROWN

Young Goodman Brown [1] came forth at sunset into the street at Salem village; but put his head back, after crossing the threshold, to exchange a parting kiss with his young wife. And Faith, as the wife was aptly named, thrust her own pretty head into the street, letting the wind play with the pink ribbons of her cap while she called to Goodman Brown.

"Dearest heart," whispered she, softly and rather sadly, when her lips were close to his ear, "prithee put off your journey until sunrise and sleep in your own bed to-night. A lone woman is troubled with such dreams and such thoughts that she's afeard of herself sometimes. Pray tarry with me this night, dear husband, of all nights in the year."

"My love and my Faith," replied young Goodman Brown, "of all nights in the year, this one night must I tarry away from thee. My journey, as thou callest it, forth and back again, must needs be done 'twixt now and sunrise. What, my sweet, pretty wife, dost thou doubt me already, and we but three months married?"

"Then God bless you!" said Faith, with the pink ribbons; "and may you find all well when you come back."

"Amen!" cried Goodman Brown. "Say thy prayers, dear Faith, and go to bed at dusk, and no harm will come to thee."

So they parted; and the young man pursued his way until, being about to turn the corner by the meeting-house, he looked back and saw the head of Faith still peeping after him with a melancholy air, in spite of her pink ribbons.

"Poor little Faith!" thought he, for his heart smote him. "What a wretch am I to leave her on such an errand! She talks of dreams, too. Methought as she spoke there was trouble in her face, as if a dream had warned her what work is to be done to-night. But no, no; 't would kill her to think it. Well, she's a blessed angel on earth; and after this one night I'll cling to her skirts and follow her to heaven."

With this excellent resolve for the future, Goodman Brown felt himself justified in making more haste on his present evil purpose. He had taken a dreary road, darkened by all the gloomiest trees of the forest, which barely stood aside to let the narrow path creep through, and closed immediately behind. It was all as lonely as could be; and there is this peculiarity in such a solitude, that the traveler knows not who may be concealed by the innumerable

---

1. The term "Goodman" refers to a man of substance but not of gentle birth or social standing. Hawthorne plays on its original form, "Good Man."

trunks and the thick boughs overhead; so that with lonely footsteps he may yet be passing through an unseen multitude.

"There may be a devilish Indian behind every tree," said Goodman Brown to himself; and he glanced fearfully behind him as he added, "What if the devil himself should be at my very elbow!"

His head being turned back, he passed a crook of the road, and, looking forward again, beheld the figure of a man, in grave and decent attire, seated at the foot of an old tree. He arose at Goodman Brown's approach and walked onward side by side with him.

"You are late, Goodman Brown," said he. "The clock of the Old South [2] was striking as I came through Boston, and that is full fifteen minutes agone."

"Faith kept me back a while," replied the young man, with a tremor in his voice, caused by the sudden appearance of his companion, though not wholly unexpected.

It was now deep dusk in the forest, and deepest in that part of it where these two were journeying. As nearly as could be discerned, the second traveler was about fifty years old, apparently in the same rank of life as Goodman Brown, and bearing a considerable resemblance to him, though perhaps more in expression than features. Still they might have been taken for father and son. And yet, though the elder person was as simply clad as the younger, and as simple in manner too, he had an indescribable air of one who knew the world, and who would not have felt abashed at the governor's dinner table or in King William's court,[3] were it possible that his affairs should call him thither. But the only thing about him that could be fixed upon as remarkable was his staff, which bore the likeness of a great black snake, so curiously wrought that it might almost be seen to twist and wriggle itself like a living serpent. This, of course, must have been an ocular deception, assisted by the uncertain light.

"Come, Goodman Brown," cried his fellow-traveler, "this is a dull pace for the beginning of a journey. Take my staff, if you are so soon weary."

"Friend," said the other, exchanging his slow pace for a full stop, "having kept covenant by meeting thee here, it is my purpose now to return whence I came. I have scruples touching the matter thou wot'st of."

"Sayest thou so?" replied he of the serpent, smiling apart. "Let us walk on, nevertheless, reasoning as we go; and if I convince thee not thou shalt turn back. We are but a little way in the forest yet."

"Too far! too far!" exclaimed the goodman, unconsciously resuming his walk. "My father never went into the woods on such an er-

2. A Boston church built in 1730. This is an anachronism, since the story is set in the 1690s.
3. William III, King of England from 1689 to 1702.

rand, nor his father before him. We have been a race of honest men and good Christians since the days of the martyrs; and shall I be the first of the name of Brown that ever took his path and kept"—

"Such company, thou wouldst say," observed the elder person, interpreting his pause. "Well said, Goodman Brown! I have been as well acquainted with your family as with ever a one among the Puritans; and that's no trifle to say. I helped your grandfather, the constable, when he lashed the Quaker woman so smartly through the streets of Salem; and it was I that brought your father a pitch-pine knot, kindled at my own hearth, to set fire to an Indian village, in King Philip's war.[4] They were my good friends, both; and many a pleasant walk have we had along this path, and returned merrily after midnight. I would fain be friends with you for their sake."

"If it be as thou sayest," replied Goodman Brown, "I marvel they never spoke of these matters; or, verily, I marvel not, seeing that the least rumor of the sort would have driven them from New England. We are a people of prayer, and good works to boot, and abide no such wickedness."

"Wickedness or not," said the traveler with the twisted staff, "I have a very general acquaintance here in New England. The deacons of many a church have drunk the communion wine with me; the selectmen of divers towns make me their chairman; and a majority of the Great and General Court[5] are firm supporters of my interest. The governor and I, too— But these are state secrets."

"Can this be so?" cried Goodman Brown, with a stare of amazement at his undisturbed companion. "Howbeit, I have nothing to do with the governor and council; they have their own ways, and are no rule for a simple husbandman like me. But, were I to go on with thee, how should I meet the eye of that good old man, our minister, at Salem village? Oh, his voice would make me tremble both Sabbath day and lecture day."[6]

Thus far the elder traveler had listened with due gravity; but now burst into a fit of irrepressible mirth, shaking himself so violently that his snake-like staff actually seemed to wriggle in sympathy.

"Ha! ha! ha!" shouted he again and again; then composing himself, "Well, go on, Goodman Brown, go on; but, prithee, don't kill me with laughing."

"Well, then, to end the matter at once," said Goodman Brown, considerably nettled, "there is my wife, Faith. It would break her dear little heart; and I'd rather break my own."

"Nay, if that be the case," answered the other, "e'en go thy ways,

---

4. King Philip (also called Metacomet) led the last Indian uprising against the white man in southern New England. He was defeated and killed in 1676.
5. The colonial legislature of Massachusetts.
6. Thursday, the usual day for the midweek sermon.

Goodman Brown. I would not for twenty old women like the one hobbling before us that Faith should come to any harm."

As he spoke he pointed his staff at a female figure on the path, in whom Goodman Brown recognized a very pious and exemplary dame, who had taught him his catechism in youth, and was still his moral and spiritual adviser, jointly with the minister and Deacon Gookin.

"A marvel, truly, that Goody Cloyse [7] should be so far in the wilderness at nightfall," said he. "But with your leave, friend, I shall take a cut through the woods until we have left this Christian woman behind. Being a stranger to you, she might ask whom I was consorting with and whither I was going."

"Be it so," said his fellow-traveler. "Betake you the woods, and let me keep the path."

Accordingly the young man turned aside, but took care to watch his companion, who advanced softly along the road until he had come within a staff's length of the old dame. She, meanwhile, was making the best of her way, with singular speed for so aged a woman, and mumbling some indistinct words—a prayer, doubtless—as she went. The traveler put forth his staff and touched her withered neck with what seemed the serpent's tail.

"The devil!" screamed the pious old lady.

"Then Goody Cloyse knows her old friend?" observed the traveler, confronting her and leaning on his writhing stick.

"Ah, forsooth, and is it your worship indeed?" cried the good dame. "Yea, truly is it, and in the very image of my old gossip, Goodman Brown, the grandfather of the silly fellow that now is. But—would your worship believe it?—my broomstick hath strangely disappeared, stolen, as I suspect, by that unhanged witch, Goody Cory, and that, too, when I was all anointed with the juice of smallage, and cinquefoil, and wolf's bane"—[8]

"Mingled with fine wheat and the fat of a new-born babe," said the shape of old Goodman Brown.

"Ah, your worship knows the recipe," cried the old lady, cackling aloud. "So, as I was saying, being all ready for the meeting, and no horse to ride on, I made up my mind to foot it; for they tell me there is a nice young man to be taken into communion to-night. But now your good worship will lend me your arm, and we shall be there in a twinkling."

"That can hardly be," answered her friend. "I may not spare you my arm, Goody Cloyse; but here is my staff, if you will."

7. Goody Cloyse and Goody Cory were historical figures who (along with Martha Carrier) were sentenced to death for witchcraft in 1692 by a court that included Hawthorne's great-great-grandfather. "Goody" is a contraction of "Goodwife."
8. Plants believed to have magical power against evil.

So saying, he threw it down at her feet, where, perhaps, it assumed life, being one of the rods which its owner had formerly lent to the Egyptian magi.[9] Of this fact, however, Goodman Brown could not take cognizance. He had cast up his eyes in astonishment, and, looking down again, beheld neither Goody Cloyse nor the serpentine staff, but this fellow-traveler alone, who waited for him as calmly as if nothing had happened.

"That old woman taught me my catechism," said the young man; and there was a world of meaning in this simple comment.

They continued to walk onward, while the elder traveler exhorted his companion to make good speed and persevere in the path, discoursing so aptly that his arguments seemed rather to spring up in the bosom of his auditor than to be suggested by himself. As they went, he plucked a branch of maple to serve for a walking stick, and began to strip it of the twigs and little boughs, which were wet with evening dew. The moment his fingers touched them they became strangely withered and dried up as with a week's sunshine. Thus the pair proceeded, at a good free pace, until suddenly, in a gloomy hollow of the road, Goodman Brown sat himself down on the stump of a tree and refused to go any farther.

"Friend," said he, stubbornly, "my mind is made up. Not another step will I budge on this errand. What if a wretched old woman do choose to go to the devil when I thought she was going to heaven: is that any reason why I should quit my dear Faith and go after her?"

"You will think better of this by and by," said his acquaintance, composedly. "Sit here and rest yourself a while; and when you feel like moving again, there is my staff to help you along."

Without more words, he threw his companion the maple stick, and was as speedily out of sight as if he had vanished into the deepening gloom. The young man sat a few moments by the roadside, applauding himself greatly, and thinking with how clear a conscience he should meet the minister in his morning walk, nor shrink from the eye of good old Deacon Gookin. And what calm sleep would be his that very night, which was to have been spent so wickedly, but so purely and sweetly now, in the arms of Faith! Amidst these pleasant and praiseworthy meditations, Goodman Brown heard the tramp of horses along the road, and deemed it advisable to conceal himself within the verge of the forest, conscious

9. The reference is to the biblical story of Aaron's rod (Exodus 7). "And Moses and Aaron went in unto Pharaoh, and they did so as the Lord had commanded: and Aaron cast down his rod before Pharaoh, and before his servants, and it became a serpent. Then Pharaoh also called the wise men [magi] and the sorcerers: now the magicians of Egypt, they also did in like manner with their enchantments. For they cast down every man his rod, and they became serpents: but Aaron's rod swallowed up their rods."

of the guilty purpose that had brought him thither, though now so happily turned from it.

On came the hoof tramps and the voices of the riders, two grave old voices, conversing soberly as they drew near. These mingled sounds appeared to pass along the road, within a few yards of the young man's hiding-place; but, owing doubtless to the depth of the gloom at that particular spot, neither the travelers nor their steeds were visible. Though their figures brushed the small boughs by the wayside, it could not be seen that they intercepted, even for a moment, the faint gleam from the strip of bright sky athwart which they must have passed. Goodman Brown alternately crouched and stood on tiptoe, pulling aside the branches and thrusting forth his head as far as he durst without discerning so much as a shadow. It vexed him the more, because he could have sworn, were such a thing possible, that he recognized the voices of the minister and Deacon Gookin, jogging along quietly, as they were wont to do, when bound to some ordination or ecclesiastical council. While yet within hearing, one of the riders stopped to pluck a switch.

"Of the two, reverend sir," said the voice like the deacon's, "I had rather miss an ordination dinner than to-night's meeting. They tell me that some of our community are to be here from Falmouth and beyond, and others from Connecticut and Rhode Island, besides several of the Indian powwows, who, after their fashion, know almost as much deviltry as the best of us. Moreover, there is a goodly young woman to be taken into communion."

"Mighty well, Deacon Gookin!" replied the solemn old tones of the minister. "Spur up, or we shall be late. Nothing can be done, you know, until I get on the ground."

The hoofs clattered again; and the voices, talking so strangely in the empty air, passed on through the forest, where no church had ever been gathered or solitary Christian prayed. Whither, then, could these holy men be journeying so deep into the heathen wilderness? Young Goodman Brown caught hold of a tree for support, being ready to sink down on the ground, faint and overburdened with the heavy sickness of his heart. He looked up to the sky, doubting whether there really was a heaven above him. Yet there was the blue arch, and the stars brightening in it.

"With heaven above and Faith below, I will yet stand firm against the devil!" cried Goodman Brown.

While he still gazed upward into the deep arch of the firmament and had lifted his hands to pray, a cloud, though no wind was stirring, hurried across the zenith and hid the brightening stars. The blue sky was still visible, except directly overhead, where this black mass of cloud was sweeping swiftly northward. Aloft in the air, as if from the depths of the cloud, came a confused and doubtful sound of voices. Once the listener fancied that he could distinguish the accents of towns-people of his own, men and women, both pious and ungodly, many of whom he had met at the communion table, and had seen others rioting at the tavern. The next moment, so indistinct were the sounds, he doubted whether he had heard aught but the murmur of the old forest, whispering without a wind. Then came a stronger swell of those familiar tones, heard daily in the sunshine at Salem village, but never until now from a cloud of night. There was one voice, of a young woman, uttering lamentations, yet with an uncertain sorrow, and entreating for some favor, which, perhaps, it would grieve her to obtain; and all the unseen multitude, both saints and sinners, seemed to encourage her onward.

"Faith!" shouted Goodman Brown, in a voice of agony and desperation; and the echoes of the forest mocked him, crying, "Faith! Faith!" as if bewildered wretches were seeking her all through the wilderness.

The cry of grief, rage, and terror was yet piercing the night, when the unhappy husband held his breath for a response. There was a scream, drowned immediately in a louder murmur of voices, fading into far-off laughter, as the dark cloud swept away, leaving the clear and silent sky above Goodman Brown. But something fluttered lightly down through the air and caught on the branch of a tree. The young man seized it, and beheld a pink ribbon.

"My Faith is gone!" cried he, after one stupefied moment. "There is no good on earth; and sin is but a name. Come, devil; for to thee is this world given."

And, maddened with despair, so that he laughed loud and long, did Goodman Brown grasp his staff and set forth again, at such a rate that he seemed to fly along the forest path rather than to walk or run. The road grew wilder and drearier and more faintly traced, and vanished at length, leaving him in the heart of the dark wilderness, still rushing onward with the instinct that guides mortal man to evil. The whole forest was peopled with frightful sounds—the creaking of the trees, the howling of wild beasts, and the yell of Indians; while sometimes the wind tolled like a distant church bell, and sometimes gave a broad roar around the traveler, as if all Nature were laughing him to scorn. But he was himself the chief horror of the scene, and shrank not from its other horrors.

"Ha! ha! ha!" roared Goodman Brown when the wind laughed at him. "Let us hear which will laugh loudest. Think not to frighten me with your deviltry. Come witch, come wizard, come Indian powwow, come devil himself, and here comes Goodman Brown. You may as well fear him as he fear you."

In truth, all through the haunted forest there could be nothing

more frightful than the figure of Goodman Brown. On he flew
among the black pines, brandishing his staff with frenzied gestures,
now giving vent to an inspiration of horrid blasphemy, and now
shouting forth such laughter as set all the echoes of the forest laughing like demons around him. The fiend in his own shape is less hideous than when he rages in the breast of man. Thus sped the de-
moniac on his course, until, quivering among the trees, he saw a
red light before him, as when the felled trunks and branches of a
clearing have been set on fire, and throw up their lurid blaze
against the sky, at the hour of midnight. He paused, in a lull of the
tempest that had driven him onward, and heard the swell of what
seemed a hymn, rolling solemnly from a distance with the weight of
many voices. He knew the tune; it was a familiar one in the choir of
the village meeting-house. The verse died heavily away, and was
lengthened by a chorus, not of human voices, but of all the sounds
of the benighted wilderness pealing in awful harmony together.
Goodman Brown cried out, and his cry was lost to his own ear by its
unison with the cry of the desert.

In the interval of silence he stole forward until the light glared
full upon his eyes. At one extremity of an open space, hemmed in
by the dark wall of the forest, arose a rock, bearing some rude, natural resemblance either to an altar or a pulpit, and surrounded by
four blazing pines, their tops aflame, their stems untouched, like
candles at an evening meeting. The mass of foliage that had overgrown the summit of the rock was all on fire, blazing high into the
night and fitfully illuminating the whole field. Each pendent twig
and leafy festoon was in a blaze. As the red light arose and fell, a
numerous congregation alternately shone forth, then disappeared in
shadow, and again grew, as it were, out of the darkness, peopling
the heart of the solitary woods at once.

"A grave and dark-clad company," quoth Goodman Brown.

In truth they were such. Among them, quivering to and fro between gloom and splendor, appeared faces that would be seen next
day at the council board of the province, and others which, Sabbath
after Sabbath, looked devoutly heavenward, and benignantly over
the crowded pews, from the holiest pulpits in the land. Some affirm
that the lady of the governor was there. At least there were high
dames well known to her, and wives of honored husbands, and
widows, a great multitude, and ancient maidens, all of excellent
repute, and fair young girls, who trembled lest their mothers should
espy them. Either the sudden gleams of light flashing over the obscure field bedazzled Goodman Brown, or he recognized a score of
the church members of Salem village famous for their especial
sanctity. Good old Deacon Gookin had arrived, and waited at the
skirts of that venerable saint, his revered pastor. But, irreverently

consorting with these grave, reputable, and pious people, these elders of the church, these chaste dames and dewy virgins, there were men of dissolute lives and women of spotted fame, wretches given over to all mean and filthy vice, and suspected even of horrid crimes. It was strange to see that the good shrank not from the wicked, nor were the sinners abashed by the saints. Scattered also among their pale-faced enemies were the Indian priests, or pow-wows, who had often scared their native forest with more hideous incantations than any known to English witchcraft.

"But where is Faith?" thought Goodman Brown; and, as hope came into his heart, he trembled.

Another verse of the hymn arose, a slow and mournful strain, such as the pious love, but joined to words which expressed all that our nature can conceive of sin, and darkly hinted at far more. Unfathomable to mere mortals is the lore of fiends. Verse after verse was sung; and still the chorus of the desert swelled between like the deepest tone of a mighty organ; and with the final peal of that dreadful anthem there came a sound, as if the roaring wind, the rushing streams, the howling beasts, and every other voice of the unconcerted wilderness were mingling and according with the voice of guilty man in homage to the prince of all. The four blazing pines threw up a loftier flame, and obscurely discovered shapes and visages of horror on the smoke wreaths above the impious assembly. At the same moment the fire on the rock shot redly forth and formed a glowing arch above its base, where now appeared a figure. With reverence be it spoken, the figure bore no slight similitude, both in garb and manner, to some grave divine of the New England churches.

"Bring forth the converts!" cried a voice that echoed through the field and rolled into the forest.

At the word, Goodman Brown stepped forth from the shadow of the trees and approached the congregation, with whom he felt a loathful brotherhood by the sympathy of all that was wicked in his heart. He could have well-nigh sworn that the shape of his own dead father beckoned him to advance, looking downward from a smoke wreath, while a woman, with dim features of despair, threw out her hand to warn him back. Was it his mother? But he had no power to retreat one step, nor to resist, even in thought, when the minister and good old Deacon Gookin seized his arms and led him to the blazing rock. Thither came also the slender form of a veiled female, led between Goody Cloyse, that pious teacher of the catechism, and Martha Carrier,[10] who had received the devil's promise

10. See note 7.

to be queen of hell. A rampant hag was she. And there stood the proselytes beneath the canopy of fire.

"Welcome, my children," said the dark figure, "to the communion of your race. Ye have found thus young your nature and your destiny. My children, look behind you!"

They turned; and flashing forth, as it were, in a sheet of flame, the fiend worshippers were seen; the smile of welcome gleamed darkly on every visage.

"There," resumed the sable form, "are all whom ye have reverenced from youth. Ye deemed them holier than yourselves, and shrank from your own sin, contrasting it with their lives of righteousness and prayerful aspirations heavenward. Yet here are they all in my worshipping assembly. This night it shall be granted you to know their secret deeds: how hoary-bearded elders of the church have whispered wanton words to the young maids of their households; how many a woman, eager for widows' weeds, has given her husband a drink at bedtime and let him sleep his last sleep in her bosom; how beardless youths have made haste to inherit their fathers' wealth; and how fair damsels—blush not, sweet ones—have dug little graves in the garden, and bidden me, the sole guest, to an infant's funeral. By the sympathy of your human hearts for sin ye shall scent out all the places—whether in church, bed-chamber, street, field, or forest—where crime has been committed, and shall exult to behold the whole earth one stain of guilt, one mighty blood spot. Far more than this. It shall be yours to penetrate, in every bosom, the deep mystery of sin, the fountain of all wicked arts, and which inexhaustibly supplies more evil impulses than human power—than my power at its utmost—can make manifest in deeds. And now, my children, look upon each other."

They did so; and, by the blaze of the hell-kindled torches, the wretched man beheld his Faith, and the wife her husband, trembling before that unhallowed altar.

"Lo, there ye stand, my children," said the figure, in a deep and solemn tone, almost sad with its despairing awfulness, as if his once angelic nature could yet mourn for our miserable race. "Depending upon one another's hearts, ye had still hoped that virtue were not all a dream. Now are ye undeceived. Evil is the nature of mankind. Evil must be your only happiness. Welcome again, my children, to the communion of your race."

"Welcome," repeated the fiend worshippers, in one cry of despair and triumph.

And there they stood, the only pair, as it seemed, who were yet hesitating on the verge of wickedness in this dark world. A basin was hollowed, naturally, in the rock. Did it contain water, reddened by the lurid light? or was it blood? or, perchance, a liquid flame? Herein did the shape of evil dip his hand and prepare to lay the mark of baptism upon their foreheads, that they might be partakers of the mystery of sin, more conscious of the secret guilt of others, both in deed and thought, than they could now be of their own. The husband cast one look at his pale wife, and Faith at him. What polluted wretches would the next glance show them to each other, shuddering alike at what they disclosed and what they saw!

"Faith! Faith!" cried the husband, "look up to heaven, and resist the wicked one."

Whether Faith obeyed he knew not. Hardly had he spoken when he found himself amid calm night and solitude, listening to a roar of the wind which died heavily away through the forest. He staggered against the rock, and felt it chill and damp; while a hanging twig, that had been all on fire, besprinkled his cheek with the coldest dew.

The next morning young Goodman Brown came slowly into the street of Salem village, staring around him like a bewildered man. The good old minister was taking a walk along the graveyard to get an appetite for breakfast and meditate his sermon, and bestowed a blessing, as he passed, on Goodman Brown. He shrank from the venerable saint as if to avoid an anathema. Old Deacon Gookin was at domestic worship, and the holy words of his prayer were heard through the open window. "What God doth the wizard pray to?" quoth Goodman Brown. Goody Cloyse, that excellent old Christian, stood in the early sunshine at her own lattice, catechizing a little girl who had brought her a pint of morning's milk. Goodman Brown snatched away the child as from the grasp of the fiend himself. Turning the corner by the meeting-house, he spied the head of Faith, with the pink ribbons, gazing anxiously forth, and bursting into such joy at sight of him that she skipped along the street and almost kissed her husband before the whole village. But Goodman Brown looked sternly and sadly into her face, and passed on without a greeting.

Had Goodman Brown fallen asleep in the forest and only dreamed a wild dream of a witch-meeting?

Be it so if you will; but, alas! it was a dream of evil omen for young Goodman Brown. A stern, a sad, a darkly meditative, a distrustful, if not a desperate man did he become from the night of that fearful dream. On the Sabbath day, when the congregation were singing a holy psalm, he could not listen because an anthem of sin rushed loudly upon his ear and drowned all the blessed strain. When the minister spoke from the pulpit with power and fervid eloquence, and, with his hand on the open Bible, of the sacred truths of our religion, and of saint-like lives and triumphant deaths, and of future bliss or misery unutterable, then did Goodman Brown turn pale, dreading lest the roof should thunder down upon the gray blasphemer and his hearers. Often, awaking suddenly at midnight, he shrank from the bosom of Faith; and at morning or eventide, when the family knelt down at prayer, he scowled and muttered to himself, and gazed sternly at his wife, and turned away. And when he had lived long, and was borne to his grave a hoary corpse, followed by Faith, an aged woman, and children and grandchildren, a goodly procession, besides neighbors not a few, they carved no hopeful verse upon his tombstone, for his dying hour was gloom.

From *Mosses from an Old Manse* (1846; first published in 1835)

WAKEFIELD

In some old magazine or newspaper I recollect a story, told as truth, of a man—let us call him Wakefield—who absented himself for a long time from his wife. The fact, thus abstractedly stated, is not very uncommon, nor—without a proper distinction of circumstances—to be condemned either as naughty or nonsensical. Howbeit, this, though far from the most aggravated, is perhaps the strangest, instance on record, of marital delinquency; and, moreover, as remarkable a freak as may be found in the whole list of human oddities. The wedded couple lived in London. The man, under pretence of going a journey, took lodgings in the next street to his own house, and there, unheard of by his wife or friends, and without the shadow of a reason for such self-banishment, dwelt upwards of twenty years. During that period, he beheld his home every day, and frequently the forlorn Mrs. Wakefield. And after so great a gap in his matrimonial felicity—when his death was reckoned certain, his estate settled, his name dismissed from memory, and his wife, long, long ago, resigned to her autumnal widowhood—he entered the door one evening, quietly, as from a day's absence, and became a loving spouse till death.

This outline is all that I remember. But the incident, though of the purest originality, unexampled, and probably never to be repeated, is one, I think, which appeals to the generous sympathies of mankind. We know, each for himself, that none of us would perpetrate such a folly, yet feel as if some other might. To my own contemplations, at least, it has often recurred, always exciting wonder, but with a sense that the story must be true, and a conception of its hero's character. Whenever any subject so forcibly affects the mind, time is well spent in thinking of it. If the reader choose, let him do his own meditation; or if he prefer to ramble with me through the twenty years of Wakefield's vagary, I bid him welcome; trusting that there will be a pervading spirit and a moral, even should we fail to find them, done up neatly, and condensed into the final sentence. Thought has always its efficacy, and every striking incident its moral.

What sort of a man was Wakefield? We are free to shape out our own idea, and call it by his name. He was now in the meridian of life; his matrimonial affections, never violent, were sobered into a calm, habitual sentiment; of all husbands, he was likely to be the most constant, because a certain sluggishness would keep his heart at rest, wherever it might be placed. He was intellectual, but not actively so; his mind occupied itself in long and lazy musings, that ended to no purpose, or had not vigor to attain it; his thoughts were seldom so energetic as to seize hold of words. Imagination, in the proper meaning of the term, made no part of Wakefield's gifts. With a cold but not depraved nor wandering heart, and a mind never feverish with riotous thoughts, nor perplexed with originality, who could have anticipated that our friend would entitle himself to a foremost place among the doers of eccentric deeds? Had his acquaintances been asked, who was the man in London the surest to perform nothing to-day which should be remembered on the morrow, they would have thought of Wakefield. Only the wife of his bosom might have hesitated. She, without having analyzed his character, was partly aware of a quiet selfishness, that had rusted into his inactive mind; of a peculiar sort of vanity, the most uneasy attribute about him; of a disposition to craft, which had seldom produced more positive effects than the keeping of petty secrets, hardly worth revealing; and, lastly, of what she called a little strangeness, sometimes, in the good man. This latter quality is indefinable, and perhaps non-existent.

Let us now imagine Wakefield bidding adieu to his wife. It is the dusk of an October evening. His equipment is a drab great-coat, a hat covered with an oilcloth, top-boots, an umbrella in one hand and a small portmanteau in the other. He has informed Mrs. Wakefield that he is to take the night coach into the country. She would fain inquire the length of his journey, its object, and the probable time of his return; but, indulgent to his harmless love of mystery, interrogates him only by a look. He tells her not to expect him positively by the return coach, nor to be alarmed should he tarry three or four days; but, at all events, to look for him at supper on Friday evening. Wakefield himself, be it considered, has no suspicion of what is before him. He holds out his hand, she gives her own, and meets his parting kiss in the matter-of-course way of a ten years' matrimony; and forth goes the middle-aged Mr. Wakefield, almost resolved to perplex his good lady by a whole week's absence. After the door has closed behind him, she perceives it thrust partly open, and a vision of her husband's face, through the aperture, smiling on her, and gone in a moment. For the time, this little incident is dismissed without a thought. But, long afterwards, when she has been more years a widow than a wife, that smile recurs, and flickers across all her reminiscences of Wakefield's visage. In her many musings, she surrounds the original smile with a multitude of fantasies, which make it strange and awful: as, for instance, if she imagines him in a coffin, that parting look is frozen on his pale features; or, if she dreams of him in heaven, still his blessed spirit wears a quiet and crafty smile. Yet, for its sake, when all others have given him up for dead, she sometimes doubts whether she is a widow.

But our business is with the husband. We must hurry after him along the street, ere he lose his individuality, and melt into the great mass of London life. It would be vain searching for him there. Let us follow close at his heels, therefore, until, after several super-fluous turns and doublings, we find him comfortably established by the fireside of a small apartment, previously bespoken. He is in the next street to his own, and at his journey's end. He can scarcely trust his good fortune, in having got thither unperceived—recollect-ing that, at one time, he was delayed by the throng, in the very focus of a lighted lantern; and, again, there were footsteps that seemed to tread behind his own, distinct from the multitudinous tramp around him; and, anon, he heard a voice shouting afar, and fancied that it called his name. Doubtless, a dozen busybodies had been watching him, and told his wife the whole affair. Poor Wake-field! Little knowest thou thine own insignificance in this great world! No mortal eye but mine has traced thee. Go quietly to thy bed, foolish man; and, on the morrow, if thou wilt be wise, get thee home to good Mrs. Wakefield, and tell her the truth. Remove not thyself, even for a little week, from thy place in her chaste bosom. Were she, for a single moment, to deem thee dead, or lost, or last-ingly divided from her, thou wouldst be wofully conscious of a change in thy true wife forever after. It is perilous to make a chasm in human affections; not that they gape so long and wide—but so quickly close again!

Almost repenting of his frolic, or whatever it may be termed, Wakefield lies down betimes, and starting from his first nap, spreads forth his arms into the wide and solitary waste of the unac-customed bed. "No,"—thinks he, gathering the bedclothes about him,—"I will not sleep alone another night."

In the morning he rises earlier than usual, and sets himself to consider what he really means to do. Such are his loose and ram-bling modes of thought that he has taken this very singular step with the consciousness of a purpose, indeed, but without being able to define it sufficiently for his own contemplation. The vagueness of the project, and the convulsive effort with which he plunges into the execution of it, are equally characteristic of a feeble-minded man. Wakefield sifts his ideas, however, as minutely as he may, and finds himself curious to know the progress of mat-ters at home—how his exemplary wife will endure her widowhood of a week; and, briefly, how the little sphere of creatures and cir-cumstances, in which he was a central object, will be affected by his removal. A morbid vanity, therefore, lies nearest the bottom of the affair. But, how is he to attain his ends? Not, certainly, by keep-ing close in this comfortable lodging, where, though he slept and awoke in the next street to his home, he is as effectually abroad as if the stage-coach had been whirling him away all night. Yet, should he reappear, the whole project is knocked in the head. His poor brains being hopelessly puzzled with this dilemma, he at length ventures out, partly resolving to cross the head of the street, and send one hasty glance towards his forsaken domicile. Habit—for he is a man of habits—takes him by the hand, and guides him, wholly unaware, to his own door, where, just at the critical moment, he is aroused by the scraping of his foot upon the step. Wakefield! whither are you going?

At that instant his fate was turning on the pivot. Little dreaming of the doom to which his first backward step devotes him, he hurries away, breathless with agitation hitherto unfelt, and hardly dares turn his head at the distant corner. Can it be that nobody caught sight of him? Will not the whole household—the decent Mrs. Wakefield, the smart maid servant, and the dirty little footboy—raise a hue and cry, through London streets, in pursuit of their fugitive lord and master? Wonderful escape! He gathers courage to pause and look homeward, but is perplexed with a sense of change about the familiar edifice, such as affects us all, when, after a separation of months or years, we again see some hill or lake, or work of art, with which we were friends of old. In ordinary cases, this indescribable impression is caused by the comparison and contrast between our imperfect reminiscences and the reality. In Wakefield, the magic of a single night has wrought a similar transformation, because, in that brief period, a great moral change has been effected. But this is a secret from himself. Before leaving the spot, he catches a far and momentary glimpse of his wife, passing athwart the front window, with her face turned towards the head of the street. The crafty nincompoop takes to his heels, scared with the idea that, among a thousand such atoms of mortality, her eye must have detected him. Right glad is his heart, though his brain be somewhat dizzy, when he finds himself by the coal fire of his lodgings.

So much for the commencement of this long whim-wham. After the initial conception, and the stirring up of the man's sluggish temperament to put it in practice, the whole matter evolves itself in a natural train. We may suppose him, as the result of deep deliberation, buying a new wig, of reddish hair, and selecting sundry garments, in a fashion unlike his customary suit of brown, from a Jew's old-clothes bag. It is accomplished. Wakefield is another man. The new system being now established, a retrograde movement to the old would be almost as difficult as the step that placed him in his unparalleled position. Furthermore, he is rendered obstinate by a sulkiness occasionally incident to his temper, and brought on at present by the inadequate sensation which he conceives to have been produced in the bosom of Mrs. Wakefield. He will not go back until she be frightened half to death. Well; twice or thrice has she passed before his sight, each time with a heavier step, a paler cheek, and more anxious brow; and in the third week of his non-appearance he detects a portent of evil entering the house, in the guise of an apothecary. Next day the knocker is muffled. Towards nightfall comes the chariot of a physician, and deposits its big-wigged and solemn burden at Wakefield's door, whence, after a quarter of an hour's visit, he emerges, perchance the herald of a funeral. Dear woman! Will she die? By this time, Wakefield is excited to something like energy of feeling, but still lingers away from his wife's bedside, pleading with his conscience that she must not be disturbed at such a juncture. If aught else restrains him, he does not know it. In the course of a few weeks she gradually recovers; the crisis is over; her heart is sad, perhaps, but quiet; and, let him return soon or late, it will never be feverish for him again. Such ideas glimmer through the mist of Wakefield's mind, and render him indistinctly conscious that an almost impassable gulf divides his hired apartment from his former home. "It is but in the next street!" he sometimes says. Fool! it is in another world. Hitherto, he has put off his return from one particular day to another; henceforward, he leaves the precise time undetermined. Not to-morrow—probably next week—pretty soon. Poor man! The dead have nearly as much chance of revisiting their earthly homes as the self-banished Wakefield.

Would that I had a folio [1] to write, instead of an article of a dozen pages! Then might I exemplify how an influence beyond our control lays its strong hand on every deed which we do, and weaves its consequences into an iron tissue of necessity. Wakefield is spellbound. We must leave him, for ten years or so, to haunt around his house, without once crossing the threshold, and to be faithful to his wife, with all the affection of which his heart is capable, while he is slowly fading out of hers. Long since, it must be remarked, he had lost the perception of singularity in his conduct.

Now for a scene! Amid the throng of a London street we distinguish a man, now waxing elderly, with few characteristics to attract careless observers, yet bearing, in his whole aspect, the handwriting of no common fate, for such as have the skill to read it. He is meagre; his low and narrow forehead is deeply wrinkled; his eyes, small and lustreless, sometimes wander apprehensively about him, but oftener seem to look inward. He bends his head, and moves with an indescribable obliquity of gait, as if unwilling to display his full front to the world. Watch him long enough to see what we have described, and you will allow that circumstances—which often pro-

1. A book of the largest size.

duce remarkable men from nature's ordinary handiwork—have produced one such here. Next, leaving him to sidle along the footwalk, cast your eyes in the opposite direction, where a portly female, considerably in the wane of life, with a prayer-book in her hand, is proceeding to yonder church. She has the placid mien of settled widowhood. Her regrets have either died away, or have become so essential to her heart, that they would be poorly exchanged for joy. Just as the lean man and well-conditioned woman are passing, a slight obstruction occurs, and brings these two figures directly in contact. Their hands touch; the pressure of the crowd forces her bosom against his shoulder; they stand, face to face, staring into each other's eyes. After a ten years' separation, thus Wakefield meets his wife!

The throng eddies away, and carries them asunder. The sober widow, resuming her former pace, proceeds to church, but pauses in the portal, and throws a perplexed glance along the street. She passes in, however, opening her prayer-book as she goes. And the man! with so wild a face that busy and selfish London stands to gaze after him, he hurries to his lodgings, bolts the door, and throws himself upon the bed. The latent feelings of years break out; his feeble mind acquires a brief energy from their strength; all the miserable strangeness of his life is revealed to him at a glance: and he cries out, passionately, "Wakefield! Wakefield! You are mad!"

Perhaps he was so. The singularity of his situation must have so moulded him to himself, that, considered in regard to his fellow-creatures and the business of life, he could not be said to possess his right mind. He had contrived, or rather he had happened, to dissever himself from the world—to vanish—to give up his place and privileges with living men, without being admitted among the dead. The life of a hermit is nowise parallel to his. He was in the bustle of the city, as of old; but the crowd swept by and saw him not; he was, we may figuratively say, always beside his wife and at his hearth, yet must never feel the warmth of the one nor the affection of the other. It was Wakefield's unprecedented fate to retain his original share of human sympathies, and to be still involved in human interests, while he had lost his reciprocal influence on them. It would be a most curious speculation to trace out the effect of such circumstances on his heart and intellect, separately, and in unison. Yet, changed as he was, he would seldom be conscious of it, but deem himself the same man as ever; glimpses of the truth, indeed, would come, but only for the moment; and still he would keep saying, "I shall soon go back!"—nor reflect that he had been saying so for twenty years.

I conceive, also, that these twenty years would appear, in the retrospect, scarcely longer than the week to which Wakefield had at first limited his absence. He would look on the affair as no more than an interlude in the main business of his life. When, after a little while more, he should deem it time to reënter his parlor, his wife would clap her hands for joy, on beholding the middle-aged Mr. Wakefield. Alas, what a mistake! Would Time but await the close of our favorite follies, we should be young men, all of us, and till Doomsday.

One evening, in the twentieth year since he vanished, Wakefield is taking his customary walk towards the dwelling which he still calls his own. It is a gusty night of autumn, with frequent showers that patter down upon the pavement, and are gone before a man can put up his umbrella. Pausing near the house, Wakefield discerns, through the parlor windows of the second floor, the red glow and the glimmer and fitful flash of a comfortable fire. On the ceiling appears a grotesque shadow of good Mrs. Wakefield. The cap, the nose and chin, and the broad waist, form an admirable caricature, which dances, moreover, with the up-flickering and down-sinking blaze, almost too merrily for the shade of an elderly widow. At this instant a shower chances to fall, and is driven, by the unmannerly gust, full into Wakefield's face and bosom. He is quite penetrated with its autumnal chill. Shall he stand, wet and shivering here, when his own hearth has a good fire to warm him, and his own wife will run to fetch the gray coat and small-clothes, which, doubtless, she has kept carefully in the closet of their bed chamber? No! Wakefield is no such fool. He ascends the steps—heavily!—for twenty years have stiffened his legs since he came down—but he knows it not. Stay, Wakefield! Would you go to the sole home that is left you? Then step into your grave! The door opens. As he passes in, we have a parting glimpse of his visage, and recognize the crafty smile, which was the precursor of the little joke that he has ever since been playing off at his wife's expense. How unmercifully has he quizzed [2] the poor woman! Well, a good night's rest to Wakefield!

This happy event—supposing it to be such—could only have occurred at an unpremeditated moment. We will not follow our friend across the threshold. He has left us much food for thought, a portion of which shall lend its wisdom to a moral, and be shaped into a figure.[3] Amid the seeming confusion of our mysterious world, individuals are so nicely adjusted to a system, and systems to one another and to a whole, that, by stepping aside for a moment, a man exposes himself to a fearful risk of losing his place forever. Like Wakefield, he may become, as it were, the Outcast of the Universe.

From *Twice-Told Tales* (1837)

2. Mocked or made sport of.
3. Emblem or symbolic illustration.

RAPPACCINI'S DAUGHTER

A young man, named Giovanni Guasconti, came, very long ago, from the more southern region of Italy, to pursue his studies at the University of Padua. Giovanni, who had but a scanty supply of gold ducats in his pocket, took lodgings in a high and gloomy chamber of an old edifice which looked not unworthy to have been the palace of a Paduan noble, and which, in fact, exhibited over its entrance the armorial bearings of a family long since extinct. The young stranger, who was not unstudied in the great poem of his country, recollected that one of the ancestors of this family, and perhaps an occupant of this very mansion, had been pictured by Dante as a partaker of the immortal agonies of his Inferno. These reminiscences and associations, together with the tendency to heartbreak natural to a young man for the first time out of his native sphere, caused Giovanni to sigh heavily as he looked around the desolate and ill-furnished apartment.

"Holy Virgin, signor!" cried old Dame Lisabetta, who, won by the youth's remarkable beauty of person, was kindly endeavoring to give the chamber a habitable air, "what a sigh was that to come out of a young man's heart! Do you find this old mansion gloomy? For the love of Heaven, then, put your head out of the window, and you will see as bright sunshine as you have left in Naples."

Guasconti mechanically did as the old woman advised, but could not quite agree with her that the Paduan sunshine was as cheerful as that of southern Italy. Such as it was, however, it fell upon a garden beneath the window and expended its fostering influences on a variety of plants, which seemed to have been cultivated with exceeding care.

"Does this garden belong to the house?" asked Giovanni.

"Heaven, forbid, signor unless it were fruitful of better pot herbs than any that grow there now," answered old Lisabetta. "No; that garden is cultivated by the own hands of Signor Giacomo Rappaccini, the famous doctor, who, I warrant him, has been heard of as far as Naples. It is said that he distils these plants into medicines that are as potent as a charm. Oftentimes you may see the signor doctor at work, and perchance the signora, his daughter, too, gathering the strange flowers that grow in the garden."

The old woman had now done what she could for the aspect of the chamber; and, commending the young man to the protection of the saints, took her departure.

Giovanni still found no better occupation than to look down into the garden beneath his window. From its appearance, he judged it to be one of those botanic gardens which were of earlier date in

Padua than elsewhere in Italy or in the world. Or, not improbably, it might once have been the pleasure-place of an opulent family; for there was the ruin of a marble fountain in the centre, sculptured with rare art but so wofully shattered that it was impossible to trace the original design from the chaos of remaining fragments. The water, however, continued to gush and sparkle into the sunbeams as cheerfully as ever. A little gurgling sound ascended to the young man's window, and made him feel as if the fountain were an immortal spirit that sung its song unceasingly and without heeding the vicissitudes around it, while one century imbodied it in marble and another scattered the perishable garniture on the soil. All about the pool into which the water subsided grew various plants, that seemed to require a plentiful supply of moisture for the nourishment of gigantic leaves, and, in some instances, flowers gorgeously magnificent. There was one shrub in particular, set in a marble vase in the midst of the pool, that bore a profusion of purple blossoms, each of which had the lustre and richness of a gem; and the whole together made a show so resplendent that it seemed enough to illuminate the garden, even had there been no sunshine. Every portion of the soil was peopled with plants and herbs, which, if less beautiful, still bore tokens of assiduous care, as if all had their individual virtues, known to the scientific mind that fostered them. Some were placed in urns, rich with old carving, and others in common garden pots; some crept serpent-like along the ground or climbed on high, using whatever means of ascent was offered them. One plant had wreathed itself round a statue of Vertumnus,[1] which was thus quite veiled and shrouded in a drapery of hanging foliage, so happily arranged that it might have served a sculptor for a study.

While Giovanni stood at the window he heard a rustling behind a screen of leaves, and became aware that a person was at work in the garden. His figure soon emerged into view, and showed itself to be that of no common laborer, but a tall, emaciated, sallow, and sickly-looking man, dressed in a scholar's garb of black. He was beyond the middle term of life, with grey hair, a thin, grey beard, and a face singularly marked with intellect and cultivation, but which could never, even in his more youthful days, have expressed much warmth of heart.

Nothing could exceed the intentness with which this scientific gardener examined every shrub which grew in his path: it seemed as if he was looking into their inmost nature, making observations in regard to their creative essence, and discovering why one leaf grew in this shape and another in that, and wherefore such and such flowers differed among themselves in hue and perfume. Nev-

1. The Roman god of gardens and of the changing seasons.

ertheless, in spite of this deep intelligence on his part, there was no
approach to intimacy between himself and these vegetable existences. On the contrary, he avoided their actual touch or the direct
inhaling of their odors with a caution that impressed Giovanni most
disagreeably; for the man's demeanor was that of one walking
among malignant influences, such as savage beasts, or deadly
snakes, or evil spirits, which, should he allow them one moment of
license, would wreak upon him some terrible fatality. It was
strangely frightful to the young man's imagination to see this air of
insecurity in a person cultivating a garden, that most simple and innocent of human toils, and which had been alike the joy and labor
of the unfallen parents of the race. Was this garden, then, the Eden
of the present world? And this man, with such a perception of harm
in what his own hands caused to grow,—was he the Adam?

The distrustful gardener, while plucking away the dead leaves or
pruning the too luxuriant growth of the shrubs, defended his hands
with a pair of thick gloves. Nor were these his only armor. When, in
his walk through the garden, he came to the magnificent plant that
hung its purple gems beside the marble fountain, he placed a kind
of mask over his mouth and nostrils, as if all this beauty did but
conceal a deadlier malice; but, finding his task still too dangerous,
he drew back, removed the mask, and called loudly, but in the in-
firm voice of a person affected with inward disease,—

"Beatrice! Beatrice!"

"Here am I, my father. What would you?" cried a rich and youthful voice from the window of the opposite house—a voice as rich as
a tropical sunset, and which made Giovanni, though he knew not
why, think of deep hues of purple or crimson and of perfumes heavily delectable. "Are you in the garden?"

"Yes, Beatrice," answered the gardener, "and I need your help."

Soon there emerged from under a sculptured portal the figure of a
young girl, arrayed with as much richness of taste as the most splendid of the flowers, beautiful as the day, and with a bloom so deep
and vivid that one shade more would have been too much. She
looked redundant with life, health, and energy; all of which attributes were bound down and compressed, as it were, and girdled
tensely, in their luxuriance, by her virgin zone.[2] Yet Giovanni's
fancy must have grown morbid while he looked down into the garden; for the impression which the fair stranger made upon him was
as if here were another flower, the human sister of those vegetable
ones, as beautiful as they, more beautiful than the richest of them,
but still to be touched only with a glove, nor to be approached
without a mask. As Beatrice came down the garden path, it was ob-

2. A belt or cincture worn by a maiden.

servable that she handled and inhaled the odor of several of the plants which her father had most sedulously avoided.

"Here, Beatrice," said the latter, "see how many needful offices require to be done to our chief treasure. Yet, shattered as I am, my life might pay the penalty of approaching it so closely as circumstances demand. Henceforth, I fear, this plant must be consigned to your sole charge."

"And gladly will I undertake it," cried again the rich tones of the young lady, as she bent towards the magnificent plant and opened her arms as if to embrace it. "Yes, my sister, my splendor, it shall be Beatrice's task to nurse and serve thee; and thou shalt reward her with thy kisses and perfumed breath, which to her is as the breath of life."

Then, with all the tenderness in her manner that was so strikingly expressed in her words, she busied herself with such attentions as the plant seemed to require; and Giovanni, at his lofty window, rubbed his eyes and almost doubted whether it were a girl tending her favorite flower, or one sister performing the duties of affection to another. The scene soon terminated. Whether Dr. Rappaccini had finished his labors in the garden, or that his watchful eye had caught the stranger's face, he now took his daughter's arm and retired. Night was already closing in; oppressive exhalations seemed to proceed from the plants and steal upward past the open window; and Giovanni, closing the lattice, went to his couch and dreamed of a rich flower and beautiful girl. Flower and maiden were different, and yet the same, and fraught with some strange peril in either shape.

But there is an influence in the light of morning that tends to rectify whatever errors of fancy, or even of judgment, we may have incurred during the sun's decline, or among the shadows of the night, or in the less wholesome glow of moonshine. Giovanni's first movement, on starting from sleep, was to throw open the window and gaze down into the garden which his dreams had made so fertile of mysteries. He was surprised and a little ashamed to find how real and matter-of-fact an affair it proved to be, in the first rays of the sun which gilded the dew-drops that hung upon leaf and blossom, and, while giving a brighter beauty to each rare flower, brought everything within the limits of ordinary experience. The young man rejoiced that, in the heart of the barren city, he had the privilege of overlooking this spot of lovely and luxuriant vegetation. It would serve, he said to himself, as a symbolic language to keep him in communion with Nature. Neither the sickly and thought-worn Dr. Giacomo Rappaccini, it is true, nor his brilliant daughter, were now visible; so that Giovanni could not determine how much of the singularity which he attributed to both was due to their own qualities and how much to his wonder-working fancy; but he was inclined to take a most rational view of the whole matter.

In the course of the day he paid his respects to Signor Pietro Baglioni, professor of medicine in the university, a physician of eminent repute, to whom Giovanni had brought a letter of introduction. The professor was an elderly personage, apparently of genial nature, and habits that might almost be called jovial. He kept the young man to dinner, and made himself very agreeable by the freedom and liveliness of his conversation, especially when warmed by a flask or two of Tuscan wine. Giovanni, conceiving that men of science, inhabitants of the same city, must needs be on familiar terms with one another, took an opportunity to mention the name of Dr. Rappaccini. But the professor did not respond with so much cordiality as he had anticipated.

"Ill would it become a teacher of the divine art of medicine," said Professor Pietro Baglioni, in answer to a question of Giovanni, "to withhold due and well-considered praise of a physician so eminently skilled as Rappaccini; but, on the other hand, I should answer it but scantily to my conscience were I to permit a worthy youth like yourself, Signor Giovanni, the son of an ancient friend, to imbibe erroneous ideas respecting a man who might hereafter chance to hold your life and death in his hands. The truth is, our worshipful Dr. Rappaccini has as much science as any member of the faculty—with perhaps one single exception—in Padua, or all Italy; but there are certain grave objections to his professional character."

"And what are they?" asked the young man.

"Has my friend Giovanni any disease of body or heart, that he is so inquisitive about physicians?" said the professor, with a smile. "But as for Rappaccini, it is said of him—and I, who know the man well, can answer for its truth—that he cares infinitely more for science than for mankind. His patients are interesting to him only as subjects for some new experiment. He would sacrifice human life, his own among the rest, or whatever else was dearest to him, for the sake of adding so much as a grain of mustard seed to the great heap of his accumulated knowledge."

"Methinks he is an awful man indeed," remarked Guasconti, mentally recalling the cold and purely intellectual aspect of Rappaccini. "And yet, worshipful professor, is it not a noble spirit? Are there many men capable of so spiritual a love of science?"

"God forbid," answered the professor, somewhat testily; "at least, unless they take sounder views of the healing art than those adopted by Rappaccini. It is his theory that all medicinal virtues are comprised within those substances which we term vegetable poisons. These he cultivates with his own hands, and is said even to have produced new varieties of poison, more horribly deleterious than Nature, without the assistance of this learned person, would ever have plagued the world withal. That the signor doctor does less mischief than might be expected with such dangerous substances is undeniable. Now and then, it must be owned, he has effected, or seemed to effect, a marvellous cure; but, to tell you my private mind, Signor Giovanni, he should receive little credit for such instances of success,—they being probably the work of chance,—but should be held strictly accountable for his failures, which may justly be considered his own work."

The youth might have taken Baglioni's opinions with many grains of allowance had he known that there was a professional warfare of long continuance between him and Dr. Rappaccini, in which the latter was generally thought to have gained the advantage. If the reader be inclined to judge for himself, we refer him to certain black-letter [3] tracts on both sides, preserved in the medical department of the University of Padua.

"I know not, most learned professor," returned Giovanni, after musing on what had been said of Rappaccini's exclusive zeal for science,—"I know not how dearly this physician may love his art; but surely there is one object more dear to him. He has a daughter."

"Aha!" cried the professor, with a laugh. "So now our friend Giovanni's secret is out. You have heard of this daughter, whom all the young men in Padua are wild about, though not half a dozen have ever had the good hap to see her face. I know little of the Signora Beatrice save that Rappaccini is said to have instructed her deeply in his science, and that, young and beautiful as fame reports her, she is already qualified to fill a professor's chair. Perchance her father destines her for mine! Other absurd rumors there be, not worth talking about or listening to. So now, Signor Giovanni, drink off your glass of lachryma." [4]

Guasconti returned to his lodgings somewhat heated with the wine he had quaffed, and which caused his brain to swim with strange fantasies in reference to Dr. Rappaccini and the beautiful Beatrice. On his way, happening to pass by a florist's, he bought a fresh bouquet of flowers.

Ascending to his chamber, he seated himself near the window, but within the shadow thrown by the depth of the wall, so that he could look down into the garden with little risk of being discovered. All beneath his eye was a solitude. The strange plants were basking in the sunshine, and now and then nodding gently to one another, as if in acknowledgment of sympathy and kindred. In the

3. A heavy type face, often called "Gothic" or "Old English," used by the early printers.
4. Lachryma Christi ("Tears of Christ"), a famous Italian wine.

midst, by the shattered fountain, grew the magnificent shrub, with
its purple gems clustering all over it; they glowed in the air, and
gleamed back again out of the depths of the pool, which thus
seemed to overflow with colored radiance from the rich reflection
that was steeped in it. At first, as we have said, the garden was a solitude. Soon, however,—as Giovanni had half hoped, half feared,
would be the case,—a figure appeared beneath the antique sculptured portal, and came down between the rows of plants, inhaling
their various perfumes as if she were one of those beings of old
classic fable that lived upon sweet odors. On again beholding Beatrice, the young man was even startled to perceive how much her
beauty exceeded his recollection of it; so brilliant, so vivid, was its
character, that she glowed amid the sunlight, and, as Giovanni
whispered to himself, positively illuminated the more shadowy intervals of the garden path. Her face being now more revealed than
on the former occasion, he was struck by its expression of simplicity
and sweetness—qualities that had not entered into his idea of her
character, and which made him ask anew what manner of mortal
she might be. Nor did he fail again to observe, or imagine, an analogy between the beautiful girl and the gorgeous shrub that hung its
gem-like flowers over the fountain,—a resemblance which Beatrice
seemed to have indulged a fantastic humor in heightening, both by
the arrangement of her dress and the selection of its hues.

Approaching the shrub, she threw open her arms, as with a passionate ardor, and drew its branches into an intimate embrace—so
intimate that her features were hidden in its leafy bosom and her
glistening ringlets all intermingled with the flowers.

"Give me thy breath, my sister," exclaimed Beatrice; "for I am
faint with common air. And give me this flower of thine, which I
separate with gentlest fingers from the stem and place it close beside my heart."

With these words the beautiful daughter of Rappaccini plucked
one of the richest blossoms of the shrub, and was about to fasten it
in her bosom. But now, unless Giovanni's draughts of wine had
bewildered his senses, a singular incident occurred. A small
orange-colored reptile, of the lizard or chameleon species, chanced
to be creeping along the path, just at the feet of Beatrice. It appeared to Giovanni,—but, at the distance from which he gazed, he
could scarcely have seen anything so minute,—it appeared to him,
however, that a drop or two of moisture from the broken stem of the
flower descended upon the lizard's head. For an instant the reptile
contorted itself violently, and then lay motionless in the sunshine.
Beatrice observed this remarkable phenomenon, and crossed herself, sadly, but without surprise; nor did she therefore hesitate to arrange the fatal flower in her bosom. There it blushed, and almost

glimmered with the dazzling effect of a precious stone, adding to her dress and aspect the one appropriate charm which nothing else in the world could have supplied. But Giovanni, out of the shadow of his window, bent forward and shrank back, and murmured and trembled.

"Am I awake? Have I my senses?" said he to himself. "What is this being? Beautiful shall I call her, or inexpressibly terrible?"

Beatrice now strayed carelessly through the garden, approaching closer beneath Giovanni's window, so that he was compelled to thrust his head quite out of its concealment in order to gratify the intense and painful curiosity which she excited. At this moment there came a beautiful insect over the garden wall; it had, perhaps, wandered through the city, and found no flowers or verdure among those antique haunts of men until the heavy perfumes of Dr. Rappaccini's shrubs had lured it from afar. Without alighting on the flowers, this winged brightness seemed to be attracted by Beatrice, and lingered in the air and fluttered about her head. Now, here it could not be but that Giovanni Guasconti's eyes deceived him. Be that as it might, he fancied that, while Beatrice was gazing at the insect with childish delight, it grew faint and fell at her feet; its bright wings shivered; it was dead—from no cause that he could discern, unless it were the atmosphere of her breath. Again Beatrice crossed herself and sighed heavily as she bent over the dead insect.

An impulsive movement of Giovanni drew her eyes to the window. There she beheld the beautiful head of the young man— rather a Grecian than an Italian head, with fair, regular features, and a glistening of gold among his ringlets—gazing down upon her like a being that hovered in mid air. Scarcely knowing what he did, Giovanni threw down the bouquet which he had hitherto held in his hand.

"Signora," said he, "there are pure and healthful flowers. Wear them for the sake of Giovanni Guasconti."

Thanks, signor," replied Beatrice, with her rich voice, that came forth as it were like a gush of music, and with a mirthful expression half childish and half woman-like. "I accept your gift, and would fain recompense it with this precious purple flower; but if I toss it into the air it will not reach you. So Signor Guasconti must even content himself with my thanks."

She lifted the bouquet from the ground, and then, as if inwardly ashamed at having stepped aside from her maidenly reserve to respond to a stranger's greeting, passed swiftly homeward through the garden. But few as the moments were, it seemed to Giovanni, when she was on the point of vanishing beneath the sculptured portal, that his beautiful bouquet was already beginning to wither in her grasp. It was an idle thought; there could be no possibility of distinguishing a faded flower from a fresh one at so great a distance.

For many days after this incident the young man avoided the window that looked into Dr. Rappaccini's garden, as if something ugly and monstrous would have blasted his eyesight had he been betrayed into a glance. He felt conscious of having put himself, to a certain extent, within the influence of an unintelligible power by the communication which he had opened with Beatrice. The wisest course would have been, if his heart were in any real danger, to quit his lodgings and Padua itself at once; the next wiser, to have accustomed himself, as far as possible, to the familiar and daylight view of Beatrice—thus bringing her rigidly and systematically within the limits of ordinary experience. Least of all, while avoiding her sight, ought Giovanni to have remained so near this extraordinary being that the proximity and possibility even of intercourse should give a kind of substance and reality to the wild vagaries which his imagination ran riot continually in producing. Guasconti had not a deep heart—or, at all events, its depths were not sounded now; but he had a quick fancy and an ardent southern temperament, which rose every instant to a higher fever pitch. Whether or no Beatrice possessed those terrible attributes, that fatal breath, the affinity with those so beautiful and deadly flowers which were indicated by what Giovanni had witnessed, she had at least instilled a fierce and subtle poison into his system. It was not love, although her rich beauty was a madness to him; nor horror, even while he fancied her spirit to be imbued with the same baneful essence that seemed to pervade her physical frame; but a wild offspring of both love and horror that had each parent in it, and burned like one and shivered like the other. Giovanni knew not what to dread; still less did he know what to hope; yet hope and dread kept a continual warfare in his breast, alternately vanquishing one another and starting up afresh to renew the contest. Blessed are all simple emotions, be they dark or bright! It is the lurid intermixture of the two that produces the illuminating blaze of the infernal regions.

Sometimes he endeavored to assuage the fever of his spirit by a rapid walk through the streets of Padua or beyond its gates; his footsteps kept time with the throbbings of his brain, so that the walk was apt to accelerate itself to a race. One day he found himself arrested; his arm was seized by a portly personage, who had turned back on recognizing the young man and expended much breath in overtaking him.

"Signor Giovanni! Stay, my young friend!" cried he. "Have you forgotten me? That might well be the case if I were as much altered as yourself."

It was Baglioni, whom Giovanni had avoided ever since their first meeting, from a doubt that the professor's sagacity would look too deeply into his secrets. Endeavoring to recover himself, he stared forth wildly from his inner world into the outer one and spoke like a man in a dream.

"Yes; I am Giovanni Guasconti. You are Professor Pietro Baglioni. Now let me pass!"

"Not yet, not yet, Signor Giovanni Guasconti," said the professor, smiling, but at the same time scrutinizing the youth with an earnest glance. "What! did I grow up side by side with your father? and shall his son pass me like a stranger in these old streets of Padua? Stand still, Signor Giovanni; for we must have a word or two before we part."

"Speedily, then, most worshipful professor, speedily," said Giovanni, with feverish impatience. "Does not your worship see that I am in haste?"

Now, while he was speaking there came a man in black along the street, stooping and moving feebly like a person in inferior health. His face was all overspread with a most sickly and sallow hue, but yet so pervaded with an expression of piercing and active intellect that an observer might easily have overlooked the merely physical attributes and have seen only this wonderful energy. As he passed, this person exchanged a cold and distant salutation with Baglioni, but fixed his eyes upon Giovanni with an intentness that seemed to bring out whatever was within him worthy of notice. Nevertheless, there was a peculiar quietness in the look, as if taking merely a speculative, not a human, interest in the young man.

"It is Dr. Rappaccini!" whispered the professor when the stranger had passed. "Has he ever seen your face before?"

"Not that I know," answered Giovanni, starting at the name.

"He *has* seen you! he must have seen you!" said Baglioni, hastily. "For some purpose or other, this man of science is making a study of you. I know that look of his! It is the same that coldly illuminates his face as he bends over a bird, a mouse, or a butterfly, which, in pursuance of some experiment, he has killed by the perfume of a flower; a look as deep as Nature itself, but without Nature's warmth of love. Signor Giovanni, I will stake my life upon it, you are the subject of one of Rappaccini's experiments!"

"Will you make a fool of me?" cried Giovanni, passionately. "*That*, signor professor, were an untoward experiment."

"Patience! patience!" replied the imperturbable professor. "I tell thee, my poor Giovanni, that Rappaccini has a scientific interest in thee. Thou hast fallen into fearful hands! And the Signora Beatrice,—what part does she act in this mystery?"

But Guasconti, finding Baglioni's pertinacity intolerable, here broke away, and was gone before the professor could again seize his arm. He looked after the young man intently and shook his head.

"This must not be," said Baglioni to himself. "The youth is the son of my old friend, and shall not come to any harm from which the arcana of medical science can preserve him. Besides, it is too insufferable an impertinence in Rappaccini, thus to snatch the lad out of my own hands, as I may say, and make use of him for his infernal experiments. This daughter of his! It shall be looked to. Perchance, most learned Rappaccini, I may foil you where you little dream of it!"

Meanwhile Giovanni had pursued a circuitous route, and at length found himself at the door of his lodgings. As he crossed the threshold he was met by old Lisabetta, who smirked and smiled, and was evidently desirous to attract his attention; vainly, however, as the ebullition of his feelings had momentarily subsided into a cold and dull vacuity. He turned his eyes full upon the withered face that was puckering itself into a smile, but seemed to behold it not. The old dame, therefore, laid her grasp upon his cloak.

"Signor! signor!" whispered she, still with a smile over the whole breadth of her visage, so that it looked not unlike a grotesque carving in wood, darkened by centuries. "Listen, signor! There is a private entrance into the garden!"

"What do you say?" exclaimed Giovanni, turning quickly about, as if an inanimate thing should start into feverish life. "A private entrance into Dr. Rappaccini's garden?"

"Hush! hush! not so loud!" whispered Lisabetta, putting her hand over his mouth. "Yes; into the worshipful doctor's garden, where you may see all his fine shrubbery. Many a young man in Padua would give gold to be admitted among those flowers."

Giovanni put a piece of gold into her hand.

"Show me the way," said he.

A surmise, probably excited by his conversation with Baglioni, crossed his mind, that this interposition of old Lisabetta might perchance be connected with the intrigue, whatever were its nature, in which the professor seemed to suppose that Dr. Rappaccini was involving him. But such a suspicion, though it disturbed Giovanni, was inadequate to restrain him. The instant that he was aware of the possibility of approaching Beatrice, it seemed an absolute necessity of his existence to do so. It mattered not whether she were angel or demon; he was irrevocably within her sphere, and must obey the law that whirled him onward, in ever-lessening circles, towards a result which he did not attempt to foreshadow; and yet, strange to say, there came across him a sudden doubt whether this intense interest on his part were not delusory; whether it were really of so deep and positive a nature as to justify him in now thrust-ing himself into an incalculable position; whether it were not merely the fantasy of a young man's brain, only slightly or not at all connected with his heart.

He paused, hesitated, turned half about, but again went on. His withered guide led him along several obscure passages, and finally undid a door, through which, as it was opened, there came the sight and sound of rustling leaves, with the broken sunshine glimmering among them. Giovanni stepped forth, and, forcing himself through the entanglement of a shrub that wreathed its tendrils over the hid-den entrance, stood beneath his own window in the open area of Dr. Rappaccini's garden.

How often is it the case that, when impossibilities have come to pass and dreams have condensed their misty substance into tangi-ble realities, we find ourselves calm, and even coldly self-pos-sessed, amid circumstances which it would have been a delirium of joy or agony to anticipate! Fate delights to thwart us thus. Passion will choose his own time to rush upon the scene, and lingers sluggishly behind when an appropriate adjustment of events would seem to summon his appearance. So was it now with Giovanni. Day after day his pulses had throbbed with feverish blood at the im-probable idea of an interview with Beatrice, and of standing with her, face to face, in this very garden, basking in the Oriental sun-shine of her beauty, and snatching from her full gaze the mystery which he deemed the riddle of his own existence. But now there was a singular and untimely equanimity within his breast. He threw a glance around the garden to discover if Beatrice or her fa-ther were present, and, perceiving that he was alone, began a criti-cal observation of the plants.

The aspect of one and all of them dissatisfied him; their gorgeousness seemed fierce, passionate, and even unnatural. There was hardly an individual shrub which a wanderer, straying by him-self through a forest, would not have been startled to find growing wild, as if an unearthly face had glared at him out of the thicket. Several also would have shocked a delicate instinct by an appear-ance of artificialness indicating that there had been such commix-ture, and, as it were, adultery, of various vegetable species, that the production was no longer of God's making, but the monstrous off-spring of man's depraved fancy, glowing with only an evil mockery of beauty. They were probably the result of experiment, which in one or two cases had succeeded in mingling plants individually lovely into a compound possessing the questionable and ominous character that distinguished the whole growth of the garden. In fine, Giovanni recognized but two or three plants in the collection, and those of a kind that he well knew to be poisonous. While busy with these contemplations he heard the rustling of a silken garment, and, turning, beheld Beatrice emerging from beneath the sculptured portal.

Giovanni had not considered with himself what should be his deportment; whether he should apologize for his intrusion into the garden, or assume that he was there with the privity at least, if not by the desire, of Dr. Rappaccini or his daughter; but Beatrice's manner placed him at his ease, though leaving him still in doubt by what agency he had gained admittance. She came lightly along the path and met him near the broken fountain. There was surprise in her face, but brightened by a simple and kind expression of pleasure.

"You are a connoisseur in flowers, signor," said Beatrice, with a smile, alluding to the bouquet which he had flung her from the window. "It is no marvel, therefore, if the sight of my father's rare collection has tempted you to take a nearer view. If he were here, he could tell you many strange and interesting facts as to the nature and habits of these shrubs; for he has spent a lifetime in such studies, and this garden is his world."

"And yourself, lady," observed Giovanni, "if fame says true,— you likewise are deeply skilled in the virtues indicated by these rich blossoms and these spicy perfumes. Would you deign to be my instructress, I should prove an apter scholar than if taught by Signor Rappaccini himself."

"Are there such idle rumors?" asked Beatrice, with the music of a pleasant laugh. "Do people say that I am skilled in my father's science of plants? What a jest is there! No; though I have grown up among these flowers, I know no more of them than their hues and perfume; and sometimes methinks I would fain rid myself of even that small knowledge. There are many flowers here, and those not the least brilliant, that shock and offend me when they meet my eye. But pray, signor, do not believe these stories about my science. Believe nothing of me save what you see with your own eyes."

"And must I believe all that I have seen with my own eyes?" asked Giovanni, pointedly, while the recollection of former scenes made him shrink. "No, signora; you demand too little of me. Bid me believe nothing save what comes from your own lips."

It would appear that Beatrice understood him. There came a deep flush to her cheek; but she looked full into Giovanni's eyes, and responded to his gaze of uneasy suspicion with a queenlike haughtiness.

"I do so bid you, signor," she replied. "Forget whatever you may have fancied in regard to me. If true to the outward senses, still it may be false in its essence; but the words of Beatrice Rappaccini's lips are true from the depths of the heart outward. Those you may believe."

A fervor glowed in her whole aspect and beamed upon Giovanni's consciousness like the light of truth itself; but while she spoke there was a fragrance in the atmosphere around her, rich and delightful, though evanescent, yet which the young man, from an indefinable reluctance, scarcely dared to draw into his lungs. It might be the odor of the flowers. Could it be Beatrice's breath which thus embalmed her words with a strange richness, as if by steeping them in her heart? A faintness passed like a shadow over Giovanni and flitted away; he seemed to gaze through the beautiful girl's eyes into her transparent soul, and felt no more doubt or fear.

The tinge of passion that had colored Beatrice's manner vanished; she became gay, and appeared to derive a pure delight from her communion with the youth not unlike what the maiden of a lonely island might have felt conversing with a voyager from the civilized world. Evidently her experience of life had been confined within the limits of that garden. She talked now about matters as simple as the daylight or summer clouds, and now asked questions in reference to the city, or Giovanni's distant home, his friends, his mother, and his sisters—questions indicating such seclusion, and such lack of familiarity with modes and forms, that Giovanni responded as if to an infant. Her spirit gushed out before him like a fresh rill that was just catching its first glimpse of the sunlight and wondering at the reflections of earth and sky which were flung into its bosom. There came thoughts, too, from a deep source, and fantasies of a gemlike brilliancy, as if diamonds and rubies sparkled upward among the bubbles of the fountain. Ever and anon there gleamed across the young man's mind a sense of wonder that he should be walking side by side with the being who had so wrought upon his imagination, whom he had idealized in such hues of terror, in whom he had positively witnessed such manifestations of dreadful attributes,—that he should be conversing with Beatrice like a brother, and should find her so human and so maidenlike. But such reflections were only momentary; the effect of her character was too real not to make itself familiar at once.

In this free intercourse they had strayed through the garden, and now, after many turns among its avenues, were come to the shattered fountain, beside which grew the magnificent shrub, with its treasury of glowing blossoms. A fragrance was diffused from it which Giovanni recognized as identical with that which he had attributed to Beatrice's breath, but incomparably more powerful. As her eyes fell upon it, Giovanni beheld her press her hand to her bosom as if her heart were throbbing suddenly and painfully.

"For the first time in my life," murmured she, addressing the shrub, "I had forgotten thee."

"I remember, signora," said Giovanni, "that you once promised to reward me with one of these living gems for the bouquet which I had the happy boldness to fling to your feet. Permit me now to pluck it as a memorial of this interview."

He made a step towards the shrub with extended hand; but Beatrice darted forward, uttering a shriek that went through his heart like a dagger. She caught his hand and drew it back with the whole force of her slender figure. Giovanni felt her touch thrilling through his fibres.

"Touch it not!" exclaimed she, in a voice of agony. "Not for thy life! It is fatal!"

Then, hiding her face, she fled from him and vanished beneath the sculptured portal. As Giovanni followed her with his eyes, he beheld the emaciated figure and pale intelligence of Dr. Rappaccini, who had been watching the scene, he knew not how long, within the shadow of the entrance.

No sooner was Guasconti alone in his chamber than the image of Beatrice came back to his passionate musings, invested with all the witchery that had been gathering around it ever since his first glimpse of her, and now likewise imbued with a tender warmth of girlish womanhood. She was human; her nature was endowed with all gentle and feminine qualities; she was worthiest to be worshipped; she was capable, surely, on her part, of the height and heroism of love. Those tokens which he had hitherto considered as proofs of a frightful peculiarity in her physical and moral system were now either forgotten, or, by the subtle sophistry of passion transmitted into a golden crown of enchantment, rendering Beatrice the more admirable by so much as she was the more unique. Whatever had looked ugly was now beautiful; or, if incapable of such a change, it stole away and hid itself among those shapeless half ideas which throng the dim region beyond the daylight of our perfect consciousness. Thus did he spend the night, nor fell asleep until the dawn had begun to awake the slumbering flowers in Dr. Rappaccini's garden, whither Giovanni's dreams doubtless led him. Up rose the sun in his due season, and, flinging his beams upon the young man's eyelids, awoke him to a sense of pain. When thoroughly aroused, he became sensible of a burning and tingling agony in his hand—in his right hand—the very hand which Beatrice had grasped in her own when he was on the point of plucking one of the gemlike flowers. On the back of that hand there was now a purple print like that of four small fingers, and the likeness of a slender thumb upon his wrist.

Oh, how stubbornly does love,—or even that cunning semblance of love which flourishes in the imagination, but strikes no depth of root into the heart,—how stubbornly does it hold its faith until the moment comes when it is doomed to vanish into thin mist! Giovanni wrapped a handkerchief about his hand and wondered what evil thing had stung him, and soon forgot his pain in a reverie of Beatrice.

After the first interview, a second was in the inevitable course of what we call fate. A third; a fourth; and a meeting with Beatrice in the garden was no longer an incident in Giovanni's daily life, but the whole space in which he might be said to live; for the anticipation and memory of that ecstatic hour made up the remainder. Nor was it otherwise with the daughter of Rappaccini. She watched for the youth's appearance, and flew to his side with confidence as unreserved as if they had been playmates from early infancy—as if they were such playmates still. If, by any unwonted chance, he failed to come at the appointed moment, she stood beneath the window and sent up the rich sweetness of her tones to float around him in his chamber and echo and reverberate throughout his heart: "Giovanni! Giovanni! Why tarriest thou? Come down!" And down he hastened into that Eden of poisonous flowers.

But, with all this intimate familiarity, there was still a reserve in Beatrice's demeanor, so rigidly and invariably sustained that the idea of infringing it scarcely occurred to his imagination. By all appreciable signs, they loved; they had looked love with eyes that conveyed the holy secret from the depths of one soul into the depths of the other, as if it were too sacred to be whispered by the way; they had even spoken love in those gushes of passion when their spirits darted forth in articulated breath like tongues of long-hidden flame; and yet there had been no seal of lips, no clasp of hands, nor any slightest caress such as love claims and hallows. He had never touched one of the gleaming ringlets of her hair; her garment—so marked was the physical barrier between them—had never been waved against him by a breeze. On the few occasions when Giovanni had seemed tempted to overstep the limit, Beatrice grew so sad, so stern, and withal wore such a look of desolate separation, shuddering at itself, that not a spoken word was requisite to repel him. At such times he was startled at the horrible suspicions that rose, monster-like, out of the caverns of his heart and stared him in the face; his love grew thin and faint as the morning mist, his doubts alone had substance. But, when Beatrice's face brightened again after the momentary shadow, she was transformed at once from the mysterious, questionable being whom he had watched with so much awe and horror; she was now the beautiful and unsophisticated girl whom he felt that his spirit knew with a certainty beyond all other knowledge.

A considerable time had now passed since Giovanni's last meet-

ing with Baglioni. One morning, however, he was disagreeably surprised by a visit from the professor, whom he had scarcely thought
of for whole weeks, and would willingly have forgotten still longer.
Given up as he had long been to a pervading excitement, he could
tolerate no companions except upon condition of their perfect sympathy with his present state of feeling. Such sympathy was not to be
expected from Professor Baglioni.

The visitor chatted carelessly for a few minutes about the gossip
of the city and the university, and then took up another topic.

"I have been reading an old classic author lately," said he, "and
met with a story that strangely interested me.[5] Possibly you may
remember it. It is of an Indian prince, who sent a beautiful woman
as a present to Alexander the Great. She was as lovely as the dawn
and gorgeous as the sunset; but what especially distinguished her
was a certain rich perfume in her breath—richer than a garden of
Persian roses. Alexander, as was natural to a youthful conqueror,
fell in love at first sight with this magnificent stranger; but a certain
sage physician, happening to be present, discovered a terrible secret in regard to her."

"And what was that?" asked Giovanni, turning his eyes downward to avoid those of the professor.

"That this lovely woman," continued Baglioni, with emphasis,
"had been nourished with poisons from her birth upward, until her
whole nature was so imbued with them that she herself had become the deadliest poison in existence. Poison was her element of
life. With that rich perfume of her breath she blasted the very air.
Her love would have been poison—her embrace death. Is not this a
marvellous tale?"

"A childish fable," answered Giovanni, nervously starting from
his chair. "I marvel how your worship finds time to read such nonsense among your graver studies."

"By the by," said the professor, looking uneasily about him,
"what singular fragrance is this in your apartment? Is it the perfume
of your gloves? It is faint, but delicious; and yet, after all, by no
means agreeable. Were I to breathe it long, methinks it would make
me ill. It is like the breath of a flower; but I see no flowers in the
chamber."

"Nor are there any," replied Giovanni, who had turned pale as
the professor spoke; "nor, I think, is there any fragrance except in
your worship's imagination. Odors, being a sort of element combined of the sensual and the spiritual, are apt to deceive us in this
manner. The recollection of a perfume, the bare idea of it, may easily be mistaken for a present reality."

"Ay; but my sober imagination does not often play such tricks,"

5. The story is to be found in Sir Thomas Browne's *Pseudodoxia Epidemica* (1646),
Book VII, chap. 17. Hawthorne copied it into his *American Notebooks*.

said Baglioni; "and, were I to fancy any kind of odor, it would be
that of some vile apothecary drug, wherewith my fingers are likely
enough to be imbued. Our worshipful friend Rappaccini, as I have
heard, tinctures his medicaments with odors richer than those of
Araby. Doubtless, likewise, the fair and learned Signora Beatrice
would minister to her patients with draughts as sweet as a maiden's
breath; but woe to him that sips them!"

Giovanni's face evinced many contending emotions. The tone in
which the professor alluded to the pure and lovely daughter of Rappaccini was a torture to his soul; and yet the intimation of a view of
her character, opposite to his own, gave instantaneous distinctness
to a thousand dim suspicions, which now grinned at him like so
many demons. But he strove hard to quell them and to respond to
Baglioni with a true lover's perfect faith.

"Signor professor," said he, "you were my father's friend; perchance, too, it is your purpose to act a friendly part towards his son.
I would fain feel nothing towards you save respect and deference;
but I pray you to observe, signor, that there is one subject on which
we must not speak. You know not the Signora Beatrice. You cannot,
therefore, estimate the wrong—the blasphemy, I may even say—
that is offered to her character by a light or injurious word."

"Giovanni! my poor Giovanni!" answered the professor, with a
calm expression of pity, "I know this wretched girl far better than
yourself. You shall hear the truth in respect to the poisoner Rappaccini and his poisonous daughter; yes, poisonous as she is beautiful.
Listen; for, even should you do violence to my gray hairs, it shall
not silence me. That old fable of the Indian woman has become a
truth by the deep and deadly science of Rappaccini and in the person of the lovely Beatrice."

Giovanni groaned and hid his face.

"Her father," continued Baglioni, "was not restrained by natural
affection from offering up his child in this horrible manner as the
victim of his insane zeal for science; for, let us do him justice, he is
as true a man of science as ever distilled his own heart in an alem-
bic. What, then, will be your fate? Beyond a doubt you are selected
as the material of some new experiment. Perhaps the result is to be
death; perhaps a fate more awful still. Rappaccini, with what he
calls the interest of science before his eyes, will hesitate at nothing."

"It is a dream," muttered Giovanni to himself; "surely it is a
dream."

"But," resumed the professor, "be of good cheer, son of my
friend. It is not yet too late for the rescue. Possibly we may even ·
succeed in bringing back this miserable child within the limits of
ordinary nature, from which her father's madness has estranged her.

Behold this little silver vase! It was wrought by the hands of the renowned Benvenuto Cellini,[6] and is well worthy to be a love gift to the fairest dame in Italy. But its contents are invaluable. One little sip of this antidote would have rendered the most virulent poisons of the Borgias [7] innocuous. Doubt not that it will be as efficacious against those of Rappaccini. Bestow the vase, and the precious liquid within it, on your Beatrice, and hopefully await the result."

Baglioni laid a small, exquisitely wrought silver vial on the table and withdrew, leaving what he had said to produce its effect upon the young man's mind.

"We will thwart Rappaccini yet," thought he, chuckling to himself, as he descended the stairs; "but, let us confess the truth of him, he is a wonderful man—a wonderful man indeed; a vile empiric,[8] however, in his practice, and therefore not to be tolerated by those who respect the good old rules of the medical profession."

Throughout Giovanni's whole acquaintance with Beatrice, he had occasionally, as we have said, been haunted by dark surmises as to her character; yet so thoroughly had she made herself felt by him as a simple, natural, most affectionate, and guileless creature, that the image now held up by Professor Baglioni looked as strange and incredible as if it were not in accordance with his own original conception. True, there were ugly recollections connected with his first glimpses of the beautiful girl; he could not quite forget the bouquet that withered in her grasp, and the insect that perished amid the sunny air, by no ostensible agency save the fragrance of her breath. These incidents, however, dissolving in the pure light of her character, had no longer the efficacy of facts, but were acknowledged as mistaken fantasies, by whatever testimony of the senses they might appear to be substantiated. There is something truer and more real than what we can see with the eyes and touch with the finger. On such better evidence had Giovanni founded his confidence in Beatrice, though rather by the necessary force of her high attributes than by any deep and generous faith on his part. But now his spirit was incapable of sustaining itself at the height to which the early enthusiasm of passion had exalted it; he fell down, grovelling among earthly doubts, and defiled therewith the pure whiteness of Beatrice's image. Not that he gave her up; he did but distrust. He resolved to institute some decisive test that should sat-

6. Benvenuto Cellini (1500–71), Italian writer and artist noted for his craftsmanship in gold and silver.
7. A family whose members, influential in the papacy and Italian politics (c. 1460–1519), were often accused of poisoning their enemies.
8. Member of a sect among ancient physicians called *Empirici*, who (in opposition to the *Dogmatici* and *Methodici*) drew their rules of practice entirely from experience, to the exclusion of theory and custom.

isfy him, once for all, whether there were those dreadful peculiarities in her physical nature which could not be supposed to exist without some corresponding monstrosity of soul. His eyes, gazing down afar, might have deceived him as to the lizard, the insect, and the flowers; but if he could witness, at the distance of a few paces, the sudden blight of one fresh and healthful flower in Beatrice's hand, there would be room for no further question. With this idea he hastened to the florist's and purchased a bouquet that was still gemmed with the morning dew-drops.

It was now the customary hour of his daily interview with Beatrice. Before descending into the garden, Giovanni failed not to look at his figure in the mirror,—a vanity to be expected in a beautiful young man, yet, as displaying itself at that troubled and feverish moment, the token of a certain shallowness of feeling and insincerity of character. He did gaze, however, and said to himself that his features had never before possessed so rich a grace, nor his eyes such vivacity, nor his cheeks so warm a hue of superabundant life.

"At least," thought he, "her poison has not yet insinuated itself into my system. I am no flower to perish in her grasp."

With that thought he turned his eyes on the bouquet, which he had never once laid aside from his hand. A thrill of indefinable horror shot through his frame on perceiving that those dewy flowers were already beginning to droop; they wore the aspect of things that had been fresh and lovely yesterday. Giovanni grew white as marble, and stood motionless before the mirror, staring at his own reflection there as at the likeness of something frightful. He remembered Baglioni's remark about the fragrance that seemed to pervade the chamber. It must have been the poison in his breath! Then he shuddered—shuddered at himself. Recovering from his stupor, he began to watch with curious eye a spider that was busily at work hanging its web from the antique cornice of the apartment, crossing and recrossing the artful system of interwoven lines—as vigorous and active a spider as ever dangled from an old ceiling. Giovanni bent towards the insect, and emitted a deep, long breath. The spider suddenly ceased its toil; the web vibrated with a tremor originating in the body of the small artisan. Again Giovanni sent forth a breath, deeper, longer, and imbued with a venomous feeling out of his heart: he knew not whether he were wicked, or only desperate. The spider made a convulsive gripe with his limbs and hung dead across the window.

"Accursed! accursed!" muttered Giovanni, addressing himself. "Hast thou grown so poisonous that this deadly insect perished by thy breath?"

At that moment a rich, sweet voice came floating up from the garden.

"Giovanni! Giovanni! It is past the hour! Why tarriest thou? Come down!"

"Yes," muttered Giovanni again. "She is the only being whom my breath may not slay! Would that it might!"

He rushed down, and in an instant was standing before the bright and loving eyes of Beatrice. A moment ago his wrath and despair had been so fierce that he could have desired nothing so much as to wither her by a glance; but with her actual presence there came influences which had too real an existence to be at once shaken off: recollections of the delicate and benign power of her feminine nature, which had so often enveloped him in a religious calm; recollections of many a holy and passionate outgush of her heart, when the pure fountain had been unsealed from its depths and made visible in its transparency to his mental eye; recollections which, had Giovanni known how to estimate them, would have assured him that all this ugly mystery was but an earthly illusion, and that, whatever mist of evil might seem to have gathered over her, the real Beatrice was a heavenly angel. Incapable as he was of such high faith, still her presence had not utterly lost its magic. Giovanni's rage was quelled into an aspect of sullen insensibility. Beatrice, with a quick spiritual sense, immediately felt that there was a gulf of blackness between them which neither he nor she could pass. They walked on together, sad and silent, and came thus to the marble fountain and to its pool of water on the ground, in the midst of which grew the shrub that bore gem-like blossoms. Giovanni was affrighted at the eager enjoyment—the appetite, as it were—with which he found himself inhaling the fragrance of the flowers.

"Beatrice," asked he, abruptly, "whence came this shrub?"

"My father created it," answered she, with simplicity.

"Created it! created it!" repeated Giovanni. "What mean you, Beatrice?"

"He is a man fearfully acquainted with the secrets of Nature," replied Beatrice; "and, at the hour when I first drew breath, this plant sprang from the soil, the offspring of his science, of his intellect, while I was but his earthly child. Approach it not!" continued she, observing with terror that Giovanni was drawing nearer to the shrub. "It has qualities that you little dream of. But I, dearest Giovanni,—I grew up and blossomed with the plant and was nourished with its breath. It was my sister, and I loved it with a human affection; for, alas!—hast thou not suspected it?—there was an awful doom."

Here Giovanni frowned so darkly upon her that Beatrice paused and trembled. But her faith in his tenderness reassured her, and made her blush that she had doubted for an instant.

"There was an awful doom," she continued, "the effect of my father's fatal love of science, which estranged me from all society of my kind. Until Heaven sent thee, dearest Giovanni, oh, how lonely was thy poor Beatrice!"

"Was it a hard doom?" asked Giovanni, fixing his eyes upon her.

"Only of late have I known how hard it was," answered she, tenderly. "Oh, yes; but my heart was torpid, and therefore quiet."

Giovanni's rage broke forth from his sullen gloom like a lightning flash out of a dark cloud.

"Accursed one!" cried he, with venomous scorn and anger. "And, finding thy solitude wearisome, thou hast severed me likewise from all the warmth of life and enticed me into thy region of unspeakable horror!"

"Giovanni!" exclaimed Beatrice, turning her large bright eyes upon his face. The force of his words had not found its way into her mind; she was merely thunderstruck.

"Yes, poisonous thing!" repeated Giovanni, beside himself with passion. "Thou hast done it! Thou hast blasted me! Thou hast filled my veins with poison! Thou hast made me as hateful, as ugly, as loathsome and deadly a creature as thyself—a world's wonder of hideous monstrosity! Now, if our breath be happily as fatal to ourselves as to all others, let us join our lips in one kiss of unutterable hatred, and so die!"

"What has befallen me?" murmured Beatrice, with a low moan out of her heart. "Holy Virgin, pity me, a poor heart-broken child!"

"Thou,—dost thou pray?" cried Giovanni, still with the same fiendish scorn. "Thy very prayers, as they come from thy lips, taint the atmosphere with death. Yes, yes; let us pray! Let us to church and dip our fingers in the holy water at the portal! They that come after us will perish as by a pestilence! Let us sign crosses in the air! It will be scattering curses abroad in the likeness of holy symbols!"

"Giovanni," said Beatrice, calmly, for her grief was beyond passion, "why dost thou join thyself with me thus in those terrible words? I, it is true, am the horrible thing thou namest me. But thou,—what hast thou to do, save with one other shudder at my hideous misery to go forth out of the garden and mingle with thy race, and forget that there ever crawled on earth such a monster as poor Beatrice?"

"Dost thou pretend ignorance?" asked Giovanni, scowling upon her. "Behold! this power have I gained from the pure daughter of Rappaccini."

There was a swarm of summer insects flitting through the air in search of the food promised by the flower odors of the fatal garden. They circled round Giovanni's head, and were evidently attracted towards him by the same influence which had drawn them for an instant within the sphere of several of the shrubs. He sent forth a breath among them, and smiled bitterly at Beatrice as at least a score of the insects fell dead upon the ground.

"I see it! I see it!" shrieked Beatrice. "It is my father's fatal science! No, no, Giovanni; it was not I! Never! never! I dreamed only to love thee and be with thee a little time, and so to let thee pass away, leaving but thine image in mine heart; for, Giovanni, believe it, though my body be nourished with poison, my spirit is God's creature, and craves love as its daily food. But my father,—he has united us in this fearful sympathy. Yes; spurn me, tread upon me, kill me! Oh, what is death after such words as thine? But it was not I. Not for a world of bliss would I have done it."

Giovanni's passion had exhausted itself in its outburst from his lips. There now came across him a sense, mournful, and not without tenderness, of the intimate and peculiar relationship between Beatrice and himself. They stood, as it were, in an utter solitude, which would be made none the less solitary by the densest throng of human life. Ought not, then, the desert of humanity around them to press this insulated pair closer together? If they should be cruel to one another, who was there to be kind to them? Besides, thought Giovanni, might there not still be a hope of his returning within the limits of ordinary nature, and leading Beatrice, the redeemed Beatrice, by the hand? O, weak, and selfish, and unworthy spirit, that could dream of an earthly union and earthly happiness as possible, after such deep love had been so bitterly wronged as was Beatrice's love by Giovanni's blighting words! No, no; there could be no such hope. She must pass heavily, with that broken heart, across the borders of Time—she must bathe her hurts in some fount of paradise, and forget her grief in the light of immortality, and *there* be well.

But Giovanni did not know it.

"Dear Beatrice," said he, approaching her, while she shrank away as always at his approach, but now with a different impulse, "dearest Beatrice, our fate is not yet so desperate. Behold! there is a medicine, potent, as a wise physician has assured me, and almost divine in its efficacy. It is composed of ingredients the most opposite to those by which thy awful father has brought this calamity upon thee and me. It is distilled of blessed herbs. Shall we not quaff it together, and thus be purified from evil?"

"Give it me!" said Beatrice, extending her hand to receive the little silver vial which Giovanni took from his bosom. She added, with a peculiar emphasis, "I will drink; but do thou await the result."

She put Baglioni's antidote to her lips; and, at the same moment, the figure of Rappaccini emerged from the portal and came slowly towards the marble fountain. As he drew near, the pale man of science seemed to gaze with a triumphant expression at the beautiful youth and maiden, as might an artist who should spend his life in achieving a picture or a group of statuary and finally be satisfied with his success. He paused; his bent form grew erect with conscious power; he spread out his hands over them in the attitude of a father imploring a blessing upon his children; but those were the same hands that had thrown poison into the stream of their lives. Giovanni trembled. Beatrice shuddered nervously, and pressed her hand upon her heart.

"My daughter," said Rappaccini, "thou art no longer lonely in the world. Pluck one of those precious gems from thy sister shrub and bid thy bridegroom wear it in his bosom. It will not harm him now. My science and the sympathy between thee and him have so wrought within his system, that he now stands apart from common men, as thou dost, daughter of my pride and triumph, from ordinary women. Pass on, then, through the world, most dear to one another and dreadful to all besides!"

"My father," said Beatrice, feebly,—and still as she spoke she kept her hand upon her heart,—"wherefore didst thou inflict this miserable doom upon thy child?"

"Miserable!" exclaimed Rappaccini. "What mean you, foolish girl? Dost thou deem it misery to be endowed with marvellous gifts against which no power nor strength could avail an enemy—misery, to be able to quell the mightiest with a breath—misery, to be as terrible as thou art beautiful? Wouldst thou, then, have preferred the condition of a weak woman, exposed to all evil and capable of none?"

"I would fain have been loved, not feared," murmured Beatrice, sinking down upon the ground. "But now it matters not. I am going, father, where the evil which thou hast striven to mingle with my being will pass away like a dream—like the fragrance of these poisonous flowers, which will no longer taint my breath among the flowers of Eden. Farewell, Giovanni! Thy words of hatred are like lead within my heart; but they, too, will fall away as I ascend. Oh, was there not, from the first, more poison in thy nature than in mine?"

To Beatrice,—so radically had her earthly part been wrought upon by Rappaccini's skill,—as poison had been life, so the powerful antidote was death; and thus the poor victim of man's ingenuity and of thwarted nature, and of the fatality that attends all such efforts of perverted wisdom, perished there, at the feet of her father and Giovanni. Just at that moment Professor Pietro Baglioni looked forth from the window, and called loudly, in a tone of triumph mixed with horror, to the thunderstricken man of science,—

"Rappaccini! Rappaccini! and is *this* the upshot of your experiment!"

From *Mosses from an Old Manse* (1846)

·Edgar Allan Poe·

LIGEIA

*And the will therein lieth, which dieth not. Who
knoweth the mysteries of the will, with its vigor?
For God is but a great will pervading all things by
nature of its intentness. Man doth not yield himself to the angels, nor unto death utterly, save only
through the weakness of his feeble will.*
                                    —Joseph Glanvill [1]

I cannot, for my soul, remember how, when, or even precisely
where, I first became acquainted with the lady Ligeia. Long years
have since elapsed, and my memory is feeble through much suffering. Or, perhaps, I cannot *now* bring these points to mind, because,
in truth, the character of my beloved, her rare learning, her singular
yet placid cast of beauty, and the thrilling and enthralling eloquence of her low musical language, made their way into my heart
by paces so steadily and stealthily progressive that they have been
unnoticed and unknown. Yet I believe that I met her first and most
frequently in some large, old decaying city near the Rhine. Of her
family—I have surely heard her speak. That it is of a remotely ancient date cannot be doubted. Ligeia! Ligeia! Buried in studies of a
nature more than all else adapted to deaden impressions of the
outward world, it is by that sweet word alone—by Ligeia—that I
bring before mine eyes in fancy the image of her who is no more.

1. Joseph Glanvill (1636–1680), English ecclesiastic associated with the Cambridge Platonists, defended his belief in the pre-existence of the soul in *Lux
Orientalis* (1662).

And now, while I write, a recollection flashes upon me that I have *never known* the paternal name of her who was my friend and my betrothed, and who became the partner of my studies, and finally the wife of my bosom. Was it a playful charge on the part of my Ligeia? or was it a test of my strength of affection, that I should institute no inquiries upon this point? or was it rather a caprice of my own—a wildly romantic offering on the shrine of the most passionate devotion? I but indistinctly recall the fact myself—what wonder that I have utterly forgotten the circumstances which originated or attended it? And, indeed, if ever that spirit which is entitled *Romance*—if ever she, the wan and the misty-winged *Ashtophet* [2] of idolatrous Egypt, presided, as they tell, over marriages ill-omened, then most surely she presided over mine.

There is one dear topic, however, on which my memory fails me not. It is the *person* of Ligeia. In stature she was tall, somewhat slender, and, in her latter days, even emaciated. I would in vain attempt to portray the majesty, the quiet ease, of her demeanor, or the incomprehensible lightness and elasticity of her footfall. She came and departed as a shadow. I was never made aware of her entrance into my closed study save by the dear music of her low sweet voice, as she placed her marble hand upon my shoulder. In beauty of her face no maiden ever equalled her. It was the radiance of an opium dream—an airy and spirit-lifting vision more wildly divine than the phantasies which hovered about the slumbering souls of the daughters of Delos.[3] Yet her features were not of that regular mould which we have been falsely taught to worship in the classical labors of the heathen. "There is no exquisite beauty," says Bacon, Lord Verulam, speaking truly of all the forms and *genera* of beauty, "without some *strangeness* in the proportion." [4] Yet, although I saw that the features of Ligeia were not of a classic regularity—although I perceived that her loveliness was indeed "exquisite," and felt that there was much of "strangeness" pervading it, yet I have tried in vain to detect the irregularity and to trace home my own perception of "the strange." I examined the contour of the lofty and pale forehead—it was faultless—how cold indeed that word when applied to a majesty so divine!—the skin rivalling the purest ivory, the commanding extent and repose, the gentle prominence of the regions

2. Probably Ashtoreth (Astarte), goddess of fertility in Near Eastern cults.
3. Greek island, one of the Cyclades, and believed in Greek mythology to be the birthplace of Apollo, god of the fine arts; a great temple in his honor was erected there. Delos was so venerated that it was unlawful for a child to be born there, or for a man to die there. The "daughters of Delos" appear to be Poe's invention, but the phrase clearly imparts a mysterious and priestess-like quality to the characterization of Ligeia.
4. From the essay "Of Beauty" by Francis Bacon (1561–1626), first Baron Verulam. Bacon's exact words are "There is no excellent beauty. . . ."

above the temples; [5] and then the raven-black, the glossy, the luxuriant and naturally-curling tresses, setting forth the full force of the Homeric epithet, "hyacinthine"! [6] I looked at the delicate outlines of the nose—and nowhere but in the graceful medallions of the Hebrews had I beheld a similar perfection. There were the same luxurious smoothness of surface, the same scarcely perceptible tendency to the aquiline, the same harmoniously curved nostrils speaking the free spirit. I regarded the sweet mouth. Here was indeed the triumph of all things heavenly—the magnificent turn of the short upper lip—the soft, voluptuous slumber of the under—the dimples which sported, and the color which spoke—the teeth glancing back, with a brilliancy almost startling, every ray of the holy light which fell upon them in her serene and placid, yet most exultingly radiant of all smiles. I scrutinized the formation of the chin—and here, too, I found the gentleness of breadth, the softness and the majesty, the fullness and the spirituality, of the Greek—the contour which the God Apollo revealed but in a dream, to Cleomenes,[7] the son of the Athenian. And then I peered into the large eyes of Ligeia.

For eyes we have no models in the remotely antique. It might have been, too, that in these eyes of my beloved lay the secret to which Lord Verulam alludes. They were, I must believe, far larger than the ordinary eyes of our own race. They were even fuller than the fullest of the gazelle eyes of the tribe of the valley of Nourjahad.[8] Yet it was only at intervals—in moments of intense excitement—that this peculiarity became more than slightly noticeable in Ligeia. And at such moments was her beauty—in my heated fancy thus it appeared perhaps—the beauty of being either above or apart from the earth—the beauty of the Fabulous Houri [9] of the Turk. The hue of the orbs was the most brilliant of black, and, far over them, hung jetty lashes of great length. The brows, slightly irregular in outline, had the same tint. The "strangeness," however, which I found in the eyes, was of a nature distinct from the formation, or the color, or the brilliancy of the features, and must, after all, be referred to the *expression*. Ah, word of no meaning! behind whose vast latitude of mere sound we intrench our ignorance of so much of the spiritual. The expression of the eyes of Ligeia! How for

5. According to the principles of phrenology, the "prominence of the regions above the temples" would indicate love of life.
6. A Homeric epithet for the hair, which curls "like the hyacinth flower." Hyacinthus was the beautiful boy whom Apollo loved and accidentally killed; the hyacinth flower was said to spring annually from his blood, as an emblem of lost love.
7. Sculptor of the celebrated Venus de' Medici; Apollo was the god of artistic inspiration.
8. *The History of Nourjahad* (1767), an oriental tale by Mrs. Frances Sheridan (1724–66).
9. The beautiful nymphs of the Mohammedan paradise.

long hours have I pondered upon it! How have I, through the
whole of a midsummer night struggled to fathom it! What was it—
that something more profound than the well of Democritus [10]—
which lay far within the pupils of my beloved? What *was* it? I was
possessed with a passion to discover. Those eyes! those large, those
shining, those divine orbs! they became to me twin stars [11] of Leda
and I to them devoutest of astrologers.

There is no point, among the many incomprehensible anomalies
of the science of mind, more thrillingly exciting than the fact—
never, I believe, noticed in the schools—that, in our endeavors to
recall to memory something long forgotten, we often find ourselves
upon the very verge of remembrance, without being able, in the
end, to remember. And thus how frequently, in my intense scrutiny
of Ligeia's eyes, have I felt approaching the full knowledge of their
expression—felt it approaching—yet not quite be mine—and so at
length entirely depart! And (strange, oh strangest mystery of all!) I
found, in the commonest objects of the universe, a circle of analogies to that expression. I mean to say that, subsequently to the
period when Ligeia's beauty passed into my spirit, there dwelling
as in a shrine, I derived, from many existences in the material
world, a sentiment such as I felt always aroused within me by her
large and luminous orbs. Yet not the more could I define that sentiment, or analyze, or even steadily view it. I recognized it, let me
repeat, sometimes in the survey of a rapidly-growing vine—in the
contemplation of a moth, a butterfly, a chrysalis, a stream of running
water. I have felt it in the ocean; in the falling of a meteor. I have
felt it in the glances of unusually aged people. And there are one or
two stars in heaven—(one especially, a star of the sixth magnitude,
double and changeable, to be found near the large star in Lyra [12])
in a telescopic scrutiny of which I have been made aware of the
feeling. I have been filled with it by certain sounds from stringed
instruments, and not unfrequently by passages from books. Among
innumerable other instances, I well remember something in a volume of Joseph Glanvill, which (perhaps merely from its
quaintness—who shall say?) never failed to inspire me with the
sentiment;—"And the will therein lieth, which dieth not. Who knoweth the mysteries of the will, with its vigor? For God is but a great
will pervading all things by nature of its intentness. Man doth not
yield him to the angels, nor unto death utterly, save only through
the weakness of his feeble will."

10. Greek philosopher of the fifth century B.C., who said that truth lies deep in wells
and caves (i.e., out of human sight).
11. Castor and Pollux, named after the twin sons of Leda and Zeus, and the two
brightest stars in the constellation Gemini.
12. Epsilon Lyræ is a famous double star located near Vega, the brightest star in the
constellation Lyra.

Length of years, and subsequent reflection, have enabled me to trace, indeed, some remote connection between this passage in the English moralist and a portion of the character of Ligeia. An *intensity* in thought, action, or speech, was possibly, in her, a result, or at least an index of that gigantic volition which, during our long intercourse, failed to give other and more immediate evidence of its existence. Of all the women whom I have ever known, she, the outwardly calm, the ever-placid Ligeia, was the most violently a prey to the tumultuous vultures of stern passion. And of such passion I could form no estimate, save by the miraculous expansion of those eyes which at once so delighted and appalled me—by the almost magical melody, modulation, distinctness, and placidity of her very low voice—and by the fierce energy (rendered doubly effective by contrast with her manner of utterance) of the wild words which she habitually uttered.

I have spoken of the learning of Ligeia: it was immense—such as I have never known in woman. In the classical tongues was she deeply proficient, and as far as my own acquaintance extended in regard to the modern dialects of Europe, I have never known her at fault. Indeed upon any theme of the most admired, because simply the most abstruse of the boasted erudition of the academy, have I *ever* found Ligeia at fault? How singularly—how thrillingly, this one point in the nature of my wife forced itself, at this late period only, upon my attention! I said her knowledge was such as I have never known in woman—but where breathes the man who has traversed, and successfully, *all* the wide areas of moral, physical, and mathematical science? I saw not then what I now clearly perceive, that the acquisitions of Ligeia were gigantic, were astounding; yet I was sufficiently aware of her infinite supremacy to resign myself, with a child-like confidence, to her guidance through the chaotic world of metaphysical investigation at which I was most busily occupied during the earlier years of our marriage. With how vast a triumph—with how vivid a delight—with how much of all that is ethereal in hope—did I *feel*, as she bent over me in studies but litttle sought—but less known—that delicious vista by slow degrees expanding before me, down whose long, gorgeous, and all untrodden path, I might at length pass onward to the goal of a wisdom too divinely precious not to be forbidden!

How poignant, then, must have been the grief with which, after some years, I beheld my well-grounded expectations take wings to themselves and fly away! Without Ligeia I was but as a child groping benighted. Her presence, her readings alone, rendered vividly luminous the many mysteries of the transcendentalism in which we were immersed. Wanting the radiant lustre of her eyes, letters, lambent and golden, grew duller than Saturnian [13] lead. And now those eyes shone less and less frequently upon the pages over which I pored. Ligeia grew ill. The wild eyes blazed with a too-too glorious effulgence; the pale fingers became of the transparent waxen hue of the grave, and the blue veins upon the lofty forehead swelled and sank impetuously with the tides of the most gentle emotion. I saw that she must die—and I struggled desperately in spirit with the grim Azrael.[14] And the struggles of the passionate wife were, to my astonishment, even more energetic than my own. There had been much in her stern nature to impress me with the belief that, to her, death would have come without its terrors;—but not so. Words are impotent to convey any just idea of the fierceness of resistance with which she wrestled with the Shadow. I groaned in anguish at the pitiable spectacle. I would have soothed—I would have reasoned; but, in the intensity of her wild desire for life,—for life— *but* for life—solace and reason were alike the utmost of folly. Yet not until the last instance, amid the most convulsive writhings of her fierce spirit, was shaken the external placidity of her demeanor. Her voice grew more gentle—grew more low—yet I would not wish to dwell upon the wild meaning of the quietly uttered words. My brain reeled as I hearkened entranced, to a melody more than mortal—to assumptions and aspirations which mortality had never before known.

That she loved me I should not have doubted; and I might have been easily aware that, in a bosom such as hers, love would have reigned no ordinary passion. But in death only, was I fully impressed with the strength of her affection. For long hours, detaining my hand, would she pour out before me the overflowing of a heart whose more than passionate devotion amounted to idolatry. How had I deserved to be so blessed by such confessions?—how had I deserved to be so cursed with the removal of my beloved in the hour of her making them? But upon this subject I cannot bear to dilate. Let me say only, that in Ligeia's more than womanly abandonment to a love, alas! all unmerited, all unworthily bestowed, I at length recognized the principle of her longing with so wildly earnest a desire for the life which was now fleeing so rapidly away. It is this wild longing—it is this eager vehemence of desire for life— *but* for life—that I have no power to portray—no utterance capable of expressing.

At high noon of the night in which she departed, beckoning me, peremptorily, to her side, she bade me repeat certain verses com-

13. In alchemy, Saturn is the technical term for lead. When Ligeia disappears, the alchemical process is reversed, and gold returns to lead.
14. The angel of Death in Hebrew and Mohammedan lore.

posed by herself not many days before. I obeyed her.—They were
these:

> Lo! 'tis a gala night
> Within the lonesome latter years!
> An angel throng, bewinged, bedight
> In veils, and drowned in tears,
> Sit in a theatre, to see
> A play of hopes and fears,
> While the orchestra breathes fitfully
> The music of the spheres
>
> Mimes, in the form of God on high,
> Mutter and mumble low,
> And hither and thither fly—
> Mere puppets they, who come and go
> At bidding of vast formless things
> That shift the scenery to and fro,
> Flapping from out their Condor wings
> Invisible Woe!
>
> That motley drama!—oh, be sure
> It shall not be forgot
> With its Phantom chased forevermore,
> By a crowd that seized it not,
> Through a circle that ever returneth in
> To the self-same spot,
> And much of madness and more of Sin
> And Horror the soul of the plot.
>
> But see, amid the mimic rout,
> A crawling shape intrude!
> A blood-red thing that writhes from out
> The scenic solitude!
> It writhes!—it writhes!—with mortal pangs
> The mimes become its food,
> And the seraphs sob at vermin fangs
> In human gore imbued.
>
> Out—out are the lights—out all!
> And over each quivering form,
> The curtain, a funeral pall,
> Comes down with the rush of a storm,
> And the angels, all pallid and wan,
> Uprising, unveiling, affirm
> That the play is the tragedy, "Man,"
> And its hero the Conqueror Worm.[15]

"O God!" half shrieked Ligeia, leaping to her feet and extending
her arms aloft with a spasmodic movement, as I made an end of

15. This poem was first published separately in 1843, under the title "The Conqueror Worm," but was not incorporated into the story until 1845.

these lines—"O God! O Divine Father!—shall these things be un-deviatingly so?—shall this Conqueror be not once conquered? Are we not part and parcel of Thee? Who—who knoweth the mysteries of the will with its vigor? Man doth not yield him to the angels, *nor unto death utterly* save only through the weakness of his feeble will."

And now, as if exhausted with emotion, she suffered her white arms to fall, and returned solemnly to her bed of death. And as she breathed her last sighs, there came mingled with them a low mur-mur from her lips. I bent to them my ear and distinguished, again, the concluding words of the passage in Glanvill—*"Man doth not yield him to the angels, nor unto death utterly, save only through the weakness of his feeble will."*

She died;—and I, crushed into the very dust with sorrow, could no longer endure the lonely desolation of my dwelling in the dim and decaying city by the Rhine. I had no lack of what the world calls wealth. Ligeia had brought me far more, very far more than or-dinarily falls to the lot of mortals. After a few months, therefore, of weary and aimless wandering, I purchased, and put in some repair, an abbey, which I shall not name, in one of the wildest and least frequented portions of fair England. The gloomy and dreary gran-deur of the building, the almost savage aspect of the domain, the many melancholy and time-honored memories connected with both, had much in unison with the feelings of utter abandonment which had driven me into that remote and unsocial region of the country. Yet although the external abbey, with its verdant decay hanging about it, suffered but little alteration, I gave way, with a childlike perversity, and perchance with a faint hope of alleviating my sorrows, to a display of more than regal magnificence within.— For such follies, even in childhood, I had imbibed a taste and now they came back to me as if in the dotage of grief. Alas, I feel how much even of incipient madness might have been discovered in the gorgeous and fantastic draperies, in the solemn carvings of Egypt, in the wild cornices and furniture, in the Bedlam [16] patterns of the carpets of tufted gold! I had become a bounden slave in the tram-mels of opium, and my labors and my orders had taken a coloring from my dreams. But these absurdities I must not pause to detail. Let me speak only of that one chamber, ever accursed, whither in a moment of mental alienation, I led from the altar as my bride—as the successor of the unforgotten Ligeia—the fair-haired and blue-eyed Lady Rowena Trevanion, of Tremaine.

There is no individual portion of the architecture and decoration of that bridal chamber which is not now visibly before me. Where

16. "Crazy" patterns. The term was derived from the Hospital of St. Mary of Bethle-hem ("Bedlam"), a notorious London asylum for the insane.

were the souls of the haughty family of the bride, when, through thirst of gold, they permitted to pass the threshold of an apartment *so* bedecked, a maiden and a daughter so beloved? I have said that I minutely remember the details of the chamber—yet I am sadly forgetful on topics of deep moment—and here there was no system, no keeping, in the fantastic display, to take hold upon the memory. The room lay in a high turret of the castellated abbey, was pentagonal in shape, and of capacious size. Occupying the whole southern face of the pentagon was the sole window—an immense sheet of unbroken glass from Venice—a single pane, and tinted of a leaden hue, so that the rays of either the sun or moon, passing through it, fell with a ghastly lustre on the objects within. Over the upper portion of this huge window, extended the trellis-work of an aged vine, which clambered up the massy walls of the turret. The ceiling, of gloomy-looking oak, was excessively lofty, vaulted, and elaborately fretted with the wildest and most grotesque specimens of a semi-Gothic, semi-Druidical device. From out the most central recess of this melancholy vaulting, depended, by a single chain of gold with long links, a huge censer of the same metal, Saracenic in pattern, and with many perforations so contrived that there writhed in and out of them, as if endued with a serpent vitality, a continual succession of parti-colored fires.

Some few ottomans and golden candelabra, of Eastern figure, were in various stations about—and there was the couch, too—the bridal couch—of an Indian model, and low, and sculptured of solid ebony, with a pall-like canopy above. In each of the angles of the chamber stood on end a gigantic sarcophagus of black granite, from the tombs of the kings over against Luxor,[17] with their aged lids full of immemorial sculpture. But in draping of the apartment lay, alas! the chief phantasy of all. The lofty walls, gigantic in height—even unproportionably so—were hung from summit to foot, in vast folds, with a heavy and massive-looking tapestry—tapestry of a material which was found alike as a carpet on the floor, as a covering for the ottomans and the ebony bed, as a canopy for the bed, and as the gorgeous volutes of the curtains which partially shaded the window. The material was the richest cloth of gold. It was spotted all over, at irregular intervals, with arabesque figures, about a foot in diameter, and wrought upon the cloth in patterns of the most jetty black. But these figures partook of the true character of the arabesque only when regarded from a single point of view. By a contrivance now common, and indeed traceable to a very remote period of antiquity, they were made changeable in aspect. To one entering the room, they bore the appearance of simple monstros-

17. Site of Thebes, on the east bank of the Nile. It excited the Romantic imagination because of the startling archaeological discoveries made there.

ities; but upon a farther advance, this appearance gradually departed; and step by step, as the visitor moved his station in the chamber, he saw himself surrounded by an endless succession of the ghastly forms which belong to the superstition of the Norman, or arise in the guilty slumbers of the monk. The phantasmagoric effect was vastly heightened by the artificial introduction of a strong continual current of wind behind the draperies—giving a hideous and uneasy animation to the whole.

In halls such as these—in a bridal chamber such as this—I passed, with the lady of Tremaine, the unhallowed hours of the first month of our marriage—passed them with but little disquietude. That my wife dreaded the fierce moodiness of my temper—that she shunned me and loved me but little—I could not help perceiving; but it gave me rather pleasure than otherwise. I loathed her with a hatred belonging more to demon than to man. My memory flew back (oh, with what intensity of regret!) to Ligeia, the beloved, the august, the beautiful, the entombed. I revelled in recollections of her purity, of her wisdom, of her lofty, her ethereal nature, of her passionate, her idolatrous love. Now, then, did my spirit fully and freely burn with more than all the fires of her own. In the excitement of my opium dreams (for I was habitually fettered in the shackles of the drug) I would call aloud upon her name, during the silence of the night, or among the sheltered recesses of the glens by day, as if, through the wild eagerness, the solemn passion, the consuming ardor of my longing for the departed, I could restore her to the pathway she had abandoned—ah, *could* it be forever?—upon the earth.

About the commencement of the second month of the marriage, the Lady Rowena was attacked with sudden illness, from which her recovery was slow. The fever which consumed her rendered her nights uneasy; and in her perturbed state of half-slumber, she spoke of sounds, and of motions in and about the chamber of the turret, which I concluded had no origin save in the distemper of her fancy, or perhaps in the phantasmagoric influences of the chamber itself. She became at length convalescent—finally well. Yet but a brief period elapsed, ere a second more violent disorder again threw her upon a bed of suffering; and from this attack her frame, at all times feeble, never altogether recovered. Her illnesses were, after this epoch, of alarming character, and of more alarming recurrence, defying alike the knowledge and the great exertions of her physicians. With the increase of the chronic disease which had thus, apparently, taken too sure hold upon her constitution to be eradicated by human means, I could not fail to observe a similar increase in the nervous irritation of her temperament, and in her excitability by trivial causes of fear. She spoke again, and now more frequently and pertinaciously, of the sounds—of the slight sounds—and of the unusual motions among the tapestries, to which she had formerly alluded.

One night, near the closing in of September, she pressed this distressing subject with more than usual emphasis upon my attention. She had just awakened from an unquiet slumber, and I had been watching, with feelings half of anxiety, half of vague terror, the workings of her emaciated countenance. I sat by the side of her ebony bed, upon one of the ottomans of India. She partly arose and spoke, in an earnest low whisper, of sounds which she *then* heard, but which I could not hear—and of motions which she *then* saw, but which I could not perceive. The wind was rushing hurriedly behind the tapestries, and I wished to show her (what, let me confess it, I could not *all* believe) that those almost inarticulate breathings, and those very gentle variations of the figures upon the wall, were but the natural effects of that customary rushing of the wind. But a deadly pallor, overspreading her face, had proved to me that my exertions to reassure her would be fruitless. She appeared to be fainting, and no attendants were within call. I remembered where was deposited a decanter of light wine which had been ordered by her physicians, and hastened across the chamber to procure it. But, as I stepped beneath the light of the censer, two circumstances of a startling nature attracted my attention. I had felt that some palpable although invisible object had passed lightly by my person; and I saw that there lay upon the golden carpet, in the very middle of the rich lustre thrown from the censer, a shadow—a faint, indefinite shadow of angelic aspect—such as might be fancied for the shadow of a shade. But I was wild with the excitement of an immoderate dose of opium, and heeded these things but little, nor spoke of them to Rowena. Having found the wine, I recrossed the chamber and poured out a goblet-ful, which I held to the lips of the fainting lady. She had now partially recovered, however, and took the vessel herself, while I sank upon an ottoman near me, with my eyes fastened upon her person. It was then that I became distinctly aware of a gentle foot-fall upon the carpet, and near the couch; and in a second thereafter, as Rowena was in the act of raising the wine to her lips, I saw, or may have dreamed that I saw, fall within the goblet, as if from some invisible spring in the atmosphere of the room, three or four large drops of a brilliant and ruby colored fluid. If this I saw—not so Rowena. She swallowed the wine unhesitatingly, and I forbore to speak to her of a circumstance which must, after all, I considered, have been but the suggestion of a vivid imagination, rendered morbidly active by the terror of the lady, by the opium, and by the hour.

Yet I cannot conceal it from my own perception that, immediately subsequent to the fall of the ruby-drops, a rapid change for the worse took place in the disorder of my wife; so that, on the third subsequent night, the hands of her menials prepared her for the tomb, and on the fourth, I sat alone, with her shrouded body, in that fantastic chamber which had received her as my bride. Wild visions, opium-engendered, flitted, shadow-like, before me. I gazed with unquiet eye upon the sarcophagi in the angles of the room, upon the varying figures of the drapery, and upon the writhing of the parti-colored fires in the censer overhead. My eyes then fell, as I called to mind the circumstances of a former night, to the spot beneath the glare of the censer where I had seen the faint traces of the shadow. It was there, however, no longer; and breathing with greater freedom, I turned my glances to the pallid and rigid figure upon the bed. Then rushed upon me a thousand memories of Ligeia—and then came back upon my heart, with the turbulent violence of a flood, the whole of that unutterable woe with which I had regarded *her* thus enshrouded. The night waned; and still, with a bosom full of bitter thoughts of the one only and supremely beloved, I remained gazing upon the body of Rowena.

It might have been midnight, or perhaps earlier, or later, for I had taken no note of time, when a sob, low, gentle, but very distinct, startled me from my revery.—I *felt* that it came from the bed of ebony—the bed of death. I listened in an agony of superstitious terror—but there was no repetition of the sound. I strained my vision to detect any motion in the corpse—but there was not the slightest perceptible. Yet I could not have been deceived. I *had* heard the noise, however faint, and my soul was awakened within me. I resolutely and perseveringly kept my attention riveted upon the body. Many minutes elapsed before any circumstance occurred tending to throw light upon the mystery. At length it became evident that a slight, a very feeble, and barely noticeable tinge of color had flushed up within the cheeks, and along the sunken small veins of the eyelids. Through a species of unutterable horror and awe, for which the language of mortality has no sufficiently energetic expression, I felt my heart cease to beat, my limbs grow rigid where I sat. Yet a sense of duty finally operated to restore my self-possession. I could no longer doubt that we had been precipitate in our preparations—that Rowena still lived. It was necessary that some immediate exertion be made; yet the turret was altogether apart from the portion of the abbey tenanted by the servants—there were none within call—I had no means of summoning them to my aid without leaving the room for many minutes—and this I could not venture to do. I therefore struggled alone in my endeavors to call back the spirit still hovering. In a short period it was certain, however, that a relapse had taken place; the color disappeared from both eyelid and cheek, leaving a wanness even more than that of marble; the lips became doubly shrivelled and pinched up in the ghastly expression of death; a repulsive clamminess and coldness overspread rapidly the surface of the body; and all the usual rigorous stiffness immediately supervened. I fell back with a shudder upon the couch from which I had been so startlingly aroused, and again gave myself up to passionate waking visions of Ligeia.

An hour thus elapsed when (could it be possible?) I was a second time aware of some vague sound issuing from the region of the bed. I listened—in extremity of horror. The sound came again—it was a sigh. Rushing to the corpse, I saw—distinctly saw—a tremor upon the lips. In a minute afterward they relaxed, disclosing a bright line of the pearly teeth. Amazement now struggled in my bosom with the profound awe which had hitherto reigned there alone. I felt that my vision grew dim, that my reason wandered; and it was only by a violent effort that I at length succeeded in nerving myself to the task which duty thus once more had pointed out. There was now a partial glow upon the forehead and upon the cheek and throat; a perceptible warmth pervaded the whole frame; there was even a slight pulsation at the heart. The lady *lived;* and with redoubled ardor I betook myself to the task of restoration. I chafed and bathed the temples and the hands, and used every exertion which experience, and no little medical reading, could suggest. But in vain. Suddenly, the color fled, the pulsation ceased, the lips resumed the expression of the dead, and in an instant afterward, the whole body took upon itself the icy chilliness, the livid hue, the intense rigidity, the sunken outline, and all the loathsome peculiarities of that which has been, for many days, a tenant of the tomb.

And again I sunk into visions of Ligeia—and again (what marvel that I shudder while I write?), *again* there reached my ears a low sob from the region of the ebony bed. But why shall I minutely detail the unspeakable horrors of that night? Why shall I pause to relate how, time after time, until near the period of the gray dawn, this hideous drama of revivification was repeated; how each terrific relapse was only into a sterner and apparently more irredeemable death; how each agony wore the aspect of a struggle with some invisible foe; and how each struggle was succeeded by I know not what wild change in the personal appearance of the corpse? Let me hurry to a conclusion.

The greater part of the fearful night had worn away, and she who had been dead, once again stirred—and now more vigorously than hitherto, although arousing from a dissolution more appalling in its utter hopelessness than any. I had long ceased to struggle or to move, and remained sitting rigidly upon the ottoman, a helpless prey to a whirl of violent emotions, of which extreme awe was perhaps the least terrible, the least consuming. The corpse, I repeat, stirred and now more vigorously than before. The hues of life flushed up with unwonted energy into the countenance—the limbs relaxed—and, save that the eyelids were yet pressed heavily together, and that the bandages and draperies of the grave still imparted their charnel character to the figure, I might have dreamed that Rowena had indeed shaken off, utterly, the fetters of Death. But if this idea was not, even then, altogether adopted, I could at least doubt no longer, when arising from the bed, tottering, with feeble steps, with closed eyes, and with the manner of one bewildered in a dream, the thing that was enshrouded advanced boldly and palpably into the middle of the apartment.

I trembled not—I stirred not—for a crowd of unutterable fancies connected with the air, the stature, the demeanor of the figure, rushing hurriedly through my brain, had paralyzed—had chilled me into stone. I stirred not—but gazed upon the apparition. There was a mad disorder in my thoughts—a tumult unappeasable. Could it, indeed, be the *living* Rowena who confronted me? Could it indeed be Rowena *at all*—the fair-haired, the blue-eyed Lady Rowena Trevanion of Tremaine? Why, *why* should I doubt it? The bandage lay heavily about the mouth—but then might it not be the mouth of the breathing Lady of Tremaine? And the cheeks—there were the roses as in her noon of life—yes, these might indeed be the fair cheeks of the living Lady of Tremaine. And the chin, with its dimples, as in health, might it not be hers?—but *had she then grown taller since her malady?* What inexpressible madness seized me with that thought? One bound, and I had reached her feet! Shrinking from my touch, she let fall from her head, unloosened, the ghastly cerements which had confined it, and there streamed forth, into the rushing atmosphere of the chamber, huge masses of long and dishevelled hair; *it was blacker than the raven wings of the midnight!* And now slowly opened *the eyes* of the figure which stood before me. "Here then, at least," I shrieked aloud, "can I never—can I never be mistaken—these are the full, and the black, and the wild eyes—of my lost love—of the lady—of the LADY LIGEIA!"

From *Tales of the Grotesque and Arabesque* (1840; first published in 1838, and subsequently revised)

WILLIAM WILSON

What say of it? What say of CONSCIENCE *grim,*
That spectre in my path?
                    CHAMBERLAYNE: *Pharronida*[1]

Let me call myself, for the present, William Wilson. The fair page
now lying before me need not be sullied with my real appellation.
This has been already too much an object for the scorn—for the
horror—for the detestation of my race. To the uttermost regions of
the globe have not the indignant winds bruited its unparalleled in-
famy? Oh, outcast of all outcasts most abandoned!—to the earth art
thou forever dead? to its honors, to its flowers, to its golden aspirations?—and a cloud, dense, dismal, and limitless, does it not hang
eternally between thy hopes and heaven?

I would not, if I could, here or to-day, embody a record of my
later years of unspeakable misery and unpardonable crime. This
epoch, these later years, took unto themselves a sudden elevation
in turpitude, whose origin alone it is my present purpose to assign.
Men usually grow base by degrees. From me, in an instant, all virtue dropped bodily as a mantle. From comparatively trivial wickedness I passed, with the stride of a giant, into more than the enormi-
ties of an Elah-Gabalus.[2] What chance—what one event brought
this evil thing to pass, bear with me while I relate. Death approaches; and the shadow which foreruns him has thrown a softening influence over my spirit. I long, in passing through the dim
valley, for the sympathy—I had nearly said for the pity—of my
fellow-men. I would fain have them believe that I have been, in
some measure, the slave of circumstances beyond human control. I
would wish them to seek out, for me, in the details I am about to
give, some little oasis of *fatality* amid a wilderness of error. I would
have them allow—what they cannot refrain from allowing—that, although temptation may have erewhile existed as great, man was
never *thus*, at least, tempted before—certainly, never *thus* fell. And
is it therefore that he has never thus suffered? Have I not indeed
been living in a dream? And am I not now dying a victim to the horror and the mystery of the wildest of all sublunary visions?

I am the descendant of a race whose imaginative and easily excit-
able temperament has at all times rendered them remarkable; and,

1. William Chamberlayne (1619—89), remembered for his heroic poem *Pharonnida*
(1659), which has a romantic Eastern setting.
2. Elagabalus or Heliogabalus, Roman emperor whose reign (A.D. 218–22) was noted
for its profligacy and licentiousness.

in my earliest infancy, I gave evidence of having fully inherited the family character. As I advanced in years it was more strongly developed; becoming, for many reasons, a cause of serious disquietude to my friends, and of positive injury to myself. I grew self-willed, addicted to the wildest caprices, and a prey to the most ungovernable passions. Weak-minded, and beset with constitutional infirmities akin to my own, my parents could do but little to check the evil propensities which distinguished me. Some feeble and ill-directed efforts resulted in complete failure on their part, and, of course, in total triumph on mine. Thenceforward my voice was a household law; and at an age when few children have abandoned their leading-strings I was left to the guidance of my own will, and became, in all but name, the master of my own actions.

My earliest recollections of a school-life are connected with a large, rambling Elizabethan house, in a misty-looking village of England, where were a vast number of gigantic and gnarled trees, and where all the houses were excessively ancient. In truth, it was a dream-like and spirit-soothing place, that venerable old town. At this moment, in fancy, I feel the refreshing chilliness of its deeply-shadowed avenues, inhale the fragrance of its thousand shrubberies, and thrill anew with undefinable delight at the deep hollow note of the church-bell, breaking, each hour, with sullen and sudden roar, upon the stillness of the dusky atmosphere in which the fretted Gothic steeple lay imbedded and asleep.

It gives me, perhaps, as much of pleasure as I can now in any manner experience to dwell upon minute recollections of the school and its concerns. Steeped in misery as I am—misery, alas! only too real—I shall be pardoned for seeking relief, however slight and temporary, in the weakness of a few rambling details. These, moreover, utterly trivial, and even ridiculous in themselves, assume to my fancy adventitious importance, as connected with a period and a locality when and where I recognize the first ambiguous monitions of the destiny which afterwards so fully overshadowed me. Let me then remember.

The house, I have said, was old and irregular. The grounds were extensive, and a high and solid brick wall, topped with a bed of mortar and broken glass, encompassed the whole. This prison-like rampart formed the limit of our domain; beyond it we saw but thrice a week—once every Saturday afternoon, when, attended by two ushers, we were permitted to take brief walks in a body through some of the neighboring fields—and twice during Sunday, when we were paraded in the same formal manner to the morning and evening service in the one church of the village. Of this church the principal of our school was pastor. With how deep a spirit of wonder and perplexity was I wont to regard him from our remote pew in the gallery, as, with step solemn and slow, he ascended the pulpit! This reverend man, with countenance so demurely benign, with robes so glossy and so clerically flowing, with wig so minutely powdered, so rigid and so vast,—could this be he who, of late, with sour visage, and in snuffy habiliments, administered, ferule in hand, the Draconian Laws [3] of the academy? Oh, gigantic paradox, too utterly monstrous for solution!

At an angle of the ponderous wall frowned a more ponderous gate. It was riveted and studded with iron bolts, and surmounted with jagged iron spikes. What impressions of deep awe did it inspire! It was never opened save for the three periodical egressions and ingressions already mentioned; then, in every creak of its mighty hinges, we found a plentitude of mystery—a world of matter for solemn remark, or for more solemn meditation.

The extensive enclosure was irregular in form, having many capacious recesses. Of these, three or four of the largest constituted the play-ground. It was level, and covered with fine hard gravel. I well remember it had no trees, nor benches, nor anything similar within it. Of course it was in the rear of the house. In front lay a small parterre,[4] planted with box and other shrubs; but through this sacred division we passed only upon rare occasions indeed—such as a first advent to school or final departure thence, or perhaps when, a parent or friend having called for us, we joyfully took our way home for the Christmas or Midsummer holidays.

But the house!—how quaint an old building was this!—to me how veritably a palace of enchantment! There was really no end to its windings—to its incomprehensible subdivisions. It was difficult, at any given time, to say with certainty upon which of its two stories one happened to be. From each room to every other there were sure to be found three or four steps either in ascent or descent. Then the lateral branches were innumerable, inconceivable, and so returning in upon themselves that our most exact ideas in regard to the whole mansion were not very far different from those with which we pondered upon infinity. During the five years of my residence here I was never able to ascertain, with precision, in what remote locality lay the little sleeping apartment assigned to myself and some eighteen or twenty other scholars.

The school-room was the largest in the house—I could not help thinking, in the world. It was very long, narrow, and dismally low, with pointed Gothic windows and a ceiling of oak. In a remote and terror-inspiring angle was a square enclosure of eight or ten feet, comprising the *sanctum*,[5] "during hours," of our principal, the Rev-

3. Draco, chief magistrate of Athens in 621 B.C., promulgated an unusually severe code of laws.
4. Level plot of ground containing an ornamental arrangement of flower beds.
5. Private retreat; originally a shrine or "holy place."

erend Dr. Bransby. It was a solid structure, with massy door, sooner than open which in the absence of the "Dominie" [6] we would all have willingly perished by the *peine forte et dure*.[7] In other angles were two other similar boxes, far less reverenced, indeed, but still greatly matters of awe. One of these was the pulpit of the "classical" usher, one of the "English and mathematical." Interspersed about the room, crossing and recrossing in endless irregularity, were innumerable benches and desks, black, ancient, and time-worn, piled desperately with much-bethumbed books, and so be-seamed with initial letters, names at full length, grotesque figures, and other multiplied efforts of the knife, as to have entirely lost what little of original form might have been their portion in days long departed. A huge bucket with water stood at one extremity of the room, and a clock of stupendous dimensions at the other.

Encompassed by the massy walls of this venerable academy, I passed, yet not in tedium or disgust, the years of the third lustrum of my life. The teeming brain of childhood requires no external world of incident to occupy or amuse it; and the apparently dismal monotony of a school was replete with more intense excitement than my riper youth has derived from luxury, or my full manhood from crime. Yet I must believe that my first mental development had in it much of the uncommon—even much of the *outré*.[8] Upon mankind at large the events of very early existence rarely leave in mature age any definite impression. All is gray shadow—a weak and irregular remembrance—an indistinct regathering of feeble pleasures and phantasmagoric pains. With me this is not so. In childhood I must have felt with the energy of a man what I now find stamped upon memory in lines as vivid, as deep, and as durable as the *exergues* [9] of the Carthaginian medals.

Yet in fact—in the fact of the world's view—how little was there to remember! The morning's awakening, the nightly summons to bed; the connings, the recitations; the periodical half-holidays, and perambulations; the play-ground, with its broils, its pastimes, its intrigues;—these, by a mental sorcery long forgotten, were made to involve a wilderness of sensation, a world of rich incident, an uni-verse of varied emotion, of excitement the most passionate and spirit-stirring. *"Oh, le bon temps, que ce siècle de fer!"* [10]

In truth, the ardor, the enthusiasm, and the imperiousness of my disposition, soon rendered me a marked character among my

6. Schoolmaster.
7. "Severe and hard punishment": a form of torture in which the prisoner's body was pressed by heavy weights until he confessed or died.
8. Extravagant or outlandish quality.
9. Inscriptions on the back of ancient medallions.
10. "Oh, the best of times, this age of iron!"—from Voltaire's poem of 1736, "Le Mondain" ("The Worldly Man"), a defense of luxury and the present "Age of Iron" (as against those who look back nostalgically to a lost Golden Age).

schoolmates, and by slow but natural gradations gave me an ascendency over all not greatly older than myself: over all with a single exception. This exception was found in the person of a scholar, who, although no relation, bore the same Christian and surname as myself,—a circumstance, in fact, little remarkable; for, notwithstanding a noble descent, mine was one of those every-day appellations which seem by prescriptive right to have been, time out of mind, the common property of the mob. In this narrative I have therefore designated myself as William Wilson,—a fictitious title not very dissimilar to the real. My namesake alone, of those who in school-phraseology constituted "our set," presumed to compete with me in the studies of the class—in the sports and broils of the play-ground—to refuse implicit belief in my assertions, and submission to my will—indeed, to interfere with my arbitrary dictation in any respect whatsoever. If there is on earth a supreme and unqualified despotism, it is the despotism of a master-mind in boyhood over the less energetic spirits of its companions.

Wilson's rebellion was to me a source of the greatest embarrassment; the more so as, in spite of the bravado with which in public I made a point of treating him and his pretensions, I secretly felt that I feared him, and could not help thinking the equality, which he maintained so easily with myself, a proof of his true superiority; since not to be overcome cost me a perpetual struggle. Yet this superiority, even this equality, was in truth acknowledged by no one but myself; our associates, by some unaccountable blindness, seemed not even to suspect it. Indeed, his competition, his resistance, and especially his impertinent and dogged interference with my purposes, were not more pointed than private. He appeared to be destitute alike of the ambition which urged, and of the passionate energy of mind which enabled, me to excel. In his rivalry he might have been supposed actuated solely by a whimsical desire to thwart, astonish, or mortify myself; although there were times when I could not help observing, with a feeling made up of wonder, abasement, and pique, that he mingled with his injuries, his insults, or his contradictions, a certain most inappropriate, and assuredly most unwelcome, *affectionateness* of manner. I could only conceive this singular behavior to arise from a consummate self-conceit assuming the vulgar airs of patronage and protection.

Perhaps it was this latter trait in Wilson's conduct, conjoined with our identity of name, and the mere accident of our having entered the school upon the same day, which set afloat the notion that we were brothers, among the senior classes in the academy. These do not usually inquire with much strictness into the affairs of their juniors. I have before said, or should have said, that Wilson was not in the most remote degree connected with my family. But assuredly if we *had* been brothers we must have been twins; for, after leaving Dr. Bransby's, I casually learned that my namesake was born on the nineteenth of January, 1813; and this is a somewhat remarkable coincidence; for the day is precisely that of my own nativity.

It may seem strange that in spite of the continual anxiety occasioned me by the rivalry of Wilson, and his intolerable spirit of contradiction, I could not bring myself to hate him altogether. We had, to be sure, nearly every day a quarrel in which, yielding me publicly the palm of victory, he, in some manner, contrived to make me feel that it was he who had deserved it; yet a sense of pride on my part, and a veritable dignity on his own, kept us always upon what are called "speaking terms," while there were many points of strong congeniality in our tempers, operating to awake in me a sentiment which our position alone, perhaps, prevented from ripening into friendship. It is difficult, indeed, to define, or even to describe, my real feelings towards him. They formed a motley and heterogeneous admixture: some petulant animosity, which was not yet hatred, some esteem, more respect, much fear, with a world of uneasy curiosity. To the moralist it will be unnecessary to say, in addition, that Wilson and myself were the most inseparable of companions.

It was no doubt the anomalous state of affairs existing between us, which turned all my attacks upon him (and they were many, either open or covert) into the channel of banter or practical joke (giving pain while assuming the aspect of mere fun) rather than into a more serious and determined hostility. But my endeavors on this head were by no means uniformly successful, even when my plans were the most wittily concocted; for my namesake had much about him, in character, of that unassuming and quiet austerity which, while enjoying the poignancy of its own jokes, has no heel of Achilles in itself, and absolutely refuses to be laughed at. I could find, indeed, but one vulnerable point, and that lying in a personal peculiarity arising, perhaps, from constitutional disease, would have been spared by any antagonist less at his wit's end than myself:—my rival had a weakness in the faucial or guttural organs, which precluded him from raising his voice at any time *above a very low whisper*. Of this defect I did not fail to take what poor advantage lay in my power.

Wilson's retaliations in kind were many; and there was one form of his practical wit that disturbed me beyond measure. How his sagacity first discovered at all that so petty a thing would vex me, is a question I never could solve; but having discovered, he habitually practised the annoyance. I had always felt aversion to my uncourtly patronymic, and its very common, if not plebeian, prænomen.[11] The words were venom in my ears; and when, upon the day

11. Family name (patronymic) and first name (prænomen).

of my arrival, a second William Wilson came also to the academy, I felt angry with him for bearing the name, and doubly disgusted with the name because a stranger bore it, who would be the cause of its two-fold repetition, who would be constantly in my presence, and whose concerns, in the ordinary routine of the school business, must inevitably, on account of the detestable coincidence, be often confounded with my own.

The feeling of vexation thus engendered grew stronger with every circumstance tending to show resemblance, moral or physical, between my rival and myself. I had not then discovered the remarkable fact that we were of the same age; but I saw that we were of the same height, and I perceived that we were even singularly alike in general contour of person and outline of feature. I was galled, too, by the rumor touching a relationship, which had grown current in the upper forms. In a word, nothing could more seriously disturb me, (although I scrupulously concealed such disturbance) than any allusion to a similarity of mind, person, or condition existing between us. But, in truth, I had no reason to believe that (with the exception of the matter of relationship, and in the case of Wilson himself) this similarity had ever been made a subject of comment, or even observed at all by our schoolfellows. That *he* observed it in all its bearings, and as fixedly as I, was apparent; but that he could discover in such circumstances so fruitful a field of annoyance can only be attributed, as I said before, to his more than ordinary penetration.

His cue, which was to perfect an imitation of myself, lay both in words and in actions; and most admirably did he play his part. My dress it was an easy matter to copy; my gait and general manner were, without difficulty, appropriated; in spite of his constitutional defect, even my voice did not escape him. My louder tones were, of course, unattempted, but then the key,—it was identical; *and his singular whisper,—it grew the very echo of my own.*

How greatly this most exquisite portraiture harassed me (for it could not justly be termed a caricature) I will not now venture to describe. I had but one consolation—in the fact that the imitation, apparently, was noticed by myself alone, and that I had to endure only the knowing and strangely sarcastic smiles of my namesake himself. Satisfied with having produced in my bosom the intended effect, he seemed to chuckle in secret over the sting he had inflicted, and was characteristically disregardful of the public applause which the success of his witty endeavors might have so easily elicited. That the school, indeed, did not feel his design, perceive its accomplishment, and participate in his sneer, was, for many anxious months, a riddle I could not resolve. Perhaps the *gradation* of his copy rendered it not so readily perceptible; or, more possibly, I owed my security to the masterly air of the copyist, who, disdaining the letter, (which in a painting is all the obtuse can see) gave but the full spirit of his original for my individual contemplation and chagrin.

I have already more than once spoken of the disgusting air of patronage which he assumed toward me, and of his frequent officious interference with my will. This interference often took the ungracious character of advice; advice not openly given, but hinted or insinuated. I received it with a repugnance which gained strength as I grew in years. Yet, at this distant day, let me do him the simple justice to acknowledge that I can recall no occasion when the suggestions of my rival were on the side of those errors or follies so usual to his immature age and seeming inexperience; that his moral sense, at least, if not his general talents and worldly wisdom, was far keener than my own; and that I might, to-day, have been a better, and thus a happier man, had I less frequently rejected the counsels embodied in those meaning whispers which I then but too cordially hated and too bitterly despised.

As it was, I at length grew restive in the extreme under his distasteful supervision, and daily resented more and more openly what I considered his intolerable arrogance. I have said that, in the first years of our connection as schoolmates, my feelings in regard to him might have been easily ripened into friendship; but, in the latter months of my residence at the academy, although the intrusion of his ordinary manner had, beyond doubt, in some measure abated, my sentiments, in nearly similar proportion, partook very much of positive hatred. Upon one occasion he saw this, I think, and afterwards avoided or made a show of avoiding me.

It was about the same period, if I remember aright, that, in an altercation of violence with him, in which he was more than usually thrown off his guard, and spoke and acted with an openness of demeanor rather foreign to his nature, I discovered, or fancied I discovered, in his accent, his air and general appearance, a something which first startled, and then deeply interested me, by bringing to mind dim visions of my earliest infancy—wild, confused and thronging memories of a time when memory herself was yet unborn. I cannot better describe the sensation which oppressed me than by saying that I could with difficulty shake off the belief of my having been acquainted with the being who stood before me, at some epoch very long ago—some point of the past even infinitely remote. The delusion, however, faded rapidly as it came; and I mention it at all but to define the day of the last conversation I there held with my singular namesake.

The huge old house, with its countless subdivisions, had several large chambers communicating with each other, where slept the greater number of the students. There were, however, (as must necessarily happen in a building so awkwardly planned) many little nooks or recesses, the odds and ends of the structure; and these the economic ingenuity of Dr. Bransby had also fitted up as dormitories; although, being the merest closets, they were capable of accommodating but a single individual. One of these small apartments was occupied by Wilson.

One night, about the close of my fifth year at the school, and immediately after the altercation just mentioned, finding every one wrapped in sleep, I arose from bed, and, lamp in hand, stole through a wilderness of narrow passages from my own bedroom to that of my rival. I had long been plotting one of those ill-natured pieces of practical wit at his expense in which I had hitherto been so uniformly unsuccessful. It was my intention, now, to put my scheme in operation, and I resolved to make him feel the whole extent of the malice with which I was imbued. Having reached his closet, I noiselessly entered, leaving the lamp, with a shade over it, on the outside. I advanced a step, and listened to the sound of his tranquil breathing. Assured of his being asleep, I returned, took the light, and with it again approached the bed. Close curtains were around it, which, in the prosecution of my plan, I slowly and quietly withdrew, when the bright rays fell vividly upon the sleeper, and my eyes at the same moment upon his countenance. I looked,—and a numbness, an iciness of feeling, instantly pervaded my frame. My breast heaved, my knees tottered, my whole spirit became possessed with an objectless yet intolerable horror. Gasping for breath, I lowered the lamp in still nearer proximity to the face. Were these,—*these* the lineaments of William Wilson? I saw, indeed, that they were his, but I shook as if with a fit of the ague, in fancying they were not. What *was* there about them to confound me in this manner? I gazed,—while my brain reeled with a multitude in incoherent thoughts. Not thus he appeared—assuredly not *thus*— in the vivacity of his waking hours. The same name! the same contour of person! The same day of arrival at the academy! And then his dogged and meaningless imitation of my gait, my voice, my habits, and my manner! Was it, in truth, within the bounds of human possibility, that *what I now saw* was the result, merely, of the habitual practice of this sarcastic imitation? Awestricken, and with a creeping shudder, I extinguished the lamp, passed silently from the chamber, and left, at once, the halls of that old academy, never to enter them again.

After a lapse of some months, spent at home in mere idleness, I found myself a student at Eton.[12] The brief interval had been suf-

12. Eton College, famous English preparatory school near Windsor.

ficient to enfeeble my remembrance of the events at Dr. Bransby's
or at least to effect a material change in the nature of the feelings
with which I remembered them. The truth—the tragedy—of the
drama was no more. I could now find room to doubt the evidence of
my senses; and seldom called up the subject at all but with wonder
at the extent of human credulity, and a smile at the vivid force of
the imagination which I hereditarily possessed. Neither was this
species of scepticism likely to be diminished by the character of the
life I led at Eton. The vortex of thoughtless folly, into which I there
so immediately and so recklessly plunged, washed away all but the
froth of my past hours, engulfed at once every solid or serious impression, and left to memory only the veriest levities of a former
existence.

I do not wish, however, to trace the course of my miserable profligacy here—a profligacy which set at defiance the laws, while it
eluded the vigilance, of the institution. Three years of folly, passed
without profit, had but given me rooted habits of vice, and added,
in a somewhat unusual degree, to my bodily stature, when, after a
week of soulless dissipation, I invited a small party of the most dissolute students to a secret carousal in my chambers. We met at a
late hour of the night; for our debaucheries were to be faithfully
protracted until morning. The wine flowed freely, and there were
not wanting other and perhaps more dangerous seductions; so that
the gray dawn had already faintly appeared in the east while our
delirious extravagance was at its height. Madly flushed with cards
and intoxication, I was in the act of insisting upon a toast of more
than wonted profanity, when my attention was suddenly diverted
by the violent, although partial, unclosing of the door of the apartment, and by the eager voice of a servant from without. He said that
some person, apparently in great haste, demanded to speak with me
in the hall.

Wildly excited with wine, the unexpected interruption rather delighted than surprised me. I staggered forward at once, and a few
steps brought me to the vestibule of the building. In this low and
small room there hung no lamp; and now no light at all was admitted, save that of the exceedingly feeble dawn which made its way
through the semi-circular window. As I put my foot over the threshold, I became aware of the figure of a youth about my own height,
and habited in a white kerseymere morning frock, cut in the novel
fashion of the one I myself wore at the moment. This the faint light
enabled me to perceive; but the features of his face I could not distinguish. Upon my entering, he strode hurriedly up to me, and,
seizing me by the arm with a gesture of petulant impatience, whispered the words "William Wilson!" in my ear.

I grew perfectly sober in an instant.

There was that in the manner of the stranger, and in the tremulous shake of his uplifted finger, as he held it between my eyes and the light, which filled me with unqualified amazement; but it was not this which had so violently moved me. It was the pregnancy of solemn admonition in the singular, low, hissing utterance; and, above all, it was the character, the tone, *the key*, of those few, simple, and familiar, yet *whispered* syllables, which came with a thousand thronging memories of by-gone days, and struck upon my soul with the shock of a galvanic battery. Ere I could recover the use of my senses he was gone.

Although this event failed not of a vivid effect upon my disordered imagination, yet was it as evanescent as vivid. For some weeks, indeed, I busied myself in earnest inquiry, or was wrapped in a cloud of morbid speculation. I did not pretend to disguise from my perception the identity of the singular individual who thus perseveringly interfered with my affairs, and harassed me with his insinuated counsel. But who and what was this Wilson?—and whence came he?—and what were his purposes? Upon neither of these points could I be satisfied—merely ascertaining, in regard to him, that a sudden accident in his family had caused his removal from Dr. Bransby's academy on the afternoon of the day in which I myself had eloped. But in a brief period I ceased to think upon the subject, my attention being all absorbed in a contemplated departure for Oxford. Thither I soon went, the uncalculating vanity of my parents furnishing me with an outfit and annual establishment which would enable me to indulge at will in the luxury already so dear to my heart—to vie in profuseness of expenditure with the haughtiest heirs of the wealthiest earldoms in Great Britain.

Excited by such appliances to vice, my constitutional temperament broke forth with redoubled ardor, and I spurned even the common restraints of decency in the mad infatuation of my revels. But it were absurd to pause in the detail of my extravagance. Let it suffice, that among spendthrifts I out-Heroded Herod,[13] and that, giving name to a multitude of novel follies, I added no brief appendix to the long catalogue of vices then usual in the most dissolute university of Europe.

It could hardly be credited, however, that I had, even here, so utterly fallen from the gentlemanly estate as to seek acquaintance with the vilest arts of the gambler by profession, and, having become an adept in his despicable science, to practise it habitually as a means of increasing my already enormous income at the expense of the weak-minded among my fellow-collegians. Such, nevertheless, was the fact. And the very enormity of this offence against all

13. To outdo even the worst example. See *Hamlet*, III.ii.15.

manly and honorable sentiment proved, beyond doubt, the main if not the sole reason of the impunity with which it was committed. Who, indeed, among my most abandoned associates, would not rather have disputed the clearest evidence of his senses, than have suspected of such courses the gay, the frank, the generous William Wilson—the noblest and most liberal commoner at Oxford: him whose follies (said his parasites) were but the follies of youth and unbridled fancy—whose errors but inimitable whim—whose darkest vice but a careless and dashing extravagance?

I had been now two years successfully busied in this way, when there came to the university a young *parvenu* [14] nobleman, Glendinning—rich, said report, as Herodes Atticus [15]—his riches, too, as easily acquired. I soon found him of weak intellect, and of course marked him as a fitting subject for my skill. I frequently engaged him in play, and contrived, with the gambler's usual art, to let him win considerable sums, the more effectually to entangle him in my snares. At length, my schemes being ripe, I met him (with the full intention that this meeting should be final and decisive) at the chambers of a fellow-commoner (Mr. Preston), equally intimate with both, but who, to do him justice, entertained not even a remote suspicion of my design. To give to this a better coloring, I had contrived to have assembled a party of some eight or ten, and was solicitously careful that the introduction of cards should appear accidental, and originate in the proposal of my contemplated dupe himself. To be brief upon a vile topic, none of the low finesse was omitted, so customary upon similar occasions that it is a just matter for wonder how any are still found so besotted as to fall its victim.

We had protracted our sitting far into the night, and I had at length effected the manœuvre of getting Glendinning as my sole antagonist. The game, too, was my favorite *écarté*.[16] The rest of the company, interested in the extent of our play, had abandoned their own cards, and were standing around us as spectators. The *parvenu*, who had been induced, by my artifices in the early part of the evening, to drink deeply, now shuffled, dealt, or played, with a wild nervousness of manner for which his intoxication, I thought, might partially but could not altogether account. In a very short period he had become my debtor to a large amount, when, having taken a long draught of port, he did precisely what I had been coolly anticipating—he proposed to double our already extravagant stakes. With a well-feigned show of reluctance, and not until after my repeated refusal had seduced him into some angry words which gave a color

14. An upstart; one who has suddenly risen to wealth or position.
15. Herodes Atticus of Marathon (A.D. 101–77), a famous patron of learning, who did much through his riches and culture to enhance the glory of Athens.
16. A game for two persons, played with a pack from which the cards under seven have been discarded.

of pique to my compliance, did I finally comply. The result, of course, did but prove how entirely the prey was in my toils; in less than an hour he had quadrupled his debt. For some time his countenance had been losing the florid tinge lent it by the wine; but now, to my astonishment, I perceived that it had grown to a pallor truly fearful. I say, to my astonishment. Glendinning had been represented to my eager inquiries as immeasurably wealthy; and the sums which he had as yet lost, although in themselves vast, could not, I supposed, very seriously annoy, much less so violently affect him. That he was overcome by the wine just swallowed, was the idea which most readily presented itself; and, rather with a view to the preservation of my own character in the eyes of my associates, than from any less interested motive, I was about to insist, peremptorily, upon a discontinuance of the play, when some expressions at my elbow from among the company, and an ejaculation evincing utter despair on the part of Glendinning, gave me to understand that I had effected his total ruin under circumstances which, rendering him an object for the pity of all, should have protected him from the ill offices even of a fiend.

What now might have been my conduct it is difficult to say. The pitable condition of my dupe had thrown an air of embarrassed gloom over all; and for some moments a profound silence was maintained, during which I could not help feeling my cheeks tingle with the many burning glances of scorn or reproach cast upon my by the less abandoned of the party. I will even own that an intolerable weight of anxiety was for a brief instant lifted from my bosom by the sudden and extraordinary interruption which ensued. The wide, heavy folding-doors of the apartment were all at once thrown open, to their full extent, with a vigorous and rushing impetuosity that extinguished, as if by magic, every candle in the room. Their light, in dying, enabled us just to perceive that a stranger had entered, about my own height, and closely muffled in a cloak. The darkness, however, was now total; and we could only *feel* that he was standing in our midst. Before any one of us could recover from the extreme astonishment into which this rudeness had thrown all, we heard the voice of the intruder.

"Gentlemen," he said, in a low, distinct, and never-to-be-forgotten *whisper* which thrilled to the very marrow of my bones, "gentlemen, I make no apology for this behavior, because, in thus behaving, I am but fulfilling a duty. You are, beyond doubt, uninformed of the true character of the person who has to-night won at *écarté* a large sum of money from Lord Glendinning. I will therefore put you upon an expeditious and decisive plan of obtaining this very necessary information. Please to examine, at your leisure, the inner linings of the cuff of his left sleeve, and the several little packages which may be found in the somewhat capacious pockets of his embroidered morning wrapper."

While he spoke, so profound was the stillness that one might have heard a pin drop upon the floor. In ceasing, he departed at once, and as abruptly as he had entered. Can I—shall I describe my sensations? Must I say that I felt all the horrors of the damned? Most assuredly I had little time for reflection. Many hands roughly seized me upon the spot, and lights were immediately re-procured. A search ensued. In the lining of my sleeve were found all the court cards essential in *écarté*, and, in the pockets of my wrapper, a number of packs, fac-similes of those used at our sittings, with the single exception that mine were of the species called, technically, *arrondis*; the honors being slightly convex at the ends, the lower cards slightly convex at the sides. In this disposition, the dupe who cuts, as customary, at the length of the pack, will invariably find that he cuts his antagonist an honor; while the gambler, cutting at the breadth, will, as certainly, cut nothing for his victim which may count in the records of the game.

Any burst of indignation upon this discovery would have affected me less than the silent contempt, or the sarcastic composure, with which it was received.

"Mr. Wilson," said our host, stooping to remove from beneath his feet an exceedingly luxurious cloak of rare furs, "Mr. Wilson, this is your property." (The weather was cold; and, upon quitting my own room, I had thrown a cloak over my dressing wrapper, putting it off upon reaching the scene of play.) "I presume it is supererogatory to seek here" (eying the folds of the garment with a bitter smile) "for any farther evidence of your skill. Indeed, we have had enough. You will see the necessity, I hope, of quitting Oxford—at all events, of quitting instantly my chambers."

Abased, humbled to the dust as I then was, it is probable that I should have resented this galling language by immediate personal violence, had not my whole attention been at the moment arrested by a fact of the most startling character. The cloak which I had worn was of a rare description of fur; how rare, how extravagantly costly, I shall not venture to say. Its fashion, too, was of my own fantastic invention; for I was fastidious to an absurd degree of coxcombry, in matters of this frivolous nature. When, therefore, Mr. Preston reached me that which he had picked up upon the floor, and near the folding-doors of the apartment, it was with an astonishment nearly bordering upon terror, that I perceived my own already hanging on my arm, (where I had no doubt unwittingly placed it) and that the one presented me was but its exact counterpart in every, in even the minutest possible particular. The singular being who had so disastrously exposed me, had been muffled, I remembered, in a cloak; and none had been worn at all by any of the members of our party, with the exception of myself. Retaining some presence of mind, I took the one offered me by Preston; placed it, unnoticed, over my own; left the apartment with a resolute scowl of defiance; and, next morning ere dawn of day, commenced a hurried journey from Oxford to the continent, in a perfect agony of horror and of shame.

I fled in vain. My evil destiny pursued me as if in exultation, and proved, indeed, that the exercise of its mysterious dominion had as yet only begun. Scarcely had I set foot in Paris, ere I had fresh evidence of the detestable interest taken by this Wilson in my concerns. Years flew, while I experienced no relief. Villain!—at Rome, with how untimely, yet with how spectral an officiousness, stepped he in between me and my ambition! At Vienna, too—at Berlin—and at Moscow! Where, in truth, had I *not* bitter cause to curse him within my heart? From his inscrutable tyranny did I at length flee, panic-stricken, as from a pestilence; and to the very ends of the earth *I fled in vain.*

And again, and again, in secret communion with my own spirit, would I demand the questions, "Who is he?—whence came he?—and what are his objects?" But no answer was there found. And now I scrutinized, with a minute scrutiny, the forms, and the methods, and the leading traits of his impertinent supervision. But even here there was very little upon which to base a conjecture. It was noticeable, indeed, that, in no one of the multiplied instances in which he had of late crossed my path, had he so crossed it except to frustrate those schemes, or to disturb those actions, which, if fully carried out, might have resulted in bitter mischief. Poor justification this, in truth, for an authority so imperiously assumed! Poor indemnity of natural rights of self-agency so pertinaciously, so insultingly denied!

I had also been forced to notice that my tormentor, for a very long period of time, (while scrupulously and with miraculous dexterity maintaining his whim of an identity of apparel with myself) had so contrived it, in the execution of his varied interference with my will, that I saw not, at any moment, the features of his face. Be Wilson what he might, *this*, at least, was but the veriest of affectation, or of folly. Could he, for an instant, have supposed that, in my admonisher at Eton—in the destroyer of my honor at Oxford,—in him who thwarted my ambition at Rome, my revenge at Paris, my passionate love at Naples, or what he falsely termed my avarice in Egypt,—that in this, my arch-enemy and evil genius, I could fail to recognize the William Wilson of my school-boy days: the namesake, the companion, the rival, the hated and dreaded rival at Dr.

Bransby's? Impossible!—but let me hasten to the last eventful scene of the drama.

Thus far I had succumbed supinely to this imperious domination. The sentiment of deep awe with which I habitually regarded the elevated character, the majestic wisdom, the apparent omnipresence and omnipotence of Wilson, added to a feeling of even terror, with which certain other traits in his nature and assumptions inspired me, had operated, hitherto, to impress me with an idea of my own utter weakness and helplessness, and to suggest an implicit, although bitterly reluctant submission to his arbitrary will. But, of late days, I had given myself up entirely to wine; and its maddening influence upon my hereditary temper rendered me more and more impatient of control. I began to murmur, to hesitate, to resist. And was it only fancy which induced me to believe that, with the increase of my own firmness, that of my tormentor underwent a proportional diminution? Be this as it may, I now began to feel the inspiration of a burning hope, and at length nurtured in my secret thoughts a stern and desperate resolution that I would submit no longer to be enslaved.

It was at Rome, during the Carnival of 18—, that I attended a masquerade in the palazzo of the Neapolitan Duke Di Broglio. I had indulged more freely than usual in the excesses of the wine-table; and now the suffocating atmosphere of the crowded room irritated me beyond endurance. The difficulty, too, of forcing my way through the mazes of the company contributed not a little to the ruffling of my temper; for I was anxiously seeking (let me not say with what unworthy motive) the young, the gay, the beautiful wife of the aged and doting Di Broglio. With a too unscrupulous confidence she had previously communicated to me the secret of the costume in which she would be habited, and now, having caught a glimpse of her person, I was hurrying to make my way into her presence. At this moment I felt a light hand placed upon my shoulder, and that ever-remembered, low, damnable *whisper* within my ear.

In an absolute frenzy of wrath, I turned at once upon him who had thus interrupted me, and seized him violently by the collar. He was attired, as I had expected, in a costume altogether similar to my own; wearing a Spanish cloak of blue velvet, begirt about the waist with a crimson belt sustaining a rapier. A mask of black silk entirely covered his face.

"Scoundrel!" I said, in a voice husky with rage, while every syllable I uttered seemed as new fuel to my fury; "scoundrel! imposter! accursed villain! you shall not—you *shall not* dog me unto death! Follow me, or I stab you where you stand!"—and I broke my way from the ball-room into a small antechamber adjoining, dragging him unresistingly with me as I went.

Upon entering, I thrust him furiously from me. He staggered against the wall, while I closed the door with an oath, and commanded him to draw. He hesitated but for an instant; then, with a slight sigh, drew in silence, and put himself upon his defence.

The contest was brief indeed. I was frantic with every species of wild excitement, and felt within my single arm the energy and power of a multitude. In a few seconds I forced him by sheer strength against the wainscoting, and thus, getting him at mercy, plunged my sword, with brute ferocity, repeatedly through and through his bosom.

At that instant some person tried the latch of the door. I hastened to prevent an intrusion, and then immediately returned to my dying antagonist. But what human language can adequately portray *that* astonishment, *that* horror which possessed me at the spectacle then presented to view? The brief moment in which I averted my eyes had been sufficient to produce, apparently, a material change in the arrangements at the upper or farther end of the room. A large mirror—so at first it seemed to me in my confusion—now stood where none had been perceptible before; and, as I stepped up to it in extremity of terror, mine own image, but with features all pale and dabbled in blood, advanced to meet me with a feeble and tottering gait.

Thus it appeared, I say, but was not. It was my antagonist—it was Wilson, who then stood before me in the agonies of his dissolution. His mask and cloak lay, where he had thrown them, upon the floor. Not a thread in all his raiment—not a line in all the marked and singular lineaments of his face which was not, even in the most absolute identity, *mine own!*

It was Wilson; but he spoke no longer in a whisper, and I could have fancied that I myself was speaking while he said:—

"You have conquered, and I yield. Yet, henceforward art thou also dead—dead to the World, to Heaven and to Hope! In me didst thou exist—and, in my death, see by this image, which is thine own, how utterly thou hast murdered thyself."

From *Tales of the Grotesque and Arabesque* (1840)

THE FALL OF THE HOUSE OF USHER

Son coeur est un luth suspendu;
Sitôt qu'on le touche il résonne.
　　　　　　　　　—Béranger [1]

During the whole of a dull, dark, and soundless day in the autumn
of the year, when the clouds hung oppressively low in the heavens,
I had been passing alone, on horseback, through a singularly dreary
tract of country; and at length found myself, as the shades of the
evening drew on, within view of the melancholy House of Usher. I
know not how it was, but, with the first glimpse of the building, a
sense of insufferable gloom pervaded my spirit. I say insufferable;
for the feeling was unrelieved by any of that half pleasurable, because poetic, sentiment with which the mind usually receives even
the sternest natural images of the desolate or terrible. I looked upon
the scene before me—upon the mere house, and the simple landscape features of the domain, upon the bleak walls, upon the vacant
eyelike windows, upon a few rank sedges, and upon a few white
trunks of decayed trees—with an utter depression of soul which I
can compare to no earthly sensation more properly than to the af-
terdream of the reveler upon opium: the bitter lapse into everyday
life, the hideous dropping off of the veil. There was an iciness, a
sinking, a sickening of the heart, an unredeemed dreariness of
thought, which no goading of the imagination could torture into
aught of the sublime. What was it—I paused to think—what was it
that so unnerved me in the contemplation of the House of Usher? It
was a mystery all insoluble; nor could I grapple with the shadowy
fancies that crowded upon me as I pondered. I was forced to fall
back upon the unsatisfactory conclusion that while, beyond doubt,
there *are* combinations of very simple natural objects which have
the power of thus affecting us, still the analysis of this power lies
among considerations beyond our depth. It was possible, I reflected, that a mere different arrangement of the particulars of the
scene, of the details of the picture, would be sufficient to modify, or
perhaps to annihilate, its capacity for sorrowful impression, and,
acting upon this idea, I reined my horse to the precipitous brink of
a black and lurid tarn [2] that lay in unruffled luster by the dwelling,

1. "His heart is a suspended lute; /Whenever one touches it, it resounds." From the
poem "Le refus" by Pierre-Jean de Béranger (1780–1857), a writer of popular verse.
2. A small, stagnant body of water having no significant tributaries.

and gazed down—but with a shudder even more thrilling than before—upon the remodeled and inverted images of the gray sedge, and the ghastly tree-stems, and the vacant and eyelike windows.

Nevertheless, in this mansion of gloom I now proposed to myself a sojourn of some weeks. Its proprietor, Roderick Usher, had been one of my boon companions in boyhood; but many years had elapsed since our last meeting. A letter, however, had lately reached me in a distant part of the country—a letter from him—which in its wildly importunate nature had admitted of no other than a personal reply. The MS. gave evidence of nervous agitation. The writer spoke of acute bodily illness, of a mental disorder which oppressed him, and of an earnest desire to see me, as his best and indeed his only personal friend, with a view of attempting, by the cheerfulness of my society, some alleviation of his malady. It was the manner in which all this, and much more, was said—it was the apparent *heart* that went with his request—which allowed me no room for hesitation; and I accordingly obeyed forthwith what I still considered a very singular summons.

Although as boys we had been even intimate associates, yet I really knew little of my friend. His reserve had been always excessive and habitual. I was aware, however, that his very ancient family had been noted, time out of mind, for a peculiar sensibility of temperament, displaying itself, through long ages, in many works of exalted art, and manifested of late in repeated deeds of munificent yet unobtrusive charity, as well as in a passionate devotion to the intricacies, perhaps even more than to the orthodox and easily recognizable beauties, of musical science. I had learned, too, the very remarkable fact that the stem of the Usher race, all time-honored as it was, had put forth at no period any enduring branch; in other words, that the entire family lay in the direct line of descent, and had always, with a very trifling and very temporary variation, so lain. It was this deficiency, I considered, while running over in thought the perfect keeping of the character of the premises with the accredited character of the people, and while speculating upon the possible influence which the one, in the long lapse of centuries, might have exercised upon the other—it was this deficiency, perhaps, of collateral issue, and the consequent undeviating transmission from sire to son of the patrimony with the name, which had at length so identified the two as to merge the original title of the estate in the quaint and equivocal appellation of the "House of Usher"—an appellation which seemed to include, in the minds of the peasantry who used it, both the family and the family mansion.

I have said that the sole effect of my somewhat childish experiment, that of looking down within the tarn, had been to deepen the first singular impression. There can be no doubt that the consciousness of the rapid increase of my superstition—for why should I not so term it?—served mainly to accelerate the increase itself. Such, I have long known, is the paradoxical law of all sentiments having terror as a basis. And it might have been for this reason only, that, when I again uplifted my eyes to the house itself from its image in the pool, there grew in my mind a strange fancy—a fancy so ridiculous, indeed, that I but mention it to show the vivid force of the sensations which oppressed me. I had so worked upon my imagination as really to believe that about the whole mansion and domain there hung an atmosphere peculiar to themselves and their immediate vicinity: an atmosphere which had no affinity with the air of heaven, but which had reeked up from the decayed trees, and the gray wall, and the silent tarn; a pestilent and mystic vapor, dull, sluggish, faintly discernible, and leaden-hued.

Shaking off from my spirit what *must* have been a dream, I scanned more narrowly the real aspect of the building. Its principal feature seemed to be that of an excessive antiquity. The discoloration of ages had been great. Minute fungi overspread the whole exterior, hanging in a fine tangled webwork from the eaves. Yet all this was apart from any extraordinary dilapidation. No portion of the masonry had fallen; and there appeared to be a wild inconsistency between its still perfect adaptation of parts and the crumbling condition of the individual stones. In this there was much that reminded me of the specious totality of old woodwork which has rotted for long years in some neglected vault, with no disturbance from the breath of the external air. Beyond this indication of extensive decay, however, the fabric gave little token of instability. Perhaps the eye of a scrutinizing observer might have discovered a barely perceptible fissure, which, extending from the roof of the building in front, made its way down the wall in a zigzag direction, until it became lost in the sullen waters of the tarn.

Noticing these things, I rode over a short causeway to the house. A servant in waiting took my horse, and I entered the Gothic archway of the hall. A valet, of stealthy step, thence conducted me in silence through many dark and intricate passages in my progress to the *studio* of his master. Much that I encountered on the way contributed, I know not how, to heighten the vague sentiments of which I have already spoken. While the objects around me—while the carvings of the ceiling, the somber tapestries of the walls, the ebon blackness of the floors, and the phantasmagoric armorial trophies which rattled as I strode, were but matters to which, or to such as which, I had been accustomed from my infancy,—while I hesitated not to acknowledge how familiar was all this, I still wondered to find how unfamiliar were the fancies which ordinary images were stirring up. On one of the staircases I met the physician of the family. His countenance, I thought, wore a mingled expression of low cunning and perplexity. He accosted me with trepidation and passed on. The valet now threw open a door and ushered me into the presence of his master.

The room in which I found myself was very large and lofty. The windows were long, narrow, and pointed, and at so vast a distance from the black oaken floor as to be altogether inaccessible from within. Feeble gleams of encrimsoned light made their way through the trellised panes, and served to render sufficiently distinct the more prominent objects around; the eye, however, struggled in vain to reach the remoter angles of the chamber, or the recesses of the vaulted and fretted ceiling. Dark draperies hung upon the walls. The general furniture was profuse, comfortless, antique, and tattered. Many books and musical instruments lay scattered about, but failed to give any vitality to the scene. I felt that I breathed an atmosphere of sorrow. An air of stern, deep, and irredeemable gloom hung over and pervaded all.

Upon my entrance, Usher arose from a sofa on which he had been lying at full length, and greeted me with a vivacious warmth which had much in it, I at first thought, of an overdone cordiality—of the constrained effort of the *ennuyé* [3] man of the world. A glance, however, at his countenance, convinced me of his perfect sincerity. We sat down; and for some moments, while he spoke not, I gazed upon him with a feeling half of pity, half of awe. Surely man had never before so terribly altered, in so brief a period, as had Roderick Usher! It was with difficulty that I could bring myself to admit the identity of the wan being before me with the companion of my early boyhood. Yet the character of his face had been at all times remarkable. [4] A cadaverousness of complexion; an eye large, liquid, and luminous beyond comparison; lips somewhat thin and very pallid, but of a surpassingly beautiful curve; a nose of a delicate Hebrew model, but with a breadth of nostril unusual in similar formations; a finely-molded chin, speaking, in its want of prominence, of a want of moral energy; hair of a more than weblike softness and tenuity,—these features, with an inordinate expansion above the regions of the temple, made up altogether a countenance not easily to be forgotten. And now in the mere exaggeration of the prevailing character of these features, and of the expression they were wont to convey, lay so much of change that I doubted to whom I spoke. The now ghastly pallor of the skin, and the now miraculous luster of the

3. Bored.
4. As many critics have noted, the description of Usher is a likeness of Poe himself. Poe believed in the principles of phrenology, the popular nineteenth-century "science" based on the theory that the external conformations of the cranium are an index to mental and spiritual qualities.

eye, above all things startled and even awed me. The silken hair, too, had been suffered to grow all unheeded, and as, in its wild gossamer texture, it floated rather than fell about the face, I could not, even with effort, connect its arabesque expression with any idea of simple humanity.

In the manner of my friend I was at once struck with an incoherence, an inconsistency; and I soon found this to arise from a series of feeble and futile struggles to overcome an habitual trepidancy, an excessive nervous agitation. For something of this nature I had indeed been prepared, no less by his letter than by reminiscences of certain boyish traits, and by conclusions deduced from his peculiar physical conformation and temperament. His action was alternately vivacious and sullen. His voice varied rapidly from a tremulous indecision (when the animal spirits seemed utterly in abeyance) to that species of energetic concision—that abrupt, weighty, unhurried, and hollow-sounding enunciation, that leaden, self-balanced, and perfectly modulated guttural utterance—which may be observed in the lost drunkard, or the irreclaimable eater of opium, during the periods of his most intense excitement.

It was thus that he spoke of the object of my visit, of his earnest desire to see me, and of the solace he expected me to afford him. He entered at some length into what he conceived to be the nature of his malady. It was, he said, a constitutional and a family evil, and one for which he despaired to find a remedy—a mere nervous affection, he immediately added, which would undoubtedly soon pass off. It displayed itself in a host of unnatural sensations. Some of these, as he detailed them, interested and bewildered me; although, perhaps, the terms and the general manner of the narration had their weight. He suffered much from a morbid acuteness of the senses; the most insipid food was alone endurable; he could wear only garments of certain texture; the odors of all flowers were oppressive; his eyes were tortured by even faint light; and there were but peculiar sounds, and these from stringed instruments, which did not inspire him with horror.

To an anomalous species of terror I found him a bounden slave. "I shall perish," said he, "I *must* perish in this deplorable folly. Thus, thus, and not otherwise, shall I be lost. I dread the events of the future, not in themselves, but in their results. I shudder at the thought of any, even the most trivial, incident, which may operate upon this intolerable agitation of soul. I have, indeed, no abhorrence of danger, except in its absolute effect,—in terror. In this unnerved, in this pitiable condition, I feel that the period will sooner or later arrive when I must abandon life and reason together in some struggle with the grim phantasm, FEAR."

I learned moreover at intervals, and through broken and equivocal hints, another singular feature of his mental condition. He was enchained by certain superstitious impressions in regard to the dwelling which he tenanted, and whence for many years he had never ventured forth, in regard to an influence whose supposititious force was conveyed in terms too shadowy here to be restated,—an influence which some peculiarities in the mere form and substance of his family mansion had, by dint of long sufferance, he said, obtained over his spirit; an effect which the *physique* of the gray walls and turrets, and of the dim tarn into which they all looked down, had at length brought about upon the *morale* of his existence.

He admitted, however, although with hesitation, that much of the peculiar gloom which thus afflicted him could be traced to a more natural and far more palpable origin,—to the severe and long-continued illness, indeed to the evidently approaching dissolution, of a tenderly beloved sister, his sole companion for long years, his last and only relative on earth. "Her decease," he said, with a bitterness which I can never forget, "would leave him (him, the hopeless and the frail) the last of the ancient race of the Ushers." While he spoke, the lady Madeline (for so was she called) passed slowly through a remote portion of the apartment, and, without having noticed my presence, disappeared. I regarded her with an utter astonishment not unmingled with dread, and yet I found it impossible to account for such feelings. A sensation of stupor oppressed me, as my eyes followed her retreating steps. When a door, at length, closed upon her, my glance sought instinctively and eagerly the countenance of the brother; but he had buried his face in his hands, and I could only perceive that a far more than ordinary wanness had overspread the emaciated fingers through which trickled many passionate tears.

The disease of the lady Madeline had long baffled the skill of her physicians. A settled apathy, a gradual wasting away of the person, and frequent although transient affections of a partially cataleptical[5] character, were the unusual diagnosis. Hitherto she had steadily borne up against the pressure of her malady, and had not betaken herself finally to bed; but, on the closing-in of the evening of my arrival at the house, she succumbed (as her brother told me at night with inexpressible agitation) to the prostrating power of the destroyer; and I learned that the glimpse I had obtained of her person would thus probably be the last I should obtain,—that the lady, at least while living, would be seen by me no more.

For several days ensuing, her name was unmentioned by either Usher or myself; and during this period I was busied in earnest endeavors to alleviate the melancholy of my friend. We painted and

5. Catalepsy is an illness marked by seizure or trance, with a suspension of sensation and consciousness: suspended animation.

read together; or I listened, as if in a dream, to the wild improvisations of his speaking guitar. And thus, as a closer and still closer intimacy admitted me more unreservedly into the recesses of his spirit, the more bitterly did I perceive the futility of all attempt at cheering a mind from which darkness, as if an inherent positive quality, poured forth upon all objects of the moral and physical universe, in one unceasing radiation of gloom.

I shall ever bear about me a memory of the many solemn hours I thus spent alone with the master of the House of Usher. Yet I should fail in any attempt to convey an idea of the exact character of the studies, or of the occupations, in which he involved me, or led me the way. An excited and highly distempered ideality threw a sulphureous luster over all. His long, improvised dirges will ring forever in my ears. Among other things, I hold painfully in mind a certain singular perversion and amplification of the wild air of the last waltz of Von Weber.[6] From the paintings over which his elaborate fancy brooded, and which grew, touch by touch, into vaguenesses at which I shuddered the more thrillingly because I shuddered knowing not why,—from these paintings (vivid as their images now are before me) I would in vain endeavor to educe more than a small portion which should lie within the compass of merely written words. By the utter simplicity, by the nakedness of his designs, he arrested and over-awed attention. If ever mortal painted an idea, that mortal was Roderick Usher. For me at least, in the circumstances then surrounding me, there arose, out of the pure abstractions which the hypochondriac contrived to throw upon his canvas, an intensity of intolerable awe, no shadow of which felt I ever yet in the contemplation of the certainly glowing yet too concrete reveries of Fuseli.[7]

One of the phantasmagoric conceptions of my friend, partaking not so rigidly of the spirit of abstraction, may be shadowed forth, although feebly, in words. A small picture presented the interior of an immensely long and rectangular vault or tunnel, with low walls, smooth, white, and without interruption or device. Certain accessory points of the design served well to convey the idea that this excavation lay at an exceeding depth below the surface of the earth. No outlet was observed in any portion of its vast extent, and no torch, or other artificial source of light, was discernible; yet a flood of intense rays rolled throughout, and bathed the whole in a ghastly and inappropriate splendor.

6. Karl Maria von Weber (1786–1826) was considered the father of the Romantic School in opera. The "last waltz of Von Weber" was actually composed by Karl Gottlieb Reissiger (1798–1859), and is to be found in his *Danses brillantes* (No. 5).
7. Henry Fuseli (1741–1825), Swiss-born English painter, a master of the grotesque and the visionary.

I have just spoken of that morbid condition of the auditory nerve which rendered all music intolerable to the sufferer, with the exception of certain effects of stringed instruments. It was, perhaps, the narrow limits to which he thus confined himself upon the guitar, which gave birth, in great measure, to the fantastic character of his performances. But the fervid *facility* of his *impromptus* could not be so accounted for. They must have been, and were, in the notes as well as in the words of his wild fantasias (for he not unfrequently accompanied himself with rimed verbal improvisations), the result of that intense mental collectedness and concentration to which I have previously alluded as observable only in particular moments of the highest artificial excitement. The words of one of these rhapsodies I have easily remembered. I was, perhaps, the more forcibly impressed with it as he gave it, because, in the under or mystic current of its meaning, I fancied that I perceived, and for the first time, a full consciousness, on the part of Usher, of the tottering of his lofty reason upon her throne. The verses, which were entitled "The Haunted Palace," [8] ran very nearly, if not accurately, thus:—

I

In the greenest of our valleys
　By good angels tenanted,
Once a fair and stately palace—
　Radiant palace—reared its head.
In the monarch Thought's dominion.
　It stood there;
Never seraph spread a pinion
　Over fabric half so fair.

II

Banners yellow, glorious, golden,
　On its roof did float and flow
(This—all this—was in the olden
　Time long ago),
And every gentle air that dallied,
　In that sweet day,
Along the ramparts plumed and pallid,
　A winged odor went away.

III

Wanderers in that happy valley
　Through two luminous windows saw
Spirits moving musically
　To a lute's well-tuned law,

8. "The Haunted Palace" was published separately by Poe in 1839, before the appearance of the story.

Round about a throne, where sitting,
    Porphyrogene,[9]
In state his glory well befitting,
    The ruler of the realm was seen.

IV

And all with pearl and ruby glowing
    Was the fair palace door,
Through which came flowing, flowing, flowing,
    And sparkling evermore,
A troop of Echoes, whose sweet duty
    Was but to sing,
In voices of surpassing beauty,
    The wit and wisdom of their king.

V

But evil things, in robes of sorrow,
    Assailed the monarch's high estate;
(Ah, let us mourn, for never morrow
    Shall dawn upon him, desolate!)
And, round about his home, the glory
    That blushed and bloomed
Is but a dim-remembered story
    Of the old time entombed.

VI

And travelers now within that valley
    Through the red-litten windows see
Vast forms that move fantastically
    To a discordant melody;
While, like a ghastly rapid river,
    Through the pale door,
A hideous throng rush out forever,
    And laugh—but smile no more.

I well remember that suggestions arising from this ballad led us into a train of thought, wherein there became manifest an opinion of Usher's which I mention, not so much on account of its novelty (for other men have thought thus) as on account of the pertinacity with which he maintained it. This opinion, in its general form, was that of the sentience of all vegetable things. But in his disordered fancy, the idea had assumed a more daring character, and trespassed, under certain conditions, upon the kingdom of inorganization. I lack words to express the full extent or the earnest *abandon* of his persuasion. The belief, however, was connected (as I have previously hinted) with the gray stones of the home of his forefathers. The conditions of the sentience had been here, he imagined, fulfilled in the method of collocation of these stones,—in the order

9. Wellborn, "born to the purple."

of their arrangement, as well as in that of the many fungi which overspread them, and of the decayed trees which stood around; above all, in the long undisturbed endurance of this arrangement, and in its reduplication in the still waters of the tarn. Its evidence— the evidence of the sentience—was to be seen, he said (and I here started as he spoke), in the gradual yet certain condensation of an atmosphere of their own about the waters and the walls. The result was discoverable, he added, in that silent yet importunate and terrible influence which for centuries had molded the destinies of his family, and which made *him* what I now saw him,—what he was. Such opinions need no comment, and I will make none.

Our books—the books which for years had formed no small portion of the mental existence of the invalid—were, as might be supposed, in strict keeping with this character of phantasm. We pored together over such works as the Ververt and Chartreuse of Gresset; the Belphegor of Machiavelli; the Heaven and Hell of Swedenborg; the Subterranean Voyage of Nicholas Klimm by Holberg; the Chiromancy of Robert Flud, of Jean D'Indagine, and of De la Chambre; the Journey into the Blue Distance of Tieck; and the City of the Sun of Campanella. One favorite volume was a small octavo edition of the *Directorium Inquisitorum,* by the Dominican Eymeric de Gironne; and there were passages in Pomponius Mela, about the old African Satyrs and Aegipans, over which Usher would sit dreaming for hours. His chief delight, however, was found in the perusal of an exceedingly rare and curious book in quarto Gothic,— the manual of a forgotten church,—the *Vigiliæ Mortuorum secundum Chorum Ecclesiæ Maguntinæ.*[10]

I could not help thinking of the wild ritual of this work, and of its probable influence upon the hypochondriac, when one evening,

10. Usher's library is an image of his mind. *Ver-vert* and *La Chartreuse* are satirical, anticlerical poems by Jean-Baptiste-Louis Gresset (1709–77); *Belfagor* is an antifeminist satire by Niccolò Machiavelli (1469–1527). The next two titles suggest Usher's obsession with the relations between the world of spirit and the world of matter: *Heaven and Its Wonders and Hell,* by the philosopher-mystic Emanuel Swedenborg (1688–1772), treats of the correspondences between heaven and earth; the *Journey to the World Under Ground, Being the Subterraneous Travels of Niels Klim,* by Ludwig Holberg (1684–1754), is a Utopian fantasy cast in the form of an imaginary voyage (translated into English in 1742). Chiromancy (palmistry) is the subject of the books by Robert Fludd (1574–1637), English philosopher-alchemist; Jean D'Indaginé; and Marin Cureau de la Chambre. "Journey into the Blue Distance" is the subtitle of a fairytale novel by Johann Ludwig Tieck (*Das alte Buch,* 1834). Tommaso Campanella (1568–1639), Italian philosopher, writes of an ideal or Utopian community in his *Civitas Solis* ("City of the Sun," 1623). The *Directorium inquisitorum* of Nicolás Eymerich (1320–99) deals with the methods and tortures of the Spanish Inquisition. Pomponius Mela (first century A.D.) wrote a geography describing such fabulous creatures as the satyrs and Aegipans (goatmen) of Africa. The mysterious last item in the catalogue, *The Vigils of the Dead According to the Choir of the Church of Mayence* [Mainz], is an extremely rare book, printed c. 1500, obviously the prize of Usher's library.

having informed me abruptly that the lady Madeline was no more, he stated his intention of preserving her corpse for a fortnight, (previously to its final interment) in one of the numerous vaults within the main walls of the building. The worldly reason, however, assigned for this singular proceeding was one which I did not feel at liberty to dispute. The brother had been led to his resolution (so he told me) by consideration of the unusual character of the malady of the deceased, of certain obtrusive and eager inquiries on the part of her medical men, and of the remote and exposed situation of the burial ground of the family. I will not deny that when I called to mind the sinister countenance of the person whom I met upon the staircase, on the day of my arrival at the house, I had no desire to oppose what I regarded as at best but a harmless, and by no means an unnatural, precaution.[11]

At the request of Usher, I personally aided him in the arrangement for the temporary entombment. The body having been encoffined, we two alone bore it to its rest. The vault in which we placed it (and which had been so long unopened that our torches, half smothered in its oppressive atmosphere, gave us little opportunity for investigation) was small, damp, and entirely without means of admission for light; lying, at great depth, immediately beneath that portion of the building in which was my own sleeping apartment. It had been used apparently, in remote feudal times, for the worst purposes of a donjon keep, and in later days as a place of deposit for powder, or some other highly combustible substance, as a portion of its floor, and the whole interior of a long archway through which we reached it, were carefully sheathed with copper. The door, of massive iron, had been also similarly protected. Its immense weight caused an unusually sharp grating sound as it moved upon its hinges.

Having deposited our mournful burden upon tressels within this region of horror, we partially turned aside the yet unscrewed lid of the coffin, and looked upon the face of the tenant. A striking similitude between the brother and sister now first arrested my attention; and Usher, divining, perhaps, my thoughts, murmured out some few words from which I learned that the deceased and himself had been twins, and that sympathies existed between them. Our glances, however, rested not long upon the dead, for we could not regard her unawed. The disease which had thus entombed the lady in the maturity of youth, had left, as usual in all maladies of a strictly cataleptical character, the mockery of a faint blush upon the bosom and the face, and that suspiciously lingering smile upon the lip which is so terrible in death. We replaced and screwed down

11. "Body-snatching" for the purpose of medical experimentation was not uncommon in the early nineteenth century.

the lid, and having secured the door of iron, made our way, with toil, into the scarcely less gloomy apartments of the upper portion of the house.

And now, some days of bitter grief having elapsed, an observable change came over the features of the mental disorder of my friend. His ordinary manner had vanished. His ordinary occupations were neglected or forgotten. He roamed from chamber to chamber with hurried, unequal, and objectless step. The pallor of his countenance had assumed, if possible, a more ghastly hue, but the luminousness of his eye had utterly gone out. The once occasional huskiness of his tone was heard no more; and a tremulous quavor, as if of extreme terror, habitually characterized his utterance. There were times, indeed, when I thought his unceasingly agitated mind was laboring with some oppressive secret, to divulge which he struggled for the necessary courage. At times, again, I was obliged to resolve all into the mere inexplicable vagaries of madness, for I beheld him gazing upon vacancy for long hours, in an attitude of the profoundest attention, as if listening to some imaginary sound. It was no wonder that his condition terrified—that it infected me. I felt creeping upon me, by slow yet certain degrees, the wild influences of his own fantastic yet impressive superstitions.

It was, especially, upon retiring to bed late in the night of the seventh or eighth day after the placing of the lady Madeline within the donjon, that I experienced the full power of such feelings. Sleep came not near my couch, while the hours waned and waned away. I struggled to reason off the nervousness which had dominion over me. I endeavored to believe that much if not all of what I felt was due to the bewildering influence of the gloomy furniture of the room,—of the dark and tattered draperies which, tortured into motion by the breath of a rising tempest, swayed fitfully to and fro upon the walls, and rustled uneasily about the decorations of the bed. But my efforts were fruitless. An irrepressible tremor gradually pervaded my frame; and at length there sat upon my very heart an incubus of utterly causeless alarm. Shaking this off with a gasp and a struggle, I uplifted myself upon the pillows, and, peering earnestly within the intense darkness of the chamber, hearkened—I know not why, except that an instinctive spirit prompted me—to certain low and indefinite sounds which came, through the pauses of the storm, at long intervals, I knew not whence. Overpowered by an intense sentiment of horror, unaccountable yet unendurable, I threw on my clothes with haste (for I felt that I should sleep no more during the night), and endeavored to arouse myself from the pitiable condition to which I had fallen, by pacing rapidly to and fro through the apartment.

I had taken but few turns in this manner, when a light step on an adjoining staircase arrested my attention. I presently recognized it as that of Usher. In an instant afterward he rapped with a gentle touch at my door, and entered, bearing a lamp. His countenance was, as usual, cadaverously wan—but, moreover, there was a species of mad hilarity in his eyes,—an evidently restrained hysteria in his whole demeanor. His air appalled me—but anything was preferable to the solitude which I had so long endured, and I even welcomed his presence as a relief.

"And you have not seen it?" he said abruptly, after having stared about him for some moments in silence,—"you have not then seen it?—but, stay! you shall." Thus speaking, and having carefully shaded his lamp, he hurried to one of the casements, and threw it freely open to the storm.

The impetuous fury of the entering gust nearly lifted us from our feet. It was, indeed, a tempestuous yet sternly beautiful night, and one wildly singular in its terror and its beauty. A whirl wind had apparently collected its force in our vicinity, for there were frequent and violent alterations in the direction of the wind; and the exceeding density of the clouds (which hung so low as to press upon the turrets of the house) did not prevent our perceiving the lifelike velocity with which they flew careering from all points against each other, without passing away into the distance. I say that even their exceeding density did not prevent our perceiving this; yet we had no glimpse of the moon or stars, nor was there any flashing forth of the lightning. But the under surfaces of the huge masses of agitated vapor, as well as all terrestrial objects immediately around us, were glowing in the unnatural light of a faintly luminous and distinctly visible gaseous exhalation which hung about and enshrouded the mansion.

"You must not—you shall not behold this!" said I shudderingly, to Usher, as I led him with a gentle violence from the window to a seat. "These appearances, which bewilder you, are merely electrical phenomena not uncommon—or it may be that they have their ghastly origin in the rank miasma of the tarn. Let us close this casement; the air is chilling and dangerous to your frame. Here is one of your favorite romances. I will read, and you shall listen;—and so we will pass away this terrible night together."

The antique volume which I had taken up was the "Mad Trist" of Sir Launcelot Canning,[12] but I had called it a favorite of Usher's more in sad jest than in earnest; for, in truth, there is little in its uncouth and unimaginative prolixity which could have had interest for the lofty and spiritual ideality of my friend. It was, however, the only book immediately at hand; and I indulged a vague hope that

12. "The Mad Trist" is evidently an invention of Poe's.

the excitement which now agitated the hypochondriac might find relief (for the history of mental disorder is full of similar anomalies) even in the extremeness of the folly which I should read. Could I have judged, indeed, by the wild, overstrained air of vivacity with which he hearkened, or apparently hearkened, to the words of the tale, I might well have congratulated myself upon the success of my design.

I had arrived at that well-known portion of the story where Ethelred, the hero of the Trist, having sought in vain for peaceable admission into the dwelling of the hermit, proceeds to make good an entrance by force. Here, it will be remembered, the words of the narrative run thus:—

"And Ethelred, who was by nature of a doughty heart, and who was now mighty withal on account of the powerfulness of the wine which he had drunken, waited no longer to hold parley with the hermit, who, in sooth, was of an obstinate and maliceful turn, but, feeling the rain upon his shoulders, and fearing the rising of the tempest, uplifted his mace outright, and with blows made quickly room in the plankings of the door for his gauntleted hand; and now, pulling therewith sturdily, he so cracked, and ripped, and tore all asunder, that the noise of the dry and hollow-sounding wood alarumed and reverberated throughout the forest."

At the termination of this sentence I started, and for a moment paused; for it appeared to me (although I at once concluded that my excited fancy had deceived me)—it appeared to me that from some very remote portion of the mansion there came, indistinctly, to my ears, what might have been in its exact similarity of character the echo (but a stifled and dull one certainly) of the very cracking and ripping sound which Sir Launcelot had so particularly described. It was, beyond doubt, the coincidence alone which had arrested my attention; for amid the rattling of the sashes of the casements, and the ordinary commingled noises of the still increasing storm, the sound, in itself, had nothing, surely, which should have interested or disturbed me. I continued the story:—

"But the good champion Ethelred, now entering within the door, was sore enraged and amazed to perceive no signal of the maliceful hermit; but, in the stead thereof, a dragon of a scaly and prodigious demeanor, and of a fiery tongue, which sate in guard before a palace of gold with a floor of silver, and upon the wall there hung a shield of shining brass with this legend enwritten:—

> Who entereth herein, a conqueror hath bin;
> Who slayeth the dragon, the shield he shall win.

And Ethelred uplifted his mace, and struck upon the head of the dragon, which fell before him, and gave up his pesty breath, with a shriek so horrid and harsh, and withal so piercing, that Ethelred had fain to close his ears with his hands against the dreadful noise of it, the like whereof was never before heard."

Here again I paused abruptly, and now with a feeling of wild amazement, for there could be no doubt whatever that, in this instance, I did actually hear (although from what direction it proceeded I found it impossible to say) a low and apparently distant, but harsh, protracted, and most unusual screaming or grating sound,—the exact counterpart of what my fancy had already conjured up for the dragon's unnatural shriek as described by the romancer.

Oppressed as I certainly was, upon the occurrence of this second and most extraordinary coincidence, by a thousand conflicting sensations, in which wonder and extreme terror were predominant, I still retained sufficient presence of mind to avoid exciting, by any observation, the sensitive nervousness of my companion. I was by no means certain that he had noticed the sounds in question; although, assuredly, a strange alteration had during the last few minutes taken place in his demeanor. From a position fronting my own, he had gradually brought round his chair, so as to sit with his face to the door of the chamber; and thus I could but partially perceive his features, although I saw that his lips trembled as if he were murmuring inaudibly. His head had dropped upon his breast; yet I knew that he was not asleep, from the wide rigid opening of the eyes as I caught a glance of it in profile. The motion of his body, too, was at variance with this idea, for he rocked from side to side with a gentle yet constant and uniform sway. Having rapidly taken notice of all this, I resumed the narrative of Sir Launcelot, which thus proceeded:—

"And now the champion, having escaped from the terrible fury of the dragon, bethinking himself of the brazen shield, and of the breaking up of the enchantment which was upon it, removed the carcass from out of the way before him, and approached valorously over the silver pavement of the castle to where the shield was upon the wall; which in sooth tarried not for his full coming, but fell down at his feet upon the silver floor, with a mighty great and terrible ringing sound."

No sooner had these syllables passed my lips than—as if a shield of brass had indeed, at the moment, fallen heavily upon a floor of silver—I became aware of a distinct, hollow, metallic, and clangorous yet apparently muffled reverberation. Completely unnerved, I leaped to my feet; but the measured rocking movement of Usher was undisturbed. I rushed to the chair in which he sat. His eyes were bent fixedly before him, and throughout his whole countenance there reigned a stony rigidity. But, as I placed my hand upon his shoulder, there came a strong shudder over his whole person; a sickly smile quivered about his lips; and I saw that he spoke in a low, hurried, and gibbering murmur, as if unconscious of my presence. Bending closely over him, I at length drank in the hideous import of his words.

"Not hear it?—yes, I hear it, and *have* heard it. Long—long—long—many minutes, many hours, many days, have I heard it, yet I dared not—oh, pity me, miserable wretch that I am!—I dared not—I *dared* not speak! *We have put her living in the tomb!* Said I not that my senses were acute? I *now* tell you that I have heard her first feeble movements in the hollow coffin. I heard them—many, many days ago—yet I dared not—*I dared not speak!* And now—tonight—Ethelred— ha! ha!—the breaking of the hermit's door, and the deathcry of the dragon, and the clangor of the shield!—say, rather, the rending of her coffin, and the grating of the iron hinges of her prison, and her struggles within the coppered archway of the vault! Oh, whither shall I fly? Will she not be here anon? Is she not hurrying to upbraid me for my haste? Have I not heard her footstep on the stair? Do I not distinguish that heavy and horrible beating of her heart? Madman!"—here he sprang furiously to his feet, and shrieked out his syllables, as if in the effort he were giving up his soul—*"Madman! I tell you that she now stands without the door!"*

As if in the superhuman energy of his utterance there had been found the potency of a spell, the huge antique panels to which the speaker pointed threw slowly back, upon the instant, their ponderous and ebony jaws. It was the work of the rushing gust—but then without those doors there *did* stand the lofty and enshrouded figure of the lady Madeline of Usher! There was blood upon her white robes, and the evidence of some bitter struggle upon every portion of her emaciated frame. For a moment she remained trembling and reeling to and fro upon the threshold—then, with a low moaning cry, fell heavily inward upon the person of her brother, and in her violent and now final death agonies, bore him to the floor a corpse, and a victim to the terrors he had anticipated.

From that chamber and from that mansion I fled aghast. The storm was still abroad in all its wrath as I found myself crossing the old causeway. Suddenly there shot along the path a wild light, and I turned to see whence a gleam so unusual could have issued; for the vast house and its shadows were alone behind me. The radiance was that of the full, setting, and blood-red moon, which now shone vividly through that once barely discernible fissure, of which I have before spoken as extending from the roof of the building, in a zigzag direction, to the base. While I gazed, this fissure rapidly widened—there came a fierce breath of the whirlwind—the entire orb of the satellite burst at once upon my sight—my brain reeled as I saw the mighty walls rushing asunder—there was a long, tumultuous shouting like the voice of a thousand waters [13]—and the deep and dank tarn at my feet closed sullenly and silently over the fragments of the *"House of Usher."*

13. The voice of God is described as the "sound of many waters" in Ezek. 43:2, Rev. 1:15, and Rev. 14.2. In Rev. 14 it is followed by the fall of Babylon.

From *Tales of the Grotesque and Arabesque*
(1840; revised for the *Tales* of 1845)

THE PURLOINED LETTER

Nil sapientiæ odiosius acumine nimio.
Seneca.[1]

At Paris, just after dark one gusty evening in the autumn of 18—, I was enjoying the twofold luxury of meditation and a meerschaum,[2] in company with my friend C. Auguste Dupin, in his little back library, or book-closet, *au troisième, No. 33, Rue Dunôt, Faubourg St. Germain.* For one hour at least we had maintained a profound silence; while each, to any casual observer, might have seemed intently and exclusively occupied with the curling eddies of smoke that oppressed the atmosphere of the chamber. For myself, however, I was mentally discussing certain topics which had formed matter for conversation between us at an earlier period of the evening; I mean the affair of the Rue Morgue, and the mystery attending the murder of Marie Rogêt.[3] I looked upon it, therefore, as something of a coincidence, when the door of our apartment was thrown open and admitted our old acquaintance, Monsieur G——, the Prefect of the Parisian police.[4]

We gave him a hearty welcome; for there was nearly half as much of the entertaining as of the contemptible about the man, and we had not seen him for several years. We had been sitting in the dark, and Dupin now arose for the purpose of lighting a lamp, but sat down again, without doing so, upon G——'s saying that he had called to consult us, or rather to ask the opinion of my friend, about some official business which had occasioned a great deal of trouble.

"If it is any point requiring reflection," observed Dupin, as he forbore to enkindle the wick, "we shall examine it to better purpose in the dark."

"That is another of your odd notions," said the Prefect, who had a fashion of calling everything "odd" that was beyond his comprehension, and thus lived amid an absolute legion of "oddities."

"Very true," said Dupin, as he supplied his visitor with a pipe, and rolled towards him a comfortable chair.

1. "Too great ingenuity is the enemy of wisdom." Seneca was a Roman philosopher and tragedian of the first century A.D.
2. A pipe with a bowl made of meerschaum, a white, clay-like substance.
3. Dupin is the hero of two earlier stories by Poe, "The Murders in the Rue Morgue" and "The Mystery of Marie Rogêt." In the first, Dupin is described as living on the fourth floor (*au troisième,* three flights up) of a "time-eaten and grotesque mansion . . . in a retired and desolate portion of the Faubourg St. Germain."
4. The prefect was the chief commissioner of the Paris police.

"And what is the difficulty now?" I asked. "Nothing more in the assassination way, I hope?"

"Oh, no; nothing of that nature. The fact is, the business is *very* simple indeed, and I make no doubt that we can manage it sufficiently well ourselves; but then I thought Dupin would like to hear the details of it, because it is so excessively *odd.*"

"Simple and odd," said Dupin.

"Why, yes; and not exactly that, either. The fact is, we have all been a good deal puzzled because the affair *is* so simple, and yet baffles us altogether."

"Perhaps it is the very simplicity of the thing which puts you at fault," said my friend.

"What nonsense you *do* talk!" replied the Prefect, laughing heartily.

"Perhaps the mystery is a little *too* plain," said Dupin.

"Oh, good heavens! who ever heard of such an idea?"

"A little *too* self-evident."

"Ha! ha! ha!—ha! ha! ha!—ho! ho! ho!" roared our visitor, profoundly amused, "oh, Dupin, you will be the death of me yet!"

"And what, after all, *is* the matter on hand?" I asked

"Why, I will tell you," replied the Prefect as he gave a long, steady and contemplative puff, and settled himself in his chair. "I will tell you in a few words; but, before I begin, let me caution you that this is an affair demanding the greatest secrecy, and that I should most probably lose the position I now hold, were it known that I confided it to any one."

"Proceed," said I.

"Or not," said Dupin.

"Well, then; I have received personal information, from a very high quarter, that a certain document of the last importance has been purloined from the royal apartments. The individual who purloined it is known; this beyond a doubt; he was seen to take it. It is known, also, that it still remains in his possession."

"How is this known?" asked Dupin.

"It is clearly inferred," replied the Prefect, "from the nature of the document, and from the non-appearance of certain results which would at once arise from its passing *out* of the robber's possession; that is to say, from his employing it as he must design in the end to employ it."

"Be a little more explicit," I said.

"Well, I may venture so far as to say that the paper gives its holder a certain power in a certain quarter where such power is immensely valuable." The Prefect was fond of the cant of diplomacy.

"Still I do not quite understand," said Dupin.

"No? Well; the disclosure of the document to a third person, who shall be nameless, would bring in question the honor of a personage of most exalted station; and this fact gives the holder of the document an ascendency over the illustrious personage whose honor and peace are so jeopardized."

"But this ascendency," I interposed, "would depend upon the robber's knowledge of the loser's knowledge of the robber. Who would dare—"

"The thief," said G——, "is the Minister D——, who dares all things, those unbecoming as well as those becoming a man. The method of the theft was not less ingenious than bold. The document in question—a letter, to be frank—had been received by the personage robbed while alone in the royal boudoir. During its perusal she was suddenly interrupted by the entrance of the other exalted personage from whom especially it was her wish to conceal it. After a hurried and vain endeavor to thrust it in a drawer, she was forced to place it, open as it was, upon a table. The address, however, was uppermost, and, the contents thus unexposed, the letter escaped notice. At this juncture enters the minister D——. His lynx eye immediately perceives the paper, recognizes the handwriting of the address, observes the confusion of the personage addressed, and fathoms her secret. After some business transactions, hurried through in his ordinary manner, he produces a letter somewhat similar to the one in question, opens it, pretends to read it, and then places it in close juxtaposition to the other. Again he converses, for some fifteen minutes, upon the public affairs. At length, in taking leave, he takes also from the table the letter to which he had no claim. Its rightful owner saw, but, of course, dared not call attention to the act, in the presence of the third personage who stood at her elbow. The Minister decamped; leaving his own letter—one of no importance—upon the table."

"Here, then," said Dupin to me, "you have precisely what you demand to make the ascendency complete—the robber's knowledge of the loser's knowledge of the robber."

"Yes," replied the Prefect; "and the power thus attained has, for some months past, been wielded, for political purposes, to a very dangerous extent. The personage robbed is more thoroughly convinced, every day, of the necessity of reclaiming her letter. But this, of course, cannot be done openly. In fine, driven to despair, she has committed the matter to me."

"Than whom," said Dupin, amid a perfect whirlwind of smoke, "no more sagacious agent could, I suppose, be desired, or even imagined."

"You flatter me," replied the Prefect; "but it is possible that some such opinion may have been entertained."

"It is clear," said I, "as you observe, that the letter is still in possession of the Minister; since it is this possession, and not any employment of the letter, which bestows the power. With the employment the power departs."

"True," said G——; "and upon this conviction I proceeded. My first care was to make thorough search of the Minister's Hotel; [5] and here my chief embarrassment lay in the necessity of searching without his knowledge. Beyond all things, I have been warned of the danger which would result from giving him reason to suspect our design."

"But," said I, "you are quite *au fait* [6] in these investigations. The Parisian police have done this thing often before."

"Oh, yes; and for this reason I did not despair. The habits of the Minister gave me, too, a great advantage. He is frequently absent from home all night. His servants are by no means numerous. They sleep at a distance from their master's apartment, and, being chiefly Neapolitans, are readily made drunk. I have keys, as you know, with which I can open any chamber or cabinet in Paris. For three months a night has not passed, during the greater part of which I have not been engaged, personally, in ransacking the D—— Hotel. My honor is interested, and, to mention a great secret, the reward is enormous. So I did not abandon the search until I had become fully satisfied that the thief is a more astute man than myself. I fancy that I have investigated every nook and corner of the premises in which it is possible that the paper can be concealed."

"But is it not possible," I suggested, "that although the letter may be in possession of the Minister, as it unquestionably is, he may have concealed it elsewhere than upon his own premises?"

"This is barely possible," said Dupin. "The present peculiar condition of affairs at court, and especially of those intrigues in which D—— is known to be involved, would render the instant availability of the document—its susceptibility of being produced at a moment's notice—a point of nearly equal importance with its possession."

"Its susceptibility of being produced?" said I.

"That is to say, of being *destroyed*," said Dupin.

"True," I observed; "the paper is clearly then upon the premises. As for its being upon the person of the Minister, we may consider that as out of the question."

"Entirely," said the Prefect. "He has been twice waylaid, as if by footpads,[7] and his person rigorously searched under my own inspection."

"You might have spared yourself this trouble," said Dupin.

5. Mansion or townhouse.
6. Knowledgeable or thoroughly conversant.
7. Highwaymen who attack on foot.

"D——, I presume, is not altogether a fool, and, if not, must have anticipated these waylayings, as a matter of course."

"Not *altogether* a fool," said G——, "but then he's a poet, which I take to be only one remove from a fool."

"True," said Dupin, after a long and thoughtful whiff from his meerschaum, "although I have been guilty of certain doggerel myself."

"Suppose you detail," said I, "the particulars of your search."

"Why, the fact is, we took our time, and we searched *everywhere*. I have had long experience in these affairs. I took the entire building, room by room; devoting the nights of a whole week to each. We examined, first, the furniture of each apartment. We opened every possible drawer; and I presume you know that, to a properly trained police agent, such a thing as a *secret* drawer is impossible. Any man is a dolt who permits a 'secret' drawer to escape him in a search of this kind. The thing is *so* plain. There is a certain amount of bulk—of space—to be accounted for in every cabinet. Then we have accurate rules. The fiftieth part of a line could not escape us. After the cabinets we took the chairs. The cushions we probed with the fine long needles you have seen me employ. From the tables we removed the tops."

"Why so?"

"Sometimes the top of a table, or other similarly arranged piece of furniture, is removed by the person wishing to conceal an article; then the leg is excavated, the article deposited within the cavity, and the top replaced. The bottoms and tops of bedposts are employed in the same way."

"But could not the cavity be detected by sounding?" I asked.

"By no means, if, when the article is deposited, a sufficient wadding of cotton be placed around it. Besides, in our case, we were obliged to proceed without noise."

"But you could not have removed—you could not have taken to pieces *all* articles of furniture in which it would have been possible to make a deposit in the manner you mention. A letter may be compressed into a thin spiral roll, not differing much in shape or bulk from a large knitting-needle, and in this form it might be inserted into the rung of a chair, for example. You did not take to pieces all the chairs?"

"Certainly not; but we did better—we examined the rungs of every chair in the Hotel, and, indeed, the jointings of every description of furniture, by the aid of a most powerful microscope.[8] Had there been any traces of recent disturbance we should not have failed to detect it instantly. A single grain of gimlet-dust, for ex-

8. A powerful magnifying glass.

ample, would have been as obvious as an apple. Any disorder in the gluing—any unusual gaping in the joints—would have sufficed to insure detection."

"I presume you looked to the mirrors, between the boards and the plates, and you probed the beds and the bed-clothes, as well as the curtains and carpets."

"That, of course; and when we had absolutely completed every particle of the furniture in this way, then we examined the house itself. We divided its entire surface into compartments, which we numbered, so that none might be missed; then we scrutinized each individual square inch throughout the premises, including the two houses immediately adjoining, with the microscope, as before."

"The two houses adjoining!" I exclaimed; "you must have had a great deal of trouble."

"We had; but the reward offered is prodigious."

"You include the *grounds* about the houses?"

"All the grounds are paved with brick. They gave us comparatively little trouble. We examined the moss between the bricks, and found it undisturbed."

"You looked among D——'s papers, of course, and into the books of the library?"

"Certainly; we opened every package and parcel; we not only opened every book, but we turned over every leaf in each volume, not contenting ourselves with a mere shake, according to the fashion of some of our police officers. We also measured the thickness of every book-*cover*, with the most accurate admeasurement, and applied to each the most jealous scrutiny of the microscope. Had any of the bindings been recently meddled with, it would have been utterly impossible that the fact should have escaped observation. Some five or six volumes, just from the hands of the binder, we carefully probed, longitudinally, with the needles."

"You explored the floors beneath the carpets?"

"Beyond doubt. We removed every carpet, and examined the boards with the microscope."

"And the paper on the walls?"

"Yes."

"You looked into the cellars?"

"We did."

"Then," I said, "you have been making a miscalculation, and the letter is *not* upon the premises, as you suppose."

"I fear you are right there," said the Prefect. "And now, Dupin, what would you advise me to do?"

"To make a thorough re-search of the premises."

"That is absolutely needless," replied G——. "I am not more sure that I breathe than I am that the letter is not at the Hotel."

"I have no better advice to give you," said Dupin. "You have, of course, an accurate description of the letter?"

"Oh, yes!"—And here the Prefect, producing a memorandum-book, proceeded to read aloud a minute account of the internal, and especially of the external appearance of the missing document. Soon after finishing the perusal of this description, he took his departure, more entirely depressed in spirits than I had ever known the good gentleman before.

In about a month afterwards he paid us another visit, and found us occupied very nearly as before. He took a pipe and a chair and entered into some ordinary conversation. At length I said,—

"Well, but, G——, what of the purloined letter? I presume you have at last made up your mind that there is no such thing as over-reaching the Minister?"

"Confound him, say I—yes; I made the re-examination, however, as Dupin suggested—but it was all labor lost, as I knew it would be."

"How much was the reward offered, did you say?" asked Dupin.

"Why, a very great deal—a *very* liberal reward—I don't like to say how much, precisely; but one thing I *will* say, that I wouldn't mind giving my individual check for fifty thousand francs to any one who could obtain me that letter. The fact is, it is becoming of more and more importance every day; and the reward has been lately doubled. If it were trebled, however, I could do no more than I have done."

"Why, yes," said Dupin, drawlingly, between the whiffs of his meerschaum, "I really—think, G——, you have not exerted yourself—to the utmost in this matter. You might—do a little more, I think, eh?"

"How?—in what way?"

"Why—puff, puff—you might—puff, puff—employ counsel in the matter, eh?—puff, puff, puff. Do you remember the story they tell of Abernethy?" [9]

"No; hang Abernethy!"

"To be sure! hang him and welcome. But, once upon a time, a certain rich miser conceived the design of sponging upon this Abernethy for a medical opinion. Getting up, for this purpose, an ordinary conversation in a private company, he insinuated his case to the physician, as that of an imaginary individual.

" 'We will suppose,' said the miser, 'that his symptoms are such and such; now, doctor, what would *you* have directed him to take?'

" 'Take!' said Abernethy, 'why, take *advice*, to be sure.' "

"But," said the Prefect, a little discomposed, "I am *perfectly* will-

9. Dr. John Abernethy (1764–1831), famous British surgeon.

ing to take advice, and to pay for it. I would *really* give fifty thousand francs to any one who would aid me in the matter."

"In that case," replied Dupin, opening a drawer and producing a check-book, "you may as well fill me up a check for the amount mentioned. When you have signed it, I will hand you the letter."

I was astounded. The Prefect appeared absolutely thunderstricken. For some minutes he remained speechless and motionless, looking incredulously at my friend with open mouth, and eyes that seemed starting from their sockets; then, apparently recovering himself in some measure, he seized a pen, and after several pauses and vacant stares, finally filled up and signed a check for fifty thousand francs, and handed it across the table to Dupin. The latter examined it carefully and deposited it in his pocket-book; then, unlocking an escritoire,[10] took thence a letter and gave it to the Prefect. This functionary grasped it in a perfect agony of joy, opened it with a trembling hand, cast a rapid glance at its contents, and then, scrambling and struggling to the door, rushed at length unceremoniously from the room and from the house, without having uttered a syllable since Dupin had requested him to fill up the check.

When he had gone, my friend entered into some explanations.

"The Parisian police," he said, "are exceedingly able in their way. They are persevering, ingenious, cunning, and thoroughly versed in the knowledge which their duties seem chiefly to demand. Thus, when G—— detailed to us his mode of searching the premises at the Hotel D——, I felt entire confidence in his having made a satisfactory investigation—so far as his labors extended."

"So far as his labors extended?" said I.

"Yes," said Dupin. "The measures adopted were not only the best of their kind, but carried out to absolute perfection. Had the letter been deposited within the range of their search, these fellows would, beyond a question, have found it."

I merely laughed—but he seemed quite serious in all that he said.

"The measures, then," he continued, "were good in their kind, and well executed; their defect lay in their being inapplicable to the case, and to the man. A certain set of highly ingenious resources are, with the Prefect, a sort of Procrustean bed,[11] to which he forcibly adapts his designs. But he perpetually errs by being too deep or too shallow, for the matter in hand; and many a schoolboy is a better reasoner than he. I knew one about eight years of age, whose

10. Writing desk.
11. In mythology, Procrustes was a robber who either stretched or lopped off his victims to fit the size of his beds.

success at guessing in the game of 'even and odd' attracted universal admiration. This game is simple, and is played with marbles.
One player holds in his hand a number of these toys, and demands
of another whether that number is even or odd. If the guess is right,
the guesser wins one; if wrong, he loses one. The boy to whom I
allude won all the marbles of the school. Of course he had some
principle of guessing; and this lay in mere observation and admeasurement of the astuteness of his opponents. For example, an
arrant simpleton is his opponent, and, holding up his closed hand,
asks, 'are they even or odd?' Our schoolboy replies, 'odd,' and
loses; but upon the second trial he wins, for he then says to himself,
'the simpleton had them even upon the first trial, and his amount of
cunning is just sufficient to make him have them odd upon the second; I will therefore guess odd;'—he guesses odd, and wins. Now,
with a simpleton a degree above the first, he would have reasoned
thus: 'This fellow finds that in the first instance I guessed odd, and,
in the second, he will propose to himself, upon the first impulse, a
simple variation from even to odd, as did the first simpleton; but
then a second thought will suggest that this is too simple a variation, and finally he will decide upon putting it even as before. I will
therefore guess even;'—he guesses even, and wins. Now this mode
of reasoning in the schoolboy, whom his fellows termed 'lucky,'—
what, in its last analysis, is it?"

"It is merely," I said, "an identification of the reasoner's intellect
with that of his opponent."

"It is," said Dupin; "and, upon inquiring of the boy by what
means he effected the *thorough* identification in which his success
consisted, I received answer as follows: 'When I wish to find out
how wise, or how stupid, or how good, or how wicked is any one, or
what are his thoughts at the moment, I fashion the expression of my
face, as accurately as possible, in accordance with the expression of
his, and then wait to see what thoughts or sentiments arise in my
mind or heart, as if to match or correspond with the expression.'
This response of the schoolboy lies at the bottom of all the spurious
profundity which has been attributed to Rochefoucauld, to La
Bruyère, to Machiavelli, and to Campanella." [12]

"And the identification," I said, "of the reasoner's intellect with
that of his opponent depends, if I understand you aright, upon the
accuracy with which the opponent's intellect is admeasured."

"For its practical value it depends upon this," replied Dupin;

---

12. François, Duc de la Rochefoucauld (1613–80), was the author of cynical and
paradoxical maxims on human nature; Jean de la Bruyère (1645–96) was another
master of ironic observation; Niccolò Machiavelli (1469–1527) is notorious for his
cynical political philosophy; Tommaso Campanella (1568–1639) was an Italian philosopher noted for his subtlety.

"and the Prefect and his cohort fail so frequently, first, by default of this identification, and, secondly, by ill-admeasurement, or rather through non-admeasurement, of the intellect with which they are engaged. They consider only their *own* ideas of ingenuity; and, in searching for anything hidden, advert only to the modes in which *they* would have hidden it. They are right in this much—that their own ingenuity is a faithful representative of that of *the mass:* but when the cunning of the individual felon is diverse in character from their own, the felon foils them, of course. This always happens when it is above their own, and very usually when it is below. They have no variation of principle in their investigations; at best, when urged by some unusual emergency—by some extraordinary reward—they extend or exaggerate their old modes of *practice,* without touching their principles. What, for example, in this case of D——, has been done to vary the principle of action? What is all this boring, and probing, and sounding, and scrutinizing with the microscope, and dividing the surface of the building into registered square inches—what is it all but an exaggeration *of the application* of the one principle or set of principles of search, which are based upon the one set of notions regarding human ingenuity, to which the Prefect, in the long routine of his duty, has been accustomed? Do you not see he has taken it for granted that *all* men proceed to conceal a letter,—not exactly in a gimlet-hole bored in a chair-leg—but, at least, in *some* out-of-the-way hole or corner suggested by the same tenor of thought which would urge a man to secrete a letter in a gimlet-hole bored in a chair-leg? And do you not see, also, that such *recherchés* [13] nooks for concealment are adapted only for ordinary occasions, and would be adopted only by ordinary intellects; for, in all cases of concealment, a disposal of the article concealed—a disposal of it in this *recherché* manner—is, in the very first instance, presumable and presumed; and thus its discovery depends, not at all upon the acumen, but altogether upon the mere care, patience, and determination of the seekers; and where the case is of importance—or, what amounts to the same thing in the policial eyes, when the reward is of magnitude—the qualities in question have *never* been known to fail. You will now understand what I meant in suggesting that, had the purloined letter been hidden anywhere within the limits of the Prefect's examination—in other words, had the principle of its concealment been comprehended within the principles of the Prefect—its discovery would have been a matter altogether beyond question. This functionary, however, has been thoroughly mystified; and the remote source of his defeat lies in the supposition that the Minister is a fool, because he has

13. Obscure or overly ingenious.

acquired renown as a poet. All fools are poets; this the Prefect *feels;* and he is merely guilty of a *non distributio medii* in thence inferring that all poets are fools." [14]

"But is this really the poet?" I asked. "There are two brothers, I know; and both have attained reputation in letters. The Minister I believe has written learnedly on the Differential Calculus. He is a mathematician, and no poet."

"You are mistaken; I know him well; he is both. As poet *and* mathematician, he would reason well; as mere mathematician, he could not have reasoned at all, and thus would have been at the mercy of the Prefect."

"You surprise me," I said, "by these opinions, which have been contradicted by the voice of the world. You do not mean to set at naught the well-digested idea of centuries. The mathematical reason has long been regarded as *the* reason *par excellence.*"

" '*Il-y-a à parier,*' " replied Dupin, quoting from Chamfort, " '*que toute idée publique, toute convention reçue, est une sottise, car elle a convenue au plus grand nombre.*' [15] The mathematicians, I grant you, have done their best to promulgate the popular error to which you allude, and which is none the less an error for its promulgation as truth. With an art worthy a better cause, for example, they have insinuated the term 'analysis' into application to algebra. The French are the originators of this particular deception; but if a term is of any importance—if words derive any value from applicability—then 'analysis' conveys 'algebra' about as much as, in Latin, '*ambitus*' implies 'ambition,' '*religio*' 'religion,' or '*homines honesti*' a set of honorable men." [16]

"You have a quarrel on hand, I see," said I, "with some of the algebraists of Paris; but proceed."

"I dispute the availability, and thus the value, of that reason which is cultivated in any especial form other than the abstractly logical. I dispute, in particular, the reason educed by mathematical study. The mathematics are the science of form and quantity; mathematical reasoning is merely logic applied to observation upon form and quantity. The great error lies in supposing that even the truths of what is called *pure* algebra are abstract or general truths. And this error is so egregious that I am confounded at the universality

14. In logic, the "undistributed middle" describes a syllogistic fallacy in which neither premise conveys information about all members of the class designated by the middle term (e.g., "All men are sinners, and all weaklings are sinners; therefore all men are weaklings").

15. "The odds are that every familiar idea, every agreed-upon convention, is a piece of folly, since it is acceptable to the great majority." Nicolas-Sébastien Roch de Chamfort (1741–94) was well known for his witty maxims.

16. Dupin's argument is that the common or derived meanings of words often differ from the etymological source. Hence, in Latin, *ambitus* literally means a circle or revolution.

with which it has been received. Mathematical axioms are *not* axioms of general truth. What is true of *relation*—of form and quantity—is often grossly false in regard to morals, for example. In this latter science it is very usually *un*true that the aggregated parts are equal to the whole. In chemistry also the axiom fails. In the consideration of motive it fails; for two motives, each of a given value, have not, necessarily, a value when united, equal to the sum of their values apart. There are numerous other mathematical truths which are only truths within the limits of *relation*. But the mathematician argues, from his *finite truths*, through habit, as if they were of an absolutely general applicability—as the world indeed imagines them to be. Bryant, in his very learned 'Mythology,' mentions an analogous source of error, when he says that 'although the Pagan fables are not believed, yet we forget ourselves continually, and make inferences from them as existing realities.' [17] With the algebraists, however, who are Pagans themselves, the 'Pagan fables' *are* believed, and the inferences are made, not so much through lapse of memory, as through an unaccountable addling of the brains. In short, I never yet encountered the mere mathematician who could be trusted out of equal roots, or one who did not clandestinely hold it as a point of his faith that $x^2 + px$ was absolutely and unconditionally equal to q. Say to one of these gentlemen, by way of experiment, if you please, that you believe occasions may occur where $x^2 + px$ is *not* altogether equal to q, and, having made him understand what you mean, get out of his reach as speedily as convenient, for, beyond doubt, he will endeavor to knock you down.

"I mean to say," continued Dupin, while I merely laughed at his last observations, "that, if the Minister had been no more than a mathematician, the Prefect would have been under no necessity of giving me this check. I knew him, however, as both mathematician and poet, and my measures were adapted to his capacity, with reference to the circumstances by which he was surrounded. I knew him as a courtier, too, and as a bold *intriguant*.[18] Such a man, I considered, could not fail to be aware of the ordinary policial modes of action. He could not have failed to anticipate—and events have proved that he did not fail to anticipate—the waylayings to which he was subjected. He must have foreseen, I reflected, the secret investigations of his premises. His frequent absences from home at night, which were hailed by the Prefect as certain aids to his success, I regarded only as ruses, to afford opportunity for thorough search to the police, and thus the sooner to impress them with the

17. Jacob Bryant (1715–1804), an English antiquary, was the author of *A New System or an Analysis of Ancient Mythology.*
18. Schemer.

conviction to which G——, in fact, did finally arrive—the conviction that the letter was not upon the premises. I felt, also, that the whole train of thought, which I was at some pains in detailing to you just now, concerning the invariable principle of policial action in searches for articles concealed—I felt that this whole train of thought would necessarily pass through the mind of the Minister. It would imperatively lead him to despise all the ordinary *nooks* of concealment. *He* could not, I reflected, be so weak as not to see that the most intricate and remote recess of his Hotel would be as open as his commonest closets to the eyes, to the probes, to the gimlets, and to the microscopes of the Prefect. I saw, in fine, that he would be driven, as a matter of course, to *simplicity,* if not deliberately induced to it as a matter of choice. You will remember, perhaps, how desperately the Prefect laughed when I suggested, upon our first interview, that it was just possible this mystery troubled him so much on account of its being so *very* self-evident."

"Yes," said I, "I remember his merriment well. I really thought he would have fallen into convulsions."

"The material world," continued Dupin, "abounds with very strict analogies to the immaterial; and thus some color of truth has been given to the rhetorical dogma, that metaphor, or simile, may be made to strengthen an argument, as well as to embellish a description. The principle of the *vis inertiæ*,[19] for example, seems to be identical in physics and metaphysics. It is not more true in the former, that a large body is with more difficulty set in motion than a smaller one, and that its subsequent momentum is commensurate with this difficulty, than it is, in the latter, that intellects of the vaster capacity, while more forcible, more constant, and more eventful in their movements than those of inferior grade, are yet the less readily moved, and more embarrassed and full of hesitation in the first few steps of their progress. Again: have you ever noticed which of the street signs, over the shop-doors, are the most attractive of attention?"

"I have never given the matter a thought," I said.

"There is a game of puzzles," he resumed, "which is played upon a map. One party playing requires another to find a given word—the name of town, river, state, or empire—any word, in short, upon the motley and perplexed surface of the chart. A novice in the game generally seeks to embarrass his opponents by giving them the most minutely lettered names; but the adept selects such words as stretch, in large characters, from one end of the chart to the other. These, like the over-largely lettered signs and placards of the street,

19. Inertial force.

escape observation by dint of being excessively obvious; and here the physical oversight is precisely analogous with the moral inapprehension by which the intellect suffers to pass unnoticed those considerations which are too obtrusively and too palpably self-evident. But this is a point, it appears, somewhat above or beneath the understanding of the Prefect. He never once thought it probable, or possible, that the Minister had deposited the letter immediately beneath the nose of the whole world, by way of best preventing any portion of that world from perceiving it.

"But the more I reflected upon the daring, dashing, and discriminating ingenuity of D——; upon the fact that the document must always have been *at hand,* if he intended to use it to good purpose; and upon the decisive evidence, obtained by the Prefect, that it was not hidden within the limits of that dignitary's ordinary search—the more satisfied I became that, to conceal this letter, the Minister had resorted to the comprehensive and sagacious expedient of not attempting to conceal it at all.

"Full of these ideas, I prepared myself with a pair of green spectacles, and called one fine morning, quite by accident, at the Ministerial Hotel. I found D—— at home, yawning, lounging, and dawdling, as usual, and pretending to be in the last extremity of ennui. He is, perhaps, the most really energetic human being now alive—but that is only when nobody sees him.

"To be even with him, I complained of my weak eyes, and lamented the necessity of the spectacles, under cover of which I cautiously and thoroughly surveyed the apartment, while seemingly intent only upon the conversation of my host.

"I paid especial attention to a large writing-table near which he sat, and upon which lay confusedly some miscellaneous letters and other papers, with one or two musical instruments and a few books. Here, however, after a long and very deliberate scrutiny, I saw nothing to excite particular suspicion.

"At length my eyes, in going the circuit of the room, fell upon a trumpery filigree card-rack of pasteboard, that hung dangling by a dirty blue ribbon from a little brass knob just beneath the middle of the mantel-piece. In this rack, which had three or four compartments, were five or six visiting cards and a solitary letter. This last was much soiled and crumpled. It was torn nearly in two, across the middle—as if a design, in the first instance, to tear it entirely up as worthless, had been altered, or stayed, in the second. It had a large black seal, bearing the D—— cipher *very* conspicuously, and was addressed, in a diminutive female hand, to D——, the Minister, himself. It was thrust carelessly, and even, as it seemed, contemptuously, into one of the upper divisions of the rack.

"No sooner had I glanced at this letter, than I concluded it to be that of which I was in search. To be sure, it was, to all appearance, radically different from the one of which the Prefect had read us so minute a description. Here the seal was large and black, with the D—— cipher; there it was small and red, with the ducal arms of the S—— family. Here the address, to the Minister, was diminutive and feminine; there the superscription, to a certain royal personage, was markedly bold and decided; the size alone formed a point of correspondence. But then, the *radicalness* of these differences, which was excessive; the dirt; the soiled and torn condition of the paper, so inconsistent with the *true* methodical habits of D——, and so suggestive of a design to delude the beholder into an idea of the worthlessness of the document; these things, together with the hyperobtrusive situation of this document, full in the view of every visitor, and thus exactly in accordance with the conclusions to which I had previously arrived; these things, I say, were strongly corroborative of suspicion, in one who came with the intention to suspect.

"I protracted my visit as long as possible, and, while I maintained a most animated discussion with the Minister, on a topic which I knew well had never failed to interest and excite him, I kept my attention really riveted upon the letter. In this examination, I committed to memory its external appearance and arrangement in the rack; and also fell, at length, upon a discovery which set at rest whatever trivial doubt I might have entertained. In scrutinizing the edges of the paper, I observed them to be more *chafed* than seemed necessary. They presented the *broken* appearance which is manifested when a stiff paper, having been once folded and pressed with a folder, is refolded in a reversed direction, in the same creases or edges which had formed the original fold. This discovery was sufficient. It was clear to me that the letter had been turned, as a glove, inside out, re-directed, and re-sealed. I bade the Minister good-morning, and took my departure at once, leaving a gold snuff-box upon the table.

"The next morning I called for the snuff-box, when we resumed, quite eagerly, the conversation of the preceding day. While thus engaged, however, a loud report, as if of a pistol, was heard immediately beneath the windows of the Hotel, and was succeeded by a series of fearful screams, and the shoutings of a mob. D—— rushed to a casement, threw it open, and looked out. In the meantime, I stepped to the card-rack, took the letter, put it in my pocket, and re-placed it by a fac-simile (so far as regards externals), which I had carefully prepared at my lodgings—imitating the D—— cipher, very readily, by means of a seal formed of bread.

"The disturbance in the street had been occasioned by the frantic behavior of a man with a musket. He had fired it among a crowd of women and children. It proved, however, to have been without ball, and the fellow was suffered to go his way as a lunatic or a drunkard. When he had gone, D—— came from the window, whither I had followed him immediately upon securing the object in view. Soon afterwards I bade him farewell. The pretended lunatic was a man in my own pay."

"But what purpose had you," I asked, "in replacing the letter by a fac-simile? Would it not have been better, at the first visit, to have seized it openly, and departed?"

"D——," replied Dupin, "is a desperate man, and a man of nerve. His Hotel, too, is not without attendants devoted to his interests. Had I made the wild attempt you suggest, I might never have left the Ministerial presence alive. The good people of Paris might have heard of me no more. But I had an object apart from these considerations. You know my political prepossessions. In this matter, I act as a partisan of the lady concerned. For eighteen months the Minister has had her in his power. She has now him in hers—since, being unaware that the letter is not in his possession, he will proceed with his exactions as if it was. Thus will he inevitably commit himself, at once, to his political destruction. His downfall, too, will not be more precipitate than awkward. It is all very well to talk about the *facilis descensus Averni;* [20] but in all kinds of climbing, as Catalani [21] said of singing, it is far more easy to get up than to come down. In the present instance I have no sympathy—at least no pity—for him who descends. He is that *monstrum horrendum*,[22] an unprincipled man of genius. I confess, however, that I should like very well to know the precise character of his thoughts, when, being defied by her whom the Prefect terms 'a certain personage,' he is reduced to opening the letter which I left for him in the card-rack."

"How? did you put anything particular in it?"

"Why—it did not seem altogether right to leave the interior blank—that would have been insulting. D——, at Vienna once, did me an evil turn, which I told him, quite good-humoredly, that I should remember. So, as I knew he would feel some curiosity in regard to the identity of the person who had outwitted him, I thought it a pity not to give him a clew. He is well acquainted with my MSS.,[23] and I just copied into the middle of the blank sheet the words—

20. Actually "facilis descensus Averno" ("easy is the descent to Avernus [Hell]"). Virgil *Aeneid* VI.126.
21. Angelica Catalani was a famous opera singer of Poe's day.
22. "Horrible monster." Virgil *Aeneid* III.658.
23. Manuscripts; i.e., handwriting.

'——Un dessein si funeste,
S'il n'est digne d'Atrée, est digne de Thyeste.'

They are to be found in Crébillon's *Atrée*." [24]

24. "A scheme so deadly / If it is not worthy of Atreus, is quite worthy of Thyestes."
Prosper Jolyot de Crébillon (1674–1762), *Atrée et Thyeste*, V.v.13—14. Crébillon was
a famous tragic dramatist and rival of Voltaire. These lines from a soliloquy by
Atreus refer to his scheme for obtaining revenge on his brother Thyestes, who had
seduced Atreus's wife. Atreus gained revenge by murdering the children of Thyestes
and serving them to him at a feast. The implication is that Dupin and the Minister
are linked together psychologically as rival "brothers."

From *Tales* (1845)

·Herman Melville·

BARTLEBY THE SCRIVENER
A Story of Wall Street

I am a rather elderly man. The nature of my avocations, for the last thirty years, has brought me into more than ordinary contact with what would seem an interesting and somewhat singular set of men, of whom, as yet, nothing, that I know of, has ever been written—I mean, the law-copyists, or scriveners.[1] I have known very many of them, professionally and privately, and, if I pleased, could relate divers histories, at which good-natured gentlemen might smile, and sentimental souls might weep. But I waive the biographies of all other scriveners, for a few passages in the life of Bartleby, who was a scrivener, the strangest I ever saw, or heard of. While, of other law-copyists, I might write the complete life, of Bartleby nothing of that sort can be done. I believe that no materials exist, for a full and satisfactory biography of this man. It is an irreparable loss to literature. Bartleby was one of those beings of whom nothing is ascertainable, except from the original sources, and, in his case, those are very small. What my own astonished eyes saw of Bartleby, *that* is all I know of him, except, indeed, one vague report, which will appear in the sequel.

Ere introducing the scrivener, as he first appeared to me, it is fit I make some mention of myself, my *employés,* my business, my chambers, and general surroundings; because some such description is indispensable to an adequate understanding of the chief

1. The scriveners copied out legal documents by hand.

character about to be presented. Imprimis:[2] I am a man who, from his youth upwards, has been filled with a profound conviction that the easiest way of life is the best. Hence, though I belong to a profession proverbially energetic and nervous, even to turbulence, at times, yet nothing of that sort have I ever suffered to invade my peace. I am one of those unambitious lawyers who never addresses a jury, or in any way draws down public applause; but, in the cool tranquillity of a snug retreat, do a snug business among rich men's bonds, and mortgages, and title-deeds. All who know me, consider me an eminently *safe* man. The late John Jacob Astor,[3] a personage little given to poetic enthusiasm, had no hesitation in pronouncing my first grand point to be prudence; my next, method. I do not speak it in vanity, but simply record the fact, that I was not unemployed in my profession by the late John Jacob Astor; a name which, I admit, I love to repeat; for it hath a rounded and orbicular sound to it, and rings like unto bullion. I will freely add, that I was not insensible to the late John Jacob Astor's good opinion.

Some time prior to the period at which this little history begins, my avocations had been largely increased. The good old office, now extinct in the State of New York, of a Master in Chancery,[4] had been conferred upon me. It was not a very arduous office, but very pleasantly remunerative. I seldom lose my temper; much more seldom indulge in dangerous indignation at wrongs and outrages; but I must be permitted to be rash here and declare, that I consider the sudden and violent abrogation of the office of Master in Chancery, by the new Constitution, as a ———— premature act; inasmuch as I had counted upon a life-lease of the profits, whereas I only received those of a few short years. But this is by the way.

My chambers were up stairs, at No. — Wall Street. At one end, they looked upon the white wall of the interior of a spacious skylight shaft, penetrating the building from top to bottom.

This view might have been considered rather tame than otherwise, deficient in what landscape painters call "life." But, if so, the view from the other end of my chambers offered, at least, a contrast, if nothing more. In that direction, my windows commanded an unobstructed view of a lofty brick wall, black by age and everlasting shade; which wall required no spy-glass to bring out its lurking beauties, but, for the benefit of all near-sighted spectators, was

2. "In the first place." Often used to introduce the first of a number of items in a legal document.
3. John Jacob Astor (1763–1848), merchant and financier, amassed an enormous fortune—the largest in America up to that time.
4. Courts of chancery had jurisdiction in equity, rather than in common law; i.e., they dealt with matters of fairness and natural justice, rather than with matters prescribed by law. In view of his later treatment of Bartleby, it is ironic that the narrator should be a Master in Chancery.

pushed up to within ten feet of my window panes. Owing to the great height of the surrounding buildings, and my chambers being on the second floor, the interval between this wall and mine not a little resembled a huge square cistern.

At the period just preceding the advent of Bartleby, I had two persons as copyists in my employment, and a promising lad as an office-boy. First Turkey; second, Nippers; third, Ginger Nut. These may seem names, the like of which are not usually found in the Directory. In truth, they were nicknames, mutually conferred upon each other by my three clerks, and were deemed expressive of their respective persons or characters. Turkey was a short, pursy Englishman, of about my age—that is, somewhere not far from sixty. In the morning, one might say, his face was of a fine florid hue, but after twelve o'clock, meridian—his dinner hour—it blazed like a grate full of Christmas coals; and continued blazing—but, as it were, with a gradual wane—till six o'clock, P.M., or thereabouts; after which, I saw no more of the proprietor of the face, which, gaining its meridian with the sun, seemed to set with it, to rise, culminate, and decline the following day, with the like regularity and undiminished glory. There are many singular coincidences I have known in the course of my life, not the least among which was the fact, that, exactly when Turkey displayed his fullest beams from his red and radiant countenance, just then, too, at that critical moment, began the daily period when I considered his business capacities as seriously disturbed for the remainder of the twenty-four hours. Not that he was absolutely idle, or averse to business, then; far from it. The difficulty was, he was apt to be altogether too energetic. There was a strange, inflamed, flurried, flighty recklessness of activity about him. He would be incautious in dipping his pen into his inkstand. All his blots upon my documents were dropped there after twelve o'clock, meridian. Indeed, not only would he be reckless, and sadly given to making blots in the afternoon, but, some days, he went further, and was rather noisy. At such times, too, his face flamed with augmented blazonry, as if cannel coal had been heaped on anthracite.[5] He made an unpleasant racket with his chair; spilled his sand-box; in mending his pens, impatiently split them all to pieces, and threw them on the floor in a sudden passion; stood up, and leaned over his table, boxing his papers about in a most indecorous manner, very sad to behold in an elderly man like him. Nevertheless, as he was in many ways a most valuable person to me, and all the time before twelve o'clock meridian, was the quickest, steadiest creature, too, accomplishing a great deal of work in a style not easily to be matched—for these reasons, I was willing to

5. Cannel (bituminous) coal burns brightly with much smoke; anthracite (hard) coal burns slowly with a clean flame.

overlook his eccentricities, though, indeed, occasionally, I remonstrated with him. I did this very gently, however, because, though the civilest, nay, the blandest and most reverential of men in the morning, yet, in the afternoon, he was disposed, upon provocation, to be slightly rash with his tongue—in fact, insolent. Now, valuing his morning services as I did, and resolved not to lose them—yet, at the same time, made uncomfortable by his inflamed ways after twelve o'clock—and being a man of peace, unwilling by my admonitions to call forth unseemly retorts from him, I took upon me, one Saturday noon (he was always worse on Saturdays) to hint to him, very kindly, that, perhaps, now that he was growing old, it might be well to abridge his labors; in short, he need not come to my chambers after twelve o'clock, but, dinner over, had best go home to his lodgings, and rest himself till tea-time. But no; he insisted upon his afternoon devotions. His countenance became intolerably fervid, as he oratorically assured me—gesticulating with a long ruler at the other end of the room—that if his services in the morning were useful, how indispensable, then, in the afternoon?

"With submission, sir," said Turkey, on this occasion, "I consider myself your right-hand man. In the morning I but marshal and deploy my columns; but in the afternoon I put myself at their head, and gallantly charge the foe, thus"—and he made a violent thrust with the ruler.

"But the blots, Turkey," intimated I.

"True; but, with submission, sir, behold these hairs! I am getting old. Surely, sir, a blot or two of a warm afternoon is not to be severely urged against gray hairs. Old age—even if it blot the page—is honorable. With submission, sir, we *both* are getting old."

This appeal to my fellow-feeling was hardly to be resisted. At all events, I saw that go he would not. So, I made up my mind to let him stay, resolving, nevertheless, to see to it that, during the afternoon, he had to do with my less important papers.

Nippers, the second on my list, was a whiskered, sallow, and, upon the whole, rather piratical-looking young man, of about five-and-twenty. I always deemed him the victim of two evil powers—ambition and indigestion. The ambition was evinced by a certain impatience of the duties of a mere copyist, and unwarrantable usurpation of strictly professional affairs, such as the original drawing up of legal documents. The indigestion seemed betokened in an occasional nervous testiness and grinning irritability, causing the teeth to audibly grind together over mistakes committed in copying; unnecessary maledictions, hissed, rather than spoken, in the heat of business; and especially by a continual discontent with the height of the table where he worked. Though of a very ingenious mechanical turn, Nippers could never get this table to suit him. He put chips under it, blocks of various sorts, bits of pasteboard, and at last went so far as to attempt an exquisite adjustment, by final pieces of folded blotting-paper. But no invention would answer. If, for the sake of easing his back, he brought the table-lid at a sharp angle well up towards his chin, and wrote there like a man using the steep roof of a Dutch house for his desk, then he declared that it stopped the circulation in his arms. If now he lowered the table to his waistbands, and stooped over it in writing, then there was a sore aching in his back. In short, the truth of the matter was, Nippers knew not what he wanted. Or, if he wanted anything, it was to be rid of a scrivener's table altogether. Among the manifestations of his diseased ambition was a fondness he had for receiving visits from certain ambiguous-looking fellows in seedy coats, whom he called his clients. Indeed, I was aware that not only was he, at times, considerable of a ward-politician, but he occasionally did a little business at the Justices' courts, and was not unknown on the steps of the Tombs.[6] I have good reason to believe, however, that one individual who called upon him at my chambers, and who, with a grand air, he insisted was his client, was no other than a dun,[7] and the alleged title-deed, a bill. But, with all his failings, and the annoyances he caused me, Nippers, like his compatriot Turkey, was a very useful man to me; wrote a neat, swift hand; and, when he chose, was not deficient in a gentlemanly sort of deportment. Added to this, he always dressed in a gentlemanly sort of way; and so, incidentally, reflected credit upon my chambers. Whereas, with respect to Turkey, I had much ado to keep him from being a reproach to me. His clothes were apt to look oily, and smell of eating-houses. He wore his pantaloons very loose and baggy in summer. His coats were execrable; his hat not to be handled. But while the hat was a thing of indifference to me, inasmuch as his natural civility and deference, as a dependent Englishman, always led him to doff it the moment he entered the room, yet his coat was another matter. Concerning his coats, I reasoned with him; but with no effect. The truth was, I suppose, that a man with so small an income could not afford to sport such a lustrous face and a lustrous coat at one and the same time. As Nippers once observed, Turkey's money went chiefly for red ink. One winter day, I presented Turkey with a highly respectable-looking coat of my own—a padded gray coat, of a most comfortable warmth, and which buttoned straight up from the knee to the neck. I thought Turkey would appreciate the favor, and abate his rashness and obstreperousness of afternoons. But no; I verily believe that buttoning himself up in so downy and blanket-like a coat had a pernicious effect upon him—upon the same princi-

6. The old prison in New York.
7. Bill collector.

ple that too much oats are bad for horses. In fact, precisely as a rash, restive horse is said to feel his oats, so Turkey felt his coat. It made him insolent. He was a man whom prosperity harmed.

Though, concerning the self-indulgent habits of Turkey, I had my own private surmises, yet, touching Nippers, I was well persuaded that, whatever might be his faults in other respects, he was, at least, a temperate young man. But, indeed, nature herself seemed to have been his vintner, and, at his birth, charged him so thoroughly with an irritable, brandy-like disposition, that all subsequent potations were needless. When I consider how, amid the stillness of my chambers, Nippers would sometimes impatiently rise from his seat, and stooping over his table, spread his arms wide apart, seize the whole desk, and move it, and jerk it, with a grim, grinding motion on the floor, as if the table were a perverse voluntary agent, intent on thwarting and vexing him, I plainly perceive that, for Nippers, brandy-and-water were altogether superfluous.

It was fortunate for me that, owing to its peculiar cause—indigestion—the irritability and consequent nervousness of Nippers were mainly observable in the morning, while in the afternoon he was comparatively mild. So that, Turkey's paroxysms only coming on about twelve o'clock, I never had to do with their eccentricities at one time. Their fits relieved each other, like guards. When Nippers's was on, Turkey's was off; and *vice versa*. This was a good natural arrangement, under the circumstances.

Ginger Nut, the third on my list, was a lad, some twelve years old. His father was a carman, ambitious of seeing his son on the bench instead of a cart, before he died. So he sent him to my office, as student at law, errand-boy, cleaner and sweeper, at the rate of one dollar a week. He had a little desk to himself, but he did not use it much. Upon inspection, the drawer exhibited a great array of the shells of various sorts of nuts. Indeed, to this quick-witted youth, the whole noble science of the law was contained in a nutshell. Not the least among the employments of Ginger Nut, as well as one which he discharged with the most alacrity, was his duty as cake and apple purveyor for Turkey and Nippers. Copying law-papers being proverbially a dry, husky sort of business, my two scriveners were fain to moisten their mouths very often with Spitzenbergs,[8] to be had at the numerous stalls nigh the Custom House and Post Office. Also, they sent Ginger Nut very frequently for that peculiar cake—small, flat, round, and very spicy—after which he had been named by them. Of a cold morning, when business was but dull, Turkey would gobble up scores of these cakes, as if they

8. A variety of apple.

were mere wafers—indeed, they sell them at the rate of six or eight for a penny—the scrape of his pen blending with the crunching of the crisp particles in his mouth. Rashest of all the fiery afternoon blunders and flurried rashnesses of Turkey, was his once moistening a ginger-cake between his lips, and clapping it on to a mortgage, for a seal. I came within an ace of dismissing him then. But he mollified me by making an oriental bow, and saying—

"With submission, sir, it was generous of me to find [9] you in stationery on my own account."

Now my original business—that of a conveyancer and title hunter, and drawer-up of recondite documents of all sorts—was considerably increased by receiving the master's office. There was now great work for scriveners. Not only must I push the clerks already with me, but I must have additional help.

In answer to my advertisement, a motionless young man one morning stood upon my office threshold, the door being open, for it was summer. I can see that figure now—pallidly neat, pitiably respectable, incurably forlorn! It was Bartleby.

After a few words touching his qualifications, I engaged him, glad to have among my corps of copyists a man of so singularly sedate an aspect, which I thought might operate beneficially upon the flighty temper of Turkey, and the fiery one of Nippers.

I should have stated before that ground-glass folding-doors divided my premises into two parts, one of which was occupied by my scriveners, the other by myself. According to my humor, I threw open these doors, or closed them. I resolved to assign Bartleby a corner by the folding-doors, but on my side of them, so as to have this quiet man within easy call, in case any trifling thing was to be done. I placed his desk close up to a small side-window in that part of the room, a window which originally had afforded a lateral view of certain grimy back-yards and bricks, but which, owing to subsequent erections, commanded at present no view at all, though it gave some light. Within three feet of the panes was a wall, and the light came down from far above, between two lofty buildings, as from a very small opening in a dome. Still further to a satisfactory arrangement, I procured a high green folding screen, which might entirely isolate Bartleby from my sight, though not remove him from my voice. And thus, in a manner, privacy and society were conjoined.

At first, Bartleby did an extraordinary quantity of writing. As if long famishing for something to copy, he seemed to gorge himself on my documents. There was no pause for digestion. He ran a day

9. To supply or provide.

and night line, copying by sun-light and by candle-light. I should have been quite delighted with his application, had he been cheerfully industrious. But he wrote on silently, palely, mechanically.

It is, of course, an indispensable part of a scrivener's business to verify the accuracy of his copy, word by word. Where there are two or more scriveners in an office, they assist each other in this examination, one reading from the copy, the other holding the original. It is a very dull, wearisome, and lethargic affair. I can readily imagine that, to some sanguine temperaments, it would be altogether intolerable. For example, I cannot credit that the mettlesome poet, Byron, would have contentedly sat down with Bartleby to examine a law document of, say five hundred pages, closely written in a crimpy hand.

Now and then, in the haste of business, it had been my habit to assist in comparing some brief document myself, calling Turkey or Nippers for this purpose. One object I had, in placing Bartleby so handy to me behind the screen, was, to avail myself of his services on such trivial occasions. It was on the third day, I think, of his being with me, and before any necessity had arisen for having his own writing examined, that, being much hurried to complete a small affair I had in hand, I abruptly called to Bartleby. In my haste and natural expectancy of instant compliance, I sat with my head bent over the original on my desk, and my right hand sideways, and somewhat nervously extended with the copy, so that, immediately upon emerging from his retreat, Bartleby might snatch it and proceed to business without the least delay.

In this very attitude did I sit when I called to him, rapidly stating what it was I wanted him to do—namely, to examine a small paper with me. Imagine my surprise, nay, my consternation, when, without moving from his privacy, Bartleby, in a singularly mild, firm voice, replied, "I would prefer not to."

I sat awhile in perfect silence, rallying my stunned faculties. Immediately it occurred to me that my ears had deceived me, or Bartleby had entirely misunderstood my meaning. I repeated my request in the clearest tone I could assume; but in quite as clear a one came the previous reply, "I would prefer not to."

"Prefer not to," echoed I, rising in high excitement, and crossing the room with a stride. "What do you mean? Are you moon-struck? I want you to help me compare this sheet here—take it," and I thrust it towards him.

"I would prefer not to," said he.

I looked at him steadfastly. His face was leanly composed; his gray eye dimly calm. Not a wrinkle of agitation rippled him. Had there been the least uneasiness, anger, impatience or impertinence in his manner; in other words, had there been anything ordinarily human about him, doubtless I should have violently dismissed him from the premises. But as it was, I should have as soon thought of turning my pale plaster-of-paris bust of Cicero [10] out of doors. I stood gazing at him awhile, as he went on with his own writing, and then reseated myself at my desk. This is very strange, thought I. What had one best do? But my business hurried me. I concluded to forget the matter for the present, reserving it for my future leisure. So, calling Nippers from the other room, the paper was speedily examined.

A few days after this, Bartleby concluded four lengthy documents, being quadruplicates of a week's testimony taken before me in my High Court of Chancery. It became necessary to examine them. It was an important suit, and great accuracy was imperative. Having all things arranged, I called Turkey, Nippers and Ginger Nut, from the next room, meaning to place the four copies in the hands of my four clerks, while I should read from the original. Accordingly, Turkey, Nippers, and Ginger Nut had taken their seats in a row, each with his document in his hand, when I called to Bartleby to join this interesting group.

"Bartleby! quick, I am waiting."

I heard a slow scrape of his chair legs on the uncarpeted floor, and soon he appeared standing at the entrance of his hermitage.

"What is wanted?" said he, mildly.

"The copies, the copies," said I, hurriedly. "We are going to examine them. There"—and I held towards him the fourth quadruplicate.

"I would prefer not to," he said, and gently disappeared behind the screen.

For a few moments I was turned into a pillar of salt,[11] standing at the head of my seated column of clerks. Recovering myself, I advanced towards the screen, and demanded the reason for such extraordinary conduct.

"*Why* do you refuse?"

"I would prefer not to."

With any other man I should have flown outright into a dreadful passion, scorned all further words, and thrust him ignominiously from my presence. But there was something about Bartleby that not only strangely disarmed me, but, in a wonderful manner, touched and disconcerted me. I began to reason with him.

"These are your own copies we are about to examine. It is labor saving to you, because one examination will answer for your four

10. Marcus Tullius Cicero (106–43 B.C.), Roman writer and orator, a traditional model for lawyers.
11. See Gen. 19:26. Lot's wife defied the will of God and, looking behind her, was turned into a pillar of salt.

papers. It is common usage. Every copyist is bound to help examine his copy. Is it not so? Will you not speak? Answer!"

"I prefer not to," he replied in a flute-like tone. It seemed to me
that, while I had been addressing him, he carefully revolved every
statement that I made; fully comprehended the meaning; could not
gainsay the irresistible conclusion; but, at the same time, some par-
amount consideration prevailed with him to reply as he did.

"You are decided, then, not to comply with my request—a
request made according to common usage and common sense?"

He briefly gave me to understand, that on that point my judgment
was sound. Yes: his decision was irreversible.

It is not seldom the case that, when a man is browbeaten in some
unprecedented and violently unreasonable way, he begins to stag-
ger in his own plainest faith. He begins, as it were, vaguely to surmise that, wonderful as it may be, all the justice and all the reason
is on the other side. Accordingly, if any disinterested persons are
present, he turns to them for some reinforcement for his own faltering mind.

"Turkey," said I, "what do you think of this? Am I not right?"

"With submission, sir," and Turkey, in his blandest tone, "I think
that you are."

"Nippers," said I, "what do *you* think of it?"

"I think I should kick him out of the office."

(The reader of nice perceptions will here perceive that, it being
morning, Turkey's answer is couched in polite and tranquil terms,
but Nippers replies in ill-tempered ones. Or, to repeat a previous
sentence, Nippers's ugly mood was on duty, and Turkey's off.)

"Ginger Nut," said I, willing to enlist the smallest suffrage in my
behalf, "what do *you* think of it?"

"I think, sir, he's a little *luny*," replied Ginger Nut, with a grin.

"You hear what they say," said I, turning towards the screen,
"come forth and do your duty."

But he vouchsafed no reply. I pondered a moment in sore perplexity. But once more business hurried me. I determined again to
postpone the consideration of this dilemma to my future leisure.
With a little trouble we made out to examine the papers without
Bartleby, though at every page or two Turkey deferentially dropped
his opinion, that this proceeding was quite out of the common;
while Nippers, twitching in his chair with a dyspeptic nervousness,
ground out, between his set teeth, occasional hissing maledictions
against the stubborn oaf behind the screen. And for his (Nippers's)
part, this was the first and the last time he would do another man's
business without pay.

Meanwhile Bartleby sat in his hermitage, oblivious to everything
but his own peculiar business there.

Some days passed, the scrivener being employed upon another lengthy work. His late remarkable conduct led me to regard his ways narrowly. I observed that he never went to dinner; indeed, that he never went anywhere. As yet I had never, of my personal knowledge, known him to be outside of my office. He was a perpetual sentry in the corner. At about eleven o'clock though, in the morning, I noticed that Ginger Nut would advance toward the opening in Bartleby's screen, as if silently beckoned thither by a gesture invisible to me where I sat. The boy would then leave the office, jingling a few pence, and reappear with a handful of ginger-nuts, which he delivered in the hermitage, receiving two of the cakes for his trouble.

He lives, then, on ginger-nuts, thought I; never eats a dinner, properly speaking; he must be a vegetarian, then, but no; he never eats even vegetables, he eats nothing but ginger-nuts. My mind then ran on in reveries concerning the probable effects upon the human constitution of living entirely on ginger-nuts. Ginger-nuts are so called, because they contain ginger as one of their peculiar constituents, and the final flavoring one. Now, what was ginger? A hot, spicy thing. Was Bartleby hot and spicy? Not at all. Ginger, then, had no effect upon Bartleby. Probably he preferred it should have none.

Nothing so aggravates an earnest person as a passive resistance. If the individual so resisted be of a not inhumane temper, and the resisting one perfectly harmless in his passivity, then, in the better moods of the former, he will endeavor charitably to construe to his imagination what proves impossible to be solved by his judgment. Even so, for the most part, I regarded Bartleby and his ways. Poor fellow! thought I, he means no mischief; it is plain he intends no insolence; his aspect sufficiently evinces that his eccentricities are involuntary. He is useful to me. I can get along with him. If I turn him away, the chances are he will fall in with some less-indulgent employer, and then he will be rudely treated, and perhaps driven forth miserably to starve. Yes. Here I can cheaply purchase a delicious self-approval. To befriend Bartleby; to humor him in his strange willfulness, will cost me little or nothing, while I lay up in my soul what will eventually prove a sweet morsel for my conscience. But this mood was not invariable with me. The passiveness of Bartleby sometimes irritated me. I felt strangely goaded on to encounter him in new opposition—to elicit some angry spark from him answerable to my own. But, indeed, I might as well have essayed to strike fire with my knuckles against a bit of Windsor soap.[12] But one afternoon the evil impulse in me mastered me, and the following little scene ensued:

12. A kind of scented soap, usually brown.

"Bartleby," said I, "when those papers are all copied, I will compare them with you."

"I would prefer not to."

"How? Surely you do not mean to persist in that mulish vagary?"

No answer.

I threw open the folding-doors near by, and, turning upon Turkey and Nippers, exclaimed:

"Bartleby a second time says, he won't examine his papers. What do you think of it, Turkey?"

It was afternoon, be it remembered. Turkey sat glowing like a brass boiler; his bald head steaming; his hands reeling among his blotted papers.

"Think of it?" roared Turkey. "I think I'll just step behind his screen, and black his eyes for him!"

So saying, Turkey rose to his feet and threw his arms into a pugilistic position. He was hurrying away to make good his promise, when I detained him, alarmed at the effect of incautiously rousing Turkey's combativeness after dinner.

"Sit down, Turkey," said I, "and hear what Nippers has to say. What do you think of it, Nippers? Would I not be justified in immediately dismissing Bartleby?"

"Excuse me, that is for you to decide, sir. I think his conduct quite unusual, and, indeed, unjust, as regards Turkey and myself. But it may only be a passing whim."

"Ah," exclaimed I, "you have strangely changed your mind, then—you speak very gently of him now."

"All beer," cried Turkey; "gentleness is effects of beer—Nippers and I dined together to-day. You see how gentle *I* am, sir. Shall I go and black his eyes?"

"You refer to Bartleby, I suppose. No, not to-day, Turkey," I replied; "pray, put up your fists."

I closed the doors, and again advanced towards Bartleby. I felt additional incentives tempting me to my fate. I burned to be rebelled against again. I remembered that Bartleby never left the office.

"Bartleby," said I, "Ginger Nut is away; just step around to the Post Office, won't you?" (it was but a three minutes' walk) "and see if there is anything for me."

"I would prefer not to."

"You *will* not?"

"I *prefer* not."

I staggered to my desk, and sat there in a deep study. My blind inveteracy returned. Was there any other thing in which I could procure myself to be ignominiously repulsed by this lean, penniless wight?—my hired clerk? What added thing is there, perfectly reasonable, that he will be sure to refuse to do?

"Bartleby!"

No answer.

"Bartleby," in a louder tone.

No answer.

"Bartleby," I roared.

Like a very ghost, agreeably to the laws of magical invocation, at the third summons, he appeared at the entrance of his hermitage.

"Go to the next room, and tell Nippers to come to me."

"I prefer not to," he respectfully and slowly said, and mildly disappeared.

"Very good, Bartleby," said I, in a quiet sort of serenely-severe self-possessed tone, intimating the unalterable purpose of some terrible retribution very close at hand. At the moment I half intended something of the kind. But upon the whole, as it was drawing towards my dinner-hour, I thought it best to put on my hat and walk home for the day, suffering much from perplexity and distress of mind.

Shall I acknowledge it? The conclusion of this whole business was, that it soon became a fixed fact of my chambers, that a pale young scrivener, by the name of Bartleby, had a desk there; that he copied for me at the usual rate of four cents a folio (one hundred words); but he was permanently exempt from examining the work done by him, that duty being transferred to Turkey and Nippers, out of compliment, doubtless, to their superior acuteness; moreover, said Bartleby was never, on any account, to be dispatched on the most trivial errand of any sort; and that even if entreated to take upon him such a matter, it was generally understood that he would "prefer not to"—in other words, that he would refuse point-blank.

As days passed on, I became considerably reconciled to Bartleby. His steadiness, his freedom from all dissipation, his incessant industry (except when he chose to throw himself into a standing revery behind his screen), his great stillness, his unalterableness of demeanor under all circumstances, made him a valuable acquisition. One prime thing was this—*he was always there*—first in the morning, continually through the day, and the last at night. I had a singular confidence in his honesty. I felt my most precious papers perfectly safe in his hands. Sometimes, to be sure, I could not, for the very soul of me, avoid falling into sudden spasmodic passions with him. For it was exceeding difficult to bear in mind all the time those strange peculiarities, privileges, and unheard-of exemptions, forming the tacit stipulations on Bartleby's part under which he remained in my office. Now and then, in the eagerness of dispatching pressing business, I would inadvertently summon Bartleby, in a short, rapid tone, to put his finger, say, on the incipient tie of a bit of red tape with which I was about compressing some papers. Of course, from behind the screen the usual answer, "I prefer not to," was sure to come; and then, how could a human creature, with the common infirmities of our nature, refrain from bitterly exclaiming upon such perverseness—such unreasonableness? However, every added repulse of this sort which I received only tended to lessen the probability of my repeating the inadvertence.

Here it must be said, that, according to the custom of most legal gentlemen occupying chambers in densely-populated law buildings, there were several keys to my door. One was kept by a woman residing in the attic, which person weekly scrubbed and daily swept and dusted my apartments. Another was kept by Turkey for convenience sake. The third I sometimes carried in my own pocket. The fourth I knew not who had.

Now, one Sunday morning I happened to go to Trinity Church, to hear a celebrated preacher, and finding myself rather early on the ground I thought I would walk round to my chambers for a while. Luckily I had my key with me; but upon applying it to the lock, I found it resisted by something inserted from the inside. Quite surprised, I called out; when to my consternation a key was turned from within; and thrusting his lean visage at me, and holding the door ajar, the apparition of Bartleby appeared, in his shirtsleeves, and otherwise in a strangely tattered *déshabillé*,[12a] saying quietly that he was sorry, but he was deeply engaged just then, and—preferred not admitting me at present. In a brief word or two, he moreover added, that perhaps I had better walk round the block two or three times, and by that time he would probably have concluded his affairs.

Now, the utterly unsurmised appearance of Bartleby, tenanting my law-chambers of a Sunday morning, with his cadaverously gentlemanly *nonchalance*, yet withal firm and self-possessed, had such a strange effect upon me, that incontinently I slunk away from my own door, and did as desired. But not without sundry twinges of impotent rebellion against the mild effrontery of this unaccountable scrivener. Indeed, it was his wonderful mildness chiefly, which not only disarmed me, but unmanned me as it were. For I consider that one, for the time, is sort of unmanned when he tranquilly permits his hired clerk to dictate to him, and order him away from his own premises. Furthermore, I was full of uneasiness as to what Bartleby could possibly be doing in my office in his shirt sleeves, and in an otherwise dismantled condition of a Sunday morning. Was anything

12a. Negligently or partly dressed state.

amiss going on? Nay, that was out of the question. It was not to be thought of for a moment that Bartleby was an immoral person. But what could he be doing there?—copying? Nay again, whatever might be his eccentricities, Bartleby was an eminently decorous person. He would be the last man to sit down to his desk in any state approaching to nudity. Besides, it was Sunday; and there was something about Bartleby that forbade the supposition that he would by any secular occupation violate the proprieties of the day.

Nevertheless, my mind was not pacified; and full of a restless curiosity, at last I returned to the door. Without hindrance I inserted my key, opened it, and entered. Bartleby was not to be seen. I looked round anxiously, peeped behind his screen; but it was very plain that he was gone. Upon more closely examining the place, I surmised that for an indefinite period Bartleby must have eaten, dressed, and slept in my office, and that too without plate, mirror, or bed. The cushioned seat of a rickety old sofa in one corner bore the faint impress of a lean, reclining form. Rolled away under his desk, I found a blanket; under the empty grate, a blacking box and brush; on a chair, a tin basin, with soap and a ragged towel; in a newspaper a few crumbs of ginger-nuts and a morsel of cheese. Yes, thought I, it is evident enough that Bartleby has been making his home here, keeping bachelor's hall all by himself. Immediately then the thought came sweeping across me, what miserable friendlessness and loneliness are here revealed! His poverty is great; but his solitude, how horrible! Think of it. Of a Sunday, Wall Street is deserted as Petra;[13] and every night of every day it is an emptiness. This building, too, which of week-days hums with industry and life, at nightfall echoes with sheer vacancy, and all through Sunday is forlorn. And here Bartleby makes his home; sole spectator of a solitude which he has seen all populous—a sort of innocent and transformed Marius brooding among the ruins of Carthage! [14]

For the first time in my life a feeling of overpowering stinging melancholy seized me. Before, I had never experienced aught but a not unpleasing sadness. The bond of a common humanity now drew me irresistibly to gloom. A fraternal melancholy! For both I and Bartleby were sons of Adam. I remembered the bright silks and sparkling faces I had seen that day, in gala trim, swan-like sailing down the Mississippi of Broadway; and I contrasted them with the pallid copyist, and thought to myself, Ah, happiness courts the

---

13. A deserted ruin near the Dead Sea, once the center of caravan trade. It is walled in by towering rocks, thus suggesting Wall Street to Melville.
14. Gaius Marius (155–86 B.C.), Roman general. Although the most successful warrior of his day, Marius—who was of plebeian descent—lacked the intellectual and cultural gifts needed for successful politics. He was defeated by Sulla, and subsequently pictured himself as a fugitive among the ruins of Carthage.

light, so we deem the world is gay; but misery hides aloof, so we deem that misery there is none. These sad fancyings—chimeras, doubtless, of a sick and silly brain—led on to other and more special thoughts, concerning the eccentricities of Bartleby. Presentiments of strange discoveries hovered round me. The scrivener's pale form appeared to me laid out, among uncaring strangers, in its shivering winding-sheet.

Suddenly I was attracted by Bartleby's closed desk, the key in open sight left in the lock.

I mean no mischief, seek the gratification of no heartless curiosity, thought I; besides, the desk is mine, and its contents, too, so I will make bold to look within. Everything was methodically arranged, the papers smoothly placed. The pigeon holes were deep, and removing the files of documents, I groped into their recesses. Presently I felt something there, and dragged it out. It was an old bandana handkerchief, heavy and knotted. I opened it, and saw it was a savings' bank.

I now recalled all the quiet mysteries which I had noted in the man. I remembered that he never spoke but to answer; that, though at intervals he had considerable time to himself, yet I had never seen him reading—no, not even a newspaper; that for long periods he would stand looking out, at his pale window behind the screen, upon the dead brick wall; I was quite sure he never visited any refectory or eating house; while his pale face clearly indicated that he never drank beer like Turkey, or tea and coffee even, like other men; that he never went anywhere in particular that I could learn; never went out for a walk, unless, indeed, that was the case at present; that he had declined telling who he was, or whence he came, or whether he had any relatives in the world; that though so thin and pale, he never complained of ill health. And more than all, I remembered a certain unconscious air of pallid—how shall I call it?—of pallid haughtiness, say, or rather an austere reserve about him, which had positively awed me into my tame compliance with his eccentricities, when I had feared to ask him to do the slightest incidental thing for me, even though I might know, from his long-continued motionlessness, that behind his screen he must be standing in one of those dead-wall reveries of his.

Revolving all these things, and coupling them with the recently discovered fact, that he made my office his constant abiding place and home, and not forgetful of his morbid moodiness; revolving all these things, a prudential feeling began to steal over me. My first emotions had been those of pure melancholy and sincerest pity; but just in proportion as the forlornness of Bartleby grew and grew to my imagination, did that same melancholy merge into fear, that pity into repulsion. So true it is, and so terrible, too, that up to a certain point the thought or sight of misery enlists our best affections; but, in certain special cases, beyond that point it does not. They err who would assert that invariably this is owing to the inherent selfishness of the human heart. It rather proceeds from a certain hopelessness of remedying excessive and organic ill. To a sensitive being, pity is not seldom pain. And when at last it is perceived that such pity cannot lead to effectual succor, common sense bids the soul be rid of it. What I saw that morning persuaded me that the scrivener was the victim of innate and incurable disorder. I might give alms to his body; but his body did not pain him; it was his soul that suffered, and his soul I could not reach.

I did not accomplish the purpose of going to Trinity Church that morning. Somehow, the things I had seen disqualified me for the time from church-going. I walked homeward, thinking what I would do with Bartleby. Finally, I resolved upon this—I would put certain calm questions to him the next morning, touching his history, etc., and if he declined to answer them openly and unreservedly (and I supposed he would prefer not), then to give him a twenty dollar bill over and above whatever I might owe him, and tell him his services were no longer required; but that if in any other way I could assist him, I would be happy to do so, especially if he desired to return to his native place, wherever that might be, I would willingly help to defray the expenses. Moreover, if, after reaching home, he found himself at any time in want of aid, a letter from him would be sure of a reply.

The next morning came.

"Bartleby," said I, gently calling to him behind his screen.

No reply.

"Bartleby," said I, in a still gentler tone, "come here; I am not going to ask you to do anything you would prefer not to do—I simply wish to speak to you."

Upon this he noiselessly slid into view.

"Will you tell me, Bartleby, where you were born?"

"I would prefer not to."

"Will you tell me *anything* about yourself?"

"I would prefer not to."

"But what reasonable objection can you have to speak to me? I feel friendly towards you."

He did not look at me while I spoke, but kept his glance fixed upon my bust of Cicero, which, as I then sat, was directly behind me, some six inches above my head.

"What is your answer, Bartleby?" said I, after waiting a considerable time for a reply, during which his countenance remained immovable, only there was the faintest conceivable tremor of the white attenuated mouth.

"At present I prefer to give no answer," he said, and retired into his hermitage.

It was rather weak in me I confess, but his manner, on this occasion, nettled me. Not only did there seem to lurk in it a certain calm disdain, but his perverseness seemed ungrateful, considering the undeniable good usage and indulgence he had received from me.

Again I sat ruminating what I should do. Mortified as I was at his behavior, and resolved as I had been to dismiss him when I entered my office, nevertheless I strangely felt something superstitious knocking at my heart, and forbidding me to carry out my purpose, and denouncing me for a villain if I dared to breathe one bitter word against this forlornest of mankind. At last, familiarly drawing my chair behind his screen, I sat down and said: "Bartleby, never mind, then, about revealing your history; but let me entreat you, as a friend, to comply as far as may be with the usages of this office. Say now, you will help to examine papers to-morrow or next day: in short, say now, that in a day or two you will begin to be a little reasonable:—say so, Bartleby."

"At present I would prefer not to be a little reasonable," was his mildly cadaverous reply.

Just then the folding-doors opened, and Nippers approached. He seemed suffering from an unusually bad night's rest, induced by severer indigestion than common. He overheard those final words of Bartleby.

"*Prefer not*, eh?" gritted Nippers—"I'd *prefer* him, if I were you, sir," addressing me—"I'd *prefer* him; I'd give him preferences, the stubborn mule! What is it, sir, pray, that he *prefers* not to do now?"

Bartleby moved not a limb.

"Mr. Nippers," said I, "I'd prefer that you would withdraw for the present."

Somehow, of late, I had got into the way of involuntarily using this word "prefer" upon all sorts of not exactly suitable occasions. And I trembled to think that my contact with the scrivener had already and seriously affected me in a mental way. And what further and deeper aberration might it not yet produce? This apprehension had not been without efficacy in determining me to summary measures.

As Nippers, looking very sour and sulky, was departing, Turkey blandly and deferentially approached.

"With submission, sir," said he, "yesterday I was thinking about Bartleby here, and I think that if he would but prefer to take a quart of good ale every day, it would do much towards mending him, and enabling him to assist in examining his papers."

"So you have got the word, too," said I, slightly excited.

"With submission, what word, sir?" asked Turkey, respectfully crowding himself into the contracted space behind the screen, and by so doing, making me jostle the scrivener. "What word, sir?"

"I would prefer to be left alone here," said Bartleby, as if offended at being mobbed in his privacy.

"That's the word, Turkey," said I—*"that's* it."

"Oh, *prefer?* oh yes—queer word. I never use it myself. But, sir, as I was saying, if he would but prefer—"

"Turkey," interrupted I, "you will please withdraw."

"Oh certainly, sir, if you prefer that I should."

As he opened the folding-door to retire, Nippers at his desk caught a glimpse of me, and asked whether I would prefer to have a certain paper copied on blue paper or white. He did not in the least roguishly accent the word "prefer." It was plain that it involuntarily rolled from his tongue. I thought to myself, surely I must get rid of a demented man, who already has in some degree turned the tongues, if not the heads, of myself and clerks. But I thought it prudent not to break the dismission at once.

The next day I noticed that Bartleby did nothing but stand at his window in his dead-wall revery. Upon asking him why he did not write, he said that he had decided upon doing no more writing.

"Why, how now? what next?" exclaimed I, "do no more writing?"

"No more."

"And what is the reason?"

"Do you not see the reason for yourself?" he indifferently replied.

I looked steadfastly at him, and perceived that his eyes looked dull and glazed. Instantly it occurred to me, that his unexampled diligence in copying by his dim window for the first few weeks of his stay with me might have temporarily impaired his vision.

I was touched. I said something in condolence with him. I hinted that of course he did wisely in abstaining from writing for a while; and urged him to embrace that opportunity of taking wholesome exercise in the open air. This, however, he did not do. A few days after this, my other clerks being absent, and being in a great hurry to dispatch certain letters by the mail, I thought that, having nothing else earthly to do, Bartleby would surely be less inflexible than usual, and carry these letters to the post-office. But he blankly declined. So, much to my inconvenience, I went myself.

Still added days went by. Whether Bartleby's eyes improved or not, I could not say. To all appearance, I thought they did. But when I asked him if they did, he vouchsafed no answer. At all events, he would do no copying. At last, in reply to my urgings, he informed me that he had permanently given up copying.

"What!" exclaimed I; "suppose your eyes should get entirely well—better than ever before—would you not copy then?"

"I have given up copying," he answered, and slid aside.

He remained as ever, a fixture in my chamber. Nay—if that were possible—he became still more of a fixture than before. What was to be done? He would do nothing in the office; why should he stay there? In plain fact, he had now become a millstone to me,[15] not only useless as a necklace, but afflictive to bear. Yet I was sorry for him. I speak less than truth when I say that, on his own account, he occasioned me uneasiness. If he would but have named a single relative or friend, I would instantly have written, and urged their taking the poor fellow away to some convenient retreat. But he seemed alone, absolutely alone in the universe. A bit of wreck in the mid Atlantic. At length, necessities connected with my business tyrannized over all other considerations. Decently as I could, I told Bartleby that in six days' time he must unconditionally leave the office. I warned him to take measures, in the interval, for procuring some other abode. I offered to assist him in this endeavor, if he himself would but take the first step towards a removal. "And when you finally quit me, Bartleby," added I, "I shall see that you go not away entirely unprovided. Six days from this hour, remember."

At the expiration of that period, I peeped behind the screen, and lo! Bartleby was there.

I buttoned up my coat, balanced myself; advanced slowly towards him, touched his shoulder, and said, "The time has come; you must quit this place; I am sorry for you; here is money; but you must go."

"I would prefer not," he replied, with his back still towards me.

"You *must*."

He remained silent.

Now I had an unbounded confidence in this man's common honesty. He had frequently restored to me sixpences and shillings carelessly dropped upon the floor, for I am apt to be very reckless in such shirt-button affairs. The proceeding, then, which followed will not be deemed extraordinary.

"Bartleby," said I, "I owe you twelve dollars on account; here are thirty-two; the odd twenty are yours— Will you take it?" and I handed the bills towards him.

But he made no motion.

"I will leave them here, then," putting them under a weight on

15. Matt. 18: 4–6. "Whosoever therefore shall humble himself as this little child, the same is greatest in the kingdom of heaven. And whoso shall receive one such little child in my name receiveth me. But whoso shall offend one of these little ones which believe in me, it were better for him that a millstone were hanged about his neck, and *that* he were drowned in the depth of the sea."

the table. Then taking my hat and cane and going to the door, I tranquilly turned and added—"After you have removed your things from these offices, Bartleby, you will of course lock the door—since every one is now gone for the day but you—and if you please, slip your key underneath the mat, so that I may have it in the morning. I shall not see you again; so good-by to you. If, hereafter, in your new place of abode, I can be of any service to you, do not fail to advise me by letter. Good-by, Bartleby, and fare you well."

But he answered not a word; like the last column of some ruined temple, he remained standing mute and solitary in the middle of the otherwise deserted room.

As I walked home in a pensive mood, my vanity got the better of my pity. I could not but highly plume myself on my masterly management in getting rid of Bartleby. Masterly I call it, and such it must appear to any dispassionate thinker. The beauty of my procedure seemed to consist in its perfect quietness. There was no vulgar bullying, no bravado of any sort, no choleric hectoring, and striding to and fro across the apartment, jerking out vehement commands for Bartleby to bundle himself off with his beggarly traps. Nothing of the kind. Without loudly bidding Bartleby depart—as an inferior genius might have done—I *assumed* the ground that depart he must; and upon that assumption built all I had to say. The more I thought over my procedure, the more I was charmed with it. Nevertheless, next morning, upon awakening, I had my doubts—I had somehow slept off the fumes of vanity. One of the coolest and wisest hours a man has, is just after he awakes in the morning. My procedure seemed as sagacious as ever—but only in theory. How it would prove in practice—there was the rub. It was truly a beautiful thought to have assumed Bartleby's departure; but, after all, that assumption was simply my own, and none of Bartleby's. The great point was, not whether I had assumed that he would quit me, but whether he would prefer so to do. He was more a man of preferences than assumptions.

After breakfast, I walked down town, arguing the probabilities *pro* and *con.* One moment I thought it would prove a miserable failure, and Bartleby would be found all alive at my office as usual; the next moment it seemed certain that I should find his chair empty. And so I kept veering about. At the corner of Broadway and Canal Street, I saw quite an excited group of people standing in earnest conversation.

"I'll take odds he doesn't," said a voice as I passed.

"Doesn't go?—done!" said I, "put up your money."

I was instinctively putting my hand in my pocket to produce my own, when I remembered that this was an election day. The words I had overheard bore no reference to Bartleby, but to the success or non-success of some candidate for the mayoralty. In my intent frame of mind, I had, as it were, imagined that all Broadway shared in my excitement, and were debating the same question with me. I passed on, very thankful that the uproar of the street screened my momentary absent-mindedness.

As I had intended, I was earlier than usual at my office door. I stood listening for a moment. All was still. He must be gone. I tried the knob. The door was locked. Yes, my procedure had worked to a charm; he indeed must be vanished. Yet a certain melancholy mixed with this: I was almost sorry for my brilliant success. I was fumbling under the door mat for the key, which Bartleby was to have left there for me, when accidentally my knee knocked against a panel, producing a summoning sound, and in response a voice came to me from within—"Not yet; I am occupied."

It was Bartleby.

I was thunderstruck. For an instant I stood like the man who, pipe in mouth, was killed one cloudless afternoon long ago in Virginia, by summer lightning; at his own warm open window he was killed, and remained leaning out there upon the dreamy afternoon, till some one touched him, when he fell.

"Not gone!" I murmured at last. But again obeying that wondrous ascendancy which the inscrutable scrivener had over me, and from which ascendancy, for all my chafing, I could not completely escape, I slowly went down stairs and out into the street, and while walking round the block, considered what I should next do in this unheard-of perplexity. Turn the man out by an actual thrusting I could not; to drive him away by calling him hard names would not do; calling in the police was an unpleasant idea; and yet, permit him to enjoy his cadaverous triumph over me—this, too, I could not think of. What was to be done? or, if nothing could be done, was there anything further that I could *assume* in the matter? Yes, as before I had prospectively assumed that Bartleby would depart, so now I might retrospectively assume that departed he was. In the legitimate carrying out of this assumption, I might enter my office in a great hurry, and pretending not to see Bartleby at all, walk straight against him as if he were air. Such a proceeding would in a singular degree have the appearance of a home-thrust. It was hardly possible that Bartleby could withstand such an application of the doctrine of assumptions. But upon second thoughts the success of the plan seemed rather dubious. I resolved to argue the matter over with him again.

"Bartleby," said I, entering the office, with a quietly severe expression, "I am seriously displeased. I am pained, Bartleby. I had thought better of you. I had imagined you of such a gentlemanly organization, that in any delicate dilemma a slight hint would suffice—in short, an assumption. But it appears I am deceived. Why," I added, unaffectedly starting, "you have not even touched that money yet," pointing to it, just where I had left it the evening previous.

He answered nothing.

"Will you, or will you not, quit me?" I now demanded in a sudden passion, advancing close to him.

"I would prefer *not* to quit you," he replied, gently emphasizing the *not*.

"What earthly right have you to stay here? Do you pay any rent? Do you pay my taxes? Or is this property yours?"

He answered nothing.

"Are you ready to go on and write now? Are your eyes recovered? Could you copy a small paper for me this morning? or help examine a few lines? or step round to the post-office? In a word, will you do anything at all, to give a coloring to your refusal to depart the premises?"

He silently retired into his hermitage.

I was now in such a state of nervous resentment that I thought it but prudent to check myself at present from further demonstrations. Bartleby and I were alone. I remembered the tragedy of the unfortunate Adams and the still more unfortunate Colt [16] in the solitary office of the latter; and how poor Colt, being dreadfully incensed by Adams, and imprudently permitting himself to get wildly excited, was at unawares hurried into his fatal act—an act which certainly no man could possibly deplore more than the actor himself. Often it had occurred to me in my ponderings upon the subject that had that altercation taken place in the public street, or at a private residence, it would not have terminated as it did. It was the circumstance of being alone in a solitary office, up stairs, of a building entirely unhallowed by humanizing domestic associations—an uncarpeted office, doubtless, of a dusty, haggard sort of appearance—this it must have been, which greatly helped to enhance the irritable desperation of the hapless Colt.

But when this old Adam [17] of resentment rose in me and tempted me concerning Bartleby, I grappled him and threw him. How? Why, simply by recalling the divine injunction: "A new commandment give I unto you, that ye love one another." [18] Yes, this it was

16. A notorious murder case of 1841, in which John C. Colt killed Samuel Adams with an unpremeditated blow to the head.
17. The first man, who fell through sin; "this old Adam" therefore represents the unregenerate condition of man (see Rom. 6:6). Christ is the "new Adam," who will redeem man from sin.
18. John 15:12–13. "This is my commandment, that ye love one another, as I have loved you. Greater love hath no man than this, that a man lay down his life for his friends."

that saved me. Aside from higher considerations, charity often operates as a vastly wise and prudent principle—a great safeguard to its possessor. Men have committed murder for jealousy's sake, and anger's sake, and hatred's sake, and selfishness' sake, and spiritual pride's sake; but no man, that ever I heard of, ever committed a diabolical murder for sweet charity's sake. Mere self-interest, then, if no better motive can be enlisted, should, especially with high-tempered men, prompt all beings to charity and philanthropy. At any rate, upon the occasion in question, I strove to drown my exasperated feelings towards the scrivener by benevolently construing his conduct. Poor fellow, poor fellow! thought I, he don't mean anything; and besides, he has seen hard times, and ought to be indulged.

I endeavored, also, immediately to occupy myself, and at the same time to comfort my despondency. I tried to fancy, that in the course of the morning, at such time as might prove agreeable to him, Bartleby, of his own free accord, would emerge from his hermitage and take up some decided line of march in the direction of the door. But no. Half-past twelve o'clock came; Turkey began to glow in the face, overturn his inkstand, and become generally obstreperous; Nippers abated down into quietude and courtesy; Ginger Nut munched his noon apple; and Bartleby remained standing at his window in one of his profoundest dead-wall reveries. Will it be credited? Ought I to acknowledge it? That afternoon I left the office without saying one further word to him.

Some days now passed, during which, at leisure intervals I looked a little into "Edwards on the Will," [19] and "Priestley on Necessity." [20] Under the circumstances, those books induced a salutary feeling. Gradually I slid into the persuasion that these troubles of mine, touching the scrivener, had been all predestinated from eternity, and Bartleby was billeted upon me for some mysterious purpose of an allwise Providence, which it was not for a mere mortal like me to fathom. Yes, Bartleby, stay there behind your screen, thought I; I shall persecute you no more; you are harmless and noiseless as any of these old chairs; in short, I never feel so private as when I know you are here. At last I see it, I feel it; I penetrate to the predestinated purpose of my life. I am content. Others may have loftier parts to enact; but my mission in this world, Bartleby, is to furnish you with office-room for such period as you may see fit to remain.

19. In his *Freedom of the Will,* the Calvinist theologian Jonathan Edwards (1703–58) argued that the doctrine of free will is false, since all our actions are bound by the laws of causation.
20. Joseph Priestley (1733–1804), the English chemist who discovered oxygen, was a voluminous writer on theological subjects. He defended the necessitarian doctrine that all events are determined by preceding causes.

I believe that this wise and blessed frame of mind would have continued with me, had it not been for the unsolicited and uncharitable remarks obtruded upon me by my professional friends who visited the rooms. But thus it often is, that the constant friction of illiberal minds wears out at last the best resolves of the more generous. Though to be sure, when I reflected upon it, it was not strange that people entering my office should be struck by the peculiar aspect of the unaccountable Bartleby, and so be tempted to throw out some sinister observations concerning him. Sometimes an attorney, having business with me, and calling at my office, and finding no one but the scrivener there, would undertake to obtain some sort of precise information from him touching my whereabouts; but without heeding his idle talk, Bartleby would remain standing immovable in the middle of the room. So after contemplating him in that position for a time, the attorney would depart, no wiser than he came.

Also, when a Reference [21] was going on, and the room full of lawyers and witnesses, and business driving fast, some deeply-occupied legal gentleman present, seeing Bartleby wholly unemployed, would request him to run round to his (the legal gentleman's) office and fetch some papers for him. Thereupon, Bartleby would tranquilly decline, and yet remain idle as before. Then the lawyer would give a great stare, and turn to me. And what could I say? At last I was made aware that all through the circle of my professional acquaintance, a whisper of wonder was running round, having reference to the strange creature I kept at my office. This worried me very much. And as the idea came upon me of his possibly turning out a long-lived man, and keep occupying my chambers, and denying my authority; and perplexing my visitors; and scandalizing my professional reputation; and casting a general gloom over the premises; keeping soul and body together to the last upon his savings (for doubtless he spent but half a dime a day), and in the end perhaps outlive me, and claim possession of my office by right of his perpetual occupancy: as all these dark anticipations crowded upon me more and more, and my friends continually intruded their relentless remarks upon the apparition in my room; a great change was wrought in me. I resolved to gather all my faculties together, and forever rid me of this intolerable incubus.

Ere revolving any complicated project, however, adapted to this end, I first simply suggested to Bartleby the propriety of his permanent departure. In a calm and serious tone, I commended the idea to his careful and mature consideration. But, having taken three days to meditate upon it, he apprised me, that his original determi-

21. The act of submitting or referring a dispute or controversy to the Masters of the Court of Chancery.

nation remained the same; in short, that he still preferred to abide with me.

What shall I do? I now said to myself, buttoning up my coat to the last button. What shall I do? what ought I to do? what does conscience say I *should* do with this man, or, rather, ghost. Rid myself of him, I must; go, he shall. But how? You will not thrust him, the poor, pale, passive mortal—you will not thrust such a helpless creature out of you door? you will not dishonor yourself by such cruelty? No, I will not, I cannot do that. Rather would I let him live and die here, and then mason up his remains in the wall. What, then, will you do? For all your coaxing, he will not budge. Bribes he leaves under your own paperweight on your table; in short, it is quite plain that he prefers to cling to you.

Then something severe, something unusual must be done. What! surely you will not have him collared by a constable, and commit his innocent pallor to the common jail? And upon what ground could you procure such a thing to be done?—a vagrant, is he? What! he a vagrant, a wanderer, who refuses to budge? It is because he will *not* be a vagrant, then, that you seek to count him *as* a vagrant. That is too absurd. No visible means of support: there I have him. Wrong again: for indubitably he *does* support himself, and that is the only unanswerable proof that any man can show of his possessing the means so to do. No more, then. Since he will not quit me, I must quit him. I will change my offices; I will move elsewhere, and give him fair notice, that if I find him on my new premises I will then proceed against him as a common trespasser.

Acting accordingly, next day I thus addressed him: "I find these chambers too far from the City Hall; the air is unwholesome. In a word, I propose to remove my offices next week, and shall no longer require your services. I tell you this now, in order that you may seek another place."

He made no reply, and nothing more was said.

On the appointed day I engaged carts and men, proceeded to my chambers, and, having but little furniture, everything was removed in a few hours. Throughout, the scrivener remained standing behind the screen, which I directed to be removed the last thing. It was withdrawn; and, being folded up like a huge folio, left him the motionless occupant of a naked room. I stood in the entry watching him a moment, while something from within me upbraided me.

I re-entered, with my hand in my pocket—and—and my heart in my mouth.

"Good-by, Bartleby; I am going—good-by, and God some way bless you; and take that," slipping something in his hand. But it dropped upon the floor, and then—strange to say—I tore myself from him whom I had so longed to be rid of.

Established in my new quarters, for a day or two I kept the door locked, and started at every footfall in the passages. When I returned to my rooms, after any little absence, I would pause at the threshold for an instant, and attentively listen, ere applying my key. But these fears were needless. Bartleby never came nigh me.

I thought all was going well, when a perturbed-looking stranger visited me, inquiring whether I was the person who had recently occupied rooms at No. — Wall Street.

Full of forebodings, I replied that I was.

"Then, sir," said the stranger, who proved a lawyer, "you are responsible for the man you left there. He refuses to do any copying; he refuses to do anything; he says he prefers not to; and he refuses to quit the premises."

"I am very sorry, sir," said I, with assumed tranquillity, but an inward tremor, "but, really, the man you allude to is nothing to me—he is no relation or apprentice of mine, that you should hold me responsible for him."

"In mercy's name, who is he?"

"I certainly cannot inform you. I know nothing about him. Formerly I employed him as a copyist; but he has done nothing for me now for some time past."

"I shall settle him, then—good morning, sir."

Several days passed, and I heard nothing more; and, though I often felt a charitable prompting to call at the place and see poor Bartleby, yet a certain squeamishness, of I know not what, withheld me.

All is over with him, by this time, thought I, at last, when, through another week, no further intelligence reached me. But, coming to my room the day after, I found several persons waiting at my door in a high state of nervous excitement.

"That's the man—here he comes," cried the foremost one, whom I recognized as the lawyer who had previously called upon me alone.

"You must take him away, sir, at once," cried a portly person among them, advancing upon me, and whom I knew to be the landlord of No. — Wall Street. "These gentlemen, my tenants, cannot stand it any longer; Mr. B——," pointing to the lawyer, "has turned him out of his room, and he now persists in haunting the building generally, sitting upon the banisters of the stairs by day, and sleeping in the entry by night. Everybody is concerned; clients are leaving the offices; some fears are entertained of a mob; something you must do, and that without delay."

Aghast at this torrent, I fell back before it, and would fain have locked myself in my new quarters. In vain I persisted that Bartleby was nothing to me—no more than to any one else. In vain—I was the last person known to have anything to do with him, and they held me to the terrible account. Fearful, then, of being exposed in the papers (as one person present obscurely threatened), I considered the matter, and, at length, said, that if the lawyer would give me a confidential interview with the scrivener, in his (the lawyer's) own room, I would, that afternoon, strive my best to rid them of the nuisance they complained of.

Going up stairs to my old haunt, there was Bartleby silently sitting upon the banister at the landing.

"What are you doing here, Bartleby?" said I.

"Sitting upon the banister," he mildly replied.

I motioned him into the lawyer's room, who then left us.

"Bartleby," said I, "are you aware that you are the cause of great tribulation to me, by persisting in occupying the entry after being dismissed from the office?"

No answer.

"Now one of two things must take place. Either you must do something, or something must be done to you. Now what sort of business would you like to engage in? Would you like to re-engage in copying for some one?"

"No; I would prefer not to make any change."

"Would you like a clerkship in a dry-goods store?"

"There is too much confinement about that. No, I would not like a clerkship; but I am not particular."

"Too much confinement," I cried, "why, you keep yourself confined all the time!"

"I would prefer not to take a clerkship," he rejoined, as if to settle that little item at once.

"How would a bar-tender's business suit you? There is no trying of the eye-sight in that."

"I would not like it at all; though, as I said before, I am not particular."

His unwonted wordiness inspirited me. I returned to the charge.

"Well, then, would you like to travel through the country collecting bills for the merchants? That would improve your health."

"No, I would prefer to be doing something else."

"How, then, would going as a companion to Europe, to entertain some young gentleman with your conversation—how would that suit you?"

"Not at all. It does not strike me that there is anything definite about that. I like to be stationary. But I am not particular."

"Stationary you shall be, then," I cried, now losing all patience, and, for the first time in all my exasperating connection with him, fairly flying into a passion. "If you do not go away from these premises before night, I shall feel bound—indeed, I *am* bound—to—to—

to quit the premises myself!" I rather absurdly concluded, knowing not with what possible threat to try to frighten his immobility into compliance. Despairing of all further efforts, I was precipitately leaving him, when a final thought occurred to me—one which had not been wholly unindulged before.

"Bartleby," said I, in the kindest tone I could assume under such exciting circumstances, "will you go home with me now—not to my office, but my dwelling—and remain there till we can conclude upon some convenient arrangement for you at our leisure? Come, let us start now, right away."

"No: at present I would prefer not to make any change at all."

I answered nothing; but, effectually dodging every one by the suddenness and rapidity of my flight, rushed from the building, ran up Wall Street towards Broadway, and, jumping into the first omnibus, was soon removed from pursuit. As soon as tranquillity returned, I distinctly perceived that I had now done all that I possibly could, both in respect to the demands of the landlord and his tenants, and with regard to my own desire and sense of duty, to benefit Bartleby, and shield him from rude persecution. I now strove to be entirely care-free and quiescent; and my conscience justified me in the attempt; though, indeed, it was not so successful as I could have wished. So fearful was I of being again hunted out by the incensed landlord and his exasperated tenants, that, surrendering my business to Nippers, for a few days, I drove about the upper part of the town and through the suburbs, in my rockaway; crossed over to Jersey City and Hoboken, and paid fugitive visits to Manhattanville and Astoria. In fact, I almost lived in my rockaway for the time.

When again I entered my office, lo, a note from the landlord lay upon the desk. I opened it with trembling hands. It informed me that the writer had sent to the police, and had Bartleby removed to the Tombs as a vagrant. Moreover, since I knew more about him than any one else, he wished me to appear at that place, and make a suitable statement of the facts. These tidings had a conflicting effect upon me. At first I was indignant; but, at last, almost approved. The landlord's energetic, summary disposition, had led him to adopt a procedure which I do not think I would have decided upon myself; and yet, as a last resort, under such peculiar circumstances, it seemed the only plan.

As I afterwards learned, the poor scrivener, when told that he must be conducted to the Tombs, offered not the slightest obstacle, but, in his pale, unmoving way, silently acquiesced.

Some of the compassionate and curious bystanders joined the party; and headed by one of the constables arm-in-arm with Bartleby, the silent procession filed its way through all the noise, and heat, and joy of the roaring thoroughfares at noon.

The same day I received the note, I went to the Tombs, or, to speak more properly, the Halls of Justice. Seeking the right officer, I stated the purpose of my call, and was informed that the individual I described was, indeed, within. I then assured the functionary that Bartleby was a perfectly honest man, and greatly to be compassionated, however unaccountably eccentric. I narrated all I knew, and closed by suggesting the idea of letting him remain in as indulgent confinement as possible, till something less harsh might be done—though, indeed, I hardly knew what. At all events, if nothing else could be decided upon, the alms-house must receive him. I then begged to have an interview.

Being under no disgraceful charge, and quite serene and harmless in all his ways, they had permitted him freely to wander about the prison, and, especially, in the inclosed grass-platted yards thereof. And so I found him there, standing all alone in the quietest of the yards, his face towards a high wall, while all around, from the narrow slits of the jail windows, I thought I saw peering out upon him the eyes of murderers and thieves.

"Bartleby!"

"I know you," he said, without looking round—"and I want nothing to say to you."

"It was not I that brought you here, Bartleby," said I, keenly pained at his implied suspicion. "And to you, this should not be so vile a place. Nothing reproachful attaches to you by being here. And see, it is not so sad a place as one might think. Look, there is the sky, and here is the grass."

"I know where I am," he replied, but would say nothing more, and so I left him.

As I entered the corridor again, a broad meat-like man, in an apron, accosted me, and, jerking his thumb over his shoulder, said—"Is that your friend?"

"Yes."

"Does he want to starve? If he does, let him live on the prison fare, that's all."

"Who are you?" asked I, not knowing what to make of such an unofficially speaking person in such a place.

"I am the grub-man. Such gentlemen as have friends here, hire me to provide them with something good to eat."

"Is this so?" said I, turning to the turnkey.

He said it was.

"Well, then," said I, slipping some silver into the grub-man's hands (for so they called him), "I want you to give particular attention to my friend there; let him have the best dinner you can get. And you must be as polite to him as possible."

"Introduce me, will you?" said the grub-man, looking at me with an expression which seemed to say he was all impatience for an opportunity to give a specimen of his breeding.

Thinking it would prove of benefit to the scrivener, I acquiesced; and, asking the grub-man his name, went up with him to Bartleby.

"Bartleby, this is a friend; you will find him very useful to you."

"Your sarvant, sir, your sarvant," said the grub-man, making a low salutation behind his apron. "Hope you find it pleasant here, sir; nice grounds—cool apartments—hope you'll stay with us some time—try to make it agreeable. What will you have for dinner to-day?"

"I prefer not to dine to-day," said Bartleby, turning away. "It would disagree with me; I am unused to dinners." So saying, he slowly moved to the other side of the inclosure, and took up a position fronting the dead-wall.

"How's this?" said the grub-man, addressing me with a stare of astonishment. "He's odd, ain't he?"

"I think he is a little deranged," said I, sadly.

"Deranged? deranged is it? Well, now, upon my word, I thought that friend of yourn was a gentleman forger; they are always pale and genteel-like, them forgers. I can't help pity 'em—can't help it, sir. Did you know Monroe Edwards?" he added, touchingly, and paused. Then, laying his hand piteously on my shoulder, sighed, "he died of consumption at Sing-Sing. So you weren't acquainted with Monroe?"

"No, I was never socially acquainted with any forgers. But I cannot stop longer. Look to my friend yonder. You will not lose by it. I will see you again."

Some few days after this, I again obtained admission to the Tombs, and went through the corridors in quest of Bartleby; but without finding him.

"I saw him coming from his cell not long ago," said a turnkey, "may be he's gone to loiter in the yards."

So I went in that direction.

"Are you looking for the silent man?" said another turnkey, passing me. "Yonder he lies—sleeping in the yard there. 'Tis not twenty minutes since I saw him lie down."

The yard was entirely quiet. It was not accessible to the common prisoners. The surrounding walls, of amazing thickness, kept off all sounds behind them. The Egyptian character of the masonry weighed upon me with its gloom. But a soft imprisoned turf grew under foot. The heart of the eternal pyramids, it seemed, wherein, by some strange magic, through the clefts, grass-seed, dropped by birds, had sprung.

Strangely huddled at the base of the wall, his knees drawn up, and lying on his side, his head touching the cold stones, I saw the wasted Bartleby. But nothing stirred. I paused; then went close up to him; stooped over, and saw that his dim eyes were open; otherwise he seemed profoundly sleeping. Something prompted me to touch him. I felt his hand, when a tingling shiver ran up my arm and down my spine to my feet,

The round face of the grub-man peered upon me now. "His dinner is ready. Won't he dine to-day, either? Or does he live without dining?"

"Lives without dining," said I, and closed the eyes.

"Eh!—He's asleep, ain't he?"

"With kings and counselors," [22] murmured I.

There would seem little need for proceeding further in this history. Imagination will readily supply the meagre recital of poor Bartleby's interment. But, ere parting with the reader, let me say, that if this little narrative has sufficiently interested him, to awaken curiosity as to who Bartleby was, and what manner of life he led prior to the present narrator's making his acquaintance, I can only reply, that in such curiosity I fully share, but am wholly unable to gratify it. Yet here I hardly know whether I should divulge one little item of rumor, which came to my ear a few months after the scrivener's decease. Upon what basis it rested, I could never ascertain; and hence, how true it is I cannot now tell. But, inasmuch as this vague report has not been without a certain suggestive interest to me, however sad, it may prove the same with some others; and so I will briefly mention it. The report was this: that Bartleby had been a subordinate clerk in the Dead Letter Office at Washington, from which he had been suddenly removed by a change in the administration. When I think over this rumor, hardly can I express the emotions which seize me. Dead letters! does it not sound like dead men? Conceive a man by nature and misfortune prone to a pallid hopelessness, can any business seem more fitted to heighten it than that of continually handling these dead letters, and assorting them for the flames? For by the cartload they are annually burned. Sometimes from out the folded paper the pale clerk takes a ring—the finger it was meant for, perhaps, moulders in the grave; a bank-note sent in swiftest charity—he whom it would relieve, nor eats nor hungers any more; pardon for those who died despairing; hope for those who died unhoping; good tidings for those who died stifled

22. See the complaint of the afflicted Job (Job 3:11–16). "Why died I not from the womb? *why* did I *not* give up the ghost when I came out of the belly? Why did the knees prevent me? or why the breasts that I should suck? For now should I have lain still and been quiet, I should have slept: then had I been at rest, With kings and counselors of the earth, which built desolate places for themselves; Or with princes that had gold, who filled their houses with silver: Or as a hidden untimely birth I had not been; as infants *which* never saw light."

by unrelieved calamities. On errands of life, these letters speed to death.

Ah, Bartleby! Ah, humanity!

From *Piazza Tales* (1856)

BENITO CERENO [1]

In the year 1799, Captain Amasa Delano, of Duxbury, in Massachusetts, commanding a large sealer and general trader, lay at anchor with a valuable cargo, in the harbour of St. Maria—a small, desert, uninhabited island toward the southern extremity of the long coast of Chili. There he had touched for water.

On the second day, not long after dawn, while lying in his berth, his mate came below, informing him that a strange sail was coming into the bay. Ships were then not so plenty in those waters as now. He rose, dressed, and went on deck.

The morning was one peculiar to that coast. Everything was mute and calm; everything gray. The sea, though undulated into long roods [2] of swells, seemed fixed, and was sleeked at the surface like waved lead that has cooled and set in the smelter's mould. The sky seemed a gray surtout.[3] Flights of troubled gray fowl, kith and kin with flights of troubled gray vapours among which they were mixed, skimmed low and fitfully over the waters, as swallows over meadows before storms. Shadows present, foreshadowing deeper shadows to come.

To Captain Delano's surprise, the stranger, viewed through the glass,[4] showed no colours; though to do so upon entering a haven, however uninhabited in its shores, where but a single other ship might be lying, was the custom among peaceful seamen of all nations. Considering the lawlessness and loneliness of the spot, and the sort of stories, at that day, associated with those seas, Captain Delano's surprise might have deepened into some uneasiness had he not been a person of a singularly undistrustful good-nature, not liable, except on extraordinary and repeated incentives, and hardly then, to indulge in personal alarms, any way involving the imputation of malign evil in man. Whether, in view of what humanity is capable, such a trait implies, along with a benevolent heart, more

1. The name "Benito Cereno" is richly suggestive. "Benito" has overtones of the Spanish *bonito*, "nice," and "Cereno" echoes *sereno* ("calm," "serene"). "Benito" is also a form of *benedictino*, "Benedictine." The Benedictine Order of monks, known as the "Black Monks," was founded by St. Benedict about the year 529. There is also a suggestion of the Latin *benedictus*, "blessed."
Although Melville found the substance of his story in Chapter XVIII of Amasa Delano's *Narrative of Voyages and Travels, in the Northern and Southern Hemispheres* . . . (Boston, 1817), Delano's account was radically transformed in his imagination. For a discussion of this source, see Harold H. Scudder, "Melville's *Benito Cereno* and Captain Delano's Voyages" (which reprints Delano's chapter), *PMLA* 43 (1928), 502–32.
2. A rood, a distance of 6–8 yards, originally meant "stick" or "rod," and is applied especially to a gallows or to the Cross on which Christ was crucified.
3. Hooded cloak.
4. Telescope.

than ordinary quickness and accuracy of intellectual perception, may be left to the wise to determine.

But whatever misgivings might have obtruded on first seeing the stranger, would almost, in any seaman's mind, have been dissipated by observing that the ship, in navigating into the harbour, was drawing too near the land; a sunken reef making out off her bow. This seemed to prove her a stranger, indeed, not only to the sealer, but the island; consequently, she could be no wonted freebooter on that ocean. With no small interest, Captain Delano continued to watch her—a proceeding not much facilitated by the vapours partly mantling the hull, through which the far matin light from her cabin streamed equivocally enough; much like the sun—by this time hemisphered on the rim of the horizon, and, apparently, in company with the strange ship entering the harbour—which, wimpled by the same low, creeping clouds, showed not unlike a Lima intriguante's [5] one sinister eye peering across the Plaza from the Indian loop-hole of her dusk *saya-y-manta*.[6]

It might have been but a deception of the vapours, but the longer the stranger was watched the more singular appeared her manœuvres. Ere long it seemed hard to decide whether she meant to come in or no—what she wanted, or what she was about. The wind, which had breezed up a little during the night, was now extremely light and baffling, which the more increased the apparent uncertainty of her movements.

Surmising, at last, that it might be a ship in distress, Captain Delano ordered his whale-boat to be dropped, and, much to the wary opposition of his mate, prepared to board her, and, at the least, pilot her in. On the night previous, a fishing-party of the seamen had gone a long distance to some detached rocks out of sight from the sealer, and, an hour or two before daybreak, had returned, having met with no small success. Presuming that the stranger might have been long off soundings,[7] the good captain put several baskets of the fish, for presents, into his boat, and so pulled away. From her continuing too near the sunken reef, deeming her in danger, calling to his men, he made all haste to apprise those on board of their situation. But, some time ere the boat came up, the wind, light though it was, having shifted, had headed the vessel off, as well as partly broken the vapours from about her.

Upon gaining a less remote view, the ship, when made signally visible on the verge of the leaden-hued swells, with the shreds of fog here and there raggedly furring her, appeared like a

5. A seductive woman.
6. Skirt-and-shawl.
7. That is, long away from a shore where soundings (depth measurements) could be taken.

whitewashed monastery after a thunder-storm, seen perched upon some dun cliff among the Pyrenees. But it was no purely fanciful resemblance which now, for a moment, almost led Captain Delano to think that nothing less than a ship-load of monks was before him. Peering over the bulwarks were what really seemed, in the hazy distance, throngs of dark cowls; while, fitfully revealed through the open port-holes, other dark moving figures were dimly descried, as of Black Friars pacing the cloisters.

Upon a still nigher approach, this appearance was modified, and the true character of the vessel was plain—a Spanish merchantman of the first class, carrying negro slaves, amongst other valuable freight, from one colonial port to another. A very large, and, in its time, a very fine vessel, such as in those days were at intervals encountered along that main; sometimes superseded Acapulco treasure-ships,[8] or retired frigates of the Spanish king's navy, which, like superannuated Italian palaces, still, under a decline of masters, preserved signs of former state.

As the whale-boat drew more and more nigh, the cause of the peculiar pipe-clayed aspect of the stranger was seen in the slovenly neglect pervading her. The spars, ropes, and great part of the bulwarks, looked woolly, from long unacquaintance with the scraper, tar, and the brush. Her keel seemed laid, her ribs put together, and she launched, from Ezekiel's Valley of Dry Bones.[9]

In the present business in which she was engaged, the ship's general model and rig appeared to have undergone no material change from their original warlike and Froissart pattern.[10] However, no guns were seen.

The tops [11] were large, and were railed about with what had once been octagonal net-work, all now in sad disrepair. These tops hung overhead like three ruinous aviaries, in one of which was seen perched, on a ratlin, a white noddy, a strange fowl, so called from its lethargic, somnambulistic character, being frequently caught by hand at sea. Battered and mouldy, the castellated forecastle seemed some ancient turret, long ago taken by assault, and then left to decay. Toward the stern, two high-raised quarter-galleries—the balustrades here and there covered with dry, tindery sea-moss—opening out from the unoccupied state-cabin, whose dead-lights,[12] for all the mild weather, were hermetically closed and caulked—these tenantless balconies hung over the sea as if it were the grand Venetian canal. But the principal relic of faded grandeur was the ample

8. Mexican gold was shipped to Spain from the port of Acapulco.
9. Ezekiel 37.
10. Jean Froissart (1338–1410), French chronicler of fourteenth-century life. Melville implies that the ship resembled a medieval vessel.
11. Platforms near the heads of the lower masts.
12. Shutters that fasten over the portholes and cabin windows.

oval of the shield-like stern-piece, intricately carved with the arms of Castile and Leon,[13] medallioned about by groups of mythological or symbolical devices; uppermost and central of which was a dark satyr in a mask, holding his foot on the prostrate neck of a writhing figure, likewise masked.

Whether the ship had a figure-head, or only a plain beak, was not quite certain, owing to canvas wrapped about that part, either to protect it while undergoing a refurbishing, or else decently to hide its decay. Rudely painted or chalked, as in a sailor freak, along the forward side of a sort of pedestal below the canvas, was the sentence, *"Seguid vuestro jefe"* (follow your leader); while upon the tarnished head-boards, near by, appeared, in stately capitals, once gilt, the ship's name, "SAN DOMINICK," each letter streakingly corroded with tricklings of copper-spike rust; while, like mourning weeds, dark festoons of sea-grass slimily swept to and fro over the name, with every hearse-like roll of the hull.

As, at last, the boat was hooked from the bow along toward the gangway amidship, its keel, while yet some inches separated from the hull, harshly grated as on a sunken coral reef. It proved a huge bunch of conglobated barnacles adhering below the water to the side like a wen—a token of baffling airs and long calms passed somewhere in those seas.

Climbing the side, the visitor was at once surrounded by a clamorous throng of whites and blacks, but the latter outnumbering the former more than could have been expected, negro transportation-ship as the stranger in port was. But, in one language, and as with one voice, all poured out a common tale of suffering; in which the negresses, of whom there were not a few, exceeded the others in their dolorous vehemence. The scurvy, together with the fever, had swept off a great part of their number, more especially the Spaniards. Off Cape Horn they had narrowly escaped shipwreck; then, for days together, they had lain tranced without wind; their provisions were low; their water next to none; their lips that moment were baked.

While Captain Delano was thus made the mark of all eager tongues, his one eager glance took in all faces, with every other object about him.

Always upon first boarding a large and populous ship at sea, especially a foreign one, with a nondescript crew such as Lascars or Manilla men,[14] the impression varies in a peculiar way from that produced by first entering a strange house with strange inmates in a strange land. Both house and ship—the one by its walls and blinds,

13. The kingdom of Castile and León joined with Aragon to form the united Spain of the sixteenth century.
14. East Indian sailors.

the other by its high bulwarks like ramparts—hoard from view their interiors till the last moment; but in the case of the ship there is this addition: that the living spectacle it contains, upon its sudden and complete disclosure, has, in contrast with the blank ocean which zones it, something of the effect of enchantment. The ship seems unreal; these strange costumes, gestures, and faces, but a shadowy tableau just emerged from the deep, which directly must receive back what it gave.

Perhaps it was some such influence, as above is attempted to be described, which, in Captain Delano's mind, heightened whatever, upon a staid scrutiny, might have seemed unusual; especially the conspicuous figures of four elderly grizzled negroes, their heads like black, doddered [15] willow-tops, who, in venerable contrast to the tumult below them, were couched, sphinx-like, one on the starboard cat-head,[16] another on the larboard, and the remaining pair face to face on the opposite bulwarks above the main-chains. They each had bits of un-stranded old junk in their hands, and, with a sort of stoical self-content, were picking the junk into oakum,[17] a small heap of which lay by their sides. They accompanied the task with a continuous, low, monotonous chant; droning and druling away like so many gray-headed bagpipers playing a funeral march.

The quarter-deck rose into an ample elevated poop, upon the forward verge of which, lifted, like the oakum-pickers, some eight feet above the general throng, sat along in a row, separated by regular spaces, the crosslegged figures of six other blacks; each with a rusty hatchet in his hand, which, with a bit of brick and a rag, he was engaged like a scullion [18] in scouring; while between each two was a small stack of hatchets, their rusted edges turned forward awaiting a like operation. Though occasionally the four oakum-pickers would briefly address some person or persons in the crowd below, yet the six hatchet-polishers neither spoke to others, nor breathed a whisper among themselves, but sat intent upon their task, except at intervals, when, with the peculiar love in negroes of uniting industry with pastime, two and two they sideways clashed their hatchets together, like cymbals, with a barbarous din. All six, unlike the generality, had the raw aspect of unsophisticated Africans.

But that first comprehensive glance which took in those ten figures, with scores less conspicuous, rested but an instant upon them,

15. Having lost the top branches through age or decay.
16. A beam projecting from the bow of the ship, and used as a support to lift the anchor.
17. Picking the loose hemp fibers from pieces of old rope; the loose fibers, called oakum, were used to caulk the seams in a wooden ship.
18. Kitchen boy.

as, impatient of the hubbub of voices, the visitor turned in quest of whomsoever it might be that commanded the ship.

But as if not unwilling to let nature make known her own case among his suffering charge, or else in despair of restraining it for the time, the Spanish captain, a gentlemanly, reserved-looking, and rather young man to a stranger's eye, dressed with singular richness, but bearing plain traces of recent sleepless cares and disquietudes, stood passively by, leaning against the mainmast, at one moment casting a dreary, spiritless look upon his excited people, at the next an unhappy glance toward his visitor. By his side stood a black of small stature, in whose rude face, as occasionally, like a shepherd's dog, he mutely turned it up into the Spaniard's, sorrow and affection were equally blended.

Struggling through the throng, the American advanced to the Spaniard, assuring him of his sympathies, and offering to render whatever assistance might be in his power. To which the Spaniard returned for the present but grave and ceremonious acknowledgments, his national formality dusked by the saturnine mood of ill-health.

But losing no time in mere compliments, Captain Delano, returning to the gangway, had his basket of fish brought up; and as the wind still continued light, so that some hours at least must elapse ere the ship could be brought to the anchorage, he bade his men return to the sealer, and fetch back as much water as the whale-boat could carry, with whatever soft bread the steward might have, all the remaining pumpkins on board, with a box of sugar, and a dozen of his private bottles of cider.

Not many minutes after the boat's pushing off, to the vexation of all, the wind entirely died away, and the tide turning, began drifting back the ship helplessly seaward. But trusting this would not last long, Captain Delano sought, with good hopes, to cheer up the strangers, feeling no small satisfaction that, with persons in their condition, he could—thanks to his frequent voyages along the Spanish main—converse with some freedom in their native tongue.

While left alone with them, he was not long in observing some things tending to heighten his first impressions; but surprise was lost in pity, both for the Spaniards and blacks, alike evidently reduced from scarcity of water and provisions; while long-continued suffering seemed to have brought out the less good-natured qualities of the negroes, besides, at the same time, impairing the Spaniard's authority over them. But, under the circumstances, precisely this condition of things was to have been anticipated. In armies, navies, cities, or families, in nature herself, nothing more relaxes good order than misery. Still, Captain Delano was not without the idea, that had Benito Cereno been a man of greater energy, misrule would hardly have come to the present pass. But the debility, constitutional or induced by hardships, bodily and mental, of the Spanish captain, was too obvious to be overlooked. A prey to settled dejection, as if long mocked with hope he would not now indulge it, even when it had ceased to be a mock, the prospect of that day, or evening at furthest, lying at anchor, with plenty of water for his people, and a brother captain to counsel and befriend, seemed in no perceptible degree to encourage him. His mind appeared unstrung, if not still more seriously affected. Shut up in these oaken walls, chained to one dull round of command, whose unconditionality cloyed him, like some hypochondriac abbot he moved slowly about, at times suddenly pausing, starting, or staring, biting his lip, biting his finger-nail, flushing, paling, twitching his beard, with other symptoms of an absent or moody mind. This distempered spirit was lodged, as before hinted, in as distempered a frame. He was rather tall, but seemed never to have been robust, and now with nervous suffering was almost worn to a skeleton. A tendency to some pulmonary complaint appeared to have been lately confirmed. His voice was like that of one with lungs half gone—hoarsely suppressed, a husky whisper. No wonder that, as in this state he tottered about, his private servant apprehensively followed him. Sometimes the negro gave his master his arm, or took his handkerchief out of his pocket for him; performing these and similar offices with that affectionate zeal which transmutes into something filial or fraternal acts in themselves but menial; and which has gained for the negro the repute of making the most pleasing body-servant in the world; one, too, whom a master need be on no stiffly superior terms with, but may treat with familiar trust; less a servant than a devoted companion.

Marking the noisy indocility of the blacks in general, as well as what seemed the sullen inefficiency of the whites, it was not without humane satisfaction that Captain Delano witnessed the steady good conduct of Babo.

But the good conduct of Babo, hardly more than the ill-behaviour of others, seemed to withdraw the half-lunatic Don Benito from his cloudy languor. Not that such precisely was the impression made by the Spaniard on the mind of his visitor. The Spaniard's individual unrest was, for the present, but noted as a conspicuous feature in the ship's general affliction. Still, Captain Delano was not a little concerned at what he could not help taking for the time to be Don Benito's unfriendly indifference toward himself. The Spaniard's manner, too, conveyed a sort of sour and gloomy disdain, which he seemed at no pains to disguise. But this the American in charity ascribed to the harassing effects of sickness, since, in former instances, he had noted that there are peculiar natures on whom prolonged physical suffering seems to cancel every social instinct of kindness; as if, forced to black bread themselves, they deemed it but equity that each person coming nigh them should, indirectly, by some slight or affront, be made to partake of their fare.

But ere long Captain Delano bethought him that, indulgent as he was at the first, in judging the Spaniard, he might not, after all, have exercised charity enough. At bottom it was Don Benito's reserve which displeased him; but the same reserve was shown toward all but his faithful personal attendant. Even the formal reports which, according to sea-usage, were, at stated times, made to him by some petty underling, either a white, mulatto, or black, he hardly had patience enough to listen to, without betraying contemptuous aversion. His manner upon such occasions was, in its degree, not unlike that which might be supposed to have been his imperial countryman's, Charles V.,[19] just previous to the anchoritish retirement of that monarch from the throne.

This splenetic disrelish of his place was evinced in almost every function pertaining to it. Proud as he was moody, he condescended to no personal mandate. Whatever special orders were necessary, their delivery was delegated to his body-servant, who in turn transferred them to their ultimate destination, through runners, alert Spanish boys or slave-boys, like pages or pilot-fish [20] within easy call continually hovering round Don Benito. So that to have beheld this undemonstrative invalid gliding about, apathetic and mute, no landsman could have dreamed that in him was lodged a dictatorship beyond which, while at sea, there was no earthly appeal.

Thus, the Spaniard, regarded in his reserve, seemed the involuntary victim of mental disorder. But, in fact, his reserve might, in some degree, have proceeded from design. If so, then here was evinced the unhealthy climax of that icy though conscientious policy, more or less adopted by all commanders of large ships, which, except in signal emergencies, obliterates alike the manifestation of sway with every trace of sociality; transforming the man into a block, or rather into a loaded cannon, which, until there is call for thunder, has nothing to say.

Viewing him in this light, it seemed but a natural token of the perverse habit induced by a long course of such hard self-restraint, that, notwithstanding the present condition of his ship, the Spaniard should still persist in a demeanour, which, however harmless, or, it may be, appropriate, in a well-appointed vessel, such as the *San Dominick* might have been at the outset of the voyage, was

19. Charles V (1500–58), emperor of the Holy Roman Empire and (as Charles I) king of Spain, retired to a little house attached to a monastery. An anchorite is a hermit or recluse.
20. Pilot fish swim in company with larger fish, especially sharks.

anything but judicious now. But the Spaniard, perhaps, thought that it was with captains as with gods: reserve, under all events, must still be their cue. But probably this appearance of slumbering dominion might have been but an attempted disguise to conscious imbecility—not deep policy, but shallow device. But be all this as it might, whether Don Benito's manner was designed or not, the more Captain Delano noted its pervading reserve, the less he felt uneasiness at any particular manifestation of that reserve toward himself.

Neither were his thoughts taken up by the captain alone. Wonted to the quiet orderliness of the sealer's comfortable family of a crew, the noisy confusion of the San Dominick's suffering host repeatedly challenged his eye. Some prominent breaches, not only of discipline but of decency, were observed. These Captain Delano could not but ascribe, in the main, to the absence of those subordinate deck-officers to whom, along with higher duties, is entrusted what may be styled the police department of a populous ship. True, the old oakum-pickers appeared at times to act the part of monitorial constables to their countrymen, the blacks; but though occasionally succeeding in allaying trifling outbreaks now and then between man and man, they could do little or nothing toward establishing general quiet. The San Dominick was in the condition of a transatlantic emigrant ship, among whose multitude of living freight are some individuals, doubtless, as little troublesome as crates and bales; but the friendly remonstrances of such with their ruder companions are of not so much avail as the unfriendly arm of the mate. What the San Dominick wanted was, what the emigrant ship has, stern superior officers. But on these decks not so much as a fourth mate was to be seen.

The visitor's curiosity was roused to learn the particulars of those mishaps which had brought about such absenteeism, with its consequences; because, though deriving some inkling of the voyage from the wails which at the first moment had greeted him, yet of the details no clear understanding had been had. The best account would, doubtless, be given by the captain. Yet at first the visitor was loth to ask it, unwilling to provoke some distant rebuff. But plucking up courage, he at last accosted Don Benito, renewing the expression of his benevolent interest, adding, that did he (Captain Delano) but know the particulars of the ship's misfortunes, he would, perhaps, be better able in the end to relieve them. Would Don Benito favour him with the whole story.

Don Benito faltered; then, like some somnambulist suddenly interfered with, vacantly stared at his visitor, and ended by looking down on the deck. He maintained this posture so long, that Captain Delano, almost equally disconcerted, and involuntarily almost as rude, turned suddenly from him, walking forward to accost one of the Spanish seamen for the desired information. But he had hardly gone five paces, when, with a sort of eagerness, Don Benito invited him back, regretting his momentary absence of mind, and professing readiness to gratify him.

While most part of the story was being given, the two captains stood on the after part of the main-deck, a privileged spot, no one being near but the servant.

"It is now a hundred and ninety days," began the Spaniard, in his husky whisper, "that this ship, well officered and well manned, with several cabin passengers—some fifty Spaniards in all—sailed from Buenos Ayres bound to Lima, with a general cargo, hardware, Paraguay tea and the like—and," pointing forward, "that parcel of negroes, now not more than a hundred and fifty, as you see, but then numbering over three hundred souls. Off Cape Horn we had heavy gales. In one moment, by night, three of my best officers, with fifteen sailors, were lost, with the main-yard; the spar snapping under them in the slings, as they sought, with heavers,[21] to beat down the icy sail. To lighten the hull, the heavier sacks of mata were thrown into the sea, with most of the water-pipes [22] lashed on deck at the time. And this last necessity it was, combined with the prolonged detentions afterward experienced, which eventually brought about our chief causes of suffering. When — "

Here there was a sudden fainting attack of his cough, brought on, no doubt, by his mental distress. His servant sustained him, and drawing a cordial from his pocket placed it to his lips. He a little revived. But unwilling to leave him unsupported while yet imperfectly restored, the black with one arm still encircled his master, at the same time keeping his eye fixed on his face, as if to watch for the first sign of complete restoration, or relapse, as the event might prove.

The Spaniard proceeded, but brokenly and obscurely, as one in a dream.

—"Oh, my God! rather than pass through what I have, with joy I would have hailed the most terrible gales; but — "

His cough returned and with increased violence; this subsiding, with reddened lips and closed eyes he fell heavily against his supporter.

"His mind wanders. He was thinking of the plague that followed the gales," plaintively sighed the servant; "my poor, poor master!" wringing one hand, and with the other wiping the mouth. "But be patient, señor," again turning to Captain Delano, "these fits do not last long; master will soon be himself."

21. "Slings," ropes or chains for supporting a yard; "heavers," short bars used for twisting ropes.
22. Large casks.

Don Benito reviving, went on; but as this portion of the story was very brokenly delivered, the substance only will here be set down.

It appeared that after the ship had been many days tossed in storms off the Cape, the scurvy broke out, carrying off numbers of the whites and blacks. When at last they had worked round into the Pacific, their spars and sails were so damaged, and so inadequately handled by the surviving mariners, most of whom were become invalids, that, unable to lay her northerly course by the wind, which was powerful, the unmanageable ship, for successive days and nights, was blown north-westward, where the breeze suddenly deserted her, in unknown waters, to sultry calms. The absence of the water-pipes now proved as fatal to life as before their presence had menaced it. Induced, or at least aggravated, by the more than scanty allowance of water, a malignant fever followed the scurvy; with the excessive heat of the lengthened calm, making such short work of it as to sweep away, as by billows, whole families of the Africans, and a yet larger number, proportionably, of the Spaniards, including, by a luckless fatality, every remaining officer on board. Consequently, in the smart west winds eventually following the calm, the already rent sails, having to be simply dropped, not furled, at need, had been gradually reduced to the beggars' rags they were now. To procure substitutes for his lost sailors, as well as supplies of water and sails, the captain, at the earliest opportunity, had made for Baldivia, the southernmost civilised port of Chili and South America; but upon nearing the coast the thick weather had prevented him from so much as sighting that harbour. Since which period, almost without a crew, and almost without canvas, and almost without water, and, at intervals, giving its added dead to the sea, the *San Dominick* had been battledored about by contrary winds, inveigled by currents, or grown weedy in calms. Like a man lost in woods, more than once she had doubled upon her own track.

"But throughout these calamities," huskily continued Don Benito, painfully turning in the half-embrace of his servant, "I have to thank those negroes you see, who, though to your inexperienced eyes appearing unruly, have, indeed, conducted themselves with less of restlessness than even their owner could have thought possible under such circumstances."

Here he again fell faintly back. Again his mind wandered; but he rallied, and less obscurely proceeded.

"Yes, their owner was quite right in assuring me that no fetters would be needed with his blacks; so that while, as is wont in this transportation, these negroes have always remained upon deck—not thrust below, as in the Guinea-men [23]—they have, also, from the

23. Slave ships trading with the coast of West Africa.

beginning, been freely permitted to range within given bounds at their pleasure."

Once more the faintness returned—his mind roved—but, recovering, he resumed.

"But it is Babo here to whom, under God, I owe not only my own preservation, but likewise to him, chiefly, the merit is due, of pacifying his more ignorant brethren, when at intervals tempted to murmurings."

"Ah, master," sighed the black, bowing his face, "don't speak of me; Babo is nothing; what Babo has done was but duty."

"Faithful fellow!" cried Captain Delano. "Don Benito, I envy you such a friend; slave I cannot call him."

As master and man stood before him, the black upholding the white, Captain Delano could not but bethink him of the beauty of that relationship which could present such a spectacle of fidelity on the one hand and confidence on the other. The scene was heightened by the contrast in dress, denoting their relative positions. The Spaniard wore a loose Chili jacket of dark velvet; white small-clothes and stockings, with silver buckles at the knee and instep; a high-crowned sombrero, of fine grass; a slender sword, silver mounted, hung from a knot in his sash—the last being an almost invariable adjunct, more for utility than ornament, of a South American gentleman's dress to this hour. Excepting when his occasional nervous contortions brought about disarray, there was a certain precision in his attire curiously at variance with the unsightly disorder around; especially in the belittered ghetto, forward of the mainmast, wholly occupied by the blacks.

The servant wore nothing but wide trowsers, apparently, from their coarseness and patches, made out of some old topsail; they were clean, and confined at the waist by a bit of unstranded rope, which, with his composed, deprecatory air at times, made him look something like a begging friar of St. Francis.

However unsuitable for the time and place, at least in the blunt-thinking American's eyes, and however strangely surviving in the midst of all his afflictions, the toilet of Don Benito might not, in fashion at least, have gone beyond the style of the day among South Americans of his class. Though on the present voyage sailing from Buenos Ayres, he had avowed himself a native and resident of Chili, whose inhabitants had not so generally adopted the plain coat and once plebeian pantaloons; but, with a becoming modification, adhered to their provincial costume, picturesque as any in the world. Still, relatively to the pale history of the voyage, and his own pale face, there seemed something so incongruous in the Spaniard's apparel, as almost to suggest the image of an invalid courtier tottering about London streets in the time of the plague.

The portion of the narrative which, perhaps, most excited interest, as well as some surprise, considering the latitudes in question, was the long calms spoken of, and more particularly the ship's so long drifting about. Without communicating the opinion, of course, the American could not but impute at least part of the detentions both to clumsy seamanship and faulty navigation. Eyeing Don Benito's small, yellow hands, he easily inferred that the young captain had not got into command at the hawse-hole,[24] but the cabin window; and if so, why wonder at incompetence, in youth, sickness, and gentility united?

But drowning criticism in compassion, after a fresh repetition of his sympathies, Captain Delano, having heard out his story, not only engaged, as in the first place, to see Don Benito and his people supplied in their immediate bodily needs, but, also, now further promised to assist him in procuring a large permanent supply of water, as well as some sails and rigging; and, though it would involve no small embarrassment to himself, yet he would spare three of his best seamen for temporary deck officers; so that without delay the ship might proceed to Conception, there fully to refit for Lima, her destined port.

Such generosity was not without its effect, even upon the invalid. His face lighted up; eager and hectic, he met the honest glance of his visitor. With gratitude he seemed overcome.

"This excitement is bad for master," whispered the servant, taking his arm, and with soothing words gently drawing him aside.

When Don Benito returned, the American was pained to observe that his hopefulness, like the sudden kindling in his cheek, was but febrile and transient.

Ere long, with a joyless mien, looking up toward the poop, the host invited his guest to accompany him there, for the benefit of what little breath of wind might be stirring.

As, during the telling of the story, Captain Delano had once or twice started at the occasional cymballing of the hatchet-polishers, wondering why such an interruption should be allowed, especially in that part of the ship, and in the ears of an invalid; and moreover, as the hatchets had anything but an attractive look, and the handlers of them still less so, it was, therefore, to tell the truth, not without some lurking reluctance, or even shrinking, it may be, that Captain Delano, with apparent complaisance, acquiesced in his host's invitation. The more so, since, with an untimely caprice of punctilio, rendered distressing by his cadaverous aspect, Don Benito, with Castilian bows, solemnly insisted upon his guest's preceding him

24. One of the holes in the bow of a ship, through which a cable passes. Don Benito had no experience as an ordinary seaman, but came in through the "cabin window."

up the ladder leading to the elevation; where, one on each side of the last step, sat for armorial supporters and sentries two of the ominous file. Gingerly enough stepped good Captain Delano between them, and in the instant of leaving them behind, like one running the gauntlet, he felt an apprehensive twitch in the calves of his legs.

But when, facing about, he saw the whole file, like so many organ-grinders, still stupidly intent on their work, unmindful of everything besides, he could not but smile at his late fidgety panic.

Presently, while standing with his host, looking forward upon the decks below, he was struck by one of those instances of insubordination previously alluded to. Three black boys, with two Spanish boys, were sitting together on the hatches, scraping a rude wooden platter, in which some scanty mess had recently been cooked. Suddenly, one of the black boys, enraged at a word dropped by one of his white companions, seized a knife, and, though called to forbear by one of the oakum-pickers, struck the lad over the head, inflicting a gash from which blood flowed.

In amazement, Captain Delano inquired what this meant. To which the pale Don Benito dully muttered, that it was merely the sport of the lad.

"Pretty serious sport, truly," rejoined Captain Delano. "Had such a thing happened on board the *Bachelor's Delight*, instant punishment would have followed."

At these words the Spaniard turned upon the American one of his sudden, staring, half-lunatic looks; then, relapsing into his torpor, answered, "Doubtless, doubtless, señor."

Is it, thought Captain Delano, that this hapless man is one of those paper captains I've known, who by policy wink at what by power they cannot put down? I know no sadder sight than a commander who has little of command but the name.

"I should think, Don Benito," he now said, glancing toward the oakum-picker who had sought to interfere with the boys, "that you would find it advantageous to keep all your blacks employed, especially the younger ones, no matter at what useless task, and no matter what happens to the ship. Why, even with my little band, I find such a course indispensable. I once kept a crew on my quarter-deck thrumming [25] mats for my cabin, when, for three days, I had given up my ship—mats, men, and all—for a speedy loss, owing to the violence of a gale, in which we could do nothing but helplessly drive before it."

"Doubtless, doubtless," muttered Don Benito.

25. Sewing bunches of rope yarn over a mat so as to produce a shaggy surface, suitable for preventing chafing or stopping a leak.

"But," continued Captain Delano, again glancing upon the oakum-pickers and then at the hatchet-polishers, near by, "I see you keep some, at least, of your host employed."

"Yes," was again the vacant response.

"Those old men there, shaking their pows [26] from their pulpits," continued Captain Delano, pointing to the oakum-pickers, "seem to act the part of old dominies [27] to the rest, little heeded as their admonitions are at times. Is this voluntary on their part, Don Benito, or have you appointed them shepherds to your flock of black sheep?"

"What posts they fill, I appointed them," rejoined the Spaniard, in an acrid tone, as if resenting some supposed satiric reflection.

"And these others, these Ashantee [28] conjurers here," continued Captain Delano, rather uneasily eyeing the brandished steel of the hatchet-polishers, where, in spots, it had been brought to a shine, "this seems a curious business they are at, Don Benito?"

"In the gales we met," answered the Spaniard, "what of our general cargo was not thrown overboard was much damaged by the brine. Since coming into calm weather, I have had several cases of knives and hatchets daily brought up for overhauling and cleaning."

"A prudent idea, Don Benito. You are part owner of ship and cargo, I presume; but none of the slaves, perhaps?"

"I am owner of all you see," impatiently returned Don Benito, "except the main company of blacks, who belonged to my late friend, Alexandro Aranda."

As he mentioned this name, his air was heart-broken; his knees shook; his servant supported him.

Thinking he divined the cause of such unusual emotion, to confirm his surmise, Captain Delano, after a pause, said: "And may I ask, Don Benito, whether—since a while ago you spoke of some cabin passengers—the friend, whose loss so afflicts you, at the outset of the voyage accompanied his blacks?"

"Yes."

"But died of the fever?"

"Died of the fever. Oh, could I but — "

Again quivering, the Spaniard paused.

"Pardon me," said Captain Delano lowly, "but I think that, by a sympathetic experience, I conjecture, Don Benito, what it is that gives the keener edge to your grief. It was once my hard fortune to lose, at sea, a dear friend, my own brother, then supercargo. As-

26. Dialect form of "polls" (heads).
27. Schoolmasters.
28. A native kingdom in West Africa.

sured of the welfare of his spirit, its departure I could have borne like a man; but that honest eye, that honest hand— both of which had so often met mine—and that warm heart; all, all—like scraps to the dogs—to throw all to the sharks! It was then I vowed never to have for fellow-voyager a man I loved, unless, unbeknown to him, I had provided every requisite, in case of a fatality, for embalming his mortal part for interment on shore. Were your friend's remains now on board this ship, Don Benito, not thus strangely would the mention of his name affect you."

"On board this ship?" echoed the Spaniard. Then, with horrified gestures, as directed against some spectre, he unconsciously fell into the ready arms of his attendant, who, with a silent appeal toward Captain Delano, seemed beseeching him not again to broach a theme so unspeakably distressing to his master.

This poor fellow now, thought the pained American, is the victim of that sad superstition which associates goblins with the deserted body of man, as ghosts with an abandoned house. How unlike are we made! What to me, in like case, would have been a solemn satisfaction, the bare suggestion, even, terrifies the Spaniard into this trance. Poor Alexandro Aranda! what would you say could you here see your friend—who, on former voyages, when you, for months, were left behind, has, I dare say, often longed, and longed, for one peep at you—now transported with terror at the least thought of having you any way nigh him.

At this moment, with a dreary graveyard toll, betokening a flaw, the ship's forecastle bell, smote by one of the grizzled oakum-pickers, proclaimed ten o'clock through the leaden calm; when Captain Delano's attention was caught by the moving figure of a gigantic black, emerging from the general crowd below, and slowly advancing toward the elevated poop. An iron collar was about his neck, from which depended a chain, thrice wound round his body; the terminating links padlocked together at a broad band of iron, his girdle.

"How like a mute Atufal moves," murmured the servant.

The black mounted the steps of the poop, and, like a brave prisoner, brought up to receive sentence, stood in unquailing muteness before Don Benito, now recovered from his attack.

At the first glimpse of his approach, Don Benito had started, a resentful shadow swept over his face; and, as with the sudden memory of bootless rage, his white lips glued together.

This is some mulish mutineer, thought Captain Delano, surveying, not without a mixture of admiration, the colossal form of the negro.

"See, he waits your question, master," said the servant.

Thus reminded, Don Benito, nervously averting his glance, as if shunning, by anticipation, some rebellious response, in a disconcerted voice, thus spoke:

"Atufal, will you ask my pardon now?"

The black was silent.

"Again, master," murmured the servant, with bitter upbraiding eyeing his countryman, "again, master; he will bend to master yet."

"Answer," said Don Benito, still averting his glance, "say but the one word, *pardon,* and your chains shall be off."

Upon this, the black, slowly raising both arms, let them lifelessly fall, his links clanking, his head bowed; as much as to say, "No, I am content."

"Go," said Don Benito, with inkept and unknown emotion.

Deliberately as he had come, the black obeyed.

"Excuse me, Don Benito," said Captain Delano, "but this scene surprises me; what means it, pray?"

"It means that that negro alone, of all the band, has given me peculiar cause of offence. I have put him in chains; I — "

Here he paused; his hand to his head, as if there were a swimming there, or a sudden bewilderment of memory had come over him; but meeting his servant's kindly glance seemed reassured, and proceeded:

"I could not scourge such a form. But I told him he must ask my pardon. As yet he has not. At my command, every two hours he stands before me."

"And how long has this been?"

"Some sixty days."

"And obedient in all else? And respectful?"

"Yes."

"Upon my conscience, then," exclaimed Captain Delano impulsively, "he has a royal spirit in him, this fellow."

"He may have some right to it," bitterly returned Don Benito, "he says he was king in his own land."

"Yes," said the servant, entering a word, "those slits in Atufal's ears once held wedges of gold; but poor Babo here, in his own land, was only a poor slave; a black man's slave was Babo, who now is the white's."

Somewhat annoyed by these conversational familiarities, Captain Delano turned curiously upon the attendant, then glanced inquiringly at his master; but, as if long wonted to these little informalities, neither master nor man seemed to understand him.

"What, pray, was Atufal's offence, Don Benito?" asked Captain Delano; "if it was not something very serious, take a fool's advice, and, in view of his general docility, as well as in some natural respect for his spirit, remit him his penalty."

"No, no, master never will do that," here murmured the servant to himself, "proud Atufal must first ask master's pardon. The slave there carries the padlock, but master here carries the key."

His attention thus directed, Captain Delano now noticed for the first, that, suspended by a slender silken cord from Don Benito's neck, hung a key. At once, from the servant's muttered syllables, divining the key's purpose, he smiled and said: —"So, Don Benito—padlock and key—significant symbols, truly."

Biting his lip, Don Benito faltered.

Though the remark of Captain Delano, a man of such native simplicity as to be incapable of satire or irony, had been dropped in playful allusion to the Spaniard's singularly evidenced lordship over the black; yet the hypochondriac seemed some way to have taken it as a malicious reflection upon his confessed inability thus far to break down, at least, on a verbal summons, the entrenched will of the slave. Deploring this supposed misconception, yet despairing of correcting it, Captain Delano shifted the subject; but finding his companion more than ever withdrawn, as if still sourly digesting the lees of the presumed affront above mentioned, by and by Captain Delano likewise became less talkative, oppressed, against his own will, by what seemed the secret vindictiveness of the morbidly sensitive Spaniard. But the good sailor, himself of a quite contrary disposition, refrained, on his part, alike from the appearance as from the feeling of resentment, and if silent, was only so from contagion.

Presently the Spaniard, assisted by his servant, somewhat discourteously crossed over from his guest; a procedure which, sensibly enough, might have been allowed to pass for idle caprice of ill-humour, had not master and man, lingering round the corner of the elevated skylight, began whispering together in low voices. This was unpleasing. And more; the moody air of the Spaniard, which at times had not been without a sort of valetudinarian stateliness, now seemed anything but dignified; while the menial familiarity of the servant lost its original charm of simple-hearted attachment.

In his embarrassment, the visitor turned his face to the other side of the ship. By so doing, his glance accidentally fell on a young Spanish sailor, a coil of rope in his hand, just stepped from the deck to the first round of the mizen-rigging. Perhaps the man would not have been particularly noticed, were it not that, during his ascent to one of the yards, he, with a sort of covert intentness, kept his eye fixed on Captain Delano, from whom, presently, it passed, as if by a natural sequence, to the two whisperers.

His own attention thus redirected to that quarter, Captain Delano gave a slight start. From something in Don Benito's manner just then, it seemed as if the visitor had, at least partly, been the subject of the withdrawn consultation going on—a conjecture as little agreeable to the guest as it was little flattering to the host.

The singular alternations of courtesy and ill-breeding in the Spanish captain were unaccountable, except on one of two suppositions—innocent lunacy, or wicked imposture.

But the first idea, though it might naturally have occurred to an indifferent observer, and, in some respect, had not hitherto been wholly a stranger to Captain Delano's mind, yet, now that, in an incipient way, he began to regard the stranger's conduct something in the light of an intentional affront, of course the idea of lunacy was virtually vacated. But if not a lunatic, what then? Under the circumstances, would a gentleman, nay, any honest boor, act the part now acted by his host? The man was an impostor. Some low-born adventurer, masquerading as an oceanic grandee; yet so ignorant of the first requisites of mere gentlemanhood as to be betrayed into the present remarkable indecorum. That strange ceremoniousness, too, at other times evinced, seemed not uncharacteristic of one playing a part above his real level. Benito Cereno—Don Benito Cereno—a sounding name. One, too, at that period, not unknown, in the surname, to supercargoes [29] and sea-captains trading along the Spanish Main, as belonging to one of the most enterprising and extensive mercantile families in all those provinces; several members of it having titles; a sort of Castilian Rothschild,[30] with a noble brother, or cousin, in every great trading town of South America. The alleged Don Benito was in early manhood, about twenty-nine or thirty. To assume a sort of roving cadetship in the maritime affairs of such a house, what more likely scheme for a young knave of talent and spirit? But the Spaniard was a pale invalid. Never mind. For even to the degree of simulating mortal disease, the craft of some tricksters had been known to attain. To think that, under the aspect of infantile weakness, the most savage energies might be couched—those velvets of the Spaniard but the silky paw to his fangs.

From no train of thought did these fancies come; not from within, but from without; suddenly, too, and in one throng, like hoar frost; yet as soon to vanish as the mild sun of Captain Delano's good-nature regained its meridian.

Glancing over once more toward his host—whose side-face, revealed above the skylight, was now turned toward him—he was struck by the profile, whose clearness of cut was refined by the thinness, incident to ill-health, as well as ennobled about the chin by the beard. Away with suspicion. He was a true off-shoot of a true hidalgo [31] Cereno.

29. Officers on board ship who have charge of its cargo.
30. The Rothschilds were a family of wealthy bankers.
31. A Spanish aristocrat (literally, *hijo de algo,* "son of something").

Relieved by these and other better thoughts, the visitor, lightly humming a tune, now began indifferently pacing the poop, so as not to betray to Don Benito that he had at all mistrusted incivility, much less duplicity; for such mistrust would yet be proved illusory, and by the event; though, for the present, the circumstance which had provoked that distrust remained unexplained. But when that little mystery should have been cleared up, Captain Delano thought he might extremely regret it, did he allow Don Benito to become aware that he had indulged in ungenerous surmises. In short, to the Spaniard's black-letter [32] text, it was best, for a while, to leave open margin.

Presently, his pale face twitching and overcast, the Spaniard, still supported by his attendant, moved over toward his guest, when, with even more than his usual embarrassment, and a strange sort of intriguing intonation in his husky whisper, the following conversation began:—

"Señor, may I ask how long you have lain at this isle?"

"Oh, but a day or two, Don Benito."

"And from what port are you last?"

"Canton."

"And there, señor, you exchanged your seal-skins for teas and silks, I think you said?"

"Yes. Silks, mostly."

"And the balance you took in specie, perhaps?"

Captain Delano, fidgeting a little, answered:

"Yes; some silver; not a very great deal, though."

"Ah—well. May I ask how many men have you, señor?"

Captain Delano slightly started, but answered:

"About five-and-twenty, all told."

"And at present, señor, all on board, I suppose?"

"All on board, Don Benito," replied the captain, now with satisfaction.

"And will be to-night, señor?"

At this last question, following so many pertinacious ones, for the soul of him Captain Delano could not but look very earnestly at the questioner, who, instead of meeting the glance, with every token of craven discomposure dropped his eyes to the deck; presenting an unworthy contrast to his servant, who, just then, was kneeling at his feet, adjusting a loose shoe-buckle; his disengaged face meantime, with humble curiosity, turned openly up into his master's downcast one.

The Spaniard, still with a guilty shuffle, repeated his question:

"And—and will be to-night, señor?"

"Yes, for aught I know," returned Captain Delano—"but nay,"

32. Gothic or Old English type used by early printers. Here it signifies a puzzle or mystery upon which it would be unwise to comment ("leave open margin").

rallying himself into fearless truth, "some of them talked of going off on another fishing party about midnight."

"Your ships generally go—go more or less armed, I believe, señor?"

"Oh, a six-pounder or two, in case of emergency," was the intrepidly indifferent reply, "with a small stock of muskets, sealing-spears, and cutlasses, you know."

As he thus responded, Captain Delano again glanced at Don Benito, but the latter's eyes were averted; while abruptly and awkwardly shifting the subject, he made some peevish allusion to the calm, and then, without apology, once more, with his attendant, withdrew to the opposite bulwarks, where the whispering was resumed.

At this moment, and ere Captain Delano could cast a cool thought upon what had just passed, the young Spanish sailor, before mentioned, was seen descending from the rigging. In act of stooping over to spring inboard to the deck, his voluminous, unconfined frock, or shirt, of coarse woollen, much spotted with tar, opened out far down the chest, revealing a soiled under-garment of what seemed the finest linen, edged, about the neck, with a narrow blue ribbon, sadly faded and worn. At this moment the young sailor's eye was again fixed on the whisperers, and Captain Delano thought he observed a lurking significance in it, as if silent signs, of some Freemason sort,[33] had that instant been interchanged.

This once more impelled his own glance in the direction of Don Benito, and, as before, he could not but infer that himself formed the subject of the conference. He paused. The sound of the hatchet-polishing fell on his ears. He cast another swift side-look at the two. They had the air of conspirators. In connection with the late questionings, and the incident of the young sailor, these things now begat such return of involuntary suspicion, that the singular guilelessness of the American could not endure it. Plucking up a gay and humorous expression, he crossed over to the two rapidly, saying: "Ha, Don Benito, your black here seems high in your trust; a sort of privy-counsellor, in fact."

Upon this, the servant looked up with a good-natured grin, but the master started as from a venomous bite. It was a moment or two before the Spaniard sufficiently recovered himself to reply; which he did, at last, with cold constraint: "Yes, señor, I have trust in Babo."

Here Babo, changing his previous grin of mere animal humour into an intelligent smile, not ungratefully eyed his master.

33. Freemasonry is a private brotherhood whose members use signs and symbols known only to themselves. In its early days Freemasonry was popularly associated with secrecy and subversion.

Finding that the Spaniard now stood silent and reserved, as if involuntarily, or purposely giving hint that his guest's proximity was inconvenient just then, Captain Delano, unwilling to appear uncivil even to incivility itself, made some trivial remark and moved off; again and again turning over in his mind the mysterious demeanour of Don Benito Cereno.

He had descended from the poop, and, wrapped in thought, was passing near a dark hatchway, leading down into the steerage, when, perceiving motion there, he looked to see what moved. The same instant there was a sparkle in the shadowy hatchway, and he saw one of the Spanish sailors, prowling there, hurriedly placing his hand in the bosom of his frock, as if hiding something. Before the man could have been certain who it was that was passing, he slunk below out of sight. But enough was seen of him to make it sure that he was the same young sailor before noticed in the rigging.

What was that which so sparkled? thought Captain Delano. It was no lamp—no match—no live coal. Could it have been a jewel? But how come sailors with jewels?—or with silk-trimmed under-shirts either? Has he been robbing the trunks of the dead cabin passengers? But if so, he would hardly wear one of the stolen articles on board ship here. Ah, ah—if, now, that was, indeed, a secret sign I saw passing between this suspicious fellow and his captain a while since; if I could only be certain that, in my uneasiness, my senses did not deceive me, then —

Here, passing from one suspicious thing to another, his mind revolved the strange questions put to him concerning his ship.

By a curious coincidence, as each point was recalled, the black wizards of Ashantee would strike up with their hatchets, as in ominous comment on the white stranger's thoughts. Pressed by such enigmas and portents, it would have been almost against nature, had not, even into the least distrustful heart, some ugly misgivings obtruded.

Observing the ship, now helplessly fallen into a current, with enchanted sails, drifting with increased rapidity seaward; and noting that, from a lately intercepted projection of the land, the sealer was hidden, the stout mariner began to quake at thoughts which he barely durst confess to himself. Above all, he began to feel a ghostly dread of Don Benito. And yet, when he roused himself, dilated his chest, felt himself strong on his legs, and coolly considered it— what did all these phantoms amount to?

Had the Spaniard any sinister scheme, it must have reference not so much to him (Captain Delano) as to his ship (the *Bachelor's Delight*). Hence the present drifting away of the one ship from the other, instead of favouring any such possible scheme, was, for the time, at least, opposed to it. Clearly any suspicion, combining such contradictions, must needs be delusive. Besides, was it not absurd to think of a vessel in distress—a vessel by sickness almost dismanned of her crew—a vessel whose inmates were parched for water—was it not a thousand times absurd that such a craft should, at present, be of a piratical character; or her commander, either for himself or those under him, cherish any desire but for speedy relief and refreshment? But then, might not general distress, and thirst in particular, be affected? And might not that same undiminished Spanish crew, alleged to have perished off to a remnant, be at that very moment lurking in the hold? On heart-broken pretence of entreating a cup of cold water, fiends in human form had got into lonely dwellings, nor retired until a dark deed had been done. And among the Malay pirates, it was no unusual thing to lure ships after them into their treacherous harbours, or entice boarders from a declared enemy at sea, by the spectacle of thinly manned or vacant decks, beneath which prowled a hundred spears with yellow arms ready to upthrust them through the mats. Not that Captain Delano had entirely credited such things. He had heard of them—and now, as stories, they recurred. The present destination of the ship was the anchorage. There she would be near his own vessel. Upon gaining that vicinity, might not the *San Dominick*, like a slumbering volcano, suddenly let loose energies now hid?

He recalled the Spaniard's manner while telling his story. There was a gloomy hesitancy and subterfuge about it. It was just the manner of one making up his tale for evil purposes as he goes. But if that story was not true, what was the truth? That the ship had unlawfully come into the Spaniard's possession? But in many of its details, especially in reference to the more calamitous parts, such as the fatalities among the seamen, the consequent prolonged beating about, the past sufferings from obstinate calms, and still continued suffering from thirst; in all these points, as well as others, Don Benito's story had corroborated not only the wailing ejaculations of the indiscriminate multitude, white and black, but likewise—what seemed impossible to be counterfeit—by the very expression and play of every human feature, which Captain Delano saw. If Don Benito's story was, throughout, an invention, then every soul on board, down to the youngest negress, was his carefully drilled recruit in the plot: an incredible inference. And yet, if there was ground for mistrusting his veracity, that inference was a legitimate one.

But those questions of the Spaniard. There, indeed, one might pause. Did they not seem put with much the same object with which the burglar or assassin, by day-time, reconnoitres the walls of a house? But, with ill purposes, to solicit such information openly of the chief person endangered, and so, in effect, setting him on his guard; how unlikely a procedure was that. Absurd, then, to suppose that those questions had been prompted by evil designs. Thus, the same conduct, which, in this instance, had raised the alarm, served to dispel it. In short, scarce any suspicion or uneasiness, however apparently reasonable at the time, which was not now, with equal apparent reason, dismissed.

At last he began to laugh at his former forebodings; and laugh at the strange ship for, in its aspect, some way siding with them, as it were; and laugh, too, at the odd-looking blacks, particularly those old scissors-grinders, the Ashantees; and those bedridden old knitting women, the oakum-pickers; and almost at the dark Spaniard himself, the central hobgoblin of all.

For the rest, whatever in a serious way seemed enigmatical, was now good-naturedly explained away by the thought that, for the most part, the poor invalid scarcely knew what he was about; either sulking in black vapours, or putting idle questions without sense or object. Evidently, for the present, the man was not fit to be entrusted with the ship. On some benevolent plea withdrawing the command from him, Captain Delano would yet have to send her to Conception, in charge of his second mate, a worthy person and good navigator—a plan not more convenient for the *San Dominick* than for Don Benito; for, relieved from all anxiety, keeping wholly to his cabin, the sick man, under the good nursing of his servant, would, probably, by the end of the passage, be in a measure restored to health, and with that he should also be restored to authority.

Such were the American's thoughts. They were tranquillising. There was a difference between the idea of Don Benito's darkly preordaining Captain Delano's fate, and Captain Delano's lightly arranging Don Benito's. Nevertheless, it was not without something of relief that the good seaman presently perceived his whale-boat in the distance. Its absence had been prolonged by unexpected detention at the sealer's side, as well as its returning trip lengthened by the continual recession of the goal.

The advancing speck was observed by the blacks. Their shouts attracted the attention of Don Benito, who, with a return of courtesy, approaching Captain Delano, expressed satisfaction at the coming of some supplies, slight and temporary as they must necessarily prove.

Captain Delano responded; but while doing so, his attention was drawn to something passing on the deck below: among the crowd climbing the landward bulwarks, anxiously watching the coming boat, two blacks, to all appearances accidentally incommoded by one of the sailors, violently pushed him aside, which the sailor some way resenting, they dashed him to the deck, despite the earnest cries of the oakum-pickers.

"Don Benito," said Captain Delano quickly, "do you see what is going on there? Look!"

But, seized by his cough, the Spaniard staggered, with both hands to his face, on the point of falling. Captain Delano would have supported him, but the servant was more alert, who, with one hand sustaining his master, with the other applied the cordial. Don Benito restored, the black withdrew his support, slipping aside a little, but dutifully remaining within call of a whisper. Such discretion was here evinced as quite wiped away, in the visitor's eyes, any blemish of impropriety which might have attached to the attendant from the indecorous conferences before mentioned; showing, too, that if the servant were to blame, it might be more the master's fault than his own, since, when left to himself, he could conduct thus well.

His glance called away from the spectacle of disorder to the more pleasing one before him, Captain Delano could not avoid again congratulating his host upon possessing such a servant, who, though perhaps a little too forward now and then, must upon the whole be invaluable to one in the invalid's situation.

"Tell me, Don Benito," he added, with a smile—"I should like to have your man here, myself—what will you take for him? Would fifty doubloons be any object?"

"Master wouldn't part with Babo for a thousand doubloons," murmured the black, overhearing the offer, and taking it in earnest, and, with the strange vanity of a faithful slave, appreciated by his master, scorning to hear so paltry a valuation put upon him by a stranger. But Don Benito, apparently hardly yet completely restored, and again interrupted by his cough, made but some broken reply.

Soon his physical distress became so great, affecting his mind, too, apparently, that, as if to screen the sad spectacle, the servant gently conducted his master below.

Left to himself, the American, to while away the time till his boat should arrive, would have pleasantly accosted some one of the few Spanish seamen he saw; but recalling something that Don Benito had said touching their ill conduct, he refrained; as a shipmaster indisposed to countenance cowardice or unfaithfulness in seamen.

While, with these thoughts, standing with eye directed forward toward that handful of sailors, suddenly he thought that one or two of them returned the glance and with a sort of meaning. He rubbed his eyes, and looked again; but again seemed to see the same thing. Under a new form, but more obscure than any previous one, the old suspicions recurred, but, in the absence of Don Benito, with less of panic than before. Despite the bad account given of the sailors, Captain Delano resolved forthwith to accost one of them. Descending the poop, he made his way through the blacks, his movement drawing a queer cry from the oakum-pickers, prompted by whom, the negroes, twitching each other aside, divided before him; but, as if curious to see what was the object of this deliberate visit to their ghetto, closing in behind, in tolerable order, followed the white stranger up. His progress thus proclaimed as by mounted kings-at-arms, and escorted as by a Caffre [34] guard of honour, Captain Delano, assuming a good-humoured, off-handed air, continued to advance; now and then saying a blithe word to the negroes, and his eye curiously surveying the white faces, here and there sparsely mixed in with the blacks, like stray white pawns venturously involved in the ranks of the chessmen opposed.

While thinking which of them to select for his purpose, he chanced to observe a sailor seated on the deck engaged in tarring the strap of a large block, a circle of blacks squatted round him inquisitively eyeing the process.

The mean employment of the man was in contrast with something superior in his figure. His hand, black with continually thrusting it into the tar-pot held for him by a negro, seemed not naturally allied to his face, a face which would have been a very fine one but for its haggardness. Whether this haggardness had aught to do with criminality, could not be determined; since, as intense heat and cold, though unlike, produce like sensations, so innocence and guilt, when, through casual association with mental pain, stamping any visible impress, use one seal—a hacked one.

Not again that this reflection occurred to Captain Delano at the time, charitable man as he was. Rather another idea. Because observing so singular a haggardness combined with a dark eye, averted as in trouble and shame, and then again recalling Don Benito's confessed ill opinion of his crew, insensibly he was operated upon by certain general notions which, while disconnecting pain and abashment from virtue, invariably link them with vice.

If, indeed, there be any wickedness on board this ship, thought Captain Delano, be sure that man there has fouled his hand in it, even as now he fouls it in the pitch. I don't like to accost him. I will speak to this other, this old Jack here on the windlass.

He advanced to an old Barcelona tar, in ragged red breeches and dirty night-cap, cheeks trenched and bronzed, whiskers dense as thorn hedges. Seated between two sleepy-looking Africans, this

34. Kaffir, a South African tribe.

mariner, like his younger shipmate, was employed upon some rigging—splicing a cable—the sleepy-looking blacks performing the inferior function of holding the outer parts of the ropes for him.

Upon Captain Delano's approach, the man at once hung his head below its previous level; the one necessary for business. It appeared as if he desired to be thought absorbed, with more than common fidelity, in his task. Being addressed, he glanced up, but with what seemed a furtive, diffident air, which sat strangely enough on his weather-beaten visage, much as if a grizzly bear, instead of growling and biting, should simper and cast sheep's eyes. He was asked several questions concerning the voyage—questions purposely referring to several particulars in Don Benito's narrative, not previously corroborated by those impulsive cries greeting the visitor on first coming on board. The questions were briefly answered, confirming all that remained to be confirmed of the story. The negroes about the windlass joined in with the old sailor; but, as they became talkative, he by degrees became mute, and at length quite glum, seemed morosely unwilling to answer more questions, and yet, all the while, this ursine air was somehow mixed with his sheepish one.

Despairing of getting into unembarrassed talk with such a centaur, Captain Delano, after glancing round for a more promising countenance, but seeing none, spoke pleasantly to the blacks to make way for him; and so, amid various grins and grimaces, returned to the poop, feeling a little strange at first, he could hardly tell why, but upon the whole with regained confidence in Benito Cereno.

How plainly, thought he, did that old whiskerando yonder betray a consciousness of ill desert. No doubt, when he saw me coming, he dreaded lest I, apprised by his captain of the crew's general misbehaviour, came with sharp words for him, and so down with his head. And yet—and yet, now that I think of it, that very old fellow, if I err not, was one of those who seemed so earnestly eyeing me here a while since. Ah, these currents spin one's head round almost as much as they do the ship. Ha, there now's a pleasant sort of sunny sight; quite sociable, too.

His attention had been drawn to a slumbering negress, partly disclosed through the lacework of some rigging, lying, with youthful limbs carelessly disposed, under the lee of the bulwarks, like a doe in the shade of a woodland rock. Sprawling at her lapped breasts was her wide-awake fawn, stark naked, its black little body half lifted from the deck, crosswise with its dam's; its hands, like two paws, clambering upon her; its mouth and nose ineffectually rooting to get at the mark; and meantime giving a vexatious half-grunt, blending with the composed snore of the negress.

The uncommon vigour of the child at length roused the mother. She started up, at a distance facing Captain Delano. But as if not at all concerned at the attitude in which she had been caught, delight-edly she caught the child up, with maternal transports, covering it with kisses.

There's naked nature, now; pure tenderness and love, thought Captain Delano, well pleased.

This incident prompted him to remark the other negresses more particularly than before. He was gratified with their manners: like most uncivilised women, they seemed at once tender of heart and tough of constitution; equally ready to die for their infants or fight for them. Unsophisticated as leopardesses; loving as doves. Ah! thought Captain Delano, these, perhaps, are some of the very women whom Ledyard [35] saw in Africa, and gave such a noble account of.

These natural sights somehow insensibly deepened his confidence and ease. At last he looked to see how his boat was getting on; but it was still pretty remote. He turned to see if Don Benito had returned; but he had not.

To change the scene, as well as to please himself with a leisurely observation of the coming boat, stepping over into the mizen-chains, he clambered his way into the starboard quarter-gallery—one of those abandoned Venetian-looking water-balconies previously mentioned—retreats cut off from the deck. As his foot pressed the half-damp, half-dry sea-mosses matting the place, and a chance phantom cat's-paw—an islet of breeze, unheralded, un-followed—as this ghostly cat's-paw came fanning his cheek; as his glance fell upon the row of small, round dead-lights—all closed like coppered eyes of the coffined—and the state-cabin door, once connecting with the gallery, even as the dead-lights had once looked out upon it, but now caulked fast like a sarcophagus lid; and to a purple-black, tarred-over panel, threshold, and post; and he bethought him of the time, when that state-cabin and this state-balcony had heard the voices of the Spanish king's officers, and the forms of the Lima viceroy's daughters had perhaps leaned where he stood—as these and other images flitted through his mind, as the cat's-paw through the calm, gradually he felt rising a dreamy inquietude, like that of one who alone on the prairie feels unrest from the repose of the noon.

He leaned against the carved balustrade, again looking off toward his boat; but found his eye falling upon the ribbon grass, trailing along the ship's water-line, straight as a border of green box; and parterres of seaweed, broad ovals and crescents, floating nigh and

---

35. John Ledyard (1751–88), American traveler.

far, with what seemed long formal alleys between, crossing the terraces of swells, and sweeping round as if leading to the grottoes below. And overhanging all was the balustrade by his arm, which, partly stained with pitch and partly embossed with moss, seemed the charred ruin of some summer-house in a grand garden long running to waste.

Trying to break one charm, he was but becharmed anew. Though upon the wide sea, he seemed in some far inland country; prisoner in some deserted château, left to stare at empty grounds, and peer out at vague roads, where never wagon or wayfarer passed.

But these enchantments were a little disenchanted as his eye fell on the corroded main-chains. Of an ancient style, massy and rusty in link, shackle, and bolt, they seemed even more fit for the ship's present business than the one for which she had been built.

Presently he thought something moved nigh the chains. He rubbed his eyes, and looked hard. Groves of rigging were about the chains; and there, peering from behind a great stay, like an Indian from behind a hemlock, a Spanish sailor, a marling-spike [36] in his hand, was seen, who made what seemed an imperfect gesture toward the balcony, but immediately, as if alarmed by some advancing step along the deck within, vanished into the recesses of the hempen forest, like a poacher.

What meant this? Something the man had sought to communicate, unbeknown to anyone, even to his captain. Did the secret involve aught unfavourable to his captain? Were those previous misgivings of Captain Delano's about to be verified? Or, in his haunted mood at the moment, had some random, unintentional motion of the man, while busy with the stay, as if repairing it, been mistaken for a significant beckoning?

Not unbewildered, again he gazed off for his boat. But it was temporarily hidden by a rocky spur of the isle. As with some eagerness he bent forward, watching for the first shooting view of its beak, the balustrade gave way before him like charcoal. Had he not clutched an outreaching rope he would have fallen into the sea. The crash, though feeble, and the fall, though hollow, of the rotten fragments, must have been overheard. He glanced up. With sober curiosity peering down upon him was one of the old oakum-pickers, slipped from his perch to an outside room; while below the old negro, and, invisible to him, reconnoitring from a port-hole like a fox from the mouth of its den, crouched the Spanish sailor again. From something suddenly suggested by the man's air, the mad idea now darted into Captain Delano's mind, that Don Benito's plea of indisposition, in withdrawing below, was but a pretence: that he was

36. A pointed metal spike, used to separate strands of rope in splicing.

engaged there maturing his plot, of which the sailor, by some means gaining an inkling, had a mind to warn the stranger against; incited, it may be, by gratitude for a kind word on first boarding the ship. Was it from foreseeing some possible interference like this, that Don Benito had, beforehand, given such a bad character of his sailors, while praising the negroes; though, indeed, the former seemed as docile as the latter the contrary? The whites, too, by nature, were the shrewder race. A man with some evil design, would he not be likely to speak well of that stupidity which was blind to his depravity, and malign that intelligence from which it might not be hidden? Not unlikely, perhaps. But if the whites had dark secrets concerning Don Benito, could then Don Benito be any way in complicity with the blacks? But they were too stupid. Besides, who ever heard of a white so far a renegade as to apostatise from his very species almost, by leaguing in against it with negroes? These difficulties recalled former ones. Lost in their mazes, Captain Delano, who had now regained the deck, was uneasily advancing along it, when he observed a new face; an aged sailor seated cross-legged near the main hatchway. His skin was shrunk up with wrinkles like a pelican's empty pouch; his hair frosted; his countenance grave and composed. His hands were full of ropes, which he was working into a large knot. Some blacks were about him obligingly dipping the strands for him, here and there, as the exigencies of the operation demanded.

Captain Delano crossed over to him, and stood in silence surveying the knot; his mind, by a not uncongenial transition, passing from its own entanglements to those of the hemp. For intricacy, such a knot he had never seen in an American ship, nor indeed any other. The old man looked like an Egyptian priest, making Gordian knots for the temple of Ammon.[37] The knot seemed a combination of double-bowline-knot, treble-crown-knot, back-handed-well-knot, knot-in-and-out-knot, and jamming-knot.

At last, puzzled to comprehend the meaning of such a knot, Captain Delano addressed the knotter: —

"What are you knotting there, my man?"

"The knot," was the brief reply, without looking up.

"So it seems; but what is it for?"

"For someone else to undo," muttered back the old man, plying his fingers harder than ever, the knot being now nearly completed.

While Captain Delano stood watching him, suddenly the old man threw the knot toward him, saying in broken English—the first

---

37. Gordian Knot, an intricate knot tied by King Gordius and cut by Alexander the Great with a sword after he heard an oracle promise that whoever could undo the knot would be the ruler of Asia. Ammon, an Egyptian deity (the local god of Thebes) whose name has the root meaning "conceal."

heard in the ship—something to this effect: "Undo it, cut it, quick." It was said lowly, but with such condensation of rapidity that the long, slow words in Spanish, which had preceded and followed, almost operated as covers to the brief English between.

For a moment, knot in hand, and knot in head, Captain Delano stood mute; while, without further heeding him, the old man was now intent upon other ropes. Presently there was a slight stir behind Captain Delano. Turning, he saw the chained negro, Atufal, standing quietly there. The next moment the old sailor rose, muttering, and, followed by his subordinate negroes, removed to the forward part of the ship, where in the crowd he disappeared.

An elderly negro, in a clout like an infant's, and with a pepper-and-salt head, and a kind of attorney air, now approached Captain Delano. In tolerable Spanish, and with a good-natured, knowing wink, he informed him that the old knotter was simple-witted, but harmless; often playing his odd tricks. The negro concluded by begging the knot, for of course the stranger would not care to be troubled with it. Unconsciously, it was handed to him. With a sort of *congé*,[38] the negro received it, and, turning his back, ferreted into it like a detective custom-house officer after smuggled laces. Soon, with some African word, equivalent to pshaw, he tossed the knot overboard.

All this is very queer now, thought Captain Delano, with a qualmish sort of emotion; but, as one feeling incipient sea-sickness, he strove, by ignoring the symptoms, to get rid of the malady. Once more he looked off for his boat. To his delight, it was now again in view, leaving the rocky spur astern.

The sensation here experienced, after at first relieving his uneasiness, with unforeseen efficacy soon began to remove it. The less distant sight of that well-known boat—showing it, not as before, half blended with the haze, but with outline defined, so that its individuality, like a man's, was manifest; that boat, *Rover* by name, which, though now in strange seas, had often pressed the beach of Captain Delano's home, and, brought to its threshold for repairs, had familiarly lain there, as a Newfoundland dog; the sight of that household boat evoked a thousand trustful associations, which, contrasted with previous suspicions, filled him not only with lightsome confidence, but somehow with half-humorous self-reproaches at his former lack of it.

"What, I, Amasa Delano—Jack of the Beach, as they called me when a lad—I, Amasa; the same that, duck-satchel [39] in hand, used to paddle along the water-side to the school-house made from the old hulk—I, little Jack of the Beach, that used to go berrying with

38. Formal bow, as in leave-taking.
39. Satchel made of heavy cotton cloth (duck).

cousin Nat and the rest; I to be murdered here at the ends of the earth, on board a haunted pirate-ship by a horrible Spaniard? Too nonsensical to think of! Who would murder Amasa Delano? His conscience is clean. There is someone above. Fie, fie, Jack of the Beach! you are a child indeed; a child of the second childhood, old boy; you are beginning to dote and drule, I'm afraid."

Light of heart and foot, he stepped aft, and there was met by Don Benito's servant, who, with a pleasing expression, responsive to his own present feelings, informed him that his master had recovered from the effects of his coughing fit, and had just ordered him to go present his compliments to his good guest, Don Amasa, and say that he (Don Benito) would soon have the happiness to rejoin him.

There now, do you mark that? again thought Captain Delano, walking the poop. What a donkey I was. This kind gentleman who here sends me his kind compliments, he, but ten minutes ago, dark-lantern in hand, was dodging round some old grindstone in the hold, sharpening a hatchet for me, I thought. Well, well; these long calms have a morbid effect on the mind, I've often heard, though I never believed it before. Ha! glancing toward the boat; there's *Rover;* good dog; a white bone in her mouth. A pretty big bone though, seems to me.—What? Yes, she has fallen afoul of the bubbling tide-rip there. It sets her the other way, too, for the time. Patience.

It was now about noon, though, from the grayness of everything, it seemed to be getting toward dusk.

The calm was confirmed. In the far distance, away from the influence of land, the leaden ocean seemed laid out and leaded up, its course finished, soul gone, defunct. But the current from landward, where the ship was, increased; silently sweeping her further and further toward the tranced waters beyond.

Still, from his knowledge of those latitudes, cherishing hopes of a breeze, and a fair and fresh one, at any moment, Captain Delano, despite present prospects, buoyantly counted upon bringing the *San Dominick* safely to anchor ere night. This distance swept over was nothing; since, with a good wind, ten minutes' sailing would retrace more than sixty minutes' drifting. Meantime, one moment turning to mark *Rover* fighting the tide-rip, and the next to see Don Benito approaching, he continued walking the poop.

Gradually he felt a vexation arising from the delay of his boat; this soon merged into uneasiness; and at last—his eye falling continually, as from a stage-box into the pit, upon the strange crowd before and below him, and, by and by, recognising there the face—now composed to indifference—of the Spanish sailor who had seemed to beckon from the main-chains—something of his old trepidations returned.

Ah, thought he—gravely enough—this is like the ague: because it went off, it follows not that it won't come back.

Though ashamed of the relapse, he could not altogether subdue it; and so, exerting his good-nature to the utmost, insensibly he came to a compromise.

Yes, this is a strange craft; a strange history, too, and strange folks on board. But—nothing more.

By way of keeping his mind out of mischief till the boat should arrive, he tried to occupy it with turning over and over, in a purely speculative sort of way, some lesser peculiarities of the captain and crew. Among others, four curious points recurred: —

First, the affair of the Spanish lad assailed with a knife by the slave-boy; an act winked at by Don Benito. Second, the tyranny in Don Benito's treatment of Atufal, the black; as if a child should lead a bull of the Nile by the ring in his nose. Third, the trampling of the sailor by the two negroes; a piece of insolence passed over without so much as a reprimand. Fourth, the cringing submission to their master of all the ship's underlings, mostly blacks; as if by the least inadvertence they feared to draw down his despotic displeasure.

Coupling these points, they seemed somewhat contradictory. But what then, thought Captain Delano, glancing toward his now nearing boat—what then? Why, Don Benito is a very capricious commander. But he is not the first of the sort I have seen; though it's true he rather exceeds any other. But as a nation—continued he in his reveries—these Spaniards are all an odd set; the very word Spaniard has a curious, conspirator, Guy-Fawkish [40] twang to it. And yet, I dare say, Spaniards in the main are as good folks as any in Duxbury, Massachusetts. Ah, good! At last *Rover* has come.

As, with its welcome freight, the boat touched the side, the oakum-pickers, with venerable gestures, sought to restrain the blacks, who, at the sight of three gurried [41] water-casks in its bottom, and a pile of wilted pumpkins in its bow, hung over the bulwarks in disorderly raptures.

Don Benito, with his servant, now appeared; his coming, perhaps, hastened by hearing the noise. Of him Captain Delano sought permission to serve out the water, so that all might share alike, and none injure themselves by unfair excess. But sensible, and, on Don Benito's account, kind as this offer was, it was received with what seemed impatience; as if aware that he lacked energy as a commander, Don Benito, with the true jealousy of weakness, resented as an affront any interference. So, at least, Captain Delano inferred.

40. Guy Fawkes (1570–1606), leader of a Roman Catholic conspiracy to blow up the Houses of Parliament in the "Gunpowder Plot" of 1605, in protest against increasingly severe penal laws.
41. Coated with fish offal.

In another moment the casks were being hoisted in, when some of the eager negroes accidentally jostled Captain Delano, where he stood by the gangway; so that, unmindful of Don Benito, yielding to the impulse of the moment, with good-natured authority he bade the blacks stand back; to enforce his words making use of a half-mirthful, half-menacing gesture. Instantly the blacks paused, just where they were, each negro and negress suspended in his or her posture, exactly as the word had found them—for a few seconds continuing so—while, as between the responsive posts of a telegraph, an unknown syllable ran from man to man among the perched oakum-pickers. While the visitor's attention was fixed by this scene, suddenly the hatchet-polishers half rose, and a rapid cry came from Don Benito.

Thinking that at the signal of the Spaniard he was about to be massacred, Captain Delano would have sprung for his boat, but paused, as the oakum-pickers, dropping down into the crowd with earnest exclamations, forced every white and every negro back, at the same moment, with gestures friendly and familiar, almost jocose, bidding him, in substance, not be a fool. Simultaneously the hatchet-polishers resumed their seats, quietly as so many tailors, and at once, as if nothing had happened, the work of hoisting in the casks was resumed, whites and blacks singing at the tackle.

Captain Delano glanced toward Don Benito. As he saw his meagre form in the act of recovering itself from reclining in the servant's arms, into which the agitated invalid had fallen, he could not but marvel at the panic by which himself had been surprised, on the darting supposition that such a commander, who, upon a legitimate occasion, so trivial, too, as it now appeared, could lose all self-command, was, with energetic iniquity, going to bring about his murder.

The casks being on deck, Captain Delano was handed a number of jars and cups by one of the steward's aids, who, in the name of his captain, entreated him to do as he had proposed—dole out the water. He complied, with republican impartiality as to this republican element, which always seeks one level, serving the oldest white no better than the youngest black; excepting, indeed, poor Don Benito, whose condition, if not rank, demanded an extra allowance. To him, in the first place, Captain Delano presented a fair pitcher of the fluid; but, thirsting as he was for it, the Spaniard quaffed not a drop until after several grave bows and salutes. A reciprocation of courtesies which the sight-loving Africans hailed with clapping of hands.

Two of the less wilted pumpkins being reserved for the cabin table, the residue were minced up on the spot for the general regalement. But the soft bread, sugar, and bottled cider, Captain

Delano would have given the whites alone, and in chief Don Benito; but the latter objected; which disinterestedness not a little pleased the American; and so mouthfuls all around were given alike to whites and blacks; excepting one bottle of cider, which Babo insisted upon setting aside for his master.

Here it may be observed that as on the first visit of the boat, the American had not permitted his men to board the ship, neither did he now; being unwilling to add to the confusion of the decks.

Not uninfluenced by the peculiar good-humour at present prevailing, and for the time oblivious of any but benevolent thoughts, Captain Delano, who, from recent indications, counted upon a breeze within an hour or two at furthest, dispatched the boat back to the sealer, with orders for all the hands that could be spared immediately to set about rafting casks to the water-place and filling them. Likewise he bade word be carried to his chief officer, that if, against present expectation, the ship was not brought to anchor by sunset, he need be under no concern; for as there was to be a full moon that night, he (Captain Delano) would remain on board ready to play the pilot, come the wind soon or late.

As the two captains stood together, observing the departing boat—the servant, as it happened, having just spied a spot on his master's velvet sleeve, and silently engaged rubbing it out—the American expressed his regrets that the *San Dominick* had no boats; none, at least, but the unseaworthy old hulk of the long-boat, which, warped as a camel's skeleton in the desert, and almost as bleached, lay pot-wise inverted amidships, one side a little tipped, furnishing a subterraneous sort of den for family groups of the blacks, mostly women and small children; who, squatting on old mats below, or perched above in the dark dome, on the elevated seats, were descried, some distance within, like a social circle of bats, sheltering in some friendly cave; at intervals, ebon flights of naked boys and girls, three or four years old, darting in and out of the den's mouth.

"Had you three or four boats now, Don Benito," said Captain Delano, "I think that, by tugging at the oars, your negroes here might help along matters some. Did you sail from port without boats, Don Benito?"

"They were stove in the gales, señor."

"That was bad. Many men, too, you lost then. Boats and men. Those must have been hard gales, Don Benito."

"Past all speech," cringed the Spaniard.

"Tell me, Don Benito," continued his companion with increased interest, "tell me, were these gales immediately off the pitch of Cape Horn?"

"Cape Horn?—who spoke of Cape Horn?"

"Yourself did, when giving me an account of your voyage," answered Captain Delano, with almost equal astonishment at this eating of his own words, even as he ever seemed eating his own heart, on the part of the Spaniard. "You yourself, Don Benito, spoke of Cape Horn," he emphatically repeated.

The Spaniard turned, in a sort of stooping posture, pausing an instant, as one about to make a plunging exchange of elements, as from air to water.

At this moment a messenger-boy, a white, hurried by, in the regular performance of his function carrying the last expired half-hour forward to the forecastle, from the cabin time-piece, to have it struck at the ship's large bell.

"Master," said the servant, discontinuing his work on the coat sleeve, and addressing the rapt Spaniard with a sort of timid apprehensiveness, as one charged with a duty, the discharge of which, it was foreseen, would prove irksome to the very person who had imposed it, and for whose benefit it was intended, "master told me never mind where he was, or how engaged, always to remind him, to a minute, when shaving-time comes. Miguel has gone to strike the half-hour afternoon. It is *now*, master. Will master go into the cuddy?" [42]

"Ah—yes," answered the Spaniard, starting, as from dreams into realities; then turning upon Captain Delano, he said that ere long he would resume the conversation.

"Then if master means to talk more to Don Amasa," said the servant, "why not let Don Amasa sit by master in the cuddy, and master can talk, and Don Amasa can listen, while Babo here lathers and strops."

"Yes," said Captain Delano, not unpleased with this sociable plan, "yes, Don Benito, unless you had rather not, I will go with you."

"Be it so, señor."

As the three passed aft, the American could not but think it another strange instance of his host's capriciousness, this being shaved with such uncommon punctuality in the midddle of the day. But he deemed it more than likely that the servant's anxious fidelity had something to do with the matter; inasmuch as the timely interruption served to rally his master from the mood which had evidently been coming upon him.

The place called the cuddy was a light deck-cabin formed by the poop, a sort of attic to the large cabin below. Part of it had formerly been the quarters of the officers; but since their death all the partitionings had been thrown down, and the whole interior converted

42. Small cabin.

into one spacious and airy marine hall; for absence of fine furniture and picturesque disarray of odd appurtenances, somewhat answering to the wide, cluttered hall of some eccentric bachelor-squire in the country, who hangs his shooting-jacket and tobacco-pouch on deer antlers, and keeps his fishing-rod, tongs, and walking-stick in the same corner.

The similitude was heightened, if not originally suggested, by glimpses of the surrounding sea; since, in one aspect, the country and the ocean seem cousins-german.

The floor of the cuddy was matted. Overhead, four or five old muskets were stuck into horizontal holes along the beams. On one side was a claw-footed old table lashed to the deck; a thumbed missal on it, and over it a small, meagre crucifix attached to the bulkhead. Under the table lay a dented cutlass or two, with a hacked harpoon, among some melancholy old rigging, like a heap of poor friars' girdles. There were also two long, sharp-ribbed settees of Malacca cane, black with age, and uncomfortable to look at as inquisitors' racks, with a large, misshapen arm-chair, which, furnished with a rude barber's crotch at the back, working with a screw, seemed some grotesque engine of torment. A flag locker was in one corner, open, exposing various coloured bunting, some rolled up, others half unrolled, still others tumbled. Opposite was a cumbrous washstand, of black mahogany, all of one block, with a pedestal, like a font, and over it a railed shelf, containing combs, brushes, and other implements of the toilet. A torn hammock of stained grass swung near; the sheets tossed, and the pillow wrinkled up like a brow, as if whoever slept here slept but illy, with alternate visitations of sad thoughts and bad dreams.

The further extremity of the cuddy, overhanging the ship's stern, was pierced with three openings, windows or port-holes, according as men or cannon might peer, socially or unsocially, out of them. At present neither men nor cannon were seen, though huge ring-bolts and other rusty iron fixtures of the woodwork hinted of twenty-four-pounders.

Glancing toward the hammock as he entered, Captain Delano said, "You sleep here, Don Benito?"

"Yes, señor, since we got into mild weather."

"This seems a sort of dormitory, sitting-room, sail-loft, chapel, armoury, and private closet all together, Don Benito," added Captain Delano, looking round.

"Yes, señor; events have not been favourable to much order in my arrangements."

Here the servant, napkin on arm, made a motion as if waiting his master's good pleasure. Don Benito signified his readiness, when, seating him in the Malacca arm-chair, and for the guest's convenience drawing opposite one of the settees, the servant commenced operations by throwing back his master's collar and loosening his cravat.

There is something in the negro which, in a peculiar way, fits him for avocations about one's person. Most negroes are natural valets and hair-dressers; taking to the comb and brush congenially as to the castanets, and flourishing them apparently with almost equal satisfaction. There is, too, a smooth tact about them in this employment, with a marvellous, noiseless, gliding briskness, not ungraceful in its way, singularly pleasing to behold, and still more so to be the manipulated subject of. And above all is the great gift of good-humour. Not the mere grin or laugh is here meant. Those were unsuitable. But a certain easy cheerfulness, harmonious in every glance and gesture; as though God had set the whole negro to some pleasant tune.

When to this is added the docility arising from the unaspiring contentment of a limited mind, and that susceptibility of blind attachment sometimes inhering in indisputable inferiors, one readily perceives why those hypochondriacs, Johnson and Byron—it may be, something like the hypochondriac Benito Cereno—took to their hearts, almost to the exclusion of the entire white race, their serving-men, the negroes, Barber and Fletcher.[43] But if there be that in the negro which exempts him from the inflicted sourness of the morbid or cynical mind, how, in his most prepossessing aspects, must he appear to a benevolent one? When at ease with respect to exterior things, Captain Delano's nature was not only benign, but familiarly and humorously so. At home, he had often taken rare satisfaction in sitting in his door, watching some free man of colour at his work or play. If on a voyage he chanced to have a black sailor, invariably he was on chatty and half-gamesome terms with him. In fact, like most men of a good, blithe heart, Captain Delano took to negroes, not philanthropically, but genially, just as other men to Newfoundland dogs.

Hitherto, the circumstances in which he found the San Dominick had repressed the tendency. But in the cuddy, relieved from his former uneasiness, and, for various reasons, more sociably inclined than at any previous period of the day, and seeing the coloured servant, napkin on arm, so debonnaire about his master, in a business so familiar as that of shaving, too, all his old weakness for negroes returned.

Among other things, he was amused with an odd instance of the

43. Francis Barber, Negro servant of Dr. Samuel Johnson; William Fletcher, servant to Lord Byron.

African love of bright colours and fine shows, in the black's informally taking from the flag-locker a great piece of bunting of all hues, and lavishly tucking it under his master's chin for an apron.

The mode of shaving among the Spaniards is a little different from what it is with other nations. They have a basin, specifically called a barber's basin, which on one side is scooped out, so as accurately to receive the chin, against which it is closely held in lathering; which is done, not with a brush, but with soap dipped in the water of the basin and rubbed on the face.

In the present instance salt-water was used for lack of better; and the parts lathered were only the upper lip, and low down under the throat, all the rest being cultivated beard.

The preliminaries being somewhat novel to Captain Delano, he sat curiously eyeing them, so that no conversation took place, nor, for the present, did Don Benito appear disposed to renew any.

Setting down his basin, the negro searched among the razors, as for the sharpest, and having found it, gave it an additional edge by expertly stropping it on the firm, smooth, oily skin of his open palm; he then made a gesture as if to begin, but midway stood suspended for an instant, one hand elevating the razor, the other professionally dabbling among the bubbling suds on the Spaniard's lank neck. Not unaffected by the close sight of the gleaming steel, Don Benito nervously shuddered; his usual ghastliness was heightened by the lather, which lather, again, was intensified in its hue by the contrasting sootiness of the negro's body. Altogether the scene was somewhat peculiar, at least to Captain Delano, nor, as he saw the two thus postured, could he resist the vagary, that in the black he saw a headsman, and in the white a man at the block. But this was one of those antic conceits, appearing and vanishing in a breath, from which, perhaps, the best regulated mind is not always free.

Meantime the agitation of the Spaniard had a little loosened the bunting from around him, so that one broad fold swept curtain-like over the chair-arm to the floor, revealing, amid a profusion of armorial bars and ground-colours—black, blue and yellow—a closed castle in a blood-red field diagonal with a lion rampant in a white.

"The castle and the lion," exclaimed Captain Delano—"why, Don Benito, this is the flag of Spain you use here. It's well it's only I, and not the king, that sees this," he added, with a smile, "but"— turning toward the black—"it's all one, I suppose, so the colours be gay"; which playful remark did not fail somewhat to tickle the negro.

"Now, master," he said, readjusting the flag, and pressing the head gently further back into the crotch of the chair; "now, master," and the steel glanced nigh the throat.

Again Don Benito faintly shuddered.

"You must not shake so, master. See, Don Amasa, master always shakes when I shave him. And yet master knows I never yet have drawn blood, though it's true, if master will shake so, I may some of these times. Now, master," he continued. "And now, Don Amasa, please go on with your talk about the gale, and all that; master can hear, and, between times, master can answer."

"Ah yes, these gales," said Captain Delano; "but the more I think of your voyage, Don Benito, the more I wonder, not at the gales, terrible as they must have been, but at the disastrous interval following them. For here, by your account, have you been these two months and more getting from Cape Horn to St. Maria, a distance which I myself, with a good wind, have sailed in a few days. True, you had calms, and long ones, but to be becalmed for two months, that is, at least, unusual. Why, Don Benito, had almost any other gentleman told me such a story, I should have been half disposed to a little incredulity."

Here an involuntary expression came over the Spaniard, similar to that just before on the deck, and whether it was the start he gave, or a sudden gawky roll of the hull in the calm, or a momentary unsteadiness of the servant's hand, however it was, just then the razor drew blood, spots of which stained the creamy lather under the throat: immediately the black barber drew back his steel, and, remaining in his professional attitude, back to Captain Delano, and face to Don Benito, held up the trickling razor, saying, with a sort of half-humorous sorrow, "See, master—you shook so—here's Babo's first blood."

No sword drawn before James the First of England, no assassination in that timid king's presence, could have produced a more terrified aspect than was now presented by Don Benito.

Poor fellow, thought Captain Delano, so nervous he can't even bear the sight of barber's blood; and this unstrung, sick man, is it credible that I should have imagined he meant to spill all my blood, who can't endure the sight of one little drop of his own? Surely, Amasa Delano, you have been beside yourself this day. Tell it not when you get home, sappy Amasa. Well, well, he looks like a murderer, doesn't he? More like as if himself were to be done for. Well, well, this day's experience shall be a good lesson.

Meantime, while these things were running through the honest seaman's mind, the servant had taken the napkin from his arm, and to Don Benito had said: "But answer Don Amasa, please, master, while I wipe this ugly stuff off the razor, and strop it again."

As he said the words, his face was turned half round, so as to be alike visible to the Spaniard and the American, and seemed, by its expression, to hint, that he was desirous, by getting his master to go on with the conversation, considerably to withdraw his attention from the recent annoying accident. As if glad to snatch the offered relief, Don Benito resumed, rehearsing to Captain Delano, that not only were the calms of unusual duration, but the ship had fallen in with obstinate currents; and other things he added, some of which were but repetitions of former statements, to explain how it came to pass that the passage from Cape Horn to St. Maria had been so exceedingly long; now and then mingling with his words incidental praises, less qualified than before, to the blacks, for their general good conduct. These particulars were not given consecutively, the servant, at convenient times, using his razor, and so, between the intervals of shaving, the story and panegyric went on with more than usual huskiness.

To Captain Delano's imagination, now again not wholly at rest, there was something so hollow in the Spaniard's manner, with apparently some reciprocal hollowness in the servant's dusky comment of silence, that the idea flashed across him, that possibly master and man, for some unknown purpose, were acting out, both in word and deed, nay, to the very tremor of Don Benito's limbs, some juggling play before him. Neither did the suspicion of collusion lack apparent support, from the fact of those whispered conferences before mentioned. But then, what could be the object of enacting this play of the barber before him? At last, regarding the notion as a whimsy, insensibly suggested, perhaps, by the theatrical aspect of Don Benito in his harlequin ensign, Captain Delano speedily banished it.

The shaving over, the servant bestirred himself with a small bottle of scented waters, pouring a few drops on the head, and then diligently rubbing; the vehemence of the exercise causing the muscles of his face to twitch rather strangely.

His next operation was with comb, scissors, and brush; going round and round, smoothing a curl here, clipping an unruly whisker-hair there, giving a graceful sweep to the temple-lock, with other impromptu touches evincing the hand of a master; while, like any resigned gentleman in barber's hands, Don Benito bore all, much less uneasily, at least, than he had done the razoring; indeed, he sat so pale and rigid now, that the negro seemed a Nubian [44] sculptor finishing off a white statue-head.

All being over at last, the standard of Spain removed, tumbled up, and tossed back into the flag-locker, the negro's warm breath blowing away any stray hair which might have lodged down his master's neck; collar and cravat readjusted; a speck of lint whisked off the velvet lapel; all this being done; backing off a little space, and

44. Nubia, a region in northeast Africa. The term "Nubian" has become synonymous with "black slave."

pausing with an expression of subdued self-complacency, the servant for a moment surveyed his master, as, in toilet at least, the creature of his own tasteful hands.

Captain Delano playfully complimented him upon his achievement; at the same time congratulating Don Benito.

But neither sweet waters, nor shampooing, nor fidelity, nor sociality, delighted the Spaniard. Seeing him relapsing into forbidding gloom, and still remaining seated, Captain Delano, thinking that his presence was undesired just then, withdrew, on pretence of seeing whether, as he had prophesied, any signs of a breeze were visible.

Walking forward to the mainmast, he stood a while thinking over the scene, and not without some undefined misgivings, when he heard a noise near the cuddy, and turning, saw the negro, his hand to his cheek. Advancing, Captain Delano perceived that the cheek was bleeding. He was about to ask the cause, when the negro's wailing soliloquy enlightened him.

"Ah, when will master get better from his sickness; only the sour heart that sour sickness breeds made him serve Babo so; cutting Babo with the razor, because, only by accident, Babo had given master one little scratch; and for the first time in so many a day, too. Ah, ah, ah," holding his hand to his face.

Is it possible, thought Captain Delano; was it to wreak in private his Spanish spite against this poor friend of his, that Don Benito, by his sullen manner, impelled me to withdraw? Ah, this slavery breeds ugly passions in man.—Poor fellow!

He was about to speak in sympathy to the negro, but with a timid reluctance he now re-entered the cuddy.

Presently master and man came forth; Don Benito leaning on his servant as if nothing had happened.

But a sort of love-quarrel, after all, thought Captain Delano.

He accosted Don Benito, and they slowly walked together. They had gone but a few paces, when the steward—a tall, rajah-looking mulatto, orientally set off with a pagoda turban formed by three or four Madras handkerchiefs wound about his head, tier on tier—approaching with a salaam, announced lunch in the cabin.

On their way thither, the two captains were preceded by the mulatto, who, turning round as he advanced, with continual smiles and bows, ushered them on, a display of elegance which quite completed the insignificance of the small bare-headed Babo, who, as if not unconscious of inferiority, eyed askance the graceful steward. But in part, Captain Delano imputed his jealous watchfulness to that peculiar feeling which the full-blooded African entertains for the adulterated one. As for the steward, his manner, if not bespeaking much dignity of self-respect, yet evidenced his extreme desire to please; which is doubly meritorious, as at once Christian and Chesterfieldian.[45]

Captain Delano observed with interest that while the complexion of the mulatto was hybrid, his physiognomy was European—classically so.

"Don Benito," whispered he, "I am glad to see this usher-of-the-golden-rod [46] of yours; the sight refutes an ugly remark once made to me by a Barbados planter; that when a mulatto has a regular European face, look out for him; he is a devil. But see, your steward here has features more regular than King George's of England; and yet there he nods, and bows, and smiles; a king, indeed—the king of kind hearts and polite fellows. What a pleasant voice he has, too!"

"He has, señor."

"But tell me, has he not, so far as you have known him, always proved a good, worthy fellow?" said Captain Delano, pausing, while with a final genuflection the steward disappeared into the cabin; "come, for the reason just mentioned, I am curious to know."

"Francesco is a good man," a sort of sluggishly responded Don Benito, like a phlegmatic appreciator, who would neither find fault nor flatter.

"Ah, I thought so. For it were strange, indeed, and not very creditable to us white-skins, if a little of our blood mixed with the African's should, far from improving the latter's quality, have the sad effect of pouring vitriolic acid into black broth; improving the hue, perhaps, but not the wholesomeness."

"Doubtless, doubtless, señor, but"—glancing at Babo—"not to speak of negroes, your planter's remark I have heard applied to the Spanish and Indian intermixtures in our provinces. But I know nothing about the matter," he listlessly added.

And here they entered the cabin.

The lunch was a frugal one. Some of Captain Delano's fresh fish and pumpkins, biscuit and salt beef, the reserved bottle of cider, and the *San Dominick*'s last bottle of Canary.

As they entered, Francesco, with two or three coloured aids, was hovering over the table giving the last adjustments. Upon perceiving their master they withdrew, Francesco making a smiling *congé*, and the Spaniard, without condescending to notice it, fastidiously remarking to his companion that he relished not superfluous attendance.

45. Worldly or urbane; from the fourth Earl of Chesterfield (1694–1773), whose letters emphasized elegant and sophisticated behavior.
46. Alludes to the chief officer or servant of a court or royal household, who carries the rod of authority before his master.

Without companions, host and guest sat down, like a childless married couple, at opposite ends of the table, Don Benito waving Captain Delano to his place, and, weak as he was, insisting upon that gentleman being seated before himself.

The negro placed a rug under Don Benito's feet, and a cushion behind his back, and then stood behind, not his master's chair, but Captain Delano's. At first, this a little surprised the latter. But it was soon evident that, in taking his position, the black was still true to his master; since by facing him he could the more readily anticipate his slightest want.

"This is an uncommonly intelligent fellow of yours, Don Benito," whispered Captain Delano across the table.

"You say true, señor."

During the repast, the guest again reverted to parts of Don Benito's story, begging further particulars here and there. He inquired how it was that the scurvy and fever should have committed such wholesale havoc upon the whites, while destroying less than half of the blacks. As if this question reproduced the whole scene of plague before the Spaniard's eyes, miserably reminding him of his solitude in a cabin where before he had had so many friends and officers round him, his hand shook, his face became hueless, broken words escaped; but directly the sane memory of the past seemed replaced by insane terrors of the present. With starting eyes he stared before him at vacancy. For nothing was to be seen but the hand of his servant pushing the Canary over toward him. At length a few sips served partially to restore him. He made random reference to the different constitution of races, enabling one to offer more resistance to certain maladies than another. The thought was new to his companion.

Presently Captain Delano, intending to say something to his host concerning the pecuniary part of the business he had undertaken for him, especially—since he was strictly accountable to his owners—with reference to the new suit of sails, and other things of that sort; and naturally preferring to conduct such affairs in private, was desirous that the servant should withdraw; imagining that Don Benito for a few minutes could dispense with his attendance. He, however, waited a while; thinking that, as the conversation proceeded, Don Benito, without being prompted, would perceive the propriety of the step.

But it was otherwise. At last catching his host's eye, Captain Delano, with a slight backward gesture of his thumb, whispered, "Don Benito, pardon me, but there is an interference with the full expression of what I have to say to you."

Upon this the Spaniard changed countenance; which was imputed to his resenting the hint, as in some way a reflection upon his servant. After a moment's pause, he assured his guest that the black's remaining with them could be of no disservice; because since losing his officers he had made Babo (whose original office, it now appeared, had been captain of the slaves) not only his constant attendant and companion, but in all things his confidant.

After this, nothing more could be said; though, indeed, Captain Delano could hardly avoid some little tinge of irritation upon being left ungratified in so inconsiderable a wish, by one, too, for whom he intended such solid services. But it is only his querulousness, thought he; and so filling his glass he proceeded to business.

The price of the sails and other matters was fixed upon. But while this was being done, the American observed that, though his original offer of assistance had been hailed with hectic animation, yet now when it was reduced to a business transaction, indifference and apathy were betrayed. Don Benito, in fact, appeared to submit to hearing the details more out of regard to common propriety than from any impression that weighty benefit to himself and his voyage was involved.

Soon, his manner became still more reserved. The effort was vain to seek to draw him into social talk. Gnawed by his splenetic mood, he sat twitching his beard, while to little purpose the hand of his servant, mute as that on the wall, slowly pushed over the Canary.

Lunch being over, they sat down on the cushioned transom; the servant placing a pillow behind his master. The long continuance of the calm had now affected the atmosphere. Don Benito sighed heavily, as if for breath.

"Why not adjourn to the cuddy," said Captain Delano; "there is more air there." But the host sat silent and motionless.

Meantime his servant knelt before him, with a large fan of feathers. And Francesco, coming in on tiptoes, handed the negro a little cup of aromatic waters, with which at intervals he chafed his master's brow; smoothing the hair along the temples as a nurse does a child's. He spoke no word. He only rested his eye on his master's, as if, amid all Don Benito's distress, a little to refresh his spirit by the silent sight of fidelity.

Presently the ship's bell sounded two o'clock; and through the cabin windows a slight rippling of the sea was discerned; and from the desired direction.

"There," exclaimed Captain Delano, "I told you so, Don Benito, look!"

He had risen to his feet, speaking in a very animated tone, with a view the more to rouse his companion. But though the crimson curtain of the stern window near him that moment fluttered against his pale cheek, Don Benito seemed to have even less welcome for the breeze than the calm.

Poor fellow, thought Captain Delano, bitter experience has taught him that one ripple does not make a wind, any more than one swallow a summer. But he is mistaken for once. I will get his ship in for him, and prove it.

Briefly alluding to his weak condition, he urged his host to remain quietly where he was, since he (Captain Delano) would with pleasure take upon himself the responsibility of making the best use of the wind.

Upon gaining the deck, Captain Delano started at the unexpected figure of Atufal, monumentally fixed at the threshold, like one of those sculptured porters of black marble guarding the porches of Egyptian tombs.

But this time the start was, perhaps, purely physical. Atufal's presence, singularly attesting docility even in sullenness, was contrasted with that of the hatchet-polishers, who in patience evinced their industry; while both spectacles showed, that lax as Don Benito's general authority might be, still, whenever he chose to exert it, no man so savage or colossal but must, more or less, bow.

Snatching a trumpet which hung from the bulwarks, with a free step Captain Delano advanced to the forward edge of the poop, issuing his orders in his best Spanish. The few sailors and many negroes, all equally pleased, obediently set about heading the ship toward the harbour.

While giving some directions about setting a lower stun'-sail, suddenly Captain Delano heard a voice faithfully repeating his orders. Turning, he saw Babo, now for the time acting, under the pilot, his original part of captain of the slaves. This assistance proved valuable. Tattered sails and warped yards were soon brought into some trim. And no brace or halyard was pulled but to the blithe songs of the inspirited negroes.

Good fellows, thought Captain Delano, a little training would make fine sailors of them. Why, see, the very women pull and sing too. These must be some of those Ashantee negresses that make such capital soldiers, I've heard. But who's at the helm? I must have a good hand there.

He went to see.

The *San Dominick* steered with a cumbrous tiller, with large horizontal pulleys attached. At each pulley-end stood a subordinate black, and between them, at the tiller-head, the responsible post, a Spanish seaman, whose countenance evinced his due share in the general hopefulness and confidence at the coming of the breeze.

He proved the same man who had behaved with so shamefaced an air on the windlass.

"Ah—it is you, my man," exclaimed Captain Delano—"well, no more sheep's-eyes now;—look straight forward and keep the ship so. Good hand, I trust? And want to get into the harbour, don't you?"

The man assented with an inward chuckle, grasping the tiller-head firmly. Upon this, unperceived by the American, the two blacks eyed the sailor intently.

Finding all right at the helm, the pilot went forward to the forecastle, to see how matters stood there.

The ship now had way enough to breast the current. With the approach of evening, the breeze would be sure to freshen.

Having done all that was needed for the present, Captain Delano, giving his last orders to the sailors, turned aft to report affairs to Don Benito in the cabin; perhaps additionally incited to rejoin him by the hope of snatching a moment's private chat while the servant was engaged upon deck.

From opposite sides, there were, beneath the poop, two approaches to the cabin; one further forward than the other, and consequently communicating with a longer passage. Marking the servant still above, Captain Delano, taking the nighest entrance—the one last named, and at whose porch Atufal still stood—hurried on his way, till, arrived at the cabin threshold, he paused an instant, a little to recover from his eagerness. Then, with the words of his intended business upon his lips, he entered. As he advanced toward the seated Spaniard, he heard another footstep, keeping time with his. From the opposite door, a salver in hand, the servant was likewise advancing.

"Confound the faithful fellow," thought Captain Delano; "what a vexatious coincidence."

Possibly the vexation might have been something different, were it not for the brisk confidence inspired by the breeze. But even as it was, he felt a slight twinge, from a sudden indefinite association in his mind of Babo with Atufal.

"Don Benito," said he "I give you joy; the breeze will hold, and will increase. By the way, your tall man and time-piece, Atufal, stands without. By your order, of course?"

Don Benito recoiled, as if at some bland satirical touch, delivered with such adroit garnish of apparent good breeding as to present no handle for retort.

He is like one flayed alive, thought Captain Delano; where may one touch him without causing a shrink?

The servant moved before his master, adjusting a cushion; recalled to civility, the Spaniard stiffly replied: "You are right. The slave appears where you saw him, according to my command; which is, that if at the given hour I am below, he must take his stand and abide my coming."

"Ah now, pardon me, but that is treating the poor fellow like an ex-king indeed. Ah, Don Benito," smiling, "for all the licence you permit in some things, I fear lest, at bottom, you are a bitter hard master."

Again Don Benito shrank; and this time, as the good sailor thought, from a genuine twinge of his conscience.

Again conversation became constrained. In vain Captain Delano called attention to the now perceptible motion of the keel gently cleaving the sea; with lack-lustre eye, Don Benito returned words few and reserved.

By and by, the wind having steadily risen, and still blowing right into the harbour, bore the *San Dominick* swiftly on. Rounding a point of land, the sealer at distance came into open view.

Meantime Captain Delano had again repaired to the deck, remaining there some time. Having at last altered the ship's course, so as to give the reef a wide berth, he returned for a few moments below.

I will cheer up my poor friend this time, thought he.

"Better and better, Don Benito," he cried as he blithely re-entered: "there will soon be an end to your cares, at least for a while. For when, after a long, sad voyage, you know, the anchor drops into the haven, all its vast weight seems lifted from the captain's heart. We are getting on famously, Don Benito. My ship is in sight. Look through this side-light here; there she is; all a-taunt-o! The *Bachelor's Delight*, my good friend. Ah, how this wind braces one up. Come, you must take a cup of coffee with me this evening. My old steward will give you as fine a cup as ever any sultan tasted. What say you, Don Benito, will you?"

At first, the Spaniard glanced feverishly up, casting a longing look toward the sealer, while with mute concern his servant gazed into his face. Suddenly the old ague of coldness returned, and dropping back to his cushions he was silent.

"You do not answer. Come, all day you have been my host; would you have hospitality all on one side?"

"I cannot go," was the response.

"What? it will not fatigue you. The ships will lie together as near as they can, without swinging foul. It will be little more than stepping from deck to deck; which is but as from room to room. Come, come, you must not refuse me."

"I cannot go," decisively and repulsively repeated Don Benito.

Renouncing all but the last appearance of courtesy, with a sort of cadaverous sullenness, and biting his thin nails to the quick, he glanced, almost glared, at his guest, as if impatient that a stranger's presence should interfere with the full indulgence of his morbid hour. Meantime the sound of the parted waters came more and more gurglingly and merrily in at the windows; as reproaching him for his dark spleen; as telling him that, sulk as he might, and go mad with it, nature cared not a jot; since, whose fault was it, pray?

But the foul mood was now at its depth, as the fair wind at its height.

There was something in the man so far beyond any mere unsociality or sourness previously evinced, that even the forbearing good-nature of his guest could no longer endure it. Wholly at a loss to account for such demeanour, and deeming sickness with eccentricity, however extreme, no adequate excuse, well satisfied, too, that nothing in his own conduct could justify it, Captain Delano's pride began to be roused. Himself became reserved. But all seemed one to the Spaniard. Quitting him, therefore, Captain Delano once more went to the deck.

The ship was now within less than two miles of the sealer. The whale-boat was seen darting over the interval.

To be brief, the two vessels, thanks to the pilot's skill, ere long in neighbourly style lay anchored together.

Before returning to his own vessel, Captain Delano had intended communicating to Don Benito the smaller details of the proposed services to be rendered. But, as it was, unwilling anew to subject himself to rebuffs, he resolved, now that he had seen the *San Dominick* safely moored, immediately to quit her, without further allusion to hospitality or business. Indefinitely postponing his ulterior plans, he would regulate his future actions according to future circumstances. His boat was ready to receive him; but his host still tarried below. Well, thought Captain Delano, if he has little breeding, the more need to show mine. He descended to the cabin to bid a ceremonious, and, it may be, tacitly rebukeful adieu. But to his great satisfaction, Don Benito, as if he began to feel the weight of that treatment with which his slighted guest had, not indecorously, retaliated upon him, now supported by his servant, rose to his feet, and grasping Captain Delano's hand, stood tremulous; too much agitated to speak. But the good augury hence drawn was suddenly dashed, by his resuming all his previous reserve, with augmented gloom, as, with half-averted eyes, he silently reseated himself on his cushions. With a corresponding return of his own chilled feelings, Captain Delano bowed and withdrew.

He was hardly midway in the narrow corridor, dim as a tunnel, leading from the cabin to the stairs, when a sound, as of the tolling for execution in some jail-yard, fell on his ears. It was the echo of the ship's flawed bell, striking the hour, drearily reverberated in this subterranean vault. Instantly, by a fatality not to be withstood, his mind, responsive to the portent, swarmed with superstitious suspicions. He paused. In images far swifter than these sentences, the minutest details of all his former distrusts swept through him.

Hitherto, credulous good-nature had been too ready to furnish excuses for reasonable fears. Why was the Spaniard, so superfluously punctilious at times, now heedless of common propriety in not accompanying to the side his departing guest? Did indisposition forbid? Indisposition had not forbidden more irksome exertion that day. His last equivocal demeanour recurred. He had risen to his feet, grasped his guest's hand, motioned toward his hat; then, in an instant, all was eclipsed in sinister muteness and gloom. Did this imply one brief, repentant relenting at the final moment, from some iniquitous plot, followed by remorseless return to it? His last glance seemed to express a calamitous, yet acquiescent farewell to Captain Delano forever. Why decline the invitation to visit the sealer that evening? Or was the Spaniard less hardened than the Jew, who refrained not from supping at the board of him whom the same night he meant to betray? [47] What imported all those day-long enigmas and contradictions, except they were intended to mystify, preliminary to some stealthy blow? Atufal, the pretended rebel, but punctual shadow, that moment lurked by the threshold without. He seemed a sentry, and more. Who, by his own confession, had stationed him there? Was the negro now lying in wait?

The Spaniard behind—his creature before: to rush from darkness to light was the involuntary choice.

The next moment, with clenched jaw and hand, he passed Atufal, and stood unharmed in the light. As he saw his trim ship lying peacefully at anchor, and almost within ordinary call; as he saw his household boat, with familiar faces in it, patiently rising and falling on the short waves by the San Dominick's side; and then, glancing about the decks where he stood, saw the oakum-pickers still gravely plying their fingers; and heard the low, buzzing whistle and industrious hum of the hatchet-polishers, still bestirring themselves over their endless occupation; and more than all, as he saw the benign aspect of nature, taking her innocent repose in the evening; the screened sun in the quiet camp of the west shining out like the mild light from Abraham's tent; [48] as charmed eye and ear took in all these, with the chained figure of the black, clenched jaw and hand relaxed. Once again he smiled at the phantoms which had mocked him, and felt something like a tinge of remorse, that, by harbouring them even for a moment, he should, by implication, have betrayed an atheist doubt of the ever-watchful Providence above.

There was a few minutes' delay, while, in obedience to his orders, the boat was being hooked along to the gangway. During this interval, a sort of saddened satisfaction stole over Captain Delano, at thinking of the kindly offices he had that day discharged for a

47. Alludes to the Last Supper and Judas's betrayal of Jesus; see Matthew 26.
48. The allusion may be to Genesis 18.

stranger. Ah, thought he, after good actions one's conscience is never ungrateful, however much so the benefited party may be.

Presently, his foot, in the first act of descent into the boat, pressed the first round of the side-ladder, his face presented inward upon the deck. In the same moment, he heard his name courteously sounded; and, to his pleased surprise, saw Don Benito advancing—an unwonted energy in his air, as if, at the last moment, intent upon making amends for his recent discourtesy. With instinctive good feeling, Captain Delano, withdrawing his foot, turned and reciprocally advanced. As he did so, the Spaniard's nervous eagerness increased, but his vital energy failed; so that, the better to support him, the servant, placing his master's hand on his naked shoulder, and gently holding it there, formed himself into a sort of crutch.

When the two captains met, the Spaniard again fervently took the hand of the American, at the same time casting an earnest glance into his eyes, but, as before, too much overcome to speak.

I have done him wrong, self-reproachfully thought Captain Delano; his apparent coldness has deceived me; in no instance has he meant to offend.

Meantime, as if fearful that the continuance of the scene might too much unstring his master, the servant seemed anxious to terminate it. And so, still presenting himself as a crutch, and walking between the two captains, he advanced with them toward the gangway; while still, as if full of kindly contrition, Don Benito would not let go the hand of Captain Delano, but retained it in his, across the black's body.

Soon they were standing by the side, looking over into the boat, whose crew turned up their curious eyes. Waiting a moment for the Spaniard to relinquish his hold, the now embarrassed Captain Delano lifted his foot, to overstep the threshold of the open gangway; but still Don Benito would not let go his hand. And yet, with an agitated tone, he said, "I can go no further; here I must bid you adieu. Adieu, my dear, dear Don Amasa. Go—go!" suddenly tearing his hand loose, "go, and God guard you better than me, my best friend."

Not unaffected, Captain Delano would now have lingered; but catching the meekly admonitory eye of the servant, with a hasty farewell he descended into his boat, followed by the continual adieus of Don Benito, standing rooted in the gangway.

Seating himself in the stern, Captain Delano, making a last salute, ordered the boat shoved off. The crew had their oars on end. The bowsmen pushed the boat a sufficient distance for the oars to be lengthwise dropped. The instant that was done, Don Benito sprang over the bulwarks, falling at the feet of Captain Delano; at the same time calling toward his ship, but in tones so frenzied, that none in the boat could understand him. But, as if not equally obtuse, three sailors, from three different and distant parts of the ship, splashed into the sea, swimming after their captain, as if intent upon his rescue.

The dismayed officer of the boat eagerly asked what this meant. To which, Captain Delano, turning a disdainful smile upon the unaccountable Spaniard, answered that, for his part, he neither knew nor cared; but it seemed as if Don Benito had taken it into his head to produce the impression among his people that the boat wanted to kidnap him. "Or else—give way for your lives," he wildly added, starting at a clattering hubbub in the ship, above which rang the tocsin of the hatchet-polishers; and seizing Don Benito by the throat he added, "this plotting pirate means murder!" Here, in apparent verification of the words, the servant, a dagger in his hand, was seen on the rail overhead, poised, in the act of leaping, as if with desperate fidelity to befriend his master to the last; while, seemingly to aid the black, the three white sailors were trying to clamber into the hampered bow. Meantime, the whole host of negroes, as if inflamed at the sight of their jeopardised captain, impended in one sooty avalanche over the bulwarks.

All this, with what preceded, and what followed, occurred with such involutions of rapidity, that past, present, and future seemed one.

Seeing the negro coming, Captain Delano had flung the Spaniard aside, almost in the very act of clutching him, and, by the unconscious recoil, shifting his place, with arms thrown up, so promptly grappled the servant in his descent, that with dagger presented at Captain Delano's heart, the black seemed of purpose to have leaped there as to his mark. But the weapon was wrenched away, and the assailant dashed down into the bottom of the boat, which now, with disentangled oars, began to speed through the sea.

At this juncture, the left hand of Captain Delano, on one side, again clutched the half-reclined Don Benito, heedless that he was in a speechless faint, while his right foot, on the other side, ground the prostrate negro; and his right arm pressed for added speed on the after-oar, his eye bent forward, encouraging his men to their utmost.

But here, the officer of the boat, who had at last succeeded in beating off the towing sailors, and was now, with face turned aft, assisting the bowsman at his oar, suddenly called to Captain Delano, to see what the black was about; while a Portuguese oarsman shouted to him to give heed to what the Spaniard was saying.

Glancing down at his feet, Captain Delano saw the freed hand of the servant aiming with a second dagger—a small one, before concealed in his wool—with this he was snakishly writhing up from the boat's bottom, at the heart of his master, his countenance lividly vindictive, expressing the centred purpose of his soul; while the Spaniard, half-choked, was vainly shrinking away, with husky words, incoherent to all but the Portuguese.

That moment, across the long-benighted mind of Captain Delano, a flash of revelation swept, illuminating, in unanticipated clearness, his host's whole mysterious demeanour, with every enigmatic event of the day, as well as the entire past voyage of the *San Dominick.* He smote Babo's hand down, but his own heart smote him harder. With infinite pity he withdrew his hold from Don Benito. Not Captain Delano, but Don Benito, the black, in leaping into the boat, had intended to stab.

Both the black's hands were held, as, glancing up toward the *San Dominick,* Captain Delano, now with scales dropped from his eyes, saw the negroes, not in misrule, not in tumult, not as if frantically concerned for Don Benito, but with mask torn away, flourishing hatchets and knives, in ferocious piratical revolt. Like delirious black dervishes, the six Ashantees danced on the poop. Prevented by their foes from springing into the water, the Spanish boys were hurrying up to the topmost spars, while such of the few Spanish sailors, not already in the sea, less alert, were descried, helplessly mixed in, on deck, with the blacks.

Meantime Captain Delano hailed his own vessel, ordering the ports up, and the guns run out. But by this time the cable of the *San Dominick* had been cut; and the fag-end, in lashing out, whipped away the canvas shroud about the beak, suddenly revealing, as the bleached hull swung round toward the open ocean, death for the figure-head, in a human skeleton; chalky comment on the chalked words below, *"Follow your leader."*

At the sight, Don Benito, covering his face, wailed out: "'Tis he, Aranda! my murdered, unburied friend!"

Upon reaching the sealer, calling for ropes, Captain Delano bound the negro, who made no resistance, and had him hoisted to the deck. He would then have assisted the now almost helpless Don Benito up the side; but Don Benito, wan as he was, refused to move, or be moved, until the negro should have been first put below out of view. When, presently assured that it was done, he no more shrank from the ascent.

The boat was immediately dispatched back to pick up the three swimming sailors. Meantime, the guns were in readiness, though, owing to the *San Dominick* having glided somewhat astern of the sealer, only the aftermost one could be brought to bear. With this, they fired six times; thinking to cripple the fugitive ship by bringing down her spars. But only a few inconsiderable ropes were shot away. Soon the ship was beyond the gun's range, steering broad out of the bay; the blacks thickly clustering round the bowsprit, one moment with taunting cries toward the whites, the next with upthrown gestures hailing the now dusky moors of ocean—cawing crows escaped from the hand of the fowler.

The first impulse was to slip the cables and give chase. But, upon second thoughts, to pursue with whale-boat and yawl seemed more promising.

Upon inquiring of Don Benito what firearms they had on board the *San Dominick*, Captain Delano was answered that they had none that could be used; because, in the earlier stages of the mutiny, a cabin passenger, since dead, had secretly put out of order the locks of what few muskets there were. But with all his remaining strength, Don Benito entreated the American not to give chase, either with ship or boat; for the negroes had already proved themselves such desperadoes, that, in case of a present assault, nothing but a total massacre of the whites could be looked for. But, regarding this warning as coming from one whose spirit had been crushed by misery, the American did not give up his design.

The boats were got ready and armed. Captain Delano ordered his men into them. He was going himself when Don Benito grasped his arm.

"What! have you saved my life, señor, and are you now going to throw away your own?"

The officers also, for reasons connected with their interests and those of the voyage, and a duty owing to the owners, strongly objected against their commander's going. Weighing their remonstrances a moment, Captain Delano felt bound to remain; appointing his chief mate—an athletic and resolute man, who had been a privateer's-man—to head the party. The more to encourage the sailors, they were told, that the Spanish captain considered his ship good as lost; that she and her cargo, including some gold and silver, were worth more than a thousand doubloons. Take her, and no small part should be theirs. The sailors replied with a shout.

The fugitives had now almost gained an offing.[49] It was nearly night; but the moon was rising. After hard, prolonged pulling, the boats came up on the ship's quarters, at a suitable distance laying upon their oars to discharge their muskets. Having no bullets to return, the negroes sent their yells. But, upon the second volley, Indian-like, they hurtled their hatchets. One took off a sailor's fingers. Another struck the whaleboat's bow, cutting off the rope there, and remaining stuck in the gunwale like a woodman's axe. Snatching it, quivering from its lodgment, the mate hurled it back. The returned gauntlet now stuck in the ship's broken quarter-gallery, and so remained.

49. A safe distance from shore.

The negroes giving too hot a reception, the whites kept a more respectful distance. Hovering now just out of reach of the hurtling hatchets, they, with a view to the close encounter which must soon come, sought to decoy the blacks into entirely disarming themselves of their most murderous weapons in a hand-to-hand fight, by foolishly flinging them, as missiles, short of the mark, into the sea. But, ere long, perceiving the stratagem, the negroes desisted, though not before many of them had to replace their lost hatchets with handspikes; an exchange which, as counted upon, proved, in the end, favourable to the assailants.

Meantime, with a strong wind, the ship still clove the water; the boats alternately falling behind, and pulling up, to discharge fresh volleys.

The fire was mostly directed toward the stern, since there, chiefly, the negroes, at present, were clustering. But to kill or maim the negroes was not the object. To take them, with the ship, was the object. To do it, the ship must be boarded; which could not be done by boats while she was sailing so fast.

A thought now struck the mate. Observing the Spanish boys still aloft, high as they could get, he called to them to descend to the yards, and cut adrift the sails. It was done. About this time, owing to causes hereafter to be shown, two Spaniards, in the dress of sailors, and conspicuously showing themselves, were killed; not by volleys, but by deliberate marksman's shots; while, as it afterward appeared, by one of the general discharges, Atufal, the black, and the Spaniard at the helm likewise were killed. What now with the loss of the sails, and loss of leaders, the ship became unmanageable to the negroes.

With creaking masts, she came heavily round to the wind; the prow slowly swinging into view of the boats, its skeleton gleaming in the horizontal moonlight, and casting a gigantic ribbed shadow upon the water. One extended arm of the ghost seemed beckoning the whites to avenge it.

"Follow your leader!" cried the mate; and, one on each bow, the boats boarded. Sealing-spears and cutlasses crossed hatchets and handspikes. Huddled upon the long-boat amidships, the negresses raised a wailing chant, whose chorus was the clash of the steel.

For a time, the attack wavered; the negroes wedging themselves to beat it back; the half-repelled sailors, as yet unable to gain a footing, fighting as troopers in the saddle, one leg sideways flung over the bulwarks, and one without, plying their cutlasses like carters' whips. But in vain. They were almost overborne, when, rallying themselves into a squad as one man, with a huzza, they sprang inboard, where, entangled, they involuntarily separated again. For a few breaths' space, there was a vague, muffled, inner sound, as of submerged sword-fish rushing hither and thither through shoals of black-fish. Soon, in a reunited band, and joined by the Spanish seamen, the whites came to the surface, irresistibly driving the negroes toward the stern. But a barricade of casks and sacks, from side to side, had been thrown up by the mainmast. Here the negroes faced about, and though scorning peace or truce, yet fain would have had respite. But, without pause, overleaping the barrier, the unflagging sailors again closed. Exhausted, the blacks now fought in despair. Their red tongues lolled, wolf-like, from their black mouths. But the pale sailors' teeth were set; not a word was spoken; and, in five minutes more, the ship was won.

Nearly a score of the negroes were killed. Exclusive of those by the balls, many were mangled; their wounds—mostly inflicted by the long-edged sealing-spears—resembling those shaven ones of the English at Preston-pans, made by the poled scythes of the Highlanders.[50] On the other side, none were killed, though several were wounded; some severely, including the mate. The surviving negroes were temporarily secured, and the ship, towed back into the harbour at midnight, once more lay anchored.

Omitting the incidents and arrangements ensuing, suffice it that, after two days spent in refitting, the ships sailed in company for Conception, in Chili, and thence for Lima, in Peru; where, before the vice-regal courts, the whole affair, from the beginning, underwent investigation.

Though, midway on the passage, the ill-fated Spaniard, relaxed from constraint, showed some signs of regaining health with freewill; yet, agreeably to his own foreboding, shortly before arriving at Lima, he relapsed, finally becoming so reduced as to be carried ashore in arms. Hearing of his story and plight, one of the many religious institutions of the City of Kings opened an hospitable refuge to him, where both physician and priest were his nurses, and a member of the order volunteered to be his one special guardian and consoler, by night and by day.

The following extracts, translated from one of the official Spanish documents, will, it is hoped, shed light on the preceding narrative, as well as, in the first place, reveal the true port of departure and true history of the San Dominick's voyage, down to the time of her touching at the island of St. Maria.

But, ere the extracts come, it may be well to preface them with a remark.

The document selected, from among many others, for partial translation, contains the deposition of Benito Cereno; the first taken in the case. Some disclosures therein were, at the time, held dubi-

50. At the battle of Prestonpans (1745) the Scotch Highlanders, supporters of Bonnie Prince Charlie, gained a complete victory over the English forces.

ous for both learned and natural reasons. The tribunal inclined to the opinion that the deponent, not undisturbed in his mind by recent events, raved of some things which could never have happened. But subsequent depositions of the surviving sailors, bearing out the revelations of their captain in several of the strangest particulars, gave credence to the rest. So that the tribunal, in its final decision, rested its capital sentences upon statements which, had they lacked confirmation, it would have deemed it but duty to reject.

I, DON JOSÉ DE ABOS AND PADILLA, His Majesty's Notary for the Royal Revenue, and Register of this Province, and Notary Public of the Holy Crusade of this Bishopric, etc.

Do certify and declare, as much as is requisite in law, that, in the criminal cause commenced the twenty-fourth of the month of September, in the year seventeen hundred and ninety-nine, against the negroes of the ship *San Dominick*, the following declaration before me was made:—

Declaration of the first witness, DON BENITO CERENO.

The same day, and month, and year, His Honour, Doctor Juan Martinez de Rozas, Councillor of the Royal Audience [51] of this Kingdom, and learned in the law of this Intendency, ordered the captain of the ship *San Dominick,* Don Benito Cereno, to appear; which he did in his litter, attended by the monk Infelez; of whom he received the oath, which he took by God, our Lord, and a sign of the Cross; under which he promised to tell the truth of whatever he should know and should be asked;—and being interrogated agreeably to the tenor of the act commencing the process, he said, that on the twentieth of May last, he set sail with his ship from the port of Valparaiso, bound to that of Callao; loaded with the produce of the country besides thirty cases of hardware and one hundred and sixty blacks, of both sexes, mostly belonging to Don Alexandro Aranda, gentleman, of the city of Mendoza; that the crew of the ship consisted of thirty-six men, besides the persons who went as passengers; that the negroes were in part as follows:—

[Here, in the original, follows a list of some fifty names, descriptions, and ages, compiled from certain recovered documents of Aranda's, and also from recollections of the deponent, from which portions only are extracted.] [52]

---

51. The Spanish colonies were divided into separate territories or *audiencias*, each with its own court of justice.
52. All materials within square brackets are part of Melville's narrative.

—One, from about eighteen to nineteen years, named José, and this was the man that waited upon his master, Don Alexandro, and who speaks well the Spanish, having served him four or five years; * * * a mulatto, named Francesco, the cabin steward, of a good person and voice, having sung in the Valparaiso churches, native of the province of Buenos Ayres, aged about thirty-five years. * * * A smart negro, named Dago, who had been for many years a gravedigger among the Spaniards, aged forty-six years. * * * Four old negroes, born in Africa, from sixty to seventy, but sound, caulkers by trade, whose names are as follows:—the first was named Muri, and he was killed (as was also his son named Diamelo); the second, Nacta; the third, Yola, likewise killed; the fourth, Ghofan; and six full-grown negroes, aged from thirty to forty-five, all raw, and born among the Ashantees—Matiluqui, Yan, Lecbe, Mapenda, Yambaio, Akim; four of whom were killed; * * * a powerful negro named Atufal, who being supposed to have been a chief in Africa, his owner set great store by him. * * * And a small negro of Senegal, but some years among the Spaniards, aged about thirty, which negro's name was Babo; * * * that he does not remember the names of the others, but that still expecting the residue of Don Alexandro's papers will be found, will then take due account of them all, and remit to the court; * * * and thirty-nine women and children of all ages.

[*The catalogue over, the deposition goes on:*]

* * * That all the negroes slept upon deck, as is customary in this navigation, and none wore fetters, because the owner, his friend Aranda, told him that they were all tractable; * * * that on the seventh day after leaving port, at three o'clock in the morning, all the Spaniards being asleep except the two officers on the watch, who were the boatswain, Juan Robles, and the carpenter, Juan Bautista Gayete, and the helmsman and his boy, the negroes revolted suddenly, wounded dangerously the boatswain and the carpenter, and successively killed eighteen men of those who were sleeping upon deck, some with handspikes and hatchets, and others by throwing them alive overboard, after tying them; that of the Spaniards upon deck, they left about seven, as he thinks, alive and tied, to manœuvre the ship, and three or four more, who hid themselves, remained also alive. Although in the act of revolt the negroes made themselves masters of the hatchway, six or seven wounded went through it to the cockpit, without any hindrance on their part; that during the act of revolt, the mate and another person,

whose name he does not recollect, attempted to come up through the hatchway, but being quickly wounded, were obliged to return to the cabin; that the deponent resolved at break of day to come up the companion-way, where the negro Babo was, being the ringleader, and Atufal, who assisted him, and having spoken to them, exhorted them to cease committing such atrocities, asking them, at the same time, what they wanted and intended to do, offering, himself, to obey their commands; that notwithstanding this, they threw, in his presence, three men, alive and tied, overboard; that they told the deponent to come up, and that they would not kill him; which having done, the negro Babo asked him whether there were in these seas any negro countries where they might be carried, and he answered them, No; that the negro Babo afterward told him to carry them to Senegal,[53] or to the neighbouring islands of St. Nicholas; and he answered, that this was impossible, on account of the great distance, the necessity involved of rounding Cape Horn, the bad condition of the vessel, the want of provisions, sails, and water; but that the negro Babo replied to him he must carry them in any way; that they would do and conform themselves to everything the deponent should require as to eating and drinking; that after a long conference, being absolutely compelled to please them, for they threatened to kill all the whites if they were not, at all events, carried to Senegal, he told them that what was most wanting for the voyage was water; that they would go near the coast to take it, and thence they would proceed on their course; that the negro Babo agreed to it; and the deponent steered toward the intermediate ports, hoping to meet some Spanish or foreign vessel that would save them; that within ten or eleven days they saw the land, and continued their course by it in the vicinity of Nasca; that the deponent observed that the negroes were now restless and mutinous, because he did not effect the taking in of water, the negro Babo having required, with threats, that it should be done, without fail, the following day; he told him he saw plainly that the coast was steep, and the rivers designated in the maps were not to be found, with other reasons suitable to the circumstances; that the best way would be to go to the island of Santa Maria, where they might water easily, it being a solitary island, as the foreigners did; that the deponent did not go to Pisco, that was near, nor make any other port of the coast, because the negro Babo had intimated to him several times, that he would kill all the whites the very moment he should

53. West African country with a large Negro population.

perceive any city, town, or settlement of any kind on the shores
to which they should be carried: that having determined to go
to the island of Santa Maria, as the deponent had planned, for
the purpose of trying whether, on the passage or near the island
itself, they could find any vessel that should favour them, or
whether he could escape from it in a boat to the neighbouring
coast of Arruco, to adopt the necessary means he immediately
changed his course, steering for the island; that the negroes
Babo and Atufal held daily conferences, in which they discussed what was necessary for their design of returning to Senegal, whether they were to kill all the Spaniards, and particularly the deponent; that eight days after parting with the coast
of Nasca, the deponent being on the watch a little after daybreak, and soon after the negroes had their meeting, the negro
Babo came to the place where the deponent was, and told him
that he had determined to kill his master, Don Alexandro
Aranda, both because he and his companions could not otherwise be sure of their liberty, and that to keep the seamen in
subjection, he wanted to prepare a warning of what road they
should be made to take did they or any of them oppose him;
and that, by means of the death of Don Alexandro, that warning
would best be given; but, that what this last meant, the deponent did not at the time comprehend, nor could not, further than
that the death of Don Alexandro was intended; and moreover
the negro Babo proposed to the deponent to call the mate Raneds, who was sleeping in the cabin, before the thing was done,
for fear, as the deponent understood it, that the mate, who was
a good navigator, should be killed with Don Alexandro and the
rest; that the deponent, who was the friend, from youth, of Don
Alexandro, prayed and conjured, but all was useless; for the
negro Babo answered him that the thing could not be prevented, and that all the Spaniards risked their death if they should
attempt to frustrate his will in this matter, or any other; that, in
this conflict, the deponent called the mate, Raneds, who was
forced to go apart, and immediately the negro Babo commanded the Ashantee Matiluqui and the Ashantee Lecbe to go
and commit the murder; that those two went down with
hatchets to the berth of Don Alexandro; that, yet half alive and
mangled, they dragged him on deck; that they were going to
throw him overboard in that state, but the negro Babo stopped
them, bidding the murder be completed on the deck before
him, which was done, when, by his orders, the body was carried below, forward; that nothing more was seen of it by the
deponent for three days; * * * that Don Alonzo Sidonia, an old
man, long resident at Valparaiso, and lately appointed to a civil

office in Peru, whither he had taken passage, was at the time sleeping in the berth opposite Don Alexandro's; that awakening at his cries, surprised by them, and at the sight of the negroes with their bloody hatchets in their hands, he threw himself into the sea through a window which was near him, and was drowned, without it being in the power of the deponent to assist or take him up; * * * that a short time after killing Aranda, they brought upon deck his german-cousin, of middle-age, Don Francisco Masa, of Mendoza, and the young Don Joaquin, Marques de Aramboalaza, then lately from Spain, with his Spanish servant Ponce, and the three young clerks of Aranda, José Mozairi, Lorenzo Bargas, and Hermenegildo Gandix, all of Cadiz; that Don Joaquin and Hermenegildo Gandix, the negro Babo, for purposes hereafter to appear, preserved alive; but Don Francisco Masa José Mozairi, and Lorenzo Bargas, with Ponce the servant, besides the boatswain, Juan Robles, the boatswain's mates, Manuel Viscaya and Roderigo Hurta, and four of the sailors, the negro Babo ordered to be thrown alive into the sea, although they made no resistance, nor begged for anything else but mercy; that the boatswain, Juan Robles, who knew how to swim, kept the longest above water, making acts of contrition, and, in the last words he uttered, charged this deponent to cause mass to be said for his soul to our Lady of Succour: * * * that, during the three days which followed, the deponent, uncertain what fate had befallen the remains of Don Alexandro, frequently asked the negro Babo where they were, and, if still on board, whether they were to be preserved for interment ashore, entreating him so to order it; that the negro Babo answered nothing till the fourth day, when at sunrise, the deponent coming on deck, the negro Babo showed him a skeleton, which had been substituted for the ship's proper figurehead—the image of Christopher Colon, the discoverer of the New World; that the negro Babo asked him whose skeleton that was, and whether, from its whiteness, he should not think it a white's; that, upon discovering his face, the negro Babo, coming close, said words to this effect: 'Keep faith with the blacks from here to Senegal, or you shall in spirit, as now in body, follow your leader,' pointing to the prow; * * * that the same morning the negro Babo took by succession each Spaniard forward, and asked him whose skeleton that was, and whether, from its whiteness, he should not think it a white's; that each Spaniard covered his face; that then to each the negro Babo repeated the words in the first place said to the deponent; * * * that they (the Spaniards), being then assembled aft, the negro Babo harangued them, saying that he had now done all; that the deponent (as navigator for the negroes) might pursue his course, warning him and all of them that they should, soul and body, go the way of Don Alexandro, if he saw them (the Spaniards) speak or plot anything against them (the negroes)—a threat which was repeated every day; that, before the events last mentioned, they had tied the cook to throw him overboard, for it is not known what thing they heard him speak, but finally the negro Babo spared his life, at the request of the deponent; that a few days after, the deponent, endeavouring not to omit any means to preserve the lives of the remaining whites, spoke to the negroes peace and tranquillity, and agreed to draw up a paper, signed by the deponent and the sailors who could write, as also by the negro Babo, for himself and all the blacks, in which the deponent obliged himself to carry them to Senegal, and they not to kill any more, and he formally to make over to them the ship, with the cargo, with which they were for that time satisfied and quieted. * * * But the next day, the more surely to guard against the sailors' escape, the negro Babo commanded all the boats to be destroyed but the long-boat, which was unseaworthy, and another, a cutter in good condition, which knowing it would yet be wanted for towing the water-casks, he had it lowered down into the hold.

[*Various particulars of the prolonged and perplexed navigation ensuing here follow, with incidents of a calamitous calm, from which portion one passage is extracted, to wit:*]

—That on the fifth day of the calm, all on board suffering much from the heat, and want of water, and five having died in fits, and mad, the negroes became irritable, and for a chance gesture, which they deemed suspicious—though it was harmless—made by the mate, Raneds, to the deponent in the act of handing a quadrant, they killed him; but that for this they afterward were sorry, the mate being the only remaining navigator on board, except the deponent.

—That omitting other events, which daily happened, and which can only serve uselessly to recall past misfortunes and conflicts, after seventy-three days' navigation, reckoned from the time they sailed from Nasca, during which they navigated under a scanty allowance of water, and were afflicted with the calms beforementioned, they at last arrived at the island of Santa Maria, on the seventeenth of the month of August, at about six o'clock in the afternoon, at which hour they cast anchor very near the American ship, *Bachelor's Delight,* which lay in the same bay, commanded by the generous Captain Amasa Delano; but at six o'clock in the morning, they had already descried the port, and the negroes became uneasy, as soon as at distance they saw the ship, not having expected to see one there; that the negro Babo pacified them, assuring them that no fear need be had; that straightway he ordered the figure on the bow to be covered with canvas, as for repairs, and had the decks a little set in order; that for a time the negro Babo and the negro Atufal conferred; that the negro Atufal was for sailing away, but the negro Babo would not, and, by himself, cast about what to do; that at last he came to the deponent, proposing to him to say and do all that the deponent declares to have said and done to the American captain; * * * that the negro Babo warned him that if he varied in the least, or uttered any word, or gave any look that should give the least intimation of the past events or present state, he would instantly kill him, with all his companions, showing a dagger, which he carried hid, saying something which, as he understood it, meant that that dagger would be alert as his eye; that the negro Babo then announced the plan to all his companions, which pleased them; that he then, the better to disguise the truth, devised many expedients, in some of them uniting deceit and defence; that of this sort was the device of the six Ashantees before-named, who were his bravos; that them he stationed on the break of the poop, as if to clean certain hatchets (in cases, which were part of the cargo), but in reality to use them, and distribute them at need, and at a given word he told them; that, among other devices, was the device of presenting Atufal, his right-hand man, as chained, though in a moment the chains could be dropped; that in every particular he informed the deponent what part he was expected to enact in every device, and what story he was to tell on every occasion, always threatening him with instant death if he varied in the least; that, conscious that many of the negroes would be turbulent, the negro Babo appointed the four aged negroes, who were caulkers, to keep what domestic order they could on the decks; that again and again he harangued the Spaniards and his companions, informing them of his intent, and of his devices, and of the invented story that this deponent was to tell; charging them lest any of them varied from that story; that these arrangements were made and matured during the interval of two or three hours, between their first sighting the ship and the arrival on board of Captain Amasa Delano; that this happened about half-past seven o'clock in the morning, Captain Amasa Delano coming in his boat, and all gladly receiving him; that the deponent, as well as he could force himself, acting then the part of principal owner, and a free captain of the ship, told Captain Amasa Delano, when called upon, that he came from Buenos Ayres, bound to Lima, with three hundred negroes; that off Cape Horn, and in a subsequent fever, many negroes had died; that also, by similar casualties, all the sea-officers and the greatest part of the crew had died.

[*And so the deposition goes on, circumstantially recounting the fictitious story dictated to the deponent by Babo, and through the deponent imposed upon Captain Delano; and also recounting the friendly offers of Captain Delano, with other things, but all of which is here omitted. After the fictitious story, etc., the deposition proceeds:*]

—that the generous Captain Amasa Delano remained on board all the day, till he left the ship anchored at six o'clock in the evening, deponent speaking to him always of his pretended misfortunes, under the forementioned principles, without having had it in his power to tell a single word, or give him the least hint, that he might know the truth and state of things; because the negro Babo, performing the office of an officious servant with all the appearance of submission of the humble slave, did not leave the deponent one moment; that this was in order to observe the deponent's actions and words, for the negro Babo understands well the Spanish; and besides, there were thereabout some others who were constantly on the watch, and likewise understood the Spanish; * * * that upon one occasion, while deponent was standing on the deck conversing with Amasa Delano, by a secret sign the negro Babo drew him (the deponent) aside, the act appearing as if originating with the deponent; that then, he being drawn aside, the negro Babo proposed to him to gain from Amasa Delano full particulars about his ship, and crew, and arms; that the deponent asked "For what?" that the negro Babo answered he might conceive; that, grieved at the prospect of what might overtake the generous Captain Amasa Delano, the deponent at first refused to ask the desired questions, and used every argument to induce the negro Babo to give up this new design; that the negro Babo showed the point of his dagger; that, after the information had been obtained, the negro Babo again drew him aside, telling him that that very night he (the deponent) would be captain of two ships, instead of one, for that, great part of the American's ship's crew being to be absent fishing, the six Ashantees, without anyone else, would easily take it; that at

this time he said other things to the same purpose; that no en-
treaties availed; that, before Amasa Delano's coming on board,
no hint had been given touching the capture of the American
ship: that to prevent this project the deponent was powerless;
* * *—that in some things his memory is confused, he cannot
distinctly recall every event; * * *—that as soon as they had cast
anchor at six of the clock in the evening, as has before been stated, the American captain took leave, to return to his vessel;
that upon a sudden impulse, which the deponent believes to
have come from God and his angels, he, after the farewell had
been said, followed the generous Captain Amasa Delano as far
as the gunwale, where he stayed, under pretence of taking
leave, until Amasa Delano should have been seated in his boat;
that on shoving off, the deponent sprang from the gunwale into
the boat, and fell into it, he knows not how, God guarding him;
that—

[*Here, in the original, follows the account of what further
happened at the escape, and how the* San Dominick *was retaken, and of the passage to the coast; including in the recital
many expressions of "eternal gratitude" to the "generous Captain Amasa Delano." The deposition then proceeds with reca-
pitulatory remarks, and a partial renumeration of the negroes,
making record of their individual part in the past events, with
a view to furnishing, according to command of the court, the
data whereon to found the criminal sentences to be pronounced. From this portion is the following:*]

—That he believes that all the negroes, though not in the first
place knowing to the design of revolt, when it was accomplished, approved it. * * * That the negro, José, eighteen
years old, and in the personal service of Don Alexandro, was
the one who communicated the information to the negro Babo,
about the state of things in the cabin, before the revolt; that this
is known, because, in the preceding midnight, he used to come
from his berth, which was under his master's, in the cabin, to
the deck where the ringleader and his associates were, and had
secret conversations with the negro Babo, in which he was several times seen by the mate; that, one night, the mate drove
him away twice; * * * that this same negro José was the one
who, without being commanded to do so by the negro Babo, as
Lecbe and Matiluqui were, stabbed his master, Don Alexandro,
after he had been dragged half-lifeless to the deck; * * * that
the mulatto steward, Francesco, was of the first band of revol-
ters, that he was, in all things, the creature and tool of the negro

Babo; that, to make his court, he, just before a repast in the cabin, proposed, to the negro Babo, poisoning a dish for the generous Captain Amasa Delano; this is known and believed, because the negroes have said it; but that the negro Babo, having another design, forbade Francesco; * * * that the Ashantee Lecbe was one of the worst of them; for that, on the day the ship was retaken, he assisted in the defence of her, with a hatchet in each hand, with one of which he wounded, in the breast, the chief mate of Amasa Delano, in the first act of boarding; this all knew; that, in sight of the deponent, Lecbe struck, with a hatchet, Don Francisco Masa, when, by the negro Babo's orders, he was carrying him to throw him overboard, alive, besides participating in the murder, before mentioned, of Don Alexandro Aranda, and others of the cabin passengers; that, owing to the fury with which the Ashantees fought in the engagement with the boats, but this Lecbe and Yan survived; that Yan was bad as Lecbe; that Yan was the man who, by Babo's command, willingly prepared the skeleton of Don Alexandro, in a way the negroes afterward told the deponent, but which he, so long as reason is left him, can never divulge; that Yan and Lecbe were the two who, in a calm by night, riveted the skeleton to the bow; this also the negroes told him; that the negro Babo was he who traced the inscription below it; that the negro Babo was the plotter from first to last; he ordered every murder, and was the helm and keel of the revolt; that Atufal was his lieutenant in all; but Atufal, with his own hand, committed no murder; nor did the negro Babo; * * * that Atufal was shot, being killed in the fight with the boats, ere boarding; * * * that the negresses, of age, were knowing to the revolt, and testified themselves satisfied at the death of their master, Don Alexandro; that, had the negroes not restrained them, they would have tortured to death, instead of simply killing, the Spaniards slain by command of the negro Babo; that the negresses used their utmost influence to have the deponent made away with; that, in the various acts of murder, they sang songs and danced—not gaily, but solemnly; and before the engagement with the boats, as well as during the action, they sang melancholy songs to the negroes, and that this melancholy tone was more inflaming than a different one would have been, and was so intended; that all this is believed, because the negroes have said it.

—That of the thirty-six men of the crew, exclusive of the passengers (all of whom are now dead), which the deponent had knowledge of, six only remained alive, with four cabin-boys and ship-boys, not included with the crew; * * * —that the negroes broke an arm of one of the cabin-boys and gave him strokes with hatchets.

[*Then follow various random disclosures referring to various periods of time. The following are extracted:*]

—That during the presence of Captain Amasa Delano on board, some attempts were made by the sailors, and one by Hermenegildo Gandix, to convey hints to him of the true state of affairs; but that these attempts were ineffectual, owing to fear of incurring death, and, furthermore, owing to the devices which offered contradictions to the true state of affairs, as well as owing to the generosity and piety of Amasa Delano incapable of sounding such wickedness; * * * that Luys Galgo, a sailor about sixty years of age, and formerly of the king's navy, was one of those who sought to convey tokens to Captain Amasa Delano; but his intent, though undiscovered, being suspected, he was, on a pretence, made to retire out of sight, and at last into the hold, and there was made away with. This the negroes have since said; * * * that one of the ship-boys feeling, from Captain Amasa Delano's presence, some hopes of release, and not having enough prudence, dropped some chance word respecting his expectations, which being overheard and understood by a slave-boy with whom he was eating at the time, the latter struck him on the head with a knife, inflicting a bad wound, but of which the boy is now healing; that likewise, not long before the ship was brought to anchor, one of the seamen, steering at the time, endangered himself by letting the blacks remark some expression in his countenance, arising from a cause similar to the above; but this sailor, by his heedful after conduct, escaped; * * * that these statements are made to show the court that from the beginning to the end of the revolt, it was impossible for the deponent and his men to act otherwise than they did; * * * —that the third clerk, Hermenegildo Gandix, who before had been forced to live among the seamen, wearing a seaman's habit, and in all respects appearing to be one for the time, he, Gandix, was killed by a musket-ball fired through mistake from the boats before boarding; having in his fright run up the mizen-rigging, calling to the boats—"don't board," lest upon their boarding the negroes should kill him; that this inducing the Americans to believe he some way favoured the cause of the negroes, they fired two balls at him, so that he fell wounded from the rigging, and was drowned in the sea; * * * —that the young Don Joaquin, Marques de Aramboalaza, like Hermenegildo Gandix, the third clerk, was degraded to the of-

fice and appearance of a common seaman; that upon one occasion when Don Joaquin shrank, the negro Babo commanded
the Ashantee Lecbe to take tar and heat it, and pour it upon
Don Joaquin's hands; * * * —that Don Joaquin was killed
owing to another mistake of the Americans, but one impossible
to be avoided, as upon the approach of the boats, Don Joaquin,
with a hatchet tied edge out and upright to his hand, was made
by the negroes to appear on the bulwarks; whereupon, seen
with arms in his hands and in a questionable attitude, he was
shot for a renegade seamen; * * * —that on the person of Don
Joaquin was found secreted a jewel, which, by papers that were
discovered, proved to have been meant for the shrine of our
Lady of Mercy in Lima; a votive offering, beforehand prepared
and guarded, to attest his gratitude, when he should have
landed in Peru, his last destination, for the safe conclusion of
his entire voyage from Spain; * * * —that the jewel, with the
other effects of the late Don Joaquin, is in the custody of the
brethren of the Hospital de Sacerdotes, awaiting the disposition of the honourable court; * * * —that, owing to the condition of the deponent, as well as the haste in which the boats
departed for the attack, the Americans were not forewarned
that there were, among the apparent crew, a passenger and one
of the clerks disguised by the negro Babo; * * * —that, besides
the negroes killed in the action, some were killed after the capture and reanchoring at night, when shackled to the ring-bolts
on deck; that these deaths were committed by the sailors, ere
they could be prevented. That so soon as informed of it, Captain Amasa Delano used all his authority, and, in particular
with his own hand, struck down Martinez Gola, who, having
found a razor in the pocket of an old jacket of his, which one of
the shackled negroes had on, was aiming it at the negro's
throat; that the noble Captain Amasa Delano also wrenched
from the hand of Bartholomew Barlo a dagger, secreted at the
time of the massacre of the whites, with which he was in the
act of stabbing a shackled negro, who, the same day, with another negro, had thrown him down and jumped upon him; * * *
—that, for all the events, befalling through so long a time, during which the ship was in the hands of the negro Babo, he cannot here give account; but that, what he has said is the most
substantial of what occurs to him at present, and is the truth
under the oath which he has taken; which declaration he affirmed and ratified, after hearing it read to him.

He said that he is twenty-nine years of age, and broken in
body and mind; that when finally dismissed by the court, he
shall not return home to Chili, but betake himself to the monas-

tery on Mount Agonia without; and signed with his honour, and crossed himself, and, for the time, departed as he came, in his litter, with the monk Infelez, to the Hospital de Sacerdotes.

BENITO CERENO.

DOCTOR ROZAS.

If the Deposition have served as the key to fit into the lock of the complications which precede it, then, as a vault whose door has been flung back, the *San Dominick*'s hull lies open to-day.

Hitherto the nature of this narrative, besides rendering the intricacies in the beginning unavoidable, has more or less required that many things, instead of being set down in the order of occurrence, should be retrospectively, or irregularly given; this last is the case with the following passages, which will conclude the account:—

During the long, mild voyage to Lima, there was, as before hinted, a period during which the sufferer a little recovered his health, or, at least in some degree, his tranquillity. Ere the decided relapse which came, the two captains had many cordial conversations—their fraternal unreserve in singular contrast with former withdrawments.

Again and again it was repeated, how hard it had been to enact the part forced on the Spaniard by Babo.

"Ah, my dear friend," Don Benito once said, "at those very times when you thought me so morose and ungrateful, nay, when, as you now admit, you half thought me plotting your murder, at those very times my heart was frozen; I could not look at you, thinking of what, both on board this ship and your own, hung, from other hands, over my kind benefactor. And as God lives, Don Amasa, I know not whether desire for my own safety alone could have nerved me to that leap into your boat, had it not been for the thought that, did you, unenlightened, return to your ship, you, my best friend, with all who might be with you, stolen upon, that night, in your hammocks, would never in this world have wakened again. Do but think how you walked this deck, how you sat in this cabin, every inch of ground mined into honeycombs under you. Had I dropped the least hint, made the least advance toward an understanding between us, death, explosive death—yours as mine—would have ended the scene."

"True, true," cried Captain Delano, starting, "you have saved my life, Don Benito, more than I yours; saved it, too, against my knowledge and will."

"Nay, my friend," rejoined the Spaniard, courteous even to the point of religion, "God charmed your life, but you saved mine. To think of some things you did—those smilings and chattings, rash pointings and gesturings. For less than these, they slew my mate, Raneds; but you had the Prince of Heaven's safe-conduct through all ambuscades."

"Yes, all is owing to Providence, I know: but the temper of my mind that morning was more than commonly pleasant, while the sight of so much suffering, more apparent than real, added to my good-nature, compassion, and charity, happily interweaving the three. Had it been otherwise, doubtless, as you hint, some of my interferences might have ended unhappily enough. Besides, those feelings I spoke of enabled me to get the better of momentary distrust, at times when acuteness might have cost me my life, without saving another's. Only at the end did my suspicions get the better of me, and you know how wide of the mark they then proved."

"Wide, indeed," said Don Benito sadly; "you were with me all day; stood with me, sat with me, talked with me, looked at me, ate with me, drank with me; and yet, your last act was to clutch for a monster, not only an innocent man, but the most pitiable of all men. To such degree may malign machinations and deceptions impose. So far may even the best man err, in judging the conduct of one with the recesses of whose condition he is not acquainted. But you were forced to it; and you were in time undeceived. Would that, in both respects, it was so ever, and with all men."

"You generalise, Don Benito; and mournfully enough. But the past is past; why moralise upon it? Forget it. See, yon bright sun has forgotten it all, the blue sea, and the blue sky; these have turned over new leaves."

"Because they have no memory," he dejectedly replied; "because they are not human."

"But these mild Trades that now fan your cheek, do they not come with a human-like healing to you? Warm friends, steadfast friends are the Trades."

"With their steadfastness they but waft me to my tomb, señor," was the foreboding response.

"You are saved," cried Captain Delano, more and more astonished and pained; "you are saved: what has cast such a shadow upon you?"

"The negro."

There was silence, while the moody man sat, slowly and unconsciously gathering his mantle about him, as if it were a pall.

There was no more conversation that day.

But if the Spaniard's melancholy sometimes ended in muteness upon topics like the above, there were others upon which he never spoke at all; on which, indeed, all his old reserves were piled. Pass over the worst, and, only to elucidate, let an item or two of these be cited. The dress, so precise and costly, worn by him on the day whose events have been narrated, had not willingly been put on. And that silver-mounted sword, apparent symbol of despotic command, was not, indeed, a sword, but the ghost of one. The scabbard, artificially stiffened, was empty.

As for the black—whose brain, not body, had schemed and led the revolt, with the plot—his slight frame, inadequate to that which it held, had at once yielded to the superior muscular strength of his captor, in the boat. Seeing all was over, he uttered no sound, and could not be forced to. His aspect seemed to say, since I cannot do deeds, I will not speak words. Put in irons in the hold, with the rest, he was carried to Lima. During the passage, Don Benito did not visit him. Nor then, nor at any time after, would he look at him. Before the tribunal he refused. When pressed by the judges he fainted. On the testimony of the sailors alone rested the legal identity of Babo.

Some months after, dragged to the gibbet at the tail of a mule, the black met his voiceless end. The body was burned to ashes; but for many days the head, that hive of subtlety, fixed on a pole in the Plaza, met, unabashed, the gaze of the whites; and across the Plaza looked toward St. Bartholomew's church, in whose vaults slept then, as now, the recovered bones of Aranda: and across the Rimac bridge looked toward the monastery, on Mount Agonia without; where, three months after being dismissed by the court, Benito Cereno, borne on the bier, did, indeed, follow his leader.

From *Piazza Tales* (1856)

·Henry James·

DAISY MILLER: A STUDY

I

At the little town of Vevey, in Switzerland,[1] there is a particularly comfortable hotel; there are indeed many hotels, since the entertainment of tourists is the business of the place, which, as many travellers will remember, is seated upon the edge of a remarkably blue lake—a lake that it behoves every tourist to visit. The shore of the lake presents an unbroken array of establishments of this order, of every category, from the "grand hotel" of the newest fashion, with a chalk-white front, a hundred balconies, and a dozen flags flying from its roof, to the small Swiss pension of an elder day, with its name inscribed in German-looking lettering upon a pink or yellow wall and an awkward summer-house in the angle of the garden. One of the hotels at Vevey, however, is famous, even classical, being distinguished from many of its upstart neighbours by an air both of luxury and of maturity. In this region, through the month of June, American travellers are extremely numerous; it may be said indeed that Vevey assumes at that time some of the characteristics of an American watering-place. There are sights and sounds that evoke a vision, an echo, of Newport and Saratoga.[2] There is a flitting hither and thither of "stylish" young girls, a rustling of muslin flounces, a rattle of dance-music in the morning hours, a sound of high-pitched voices at all times. You receive an impression of these

1. Resort town at the northeast end of Lake Geneva, and the setting for Jean-Jacques Rousseau's *Nouvelle Héloise* (1761), a romance about the conflict between natural desires and social convention. James visited the area in 1872.
2. Newport, Rhode Island, and Saratoga Springs, New York, two of the most fashionable American resorts during the nineteenth century.

things at the excellent inn of the "Trois Couronnes," [3] and are transported in fancy to the Ocean House or to Congress Hall.[4] But at
the "Trois Couronnes," it must be added, there are other features
much at variance with these suggestions: neat German waiters who
look like secretaries of legation; Russian princesses sitting in the
garden; little Polish boys walking about, held by the hand, with
their governors; a view of the snowy crest of the Dent du Midi and
the picturesque towers of the Castle of Chillon.[5]

I hardly know whether it was the analogies or the differences that
were uppermost in the mind of a young American, who, two or
three years ago, sat in the garden of the "Trois Couronnes," looking
about him rather idly at some of the graceful objects I have mentioned. It was a beautiful summer morning, and in whatever fashion
the young American looked at things they must have seemed to him
charming. He had come from Geneva the day before, by the little
steamer, to see his aunt, who was staying at the hotel—Geneva having been for a long time his place of residence. But his aunt had a
headache—his aunt had almost always a headache—and she was
now shut up in her room smelling camphor, so that he was at liberty
to wander about. He was some seven-and-twenty years of age;
when his friends spoke of him they usually said that he was at
Geneva "studying." When his enemies spoke of him they said—but
after all he had no enemies: he was extremely amiable and generally liked. What I should say is simply that when certain persons
spoke of him they conveyed that the reason of his spending so
much time at Geneva was that he was extremely devoted to a lady
who lived there—a foreign lady, a person older than himself. Very
few Americans—truly I think none—had ever seen this lady, about
whom there were some singular stories. But Winterbourne had an
old attachment for the little capital of Calvinism; he had been put to
school there as a boy and had afterwards even gone, on trial—trial
of the grey old "Academy" on the steep and stony hillside—to college there; circumstances which had led to his forming a great
many youthful friendships. Many of these he had kept, and they
were a source of great satisfaction to him.

After knocking at his aunt's door and learning that she was indisposed he had taken a walk about the town and then he had come
in to his breakfast. He had now finished that repast, but was enjoying a small cup of coffee which had been served him on a little

3. "Three Crowns," a well-known hotel in Vevey.
4. Hotels in Newport and Saratoga Springs.
5. A tourist attraction on Lake Geneva. After Shelley and Byron had visited there in
1816, Byron immediately began his famous poem, "The Prisoner of Chillon." The
historic "prisoner," François Bonivard, or Bonnivard (1493–1570), was a reforming
priest who strove for the independence of Geneva. He was imprisoned in the Castle
from 1530 to 1535, and became a legendary martyr in the cause of liberty.

table in the garden by one of the waiters who looked like *attachés*. At last he finished his coffee and lit a cigarette. Presently a small boy came walking along the path—an urchin of nine or ten. The child, who was diminutive for his years, had an aged expression of countenance, a pale complexion and sharp little features. He was dressed in knickerbockers and had red stockings that displayed his poor little spindle-shanks; he also wore a brilliant red cravat. He carried in his hand a long alpenstock, the sharp point of which he thrust into everything he approached—the flower-beds, the garden-benches, the trains of the ladies' dresses. In front of Winterbourne he paused, looking at him with a pair of bright and penetrating little eyes.

"Will you give me a lump of sugar?" he asked in a small sharp hard voice—a voice immature and yet somehow not young.

Winterbourne glanced at the light table near him, on which his coffee-service rested, and saw that several morsels of sugar remained. "Yes, you may take one," he answered; "but I don't think too much sugar good for little boys."

This little boy stepped forward and carefully selected three of the coveted fragments, two of which he buried in the pocket of his knickerbockers, depositing the other as promptly in another place. He poked his alpenstock, lance-fashion, into Winterbourne's bench and tried to crack the lump of sugar with his teeth.

"Oh blazes; it's har-r-d!" he exclaimed, divesting vowel and consonants, pertinently enough, of any taint of softness.

Winterbourne had immediately gathered that he might have the honour of claiming him as a countryman. "Take care you don't hurt your teeth," he said paternally.

"I haven't [6] got any teeth to hurt. They've all come out. I've only got seven teeth. Mother counted them last night, and one came out right afterwards. She said she'd slap me if any more came out. I can't help it. It's this old Europe. It's the climate that makes them come out. In America they didn't come out. It's these hotels."

Winterbourne was much amused. "If you eat three lumps of sugar your mother will certainly slap you," he ventured.

"She's got to give me some candy then," rejoined his young interlocutor. "I can't get any candy here—any American candy. American candy's the best candy."

"And are American little boys the best little boys?" Winterbourne asked.

"I don't know. *I'm* an American boy," said the child.

"I see you're one of the best!" the young man laughed.

"Are you an American man?" pursued this vivacious infant. And

6. For the sake of consistency, James's "pure" contractions have been spliced (e.g., "have n't" becomes "haven't").

then on his friend's affirmative reply, "American men are the best,"
he declared with assurance.

His companion thanked him for the compliment, and the child,
who had now got astride of his alpenstock, stood looking about him
while he attacked another lump of sugar. Winterbourne wondered
if he himself had been like this in his infancy, for he had been
brought to Europe at about the same age.

"Here comes my sister!" cried his young compatriot. "She's an
American girl, you bet!"

Winterbourne looked along the path and saw a beautiful young
lady advancing. "American girls are the best girls," he thereupon
cheerfully remarked to his visitor.

"My sister ain't the best!" the child promptly returned. "She's
always blowing at me."

"I imagine that's your fault, not hers," said Winterbourne. The
young lady meanwhile had drawn near. She was dressed in white
muslin, with a hundred frills and flounces and knots of pale-
coloured ribbon. Bareheaded, she balanced in her hand a large parasol with a deep border of embroidery; and she was strikingly, admirably pretty. "How pretty they are!" thought our friend, who
straightened himself in his seat as if he were ready to rise.

The young lady paused in front of his bench, near the parapet of
the garden, which overlooked the lake. The small boy had now converted his alpenstock into a vaulting-pole, by the aid of which he
was springing about in the gravel and kicking it up not a little.
"Why Randolph," she freely began, "what *are* you doing?"

"I'm going up the Alps!" cried Randolph. "This is the way!" And
he gave another extravagant jump, scattering the pebbles about
Winterbourne's ears.

"That's the way they come down," said Winterbourne.

"He's an American man!" proclaimed Randolph in his harsh little
voice.

The young lady gave no heed to this circumstance, but looked
straight at her brother. "Well, I guess you'd better be quiet," she
simply observed.

It seemed to Winterbourne that he had been in a manner presented. He got up and stepped slowly toward the charming creature, throwing away his cigarette. "This little boy and I have made
acquaintance," he said with great civility. In Geneva, as he had
been perfectly aware, a young man wasn't at liberty to speak to a
young unmarried lady save under certain rarely-occurring conditions; but here at Vevey what conditions could be better than
these?—a pretty American girl coming to stand in front of you in a
garden with all the confidence in life. This pretty American girl,
whatever that might prove, on hearing Winterbourne's observation

simply glanced at him; she then turned her head and looked over the parapet, at the lake and the opposite mountains. He wondered whether he had gone too far, but decided that he must gallantly advance rather than retreat. While he was thinking of something else to say the young lady turned again to the little boy, whom she addressed quite as if they were alone together. "I should like to know where you got that pole."

"I bought it!" Randolph shouted.

"You don't mean to say you're going to take it to Italy!"

"Yes, I'm going to take it t' Italy!" the child rang out.

She glanced over the front of her dress and smoothed out a knot or two of ribbon. Then she gave her sweet eyes to the prospect again. "Well, I guess you'd better leave it somewhere," she dropped after a moment.

"Are you going to Italy?" Winterbourne now decided very respectfully to enquire.

She glanced at him with lovely remoteness. "Yes, sir," she then replied. And she said nothing more.

"And are you—a—thinking of the Simplon?" [7] he pursued with a slight drop of assurance.

"I don't know," she said. "I suppose it's some mountain. Randolph, what mountain are we thinking of?"

"Thinking of?"—the boy stared.

"Why going right over."

"Going to where?" he demanded.

"Why right down to Italy"—Winterbourne felt vague emulations.

"I don't know," said Randolph. "I don't want to go t' Italy. I want to go to America."

"Oh Italy's a beautiful place!" the young man laughed.

"Can you get candy there?" Randolph asked of all the echoes.

"I hope not," said his sister. "I guess you've had enough candy, and mother thinks so too."

"I haven't had any for ever so long—for a hundred weeks!" cried the boy, still jumping about.

The young lady inspected her flounces and smoothed her ribbons again; and Winterbourne presently risked an observation on the beauty of the view. He was ceasing to be in doubt, for he had begun to perceive that she was really not in the least embarrassed. She might be cold, she might be austere, she might even be prim; for that was apparently—he had already so generalised—what the most "distant" American girls did: they came and planted themselves straight in front of you to show how rigidly unapproachable they were. There hadn't been the slightest flush in her fresh

7. The Simplon Pass through the Alps into Italy.

fairness however; so that she was clearly neither offended nor fluttered. Only she was composed—he had seen that before too—of charming little parts that didn't match and that made no *ensemble*; and if she looked another way when he spoke to her, and seemed not particularly to hear him, this was simply her habit, her manner, the result of her having no idea whatever of "form" (with such a tell-tale appendage as Randolph where in the world would she have got it?) in any such connexion. As he talked a little more and pointed out some of the objects of interest in the view, with which she appeared wholly unacquainted, she gradually, none the less, gave him more of the benefit of her attention; and then he saw that act unqualified by the faintest shadow of reserve. It wasn't however what would have been called a "bold" front that she presented, for her expression was as decently limpid as the very cleanest water. Her eyes were the very prettiest conceivable, and indeed Winterbourne hadn't for a long time seen anything prettier than his fair country-woman's various features—her complexion, her nose, her ears, her teeth. He took a great interest generally in that range of effects and was addicted to noting and, as it were, recording them; so that in regard to this young lady's face he made several observations. It wasn't at all insipid, yet at the same time wasn't pointedly—what point, on earth, could she ever make?—expressive; and though it offered such a collection of small finenesses and neatnesses he mentally accused it—very forgivingly—of a want of finish. He thought nothing more likely than that its wearer would have had her own experience of the action of her charms, as she would certainly have acquired a resulting confidence; but even should she depend on this for her main amusement her bright sweet superficial little visage gave out neither mockery nor irony. Before long it became clear that, however these things might be, she was much disposed to conversation. She remarked to Winterbourne that they were going to Rome for the winter—she and her mother and Randolph. She asked him if he was a "real American"; she wouldn't have taken him for one; he seemed more like a German—this flower was gathered as from a large field of comparison—especially when he spoke. Winterbourne, laughing, answered that he had met Germans who spoke like Americans, but not, so far as he remembered, any American with the resemblance she noted. Then he asked her if she mightn't be more at ease should she occupy the bench he had just quitted. She answered that she liked hanging round, but she none the less resignedly, after a little, dropped to the bench. She told him she was from New York State—"if you know where that is"; but our friend really quickened this current by catching hold of her small slippery brother and making him stand a few minutes by his side.

"Tell me your honest name, my boy." So he artfully proceeded.

In response to which the child was indeed unvarnished truth. "Randolph C. Miller. And I'll tell you hers." With which he levelled his alpenstock at his sister.

"You had better wait till you're asked!" said this young lady quite at her leisure.

"I should like very much to know *your* name," Winterbourne made free to reply.

"Her name's Daisy Miller!" cried the urchin. "But that ain't her real name; that ain't her name on her cards."

"It's a pity you haven't got one of my cards!" Miss Miller quite as naturally remarked.

"Her real name's Annie P. Miller," the boy went on.

It seemed, all amazingly, to do her good. "Ask him *his* now"— and she indicated their friend.

But to this point Randolph seemed perfectly indifferent; he continued to supply information with regard to his own family. "My father's name is Ezra B. Miller. My father ain't in Europe—he's in a better place than Europe." Winterbourne for a moment supposed this the manner in which the child had been taught to intimate that Mr. Miller had been removed to the sphere of celestial rewards. But Randolph immediately added: "My father's in Schenectady. He's got a big business. My father's rich, you bet."

"Well!" ejaculated Miss Miller, lowering her parasol and looking at the embroidered border. Winterbourne presently released the child, who departed, dragging his alpenstock along the path. "He don't like Europe," said the girl as with an artless instinct for historic truth. "He wants to go back."

"To Schenectady, you mean?"

"Yes, he wants to go right home. He hasn't got any boys here. There's one boy here, but he always goes round with a teacher. They won't let him play."

"And your brother hasn't any teacher?" Winterbourne enquired.

It tapped, at a touch, the spring of confidence. "Mother thought of getting him one—to travel round with us. There was a lady told her of a very good teacher; an American lady—perhaps you know her— Mrs. Sanders. I think she came from Boston. She told her of this teacher, and we thought of getting him to travel round with us. But Randolph said he didn't want a teacher travelling round with us. He said he wouldn't have lessons when he was in the cars. And we *are* in the cars about half the time. There was an English lady we met in the cars—I think her name was Miss Featherstone; perhaps you know her. She wanted to know why I didn't give Randolph lessons—give him 'instruction,' she called it. I guess he could give me more instruction than I could give him. He's very smart."

"Yes," said Winterbourne; "he seems very smart."

"Mother's going to get a teacher for him as soon as we get t' Italy. Can you get good teachers in Italy?"

"Very good, I should think," Winterbourne hastened to reply.

"Or else she's going to find some school. He ought to learn some more. He's only nine. He's going to college." And in this way Miss Miller continued to converse upon the affairs of her family and upon other topics. She sat there with her extremely pretty hands, ornamented with very brilliant rings, folded in her lap, and with her pretty eyes now resting upon those of Winterbourne, now wandering over the garden, the people who passed before her and the beautiful view. She addressed her new acquaintance as if she had known him a long time. He found it very pleasant. It was many years since he had heard a young girl talk so much. It might have been said of this wandering maiden who had come and sat down beside him upon a bench that she chattered. She was very quiet, she sat in a charming tranquil attitude; but her lips and her eyes were constantly moving. She had a soft slender agreeable voice, and her tone was distinctly sociable. She gave Winterbourne a report of her movements and intentions, and those of her mother and brother, in Europe, and enumerated in particular the various hotels at which they had stopped. "That English lady in the cars," she said—"Miss Featherstone—asked me if we didn't all live in hotels in America. I told her I had never been in so many hotels in my life as since I came to Europe. I've never seen so many—it's nothing but hotels." But Miss Miller made this remark with no querulous accent; she appeared to be in the best humour with everything. She declared that the hotels were very good when once you got used to their ways and that Europe was perfectly entrancing. She wasn't disappointed—not a bit. Perhaps it was because she had heard so much about it before. She had ever so many intimate friends who had been there ever so many times, and that way she had got thoroughly posted. And then she had had ever so many dresses and things from Paris. Whenever she put on a Paris dress she felt as if she were in Europe.

"It was a kind of a wishing-cap," Winterbourne smiled.

"Yes," said Miss Miller at once and without examining this analogy; "it always made me wish I was here. But I needn't have done that for dresses. I'm sure they send all the pretty ones to America; you see the most frightful things here. The only thing I don't like," she proceeded, "is the society. There ain't any society—or if there is I don't know where it keeps itself. Do you? I suppose there's some society somewhere, but I haven't seen anything of it. I'm very fond of society and I've always had plenty of it. I don't mean only in Schenectady, but in New York. I used to go to New York every winter. In New York I had lots of society. Last winter I had seventeen dinners given me, and three of them were by gentlemen," added Daisy Miller. "I've more friends in New York than in Schenectady—more gentlemen friends; and more young lady friends too," she resumed in a moment. She paused again for an instant; she was looking at Winterbourne with all her prettiness in her frank gay eyes and in her clear rather uniform smile. "I've always had," she said, "a great deal of gentlemen's society."

Poor Winterbourne was amused and perplexed—above all he was charmed. He had never yet heard a young girl express herself in just this fashion; never at least save in cases where to say such things was to have at the same time some rather complicated consciousness about them. And yet was he to accuse Miss Daisy Miller of an actual or a potential *arrière-pensée*,[8] as they said at Geneva? He felt he had lived at Geneva so long as to have got morally muddled; he had lost the right sense for the young American tone. Never indeed since he had grown old enough to appreciate things had he encountered a young compatriot of so "strong" a type as this. Certainly she was very charming, but how extraordinarily communicative and how tremendously easy! Was she simply a pretty girl from New York State—were they all like that, the pretty girls who had had a good deal of gentlemen's society? Or was she also a designing, an audacious, in short an expert young person? Yes, his instinct for such a question had ceased to serve him, and his reason could but mislead. Miss Daisy Miller looked extremely innocent. Some people had told him that after all American girls *were* exceedingly innocent, and others had told him that after all they weren't. He must on the whole take Miss Daisy Miller for a flirt—a pretty American flirt. He had never as yet had relations with representatives of that class. He had known here in Europe two or three women—persons older than Miss Daisy Miller and provided, for respectability's sake, with husbands—who were great coquettes; dangerous terrible women with whom one's light commerce might indeed take a serious turn. But this charming apparition wasn't a coquette in that sense; she was very unsophisticated; she was only a pretty American flirt. Winterbourne was almost grateful for having found the formula that applied to Miss Daisy Miller. He leaned back in his seat; he remarked to himself that she had the finest little nose he had ever seen; he wondered what were the regular conditions and limitations of one's intercourse with a pretty American flirt. It presently became apparent that he was on the way to learn.

"Have you been to that old castle?" the girl soon asked, pointing with her parasol to the far-shining walls of the Château de Chillon.

8. Ulterior motive.

"Yes, formerly, more than once," said Winterbourne. "You too, I suppose, have seen it?"

"No, we haven't been there. I want to go there dreadfully. Of course I mean to go there. I wouldn't go away from here without having seen that old castle."

"It's a very pretty excursion," the young man returned, "and very easy to make. You can drive, you know, or you can go by the little steamer."

"You can go in the cars," said Miss Miller.

"Yes, you can go in the cars," Winterbourne assented.

"Our courier says they take you right up to the castle," she continued. "We were going last week, but mother gave out. She suffers dreadfully from dyspepsia. She said she couldn't any more go—!" But this sketch of Mrs. Miller's plea remained unfinished. "Randolph wouldn't go either; he says he don't think much of old castles. But I guess we'll go this week if we can get Randolph."

"Your brother isn't interested in ancient monuments?" Winterbourne indulgently asked.

He now drew her, as he guessed she would herself have said, every time. "Why no, he says he don't care much about old castles. He's only nine. He wants to stay at the hotel. Mother's afraid to leave him alone, and the courier won't stay with him; so we haven't been to many places. But it will be too bad if we don't go up there." And Miss Miller pointed again at the Château de Chillon.

"I should think it might be arranged," Winterbourne was thus emboldened to reply. "Couldn't you get some one to stay—for the afternoon—with Randolph?"

Miss Miller looked at him a moment, and then with all serenity, "I wish *you'd* stay with him!" she said.

He pretended to consider it. "I'd much rather go to Chillon with you."

"With me?" she asked without a shadow of emotion.

She didn't rise blushing, as a young person at Geneva would have done; and yet, conscious that he had gone very far, he thought it possible she had drawn back. "And with your mother," he answered very respectfully.

But it seemed that both his audacity and his respect were lost on Miss Daisy Miller. "I guess mother wouldn't go—for *you*," she smiled. "And she ain't much *bent* on going, anyway. She don't like to ride round in the afternoon." After which she familiarly proceeded: "but did you really mean what you said just now—that you'd like to go up there?"

"Most earnestly I meant it," Winterbourne declared.

"Then we may arrange it. If mother will stay with Randolph I guess Eugenio will."

"Eugenio?" the young man echoed.

"Eugenio's our courier. He doesn't like to stay with Randolph—he's the most fastidious man I ever saw. But he's a splendid courier. I guess he'll stay at home with Randolph if mother does, and then we can go to the castle."

Winterbourne reflected for an instant as lucidly as possible: "we" could only mean Miss Miller and himself. This prospect seemed almost too good to believe; he felt as if he ought to kiss the young lady's hand. Possibly he would have done so,—and quite spoiled his chance; but at this moment another person—presumably Eugenio—appeared. A tall handsome man, with superb whiskers and wearing a velvet morning-coat and voluminous watch-guard, approached the young lady, looking sharply at her companion. "Oh Eugenio!" she said with the friendliest accent.

Eugenio had eyed Winterbourne from head to foot; he now bowed gravely to Miss Miller. "I have the honour to inform Mademoiselle that luncheon's on table."

Mademoiselle slowly rose. "See here, Eugenio, I'm going to that old castle anyway."

"To the Château de Chillon, Mademoiselle?" the courier enquired. "Mademoiselle has made arrangements?" he added in a tone that struck Winterbourne as impertinent.

Eugenio's tone apparently threw, even to Miss Miller's own apprehension, a slightly ironical light on her position. She turned to Winterbourne with the slightest blush. "You won't back out?"

"I shall not be happy till we go!" he protested.

"And you're staying in this hotel?" she went on. "And you're really American?"

The courier still stood there with an effect of offence for the young man so far as the latter saw in it a tacit reflexion on Miss Miller's behaviour and an insinuation that she "picked up" acquaintances. "I shall have the honour of presenting to you a person who'll tell you all about me," he said, smiling, and referring to his aunt.

"Oh well, we'll go some day," she beautifully answered; with which she gave him a smile and turned away. She put up her parasol and walked back to the inn beside Eugenio. Winterbourne stood watching her, and as she moved away, drawing her muslin furbelows over the walk, he spoke to himself of her natural elegance.

II

He had, however, engaged to do more than proved feasible in promising to present his aunt, Mrs. Costello, to Miss Daisy Miller. As soon as that lady had got better of her headache he waited on her in her apartment and, after a show of the proper solicitude about her health, asked if she had noticed in the hotel an American family—a mamma, a daughter and an obstreperous little boy.

"An obstreperous little boy and a preposterous big courier?" said Mrs. Costello. "Oh yes, I've noticed them. Seen them, heard them and kept out of their way." Mrs. Costello was a widow of fortune, a person of much distinction and who frequently intimated that if she hadn't been so dreadfully liable to sick-headaches she would probably have left a deeper impress on her time. She had a long pale face, a high nose and a great deal of very striking white hair, which she wore in large puffs and over the top of her head. She had two sons married in New York and another who was now in Europe. This young man was amusing himself at Homburg and, though guided by his taste, was rarely observed to visit any particular city at the moment selected by his mother for her appearance there. Her nephew, who had come to Vevey expressly to see her, was therefore more attentive than, as she said, her very own. He had imbibed at Geneva the idea that one must be irreproachable in all such forms. Mrs. Costello hadn't seen him for many years and was now greatly pleased with him, manifesting her approbation by initiating him into many of the secrets of that social sway which, as he could see she would like him to think, she exerted from her stronghold in Forty-Second Street. She admitted that she was very exclusive, but if he had been better acquainted with New York he would see that one had to be. And her picture of the minutely hierarchical constitution of the society of that city, which she presented to him in many different lights, was, to Winterbourne's imagination, almost oppressively striking.

He at once recognised from her tone that Miss Daisy Miller's place in the social scale was low. "I'm afraid you don't approve of them," he pursued in reference to his new friends.

"They're horribly common"—it was perfectly simple. "They're the sort of Americans that one does one's duty by just ignoring."

"Ah you just ignore them?"—the young man took it in.

"I can't *not*, my dear Frederick. I wouldn't if I hadn't to, but I have to."

"The little girl's very pretty," he went on in a moment.

"Of course she's very pretty. But she's of the last crudity."

"I see what you mean of course," he allowed after another pause.

"She has that charming look they all have," his aunt resumed. "I can't think where they pick it up; and she dresses in perfection—no, you don't know how well she dresses. I can't think where they get their taste."

"But, my dear aunt, she's not, after all, a Comanche savage."

"She is a young lady," said Mrs. Costello, "who has an intimacy with her mamma's courier?"

"An 'intimacy' with him?" Ah there it was!

"There's no other name for such a relation. But the skinny little mother's just as bad! They treat the courier as a familiar friend—as a gentleman and a scholar. I shouldn't wonder if he dines with them. Very likely they've never seen a man with such good manners, such fine clothes, so *like* a gentleman—or a scholar. He probably corresponds to the young lady's idea of a count. He sits with them in the garden of an evening. I think he smokes in their faces."

Winterbourne listened with interest to these disclosures; they helped him to make up his mind about Miss Daisy. Evidently she was rather wild. "Well," he said, "I'm not a courier and I didn't smoke in her face, and yet she was very charming to me."

"You had better have mentioned at first," Mrs. Costello returned with dignity, "that you had made her valuable acquaintance."

"We simply met in the garden and talked a bit."

"By appointment—no? Ah that's still to come! Pray what did you say?"

"I said I should take the liberty of introducing her to my admirable aunt."

"Your admirable aunt's a thousand times obliged to you."

"It was to guarantee my respectability."

"And pray who's to guarantee hers?"

"Ah you're cruel!" said the young man. "She's a very innocent girl."

"You don't say that as if you believed it," Mrs. Costello returned.

"She's completely uneducated," Winterbourne acknowledged, "but she's wonderfully pretty, and in short she's very nice. To prove I believe it I'm going to take her to the Château de Chillon."

Mrs. Costello made a wondrous face. "You two are going off there together? I should say it proved just the contrary. How long had you known her, may I ask, when this interesting project was formed? You haven't been twenty-four hours in the house."

"I had known her half an hour!" Winterbourne smiled.

"Then she's just what I supposed."

"And what do you suppose?"

"Why that she's a horror."

Our youth was silent for some moments. "You really think then," he presently began, and with a desire for trustworthy information, "you really think that—" But he paused again while his aunt waited.

"Think what, sir?"

"That she's the sort of young lady who expects a man sooner or later to—well, we'll call it carry her off?"

"I haven't the least idea what such young ladies expect a man to do. But I really consider you had better not meddle with little

American girls who are uneducated, as you mildly put it. You've lived too long out of the country. You'll be sure to make some great mistake. You're too innocent."

"My dear aunt, not so much as that comes to!" he protested with a laugh and a curl of his moustache.

"You're too guilty then!"

He continued all thoughtfully to finger the ornament in question. "You won't let the poor girl know you then?" he asked at last.

"Is it literally true that she's going to the Château de Chillon with you?"

"I've no doubt she fully intends it."

"Then, my dear Frederick," said Mrs. Costello, "I must decline the honour of her acquaintance. I'm an old woman, but I'm not too old—thank heaven—to be honestly shocked!"

"But don't they all do these things—the little American girls at home?" Winterbourne enquired.

Mrs. Costello stared a moment. "I should like to see my grand-daughters do them!" she then grimly returned.

This seemed to throw some light on the matter, for Winterbourne remembered to have heard his pretty cousins in New York, the daughters of this lady's two daughters, called "tremendous flirts." If therefore Miss Daisy Miller exceeded the liberal licence allowed to these young women it was probable she did go even by the American allowance rather far. Winterbourne was impatient to see her again, and it vexed, it even a little humiliated him, that he shouldn't by instinct appreciate her justly.

Though so impatient to see her again he hardly knew what ground he should give for his aunt's refusal to become acquainted with her; but he discovered promptly enough that with Miss Daisy Miller there was no great need of walking on tiptoe. He found her that evening in the garden, wandering about in the warm starlight after the manner of an indolent sylph and swinging to and fro the largest fan he had ever beheld. It was ten o'clock. He had dined with his aunt, had been sitting with her since dinner, and had just taken leave of her till the morrow. His young friend frankly rejoiced to renew their intercourse; she pronounced it the stupidest evening she had ever passed.

"Have you been all alone?" he asked with no intention of an epigram and no effect of her perceiving one.

"I've been walking round with mother. But mother gets tired walking round," Miss Miller explained.

"Has she gone to bed?"

"No, she doesn't like to go to bed. She doesn't sleep scarcely any—not three hours. She says she doesn't know how she lives. She's dreadfully nervous. I guess she sleeps more than she thinks.

She's gone somewhere after Randolph; she wants to try to get him to go to bed. He doesn't like to go to bed."

The soft impartiality of her *constatations*,[9] as Winterbourne would have termed them, was a thing by itself—exquisite little fatalist as they seemed to make her. "Let us hope she'll persuade him," he encouragingly said.

"Well, she'll talk to him all she can—but he doesn't like her to talk to him": with which Miss Daisy opened and closed her fan. "She's going to try to get Eugenio to talk to him. But Randolph ain't afraid of Eugenio. Eugenio's a splendid courier, but he can't make much impression on Randolph! I don't believe he'll go to bed before eleven." Her detachment from any invidious judgement of this was, to her companion's sense, inimitable; and it appeared that Randolph's vigil was in fact triumphantly prolonged, for Winterbourne attended her in her stroll for some time without meeting her mother. "I've been looking round for that lady you want to introduce me to," she resumed—"I guess she's your aunt." Then on his admitting the fact and expressing some curiosity as to how she had learned it, she said she had heard all about Mrs. Costello from the chambermaid. She was very quiet and very *comme il faut*; [10] she wore white puffs; she spoke to no one and she never dined at the common table. Every two days she had a headache. "I think that's a lovely description, headache and all!" said Miss Daisy, chattering along in her thin gay voice. "I want to know her ever so much. I know just what *your* aunt would be; I know I'd like her. She'd be very exclusive. I like a lady to be exclusive; I'm dying to be exclusive myself. Well, I guess we *are* exclusive, mother and I. We don't speak to any one—or they don't speak to us. I suppose it's about the same thing. Anyway, I shall be ever so glad to meet your aunt."

Winterbourne was embarrassed—he could but trump up some evasion. "She'd be most happy, but I'm afraid those tiresome headaches are always to be reckoned with."

The girl looked at him through the fine dusk. "Well, I suppose she doesn't have a headache every day."

He had to make the best of it. "She tells me she wonderfully does." He didn't know what else to say.

Miss Miller stopped and stood looking at him. Her prettiness was still visible in the darkness; she kept flapping to and fro her enormous fan. "She doesn't want to know me!" she then lightly broke out. "Why don't you say so? You needn't be afraid. *I'm* not afraid!" And she quite crowed for the fun of it.

Winterbourne distinguished however a wee false note in this: he

9. Declarations, statements.
10. Proper, decorous.

was touched, shocked, mortified by it. "My dear young lady, she knows no one. She goes through life immured. It's her wretched health."

The young girl walked on a few steps in the glee of the thing. "You needn't be afraid," she repeated. "Why should she want to know me?" Then she paused again; she was close to the parapet of the garden, and in front of her was the starlit lake. There was a vague sheen on its surface, and in the distance were dimly-seen mountain forms. Daisy Miller looked out at these great lights and shades and again proclaimed a gay indifference—"Gracious! she *is* exclusive!" Winterbourne wondered if she were seriously wounded and for a moment almost wished her sense of injury might be such as to make it becoming in him to reassure and comfort her. He had a pleasant sense that she would be all accessible to a respectful tenderness at that moment. He felt quite ready to sacrifice his aunt— conversationally; to acknowledge she was a proud rude woman and to make the point that they needn't mind her. But before he had time to commit himself to this questionable mixture of gallantry and impiety, the young lady, resuming her walk, gave an exclamation in quite another tone. "Well, here's mother! I guess she *hasn't* got Randolph to go to bed." The figure of a lady appeared, at a distance, very indistinct in the darkness; it advanced with a slow and wavering step and then suddenly seemed to pause.

"Are you sure it's your mother? Can you make her out in this thick dusk?" Winterbourne asked.

"Well," the girl laughed, "I guess I know my own mother! And when she has got on my shawl too. She's always wearing my things."

The lady in question, ceasing now to approach, hovered vaguely about the spot at which she had checked her steps.

"I'm afraid your mother doesn't see you," said Winterbourne. "Or perhaps," he added—thinking, with Miss Miller, the joke permissible—"perhaps she feels guilty about your shawl."

"Oh, it's a fearful old thing!" his companion placidly answered. "I told her she could wear it if she didn't mind looking like a fright. She won't come here because she sees you."

"Ah then," said Winterbourne, "I had better leave you."

"Oh no—come on!" the girl insisted.

"I'm afraid your mother doesn't approve of my walking with you."

She gave him, he thought, the oddest glance. "It isn't for me; it's for you—that is it's for *her*. Well, I don't know who it's for! But mother doesn't like any of my gentlemen friends. She's right down timid. She always makes a fuss if I introduce a gentleman. But I *do* introduce them—almost always. If I didn't introduce my gentle-

men friends to mother," Miss Miller added, in her small flat mono-
tone, "I shouldn't think I was natural."

"Well, to introduce me," Winterbourne remarked, "you must
know my name." And he proceeded to pronounce it.

"Oh my—I can't say all that!" cried his companion, much
amused. But by this time they had come up to Mrs. Miller, who, as
they drew near, walked to the parapet of the garden and leaned on
it, looking intently at the lake and presenting her back to them.
"Mother!" said the girl in a tone of decision—upon which the elder
lady turned round. "Mr. Frederick Forsyth Winterbourne," said the
latter's young friend, repeating his lesson of a moment before and
introducing him very frankly and prettily. "Common" she might be,
as Mrs. Costello had pronounced her; yet what provision was made
by that epithet for her queer little native grace?

Her mother was a small spare light person, with a wandering eye,
a scarce perceptible nose, and, as to make up for it, an unmistakeable forehead, decorated—but too far back, as Winterbourne mentally described it—with thin much-frizzled hair. Like her daughter
Mrs. Miller was dressed with extreme elegance; she had enormous
diamonds in her ears. So far as the young man could observe, she
gave him no greeting—she certainly wasn't looking at him. Daisy
was near her, pulling her shawl straight. "What are you doing, poking round here?" this young lady enquired—yet by no means with
the harshness of accent her choice of words might have implied.

"Well, I don't know"—and the new-comer turned to the lake
again.

"I shouldn't think you'd want that shawl!" Daisy familiarly proceeded.

"Well—I do!" her mother answered with a sound that partook for
Winterbourne of an odd strain between mirth and woe.

"Did you get Randolph to go to bed?" Daisy asked.

"No, I couldn't induce him"—and Mrs. Miller seemed to confess
to the same mild fatalism as her daughter. "He wants to talk to the
waiter. He *likes* to talk to that waiter."

"I was just telling Mr. Winterbourne," the girl went on; and to
the young man's ear her tone might have indicated that she had
been uttering his name all her life.

"Oh yes!" he concurred—"I've the pleasure of knowing your
son."

Randolph's mamma was silent; she kept her attention on the lake.
But at last a sigh broke from her. "Well, I don't see how he lives!"

"Anyhow, it isn't so bad as it was at Dover," Daisy at least
opined.

"And what occurred at Dover?" Winterbourne desired to know.

"He wouldn't go to bed at all. I guess he sat up all night—in the public parlour. He wasn't in bed at twelve o'clock: it seemed as if he couldn't budge."

"It was half-past twelve when *I* gave up," Mrs. Miller recorded with passionless accuracy.

It was of great interest to Winterbourne. "Does he sleep much during the day?"

"I guess he doesn't sleep *very* much," Daisy rejoined.

"I wish he just *would!*" said her mother. "It seems as if he *must* make it up somehow."

"Well, I guess it's we that make it up. I think he's real tiresome," Daisy pursued.

After which, for some moments, there was silence. "Well, Daisy Miller," the elder lady then unexpectedly broke out, "I shouldn't think you'd want to talk against you own brother!"

"Well, he *is* tiresome, mother," said the girl, but with no sharpness of insistence.

"Well, he's only nine," Mrs. Miller lucidly urged.

"Well, he wouldn't go up to that castle, anyway," her daughter replied as for accommodation. "I'm going up there with Mr. Winterbourne."

To this announcement, very placidly made, Daisy's parent offered no response. Winterbourne took for granted on this that she opposed such a course; but he said to himself at the same time that she was a simple easily-managed person and that a few deferential protestations would modify her attitude. "Yes," he therefore interposed, "your daughter has kindly allowed me the honour of being her guide."

Mrs. Miller's wandering eyes attached themselves with an appealing air to her other companion, who, however, strolled a few steps further, gently humming to herself. "I presume you'll go in the cars," she then quite colourlessly remarked.

"Yes, or in the boat," said Winterbourne.

"Well, of course I don't know," Mrs. Miller returned. "I've never been up to that castle."

"It is a pity you shouldn't go," he observed, beginning to feel reassured as to her opposition. And yet he was quite prepared to find that as a matter of course she meant to accompany her daughter.

It was on this view accordingly that light was projected for him. "We've been thinking ever so much about going, but it seems as if we couldn't. Of course Daisy—she wants to go round everywhere. But there's a lady here—I don't know her name—she says she shouldn't think we'd want to go to see castles *here;* she should think we'd want to wait till we got t' Italy. It seems as if there would be so many there," continued Mrs. Miller with an air of increasing confidence. "Of course we only want to see the principal ones. We visited several in England," she presently added.

"Ah yes, in England there are beautiful castles," said Winterbourne. "But Chillon here is very well worth seeing."

"Well, if Daisy feels up to it—" said Mrs. Miller in a tone that seemed to break under the burden of such conceptions. "It seems as if there's nothing she won't undertake."

"Oh I'm pretty sure she'll enjoy it!" Winterbourne declared. And he desired more and more to make it a certainty that he was to have the privilege of a *tête-à-tête* [11] with the young lady who was still strolling along in front of them and softly vocalising. "You're not disposed, madam," he enquired, "to make the so interesting excursion yourself?"

So addressed Daisy's mother looked at him an instant with a certain scared obliquity and then walked forward in silence. Then, "I guess she had better go alone," she said simply.

It gave him occasion to note that this was a very different type of maternity from that of the vigilant matrons who massed themselves in the forefront of social intercourse in the dark old city at the other end of the lake. But his meditations were interrupted by hearing his name very distinctly pronounced by Mrs. Miller's unprotected daughter. "Mr. Winterbourne!" she piped from a considerable distance.

"Mademoiselle!" said the young man.

"Don't you want to take me out in a boat?"

"At present?" he asked.

"Why of course!" she gaily returned.

"Well, Annie Miller!" exclaimed her mother.

"I beg you, madam, to let her go," he hereupon eagerly pleaded; so instantly had he been struck with the romantic side of this chance to guide through the summer starlight a skiff freighted with a fresh and beautiful young girl.

"I shouldn't think she'd want to," said her mother. "I should think she'd rather go indoors."

"I'm sure Mr. Winterbourne wants to *take* me," Daisy declared. "He's so awfully devoted!"

"I'll row you over to Chillon under the stars."

"I don't believe it!" Daisy laughed.

"Well!" the elder lady again gasped, as in rebuke of this freedom.

"You haven't spoken to me for half an hour," her daughter went on.

"I've been having some very pleasant conversation with your mother," Winterbourne replied.

11. Private conversation.

"Oh pshaw! I want you to take me out in a boat!" Daisy went on as if nothing else had been said. They had all stopped and she had turned round and was looking at her friend. Her face wore a charming smile, her pretty eyes gleamed in the darkness, she swung her great fan about. No, he felt, it was impossible to be prettier than that.

"There are half a dozen boats moored at that landing-place," and he pointed to a range of steps that descended from the garden to the lake. "If you'll do me the honour to accept my arm we'll go and select one of them."

She stood there smiling; she threw back her head; she laughed as for the drollery of this. "I like a gentleman to be formal!"

"I assure you it's a formal offer."

"I was bound I'd make you say something," Daisy agreeably mocked.

"You see it's not very difficult," said Winterbourne. "But I'm afraid you're chaffing me."

"I think not, sir," Mrs. Miller shyly pleaded.

"Do then let me give you a row," he persisted to Daisy.

"It's quite lovely, the way you say that!" she cried in reward.

"It will be still more lovely to do it."

"Yes, it would be lovely!" But she made no movement to accompany him; she only remained an elegant image of free light irony.

"I guess you'd better find out what time it is," her mother impartially contributed.

"It's eleven o'clock, Madam," said a voice with a foreign accent out of the neighbouring darkness; and Winterbourne, turning, recognised the florid personage he had already seen in attendance. He had apparently just approached.

"Oh Eugenio," said Daisy, "I'm going out with Mr. Winterbourne in a boat!"

Eugenio bowed. "At this hour of the night, Mademoiselle?"

"I'm going with Mr. Winterbourne," she repeated with her shining smile. "I'm going this very minute."

"Do tell her she can't, Eugenio," Mrs. Miller said to the courier.

"I think you had better not go out in a boat, Mademoiselle," the man declared.

Winterbourne wished to goodness this pretty girl were not on such familiar terms with her courier; but he said nothing, and she meanwhile added to his ground. "I suppose you don't think it's proper! My!" she wailed; "Eugenio doesn't think anything's proper."

"I'm nevertheless quite at your service," Winterbourne hastened to remark.

"Does Mademoiselle propose to go alone?" Eugenio asked of Mrs. Miller.

"Oh no, with this gentleman!" cried Daisy's mamma for reassurance.

"I *meant* alone with the gentleman." The courier looked for a moment at Winterbourne—the latter seemed to make out in his face a vague presumptuous intelligence as at the expense of their companions—and then solemnly and with a bow, "As Mademoiselle pleases!" he said.

But Daisy broke off at this. "Oh I hoped you'd make a fuss! I don't care to go now."

"Ah but I myself shall make a fuss if you don't go," Winterbourne declared with spirit.

"That's all I want—a little fuss!" With which she began to laugh again.

"Mr. Randolph has retired for the night!" the courier hereupon importantly announced.

"Oh Daisy, now we can go then!" cried Mrs. Miller.

Her daughter turned away from their friend, all lighted with her odd perversity. "Good-night—I hope you're disappointed or disgusted or something!"

He looked at her gravely, taking her by the hand she offered. "I'm puzzled, if you want to know!" he answered.

"Well, I hope it won't keep you awake!" she said very smartly; and, under the escort of the privileged Eugenio, the two ladies passed toward the house.

Winterbourne's eyes followed them; he was indeed quite mystified. He lingered beside the lake a quarter of an hour, baffled by the question of the girl's sudden familiarities and caprices. But the only very definite conclusion he came to was that he should enjoy deucedly "going off" with her somewhere.

Two days later he went off with her to the Castle of Chillon. He waited for her in the large hall of the hotel, where the couriers, the servants, the foreign tourists were lounging about and staring. It wasn't the place he would have chosen for a tryst, but she had placidly appointed it. She came tripping downstairs, buttoning her long gloves, squeezing her folded parasol against her pretty figure, dressed exactly in the way that consorted best, to his fancy, with their adventure. He was a man of imagination and, as our ancestors used to say, of sensibility; as he took in her charming air and caught from the great staircase her impatient confiding step the note of some small sweet strain of romance, not intense but clear and sweet, seemed to sound for their start. He could have believed he was *really* going "off" with her. He led her out through all the idle people assembled—they all looked at her straight and hard: she had begun to chatter as soon as she joined him. His preference had been that they should be conveyed to Chillon in a carriage, but she expressed a lively wish to go in the little steamer—there would be such a lovely breeze upon the water and they should see such lots of people. The sail wasn't long, but Winterbourne's companion found time for many characteristic remarks and other demonstrations, not a few of which were, from the extremity of their candour, slightly disconcerting. To the young man himself their small excursion showed so far delightfully irregular and incongruously intimate that, even allowing for her habitual sense of freedom, he had some expectation of seeing her appear to find in it the same savour. But it must be confessed that he was in this particular rather disappointed. Miss Miller was highly animated, she was in the brightest spirits; but she was clearly not at all in a nervous flutter— as she should have been to match *his* tension; she avoided neither his eyes nor those of any one else; she neither coloured from an awkward consciousness when she looked at him nor when she saw that people were looking at herself. People continued to look at her a great deal, and Winterbourne could at least take pleasure in his pretty companion's distinguished air. He had been privately afraid she would talk loud, laugh overmuch, and even perhaps desire to move extravagantly about the boat. But he quite forgot his fears; he sat smiling with his eyes on her face while, without stirring from her place, she delivered herself of a great number of original reflexions. It was the most charming innocent prattle he had ever heard, for, by his own experience hitherto, when young persons were so ingenuous they were less articulate and when they were so confident were more sophisticated. If he had assented to the idea that she was "common," at any rate, *was* she proving so, after all, or was he simply getting used to her commonness? Her discourse was for the most part of what immediately and superficially surrounded them, but there were moments when it threw out a longer look or took a sudden straight plunge.

"What on *earth* are you so solemn about?" she suddenly demanded, fixing her agreeable eyes on her friend's.

"*Am* I solemn?" he asked. "I had an idea I was grinning from ear to ear."

"You look as if you were taking me to a prayer-meeting or a funeral. If that's a grin your ears are very near together."

"Should you like me to dance a hornpipe on the deck?"

"Pray do, and I'll carry round your hat. It will pay the expenses of our journey."

"I never was better pleased in my life," Winterbourne returned.

She looked at him a moment, then let it renew her amusement. "I like to make you say those things. You're a queer mixture!"

In the castle, after they had landed, nothing could exceed the light independence of her humour. She tripped about the vaulted chambers, rustled her skirts in the corkscrew staircases, flirted back with a pretty little cry and a shudder from the edge of the oubliettes [12] and turned a singularly well-shaped ear to everything Winterbourne told her about the place. But he saw she cared little for mediæval history and that the grim ghosts of Chillon loomed but faintly before her. They had the good fortune to have been able to wander without other society than that of their guide; and Winterbourne arranged with this companion that they shouldn't be hurried—that they should linger and pause wherever they chose. He interpreted the bargain generously—Winterbourne on his side had been generous—and ended by leaving them quite to themselves. Miss Miller's observations were marked by no logical consistency; for anything she wanted to say she was sure to find a pretext. She found a great many, in the tortuous passages and rugged embrasures of the place, for asking her young man sudden questions about himself, his family, his previous history, his tastes, his habits, his designs, and for supplying information on corresponding points in her own situation. Of her own tastes, habits and designs the charming creature was prepared to give the most definite and indeed the most favourable account.

"Well, I hope you know enough!" she exclaimed after Winterbourne had sketched for her something of the story of the unhappy Bonnivard. "I never saw a man that knew so much!" The history of Bonnivard had evidently, as they say, gone into one ear and out of the other. But this easy erudition struck her none the less as wonderful, and she was soon quite sure she wished Winterbourne would travel with them and "go round" with them: they too in that case might learn something about something. "Don't you want to come and teach Randolph?" she asked; "I guess he'd improve with a gentleman teacher." Winterbourne was certain that nothing could possibly please him so much, but that he had unfortunately other occupations. "Other occupations? I don't believe a speck of it!" she protested. "What do you mean now? You're not in business." The young man allowed that he was not in business, but he had engagements which even within a day or two would necessitate his return to Geneva. "Oh bother!" she panted, "I don't believe it!" and she began to talk about something else. But a few moments later, when he was pointing out to her the interesting design of an antique

12. Dungeons.

fireplace, she broke out irrelevantly: "You don't mean to say you're going back to Geneva?"

"It is a melancholy fact that I shall have to report myself there to-morrow."

She met it with a vivacity that could only flatter him. "Well, Mr. Winterbourne, I think you're horrid!"

"Oh don't say such dreadful things!" he quite sincerely pleaded—"just at the last."

"The last?" the girl cried; "I call it the very first! I've half a mind to leave you here and go straight back to the hotel alone." And for the next ten minutes she did nothing but call him horrid. Poor Winterbourne was fairly bewildered; no young lady had as yet done him the honour to be so agitated by the mention of his personal plans. His companion, after this, ceased to pay any attention to the curiosities of Chillon or the beauties of the lake; she opened fire on the special charmer in Geneva whom she appeared to have instantly taken it for granted that he was hurrying back to see. How did Miss Daisy Miller know of that agent of his fate in Geneva? Winterbourne, who denied the existence of such a person, was quite unable to discover; and he was divided between amazement at the rapidity of her induction and amusement at the directness of her criticism. She struck him afresh, in all this, as an extraordinary mixture of innocence and crudity. "Does she never allow you more than three days at a time?" Miss Miller wished ironically to know. "Doesn't she give you a vacation in summer? there's no one so hard-worked but they can get leave to go off somewhere at this season. I suppose if you stay another day she'll come right after you in the boat. Do wait over till Friday and I'll go down to the landing to see her arrive!" He began at last even to feel he had been wrong to be disappointed in the temper in which his young lady had embarked. If he had missed the personal accent, the personal accent was now making its appearance. It sounded very distinctly, toward the end, in her telling him she'd stop "teasing" him if he'd promise her solemnly to come down to Rome that winter.

"That's not a difficult promise to make," he hastened to acknowledge. "My aunt has taken an apartment in Rome from January and has already asked me to come and see her."

"I don't want you to come for your aunt," said Daisy; "I want you just to come for me." And this was the only allusion he was ever to hear her make again to his invidious kinswoman. He promised her that at any rate he would certainly come, and after this she forbore from teasing. Winterbourne took a carriage and they drove back to Vevey in the dusk; the girl at his side, her animation a little spent, was now quite distractingly passive.

In the evening he mentioned to Mrs. Costello that he had spent the afternoon at Chillon with Miss Daisy Miller.

"The Americans—of the courier?" asked this lady.

"Ah happily the courier stayed at home."

"She went with you all alone?"

"All alone."

Mrs. Costello sniffed a little at her smelling-bottle. "And that," she exclaimed, "is the little abomination you wanted me to know!"

III

Winterbourne, who had returned to Geneva the day after his excursion to Chillon, went to Rome toward the end of January. His aunt had been established there a considerable time and he had received from her a couple of characteristic letters. "Those people you were so devoted to last summer at Vevey have turned up here, courier and all," she wrote. "They seem to have made several acquaintances, but the courier continues to be the most *intime*. The young lady, however, is also very intimate with various third-rate Italians, with whom she rackets about in a way that makes much talk. Bring me that pretty novel of Cherbuliez's—'Paule Méré' [13]— and don't come later than the 23d."

Our friend would in the natural course of events, on arriving in Rome, have presently ascertained Mrs. Miller's address at the American banker's and gone to pay his compliments to Miss Daisy. "After what happened at Vevey I certainly think I may call upon them," he said to Mrs. Costello.

"If after what happens—at Vevey and everywhere—you desire to keep up the acquaintance, you're very welcome. Of course you're not squeamish—a man may know every one. Men are welcome to the privilege!"

"Pray what is it then that 'happens'—here for instance?" Winterbourne asked.

"Well, the girl tears about alone with her unmistakeably low foreigners. As to what happens further you must apply elsewhere for information. She has picked up half a dozen of the regular Roman fortune-hunters of the inferior sort and she takes them about to such houses as she may put *her* nose into. When she comes to a party— such a party as she can come to—she brings with her a gentleman with a good deal of manner and a wonderful moustache."

"And where's the mother?"

"I haven't the least idea. They're very dreadful people."

Winterbourne thought them over in these new lights. "They're

13. Victor Cherbuliez (1829–99), Swiss-born novelist of manners, author of the epistolary novel *Paule Méré* (1864). Mrs. Costello is asking for a popular work of the day.

very ignorant—very innocent only, and utterly uncivilised. Depend on it they're not 'bad.' "

"They're hopelessly vulgar," said Mrs. Costello. "Whether or no being hopelessly vulgar is being 'bad' is a question for the metaphysicians. They're bad enough to blush for, at any rate; and for this short life that's quite enough."

The news that his little friend the child of nature of the Swiss lakeside was now surrounded by half a dozen wonderful moustaches checked Winterbourne's impulse to go straightway to see her. He had perhaps not definitely flattered himself that he had made an ineffaceable impression upon her heart, but he was annoyed at hearing of a state of affairs so little in harmony with an image that had lately flitted in and out of his own meditations; the image of a very pretty girl looking out of an old Roman window and asking herself urgently when Mr. Winterbourne would arrive. If, however, he determined to wait a little before reminding this young lady of his claim to her faithful remembrance, he called with more promptitude on two or three other friends. One of these friends was an American lady who had spent several winters at Geneva, where she had placed her children at school. She was a very accomplished woman and she lived in Via Gregoriana. Winterbourne found her in a little crimson drawing-room on a third floor; the room was filled with southern sunshine. He hadn't been there ten minutes when the servant, appearing in the doorway, announced complacently "Madame Mila!" This announcement was presently followed by the entrance of little Randolph Miller, who stopped in the middle of the room and stood staring at Winterbourne. An instant later his pretty sister crossed the threshold; and then, after a considerable interval, the parent of the pair slowly advanced.

"I guess I know you!" Randolph broke ground without delay.

"I'm sure you know a great many things"—and his old friend clutched him all interestedly by the arm. "How's your education coming on?"

Daisy was engaged in some pretty babble with her hostess, but when she heard Winterbourne's voice she quickly turned her head with a "Well, I declare!" which he met smiling. "I told you I should come, you know."

"Well, I didn't believe it," she answered.

"I'm much obliged to you for that," laughed the young man.

"You might have come to see me then," Daisy went on as if they had parted the week before.

"I arrived only yesterday."

"I don't believe any such thing!" the girl declared afresh.

Winterbourne turned with a protesting smile to her mother, but this lady evaded his glance and, seating herself, fixed her eyes on her son. "We've got a bigger place than this," Randolph hereupon broke out. "It's all gold on the walls."

Mrs. Miller, more of a fatalist apparently than ever, turned uneasily in her chair. "I told you if I was to bring you you'd say something!" she stated as for the benefit of such of the company as might hear it.

"I told *you!*" Randolph retorted. "I tell *you*, sir!" he added jocosely, giving Winterbourne a thump on the knee. "It *is* bigger too!"

As Daisy's conversation with her hostess still occupied her Winterbourne judged it becoming to address a few words to her mother—such as "I hope you've been well since we parted at Vevey."

Mrs. Miller now certainly looked at him—at his chin. "Not very well, sir," she answered.

"She's got the dyspepsia," said Randolph. "I've got it too. Father's got it bad. But I've got it worst!"

This proclamation, instead of embarrassing Mrs. Miller, seemed to soothe her by reconstituting the environment to which she was most accustomed. "I suffer from the liver," she amiably whined to Winterbourne. "I think it's this climate; it's less bracing than Schenectady, especially in the winter season. I don't know whether you know we reside at Schenectady. I was saying to Daisy that I certainly hadn't found any one like Dr. Davis and I didn't believe I *would*. Oh up in Schenectady, he stands first; they think everything of Dr. Davis. He has so much to do, and yet there was nothing he wouldn't do for *me*. He said he never saw anything like my dyspepsia, but he was bound to get at it. I'm sure there was nothing he wouldn't try, and I didn't care what he did to me if he only brought me relief. He was just going to try something new, and I just longed for it, when we came right off. Mr. Miller felt as if he wanted Daisy to see Europe for herself. But I couldn't help writing the other day that I supposed it was all right for Daisy, but that I didn't know as I *could* get on much longer without Dr. Davis. At Schenectady he stands at the very top; and there's a great deal of sickness there too. It affects my sleep."

Winterbourne had a good deal of pathological gossip with Dr. Davis's patient, during which Daisy chattered unremittingly to her own companion. The young man asked Mrs. Miller how she was pleased with Rome. "Well, I must say I'm disappointed," she confessed. "We had heard so much about it—I suppose we had heard too much. But we couldn't help that. We had been led to expect something different."

Winterbourne, however, abounded in reassurance. "Ah wait a little, and you'll grow very fond of it."

"I hate it worse and worse every day!" cried Randolph.

"You're like the infant Hannibal," [14] his friend laughed.

"No I ain't—like any infant!" Randolph declared at a venture.

"Well, that's so—and you never *were!*" his mother concurred. "But we've seen places," she resumed, "that I'd put a long way ahead of Rome." And in reply to Winterbourne's interrogation, "There's Zürich—up there in the mountains," she instanced; "I think Zürich's real lovely, and we hadn't heard half so much about it."

"The best place we've seen's the *City of Richmond!*" said Randolph.

"He means the ship," Mrs. Miller explained. "We crossed in that ship. Randolph had a good time on the *City of Richmond.*"

"It's the best place *I've* struck," the child repeated. "Only it was turned the wrong way."

"Well, we've got to turn the right way sometime," said Mrs. Miller with strained but weak optimism. Winterbourne expressed the hope that her daughter at least appreciated the so various interest of Rome, and she declared with some spirit that Daisy was quite carried away. "It's on account of the society—the society's splendid. She goes round everywhere; she has made a great number of acquaintances. Of course she goes round more than I do. I must say they've all been very sweet—they've taken her right in. And then she knows a great many gentlemen. Oh she thinks there's nothing like Rome. Of course it's a great deal pleasanter for a young lady if she knows plenty of gentlemen."

By this time Daisy had turned her attention again to Winterbourne, but in quite the same free form. "I've been telling Mrs. Walker how mean you were!"

"And what's the evidence you've offered?" he asked, a trifle disconcerted, for all his superior gallantry, by her inadequate measure of the zeal of an admirer who on his way down to Rome had stopped neither at Bologna nor at Florence, simply because of a certain sweet appeal to his fond fancy, not to say to his finest curiosity. He remembered how a cynical compatriot had once told him that American women—the pretty ones, and this gave a largeness to the axiom—were at once the most exacting in the world and the least endowed with a sense of indebtedness.

"Why you were awfully mean up at Vevey," Daisy said. "You wouldn't do most anything. You wouldn't stay there when I asked you."

"Dearest young lady," cried Winterbourne, with generous passion, "have I come all the way to Rome only to be riddled by your silver shafts?"

14. Hannibal, Carthaginian general (247–183 B.C.) brought up to have an undying hatred of Rome.

"Just hear him say that!"—and she gave an affectionate twist to a bow on her hostess's dress. "Did you ever hear anything so quaint?"

"So 'quaint,' my dear?" echoed Mrs. Walker more critically—quite in the tone of a partisan of Winterbourne.

"Well, I don't know"—and the girl continued to finger her ribbons. "Mrs. Walker, I want to tell you something."

"Say, mother-r," broke in Randolph with his rough ends to his words, "I tell you you've got to go. Eugenio 'll raise something!"

"I'm not afraid of Eugenio," said Daisy with a toss of her head. "Look here, Mrs. Walker," she went on, "you know I'm coming to your party."

"I'm delighted to hear it."

"I've got a lovely dress."

"I'm very sure of that."

"But I want to ask a favour—permission to bring a friend."

"I shall be happy to see any of your friends," said Mrs. Walker, who turned with a smile to Mrs. Miller.

"Oh they're not my friends," cried that lady, squirming in shy repudiation. "It seems as if they didn't take to *me*—I never spoke to one of them!"

"It's an intimate friend of mine, Mr. Giovanelli," Daisy pursued without a tremor in her young clearness or a shadow on her shining bloom.

Mrs. Walker had a pause and gave a rapid glance at Winterbourne. "I shall be glad to see Mr. Giovanelli," she then returned.

"He's just the finest kind of Italian," Daisy pursued with the prettiest serenity. "He's a great friend of mine and the handsomest man in the world—except Mr. Winterbourne! He knows plenty of Italians, but he wants to know some Americans. It seems as if he was crazy about Americans. He's tremendously bright. He's perfectly lovely!"

It was settled that this paragon should be brought to Mrs. Walker's party, and then Mrs. Miller prepared to take her leave. "I guess we'll go right back to the hotel," she remarked with a confessed failure of the larger imagination.

"You may go back to the hotel, mother," Daisy replied, "but I'm just going to walk round."

"She's going to go it with Mr. Giovanelli," Randolph unscrupulously commented.

"I'm going to go it on the Pincio," [15] Daisy peaceably smiled, while the way that she "condoned" these things almost melted Winterbourne's heart.

"Alone, my dear—at this hour?" Mrs. Walker asked. The after-

15. One of the hills of Rome.

noon was drawing to a close—it was the hour for the throng of carriages and of contemplative pedestrians. "I don't consider it's safe, Daisy," her hostess firmly asserted.

"Neither do I then," Mrs. Miller thus borrowed confidence to add. "You'll catch the fever as sure as you live. Remember what Dr. Davis told you!"

"Give her some of that medicine before she starts in," Randolph suggested.

The company had risen to its feet; Daisy, still showing her pretty teeth, bent over and kissed her hostess. "Mrs. Walker, you're too perfect," she simply said. "I'm not going alone; I'm going to meet a friend."

"Your friend won't keep you from catching the fever even if it *is* his own second nature," Mrs. Miller observed.

"Is it Mr. Giovanelli that's the dangerous attraction?" Mrs. Walker asked without mercy.

Winterbourne was watching the challenged girl; at this question his attention quickened. She stood there smiling and smoothing her bonnet-ribbons; she glanced at Winterbourne. Then, while she glanced and smiled, she brought out all affirmatively and without a shade of hesitation: "Mr. Giovanelli—the beautiful Giovanelli."

"My dear young friend"—and, taking her hand, Mrs. Walker turned to pleading—"don't prowl off to the Pincio at this hour to meet a beautiful Italian."

"Well, he speaks first-rate English," Mrs. Miller incoherently mentioned.

"Gracious me," Daisy piped up, "I don't want to do anything that's going to affect my health—or my character either! There's an easy way to settle it." Her eyes continued to play over Winterbourne. "The Pincio's only a hundred yards off, and if Mr. Winterbourne were as polite as he pretends he'd offer to walk right in with me!"

Winterbourne's politeness hastened to proclaim itself, and the girl gave him gracious leave to accompany her. They passed downstairs before her mother, and at the door he saw Mrs. Miller's carriage drawn up, with the ornamental courier whose acquaintance he had made at Vevey seated within. "Good-bye, Eugenio," cried Daisy; "I'm going to take a walk!" The distance from Via Gregoriana to the beautiful garden at the other end of the Pincian Hill is in fact rapidly traversed. As the day was splendid, however, and the concourse of vehicles, walkers and loungers numerous, the young Americans found their progress much delayed. This fact was highly agreeable to Winterbourne, in spite of his consciousness of his singular situation. The slow-moving, idly-gazing Roman crowd bestowed much attention on the extremely pretty young woman of

English race who passed through it, with some difficulty, on his arm; and he wondered what on earth had been in Daisy's mind when she proposed to exhibit herself unattended to its appreciation. His own mission, to her sense, was apparently to consign her to the hands of Mr. Giovanelli; but, at once annoyed and gratified, he resolved that he would do no such thing.

"Why haven't you been to see me?" she meanwhile asked. "You can't get out of that."

"I've had the honour of telling you that I've only just stepped out of the train."

"You must have stayed in the train a good while after it stopped!" she derisively cried. "I suppose you were asleep. You've had time to go to see Mrs. Walker."

"I knew Mrs. Walker—" Winterbourne began to explain.

"I know where you knew her. You knew her at Geneva. She told me so. Well, you knew me at Vevey. That's just as good. So you ought to have come." She asked him no other question than this; she began to prattle about her own affairs. "We've got splendid rooms at the hotel; Eugenio says they're the best rooms in Rome. We're going to stay all winter—if we don't die of the fever; and I guess we'll stay then! It's a great deal nicer than I thought; I thought it would be fearfully quiet—in fact I was sure it would be deadly pokey. I foresaw we should be going round all the time with one of those dreadful old men who explain about the pictures and things. But we only had about a week of that, and now I'm enjoying myself. I know ever so many people, and they're all so charming. The society's extremely select. There are all kinds—English and Germans and Italians. I think I like the English best. I like their style of conversation. But there are some lovely Americans. I never saw anything so hospitable. There's something or other every day. There's not much dancing—but I must say I never thought dancing was everything. I was always fond of conversation. I guess I'll have plenty at Mrs. Walker's—her rooms are so small." When they had passed the gate of the Pincian Gardens Miss Miller began to wonder where Mr. Giovanelli might be. "We had better go straight to that place in front, where you look at the view."

Winterbourne at this took a stand. "I certainly shan't help you to find him."

"Then I shall find him without you," Daisy said with spirit.

"You certainly won't leave me!" he protested.

She burst into her familiar little laugh. "Are you afraid you'll get lost—or run over? But there's Giovanelli leaning against that tree. He's staring at the women in the carriages: did you ever see anything so cool?"

Winterbourne descried hereupon at some distance a little figure that stood with folded arms and nursing its cane. It had a handsome face, a hat artfully poised, a glass in one eye and a nosegay in its buttonhole. Daisy's friend looked at it a moment and then said: "Do you mean to speak to that thing?"

"Do I mean to speak to him? Why you don't suppose I mean to communicate by signs!"

"Pray understand then," the young man returned, "that I intend to remain with you."

Daisy stopped and looked at him without a sign of troubled consciousness, with nothing in her face but her charming eyes, her charming teeth and her happy dimples. "Well, she's a cool one!" he thought.

"I don't like the way you say that," she declared. "It's too imperious."

"I beg your pardon if I say it wrong. The main point's to give you an idea of my meaning."

The girl looked at him more gravely, but with eyes that were prettier than ever. "I've never allowed a gentleman to dictate to me or to interfere with anything I do."

"I think that's just where your mistake has come in," he retorted. "You should sometimes listen to a gentleman—the right one."

At this she began to laugh again. "I do nothing but listen to gentlemen! Tell me if Mr. Giovanelli is the right one."

The gentleman with the nosegay in his bosom had now made out our two friends and was approaching Miss Miller with obsequious rapidity. He bowed to Winterbourne as well as to the latter's compatriot; he seemed to shine, in his coxcombical way, with the desire to please and the fact of his own intelligent joy, though Winterbourne thought him not a bad-looking fellow. But he nevertheless said to Daisy: "No, he's not the right one."

She had clearly a natural turn for free introductions; she mentioned with the easiest grace the name of each of her companions to the other. She strolled forward with one of them on either hand; Mr. Giovanelli, who spoke English very cleverly—Winterbourne afterwards learned that he had practised the idiom upon a great many American heiresses—addressed her a great deal of very polite nonsense. He had the best possible manners, and the young American, who said nothing, reflected on that depth of Italian subtlety, so strangely opposed to Anglo-Saxon simplicity, which enables people to show a smoother surface in proportion as they're more acutely displeased. Giovanelli of course had counted upon something more intimate—he had not bargained for a party of three; but he kept his temper in a manner that suggested far-stretching intentions. Winterbourne flattered himself he had taken his measure. "He's anything but a gentleman," said the young American; "he isn't even a very plausible imitation of one. He's a music-master or a penny-a-liner or a third-rate artist. He's awfully on his good behaviour, but damn his fine eyes!" Mr. Giovanelli had indeed great advantages; but it was deeply disgusting to Daisy's other friend that something in her shouldn't have instinctively discriminated against such a type. Giovanelli chattered and jested and made himself agreeable according to his honest Roman lights. It was true that if he was an imitation the imitation was studied. "Nevertheless," Winterbourne said to himself, "a nice girl ought to know!" And then he came back to the dreadful question of whether this *was* in fact a nice girl. Would a nice girl—even allowing for her being a little American flirt—make a rendezvous with a presumably low-lived foreigner? The rendezvous in this case indeed had been in broad daylight and in the most crowded corner of Rome; but wasn't it possible to regard the choice of these very circumstances as a proof more of vulgarity than of anything else? Singular though it may seem, Winterbourne was vexed that the girl, in joining her *amoroso*,[16] shouldn't appear more impatient of his own company, and he was vexed precisely because of his inclination. It was impossible to regard her as a wholly unspotted flower—she lacked a certain indispensable fineness; and it would therefore much simplify the situation to be able to treat her as the subject of one of the visitations known to romancers as "lawless passions." That she should seem to wish to get rid of him would have helped him to think more lightly of her, just as to be able to think more lightly of her would have made her less perplexing. Daisy at any rate continued on this occasion to present herself as an inscrutable combination of audacity and innocence.

She had been walking some quarter of an hour, attended by her two cavaliers and responding in a tone of very childish gaiety, as it after all struck one of them, to the pretty speeches of the other, when a carriage that had detached itself from the revolving train drew up beside the path. At the same moment Winterbourne noticed that his friend Mrs. Walker—the lady whose house he had lately left—was seated in the vehicle and was beckoning to him. Leaving Miss Miller's side, he hastened to obey her summons—and all to find her flushed, excited, scandalised. "It's really too dreadful"—she earnestly appealed to him. "That crazy girl mustn't do this sort of thing. She mustn't walk here with you two men. Fifty people have remarked her."

Winterbourne—suddenly and rather oddly rubbed the wrong way by this—raised his grave eyebrows. "I think it's a pity to make too much fuss about it."

"It's a pity to let the girl ruin herself!"

16. Lover.

"She's very innocent," he reasoned in his own troubled interest.

"She's very reckless," cried Mrs. Walker, "and goodness knows how far—left to itself—it may go. Did you ever," she proceeded to enquire, "see anything so blatantly imbecile as the mother? After you had all left me just now I couldn't sit still for thinking of it. It seemed too pitiful not even to attempt to save them. I ordered the carriage and put on my bonnet and came here as quickly as possible. Thank heaven I've found you!"

"What do you propose to do with us?" Winterbourne uncomfortably smiled.

"To ask her to get in, to drive her about here for half an hour—so that the world may see she's not running absolutely wild—and then take her safely home."

"I don't think it's a very happy thought," he said after reflexion, "but you're at liberty to try."

Mrs. Walker accordingly tried. The young man went in pursuit of their young lady who had simply nodded and smiled, from her distance, at her recent patroness in the carriage and then had gone her way with her own companion. On learning, in the event, that Mrs. Walker had followed her, she retraced her steps, however, with a perfect good grace and with Mr. Giovanelli at her side. She professed herself "enchanted" to have a chance to present this gentleman to her good friend, and immediately achieved the introduction; declaring with it, and as if it were of as little importance, that she had never in her life seen anything so lovely as that lady's carriage-rug.

"I'm glad you admire it," said her poor pursuer, smiling sweetly. "Will you get in and let me put it over you?"

"Oh no, thank you!"—Daisy knew her mind. "I'll admire it ever so much more as I see you driving round with it."

"Do get in and drive round *with* me," Mrs. Walker pleaded.

"That would be charming, but it's so fascinating just as I am!"—with which the girl radiantly took in the gentlemen on either side of her.

"It may be fascinating, dear child, but it's not the custom here," urged the lady of the victoria, leaning forward in this vehicle with her hands devoutly clasped.

"Well, it ought to be then!" Daisy imperturbably laughed. "If I didn't walk I'd expire."

"You should walk with your mother, dear," cried Mrs. Walker with a loss of patience.

"With my mother dear?" the girl amusedly echoed. Winterbourne saw she scented interference. "My mother never walked ten steps in her life. And then, you know," she blandly added, "I'm more than five years old."

"You're old enough to be more reasonable. You're old enough, dear Miss Miller, to be talked about."

Daisy wondered to extravagance. "Talked about? What do you mean?"

"Come into my carriage and I'll tell you."

Daisy turned shining eyes again from one of the gentlemen beside her to the other. Mr. Giovanelli was bowing to and fro, rubbing down his gloves and laughing irresponsibly; Winterbourne thought the scene the most unpleasant possible. "I don't think I want to know what you mean," the girl presently said. "I don't think I should like it."

Winterbourne only wished Mrs. Walker would tuck up her carriage-rug and drive away; but this lady, as she afterwards told him, didn't feel she could "rest there." "Should you prefer being thought a very reckless girl?" she accordingly asked.

"Gracious me!" exclaimed Daisy. She looked again at Mr. Giovanelli, then she turned to her other companion. There was a small pink flush in her cheek; she was tremendously pretty. "Does Mr. Winterbourne think," she put to him with a wonderful bright intensity of appeal, "that—to save my reputation—I ought to get into the carriage?"

It really embarrassed him; for an instant he cast about—so strange was it to hear her speak that way of her "reputation." But he himself in fact had to speak in accordance with gallantry. The finest gallantry here was surely just to tell her the truth; and the truth, for our young man, as the few indications I have been able to give have made him known to the reader, was that his charming friend should listen to the voice of civilised society. He took in again her exquisite prettiness and then said the more distinctly: "I think you should get into the carriage."

Daisy gave the rein to her amusement. "I never heard anything so stiff! If this is improper, Mrs. Walker," she pursued, "then I'm *all* improper, and you had better give me right up. Good-bye; I hope you'll have a lovely ride!"—and with Mr. Giovanelli, who made a triumphantly obsequious salute, she turned away.

Mrs. Walker sat looking after her, and there were tears in Mrs. Walker's eyes. "Get in here, sir," she said to Winterbourne, indicating the place beside her. The young man answered that he felt bound to accompany Miss Miller; whereupon the lady of the victoria declared that if he refused her this favour she would never speak to him again. She was evidently wound up. He accordingly hastened to overtake Daisy and her more faithful ally, and, offering her his hand, told her that Mrs. Walker had made a stringent claim on his presence. He had expected her to answer with something rather free, something still more significant of the perversity from which the voice of society, through the lips of their distressed friend, had so earnestly endeavoured to dissuade her. But she only let her hand slip, as she scarce looked at him, through his slightly awkward grasp; while Mr. Giovanelli, to make it worse, bade him farewell with too emphatic a flourish of the hat.

Winterbourne was not in the best possible humour as he took his seat beside the author of his sacrifice. "That was not clever of you," he said candidly, as the vehicle mingled again with the throng of carriages.

"In such a case," his companion answered, "I don't want to be clever—I only want to be *true!*"

"Well, your truth has only offended the strange little creature—it has only put her off."

"It has happened very well"—Mrs. Walker accepted her work. "If she's so perfectly determined to compromise herself the sooner one knows it the better—one can act accordingly."

"I suspect she meant no great harm, you know," Winterbourne maturely opined.

"So I thought a month ago. But she has been going too far."

"What has she been doing?"

"Everything that's not done here. Flirting with any man she can pick up; sitting in corners with mysterious Italians; dancing all the evening with the same partners; receiving visits at eleven o'clock at night. Her mother melts away when the visitors come."

"But her brother," laughed Winterbourne, "sits up till two in the morning."

"He must be edified by what he sees. I'm told that at their hotel every one's talking about her and that a smile goes round among the servants when a gentleman comes and asks for Miss Miller."

"Ah we needn't mind the servants!" Winterbourne compassionately signified. "The poor girl's only fault," he presently added, "is her complete lack of education."

"She's naturally indelicate," Mrs. Walker, on her side, reasoned. "Take that example this morning. How long had you known her at Vevey?"

"A couple of days."

"Imagine then the taste of her making it a personal matter that you should have left the place!"

He agreed that taste wasn't the strong point of the Millers—after which he was silent for some moments; but only at last to add: "I suspect, Mrs. Walker, that you and I have lived too long at Geneva!" And he further noted that he should be glad to learn with what particular design she had made him enter her carriage.

"I wanted to enjoin on you the importance of your ceasing your relations with Miss Miller; that of your not appearing to flirt with her; that of your giving her no further opportunity to expose herself; that of your in short letting her alone."

"I'm afraid I can't do anything quite so enlightened as *that*," he returned. "I like her awfully, you know."

"All the more reason you shouldn't help her to make a scandal."

"Well, there shall be nothing scandalous in my attentions to her," he was willing to promise.

"There certainly will be in the way she takes them. But I've said what I had on my conscience," Mrs. Walker pursued. "If you wish to rejoin the young lady I'll put you down. Here, by the way, you have a chance."

The carriage was engaged in that part of the Pincian drive which overhangs the wall of Rome and overlooks the beautiful Villa Borghese. It is bordered by a large parapet, near which are several seats. One of these, at a distance, was occupied by a gentleman and a lady, toward whom Mrs. Walker gave a toss of her head. At the same moment these persons rose and walked to the parapet. Winterbourne had asked the coachman to stop; he now descended from the carriage. His companion looked at him a moment in silence and then, while he raised his hat, drove majestically away. He stood where he had alighted; he had turned his eyes toward Daisy and her cavalier. They evidently saw no one; they were too deeply occupied with each other. When they reached the low garden-wall they remained a little looking off at the great flat-topped pine-clusters of Villa Borghese; then the girl's attendant admirer seated himself familiarly on the broad ledge of the wall. The western sun in the opposite sky sent out a brilliant shaft through a couple of cloud-bars; whereupon the gallant Giovanelli took her parasol out of her hands and opened it. She came a little nearer and he held the parasol over her; then, still holding it, he let it so rest on her shoulder that both of their heads were hidden from Winterbourne. This young man stayed but a moment longer; then he began to walk. But he walked—not toward the couple united beneath the parasol, rather toward the residence of his aunt Mrs. Costello.

IV

He flattered himself on the following day that there was no smiling among the servants when he at least asked for Mrs. Miller at her hotel. This lady and her daughter, however, were not at home; and on the next day after, repeating his visit, Winterbourne again was met by a denial. Mrs. Walker's party took place on the evening of the third day, and in spite of the final reserves that had marked his last interview with that social critic our young man was among the guests. Mrs. Walker was one of those pilgrims from the younger world who, while in contact with the elder, make a point, in their own phrase, of studying European society; and she had on this occasion collected several specimens of diversely-born humanity to serve, as might be, for text-books. When Winterbourne arrived the little person he desired most to find wasn't there; but in a few moments he saw Mrs. Miller come in alone, very shyly and ruefully. This lady's hair, above the dead waste of her temples, was more frizzled than ever. As she approached their hostess Winterbourne also drew near.

"You see I've come all alone," said Daisy's unsupported parent. "I'm so frightened I don't know what to do; it's the first time I've ever been to a party alone—especially in this country. I wanted to bring Randolph or Eugenio or some one, but Daisy just pushed me off by myself. I ain't used to going round alone."

"And doesn't your daughter intend to favour us with her society?" Mrs. Walker impressively enquired.

"Well, Daisy's all dressed," Mrs. Miller testified with that accent of the dispassionate, if not of the philosophic, historian with which she always recorded the current incidents of her daughter's career. "She got dressed on purpose before dinner. But she has a friend of hers there; that gentleman—the handsomest of the Italians—that she wanted to bring. They've got going at the piano—it seems as if they couldn't leave off. Mr. Giovanelli does sing splendidly. But I guess they'll come before very long," Mrs. Miller hopefully concluded.

"I'm sorry she should come—in that particular way," Mrs. Walker permitted herself to observe.

"Well, I told her there was no use in her getting dressed before dinner if she was going to wait three hours," returned Daisy's mamma. "I didn't see the use of her putting on such a dress as that to sit round with Mr. Giovanelli."

"This is most horrible!" said Mrs. Walker, turning away and addressing herself to Winterbourne. "*Elle s'affiche, la malheureuse.*[17] It's her revenge for my having ventured to remonstrate with her. When she comes I shan't speak to her."

Daisy came after eleven o'clock, but she wasn't, on such an occasion, a young lady to wait to be spoken to. She rustled forward in radiant loveliness, smiling and chattering, carrying a large bouquet and attended by Mr. Giovanelli. Every one stopped talking and turned and looked at her while she floated up to Mrs. Walker. "I'm afraid you thought I never was coming, so I sent mother off to tell you. I wanted to make Mr. Giovanelli practise some things before he came; you know he sings beautifully, and I want you to ask him

17. "She's making a display of herself, the poor wretch."

to sing. This is Mr. Giovanelli; you know I introduced him to you; he's got the most lovely voice and he knows the most charming set of songs. I made him go over them this evening on purpose; we had the greatest time at the hotel." Of all this Daisy delivered herself with the sweetest brightest loudest confidence, looking now at her hostess and now at all the room, while she gave a series of little pats, round her very white shoulders, to the edges of her dress. "Is there any one I know?" she as undiscourageably asked.

"I think every one knows you!" said Mrs. Walker as with a grand intention; and she gave a very cursory greeting to Mr. Giovanelli. This gentleman bore himself gallantly; he smiled and bowed and showed his white teeth, he curled his moustaches and rolled his eyes and performed all the proper functions of a handsome Italian at an evening party. He sang, very prettily, half a dozen songs, though Mrs. Walker afterwards declared that she had been quite unable to find out who asked him. It was apparently not Daisy who had set him in motion—this young lady being seated a distance from the piano and though she had publicly, as it were, professed herself his musical patroness or guarantor, giving herself to gay and audible discourse while he warbled.

"It's a pity these rooms are so small; we can't dance," she remarked to Winterbourne as if she had seen him five minutes before.

"I'm not sorry we can't dance," he candidly returned. "I'm incapable of a step."

"Of course you're incapable of a step," the girl assented. "I should think your legs *would* be stiff cooped in there so much of the time in that victoria."

"Well, they were very restless there three days ago," he amicably laughed; "all they really wanted was to dance attendance on you."

"Oh my other friend—my friend in need—stuck to me; he seems more at one with his limbs than you are—I'll say that for him. But did you ever hear anything so cool," Daisy demanded, "as Mrs. Walker's wanting me to get into her carriage and drop poor Mr. Giovanelli, and under the pretext that it was proper? People have different ideas! It would have been most unkind; he had been talking about that walk for ten days."

"He shouldn't have talked about it at all," Winterbourne decided to make answer on this: "he would never have proposed to a young lady of this country to walk about the streets of Rome with him."

"About the streets?" she cried with her pretty stare. "Where then would he have proposed to her to walk? The Pincio ain't the streets either, I guess; and I besides, thank goodness, am not a young lady of this country. The young ladies of this country have a dreadfully pokey time of it, by what I can discover; I don't see why I should change my habits for *such* stupids."

"I'm afraid your habits are those of a ruthless flirt," said Winterbourne with studied severity.

"Of course they are!"—and she hoped, evidently, by the manner of it, to take his breath away. "I'm a fearful frightful flirt! Did you ever hear of a nice girl that wasn't? But I suppose you'll tell me now I'm not a nice girl."

He remained grave indeed under the shock of her cynical profession. "You're a very nice girl, but I wish you'd flirt with me, and me only."

"Ah thank you, thank you very much: you're the last man I should think of flirting with. As I've had the pleasure of informing you, you're too stiff."

"You say that too often," he resentfully remarked.

Daisy gave a delighted laugh. "If I could have the sweet hope of making you angry I'd say it again."

"Don't do that—when I'm angry I'm stiffer than ever. But if you won't flirt with me do cease at least to flirt with your friend at the piano. They don't," he declared as in full sympathy with "them," "understand that sort of thing here."

"I thought they understood nothing else!" Daisy cried with startling world-knowledge.

"Not in young unmarried women."

"It seems to me much more proper in young unmarried than in old married ones," she retorted.

"Well," said Winterbourne, "when you deal with natives you must go by the custom of the country. American flirting is a purely American silliness; it has—in its ineptitude of innocence—no place in *this* system. So when you show yourself in public with Mr. Giovanelli and without your mother—"

"Gracious, poor mother!"—and she made it beautifully unspeakable.

Winterbourne had a touched sense for this, but it didn't alter his attitude. "Though *you* may be flirting Mr. Giovanelli isn't—he means something else."

"He isn't preaching at any rate," she returned. "And if you want very much to know, we're neither of us flirting—not a little speck. We're too good friends for that. We're real intimate friends."

He was to continue to find her thus at moments inimitable. "Ah," he then judged, "if you're in love with each other it's another affair altogether!"

She had allowed him up to this point to speak so frankly that he had no thought of shocking her by the force of his logic; yet she now none the less immediately rose, blushing visibly and leaving him mentally to exclaim that the name of little American flirts was incoherence. "Mr. Giovanelli at least," she answered, sparing but a

single small queer glance for it, a queerer small glance, he felt, than
he had ever yet had from her—"Mr. Giovanelli never says to me
such very disagreeable things."

It had an effect on him—he stood staring. The subject of their
contention had finished singing; he left the piano, and his recognition of what—a little awkwardly—didn't take place in celebration of
this might nevertheless have been an acclaimed operatic tenor's
series of repeated ducks before the curtain. So he bowed himself
over to Daisy. "Won't you come to the other room and have some
tea?" he asked—offering Mrs. Walker's slightly thin refreshment as
he might have done all the kingdoms of the earth.

Daisy at last turned on Winterbourne a more natural and calculable light. He was but the more muddled by it, however, since so in-
consequent a smile 'made nothing clear—it seemed at the most to
prove in her a sweetness and softness that reverted instinctively to
the pardon of offences. "It has never occurred to Mr. Winterbourne
to offer me any tea," she said with her finest little intention of torment and triumph.

"I've offered you excellent advice," the young man permitted
himself to growl.

"I prefer weak tea!" cried Daisy, and she went off with the brilliant Giovanelli. She sat with him in the adjoining room, in the
embrasure of the window, for the rest of the evening. There was an
interesting performance at the piano, but neither of these con-
versers gave heed to it. When Daisy came to take leave of Mrs.
Walker this lady conscientiously repaired the weakness of which
she had been guilty at the moment of the girl's arrival—she turned
her back straight on Miss Miller and left her to depart with what
grace she might. Winterbourne happened to be near the door; he
saw it all. Daisy turned very pale and looked at her mother, but
Mrs. Miller was humbly unconscious of any rupture of any law or of
any deviation from any custom. She appeared indeed to have felt an
incongruous impulse to draw attention to her own striking confor-
mity. "Good-night, Mrs. Walker," she said; "we've had a beautiful
evening. You see if I let Daisy come to parties without me I don't
want her to go away without me." Daisy turned away, looking with
a small white prettiness, a blighted grace, at the circle near the
door: Winterbourne saw that for the first moment she was too much
shocked and puzzled even for indignation. He on his side was
greatly touched.

"That was very cruel," he promptly remarked to Mrs. Walker.

But this lady's face was also as a stone. "She never enters my
drawing-room again."

Since Winterbourne then, hereupon, was not to meet her in Mrs.
Walker's drawing-room he went as often as possible to Mrs. Miller's

hotel. The ladies were rarely at home, but when he found them the devoted Giovanelli was always present. Very often the glossy little Roman, serene in success, but not unduly presumptuous, occupied with Daisy alone the florid salon enjoyed by Eugenio's care, Mrs. Miller being apparently ever of the opinion that discretion is the better part of solicitude. Winterbourne noted, at first with surprise, that Daisy on these occasions was neither embarrassed nor annoyed by his own entrance; but he presently began to feel that she had no more surprises for him and that he really liked, after all, not making out what she was "up to." She showed no displeasure for the interruption of her *tête-à-tête* with Giovanelli; she could chatter as freshly and freely with two gentlemen as with one, and this easy flow had ever the same anomaly for her earlier friend that it was so free without availing itself of its freedom. Winterbourne reflected that if she was seriously interested in the Italian it was odd she shouldn't take more trouble to preserve the sanctity of their interviews, and he liked her the better for her innocent-looking indifference and her inexhaustible gaiety. He could hardly have said why, but she struck him as a young person not formed for a troublesome jealousy. Smile at such a betrayal though the reader may, it was a fact with regard to the women who had hitherto interested him that, given certain contingencies, Winterbourne could see himself afraid—literally afraid—of these ladies. It pleased him to believe that even were twenty other things different and Daisy should love him and he should know it and like it, he would still never be afraid of Daisy. It must be added that this conviction was not altogether flattering to her: it represented that she was nothing every way if not light.

But she was evidently very much interested in Giovanelli. She looked at him whenever he spoke; she was perpetually telling him to do this and to do that; she was constantly chaffing and abusing him. She appeared completely to have forgotten that her other friend had said anything to displease her at Mrs. Walker's entertainment. One Sunday afternoon, having gone to Saint Peter's with his aunt, Winterbourne became aware that the young woman held in horror by that lady was strolling about the great church under escort of her coxcomb of the Corso. It amused him, after a debate, to point out the exemplary pair—even at the cost, as it proved, of Mrs. Costello's saying when she had taken them in through her eye-glass: "That's what makes you so pensive in these days, eh?"

"I hadn't the least idea I was pensive," he pleaded.

"You're very much preoccupied; you're always thinking of something."

"And what is it," he asked, "that you accuse me of thinking of?"

"Of that young lady's, Miss Baker's, Miss Chandler's—what's her name?—Miss Miller's intrigue with that little barber's block."

"Do you call it an intrigue," he asked—"an affair that goes on with such peculiar publicity?"

"That's their folly," said Mrs. Costello, "it's not their merit."

"No," he insisted with a hint perhaps of the preoccupation to which his aunt had alluded—"I don't believe there's anything to be called an intrigue."

"Well"—and Mrs. Costello dropped her glass—"I've heard a dozen people speak of it: they say she's quite carried away by him."

"They're certainly as thick as thieves," our embarrassed young man allowed.

Mrs. Costello came back to them, however, after a little; and Winterbourne recognised in this a further illustration—than that supplied by his own condition—of the spell projected by the case. "He's certainly very handsome. One easily sees how it is. She thinks him the most elegant man in the world, the finest gentleman possible. She has never seen anything like him—he's better even than the courier. It was the courier probably who introduced him, and if he succeeds in marrying the young lady the courier will come in for a magnificent commission."

"I don't believe she thinks of marrying him," Winterbourne reasoned, "and I don't believe he hopes to marry her."

"You may be very sure she thinks of nothing at all. She romps on from day to day, from hour to hour, as they did in the Golden Age. I can imagine nothing more vulgar," said Mrs. Costello, whose figure of speech scarcely went on all fours. "And at the same time," she added, "depend upon it she may tell you any moment that she is 'engaged.'"

"I think that's more than Giovanelli really expects," said Winterbourne.

"And who is Giovanelli?"

"The shiny—but, to do him justice, not greasy—little Roman. I've asked questions about him and learned something. He's apparently a perfectly respectable little man. I believe he's in a small way a *cavaliere avvocato*.[18] But he doesn't move in what are called the first circles. I think it really not absolutely impossible the courier introduced him. He's evidently immensely charmed with Miss Miller. If she thinks him the finest gentleman in the world, he, on his side, has never found himself in personal contact with such splendour, such opulence, such personal daintiness, as this young lady's. And then she must seem to him wonderfully pretty and in-

18. A fairly common title of distinction given to lawyers.

teresting. Yes, he can't really hope to pull it off. That must appear to him too impossible a piece of luck. He has nothing but his handsome face to offer, and there's a substantial, a possibly explosive Mr. Miller in that mysterious land of dollars and six-shooters. Giovanelli's but too conscious that he hasn't a title to offer. If he were only a count or a *marchese!* What on earth can he make of the way they've taken him up?"

"He accounts for it by his handsome face and thinks Miss Miller a young lady *qui se passe ses fantaisies!*" [19]

"It's very true," Winterbourne pursued, "that Daisy and her mamma haven't yet risen to that stage of—what shall I call it?—of culture, at which the idea of catching a count or a *marchese* begins. I believe them intellectually incapable of that conception."

"Ah but the *cavaliere avvocato* doesn't believe them!" cried Mrs. Costello.

Of the observation excited by Daisy's "intrigue" Winterbourne gathered that day at Saint Peter's sufficient evidence. A dozen of the American colonists in Rome came to talk with his relative, who sat on a small portable stool at the base of one of the great pilasters. The vesper-service was going forward in splendid chants and organ-tones in the adjacent choir, and meanwhile, between Mrs. Costello and her friends, much was said about poor little Miss Miller's going really "too far." Winterbourne was not pleased with what he heard; but when, coming out upon the great steps of the church, he saw Daisy, who had emerged before him, get into an open cab with her accomplice and roll away through the cynical streets of Rome, the measure of her course struck him as simply there to take. He felt very sorry for her—not exactly that he believed she had completely lost her wits, but because it was painful to see so much that was pretty and undefended and natural sink so low in human estimation. He made an attempt after this to give a hint to Mrs. Miller. He met one day in the Corso a friend—a tourist like himself—who had just come out of the Doria Palace, where he had been walking through the beautiful gallery. His friend "went on" for some moments about the great portrait of Innocent X, by Velasquez,[20] suspended in one of the cabinets of the palace, and then said: "And in the same cabinet, by the way, I enjoyed sight of an image of a different kind; that little American who's so much more a work of nature than of art and whom you pointed out to me last week." In answer to Winterbourne's enquiries his friend narrated that the little American—prettier now than ever—was seated

19. "Who is satisfying her whims."
20. Diego Rodriguez de Silva y Velásquez (1599–1660), Spanish painter; the portrait is of Pope Innocent X (1574–1655).

with a companion in the secluded nook in which the papal presence is enshrined.

"All alone?" the young man heard himself disingenuously ask.

"Alone with a little Italian who sports in his button-hole a stack of flowers. The girl's a charming beauty, but I thought I understood from you the other day that she's a young lady *du meilleur monde*." [21]

"So she is!" said Winterbourne; and having assured himself that his informant had seen the interesting pair but ten minutes before, he jumped into a cab and went to call on Mrs. Miller. She was at home, but she apologised for receiving him in Daisy's absence.

"She's gone out somewhere with Mr. Giovanelli. She's always going round with Mr. Giovanelli."

"I've noticed they're intimate indeed," Winterbourne concurred.

"Oh it seems as if they couldn't live without each other!" said Mrs. Miller. "Well, he's a real gentleman anyhow. I guess I have the joke on Daisy—that she *must* be engaged!"

"And how does your daughter *take* the joke?"

"Oh she just says she ain't. But she might as *well* be!" this philosophic parent resumed. "She goes on as if she was. But I've made Mr. Giovanelli promise to tell me if Daisy don't. I'd want to write to Mr. Miller about it—wouldn't you?"

Winterbourne replied that he certainly should; and the state of mind of Daisy's mamma struck him as so unprecedented in the annals of parental vigilance that he recoiled before the attempt to educate at a single interview either her conscience or her wit.

After this Daisy was never at home and he ceased to meet her at the houses of their common acquaintance, because, as he perceived, these shrewd people had quite made up their minds as to the length she must have gone. They ceased to invite her, intimating that they wished to make, and make strongly, for the benefit of observant Europeans, the point that though Miss Daisy Miller was a pretty American girl all right, her behaviour wasn't pretty at all—was in fact regarded by her compatriots as quite monstrous. Winterbourne wondered how she felt about all the cold shoulders that were turned upon her, and sometimes found himself suspecting with impatience that she simply didn't feel and didn't know. He set her down as hopelessly childish and shallow, as such mere giddiness and ignorance incarnate as was powerless either to heed or to suffer. Then at other moments he couldn't doubt that she carried about in her elegant and irresponsible little organism a defiant, passionate, perfectly observant consciousness of the impression she

21. "Of the best society."

produced. He asked himself whether the defiance would come from the consciousness of innocence or from her being essentially a young person of the reckless class. Then it had to be admitted, he felt, that holding fast to a belief in her "innocence" was more and more but a matter of gallantry too fine-spun for use. As I have already had occasion to relate, he was reduced without pleasure to this chopping of logic and vexed at his poor fallibility, his want of instinctive certitude as to how far her extravagance was generic and national and how far it was crudely personal. Whatever it was he had helplessly missed her, and now it was too late. She was "carried away" by Mr. Giovanelli.

A few days after his brief interview with her mother he came across her at that supreme seat of flowering desolation known as the Palace of the Caesars. The early Roman spring had filled the air with bloom and perfume, and the rugged surface of the Palatine [22] was muffled with tender verdure. Daisy moved at her ease over the great mounds of ruin that are embanked with mossy marble and paved with monumental inscriptions. It seemed to him he had never known Rome so lovely as just then. He looked off at the enchanting harmony of line and colour that remotely encircles the city—he inhaled the softly humid odours and felt the freshness of the year and the antiquity of the place reaffirm themselves in deep interfusion. It struck him also that Daisy had never showed to the eye for so utterly charming; but this had been his conviction on every occasion of their meeting. Giovanelli was of course at her side, and Giovanelli too glowed as never before with something of the glory of his race.

"Well," she broke out upon the friend it would have been such mockery to designate as the latter's rival, "I should think you'd be quite lonesome!"

"Lonesome?" Winterbourne resignedly echoed.

"You're always going round by yourself. Can't you get any one to walk with you?"

"I'm not so fortunate," he answered, "as your gallant companion."

Giovanelli had from the first treated him with distinguished politeness; he listened with a deferential air to his remarks; he laughed punctiliously at his pleasantries; he attached such importance as he could find terms for to Miss Miller's cold compatriot. He carried himself in no degree like a jealous wooer; he had obviously a great deal of tact; he had no objection to any one's expecting a little humility of him. It even struck Winterbourne that he almost yearned at times for some private communication in the interest of

22. Roman hill to the south of the Forum.

his character for common sense; a chance to remark to him as another intelligent man that, bless him, *he* knew how extraordinary
was their young lady and didn't flatter himself with confident—at
least *too* confident and too delusive—hopes of matrimony and dollars. On this occasion he strolled away from his charming charge to
pluck a sprig of almond-blossom which he carefully arranged in his
button-hole.

"I know why you say that," Daisy meanwhile observed. "Because you think I go round too much with *him!*" And she nodded at
her discreet attendant.

"Every one thinks so—if you care to know," was all Winterbourne found to reply.

"Of course I care to know!"—she made this point with much
expression. "But I don't believe a word of it. They're only pretending to be shocked. They don't really care a straw what I do. Besides, I don't go round so much."

"I think you'll find they do care. They'll show it—disagreeably,"
he took on himself to state.

Daisy weighed the importance of that idea. "How—
disagreeably?"

"Haven't you noticed anything?" he compassionately asked.

"I've noticed *you*. But I noticed you've no more 'give' than a
ramrod the first time ever I saw you."

"You'll find at least that I've more 'give' than several others," he
patiently smiled.

"How shall I find it?"

"By going to see the others."

"What will they do to me?"

"They'll show you the cold shoulder. Do you know what that
means?"

Daisy was looking at him intently; she began to colour. "Do you
mean as Mrs. Walker did the other night?"

"Exactly as Mrs. Walker did the other night."

She looked away at Giovanelli, still titivating with his almond-
blossom. Then with her attention again on the important subject: "I
shouldn't think you'd let people be so unkind!"

"How can I help it?"

"I should think you'd want to say something."

"I do want to say something"—and Winterbourne paused a moment. "I want to say that your mother tells me she believes you
engaged."

"Well, I guess she does," said Daisy very simply.

The young man began to laugh. "And does Randolph believe it?"

"I guess Randolph doesn't believe anything." This testimony to
Randolph's scepticism excited Winterbourne to further mirth, and

he noticed that Giovanelli was coming back to them. Daisy, observing it as well, addressed herself again to her countryman. "Since you've mentioned it," she said, "I *am* engaged." He looked at her hard—he had stopped laughing. "You don't believe it!" she added.

He asked himself, and it was for a moment like testing a heartbeat; after which, "Yes, I believe it!" he said.

"Oh no, you don't," she answered. "But *if* you possibly do," she still more perversely pursued—"well, I ain't!"

Miss Miller and her constant guide were on their way to the gate of the enclosure, so that Winterbourne, who had but lately entered, presently took leave of them. A week later on he went to dine at a beautiful villa on the Cælian Hill, and, on arriving, dismissed his hired vehicle. The evening was perfect and he promised himself the satisfaction of walking home beneath the Arch of Constantine and past the vaguely-lighted monuments of the Forum. Above was a moon half-developed, whose radiance was not brilliant but veiled in a thin cloud-curtain that seemed to diffuse and equalise it. When on his return from the villa at eleven o'clock he approached the dusky circle of the Colosseum [23] the sense of the romantic in him easily suggested that the interior, in such an atmosphere, would well repay a glance. He turned aside and walked to one of the empty arches, near which, as he observed, an open carriage—one of the little Roman street-cabs—was stationed. Then he passed in among the cavernous shadows of the great structure and emerged upon the clear and silent arena. The place had never seemed to him more impressive. One half of the gigantic circus was in deep shade while the other slept in the luminous dusk. As he stood there he began to murmur Byron's famous lines out of "Manfred"; [24] but

23. Huge amphitheatre, completed by Titus A.D. 80. It seated 87,000 spectators, and was the scene of gladiatorial contests.
24. Lord Byron's dramatic poem *Manfred* (1817) contains a soliloquy on the Colosseum by the hero.

> I do remember me, that in my youth,
> When I was wandering,—upon such a night
> I stood within the Coliseum's wall,
> 'Midst the chief relics of almighty Rome . . .
> And thou didst shine, thou rolling moon, upon
> All this, and cast a wide and tender light,
> Which softened down the hoar austerity
> Of rugged desolation, and filled up,
> As 't were anew, the gaps of centuries;
> Leaving that beautiful which still was so,
> And making that which was not, till the place
> Became religion, and the heart ran o'er
> With silent worship of the great of old . . .

Winterbourne's sentimental admiration for *Manfred,* a tale of incest and Promethean defiance, stands in ironic contrast to his prudent intention to make a "hasty retreat" from the Colosseum. Throughout *Daisy Miller* James uses the Romantic-Byronic themes associated with the Alps and Rome as delicate counterpoints to his story of brash American innocence.

before he had finished his quotation he remembered that if nocturnal meditation thereabouts was the fruit of a rich literary culture it was none the less deprecated by medical science. The air of other ages surrounded one; but the air of other ages, coldly analysed, was no better than a villainous miasma. Winterbourne sought, however, toward the middle of the arena, a further reach of vision, intending the next moment a hasty retreat. The great cross in the centre was almost obscured; only as he drew near did he make it out distinctly. He thus also distinguished two persons stationed on the low steps that formed its base. One of these was a woman seated; her companion hovered before her.

Presently the sound of the woman's voice came to him distinctly in the warm night-air. "Well, he looks at us as one of the old lions or tigers may have looked at the Christian martyrs!" These words were winged with their accent, so that they fluttered and settled about him in the darkness like vague white doves. It was Miss Daisy Miller who had released them for flight.

"Let us hope he's not very hungry"—the bland Giovanelli fell in with her humour. "He'll have to take *me* first; you'll serve for dessert."

Winterbourne felt himself pulled up with final horror now—and, it must be added, with final relief. It was as if a sudden clearance had taken place in the ambiguity of the poor girl's appearances and the whole riddle of her contradictions had grown easy to read. She was a young lady about the *shades* of whose perversity a foolish puzzled gentleman need no longer trouble his head or his heart. That once questionable quantity *had* no shades—it was a mere black little blot. He stood there looking at her, looking at her companion too, and not reflecting that though he saw them vaguely he himself must have been more brightly presented. He felt angry at all his shiftings of view—he felt ashamed of all his tender little scruples and all his witless little mercies. He was about to advance again, and then again checked himself; not from the fear of doing her injustice, but from a sense of the danger of showing undue exhilaration for this disburdenment of cautious criticism. He turned away toward the entrance of the place; but as he did so he heard Daisy speak again.

"Why it was Mr. Winterbourne! He saw me and he cuts me dead!"

What a clever little reprobate she was, he was amply able to reflect at this, and how smartly she feigned, how promptly she sought to play off on him, a surprised and injured innocence! But nothing would induce him to cut her either "dead" or to within any measurable distance even of the famous "inch" of her life. He came forward again and went toward the great cross. Daisy had got up and Giovanelli lifted his hat. Winterbourne had now begun to think simply of the madness, on the ground of exposure and infection, of a frail young creature's lounging away such hours in a nest of malaria. What if she *were* the most plausible of little reprobates? That was no reason for her dying of the *perniciosa*.[25] "How long have you been 'fooling round' here?" he asked with conscious roughness.

Daisy, lovely in the sinister silver radiance, appraised him a moment, roughness and all. "Well, I guess all the evening." She answered with spirit and, he could see even then, with exaggeration. "I never saw anything so quaint."

"I'm afraid," he returned, "you'll not think a bad attack of Roman fever very quaint. This is the way people catch it. I wonder," he added to Giovanelli, "that you, a native Roman, should countenance such extraordinary rashness."

"Ah," said this seasoned subject, "for myself I have no fear."

"Neither have I—for you!" Winterbourne retorted in French. "I'm speaking for this young lady."

Giovanelli raised his well-shaped eyebrows and showed his shining teeth, but took his critic's rebuke with docility. "I assured Mademoiselle it was a grave indiscretion, but when was Mademoiselle ever prudent?"

"I never was sick, and I don't mean to be!" Mademoiselle declared. "I don't look like much, but I'm healthy! I was bound to see the Colosseum by moonlight—I wouldn't have wanted to go home without *that*; and we've had the most beautiful time, haven't we, Mr. Giovanelli? If there has been any danger Eugenio can give me some pills. Eugenio has got some splendid pills."

"*I* should advise you then," said Winterbourne, "to drive home as fast as possible and take one!"

Giovanelli smiled as for the striking happy thought. "What you say is very wise. I'll go and make sure the carriage is at hand." And he went forward rapidly.

Daisy followed with Winterbourne. He tried to deny himself the small fine anguish of looking at her, but his eyes themselves refused to spare him, and she seemed moreover not in the least embarrassed. He spoke no word; Daisy chattered over the beauty of the place: "Well, I *have* seen the Colosseum by moonlight—that's one thing I can rave about!" Then noticing her companion's silence she asked him why he was so stiff—it had always been her great word. He made no answer, but he felt his laugh an immense negation of stiffness. They passed under one of the dark archways; Giovanelli was in front with the carriage. Here Daisy stopped a moment, looking at her compatriot. "*Did* you believe I was engaged the other day?"

25. Malignant fever (malaria).

"It doesn't matter now what I believed the other day!" he replied with infinite point.

It was a wonder how she didn't wince for it. "Well, what do you believe now?"

"I believe it makes very little difference whether you're engaged or not!"

He felt her lighted eyes fairly penetrate the thick gloom of the vaulted passage—as if to seek some access to him she hadn't yet compassed. But Giovanelli, with a graceful inconsequence, was at present all for retreat. "Quick, quick; if we get in by midnight we're quite safe!"

Daisy took her seat in the carriage and the fortunate Italian placed himself beside her. "Don't forget Eugenio's pills!" said Winterbourne as he lifted his hat.

"I don't care," she unexpectedly cried out for this, "whether I have Roman fever or not!" On which the cab-driver cracked his whip and they rolled across the desultory patches of antique pavement.

Winterbourne—to do him justice, as it were—mentioned to no one that he had encountered Miss Miller at midnight in the Colosseum with a gentleman; in spite of which deep discretion, however, the fact of the scandalous adventure was known a couple of days later, with a dozen vivid details, to every member of the little American circle, and was commented accordingly. Winterbourne judged thus that the people about the hotel had been thoroughly empowered to testify, and that after Daisy's return there would have been an exchange of jokes between the porter and the cab-driver. But the young man became aware at the same moment of how thoroughly it had ceased to ruffle him that the little American flirt should be "talked about" by low-minded menials. These sources of current criticism a day or two later abounded still further: the little American flirt was alarmingly ill and the doctors now in possession of the scene. Winterbourne, when the rumour came to him, immediately went to the hotel for more news. He found that two or three charitable friends had preceded him and that they were being entertained in Mrs. Miller's salon by the all-efficient Randolph.

"It's going round at night that way, you bet—that's what has made her so sick. She's always going round at night. I shouldn't think she'd want to—it's so plaguey dark over here. You can't see anything over here without the moon's right up. In America they don't go round by the moon!" Mrs. Miller meanwhile wholly surrendered to her genius for unapparent uses; her salon knew her less than ever, and she was presumably now at least giving her daughter the advantage of her society. It was clear that Daisy was dangerously ill.

Winterbourne constantly attended for news from the sick-room, which reached him, however, but with worrying indirectness, though he once had speech, for a moment, of the poor girl's physician and once saw Mrs. Miller, who, sharply alarmed, struck him as thereby more happily inspired than he could have conceived and indeed as the most noiseless and light-handed of nurses. She invoked a good deal the remote shade of Dr. Davis, but Winterbourne paid her the compliment of taking her after all for less monstrous a goose. To this indulgence indeed something she further said perhaps even more insidiously disposed him. "Daisy spoke of you the other day quite pleasantly. Half the time she doesn't know what she's saying, but that time I think she did. She gave me a message—she told me to tell you. She wanted you to know she never was engaged to that handsome Italian who was always round. I'm sure I'm very glad; Mr. Giovanelli hasn't been near us since she was taken ill. I thought he was so much of a gentleman, but I don't call that very polite! A lady told me he was afraid I hadn't approved of his being round with her so much evenings. Of course it ain't as if their evenings were as pleasant as ours—since *we* don't seem to feel that way about the poison. I guess I *don't* see the point now; but I suppose he knows I'm a lady and I'd scorn to raise a fuss. Anyway, she wants you to realise she ain't engaged. I don't know why she makes so much of it, but she said to me three times 'Mind you tell Mr. Winterbourne.' And then she told me to ask if you remembered the time you went up to that castle in Switzerland. But I said I wouldn't give any such messages as *that*. Only if she ain't engaged I guess I'm glad to realise it too."

But, as Winterbourne had originally judged, the truth on this question had small actual relevance. A week after this the poor girl died; it had been indeed a terrible case of the *perniciosa*. A grave was found for her in the little Protestant cemetery, by an angle of the wall of imperial Rome, beneath the cypresses and the thick spring-flowers. Winterbourne stood there beside it with a number of other mourners; a number larger than the scandal excited by the young lady's career might have made probable. Near him stood Giovanelli, who came nearer still before Winterbourne turned away. Giovanelli, in decorous mourning, showed but a whiter face; his button-hole lacked its nosegay and he had visibly something urgent—and even to distress—to say, which he scarce knew how to "place." He decided at last to confide it with a pale convulsion to Winterbourne. "She was the most beautiful young lady I ever saw, and the most amiable." To which he added in a moment: "Also—naturally!—the most innocent."

Winterbourne sounded him with hard dry eyes, but presently repeated his words, "The most innocent?"

"The most innocent!"

It came somehow so much too late that our friend could only glare at its having come at all. "Why the devil," he asked, "did you take her to that fatal place?"

Giovanelli raised his neat shoulders and eyebrows to within suspicion of a shrug. "For myself I had no fear; and *she*—she did what she liked."

Winterbourne's eyes attached themselves to the ground. "She did what she liked!"

It determined on the part of poor Giovanelli a further pious, a further candid, confidence. "If she had lived I should have got nothing. She never would have married me."

It had been spoken as if to attest, in all sincerity, his disinterestedness, but Winterbourne scarce knew what welcome to give it. He said, however, with a grace inferior to his friend's: "I dare say not."

The latter was even by this not discouraged. "For a moment I hoped so. But no. I'm convinced."

Winterbourne took it in; he stood staring at the raw protuberance among the April daisies. When he turned round again his fellow mourner had stepped back.

He almost immediately left Rome, but the following summer he again met his aunt Mrs. Costello at Vevey. Mrs. Costello extracted from the charming old hotel there a value that the Miller family hadn't mastered the secret of. In the interval Winterbourne had often thought of the most interesting member of that trio—of her mystifying manners and her queer adventure. One day he spoke of her to his aunt—said it was on his conscience he had done her injustice.

"I'm sure I don't know"—that lady showed caution. "How did your injustice affect her?"

"She sent me a message before her death which I didn't understand at the time. But I've understood it since. She would have appreciated one's esteem."

"She took an odd way to gain it! But do you mean by what you say," Mrs. Costello asked, "that she would have reciprocated one's affection?"

As he made no answer to this she after a little looked round at him—he hadn't been directly within sight; but the effect of that wasn't to make her repeat her question. He spoke, however, after a while. "You were right in that remark that you made last summer. I was booked to make a mistake. I've lived too long in foreign parts." And this time she herself said nothing.

Nevertheless he soon went back to live at Geneva, whence there continue to come the most contradictory accounts of his motives of sojourn: a report that he's "studying" hard—an intimation that he's much interested in a very clever foreign lady.

The present text was revised for *The Novels and Tales of Henry James* (New York Edition, 1907–9). *Daisy Miller* was first published in 1878.

FROM THE PREFACE TO
DAISY MILLER [1]

It was in Rome during the autumn of 1877; a friend then living
there but settled now in a South less weighted with appeals and
memories happened to mention—which she might perfectly not
have done—some simple and uninformed American lady of the previous winter, whose young daughter, a child of nature and of freedom, accompanying her from hotel to hotel, had "picked up" by the
wayside, with the best conscience in the world, a good-looking
Roman, of vague identity, astonished at his luck, yet (so far as might
be, by the pair) all innocently, all serenely exhibited and introduced: this at least till the occurrence of some small social check,
some interrupting incident, of no great gravity or dignity, and
which I forget. I had never heard, save on this showing, of the amiable but not otherwise eminent ladies, who weren't in fact named, I
think, and whose case had merely served to point a familiar moral;
and it must have been just their want of salience that left a margin
for the small pencil-mark inveterately signifying, in such connex-
ions, "Dramatise, dramatise!" The result of my recognising a few
months later the sense of my pencil-mark was the short chronicle of
"Daisy Miller," which I indited in London the following spring and
then addressed, with no conditions attached, as I remember, to the
editor of a magazine that had its seat of publication at Philadelphia
and had lately appeared to appreciate my contributions. That gentleman however (an historian of some repute) promptly returned
me my missive, and with an absence of comment that struck me at
the time as rather grim—as, given the circumstances, requiring indeed some explanation: till a friend to whom I appealed for light,
giving him the thing to read, declared it could only have passed
with the Philadelphian critic for "an outrage on American girl-
hood." This was verily a light, and of bewildering intensity; though
I was presently to read into the matter a further helpful inference.
To the fault of being outrageous this little composition added that
of being essentially and pre-eminently a *nouvelle;* a signal example
in fact of that type, foredoomed at the best, in more cases than not,
to editorial disfavour. If accordingly I was afterwards to be cradled,
almost blissfully, in the conception that "Daisy" at least, among my
productions, might approach "success," such success for example,
on her eventual appearance, as the state of being promptly pirated
in Boston—a sweet tribute I hadn't yet received and was never
again to know—the irony of things yet claimed its rights, I couldn't

1. This first appeared in the New York Edition of James's works, published during
the years 1907-9.

but long continue to feel, in the circumstance that quite a special reprobation had waited on the first appearance in the world of the ultimately most prosperous child of my invention. So doubly discredited, at all events, this bantling met indulgence, with no great delay, in the eyes of my admirable friend the late Leslie Stephen and was published in two numbers of *The Cornhill Magazine* (1878).

It qualified itself in that publication and afterwards as "a Study"; for reasons which I confess I fail to recapture unless they may have taken account simply of a certain flatness in my poor little heroine's literal denomination. Flatness indeed, one must have felt, was the very sum of her story; so that perhaps after all the attached epithet was meant but as a deprecation, addressed to the reader, of any great critical hope of stirring scenes. It provided for mere concentration, and on an object scant and superficially vulgar—from which, however, a sufficiently brooding tenderness might eventually extract a shy incongruous charm. I suppress at all events here the appended qualification—in view of the simple truth, which ought from the first to have been apparent to me, that my little exhibition is made to no degree whatever in critical but, quite inordinately and extravagantly, in poetical terms. It comes back to me that I was at a certain hour long afterwards to have reflected, in this connexion, on the characteristic free play of the whirligig of time. It was in Italy again—in Venice and in the prized society of an interesting friend, now dead, with whom I happened to wait, on the Grand Canal, at the animated water-steps of one of the hotels. The considerable little terrace there was so disposed as to make a salient stage for certain demonstrations on the part of two young girls, children *they*, if ever, of nature and of freedom, whose use of those resources, in the general public eye, and under our own as we sat in the gondola, drew from the lips of a second companion, sociably afloat with us, the remark that there before us, with no sign absent, were a couple of attesting Daisy Millers. Then it was that, in my charming hostess's prompt protest, the whirligig, as I have called it, at once betrayed itself. "How can you liken *those* creatures to a figure of which the only fault is touchingly to have transmuted so sorry a type and to have, by a poetic artifice, not only led our judgement of it astray, but made *any* judgement quite impossible?" With which this gentle lady and admirable critic turned on the author himself. "You *know* you quite falsified, by the turn you gave it, the thing you had begun with having in mind, the thing you had had, to satiety, the chance of 'observing': your pretty perversion of it, or your unprincipled mystification of our sense of it, does it really too much honour—in spite of which, none the less, as anything charming or touching always to that extent justifies itself, we after a fashion forgive and understand you. But why *waste* your romance? There are cases, too many, in which you've done it again; in which, provoked by a spirit of observation at first no doubt sufficiently sincere, and with the measured and felt truth fairly twitching your sleeve, you have yielded to your incurable prejudice in favour of grace—to whatever it is in you that makes so inordinately for form and prettiness and pathos; not to say sometimes for misplaced drolling. Is it that you've after all too much imagination? Those awful young women capering at the hotel-door, *they* are the real little Daisy Millers that were; whereas yours in the tale is such a one, more's the pity, as—for pitch of the ingenuous, for quality of the artless—couldn't possibly have been at all." My answer to all which bristled of course with more professions than I can or need report here; the chief of them inevitably to the effect that my supposedly typical little figure was of course pure poetry, and had never been anything else; since this is what helpful imagination, in however slight a dose, ever directly makes for. As for the original grossness of readers, I dare say I added, that was another matter—but one which at any rate had then quite ceased to signify.

THE REAL THING

When the porter's wife, who used to answer the house-bell, announced "A gentleman and a lady, sir," I had, as I often had in those days—the wish being father to the thought—an immediate vision of sitters. Sitters my visitors in this case proved to be; but not in the sense I should have preferred. There was nothing at first however to indicate that they mightn't have come for a portrait. The gentleman, a man of fifty, very high and very straight, with a moustache slightly grizzled and a dark grey walking-coat admirably fitted, both of which I noted professionally—I don't mean as a barber or yet a tailor—would have struck me as a celebrity if celebrities often were striking. It was a truth of which I had for some time been conscious that a figure with a good deal of frontage was, as one might say, almost never a public institution. A glance at the lady helped to remind me of this paradoxical law: she also looked too distinguished to be a "personality." Moreover one would scarcely come across two variations together.

Neither of the pair immediately spoke—they only prolonged the preliminary gaze suggesting that each wished to give the other a chance. They were visibly shy; they stood there letting me take them in—which, as I afterwards perceived, was the most practical thing they could have done. In this way their embarrassment served their cause. I had seen people painfully reluctant to mention that they desired anything so gross as to be represented on canvas; but the scruples of my new friends appeared almost insurmountable. Yet the gentleman might have said "I should like a portrait of my wife," and the lady might have said "I should like a portrait of my husband." Perhaps they weren't husband and wife—this naturally would make the matter more delicate. Perhaps they wished to be done together—in which case they ought to have brought a third person to break the news.

"We come from Mr. Rivet," the lady finally said with a dim smile that had the effect of a moist sponge passed over a "sunk" piece of painting, as well as of a vague allusion to vanished beauty. She was as tall and straight, in her degree, as her companion, and with ten years less to carry. She looked as sad as a woman could look whose face was not charged with expression; that is her tinted oval mask showed waste as an exposed surface shows friction. The hand of time had played over her freely, but to an effect of elimination. She was slim and stiff, and so well-dressed, in dark blue cloth, with lappets and pockets and buttons, that it was clear she employed the same tailor as her husband. The couple had an indefinable air of prosperous thrift—they evidently got a good deal of luxury for their money. If I was to be one of their luxuries it would behove me to consider my terms.

"Ah Claude Rivet recommended me?" I echoed; and I added that it was very kind of him, though I could reflect that, as he only painted landscape, this wasn't a sacrifice.

The lady looked very hard at the gentleman, and the gentleman looked round the room. Then staring at the floor a moment and stroking his moustache, he rested his pleasant eyes on me with the remark; "He said you were the right one."

"I try to be, when people want to sit."

"Yes, we should like to," said the lady anxiously.

"Do you mean together?"

My visitors exchanged a glance. "If you could do anything with *me* I suppose it would be double," the gentleman stammered.

"Oh yes, there's naturally a higher charge for two figures than for one."

"We should like to make it pay," the husband confessed.

"That's very good of you," I returned, appreciating so unwonted a sympathy—for I supposed he meant pay the artist.

A sense of strangeness seemed to dawn on the lady. "We mean for the illustrations—Mr. Rivet said you might put one in."

"Put in—an illustration?" I was equally confused.

"Sketch her off, you know," said the gentleman, colouring.

It was only then that I understood the service Claude Rivet had rendered me; he had told them how I worked in black-and-white, for magazines, for story-books, for sketches of contemporary life, and consequently had copious employment for models. These things were true, but it was not less true—I may confess it now; whether because the aspiration was to lead to everything or to nothing I leave the reader to guess—that I couldn't get the honours, to say nothing of the emoluments, of a great painter of portraits out of my head. My "illustrations" were my pot-boilers; I looked to a different branch of art—far and away the most interesting it had always seemed to me—to perpetuate my fame. There was no shame in looking to it also to make my fortune; but that fortune was by so much further from being made from the moment my visitors wished to be "done" for nothing. I was disappointed; for in the pictorial sense I had immediately *seen* them. I had seized their type—I had already settled what I would do with it. Something that wouldn't absolutely have pleased them, I afterwards reflected.

"Ah you're—you're—a—?" I began as soon as I had mastered my surprise. I couldn't bring out the dingy word "models": it seemed so little to fit the case.

"We haven't had much practice," said the lady.

"We've got to *do* something, and we've thought that an artist in your line might perhaps make something of us," her husband threw off. He further mentioned that they didn't know many artists and that they had gone first, on the off-chance—he painted views of course, but sometimes put in figures; perhaps I remembered—to Mr. Rivet, whom they had met a few years before at a place in Norfolk where he was sketching.

"We used to sketch a little ourselves," the lady hinted.

"It's very awkward, but we absolutely *must* do something," her husband went on.

"Of course we're not so *very* young," she admitted with a wan smile.

With the remark that I might as well know something more about them the husband had handed me a card extracted from a neat new pocket-book—their appurtenances were all of the freshest—and inscribed with the words "Major Monarch." Impressive as these words were they didn't carry my knowledge much further; but my visitor presently added: "I've left the army and we've had the misfortune to lose our money. In fact our means are dreadfully small."

"It's awfully trying—a regular strain," said Mrs. Monarch.

They evidently wished to be discreet—to take care not to swagger because they were gentlefolk. I felt them willing to recognize this as something of a drawback, at the same time that I guessed at an underlying sense—their consolation in adversity—that they *had* their points. They certainly had; but these advantages struck me as preponderantly social; such for instance as would help to make a drawing-room look well. However, a drawing-room was always, or ought to be, a picture.

In consequence of his wife's allusion to their age Major Monarch observed: "Naturally it's more for the figure that we thought of going in. We can still hold ourselves up." On the instant I saw that the figure was indeed their strong point. His "naturally" didn't sound vain, but it lighted up the question. "*She* has the best one," he continued, nodding at his wife with a pleasant after-dinner absence of circumlocution. I could only reply, as if we were in fact sitting over our wine, that this didn't prevent his own from being very good; which led him in turn to make answer: "We thought that if you ever have to do people like us we might be something like it. *She* particularly—for a lady in a book, you know."

I was so amused by them that, to get more of it, I did my best to take their point of view; and though it was an embarrassment to find myself appraising physically, as if they were animals on hire or useful blacks, a pair whom I should have expected to meet only in one of the relations in which criticism is tacit, I looked at Mrs. Monarch judicially enough to be able to exclaim after a moment with conviction: "Oh yes, a lady in a book!" She was singularly like a bad illustration.

"We'll stand up, if you like," said the Major; and he raised himself before me with a really grand air.

I could take his measure at a glance—he was six feet two and a perfect gentleman. It would have paid any club in process of formation and in want of a stamp to engage him at a salary to stand in the principal window. What struck me at once was that in coming to me they had rather missed their vocation; they could surely have been turned to better account for advertising purposes. I couldn't of course see the thing in detail, but I could see them make somebody's fortune—I don't mean their own. There was something in them for a waistcoat-maker, an hotel-keeper or a soap-vendor. I could imagine "We always use it" pinned on their bosoms with the greatest effect; I had a vision of the brilliancy with which they would launch a table d'hôte.

Mrs. Monarch sat still, not from pride but from shyness, and presently her husband said to her: "Get up, my dear, and show how smart you are." She obeyed, but she had no need to get up to show it. She walked to the end of the studio and then came back blushing, her fluttered eyes on the partner of her appeal. I was reminded of an incident I had accidentally had a glimpse of in Paris—being with a friend there, a dramatist about to produce a play, when an actress came to him to ask to be entrusted with a part. She went through her paces before him, walked up and down as Mrs. Monarch was doing. Mrs. Monarch did it quite as well, but I abstained from applauding. It was very odd to see such people apply for such poor pay. She looked as if she had ten thousand a year. Her husband had used the word that described her: she was in the London current jargon essentially and typically "smart." Her figure was, in the same order of ideas, conspicuously and irreproachably "good." For a woman of her age her waist was surprisingly small; her elbow moreover had the orthodox crook. She held her head at the conventional angle, but why did she come to *me?* She ought to have tried on jackets at a big shop. I feared my visitors were not only destitute but "artistic"—which would be a great complication. When she sat down again I thanked her, observing that what a draughtsman most valued in his model was the faculty of keeping quiet.

"Oh *she* can keep quiet," said Major Monarch. Then he added jocosely: "I've always kept her quiet."

"I'm not a nasty fidget, am I?" It was going to wring tears from me, I felt, the way she hid her head, ostrich-like, in the other broad bosom.

The owner of this expanse addressed his answer to me. "Perhaps it isn't out of place to mention—because we ought to be quite business-like, oughtn't we?—that when I married her she was known as the Beautiful Statue."

"Oh dear!" said Mrs. Monarch ruefully.

"Of course I should want a certain amount of expression," I rejoined.

"Of *course!*"—and I had never heard such unanimity.

"And then I suppose you know that you'll get awfully tired."

"Oh we *never* get tired!" they eagerly cried.

"Have you had any kind of practice?"

They hesitated—they looked at each other. "We've been photographed—*immensely*," said Mrs. Monarch.

"She means the fellows have asked us themselves," added the Major.

"I see—because you're so good-looking."

"I don't know what they thought, but they were always after us."

"We always got our photographs for nothing," smiled Mrs. Monarch.

"We might have brought some, my dear," her husband remarked.

"I'm not sure we have any left. We've given quantities away," she explained to me.

"With our autographs and that sort of thing," said the Major.

"Are they to be got in the shops?" I enquired as a harmless pleasantry.

"Oh yes, *hers*—they used to be."

"Not now," said Mrs. Monarch with her eyes on the floor.

II

I could fancy the "sort of thing" they put on the presentation copies of their photographs, and I was sure they wrote a beautiful hand. It was odd how quickly I was sure of everything that concerned them. If they were now so poor as to have to earn shillings and pence they could never have had much of a margin. Their good looks had been their capital, and they had good-humouredly made the most of the career that this resource marked out for them. It was in their faces, the blankness, the deep intellectual repose of the twenty years of country-house visiting that had given them pleasant intonations. I could see the sunny drawing-rooms, sprinkled with periodicals she didn't read, in which Mrs. Monarch had continuously sat; I could see the wet shrubberies in which she had walked, equipped to admiration for either exercise. I could see the rich covers the Major had helped to shoot and the wonderful garments in which, late at night, he repaired to the smoking-room to talk about them. I could imagine their leggings and waterproofs, their knowing tweeds and rugs, their rolls of sticks and cases of tackle and neat umbrellas; and I could evoke the exact appearance of their servants and the compact variety of their luggage on the platforms of country stations.

They gave small tips, but they were liked; they didn't do anything themselves, but they were welcome. They looked so well everywhere; they gratified the general relish for stature, complexion and "form." They knew it without fatuity or vulgarity, and they respected themselves in consequence. They weren't superficial; they were thorough and kept themselves up—it had been their line. People with such a taste for activity had to have some line. I could feel how even in a dull house they could have been counted on for the joy of life. At present something had happened—it didn't matter what, their little income had grown less, it had grown least—and they had to do something for pocket-money. Their friends could like them, I made out, without liking to support them. There was something about them that represented credit—their clothes, their manners, their type; but if credit is a large empty pocket in which an occasional chink reverberates, the chink at least must be audible. What they wanted of me was to help to make it so. Fortunately they had no children—I soon divined that. They would also perhaps wish our relations to be kept secret: this was why it was "for the figure"—the reproduction of the face would betray them.

I liked them—I felt, quite as their friends must have done—they were so simple; and I had no objection to them if they would suit. But somehow with all their perfections I didn't easily believe in them. After all they were amateurs, and the ruling passion of my life was the detestation of the amateur. Combined with this was another perversity—an innate preference for the represented subject over the real one: the defect of the real one was so apt to be a lack of representation. I liked things that appeared; then one was sure. Whether they *were* or not was a subordinate and almost always a profitless question. There were other considerations, the first of which was that I already had two or three recruits in use, notably a young person with big feet, in alpaca, from Kilburn, who for a couple of years had come to me regularly for my illustrations and with whom I was still—perhaps ignobly—satisfied. I frankly explained to my visitors how the case stood, but they had taken more precautions than I supposed. They had reasoned out their opportunity, for Claude Rivet had told them of the projected *édition de luxe* of one of the writers of our day—the rarest of the novelists—who, long neglected by the multitudinous vulgar and dearly prized by the attentive (need I mention Philip Vincent?), had had the happy fortune of seeing, late in life, the dawn and then the full light of a higher criticism; an estimate in which on the part of the public there was something really of expiation. The edition preparing,

planned by a publisher of taste, was practically an act of high repa-
ration; the wood-cuts with which it was to be enriched were the
homage of English art to one of the most independent representatives of English letters. Major and Mrs. Monarch confessed to me
they had hoped I might be able to work *them* into my branch of the
enterprise. They knew I was to do the first of the books, "Rutland
Ramsay," but I had to make clear to them that my participation in
the rest of the affair—this first book was to be a test—must depend
on the satisfaction I should give. If this should be limited my em-
ployers would drop me with scarce common forms. It was therefore
a crisis for me, and naturally I was making special preparations,
looking about for new people, should they be necessary, and securing the best types. I admitted however that I should like to settle
down to two or three good models who would do for everything.

"Should we have often to—a—put on special clothes?" Mrs. Monarch timidly demanded.

"Dear yes—that's half the business."

"And should we be expected to supply our own costumes?"

"Oh no; I've got a lot of things. A painter's models put on—or put
off—anything he likes."

"And you mean—a—the same?"

"The same?"

Mrs. Monarch looked at her husband again.

"Oh she was just wondering," he explained, "if the costumes are
in *general* use." I had to confess that they were, and I mentioned
further that some of them—I had a lot of genuine greasy last-cen-
tury things—had served their time, a hundred years ago, on living
world-stained men and women; on figures not perhaps so far removed, in that vanished world, from *their* type, the Monarchs',
quoi! of a breeched and bewigged age. "We'll put on anything that
fits," said the Major.

"Oh I arrange that—they fit in the pictures."

"I'm afraid I should do better for the modern books. I'd come as
you like," said Mrs. Monarch.

"She has got a lot of clothes at home: they might do for contemporary life," her husband continued.

"Oh I can fancy scenes in which you'd be quite natural." And
indeed I could see the slipshod rearrangements of stale proper-
ties—the stories I tried to produce pictures for without the exasperation of reading them—whose sandy tracts the good lady might help
to people. But I had to return to the fact that for this sort of work—
the daily mechanical grind—I was already equipped: the people I
was working with were fully adequate.

"We only thought we might be more like *some* characters," said
Mrs. Monarch mildly, getting up.

Her husband also rose; he stood looking at me with a dim wistfulness that was touching in so fine a man. "Wouldn't it be rather a pull sometimes to have—a—to have—?" He hung fire; he wanted me to help him by phrasing what he meant. But I couldn't—I didn't know. So he brought it out awkwardly: "The *real* thing; a gentleman, you know, or a lady." I was quite ready to give a general assent—I admitted that there was a great deal in that. This encouraged Major Monarch to say, following up his appeal with an unacted gulp: "It's awfully hard—we've tried everything." The gulp was communicative; it proved too much for his wife. Before I knew it Mrs. Monarch had dropped again upon a divan and burst into tears. Her husband sat down beside her, holding one of her hands; whereupon she quickly dried her eyes with the other, while I felt embarrassed as she looked up at me. "There isn't a confounded job I haven't applied for—waited for—prayed for. You can fancy we'd be pretty bad first. Secretaryships and that sort of thing? You might as well ask for a peerage. I'd be *anything*—I'm strong; a messenger or a coal-heaver. I'd put on a gold-laced cap and open carriage-doors in front of the haberdasher's; I'd hang about a station to carry portmanteaux; I'd be a postman. But they won't *look* at you; there are thousands as good as yourself already on the ground. *Gentlemen,* poor beggars, who've drunk their wine, who've kept their hunters!"

I was as reassuring as I knew how to be, and my visitors were presently on their feet again while, for the experiment, we agreed on an hour. We were discussing it when the door opened and Miss Churm came in with a wet umbrella. Miss Churm had to take the omnibus to Maida Vale and then walk half a mile. She looked a trifle blowsy and slightly splashed. I scarcely ever saw her come in without thinking afresh how odd it was that, being so little in herself, she should yet be so much in others. She was a meagre little Miss Churm, but was such an ample heroine of romance. She was only a freckled cockney,[1] but she could represent everything, from a fine lady to a shepherdess; she had the faculty as she might have had a fine voice or long hair. She couldn't spell and she loved beer, but she had two or three "points," and practice, and a knack, and mother-wit, and a whimsical sensibility, and a love of the theatre, and seven sisters, and not an ounce of respect, especially for the "h." The first thing my visitors saw was that her umbrella was wet, and in their spotless perfection they visibly winced at it. The rain had come on since their arrival.

"I'm all in a soak; there *was* a mess of people in the 'bus. I wish

1. A native of the East End of London, speaking a local dialect marked by the dropping of the letter *h*. Usually a contemptuous or bantering term, implying lower-class origins.

you lived near a stytion," said Miss Churm. I requested her to get ready as quickly as possible, and she passed into the room in which she always changed her dress. But before going out she asked me what she was to get into this time.

"It's the Russian princess, don't you know?" I answered; "the one with the 'golden eyes,' in black velvet, for the long thing in the *Cheapside*." [2]

"Golden eyes? I *say!*" cried Miss Churm, while my companions watched her with intensity as she withdrew. She always arranged herself, when she was late, before I could turn round; and I kept my visitors a little on purpose, so that they might get an idea, from seeing her, what would be expected of themselves. I mentioned that she was quite my notion of an excellent model—she was really very clever.

"Do you think she looks like a Russian princess?" Major Monarch asked with lurking alarm.

"When I make her, yes."

"Oh if you have to *make* her—!" he reasoned, not without point.

"That's the most you can ask. There are so many who are not makeable."

"Well now, *here's* a lady"—and with a persuasive smile he passed his arm into his wife's—"who's already made!"

"Oh I'm not a Russian princess," Mrs. Monarch protested a little coldly. I could see she had known some and didn't like them. There at once was a complication of a kind I never had to fear with Miss Churm.

This young lady came back in black velvet—the gown was rather rusty and very low on her lean shoulders—and with a Japanese fan in her red hands. I reminded her that in the scene I was doing she had to look over some one's head. "I forget whose it is; but it doesn't matter. Just look over a head."

"I'd rather look over a stove," said Miss Churm; and she took her station near the fire. She fell into position, settled herself into a tall attitude, gave a certain backward inclination to her head and a certain forward droop to her fan, and looked, at least to my prejudiced sense, distinguished and charming, foreign and dangerous. We left her looking so while I went downstairs with Major and Mrs. Monarch.

"I believe I could come about as near it as that," said Mrs. Monarch.

"Oh you think she's shabby, but you must allow for the alchemy of art."

2. The name of the journal is suggestive. Cheapside, a thoroughfare in the City of London, was originally a marketplace with an area set aside for popular entertainment.

However, they went off with an evident increase of comfort founded on their demonstrable advantage in being the real thing. I could fancy them shuddering over Miss Churm. She was very droll about them when I went back, for I told her what they wanted.

"Well, if *she* can sit I'll tyke to bookkeeping," said my model.

"She's very ladylike," I replied as an innocent form of aggravation.

"So much the worse for *you*. That means she can't turn round."

"She'll do for the fashionable novels."

"Oh yes, she'll *do* for them!" my model humorously declared. "Ain't they bad enough without her?" I had often sociably denounced them to Miss Churm.

III

It was for the elucidation of a mystery in one of these works that I first tried Mrs. Monarch. Her husband came with her, to be useful if necessary—it was sufficiently clear that as a general thing he would prefer to come with her. At first I wondered if this were for "propriety's" sake—if he were going to be jealous and meddling. The idea was too tiresome, and if it had been confirmed it would speedily have brought our acquaintance to a close. But I soon saw there was nothing in it and that if he accompanied Mrs. Monarch it was—in addition to the chance of being wanted—simply because he had nothing else to do. When they were separate his occupation was gone and they never *had* been separate. I judged rightly that in their awkward situation their close union was their main comfort and that this union had no weak spot. It was a real marriage, an encouragement to the hesitating, a nut for pessimists to crack. Their address was humble—I remember afterwards thinking it had been the only thing about them that was really professional—and I could fancy the lamentable lodgings in which the Major would have been left alone. He could sit there more or less grimly with his wife—he couldn't sit there anyhow without her.

He had too much tact to try and make himself agreeable when he couldn't be useful; so when I was too absorbed in my work to talk he simply sat and waited. But I liked to hear him talk—it made my work, when not interrupting it, less mechanical, less special. To listen to him was to combine the excitement of going out with the economy of staying at home. There was only one hindrance—that I seemed not to know any of the people this brilliant couple had known. I think he wondered extremely, during the term of our intercourse, whom the deuce I *did* know. He hadn't a stray sixpence of an idea to fumble for, so we didn't spin it very fine; we confined ourselves to questions of leather and even of liquor—saddlers and breeches-makers and how to get excellent claret cheap—and matters like "good trains" and the habits of small game. His lore on these last subjects was astonishing—he managed to interweave the station-master with the ornithologist. When he couldn't talk about greater things he could talk cheerfully about smaller, and since I couldn't accompany him into reminiscences of the fashionable world he could lower the conversation without a visible effort to my level.

So earnest a desire to please was touching in a man who could so easily have knocked one down. He looked after the fire and had an opinion on the draught of the stove without my asking him, and I could see that he thought many of my arrangements not half knowing. I remember telling him that if I were only rich I'd offer him a salary to come and teach me how to live. Sometimes he gave a random sigh of which the essence might have been: "Give me even such a bare old barrack as *this,* and I'd do something with it!" When I wanted to use him he came alone; which was an illustration of the superior courage of women. His wife could bear her solitary second floor, and she was in general more discreet; showing by various small reserves that she was alive to the propriety of keeping our relations markedly professional—not letting them slide into sociability. She wished it to remain clear that she and the Major were employed, not cultivated, and if she approved of me as a superior, who could be kept in his place, she never thought me quite good enough for an equal.

She sat with great intensity, giving the whole of her mind to it, and was capable of remaining for an hour almost as motionless as before a photographer's lens. I could see she had been photographed often, but somehow the very habit that made her good for that purpose unfitted her for mine. At first I was extremely pleased with her ladylike air, and it was a satisfaction, on coming to follow her lines, to see how good they were and how far they could lead the pencil. But after a little skirmishing I began to find her too insurmountably stiff; do what I would with it my drawing looked like a photograph or a copy of a photograph. Her figure had no variety of expression—she herself had no sense of variety. You may say that this was my business and was only a question of placing her. Yet I placed her in every conceivable position and she managed to obliterate their differences. She was always a lady certainly, and into the bargain was always the same lady. She was the real thing, but always the same thing. There were moments when I rather writhed under the serenity of her confidence that she *was* the real thing. All her dealings with me and all her husband's were an implication that this was lucky for *me.* Meanwhile I found myself trying to invent types that approached her own, instead of making her own transform itself—in the clever way that was not impossible for instance to poor Miss Churm. Arrange as I would and take the precautions I would, she always came out, in my pictures, too tall—landing me in the dilemma of having represented a fascinating woman as seven feet high, which (out of respect perhaps to my own very much scantier inches) was far from my idea of such a personage.

The case was worse with the Major—nothing I could do would keep *him* down, so that he became useful only for the representation of brawny giants. I adored variety and range, I cherished human accidents, the illustrative note; I wanted to characterise closely, and the thing in the world I most hated was the danger of being ridden by a type. I had quarrelled with some of my friends about it; I had parted company with them for maintaining that one *had* to be, and that if the type was beautiful—witness Raphael and Leonardo—the servitude was only a gain. I was neither Leonardo nor Raphael—I might only be a presumptuous young modern searcher; but I held that everything was to be sacrificed sooner than character. When they claimed that the obsessional form could easily *be* character I retorted, perhaps superficially, "Whose?" It couldn't be everybody's—it might end in being nobody's.

After I had drawn Mrs. Monarch a dozen times I felt surer even than before that the value of such a model as Miss Churm resided precisely in the fact that she had no positive stamp, combined of course with the other fact that what she did have was a curious and inexplicable talent for imitation. Her usual appearance was like a curtain which she could draw up at request for a capital performance. This performance was simply suggestive; but it was a word to the wise—it was vivid and pretty. Sometimes even I thought it, though she was plain herself, too insipidly pretty; I made it a reproach to her that the figures drawn from her were monotonously (*bêtement,*[3] as we used to say) graceful. Nothing made her more angry: it was so much her pride to feel she could sit for characters that had nothing in common with each other. She would accuse me at such moments of taking away her "reputytion."

It suffered a certain shrinkage, this queer quantity, from the repeated visits of my new friends. Miss Churm was greatly in demand, never in want of employment, so I had no scruple in putting her off occasionally, to try them more at my ease. It was certainly amusing at first to do the real thing—it was amusing to do Major Monarch's trousers. They *were* the real thing, even if he did come out colossal. It was amusing to do his wife's back hair—it was so mathematically neat—and the particular "smart" tension of her tight stays. She lent herself especially to positions in which the face

3. "Foolishly" or "stupidly."

was somewhat averted or blurred; she abounded in ladylike back views and *profils perdus*.[4] When she stood erect she took naturally one of the attitudes in which court-painters represent queens and princesses; so that I found myself wondering whether, to draw out this accomplishment, I couldn't get the editor of the *Cheapside* to publish a really royal romance, "A Tale of Buckingham Palace." Sometimes however the real thing and the make-believe came into contact; by which I mean that Miss Churm, keeping an appointment or coming to make one on days when I had much work in hand, encountered her invidious rivals. The encounter was not on their part, for they noticed her no more than if she had been the housemaid; not from intentional loftiness, but simply because as yet, professionally, they didn't know how to fraternise, as I could imagine they would have liked—or at least that the Major would. They couldn't talk about the omnibus—they always walked; and they didn't know what else to try—she wasn't interested in good trains or cheap claret. Besides, they must have felt—in the air—that she was amused at them, secretly derisive of their ever knowing how. She wasn't a person to conceal the limits of her faith if she had had a chance to show them. On the other hand Mrs. Monarch didn't think her tidy; for why else did she take pains to say to me—it was going out of the way, for Mrs. Monarch—that she didn't like dirty women?

One day when my young lady happened to be present with my other sitters—she even dropped in, when it was convenient, for a chat—I asked her to be so good as to lend a hand in getting tea, a service with which she was familiar and which was one of a class that, living as I did in a small way, with slender domestic resources, I often appealed to my models to render. They liked to lay hands on my property, to break the sitting, and sometimes the china—it made them feel Bohemian. The next time I saw Miss Churm after this incident she surprised me greatly by making a scene about it—she accused me of having wished to humiliate her. She hadn't resented the outrage at the time, but had seemed obliging and amused, enjoying the comedy of asking Mrs. Monarch, who sat vague and silent, whether she would have cream and sugar, and putting an exaggerated simper into the question. She had tried intonations—as if she too wished to pass for the real thing—till I was afraid my other visitors would take offence.

Oh they were determined not to do this, and their touching patience was the measure of their great need. They would sit by the hour, uncomplaining, till I was ready to use them; they would come back on the chance of being wanted and would walk away cheer-

4. Oblique views "losing" most of the profile.

fully if it failed. I used to go to the door with them to see in what magnificent order they retreated. I tried to find other employment for them—I introduced them to several artists. But they didn't "take," for reasons I could appreciate, and I became rather anxiously aware that after such disappointments they fell back upon me with a heavier weight. They did me the honour to think me most *their* form. They weren't romantic enough for the painters, and in those days there were few serious workers in black-and-white. Besides, they had an eye to the great job I had mentioned to them—they had secretly set their hearts on supplying the right essence for my pictorial vindication of our fine novelist. They knew that for this undertaking I should want no costume-effects, none of the frippery of past ages—that it was a case in which everything would be contemporary and satirical and presumably genteel. If I could work them into it their future would be assured, for the labour would of course be long and the occupation steady.

One day Mrs. Monarch came without her husband—she explained his absence by his having had to go to the City. While she sat there in her usual relaxed majesty there came at the door a knock which I immediately recognised as the subdued appeal of a model out of work. It was followed by the entrance of a young man whom I at once saw to be a foreigner and who proved in fact an Italian acquainted with no English word but my name, which he uttered in a way that made it seem to include all others. I hadn't then visited his country, nor was I proficient in his tongue; but as he was not so meanly constituted—what Italian is?—as to depend only on that member for expression he conveyed to me, in familiar but graceful mimicry, that he was in search of exactly the employment in which the lady before me was engaged. I was not struck with him at first, and while I continued to draw I dropped few signs of interest or encouragement. He stood his ground however—not importunately, but with a dumb dog-like fidelity in his eyes that amounted to innocent impudence, the manner of a devoted servant—he might have been in the house for years—unjustly suspected. Suddenly it struck me that this very attitude and expression made a picture; whereupon I told him to sit down and wait till I should be free. There was another picture in the way he obeyed me, and I observed as I worked that there were others still in the way he looked wonderingly, with his head thrown back, about the high studio. He might have been crossing himself in Saint Peter's. Before I finished I said to myself "The fellow's a bankrupt orange-monger, but a treasure."

When Mrs. Monarch withdrew he passed across the room like a flash to open the door for her, standing there with the rapt pure gaze of the young Dante spellbound by the young Beatrice. As I never insisted, in such situations, on the blankness of the British domestic, I reflected that he had the making of a servant—and I needed one, but couldn't pay him to be only that—as well as of a model; in short I resolved to adopt my bright adventurer if he would agree to officiate in the double capacity. He jumped at my offer, and in the event my rashness—for I had really known nothing about him—wasn't brought home to me. He proved a sympathetic though a desultory ministrant, and had in a wonderful degree the *sentiment de la pose.*[5] It was uncultivated, instinctive, a part of the happy instinct that had guided him to my door and helped him to spell out my name on the card nailed to it. He had had no other introduction to me than a guess, from the shape of my high north window, seen outside, that my place was a studio and that as a studio it would contain an artist. He had wandered to England in search of fortune, like other intinerants, and had embarked, with a partner and a small green hand-cart, on the sale of penny ices. The ices had melted away and the partner had dissolved in their train. My young man wore tight yellow trousers with reddish stripes and his name was Oronte. He was sallow but fair, and when I put him into some old clothes of my own he looked like an Englishman. He was as good as Miss Churm, who could look, when requested, like an Italian.

IV

I thought Mrs. Monarch's face slightly convulsed when, on her coming back with her husband, she found Oronte installed. It was strange to have to recognise in a scrap of a lazzarone [6] a competitor to her magnificent Major. It was she who scented danger first, for the Major was anecdotically unconscious. But Oronte gave us tea, with a hundred eager confusions—he had never been concerned in so queer a process—and I think she thought better of me for having at last an "establishment." They saw a couple of drawings that I had made of the establishment, and Mrs. Monarch hinted that it never would have struck her he had sat for them. "Now the drawings you make from *us*, they look exactly like us," she reminded me, smiling in triumph; and I recognised that this was indeed just their defect. When I drew the Monarchs I couldn't anyhow get away from them—get into the character I wanted to represent; and I hadn't the least desire my model should be discoverable in my picture. Miss Churm never was, and Mrs. Monarch thought I hid her, very properly, because she was vulgar; whereas if she was lost it

5. "Feeling for a correct pose (or position)."
6. Neapolitan street-lounger, who lives by means of odd jobs and begging.

was only as the dead who go to heaven are lost—in the gain of an angel the more.

By this time I had got a certain start with "Rutland Ramsay," the first novel in the great projected series; that is I had produced a dozen drawings, several with the help of the Major and his wife, and I had sent them in for approval. My understanding with the publishers, as I have already hinted, had been that I was to be left to do my work, in this particular case, as I liked, with the whole book committed to me; but my connexion with the rest of the series was only contingent. There were moments when, frankly, it *was* a comfort to have the real thing under one's hand; for there were characters in "Rutland Ramsay" that were very much like it. There were people presumably as erect as the Major and women of as good a fashion as Mrs. Monarch. There was a great deal of country-house life—treated, it is true, in a fine fanciful ironical generalised way—and there was a considerable implication of knickerbockers and kilts. There were certain things I had to settle at the outset; such things for instance as the exact appearance of the hero and the particular bloom and figure of the heroine. The author of course gave me a lead, but there was a margin for interpretation. I took the Monarchs into my confidence, I told them frankly what I was about, I mentioned my embarrassments and alternatives. "Oh take *him!*" Mrs. Monarch murmured sweetly, looking at her husband; and "What could you want better than my wife?" the Major enquired with the comfortable candour that now prevailed between us.

I wasn't obliged to answer these remarks—I was only obliged to place my sitters. I wasn't easy in mind, and I postponed a little timidly perhaps the solving of my question. The book was a large canvas, the other figures were numerous, and I worked off at first some of the episodes in which the hero and the heroine were not concerned. When once I had set *them* up I should have to stick to them—I couldn't make my young man seven feet high in one place and five feet nine in another. I inclined on the whole to the latter measurement, though the Major more than once reminded me that *he* looked about as young as any one. It was indeed quite possible to arrange him, for the figure, so that it would have been difficult to detect his age. After the spontaneous Oronte had been with me a month, and after I had given him to understand several times over that his native exuberance would presently constitute an insurmountable barrier to our further intercourse, I waked to a sense of his heroic capacity. He was only five feet seven, but the remaining inches were latent. I tried him almost secretly at first, for I was really rather afraid of the judgement my other models would pass on such a choice. If they regarded Miss Churm as little better than a snare what would they think of the representation by a person so little the real thing as an Italian street-vendor of a protagonist formed by a public school?

If I went a little in fear of them it wasn't because they bullied me, because they had got an oppressive foothold, but because in their really pathetic decorum and mysteriously permanent newness they counted on me so intensely. I was therefore very glad when Jack Hawley came home: he was always of such good counsel. He painted badly himself, but there was no one like him for putting his finger on the place. He had been absent from England for a year; he had been somewhere—I don't remember where—to get a fresh eye. I was in a good deal of dread of any such organ, but we were old friends; he had been away for months and a sense of emptiness was creeping into my life. I hadn't dodged a missile for a year.

He came back with a fresh eye, but with the same old black velvet blouse, and the first evening he spent in my studio we smoked cigarettes till the small hours. He had done no work himself, he had only got the eye; so the field was clear for the production of my little things. He wanted to see what I had produced for the *Cheapside*, but he was disappointed in the exhibition. That at least seemed the meaning of two or three comprehensive groans which, as he lounged on my big divan, his leg folded under him, looking at my latest drawings, issued from his lips with the smoke of the cigarette.

"What's the matter with you?" I asked.

"What's the matter with *you?*"

"Nothing save that I'm mystified."

"You are indeed. You're quite off the hinge. What's the meaning of this new fad?" And he tossed me, with visible irreverence, a drawing in which I happened to have depicted both my elegant models. I asked if he didn't think it good, and he replied that it struck him as execrable, given the sort of thing I had always represented myself to him as wishing to arrive at; but I let that pass—I was so anxious to see exactly what he meant. The two figures in the picture looked colossal, but I supposed this was *not* what he meant, inasmuch as, for aught he knew to the contrary, I might have been trying for some such effect. I maintained that I was working exactly in the same way as when he last had done me the honour to tell me I might do something some day. "Well, there's a screw loose somewhere," he answered; "wait a bit and I'll discover it." I depended upon him to do so: where else was the fresh eye? But he produced at last nothing more luminous than "I don't know—I don't like your types." This was lame for a critic who had never consented to discuss with me anything but the question of execution, the direction of strokes and the mystery of values.

"In the drawings you've been looking at I think my types are very handsome."

"Oh they won't do!"

"I've been working with new models."

"I see you have. *They* won't do."

"Are you very sure of that?"

"Absolutely—they're stupid."

"You mean *I* am—for I ought to get round that."

"You *can't*—with such people. Who are they?"

I told him, so far as was necessary, and he concluded heartlessly: *"Ce sont des gens qu'il faut mettre à la porte."* [7]

"You've never seen them; they're awfully good"—I flew to their defence.

"Not seen them? Why all this recent work of yours drops to pieces with them. It's all I want to see of them."

"No one else has said anything against it—the *Cheapside* people are pleased."

"Every one else is an ass, and the *Cheapside* people the biggest asses of all. Come, don't pretend at this time of day to have pretty illusions about the public, especially about publishers and editors. It's not for *such* animals you work—it's for those who know, *coloro che sanno;* [8] so keep straight for *me* if you can't keep straight for yourself. There was a certain sort of thing you used to try for—and a very good thing it was. But this twaddle isn't *in* it." When I talked with Hawley later about "Rutland Ramsay" and its possible successors he declared that I must get back into my boat again or I should go to the bottom. His voice in short was the voice of warning.

I noted the warning, but I didn't turn my friends out of doors. They bored me a good deal; but the very fact that they bored me admonished me not to sacrifice them—if there was anything to be done with them—simply to irritation. As I looked back at this phase they seem to me to have pervaded my life not a little. I have a vision of them as most of the time in my studio, seated against the wall on an old velvet bench to be out of the way, and resembling the while a pair of patient courtiers in a royal ante-chamber. I'm convinced that during the coldest weeks of the winter they held their ground because it saved them fire. Their newness was losing its gloss, and it was impossible not to feel them objects of charity. Whenever Miss Churm arrived they went away, and after I was fairly launched in "Rutland Ramsay" Miss Churm arrived pretty often. They managed to express to me tacitly that they supposed I wanted her for the low life of the book, and I let them suppose it,

7. "They are the sort of people one must get rid of (show to the door)."
8. In the *Inferno* (4:131) Dante refers to Aristotle as *il maestro di color che sanno* ("the master of those that know").

since they had attempted to study the work—it was lying about the studio—without discovering that it dealt only with the highest circles. They had dipped into the most brilliant of our novelists without deciphering many passages. I still took an hour from them, now and again, in spite of Jack Hawley's warning: it would be time enough to dismiss them, if dismissal should be necessary, when the rigour of the season was over. Hawley had made their acquaintance—he had met them at my fireside—and thought them a ridiculous pair. Learning that he was a painter they tried to approach him, to show him too that they were the real thing; but he looked at them, across the big room, as if they were miles away: they were a compendium of everything he most objected to in the social system of his country. Such people as that, all convention and patent-leather, with ejaculations that stopped conversation, had no business in a studio. A studio was a place to learn to see, and how could you see through a pair of feather-beds?

The main inconvenience I suffered at their hands was that at first I was shy of letting it break upon them that my artful little servant had begun to sit to me for "Rutland Ramsay." They knew I had been odd enough—they were prepared by this time to allow oddity to artists—to pick a foreign vagabond out of the streets when I might have had a person with whiskers and credentials; but it was some time before they learned how high I rated his accomplishments. They found him in an attitude more than once, but they never doubted I was doing him as an organ-grinder. There were several things they never guessed, and one of them was that for a striking scene in the novel, in which a footman briefly figured, it occurred to me to make use of Major Monarch as the menial. I kept putting this off, I didn't like to ask him to don the livery—besides the difficulty of finding a livery to fit him. At last, one day late in the winter, when I was at work on the despised Oronte, who caught one's idea on the wing, and was in the glow of feeling myself go very straight, they came in, the Major and his wife, with their society laugh about nothing (there was less and less to laugh at); came in like country-callers—they always reminded me of that—who have walked across the park after church and are presently persuaded to stay to luncheon. Luncheon was over, but they could stay to tea—I knew they wanted it. The fit was on me, however, and I couldn't let my ardour cool and my work wait, with the fading daylight, while my model prepared it. So I asked Mrs. Monarch if she would mind laying it out—a request which for an instant brought all the blood to her face. Her eyes were on her husband's for a second, and some mute telegraphy passed between them. Their folly was over the next instant; his cheerful shrewdness put an end to it. So far from pitying their wounded pride, I must add, I was moved to give it as complete a lesson as I could. They bustled about together and got out the cups and saucers and made the kettle boil. I know they felt as if they were waiting on my servant, and when the tea was prepared I said: "He'll have a cup, please—he's tired." Mrs. Monarch brought him one where he stood, and he took it from her as if he had been a gentleman at a party squeezing a crush-hat with an elbow.

Then it came over me that she had made a great effort for me—made it with a kind of nobleness—and that I owed her a compensation. Each time I saw her after this I wondered what the compensation could be. I couldn't go on doing the wrong thing to oblige them. Oh it *was* the wrong thing, the stamp of the work for which they sat—Hawley was not the only person to say it now. I sent in a large number of the drawings I had made for "Rutland Ramsey," and I received a warning that was more to the point than Hawley's. The artistic adviser of the house for which I was working was of opinion that many of my illustrations were not what had been looked for. Most of these illustrations were the subjects in which the Monarchs had figured. Without going into the question of what *had* been looked for, I had to face the fact that at this rate I shouldn't get the other books to do. I hurled myself in despair on Miss Churm—I put her through all her paces. I not only adopted Oronte publicly as my hero, but one morning when the Major looked in to see if I didn't require him to finish a *Cheapside* figure for which he had begun to sit the week before, I told him I had changed my mind—I'd do the drawing from my man. At this my visitor turned pale and stood looking at me. "Is *he* your idea of an English gentleman?" he asked.

I was disappointed, I was nervous, I wanted to get on with my work; so I replied with irritation: "Oh my dear Major—I can't be ruined for *you!*"

It was a horrid speech, but he stood another moment—after which, without a word, he quitted the studio. I drew a long breath, for I said to myself that I shouldn't see him again. I hadn't told him definitely that I was in danger of having my work rejected, but I was vexed at his not having felt the catastrophe in the air, read with me the moral of our fruitless collaboration, the lesson that in the deceptive atmosphere of art even the highest respectability may fail of being plastic.

I didn't owe my friends money, but I did see them again. They reappeared together three days later, and, given all the other facts, there was something tragic in that one. It was a clear proof they could find nothing else in life to do. They had threshed the matter out in a dismal conference—they had digested the bad news that they were not in for the series. If they weren't useful to me even for the *Cheapside* their function seemed difficult to determine, and I could only judge at first that they had come, forgivingly, decorously, to take a last leave. This made me rejoice in secret that I had little leisure for a scene; for I had placed both my other models in position together and I was pegging away at a drawing from which I hoped to derive glory. It had been suggested by the passage in which Rutland Ramsay, drawing up a chair to Artemisia's piano-stool, says extraordinary things to her while she ostensibly fingers out a difficult piece of music. I had done Miss Churm at the piano before—it was an attitude in which she knew how to take on an absolutely poetic grace. I wished the two figures to "compose" together with intensity, and my little Italian had entered perfectly into my conception. The pair were vividly before me, the piano had been pulled out; it was a charming show of blended youth and murmured love, which I had only to catch and keep. My visitors stood and looked at it, and I was friendly to them over my shoulder.

They made no response, but I was used to silent company 'and went on with my work, only a little disconcerted—even though exhilarated by the sense that *this* was at least the ideal thing—at not having got rid of them after all. Presently I heard Mrs. Monarch's sweet voice beside or rather above me: "I wish her hair were a little better done." I looked up and she was staring with a strange fixedness at Miss Churm, whose back was turned to her. "Do you mind my just touching it?" she went on—a question which made me spring up for an instant as with the instinctive fear that she might do the young lady a harm. But she quieted me with a glance I shall never forget—I confess I should like to have been able to paint *that*—and went for a moment to my model. She spoke to her softly, laying a hand on her shoulder and bending over her; and as the girl, understanding, gratefully assented, she disposed her rough curls, with a few quick passes, in such a way as to make Miss Churm's head twice as charming. It was one of the most heroic personal services I've ever seen rendered. Then Mrs. Monarch turned away with a low sigh and, looking about her as if for something to do, stooped to the floor with a noble humility and picked up a dirty rag that had dropped out of my paint-box.

The Major meanwhile had also been looking for something to do, and, wandering to the other end of the studio, saw before him my breakfast-things neglected, unremoved, "I say, can't I be useful *here?*" he called out to me with an irrepressible quaver. I assented with a laugh that I fear was awkward, and for the next ten minutes, while I worked, I heard the light clatter of china and the tinkle of spoons and glass. Mrs. Monarch assisted her husband—they washed up my crockery, they put it away. They wandered off into my little scullery, and I afterwards found that they had cleaned my knives and that my slender stock of plate had an unprecedented surface. When it came over me, the latent eloquence of what they were doing, I confess that my drawing was blurred for a moment—the picture swam. They had accepted their failure, but they couldn't accept their fate. They had bowed their heads in bewilderment to the perverse and cruel law in virtue of which the real thing could be so much less precious than the unreal; but they didn't want to starve. If my servants were my models, then my models might be my servants. They would reverse the parts—the others would sit for the ladies and gentlemen and *they* would do the work. They would still be in the studio—it was an intense dumb appeal to me not to turn them out. "Take us on," they wanted to say—"we'll do anything."

My pencil dropped from my hand; my sitting was spoiled and I got rid of my sitters, who were also evidently rather mystified and awestruck. Then, alone with the Major and his wife I had a most uncomfortable moment. He put their prayer into a single sentence: "I say, you know—just let *us* do for you, can't you?" I couldn't—it was dreadful to see them emptying my slops; but I pretended I could, to oblige them, for about a week. Then I gave them a sum of money to go away, and I never saw them again. I obtained the remaining books, but my friend Hawley repeats that Major and Mrs. Monarch did me a permanent harm, got me into false ways. If it be true I'm content to have paid the price—for the memory.

From *The Real Thing and Other Tales* (1893)

THE JOLLY CORNER

I

"Every one asks me what I 'think' of everything," said Spencer Brydon; "and I make answer as I can—begging or dodging the question, putting them off with any nonsense. It wouldn't matter to any of them really," he went on, "for, even were it possible to meet in that stand-and-deliver way so silly a demand on so big a subject, my 'thoughts' would still be almost altogether about something that concerns only myself." He was talking to Miss Staverton, with whom for a couple of months now he had availed himself of every possible occasion to talk; this disposition and this resource, this comfort and support, as the situation in fact presented itself, having promptly enough taken the first place in the considerable array of rather unattenuated surprises attending his so strangely belated return to America. Everything was somehow a surprise; and that might be natural when one had so long and so consistently neglected everything, taken pains to give surprises so much margin for play. He had given them more than thirty years—thirty-three, to be exact; and they now seemed to him to have organised their performance quite on the scale of that license. He had been twenty-three on leaving New York—he was fifty-six today: unless indeed he were to reckon as he had sometimes, since his repatriation, found himself feeling; in which case he would have lived longer than is often allotted to man. It would have taken a century, he repeatedly said to himself, and said also to Alice Staverton, it would have taken a longer absence and a more averted mind than those even of which he had been guilty, to pile up the differences, the newnesses, the queernesses, above all the bignesses, for the better or the worse, that at present assaulted his vision wherever he looked.

The great fact all the while however had been the incalculability; since he *had* supposed himself, from decade to decade, to be allowing, and in the most liberal and intelligent manner, for brilliancy of change. He actually saw that he had allowed for nothing; he missed what he would have been sure of finding, he found what he would never have imagined. Proportions and values were upside-down; the ugly things he had expected, the ugly things of his far-away youth, when he had too promptly waked up to a sense of the ugly— these uncanny phenomena placed him rather, as it happened, under the charm; whereas the "swagger" things, the modern, the monstrous, the famous things, those he had more particularly, like thousands of ingenuous enquirers every year, come over to see, were exactly his sources of dismay. They were as so many set traps for displeasure, above all for reaction, of which his restless tread was constantly pressing the spring. It was interesting, doubtless, the whole show, but it would have been too disconcerting hadn't a certain finer truth saved the situation. He had distinctly not, in this steadier light, come over *all* for the monstrosities; he had come, not only in the last analysis but quite on the face of the act, under an impulse with which they had nothing to do. He had come—putting the thing pompously—to look at his "property," which he had thus for a third of a century not been within four thousand miles of; or, expressing it less sordidly, he had yielded to the humour of seeing again his house on the jolly corner, as he usually, and quite fondly, described it—the one in which he had first seen the light, in which various members of his family had lived and had died, in which the holidays of his overschooled boyhood had been passed and the few social flowers of his chilled adolescence gathered, and which, alien-ated then for so long a period, had, through the successive deaths of his two brothers and the termination of old arrangements, come wholly into his hands. He was the owner of another, not quite so "good"—the jolly corner having been, from far back, superlatively extended and consecrated; and the value of the pair represented his main capital, with an income consisting, in these later years, of their respective rents which (thanks precisely to their original ex-cellent type) had never been depressingly low. He could live in "Europe," as he had been in the habit of living, on the product of these flourishing New York leases, and all the better since, that of the second structure, the mere number in its long row, having within a twelvemonth fallen in, renovation at a high advance had proved beautifully possible.

These were items of property indeed, but he had found himself since his arrival distinguishing more than ever between them. The house within the street, two bristling blocks westward, was already in course of reconstruction as a tall mass of flats; he had acceded, some time before, to overtures for this conversion—in which, now that it was going forward, it had been not the least of his astonish-ments to find himself able, on the spot, and though without a pre-vious ounce of such experience, to participate with a certain in-telligence, almost with a certain authority. He had lived his life with his back so turned to such concerns and his face addressed to those of so different an order that he scarce knew what to make of this lively stir, in a compartment of his mind never yet penetrated, of a capacity for business and a sense for construction. These virtues, so common all round him now, had been dormant in his own organism—where it might be said of them perhaps that they had slept the sleep of the just. At present, in the splendid autumn weather—the autumn at least was a pure boon in the terrible place—he loafed about his "work" undeterred, secretly agitated; not in the least "minding" that the whole proposition, as they said, was vulgar and sordid, and ready to climb ladders, to walk the plank, to handle materials and look wise about them, to ask questions, in fine, and challenge explanations and really "go into" figures.

It amused, it verily quite charmed him; and, by the same stroke, it amused, and even more, Alice Staverton, though perhaps charming her perceptibly less. She wasn't however going to be better off for it, as *he* was—and so astonishingly much: nothing was now likely, he knew, ever to make her better off than she found herself, in the afternoon of life, as the delicately frugal possessor and tenant of the small house in Irving Place to which she had subtly managed to cling through her almost unbroken New York career. If he knew the way to it now better than to any other address among the dreadful multiplied numberings which seemed to him to reduce the whole place to some vast ledger-page, overgrown, fantastic, of ruled and criss-crossed lines and figures—if he had formed, for his consolation, that habit, it was really not a little because of the charm of his having encountered and recognised, in the vast wilderness of the wholesale, breaking through the mere gross generalisation of wealth and force and success, a small still scene where items and shades, all delicate things, kept the sharpness of the notes of a high voice perfectly trained, and where economy hung about like the scent of a garden. His old friend lived with one maid and herself dusted her relics and trimmed her lamps and polished her silver; she stood off, in the awful modern crush, when she could, but she sallied forth and did battle when the challenge was really to "spirit," the spirit she after all confessed to, proudly and a little shyly, as to that of the better time, that of *their* common, their quite far-away and antediluvian social period and order. She made use of the street-cars when need be, the terrible things that people scrambled for as the panic-stricken at sea scramble for the boats; she affronted, inscrutably, under stress, all the public concussions and ordeals; and yet, with that slim mystifying grace of her appearance, which defied you to say if she were a fair young woman who looked older through trouble, or a fine smooth older one who looked young through successful indifference; with her precious reference, above all, to memories and histories into which he could enter, she was as exquisite for him as some pale pressed flower (a rarity to begin with), and, failing other sweetnesses, she was a sufficient reward of his effort. They had communities of knowledge, "their" knowledge (this discriminating possessive was always on her lips) of presences of the other age, presences all overlaid, in his case, by the experience of a man and the freedom of a wanderer, overlaid by pleasure, by infidelity, by passages of life that were strange and dim to her, just by "Europe" in short, but still unobscured, still exposed and cherished, under that pious visitation of the spirit from which she had never been diverted.

She had come with him one day to see how his "apartment-house" was rising; he had helped her over gaps and explained to her plans, and while they were there had happened to have, before her, a brief but lively discussion with the man in charge, the representative of the building-firm that had undertaken his work. He had found himself quite "standing-up" to this personage over a failure on the latter's part to observe some detail of one of their noted conditions, and had so lucidly urged his case that, besides ever so prettily flushing, at the time, for sympathy in his triumph, she had afterwards said to him (though to a slightly greater effect of irony) that he had clearly for too many years neglected a real gift. If he had but stayed at home he would have anticipated the inventor of the sky-scraper. If he had but stayed at home he would have discovered his genius in time really to start some new variety of awful architectural hare and run it till it burrowed in a gold-mine. He was to remember these words, while the weeks elapsed, for the small silver ring they had sounded over the queerest and deepest of his own lately most disguised and most muffled vibrations.

It had begun to be present to him after the first fortnight, it had broken out with the oddest abruptness, this particular wanton wonderment: it met him there—and this was the image under which he himself judged the matter, or at least, not a little, thrilled and flushed with it—very much as he might have been met by some strange figure, some unexpected occupant, at a turn of one of the dim passages of an empty house. The quaint analogy quite hauntingly remained with him, when he didn't indeed rather improve it by a still intenser form: that of his opening a door behind which he would have made sure of finding nothing, a door into a room shuttered and void, and yet so coming, with a great suppressed start, on some quite erect confronting presence, something planted in the middle of the place and facing him through the dusk. After that visit to the house in construction he walked with his companion to see the other and always so much the better one, which in the eastward direction formed one of the corners, the "jolly" one precisely, of the street now so generally dishonoured and disfigured in its westward reaches, and of the comparatively conservative Avenue. The Avenue still had pretensions, as Miss Staverton said, to decency; the old people had mostly gone, the old names were unknown, and here and there an old association seemed to stray, all vaguely, like some very aged person, out too late, whom you might meet and feel the impulse to watch or follow, in kindness, for safe restoration to shelter.

They went in together, our friends; he admitted himself with his key, as he kept no one there, he explained, preferring, for his reasons, to leave the place empty, under a simple arrangement with a good woman living in the neighbourhood and who came for a daily hour to open windows and dust and sweep. Spencer Brydon had his reasons and was growingly aware of them; they seemed to him better each time he was there, though he didn't name them all to his companion, any more than he told her as yet how often, how quite absurdly often, he himself came. He only let her see for the present, while they walked through the great blank rooms, that absolute vacancy reigned and that, from top to bottom, there was nothing but Mrs. Muldoon's broomstick, in a corner, to tempt the burglar. Mrs. Muldoon was then on the premises, and she loquaciously attended the visitors, preceding them from room to room and pushing back shutters and throwing up sashes—all to show them, as she remarked, how little there was to see. There was little indeed to see in the great gaunt shell where the main dispositions and the general apportionment of space, the style of an age of ampler allowances, had nevertheless for its master their honest pleading message, affecting him as some good old servant's, some lifelong retainer's appeal for a character, or even for a retiring-pension; yet it was also a remark of Mrs. Muldoon's that, glad as she was to oblige him by her noonday round, there was a request she greatly hoped he would never make of her. If he should wish her for any reason to come in after dark she would just tell him, if he "plased," that he must ask it of somebody else.

The fact that there was nothing to see didn't militate for the worthy woman against what one *might* see, and she put it frankly to Miss Staverton that no lady could be expected to like, could she? "craping [1] up to thim top storeys in the ayvil hours." The gas and the electric light were off the house, and she fairly evoked a gruesome vision of her march through the great grey rooms—so many of them as there were too!—with her glimmering taper. Miss Staverton met her honest glare with a smile and the profession that she herself certainly would recoil from such an adventure. Spencer Brydon meanwhile held his peace—for the moment; the question of the "evil" hours in his old home had already become too grave for him. He had begun some time since to "crape," and he knew just why a packet of candles addressed to that pursuit had been stowed by his own hand, three weeks before, at the back of a drawer of the

1. "Creeping."

fine old sideboard that occupied, as a "fixture," the deep recess in the dining-room. Just now he laughed at his companions—quickly however changing the subject; for the reason that, in the first place, his laugh struck him even at that moment as starting the odd echo, the conscious human resonance (he scarce knew how to qualify it) that sounds made while he was there alone sent back to his ear or his fancy; and that, in the second, he imagined Alice Staverton for the instant on the point of asking him, with a divination, if he ever so prowled. There were divinations he was unprepared for, and he had at all events averted enquiry by the time Mrs. Muldoon had left them, passing on to other parts.

There was happily enough to say, on so consecrated a spot, that could be said freely and fairly; so that a whole train of declarations was precipitated by his friend's having herself broken out, after a yearning look round: "But I hope you don't mean they want you to pull *this* to pieces!" His answer came, promptly, with his re-awakened wrath: it was of course exactly what they wanted, and what they were "at" him for, daily, with the iteration of people who couldn't for their life understand a man's liability to decent feelings. He had found the place, just as it stood and beyond what he could express, an interest and a joy. There were values other than the beastly rent-values, and in short, in short—! But it was thus Miss Staverton took him up. "In short you're to make so good a thing of your sky-scraper that, living in luxury on *those* ill-gotten gains, you can afford for a while to be sentimental here!" Her smile had for him, with the words, the particular mild irony with which he found half her talk suffused; an irony without bitterness and that came, exactly, from her having so much imagination—not, like the cheap sarcasms with which one heard most people, about the world of "society," bid for the reputation of cleverness, from nobody's really having any. It was agreeable to him at this very moment to be sure that when he had answered, after a brief demur, "Well yes: so, precisely, you may put it!" her imagination would still do him justice. He explained that even if never a dollar were to come to him from the other house he would nevertheless cherish this one; and he dwelt, further, while they lingered and wandered, on the fact of the stupefaction he was already exciting, the positive mystification he felt himself create.

He spoke of the value of all he read into it, into the mere sight of the walls, mere shapes of the rooms, mere sound of the floors, mere feel, in his hand, of the old silver-plated knobs of the several mahogany doors, which suggested the pressure of the palms of the dead; the seventy years of the past in fine that these things represented, the annals of nearly three generations, counting his grandfather's, the one that had ended there, and the impalpable ashes of his long-extinct youth, afloat in the very air like microscopic motes. She listened to everything; she was a woman who answered intimately but who utterly didn't chatter. She scattered abroad therefore no cloud of words; she could assent, she could agree, above all she could encourage, without doing that. Only at the last she went a little further than he had done himself. "And then how do you know? You may still, after all, want to live here." It rather indeed pulled him up, for it wasn't what he had been thinking, at least in her sense of the words. "You mean I may decide to stay on for the sake of it?"

"Well, *with* such a home—!" But, quite beautifully, she had too much tact to dot so monstrous an *i*, and it was precisely an illustration of the way she didn't rattle. How could any one—of any wit—insist on any one else's "wanting" to live in New York?

"Oh," he said, "I *might* have lived here (since I had my opportunity early in life); I might have put in here all these years. Then everything would have been different enough—and, I dare say, 'funny' enough. But that's another matter. And then the beauty of it—I mean of my perversity, of my refusal to agree to a 'deal'—is just in the total absence of a reason. Don't you see that if I had a reason about the matter at all it would *have* to be the other way, and would then be inevitably a reason of dollars? There are no reasons here *but* of dollars. Let us therefore have none whatever—not the ghost of one."

They were back in the hall then for departure, but from where they stood the vista was large, through an open door, into the great square main saloon, with its almost antique felicity of brave spaces between windows. Her eyes came back from that reach and met his own a moment. "Are you very sure the 'ghost' of one doesn't, much rather, serve—?"

He had a positive sense of turning pale. But it was as near as they were then to come. For he made answer, he believed, between a glare and a grin: "Oh ghosts—of course the place must swarm with them! I should be ashamed of it if it didn't. Poor Mrs. Muldoon's right, and it's why I haven't asked her to do more than look in."

Miss Staverton's gaze again lost itself, and things she didn't utter, it was clear, came and went in her mind. She might even for the minute, off there in the fine room, have imagined some element dimly gathering. Simplified like the death-mask of a handsome face, it perhaps produced for her just then an effect akin to the stir of an expression in the "set" commemorative plaster. Yet whatever her impression may have been she produced instead a vague platitude. "Well, if it were only furnished and lived in—!"

She appeared to imply that in case of its being still furnished he might have been a little less opposed to the idea of a return. But

she passed straight into the vestibule, as if to leave her words behind her, and the next moment he had opened the house-door and
was standing with her on the steps. He closed the door and, while
he re-pocketed his key, looking up and down, they took in the comparatively harsh actuality of the Avenue, which reminded him of
the assault of the outer light of the Desert on the traveller emerging
from an Egyptian tomb. But he risked before they stepped into the
street his gathered answer to her speech. "For me it *is* lived in. For
me it *is* furnished." At which it was easy for her to sigh "Ah yes—!"
all vaguely and discreetly; since his parents and his favourite sister,
to say nothing of other kin, in numbers, had run their course and
met their end there. That represented, within the walls, ineface-
able life.

It was a few days after this that, during an hour passed with her
again, he had expressed his impatience of the too flattering curiosity—among the people he met—about his appreciation of New
York. He had arrived at none at all that was socially producible, and
as for that matter of his "thinking" (thinking the better or the worse
of anything there) he was wholly taken up with one subject of
thought. It was mere vain egoism, and it was moreover, if she liked,
a morbid obsession. He found all things come back to the question
of what he personally might have been, how he might have led his
life and "turned out," if he had not so, at the outset, given it up.
And confessing for the first time to the intensity within him of this
absurd speculation—which but proved also, no doubt, the habit of
too selfishly thinking—he affirmed the impotence there of any other
source of interest, any other native appeal. "What would it have
made of me, what would it have made of me? I keep for ever wondering, all idiotically; as if I could possibly know! I see what it has
made of dozen of others, those I meet, and it positively aches
within me, to the point of exasperation, that it would have made
something of me as well. Only I can't make out *what,* and the worry
of it, the small rage of curiosity never to be satisfied, brings back
what I remember to have felt, once or twice, after judging best, for
reasons, to burn some important letter unopened. I've been sorry,
I've hated it—I've never known what was in the letter. You may of
course say it's a trifle—!"

"I don't say it's a trifle," Miss Staverton gravely interrupted.

She was seated by her fire, and before her, on his feet and
restless, he turned to and fro between this intensity of his idea and
a fitful and unseeing inspection, through his single eye-glass, of the
dear little old objects on her chimney-piece. Her interruption made
him for an instant look at her harder. "I shouldn't care if you did!"
he laughed, however; "and it's only a figure, at any rate, for the way
I now feel. *Not* to have followed my perverse young course—and

almost in the teeth of my father's curse, as I may say; not to have kept it up, so, 'over there,' from that day to this, without a doubt or a pang; not, above all, to have liked it, to have loved it, so much, loved it, no doubt, with such an abysmal conceit of my own preference: some variation from *that*, I say, must have produced some different effect for my life and for my 'form.' I should have stuck here—if it had been possible; and I was too young, at twenty-three, to judge, *pour deux sous*, [2] whether it *were* possible. If I had waited I might have seen it was, and then I might have been, by staying here, something nearer to one of these types who have been hammered so hard and made so keen by their conditions. It isn't that I admire them so much—the question of any charm in them, or of any charm, beyond that of the rank money-passion, exerted by their conditions *for* them, has nothing to do with the matter: it's only a question of what fantastic, yet perfectly possible, development of my own nature I mayn't have missed. It comes over me that I had then a strange *alter ego* [3] deep down somewhere within me, as the full-blown flower is in the small tight bud, and that I just took the course, I just transferred him to the climate, that blighted him for once and for ever."

"And you wonder about the flower," Miss Staverton said. "So do I, if you want to know; and so I've been wondering these several weeks. I believe in the flower," she continued, "I feel it would have been quite splendid, quite huge and monstrous."

"Monstrous above all!" her visitor echoed; "and I imagine, by the same stroke, quite hideous and offensive."

"You don't believe that," she returned; "if you did you wouldn't wonder. You'd know, and that would be enough for you. What you feel—and what I feel *for* you—is that you'd have had power."

"You'd have liked me that way?" he asked.

She barely hung fire. "How should I not have liked you?"

"I see. You'd have liked me, have preferred me, a billionaire!"

"How should I not have liked you?" she simply again asked.

He stood before her still—her question kept him motionless. He took it in, so much there was of it; and indeed his not otherwise meeting it testified to that. "I know at least what I am," he simply went on; "the other side of the medal's clear enough. I've not been edifying—I believe I'm thought in a hundred quarters to have been barely decent. I've followed strange paths and worshipped strange gods; it must have come to you again and again—in fact you've admitted to me as much—that I was leading, at any time these thirty

2. "For two cents."
3. Originally, "another I"—an intimate and trusted friend, a "second self." But James is using the term in the modern sense, as a psychological double.

years, a selfish frivolous scandalous life. And you see what it has
made of me."

She just waited, smiling at him. "You see what it has made of
me."

"Oh you're a person whom nothing can have altered. You were
born to be what you are, anywhere, anyway: you've the perfection
nothing else could have blighted. And don't you see how, without
my exile, I shouldn't have been waiting till now—?" But he pulled
up for the strange pang.

"The great thing to see," she presently said, "seems to me to be
that it has spoiled nothing. It hasn't spoiled your being here at last.
It hasn't spoiled this. It hasn't spoiled your speaking—" She also
however faltered.

He wondered at everything her controlled emotion might mean.
"Do you believe then—too dreadfully!—that I *am* as good as I
might ever have been?"

"Oh no! Far from it!" With which she got up from her chair and
was nearer to him. "But I don't care," she smiled.

"You mean I'm good enough?"

She considered a little. "Will you believe it if I say so? I mean
will you let that settle your question for you?" And then as if making out in his face that he drew back from this, that he had some
idea which, however absurd, he couldn't yet bargain away: "Oh
you don't care either—but very differently: you don't care for anything but yourself."

Spencer Brydon recognised it—it was in fact what he had absolutely professed. Yet he importantly qualified. "*He* isn't myself.
He's the just so totally other person. But I do want to see him," he
added. "And I can. And I shall."

Their eyes met for a minute while he guessed from something in
hers that she divined his strange sense. But neither of them otherwise expressed it, and her apparent understanding, with no protesting shock, no easy derision, touched him more deeply than anything yet, constituting for his stifled perversity, on the spot, an
element that was like breatheable air. What she said however was
unexpected. "Well, *I've* seen him."

"You—?"

"I've seen him in a dream."

"Oh a 'dream'—!" It let him down.

"But twice over," she continued. "I saw him as I see you now."

"You've dreamed the same dream—"

"Twice over," she repeated. "The very same."

This did somehow a little speak to him, as it also gratified him.
"You dream about me at that rate?"

"Ah about *him!*" she smiled.

His eyes again sounded her. "Then you know all about him." And as she said nothing more: "What's the wretch like?"

She hesitated, and it was as if he were pressing her so hard that, resisting for reasons of her own, she had to turn away. "I'll tell you some other time!"

II

It was after this that there was most of a virtue for him, most of a cultivated charm, most of a preposterous secret thrill, in the particular form of surrender to his obsession and of address to what he more and more believed to be his privilege. It was what in these weeks he was living for—since he really felt life to begin but after Mrs. Muldoon had retired from the scene and, visiting the ample house from attic to cellar, making sure he was alone, he knew himself in safe possession and, as he tacitly expressed it, let himself go. He sometimes came twice in the twenty-four hours; the moments he liked best were those of gathering dusk, of the short autumn twilight; this was the time of which, again and again, he found himself hoping most. Then he could, as seemed to him, most intimately wander and wait, linger and listen, feel his fine attention, never in his life before so fine, on the pulse of the great vague place: he preferred the lampless hour and only wished he might have prolonged each day the deep crepuscular spell. Later—rarely much before midnight, but then for a considerable vigil—he watched with his glimmering light; moving slowly, holding it high, playing it far, rejoicing above all, as much as he might, in open vistas, reaches of communication between rooms and by passages; the long straight chance or show, as he would have called it, for the revelation he pretended to invite. It was practice he found he could perfectly "work" without exciting remark; no one was in the least the wiser for it; even Alice Staverton, who was moreover a well of discretion, didn't quite fully imagine.

He let himself in and let himself out with the assurance of calm proprietorship; and accident so far favoured him that, if a fat Avenue "officer" had happened on occasion to see him entering at eleven-thirty, he had never yet, to the best of his belief, been noticed as emerging at two. He walked there on the crisp November night, arrived regularly at the evening's end; it was as easy to do this after dining out as to take his way to a club or to his hotel. When he left his club, if he hadn't been dining out, it was ostensibly to go to his hotel; and when he left his hotel, if he had spent a part of the evening there, it was ostensibly to go to his club. Everything was easy in fine; everything conspired and promoted: there

was truly even in the strain of his experience something that
glossed over, something that salved and simplified, all the rest of
consciousness. He circulated, talked, renewed, loosely and pleasantly, old relations—met indeed, so far as he could, new expectations and seemed to make out on the whole that in spite of the career, of such different contacts, which he had spoken of to Miss
Staverton as ministering so little, for those who might have watched
it, to edification, he was positively rather liked than not. He was a
dim secondary social success—and all with people who had truly
not an idea of him. It was all mere surface sound, this murmur of
their welcome, this popping of their corks—just as his gestures of
response were the extravagant shadows, emphatic in proportion as
they meant little, of some game of *ombres chinoises*.[4] He projected
himself all day, in thought, straight over the bristling line of hard
unconscious heads and into the other, the real, the waiting life; the
life that, as soon as he had heard behind him the click of his great
house-door, began for him, on the jolly corner, as beguilingly as the
slow opening bars of some rich music follows the tap of the conductor's wand.

He always caught the first effect of the steel point of his stick on
the old marble of the hall pavement, large black-and-white squares
that he remembered as the admiration of his childhood and that had
then made in him, as he now saw, for the growth of an early conception of style. This effect was the dim reverberating tinkle as of
some faroff bell hung who should say where?—in the depths of the
house, of the past, of that mystical other world that might have
flourished for him had he not, for weal or woe, abandoned it. On
this impression he did ever the same thing; he put his stick noiselessly away in a corner—feeling the place once more in the likeness
of some great glass bowl, all precious concave crystal, set delicately
humming by the play of a moist finger round its edge. The concave
crystal held, as it were, this mystical other world, and the indescribably fine murmur of its rim was the sigh there, the scarce audible
pathetic wail to his strained ear, of all the old baffled forsworn possibilities. What he did therefore by this appeal of his hushed presence was to wake them into such measure of ghostly life as they
might still enjoy. They were shy, all but unappeasably shy, but they
weren't really sinister; at least they weren't as he had hitherto felt
them—before they had taken the Form he so yearned to make them
take, the Form he at moments saw himself in the light of fairly
hunting on tiptoe, the points of his evening-shoes, from room to
room and from storey to storey.

That was the essence of his vision—which was all rank folly, if

4. Charades.

one would, while he was out of the house and otherwise occupied, but which took on the last verisimilitude as soon as he was placed and posted. He knew what he meant and what he wanted; it was as clear as the figure on a cheque presented in demand for cash. His *alter ego* "walked"—that was the note of his image of him, while his image of his motive for his own odd pastime was the desire to waylay him and meet him. He roamed, slowly, warily, but all restlessly, he himself did—Mrs. Muldoon had been right, absolutely, with her figure of their "craping"; and the presence he watched for would roam restlessly too. But it would be as cautious and as shifty; the conviction of its probable, in fact its already quite sensible, quite audible evasion of pursuit grew for him from night to night, laying on him finally a rigour to which nothing in his life had been comparable. It had been the theory of many superficially-judging persons, he knew, that he was wasting that life in a surrender to sensations, but he had tasted of no pleasure so fine as his actual tension, had been introduced to no sport that demanded at once the patience and the nerve of this stalking of a creature more subtle, yet at bay perhaps more formidable, than any beast of the forest. The terms, the comparisons, the very practices of the chase positively came again into play; there were even moments when passages of his occasional experience as a sportsman, stirred memories, from his younger time, of moor and mountain and desert, revived for him—and to the increase of his keenness—by the tremendous force of analogy. He found himself at moments—once he had placed his single light on some mantel-shelf or in some recess—stepping back into shelter or shade, effacing himself behind a door or in an embrasure, as he had sought of old the vantage of rock and tree; he found himself holding his breath and living in the joy of the instant, the supreme suspense created by big game alone.

He wasn't afraid (though putting himself the question as he believed gentlemen on Bengal tiger-shoots or in close quarters with the great bear of the Rockies had been known to confess to having put it); and this indeed—since here at least he might be frank!—because of the impression, so intimate and so strange, that he himself produced as yet a dread, produced certainly a strain, beyond the liveliest he was likely to feel. They fell for him into categories, they fairly became familiar, the signs, for his own perception, of the alarm his presence and his vigilance created; though leaving him always to remark, portentously, on his probably having formed a relation, his probably enjoying a consciousness, unique in the experience of man. People enough, first and last, had been in terror of apparitions, but who had ever before so turned the tables and become himself, in the apparitional world, an incalculable terror? He might have found this sublime had he quite dared to think of it;

but he didn't too much insist, truly, on that side of his privilege. With habit and repetition he gained to an extraordinary degree the power to penetrate the dusk of distances and the darkness of corners, to resolve back into their innocence the treacheries of uncertain light, the evil-looking forms taken in the gloom by mere shadows, by accidents of the air, by shifting effects of perspective; putting down his dim luminary he could still wander on without it, pass into other rooms and, only knowing it was there behind him in case of need, see his way about, visually project for his purpose a comparative clearness. It made him feel, this acquired faculty, like some monstrous stealthy cat; he wondered if he would have glared at these moments with large shining yellow eyes, and what it mightn't verily be, for the poor hard-pressed *alter ego,* to be confronted with such a type.

He liked however the open shutters; he opened everywhere those Mrs. Muldoon had closed, closing them as carefully afterwards, so that she shouldn't notice: he liked—oh this he did like, and above all in the upper rooms!—the sense of the hard silver of the autumn stars through the window-panes, and scarcely less the flare of the street-lamps below, the white electric lustre which it would have taken curtains to keep out. This was human actual social; this was of the world he had lived in, and he was more at his ease certainly for the countenance, coldly general and impersonal, that all the while and in spite of his detachment it seemed to give him. He had support of course mostly in the rooms at the wide front and the prolonged side; it failed him considerably in the central shades and the parts at the back. But if he sometimes, on his rounds, was glad of his optical reach, so none the less often the rear of the house affected him as the very jungle of his prey. The place was there more subdivided; a large "extension" in particular, where small rooms for servants had been multiplied, abounded in nooks and corners, in closets and passages, in the ramifications especially of an ample back staircase over which he leaned, many a time, to look far down—not deterred from his gravity even while aware that he might, for a spectator, have figured some solemn simpleton playing at hide-and-seek. Outside in fact he might himself make that ironic *rapprochement;* [5] but within the walls, and in spite of the clear windows, his consistency was proof against the cynical light of New York.

It had belonged to that idea of the exasperated consciousness of his victim to become a real test for him; since he had quite put it to himself from the first that, oh distinctly! he could "cultivate" his whole perception. He had felt it as above all open to cultivation—

5. Comparison.

which indeed was but another name for his manner of spending his time. He was bringing it on, bringing it to perfection, by practice; in consequence of which it had grown so fine that he was now aware of impressions, attestations of his general postulate, that couldn't have broken upon him at once. This was the case more specifically with a phenomenon at last quite frequent for him in the upper rooms, the recognition—absolutely unmistakeable, and by a turn dating from a particular hour, his resumption of his campaign after a diplomatic drop, a calculated absence of three nights—of his being definitely followed, tracked at a distance carefully taken and to the express end that he should the less confidently, less arrogantly, appear to himself merely to pursue. It worried, it finally quite broke him up, for it proved, of all the conceivable impressions, the one least suited to his book. He was kept in sight while remaining himself—as regards the essence of his position—sightless, and his only recourse then was in abrupt turns, rapid recoveries of ground. He wheeled about, retracing his steps, as if he might so catch in his face at least the stirred air of some other quick revolution. It was indeed true that his fully dislocalised thought of these manœuvres recalled to him Pantaloon, at the Christmas farce, buffeted and tricked from behind by ubiquitous Harlequin; [6] but it left intact the influence of the conditions themselves each time he was re-exposed to them, so that in fact this association, had he suffered it to become constant, would on a certain side have but ministered to his intenser gravity. He had made, as I have said, to create on the premises the baseless sense of a reprieve, his three absences; and the result of the third was to confirm the after-effect of the second.

On his return, that night—the night succeeding his last intermission—he stood in the hall and looked up the staircase with a certainty more intimate than any he had yet known. "He's *there*, at the top, and waiting—not, as in general, falling back for disappearance. He's holding his ground, and it's the first time—which is a proof, isn't it? that something has happened for him." So Brydon argued with his hand on the banister and his foot on the lowest stair; in which position he felt as never before the air chilled by his logic. He himself turned cold in it, for he seemed of a sudden to know what now was involved. "Harder pressed?—yes, he takes it in, with its thus making clear to him that I've come, as they say, 'to stay.' He finally doesn't like and can't bear it, in the sense, I mean, that his wrath, his menaced interest, now balances with his dread. I've hunted him till he has 'turned': that, up there, is what has hap-

---

6. In the Italian *commedia dell'arte*, Pantaloon is the foolish old man; Harlequin, the conventional clown. Both characters figure in the traditional Christmas pantomime, or farce for children.

pened—he's the fanged or the antlered animal brought at last to bay." There came to him, as I say—but determined by an influence beyond my notation!—the acuteness of this certainty; under which however the next moment he had broken into a sweat that he would as little have consented to attribute to fear as he would have dared immediately to act upon it for enterprise. It marked none the less a prodigious thrill, a thrill that represented sudden dismay, no doubt, but also represented, and with the selfsame throb, the strangest, the most joyous, possibly the next minute almost the proudest, duplication of consciousness.

"He has been dodging, retreating, hiding, but now, worked up to anger, he'll fight!"—this intense impression made a single mouthful, as it were, of terror and applause. But what was wondrous was that the applause, for the felt fact, was so eager, since, if it was his other self he was running to earth, this ineffable identity was thus in the last resort not unworthy of him. It bristled there—somewhere near at hand, however unseen still—as the hunted thing, even as the trodden worm of the adage *must* at last bristle; and Brydon at this instant tasted probably of a sensation more complex than had ever before found itself consistent with sanity. It was as if it would have shamed him that a character so associated with his own should triumphantly succeed in just skulking, should to the end not risk the open, so that the drop of this danger was, on the spot, a great lift of the whole situation. Yet with another rare shift of the same subtlety he was already trying to measure by how much more he himself might now be in peril of fear; so rejoicing that he could, in another form, actively inspire that fear, and simultaneously quaking for the form in which he might passively know it.

The apprehension of knowing it must after a little have grown in him, and the strangest moment of his adventure perhaps, the most memorable or really most interesting, afterwards, of his crisis, was the lapse of certain instants of concentrated conscious *combat*, the sense of a need to hold on to something, even after the manner of a man slipping and slipping on some awful incline; the vivid impulse, above all, to move, to act, to charge, somehow and upon something—to show himself, in a word, that he wasn't afraid. The state of "holding-on" was thus the state to which he was momentarily reduced; if there had been anything, in the great vacancy, to seize, he would presently have been aware of having clutched it as he might under a shock at home have clutched the nearest chairback. He had been surprised at any rate—of this he *was* aware—into something unprecedented since his original appropriation of the place; he had closed his eyes, held them tight, for a long minute, as with that instinct of dismay and that terror of vision. When he opened them the room, the other contiguous rooms, extraordinarily, seemed lighter—so light, almost, that at first he took the change for day. He stood firm, however that might be, just where he had paused; his resistance had helped him—it was as if there were something he had tided over. He knew after a little what this was—it had been in the imminent danger of flight. He had stiffened his will against going; without this he would have made for the stairs, and it seemed to him that, still with his eyes closed, he would have descended them, would have known how, straight and swiftly, to the bottom.

Well, as he had held out, here he was—still at the top, among the more intricate upper rooms and with the gauntlet of the others, of all the rest of the house, still to run when it should be his time to go. He would go at his time—only at his time: didn't he go every night very much at the same hour? He took out his watch—there was light for that: it was scarcely a quarter past one, and he had never withdrawn so soon. He reached his lodgings for the most part at two—with his walk of a quarter of an hour. He would wait for the last quarter—he wouldn't stir till then; and he kept his watch there with his eyes on it, reflecting while he held it that this deliberate wait, a wait with an effort, which he recognised, would serve perfectly for the attestation he desired to make. It would prove his courage—unless indeed the latter might most be proved by his budging at last from his place. What he mainly felt now was that, since he hadn't originally scuttled, he had his dignities—which had never in his life seemed so many—all to preserve and to carry aloft. This was before him in truth as a physical image, an image almost worthy of an age of greater romance. That remark indeed glimmered for him only to glow the next instant with a finer light; since what age of romance, after all, could have matched either the state of his mind or, "objectively," as they said, the wonder of his situation? The only difference would have been that, brandishing his dignities over his head as in a parchment scroll, he might then—that is in the heroic time—have proceeded downstairs with a drawn sword in his other grasp.

At present, really, the light he had set down on the mantel of the next room would have to figure his sword; which utensil, in the course of a minute, he had taken the requisite number of steps to possess himself of. The door between the rooms was open, and from the second another door opened to a third. These rooms, as he remembered, gave all three upon a common corridor as well, but there was a fourth, beyond them, without issue save through the preceding. To have moved, to have heard his step again, was appreciably a help; though even in recognising this he lingered once more a little by the chimney-piece on which his light had rested. When he next moved, just hesitating where to turn, he found him-

self considering a circumstance that, after his first and comparatively vague apprehension of it, produced in him the start that often
attends some pang of recollection, the violent shock of having
ceased happily to forget. He had come into sight of the door in
which the brief chain of communication ended and which he now
surveyed from the nearer threshold, the one not directly facing it.
Placed at some distance to the left of this point, it would have admitted him to the last room of the four, the room without other
approach or egress, had it not, to his intimate conviction, been
closed *since* his former visitation, the matter probably of a quarter
of an hour before. He stared with all his eyes at the wonder of the
fact, arrested again where he stood and again holding his breath
while he sounded its sense. Surely it had been *subsequently*
closed—that is it had been on his previous passage indubitably
open!

He took it full in the face that something had happened between—that he couldn't not have noticed before (by which he
meant on his original tour of all the rooms that evening) that such a
barrier had exceptionally presented itself. He had indeed since that
moment undergone an agitation so extraordinary that it might have
muddled for him any earlier view; and he tried to convince himself
that he might perhaps then have gone into the room and, inadvertently, automatically, on coming out, have drawn the door after him.
The difficulty was that this exactly was what he never did; it was
against his whole policy, as he might have said, the essence of
which was to keep vistas clear. He had them from the first, as he
was well aware, quite on the brain: the strange apparition, at the far
end of one of them, of his baffled "prey" (which had become by so
sharp an irony so little the term now to apply!) was the form of success his imagination had most cherished, projecting into it always a
refinement of beauty. He had known fifty times the start of perception that had afterwards dropped; had fifty times gasped to himself
"There!" under some fond brief hallucination. The house, as the
case stood, admirably lent itself; he might wonder at the taste, the
native architecture of the particular time, which could rejoice so in
the multiplication of doors—the opposite extreme to the modern,
the actual almost complete proscription of them; but it had fairly
contributed to provoke this obsession of the presence encountered
telescopically, as he might say, focussed and studied in diminishing
perspective and as by a rest for the elbow.

It was with these considerations that his present attention was
charged—they perfectly availed to make what he saw portentous.
He *couldn't*, by any lapse, have blocked that aperture; and if he
hadn't, if it was unthinkable, why what else was clear but that there
had been another agent? Another agent?—he had been catching, as

he felt, a moment back, the very breath of him; but when had he been so close as in this simple, this logical, this completely personal act? It was so logical, that is, that one might have *taken* it for personal; yet for what did Brydon take it, he asked himself, while softly panting, he felt his eyes almost leave their socket. Ah this time at last they *were*, the two, the opposed projections of him, in presence; and this time, as much as one would, the question of danger loomed. With it rose, as not before, the question of courage—for what he knew the blank face of the door to say to him was "Show us how much you have!" It stared, it glared back at him with that challenge; it put to him the two alternatives: should he just push it open or not? Oh to have this consciousness was to *think*—and to think, Brydon knew, as he stood there, was, with the lapsing moments, not to have acted! Not to have acted—that was the misery and the pang—was even still not to act; was in fact *all* to feel the thing in another, in a new and terrible way. How long did he pause and how long did he debate? There was presently nothing to measure it; for his vibration had already changed—as just by the effect of its intensity. Shut up there, at bay, defiant, and with the prodigy of the thing palpably proveably *done,* thus giving notice like some stark signboard—under that accession of accent the situation itself had turned; and Brydon at last remarkably made up his mind on what it had turned to.

It had turned altogether to a different admonition; to a supreme hint, for him, of the value of Discretion! This slowly dawned, no doubt—for it could take its time; so perfectly, on his threshold, had he been stayed, so little as yet had he either advanced or retreated. It was the strangest of all things that now when, by his taking ten steps and applying his hand to a latch, or even his shoulder and his knee, if necessary, to a panel, all the hunger of his prime need might have been met, his high curiosity crowned, his unrest assuaged—it was amazing, but it was also exquisite and rare, that insistence should have, at a touch, quite dropped from him. Discretion—he jumped at that; and yet not, verily, at such a pitch, because it saved his nerves or his skin, but because, much more valuably, it saved the situation. When I say he "jumped" at it I feel the consonance of this term with the fact that—at the end indeed of I know not how long—he did move again, he crossed straight to the door. He wouldn't touch it—it seemed now that he might *if* he would: he would only just wait there a little, to show, to prove, that he wouldn't. He had thus another station, close to the thin partition by which revelation was denied him; but with his eyes bent and his hands held off in a mere intensity of stillness. He listened as if there had been something to hear, but this attitude, while it lasted, was his own communication. "If you won't then—good: I spare you and I give up. You affect me as by the appeal positively for pity: you convince me that for reasons rigid and sublime—what do I know?—we both of us should have suffered. I respect them then, and, though moved and privileged as, I believe, it has never been given to man, I retire, I renounce—never, on my honour, to try again. So rest for ever—and let *me!*"

That, for Brydon, was the deep sense of this last demonstration—solemn, measured, directed, as he felt it to be. He brought it to a close, he turned away; and now verily he knew how deeply he had been stirred. He retraced his steps, taking up his candle, burnt, he observed, well-nigh to the socket, and marking again, lighten it as he would, the distinctness of his footfall; after which, in a moment, he knew himself at the other side of the house. He did here what he had not yet done at these hours—he opened half a casement, one of those in the front, and let in the air of the night; a thing he would have taken at any time previous for a sharp rupture of his spell. His spell was broken now, and it didn't matter—broken by his concession and his surrender, which made it idle henceforth that he should ever come back. The empty street—its other life so marked even by the great lamplit vacancy—was within call, within touch; he stayed there as to be in it again, high above it though he was still perched; he watched as for some comforting common fact, some vulgar human note, the passage of a scavenger or a thief, some night-bird however base. He would have blessed that sign of life; he would have welcomed positively the slow approach of his friend the policeman, whom he had hitherto only sought to avoid, and was not sure that if the patrol had come into sight he mightn't have felt the impulse to get into relation with it, to hail it, on some pretext, from his fourth floor.

The pretext that wouldn't have been too silly or too compromising, the explanation that would have saved his dignity and kept his name, in such a case, out of the papers, was not definite to him: he was so occupied with the thought of recording his Discretion—as an effect of the vow he had just uttered to his intimate adversary— that the importance of this loomed large and something had overtaken all ironically his sense of proportion. If there had been a ladder applied to the front of the house, even one of the vertiginous perpendiculars employed by painters and roofers and sometimes left standing overnight, he would have managed somehow, astride of the window-sill, to compass by outstretched leg and arm that mode of descent. If there had been some such uncanny thing as he had found in his room at hotels, a workable fire-escape in the form of notched cable or a canvas shoot, he would have availed himself of it as a proof—well, of his present delicacy. He nursed that sentiment, as the question stood, a little in vain, and even—at the end of he scarce knew, once more, how long—found it, as by the action on his mind of the failure of response of the outer world, sinking back to vague anguish. It seemed to him he had waited an age for some stir of the great grim hush; the life of the town was itself under a spell—so unnaturally, up and down the whole prospect of known and rather ugly objects, the blankness and the silence lasted. Had they ever, he asked himself, the hard-faced houses, which had begun to look livid in the dim dawn, had they ever spoken so little to any need of his spirit? Great builded voids, great crowded stillnesses put on, often, in the heart of cities, for the small hours, a sort of sinister mask, and it was of this large collective negation that Brydon presently became conscious—all the more that the break of day was, almost incredibly, now at hand, proving to him what a night he had made of it.

He looked again at his watch, saw what had become of his time-values (he had taken hours for minutes—not, as in other tense situations, minutes for hours) and the strange air of the streets was but the weak, the sullen flush of a dawn in which everything was still locked up. His choked appeal from his own open window had been the sole note of life, and he could but break off at last as for a worse despair. Yet while so deeply demoralised he was capable again of an impulse denoting—at least by his present measure—extraordinary resolution; of retracing his steps to the spot where he had turned cold with the extinction of his last pulse of doubt as to there being in the place another presence than his own. This required an effort strong enough to sicken him; but he had his reason, which overmastered for the moment everything else. There was the whole of the rest of the house to traverse, and how should he screw himself to that if the door he had seen closed were at present open? He could hold to the idea that the closing had practically been for him an act of mercy, a chance offered him to descend, depart, get off the ground and never again profane it. This conception held together, it worked; but what it meant for him depended now clearly on the amount of forbearance his recent action, or rather his recent inaction, had engendered. The image of the "presence," whatever it was, waiting there for him to go—this image had not yet been so concrete for his nerves as when he stopped short of the point at which certainty would have come to him. For, with all his resolution, or more exactly with all his dread, he did stop short—he hung back from really seeing. The risk was too great and his fear too definite: it took at this moment an awful specific form.

He knew—yes, as he had never known anything—that, *should* he see the door open, it would all too abjectly be the end of him. It would mean that the agent of his shame—for his shame was the deep abjection—was once more at large and in general possession;

and what glared him thus in the face was the act that this would determine for him. It would send him straight about to the window he
had left open, and by that window, be long ladder and dangling
rope as absent as they would, he saw himself uncontrollably insanely fatally take his way to the street. The hideous chance of this
he at least could avert; but he could only avert it by recoiling in
time from assurance. He had the whole house to deal with, this fact
was still there; only he now knew that uncertainty alone could start
him. He stole back from where he had checked himself—merely to
do so was suddenly like safety—and, making blindly for the greater
staircase, left gaping rooms and sounding passages behind. Here
was the top of the stairs, with a fine large dim descent and three
spacious landings to mark off. His instinct was all for mildness, but
his feet were harsh on the floors, and, strangely, when he had in a
couple of minutes become aware of this, it counted somehow for
help. He couldn't have spoken, the tone of his voice would have
scared him, and the common conceit or resource of "whistling in
the dark" (whether literally or figuratively) have appeared basely
vulgar; yet he liked none the less to hear himself go, and when he
had reached his first landing—taking it all with no rush, but quite
steadily—that stage of success drew from him a gasp of relief.

The house, withal, seemed immense, the scale of space again inordinate; the open rooms to no one of which his eyes deflected,
gloomed in their shuttered state like mouths of caverns; only the
high skylight that formed the crown of the deep well created for
him a medium in which he could advance, but which might have
been, for queerness of colour, some watery under-world. He tried
to think of something noble, as that his property was really grand, a
splendid possession; but this nobleness took the form too of the
clear delight with which he was finally to sacrifice it. They might
come in now, the builders, the destroyers—they might come as
soon as they would. At the end of two flights he had dropped to
another zone, and from the middle of the third, with only one more
left, he recognised the influence of the lower windows, of half-
drawn blinds, of the occasional gleam of street-lamps, of the glazed
spaces of the vestibule. This was the bottom of the sea, which
showed an illumination of its own and which he even saw paved—
when at a given moment he drew up to sink a long look over the
banisters—with the marble squares of his childhood. By that time
indubitably he felt, as he might have said in a commoner cause,
better; it had allowed him to stop and draw breath, and the ease
increased with the sight of the old black-and-white slabs. But what
he most felt was that now surely, with the element of impunity
pulling him as by hard firm hands, the case was settled for what he
might have seen above had he dared that last look. The closed door,

blessedly remote now, was still closed—and he had only in short to reach that of the house.

He came down further, he crossed the passage forming the access to the last flight; and if here again he stopped an instant it was almost for the sharpness of the thrill of assured escape. It made him shut his eyes—which opened again to the straight slope of the remainder of the stairs. Here was impunity still, but impunity almost excessive; inasmuch as the side-lights and the high fan-tracery of the entrance were glimmering straight into the hall; an appearance produced, he the next instant saw, by the fact that the vestibule gaped wide, that the hinged halves of the inner door had been thrown far back. Out of that again the *question* sprang at him, making his eyes, as he felt, half-start from his head, as they had done, at the top of the house, before the sign of the other door. If he had left that one open, hadn't he left this one closed, and wasn't he now in *most* immediate presence of some inconceivable occult activity? It was as sharp, the question, as a knife in his side, but the answer hung fire still and seemed to lose itself in the vague darkness to which the thin admitted dawn, glimmering archwise over the whole outer door, made a semicircular margin, a cold silvery nimbus that seemed to play a little as he looked—to shift and expand and contract.

It was as if there had been something within it, protected by indistinctness and corresponding in extent with the opaque surface behind, the painted panels of the last barrier to his escape, of which the key was in his pocket. The indistinctness mocked him even while he stared, affected him as somehow shrouding or challenging certitude, so that after faltering an instant on his step he let himself go with the sense that here *was* at last something to meet, to touch, to take, to know—something all unnatural and dreadful, but to advance upon which was the condition for him either of liberation or of supreme defeat. The penumbra, dense and dark, was the virtual screen of a figure which stood in it as still as some image erect in a niche or as some black-vizored sentinel guarding a treasure. Brydon was to know afterwards, was to recall and make out, the particular thing he had believed during the rest of his descent. He saw, in its great grey glimmering margin, the central vagueness diminish, and he felt it to be taking the very form toward which, for so many days, the passion of his curiosity had yearned. It gloomed, it loomed, it was something, it was somebody, the prodigy of a personal presence.

Rigid and conscious, spectral yet human, a man of his own substance and stature waited there to measure himself with his power to dismay. This only could it be—this only till he recognised, with his advance, that what made the face dim was the pair of raised

hands that covered it and in which, so far from being offered in
defiance, it was buried as for dark deprecation. So Brydon, before
him, took him in; with every fact of him now, in the higher light,
hard and acute—his planted stillness, his vivid truth, his grizzled
bent head and white masking hands, his queer actuality of evening-
dress, of dangling double eye-glass, of gleaming silk lappet and
white linen, of pearl button and gold watch-guard and polished
shoe. No portrait by a great modern master could have presented
him with more intensity, thrust him out of his frame with more art,
as if there had been "treatment," of the consummate sort, in his
every shade and salience. The revulsion, for our friend, had become, before he knew it, immense—this drop, in the act of apprehension, to the sense of his adversary's inscrutable manœuvre. That
meaning at least, while he gaped, it offered him; for he could but
gape at his other self in this other anguish, gape as a proof that *he*,
standing there for the achieved, the enjoyed, the triumphant life,
couldn't be faced in his triumph. Wasn't the proof in the splendid
covering hands, strong and completely spread?—so spread and so
intentional that, in spite of a special verity that surpassed every
other, the fact that one of these hands had lost two fingers, which
were reduced to stumps, as if accidentally shot away, the face was
effectually guarded and saved.

"Saved," though, *would* it be?—Brydon breathed his wonder till
the very impunity of his attitude and the very insistence of his eyes
produced, as he felt, a sudden stir which showed the next instant as
a deeper portent, while the head raised itself, the betrayal of a
braver purpose. The hands, as he looked, began to move, to open;
then, as if deciding in a flash, dropped from the face and left it uncovered and presented. Horror, with the sight, had leaped into Brydon's throat, gasping there in a sound he couldn't utter; for the
bared identity was too hideous as *his*, and his glare was the passion
of his protest. The face, *that* face, Spencer Brydon's?—he searched
it still, but looking away from it in dismay and denial, falling
straight from his height of sublimity. It was unknown, inconceivable, awful, disconnected from any possibility—! He had been
"sold," he inwardly moaned, stalking such game as this: the presence before him was a presence, the horror within him a horror, but
the waste of his nights had been only grotesque and the success of
his adventure an irony. Such an identity fitted his at *no* point, made
its alternative monstrous. A thousand times yes, as it came upon
him nearer now—the face was the face of a stranger. It came upon
him nearer now, quite as one of those expanding fantastic images
projected by the magic lantern of childhood; for the stranger, whoever he might be, evil, odious, blatant, vulgar, had advanced as for
aggression, and he knew himself give ground. Then harder pressed

still, sick with the force of his shock, and falling back as under the
hot breath and the roused passion of a life larger than his own, a
rage of personality before which his own collapsed, he felt the
whole vision turn to darkness and his very feet give way. His head
went round; he was going; he had gone.

III

What had next brought him back, clearly—though after how
long?—was Mrs. Muldoon's voice, coming to him from quite near,
from so near that he seemed presently to see her as kneeling on the
ground before him while he lay looking up at her; himself not
wholly on the ground, but half-raised and upheld—conscious, yes,
of tenderness of support and, more particularly, of a head pillowed
in extraordinary softness and faintly refreshing fragrance. He considered, he wondered, his wit but half at his service; then another
face intervened, bending more directly over him, and he finally
knew that Alice Staverton had made her lap an ample and perfect
cushion to him, and that she had to this end seated herself on the
lowest degree of the staircase, the rest of his long person remaining
stretched on his old black-and-white slabs. They were cold, these
marble squares of his youth; but *he* somehow was not, in this rich
return of consciousness—the most wonderful hour, little by little,
that he had ever known, leaving him, as it did, so gratefully, so
abysmally passive, and yet as with a treasure of intelligence waiting
all round him for quiet appropriation; dissolved, he might call it, in
the air of the place and producing the golden glow of a late autumn
afternoon. He had come back, yes—come back from further away
than any man but himself had ever travelled; but it was strange how
with this sense what he had come back *to* seemed really the great
thing, and as if his prodigious journey had been all for the sake of it.
Slowly but surely his consciousness grew, his vision of his state
thus completing itself: he had been miraculously *carried* back—
lifted and carefully borne as from where he had been picked up,
the uttermost end of an interminable grey passage. Even with this
he was suffered to rest, and what had now brought him to knowledge was the break in the long mild motion.

It had brought him to knowledge, to knowledge—yes, this was
the beauty of his state; which came to resemble more and more that
of a man who has gone to sleep on some news of a great inheritance, and then, after dreaming it away, after profaning it with matters strange to it, has waked up again to serenity of certitude and
has only to lie and watch it grow. This was the drift of his patience—that he had only to let it shine on him. He must moreover,
with intermissions, still have been lifted and borne; since why and
how else should he have known himself, later on, with the after-

noon glow intenser, no longer at the foot of his stairs—situated as these now seemed at that dark other end of his tunnel—but on a deep window-bench of his high saloon, over which had been spread, couch-fashion, a mantle of soft stuff lined with grey fur that was familiar to his eyes and that one of his hands kept fondly feeling as for its pledge of truth. Mrs. Muldoon's face had gone, but the other, the second he had recognised, hung over him in a way that showed how he was still propped and pillowed. He took it all in, and the more he took it the more it seemed to suffice: he was as much at peace as if he had had food and drink. It was the two women who had found him, on Mrs. Muldoon's having plied, at her usual hour, her latchkey—and on her having above all arrived while Miss Staverton still lingered near the house. She had been turning away, all anxiety, from worrying the vain bell-handle—her calculation having been of the hour of the good woman's visit; but the latter, blessedly, had come up while she was still there, and they had entered together. He had then lain, beyond the vestibule, very much as he was lying now—quite, that is, as he appeared to have fallen, but all so wondrously without bruise or gash; only in a depth of stupor. What he most took in, however, at present, with the steadier clearance, was that Alice Staverton had for a long unspeakable moment not doubted he was dead.

"It must have been that I *was*." He made it out as she held him. "Yes—I can only have died. You brought me literally to life. Only," he wondered, his eyes rising to her, "only, in the name of all the benedictions, how?"

It took her but an instant to bend her face and kiss him, and something in the manner of it, and in the way her hands clasped and locked his head while he felt the cool charity and virtue of her lips, something in all this beatitude somehow answered everything. "And now I keep you," she said.

"Oh keep me, keep me!" he pleaded while her face still hung over him: in response to which it dropped again and stayed close, clingingly close. It was the seal of their situation—of which he tasted the impress for a long blissful moment in silence. But he came back. "Yet how did you know—?"

"I was uneasy. You were to have come, you remember—and you had sent no word."

"Yes, I remember—I was to have gone to you at one today." It caught on to their "old" life and relation—which were so near and so far. "I was still out there in my strange darkness—where was it, what was it? I must have stayed there so long." He could but wonder at the depth and the duration of his swoon.

"Since last night?" she asked with a shade of fear for her possible indiscretion.

"Since this morning—it must have been: the cold dim dawn of

today. Where have I been," he vaguely wailed, "where have I been?" He felt her hold him close, and it was as if this helped him now to make in all security his mild moan. "What a long dark day!"

All in her tenderness she had waited a moment. "In the cold dim dawn?" she quavered.

But he had already gone on piecing together the parts of the whole prodigy. "As I didn't turn up you came straight—?"

She barely cast about. "I went first to your hotel—where they told me of your absence. You had dined out last evening and hadn't been back since. But they appeared to know you had been at your club."

"So you had the idea of *this*—?"

"Of what?" she asked in a moment.

"Well—of what has happened."

"I believed at least you'd have been here. I've known, all along," she said, "that you've been coming."

" 'Known' it—?"

"Well, I've believed it. I said nothing to you after that talk we had a month ago—but I felt sure. I knew you *would*," she declared.

"That I'd persist, you mean?"

"That you'd see him."

"Ah but I didn't!" cried Brydon with his long wail. "There's somebody—an awful beast; whom I brought, too horribly, to bay. But it's not me."

At this she bent over him again, and her eyes were in his eyes. "No—it's not you." And it was as if, while her face hovered, he might have made out in it, hadn't it been so near, some particular meaning blurred by a smile. "No, thank heaven," she repeated—"it's not you! Of course it wasn't to have been."

"Ah but it *was*," he gently insisted. And he stared before him now as he had been staring for so many weeks. "I was to have known myself."

"You couldn't!" she returned consolingly. And then reverting, and as if to account further for what she had herself done, "But it wasn't only *that*, that you hadn't been at home," she went on. "I waited till the hour at which we had found Mrs. Muldoon that day of my going with you; and she arrived, as I've told you, while, failing to bring any one to the door, I lingered in my despair on the steps. After a little, if she hadn't come, by such a mercy, I should have found means to hunt her up. But it wasn't," said Alice Staverton, as if once more with her fine intention—"it wasn't only that."

His eyes, as he lay, turned back to her. "What more then?"

She met it, the wonder she had stirred. "In the cold dim dawn, you say? Well, in the cold dim dawn of this morning I too saw you."

"Saw *me*—?"

"Saw *him*," said Alice Staverton. "It must have been at the same moment."

He lay an instant taking it in—as if he wished to be quite reasonable. "At the same moment?"

"Yes—in my dream again, the same one I've named to you. He came back to me. Then I knew it for a sign. He had come to you."

At this Brydon raised himself; he had to see her better. She helped him when she understood his movement, and he sat up, steadying himself beside her there on the window-bench and with his right hand grasping her left. "*He* didn't come to me."

"You came to yourself," she beautifully smiled.

"Ah I've come to myself now—thanks to you, dearest. But this brute, with his awful face—this brute's a black stranger. He's none of *me*, even as I *might* have been," Brydon sturdily declared.

But she kept the clearness that was like the breath of infallibility. "Isn't the whole point that you'd have been different?"

He almost scowled for it. "As different as *that*—?"

Her look again was more beautiful to him than the things of this world. "Haven't you exactly wanted to know *how* different? So this morning," she said, "you appeared to me."

"Like *him*?"

"A black stranger!"

"Then how did you know it was I?"

"Because, as I told you weeks ago, my mind, my imagination, had worked so over what you might, what you mightn't have been—to show you, you see, how I've thought of you. In the midst of that you came to me—that my wonder might be answered. So I knew," she went on; "and believed that, since the question held you too so fast, as you told me that day, you too would see for yourself. And when this morning I again saw I knew it would be because you had—and also then, from the first moment, because you somehow wanted me. *He* seemed to tell me of that. So why," she strangely smiled, "shouldn't I like him?"

It brought Spencer Brydon to his feet. "You 'like' that horror—?"

"I *could* have liked him. And to me," she said, "he was no horror. I had accepted him."

" 'Accepted'—?" Brydon oddly sounded.

"Before, for the interest of his difference—yes. And as *I* didn't disown him, as *I* knew him—which you at last, confronted with him in his difference, so cruelly didn't, my dear—well, he must have been, you see, less dreadful to me. And it may have pleased him that I pitied him."

She was beside him on her feet, but still holding his hand—still with her arm supporting him. But though it all brought for him thus a dim light, "You 'pitied' him?" he grudgingly, resentfully asked.

"He has been unhappy; he has been ravaged," she said.

"And haven't I been unhappy? Am not I—you've only to look at me!—ravaged?"

"Ah I don't say I like him *better*," she granted after a thought. "But he's grim, he's worn—and things have happened to him. He doesn't make shift, for sight, with your charming monocle."

"No"—it struck Brydon: "I couldn't have sported mine 'downtown.' They'd have guyed me there."

"His great convex pince-nez—I saw it, I recognised the kind—is for his poor ruined sight. And his poor right hand—!"

"Ah!" Brydon winced—whether for his proved identity or for his lost fingers. Then, "He has a million a year," he lucidly added. "But he hasn't you."

"And he isn't—no, he isn't—*you!*" she murmured as he drew her to his breast.

From *The Novels and Tales of Henry James*
(New York Edition, 1907–9; first published in 1908)

·REGIONALISM AND REALISM·

In the latter half of the nineteenth century, while James was experimenting with the *nouvelle* and shorter forms under the influence of his European masters—Flaubert and Maupassant and Turgenev—the native American short story was undergoing a transformation in subject matter rather than in form. The expanding frontier of the United States provided the substance for Mark Twain's early stories, Bret Harte's California sketches (*The Luck of Roaring Camp and Other Sketches,* 1871), and the Midwestern tales of Hamlin Garland. These new areas of experience invigorated the language of the short story, until by the end of the century the short-story reader had before him a fictional chronicle of New England, the South, the Middle West, and the Far West, the stories of each region providing a faithful record of local customs and dialects. This sense of America as a growing confederation of distinct regions, each with its local voice, forced the residents of the settled East to reassess their heritage, and writers such as Sarah Orne Jewett were to render the native experience in scrupulous detail. Applying to the life of the Maine Coast her favorite motto from Flaubert, "One should write of ordinary life as if one were writing history," Miss Jewett, daughter of a village doctor, wielded her pen like a scalpel.

The roll of regional writers is a long and uneven one: Harte, Mark Twain, Garland, Jewett, George Washington Cable, Joel Chandler Harris, O. Henry (William S. Porter), and many others. Often the writing is distressingly provincial, embodying all the worst aspects of "local color." But in the case of those writers with an ear for actual speech and an eye for significant detail, especially

Mark Twain, Jewett, and Garland, the colloquial style opened new literary frontiers. Sarah Orne Jewett's meticulous control of Maine dialects in "The Courting of Sister Wisby" and Hamlin Garland's command of Civil War slang in "The Return of a Private" reflect a new belief that the truth about America could not be told in a transplanted "literary" language, but only in the rhythms and figures of local speech. In their hands, as in those of the great French novelist Flaubert, the luminous local detail takes on a broad, symbolic meaning. The same is true of Mark Twain. His "Celebrated Jumping Frog of Calaveras County" may appear, on first reading, to be a piece of California folklore, but the cultural conflict between East and West (between "Daniel Webster" and "Andrew Jackson") is raised by Mark Twain's artistry to the level of a national myth.

In "How To Tell a Story" Mark Twain claimed that the tall tale was not regional but "American," and his entire career validates this belief that the most profound national truths must be expressed through the observed details of one time and one place. It was largely for this reason that Ernest Hemingway made his extravagant pronouncement, in *The Green Hills of Africa*, that "All modern American literature comes from one book by Mark Twain called *Huckleberry Finn*." Hemingway and Faulkner and Sherwood Anderson—to name but a few of Mark Twain's inheritors—found their task that much easier because the "regional" writers had broken through the genteel tradition to record the actual rhythms of everyday speech.

Most writers of regional short stories were content to use standard forms, ranging from the anecdote (as in Mark Twain's "Celebrated Jumping Frog of Calaveras County") to the symbolic tale adapted from Poe or Hawthorne. The more sophisticated and self-conscious writers, however, began to explore the effects which the new subject matter and freedom of expression would have on fictional treatment, using terms such as "realism" and "naturalism." The realist position, as articulated by William Dean Howells in *Criticism and Fiction* (1891), is essentially a plea for common-sense fidelity to the realities of contemporary life. Although the imaginative "romance," in the hands of a great writer like Hawthorne, had lifted everyday reality to a level of symbolic truth, Howells felt that the "practice of romance" by the ordinary artist was an evasion of reality, leading to melodrama and sentimentality. While his argument may strike the contemporary reader as a defense of blandness and mediocrity, Howells simply wished that fiction be true to his accurate—although limited—observation of the American scene.

Whatever their deserts, very few American novelists have been led out to be shot, or finally exiled to the rigors of a winter at Duluth; and

Mark Twain   (The Bettmann Archive)

Sarah Orne Jewett   (Culver Pictures)

Hamlin Garland   (The Bettmann Archive)

William Dean Howells   (The Bettmann Archive)

in a land where journeyman carpenters and plumbers strike for four dollars a day the sum of hunger and cold is comparatively small, and the wrong from class to class has been almost inappreciable, though all this is changing for the worse. Our novelists, therefore, concern themselves with the more smiling aspects of life, which are the more American, and seek the universal in the individual rather than the social interests. It is worth while, even at the risk of being called commonplace, to be true to our well-to-do actualities; the very passions themselves seem to be softened and modified by conditions which formerly at least could not be said to wrong any one, to cramp endeavor, or to cross lawful desire. Sin and suffering and shame there must always be in the world, I suppose, but I believe that in this new world of ours it is still mainly from one to another one, and oftener still from one to one's self. We have death, too, in America, and a great deal of disagreeable and painful disease, which the multiplicity of our patent medicines does not seem to cure; but this is tragedy that comes in the very nature of things, and is not peculiarly American, as the large, cheerful average of health and success and happy life is. It will not do to boast, but it is well to be true to the facts, and to see that, apart from these purely mortal troubles, the race here has enjoyed conditions in which most of the ills that have darkened its annals might be averted by honest work and unselfish behavior.

Howells's relentless devotion to the middle ground will not allow for a Hawthorne or a Faulkner, but if his ideas had been enforced we would have been spared a great deal of pretentious and false writing. His caution is especially relevant to the short story, where the risks are proportionately larger than in the novel; and many of his sensible caveats have been observed by those twentieth-century short story writers who have taken suburban life and everyday matters as their chosen field. Whether dispassionate or ironic in its viewpoint, the standard New Yorker story stays within the limits set by Howells, and in the works of John Cheever and John Updike we see what a master craftsman can accomplish in a fictional world where "sin and suffering and shame" are given a local habitation.

Other writers more systematic than Howells buttressed the argument for realism with theories drawn from Social Darwinism and from the writings of the French novelist Emile Zola, who sought to portray social and psychological forces with "scientific" accuracy. These "philosophic" realists, under the banner of "naturalism" or "veritism," based their art on a deterministic view of human behavior, in which environment and heredity leave little room for free choice. Among the "naturalists" or "veritists" Hamlin Garland was the finest writer of short fiction, as well as one of the least doctrinaire theorists. His essays in Crumbling Idols (1894) provide a persuasive theoretical basis for the prairie stories of Main-Travelled

Roads (1891). Like Howells, Garland was reacting against the popularity of "romantic" fiction, and for reasons well described by Jane Johnson in her preface to *Crumbling Idols:*

The literary nationalism which condemned Sir Walter Scott and his imitators because—as Mark Twain suggested in discussing the South's castles and culture—the romance fostered a feudal frame of mind that led to war is, of course, a way of saying Americans had not fought brothers but pseudo-Europeans [in the Civil War]. The local color movement was a form of literary nationalism which magnified the sectional differences dramatized by the Civil War, but minimized the element of foreign influence. A "scientific" outlook, whether adapted from Taine, Darwin, or Spencer, seemed consistent with local color and other forms of realism not only because it invited close attention to the facts of natural setting or regional dialect, but also because it invalidated emotional extremes like Villainy or Perfect Love—so often found in romances and so rarely in American life. Advocates of literary realism contended that the romance was responsible for many of the social ills of America. Both the old feudalism of the defeated South and the new feudalism of the robber barons . . . reflected the degenerate morality of the romance. Fiction which did not portray men within their real "social and physiological limits" led to "suicidal extremes" of moral judgment—such extremes, indeed, as once seemed to justify internecine war. Emotional, imaginative tales at last destroyed the readers' "power to recognize truth" and undermined their ability "to make independent ethical judgments," thus virtually disqualifying them for democratic citizenship.

Many of the essays in *Crumbling Idols* were written at the time of the Columbian Exposition in Chicago, and they are infused with the conviction that local color, "the native element, the differentiating element," is the "life of fiction." Garland stands at the opposite extreme from Henry James: to him provincialism is not local vision, but "dependence upon a mother country for models of art production." Like Whitman or the Impressionist painters, Garland wished the artist to work in the open air. The Chicago Exposition had introduced him to the works of the Impressionists, particularly Monet, and Garland's aesthetic is avowedly theirs: the work of art should be a unified impression, not a mosaic; it should have a commanding center of interest; and its success should be judged by the effect it has upon the viewer or reader. This is the aesthetic of Poe's tale and the picturesque sketch, recast in more modern terms and announced with the confidence derived from an expanding nation. The anecdote with which Garland closes his "Personal Word" in *Crumbling Idols* sums up the attitude of the most aggressive realists:

There came a young man to Monet, saying, "Master, teach me to paint." To which Monet replied, "I do not teach painting; I make paintings. There never has been, and there never will be, but one teacher: there she is!" and with one sweep of his arm he showed the young man the splendor of meadow and sunlight. "Go, learn of her, and listen to all she will say to you. If she says nothing, enter a notary's office and copy papers; that, at least, is not dishonorable, and is better than copying nymphs."

·Mark Twain·

THE
CELEBRATED JUMPING FROG
OF CALAVERAS COUNTY

In compliance with the request of a friend of mine, who wrote me from the East, I called on good-natured, garrulous old Simon Wheeler, and inquired after my friend's friend, Leonidas W. Smiley, as requested to do, and I hereunto append the result. I have a lurking suspicion that *Leonidas W.* Smiley is a myth; that my friend never knew such a personage; and that he only conjectured that if I asked old Wheeler about him, it would remind him of his infamous *Jim* Smiley, and he would go to work and bore me to death with some exasperating reminiscence of him as long and as tedious as it should be useless to me. If that was the design, it succeeded.

I found Simon Wheeler dozing comfortably by the bar-room stove of the dilapidated tavern in the decayed mining camp of Angel's, and I noticed that he was fat and bald-headed, and had an expression of winning gentleness and simplicity upon his tranquil countenance. He roused up, and gave me good day. I told him that a friend of mine had commissioned me to make some inquiries about a cherished companion of his boyhood named *Leonidas W.* Smiley—*Rev. Leonidas W.* Smiley, a young minister of the Gospel, who he had heard was at one time a resident of Angel's Camp. I added that if Mr. Wheeler could tell me anything about this Rev. Leonidas W. Smiley, I would feel under many obligations to him.

Simon Wheeler backed me into a corner and blockaded me there with his chair, and then sat down and reeled off the monotonous narrative which follows this paragraph. He never smiled, he never frowned, he never changed his voice from the gentle-flowing key to which he tuned his initial sentence, he never betrayed the slightest suspicion of enthusiasm; but all through the interminable narrative there ran a vein of impressive earnestness and sincerity, which showed me plainly that, so far from his imagining that there was anything ridiculous or funny about his story, he regarded it as a really important matter, and admired its two heroes as men of transcendent genius in *finesse*. I let him go on in his own way, and never interrupted him once.

"Rev. Leonidas W. H'm, Reverend Le—well, there was a feller here once by the name of *Jim* Smiley, in the winter of '49—or maybe it was the spring of '50—I don't recollect exactly, somehow, though what makes me think it was one or the other is because I remember the big flume warn't finished when he first come to camp; but anyway, he was the curiousest man about always betting on anything that turned up you ever see, if he could get anybody to bet on the other side; and if he couldn't he'd change sides. Any way that suited the other man would suit *him*—any way just so's he got a bet, *he* was satisfied. But still he was lucky, uncommon lucky; he most always come out winner. He was always ready and laying for a chance; there couldn't be no solit'ry thing mentioned but that feller'd offer to bet on it, and take ary side you please, as I was just telling you. If there was a horse-race, you'd find him flush or you'd find him busted at the end of it; if there was a dog-fight, he'd bet on it; if there was a cat-fight, he'd bet on it; if there was a chicken-fight, he'd bet on it; why, if there was two birds setting on a fence, he would bet you which one would fly first; or if there was a camp-meeting, he would be there reg'lar to bet on Parson Walker, which he judged to be the best exhorter about here, and so he was too, and a good man. If he even see a straddle-bug start to go anywheres, he would bet you how long it would take him to get to—to wherever he was going to, and if you took him up, he would foller that straddle-bug to Mexico but what he would find out where he was bound for and how long he was on the road. Lots of the boys here has seen that Smiley, and can tell you about him. Why, it never made no difference to *him*—he'd bet on *any* thing—the dangdest feller. Parson Walker's wife laid very sick once, for a good while, and it seemed as if they warn't going to save her; but one morning he come in, and Smiley up and asked him how she was, and he said she was considerable better—thank the Lord for his inf'nite mercy—and coming on so smart that with the blessing of Prov'dence she'd get well yet; and Smiley, before he thought, says, 'Well, I'll resk two-and-a-half she don't anyway.'

"Thish-yer Smiley had a mare—the boys called her the fifteen-minute nag, but that was only in fun, you know, because of course she was faster than that—and he used to win money on that horse, for all she was so slow and always had the asthma, or the distemper, or the consumption, or something of that kind. They used to give her two or three hundred yards' start, and then pass her under way; but always at the fag end of the race she'd get excited and desperate like, and come cavorting and straddling up, and scattering her legs around limber, sometimes in the air, and sometimes out to one side among the fences, and kicking up m-o-r-e dust and raising m-o-r-e racket with her coughing and sneezing and blowing her nose—and *always* fetch up at the stand just about a neck ahead, as near as you could cipher it down.

"And he had a little small bull-pup, that to look at him you'd think he warn't worth a cent but to set around and look ornery and lay for a chance to steal something. But as soon as money was up on him he was a different dog; his under-jaw'd begin to stick out like the fo'castle of a steamboat, and his teeth would uncover and shine like the furnaces. And a dog might tackle him and bully-rag him, and bite him, and throw him over his shoulder two or three times, and Andrew Jackson—which was the name of the pup—Andrew Jackson would never let on but what *he* was satisfied, and hadn't expected nothing else—and the bets being doubled and doubled on the other side all the time, till the money was all up; and then all of a sudden he would grab that other dog jest by the j'int of his hind leg and freeze to it—not chaw, you understand, but only just grip and hang on till they throwed up the sponge, if it was a year. Smiley always come out winner on that pup, till he harnessed a dog once that didn't have no hind legs, because they'd been sawed off in a circular saw, and when the thing had gone along far enough, and the money was all up, and he come to make a snatch for his pet holt, he see in a minute how he'd been imposed on, and how the other dog had him in the door, so to speak, and he 'peared surprised, and then he looked sorter discouraged-like, and didn't try no more to win the fight, and so he got shucked out bad. He give Smiley a look, as much as to say his heart was broke, and it was *his* fault, for putting up a dog that hadn't no hind legs for him to take holt of, which was his main dependence in a fight, and then he limped off a piece and laid down and died. It was a good pup, was that Andrew Jackson, and would have made a name for hisself if he'd lived, for the stuff was in him and he had genius—I know it, because he hadn't no opportunities to speak of, and it don't stand to reason that a dog could make such a fight as he could under them circumstances if he hadn't no talent. It always makes me feel sorry when I think of that last fight of his'n, and the way it turned out.

"Well, thish-yer Smiley had rat-tarriers, and chicken cocks, and tom-cats and all them kind of things, till you couldn't rest, and you couldn't fetch nothing for him to bet on but he'd match you. He ketched a frog one day, and took him home, and said he cal'lated to educate him; and so he never done nothing for three months but set in his back yard and learn that frog to jump. And you bet you he *did* learn him, too. He'd give him a little punch behind, and the next minute you'd see that frog whirling in the air like a doughnut—see him turn one summerset, or maybe a couple, if he got a good start, and come down flat-footed and all right, like a cat. He got him up so in the matter of ketching flies, and kep' him in practice so constant, that he'd nail a fly every time as fur as he could see him. Smiley said all a frog wanted was education, and he could do 'most any-thing—and I believe him. Why, I've seen him set Dan'l Webster down here on this floor—Dan'l Webster was the name of the frog—and sing out, 'Flies, Dan'l, flies!' and quicker'n you could wink he'd spring straight up and snake a fly off'n the counter there, and flop down on the floor ag'in as solid as a gob of mud, and fall to scratch-ing the side of his head with his hind foot as indifferent as if he hadn't no idea he'd been doin' any more'n any frog might do. You never see a frog so modest and straightfor'ard as he was, for all he was so gifted. And when it come to fair and square jumping on a dead level, he could get over more ground at one straddle than any animal of his breed you ever see. Jumping on a dead level was his strong suit, you understand; and when it come to that, Smiley would ante up money on him as long as he had a red.[1] Smiley was monstrous proud of his frog, and well he might be, for fellers that had traveled and been everywheres all said he laid over any frog that ever *they* see.

"Well, Smiley kep' the beast in a little lattice box, and he used to fetch him down-town sometimes and lay for a bet. One day a feller—a stranger in the camp, he was—come acrost him with his box, and says:

" 'What might it be that you've got in the box?'

"And Smiley says, sorter indifferent-like, 'It might be a parrot, or it might be a canary, maybe, but it ain't—it's only just a frog.'

"And the feller took it, and looked at it careful, and turned it round this way and that, and says, 'H'm—so 'tis. Well, what's *he* good for?'

" 'Well,' Smiley says, easy and careless, 'he's good enough for *one* thing, I should judge—he can outjump any frog in Calaveras County.'

"The feller took the box again, and took another long, particular look, and give it back to Smiley, and says, very deliberate, 'Well,'

---

1. A penny, a "red cent."

he says, 'I don't see no p'ints about that frog that's any better'n any other frog.'

" 'Maybe you don't,' Smiley says. 'Maybe you understand frogs and maybe you don't understand 'em; maybe you've had experience, and maybe you ain't only a amature, as it were. Anyways, I've got *my* opinion, and I'll resk forty dollars that he can outjump any frog in Calaveras County.'

"And the feller studied a minute, and then says, kinder sad-like, 'Well, I'm only a stranger here, and I ain't got no frog; but if I had a frog, I'd bet you.'

"And then Smiley says, 'That's all right—that's all right—if you'll hold my box a minute, I'll go and get you a frog.' And so the feller took the box, and put up his forty dollars along with Smiley's, and set down to wait.

"So he set there a good while thinking and thinking to himself, and then he got the frog out and prized his mouth open and took a teaspoon and filled him full of quail-shot—filled him pretty near up to his chin—and set him on the floor. Smiley he went to the swamp and slopped around in the mud for a long time, and finally he ketched a frog, and fetched him in, and give him to this feller, and says:

" 'Now, if you're ready, set him alongside of Dan'l, with his fore paws just even with Dan'l's, and I'll give the word.' Then he says, 'One—two—three—*git!*' and him and the feller touched up the frogs from behind, and the new frog hopped off lively, but Dan'l give a heave, and hysted up his shoulders—so—like a Frenchman, but it warn't no use—he couldn't budge; he was planted as solid as a church, and he couldn't no more stir than if he was anchored out. Smiley was a good deal surprised, and he was disgusted too, but he didn't have no idea what the matter was, of course.

"The feller took the money and started away; and when he was going out at the door, he sorter jerked his thumb over his shoulder—so—at Dan'l, and says again, very deliberate, 'Well,' he says, '*I* don't see no p'ints about that frog that's any better'n any other frog.'

"Smiley he stood scratching his head and looking down at Dan'l a long time, and at last he says, 'I do wonder what in the nation that frog throw'd off for—I wonder if there ain't something the matter with him—he 'pears to look mighty baggy, somehow.' And he ketched Dan'l by the nap of the neck, and hefted him, and says, 'Why blame my cats if he don't weigh five pound!' and turned him upside down and he belched out a double handful of shot. And then he see how it was, and he was the maddest man—he set the frog down and took out after that feller, but he never ketched him. And—"

[Here Simon Wheeler heard his name called from the front yard, and got up to see what was wanted.] And turning to me as he moved away, he said: "Just set where you are, stranger, and rest easy—I ain't going to be gone a second."

But, by your leave, I did not think that a continuation of the history of the enterprising vagabond *Jim* Smiley would be likely to afford me much information concerning the Rev. *Leonidas* W. Smiley, and so I started away.

At the door I met the sociable Wheeler returning, and he buttonholed me and recommenced.

"Well, thish-yer Smiley had a yaller one-eyed cow that didn't have no tail, only just a short stump like a bannanner, and—"

However, lacking both time and inclination, I did not wait to hear about the afflicted cow, but took my leave.

From *The Celebrated Jumping Frog of Calaveras County and Other Sketches* (1867)

·William Dean Howells·

EDITHA

The air was thick with the war feeling, like the electricity of a storm which has not yet burst. Editha sat looking out into the hot spring afternoon, with her lips parted, and panting with the intensity of the question whether she could let him go. She had decided that she could not let him stay, when she saw him at the end of the still leafless avenue, making slowly up towards the house, with his head down and his figure relaxed. She ran impatiently out on the veranda, to the edge of the steps, and imperatively demanded greater haste of him with her will before she called aloud to him: "George!"

He had quickened his pace in mystical response to her mystical urgence, before he could have heard her; now he looked up and answered, "Well?"

"Oh, how united we are!" she exulted, and then she swooped down the steps to him. "What is it?" she cried.

"It's war," he said, and he pulled her up to him and kissed her.

She kissed him back intensely, but irrelevantly, as to their passion, and uttered from deep in her throat. "How glorious!"

"It's war," he repeated, without consenting to her sense of it; and she did not know just what to think at first. She never knew what to think of him; that made his mystery, his charm. All through their courtship, which was contemporaneous with the growth of the war feeling, she had been puzzled by his want of seriousness about it. He seemed to despise it even more than he abhorred it. She could have understood his abhorring any sort of bloodshed; that would have been a survival of his old life when he thought he would be a minister, and before he changed and took up the law. But making

light of a cause so high and noble seemed to show a want of earnestness at the core of his being. Not but that she felt herself able to
cope with a congenital defect of that sort, and make his love for her
save him from himself. Now perhaps the miracle was already
wrought in him. In the presence of the tremendous fact that he announced, all triviality seemed to have gone out of him; she began to
feel that. He sank down on the top step, and wiped his forehead
with his handkerchief, while she poured out upon him her question
of the origin and authenticity of his news.

All the while, in her duplex emotioning, she was aware that now
at the very beginning she must put a guard upon herself against
urging him, by any word or act, to take the part that her whole soul
willed him to take, for the completion of her ideal of him. He was
very nearly perfect as he was, and he must be allowed to perfect
himself. But he was peculiar, and he might very well be reasoned
out of his peculiarity. Before her reasoning went her emotioning:
her nature pulling upon his nature, her womanhood upon his manhood, without her knowing the means she was using to the end she
was willing. She had always supposed that the man who won her
would have done something to win her; she did not know what, but
something. George Gearson had simply asked her for her love, on
the way home from a concert, and she gave her love to him, without, as it were, thinking. But now, it flashed upon her, if he could
do something worthy to *have* won her—be a hero, *her* hero—it
would be even better than if he had done it before asking her; it
would be grander. Besides, she had believed in the war from the
beginning.

"But don't you see, dearest," she said, "that it wouldn't have
come to this if it hadn't been in the order of Providence? And I call
any war glorious that is for the liberation of people who have been
struggling for years against the cruelest oppression. Don't you think
so, too?"

"I suppose so," he returned, languidly. "But war! Is it glorious to
break the peace of the world?"

"That ignoble peace! It was no peace at all, with that crime and
shame at our very gates." She was conscious of parroting the current phrases of the newspapers, but it was no time to pick and
choose her words. She must sacrifice anything to the high ideal she
had for him, and after a good deal of rapid argument she ended with
the climax: "But now it doesn't matter about the how or why. Since
the war has come, all that is gone. There are no two sides any more.
There is nothing now but our country."

He sat with his eyes closed and his head leant back against the
veranda, and he remarked, with a vague smile, as if musing aloud,
"Our country—right or wrong."

"Yes, right or wrong!" she returned, fervidly. "I'll go and get you some lemonade." She rose rustling, and whisked away; when she came back with two tall glasses of clouded liquid on a tray, and the ice clucking in them, he still sat as she had left him, and she said, as if there had been no interruption: "But there is no question of wrong in this case. I call it a sacred war. A war for liberty and humanity, if ever there was one. And I know you will see it just as I do, yet."

He took half the lemonade at a gulp, and he answered as he set the glass down: "I know you always have the highest ideal. When I differ from you I ought to doubt myself."

A generous sob rose in Editha's throat for the humility of a man, so very nearly perfect, who was willing to put himself below her.

Besides, she felt, more subliminally, that he was never so near slipping through her fingers as when he took that meek way.

"You shall not say that! Only, for once I happen to be right." She seized his hand in her two hands, and poured her soul from her eyes into his. "Don't you think so?" she entreated him.

He released his hand and drank the rest of his lemonade, and she added, "Have mine, too," but he shook his head in answering, "I've no business to think so, unless I act so, too."

Her heart stopped a beat before it pulsed on with leaps that she felt in her neck. She had noticed that strange thing in men: they seemed to feel bound to do what they believed, and not think a thing was finished when they said it, as girls did. She knew what was in his mind, but she pretended not, and she said, "Oh, I am not sure," and then faltered.

He went on as if to himself, without apparently heeding her: "There's only one way of proving one's faith in a thing like this."

She could not say that she understood, but she did understand.

He went on again. "If I believed—if I felt as you do about this war— Do you wish me to feel as you do?"

Now she was really not sure; so she said: "George, I don't know what you mean."

He seemed to muse away from her as before. "There is a sort of fascination in it. I suppose that at the bottom of his heart every man would like at times to have his courage tested, to see how he would act."

"How can you talk in that ghastly way?"

"It *is* rather morbid. Still, that's what it comes to, unless you're swept away by ambition or driven by conviction. I haven't the conviction or the ambition, and the other thing is what it comes to with me. I ought to have been a preacher, after all; then I couldn't have asked it of myself, as I must, now I'm a lawyer. And you believe it's a holy war, Editha?" he suddenly addressed her. "Oh, I know you do! But you wish me to believe so, too?"

She hardly knew whether he was mocking or not, in the ironical way he always had with her plainer mind. But the only thing was to be outspoken with him.

"George, I wish you to believe whatever you think is true, at any and every cost. If I've tried to talk you into anything, I take it all back."

"Oh, I know that, Editha. I know how sincere you are, and how— I wish I had your undoubting spirit! I'll think it over; I'd like to believe as you do. But I don't, now; I don't, indeed. It isn't this war alone; though this seems peculiarly wanton and needless; but it's every war—so stupid; it makes me sick. Why shouldn't this thing have been settled reasonably?"

"Because," she said, very throatily again, "God meant it to be war."

"You think it was God? Yes, I suppose that is what people will say."

"Do you suppose it would have been war if God hadn't meant it?"

"I don't know. Sometimes it seems as if God had put this world into men's keeping to work it as they pleased."

"Now, George, that is blasphemy."

"Well, I won't blaspheme. I'll try to believe in your pocket Providence," he said, and then he rose to go.

"Why don't you stay to dinner?" Dinner at Balcom's Works was at one o'clock.

"I'll come back to supper, if you'll let me. Perhaps I shall bring you a convert."

"Well, you may come back, on that condition."

"All right. If I don't come, you'll understand."

He went away without kissing her, and she felt it a suspension of their engagement. It all interested her intensely; she was undergoing a tremendous experience, and she was being equal to it. While she stood looking after him, her mother came out through one of the long windows onto the veranda, with a catlike softness and vagueness.

"Why didn't he stay to dinner?"

"Because—because—war has been declared," Editha pronounced, without turning.

Her mother said, "Oh, my!" and then said nothing more until she had sat down in one of the large Shaker chairs and rocked herself for some time. Then she closed whatever tacit passage of thought there had been in her mind with the spoken words: "Well, I hope *he* won't go."

"And *I* hope he *will*," the girl said, and confronted her mother with a stormy exaltation that would have frightened any creature less unimpressionable than a cat.

Her mother rocked herself again for an interval of cogitation. What she arrived at in speech was: "Well, I guess you've done a wicked thing, Editha Balcom."

The girl said, as she passed indoors through the same window her mother had come out by: "I haven't done anything—yet."

In her room, she put together all her letters and gifts from Gearson, down to the withered petals of the first flower he had offered, with that timidity of his veiled in that irony of his. In the heart of the packet she enshrined her engagement ring which she had restored to the pretty box he had brought it her in. Then she sat down, if not calmly yet strongly, and wrote:

GEORGE:—I understood when you left me. But I think we had better emphasize your meaning that if we cannot be one in everything we had better be one in nothing. So I am sending these things for your keeping till you have made up your mind.

I shall always love you, and therefore I shall never marry any one else. But the man I marry must love his country first of all, and be able to say to me,

"I could not love thee, dear, so much,
Loved I not honor more." [1]

There is no honor above America with me. In this great hour there is no other honor.

Your heart will make my words clear to you. I had never expected to say so much, but it has come upon me that I must say the utmost.

EDITHA.

She thought she had worded her letter well, worded it in a way that could not be bettered; all had been implied and nothing expressed.

She had it ready to send with the packet she had tied with red, white, and blue ribbon, when it occurred to her that she was not

---

1. From "To Lucasta, Going to the Wars," by the English poet Richard Lovelace (1618–57).

Tell me not, sweet, I am unkind,
  That from the nunnery
Of thy chaste breast and quiet mind,
  To war and arms I fly.

True, a new mistress now I chase,
  The first foe in the field;
And with a stronger faith embrace
  A sword, a horse, a shield.

Yet this inconstancy is such
  As you too shall adore;
I could not love thee, dear, so much,
  Loved I not honour more.

just to him, that she was not giving him a fair chance. He had said he would go and think it over, and she was not waiting. She was pushing, threatening, compelling. That was not a woman's part. She must leave him free, free, free. She could not accept for her country or herself a forced sacrifice.

In writing her letter she had satisfied the impulse from which it sprang; she could well afford to wait till he had thought it over. She put the packet and the letter by, and rested serene in the conscious-ness of having done what was laid upon her by her love itself to do, and yet used patience, mercy, justice.

She had her reward. Gearson did not come to tea, but she had given him till morning, when, late at night there came up from the village the sound of a fife and drum, with a tumult of voices, in shouting, singing, and laughing. The noise drew nearer and nearer; it reached the street end of the avenue; there it silenced itself, and one voice, the voice she knew best, rose over the silence. It fell; the air was filled with cheers; the fife and drum struck up, with the shouting, singing, and laughing again, but now retreating; and a single figure came hurrying up the avenue.

She ran down to meet her lover and clung to him. He was very gay, and he put his arm round her with a boisterous laugh. "Well, you must call me Captain now; or Cap, if you prefer; that's what the boys call me. Yes, we've had a meeting at the town-hall, and every-body has volunteered; and they selected me for captain, and I'm going to the war, the big war, the glorious war, the holy war or-dained by the pocket Providence that blesses butchery. Come along; let's tell the whole family about it. Call them from their downy beds, father, mother, Aunt Hitty, and all the folks!"

But when they mounted the veranda steps he did not wait for a larger audience; he poured the story out upon Editha alone.

"There was a lot of speaking, and then some of the fools set up a shout for me. It was all going one way, and I thought it would be a good joke to sprinkle a little cold water on them. But you can't do that with a crowd that adores you. The first thing I knew I was sprinkling hell-fire on them. 'Cry havoc, and let slip the dogs of war.' [2] That was the style. Now that it had come to the fight, there were no two parties; there was one country, and the thing was to fight to a finish as quick as possible. I suggested volunteering then and there, and I wrote my name first of all on the roster. Then they elected me—that's all. I wish I had some ice-water."

She left him walking up and down the veranda, while she ran for the ice-pitcher and a goblet, and when she came back he was still walking up and down, shouting the story he had told her to her fa-

2. Spoken by Mark Antony in *Julius Caesar*, III.i.273.

ther and mother, who had come out more sketchily dressed than they commonly were by day. He drank goblet after goblet of the ice-water without noticing who was giving it, and kept on talking, and laughing through his talk wildly. "It's astonishing," he said, "how well the worse reason looks when you try to make it appear the better. Why, I believe I was the first convert to the war in that crowd to-night! I never thought I should like to kill a man; but now I shouldn't care; and the smokeless powder lets you see the man drop that you kill. It's all for the country! What a thing it is to have a country that *can't* be wrong, but if it is, is right, anyway!"

Editha had a great, vital thought, an inspiration. She set down the ice-pitcher on the veranda floor, and ran up-stairs and got the letter she had written him. When at last he noisily bade her father and mother, "Well, good-night. I forgot I woke you up; I sha'n't want any sleep myself," she followed him down the avenue to the gate. There, after the whirling words that seemed to fly away from her thoughts and refuse to serve them, she made a last effort to solemnize the moment that seemed so crazy, and pressed the letter she had written upon him.

"What's this?" he said. "Want me to mail it?"

"No, no. It's for you. I wrote it after you went this morning. Keep it—keep it—and read it sometime—" She thought, and then her inspiration came: "Read it if ever you doubt what you've done, or fear that I regret your having done it. Read it after you've started."

They strained each other in embraces that seemed as ineffective as their words, and he kissed her face with quick, hot breaths that were so unlike him, that made her feel as if she had lost her old lover and found a stranger in his place. The stranger said: "What a gorgeous flower you are, with your red hair, and your blue eyes that look black now, and your face with the color painted out by the white moonshine! Let me hold you under the chin, to see whether I love blood, you tiger-lily!" Then he laughed Gearson's laugh, and released her, scared and giddy. Within her wilfulness she had been frightened by a sense of subtler force in him, and mystically mastered as she had never been before.

She ran all the way back to the house, and mounted the steps panting. Her mother and father were talking of the great affair. Her mother said: "Wa'n't Mr. Gearson in rather of an excited state of mind? Didn't you think he acted curious?"

"Well, not for a man who'd just been elected captain and had set 'em up for the whole of Company A," her father chuckled back.

"What in the world do you mean, Mr. Balcom? Oh! There's Editha!" She offered to follow the girl indoors.

"Don't come, mother!" Editha called, vanishing.

Mrs. Balcom remained to reproach her husband. "I don't see much of anything to laugh at."

"Well, it's catching. Caught it from Gearson. I guess it won't be much of a war, and I guess Gearson don't think so, either. The other fellows will back down as soon as they see we mean it. I wouldn't lose any sleep over it. I'm going back to bed, myself."

Gearson came again next afternoon, looking pale and rather sick, but quite himself, even to his languid irony. "I guess I'd better tell you, Editha, that I consecrated myself to your god of battles last night by pouring too many libations to him down my own throat. But I'm all right now. One has to carry off the excitement, somehow."

"Promise me," she commanded, "that you'll never touch it again!"

"What! Not let the cannikin [3] clink? Not let the soldier drink? Well, I promise."

"You don't belong to yourself now; you don't even belong to *me*. You belong to your country, and you have a sacred charge to keep yourself strong and well for your country's sake. I have been thinking, thinking all night and all day long."

"You look as if you had been crying a little, too," he said, with his queer smile.

"That's all past. I've been thinking, and worshipping *you*. Don't you suppose I know all that you've been through, to come to this? I've followed you every step from your old theories and opinions."

"Well, you've had a long row to hoe."

"And I know you've done this from the highest motives—"

"Oh, there won't be much pettifogging to do till this cruel war is—"

"And you haven't simply done it for my sake. I couldn't respect you if you had."

"Well, then we'll say I haven't. A man that hasn't got his own respect intact wants the respect of all the other people he can corner. But we won't go into that. I'm in for the thing now, and we've got to face our future. My idea is that this isn't going to be a very protracted struggle; we shall just scare the enemy to death before it comes to a fight at all. But we must provide for contingencies, Editha. If anything happens to me—"

"Oh, George!" She clung to him, sobbing.

"I don't want you to feel foolishly bound to my memory. I should hate that, wherever I happened to be."

3. Small metal drinking vessel.

"I am yours, for time and eternity—time and eternity." She liked the words; they satisfied her famine for phrases.

"Well, say eternity; that's all right; but time's another thing; and I'm talking about time. But there is something! My mother! If anything happens—"

She winced, and he laughed. "You're not the bold soldier-girl of yesterday!" Then he sobered. "If anything happens, I want you to help my mother out. She won't like my doing this thing. She brought me up to think war a fool thing as well as a bad thing. My father was in the Civil War; all through it; lost his arm in it." She thrilled with the sense of the arm round her; what if that should be lost? He laughed as if divining her: "Oh, it doesn't run in the family, as far as I know!" Then he added, gravely: "He came home with misgivings about war, and they grew on him. I guess he and mother agreed between them that I was to be brought up in his final mind about it; but that was before my time. I only knew him from my mother's report of him and his opinions; I don't know whether they were hers first; but they were hers last. This will be a blow to her. I shall have to write and tell her—"

He stopped, and she asked: "Would you like me to write, too, George?"

"I don't believe that would do. No, I'll do the writing. She'll understand a little if I say that I thought the way to minimize it was to make war on the largest possible scale at once—that I felt I must have been helping on the war somehow if I hadn't helped keep it from coming, and I knew I hadn't; when it came, I had no right to stay out of it."

Whether his sophistries satisfied him or not, they satisfied her. She clung to his breast, and whispered, with closed eyes and quivering lips: "Yes, yes, yes!"

"But if anything should happen, you might go to her and see what you could do for her. You know? It's rather far off; she can't leave her chair—"

"Oh, I'll go, if it's the ends of the earth! But nothing will happen! Nothing *can!* I—"

She felt herself lifted with his rising, and Gearson was saying, with his arm still round her, to her father: "Well, we're off at once, Mr. Balcom. We're to be formally accepted at the capital, and then bunched up with the rest somehow, and sent into camp somewhere, and got to the front as soon as possible. We all want to be in the van, of course; we're the first company to report to the Governor. I came to tell Editha, but I hadn't got round to it."

She saw him again for a moment at the capital, in the station, just before the train started southward with his regiment. He looked well, in his uniform, and very soldierly, but somehow girlish, too, with his clean-shaven face and slim figure. The manly eyes and the strong voice satisfied her, and his preoccupation with some unexpected details of duty flattered her. Other girls were weeping and bemoaning themselves, but she felt a sort of noble distinction in the abstraction, the almost unconsciousness, with which they parted. Only at the last moment he said: "Don't forget my mother. It mayn't be such a walk-over as I supposed," and he laughed at the notion.

He waved his hand to her as the train moved off—she knew it among a score of hands that were waved to other girls from the platform of the car, for it held a letter which she knew was hers. Then he went inside the car to read it, doubtless, and she did not see him again. But she felt safe for him through the strength of what she called her love. What she called her God, always speaking the name in a deep voice and with the implication of a mutual understanding, would watch over him and keep him and bring him back to her. If with an empty sleeve, then he should have three arms instead of two, for both of hers should be his for life. She did not see, though, why she should always be thinking of the arm his father had lost.

There were not many letters from him, but they were such as she could have wished, and she put her whole strength into making hers such as she imagined he could have wished, glorifying and supporting him. She wrote to his mother glorifying him as their hero, but the brief answer she got was merely to the effect that Mrs. Gearson was not well enough to write herself, and thanking her for her letter by the hand of someone who called herself "Yrs truly, Mrs. W. J. Andrews."

Editha determined not to be hurt, but to write again quite as if the answer had been all she expected. Before it seemed as if she could have written, there came news of the first skirmish, and in the list of the killed, which was telegraphed as a trifling loss on our side, was Gearson's name. There was a frantic time of trying to make out that it might be, must be, some other Gearson; but the name and the company and the regiment and the State were too definitely given.

Then there was a lapse into depths out of which it seemed as if she never could rise again; then a lift into clouds far above all grief, black clouds, that blotted out the sun, but where she soared with him, with George—George! She had the fever that she expected of herself, but she did not die in it; she was not even delirious, and it did not last long. When she was well enough to leave her bed, her one thought was of George's mother, of his strangely worded wish that she should go to her and see what she could do for her. In the exaltation of the duty laid upon her—it buoyed her up instead of burdening her—she rapidly recovered.

Her father went with her on the long railroad journey from northern New York to western Iowa; he had business out at Davenport, and he said he could just as well go then as any other time; and he went with her to the little country town where George's mother lived in a little house on the edge of the illimitable cornfields, under trees pushed to a top of the rolling prairie. George's father had settled there after the Civil War, as so many other old soldiers had done; but they were Eastern people, and Editha fancied touches of the East in the June rose overhanging the front door, and the garden with early summer flowers stretching from the gate of the paling fence.

It was very low inside the house, and so dim, with the closed blinds, that they could scarcely see one another: Editha tall and black in her crapes which filled the air with the smell of their dyes; her father standing decorously apart with his hat on his forearm, as at funerals; a woman rested in a deep arm-chair, and the woman who had let the strangers in stood behind the chair.

The seated woman turned her head round and up, and asked the woman behind her chair: "*Who* did you say?"

Editha, if she had done what she expected of herself, would have gone down on her knees at the feet of the seated figure and said, "I am George's Editha," for answer.

But instead of her own voice she heard that other woman's voice, saying: "Well, I don't know as I *did* get the name just right. I guess I'll have to make a little more light in here," and she went and pushed two of the shutters ajar.

Then Editha's father said, in his public will-now-address-a-few-remarks tone: "My name is Balcom, ma'am—Junius H. Balcom, of Balcom's Works, New York; my daughter—"

"Oh!" the seated woman broke in, with a powerful voice, the voice that always surprised Editha from Gearson's slender frame. "Let me see you. Stand round where the light can strike on your face," and Editha dumbly obeyed. "So, you're Editha Balcom," she sighed.

"Yes," Editha said, more like a culprit than a comforter.

"What did you come for?" Mrs. Gearson asked.

Editha's face quivered and her knees shook. "I came—because—because George—" She could go no further.

"Yes," the mother said, "he told me he had asked you to come if he got killed. You didn't expect that, I suppose, when you sent him."

"I would rather have died myself than done it!" Editha said, with more truth in her deep voice than she ordinarily found in it. "I tried to leave him free—"

"Yes, that letter of yours, that came back with his other things, left him free."

Editha saw now where George's irony came from.

"It was not to be read before—unless—until— I told him so," she faltered.

"Of course, he wouldn't read a letter of yours, under the circumstances, till he thought you wanted him to. Been sick?" the woman abruptly demanded.

"Very sick," Editha said, with self-pity.

"Daughter's life," her father interposed, "was almost despaired of, at one time."

Mrs. Gearson gave him no heed. "I suppose you would have been glad to die, such a brave person as you! I don't believe *he* was glad to die. He was always a timid boy, that way; he was afraid of a good many things; but if he was afraid he did what he made up his mind to. I suppose he made up his mind to go, but I knew what it cost him by what it cost me when I heard of it. I had been through *one* war before. When you sent him you didn't expect he would get killed."

The voice seemed to compassionate Editha, and it was time. "No," she huskily murmured.

"No, girls don't; women don't, when they give their men up to their country. They think they'll come marching back, somehow, just as gay as they went, or if it's an empty sleeve, or even an empty pantaloon, it's all the more glory, and they're so much the prouder of them, poor things!"

The tears began to run down Editha's face; she had not wept till then; but it was now such a relief to be understood that the tears came.

"No, you didn't expect him to get killed," Mrs. Gearson repeated, in a voice which was startlingly like George's again. "You just expected him to kill some one else, some of those foreigners, that weren't there because they had any say about it, but because they had to be there, poor wretches—conscripts, or whatever they call 'em. You thought it would be all right for my George, *your* George, to kill the sons of those miserable mothers and the husbands of those girls that you would never see the faces of." The woman lifted her powerful voice in a psalmlike note. "I thank my God he didn't live to do it! I thank my God they killed him first, and that he ain't livin' with their blood on his hands!" She dropped her eyes, which she had raised with her voice, and glared at Editha. "What you got that black on for?" She lifted herself by her powerful arms so high that her helpless body seemed to hang limp its full length. "Take it off, take it off, before I tear it from your back!"

The lady who was passing the summer near Balcom's Works was sketching Editha's beauty, which lent itself wonderfully to the effects of a colorist. It had come to that confidence which is rather apt to grow between artist and sitter, and Editha had told her everything.

"To think of your having such a tragedy in your life!" the lady said. She added: "I suppose there are people who feel that way about war. But when you consider the good this war has done—how much it has done for the country! I can't understand such people, for my part. And when you had come all the way out there to console her—got up out of a sick-bed! Well!"

"I think," Editha said, magnanimously, "she wasn't quite in her right mind; and so did papa."

"Yes," the lady said, looking at Editha's lips in nature and then at her lips in art, and giving an empirical touch to them in the picture. "But how dreadful of her! How perfectly—excuse me—how *vulgar!*"

A light broke upon Editha in the darkness which she felt had been without a gleam of brightness for weeks and months. The mystery that had bewildered her was solved by the word; and from that moment she rose from grovelling in shame and self-pity, and began to live again in the ideal.

From *Between the Dark and the Daylight*
(1907; first published in 1905)

·Sarah Orne Jewett·

THE COURTING OF
SISTER WISBY

All the morning there had been an increasing temptation to take an
out-door holiday, and early in the afternoon the temptation outgrew
my power of resistance. A far-away pasture on the long southwestern slope of a high hill was persistently present to my mind, yet
there seemed to be no particular reason why I should think of it. I
was not sure that I wanted anything from the pasture, and there was
no sign, except the temptation, that the pasture wanted anything of
me. But I was on the farther side of as many as three fences before I
stopped to think again where I was going, and why.

There is no use in trying to tell another person about that afternoon unless he distinctly remembers weather exactly like it. No
number of details concerning an Arctic ice-blockade will give a
single shiver to a child of the tropics. This was one of those perfect
New England days in late summer, when the spirit of autumn takes
a first stealthy flight, like a spy, through the ripening country-side,
and, with feigned sympathy for those who droop with August heat,
puts her cool cloak of bracing air about leaf and flower and human
shoulders. Every living thing grows suddenly cheerful and strong;
it is only when you catch sight of a horror-stricken little maple in
swampy soil,—a little maple that has second sight and foreknowledge of coming disaster to her race,—only then does a distrust of
autumn's friendliness dim your joyful satisfaction.

In midwinter there is always a day when one has the first fore-
taste of spring; in late August there is a morning when the air is for
the first time autumn like. Perhaps it is a hint to the squirrels to get

in their first supplies for the winter hoards, or a reminder that summer will soon end, and everybody had better make the most of it. We are always looking forward to the passing and ending of winter, but when summer is here it seems as if summer must always last. As I went across the fields that day, I found myself half lamenting that the world must fade again, even that the best of her budding and bloom was only a preparation for another spring-time, for an awakening beyond the coming winter's sleep.

The sun was slightly veiled; there was a chattering group of birds, which had gathered for a conference about their early migration. Yet, oddly enough, I heard the voice of a belated bobolink, and presently saw him rise from the grass and hover leisurely, while he sang a brief tune. He was much behind time if he were still a housekeeper; but as for the other birds, who listened, they cared only for their own notes. An old crow went sagging by, and gave a croak at his despised neighbor, just as a black reviewer croaked at Keats:[1] so hard it is to be just to one's contemporaries. The bobolink was indeed singing out of season, and it was impossible to say whether he really belonged most to this summer or to the next. He might have been delayed on his northward journey; at any rate, he had a light heart now, to judge from his song, and I wished that I could ask him a few questions,—how he liked being the last man among the bobolinks, and where he had taken singing lessons in the South.

Presently I left the lower fields, and took a path that led higher, where I could look beyond the village to the northern country mountainward. Here the sweet fern grew, thick and fragrant, and I also found myself heedlessly treading on pennyroyal. Near by, in a field corner, I long ago made a most comfortable seat by putting a stray piece of board and bit of rail across the angle of the fences. I have spent many a delightful hour there, in the shade and shelter of a young pitch-pine and a wild-cherry tree, with a lovely outlook toward the village, just far enough away beyond the green slopes and tall elms of the lower meadows. But that day I still had the feeling of being outward bound, and did not turn aside nor linger. The high pasture land grew more and more enticing.

I stopped to pick some blackberries that twinkled at me like beads among their dry vines, and two or three yellow-birds fluttered up from the leaves of a thistle, and then came back again, as if they had complacently discovered that I was only an overgrown yellow-bird, in strange disguise but perfectly harmless. They made me feel as if I were an intruder, though they did not offer to peck at me, and we parted company very soon. It was good to stand at last

1. John Keats (1795–1821) was severely criticized during his lifetime by the reviewers for *Blackwood's Edinburgh Magazine* and *The Quarterly Review*.

on the great shoulder of the hill. The wind was coming in from the sea, there was a fine fragrance from the pines, and the air grew sweeter every moment. I took new pleasure in the thought that in a piece of wild pasture land like this one may get closest to Nature, and subsist upon what she gives of her own free will. There have been no drudging, heavy-shod ploughmen to overturn the soil, and vex it into yielding artificial crops. Here one has to take just what Nature is pleased to give, whether one is a yellow-bird or a human being. It is very good entertainment for a summer wayfarer, and I am asking my reader now to share the winter provision which I harvested that day. Let us hope that the small birds are also faring well after their fashion, but I give them an anxious thought while the snow goes hurrying in long waves across the buried fields, this windy winter night.

I next went farther down the hill, and got a drink of fresh cool water from the brook, and pulled a tender sheaf of sweet flag beside it. The mossy old fence just beyond was the last barrier between me and the pasture which had sent an invisible messenger earlier in the day, but I saw that somebody else had come first to the rendezvous: there was a brown gingham cape-bonnet and a sprigged shoulder-shawl bobbing up and down, a little way off among the junipers. I had taken such uncommon pleasure in being alone that I instantly felt a sense of disappointment; then a warm glow of pleasant satisfaction rebuked my selfishness. This could be no one but dear old Mrs. Goodsoe, the friend of my childhood and fond dependence of my maturer years. I had not seen her for many weeks, but here she was, out on one of her famous campaigns for herbs, or perhaps just returning from a blueberrying expedition. I approached with care, so as not to startle the gingham bonnet; but she heard the rustle of the bushes against my dress, and looked up quickly, as she knelt, bending over the turf. In that position she was hardly taller than the luxuriant junipers themselves.

"I'm a-gittin' in my mulleins,"[2] she said briskly, "an' I've been thinking o' you these twenty times since I come out o' the house. I begun to believe you must ha' forgot me at last."

"I have been away from home," I explained. "Why don't you get in your pennyroyal too? There's a great plantation of it beyond the next fence but one."

"Pennyr'yal!" repeated the dear little old woman, with an air of compassion for inferior knowledge; " 't ain't the right time, darlin'. Pennyr'yal's too rank now. But for mulleins this day is prime. I've got a dreadful graspin' fit for 'em this year; seems if I must be goin'

2. Herb with large, woolly leaves. All the plants mentioned in the following pages—pennyroyal, masterwort, liverwort, thoroughwort, camomile, yellow dock—are valued either as medicinal herbs or as pot-herbs.

to need 'em extry. I feel like the squirrels must when they know a hard winter's comin'." And Mrs. Goodsoe bent over her work again, while I stood by and watched her carefully cut the best full-grown leaves with a clumsy pair of scissors, which might have served through at least half a century of herb-gathering. They were fastened to her apron-strings by a long piece of list.

"I'm going to take my jack-knife and help you," I suggested, with some fear of refusal. "I just passed a flourishing family of six or seven heads that must have been growing on purpose for you."

"Now be keerful, dear heart," was the anxious response; "choose 'em well. There's odds in mulleins same's there is in angels. Take a plant that's all run up to stalk, and there ain't but little goodness in the leaves. This one I'm at now must ha' been stepped on by some creatur' and blighted of its bloom, and the leaves is han'some! When I was small I used to have a notion that Adam an' Eve must a took mulleins fer their winter wear. Ain't they just like flannel, for all the world? I've had experience, and I know there's plenty of sickness might be saved to folks if they'd quit horse-radish and such fiery, exasperating things, and use mullein drarves in proper season. Now I shall spread these an' dry 'em nice on my spare floor in the garrit, an' come to steam 'em for use along in the winter there'll be the vally of the whole summer's goodness in 'em, sartin." And she snipped away with the dull scissors, while I listened respectfully, and took great pains to have my part of the harvest present a good appearance.

"This is most too dry a head," she added presently, a little out of breath. "There! I can tell you there's win'rows o' young doctors, bilin' over with book-larnin', that is truly ignorant of what to do for the sick, or how to p'int out those paths that well people foller toward sickness. Book-fools I call 'em, them young men, an' some on 'em never'll live to know much better, if they git to be Methuselahs. In my time every middle-aged woman, who had brought up a family, had some proper ideas o' dealin' with complaints. I won't say but there was some fools amongst *them*, but I'd rather take my chances, unless they'd forsook herbs and gone to dealin' with patent stuff. Now my mother really did sense the use of herbs and roots. I never see anybody that come up to her. She was a meek-looking woman, but very understandin', mother was."

"Then that's where you learned so much yourself, Mrs. Goodsoe," I ventured to say.

"Bless your heart, I don't hold a candle to her; 't is but little I can recall of what she used to say. No, her l'arnin' died with her," said my friend, in a self-depreciating tone. "Why, there was as many as twenty kinds of roots alone that she used to keep by her, that I forget the use of; an' I'm sure I shouldn't know where to find the most of 'em, any. There was an herb"—*airb*, she called it—"an herb called masterwort, that she used to get way from Pennsylvany; and she used to think everything of noble-liverwort, but I never could seem to get the right effects from it as she could. Though I don't know as she ever really did use masterwort where somethin' else wouldn't a served. She had a cousin married out in Pennsylvany that used to take pains to get it to her every year or two, and so she felt 't was important to have it. Some set more by such things as come from a distance, but I rec'lect mother always used to maintain that folks was meant to be doctored with the stuff that grew right about 'em; 't was sufficient, an' so ordered. That was before the whole population took to livin' on wheels, the way they do now. 'T was never my idee that we was meant to know what's goin' on all over the world to once. There's goin' to be some sort of a set-back one o' these days, with these telegraphs an' things, an' letters comin' every hand's turn, and folks leavin' their proper work to answer 'em. I may not live to see it. 'T was allowed to be difficult for folks to git about in old times, or to git word across the country, and they stood in their lot an' place, and weren't all just alike, either, same as pine-spills."

We were kneeling side by side now, as if in penitence for the march of progress, but we laughed as we turned to look at each other.

"Do you think it did much good when everybody brewed a cracked quart mug of herb-tea?" I asked, walking away on my knees to a new mullein.

"I've always lifted my voice against the practice, far's I could," declared Mrs. Goodsoe; "an' I won't deal out none o' the herbs I save for no such nonsense. There was three houses along our road,—I call no names,—where you couldn't go into the livin' room without findin' a mess o' herb-tea drorin' on the stove or side o' the fireplace, winter or summer, sick or well. One was thoroughwut, one would be camomile, and the other, like as not, yellow dock; but they all used to put in a little new rum to git out the goodness, or keep it from spilin'." (Mrs. Goodsoe favored me with a knowing smile.) "Land, how mother used to laugh! But, poor creaturs, they had to work hard, and I guess it never done 'em a mite o' harm; they was all good herbs. I wish you could hear the squawkin' there used to be when they was indulged with a real case o' sickness. Everybody would collect from far an' near; you'd see 'em coming along the road and across the pastures then; everybody clamorin' that nothin' wouldn't do no kind o' good but her choice o' teas or drarves to the feet. I wonder there was a babe lived to grow up in the whole lower part o' the town; an' if nothin' else 'peared to ail 'em, word was passed about that 't was likely Mis' So-and-So's last young one was goin' to be foolish. Land, how they'd gather! I know one day the doctor come to Widder Peck's and the house was crammed so 't he could scercely git inside the door; and he says, just as polite, 'Do send for some of the neighbors!' as if there wa'n't a soul to turn to, right or left. You'd ought to seen 'em begin to scatter."

"But don't you think the cars and telegraphs have given people more to interest them, Mrs. Goodsoe? Don't you believe people's lives were narrower then, and more taken up with little things?" I asked, unwisely, being a product of modern times.

"Not one mite, dear," said my companion stoutly. "There was as big thoughts then as there is now; these times was born o' them. The difference is in folks themselves; but now, instead o' doin' their own housekeepin' and watchin' their own neighbors,—though that was carried to excess,—they git word that a niece's child is ailin' the other side o' Massachusetts, and they drop everything and git on their best clothes, and off they jiggit in the cars. 'Tis a bad sign when folks wears out their best clothes faster 'n they do their every-day ones. The other side o' Massachusetts has got to look after itself by rights. An' besides that, Sunday-keepin' 's all gone out o' fashion. Some lays it to one thing an' some another, but some o' them old ministers that folks are all a-sighin' for did preach a lot o' stuff that wa'n't nothin' but chaff; 't wa'n't the word o' God out o' either Old Testament or New. But everybody went to meetin' and heard it, and come home, and was set to fightin' with their next door neighbor over it. Now I'm a believer, and I try to live a Christian life, but I'd as soon hear a surveyor's book read out, figgers an' all, as try to get any simple truth out o' most sermons. It's them as is most to blame."

"What was the matter that day at Widow Peck's?" I hastened to ask, for I knew by experience that the good, clear-minded soul beside me was apt to grow unduly vexed and distressed when she contemplated the state of religious teaching.

"Why, there wa'n't nothin' the matter, only a gal o' Miss Peck's had met with a dis'pintment and had gone into screechin' fits. 'T was a rovin' creatur' that had come along hayin' time, and he'd gone off an' forsook her betwixt two days; nobody ever knew what become of him. Them Pecks was 'Good Lord, anybody!' kind o' gals, and took up with whoever they could get. One of 'em married Heron, the Irishman; they lived in that little house that was burnt this summer, over on the edge o' the plains. He was a good-hearted creatur', with a laughin' eye and a clever word for everybody. He was the first Irishman that ever came this way, and we was all for gettin' a look at him, when he first used to go by. Mother's folks was what they call Scotch-Irish, though; there was an old race of 'em settled about here. They could foretell events, some on 'em, and had the second sight. I know folks used to say mother's grand-mother had them gifts, but mother was never free to speak about it to us. She remembered her well, too."

"I suppose that you mean old Jim Heron, who was such a famous fiddler?" I asked with great interest, for I am always delighted to know more about that rustic hero, parochial Orpheus[3] that he must have been!

"Now, dear heart, I suppose you don't remember him, do you?" replied Mrs. Goodsoe, earnestly. "Fiddle! He'd about break your heart with them tunes of his, or else set your heels flying up the floor in a jig, though you was minister o' the First Parish and all wound up for a funeral prayer. I tell ye there ain't no tunes sounds like them used to. It used to seem to me summer nights when I was comin' along the plains road, and he set by the window playin', as if there was a bewitched human creatur' in that old red fiddle o' his. He could make it sound just like a woman's voice tellin' somethin' over and over, as if folks could help her out o' her sorrows if she could only make 'em understand. I've set by the stone-wall and cried as if my heart was broke, and dear knows it wa'n't in them days. How he would twirl off them jigs and dance tunes! He used to make somethin' han'some out of 'em in fall an' winter, playin' at huskins and dancin' parties; but he was unstiddy by spells, as he got along in years, and never knew what it was to be forehanded. Everybody felt bad when he died; you couldn't help likin' the crea-tur'. He'd got the gift—that's all you could say about it.

"There was a Mis' Jerry Foss, that lived over by the brook bridge, on the plains road, that had lost her husband early, and was left with three child'n. She set the world by 'em, and was a real pleas-ant, ambitious little woman, and was workin' on as best she could with that little farm, when there come a rage o' scarlet fever, and her boy and two girls was swept off and laid dead within the same week. Every one o' the neighbors did what they could, but she'd had no sleep since they was taken sick, and after the funeral she set there just like a piece o' marble, and would only shake her head when you spoke to her. They all thought her reason would go; and 't would certain, if she couldn't have shed tears. An' one o' the neighbors—'t was like mother's sense, but it might have been somebody else—spoke o' Jim Heron. Mother an' one or two o' the women that knew her best was in the house with her. 'T was right in the edge o' the woods and some of us younger ones was over by the wall on the other side of the road where there was a couple of old willows,—I remember just how the brook damp felt; and we

3. In Greek mythology, a poet-musician whose lyre could charm beasts and make trees and rocks move.

kept quiet 's we could, and some other folks come along down the
road, and stood waitin' on the little bridge, hopin' somebody'd
come out, I suppose, and they'd git news. Everybody was wrought
up, and felt a good deal for her, you know. By an' by Jim Heron
come stealin' right out o' the shadows an' set down on the doorstep,
an' 't was a good while before we heard a sound; then, oh, dear me!
't was what the whole neighborhood felt for that mother all spoke in
the notes, an' they told me afterwards that Mis' Foss's face changed
in a minute, and she come right over an' got into my mother's lap,—
she was a little woman,—an' laid her head down, and there she
cried herself into a blessed sleep. After awhile one o' the other
women stole out an' told the folks, and we all went home. He only
played that one tune.

"But there!" resumed Mrs. Goodsoe, after a silence, during
which my eyes were filled with tears. "His wife always complained
that the fiddle made her nervous. She never 'peared to think nothin'
o' poor Heron after she'd once got him."

"That's often the way," said I, with harsh cynicism, though I had
no guilty person in my mind at the moment; and we went straying
off, not very far apart, up through the pasture. Mrs. Goodsoe cautioned me that we must not get so far off that we could not get back
the same day. The sunshine began to feel very hot on our backs,
and we both turned toward the shade. We had already collected a
large bundle of mullein leaves, which were carefully laid into a
clean, calico apron, held together by the four corners, and proudly
carried by me, though my companion regarded them with anxious
eyes. We sat down together at the edge of the pine woods, and Mrs.
Goodsoe proceeded to fan herself with her limp cape-bonnet.

"I declare, how hot it is! The east wind's all gone again," she
said. "It felt so cool this forenoon that I overburdened myself with
as thick a petticoat as any I've got. I'm despri't afeared of having a
chill, now that I ain't so young as once. I hate to be housed up."

"It's only August, after all," I assured her unnecessarily, confirming my statement by taking two peaches out of my pocket, and laying them side by side on the brown pine needles between us.

"Dear sakes alive!" exclaimed the old lady, with evident pleasure. "Where did you get them, now? Doesn't anything taste twice
better out-o'-doors? I ain't had such a peach for years. Do le's keep
the stones, an' I'll plant 'em; it only takes four year for a peach pit
to come to bearing, an' I guess I'm good for four year, 'thout I meet
with some accident."

I could not help agreeing, or taking a fond look at the thin little
figure, and her wrinkled brown face and kind, twinkling eyes. She
looked as if she had properly dried herself, by mistake, with some
of her mullein leaves, and was likely to keep her goodness, and to

last the longer in consequence. There never was a truer, simple-hearted soul made out of the old-fashioned country dust than Mrs. Goodsoe. I thought, as I looked away from her across the wide country, that nobody was left in any of the farm-houses so original, so full of rural wisdom and reminiscence, so really able and depend-able, as she. And nobody had made better use of her time in a world foolish enough to sometimes under-value medicinal herbs.

When we had eaten our peaches we still sat under the pines, and I was not without pride when I had poked about in the ground with a little twig, and displayed to my crony a long fine root, bright yellow to the eye, and a wholesome bitter to the taste.

"Yis, dear, goldthread," she assented indulgently. "Seems to me there's more of it than anything except grass an' hardhack. Good for canker,[4] but no better than two or three other things I can call to mind; but I always lay in a good wisp of it, for old times' sake. Now, I want to know why you should a bit it, and took away all the taste o' your nice peach? I was just thinkin' what a han'some entertain-ment we've had. I've got so I 'sociate certain things with certain folks, and goldthread was somethin' Lizy Wisby couldn't keep house without, no ways whatever. I believe she took so much it kind o' puckered her disposition."

"Lizy Wisby?" I repeated inquiringly.

"You knew her, if ever, by the name of Mis' Deacon Brimble-com," answered my friend, as if this were only a brief preface to further information, so I waited with respectful expectation. Mrs. Goodsoe had grown tired out in the sun, and a good story would be an excuse for sufficient rest. It was a most lovely place where we sat, half-way up the long hillside; for my part, I was perfectly con-tented and happy. "You've often heard of Deacon Brimblecom?" she asked, as if a great deal depended upon his being properly in-troduced.

"I remember him," said I. "They called him Deacon Brimfull, you know, and he used to go about with a witch-hazel branch to show people where to dig wells."

"That's the one," said Mrs. Goodsoe, laughing. "I didn't know's you could go so far back. I'm always divided between whether you can remember everything I can, or are only a babe in arms."

"I have a dim recollection of there being something strange about their marriage," I suggested, after a pause, which began to appear dangerous. I was so much afraid the subject would be changed.

"I can tell you all about it," I was quickly answered. "Deacon Brimblecom was very pious accordin' to his lights in his early years. He lived way back in the country then, and there come a rovin'

4. Ulcers or cancer.

preacher along, and set everybody up that way all by the ears. I've heard the old folks talk it over, but I forget most of his doctrine, except some of his followers was persuaded they could dwell among the angels while yet on airth, and this Deacon Brimfull, as you call him, felt sure he was called by the voice of a spirit bride. So he left a good, deservin' wife he had, an' four children, and built him a new house over to the other side of the land he'd had from his father. They didn't take much pains with the buildin', because they expected to be translated before long, and then the spirit brides and them folks was goin' to appear and divide up the airth amongst 'em, and the world's folks and on-believers was goin' to serve 'em or be sent to torments. They had meetin's about in the school-houses, an' all sorts o' goins on; some on 'em went crazy, but the deacon held on to what wits he had, an' by an' by the spirit bride didn't turn out to be much of a housekeeper, an' he had always been used to good livin', so he sneaked home ag'in. One o' mother's sisters married up to Ash Hill, where it all took place; that's how I come to have the particulars."

"Then how did he come to find his Eliza Wisby?" I inquired. "Do tell me the whole story; you've got mullein leaves enough."

"There's all yesterday's at home, if I haven't," replied Mrs. Goodsoe. "The way he come a-courtin' o' Sister Wisby was this: she went a-courtin' o' him.

"There was a spell he lived to home, and then his poor wife died, and he had a spirit bride in good earnest, an' the child'n was placed about with his folks and hers, for they was both out o' good families; and I don't know what come over him, but he had another pious fit that looked for all the world like the real thing. He hadn't no family cares, and he lived with his brother's folks, and turned his land in with theirs. He used to travel to every meetin' an' conference that was within reach of his old sorrel hoss's feeble legs; he j'ined the Christian Baptists that was just in their early prime, and he was a great exhorter, and got to be called deacon, though I guess he wa'n't deacon, 'less it was for a spare hand when deacon timber was scercer'n usual. An' one time there was a four days' protracted meetin' to the church in the lower part of the town. 'T was a real solemn time; something more'n usual was goin' forward, an' they collected from the whole country round. Women folks liked it, an' the men too; it give 'em a change, an' they was quartered round free, same as conference folks now. Some on 'em, for a joke, sent Silas Brimblecom up to Lizy Wisby's, though she'd give out she couldn't accommodate nobody, because of expectin' her cousin's folks. Everybody knew 't was a lie; she was amazin' close considerin' she had plenty to do with. There was a streak that wa'n't just right somewheres in Lizy's wits, I always thought. She was very kind in case o' sickness, I'll say that for her.

"You know where the house is, over there on what they call Windy Hill? There the deacon went, all unsuspectin', and 'stead o' Lizy's resentin' of him she put in her own hoss, and they come back together to evenin' meetin'. She was prominent among the sect herself, an' he bawled and talked, and she bawled and talked, an' took up more 'n the time allotted in the exercises, just as if they was showin' off to each other what they was able to do at expoundin'. Everybody was laughin' at 'em after the meetin' broke up, and that next day an' the next, an' all through, they was constant, and seemed to be havin' a beautiful occasion. Lizy had always give out she scorned the men, but when she got a chance at a particular one 't was altogether different, and the deacon seemed to please her somehow or 'nother, and— There! you don't want to listen to this old stuff that's past an' gone?"

"Oh yes, I do," said I.

"I run on like a clock that's onset her striking hand," said Mrs. Goodsoe mildly. "Sometimes my kitchen timepiece goes on half the forenoon, and I says to myself the day before yisterday I would let it be a warnin', and keep it in mind for a check on my own speech. The next news that was heard was that the deacon an' Lizy—well, opinions differed which of 'em had spoke first, but them fools settled it before the protracted meetin' was over, and give away their hearts before he started for home. They considered 't would be wise, though, considerin' their short acquaintance, to take one another on trial a spell; 't was Lizy's notion, and she asked him why he wouldn't come over and stop with her till spring, and then, if they both continued to like, they could git married any time 't was convenient. Lizy, she come and talked it over with mother, and mother disliked to offend her, but she spoke pretty plain; and Lizy felt hurt, an' thought they was showin' excellent judgment, so much harm come from hasty unions and folks comin' to a realizin' sense of each other's failin's when 't was too late.

"So one day our folks saw Deacon Brimfull a-ridin' by with a gre't coopful of hens in the back o' his wagon, and bundles o' stuff tied on top and hitched to the exes underneath; and he riz a hymn just as he passed the house, and was speedin' the old sorrel with a willer switch. 'T was most Thanksgivin' time, an' sooner 'n she expected him. New Year's was the time she set; but he thought he'd better come while the roads was fit for wheels. They was out to meetin' together Thanksgivin' Day, an' that used to be a gre't season for marryin'; so the young folks nudged each other, and some on' 'em ventured to speak to the couple as they come down the aisle. Lizy carried it off real well; she wa'n't afraid o' what nobody said or thought, and so home they went. They'd got out her yaller sleigh and her hoss; she never would ride after the deacon's poor

old creatur', and I believe it died long o' the winter from stiffenin'
up.

"Yes," said Mrs. Goodsoe emphatically, after we had silently considered the situation for a short space of time,—"yes, there was consider'ble talk, now I tell you! The raskil boys pestered 'em just
about to death for a while. They used to collect up there an' rap on
the winders, and they'd turn out all the deacon's hens 'long at nine
o'clock 'o night, and chase 'em all over the dingle; an' one night
they even lugged the pig right out o' the sty, and shoved it into the
back entry, an' run for their lives. They'd stuffed its mouth full o'
somethin', so it couldn't squeal till it got there. There wa'n't a sign
o' nobody to be seen when Lizy hasted out with the light, and she
an' the deacon had to persuade the creatur' back as best they could;
't was a cold night, and they said it took 'em till towards mornin'.
You see the deacon was just the kind of a man that a hog wouldn't
budge for; it takes a masterful man to deal with a hog. Well, there
was no end to the works nor the talk, but Lizy left 'em pretty much
alone. She did 'pear kind of dignified about it, I must say!"

"And then, were they married in the spring?"

"I was tryin' to remember whether it was just before Fast Day [5]
or just after," responded my friend, with a careful look at the sun,
which was nearer the west than either of us had noticed. "I think
likely 't was along in the last o' April, any way some of us looked
out o' the window one Monday mornin' early, and says, 'For goodness' sake! Lizy's sent the deacon home again!' His old sorrel
havin' passed away, he was ridin' in Ezry Welsh's hoss-cart, with
his hen-coop and more bundles than he had when he come, and he
looked as meechin' as ever you see. Ezry was drivin', and he let a
glance fly swiftly round to see if any of us was lookin' out; an' then
I declare if he didn't have the malice to turn right in towards the
barn, where he see my oldest brother, Joshuay, an' says he real natural, 'Joshuay, just step out with your wrench. I believe I hear my
kingbolt rattlin' kind o' loose.' Brother, he went out an' took in the
sitooation, an' the deacon bowed kind of stiff. Joshuay was so full o'
laugh, and Ezry Welsh, that they couldn't look one another in the
face. There wa'n't nothing ailed the kingbolt, you know, an' when
Josh riz up he says, 'Goin' up country for a spell, Mr. Brimblecom?'

" 'I be,' says the deacon, lookin' dreadful mortified and cast
down.

" 'Ain't things turned out well with you an' Sister Wisby?' says
Joshuay. 'You had ought to remember that the woman is the weaker
vessel.'

" 'Hang her, let her carry less sail, then!' the deacon bu'st out,

5. A spring day formerly designated in some New England states as a time for fasting and prayer (usually associated with planting time).

and he stood right up an' shook his fist there by the hen-coop, he was so mad; an' Ezry's hoss was a young creatur', an' started up an set the deacon right over backwards into the chips. We didn't know but he'd broke his neck; but when he see the women folks runnin' out, he jumped up quick as a cat, an' clim' into the cart, an' off they went. Ezry said he told him that he couldn't git along with Lizy, she was so fractious in thundery weather; if there was a rumble in the day-time she must go right to bed an' screech, and if 't was night she must git right up an' go an' call him out of a sound sleep. But everybody knew he'd never a gone home unless she'd sent him.

"Somehow they made it up agin right away, him an' Lizy, and she had him back. She'd been countin' all along on not havin' to hire nobody to work about the gardin an' so on, an' she said she wa'n't goin' to let him have a whole winter's board for nothin'. So the old hens was moved back, and they was married right off fair an' square, an' I don't know but they got along well as most folks. He brought his youngest girl down to live with 'em after a while, an' she was a real treasure to Lizy; everybody spoke well o' Phebe Brimblecom. The deacon got over his pious fit, and there was consider'ble work in him if you kept right after him. He was an amazin' cider-drinker, and he airnt the name you know him by in his latter days. Lizy never trusted him with nothin', but she kep' him well. She left everything she owned to Phebe, when she died, 'cept somethin' to satisfy the law. There, they're all gone now: seems to me sometimes, when I get thinkin', as if I'd lived a thousand years!"

I laughed, but I found that Mrs. Goodsoe's thoughts had taken a serious turn.

"There, I come by some old graves down here in the lower edge of the pasture," she said as we rose to go. "I couldn't help thinking how I should like to be laid right out in the pasture ground, when my time comes; it looked sort o' comfortable, and I have ranged these slopes so many summers. Seems as if I could see right up through the turf and tell when the weather was pleasant, and get the goodness o' the sweet fern. Now, dear, just hand me my apernful o' mulleins out o' the shade. I hope you won't come to need none this winter, but I'll dry some special for you."

"I'm going home by the road," said I, "or else by the path across the meadows, so I will walk as far as the house with you. Aren't you pleased with my company?" for she demurred at my going the least bit out of the way.

So we strolled toward the little gray house, with our plunder of mullein leaves slung on a stick which we carried between us. Of course I went in to make a call, as if I had not seen my hostess before; she is the last maker of muster-gingerbread, and before I came away I was kindly measured for a pair of mittens.

"You'll be sure to come an' see them two peach-trees after I get 'em well growin'?" Mrs. Goodsoe called after me when I had said good-by, and was almost out of hearing down the road.

From *The King of Folly Island and Other People* (1888)

·Hamlin Garland·

THE RETURN OF A PRIVATE

I

The nearer the train drew toward La Crosse, the soberer the little group of "vets" [1] became. On the long way from New Orleans they had beguiled tedium with jokes and friendly chaff; or with planning with elaborate detail what they were going to do now, after the war.[2] A long journey, slowly, irregularly, yet persistently pushing northward. When they entered on Wisconsin territory they gave a cheer, and another when they reached Madison, but after that they sank into a dumb expectancy. Comrades dropped off at one or two points beyond, until there were only four or five left who were bound for La Crosse County.

Three of them were gaunt and brown, the fourth was gaunt and pale, with signs of fever and ague upon him. One had a great scar down his temple, one limped, and they all had unnaturally large, bright eyes, showing emaciation. There were no hands greeting them at the station, no banks of gayly dressed ladies waving handkerchiefs and shouting "Bravo!" as they came in on the caboose of a freight train into the towns that had cheered and blared at them on their way to war. As they looked out or stepped upon the platform for a moment, while the train stood at the station, the loafers looked

1. Veterans of the Civil War. Throughout the story Garland makes skillful use of the jargon of the recent war, with expressions like "comrades," "squad," "skirmishin'," "foraged," "marched."
2. The story is set in Wisconsin at the end of the Civil War (the volume in which it first appeared was subtitled "Six Mississippi Valley Stories"). Like Stephen Crane, Garland was too young to know much of the war at first hand, and had to re-create the events in his imagination.

at them indifferently. Their blue coats, dusty and grimy, were too familiar now to excite notice, much less a friendly word. They were the last of the army to return, and the loafers were surfeited with such sights.

The train jogged forward so slowly that it seemed likely to be midnight before they should reach La Crosse. The little squad grumbled and swore, but it was no use; the train would not hurry, and, as a matter of fact, it was nearly two o'clock when the engine whistled "down brakes."

All of the group were farmers, living in districts several miles out of the town, and all were poor.

"Now, boys," said Private Smith, he of the fever and ague, "we are landed in La Crosse in the night. We've got to stay somewhere till mornin'. Now I ain't got no two dollars to waste on a hotel. I've got a wife and children, so I'm goin' to roost on a bench and take the cost of a bed out of my hide."

"Same here," put in one of the other men. "Hide'll grow on again, dollars'll come hard. It's going to be mighty hot skirmishin' to find a dollar these days."

"Don't think they'll be a deputation of citizens waitin' to 'scort us to a hotel, eh?" said another. His sarcasm was too obvious to require an answer.

Smith went on, "Then at daybreak we'll start for home—at least, I will."

"Well, I'll be dummed if I'll take two dollars out o' *my* hide," one of the younger men said. "I'm goin' to a hotel, ef I don't never lay up a cent."

"That'll do f'r you," said Smith; "but if you had a wife an' three young uns dependin' on yeh—"

"Which I ain't, thank the Lord! and don't intend havin' while the court knows itself." [3]

The station was deserted, chill, and dark, as they came into it at exactly a quarter to two in the morning. Lit by the oil lamps that flared a dull red light over the dingy benches, the waiting room was not an inviting place. The younger man went off to look up a hotel, while the rest remained and prepared to camp down on the floor and benches. Smith was attended to tenderly by the other men, who spread their blankets on the bench for him, and, by robbing themselves, made quite a comfortable bed, though the narrowness of the bench made his sleeping precarious.

It was chill, though August, and the two men, sitting with bowed heads, grew stiff with cold and weariness, and were forced to rise now and again and walk about to warm their stiffened limbs. It did not occur to them, probably, to contrast their coming home with

3. While reason prevails.

their going forth, or with the coming home of the generals, colonels, or even captains—but to Private Smith, at any rate, there came a sickness at heart almost deadly as he lay there on his hard bed and went over his situation.

In the deep of the night, lying on a board in the town where he had enlisted three years ago, all elation and enthusiasm gone out of him, he faced the fact that with the joy of home-coming was already mingled the bitter juice of care. He saw himself sick, worn out, taking up the work on his half-cleared farm, the inevitable mortgage standing ready with open jaw to swallow half his earnings. He had given three years of his life for a mere pittance of pay, and now!—

Morning dawned at last, slowly, with a pale yellow dome of light rising silently above the bluffs, which stand like some huge storm-devastated castle, just east of the city. Out to the left the great river swept on its massive yet silent way to the south. Bluejays called across the water from hillside to hillside through the clear, beautiful air, and hawks began to skim the tops of the hills. The older men were astir early, but Private Smith had fallen at last into a sleep, and they went out without waking him. He lay on his knapsack, his gaunt face turned toward the ceiling, his hands clasped on his breast, with a curious pathetic effect of weakness and appeal.

An engine switching near woke him at last, and he slowly sat up and stared about. He looked out of the window and saw that the sun was lightening the hills across the river. He rose and brushed his hair as well as he could, folded his blankets up, and went out to find his companions. They stood gazing silently at the river and at the hills.

"Looks natcher'l, don't it?" they said, as he came out.

"That's what it does," he replied. "An' it looks good. D' yeh see that peak?" He pointed at a beautiful symmetrical peak, rising like a slightly truncated cone, so high that it seemed the very highest of them all. It was touched by the morning sun and it glowed like a beacon, and a light scarf of gray morning fog was rolling up its shadowed side.

"My farm's just beyond that. Now, if I can only ketch a ride, we'll be home by dinner-time."

"I'm talkin' about breakfast," said one of the others.

"I guess it's one more meal o' hardtack[4] f'r me," said Smith.

They foraged around, and finally found a restaurant with a sleepy old German behind the counter, and procured some coffee, which they drank to wash down their hardtack.

"Time'll come," said Smith, holding up a piece by the corner, "when this'll be a curiosity."

"I hope to God it will! I bet I've chawed hardtack enough to

4. Hard biscuits, originally prepared for use aboard ship.

shingle every house in the coolly.[5] I've chawed it when my lampers was down, and when they wasn't. I've took it dry, soaked, and mashed. I've had it wormy, musty, sour, and blue-mouldy. I've had it in little bits and big bits; 'fore coffee an' after coffee. I'm ready f'r a change. I'd like t' git holt jest about now o' some of the hot biscuits my wife c'n make when she lays herself out f'r company."

"Well, if you set there gabblin', you'll never *see* yer wife."

"Come on," said Private Smith. "Wait a moment, boys; less take suthin'. It's on me." He led them to the rusty tin dipper which hung on a nail beside the wooden water-pail, and they grinned and drank. Then shouldering their blankets and muskets, which they were "takin' home to the boys," they struck out on their last march.

"They called that coffee Jayvy," grumbled one of them, "but it never went by the road where government Jayvy resides. I reckon I know coffee from peas."

They kept together on the road along the turnpike, and up the winding road by the river, which they followed for some miles. The river was very lovely, curving down along its sandy beds, pausing now and then under broad basswood trees, or running in dark, swift, silent currents under tangles of wild grapevines, and drooping alders, and haw trees. At one of these lovely spots the three vets sat down on the thick green sward to rest, "on Smith's account." The leaves of the trees were as fresh and green as in June, the jays called cheery greetings to them, and kingfishers darted to and fro with swooping, noiseless flight.

"I tell yeh, boys, this knocks the swamps of Loueesiana into kingdom come."

"You bet. All they c'n raise down there is snakes, niggers, and p'rticler hell."

"An' fighting men," put in the older man.

"An' fightin' men. If I had a good hook an' line I'd sneak a pick'rel out o' that pond. Say, remember that time I shot that alligator—"

"I guess we'd better be crawlin' along," interrupted Smith, rising and shouldering his knapsack, with considerable effort, which he tried to hide.

"Say, Smith, lemme give you a lift on that."

"I guess I c'n manage," said Smith, grimly.

"Course. But, yo' see, I may not have a chance right off to pay yeh back for the times you've carried my gun and hull caboodle. Say, now, gimme that gun, anyway."

"All right, if yeh feel like it, Jim," Smith replied, and they trudged along doggedly in the sun, which was getting higher and hotter each half-mile.

5. Regional pronunciation of *coulée*, Western U.S. term for the deep valley or ravine characteristic of Upper Mississippi Valley topography.

"Ain't it queer there ain't no teams comin' along," said Smith, after a long silence.

"Well, no, seein's it's Sunday."

"By jinks, that's a fact. It *is* Sunday. I'll git home in time f'r dinner, sure!" he exulted. "She don't hev dinner usially till about *one* on Sundays." And he fell into a muse, in which he smiled.

"Well, I'll git home jest about six o'clock, jest about when the boys are milkin' the cows," said old Jim Cranby. "I'll step into the barn, an' then I'll say: '*Heah!* why ain't this milkin' done before this time o' day?' An' then won't they yell!" he added, slapping his thigh in great glee.

Smith went on. "I'll jest go up the path. Old Rover'll come down the road to meet me. He won't bark; he'll know me, an' he'll come down waggin' his tail an' showin' his teeth. That's his way of laughin'. An' so I'll walk up to the kitchen door, an' I'll say, '*Dinner f'r a hungry man!*' An' then she'll jump up, an'—"

He couldn't go on. His voice choked at the thought of it. Saunders, the third man, hardly uttered a word, but walked silently behind the others. He had lost his wife the first year he was in the army. She died of pneumonia, caught in the autumn rains while working in the fields in his place.

They plodded along till at last they came to a parting of the ways. To the right the road continued up the main valley; to the left it went over the big ridge.

"Well, boys," began Smith, as they grounded their muskets and looked away up the valley, "here's where we shake hands. We've marched together a good many miles, an' now I s'pose we're done."

"Yes, I don't think we'll do any more of it f'r a while. I don't want to, I know."

"I hope I'll see yeh once in a while, boys, to talk over old times."

"Of course," said Saunders, whose voice trembled a little, too. "It ain't *exactly* like dyin'." They all found it hard to look at each other.

"But we'd ought'r go home with you," said Cranby. "You'll never climb that ridge with all them things on yer back."

"Oh, I'm all right! Don't worry about me. Every step takes me nearer home, yeh see. Well, good-by, boys."

They shook hands. "Good-by. Good luck!"

"Same to you. Lemme know how you find things at home."

"Good-by."

"Good-by."

He turned once before they passed out of sight, and waved his cap, and they did the same, and all yelled. Then all marched away with their long, steady, loping, veteran step. The solitary climber in blue walked on for a time, with his mind filled with the kindness of his comrades, and musing upon the many wonderful days they had had together in camp and field.

He thought of his chum, Billy Tripp. Poor Billy! A "minie" ball [6] fell into his breast one day, fell wailing like a cat, and tore a great ragged hole in his heart. He looked forward to a sad scene with Billy's mother and sweetheart. They would want to know all about it. He tried to recall all that Billy had said, and the particulars of it, but there was little to remember, just that wild wailing sound high in the air, a dull slap, a short, quick, expulsive groan, and the boy lay with his face in the dirt in the ploughed field they were marching across.

That was all. But all the scenes he had since been through had not dimmed the horror, the terror of that moment, when his boy comrade fell, with only a breath between a laugh and a death-groan. Poor handsome Billy! Worth millions of dollars was his young life.

These sombre recollections gave way at length to more cheerful feelings as he began to approach his home coolly. The fields and houses grew familiar, and in one or two he was greeted by people seated in the doorways. But he was in no mood to talk, and pushed on steadily, though he stopped and accepted a drink of milk once at the well-side of a neighbor.

The sun was burning hot on that slope, and his step grew slower, in spite of his iron resolution. He sat down several times to rest. Slowly he crawled up the rough, reddish-brown road, which wound along the hillside, under great trees, through dense groves of jack oaks, with tree-tops far below him on his left hand, and the hills far above him on his right. He crawled along like some minute, wingless variety of fly.

He ate some hardtack, sauced with wild berries, when he reached the summit of the ridge, and sat there for some time, looking down into his home coolly.

Sombre, pathetic figure! His wide, round, gray eyes gazing down into the beautiful valley, seeing and not seeing, the splendid cloud-shadows sweeping over the western hills and across the green and yellow wheat far below. His head drooped forward on his palm, his shoulders took on a tired stoop, his cheek-bones showed painfully. An observer might have said, "He is looking down upon his own grave."

II

Sunday comes in a Western wheat harvest with such sweet and sudden relaxation to man and beast that it would be holy for that reason, if for no other, and Sundays are usually fair in harvest-time. As one goes out into the field in the hot morning sunshine, with no

6. Elongated bullet invented by Capt. C. E. Minié in 1853. When fired, the bullet was expanded by powder contained in a cavity at its base.

sound abroad save the crickets and the indescribably pleasant silken rustling of the ripened grain, the reaper and the very sheaves in the stubble seem to be resting, dreaming.

Around the house, in the shade of the trees, the men sit, smoking, dozing, or reading the papers, while the women, never resting, move about at the housework. The men eat on Sundays about the same as on other days, and breakfast is no sooner over and out of the way than dinner begins.

But at the Smith farm there were no men dozing or reading. Mrs. Smith was alone with her three children, Mary, nine, Tommy, six, and little Ted, just past four. Her farm, rented to a neighbor, lay at the head of a coolly or narrow gully, made at some far-off post-glacial period by the vast and angry floods of water which gullied these tremendous furrows in the level prairie—furrows so deep that undisturbed portions of the original level rose like hills on either side, rose to quite considerable mountains.

The chickens wakened her as usual that Sabbath morning from dreams of her absent husband, from whom she had not heard for weeks. The shadows drifted over the hills, down the slopes, across the wheat, and up the opposite wall in leisurely way, as if, being Sunday, they could take it easy also. The fowls clustered about the housewife as she went out into the yard. Fuzzy little chickens swarmed out from the coops, where their clucking and perpetually disgruntled mothers tramped about, petulantly thrusting their heads through the spaces between the slats.

A cow called in a deep, musical bass, and a calf answered from a little pen near by, and a pig scurried guiltily out of the cabbages. Seeing all this, seeing the pig in the cabbages, the tangle of grass in the garden, the broken fence which she had mended again and again—the little woman, hardly more than a girl, sat down and cried. The bright Sabbath morning was only a mockery without him!

A few years ago they had bought this farm, paying part, mortgaging the rest in the usual way. Edward Smith was a man of terrible energy. He worked "nights and Sundays," as the saying goes, to clear the farm of its brush and of its insatiate mortgage! In the midst of his Herculean struggle came the call for volunteers, and with the grim and unselfish devotion to his country which made the Eagle Brigade able to "whip its weight in wild-cats," he threw down his scythe and grub-axe, turned his cattle loose, and became a blue-coated cog in a vast machine for killing men, and not thistles. While the millionaire sent his money to England for safe-keeping, this man, with his girl-wife and three babies, left them on a mortgaged farm, and went away to fight for an idea. It was foolish, but it was sublime for all that.

That was three years before, and the young wife, sitting on the well-curb on this bright Sabbath harvest morning, was righteously rebellious. It seemed to her that she had borne her share of the country's sorrow. Two brothers had been killed, the renter in whose hands her husband had left the farm had proved a villain; one year the farm had been without crops, and now the overripe grain was waiting the tardy hand of the neighbor who had rented it, and who was cutting his own grain first.

About six weeks before, she had received a letter saying, "We'll be discharged in a little while." But no other word had come from him. She had seen by the papers that his army was being discharged, and from day to day other soldiers slowly percolated in blue streams back into the State and county, but still *her* hero did not return.

Each week she had told the children that he was coming, and she had watched the road so long that it had become unconscious; and as she stood at the well, or by the kitchen door, her eyes were fixed unthinkingly on the road that wound down the coolly.

Nothing wears on the human soul like waiting. If the stranded mariner, searching the sun-bright seas, could once give up hope of a ship, that horrible grinding on his brain would cease. It was this waiting, hoping, on the edge of despair, that gave Emma Smith no rest.

Neighbors said, with kind intentions: "He's sick, maybe, an' can't start north just yet. He'll come along one o' these days."

"Why don't he write?" was her question, which silenced them all. This Sunday morning it seemed to her as if she could not stand it longer. The house seemed intolerably lonely. So she dressed the little ones in their best calico dresses and home-made jackets, and, closing up the house, set off down the coolly to old Mother Gray's.

"Old Widder Gray" lived at the "mouth of the coolly." She was a widow woman with a large family of stalwart boys and laughing girls. She was the visible incarnation of hospitality and optimistic poverty. With Western open-heartedness she fed every mouth that asked food of her, and worked herself to death as cheerfully as her girls danced in the neighborhood harvest dances.

She waddled down the path to meet Mrs. Smith with a broad smile on her face.

"Oh, you little dears! Come right to your granny. Gimme me a kiss! Come right in, Mis' Smith. How are yeh, anyway? Nice mornin', ain't it? Come in an' set down. Everything's in a clutter, but that won't scare you any."

She led the way into the best room, a sunny, square room, carpeted with a faded and patched rag carpet, and papered with white-and-green wall-paper, where a few faded effigies of dead members of the family hung in variously sized oval walnut frames. The house resounded with singing, laughter, whistling, tramping of heavy boots, and riotous scufflings. Half-grown boys came to the door and crooked their fingers at the children, who ran out, and were soon heard in the midst of the fun.

"Don't s'pose you've heard from Ed?" Mrs. Smith shook her head. "He'll turn up some day, when you ain't lookin' for 'm." The good old soul had said that so many times that poor Mrs. Smith derived no comfort from it any longer.

"Liz heard from Al the other day. He's comin' some day this week. Anyhow, they expect him."

"Did he say anything of—"

"No, he didn't," Mrs. Gray admitted. "But then it was only a short letter, anyhow. Al ain't much for writin', anyhow.—But come out and see my new cheese. I tell yeh, I don't believe I ever had better luck in my life. If Ed should come, I want you should take him up a piece of this cheese."

It was beyond human nature to resist the influence of that noisy, hearty, loving household, and in the midst of the singing and laughing the wife forgot her anxiety, for the time at least, and laughed and sang with the rest.

About eleven o'clock a wagon-load more drove up to the door, and Bill Gray, the widow's oldest son, and his whole family, from Sand Lake Coolly, piled out amid a good-natured uproar. Every one talked at once, except Bill, who sat in the wagon with his wrists on his knees, a straw in his mouth, and an amused twinkle in his blue eyes.

"Ain't heard nothin' o' Ed, I s'pose?" he asked in a kind of bellow. Mrs. Smith shook her head. Bill, with a delicacy very striking in such a great giant, rolled his quid in his mouth, and said:

"Didn't know but you had. I hear two or three of the Sand Lake boys are comin'. Left New Orleenes some time this week. Didn't write nothin' about Ed, but no news is good news in such cases, mother always says."

"Well, go put out yer team," said Mrs. Gray, "an' go'n bring me in some taters, an', Sim, you go see if you c'n find some corn. Sadie, you put on the water to bile. Come now, hustle yer boots, all o' yeh. If I feed this yer crowd, we've got to have some raw materials. If y' think I'm goin' to feed yeh on pie—you're just mightily mistaken."

The children went off into the field, the girls put dinner on to boil, and then went to change their dresses and fix their hair. "Somebody might come," they said.

"Land sakes, I hope not! I don't know where in time I'd set 'em, 'less they'd eat at the second table," Mrs. Gray laughed, in pretended dismay.

The two older boys, who had served their time in the army, lay out on the grass before the house, and whittled and talked desultorily about the war and the crops, and planned buying a threshing-machine. The older girls and Mrs. Smith helped enlarge the table and put on the dishes, talking all the time in that cheery, incoherent, and meaningful way a group of such women have,—a conversation to be taken for its spirit rather than for its letter, though Mrs. Gray at last got the ear of them all and dissertated at length on girls.

"Girls in love ain' no use in the whole blessed week," she said. "Sundays they're a-lookin' down the road, expectin' he'll *come.* Sunday afternoons they can't think o' nothin' else, 'cause he's *here.* Monday mornin's they're sleepy and kind o' dreamy and slimpsy, and good f'r nothin' on Tuesday and Wednesday. Thursday they git absent-minded, an' begin to look off toward Sunday agin, an' mope aroun' and let the dishwater git cold, right under their noses. Friday they break dishes, an' go off in the best room an' snivel, an' look out o' the winder. Saturdays they have queer spurts o' workin' like all p'ssessed, an' spurts o' frizzin' their hair. An' Sunday they begin it all over agin."

The girls giggled and blushed, all through this tirade from their mother, their broad faces and powerful frames anything but suggestive of lackadaisical sentiment. But Mrs. Smith said:

"Now, Mrs. Gray, I hadn't ought to stay to dinner. You've got—"

"Now you set right down! If any of them girls' beaus comes, they'll have to take what's left, that's all. They ain't s'posed to have much appetite, nohow. No, you're goin' to stay if they starve, an' they ain't no danger o' that."

At one o'clock the long table was piled with boiled potatoes, cords of boiled corn on the cob, squash and pumpkin pies, hot biscuit, sweet pickles, bread and butter, and honey. Then one of the girls took down a conch-shell from a nail, and going to the door, blew a long, fine, free blast, that showed there was no weakness of lungs in her ample chest.

Then the children came out of the forest of corn, out of the creek, out of the loft of the barn, and out of the garden.

"They come to their feed f'r all the world jest like the pigs when y' holler 'poo-ee!' See 'em scoot!" laughed Mrs. Gray, every wrinkle on her face shining with delight.

The men shut up their jack-knives, and surrounded the horse-trough to souse their faces in the cold, hard water, and in a few moments the table was filled with a merry crowd, and a row of wistful-eyed youngsters circled the kitchen wall, where they stood first on one leg and then on the other, in impatient hunger.

"Now pitch in, Mrs. Smith," said Mrs. Gray, presiding over the table. "You know these men critters. They'll eat every grain of it, if yeh give 'em a chance. I swan, they're made o' India-rubber, their stomachs is, I know it."

"Haf to eat to work," said Bill, gnawing a cob with a swift, circular motion that rivalled a corn-sheller in results.

"More like workin' to eat," put in one of the girls, with a giggle. "More eat 'n work with you."

"*You* needn't say anything, Net. Any one that'll eat seven ears—"

"I didn't, no such thing. You piled your cobs on my plate."

"That'll do to tell Ed Varney. It won't go down here where we know yeh."

"Good land! Eat all yeh want! They's plenty more in the fiel's, but I can't afford to give you young uns tea. The tea is for us women-folks, and 'specially f'r Mis' Smith an' Bill's wife. We're a-goin' to tell fortunes by it."

One by one the men filled up and shoved back, and one by one the children slipped into their places, and by two o'clock the women alone remained around the débris-covered table, sipping their tea and telling fortunes.

As they got well down to the grounds in the cup, they shook them with a circular motion in the hand, and then turned them bottom-side-up quickly in the saucer, then twirled them three or four times one way, and three or four times the other, during a breathless pause. Then Mrs. Gray lifted the cup, and, gazing into it with profound gravity, pronounced the impending fate.

It must be admitted that, to a critical observer, she had abundant preparation for hitting close to the mark, as when she told the girls that "somebody was comin'.'" "It's a man," she went on gravely. "He is cross-eyed—"

"Oh, you hush!" cried Nettie.

"He has red hair, and is death on b'iled corn and hot biscuit."

The others shrieked with delight.

"But he's goin' to get the mitten, that red-headed feller is, for I see another feller comin' up behind him."

"Oh, lemme see, lemme see!" cried Nettie.

"Keep off," said the priestess, with a lofty gesture. "His hair is black. He don't eat so much, and he works more."

The girls exploded in a shriek of laughter, and pounded their sister on the back.

At last came Mrs. Smith's turn, and she was trembling with excitement as Mrs. Gray again composed her jolly face to what she considered a proper solemnity of expression.

"Somebody is comin' to *you*," she said, after a long pause. "He's got a musket on his back. He's a soldier. He's almost here. See?"

She pointed at two little tea-stems, which really formed a faint suggestion of a man with a musket on his back. He had climbed nearly to the edge of the cup. Mrs. Smith grew pale with excitement. She trembled so she could hardly hold the cup in her hand as she gazed into it.

"It's Ed," cried the old woman. "He's on the way home. Heavens an' earth! There he is now!" She turned and waved her hand out toward the road. They rushed to the door to look where she pointed.

A man in a blue coat, with a musket on his back, was toiling slowly up the hill on the sun-bright, dusty road, toiling slowly, with bent head half hidden by a heavy knapsack. So tired it seemed that walking was indeed a process of falling. So eager to get home he would not stop, would not look aside, but plodded on, amid the cries of the locusts, the welcome of the crickets, and the rustle of the yellow wheat. Getting back to God's country, and his wife and babies!

Laughing, crying, trying to call him and the children at the same time, the little wife, almost hysterical, snatched her hat and ran out into the yard. But the soldier had disappeared over the hill into the hollow beyond, and, by the time she had found the children, he was too far away for her voice to reach him. And, besides, she was not sure it was her husband, for he had not turned his head at their shouts. This seemed so strange. Why didn't he stop to rest at his old neighbor's house? Tortured by hope and doubt, she hurried up the coolly as fast as she could push the baby wagon, the blue-coated figure just ahead pushing steadily, silently forward up the coolly.

When the excited, panting little group came in sight of the gate they saw the blue-coated figure standing, leaning upon the rough rail fence, his chin on his palms, gazing at the empty house. His knapsack, canteen, blankets, and musket lay upon the dusty grass at his feet.

He was like a man lost in a dream. His wide, hungry eyes devoured the scene. The rough lawn, the little unpainted house, the field of clear yellow wheat behind it, down across which streamed the sun, now almost ready to touch the high hill to the west, the crickets crying merrily, a cat on the fence near by, dreaming, unmindful of the stranger in blue—

How peaceful it all was. O God! How far removed from all camps, hospitals, battle lines. A little cabin in a Wisconsin coolly, but it was majestic in its peace. How did he ever leave it for those years of tramping, thirsting, killing?

Trembling, weak with emotion, her eyes on the silent figure, Mrs. Smith hurried up to the fence. Her feet made no noise in the dust and grass, and they were close upon him before he knew of them. The oldest boy ran a little ahead. He will never forget that figure, that face. It will always remain as something epic, that return of the private. He fixed his eyes on the pale face covered with a ragged beard.

"Who *are* you, sir?" asked the wife, or, rather, started to ask, for he turned, stood a moment, and then cried:

"Emma!"

"Edward!"

The children stood in a curious row to see their mother kiss this bearded, strange man, the elder girl sobbing sympathetically with her mother. Illness had left the soldier partly deaf, and this added to the strangeness of his manner.

But the youngest child stood away, even after the girl had recognized her father and kissed him. The man turned then to the baby, and said in a curiously unpaternal tone:

"Come here, my little man; don't you know me?" But the baby backed away under the fence and stood peering at him critically.

"My little man!" What meaning in those words! This baby seemed like some other woman's child, and not the infant he had left in his wife's arms. The war had come between him and his baby—he was only a strange man to him, with big eyes; a soldier, with mother hanging to his arm, and talking in a loud voice.

"And this is Tom," the private said, drawing the oldest boy to him. "*He'll* come and see me. *He* knows his poor old pap when he comes home from the war."

The mother heard the pain and reproach in his voice and hastened to apologize.

"You've changed so, Ed. He can't know yeh. This is papa, Teddy; come and kiss him—Tom and Mary do. Come, won't you?" But Teddy still peered through the fence with solemn eyes, well out of reach. He resembled a half-wild kitten that hesitates, studying the tones of one's voice.

"I'll fix him," said the soldier, and sat down to undo his knapsack, out of which he drew three enormous and very red apples. After giving one to each of the older children, he said:

"*Now* I guess he'll come. Eh, my little man? Now come see your pap."

Teddy crept slowly under the fence, assisted by the overzealous Tommy, and a moment later was kicking and squalling in his father's arms. Then they entered the house, into the sitting room, poor, bare, art-forsaken little room, too, with its rag carpet, its square clock, and its two or three chromos and pictures from *Harper's Weekly* [7] pinned about.

"Emma, I'm all tired out," said Private Smith, as he flung himself down on the carpet as he used to do, while his wife brought a

7. The most popular illustrated magazine reporting the events of the Civil War.

pillow to put under his head, and the children stood about munching their apples.

"Tommy, you run and get me a pan of chips, and Mary, you get the tea-kettle on, and I'll go and make some biscuit."

And the soldier talked. Question after question he poured forth about the crops, the cattle, the renter, the neighbors. He slipped his heavy government brogan shoes off his poor, tired, blistered feet, and lay out with utter, sweet relaxation. He was a free man again, no longer a soldier under a command. At supper he stopped once, listened and smiled. "That's old Spot. I know her voice. I s'pose that's her calf out there in the pen. I can't milk her to-night, though. I'm too tired. But I tell you, I'd like a drink of her milk. What's become of old Rove?"

"He died last winter. Poisoned, I guess." There was a moment of sadness for them all. It was some time before the husband spoke again, in a voice that trembled a little.

"Poor old feller! He'd 'a' known me half a mile away. I expected him to come down the hill to meet me. It 'ud 'a' been more like comin' home if I could 'a' seen him comin' down the road an' waggin' his tail, an' laughin' that way he has. I tell yeh, it kind o' took hold o' me to see the blinds down an' the house shut up."

"But, yeh see, we—we expected you'd write again 'fore you started. And then we thought we'd see you if you *did* come," she hastened to explain.

"Well, I ain't worth a cent on writin'. Besides, it's just as well yeh didn't know when I was comin'. I tell you, it sounds good to hear them chickens out there, an' turkeys, an' the crickets. Do you know they don't have just the same kind o' crickets down South? Who's Sam hired t' help cut yer grain?"

"The Ramsey boys."

"Looks like a good crop; but I'm afraid I won't do much gettin' it cut. This cussed fever an' ague has got me down pretty low. I don't know when I'll get rid of it. I'll bet I've took twenty-five pounds of quinine if I've taken a bit. Gimme another biscuit. I tell yeh, they taste good, Emma. I ain't had anything·like it— Say, if you'd 'a' hear'd me braggin' to th' boys about your butter 'n' biscuits I'll bet your ears 'ud 'a' burnt."

The private's wife colored with pleasure. "Oh, you're always a braggin' about your things. Everybody makes good butter."

"Yes; old lady Snyder, for instance."

"Oh, well, she ain't to be mentioned. She's Dutch."

"Or old Mis' Snively. One more cup o' tea, Mary. That's my girl! I'm feeling better already. I just b'lieve the matter with me is, I'm *starved.*"

This was a delicious hour, one long to be remembered. They

were like lovers again. But their tenderness, like that of a typical American family, found utterance in tones, rather than in words. He was praising her when praising her biscuit, and she knew it. They grew soberer when he showed where he had been struck, one ball burning the back of his hand, one cutting away a lock of hair from his temple, and one passing through the calf of his leg. The wife shuddered to think how near she had come to being a soldier's widow. Her waiting no longer seemed hard. This sweet, glorious hour effaced it all.

Then they rose, and all went out into the garden and down to the barn. He stood beside her while she milked old Spot. They began to plan fields and crops for next year.

His farm was weedy and encumbered, a rascally renter had run away with his machinery (departing between two days), his children needed clothing, the years were coming upon him, he was sick and emaciated, but his heroic soul did not quail. With the same courage with which he had faced his Southern march he entered upon a still more hazardous future.

Oh, that mystic hour! The pale man with big eyes standing there by the well, with his young wife by his side. The vast moon swinging above the eastern peaks, the cattle winding down the pasture slopes with jangling bells, the crickets singing, the stars blooming out sweet and far and serene, the katydids rhythmically calling, the little turkeys crying querulously, as they settled to roost in the poplar tree near the open gate. The voices at the well drop lower, the little ones nestle in their father's arms at last, and Teddy falls asleep there.

The common soldier of the American volunteer army had returned. His war with the South was over, and his fight, his daily running fight with nature and against the injustice of his fellow-men, was begun again.

From *Main-Travelled Roads* (1891)

·A NATIONAL ART FORM·

The short story, an orphan without a name at the beginning of the nineteenth century, entered the twentieth century as the most popular of fictional forms. This was especially true in the United States, and the achievements of major American short story writers during the succeeding half-century would lead Frank O'Connor to declare, in 1963, that "the Americans have handled the short story so wonderfully that one can say that it is a national art form." This sense of the short story as an "American" form was even a commonplace in William Dean Howells's time, and it initiates one of the most interesting passages in his *Criticism and Fiction* (1891):

I am not sure that the Americans have not brought the short story nearer perfection in the all-round sense than almost any other people, and for reasons very simple and near at hand. It might be argued from the national hurry and impatience that it was a literary form peculiarly adapted to the American temperament, but I suspect that its extraordinary development among us is owing much more to more tangible facts. The success of American magazines, which is nothing less than prodigious, is only commensurate with their excellence. Their sort of success is not only from the courage to decide which ought to please, but from the knowledge of what does please; and it is probable that, aside from the pictures, it is the short stories which please the readers of our best magazines. The serial novels they must have, of course; but rather more of course they must have short stories, and by operation of the law of supply and demand, the short stories, abundant in quantity and excellent in quality, are forthcoming because they are wanted. By another operation of the same law, which political economists have more recently taken account of, the demand follows the supply, and short stories are sought for because there is a proven ability to furnish them, and people read them willingly because they are usually very good. The art of writing them is now so disciplined and diffused with us that there is no lack either for the magazines or for the newspaper "syndicates" which deal in them almost to the exclusion of the serials.

Howells, as always, has a nice sense of the literary marketplace, but if he had written this passage a few years later he could have extended his economic argument to a literary consideration of Gresham's Law, which might be summarized as "Bad stories drive out good ones, especially when the demand is heavy." The popular magazines paid more for stories by successful writers like O. Henry than many novelists received for the work of months. The conditions of journal publication, and the increasing demand for "action" stories in an age of political imperialism, produced a whole generation of reporter-writers. The newspaper office became the training ground for short story writers, but the academic world was not far behind, and handbooks on the criticism and writing of short stories proliferated. Frank Norris read the future exactly when he commented, in 1902, that a successful story "would create a demand for another short story by the same author, but that one particular contribution, the original one, is irretrievably and hopelessly dead." Therefore if the writer is "one of the 'best men' working for a 'permanent place,'" he will

> turn his attention and time, his best efforts, to the writing of novels, reverting to the short story only when necessary for the sake of boiling the Pot or chasing the Wolf. He will abandon the field to the inferior men, or enter it only to dispose of 'copy' which does not represent him at his best. And, as a result, the quality of the short story will decline.

This "decline" continued, with some notable exceptions, until the end of World War I, when a generation of great writers—Fitzgerald, Hemingway, and Faulkner among them—turned its attention to the genre, and created the golden age of the American short story. These writers may be thought of as redeeming the genre from "journalization" through sheer talent and the imitation of European masters, and this is partly true; in a nice paradox, however, journalism itself played a role in the revitalization of the form. Among the earlier journalist-writers Stephen Crane had demonstrated that great short stories could be made of the same stuff as a news story, and with many of the same methods. A comparison of "The Open Boat" with the original newspaper account of the disaster (which appears following the story in this anthology) shows how Crane had already begun, in his newspaper article, to "lift" the bare details of the event to a level of compressed and unified symbolism. Joseph Conrad said of "The Open Boat" that "by the deep and simple humanity of its presentation [the story] seems somehow to illustrate the essentials of life itself, like a symbolic tale."

This ability to write a pure and economical descriptive prose which has the impact of "a symbolic tale," but without the trappings of overt symbolism, marks the early stories of Ernest Hemingway, and we may attribute it in large measure to his training as a journalist. When "Big Two-Hearted River" was first published, Scott Fitzgerald and a friend accused Hemingway of writing "a story in which nothing happened," with the result that it was "lacking in human interest." Hemingway replied that they "hadn't even taken the trouble to find out what he had been trying to do," and what he was trying to do is beautifully illustrated by his last-minute decision to cut a three-thousand-word coda in which Nick Adams mused upon life, painting, and the writer's craft. With this coda "Big Two-Hearted River" would have been embarrassingly personal and didactic; without it the story stands in splendid purity, a completely satisfying description of a fishing trip that nonetheless "seems somehow to illustrate the essentials of life itself, like a symbolic tale." Hemingway obviously learned the lesson of discretion and exactness from many sources, including the new poetry of 1909–22, but it was his journalistic experience that taught him to record the sequence of motion and fact, leaving the reader with the task of inferring the larger meanings.

SHERWOOD ANDERSON

The work of Sherwood Anderson, especially the related sketches of *Winesburg, Ohio* (1919), provides one bridge between the major short story writers of the late nineteenth century and the world of Hemingway and Faulkner, both of whom were befriended and encouraged by Anderson at the start of their careers. There are some signs of Anderson's influence in the apprentice works of Faulkner and Hemingway, but with the exception of "I Want To Know Why," a story of a young boy's initiation into adult experience which links *Huckleberry Finn* with Hemingway's early Nick Adams stories, Anderson's impact upon his successors was general rather than specific. To the younger generation he stood as a symbol of artistic independence, since he had begun his career as a disciple of naturalism and fought his way through to a personal and idiosyncratic style. The related sketches of *Winesburg, Ohio*, which describe the "misfits, mutterers, crazy rebels, bedroom boarders, life-starved Americans" of a Midwestern town, are lacking in a strong sense of design, but Anderson is extraordinarily deft in building up a character or "grotesque" through revealing details. "Grotesque"

Stephen Crane   (The Bettmann Archive)

is Anderson's own term (the first sketch in *Winesburg* is called
"The Book of the Grotesque"); it is as though Poe's powerful
Gothic imagination, softened and domesticated through the influence of naturalism and psychoanalysis, were applied to the desperate prisoners of provincial life. Anderson's gallery of compulsive
and obsessed figures stands out with moving clarity, but he is unable—unlike the great masters of the short story—to give them a
place in some complete and orderly fictional world. Even the interrelated *Winesburg* stories, which may have set the pattern for
Hemingway's Nick Adams cycle or Faulkner's volumes of related
short fictions, lack a commanding structure. There is no myth or historical vision to support the scattered insights, only a common setting and a deep sense of psychological frustration.

Anderson's greatest gift to his more talented successors has been
called by one critic "The Liberation of the Short Story." He attacked the formula magazine story, what he called the "plot story,"

·446·

Edith Wharton   (The Bettmann Archive)

Sherwood Anderson   (Wide World Photos)

with considerable effect, always stressing the unique relation between the "seed" of a story and its final form. Whatever their de-
fects, his stories were a constant rebuke to the bland and "well-
made" fictions of the popular magazine, which fitted so snugly into
a few academic patterns. As he implies in *A Story Teller's Story,*
Anderson found the world a mysterious and uncertain place, where

insight comes by fits and starts, but of one thing he was sure: that no Americans "lived felt or talked as the average American novel made them live feel and talk and as for the plot short stories of the magazines—those bastard children of De Maupassant, Poe, and O. Henry—it was certain that there were no plot short stories ever lived in any life" he had known anything about. In his muddled way, Anderson restored to the American short story its original promise of vitality and elasticity.

F. SCOTT FITZGERALD

With Fitzgerald, Hemingway, and Faulkner, as with Poe, Hawthorne, and James, the short story became once more the agent of powerful artistic vision. Many of Fitzgerald's lesser stories strike the minor note of O. Henry or Booth Tarkington, but in his major short fictions—"The Rich Boy," "Winter Dreams," "Babylon Revisited," and a half-dozen others—the novelist's feeling for social nuance and moral scruple is developed within a few pages. Fitzgerald's persistent theme is the loss of innocence, the sad erosions of time; and even in *The Great Gatsby,* his best-constructed novel, the episodic structure can be broken down into a series of stories illustrating this obsessive theme. Whether the paradise lost is a Midwestern boyhood, or Paris in the 1920s, or Gatsby's Platonic idea of Daisy, or the unspoiled Long Island that once greeted Dutch sailors' eyes, Fitzgerald is able to convey a moral idea through the interplay of social forces. At his best, as in "Babylon Revisited," he can combine a complex drama of character and incident with a unifying mood or "tone," in this case the elegiac atmosphere of lost grandeur and gaiety. Like Henry James, he is able to evoke a rich novelistic world as the background for his condensed stories of lost freshness.

Much of Fitzgerald's life and art is concentrated in the moving pages of "Babylon Revisited." Set in the opening years of the Great Depression, when Fitzgerald's own career was in decline, the story traces a delicate counterpoint between present-day reality and the lost illusions of the 1920s. Like Hemingway, the youthful Fitzgerald thought of postwar Paris as a "moveable feast," a romantic image of life's possibilities; but the author and the hero of "Babylon Revisited" know, at age thirty-five, that Paris is simply a state of mind. What matters is not place or circumstance, but character. Charlie Wales "believed in character; he wanted to jump back a whole generation and trust in character again as the eternally valuable element." At the end of the story he realizes that he "lost a lot in the crash" but more in the years of unthinking illusion: "I lost everything I wanted in the boom." It is this sense of destruction from within that separates Fitzgerald from the other writers of his time. Although often described as a chronicler of tastes and manners, Fitzgerald is at bottom a moral writer: his great power lies in his tragic sense, his deep feeling for lost opportunities and wasted talent. "Babylon Revisited" takes place in the Paris of 1931, but it is a direct commentary on the American personality. In it the grand designs of *The Great Gatsby* have given way to a more urgent "fact": the fear of being alone.

ERNEST HEMINGWAY

The difference between Fitzgerald and Hemingway is the difference between a born novelist and a born poet. Fitzgerald's characters define themselves in relation to each other; Hemingway's characters are solitary figures, measured against a natural landscape or an instinctive ideal of personal heroism. Hemingway has no language for the direct description of emotions; and when he tries to speak abstractly of honor, glory, courage—as in his later works—he collapses into the banal or the sentimental. But when he is describing "what really happened in action"—the "real thing, the sequence of motion and fact which made the emotion"—he can achieve effects of concentration and immediacy which add a new dimension to the short story. Like the young bullfighter in *The Sun Also Rises*, the young Hemingway could hold "his purity of line through the maximum of exposure"; and the stories of his first three collections—*In Our Time, Men Without Women,* and *Winner Take Nothing*—are the foundation of his lasting reputation. The stories of the mid-1930s, "The Short Happy Life of Francis Macomber" and "The Snows of Kilimanjaro," are much praised, but they are at bottom highly successful examples of a popular "formula," the motion picture scenario. The real dividing line in Hemingway's career comes with his two books of travel and aesthetics, *Death in the Afternoon* (1932) and *The Green Hills of Africa* (1935), where he presents the "poetics" of the early stories in the self-indulgent language of his later works. In *The Green Hills of Africa* Hemingway remembers his early career as a short story writer with a precision and concreteness that suggest the Flaubertian density of his best fiction.

> Notre Dame des Champs in the courtyard with the sawmill (*and the sudden whine of the saw, the smell of sawdust and the chestnut tree over the roof with a mad woman downstairs*) and the year worrying about money (*all of the stories back in the mail that came in through a slit in the sawmill door, with notes of rejection that would never call them stories, but always anecdotes, sketches, contes, etc. They did not want them, and we lived on poireaux and drank cahors and water*) and

how fine the fountains were at the Place de L'Observatoire (*water sheen rippling on the bronze of horses' manes, bronze breasts and shoulders, green under thin-flowing water*) and when they put up the bust of Flaubert in the Luxembourg on the short cut through the gardens on the way to the rue Soufflot (*one that we believed in, loved without criticism, heavy now in stone as an idol should be*).

The language of Hemingway's rejection slips—anecdotes, sketches, contes—reflects the passion for irrelevant definition that marked the handbooks of his day. But his stories were too powerful to be restrained by these academic distinctions, and he completed the process Anderson had begun: the liberation of the short story from preconceived patterns.

Edgar Allan Poe derived the symbolic tale from the aesthetics of Romantic poetry; a hundred years later, Ernest Hemingway brought to American short fiction the density and precision of the best modern poetry. His friend and mentor Ezra Pound had long before coined the motto, "Poetry should be at least as well written as prose," by which he meant that English and American poets should imitate the economy and control of Flaubert or Joyce. In Hemingway's early stories the debt is repaid, and one can sense the influence of those modern poets who followed Pound's "prose tradition." In stories such as "Big Two-Hearted River" and "A Clean, Well-Lighted Place" the leading tenets of Imagist poetry, as announced by Pound in his 1913 essays, are completely applicable:

1. Direct treatment of the "thing," without evasion or cliché.
2. The use of absolutely no word that does not contribute to the general design.
3. Fidelity to the rhythms of natural speech.
4. The natural object is always the adequate symbol.

This drive toward a condensed and suggestive form is perhaps best displayed in "A Clean, Well-Lighted Place," where Hemingway manages to characterize three people and establish a complex emotional situation within the compass of two thousand words, and without any authorial intrusion: all is accomplished by natural dialogue and discreet symbolism. The same tact and discretion is evident in "Big Two-Hearted River," where Hemingway's instinct for the luminous natural detail is developed in a story of scrupulous realism. Like so many of Hemingway's stories and vignettes, it belongs to a larger pattern, in this case the autobiographical account of Nick Adams's life which is developed in a dozen or more stories over a period of ten years (see the headnote to the story).

"Big Two-Hearted River" is the keystone of a story cycle recounting a young American's growth into manhood, his initiation into the dark complexities of adult life "in our time." As we know from one

Ernest Hemingway   (Bettmann/Springer Film Archive)

F. Scott Fitzgerald (The Bettmann Archive)

William Faulkner (Wide World Photos)

of the short interchapters of *In Our Time,* and from the preceding story in the Nick Adams cycle, "A Way You'll Never Be," the hero of "Big Two-Hearted River" has returned from the traumatic experience of World War I, and is seeking to regain his psychological poise by revisiting a familiar landscape, itself now transformed by recent events. But this novelistic "frame" has little to do with the integrity of the story. Taken in isolation, "Big Two-Hearted River" suggests the anxieties of a life balanced between two worlds. Poised between past and present, between the burned-over land and the swamp, where fishing would be a "tragic adventure," Nick Adams can keep his equilibrium only through an elaborate devotion to the here-and-now, the customary demands of camping and fishing. Like the trout in the stream, he must not fight the current but balance himself against it.

> Nick looked down into the pool from the bridge. It was a hot day. A kingfisher flew up the stream. It was a long time since Nick had looked into a stream and seen trout. They were very satisfactory. As the shadow of the kingfisher moved up the stream, a big trout shot upstream in a long angle, only his shadow marking the angle, then lost his shadow as he came through the surface of the water, caught the sun, and then, as he went back into the stream under the surface, his shadow seemed to float down the stream with the current, unresisting, to his post under the bridge where he tightened facing up into the current.
>
> Nick's heart tightened as the trout moved. He felt all the old feeling.

The language of this early passage is starkly simple, composed largely of monosyllables, yet the complex visual image which it creates becomes a correlative for Nick's emotions, which "tighten" as the trout tightens "facing up into the current." The one evaluative word in the descriptive paragraph, "satisfactory," is deliberately bland and open; all depends on the concrete picture, which conveys a complex structure of feeling. Much is implied, almost nothing is stated. In stories like "Big Two-Hearted River" and "A Clean, Well-Lighted Place" form and psychology are inseparable, and the stylistic ideals—dignity, restraint, economy of movement— become the unstated ideals of human behavior.

WILLIAM FAULKNER

The impact of Hemingway and Fitzgerald on the modern American short story was mainly a formal one; their gift was their language. William Faulkner, on the other hand, opened up a whole world of cultural and moral experience, and it was largely due to his example that Southern writers dominated the development of the short story during the years before and after World War II. The range of Faulkner's achievement in the short form is evident in his *Collected Stories* (1950), where the stories are carefully grouped according to subject and narrative perspective. The first section, "The Country," shows Faulkner's mastery of the hunting story and the tall tale, his ability to recast the subjects of Mark Twain and the regionalists in a modern form. Part Two, "The Village," explores the broad expanse of modern Southern life, in techniques which range from Anderson's grotesque anecdotes to Hemingway's taut narratives. In Part Three, "The Wilderness," Faulkner's feeling for the semi-legendary past leads to some of his most original effects. In evoking the lost world of the Indians (as in "Red Leaves") Faulkner employs a dignified, almost ritualistic style, one that reflects his respect for his subjects. Even the humor is formal and bizarre, giving us a sense of the gap in time and sensibility between our world and theirs. Part Four, "The Wasteland," comments on World War I and its bitter aftermath, but in forms that come dangerously close to the conventions of magazine fiction. As always, Faulkner loses his sureness and originality when he ventures outside the life of his mythical Yoknapatawpha Country.

In "The Middle Ground" (Part Five) we edge toward the realm of death and nightmare, and in the final Part Six ("Beyond") the stories are all of the supernatural and the bizarre, of death and dreams. Thus the direction of the volume's forty-odd stories is from the commonplace to the supernatural, from the local to the universal. In reading *Collected Stories* we are overpowered by that sense of a self-contained imaginary world which is the hallmark of Faulkner's art. But we are also struck by his many affinities, in subject and form, with the major writers of American short fiction. The Gothicism of Poe, the moral allegory of Hawthorne, the colloquial humor of Mark Twain, the realistic precision of Garland, the grotesque psychology of Anderson, the absolute precision of the early Hemingway—all these elements and many more are recalled during our reading, but in most cases Faulkner has assimilated them and made them his own.

Although Faulkner's *Collected Stories* is one of the richest volumes in the history of the American short story, it does not indicate his full achievement in the genre. Faulkner was by temperament and inheritance a teller of tales, and even his most carefully constructed novels—*The Sound and the Fury* and *Absalom, Absalom!*—grew out of short stories. From the time of his earliest Yoknapatawpha stories (1928–30) Faulkner seems to have had a full grasp of his imaginary Southern country, its history and its people: as the map he appended to *Absalom, Absalom!* suggests, Faulkner visualized the world of Yoknapatawpha as a vast mosaic of interrelated

Flannery O'Connor   (De Casseres)

anecdotes and tales. These stories tended to group themselves around certain themes or family situations, sometimes fusing themselves into a unified novel, at other times retaining their separate identities. Thus the stories of the Civil War and Reconstruction collected as *The Unvanquished* are loosely bound together by common themes and characters, while the stories of *Go Down, Moses* have a far greater symbolic unity and might be taken as an historical "novel" of guilt and expiation. The rhythms of the traditional storyteller came naturally to Faulkner, and even in those novels where he is exploiting the most sophisticated techniques of the modern novel we can discover the outlines of one short story after another.

The careers of Faulkner and Hemingway spanned the great period of the American short story. Never before had so many talented writers turned their energies to the form, and each year between 1930 and 1960 could yield a collection of impressive works.

Richard Wright   (Culver Pictures)

Especially prominent were the Southern writers of these years,
who alone produced a substantial body of major fiction. Most of
them followed the example of William Faulkner, who had shown
how local history and social behavior could be turned into universal

metaphors. Reading the stories of Katherine Anne Porter, Caroline Gordon, Robert Penn Warren, Eudora Welty, Flannery O'Connor, Peter Taylor, and other Southern writers, we are struck by how well suited the short form is to the treatment of a fragmented social order. The Southern landscape, filled with symbolic reminders of a failed culture, provides the perfect enlarging backdrop for the isolated incidents and characters that germinate a short story. But the major achievements of these years were by no means confined to Southern writers; and in the works of Bellow, Malamud, and Cheever we see the short story's power to crystallize the personal conflicts in any cultural setting.

Many of the writers just mentioned are "minor" artists, but only in contrast to the likes of Hawthorne or James or Faulkner. There should be nothing pejorative in the term "minor" when applied to the writers of a great literary period, since one of the signs of a great age is the proliferation of powerful and moving works by secondary figures. Any of the well-known short story writers publishing between 1930 and 1960 would have stood out as a major artist in the lean days before World War I. Within the space available in this anthology I have tried to represent the various subjects and forms which were characteristic of the American short story in the years before and after World War II, realizing that no anthology can do justice to the richness of these years. Yet even in the few stories reproduced here we get a clear impression of one reason for the high level of artistic accomplishment.

The "minor" short story writers who followed Hemingway and Faulkner were, quite simply, better informed and more intelligent about their craft than any of their predecessors. Many of them were literary critics, and all had a highly developed critical sense. They went to school to their predecessors, both the great American writers of short fiction and the European masters: Flaubert, Chekhov, Turgenev, Joyce. Their writings on the craft of the story reveal a detailed knowledge of the major theorists, and a close familiarity with the language of modern criticism: setting, tone, and point-of-view are their concerns. Anyone reading the criticism of Robert Penn Warren, or the more scattered comments of Eudora Welty and Katherine Anne Porter, must be struck by one fact: the modern craftsman knows the history of his form, its limitations and potentialities. This critical sense is very different from the "formula" criticism of an earlier generation, and reminds us of James's subtle prefaces to his novels and tales. The best modern writers of the short story know how to talk to us—and themselves—about the practical and theoretical bases of their work. Self-consciousness was the great strength of the "minor" writers in the generation following Hemingway and Faulkner, but it was also a limitation. Theirs was an art of consolidation. There were no startling breakthroughs in subject or style, as with the early Hemingway, and gradually the modern short story established its own stereotypes and monotonies, although at a much more interesting and intelligent level than the "journalistic" stories against which Anderson rebelled. By the end of the 1950s the time had come for new departures, a shattering and reforming of accepted methods.

·Stephen Crane·

THE OPEN BOAT

A Tale Intended to be after the Fact: Being the Experience of Four Men from the Sunk Steamer *Commodore* [1]

I

None of them knew the color of the sky. Their eyes glanced level, and were fastened upon the waves that swept toward them. These waves were of the hue of slate, save for the tops, which were of foaming white, and all of the men knew the colors of the sea. The horizon narrowed and widened, and dipped and rose, and at all times its edge was jagged with waves that seemed thrust up in points like rocks.

Many a man ought to have a bathtub larger than the boat which here rode upon the sea. These waves were most wrongfully and barbarously abrupt and tall, and each froth-top was a problem in small-boat navigation.

The cook squatted in the bottom, and looked with both eyes at the six inches of gunwale which separated him from the ocean. His

1. On January 1, 1897, Crane sailed as a war correspondent on the steamer *Commodore*, which was running arms from Florida to the Cuban rebels (in an effort to weaken the insurgents, Spain had established a blockade around the island). The steamer foundered (possibly as a result of sabotage), and Crane was cast adrift in an open boat with three or four crew members, including the captain, Edward Murphy, and the oiler, Billy Higgins. After a harrowing day and night the ten-foot dinghy reached the Florida shore, but the oiler was drowned in the surf.

Crane's newspaper account of the ordeal is printed at the end of the story. It is fascinating to compare this reportorial version, which utilizes so many of the techniques of Crane's fiction, with the tale that evolved from it.

sleeves were rolled over his fat forearms, and the two flaps of his unbuttoned vest dangled as he bent to bail out the boat. Often he said, "Gawd! that was a narrow clip." As he remarked it he invariably gazed eastward over the broken sea.

The oiler, steering with one of the two oars in the boat, sometimes raised himself suddenly to keep clear of water that swirled in over the stern. It was a thin little oar, and it seemed often ready to snap.

The correspondent, pulling at the other oar, watched the waves and wondered why he was there.

The injured captain, lying in the bow, was at this time buried in that profound dejection and indifference which comes, temporarily at least, to even the bravest and most enduring when, willy-nilly, the firm fails, the army loses, the ship goes down. The mind of the master of a vessel is rooted deep in the timbers of her, though he command for a day or a decade; and this captain had on him the stern impression of a scene in the grays of dawn of seven turned faces, and later a stump of a topmast with a white ball on it, that slashed to and fro at the waves, went low and lower, and down. Thereafter there was something strange in his voice. Although steady, it was deep with mourning, and of a quality beyond oration or tears.

"Keep'er a little more south, Billie," said he.

"A little more south, sir," said the oiler in the stern.

A seat in this boat was not unlike a seat upon a bucking broncho, and by the same token a broncho is not much smaller. The craft pranced and reared and plunged like an animal. As each wave came, and she rose for it, she seemed like a horse making at a fence outrageously high. The manner of her scramble over these walls of water is a mystic thing, and, moreover, at the top of them were ordinarily these problems in white water, the foam racing down from the summit of each wave requiring a new leap, and a leap from the air. Then, after scornfully bumping a crest, she would slide and race and splash down a long incline, and arrive bobbing and nodding in front of the next menace.

A singular disadvantage of the sea lies in the fact that after successfully surmounting one wave you discover that there is another behind it just as important and just as nervously anxious to do something effective in the way of swamping boats. In a ten-foot dinghy one can get an idea of the resources of the sea in the line of waves that is not probable to the average experience, which is never at sea in a dinghy. As each slaty wall of water approached, it shut all else from the view of the men in the boat, and it was not difficult to imagine that this particular wave was the final outburst of the ocean, the last effort of the grim water. There was a terrible grace in the move of the waves, and they came in silence, save for the snarling of the crests.

In the wan light the faces of the men must have been gray. Their eyes must have glinted in strange ways as they gazed steadily astern. Viewed from a balcony, the whole thing would doubtless have been weirdly picturesque. But the men in the boat had no time to see it, and if they had had leisure, there were other things to occupy their minds. The sun swung steadily up the sky, and they knew it was broad day because the color of the sea changed from slate to emerald-green streaked with amber lights, and the foam was like tumbling snow. The process of the breaking day was unknown to them. They were aware only of this effect upon the color of the waves that rolled toward them.

In disjointed sentences the cook and the correspondent argued as to the difference between a life-saving station and a house of refuge. The cook had said: "There's a house of refuge just north of the Mosquito Inlet Light, and as soon as they see us they'll come off in their boat and pick us up."

"As soon as who see us?" said the correspondent.

"The crew," said the cook.

"Houses of refuge don't have crews," said the correspondent. "As I understand them, they are only places where clothes and grub are stored for the benefit of shipwrecked people. They don't carry crews."

"Oh, yes, they do," said the cook.

"No, they don't," said the correspondent.

"Well, we're not there yet, anyhow," said the oiler, in the stern.

"Well," said the cook, "perhaps it's not a house of refuge that I'm thinking of as being near Mosquito Inlet Light; perhaps it's a life-saving station."

"We're not there yet," said the oiler in the stern.

II

As the boat bounced from the top of each wave the wind tore through the hair of the hatless men, and as the craft plopped her stern down again the spray slashed past them. The crest of each of these waves was a hill, from the top of which the men surveyed for a moment a broad tumultuous expanse, shining and wind-riven. It was probably splendid, it was probably glorious, this play of the free sea, wild with lights of emerald and white and amber.

"Bully good thing it's an onshore wind," said the cook. "If not, where would we be? Wouldn't have a show."

"That's right," said the correspondent.

The busy oiler nodded his assent.

Then the captain, in the bow, chuckled in a way that expressed humor, contempt, tragedy, all in one. "Do you think we've got much of a show now, boys?" said he.

Whereupon the three were silent, save for a trifle of hemming and hawing. To express any particular optimism at this time they felt to be childish and stupid, but they all doubtless possessed this sense of the situation in their minds. A young man thinks doggedly at such times. On the other hand, the ethics of their condition was decidedly against any open suggestion of hopelessness. So they were silent.

"Oh, well," said the captain, soothing his children, "we'll get ashore all right."

But there was that in his tone which made them think; so the oiler quoth, "Yes! if this wind holds."

The cook was bailing. "Yes! if we don't catch hell in the surf."

Canton-flannel gulls flew near and far. Sometimes they sat down on the sea, near patches of brown seaweed that rolled over the waves with a movement like carpets on a line in a gale. The birds sat comfortably in groups, and they were envied by some in the dinghy, for the wrath of the sea was no more to them than it was to a covey of prairie chickens a thousand miles inland. Often they came very close and stared at the men with black bead-like eyes. At these times they were uncanny and sinister in their unblinking scrutiny, and the men hooted angrily at them, telling them to be gone. One came, and evidently decided to alight on the top of the captain's head. The bird flew parallel to the boat and did not circle, but made short sidelong jumps in the air in chicken fashion. His black eyes were wistfully fixed upon the captain's head. "Ugly brute," said the oiler to the bird. "You look as if you were made with a jackknife." The cook and the correspondent swore darkly at the creature. The captain naturally wished to knock it away with the end of the heavy painter, but he did not dare do it, because anything resembling an emphatic gesture would have capsized this freighted boat; and so, with his open hand, the captain gently and carefully waved the gull away. After it had been discouraged from the pursuit the captain breathed easier on account of his hair, and others breathed easier because the bird struck their minds at this time as being somehow gruesome and ominous.

In the meantime the oiler and the correspondent rowed. And also they rowed. They sat together in the same seat, and each rowed an oar. Then the oiler took both oars; then the correspondent took both oars; then the oiler; then the correspondent. They rowed and they rowed. The very ticklish part of the business was when the time came for the reclining one in the stern to take his turn at the oars. By the very last star of truth, it is easier to steal eggs from under a hen than it was to change seats in the dinghy. First the man in the stern slid his hand along the thwart and moved with care, as if he were of Sèvres.[2] Then the man in the rowing-seat slid his hand along the other thwart. It was all done with the most extraordinary care. As the two sidled past each other, the whole party kept watchful eyes on the coming wave, and the captain cried: "Look out, now! Steady, there!"

The brown mats of seaweed that appeared from time to time were like islands, bits of earth. They were traveling, apparently, neither one way nor the other. They were, to all intents, stationary. They informed the men in the boat that it was making progress slowly toward the land.

The captain, rearing cautiously in the bow after the dinghy soared on a great swell, said that he had seen the lighthouse at Mosquito Inlet. Presently the cook remarked that he had seen it. The correspondent was at the oars then, and for some reason he too wished to look at the lighthouse; but his back was toward the far shore, and the waves were important, and for some time he could not seize an opportunity to turn his head. But at last there came a wave more gentle than the others, and when at the crest of it he swiftly scoured the western horizon.

"See it?" said the captain.

"No," said the correspondent, slowly; "I didn't see anything."

"Look again," said the captain. He pointed. "It's exactly in that direction."

At the top of another wave the correspondent did as he was bid, and this time his eyes chanced on a small, still thing on the edge of the swaying horizon. It was precisely like the point of a pin. It took an anxious eye to find a lighthouse so tiny.

"Think we'll make it, Captain?"

"If this wind holds and the boat don't swamp, we can't do much else," said the captain.

The little boat, lifted by each towering sea and splashed viciously by the crests, made progress that in the absence of seaweed was not apparent to those in her. She seemed just a wee thing wallowing, miraculously top up, at the mercy of five oceans. Occasionally a great spread of water, like white flames, swarmed into her.

"Bail her, cook," said the captain, serenely.

"All right, Captain," said the cheerful cook.

III

It would be difficult to describe the subtle brotherhood of men that was here established on the seas. No one said that it was so. No

2. Delicate porcelain made in Sèvres, France.

one mentioned it. But it dwelt in the boat, and each man felt it warm him. They were a captain, an oiler, a cook, and a correspondent, and they were friends—friends in a more curiously ironbound degree than may be common. The hurt captain, lying against the water jar in the bow, spoke always in a low voice and calmly; but he could never command a more ready and swiftly obedient crew than the motley three of the dinghy. It was more than a mere recognition of what was best for the common safety. There was surely in it a quality that was personal and heartfelt. And after this devotion to the commander of the boat, there was this comradeship, that the correspondent, for instance, who had been taught to be cynical of men, knew even at the time was the best experience of his life. But no one said that it was so. No one mentioned it.

"I wish we had a sail," remarked the captain. "We might try my overcoat on the end of an oar, and give you two boys a chance to rest." So the cook and the correspondent held the mast and spread wide the overcoat; the oiler steered; and the little boat made good way with her new rig. Sometimes the oiler had to scull sharply to keep a sea from breaking into the boat, but otherwise sailing was a success.

Meanwhile the lighthouse had been growing slowly larger. It had now almost assumed color, and appeared like a little gray shadow on the sky. The man at the oars could not be prevented from turning his head rather often to try for a glimpse of this little gray shadow.

At last, from the top of each wave, the men in the tossing boat could see land. Even as the lighthouse was an upright shadow on the sky, this land seemed but a long black shadow on the sea. It certainly was thinner than paper. "We must be about opposite New Smyrna," said the cook, who had coasted this shore often in schooners. "Captain, by the way, I believe they abandoned that lifesaving station there about a year ago."

"Did they?" said the captain.

The wind slowly died away. The cook and the correspondent were not now obliged to slave in order to hold high the oar. But the waves continued their old impetuous swooping at the dinghy, and the little craft, no longer under way, struggled woundily over them. The oiler or the correspondent took the oars again.

Shipwrecks are *apropos* of nothing. If men could only train for them and have them occur when the men had reached pink condition, there would be less drowning at sea. Of the four in the dinghy none had slept any time worth mentioning for two days and two nights previous to embarking in the dinghy, and in the excitement of clambering about the deck of a foundering ship they had also forgotten to eat heartily.

For these reasons, and for others, neither the oiler nor the corre-

spondent was fond of rowing at this time. The correspondent wondered ingenuously how in the name of all that was sane could there
be people who thought it amusing to row a boat. It was not an
amusement; it was a diabolical punishment, and even a genius of
mental aberrations could never conclude that it was anything but a
horror to the muscles and a crime against the back. He mentioned
to the boat in general how the amusement of rowing struck him,
and the weary-faced oiler smiled in full sympathy. Previously to the
foundering, by the way, the oiler had worked a double watch in the
engine room of the ship.

"Take her easy now, boys," said the captain. "Don't spend yourselves. If we have to run a surf you'll need all your strength, because we'll sure have to swim for it. Take your time."

Slowly the land arose from the sea. From a black line it became a
line of black and a line of white—trees and sand. Finally the captain said that he could make out a house on the shore. "That's the
house of refuge, sure," said the cook. "They'll see us before long,
and come out after us."

The distant lighthouse reared high. "The keeper ought to be able
to make us out now, if he's looking through a glass," said the captain. "He'll notify the lifesaving people."

"None of those other boats could have got ashore to give word of
this wreck," said the oiler, in a low voice, "else the lifeboat would
be out hunting us."

Slowly and beautifully the land loomed out of the sea. The wind
came again. It had veered from the northeast to the southeast. Finally a new sound struck the ears of the men in the boat. It was the
low thunder of the surf on the shore. "We'll never be able to make
the lighthouse now," said the captain. "Swing her head a little
more north, Billie."

"A little more north, sir," said the oiler.

Whereupon the little boat turned her nose once more down the
wind, and all but the oarsman watched the shore grow. Under the
influence of this expansion doubt and direful apprehension were
leaving the minds of the men. The management of the boat was still
most absorbing, but it could not prevent a quiet cheerfulness. In an
hour, perhaps, they would be ashore.

Their backbones had become thoroughly used to balancing in the
boat, and they now rode this wild colt of a dinghy like circus men.
The correspondent thought that he had been drenched to the skin,
but happening to feel in the top pocket of his coat, he found therein
eight cigars. Four of them were soaked with seawater; four were
perfectly scatheless. After a search, somebody produced three dry
matches; and thereupon the four waifs rode impudently in their
little boat and, with an assurance of an impending rescue shining in

their eyes, puffed at the big cigars, and judged well and ill of all men. Everybody took a drink of water.

IV

"Cook," remarked the captain, "there don't seem to be any signs of life about your house of refuge."

"No," replied the cook. "Funny they don't see us!"

A broad stretch of lowly coast lay before the eyes of the men. It was of low dunes topped with dark vegetation. The roar of the surf was plain, and sometimes they could see the white lip of a wave as it spun up the beach. A tiny house was blocked out black upon the sky. Southward, the slim lighthouse lifted its little gray length.

Tide, wind, and waves were swinging the dinghy northward. "Funny they don't see us," said the men.

The surf's roar was here dulled, but its tone was nevertheless thunderous and mighty. As the boat swam over the great rollers the men sat listening to this roar. "We'll swamp sure," said everybody.

It is fair to say here that there was not a lifesaving station within twenty miles in either direction; but the men did not know this fact, and in consequence they made dark and opprobrious remarks concerning the eyesight of the nation's lifesavers. Four scowling men sat in the dinghy and surpassed records in the invention of epithets.

"Funny they don't see us."

The light-heartedness of a former time had completely faded. To their sharpened minds it was easy to conjure pictures of all kinds of incompetency and blindness and, indeed, cowardice. There was the shore of the populous land, and it was bitter and bitter to them that from it came no sign.

"Well," said the captain, ultimately, "I suppose we'll have to make a try for ourselves. If we stay out here too long, we'll none of us have strength left to swim after the boat swamps."

And so the oiler, who was at the oars, turned the boat straight for the shore. There was a sudden tightening of muscles. There was some thinking.

"If we don't all get ashore," said the captain—"if we don't all get ashore, I suppose you fellows know where to send news of my finish?"

They then briefly exchanged some addresses and admonitions. As for the reflections of the men, there was a great deal of rage in them. Perchance they might be formulated thus: "If I am going to be drowned—if I am going to be drowned—if I am going to be drowned, why, in the name of the seven mad gods who rule the sea,[3] was I allowed to come thus far and contemplate sand and

3. Crane apparently assumes that each of the Seven Seas has its local god.

trees? Was I brought here merely to have my nose dragged away as I was about to nibble the sacred cheese of life? It is preposterous. If this old ninny-woman, Fate, cannot do better than this, she should be deprived of the management of men's fortunes. She is an old hen who knows not her intention. If she has decided to drown me, why did she not do it in the beginning and save me all this trouble? The whole affair is absurd. . . . But no; she cannot mean to drown me. She dare not drown me. She cannot drown me. Not after all this work." Afterward the man might have had an impulse to shake his fist at the clouds. "Just you drown me, now, and then hear what I call you!"

The billows that came at this time were more formidable. They seemed always just about to break and roll over the little boat in a turmoil of foam. There was a preparatory and long growl in the speech of them. No mind unused to the sea would have concluded that the dinghy could ascend these sheer heights in time. The shore was still afar. The oiler was a wily surfman. "Boys," he said swiftly, "she won't live three minutes more, and we're too far out to swim. Shall I take her to sea again, Captain?"

"Yes; go ahead!" said the captain.

This oiler, by a series of quick miracles and fast and steady oarsmanship, turned the boat in the middle of the surf and took her safely to sea again.

There was a considerable silence as the boat bumped over the furrowed sea to deeper water. Then somebody in gloom spoke: "Well, anyhow, they must have seen us from the shore by now."

The gulls went in slanting flight up the wind toward the gray, desolate east. A squall, marked by dingy clouds and clouds brickred, like smoke from a burning building, appeared from the southeast.

"What do you think of those lifesaving people? Ain't they peaches?"

"Funny they haven't seen us."

"Maybe they think we're out here for sport! Maybe they think we're fishin'. Maybe they think we're damned fools."

It was a long afternoon. A changed tide tried to force them southward, but wind and wave said northward. Far ahead, where coastline, sea, and sky formed their mighty angle, there were little dots which seemed to indicate a city on the shore.

"St. Augustine?"

The captain shook his head. "Too near Mosquito Inlet."

And the oiler rowed, and then the correspondent rowed; then the oiler rowed. It was a weary business. The human back can become the seat of more aches and pains than are registered in books for the composite anatomy of a regiment. It is a limited area, but it can become the theater of innumerable muscular conflicts, tangles, wrenches, knots, and other comforts.

"Did you ever like to row, Billie?" asked the correspondent.

"No," said the oiler; "hang it!"

When one exchanged the rowing-seat for a place in the bottom of the boat, he suffered a bodily depression that caused him to be careless of everything save an obligation to wiggle one finger. There was cold seawater swashing to and fro in the boat, and he lay in it. His head, pillowed on a thwart, was within an inch of the swirl of a wave-crest, and sometimes a particularly obstreperous sea came inboard and drenched him once more. But these matters did not annoy him. It is almost certain that if the boat had capsized he would have tumbled comfortably out upon the ocean as if he felt sure that it was a great soft mattress.

"Look! There's a man on the shore!"

"Where?"

"There! See 'im? See 'im?"

"Yes, sure! He's walking along."

"Now he's stopped. Look! He's facing us!"

"He's waving at us!"

"So he is! By thunder!"

"Ah, now we're all right! Now we're all right! There'll be a boat out here for us in half an hour."

"He's going on. He's running. He's going up to that house there."

The remote beach seemed lower than the sea, and it required a searching glance to discern the little black figure. The captain saw a floating stick, and they rowed to it. A bath towel was by some weird chance in the boat, and, tying this on the stick, the captain waved it. The oarsman did not dare turn his head, so he was obliged to ask questions.

"What's he doing now?"

"He's standing still again. He's looking, I think. . . . There he goes again—toward the house. . . . Now he's stopped again."

"Is he waving at us?"

"No, not now; he was, though."

"Look! There comes another man!"

"He's running."

"Look at him go, would you!"

"Why, he's on a bicycle. Now he's met the other man. They're both waving at us. Look!"

"There comes something up the beach."

"What the devil is that thing?"

"Why, it looks like a boat."

"Why, certainly, it's a boat."

"No; it's on wheels."

"Yes, so it is. Well, that must be the lifeboat. They drag them along shore on a wagon."

"That's the lifeboat, sure."

"No, by God, it's—it's an omnibus."

"I tell you it's a lifeboat."

"It is not! It's an omnibus. I can see it plain. See? One of these big hotel omnibuses."

"By thunder, you're right. It's an omnibus, sure as fate. What do you suppose they are doing with an omnibus? Maybe they are going around collecting the life-crew, hey?"

"That's it, likely. Look! There's a fellow waving a little black flag. He's standing on the steps of the omnibus. There come those other two fellows. Now they're all talking together. Look at the fellow with the flag. Maybe he ain't waving it!"

"That ain't a flag, is it? That's his coat. Why, certainly, that's his coat."

"So it is; it's his coat. He's taken it off and is waving it around his head. But would you look at him swing it!"

"Oh, say, there isn't any lifesaving station there. That's just a winter-resort hotel omnibus that has brought over some of the boarders to see us drown."

"What's that idiot with the coat mean? What's he signaling, any-how?"

"It looks as if he were trying to tell us to go north. There must be a lifesaving station up there."

"No; he thinks we're fishing. Just giving us a merry hand. See? Ah, there, Willie!"

"Well, I wish I could make something out of those signals. What do you suppose he means?"

"He don't mean anything; he's just playing."

"Well, if he'd just signal us to try the surf again, or to go to sea and wait, or go north, or go south, or go to hell, there would be some reason in it. But look at him! He just stands there and keeps his coat revolving like a wheel. The ass!"

"There come more people."

"Now there's quite a mob. Look! Isn't that a boat?"

"Where? Oh, I see where you mean. No, that's no boat."

"That fellow is still waving his coat."

"He must think we like to see him do that. Why don't he quit it? It don't mean anything."

"I don't know. I think he is trying to make us go north. It must be that there's a lifesaving station there somewhere."

"Say, he ain't tired yet. Look at 'im wave!"

"Wonder how long he can keep that up. He's been revolving his coat ever since he caught sight of us. He's an idiot. Why aren't they getting men to bring a boat out? A fishing boat—one of those big yawls—could come out here all right. Why don't he do something?"

"Oh, it's all right now."

"They'll have a boat out here for us in less than no time, now that they've seen us."

A faint yellow tone came into the sky over the low land. The shadows on the sea slowly deepened. The wind bore coldness with it, and the men began to shiver.

"Holy smoke!" said one, allowing his voice to express his impious mood, "if we keep on monkeying out here! If we've got to flounder out here all night!"

"Oh, we'll never have to stay here all night! Don't you worry. They've seen us now, and it won't be long before they'll come chasing out after us."

The shore grew dusky. The man waving a coat blended gradually into this gloom, and it swallowed in the same manner the omnibus and the group of people. The spray, when it dashed uproariously over the side, made the voyagers shrink and swear like men who were being branded.

"I'd like to catch the chump who waved the coat. I feel like socking him one, just for luck."

"Why? What did he do?"

"Oh, nothing, but then he seemed so damned cheerful."

In the meantime the oiler rowed, and then the correspondent rowed, and then the oiler rowed. Gray-faced and bowed forward, they mechanically, turn by turn, plied the leaden oars. The form of the lighthouse had vanished from the southern horizon, but finally a pale star appeared, just lifting from the sea. The streaked saffron in the west passed before the all-merging darkness, and the sea to the east was black. The land had vanished, and was expressed only by the low and drear thunder of the surf.

"If I am going to be drowned—if I am going to be drowned—if I am going to be drowned, why, in the name of the seven mad gods who rule the sea, was I allowed to come thus far and contemplate sand and trees? Was I brought here merely to have my nose dragged away as I was about to nibble the sacred cheese of life?"

The patient captain, drooped over the water jar, was sometimes obliged to speak to the oarsman.

"Keep her head up! Keep her head up!"

"Keep her head up, sir." The voices were weary and low.

This was surely a quiet evening. All save the oarsman lay heavily and listlessly in the boat's bottom. As for him, his eyes were just capable of noting the tall black waves that swept forward in a most sinister silence, save for an occasional subdued growl of a crest.

The cook's head was on a thwart, and he looked without interest at the water under his nose. He was deep in other scenes. Finally he spoke. "Billie," he murmured, dreamfully, "what kind of pie do you like best?"

V

"Pie!" said the oiler and the correspondent, agitatedly. "Don't talk about those things, blast you!"

"Well," said the cook, "I was just thinking about ham sandwiches, and—"

A night on the sea in an open boat is a long night. As darkness settled finally, the shine of the light, lifting from the sea in the south, changed to full gold. On the northern horizon a new light appeared, a small bluish gleam on the edge of the waters. These two lights were the furniture of the world. Otherwise there was nothing but waves.

Two men huddled in the stern, and distances were so magnificent in the dinghy that the rower was enabled to keep his feet partly warm by thrusting them under his companions. Their legs indeed extended far under the rowing-seat until they touched the feet of the captain forward. Sometimes, despite the efforts of the tired oarsman, a wave came piling into the boat, an icy wave of the night, and the chilling water soaked them anew. They would twist their bodies for a moment and groan, and sleep the dead sleep once more, while the water in the boat gurgled about them as the craft rocked.

The plan of the oiler and the correspondent was for one to row until he lost the ability, and then arouse the other from his seawater couch in the bottom of the boat.

The oiler plied the oars until his head drooped forward and the overpowering sleep blinded him; and he rowed yet afterward. Then he touched a man in the bottom of the boat, and called his name. "Will you spell me for a little while?" he said meekly.

"Sure, Billie," said the correspondent, awaking and dragging himself to a sitting position. They exchanged places carefully, and the oiler, cuddling down in the seawater at the cook's side, seemed to go to sleep instantly.

The particular violence of the sea had ceased. The waves came without snarling. The obligation of the man at the oars was to keep the boat headed so that the tilt of the rollers would not capsize her, and to preserve her from filling when the crests rushed past. The black waves were silent and hard to be seen in the darkness. Often one was almost upon the boat before the oarsman was aware.

In a low voice the correspondent addressed the captain. He was not sure that the captain was awake, although this iron man seemed to be always awake. "Captain, shall I keep her making for that light north, sir?"

The same steady voice answered him. "Yes. Keep it about two points off the port bow."

The cook had tied a lifebelt around himself in order to get even the warmth which this clumsy cork contrivance could donate, and he seemed almost stove-like when a rower, whose teeth invariably chattered wildly as soon as he ceased his labor, dropped down to sleep.

The correspondent, as he rowed, looked down at the two men sleeping underfoot. The cook's arm was around the oiler's shoulders, and, with their fragmentary clothing and haggard faces, they were the babes of the sea—a grotesque rendering of the old babes in the wood.

Later he must have grown stupid at his work, for suddenly there was a growling of water, and a crest came with a roar and a swash into the boat, and it was a wonder that it did not set the cook afloat in his lifebelt. The cook continued to sleep, but the oiler sat up, blinking his eyes and shaking with the new cold.

"Oh, I'm awful sorry, Billie," said the correspondent, contritely.

"That's all right, old boy," said the oiler, and lay down again and was asleep.

Presently it seemed that even the captain dozed, and the correspondent thought that he was the one man afloat on all the oceans. The wind had a voice as it came over the waves, and it was sadder than the end.

There was a long, loud swishing astern of the boat, and a gleaming trail of phosphorescence, like blue flame, was furrowed on the black waters. It might have been made by a monstrous knife.

Then there came a stillness, while the correspondent breathed with open mouth and looked at the sea.

Suddenly there was another swish and another long flash of bluish light, and this time it was alongside the boat, and might almost have been reached with an oar. The correspondent saw an enormous fin speed like a shadow through the water, hurling the crystalline spray and leaving the long glowing trail.

The correspondent looked over his shoulder at the captain. His face was hidden, and he seemed to be asleep. He looked at the babes of the sea. They certainly were asleep. So, being bereft of sympathy, he leaned a little way to one side and swore softly into the sea.

But the thing did not then leave the vicinity of the boat. Ahead or astern, on one side or the other, at intervals long or short, fled the long sparkling streak, and there was to be heard the *whirroo* of the dark fin. The speed and power of the thing was greatly to be admired. It cut the water like a gigantic and keen projectile.

The presence of this biding thing did not affect the man with the same horror that it would if he had been a picnicker. He simply looked at the sea dully and swore in an undertone.

Nevertheless, it is true that he did not wish to be alone with the thing. He wished one of his companions to awake by chance and keep him company with it. But the captain hung motionless over the water jar, and the oiler and the cook in the bottom of the boat were plunged in slumber.

VI

"If I am going to be drowned—if I am going to be drowned—if I am going to be drowned, why, in the name of the seven mad gods who rule the sea, was I allowed to come thus far and comtemplate sand and trees?"

During this dismal night, it may be remarked that a man would conclude that it was really the intention of the seven mad gods to drown him, despite the abominable injustice of it. For it was certainly an abominable injustice to drown a man who had worked so hard, so hard. The man felt it would be a crime most unnatural. Other people had drowned at sea since galleys swarmed with painted sails, but still—

When it occurs to a man that nature does not regard him as important, and that she feels she would not maim the universe by disposing of him, he at first wishes to throw bricks at the temple, and he hates deeply the fact that there are no bricks and no temples. Any visible expression of nature would surely be pelleted with his jeers.

Then, if there be no tangible thing to hoot, he feels, perhaps, the desire to confront a personification and indulge in pleas, bowed to one knee, and with hands supplicant, saying, "Yes, but I love myself."

A high cold star on a winter's night is the word he feels that she says to him. Thereafter he knows the pathos of his situation.

The men in the dinghy had not discussed these matters, but each had, no doubt, reflected upon them in silence and according to his mind. There was seldom any expression upon their faces save the general one of complete weariness. Speech was devoted to the business of the boat.

To chime the notes of his emotion, a verse mysteriously entered the correspondent's head. He had even forgotten that he had forgotten this verse, but it suddenly was in his mind.

A soldier of the Legion lay dying in Algiers;
There was lack of woman's nursing, there was dearth of woman's tears;

But a comrade stood beside him, and he took that comrade's hand,
And he said, "I never more shall see my own, my native land." [4]

In his childhood the correspondent had been made acquainted
with the fact that a soldier of the Legion lay dying in Algiers, but he
had never regarded the fact as important. Myriads of his schoolfellows had informed him of the soldier's plight, but the dinning
had naturally ended by making him perfectly indifferent. He had
never considered it his affair that a soldier of the Legion lay dying
in Algiers, nor had it appeared to him as a matter for sorrow. It was
less to him than the breaking of a pencil's point.

Now, however, it quaintly came to him as a human, living thing.
It was no longer merely a picture of a few throes in the breast of a
poet, meanwhile drinking tea and warming his feet at the grate; it
was an actuality—stern, mournful, and fine.

The correspondent plainly saw the soldier. He lay on the sand
with his feet out straight and still. While his pale left hand was
upon his chest in an attempt to thwart the going of his life, the
blood came between his fingers. In the far Algerian distance, a city
of low square forms was set against a sky that was faint with the last
sunset hues. The correspondent, plying the oars and dreaming of
the slow and slower movements of the lips of the soldier, was
moved by a profound and perfectly impersonal comprehension. He
was sorry for the soldier of the Legion who lay dying in Algiers.

The thing which had followed the boat and waited had evidently
grown bored at the delay. There was no longer to be heard the slash
of the cut-water, and there was no longer the flame of the long trail.
The light in the north still glimmered, but it was apparently no
nearer to the boat. Sometimes the boom of the surf rang in the correspondent's ears, and he turned the craft seaward then and rowed
harder. Southward, some one had evidently built a watch fire on the
beach. It was too low and too far to be seen, but it made a shimmer-
ing, roseate reflection upon the bluff in back of it, and this could be
discerned from the boat. The wind came stronger, and sometimes a
wave suddenly raged out like a mountain cat, and there was to be
seen the sheen and sparkle of a broken crest.

4. From "Bingen on the Rhine," an immensely popular poem by Caroline Sheridan
Norton (1808–77). Either Crane or the "correspondent" has compressed the opening lines of the poem:

> A soldier of the Legion lay dying in Algiers,
> There was lack of woman's nursing, there was dearth of woman's tears;
> But a comrade stood beside him, while his life-blood ebbed away,
> And bent with pitying glances, to hear what he might say.
> The dying soldier faltered, as he took that comrade's hand,
> And he said, "I nevermore shall see my own, my native land. . . ."

"Bingen on the Rhine" was a favorite recitation piece in the schoolrooms of late
nineteenth-century America.

The captain, in the bow, moved on his water jar and sat erect. "Pretty long night," he observed to the correspondent. He looked at the shore. "Those lifesaving people take their time."

"Did you see that shark playing around?"

"Yes, I saw him. He was a big fellow, all right."

"Wish I had known you were awake."

Later the correspondent spoke into the bottom of the boat. "Billie!" There was a slow and gradual disentanglement. "Billie, will you spell me?"

"Sure," said the oiler.

As soon as the correspondent touched the cold, comfortable sea-water in the bottom of the boat and had huddled close to the cook's lifebelt he was deep in sleep, despite the fact that his teeth played all the popular airs. This sleep was so good to him that it was but a moment before he heard a voice call his name in a tone that demonstrated the last stages of exhaustion. "Will you spell me?"

"Sure, Billie."

The light in the north had mysteriously vanished, but the correspondent took his course from the wide-awake captain.

Later in the night they took the boat farther out to sea, and the captain directed the cook to take one oar at the stern and keep the boat facing the seas. He was to call out if he should hear the thunder of the surf. This plan enabled the oiler and the correspondent to get respite together. "We'll give those boys a chance to get into shape again," said the captain. They curled down and, after a few preliminary chatterings and trembles, slept once more the dead sleep. Neither knew they had bequeathed to the cook the company of another shark, or perhaps the same shark.

As the boat caroused on the waves, spray occasionally bumped over the side and gave them a fresh soaking, but this had no power to break their repose. The ominous slash of the wind and the water affected them as it would have affected mummies.

"Boys," said the cook, with the notes of every reluctance in his voice, "she's drifted in pretty close. I guess one of you had better take her to sea again." The correspondent, aroused, heard the crash of the toppled crests.

As he was rowing, the captain gave him some whiskey-and-water, and this steadied the chills out of him. "If I ever get ashore and anybody shows me even a photograph of an oar—"

At last there was a short conversation.

"Billie! . . . Billie, will you spell me?"

"Sure," said the oiler.

VII

When the correspondent again opened his eyes, the sea and the sky were each of the gray hue of the dawning. Later, carmine and gold was painted upon the waters. The morning appeared finally, in its splendor, with a sky of pure blue, and the sunlight flamed on the tips of the waves.

On the distant dunes were set many little black cottages, and a tall white windmill reared above them. No man, nor dog, nor bicycle appeared on the beach. The cottages might have formed a deserted village.

The voyagers scanned the shore. A conference was held in the boat. "Well," said the captain, "if no help is coming, we might better try a run through the surf right away. If we stay out here much longer we will be too weak to do anything for ourselves at all." The others silently acquiesced in this reasoning. The boat was headed for the beach. The correspondent wondered if none ever ascended the tall wind-tower, and if then they never looked seaward. This tower was a giant, standing with its back to the plight of the ants. It represented in a degree, to the correspondent, the serenity of nature amid the struggles of the individual—nature in the wind, and nature in the vision of men. She did not seem cruel to him then, nor beneficent, nor treacherous, nor wise. But she was indifferent, flatly indifferent. It is, perhaps, plausible that a man in this situation, impressed with the unconcern of the universe, should see the innumerable flaws of his life, and have them taste wickedly in his mind, and wish for another chance. A distinction between right and wrong seems absurdly clear to him, then, in this new ignorance of the grave-edge, and he understands that if he were given another opportunity he would mend his conduct and his words, and be better and brighter during an introduction or at a tea.

"Now, boys," said the captain, "she is going to swamp sure. All we can do is to work her in as far as possible, and then when she swamps, pile out and scramble for the beach. Keep cool now, and don't jump until she swamps sure."

The oiler took the oars. Over his shoulders he scanned the surf. "Captain," he said, "I think I'd better bring her about and keep her head-on to the seas and back her in."

"All right, Billie," said the captain. "Back her in." The oiler swung the boat then, and, seated in the stern, the cook and the correspondent were obliged to look over their shoulders to contemplate the lonely and indifferent shore.

The monstrous inshore rollers heaved the boat high until the men were again enabled to see the white sheets of water scudding up the slanted beach. "We won't get in very close," said the captain. Each time a man could wrest his attention from the rollers, he turned his glance toward the shore, and in the expression of the eyes during this contemplation there was a singular quality. The correspondent, observing the others, knew that they were not afraid, but the full meaning of their glances was shrouded.

As for himself, he was too tired to grapple fundamentally with the fact. He tried to coerce his mind into thinking of it, but the mind was dominated at this time by the muscles, and the muscles said they did not care. It merely occurred to him that if he should drown it would be a shame.

There were no hurried words, no pallor, no plain agitation. The men simply looked at the shore. "Now, remember to get well clear of the boat when you jump," said the captain.

Seaward the crest of a roller suddenly fell with a thunderous crash, and the long white comber came roaring down upon the boat.

"Steady now," said the captain. The men were silent. They turned their eyes from the shore to the comber and waited. The boat slid up the incline, leaped at the furious top, bounced over it, and swung down the long back of the wave. Some water had been shipped, and the cook bailed it out.

But the next crest crashed also. The tumbling, boiling flood of white water caught the boat and whirled it almost perpendicular. Water swarmed in from all sides. The correspondent had his hands on the gunwale at this time, and when the water entered at that place he swiftly withdrew his fingers, as if he objected to wetting them.

The little boat, drunken with this weight of water, reeled and snuggled deeper into the sea.

"Bail her out, cook! Bail her out!" said the captain.

"All right, Captain," said the cook.

"Now boys, the next one will do for us sure," said the oiler. "Mind to jump clear of the boat."

The third wave moved forward, huge, furious, implacable. It fairly swallowed the dinghy, and almost simultaneously the men tumbled into the sea. A piece of lifebelt had lain in the bottom of the boat, and as the correspondent went overboard he held this to his chest with his left hand.

The January water was icy, and he reflected immediately that it was colder than he had expected to find it off the coast of Florida. This appeared to his dazed mind as a fact important enough to be noted at the time. The coldness of the water was sad; it was tragic. This fact was somehow mixed and confused with his opinion of his own situation, so that it seemed almost a proper reason for tears. The water was cold.

When he came to the surface he was conscious of little but the noisy water. Afterward he saw his companions in the sea. The oiler was ahead in the race. He was swimming strongly and rapidly. Off to the correspondent's left, the cook's great white and corked back bulged out of the water; and in the rear the captain was hanging with his one good hand to the keel of the overturned dinghy.

There is a certain immovable quality to a shore, and the correspondent wondered at it amid the confusion of the sea.

It seemed also very attractive; but the correspondent knew that it was a long journey, and he paddled leisurely. The piece of life preserver lay under him, and sometimes he whirled down the incline of a wave as if he were on a hand-sled.

But finally he arrived at a place in the sea where travel was beset with difficulty. He did not pause swimming to inquire what manner of current had caught him, but there his progress ceased. The shore was set before him like a bit of scenery on a stage, and he looked at it and understood with his eyes each detail of it.

As the cook passed, much farther to the left, the captain was calling to him, "Turn over on your back, cook! Turn over on your back and use the oar."

"All right, sir." The cook turned on his back, and, paddling with an oar, went ahead as if he were a canoe.

Presently the boat also passed to the left of the correspondent, with the captain clinging with one hand to the keel. He would have appeared like a man raising himself to look over a board fence if it were not for the extraordinary gymnastics of the boat. The correspondent marveled that the captain could still hold to it.

They passed on nearer to shore—the oiler, the cook, the captain—and following them went the water jar, bouncing gaily over the seas.

The correspondent remained in the grip of this strange new enemy—a current. The shore, with its white slope of sand and its green bluff topped with little silent cottages, was spread like a picture before him. It was very near to him then, but he was impressed as one who, in a gallery, looks at a scene from Brittany or Algiers.

He thought: "I am going to drown? Can it be possible? Can it be possible? Can it be possible?" Perhaps an individual must consider his own death to be the final phenomenon of nature.

But later a wave perhaps whirled him out of this small deadly current, for he found suddenly that he could again make progress toward the shore. Later still he was aware that the captain, clinging with one hand to the keel of the dinghy, had his face turned away from the shore and toward him, and was calling his name. "Come to the boat! Come to the boat!"

In his struggle to reach the captain and the boat, he reflected that when one gets properly wearied drowning must really be a comfortable arrangement—a cessation of hostilities accompanied by a large degree of relief; and he was glad of it, for the main thing in his mind for some moments had been horror of the temporary agony. He did not wish to be hurt.

Presently he saw a man running along the shore. He was undressing with most remarkable speed. Coat, trousers, shirt, everything flew magically off him.

"Come to the boat!" called the captain.

"All right, Captain." As the correspondent paddled, he saw the captain let himself down to bottom and leave the boat. Then the correspondent performed his one little marvel of the voyage. A large wave caught him and flung him with ease and supreme speed completely over the boat and far beyond it. It struck him even then as an event in gymnastics and a true miracle of the sea. An overturned boat in the surf is not a plaything to a swimming man.

The correspondent arrived in water that reached only to his waist, but his condition did not enable him to stand for more than a moment. Each wave knocked him into a heap, and the undertow pulled at him.

Then he saw the man who had been running and undressing, and undressing and running, come bounding into the water. He dragged ashore the cook, and then waded toward the captain; but the captain waved him away and sent him to the correspondent. He was naked—naked as a tree in winter; but a halo was about his head, and he shone like a saint. He gave a strong pull, and a long drag, and a bully heave at the correspondent's hand. The correspondent, schooled in the minor formulae, said, "Thanks, old man." But suddenly the man cried, "What's that?" He pointed a swift finger. The correspondent said, "Go."

In the shallows, face downward, lay the oiler. His forehead touched sand that was periodically, between each wave, clear of the sea.

The correspondent did not know all that transpired afterward. When he achieved safe ground he fell, striking the sand with each particular part of his body. It was as if he had dropped from a roof, but the thud was grateful to him.

It seems that instantly the beach was populated with men with blankets, clothes, and flasks, and women with coffeepots and all the remedies sacred to their minds. The welcome of the land to the men from the sea was warm and generous; but a still and dripping shape was carried slowly up the beach, and the land's welcome for it could only be the different and sinister hospitality of the grave.

When it came night, the white waves paced to and fro in the moonlight, and the wind brought the sound of the great sea's voice to the men on the shore, and they felt that they could then be interpreters.

From *The Open Boat and Other Tales of Adventure* (1898)

STEPHEN CRANE'S OWN STORY
From the *New York Press*, January 7, 1897

JACKSONVILLE, FLA., Jan. 6—It was the afternoon of New Year's. The *Commodore* lay at her dock in Jacksonville and negro stevedores processioned steadily toward her with box after box of ammunition and bundle after bundle of rifles. Her hatch, like the mouth of a monster, engulfed them. It might have been the feeding time of some legendary creature of the sea. It was in broad daylight and the crowd of gleeful Cubans on the pier did not forbear to sing the strange patriotic ballads of their island.

Everything was perfectly open. The *Commodore* was cleared with a cargo of arms and munitions for Cuba. There was none of that extreme modesty about the proceeding which had marked previous departures of the famous tug. She loaded up as placidly as if she were going to carry oranges to New York, instead of Remingtons to Cuba. Down the river, furthermore, the revenue cutter *Boutwell*, the old isosceles triangle that protects United States interests in the St. Johns, lay at anchor, with no sign of excitement aboard her.

On the decks of the *Commodore* there were exchanges of farewells in two languages. Many of the men who were to sail upon her had many intimates in the old Southern town, and we who had left our friends in the remote North received our first touch of melancholy on witnessing these strenuous and earnest good-bys.

It seems, however, that there was more difficulty at the custom house. The officers of the ship and the Cuban leaders were detained there until a mournful twilight settled upon the St. Johns, and through a heavy fog the lights of Jacksonville blinked dimly.

Then at last the *Commodore* swung clear of the dock, amid a tumult of good-bys. As she turned her bow toward the distant sea the Cubans ashore cheered and cheered. In response the *Commodore* gave three long blasts of her whistle, which even to this time impressed me with their sadness. Somehow they sounded as wails.

Then at last we began to feel like filibusters. I don't suppose that the most stolid brain could contrive to believe that there is not a mere trifle of danger in filibustering, and so as we watched the lights of Jacksonville swing past us and heard the regular thump, thump, thump of the engines we did considerable reflecting.

But I am sure that there was no hifalutin emotions visible upon any of the faces which fronted the speeding shore. In fact, from cook's boy to captain, we were all enveloped in a gentle satisfaction and cheerfulness.

But less than two miles from Jacksonville this atrocious fog caused the pilot to ram the bow of the *Commodore* hard upon the mud, and in this ignominious position we were compelled to stay until daybreak.

It was to all of us more than a physical calamity. We were now no longer filibusters. We were men on a ship stuck in the mud. A certain mental somersault was made once more necessary. But word had been sent to Jacksonville to the captain of the revenue cutter *Boutwell*, and Captain Kilgore turned out promptly and generously fired up his old triangle and came at full speed to our assistance. She dragged us out of the mud and again we headed for the mouth of the river. The revenue cutter pounded along a half mile astern of us, to make sure that we did not take on board at some place along the river men for the Cuban army.

This was the early morning of New Year's Day, and the fine golden Southern sunlight fell full upon the river. It flashed over the ancient *Boutwell* until her white sides gleamed like pearl and her rigging was spun into little threads of gold. Cheers greeted the old *Commodore* from passing ships and from the shore. It was a cheerful, almost merry, beginning to our voyage.

At Mayport, however, we changed our river pilot for a man who could take her to open sea, and again the *Commodore* was beached. The *Boutwell* was fussing around us in her venerable way, and, upon seeing our predicament, she came again to assist us, but this time with engines reversed the *Commodore* dragged herself away from the grip of the sand and again the *Commodore* headed for the open sea.

The captain of the revenue cutter grew curious. He hailed the *Commodore:* "Are you fellows going to sea to-day?"

Captain Murphy of the *Commodore* called back: "Yes, sir." And then as the whistle of the *Commodore* saluted him Captain Kilgore doffed his cap and said: "Well, gentlemen, I hope you have a pleasant cruise," and this was our last words from shore.

When the *Commodore* came to the enormous rollers that flee over the bar, a certain light-heartedness departed from the throats of the ship's company. The *Commodore* began to turn handsprings, and by the time she had gotten fairly to sea and turned into the eye of the roaring breeze that was blowing from the southeast there was an almost general opinion on board the vessel that a life on the rolling wave was not the finest thing in the world. On deck amidships lay five or six Cubans, limp, forlorn and infinitely depressed. In the bunks below lay more Cubans, also limp, forlorn and infinitely depressed. In the captain's quarters, back of the pilot house, the Cuban leaders were stretched out in postures of complete contentment to this terrestrial realm of their stomachs.

The *Commodore* was heavily laden and in this strong sea she rolled like a rubber ball. She appeared to be a gallant sea boat and bravely flung off the waves that swarmed over her bow. At this time the first mate was at the wheel, and I remember how proud he was of the ship as she dashed the white foaming waters aside and arose to the swells like a duck.

"Ain't she a daisy?" said he. But she certainly did do a remarkable lot of pitching and presently even some American seamen were made ill by the long wallowing motion of the ship. A squall confronted us dead ahead and in the impressive twilight of this New Year's Day the *Commodore* steamed sturdily toward a darkened part of the horizon. The State of Florida is very large when you look at it from an airship, but it is as narrow as a sheet of paper when you look at it sideways. The coast was merely a faint streak.

As darkness came upon the waters the *Commodore*'s wake was a broad, flaming path of blue and silver phosphorescence, and as her stout bow lunged at the great black waves she threw flashing, roaring cascades to either side. And all that was to be heard was the rhythmical and mighty pounding of the engines.

Being an inexperienced filibuster, the writer had undergone considerable mental excitement since the starting of the ship, and consequently he had not yet been to sleep, and so I went to the first mate's bunk to indulge myself in all the physical delights of holding one's self in bed. Every time the ship lurched I expected to be fired through a bulkhead, and it was neither amusing nor instructive to see in the dim light a certain accursed valise aiming itself at the top of my stomach with every lurch of the ship.

The cook was asleep on a bench in the galley. He was of a portly and noble exterior, and by means of a checker board he had himself wedged on this bench in such a manner that the motion of the ship would be unable to dislodge him. He awoke as I entered the galley, and, feeling moved, he delivered himself of some dolorous sentiments. "God," he said, in the course of his observations, "I don't feel right about this ship somehow. It strikes me that something is going to happen to us. I don't know what it is, but the old ship is going to get it in the neck, I think."

"Well, how about the men on board of her?" said I. "Are any of us going to get out, prophet?"

"Yes," said the cook, "sometimes I have these damned feelings come over me, and they are always right, and it seems to me somehow that you and I will both get out and meet again somewhere, down at Coney Island, perhaps, or some place like that."

Finding it impossible to sleep, I went back to the pilot house. An old seaman named Tom Smith, from Charleston, was then at the wheel. In the darkness I could not see Tom's face, except at those times when he leaned forward to scan the compass and the dim light from the box came upon his weather-beaten features.

"Well, Tom," said I, "how do you like filibustering?"

He said: "I think I am about through with it. I've been in a number of these expeditions, and the pay is good, but I think if I ever get back safe this time I will cut it."

I sat down in the corner of the pilot house and went almost to sleep. In the meantime the captain came on duty and he was standing near me when the chief engineer rushed up the stairs and cried hurriedly to the captain that there was something wrong in the engine room. He and the captain departed swiftly. I was drowsing there in my corner when the captain returned, and, going to the door of the little room directly back of the pilot house, cried to the Cuban leader:

"Say, can't you get those fellows to work? I can't talk their language and I can't get them started. Come on and get them going."

The Cuban leader turned to me then and said: "Go help in the fire-room. They are going to bail with buckets."

The engine room, by the way, represented a scene at this time taken from the middle kitchen of hades. In the first place, it was insufferably warm, and the lights burned faintly in a way to cause mystic and grewsome shadows. There was a quantity of soapish sea water swirling and sweeping and swishing among machinery that roared and banged and clattered and steamed, and in the second place, it was a devil of a ways down below.

Here I first came to know a certain young oiler named Billy Higgins. He was sloshing around this inferno filling buckets with water and passing them to a chain of men that extended up to the ship's side. Afterward we got orders to change our point of attack on the water and to operate through a little door on the windward side of the ship that led into the engine room.

During this time there was much talk of pumps out of order and many other statements of a mechanical kind, which I did not altogether comprehend, but understood to mean that there was a general and sudden ruin in the engine room.

There was no particular agitation at this time, and even later there was never a panic on board the *Commodore*. The party of men who worked with Higgins and me at this time were all Cubans, and we were under the direction of the Cuban leaders. Presently we were ordered again to the afterhold, and there was some hesitation about going into the abominable fireroom again, but Higgins dashed down the companionway with a bucket.

The heat and hard work in the fire-room affected me and I was obliged to come on deck again. Going forward I heard as I went talk of lowering the boats. Near the corner of the galley the mate was talking with a man.

"Why don't you send up a rocket?" said this unknown person. And the mate replied: "What the hell do we want to send up a rocket for? The ship is all right."

Returning with a little rubber and cloth overcoat, I saw the first boat about to be lowered. A certain man was the first person in this first boat, and they were handing him in a valise about as large as a hotel. I had not entirely recovered from my astonishment and pleasure in witnessing this noble deed, when I saw another valise go to him. This valise was not perhaps so large as a hotel, but it was a big valise anyhow. Afterward there went to him something which looked to me like an overcoat.

Seeing the chief engineer leaning out of his little window, I remarked to him: "What do you think of that blank, blank, blank?"

"Oh, he's a bird," said the old chief.

It was now that was heard the order to get away the lifeboat, which was stowed on top of the deckhouse. The deckhouse was a mighty slippery place, and with each roll of the ship the men there thought themselves likely to take headers into the deadly black sea. Higgins was on top of the deckhouse, and, with the first mate and two colored stokers, we wrestled with that boat, which I am willing to swear weighed as much as a Broadway cable car. She might have been spiked to the deck. We could have pushed a little brick schoolhouse along a corduroy road as easily as we could have moved this boat. But the first mate got a tackle to her from a leaward davit, and on the deck below the captain corralled enough men to make an impression upon the boat. We were ordered to cease hauling then, and in this lull the cook of the ship came to me and said: "What are you going to do?"

I told him of my plans, and he said: "Well, my God, that's what I am going to do."

Now the whistle of the *Commodore* had been turned loose, and if there ever was a voice of despair and death it was in the voice of this whistle. It had gained a new tone. It was as if its throat was already choked by the water, and this cry on the sea at night, with a wind blowing the spray over the ship, and the waves roaring over the bow, and swirling white along the decks, was to each of us probably a song of man's end.

It was now that the first mate showed a sign of losing his grip. To us who were trying in all stages of competence and experience to launch the lifeboat he raged in all terms of fiery satire and hammerlike abuse. But the boat moved at last and swung down toward the water.

Afterward when I went aft I saw the captain standing with his arm in a sling, holding on to a stay with his one good hand and directing the launching of the boat. He gave me a five-gallon jug of water to hold, and asked me what I was going to do. I told him what I thought was about the proper thing, and he told me then that the cook had the same idea, and ordered me to go forward and be ready to launch the ten-foot dingy. I remember very well that he turned then to swear at a colored stoker who was prowling around, done up in life preservers until he looked like a feather bed.

I went forward with my five-gallon jug of water, and when the captain came we launched the dingy, and they put me over the side to fend her off from the ship with an oar.

They handed me down the water jug, and then the cook came into the boat, and we sat there in the darkness, wondering why, by all our hopes of future happiness, the captain was so long in coming over the side and ordering us away from the doomed ship.

The captain was waiting for the other boat to go. Finally he hailed in the darkness: "Are you all right, Mr. Graines?"

The first mate answered: "All right, sir."

"Shove off then," cried the captain. The captain was just about to swing over the rail when a dark form came forward and a voice said: "Captain, I go with you."

The captain answered: "Yes, Billy; get in."

It was Billy Higgins, the oiler. Billy dropped into the boat and a moment later the captain followed, bringing with him an end of about forty yards of lead line. The other end was attached to the rail of the ship. As we swung back to leaward the captain said: "Boys, we will stay right near the ship till she goes down."

This cheerful information, of course, filled us all with glee. The line kept us headed properly into the wind and as we rode over the monstrous roarers we saw upon each rise the swaying lights of the dying *Commodore*.

When came the gray shade of dawn, the form of the *Commodore* grew slowly clear to us as our little ten-foot boat rose over each swell. She was floating with such an air of buoyancy that we laughed when we had time, and said: "What a guy it would be on those other fellows if she didn't sink at all."

But later we saw men aboard of her, and later still they began to hail us. I had forgotten to mention that previously we had loosened the end of the lead line and dropped much further to leaward. The men on board were a mystery to us, of course, as we had seen all the boats leave the ship. We rowed back to the ship, but did not approach too near, because we were four men in a ten-foot boat, and we knew that the touch of a hand on our gunwale would as-suredly swamp us.

The first mate cried out from the ship that the third boat had foundered alongside. He cried that they had made rafts and wished us to tow them. The captain said: "All right."

Their rafts were floating astern.

"Jump in," cried the captain, but here was a singular and most harrowing hesitation. There were five white men and two negroes. This scene in the gray light of morning impressed one as would a view into some place where ghosts move slowly. These seven men on the stern of the sinking *Commodore* were silent. Save the words of the mate to the captain there was no talk. Here was death, but here also was a most singular and indefinable kind of fortitude.

Four men, I remember, clambered over the railing and stood there watching the cold, steely sheen of the sweeping waves.

"Jump," cried the captain again. The old chief engineer first obeyed the order. He landed on the outside raft and the captain told him how to grip the raft, and he obeyed as promptly and as docilely as a scholar in riding school.

A stoker followed him, and then the first mate threw his hands over his head and plunged into the sea. He had no life belt, and for my part, even when he did this horrible thing, I somehow felt that I could see in the expression of his hands, and in the very toss of his head, as he leaped thus to death, that it was rage, rage, rage unspeakable that was in his heart at the time.

And then I saw Tom Smith, the man who was going to quit filibustering after this expedition, jump to a raft and turn his face toward us. On board the *Commodore* three men strode, still in silence and with their faces turned toward us. One man had his arms folded and was leaning against the deckhouse. His feet were crossed, so that the toe of his left foot pointed downward. There they stood gazing at us, and neither from the deck nor from the rafts was a voice raised. Still was there this silence.

The colored stoker on the first raft threw us a line and we began to tow. Of course, we perfectly understood the absolute impossibility of any such thing; our dingy was within six inches of the water's edge, there was an enormous sea running, and I knew that under the circumstances a tugboat would have no light task in moving these rafts. But we tried it, and would have continued to try it indefinitely, but that something critical came to pass. I was at an oar and so faced the rafts. The cook controlled the line. Suddenly the boat began to go backward, and then we saw this negro on the first raft pulling on the line hand over hand and drawing us to him.

He had turned into a demon. He was wild, wild as a tiger. He was crouched on this raft and ready to spring. Every muscle of him seemed to be turned into an elastic spring. His eyes were almost white. His face was the face of a lost man reaching upward, and we knew that the weight of his hand on our gunwale doomed us. The cook let go of the line.

We rowed around to see if we could not get a line from the chief engineer, and all this time, mind you, there were no shrieks, no groans, but silence, silence and silence, and then the *Commodore* sank. She lurched to windward, then swung afar back, righted and dove into the sea, and the rafts were suddenly swallowed by this frightful maw of the ocean. And then by the men on the ten-foot dingy were words said that were still not words, something far beyond words.

The lighthouse of Mosquito Inlet stuck up above the horizon like the point of a pin. We turned our dingy toward the shore. The history of life in an open boat for thirty hours would no doubt be very instructive for the young, but none is to be told here now. For my part I would prefer to tell the story at once, because from it would shine the splendid manhood of Captain Edward Murphy and of William Higgins, the oiler, but let it suffice at this time to say that when we were swamped in the surf and making the best of our way toward the shore the captain gave orders amid the wildness of the breakers as clearly as if he had been on the quarterdeck of a battleship.

John Kitchell of Daytona came running down the beach, and as he ran the air was filled with clothes. If he had pulled a single lever and undressed, even as the fire horses harness, he could not to me seem to have stripped with more speed. He dashed into the water and grabbed the cook. Then he went after the captain, but the captain sent him to me, and then it was that we saw Billy Higgins lying with his forehead on sand that was clear of the water, and he was dead.

THE BRIDE COMES TO YELLOW SKY

The great Pullman was whirling onward with such dignity of motion that a glance from the window seemed simply to prove that the plains of Texas were pouring eastward. Vast flats of green grass, dull-hued spaces of mesquite and cactus, little groups of frame houses, woods of light and tender trees, all were sweeping into the east, sweeping over the horizon, a precipice.

A newly married pair had boarded this coach at San Antonio.[1] The man's face was reddened from many days in the wind and sun, and a direct result of his new black clothes was that his brick-colored hands were constantly performing in a most conscious fashion. From time to time he looked down respectfully at his attire. He sat with a hand on each knee, like a man waiting in a barber's shop. The glances he devoted to other passengers were furtive and shy.

The bride was not pretty, nor was she very young. She wore a dress of blue cashmere, with small reservations of velvet here and there, and with steel buttons abounding. She continually twisted her head to regard her puff sleeves, very stiff, straight, and high. They embarrassed her. It was quite apparent that she had cooked, and that she expected to cook, dutifully. The blushes caused by the careless scrutiny of some passengers as she had entered the car were strange to see upon this plain, underclass countenance, which was drawn in placid, almost emotionless lines.

They were evidently very happy. "Ever been in a parlor car before?" he asked, smiling with delight.

"No," she answered. "I never was. It's fine, ain't it?"

"Great! And then after a while we'll go forward to the diner, and get a big layout. Finest meal in the world. Charge a dollar."

"Oh, do they?" cried the bride. "Charge a dollar? Why, that's too much—for us—ain't it, Jack?"

"Not this trip, anyhow," he answered bravely. "We're going to go the whole thing."

Later, he explained to her about the trains. "You see, it's a thousand miles from one end of Texas to the other; and this train runs right across it, and never stops but four times." He had the pride of an owner. He pointed out to her the dazzling fittings of the coach; and in truth her eyes opened wider as she contemplated the sea-green figured velvet, the shining brass, silver, and glass, the wood that gleamed as darkly brilliant as the surface of a pool of oil. At one

1. Crane traveled through the American West and Mexico in 1895.

end a bronze figure sturdily held a support for a separated chamber, and at convenient places on the ceiling were frescoes in olive and silver.

To the minds of the pair, their surroundings reflected the glory of their marriage that morning in San Antonio. This was the environment of their new estate, and the man's face in particular beamed with an elation that made him appear ridiculous to the negro porter. This individual at times surveyed them from afar with an amused and superior grin. On other occasions he bullied them with skill in ways that did not make it exactly plain to them that they were being bullied. He subtly used all the manners of the most unconquerable kind of snobbery. He oppressed them; but of this oppression they had small knowledge, and they speedily forgot that infrequently a number of travelers covered them with stares of derisive enjoyment. Historically there was supposed to be something infinitely humorous in their situation.

"We are due in Yellow Sky at 3:42," he said, looking tenderly into her eyes.

"Oh, are we?" she said, as if she had not been aware of it. To evince surprise at her husband's statement was part of her wifely amiability. She took from a pocket a little silver watch; and as she held it before her, and stared at it with a frown of attention, the new husband's face shone.

"I bought it in San Anton' from a friend of mine," he told her gleefully.

"It's seventeen minutes past twelve," she said, looking up at him with a kind of shy and clumsy coquetry. A passenger, noting this play, grew excessively sardonic, and winked at himself in one of the numerous mirrors.

At last they went to the dining car. Two rows of negro waiters, in glowing white suits, surveyed their entrance with the interest, and also the equanimity, of men who had been forewarned. The pair fell to the lot of a waiter who happened to feel pleasure in steering them through their meal. He viewed them with the manner of a fatherly pilot, his countenance radiant with benevolence. The patronage, entwined with the ordinary deference, was not plain to them. And yet, as they returned to their coach, they showed in their faces a sense of escape.

To the left, miles down a long purple slope, was a little ribbon of mist where moved the keening Rio Grande. The train was approaching it at an angle, and the apex was Yellow Sky. Presently it was apparent that, as the distance from Yellow Sky grew shorter, the husband became commensurately restless. His brick-red hands were more insistent in their prominence. Occasionally he was even rather absent-minded and faraway when the bride leaned forward and addressed him.

As a matter of truth, Jack Potter was beginning to find the shadow of a deed weigh upon him like a leaden slab. He, the town marshal of Yellow Sky, a man known, liked, and feared in his corner, a prominent person, had gone to San Antonio to meet a girl he believed he loved, and there, after the usual prayers, had actually induced her to marry him, without consulting Yellow Sky for any part of the transaction. He was now bringing his bride before an innocent and unsuspecting community.

Of course people in Yellow Sky married as it pleased them, in accordance with a general custom; but such was Potter's thought of his duty to his friends, or of their idea of his duty, or of an unspoken form which does not control men in these matters, that he felt he was heinous. He had committed an extraordinary crime. Face to face with this girl in San Antonio, and spurred by his sharp impulse, he had gone headlong over all the social hedges. At San Antonio he was like a man hidden in the dark. A knife to sever any friendly duty, any form, was easy to his hand in that remote city. But the hour of Yellow Sky—the hour of daylight—was approaching.

He knew full well that his marriage was an important thing to his town. It could only be exceeded by the burning of the new hotel. His friends could not forgive him. Frequently he had reflected on the advisability of telling them by telegraph, but a new cowardice had been upon him. He feared to do it. And now the train was hurrying him toward a scene of amazement, glee, and reproach. He glanced out of the window at the line of haze swinging slowly in toward the train.

Yellow Sky had a kind of brass band, which played painfully, to the delight of the populace. He laughed without heart as he thought of it. If the citizens could dream of his prospective arrival with his bride, they would parade the band at the station and escort them, amid cheers and laughing congratulations, to his adobe home.

He resolved that he would use all the devices of speed and plains-craft in making the journey from the station to his house. Once within that safe citadel, he could issue some sort of a vocal bulletin, and then not go among the citizens until they had time to wear off a little of their enthusiasm.

The bride looked anxiously at him. "What's worrying you, Jack?"

He laughed again. "I'm not worrying, girl. I'm only thinking of Yellow Sky."

She flushed in comprehension.

A sense of mutual guilt invaded their minds and developed a

finer tenderness. They looked at each other with eyes softly aglow. But Potter often laughed the same nervous laugh. The flush upon the bride's face seemed quite permanent.

The traitor to the feelings of Yellow Sky narrowly watched the speeding landscape. "We're nearly there," he said.

Presently the porter came and announced the proximity of Potter's home. He held a brush in his hand, and, with all his airy superiority gone, he brushed Potter's new clothes as the latter slowly turned this way and that way. Potter fumbled out a coin and gave it to the porter, as he had seen others do. It was a heavy and muscle-bound business, as that of a man shoeing his first horse.

The porter took their bag, and as the train began to slow they moved forward to the hooded platform of the car. Presently the two engines and their long string of coaches rushed into the station of Yellow Sky.

"They have to take water here," said Potter, from a constricted throat and in mournful cadence, as one announcing death. Before the train stopped, his eye had swept the length of the platform, and he was glad and astonished to see there was none upon it but the station-agent, who, with a slightly hurried and anxious air, was walking toward the water tanks. When the train had halted, the porter alighted first, and placed in position a little temporary step.

"Come on, girl," said Potter, hoarsely. As he helped her down they each laughed on a false note. He took the bag from the negro, and bade his wife cling to his arm. As they slunk rapidly away, his hangdog glance perceived that they were unloading the two trunks, and also that the station-agent, far ahead near the baggage car, had turned and was running toward him, making gestures. He laughed, and groaned as he laughed, when he noted the first effect of his marital bliss upon Yellow Sky. He gripped his wife's arm firmly to his side, and they fled. Behind them the porter stood, chuckling fatuously.

II

The California express on the Southern Railway was due at Yellow Sky in twenty-one minutes. There were six men at the bar of the Weary Gentleman saloon. One was a drummer [2] who talked a great deal and rapidly; three were Texans who did not care to talk at that time; and two were Mexican sheepherders, who did not talk as a general practice in the Weary Gentleman saloon. The barkeeper's dog lay on the boardwalk that crossed in front of the door. His head was on his paws, and he glanced drowsily here and there

2. A commercial traveler.

with the constant vigilance of a dog that is kicked on occasion. Across the sandy street were some vivid green grass-plots, so wonderful in appearance, amid the sands that burned near them in a blazing sun, that they caused a doubt in the mind. They exactly resembled the grass mats used to represent lawns on the stage. At the cooler end of the railway station, a man without a coat sat in a tilted chair and smoked his pipe. The fresh-cut bank of the Rio Grande circled near the town, and there could be seen beyond it a great plum-colored plain of mesquite.

Save for the busy drummer and his companions in the saloon, Yellow Sky was dozing. The newcomer leaned gracefully upon the bar, and recited many tales with the confidence of a bard who has come upon a new field.

"—and at the moment that the old man fell downstairs with the bureau in his arms, the old woman was coming up with two scuttles of coal, and of course—"

The drummer's tale was interrupted by a young man who suddenly appeared in the open door. He cried: "Scratchy Wilson's drunk, and has turned loose with both hands." The two Mexicans at once set down their glasses and faded out of the rear entrance of the saloon.

The drummer, innocent and jocular, answered: "All right, old man. S'pose he has? Come in and have a drink, anyhow."

But the information had made such an obvious cleft in every skull in the room that the drummer was obliged to see its importance. All had become instantly solemn. "Say," said he, mystified, "what is this?" His three companions made the introductory gesture of eloquent speech, but the young man at the door forestalled them.

"It means, my friend," he answered, as he came into the saloon, "that for the next two hours this town won't be a health resort."

The barkeeper went to the door and locked and barred it. Reaching out of the window, he pulled in heavy wooden shutters and barred them. Immediately a solemn, chapel-like gloom was upon the place. The drummer was looking from one to another.

"But say," he cried, "what is this, anyhow? You don't mean there is going to be a gunfight?"

"Don't know whether there'll be a fight or not," answered one man, grimly. "But there'll be some shootin'—some good shootin'."

The young man who had warned them waved his hand. "Oh, there'll be a fight fast enough, if any one wants it. Anybody can get a fight out there in the street. There's a fight just waiting."

The drummer seemed to be swayed between the interest of a foreigner and a perception of personal danger.

"What did you say his name was?" he asked.

"Scratchy Wilson," they answered in chorus.

"And will he kill anybody? What are you going to do? Does this happen often? Does he rampage around like this once a week or so? Can he break in that door?"

"No; he can't break down that door," replied the barkeeper. "He's tried it three times. But when he comes you'd better lay down on the floor, stranger. He's dead sure to shoot at it, and a bullet may come through."

Thereafter the drummer kept a strict eye upon the door. The time had not yet been called for him to hug the floor, but, as a minor precaution, he sidled near to the wall. "Will he kill anybody?" he said again.

The men laughed low and scornfully at the question.

"He's out to shoot, and he's out for trouble. Don't see any good in experimentin' with him."

"But what do you do in a case like this? What do you do?"

A man responded: "Why, he and Jack Potter—"

"But," in chorus the other men interrupted, "Jack Potter's in San Anton'."

"Well, who is he? What's he got to do with it?"

"Oh, he's the town marshal. He goes out and fights Scratchy when he gets on one of these tears."

"Wow!" said the drummer, mopping his brow. "Nice job he's got."

The voices had toned away to mere whisperings. The drummer wished to ask further questions, which were born of an increasing anxiety and bewilderment; but when he attempted them, the men merely looked at him in irritation and motioned him to remain silent. A tense waiting hush was upon them. In the deep shadows of the room their eyes shone as they listened for sounds from the street. One man made three gestures at the barkeeper; and the latter, moving like a ghost, handed him a glass and a bottle. The man poured a full glass of whiskey, and set down the bottle noiselessly. He gulped the whiskey in a swallow, and turned again toward the door in immovable silence. The drummer saw that the barkeeper, without a sound, had taken a Winchester from beneath the bar. Later he saw this individual beckoning to him, so he tiptoed across the room.

"You better come with me back of the bar."

"No, thanks," said the drummer, perspiring. "I'd rather be where I can make a break for the back door."

Whereupon the man of bottles made a kindly but peremptory gesture. The drummer obeyed it, and, finding himself seated on a box with his head below the level of the bar, balm was laid upon his soul at sight of various zinc and copper fittings that bore a resemblance to armor plate. The barkeeper took a seat comfortably upon an adjacent box.

"You see," he whispered, "this here Scratchy Wilson is a wonder with a gun—a perfect wonder—and when he goes on the war trail, we hunt our holes—naturally. He's about the last one of the old gang that used to hang out along the river here. He's a terror when he's drunk. When he's sober he's all right—kind of simple—wouldn't hurt a fly—nicest fellow in town. But when he's drunk—whoo!"

There were periods of stillness. "I wish Jack Potter was back from San Anton'," said the barkeeper. "He shot Wilson up once—in the leg—and he would sail in and pull out the kinks in this thing."

Presently they heard from a distance the sound of a shot, followed by three wild yowls. It instantly removed a bond from the men in the darkened saloon. There was a shuffling of feet. They looked at each other. "Here he comes," they said.

III

A man in a maroon-colored flannel shirt, which had been purchased for purposes of decoration, and made principally by some Jewish women on the East Side of New York, rounded a corner and walked into the middle of the main street of Yellow Sky. In either hand the man held a long, heavy, blue-black revolver. Often he yelled, and these cries rang through a semblance of a deserted village, shrilly flying over the roofs in a volume that seemed to have no relation to the ordinary vocal strength of a man. It was as if the surrounding stillness formed the arch of a tomb over him. These cries of ferocious challenge rang against walls of silence. And his boots had red tops with gilded imprints, of the kind beloved in winter by little sledding boys on the hillsides of New England.

The man's face flamed in a rage begot of whiskey. His eyes, rolling, and yet keen for ambush, hunted the still doorways and windows. He walked with the creeping movement of the midnight cat. As it occurred to him, he roared menacing information. The long revolvers in his hands were as easy as straws; they were moved with an electric swiftness. The little fingers of each hand played sometimes in a musician's way. Plain from the low collar of the shirt, the cords of his neck straightened and sank, straightened and sank, as passion moved him. The only sounds were his terrible invitations. The calm adobes preserved their demeanor at the passing of this small thing in the middle of the street.

There was no offer of fight—no offer of fight. The man called to the sky. There were no attractions. He bellowed and fumed and swayed his revolvers here and everywhere.

The dog of the barkeeper of the Weary Gentleman saloon had not appreciated the advance of events. He yet lay dozing in front of his master's door. At sight of the dog, the man paused and raised his revolver humorously. At sight of the man, the dog sprang up and walked diagonally away, with a sullen head, and growling. The man yelled, and the dog broke into a gallop. As it was about to enter an alley, there was a loud noise, a whistling, and something spat the ground directly before it. The dog screamed, and, wheeling in terror, galloped headlong in a new direction. Again there was a noise, a whistling, and sand was kicked viciously before it. Fear-stricken, the dog turned and flurried like an animal in a pen. The man stood laughing, his weapons at his hips.

Ultimately the man was attracted by the closed door of the Weary Gentleman saloon. He went to it and, hammering with a revolver, demanded drink.

The door remaining imperturbable, he picked a bit of paper from the walk, and nailed it to the framework with a knife. He then turned his back contemptuously upon this popular resort and, walking to the opposite side of the street and spinning there on his heel quickly and lithely, fired at the bit of paper. He missed it by a half-inch. He swore at himself, and went away. Later, he comfortably fusilladed the windows of his most intimate friend. The man was playing with this town. It was a toy for him.

But still there was no offer of fight. The name of Jack Potter, his ancient antagonist, entered his mind, and he concluded that it would be a glad thing if he should go to Potter's house, and by bombardment induce him to come out and fight. He moved in the direction of his desire, chanting Apache scalp-music.

When he arrived at it, Potter's house presented the same still front as had the other adobes. Taking up a strategic position, the man howled a challenge. But this house regarded him as might a great stone god. It gave no sign. After a decent wait, the man howled further challenges, mingling with them wonderful epithets.

Presently there came the spectacle of a man churning himself into deepest rage over the immobility of a house. He fumed at it as the winter wind attacks a prairie cabin in the North. To the distance there should have gone the sound of a tumult like the fighting of two hundred Mexicans. As necessity bade him, he paused for breath or to reload his revolvers.

IV

Potter and his bride walked sheepishly and with speed. Sometimes they laughed together shamefacedly and low.

"Next corner, dear," he said finally.

They put forth the efforts of a pair walking bowed against a strong wind. Potter was about to raise a finger to point the first appearance of the new home when, as they circled the corner, they came face to face with a man in a maroon-colored shirt, who was feverishly pushing cartridges into a large revolver. Upon the instant the man dropped his revolver to the ground, and, like lightning, whipped another from its holster. The second weapon was aimed at the bridegroom's chest.

There was a silence. Potter's mouth seemed to be merely a grave for his tongue. He exhibited an instinct to at once loosen his arm from the woman's grip, and he dropped the bag to the sand. As for the bride, her face had gone as yellow as old cloth. She was a slave to hideous rites, gazing at the apparitional snake.

The two men faced each other at a distance of three paces. He of the revolver smiled with a new and quiet ferocity.

"Tried to sneak up on me," he said. "Tried to sneak up on me!" His eyes grew more baleful. As Potter made a slight movement, the man thrust his revolver venomously forward. "No; don't you do it, Jack Potter. Don't you move a finger toward a gun just yet. Don't you move an eyelash. The time has come for me to settle with you, and I'm goin' to do it my own way, and loaf along with no interferin'. So if you don't want a gun bent on you, just mind what I tell you."

Potter looked at his enemy. "I ain't got a gun on me, Scratchy," he said. "Honest, I ain't." He was stiffening and steadying, but yet somewhere at the back of his mind a vision of the Pullman floated: the sea-green figured velvet, the shining brass, silver, and glass, the wood that gleamed as darkly brilliant as the surface of a pool of oil—all the glory of the marriage, the environment of the new estate. "You know I fight when it comes to fighting, Scratchy Wilson; but I ain't got a gun on me. You'll have to do all the shootin' yourself."

His enemy's face went livid. He stepped forward, and lashed his weapon to and fro before Potter's chest. "Don't you tell me you ain't got no gun on you, you whelp. Don't tell me no lie like that. There ain't a man in Texas ever seen you without no gun. Don't take me for no kid." His eyes blazed with light, and his throat worked like a pump.

"I ain't takin' you for no kid," answered Potter. His heels had not moved an inch backward. "I'm takin' you for a damn fool. I tell you I ain't got a gun, and I ain't. If you're goin' to shoot me up, you better begin now. You'll never get a chance like this again."

So much enforced reasoning had told on Wilson's rage. He was calmer. "If you ain't got a gun, why ain't you got a gun?" he sneered. "Been to Sunday school?"

"I ain't got a gun because I've just come from San Anton' with my wife. I'm married," said Potter. "And if I'd thought there was going to be any galoots like you prowling around when I brought my wife home, I'd had a gun, and don't you forget it."

"Married!" said Scratchy, not at all comprehending.

"Yes, married. I'm married," said Potter, distinctly.

"Married?" said Scratchy. Seemingly for the first time, he saw the drooping, drowning woman at the other man's side. "No!" he said. He was like a creature allowed a glimpse of another world. He moved a pace backward, and his arm, with the revolver, dropped to his side. "Is this the lady?" he asked.

"Yes; this is the lady," answered Potter.

There was another period of silence.

"Well," said Wilson at last, slowly, "I s'pose it's all off now."

"It's all off if you say so, Scratchy. You know I didn't make the trouble." Potter lifted his valise.

"Well, I 'low it's off, Jack," said Wilson. He was looking at the ground. "Married!" He was not a student of chivalry; it was merely that in the presence of this foreign condition he was a simple child of the earlier plains. He picked up his starboard revolver, and, placing both weapons in their holsters, he went away. His feet made funnel-shaped tracks in the heavy sand.

From *The Open Boat and Other Tales of
Adventure* (1898)

·Edith Wharton·

ROMAN FEVER

I

From the table at which they had been lunching two American ladies of ripe but well-cared-for middle age moved across the lofty terrace of the Roman restaurant and, leaning on its parapet, looked first at each other, and then down on the outspread glories of the Palatine and the Forum, with the same expression of vague but benevolent approval.

As they leaned there a girlish voice echoed up gaily from the stairs leading to the court below. "Well, come along, then," it cried, not to them but to an invisible companion, "and let's leave the young things to their knitting"; and a voice as fresh laughed back: "Oh, look here, Babs, not actually *knitting*—" "Well, I mean figuratively," rejoined the first. "After all, we haven't left our poor parents much else to do. . . ." and at that point the turn of the stairs engulfed the dialogue.

The two ladies looked at each other again, this time with a tinge of smiling embarrassment, and the smaller and paler one shook her head and colored slightly.

"Barbara!" she murmured, sending an unheard rebuke after the mocking voice in the stairway.

The other lady, who was fuller, and higher in color, with a small determined nose supported by vigorous black eyebrows, gave a good-humored laugh. "That's what our daughters think of us!"

Her companion replied by a deprecating gesture. "Not of us individually. We must remember that. It's just the collective modern idea of Mothers. And you see—" Half-guiltily she drew from her handsomely mounted black handbag a twist of crimson silk run through by two fine knitting needles. "One never knows," she murmured. "The new system has certainly given us a good deal of time to kill; and sometimes I get tired just looking—even at this." Her gesture was now addressed to the stupendous scene at their feet.

The dark lady laughed again, and they both relapsed upon the view, contemplating it in silence, with a sort of diffused serenity which might have been borrowed from the spring effulgence of the Roman skies. The luncheon hour was long past, and the two had their end of the vast terrace to themselves. At its opposite extremity a few groups, detained by a lingering look at the outspread city, were gathering up guide-books and fumbling for tips. The last of them scattered, and the two ladies were alone on the air-washed height.

"Well, I don't see why we shouldn't just stay here," said Mrs. Slade, the lady of the high color and energetic brows. Two derelict basket chairs stood near, and she pushed them into the angle of the parapet, and settled herself in one, her gaze upon the Palatine. "After all, it's still the most beautiful view in the world."

"It always will be, to me," assented her friend Mrs. Ansley, with so slight a stress on the "me" that Mrs. Slade, though she noticed it, wondered if it were not merely accidental, like the random underlinings of old-fashioned letter writers.

"Grace Ansley was always old-fashioned," she thought; and added aloud, with a retrospective smile: "It's a view we've both been familiar with for a good many years. When we first met here we were younger than our girls are now. You remember?"

"Oh, yes, I remember," murmured Mrs. Ansley, with the same undefinable stress. "There's that headwaiter wondering," she interpolated. She was evidently far less sure than her companion of herself and of her rights in the world.

"I'll cure him of wondering," said Mrs. Slade, stretching her hand toward a bag as discreetly opulent-looking as Mrs. Ansley's. Signing to the headwaiter, she explained that she and her friend were old lovers of Rome, and would like to spend the end of the afternoon looking down on the view—that is, if it did not disturb the service? The headwaiter, bowing over her gratuity, assured her that the ladies were most welcome, and would be still more so if they would condescend to remain for dinner. A full-moon night, they would remember. . . .

Mrs. Slade's black brows drew together, as though references to the moon were out of place and even unwelcome. But she smiled away her frown as the headwaiter retreated. "Well, why not? We might do worse. There's no knowing, I suppose, when the girls will be back. Do you even know back from *where*? I don't!"

Mrs. Ansley again colored slightly. "I think those young Italian aviators we met at the Embassy invited them to fly to Tarquinia for tea. I suppose they'll want to wait and fly back by moonlight."

"Moonlight—moonlight! What a part it still plays. Do you suppose they're as sentimental as we were?"

"I've come to the conclusion that I don't in the least know what they are," said Mrs. Ansley. "And perhaps we didn't know much more about each other."

"No; perhaps we didn't."

Her friend gave her a shy glance. "I never should have supposed you were sentimental, Alida."

"Well, perhaps I wasn't." Mrs. Slade drew her lids together in retrospect; and for a few moments the two ladies, who had been intimate since childhood, reflected how little they knew each other. Each one, of course, had a label ready to attach to the other's name; Mrs. Delphin Slade, for instance, would have told herself, or anyone who asked her, that Mrs. Horace Ansley, twenty-five years ago, had been exquisitely lovely—no, you wouldn't believe it, would you? . . . though, of course, still charming, distinguished. . . . Well, as a girl she had been exquisite; far more beautiful than her daughter Barbara, though certainly Babs, according to the new standards at any rate, was more effective—had more *edge*, as they say. Funny where she got it, with those two nullities as parents. Yes; Horace Ansley was—well, just the duplicate of his wife. Museum specimens of old New York. Good-looking, irreproachable, exemplary. Mrs. Slade and Mrs. Ansley had lived opposite each other— actually as well as figuratively—for years. When the drawing-room curtains in No. 20 East 73rd Street were renewed, No. 23, across the way, was always aware of it. And of all the movings, buyings, travels, anniversaries, illnesses—the tame chronicle of an estimable pair. Little of it escaped Mrs. Slade. But she had grown bored with it by the time her husband made his big *coup* in Wall Street, and when they bought in upper Park Avenue had already begun to think: "I'd rather live opposite a speakeasy for a change; at least one might see it raided." The idea of seeing Grace raided was so amusing that (before the move) she launched it at a woman's lunch. It made a hit, and went the rounds—she sometimes wondered if it had crossed the street, and reached Mrs. Ansley. She hoped not, but didn't much mind. Those were the days when respectability was at a discount, and it did the irreproachable no harm to laugh at them a little.

A few years later, and not many months apart, both ladies lost their husbands. There was an appropriate exchange of wreaths and condolences, and a brief renewal of intimacy in the half-shadow of their mourning; and now, after another interval, they had run across each other in Rome, at the same hotel, each of them the modest appendage of a salient daughter. The similarity of their lot had again drawn them together, lending itself to mild jokes, and the mutual confession that, if in old days it must have been tiring to "keep up" with daughters, it was now, at times, a little dull not to.

No doubt, Mrs. Slade reflected, she felt her unemployment more than poor Grace ever would. It was a big drop from being the wife of Delphin Slade to being his widow. She had always regarded herself (with a certain conjugal pride) as his equal in social gifts, as contributing her full share to the making of the exceptional couple they were: but the difference after his death was irremediable. As the wife of the famous corporation lawyer, always with an international case or two on hand, every day brought its exciting and unexpected obligation: the impromptu entertaining of eminent colleagues from abroad, the hurried dashes on legal business to London, Paris or Rome, where the entertaining was so handsomely reciprocated; the amusement of hearing in her wake: "What, that handsome woman with the good clothes and the eyes is Mrs. Slade—*the* Slade's wife? Really? Generally the wives of celebrities are such frumps."

Yes; being *the* Slade's widow was a dullish business after that. In living up to such a husband all her faculties had been engaged; now she had only her daughter to live up to, for the son who seemed to have inherited his father's gifts had died suddenly in boyhood. She had fought through that agony because her husband was there, to be helped and to help; now, after the father's death, the thought of the boy had become unbearable. There was nothing left but to mother her daughter; and dear Jenny was such a perfect daughter that she needed no excessive mothering. "Now with Babs Ansley I don't know that I *should* be so quiet," Mrs. Slade sometimes half-enviously reflected; but Jenny, who was younger than her brilliant friend, was that rare accident, an extremely pretty girl who somehow made youth and prettiness seem as safe as their absence. It was all perplexing—and to Mrs. Slade a little boring. She wished that Jenny would fall in love—with the wrong man, even; that she might have to be watched, out-maneuvered, rescued. And instead, it was Jenny who watched her mother, kept her out of drafts, made sure that she had taken her tonic. . . .

Mrs. Ansley was much less articulate than her friend, and her mental portrait of Mrs. Slade was slighter, and drawn with fainter touches. "Alida Slade's awfully brilliant; but not as brilliant as she thinks," would have summed it up; though she would have added, for the enlightenment of strangers, that Mrs. Slade had been an extremely dashing girl; much more so than her daughter, who was pretty, of course, and clever in a way, but had none of her mother's—well, "vividness," someone had once called it. Mrs. Ansley would take up current words like this, and cite them in quotation marks, as unheard-of audacities. No; Jenny was not like her mother. Sometimes Mrs. Ansley thought Alida Slade was disappointed; on the whole she had had a sad life. Full of failures and mistakes; Mrs. Ansley had always been rather sorry for her. . . .

So these two ladies visualized each other, each through the wrong end of her little telescope.

II

For a long time they continued to sit side by side without speaking. It seemed as though, to both, there was a relief in laying down their somewhat futile activities in the presence of the vast Memento Mori[1] which faced them. Mrs. Slade sat quite still, her eyes fixed on the golden slope of the Palace of the Caesars, and after a while Mrs. Ansley ceased to fidget with her bag, and she too sank into meditation. Like many intimate friends, the two ladies had never before had occasion to be silent together, and Mrs. Ansley was slightly embarrassed by what seemed, after so many years, a new stage in their intimacy, and one with which she did not yet know how to deal.

Suddenly the air was full of that deep clangor of bells which periodically covers Rome with a roof of silver. Mrs. Slade glanced at her wristwatch. "Five o'clock already," she said, as though surprised.

Mrs. Ansley suggested interrogatively: "There's bridge at the Embassy at five." For a long time Mrs. Slade did not answer. She appeared to be lost in contemplation, and Mrs. Ansley thought the remark had escaped her. But after a while she said, as if speaking out of a dream: "Bridge, did you say? Not unless you want to. . . . But I don't think I will, you know."

"Oh, no," Mrs. Ansley hastened to assure her. "I don't care to at all. It's so lovely here; and so full of old memories, as you say." She settled herself in her chair, and almost furtively drew forth her knitting. Mrs. Slade took sideway note of this activity, but her own beautifully cared-for hands remained motionless on her knee.

"I was just thinking," she said slowly, "what different things Rome stands for to each generation of travelers. To our grandmothers, Roman fever; to our mothers, sentimental dangers—how we used to be guarded!—to our daughters, no more dangers than the middle of Main Street. They don't know it—but how much they're missing!"

The long golden light was beginning to pale, and Mrs. Ansley

1. Latin for "Remember that you die." The phrase is applied to any symbolic reminder of death or the passage of time, in this instance the landscape and monuments of ancient Rome.

lifted her knitting a little closer to her eyes. "Yes; how we were guarded!"

"I always used to think," Mrs. Slade continued, "that our mothers had a much more difficult job than our grandmothers. When Roman fever stalked the streets it must have been comparatively easy to gather in the girls at the danger hour; but when you and I were young, with such beauty calling us, and the spice of disobedience thrown in, and no worse risk than catching cold during the cool hour after sunset, the mothers used to be put to it to keep us in—didn't they?"

She turned again toward Mrs. Ansley, but the latter had reached a delicate point in her knitting. "One, two, three—slip two; yes, they must have been," she assented, without looking up.

Mrs. Slade's eyes rested on her with a deepened attention. "She can knit—in the face of *this!* How like her. . . ."

Mrs. Slade leaned back, brooding, her eyes ranging from the ruins which faced her to the long green hollow of the Forum, the fading glow of the church fronts beyond it, and the outlying immensity of the Colosseum. Suddenly she thought: "It's all very well to say that our girls have done away with sentiment and moonlight. But if Babs Ansley isn't out to catch the young aviator—the one who's a Marchese—then I don't know anything. And Jenny has no chance beside her. I know that too. I wonder if that's why Grace Ansley likes the two girls to go everywhere together? My poor Jenny as a foil—!" Mrs. Slade gave a hardly audible laugh, and at the sound Mrs. Ansley dropped her knitting.

"Yes—?"

"I—oh, nothing. I was only thinking how your Babs carries everything before her. That Campolieri boy is one of the best matches in Rome. Don't look so innocent, my dear—you know he is. And I was wondering, ever so respectfully, you understand . . . wondering how two such exemplary characters as you and Horace had managed to produce anything quite so dynamic." Mrs. Slade laughed again, with a touch of asperity.

Mrs. Ansley's hands lay inert across her needles. She looked straight out at the great accumulated wreckage of passion and splendor at her feet. But her small profile was almost expressionless. At length she said: "I think you overrate Babs, my dear."

Mrs. Slade's tone grew easier. "No; I don't. I appreciate her. And perhaps envy you. Oh, my girl's perfect; if I were a chronic invalid I'd—well, I think I'd rather be in Jenny's hands. There must be times . . . but there! I always wanted a brilliant daughter . . . and never quite understood why I got an angel instead."

Mrs. Ansley echoed her laugh in a faint murmur. "Babs is an angel too."

"Of course—of course! But she's got rainbow wings. Well, they're wandering by the sea with their young men; and here we sit . . . and it all brings back the past a little too acutely."

Mrs. Ansley had resumed her knitting. One might almost have imagined (if one had known her less well, Mrs. Slade reflected) that, for her also, too many memories rose from the lengthening shadows of those august ruins. But no; she was simply absorbed in her work. What was there for her to worry about? She knew that Babs would almost certainly come back engaged to the extremely eligible Campolieri. "And she'll sell the New York house, and settle down near them in Rome, and never be in their way . . . she's much too tactful. But she'll have an excellent cook, and just the right people in for bridge and cocktails . . . and a perfectly peaceful old age among her grandchildren."

Mrs. Slade broke off this prophetic flight with a recoil of self-disgust. There was no one of whom she had less right to think unkindly than of Grace Ansley. Would she never cure herself of envying her? Perhaps she had begun too long ago.

She stood up and leaned against the parapet, filling her troubled eyes with the tranquilizing magic of the hour. But instead of tranquilizing her the sight seemed to increase her exasperation. Her gaze turned toward the Colosseum. Already its golden flank was drowned in purple shadow, and above it the sky curved crystal clear, without light or color. It was the moment when afternoon and evening hang balanced in mid-heaven.

Mrs. Slade turned back and laid her hand on her friend's arm. The gesture was so abrupt that Mrs. Ansley looked up, startled.

"The sun's set. You're not afraid, my dear?"

"Afraid—?"

"Of Roman fever or pneumonia? I remember how ill you were that winter. As a girl you had a very delicate throat, hadn't you?"

"Oh, we're all right up here. Down below, in the Forum, it does get deathly cold, all of a sudden . . . but not here."

"Ah, of course you know because you had to be so careful." Mrs. Slade turned back to the parapet. She thought: "I must make one more effort not to hate her." Aloud she said: "Whenever I look at the Forum from up here, I remember that story about a great-aunt of yours, wasn't she? A dreadfully wicked great-aunt?"

"Oh, yes; great-aunt Harriet. The one who was supposed to have sent her young sister out to the Forum after sunset to gather a night-blooming flower for her album. All our great-aunts and grandmothers used to have albums of dried flowers."

Mrs. Slade nodded. "But she really sent her because they were in love with the same man—"

"Well, that was the family tradition. They said Aunt Harriet confessed it years afterward. At any rate, the poor little sister caught the fever and died. Mother used to frighten us with the story when we were children."

"And you frightened *me* with it, that winter when you and I were here as girls. The winter I was engaged to Delphin."

Mrs. Ansley gave a faint laugh. "Oh, did I? Really frightened you? I don't believe you're easily frightened."

"Not often; but I was then. I was easily frightened because I was too happy. I wonder if you know what that means?"

"I—yes . . ." Mrs. Ansley faltered.

"Well, I suppose that was why the story of your wicked aunt made such an impression on me. And I thought: 'There's no more Roman fever, but the Forum is deathly cold after sunset—especially after a hot day. And the Colosseum's even colder and damper'."

"The Colosseum—?"

"Yes. It wasn't easy to get in, after the gates were locked for the night. Far from easy. Still, in those days it could be managed; it *was* managed, often. Lovers met there who couldn't meet elsewhere. You knew that?"

"I—I dare say. I don't remember."

"You don't remember? You don't remember going to visit some ruins or other one evening, just after dark, and catching a bad chill? You were supposed to have gone to see the moon rise. People always said that expedition was what caused your illness."

There was a moment's silence; then Mrs. Ansley rejoined: "Did they? It was all so long ago."

"Yes. And you got well again—so it didn't matter. But I suppose it struck your friends—the reason given for your illness. I mean— because everybody knew you were so prudent on account of your throat, and your mother took such care of you. . . . You *had* been out late sight-seeing, hadn't you, that night?"

"Perhaps I had. The most prudent girls aren't always prudent. What made you think of it now?"

Mrs. Slade seemed to have no answer ready. But after a moment she broke out: "Because I simply can't bear it any longer—!"

Mrs. Ansley lifted her head quickly. Her eyes were wide and very pale. "Can't bear what?"

"Why—your not knowing that I've always known why you went."

"Why I went—?"

"Yes. You think I'm bluffing, don't you? Well, you went to meet the man I was engaged to—and I can repeat every word of the letter that took you there."

While Mrs. Slade spoke Mrs. Ansley had risen unsteadily to her feet. Her bag, her knitting and gloves, slid in a panic-stricken heap to the ground. She looked at Mrs. Slade as though she were looking at a ghost.

"No, no—don't," she faltered out.

"Why not? Listen, if you don't believe me. 'My one darling, things can't go on like this. I must see you alone. Come to the Colosseum immediately after dark tomorrow. There will be somebody to let you in. No one whom you need fear will suspect'—but perhaps you've forgotten what the letter said?"

Mrs. Ansley met the challenge with an unexpected composure. Steadying herself against the chair she looked at her friend, and replied: "No; I know it by heart too."

"And the signature? 'Only *your* D.S.' Was that it? I'm right, am I? That was the letter that took you out that evening after dark?"

Mrs. Ansley was still looking at her. It seemed to Mrs. Slade that a slow struggle was going on behind the voluntarily controlled mask of her small quiet face. "I shouldn't have thought she had herself so well in hand," Mrs. Slade reflected, almost resentfully. But at this moment Mrs. Ansley spoke. "I don't know how you knew. I burnt that letter at once."

"Yes; you would, naturally—you're so prudent!" The sneer was open now. "And if you burnt the letter you're wondering how on earth I know what was in it. That's it, isn't it?"

Mrs. Slade waited, but Mrs. Ansley did not speak.

"Well, my dear, I know what was in that letter because I wrote it!"

"You wrote it?"

"Yes."

The two women stood for a minute staring at each other in the last golden light. Then Mrs. Ansley dropped back into her chair. "Oh," she murmured, and covered her face with her hands.

Mrs. Slade waited nervously for another word or movement. None came, and at length she broke out: "I horrify you."

Mrs. Ansley's hands dropped to her knee. The face they uncovered was streaked with tears. "I wasn't thinking of you. I was thinking—it was the only letter I ever had from him!"

"And I wrote it. Yes; I wrote it! But I was the girl he was engaged to. Did you happen to remember that?"

Mrs. Ansley's head drooped again. "I'm not trying to excuse myself . . . I remembered. . . ."

"And still you went?"

"Still I went."

Mrs. Slade stood looking down on the small bowed figure at her side. The flame of her wrath had already sunk, and she wondered why she had ever thought there would be any satisfaction in inflicting so purposeless a wound on her friend. But she had to justify herself.

"You do understand? I'd found out—and I hated you, hated you. I knew you were in love with Delphin—and I was afraid; afraid of you, of your quiet ways, your sweetness . . . your . . . well, I wanted you out of the way, that's all. Just for a few weeks; just till I was sure of him. So in a blind fury I wrote that letter. . . . I don't know why I'm telling you now."

"I suppose," said Mrs. Ansley slowly, "it's because you've always gone on hating me."

"Perhaps. Or because I wanted to get the whole thing off my mind." She paused. "I'm glad you destroyed the letter. Of course I never thought you'd die."

Mrs. Ansley relapsed into silence, and Mrs. Slade, leaning above her, was conscious of a strange sense of isolation, of being cut off from the warm current of human communion. "You think me a monster!"

"I don't know. . . . It was the only letter I had, and you say he didn't write it?"

"Ah, how you care for him still!"

"I cared for that memory," said Mrs. Ansley.

Mrs. Slade continued to look down on her. She seemed physically reduced by the blow—as if, when she got up, the wind might scatter her like a puff of dust. Mrs. Slade's jealousy suddenly leapt up again at the sight. All these years the woman had been living on that letter. How she must have loved him, to treasure the mere memory of its ashes! The letter of the man her friend was engaged to. Wasn't it she who was the monster?

"You tried your best to get him away from me, didn't you? But you failed; and I kept him. That's all."

"Yes. That's all."

"I wish now I hadn't told you. I'd no idea you'd feel about it as you do; I thought you'd be amused. It all happened so long ago, as you say; and you must do me the justice to remember that I had no reason to think you'd ever taken it seriously. How could I, when you were married to Horace Ansley two months afterward? As soon as you could get out of bed your mother rushed you off to Florence and married you. People were rather surprised—they wondered at its being done so quickly; but I thought I knew. I had an idea you did it out of *pique*—to be able to say you'd got ahead of Delphin and me. Girls have such silly reasons for doing the most serious things. And your marrying so soon convinced me that you'd never really cared."

"Yes. I suppose it would," Mrs. Ansley assented.

The clear heaven overhead was emptied of all its gold. Dusk

spread over it, abruptly darkening the Seven Hills. Here and there lights began to twinkle through the foliage at their feet. Steps were coming and going on the deserted terrace—waiters looking out of the doorway at the head of the stairs, then reappearing with trays and napkins and flasks of wine. Tables were moved, chairs straightened. A feeble string of electric lights flickered out. Some vases of faded flowers were carried away, and brought back replenished. A stout lady in a dust coat suddenly appeared, asking in broken Italian if anyone had seen the elastic band which held together her tattered Baedeker.[2] She poked with her stick under the table at which she had lunched, the waiters assisting.

The corner where Mrs. Slade and Mrs. Ansley sat was still shadowy and deserted. For a long time neither of them spoke. At length Mrs. Slade began again: "I suppose I did it as a sort of joke—"

"A joke?"

"Well, girls are ferocious sometimes, you know. Girls in love especially. And I remember laughing to myself all that evening at the idea that you were waiting around there in the dark, dodging out of sight, listening for every sound, trying to get in— Of course I was upset when I heard you were so ill afterward."

Mrs. Ansley had not moved for a long time. But now she turned slowly toward her companion. "But I didn't wait. He'd arranged everything. He was there. We were let in at once," she said.

Mrs. Slade sprang up from her leaning position. "Delphin there? They let you in?—Ah, now you're lying!" she burst out with violence.

Mrs. Ansley's voice grew clearer, and full of surprise. "But of course he was there. Naturally he came—"

"Came? How did he know he'd find you there? You must be raving!"

Mrs. Ansley hesitated, as though reflecting. "But I answered the letter. I told him I'd be there. So he came."

Mrs. Slade flung her hands up to her face. "Oh, God—you answered! I never thought of your answering. . . ."

"It's odd you never thought of it, if you wrote the letter."

"Yes. I was blind with rage."

Mrs. Ansley rose, and drew her fur scarf about her. "It is cold here. We'd better go. . . . I'm sorry for you," she said, as she clasped the fur about her throat.

The unexpected words sent a pang through Mrs. Slade. "Yes; we'd better go." She gathered up her bag and cloak. "I don't know why you should be sorry for me," she muttered.

2. Karl Baedeker (1801–59), a German publisher, produced a series of guidebooks to European countries and cities. These "Baedekers" were immensely popular in the nineteenth and early twentieth centuries, and went through many editions.

Mrs. Ansley stood looking away from her toward the dusky secret mass of the Colosseum. "Well—because I didn't have to wait that night."

Mrs. Slade gave an unquiet laugh. "Yes; I was beaten there. But I oughtn't to begrudge it to you, I suppose. At the end of all these years. After all, I had everything; I had him for twenty-five years. And you had nothing but that one letter that he didn't write."

Mrs. Ansley was again silent. At length she turned toward the door of the terrace. She took a step, and turned back, facing her companion.

"I had Barbara," she said, and began to move ahead of Mrs. Slade toward the stairway.

From *The World Over* (1936)

·Sherwood Anderson·

I WANT TO KNOW WHY

We got up at four in the morning, that first day in the east. On the evening before we had climbed off a freight train at the edge of town, and with the true instinct of Kentucky boys had found our way across town and to the race track and the stables at once. Then we knew we were all right. Hanley Turner right away found a nigger we knew. It was Bildad Johnson who in the winter works at Ed Becker's livery barn in our home town, Beckersville. Bildad is a good cook as almost all our niggers are and of course he, like everyone in our part of Kentucky who is anyone at all, likes the horses. In the spring Bildad begins to scratch around. A nigger from our country can flatter and wheedle anyone into letting him do most anything he wants. Bildad wheedles the stable men and the trainers from the horse farms in our country around Lexington. The trainers come into town in the evening to stand around and talk and maybe get into a poker game. Bildad gets in with them. He is always doing little favors and telling about things to eat, chicken browned in a pan, and how is the best way to cook sweet potatoes and corn bread. It makes your mouth water to hear him.

When the racing season comes on and the horses go to the races and there is all the talk on the streets in the evenings about the new colts, and everyone says when they are going over to Lexington or to the spring meeting at Churchhill Downs or to Latonia, and the horsemen that have been down to New Orleans or maybe at the winter meeting at Havana in Cuba come home to spend a week before they start out again, at such a time when everything talked about in Beckersville is just horses and nothing else and the outfits start out and horse racing is in every breath of air you breathe, Bildad shows up with a job as cook for some outfit. Often when I think about it, his always going all season to the races and working in the livery barn in the winter where horses are and where men like to come and talk about horses, I wish I was a nigger. It's a foolish thing to say, but that's the way I am about being around horses, just crazy. I can't help it.

Well, I must tell you about what we did and let you in on what I'm talking about. Four of us boys from Beckersville, all whites and sons of men who live in Beckersville regular, made up our minds we were going to the races, not just to Lexington or Louisville, I don't mean, but to the big eastern track we were always hearing our Beckersville men talk about, to Saratoga. We were all pretty young then. I was just turned fifteen and I was the oldest of the four. It was my scheme, I admit that and I talked the others into trying it. There was Hanley Turner and Henry Rieback and Tom Tumberton and•myself. I had thirty-seven dollars I had earned during the winter working nights and Saturdays in Enoch Myer's grocery. Henry Rieback had eleven dollars and the others, Hanley and Tom had only a dollar or two each. We fixed it all up and laid low until the Kentucky spring meetings were over and some of our men, the sportiest ones, the ones we envied the most, had cut out—then we cut out too.

I won't tell you the trouble we had beating our way on freights and all. We went through Cleveland and Buffalo and other cities and saw Niagara Falls. We bought things there, souvenirs and spoons and cards and shells with pictures of the falls on them for our sisters and mothers, but thought we had better not send any of the things home. We didn't want to put the folks on our trail and maybe be nabbed.

We got into Saratoga as I said at night and went to the track. Bildad fed us up. He showed us a place to sleep in hay over a shed and promised to keep still. Niggers are all right about things like that. They won't squeal on you. Often a white man you might meet, when you had run away from home like that, might appear to be all right and give you a quarter or a half dollar or something, and then go right and give you away. White men will do that, but not a nigger. You can trust them. They are squarer with kids. I don't know why.

At the Saratoga meeting that year there were a lot of men from home. Dave Williams and Arthur Mulford and Jerry Myers and others. Then there was a lot from Louisville and Lexington Henry Rieback knew but I didn't. They were professional gamblers and Henry Rieback's father is one too. He is what is called a sheet writer and goes away most of the year to tracks. In the winter when he is home in Beckersville he don't stay there much but goes away to cities and deals faro. He is a nice man and generous, is always sending Henry presents, a bicycle and a gold watch and a boy scout suit of clothes and things like that.

My own father is a lawyer. He's all right, but don't make much money and can't buy me things and anyway I'm getting so old now I don't expect it. He never said nothing to me against Henry, but Hanley Turner and Tom Tumberton's fathers did. They said to their boys that money so come by is no good and they didn't want their boys brought up to hear gamblers' talk and be thinking about such things and maybe embrace them.

That's all right and I guess the men know what they are talking about, but I don't see what it's got to do with Henry or with horses either. That's what I'm writing this story about. I'm puzzled. I'm getting to be a man and want to think straight and be O.K., and there's something I saw at the race meeting at the eastern track I can't figure out.

I can't help it. I'm crazy about thoroughbred horses. I've always been that way. When I was ten years old and saw I was growing to be big and couldn't be a rider I was so sorry I nearly died. Harry Hellinfinger in Beckersville, whose father is Postmaster, is grown up and too lazy to work, but likes to stand around in the street and get up jokes on boys like sending them to a hardware store for a gimlet to bore square holes and other jokes like that. He played one on me. He told me that if I would eat a half a cigar I would be stunted and not grow any more and maybe could be a rider. I did it. When father wasn't looking I took a cigar out of his pocket and gagged it down some way. It made me awful sick and the doctor had to be sent for, and then it did no good. I kept right on growing. It was a joke. When I told what I had done and why most fathers would have whipped me but mine didn't.

Well, I didn't get stunted and didn't die. It serves Harry Hellinfinger right. Then I made up my mind I would like to be a stable boy, but had to give that up too. Mostly niggers do that work and I knew father wouldn't let me go into it. No use to ask him.

If you've never been crazy about thoroughbreds it's because you've never been around where they are much and don't know any better. They're beautiful. There isn't anything so lovely and clean and full of spunk and honest and everything as some race horses. On the big horse farms that are all around our town Beckersville there are tracks and the horses run in the early morning. More than a thousand times I've got out of bed before daylight and walked two or three miles to the tracks. Mother wouldn't of let me go but father always says, "Let him alone." So I got some bread out of the bread box and some butter and jam, gobbled it and lit out.

At the tracks you sit on the fence with men, whites and niggers, and they chew tobacco and talk, and then the colts are brought out. It's early and the grass is covered with shiny dew and in another field a man is plowing and they are frying things in a shed where the track niggers sleep, and you know how a nigger can giggle and laugh and say things that make you laugh. A white man can't do it and some niggers can't but a track nigger can every time.

And so the colts are brought out and some are just galloped by stable boys, but almost every morning on a big track owned by a rich man who lives maybe in New York, there are always, nearly every morning, a few colts and some of the old race horses and geldings and mares that are cut loose.

It brings a lump up into my throat when a horse runs. I don't mean all horses but some. I can pick them nearly every time. It's in my blood like in the blood of race track niggers and trainers. Even when they just go slop-jogging along with a little nigger on their backs I can tell a winner. If my throat hurts and it's hard for me to swallow, that's him. He'll run like Sam Hill when you let him out. If he don't win every time it'll be a wonder and because they've got him in a pocket behind another or he was pulled or got off bad at the post or something. If I wanted to be a gambler like Henry Rieback's father I could get rich. I know I could and Henry says so too. All I would have to do is to wait 'til that hurt comes when I see a horse and then bet every cent. That's what I would do if I wanted to be a gambler, but I don't.

When you're at the tracks in the morning—not the race tracks but the training tracks around Beckersville—you don't see a horse, the kind I've been talking about, very often, but it's nice anyway. Any thoroughbred, that is sired right and out of a good mare and trained by a man that knows how, can run. If he couldn't what would he be there for and not pulling a plow?

Well, out of the stables they come and the boys are on their backs and it's lovely to be there. You hunch down on top of the fence and itch inside you. Over in the sheds the niggers giggle and sing. Bacon is being fried and coffee made. Everything smells lovely. Nothing smells better than coffee and manure and horses and niggers and bacon frying and pipes being smoked out of doors on a morning like that. It just gets you, that's what it does.

But about Saratoga. We was there six days and not a soul from home seen us and everything came off just as we wanted it to, fine weather and horses and races and all. We beat our way home and Bildad gave us a basket with fried chicken and bread and other eatables in, and I had eighteen dollars when we got back to Beckersville. Mother jawed and cried but Pop didn't say much. I told everything we done except one thing. I did and saw that alone. That's what I'm writing about. It got me upset. I think about it at night. Here it is.

At Saratoga we laid up nights in the hay in the shed Bildad had showed us and ate with the niggers early and at night when the race people had all gone away. The men from home stayed mostly in the grandstand and betting field, and didn't come out around the places where the horses are kept except to the paddocks just before a race when the horses are saddled. At Saratoga they don't have paddocks under an open shed as at Lexington and Churchill Downs and other tracks down in our country, but saddle the horses right out in an open place under trees on a lawn as smooth and nice as Banker Bohon's front yard here in Beckersville. It's lovely. The horses are sweaty and nervous and shine and the men come out and smoke cigars and look at them and the trainers are there and the owners, and your heart thumps so you can hardly breathe.

Then the bugle blows for post and the boys that ride come running out with their silk clothes on and you run to get a place by the fence with the niggers.

I always am wanting to be a trainer or owner, and at the risk of being seen and caught and sent home I went to the paddocks before every race. The other boys didn't but I did.

We got to Saratoga on a Friday and on Wednesday the next week the big Mullford Handicap was to be run. Middlestride was in it and Sunstreak. The weather was fine and the track fast. I couldn't sleep the night before.

What had happened was that both these horses are the kind it makes my throat hurt to see. Middlestride is long and looks awkward and is a gelding. He belongs to Joe Thompson, a little owner from home who only has a half dozen horses. The Mullford Handicap is for a mile and Middlestride can't untrack fast. He goes away slow and is always way back at the half, then he begins to run and if the race is a mile and a quarter he'll just eat up everything and get there.

Sunstreak is different. He is a stallion and nervous and belongs on the biggest farm we've got in our country, the Van Riddle place that belongs to Mr. Van Riddle of New York. Sunstreak is like a girl you think about sometimes but never see. He is hard all over and lovely too. When you look at his head you want to kiss him. He is trained by Jerry Tillford who knows me and has been good to me lots of times, lets me walk into a horse's stall to look at him close and other things. There isn't anything as sweet as that horse. He stands at the post quiet and not letting on, but he is just burning up inside. Then when the barrier goes up he is off like his name, Sunstreak. It makes you ache to see him. It hurts you. He just lays down and runs like a bird dog. There can't anything I ever see run like him except Middlestride when he gets untracked and stretches himself.

Gee! I ached to see that race and those two horses run, ached and dreaded it too. I didn't want to see either of our horses beaten. We had never sent a pair like that to the races before. Old men in Beckersville said so and the niggers said so. It was a fact.

Before the race I went over to the paddocks to see. I looked a last look at Middlestride, who isn't such a much standing in a paddock that way, then I went to see Sunstreak.

It was his day. I knew when I see him. I forgot all about being seen myself and walked right up. All the men from Beckersville were there and no one noticed me except Jerry Tillford. He saw me and something happened. I'll tell you about that.

I was standing looking at that horse and aching. In some way, I can't tell how, I knew just how Sunstreak felt inside. He was quiet and letting the niggers rub his legs and Mr. Van Riddle himself put the saddle on, but he was just a raging torrent inside. He was like the water in the river at Niagara Falls just before it goes plunk down. That horse wasn't thinking about running. He don't have to think about that. He was just thinking about holding himself back 'til the time for the running came. I knew that. I could just in a way see right inside him. He was going to do some awful running and I knew it. He wasn't bragging or letting on much or prancing or making a fuss, but just waiting. I knew it and Jerry Tillford his trainer knew. I looked up and then that man and I looked into each other's eyes. Something happened to me. I guess I loved the man as much as I did the horse because he knew what I knew. Seemed to me there wasn't anything in the world but that man and the horse and me. I cried and Jerry Tillford had a shine in his eyes. Then I came away to the fence to wait for the race. The horse was better than me, more steadier, and now I know better than Jerry. He was the quietest and he had to do the running.

Sunstreak ran first of course and he busted the world's record for a mile. I've seen that if I never see anything more. Everything came out just as I expected. Middlestride got left at the post and was way back and closed up to be second, just as I knew he would. He'll get a world's record too some day. They can't skin the Beckersville country on horses.

I watched the race calm because I knew what would happen. I was sure. Hanley Turner and Henry Rieback and Tom Tumberton were all more excited than me.

A funny thing had happened to me. I was thinking about Jerry Tillford the trainer and how happy he was all through the race. I liked him that afternoon even more than I ever liked my own father. I almost forgot the horses thinking that way about him. It was because of what I had seen in his eyes as he stood in the paddocks beside Sunstreak before the race started. I knew he had been watching and working with Sunstreak since the horse was a baby colt, had taught him to run and be patient and when to let himself out and not to quit, never. I knew that for him it was like a mother seeing her child do something brave or wonderful. It was the first time I ever felt for a man like that.

After the race that night I cut out from Tom and Hanley and Henry. I wanted to be by myself and I wanted to be near Jerry Tillford if I could work it. Here is what happened.

The track in Saratoga is near the edge of town. It is all polished up and trees around, the evergreen kind, and grass and everything painted and nice. If you go past the track you get to a hard road made of asphalt for automobiles, and if you go along this for a few miles there is a road turns off to a little rummy-looking farm house set in a yard.

That night after the race I went along that road because I had seen Jerry and some other men go that way in an automobile. I didn't expect to find them. I walked for a ways and then sat down by a fence to think. It was the direction they went in. I wanted to be as near Jerry as I could. I felt close to him. Pretty soon I went up the side road—I don't know why—and came to the rummy farm house. I was just lonesome to see Jerry, like wanting to see your father at night when you are a young kid. Just then an automobile came along and turned in. Jerry was in it and Henry Rieback's father, and Arthur Bedford from home, and Dave Williams and two other men I didn't know. They got out of the car and went into the house, all but Henry Rieback's father who quarreled with them and said he wouldn't go. It was only about nine o'clock, but they were all drunk and the rummy looking farm house was a place for bad women to stay in. That's what it was. I crept up along a fence and looked through a window and saw.

It's what give me the fantods.[1] I can't make it out. The women in the house were all ugly mean-looking women, not nice to look at or be near. They were homely too, except one who was tall and looked a little like the gelding Middlestride, but not clean like him, but with a hard ugly mouth. She had red hair. I saw everything plain. I got up by an old rose bush by an open window and looked. The women had on loose dresses and sat around in chairs. The men came in and some sat on the women's laps. The place smelled rotten and there was rotten talk, the kind a kid hears around a livery stable in a town like Beckersville in the winter but don't ever ex-

---

1. A state of acute worry and irritability.

pect to hear talked when there are women around. It was rotten. A
nigger wouldn't go into such a place.

I looked at Jerry Tillford. I've told you how I had been feeling
about him on account of his knowing what was going on inside of
Sunstreak in the minute before he went to the post for the race in
which he made a world's record.

Jerry bragged in that bad woman house as I know Sunstreak
wouldn't never have bragged. He said that he made that horse, that
it was him that won the race and made the record. He lied and
bragged like a fool. I never heard such silly talk.

And then, what do you suppose he did! He looked at the woman
in there, the one that was lean and hard-mouthed and looked a little
like the gelding Middlestride, but not clean like him, and his eyes
began to shine just as they did when he looked at me and at Sunstreak in the paddocks at the track in the afternoon. I stood there by
the window—gee!—but I wished I hadn't gone away from the
tracks, but had stayed with the boys and the niggers and the horses.
The tall rotten looking woman was between us just as Sunstreak
was in the paddocks in the afternoon.

Then, all of a sudden, I began to hate that man. I wanted to
scream and rush in the room and kill him. I never had such a feeling before. I was so mad clean through that I cried and my fists
were doubled up so my finger nails cut my hands.

And Jerry's eyes kept shining and he waved back and forth, and
then he went and kissed that woman and I crept away and went
back to the tracks and to bed and didn't sleep hardly any, and then
next day I got the other kids to start home with me and never told
them anything I seen.

I been thinking about it ever since. I can't make it out. Spring has
come again and I'm nearly sixteen and go to the tracks mornings
same as always, and I see Sunstreak and Middlestride and a new
colt named Strident I'll bet will lay them all out, but no one thinks
so but me and two or three niggers.

But things are different. At the tracks the air don't taste as good or
smell as good. It's because a man like Jerry Tillford, who knows
what he does, could see a horse like Sunstreak run, and kiss a
woman like that the same day. I can't make it out. Darn him, what
did he want to do like that for? I keep thinking about it and it spoils
looking at horses and smelling things and hearing niggers laugh
and everything. Sometimes I'm so mad about it I want to fight
someone. It gives me the fantods. What did he do it for? I want to
know why.

From *The Triumph of the Egg* (1921;
first published in 1918)

·F. Scott Fitzgerald·

BABYLON REVISITED

I

"And where's Mr. Campbell?" Charlie asked.

"Gone to Switzerland. Mr. Campbell's a pretty sick man, Mr. Wales."

"I'm sorry to hear that. And George Hardt?" Charlie inquired.

"Back in America, gone to work."

"And where is the Snow Bird?"

"He was in here last week. Anyway, his friend, Mr. Schaeffer, is in Paris."

Two familiar names from the long list of a year and a half ago. Charlie scribbled an address in his notebook and tore out the page.

"If you see Mr. Schaeffer, give him this," he said. "It's my brother-in-law's address. I haven't settled on a hotel yet."

He was not really disappointed to find Paris was so empty. But the stillness in the Ritz bar was strange and portentous. It was not an American bar any more—he felt polite in it, and not as if he owned it. It had gone back into France. He felt the stillness from the moment he got out of the taxi and saw the doorman, usually in a frenzy of activity at this hour, gossiping with a *chasseur* [1] by the servants' entrance.

Passing through the corridor, he heard only a single, bored voice in the once-clamorous women's room. When he turned into the bar he travelled the twenty feet of green carpet with his eyes fixed straight ahead by old habit; and then, with his foot firmly on the rail, he turned and surveyed the room, encountering only a single

1. Hotel porter.

pair of eyes that fluttered up from a newspaper in the corner. Charlie asked for the head barman, Paul, who in the latter days of the
bull market had come to work in his own custom-built car—disembarking, however, with due nicety at the nearest corner. But Paul
was at his country house today and Alix giving him information.

"No, no more," Charlie said, "I'm going slow these days."

Alix congratulated him: "You were going pretty strong a couple of
years ago."

"I'll stick to it all right," Charlie assured him. "I've stuck to it for
over a year and a half now."

"How do you find conditions in America?"

"I haven't been to America for months. I'm in business in Prague,
representing a couple of concerns there. They don't know about me
down there."

Alix smiled.

"Remember the night of George Hardt's bachelor dinner here?"
said Charlie. "By the way, what's become of Claude Fessenden?"

Alix lowered his voice confidentially: "He's in Paris, but he
doesn't come here any more. Paul doesn't allow it. He ran up a bill
of thirty thousand francs, charging all his drinks and his lunches,
and usually his dinner, for more than a year. And when Paul finally
told him he had to pay, he gave him a bad check."

Alix shook his head sadly.

"I don't understand it, such a dandy fellow. Now he's all bloated
up—" He made a plump apple of his hands.

Charlie watched a group of strident queens [2] installing themselves in a corner.

"Nothing affects them," he thought. "Stocks rise and fall, people
loaf or work, but they go on forever." The place oppressed him. He
called for the dice and shook with Alix for the drink.

"Here for long, Mr. Wales?"

"I'm here for four or five days to see my little girl."

"Oh-h! You have a little girl?"

Outside, the fire-red, gas-blue, ghost-green signs shone smokily
through the tranquil rain. It was late afternoon and the streets were
in movement; the *bistros* [3] gleamed. At the corner of the Boulevard
des Capucines he took a taxi. The Place de la Concorde moved by
in pink majesty; they crossed the logical Seine, and Charlie felt the
sudden provincial quality of the left bank.

Charlie directed his taxi to the Avenue de l'Opera, which was out
of his way. But he wanted to see the blue hour spread over the magnificent facade, and imagine that the cab horns, playing endlessly
the first few bars of *Le Plus que Lent*, were the trumpets of the Sec-

2. Homosexuals.
3. Small bars or restaurants.

ond Empire.[4] They were closing the iron grill in front of Brentano's Book-store, and people were already at dinner behind the trim little bourgeois hedge of Duval's. He had never eaten at a really cheap restaurant in Paris. Five-course dinner, four francs fifty, eighteen cents, wine included. For some odd reason he wished that he had.

As they rolled on to the Left Bank and he felt its sudden provincialism, he thought, "I spoiled this city for myself. I didn't realize it, but the days came along one after another, and then two years were gone, and everything was gone, and I was gone."

He was thirty-five, and good to look at. The Irish mobility of his face was sobered by a deep wrinkle between his eyes. As he rang his brother-in-law's bell in the Rue Palatine, the wrinkle deepened till it pulled down his brows; he felt a cramping sensation in his belly. From behind the maid who opened the door darted a lovely little girl of nine who shrieked "Daddy!" and flew up, struggling like a fish, into his arms. She pulled his head around by one ear and set her cheek against his.

"My old pie," he said.

"Oh, daddy, daddy, daddy, daddy, dads, dads, dads!"

She drew him into the salon, where the family waited, a boy and girl his daughter's age, his sister-in-law and her husband. He greeted Marion with his voice pitched carefully to avoid either feigned enthusiasm or dislike, but her response was more frankly tepid, though she minimized her expression of unalterable distrust by directing her regard toward his child. The two men clasped hands in a friendly way and Lincoln Peters rested his for a moment on Charlie's shoulder.

The room was warm and comfortably American. The three children moved intimately about, playing through the yellow oblongs that led to other rooms; the cheer of six o'clock spoke in the eager smacks of the fire and the sounds of French activity in the kitchen. But Charlie did not relax; his heart sat up rigidly in his body and he drew confidence from his daughter, who from time to time came close to him, holding in her arms the doll he had brought.

"Really extremely well," he declared in answer to Lincoln's question. "There's a lot of business there that isn't moving at all, but we're doing even better than ever. In fact, damn well. I'm bringing my sister over from America next month to keep house for me. My income last year was bigger than it was when I had money. You see, the Czechs—"

4. *Le Plus que Lent,* "The Slowest of the Slow," is probably a reference to the well-known waltz "La plus que lent" by Claude Debussy (1862–1918). Debussy said of his melody: "Let us think of cabarets, let us think also of the numerous 'five o'clocks' where the beautiful feminine listeners of whom I thought, meet." The Second Empire of Napoleon III (1851–70) was in its early days a time of great stability and luxury. The entire passage is a fantasy of lost romance and confidence.

His boasting was for a specific purpose; but after a moment, seeing a faint restiveness in Lincoln's eye, he changed the subject:

"Those are fine children of yours, well brought up, good manners."

"We think Honoria's a great little girl too."

Marion Peters came back from the kitchen. She was a tall woman with worried eyes, who had once possessed a fresh American loveliness. Charlie had never been sensitive to it and was always surprised when people spoke of how pretty she had been. From the first there had been an instinctive antipathy between them.

"Well, how do you find Honoria?" she asked.

"Wonderful. I was astonished how much she's grown in ten months. All the children are looking well."

"We haven't had a doctor for a year. How do you like being back in Paris?"

"It seems very funny to see so few Americans around."

"I'm delighted," Marion said vehemently. "Now at least you can go into a store without their assuming you're a millionaire. We've suffered like everybody, but on the whole it's a good deal pleasanter."

"But it was nice while it lasted," Charlie said. "We were a sort of royalty, almost infallible, with a sort of magic around us. In the bar this afternoon"—he stumbled, seeing his mistake—"there wasn't a man I knew."

She looked at him keenly. "I should think you'd have had enough of bars."

"I only stayed a minute. I take one drink every afternoon, and no more."

"Don't you want a cocktail before dinner?" Lincoln asked.

"I take only one drink every afternoon, and I've had that."

"I hope you keep to it," said Marion.

Her dislike was evident in the coldness with which she spoke, but Charlie only smiled; he had larger plans. Her very aggressiveness gave him an advantage, and he knew enough to wait. He wanted them to initiate the discussion of what they knew had brought him to Paris.

At dinner he couldn't decide whether Honoria was most like him or her mother. Fortunate if she didn't combine the traits of both that had brought them to disaster. A great wave of protectiveness went over him. He thought he knew what to do for her. He believed in character; he wanted to jump back a whole generation and trust in character again as the eternally valuable element. Everything wore out.

He left soon after dinner, but not to go home. He was curious to see Paris by night with clearer and more judicious eyes than those of other days. He bought a *strapontin* [5] for the Casino and watched Josephine Baker [6] go through her chocolate arabesques.

After an hour he left and strolled toward Montmartre, up the Rue Pigalle into the Place Blanche. The rain had stopped and there were a few people in evening clothes disembarking from taxis in front of cabarets, and *cocottes* [7] prowling singly or in pairs, and many Negroes. He passed a lighted door from which issued music, and stopped with the sense of familiarity; it was Bricktop's, where he had parted with so many hours and so much money. A few doors farther on he found another ancient rendezvous and incautiously put his head inside. Immediately an eager orchestra burst into sound, a pair of professional dancers leaped to their feet and a maître d'hôtel [8] swooped toward him, crying, "Crowd just arriving, sir!" But he withdrew quickly.

"You have to be damn drunk," he thought.

Zelli's was closed, the bleak and sinister cheap hotels surrounding it were dark; up in the Rue Blanche there was more light and a local, colloquial French crowd. The Poet's Cave had disappeared, but the two great mouths of the Café of Heaven and the Café of Hell still yawned—even devoured, as he watched, the meagre contents of a tourist bus—a German, a Japanese, and an American couple who glanced at him with frightened eyes.

So much for the effort and ingenuity of Montmartre. All the catering to vice and waste was on an utterly childish scale, and he suddenly realized the meaning of the word "dissipate"—to dissipate into thin air; to make nothing out of something. In the little hours of the night every move from place to place was an enormous human jump, an increase of paying for the privilege of slower and slower motion.

He remembered thousand-franc notes given to an orchestra for playing a single number, hundred-franc notes tossed to a doorman for calling a cab.

But it hadn't been given for nothing.

It had been given, even the most wildly squandered sum, as an offering to destiny that he might not remember the things most worth remembering, the things that now he would always remember—his child taken from his control, his wife escaped to a grave in Vermont.

In the glare of a *brasserie* [9] a woman spoke to him. He bought her

---

5. Folding seat.
6. Josephine Baker (1906—), Black American singer and dancer, was a sensation in the Paris of the 1920s, performing at the Folies Bergère and the Casino de Paris.
7. Prostitutes.
8. Headwaiter.
9. Tavern serving beer and food.

some eggs and coffee, and then, eluding her encouraging stare, gave her a twenty-franc note and took a taxi to his hotel.

II

He woke upon a fine fall day—football weather. The depression of yesterday was gone and he liked the people on the streets. At noon he sat opposite Honoria at Le Grand Vatel, the only restaurant he could think of not reminiscent of champagne dinners and long luncheons that began at two and ended in a blurred and vague twilight.

"Now, how about vegetables? Oughtn't you to have some vegetables?"

"Well, yes."

"Here's *épinards* and *chou-fleur* and carrots and *haricots*." [10]

"I'd like *chou-fleur*."

"Wouldn't you like to have two vegetables?"

"I usually only have one at lunch."

The waiter was pretending to be inordinately fond of children. *"Qu'elle est mignonne la petite! Elle parle exactement comme une française."* [11]

"How about dessert? Shall we wait and see?"

The waiter disappeared. Honoria looked at her father expectantly.

"What are we going to do?"

"First, we're going to that toy store in the Rue Saint-Honoré and buy you anything you like. And then we're going to the vaudeville at the Empire."

She hesitated. "I like it about the vaudeville, but not the toy store."

"Why not?"

"Well, you brought me this doll." She had it with her. "And I've got lots of things. And we're not rich any more, are we?"

"We never were. But today you are to have anything you want."

"All right," she agreed resignedly.

When there had been her mother and a French nurse he had been inclined to be strict; now he extended himself, reached out for a new tolerance; he must be both parents to her and not shut any of her out of communication.

"I want to get to know you," he said gravely. "First let me introduce myself. My name is Charles J. Wales, of Prague."

"Oh, daddy!" her voice cracked with laughter.

10. "Spinach and cauliflower and carrots and French beans."
11. "What a darling child! She speaks just like a native."

"And who are you, please?" he persisted, and she accepted a rôle immediately: "Honoria Wales, Rue Palatine, Paris."

"Married or single?"

"No, not married. Single."

He indicated the doll. "But I see you have a child, madame."

Unwilling to disinherit it, she took it to her heart and thought quickly: "Yes, I've been married, but I'm not married now. My husband is dead."

He went on quickly, "And the child's name?"

"Simone. That's after my best friend at school."

"I'm very pleased that you're doing so well at school."

"I'm third this month," she boasted. "Elsie"—that was her cousin—"is only about eighteenth, and Richard is about at the bottom."

"You like Richard and Elsie, don't you?"

"Oh, yes. I like Richard quite well and I like her all right."

Cautiously and casually he asked: "And Aunt Marion and Uncle Lincoln—which do you like best?"

"Oh, Uncle Lincoln, I guess."

He was increasingly aware of her presence. As they came in, a murmur of ". . . adorable" followed them, and now the people at the next table bent all their silences upon her, staring as if she were something no more conscious than a flower.

"Why don't I live with you?" she asked suddenly. "Because mama's dead?"

"You must stay here and learn more French. It would have been hard for daddy to take care of you so well."

"I don't really need much taking care of any more. I do everything for myself."

Going out of the restaurant, a man and a woman unexpectedly hailed him!

"Well, the old Wales!"

"Hello there, Lorraine. . . . Dunc."

Sudden ghosts out of the past: Duncan Schaeffer, a friend from college. Lorraine Quarrles, a lovely, pale blonde of thirty; one of a crowd who had helped them make months into days in the lavish times of three years ago.

"My husband couldn't come this year," she said, in answer to his question. "We're poor as hell. So he gave me two hundred a month and told me I could do my worst on that. . . . This your little girl?"

"What about coming back and sitting down?" Duncan asked.

"Can't do it." He was glad for an excuse. As always, he felt Lorraine's passionate, provocative attraction, but his own rhythm was different now.

"Well, how about dinner?" she asked.

"I'm not free. Give me your address and let me call you."

"Charlie, I believe you're sober," she said judicially. "I honestly believe he's sober, Dunc. Pinch him and see if he's sober."

Charlie indicated Honoria with his head. They both laughed.

"What's your address?" said Duncan sceptically.

He hesitated, unwilling to give the name of his hotel.

"I'm not settled yet. I'd better call you. We're going to see the vaudeville at the Empire."

"There! That's what I want to do," Lorraine said. "I want to see some clowns and acrobats and jugglers. That's just what we'll do, Dunc."

"We've got to do an errand first," said Charlie. "Perhaps we'll see you there."

"All right, you snob. . . . Good-by, beautiful little girl."

"Good-by."

Honoria bobbed politely.

Somehow, an unwelcome encounter. They liked him because he was functioning, because he was serious; they wanted to see him, because he was stronger than they were now, because they wanted to draw a certain sustenance from his strength.

At the Empire, Honoria proudly refused to sit upon her father's folded coat. She was already an individual with a code of her own, and Charlie was more and more absorbed by the desire of putting a little of himself into her before she crystallized utterly. It was hopeless to try to know her in so short a time.

Between the acts they came upon Duncan and Lorraine in the lobby where the band was playing.

"Have a drink?"

"All right, but not up at the bar. We'll take a table."

"The perfect father."

Listening abstractedly to Lorraine, Charlie watched Honoria's eyes leave their table, and he followed them wistfully about the room, wondering what they saw. He met her glance and she smiled.

"I like that lemonade," she said.

What had she said? What had he expected? Going home in a taxi afterward, he pulled her over until her head rested against his chest.

"Darling, do you ever think about your mother?"

"Yes, sometimes," she answered vaguely.

"I don't want you to forget her. Have you got a picture of her?"

"Yes, I think so. Anyhow, Aunt Marion has. Why don't you want me to forget her?"

"She loved you very much."

"I loved her too."

They were silent for a moment.

"Daddy, I want to come and live with you," she said suddenly.

His heart leaped; he had wanted it to come like this.

"Aren't you perfectly happy?"

"Yes, but I love you better than anybody. And you love me better than anybody, don't you, now that mummy's dead?"

"Of course I do. But you won't always like me best, honey. You'll grow up and meet somebody your own age and go marry him and forget you ever had a daddy."

"Yes, that's true," she agreed tranquilly.

He didn't go in. He was coming back at nine o'clock and he wanted to keep himself fresh and new for the thing he must say then.

"When you're safe inside, just show yourself in that window."

"All right. Good-by, dads, dads, dads, dads."

He waited in the dark street until she appeared, all warm and glowing, in the window above and kissed her fingers out into the night.

III

They were waiting. Marion sat behind the coffee service in a dignified black dinner dress that just faintly suggested mourning. Lincoln was walking up and down with the animation of one who had already been talking. They were as anxious as he was to get into the question. He opened it almost immediately:

"I suppose you know what I want to see you about—why I really came to Paris."

Marion played with the black stars on her necklace and frowned.

"I'm awfully anxious to have a home," he continued. "And I'm awfully anxious to have Honoria in it. I appreciate your taking in Honoria for her mother's sake, but things have changed now"—he hesitated and then continued more forcibly—"changed radically with me, and I want to ask you to reconsider the matter. It would be silly for me to deny that about three years ago I was acting badly—"

Marion looked up at him with hard eyes.

"—but all that's over. As I told you, I haven't had more than a drink a day for over a year, and I take that drink deliberately, so that the idea of alcohol won't get too big in my imagination. You see the idea?"

"No," said Marion succinctly.

"It's a sort of stunt I set myself. It keeps the matter in proportion."

"I get you," said Lincoln. "You don't want to admit it's got any attraction for you."

"Something like that. Sometimes I forget and don't take it. But I try to take it. Anyhow, I couldn't afford to drink in my position. The people I represent are more than satisfied with what I've done, and I'm bringing my sister over from Burlington to keep house for me, and I want awfully to have Honoria too. You know that even when her mother and I weren't getting along well we never let anything that happened touch Honoria. I know she's fond of me and I know I'm able to take care of her and—well, there you are. How do you feel about it?"

He knew that now he would have to take a beating. It would last an hour or two hours, and it would be difficult, but if he modulated his inevitable resentment to the chastened attitude of the reformed sinner, he might win his point in the end.

Keep your temper, he told himself. You don't want to be justified. You want Honoria.

Lincoln spoke first: "We've been talking it over ever since we got your letter last month. We're happy to have Honoria here. She's a dear little thing, and we're glad to be able to help her, but of course that isn't the question—"

Marion interrupted suddenly. "How long are you going to stay sober, Charlie?" she asked.

"Permanently, I hope."

"How can anybody count on that?"

"You know I never did drink heavily until I gave up business and came over here with nothing to do. Then Helen and I began to run around with—"

"Please leave Helen out of it. I can't bear to hear you talk about her like that."

He stared at her grimly; he had never been certain how fond of each other the sisters were in life.

"My drinking only lasted about a year and a half—from the time we came over until I—collapsed."

"It was time enough."

"It was time enough," he agreed.

"My duty is entirely to Helen," she said. "I try to think what she would have wanted me to do. Frankly, from the night you did that terrible thing you haven't really existed for me. I can't help that. She was my sister."

"Yes."

"When she was dying she asked me to look out for Honoria. If you hadn't been in a sanitarium then, it might have helped matters."

He had no answer.

"I'll never in my life be able to forget the morning when Helen knocked at my door, soaked to the skin and shivering, and said you'd locked her out."

Charlie gripped the sides of the chair. This was more difficult than he expected; he wanted to launch out into a long expostulation and explanation, but he only said: "The night I locked her out—" and she interrupted, "I don't feel up to going over that again."

After a moment's silence Lincoln said: "We're getting off the subject. You want Marion to set aside her legal guardianship and give you Honoria. I think the main point for her is whether she has confidence in you or not."

"I don't blame Marion," Charlie said slowly, "but I think she can have entire confidence in me. I had a good record up to three years ago. Of course, it's within human possibilities I might go wrong any time. But if we wait much longer I'll lose Honoria's childhood and my chance for a home." He shook his head, "I'll simply lose her, don't you see?"

"Yes, I see," said Lincoln.

"Why didn't you think of all this before?" Marion asked.

"I suppose I did, from time to time, but Helen and I were getting along badly. When I consented to the guardianship, I was flat on my back in a sanitarium and the market had cleaned me out. I knew I'd acted badly, and I thought if it would bring any peace to Helen, I'd agree to anything. But now it's different. I'm functioning, I'm behaving damn well, so far as—"

"Please don't swear at me," Marion said.

He looked at her, startled. With each remark the force of her dislike became more and more apparent. She had built up all her fear of life into one wall and faced it toward him. This trivial reproof was possibly the result of some trouble with the cook several hours before. Charlie became increasingly alarmed at leaving Honoria in this atmosphere of hostility against himself; sooner or later it would come out, in a word here, a shake of the head there, and some of that distrust would be irrevocably implanted in Honoria. But he pulled his temper down out of his face and shut it up inside him; he had won a point, for Lincoln realized the absurdity of Marion's remark and asked her lightly since when she had objected to the word "damn."

"Another thing," Charlie said: "I'm able to give her certain advantages now. I'm going to take a French governess to Prague with me. I've got a lease on a new apartment—"

He stopped, realizing that he was blundering. They couldn't be expected to accept with equanimity the fact that his income was again twice as large as their own.

"I suppose you can give her more luxuries than we can," said

Marion. "When you were throwing away money we were living along watching every ten francs. . . . I suppose you'll start doing it again."

"Oh, no," he said. "I've learned. I worked hard for ten years, you know—until I got lucky in the market, like so many people. Terribly lucky. It didn't seem any use working any more, so I quit. It won't happen again."

There was a long silence. All of them felt their nerves straining, and for the first time in a year Charlie wanted a drink. He was sure now that Lincoln Peters wanted him to have his child.

Marion shuddered suddenly; part of her saw that Charlie's feet were planted on the earth now, and her own maternal feeling recognized the naturalness of his desire; but she had lived for a long time with a prejudice—a prejudice founded on a curious disbelief in her sister's happiness, and which, in the shock of one terrible night, had turned to hatred for him. It had all happened at a point in her life where the discouragement of ill health and adverse circumstances made it necessary for her to believe in tangible villainy and a tangible villain.

"I can't help what I think!" she cried out suddenly. "How much you were responsible for Helen's death, I don't know. It's something you'll have to square with your own conscience."

An electric current of agony surged through him; for a moment he was almost on his feet, an unuttered sound echoing in his throat. He hung on to himself for a moment, another moment.

"Hold on there," said Lincoln uncomfortably. "I never thought you were responsible for that."

"Helen died of heart trouble," Charlie said dully.

"Yes, heart trouble." Marion spoke as if the phrase had another meaning for her.

Then, in the flatness that followed her outburst, she saw him plainly and she knew he had somehow arrived at control over the situation. Glancing at her husband, she found no help from him, and as abruptly as if it were a matter of no importance, she threw up the sponge.

"Do what you like!" she cried, springing up from her chair. "She's your child. I'm not the person to stand in your way. I think if it were my child I'd rather see her—" She managed to check herself. "You two decide it. I can't stand this. I'm sick. I'm going to bed."

She hurried from the room; after a moment Lincoln said:

"This has been a hard day for her. You know how strongly she feels—" His voice was almost apologetic: "When a woman gets an idea in her head."

"Of course."

"It's going to be all right. I think she sees now that you—can provide for the child, and so we can't very well stand in your way or Honoria's way."

"Thank you, Lincoln."

"I'd better go along and see how she is."

"I'm going."

He was still trembling when he reached the street, but a walk down the Rue Bonaparte to the quais set him up, and as he crossed the Seine, fresh and new by the quai lamps, he felt exultant. But back in his room he couldn't sleep. The image of Helen haunted him. Helen whom he had loved so until they had senselessly begun to abuse each other's love, tear it into shreds. On that terrible February night that Marion remembered so vividly, a slow quarrel had gone on for hours. There was a scene at the Florida, and then he attempted to take her home, and then she kissed young Webb at a table; after that there was what she had hysterically said. When he arrived home alone he turned the key in the lock in wild anger. How could he know she would arrive an hour later alone, that there would be a snowstorm in which she wandered about in slippers, too confused to find a taxi? Then the aftermath, her escaping pneumonia by a miracle, and all the attendant horror. They were "reconciled," but that was the beginning of the end, and Marion, who had seen with her own eyes and who imagined it to be one of many scenes from her sister's martyrdom, never forgot.

Going over it again brought Helen nearer, and in the white, soft light that steals upon half sleep near morning he found himself talking to her again. She said that he was perfectly right about Honoria and she wanted Honoria to be with him. She said she was glad he was being good and doing better. She said a lot of other things— very friendly things—but she was in a swing in a white dress, and swinging faster and faster all the time, so that at the end he could not hear clearly all that she said.

IV

He woke up feeling happy. The door of the world was open again. He made plans, vistas, futures for Honoria and himself, but suddenly he grew sad, remembering all the plans he and Helen had made. She had not planned to die. The present was the thing— work to do and someone to love. But not to love too much, for he knew the injury that a father can do to a daughter or a mother to a son by attaching them too closely; afterward, out in the world, the child would seek in the marriage partner the same blind tenderness and, failing probably to find it, turn against love and life.

It was another bright, crisp day. He called Lincoln Peters at the bank where he worked and asked if he could count on taking Honoria when he left for Prague. Lincoln agreed that there was no reason for delay. One thing—the legal guardianship. Marion wanted to retain that a while longer. She was upset by the whole matter, and it would oil things if she felt that the situation was still in her control for another year. Charlie agreed, wanted only the tangible, visible child.

Then the question of a governess. Charlie sat in a gloomy agency and talked to a cross Bernaise and to a buxom Breton peasant, neither of whom he could have endured. There were others whom he would see tomorrow.

He lunched with Lincoln Peters at Griffons, trying to keep down his exultation.

"There's nothing quite like your own child," Lincoln said. "But you understand how Marion feels too."

"She's forgotten how hard I worked for seven years there," Charlie said. "She just remembers one night."

"There's another thing." Lincoln hesitated. "While you and Helen were tearing around Europe throwing money away, we were just getting along. I didn't touch any of the prosperity because I never got ahead enough to carry anything but my insurance. I think Marion felt there was some kind of injustice in it—you not even working toward the end, and getting richer and richer."

"It went just as quick as it came," said Charlie.

"Yes, a lot of it stayed in the hands of *chasseurs* and saxophone players and maîtres d'hôtel—well, the big party's over now. I just said that to explain Marion's feeling about those crazy years. If you drop in about six o'clock tonight before Marion's too tired, we'll settle the details on the spot."

Back at his hotel, Charlie found a *pneumatique* [12] that had been redirected from the Ritz bar where Charlie had left his address for the purpose of finding a certain man.

> DEAR CHARLIE: You were so strange when we saw you the other day that I wondered if I did something to offend you. If so, I'm not conscious of it. In fact, I have thought about you too much for the last year, and it's always been in the back of my mind that I might see you if I came over here. We *did* have such good times that crazy spring, like the night you and I stole the butcher's tricycle, and the time we tried to call on the president and you had the old derby rim and the wire cane. Everybody seems so old lately, but I don't feel old a bit. Couldn't we get together some time today for old time's sake? I've got a vile hang-over for the moment, but will be feeling better this afternoon and will look for you about five in the sweat-shop at the Ritz.
>
> Always devotedly,
> LORRAINE.

12. Express letter delivered in Paris by a system of pneumatic tubes.

His first feeling was one of awe that he had actually, in his mature years, stolen a tricycle and pedalled Lorraine all over the Étoile between the small hours and dawn. In retrospect it was a nightmare. Locking out Helen didn't fit in with any other act of his life, but the tricycle incident did—it was one of many. How many weeks or months of dissipation to arrive at that condition of utter irresponsibility?

He tried to picture how Lorraine had appeared to him then—very attractive; Helen was unhappy about it, though she said nothing. Yesterday, in the restaurant, Lorraine had seemed trite, blurred, worn away. He emphatically did not want to see her, and he was glad Alix had not given away his hotel address. It was a relief to think, instead, of Honoria, to think of Sundays spent with her and of saying good morning to her and of knowing she was there in his house at night, drawing her breath in the darkness.

At five he took a taxi and bought presents for all the Peters—a piquant cloth doll, a box of Roman soldiers, flowers for Marion, big linen handkerchiefs for Lincoln.

He saw, when he arrived in the apartment, that Marion had accepted the inevitable. She greeted him now as though he were a recalcitrant member of the family, rather than a menacing outsider. Honoria had been told she was going; Charlie was glad to see that her tact made her conceal her excessive happiness. Only on his lap did she whisper her delight and the question "When?" before she slipped away with the other children.

He and Marion were alone for a minute in the room, and on an impulse he spoke out boldly:

"Family quarrels are bitter things. They don't go according to any rules. They're not like aches or wounds; they're more like splits in the skin that won't heal because there's not enough material. I wish you and I could be on better terms."

"Some things are hard to forget," she answered. "It's a question of confidence." There was no answer to this and presently she asked, "When do you propose to take her?"

"As soon as I can get a governess. I hoped the day after tomorrow."

"That's impossible. I've got to get her things in shape. Not before Saturday."

He yielded. Coming back into the room, Lincoln offered him a drink.

"I'll take my daily whisky," he said.

It was warm here, it was a home, people together by a fire. The children felt very safe and important; the mother and father were serious, watchful. They had things to do for the children more important than his visit here. A spoonful of medicine was, after all, more important than the strained relations between Marion and himself. They were not dull people, but they were very much in the grip of life and circumstances. He wondered if he couldn't do something to get Lincoln out of his rut at the bank.

A long peal at the door-bell; the *bonne à toute faire* [13] passed through and went down the corridor. The door opened upon another long ring, and then voices, and the three in the salon looked up expectantly; Richard moved to bring the corridor within his range of vision, and Marion rose. Then the maid came back along the corridor, closely followed by the voices, which developed under the light into Duncan Schaeffer and Lorraine Quarrles.

They were gay, they were hilarious, they were roaring with laughter. For a moment Charlie was astounded; unable to understand how they ferreted out the Peters' address.

"Ah-h-h!" Duncan wagged his finger roguishly at Charlie. "Ah-h-h!"

They both slid down another cascade of laughter. Anxious and at a loss, Charlie shook hands with them quickly and presented them to Lincoln and Marion. Marion nodded, scarcely speaking. She had drawn back a step toward the fire; her little girl stood beside her, and Marion put an arm about her shoulder.

With growing annoyance at the intrusion, Charlie waited for them to explain themselves. After some concentration Duncan said:

"We came to invite you out to dinner. Lorraine and I insist that all this shishi, cagy business 'bout your address got to stop."

Charlie came closer to them, as if to force them backward down the corridor.

"Sorry, but I can't. Tell me where you'll be and I'll phone you in half an hour."

This made no impression. Lorraine sat down suddenly on the side of a chair, and focussing her eyes on Richard, cried, "Oh, what a nice little boy! Come here, little boy." Richard glanced at his mother, but did not move. With a perceptible shrug of her shoulders, Lorraine turned back to Charlie:

"Come and dine. Sure your cousins won' mine. See you so sel'om. Or solemn."

"I can't," said Charlie sharply. "You two have dinner and I'll phone you."

Her voice became suddenly unpleasant. "All right, we'll go. But I remember once when you hammered on my door at four A.M. I was enough of a good sport to give you a drink. Come on, Dunc."

Still in slow motion, with blurred, angry faces, with uncertain feet, they retired along the corridor.

13. Maid of all work.

"Good night," Charlie said.

"Good night!" responded Lorraine emphatically.

When he went back into the salon Marion had not moved, only now her son was standing in the circle of her other arm. Lincoln was still swinging Honoria back and forth like a pendulum from side to side.

"What an outrage!" Charlie broke out. "What an absolute outrage!"

Neither of them answered. Charlie dropped into an armchair, picked up his drink, set it down again and said:

"People I haven't seen for two years having the colossal nerve—"

He broke off. Marion had made the sound "Oh!" in one swift, furious breath, turned her body from him with a jerk and left the room.

Lincoln set down Honoria carefully.

"You children go in and start your soup," he said, and when they obeyed, he said to Charlie:

"Marion's not well and she can't stand shocks. That kind of people make her really physically sick."

"I didn't tell them to come here. They wormed your name out of somebody. They deliberately—"

"Well, it's too bad. It doesn't help matters. Excuse me a minute."

Left alone, Charlie sat tense in his chair. In the next room he could hear the children eating, talking in monosyllables, already oblivious to the scene between their elders. He heard a murmur of conversation from a farther room and then the ticking bell of a telephone receiver picked up, and in a panic he moved to the other side of the room and out of earshot.

In a minute Lincoln came back. "Look here, Charlie. I think we'd better call off dinner for tonight. Marion's in bad shape."

"Is she angry with me?"

"Sort of," he said, almost roughly. "She's not strong and—"

"You mean she's changed her mind about Honoria?"

"She's pretty bitter right now. I don't know. You phone me at the bank tomorrow."

"I wish you'd explain to her I never dreamed these people would come here. I'm just as sore as you are."

"I couldn't explain anything to her now."

Charlie got up. He took his coat and hat and started down the corridor. Then he opened the door of the dining room and said in a strange voice, "Good night, children."

Honoria rose and ran around the table to hug him.

"Good night, sweetheart," he said vaguely, and then trying to make his voice more tender, trying to conciliate something, "Good night, dear children."

V

Charlie went directly to the Ritz bar with the furious idea of finding Lorraine and Duncan, but they were not there, and he realized that in any case there was nothing he could do. He had not touched his drink at the Peters', and now he ordered a whisky-and-soda. Paul came over to say hello.

"It's a great change," he said sadly. "We do about half the business we did. So many fellows I hear about back in the States lost everything, maybe not in the first crash, but then in the second. Your friend George Hardt lost every cent, I hear. Are you back in the States?"

"No, I'm in business in Prague."

"I heard that you lost a lot in the crash."

"I did," and he added grimly, "but I lost everything I wanted in the boom."

"Selling short."

"Something like that."

Again the memory of those days swept over him like a nightmare—the people they had met travelling; the people who couldn't add a row of figures or speak a coherent sentence. The little man Helen had consented to dance with at the ship's party, who had insulted her ten feet from the table; the women and girls carried screaming with drink or drugs out of public places—

—The men who locked their wives out in the snow, because the snow of twenty-nine wasn't real snow. If you didn't want it to be snow, you just paid some money.

He went to the phone and called the Peters' apartment; Lincoln answered.

"I called up because this thing is on my mind. Has Marion said anything definite?"

"Marion's sick," Lincoln answered shortly. "I know this thing isn't altogether your fault, but I can't have her go to pieces about it. I'm afraid we'll have to let it slide for six months; I can't take the chance of working her up to this state again."

"I see."

"I'm sorry, Charlie."

He went back to his table. His whisky glass was empty, but he shook his head when Alix looked at it questionably. There wasn't much he could do now except send Honoria some things; he would send her a lot of things tomorrow. He thought rather angrily that this was just money—he had given so many people money. . . .

"No, no more," he said to another waiter. "What do I owe you?"

He would come back some day; they couldn't make him pay forever. But he wanted his child, and nothing was much good now, beside that fact. He wasn't young any more, with a lot of nice thoughts and dreams to have by himself. He was absolutely sure Helen wouldn't have wanted him to be so alone.

From *Taps at Reveille* (1935; first published in 1931)

·Ernest Hemingway·

BIG TWO-HEARTED RIVER [1]

PART I

The train went on up the track out of sight, around one of the hills of burnt timber. Nick sat down on the bundle of canvas and bedding the baggage man had pitched out of the door of the baggage car. There was no town, nothing but the rails and the burned-over country. The thirteen saloons that had lined the one street of Seney had not left a trace. The foundations of the Mansion House hotel stuck up above the ground. The stone was chipped and split by the fire. It was all that was left of the town of Seney. Even the surface had been burned off the ground.

Nick looked at the burned-over stretch of hillside, where he had expected to find the scattered houses of the town and then walked down the railroad track to the bridge over the river. The river was there. It swirled against the log spiles of the bridge. Nick looked down into the clear, brown water, colored from the pebbly bottom, and watched the trout keeping themselves steady in the current with wavering fins. As he watched them they changed their positions by quick angles, only to hold steady in the fast water again. Nick watched them a long time.

1. When he wrote this story in 1924 Hemingway drew upon his personal experience of fishing the Fox (near Seney on the northern peninsula of Michigan) in 1919; but he chose for his title the name of another stream in northern Michigan, Big Two Hearted River, explaining later that the change "was made purposely, not from ignorance nor carelessness but because Big Two-Hearted River is poetry."

In the decade 1923–33 Hemingway wrote a number of stories about his fictional hero Nick Adams. Nick's adventures are based on Hemingway's own experiences, but these experiences have been transformed and rearranged so that they become

He watched them holding themselves with their noses into the current, many trout in deep, fast moving water, slightly distorted as he watched far down through the glassy convex surface of the pool, its surface pushing and swelling smooth against the resistance of the log-driven piles of the bridge. At the bottom of the pool were the big trout. Nick did not see them at first. Then he saw them at the bottom of the pool, big trout looking to hold themselves on the gravel bottom in a varying mist of gravel and sand, raised in spurts by the current.

Nick looked down into the pool from the bridge. It was a hot day. A kingfisher flew up the stream. It was a long time since Nick had looked into a stream and seen trout. They were very satisfactory. As the shadow of the kingfisher moved up the stream, a big trout shot upstream in a long angle, only his shadow marking the angle, then lost his shadow as he came through the surface of the water, caught the sun, and then, as he went back into the stream under the surface, his shadow seemed to float down the stream with the current, unresisting, to his post under the bridge where he tightened facing up into the current.

Nick's heart tightened as the trout moved. He felt all the old feeling.

He turned and looked down the stream. It stretched away, pebbly-bottomed with shallows and big boulders and a deep pool as it curved away around the foot of a bluff.

Nick walked back up the ties to where his pack lay in the cinders beside the railway track. He was happy. He adjusted the pack harness around the bundle, pulling straps tight, slung the pack on

general emblems of life "in our time." When read in the chronological order of Nick's life, not the order of publication, the stories form a loosely structured autobiographical novel of great power, which may be compared with James Joyce's *A Portrait of the Artist as a Young Man* or D. H. Lawrence's *Sons and Lovers*. Nick Adams is a typical Midwestern boy whose doctor-father teaches him to hunt and fish, and during his early adventures he is initiated into the facts of violence and death and love. Later Nick is wounded in World War I (see "A Way You'll Never Be," the immediate background for "Big Two-Hearted River"). After the war he returns home, and his new sense of reality is recorded in "Big Two-Hearted River." The final Nick Adams story, "Fathers and Sons," completes the cycle of personal development, and shows Nick coming to terms with his own son as well as the memory of his father.

The Nick Adams stories in *The Short Stories of Ernest Hemingway* should be read in the following order if one wishes to trace Nick's development: "Indian Camp," "The Doctor and the Doctor's Wife," "The Killers," "Ten Indians," "The End of Something," "The Three-Day Blow," "The Battler," "Now I Lay Me," "A Way You'll Never Be," "Big Two-Hearted River," "Cross-Country Snow," "Fathers and Sons." All these stories, and eight formerly unpublished Nick Adams pieces, are collected in *The Nick Adams Stories*, ed. Philip Young (1972). Among the new fragments is a highly personal interior monologue that was the original conclusion to "Big Two-Hearted River." It is filled with Hemingway's personal reflections on art and life, and was obviously cut to preserve the "objective" integrity of the story.

his back, got his arms through the shoulder straps and took some of the pull off his shoulders by leaning his forehead against the wide band of the tump-line. Still, it was too heavy. It was much too heavy. He had his leather rod-case in his hand and leaning forward to keep the weight of the pack high on his shoulders he walked along the road that paralleled the railway track, leaving the burned town behind in the heat, and then turned off around a hill with a high, fire-scarred hill on either side onto a road that went back into the country. He walked along the road feeling the ache from the pull of the heavy pack. The road climbed steadily. It was hard work walking up-hill. His muscles ached and the day was hot, but Nick felt happy. He felt he had left everything behind, the need for thinking, the need to write, other needs. It was all back of him.

From the time he had gotten down off the train and the baggage man had thrown his pack out of the open car door things had been different. Seney was burned, the country was burned over and changed, but it did not matter. It could not all be burned. He knew that. He hiked along the road, sweating in the sun, climbing to cross the range of hills that separated the railway from the pine plains.

The road ran on, dipping occasionally, but always climbing. Nick went on up. Finally the road after going parallel to the burnt hill-side reached the top. Nick leaned back against a stump and slipped out of the pack harness. Ahead of him, as far as he could see, was the pine plain. The burned country stopped off at the left with the range of hills. On ahead islands of dark pine trees rose out of the plain. Far off to the left was the line of the river. Nick followed it with his eye and caught glints of the water in the sun.

There was nothing but the pine plain ahead of him, until the far blue hills that marked the Lake Superior height of land. He could hardly see them, faint and far away in the heat-light over the plain. If he looked too steadily they were gone. But if he only half-looked they were there, the far-off hills of the height of land.

Nick sat down against the charred stump and smoked a cigarette. His pack balanced on the top of the stump, harness holding ready, a hollow molded in it from his back. Nick sat smoking, looking out over the country. He did not need to get his map out. He knew where he was from the position of the river.

As he smoked, his legs stretched out in front of him, he noticed a grasshopper walk along the ground and up onto his woolen sock. The grasshopper was black. As he had walked along the road, climbing, he had started many grasshoppers from the dust. They were all black. They were not the big grasshoppers with yellow and black or red and black wings whirring out from their black wing sheathing as they fly up. These were just ordinary hoppers, but all a sooty black in color. Nick had wondered about them as he walked, without really thinking about them. Now, as he watched the black hopper that was nibbling at the wool of his sock with its fourway lip, he realized that they had all turned black from living in the burned-over land. He realized that the fire must have come the year before, but the grasshoppers were all black now. He wondered how long they would stay that way.

Carefully he reached his hand down and took hold of the hopper by the wings. He turned him up, all his legs walking in the air, and looked at his jointed belly. Yes, it was black too, iridescent where the back and head were dusty.

"Go on, hopper," Nick said, speaking out loud for the first time. "Fly away somewhere."

He tossed the grasshopper up into the air and watched him sail away to a charcoal stump across the road.

Nick stood up. He leaned his back against the weight of his pack where it rested upright on the stump and got his arms through the shoulder straps. He stood with the pack on his back on the brow of the hill looking out across the country, toward the distant river and then struck down the hillside away from the road. Underfoot the ground was good walking. Two hundred yards down the hillside the fire line stopped. Then it was sweet fern, growing ankle high, to walk through, and clumps of jack pines; a long undulating country with frequent rises and descents, sandy underfoot and the country alive again.

Nick kept his direction by the sun. He knew where he wanted to strike the river and he kept on through the pine plain, mounting small rises to see other rises ahead of him and sometimes from the top of a rise a great solid island of pines off to his right or his left. He broke off some sprigs of the heathery sweet fern, and put them under his pack straps. The chafing crushed it and he smelled it as he walked.

He was tired and very hot, walking across the uneven, shadeless pine plain. At any time he knew he could strike the river by turning off to his left. It could not be more than a mile away. But he kept on toward the north to hit the river as far upstream as he could go in one day's walking.

For some time as he walked Nick had been in sight of one of the big islands of pine standing out above the rolling high ground he was crossing. He dipped down and then as he came slowly up to the crest of the bridge he turned and made toward the pine trees.

There was no underbrush in the island of pine trees. The trunks of the trees went straight up or slanted toward each other. The trunks were straight and brown without branches. The branches were high above. Some interlocked to make a solid shadow on the brown forest floor. Around the grove of trees was a bare space. It was brown and soft underfoot as Nick walked on it. This was the over-lapping of the pine needle floor, extending out beyond the width of the high branches. The trees had grown tall and the branches moved high, leaving in the sun this bare space they had once covered with shadow. Sharp at the edge of this extension of the forest floor commenced the sweet fern.

Nick slipped off his pack and lay down in the shade. He lay on his back and looked up into the pine trees. His neck and back and the small of his back rested as he stretched. The earth felt good against his back. He looked up at the sky, through the branches, and then shut his eyes. He opened them and looked up again. There was a wind high up in the branches. He shut his eyes again and went to sleep.

Nick woke stiff and cramped. The sun was nearly down. His pack was heavy and the straps painful as he lifted it on. He leaned over with the pack on and picked up the leather rod-case and started out from the pine trees across the sweet fern swale, toward the river. He knew it could not be more than a mile.

He came down a hillside covered with stumps into a meadow. At the edge of the meadow flowed the river. Nick was glad to get to the river. He walked upstream through the meadow. His trousers were soaked with the dew as he walked. After the hot day, the dew had come quickly and heavily. The river made no sound. It was too fast and smooth. At the edge of the meadow, before he mounted to a piece of high ground to make camp, Nick looked down the river at the trout rising. They were rising to insects come from the swamp on the other side of the stream when the sun went down. The trout jumped out of water to take them. While Nick walked through the little stretch of meadow alongside the stream, trout had jumped high out of water. Now as he looked down the river, the insects must be settling on the surface, for the trout were feeding steadily all down the stream. As far down the long stretch as he could see, the trout were rising, making circles all down the surface of the water, as though it were starting to rain.

The ground rose, wooded and sandy, to overlook the meadow, the stretch of river and the swamp. Nick dropped his pack and rod-case and looked for a level piece of ground. He was very hungry and he wanted to make his camp before he cooked. Between two jack pines, the ground was quite level. He took the ax out of the pack and chopped out two projecting roots. That leveled a piece of ground large enough to sleep on. He smoothed out the sandy soil with his hand and pulled all the sweet fern bushes by their roots. His hands smelled good from the sweet fern. He smoothed the uprooted earth. He did not want anything making lumps under the blankets. When he had the ground smooth, he spread his three blankets. One he folded double, next to the ground. The other two he spread on top.

With the ax he slit off a bright slab of pine from one of the stumps and split it into pegs for the tent. He wanted them long and solid to hold in the ground. With the tent unpacked and spread on the ground, the pack, leaning against a jackpine, looked much smaller. Nick tied the rope that served the tent for a ridge-pole to the trunk of one of the pine trees and pulled the tent up off the ground with the other end of the rope and tied it to the other pine. The tent hung on the rope like a canvas blanket on a clothesline. Nick poked a pole he had cut up under the back peak of the canvas and then made it a tent by pegging out the sides. He pegged the sides out taut and drove the pegs deep, hitting them down into the ground with the flat of the ax until the rope loops were buried and the canvas was drum tight.

Across the open mouth of the tent Nick fixed cheesecloth to keep out mosquitoes. He crawled inside under the mosquito bar with various things from the pack to put at the head of the bed under the slant of the canvas. Inside the tent the light came through the brown canvas. It smelled pleasantly of canvas. Already there was something mysterious and homelike. Nick was happy as he crawled inside the tent. He had not been unhappy all day. This was different though. Now things were done. There had been this to do. Now it was done. It had been a hard trip. He was very tired. That was done. He had made his camp. He was settled. Nothing could touch him. It was a good place to camp. He was there, in the good place. He was in his home where he had made it. Now he was hungry.

He came out, crawling under the cheesecloth. It was quite dark outside. It was lighter in the tent.

Nick went over to the pack and found, with his fingers, a long nail in a paper sack of nails, in the bottom of the pack. He drove it into the pine tree, holding it close and hitting it gently with the flat of the ax. He hung the pack up on the nail. All his supplies were in the pack. They were off the ground and sheltered now.

Nick was hungry. He did not believe he had ever been hungrier. He opened and emptied a can of pork and beans and a can of spaghetti into the frying pan.

"I've got a right to eat this kind of stuff, if I'm willing to carry it," Nick said. His voice sounded strange in the darkening woods. He did not speak again.

He started a fire with some chunks of pine he got with the ax from a stump. Over the fire he stuck a wire grill, pushing the four legs down into the ground with his boot. Nick put the frying pan on the grill over the flames. He was hungrier. The beans and spaghetti warmed. Nick stirred them and mixed them together. They began to bubble, making little bubbles that rose with difficulty to the surface. There was a good smell. Nick got out a bottle of tomato catchup and cut four slices of bread. The little bubbles were coming faster now. Nick sat down beside the fire and lifted the frying pan off. He poured about half the contents out into the tin plate. It spread slowly on the plate. Nick knew it was too hot. He poured on some tomato catchup. He knew the beans and spaghetti were still too hot. He looked at the fire, then at the tent, he was not going to spoil it all by burning his tongue. For years he had never enjoyed fried bananas because he had never been able to wait for them to cool. His tongue was very sensitive. He was very hungry. Across the river in the swamp, in the almost dark, he saw a mist rising. He looked at the tent once more. All right. He took a full spoonful from the plate.

"Chrise," Nick said, "Geezus Chrise," he said happily.

He ate the whole plateful before he remembered the bread. Nick finished the second plateful with the bread, mopping the plate shiny. He had not eaten since a cup of coffee and a ham sandwich in the station restaurant at St. Ignace. It had been a very fine experience. He had been that hungry before, but had not been able to satisfy it. He could have made camp hours before if he had wanted to. There were plenty of good places to camp on the river. But this was good.

Nick tucked two big chips of pine under the grill. The fire flared up. He had forgotten to get water for the coffee. Out of the pack he got a folding canvas bucket and walked down the hill, across the edge of the meadow, to the stream. The other bank was in the white mist. The grass was wet and cold as he knelt on the bank and dipped the canvas bucket into the stream. It bellied and pulled hard in the current. The water was ice cold. Nick rinsed the bucket and carried it full up to the camp. Up away from the stream it was not so cold.

Nick drove another big nail and hung up the bucket full of water. He dipped the coffee pot half full, put some more chips under the grill onto the fire and put the pot on. He could not remember which way he made coffee. He could remember an argument about it with Hopkins, but not which side he had taken. He decided to bring it to a boil. He remembered now that was Hopkins's way. He had once argued about everything with Hopkins. While he waited for the coffee to boil, he opened a small can of apricots. He liked to open cans. He emptied the can of apricots out into a tin cup. While he watched the coffee on the fire, he drank the juice syrup of the apricots, carefully at first to keep from spilling, then meditatively, sucking the apricots down. They were better than fresh apricots.

The coffee boiled as he watched. The lid came up and coffee and grounds ran down the side of the pot. Nick took it off the grill. It was a triumph for Hopkins. He put sugar in the empty apricot cup and poured some of the coffee out to cool. It was too hot to pour and he used his hat to hold the handle of the coffee pot. He would not let it steep in the pot at all. Not the first cup. It should be straight Hopkins all the way. Hop deserved that. He was a very serious coffee drinker. He was the most serious man Nick had ever known. Not heavy, serious. That was a long time ago. Hopkins spoke without moving his lips. He had played polo. He made millions of dollars in Texas. He had borrowed carfare to go to Chicago, when the wire came that his first big well had come in. He could have wired for money. That would have been too slow. They called Hop's girl the Blonde Venus. Hop did not mind because she was not his real girl. Hopkins said very confidently that none of them would make fun of his real girl. He was right. Hopkins went away when the telegram came. That was on the Black River. It took eight days for the telegram to reach him. Hopkins gave away his .22 caliber Colt automatic pistol to Nick. He gave his camera to Bill. It was to remember him always by. They were all going fishing again next summer. The Hop Head was rich. He would get a yacht and they would all cruise along the north shore of Lake Superior. He was excited but serious. They said good-bye and all felt bad. It broke up the trip. They never saw Hopkins again. That was a long time ago on the Black River.

Nick drank the coffee, the coffee according to Hopkins. The coffee was bitter. Nick laughed. It made a good ending to the story. His mind was starting to work. He knew he could choke it because he was tired enough. He spilled the coffee out of the pot and shook the grounds loose into the fire. He lit a cigarette and went inside the tent. He took off his shoes and trousers, sitting on the blankets, rolled the shoes up inside the trousers for a pillow and got in between the blankets.

Out through the front of the tent he watched the glow of the fire, when the night wind blew on it. It was a quiet night. The swamp was perfectly quiet. Nick stretched under the blanket comfortably. A mosquito hummed close to his ear. Nick sat up and lit a match. The mosquito was on the canvas, over his head. Nick moved the match quickly up to it. The mosquito made a satisfactory hiss in the flame. The match went out. Nick lay down again under the blanket. He turned on his side and shut his eyes. He was sleepy. He felt sleep coming. He curled up under the blanket and went to sleep.

PART II

In the morning the sun was up and the tent was starting to get hot. Nick crawled out under the mosquito netting stretched across the mouth of the tent, to look at the morning. The grass was wet on his hands as he came out. The sun was just up over the hill. There was the meadow, the river and the swamp. There were birch trees in the green of the swamp on the other side of the river.

The river was clear and smoothly fast in the early morning. Down about two hundred yards were three logs all the way across the stream. They made the water smooth and deep above them. As Nick watched, a mink crossed the river on the logs and went into the swamp. Nick was excited. He was excited by the early morning and the river. He was really too hurried to eat breakfast, but he knew he must. He built a little fire and put on the coffee pot.

While the water was heating in the pot he took an empty bottle and went down over the edge of the high ground to the meadow. The meadow was wet with dew and Nick wanted to catch grasshoppers for bait before the sun dried the grass. He found plenty of good grasshoppers. They were at the base of the grass stems. Sometimes they clung to a grass stem. They were cold and wet with the dew, and could not jump until the sun warmed them. Nick picked them up, taking only the medium-sized brown ones, and put them into the bottle. He turned over a log and just under the shelter of the edge were several hundred hoppers. It was a grasshopper lodging house. Nick put about fifty of the medium browns into the bottle. While he was picking up the hoppers the others warmed in the sun and commenced to hop away. They flew when they hopped. At first they made one flight and stayed stiff when they landed, as though they were dead.

Nick knew that by the time he was through with breakfast they would be as lively as ever. Without dew in the grass it would take him all day to catch a bottle full of good grasshoppers and he would have to crush many of them, slamming at them with his hat. He washed his hands at the stream. He was excited to be near it. Then he walked up to the tent. The hoppers were already jumping stiffly in the grass. In the bottle, warmed by the sun, they were jumping in a mass. Nick put in a pine stick as a cork. It plugged the mouth of the bottle enough, so the hoppers could not get out and left plenty of air passage.

He had rolled the log back and knew he could get grasshoppers there every morning.

Nick laid the bottle full of jumping grasshoppers against a pine trunk. Rapidly he mixed some buckwheat flour with water and stirred it smooth, one cup of flour, one cup of water. He put a handful of coffee in the pot and dipped a lump of grease out of a can and slid it sputtering across the hot skillet. On the smoking skillet he poured smoothly the buckwheat batter. It spread like lava, the grease spitting sharply. Around the edges the buckwheat cake began to firm, then brown, then crisp. The surface was bubbling slowly to porousness. Nick pushed under the browned under surface with a fresh pine chip. He shook the skillet sideways and the cake was loose on the surface. I won't try and flop it, he thought. He slid the chip of clean wood all the way under the cake, and flopped it over onto its face. It sputtered in the pan.

When it was cooked Nick regreased the skillet. He used all the batter. It made another big flapjack and one smaller one.

Nick ate a big flapjack and a smaller one, covered with apple butter. He put apple butter on the third cake, folded it over twice, wrapped it in oiled paper and put it in his shirt pocket. He put the apple butter jar back in the pack and cut bread for two sandwiches.

In the pack he found a big onion. He sliced it in two and peeled the silky outer skin. Then he cut one half into slices and made onion sandwiches. He wrapped them in oiled paper and buttoned them in the other pocket of his khaki shirt. He turned the skillet upside down on the grill, drank the coffee, sweetened and yellow brown with the condensed milk in it, and tidied up the camp. It was a good camp.

Nick took his fly rod out of the leather rod-case, jointed it, and shoved the rod-case back into the tent. He put on the reel and threaded the line through the guides. He had to hold it from hand to hand, as he threaded it, or it would slip back through its own weight. It was a heavy, double tapered fly line. Nick had paid eight dollars for it a long time ago. It was made heavy to lift back in the air and come forward flat and heavy and straight to make it possible to cast a fly which has no weight. Nick opened the aluminum leader box. The leaders were coiled between the damp flannel pads. Nick had wet the pads at the water cooler on the train up to St. Ignace. In the damp pads the gut leaders had softened and Nick unrolled one and tied it by a loop at the end to the heavy fly line. He fastened a hook on the end of the leader. It was a small hook; very thin and springy.

Nick took it from his hook book, sitting with the rod across his lap. He tested the knot and the spring of the rod by pulling the line taut. It was a good feeling. He was careful not to let the hook bite into his finger.

He started down to the stream, holding his rod, the bottle of grasshoppers hung from his neck by a thong tied in half hitches around the neck of the bottle. His landing net hung by a hook from his belt. Over his shoulder was a long flour sack tied at each corner into an ear. The cord went over his shoulder. The sack flapped against his legs.

Nick felt awkward and professionally happy with all his equipment hanging from him. The grasshopper bottle swung against his chest. In his shirt the breast pockets bulged against him with the lunch and his fly book.

He stepped into the stream. It was a shock. His trousers clung tight to his legs. His shoes felt the gravel. The water was a rising cold shock.

Rushing, the current sucked against his legs. Where he stepped in, the water was over his knees. He waded with the current. The gravel slid under his shoes. He looked down at the swirl of water below each leg and tipped up the bottle to get a grasshopper.

The first grasshopper gave a jump in the neck of the bottle and went out into the water. He was sucked under in the whirl by Nick's right leg and came to the surface a little way down stream. He floated rapidly, kicking. In a quick circle, breaking the smooth surface of the water, he disappeared. A trout had taken him.

Another hopper poked his face out of the bottle. His antennæ wavered. He was getting his front legs out of the bottle to jump. Nick took him by the head and held him while he threaded the slim hook under his chin, down through his thorax and into the last segments of his abdomen. The grasshopper took hold of the hook with his front feet, spitting tobacco juice on it. Nick dropped him into the water.

Holding the rod in his right hand he let out line against the pull of the grasshopper in the current. He stripped off line from the reel with his left hand and let it run free. He could see the hopper in the little waves of the current. It went out of sight.

There was a tug on the line. Nick pulled against the taut line. It was his first strike. Holding the now living rod across the current, he brought in the line with his left hand. The rod bent in jerks, the trout pumping against the current. Nick knew it was a small one. He lifted the rod straight up in the air. It bowed with the pull.

He saw the trout in the water jerking with his head and body against the shifting tangent of the line in the stream.

Nick took the line in his left hand and pulled the trout, thumping tiredly against the current, to the surface. His back was mottled the clear, water-over-gravel color, his side flashing in the sun. The rod under his right arm, Nick stooped, dipping his right hand into the current. He held the trout, never still, with his moist right hand, while he unhooked the barb from his mouth, then dropped him back into the stream.

He hung unsteadily in the current, then settled to the bottom beside a stone. Nick reached down his hand to touch him, his arm to the elbow under water. The trout was steady in the moving stream, resting on the gravel, beside a stone. As Nick's fingers touched him, touched his smooth, cool, underwater feeling he was gone, gone in a shadow across the bottom of the stream.

He's all right, Nick thought. He was only tired.

He had wet his hand before he touched the trout, so he would not disturb the delicate mucus that covered him. If a trout was touched with a dry hand, a white fungus attacked the unprotected spot. Years before when he had fished crowded streams, with fly fishermen ahead of him and behind him, Nick had again and again come on dead trout, furry with white fungus, drifted against a rock, or floating belly up in some pool. Nick did not like to fish with other men on the river. Unless they were of your party, they spoiled it.

He wallowed down the steam, above his knees in the current, through the fifty yards of shallow water above the pile of logs that crossed the stream. He did not rebait his hook and held it in his hand as he waded. He was certain he could catch small trout in the shallows, but he did not want them. There would be no big trout in the shallows this time of day.

Now the water deepened up his thighs sharply and coldly. Ahead was the smooth dammed-back flood of water above the logs. The water was smooth and dark; on the left, the lower edge of the meadow; on the right the swamp.

Nick leaned back against the current and took a hopper from the bottle. He threaded the hopper on the hook and spat on him for good luck. Then he pulled several yards of line from the reel and tossed the hopper out ahead onto the fast, dark water. It floated down towards the logs, then the weight of the line pulled the bait under the surface. Nick held the rod in his right hand, letting the line run out through his fingers.

There was a long tug. Nick struck and the rod came alive and dangerous, bent double, the line tightening, coming out of water, tightening, all in a heavy, dangerous, steady pull. Nick felt the moment when the leader would break if the strain increased and let the line go.

The reel ratcheted into a mechanical shriek as the line went out in a rush. Too fast. Nick could not check it, the line rushing out, the reel note rising as the line ran out.

With the core of the reel showing, his heart feeling stopped with the excitement, leaning back against the current that mounted icily his thighs, Nick thumbed the reel hard with his left hand. It was awkward getting his thumb inside the fly reel frame.

As he put on pressure the line tightened into sudden hardness and beyond the logs a huge trout went high out of water. As he jumped, Nick lowered the tip of the rod. But he felt, as he dropped the tip to ease the strain, the moment when the strain was too great; the hardness too tight. Of course, the leader had broken. There was no mistaking the feeling when all spring left the line and it became dry and hard. Then it went slack.

His mouth dry, his heart down, Nick reeled in. He had never seen so big a trout. There was a heaviness, a power not to be held, and then the bulk of him, as he jumped. He looked as broad as a salmon.

Nick's hand was shaky. He reeled in slowly. The thrill had been too much. He felt, vaguely, a little sick, as though it would be better to sit down.

The leader had broken where the hook was tied to it. Nick took it in his hand. He thought of the trout somewhere on the bottom, holding himself steady over the gravel, far down below the light, under the logs, with the hook in his jaw. Nick knew the trout's teeth would cut through the snell of the hook. The hook would imbed itself in his jaw. He'd bet the trout was angry. Anything that size would be angry. That was a trout. He had been solidly hooked. Solid as a rock. He felt like a rock, too, before he started off. By God, he was a big one. By God, he was the biggest one I ever heard of.

Nick climbed out onto the meadow and stood, water running down his trousers and out of his shoes, his shoes squlchy. He went over and sat on the logs. He did not want to rush his sensations any.

He wriggled his toes in the water, in his shoes, and got out a cigarette from his breast pocket. He lit it and tossed the match into the fast water below the logs. A tiny trout rose at the match, as it swung around in the fast current. Nick laughed. He would finish the cigarette.

He sat on the logs, smoking, drying in the sun, the sun warm on his back, the river shallow ahead entering the woods, curving into the woods, shallows, light glittering, big water-smooth rocks, cedars along the bank and white birches, the logs warm in the sun, smooth to sit on, without bark, gray to the touch; slowly the feeling of disappointment left him. It went away slowly, the feeling of disappointment that came sharply after the thrill that made his shoulders ache. It was all right now. His rod lying out on the logs, Nick tied a new hook on the leader, pulling the gut tight until it grimped into itself in a hard knot.

He baited up, then picked up the rod and walked to the far end of the logs to get into the water, where it was not too deep. Under and beyond the logs was a deep pool. Nick walked around the shallow shelf near the swamp shore until he came out on the shallow bed of the stream.

On the left, where the meadow ended and the woods began, a

great elm tree was uprooted. Gone over in a storm, it lay back into the woods, its roots clotted with dirt, grass growing in them, rising a solid bank beside the stream. The river cut to the edge of the uprooted tree. From where Nick stood he could see deep channels, like ruts, cut in the shallow bed of the stream by the flow of the current. Pebbly where he stood and pebbly and full of boulders beyond; where it curved near the tree roots, the bed of the stream was marly and between the ruts of deep water green weed fronds swung in the current.

Nick swung the rod back over his shoulder and forward, and the line, curving forward, laid the grasshopper down on one of the deep channels in the weeds. A trout struck and Nick hooked him.

Holding the rod far out toward the uprooted tree and sloshing backward in the current, Nick worked the trout, plunging, the rod bending alive, out of the danger of the weeds into the open river. Holding the rod, pumping alive against the current, Nick brought the trout in. He rushed, but always came, the spring of the rod yielding to the rushes, sometimes jerking under water, but always bringing him in. Nick eased downstream with the rushes. The rod above his head he led the trout over the net, then lifted.

The trout hung heavy in the net, mottled trout back and silver sides in the meshes. Nick unhooked him; heavy sides, good to hold, big undershot jaw, and slipped him, heaving and big sliding, into the long sack that hung from his shoulders in the water.

Nick spread the mouth of the sack against the current and it filled, heavy with water. He held it up, the bottom in the stream, and the water poured out through the sides. Inside at the bottom was the big trout, alive in the water.

Nick moved downstream. The sack out ahead of him sunk heavy in the water, pulling from his shoulders.

It was getting hot, the sun hot on the back of his neck.

Nick had one good trout. He did not care about getting many trout. Now the stream was shallow and wide. There were trees along both banks. The trees of the left bank made short shadows on the current in the forenoon sun. Nick knew there were trout in each shadow. In the afternoon, after the sun had crossed toward the hills, the trout would be in the cool shadows on the other side of the stream.

The very biggest ones would lie up close to the bank. You could always pick them up there on the Black. When the sun was down they all moved out into the current. Just when the sun made the water blinding in the glare before it went down, you were liable to strike a big trout anywhere in the current. It was almost impossible to fish then, the surface of the water was blinding as a mirror in the sun. Of course, you could fish upstream, but in a stream like the

Black, or this, you had to wallow against the current and in a deep place, the water piled up on you. It was no fun to fish upstream with this much current.

Nick moved along through the shallow stretch watching the banks for deep holes. A beech tree grew close beside the river, so that the branches hung down into the water. The stream went back in under the leaves. There were always trout in a place like that.

Nick did not care about fishing that hole. He was sure he would get hooked in the branches.

It looked deep though. He dropped the grasshopper so the current took it under water, back in under the overhanging branch. The line pulled hard and Nick struck. The trout threshed heavily, half out of water in the leaves and branches. The line was caught. Nick pulled hard and the trout was off. He reeled in and holding the hook in his hand, walked down the stream.

Ahead, close to the left bank, was a big log. Nick saw it was hollow; pointing up river the current entered it smoothly, only a little ripple spread each side of the log. The water was deepening. The top of the hollow log was gray and dry. It was partly in the shadow.

Nick took the cork out of the grasshopper bottle and a hopper clung to it. He picked him off, hooked him and tossed him out. He held the rod far out so that the hopper on the water moved into the current flowing into the hollow log. Nick lowered the rod and the hopper floated in. There was a heavy strike. Nick swung the rod against the pull. It felt as though he were hooked into the log itself, except for the live feeling.

He tried to force the fish out into the current. It came, heavily.

The line went slack and Nick thought the trout was gone. Then he saw him, very near, in the current, shaking his head, trying to get the hook out. His mouth was clamped shut. He was fighting the hook in the clear flowing current.

Looping in the line with his left hand, Nick swung the rod to make the line taut and tried to lead the trout toward the net, but he was gone, out of sight, the line pumping. Nick fought him against the current, letting him thump in the water against the spring of the rod. He shifted the rod to his left hand, worked the trout upstream, holding his weight, fighting on the rod, and then let him down into the net. He lifted him clear of the water, a heavy half circle in the net, the net dripping, unhooked him and slid him into the sack.

He spread the mouth of the sack and looked down in at the two big trout alive in the water.

Through the deepening water, Nick waded over to the hollow log. He took the sack off, over his head, the trout flopping as it came out of water, and hung it so the trout were deep in the water. Then he pulled himself up on the log and sat, the water from his trouser and boots running down into the stream. He laid his rod down, moved along to the shady end of the log and took the sandwiches out of his pocket. He dipped the sandwiches in the cold water. The current carried away the crumbs. He ate the sandwiches and dipped his hat full of water to drink, the water running out through his hat just ahead of his drinking.

It was cool in the shade, sitting on the log. He took a cigarette out and struck a match to light it. The match sunk into the gray wood, making a tiny furrow. Nick leaned over the side of the log, found a hard place and lit the match. He sat smoking and watching the river.

Ahead the river narrowed and went into a swamp. The river became smooth and deep and the swamp looked solid with cedar trees, their trunks close together, their branches solid. It would not be possible to walk through a swamp like that. The branches grew so low. You would have to keep almost level with the ground to move at all. You could not crash through the branches. That must be why the animals that lived in swamps were built the way they were, Nick thought.

He wished he had brought something to read. He felt like reading. He did not feel like going on into the swamp. He looked down the river. A big cedar slanted all the way across the stream. Beyond that the river went into the swamp.

Nick did not want to go in there now. He felt a reaction against deep wading with the water deepening up under his armpits, to hook big trout in places impossible to land them. In the swamp the banks were bare, the big cedars came together overhead, the sun did not come through, except in patches; in the fast deep water, in the half light, the fishing would be tragic. In the swamp fishing was a tragic adventure. Nick did not want it. He did not want to go down the stream any further today.

He took out his knife, opened it and stuck it in the log. Then he pulled up the sack, reached into it and brought out one of the trout. Holding him near the tail, hard to hold, alive, in his hand, he whacked him against the log. The trout quivered, rigid. Nick laid him on the log in the shade and broke the neck of the other fish the same way. He laid them side by side on the log. They were fine trout.

Nick cleaned them, slitting them from the vent to the tip of the jaw. All the insides and the gills and tongue came out in one piece. They were both males; long gray-white strips of milt, smooth and clean. All the insides clean and compact, coming out all together. Nick tossed the offal ashore for the minks to find.

He washed the trout in the stream. When he held them back up in the water they looked like live fish. Their color was not gone yet. He washed his hands and dried them on the log. Then he laid the trout on the sack spread out on the log, rolled them up in it, tied the bundle and put it in the landing net. His knife was still standing, blade stuck in the log. He cleaned it on the wood and put it in his pocket.

Nick stood up on the log, holding his rod, the landing net hanging heavy, then stepped into the water and splashed ashore. He climbed the bank and cut up into the woods, toward the high ground. He was going back to camp. He looked back. The river just showed through the trees. There were plenty of days coming when he could fish the swamp.

From *In Our Time* (1925)

·William Faulkner·

RED LEAVES

I

The two Indians crossed the plantation toward the slave quarters. Neat with whitewash, of baked soft brick, the two rows of houses in which lived the slaves belonging to the clan, faced one another across the mild shade of the lane marked and scored with naked feet and with a few homemade toys mute in the dust. There was no sign of life.

"I know what we will find," the first Indian said.

"What we will not find," the second said. Although it was noon, the lane was vacant, the doors of the cabins empty and quiet; no cooking smoke rose from any of the chinked and plastered chimneys.

"Yes. It happened like this when the father of him who is now the Man died." [1]

"You mean, of him who was the Man."

"Yao."

The first Indian's name was Three Basket. He was perhaps sixty. They were both squat men, a little solid, burgherlike; paunchy, with big heads, big, broad, dust-colored faces of a certain blurred serenity like carved heads on a ruined wall in Siam or Sumatra,

---

1. The genealogy of the Indian rulers given in "Red Leaves" differs considerably from that provided in other stories of "the old people" (e.g., "A Justice," "The Old People," the Appendix to *The Sound and the Fury*). But in spite of these factual discrepancies, Faulkner's vision of the Indian world—with its order and rituals—remains the same throughout his Yoknapatawpha stories.

In "Red Leaves" the original chief or Man is Doom, Issetibbeha's father. He received his name from the Frenchman de Vitry, "Doom" being a corruption of the

looming out of a mist. The sun had done it, the violent sun, the violent shade. Their hair looked like sedge grass on burnt-over land. Clamped through one ear Three Basket wore an enameled snuff-box.

"I have said all the time that this is not the good way. In the old days there were no quarters, no Negroes. A man's time was his own then. He had time. Now he must spend most of it finding work for them who prefer sweating to do."

"They are like horses and dogs."

"They are like nothing in this sensible world. Nothing contents them save sweat. They are worse than the white people."

"It is not as though the Man himself had to find work for them to do."

"You said it. I do not like slavery. It is not the good way. In the old days, there was the good way. But not now."

"You do not remember the old way either."

"I have listened to them who do. And I have tried this way. Man was not made to sweat."

"That's so. See what it has done to their flesh."

"Yes. Black. It has a bitter taste, too."

"You have eaten of it?"

"Once. I was young then, and more hardy in the appetite than now. Now it is different with me."

"Yes. They are too valuable to eat now."

"There is a bitter taste to the flesh which I do not like."

"They are too valuable to eat, anyway, when the white men will give horses for them."

They entered the lane. The mute, meager toys—the fetish-shaped objects made of wood and rags and feathers—lay in the dust about the patinaed doorsteps, among bones and broken gourd dishes. But there was no sound from any cabin, no face in any door; had not been since yesterday, when Issetibbeha died. But they already knew what they would find.

It was in the central cabin, a house a little larger than the others, where at certain phases of the moon the Negroes would gather to

French for Man (*Homme*). Issetibbeha was the Man until his death; now his fat and shiftless son, Moketubbe, is faced with the task of pursuing and capturing Issetibbeha's Negro servant. The Negro's ritual death will assure Issetibbeha comfort and companionship in the other world.

When Faulkner was once asked, "What is the significance of the title, 'Red Leaves'?" he replied: "Well, that was probably symbolism. The red leaves referred to the Indian. It was the deciduation of Nature which no one could stop that had suffocated, smothered, destroyed the Negro. That the red leaves had nothing against him when they suffocated him and destroyed him. They had nothing against him, they probably liked him, but it was normal deciduation which the red leaves, whether they regretted it or not, had nothing more to say in."—*Faulkner in the University*, ed. Frederick L. Gwynn and Joseph L. Blotner (1959), p. 39.

begin their ceremonies before removing after nightfall to the creek bottom, where they kept the drums. In this room they kept the minor accessories, the cryptic ornaments, the ceremonial records which consisted of sticks daubed with red clay in symbols. It had a hearth in the center of the floor, beneath a hole in the roof, with a few cold wood ashes and a suspended iron pot. The window shutters were closed; when the two Indians entered, after the abashless sunlight they could distinguish nothing with the eyes save a movement, shadow, out of which eyeballs rolled, so that the place appeared to be full of Negroes. The two Indians stood in the door.

"Yao," Basket said. "I said this is not the good way."

"I don't think I want to be here," the second said.

"That is black man's fear which you smell. It does not smell as ours does."

"I don't think I want to be here."

"Your fear has an odor too."

"Maybe it is Issetibbeha which we smell."

"Yao. He knows. He knows what we will find here. He knew when he died what we should find here today." Out of the rank twilight of the room the eyes, the smell, of Negroes rolled about them. "I am Three Basket, whom you know," Basket said into the room. "We are come from the Man. He whom we seek is gone?" The Negroes said nothing. The smell of them, of their bodies, seemed to ebb and flux in the still hot air. They seemed to be musing as one upon something remote, inscrutable. They were like a single octopus. They were like the roots of a huge tree uncovered, the earth broken momentarily upon the writhen, thick, fetid tangle of its lightless and outraged life. "Come," Basket said. "You know our errand. Is he whom we seek gone?"

"They are thinking something," the second said. "I do not want to be here."

"They are knowing something," Basket said.

"They are hiding him, you think?"

"No. He is gone. He has been gone since last night. It happened like this before, when the grandfather of him who is now the Man died. It took us three days to catch him. For three days Doom lay above the ground, saying, 'I see my horse and my dog. But I do not see my slave. What have you done with him that you will not permit me to lie quiet?'"

"They do not like to die."

"Yao. They cling. It makes trouble for us, always. A people without honor and without decorum. Always a trouble."

"I do not like it here."

"Nor do I. But then, they are savages; they cannot be expected to regard usage. That is why I say that this way is a bad way."

"Yao. They cling. They would even rather work in the sun than to enter the earth with a chief. But he is gone."

The Negroes had said nothing, made no sound. The white eyeballs rolled, wild, subdued; the smell was rank, violent. "Yes, they fear," the second said. "What shall we do now?"

"Let us go and talk with the Man."

"Will Moketubbe listen?"

"What can he do? He will not like to. But he is the Man now."

"Yao. He is the Man. He can wear the shoes with the red heels all the time now." They turned and went out. There was no door in the door frame. There were no doors in any of the cabins.

"He did that anyway," Basket said.

"Behind Issetibbeha's back. But now they are his shoes, since he is the Man."

"Yao. Issetibbeha did not like it. I have heard. I know that he said to Moketubbe: 'When you are the Man, the shoes will be yours. But until then, they are my shoes.' But now Moketubbe is the Man; he can wear them."

"Yao," the second said. "He is the Man now. He used to wear the shoes behind Issetibbeha's back, and it was not known if Issetibbeha knew this or not. And then Issetibbeha became dead, who was not old, and the shoes are Moketubbe's, since he is the Man now. What do you think of that?"

"I don't think about it," Basket said. "Do you?"

"No," the second said.

"Good," Basket said. "You are wise."

II

The house sat on a knoll, surrounded by oak trees. The front of it was one story in height, composed of the deck house of a steamboat which had gone ashore and which Doom, Issetibbeha's father, had dismantled with his slaves and hauled on cypress rollers twelve miles home overland. It took them five months. His house consisted at the time of one brick wall. He set the steamboat broadside on to the wall, where now the chipped and flaked gliding of the rococo cornices arched in faint splendor above the gilt lettering of the stateroom names above the jalousied doors.

Doom had been born merely a subchief, a Mingo, one of three children on the mother's side of the family. He made a journey—he was a young man then and New Orleans was a European city—from north Mississippi to New Orleans by keel boat, where he met the Chevalier Sœur Blonde de Vitry, a man whose social position, on its face, was as equivocal as Doom's own. In New Orleans, among the gamblers and cutthroats of the river front, Doom, under the tutelage of his patron, passed as the chief, the Man, the hereditary owner of that land which belonged to the male side of the family; it was the Chevalier de Vitry who spoke of him as *l'Homme* or *de l'Homme*,[2] and hence Doom.

They were seen everywhere together—the Indian, the squat man with a bold, inscrutable, underbred face, and the Parisian, the expatriate, the friend, it was said, of Carondelet and the intimate of General Wilkinson. Then they disappeared, the two of them, vanishing from their old equivocal haunts and leaving behind them the legend of the sums which Doom was believed to have won, and some tale about a young woman, daughter of a fairly well-to-do West Indian family, the son and brother of whom sought Doom with a pistol about his old haunts for some time after his disappearance.

Six months later the young woman herself disappeared, boarding the Saint Louis packet, which put in one night at a wood landing on the north Mississippi side, where the woman, accompanied by a Negro maid, got off. Four Indians met her with a horse and wagon, and they traveled for three days, slowly, since she was already big with child, to the plantation, where she found that Doom was now chief. He never told her how he accomplished it, save that his uncle and his cousin had died suddenly. Before that time the house had consisted of a brick wall built by shiftless slaves, against which was propped a thatched lean-to divided into rooms and littered with bones and refuse, set in the center of ten thousand acres of matchless parklike forest where deer grazed like domestic cattle. Doom and the woman were married there a short time before Issetibbeha was born, by a combination itinerant minister and slave trader who arrived on a mule, to the saddle of which was lashed a cotton umbrella and a three-gallon demijohn of whiskey. After that, Doom began to acquire more slaves and to cultivate some of his land, as the white people did. But he never had enough for them to do. In utter idleness the majority of them led lives transplanted whole out of African jungles, save on the occasions when, entertaining guests, Doom coursed them with dogs.

When Doom died, Issetibbeha, his son, was nineteen. He became proprietor of the land and of the quintupled herd of blacks for which he had no use at all. Though the title of Man rested with him, there was a hierarchy of cousins and uncles who ruled the clan and who finally gathered in squatting conclave over the Negro question, squatting profoundly beneath the golden names above the doors of the steamboat.

"We cannot eat them," one said.

2. Or perhaps *Du Homme* (see "The Old People" in *Go Down, Moses*).

"Why not?"

"There are too many of them."

"That's true," a third said. "Once we started, we should have to eat them all. And that much flesh diet is not good for man."

"Perhaps they will be like deer flesh. That cannot hurt you."

"We might kill a few of them and not eat them," Issetibbeha said. They looked at him for a while. "What for?" one said.

"That is true," a second said. "We cannot do that. They are too valuable; remember all the bother they have caused us, finding things for them to do. We must do as the white men do."

"How is that?" Issetibbeha said.

"Raise more Negroes by clearing more land to make corn to feed them, then sell them. We will clear the land and plant it with food and raise Negroes and sell them to the white men for money."

"But what will we do with this money?" a third said.

They thought for a while.

"We will see," the first said. They squatted, profound, grave.

"It means work," the third said.

"Let the Negroes do it," the first said.

"Yao. Let them. To sweat is bad. It is damp. It opens the pores."

"And then the night air enters."

"Yao. Let the Negroes do it. They appear to like sweating."

So they cleared the land with the Negroes and planted it in grain. Up to that time the slaves had lived in a huge pen with a lean-to roof over one corner, like a pen for pigs. But now they began to build quarters, cabins, putting the young Negroes in the cabins in pairs to mate; five years later Issetibbeha sold forty head to a Memphis trader, and he took the money and went abroad upon it, his maternal uncle from New Orleans conducting the trip. At that time the Chevalier Sœur Blonde de Vitry was an old man in Paris, in a toupee and a corset and a careful, toothless old face fixed in a grimace quizzical and profoundly tragic. He borrowed three hundred dollars from Issetibbeha and in return he introduced him into certain circles; a year later Issetibbeha returned home with a gilt bed, a pair of girandoles [3] by whose light it was said that Pompadour arranged her hair while Louis smirked at his mirrored face across her powdered shoulder,[4] and a pair of slippers with red heels. They were too small for him, since he had not worn shoes at all until he reached New Orleans on his way abroad.

He brought the slippers home in tissue paper and kept them in the remaining pocket of a pair of saddlebags filled with cedar shavings, save when he took them out on occasion for his son, Moke-

3. Large branched candleholders, sometimes backed by mirrors.
4. The Marquise de Pompadour (1721–64), mistress of Louis XV of France.

tubbe, to play with. At three years of age Moketubbe had a broad,
flat, Mongolian face that appeared to exist in a complete and unfathomable lethargy, until confronted by the slippers.

Moketubbe's mother was a comely girl whom Issetibbeha had
seen one day working in her shift in a melon patch. He stopped and
watched her for a while—the broad, solid thighs, the sound back,
the serene face. He was on his way to the creek to fish that day, but
he didn't go any farther; perhaps while he stood there watching the
unaware girl he may have remembered his own mother, the city
woman, the fugitive with her fans and laces and her Negro blood,
and all the tawdry shabbiness of that sorry affair. Within the year
Moketubbe was born; even at three he could not get his feet into
the slippers. Watching him in the still, hot afternoons as he struggled with the slippers with a certain monstrous repudiation of fact,
Issetibbeha laughed quietly to himself. He laughed at Moketubbe's
antics with the shoes for several years, because Moketubbe did not
give up trying to put them on until he was sixteen. Then he quit. Or
Issetibbeha thought he had. But he had merely quit trying in Issetibbeha's presence. Issetibbeha's newest wife told him that Moketubbe had stolen and hidden the shoes. Issetibbeha quit laughing
then, and he sent the woman away, so that he was alone. "Yao," he
said. "I too like being alive, it seems." He sent for Moketubbe. "I
give them to you," he said.

Moketubbe was twenty-five then, unmarried. Issetibbeha was not
tall, but he was taller by six inches than his son and almost a
hundred pounds lighter. Moketubbe was already diseased with
flesh, with a pale, broad, inert face and dropsical hands and feet.
"They are yours now," Issetibbeha said, watching him. Moketubbe
had looked at him once when he entered, a glance brief, discreet,
veiled.

"Thanks," he said.

Issetibbeha looked at him. He could never tell if Moketubbe saw
anything, looked at anything. "Why will it not be the same if I give
the slippers to you?"

"Thanks," Moketubbe said. Issetibbeha was using snuff at the
time; a white man had shown him how to put the powder into his
lip and scour it against his teeth with a twig of gum or of alphea.

"Well," he said, "a man cannot live forever." He looked at his
son, then his gaze went blank in turn, unseeing, and he mused for
an instant. You could not tell what he was thinking, save that he
said half aloud: "Yao. But Doom's uncle had no shoes with red
heels." He looked at his son again, fat, inert. "Beneath all that, a
man might think of doing anything and it not be known until too
late." He sat in a splint chair hammocked with deer thongs. "He

cannot even get them on; he and I are both frustrated by the same gross meat which he wears. He cannot even get them on. But is that my fault?"

He lived for five years longer, then he died. He was sick one night, and though the doctor came in a skunk-skin vest and burned sticks, Issetibbeha died before noon.

That was yesterday; the grave was dug, and for twelve hours now the People had been coming in wagons and carriages and on horseback and afoot, to eat the baked dog and the succotash and the yams cooked in ashes and to attend the funeral.

III

"It will be three days," Basket said, as he and the other Indian returned to the house. "It will be three days and the food will not be enough; I have seen it before."

The second Indian's name was Louis Berry. "He will smell too, in this weather."

"Yao. They are nothing but a trouble and a care."

"Maybe it will not take three days."

"They run far. Yao. We will smell this Man before he enters the earth. You watch and see if I am not right."

They approached the house.

"He can wear the shoes now," Berry said. "He can wear them now in man's sight."

"He cannot wear them for a while yet," Basket said. Berry looked at him. "He will lead the hunt."

"Moketubbe?" Berry said. "Do you think he will? A man to whom even talking is travail?"

"What else can he do? It is his own father who will soon begin to smell."

"That is true," Berry said. "There is even yet a price he must pay for the shoes. Yao. He has truly bought them. What do you think?"

"What do you think?"

"What do you think?"

"I think nothing."

"Nor do I. Issetibbeha will not need the shoes now. Let Moketubbe have them; Issetibbeha will not care."

"Yao. Man must die."

"Yao. Let him; there is still the Man."

The bark roof of the porch was supported by peeled cypress poles, high above the texas of the steamboat, shading an unfloored banquette where on the trodden earth mules and horses were tethered in bad weather. On the forward end of the steamboat's deck sat an old man and two women. One of the women was dressing a fowl, the other was shelling corn. The old man was talking. He was barefoot, in a long linen frock coat and a beaver hat.

"This world is going to the dogs," he said. "It is being ruined by white men. We got along fine for years and years, before the white men foisted their Negroes upon us. In the old days the old men sat in the shade and ate stewed deer's flesh and corn and smoked tobacco and talked of honor and grave affairs; now what do we do? Even the old wear themselves into the grave taking care of them that like sweating." When Basket and Berry crossed the deck he ceased and looked up at them. His eyes were querulous, bleared; his face was myriad with tiny wrinkles. "He is fled also," he said.

"Yes," Berry said, "he is gone."

"I knew it. I told them so. It will take three weeks, like when Doom died. You watch and see."

"It was three days, not three weeks," Berry said.

"Were you there?"

"No," Berry said. "But I have heard."

"Well, I was there," the old man said. "For three whole weeks, through the swamps and the briers—" They went on and left him talking.

What had been the saloon of the steamboat was now a shell, rotting slowly; the polished mahogany, the carving glinting momentarily and fading through the mold in figures cabalistic and profound; the gutted windows were like cataracted eyes. It contained a few sacks of seed or grain, and the fore part of the running gear of a barouche, to the axle of which two C-springs rusted in graceful curves, supporting nothing. In one corner a fox cub ran steadily and soundlessly up and down a willow cage; three scrawny gamecocks moved in the dust, and the place was pocked and marked with their dried droppings.

They passed through the brick wall and entered a big room of chinked logs. It contained the hinder part of the barouche, and the dismantled body lying on its side, the window slatted over with willow withes, through which protruded the heads, the still, beady, outraged eyes and frayed combs of still more game chickens. It was floored with packed clay; in one corner leaned a crude plow and two hand-hewn boat paddles. From the ceiling, suspended by four deer thongs, hung the gilt bed which Issetibbeha had fetched from Paris. It had neither mattress nor springs, the frame criss-crossed now by a neat hammocking of thongs.

Issetibbeha had tried to have his newest wife, the young one, sleep in the bed. He was congenitally short of breath himself, and he passed the nights half reclining in his splint chair. He would see her to bed and, later, wakeful, sleeping as he did but three or four hours a night, he would sit in the darkness and simulate slumber and listen to her sneak infinitesimally from the gilt and ribboned bed, to lie on a quilt pallet on the floor until just before daylight. Then she would enter the bed quietly again and in turn simulate slumber, while in the darkness beside her Issetibbeha quietly laughed and laughed.

The girandoles were lashed by thongs to two sticks propped in a corner where a ten-gallon whiskey keg lay also. There was a clay hearth; facing it, in the splint chair, Moketubbe sat. He was maybe an inch better than five feet tall, and he weighed two hundred and fifty pounds. He wore a broadcloth coat and no shirt, his round, smooth copper balloon of belly swelling above the bottom piece of a suit of linen underwear. On his feet were the slippers with the red heels. Behind his chair stood a stripling with a punkah-like fan made of fringed paper. Moketubbe sat motionless, with his broad, yellow face with its closed eyes and flat nostrils, his flipperlike arms extended. On his face was an expression profound, tragic, and inert. He did not open his eyes when Basket and Berry came in.

"He has worn them since daylight?" Basket said.

"Since daylight," the stripling said. The fan did not cease. "You can see."

"Yao," Basket said. "We can see." Moketubbe did not move. He looked like an effigy, like a Malay god in frock coat, drawers, naked chest, the trivial scarlet-heeled shoes.

"I wouldn't disturb him, if I were you," the stripling said.

"Not if I were you," Basket said. He and Berry squatted. The stripling moved the fan steadily. "O Man," Basket said, "listen." Moketubbe did not move. "He is gone," Basket said.

"I told you so," the stripling said. "I knew he would flee. I told you."

"Yao," Basket said. "You are not the first to tell us afterward what we should have known before. Why is it that some of you wise men took no steps yesterday to prevent this?"

"He does not wish to die," Berry said.

"Why should he not wish it?" Basket said.

"Because he must die some day is no reason," the stripling said. "That would not convince me either, old man."

"Hold your tongue," Berry said.

"For twenty years," Basket said, "while others of his race sweat in the fields, he served the Man in the shade. Why should he not wish to die, since he did not wish to sweat?"

"And it will be quick," Berry said. "It will not take long."

"Catch him and tell him that," the stripling said.

"Hush," Berry said. They squatted, watching Moketubbe's face. He might have been dead himself. It was as though he were cased so in flesh that even breathing took place too deep within him to show.

"Listen, O Man," Basket said. "Issetibbeha is dead. He waits. His dog and his horse we have. But his slave has fled. The one who held the pot for him, who ate of his food, from his dish, is fled. Issetibbeha waits."

"Yao," Berry said.

"This is not the first time," Basket said. "This happened when Doom, thy grandfather, lay waiting at the door of the earth. He lay waiting three days, saying, 'Where is my Negro?' And Issetibbeha, thy father, answered, 'I will find him. Rest; I will bring him to you so that you may begin the journey.'"

"Yao," Berry said.

Moketubbe had not moved, had not opened his eyes.

"For three days Issetibbeha hunted in the bottom," Basket said. "He did not even return home for food, until the Negro was with him; then he said to Doom, his father, 'Here is thy dog, thy horse, thy Negro; rest.' Issetibbeha, who is dead since yesterday, said it. And now Issetibbeha's Negro is fled. His horse and his dog wait with him, but his Negro is fled."

"Yao," Berry said.

Moketubbe had not moved. His eyes were closed; upon his supine monstrous shape there was a colossal inertia, something profoundly immobile, beyond and impervious to flesh. They watched his face, squatting.

"When thy father was newly the Man, this happened," Basket said. "And it was Issetibbeha who brought back the slave to where his father waited to enter the earth." Moketubbe's face had not moved, his eyes had not moved. After a while Basket said, "Remove the shoes."

The stripling removed the shoes. Moketubbe began to pant, his bare chest moving deep, as though he were rising from beyond his unfathomed flesh back into life, like up from the water, the sea. But his eyes had not opened yet.

Berry said, "He will lead the hunt."

"Yao," Basket said. "He is the Man. He will lead the hunt."

IV

All that day the Negro, Issetibbeha's body servant, hidden in the barn, watched Issetibbeha's dying. He was forty, a Guinea man. He had a flat nose, a close, small head; the inside corners of his eyes showed red a little, and his prominent gums were a pale bluish red above his square, broad teeth. He had been taken at fourteen by a trader off Kamerun, before his teeth had been filed. He had been Issetibbeha's body servant for twenty-three years.

On the day before, the day on which Issetibbeha lay sick, he returned to the quarters at dusk. In that unhurried hour the smoke of the cooking fires blew slowly across the street from door to door, carrying into the opposite one the smell of the identical meat and bread. The women tended them; the men were gathered at the head of the lane, watching him as he came down the slope from the house, putting his naked feet down carefully in a strange dusk. To the waiting men his eyeballs were a little luminous.

"Issetibbeha is not dead yet," the headman said.

"Not dead," the body servant said. "Who not dead?"

"In the dusk they had faces like his, the different ages, the thoughts sealed inscrutable behind faces like the death masks of apes. The smell of the fires, the cooking, blew sharp and slow across the strange dusk, as from another world, above the lane and the pickaninnies naked in the dust.

"If he lives past sundown, he will live until daybreak," one said.

"Who says?"

"Talk says."

"Yao. Talk says. We know but one thing." They looked at the body servant as he stood among them, his eyeballs a little luminous. He was breathing slow and deep. His chest was bare; he was sweating a little. "He knows. He knows it."

"Let us let the drums talk."

"Yao. Let the drums tell it."

The drums began after dark. They kept them hidden in the creek bottom. They were made of hollowed cypress knees, and the Negroes kept them hidden; why, none knew. They were buried in the mud on the bank of a slough; a lad of fourteen guarded them. He was undersized, and a mute; he squatted in the mud there all day, clouded over with mosquitoes, naked save for the mud with which he coated himself against the mosquitoes, and about his neck a fiber bag containing a pig's rib to which black shreds of flesh still adhered, and two scaly barks on a wire. He slobbered onto his clutched knees, drooling; now and then Indians came noiselessly out of the bushes behind him and stood there and contemplated him for a while and went away, and he never knew it.

From the loft of the stable where he lay hidden until dark and after, the Negro could hear the drums. They were three miles away, but he could hear them as though they were in the barn itself below him, thudding and thudding. It was as though he could see the fire too, and the black limbs turning into and out of the flames in copper gleams. Only there would be no fire. There would be no more light there than where he lay in the dusty loft, with the whispering arpeggios of rat feet along the warm and immemorial ax-squared rafters. The only fire there would be the smudge against mosquitoes where the women with nursing children crouched, their heavy, sluggish breasts nippled full and smooth into the mouths of men children; contemplative, oblivious of the drumming, since a fire would signify life.

There was a fire in the steamboat, where Issetibbeha lay dying among his wives, beneath the lashed girandoles and the suspended bed. He could see the smoke, and just before sunset he saw the doctor come out, in a waistcoat made of skunk skins, and set fire to two clay-daubed sticks at the bows of the boat deck. "So he is not dead yet," the Negro said into the whispering gloom of the loft, answering himself; he could hear the two voices, himself and himself:

"Who not dead?"

"You are dead."

"Yao, I am dead," he said quietly. He wished to be where the drums were. He imagined himself springing out of the bushes, leaping among the drums on his bare, lean, greasy, invisible limbs. But he could not do that, because man leaped past life, into where death was; he dashed into death and did not die because when death took a man, it took him just this side of the end of living. It was when death overran him from behind, still in life. The thin whisper of rat feet died in fainting gusts along the rafters. Once he had eaten rat. He was a boy then, but just come to America. They had lived ninety days in a three-foot-high 'tween deck in tropic latitudes, hearing from topside the drunken New England captain intoning aloud from a book which he did not recognize for ten years afterward to be the Bible. Squatting in the stable so, he had watched the rat, civilized, by association with man reft of its inherent cunning of limb and eye; he had caught it without difficulty, with scarce a movement of his hand, and he ate it slowly, wondering how any of the rats had escaped so long. At that time he was still wearing the single white garment which the trader, a deacon in the Unitarian church, had given him, and he spoke then only his native tongue.

He was naked now, save for a pair of dungaree pants bought by Indians from white men, and an amulet slung on a thong about his hips. The amulet consisted of one half of a mother-of-pearl lorgnon [5] which Issetibbeha had brought back from Paris, and the skull of a cottonmouth moccasin. He had killed the snake himself and eaten it, save the poison head. He lay in the loft, watching the house, the steamboat, listening to the drums, thinking of himself among the drums.

He lay there all night. The next morning he saw the doctor come out, in his skunk vest, and get on his mule and ride away, and he became quite still and watched the final dust from beneath the

5. Lorgnette; eyeglasses with a short handle.

mule's delicate feet die away, and then he found that he was still breathing and it seemed strange to him that he still breathed air, still needed air. Then he lay and watched quietly, waiting to move, his eyeballs a little luminous, but with a quiet light, and his breathing light and regular, and saw Louis Berry come out and look at the sky. It was good light then, and already five Indians squatted in their Sunday clothes along the steamboat deck; by noon there were twenty-five there. That afternoon they dug the trench in which the meat would be baked, and the yams; by that time there were almost a hundred guests—decorous, quiet, patient in their stiff European finery—and he watched Berry lead Issetibbeha's mare from the stable and tie her to a tree, and then he watched Berry emerge from the house with the old hound which lay beside Issetibbeha's chair. He tied the hound to the tree too, and it sat there, looking gravely about at the faces. Then it began to howl. It was still howling at sundown, when the Negro climbed down the back wall of the barn and entered the spring branch, where it was already dusk. He began to run then. He could hear the hound howling behind him, and near the spring, already running, he passed another Negro. The two men, the one motionless and the other running, looked for an instant at each other as though across an actual boundary between two different worlds. He ran on into full darkness, mouth closed, fists doubled, his broad nostrils bellowing steadily.

He ran on in the darkness. He knew the country well, because he had hunted it often with Issetibbeha, following on his mule the course of the fox or the cat beside Issetibbeha's mare; he knew it as well as did the men who would pursue him. He saw them for the first time shortly before sunset of the second day. He had run thirty miles then, up the creek bottom, before doubling back; lying in a pawpaw thicket he saw the pursuit for the first time. There were two of them, in shirts and straw hats, carrying their neatly rolled trousers under their arms, and they had no weapons. They were middle-aged, paunchy, and they could not have moved very fast anyway; it would be twelve hours before they could return to where he lay watching them. "So I will have until midnight to rest," he said. He was near enough to the plantation to smell the cooking fires, and he thought how he ought to be hungry, since he had not eaten in thirty hours. "But it is more important to rest," he told himself. He continued to tell himself that, lying in the pawpaw thicket, because the effort of resting, the need and the haste to rest, made his heart thud the same as the running had done. It was as though he had forgot how to rest, as though the six hours were not long enough to do it in, to remember again how to do it.

As soon as dark came he moved again. He had thought to keep going steadily and quietly through the night, since there was nowhere for him to go, but as soon as he moved he began to run at top speed, breasting his panting chest, his broad-flaring nostrils through the choked and whipping darkness. He ran for an hour, lost by then, without direction, when suddenly he stopped, and after a time his thudding heart unraveled from the sound of the drums. By the sound they were not two miles away; he followed the sound until he could smell the smudge fire and taste the acrid smoke. When he stood among them the drums did not cease; only the headman came to him where he stood in the drifting smudge, panting, his nostrils flaring and pulsing, the hushed glare of his ceaseless eyeballs in his mud-daubed face as though they were worked from lungs.

"We have expected thee," the headman said. "Go, now."

"Go?"

"Eat, and go. The dead may not consort with the living; thou knowest that."

"Yao. I know that." They did not look at one another. The drums had not ceased.

"Wilt thou eat?" the headman said.

"I am not hungry. I caught a rabbit this afternoon, and ate while I lay hidden."

"Take some cooked meat with thee, then."

He accepted the cooked meat, wrapped in leaves, and entered the creek bottom again; after a while the sound of the drums ceased. He walked steadily until daybreak. "I have twelve hours," he said. "Maybe more, since the trail was followed by night." He squatted and ate the meat and wiped his hands on his thighs. Then he rose and removed the dungaree pants and squatted again beside a slough and coated himself with mud—face, arms, body and legs— and squatted again, clasping his knees, his head bowed. When it was light enough to see, he moved back into the swamp and squatted again and went to sleep so. He did not dream at all. It was well that he moved, for, waking suddenly in broad daylight and the high sun, he saw the two Indians. They still carried their neatly rolled trousers; they stood opposite the place where he lay hidden, paunchy, thick, soft-looking, a little ludicrous in their straw hats and shirt tails.

"This is wearying work," one said.

"I'd rather be at home in the shade myself," the other said. "But there is the Man waiting at the door to the earth."

"Yao." They looked quietly about; stooping, one of them removed from his shirt tail a clot of cockle-burs. "Damn that Negro," he said.

"Yao. When have they ever been anything but a trial and a care to us?"

In the early afternoon, from the top of a tree, the Negro looked down into the plantation. He could see Issetibbeha's body in a hammock between the two trees where the horse and the dog were tethered, and the concourse about the steamboat was filled with wagons and horses and mules, with carts and saddle-horses, while in bright clumps the women and the smaller children and the old men squatted about the long trench where the smoke from the barbecuing meat blew slow and thick. The men and the big boys would all be down there in the creek bottom behind him, on the trail, their Sunday clothes rolled carefully up and wedged into tree crotches. There was a clump of men near the door to the house, to the saloon of the steamboat, though, and he watched them, and after a while he saw them bring Moketubbe out in a litter made of buckskin and persimmon poles; high hidden in his leafed nook the Negro, the quarry, looked quietly down upon his irrevocable doom with an expression as profound as Moketubbe's own. "Yao," he said quietly. "He will go then. That man whose body has been dead for fifteen years, he will go also."

In the middle of the afternoon he came face to face with an Indian. They were both on a footlog across a slough—the Negro gaunt, lean, hard, tireless and desperate; the Indian thick, soft-looking, the apparent embodiment of the ultimate and the supreme reluctance and inertia. The Indian made no move, no sound; he stood on the log and watched the Negro plunge into the slough and swim ashore and crash away into the undergrowth.

Just before sunset he lay behind a down log. Up the log in slow procession moved a line of ants. He caught them and ate them slowly, with a kind of detachment, like that of a dinner guest eating salted nuts from a dish. They too had a salt taste, engendering a salivary reaction out of all proportion. He ate them slowly, watching the unbroken line move up the log and into oblivious doom with a steady and terrific undeviation. He had eaten nothing else all day; in his caked mud mask his eyes rolled in reddened rims. At sunset, creeping along the creek bank toward where he had spotted a frog, a cottonmouth moccasin slashed him suddenly across the forearm with a thick, sluggish blow. It struck clumsily, leaving two long slashes across his arm like two razor slashes, and half sprawled with its own momentum and rage, it appeared for the moment utterly helpless with its own awkwardness and choleric anger. "Olé, Grandfather," [6] the Negro said. He touched its head and watched it

6. Salute expressing awe and reverence for the total order of nature. The salute is repeated in the Go Down, Moses stories. In "The Old People" Sam Fathers hails the phantom buck with "his right arm raised at full length, palm-outward," and speaks in the language of his Indian ancestors: " 'Oleh, Chief,' Sam said. 'Grandfather.' " And in "The Bear" Part V, Ike McCaslin confronts the rattlesnake and speaks in "the old tongue which Sam had spoken that day without premeditation either: 'Chief,' he said: 'Grandfather.' "

slash him again across his arm, and again, with thick, raking, awkward blows. "It's that I do not wish to die," he said. Then he said it again—"It's that I do not wish to die"—in a quiet tone, of slow and low amaze, as though it were something that, until the words had said themselves, he found that he had not known, or had not known the depth and extent of his desire.

V

Moketubbe took the slippers with him. He could not wear them very long while in motion, not even in the litter where he was slung reclining, so they rested upon a square of fawnskin upon his lap—the cracked, frail slippers a little shapeless now, with their scaled patent-leather surface and buckleless tongues and scarlet heels, lying upon the supine, obese shape just barely alive, carried through swamp and brier by swinging relays of men who bore steadily all day long the crime and its object, on the business of the slain. To Moketubbe it must have been as though, himself immortal, he were being carried rapidly through hell by doomed spirits which, alive, had contemplated his disaster, and, dead, were oblivious partners to his damnation.

After resting for a while, the litter propped in the center of the squatting circle and Moketubbe motionless in it, with closed eyes and his face at once peaceful for the instant and filled with inescapable foreknowledge, he could wear the slippers for a while. The stripling put them on him, forcing his big, tender, dropsical feet into them; whereupon into his face came again that expression, tragic, passive, and profoundly attentive, which dyspeptics wear. Then they went on. He made no move, no sound, inert in the rhythmic litter out of some reserve of inertia, or maybe of some kingly virtue such as courage or fortitude. After a time they set the litter down and looked at him, at the yellow face like that of an idol, beaded over with sweat. Then Three Basket or Louis Berry would say: "Take them off. Honor has been served." They would remove the shoes. Moketubbe's face would not alter, but only then would his breathing become perceptible, going in and out of his pale lips with a faint ah-ah-ah sound, and they would squat again while the couriers and the runners came up.

"Not yet?"

"Not yet. He is going east. By sunset he will reach Mouth of Tippah. Then he will turn back. We may take him tomorrow."

"Let us hope so. It will not be too soon."

"Yao. It has been three days now."

"When Doom died, it took only three days."

"But that was an old man. This one is young."

"Yao. A good race. If he is taken tomorrow, I will win a horse."

"May you win it."

"Yao. This work is not pleasant."

That was the day on which the food gave out at the plantation. The guests returned home and came back the next day with more food, enough for a week longer. On that day Issetibbeha began to smell; they could smell him for a long way up and down the bottom when it got hot toward noon and the wind blew. But they didn't capture the Negro on that day, nor on the next. It was about dusk on the sixth day when the couriers came up to the litter; they had found blood. "He has injured himself."

"Not bad, I hope," Basket said. "We cannot send with Issetibbeha one who will be of no service to him."

"Nor whom Issetibbeha himself will have to nurse and care for," Berry said.

"We do not know," the courier said. "He has hidden himself. He has crept back into the swamp. We have left pickets."

They trotted with the litter now. The place where the Negro had crept into the swamp was an hour away. In the hurry and excitement they had forgotten that Moketubbe still wore the slippers; when they reached the place Moketubbe had fainted. They removed the slippers and brought him to.

With dark, they formed a circle about the swamp. They squatted, clouded over with gnats and mosquitoes; the evening star burned low and close down the west, and the constellations began to wheel overhead. "We will give him time," they said. "Tomorrow is just another name for today."

"Yao. Let him have time." Then they ceased, and gazed as one into the darkness where the swamp lay. After a while the noise ceased, and soon the courier came out of the darkness.

"He tried to break out."

"But you turned him back?"

"He turned back. We feared for a moment, the three of us. We could smell him creeping in the darkness, and we could smell something else, which we did not know. That was why we feared, until he told us. He said to slay him there, since it would be dark and he would not have to see the face when it came. But it was not that which we smelled; he told us what it was. A snake had struck him. That was two days ago. The arm swelled, and it smelled bad. But it was not that which we smelled then, because the swelling had gone down and his arm was no larger than that of a child. He showed us. We felt the arm, all of us did; it was no larger than that of a child. He said to give him a hatchet so he could chop the arm off. But tomorrow is today also."

"Yao. Tomorrow is today."

"We feared for a while. Then he went back into the swamp."

"That is good."

"Yao. We feared. Shall I tell the Man?"

"I will see," Basket said. He went away. The courier squatted, telling again about the Negro. Basket returned. "The Man says that it is good. Return to your post."

The courier crept away. They squatted about the litter; now and then they slept. Sometime after midnight the Negro waked them. He began to shout and talk to himself, his voice coming sharp and sudden out of the darkness, then he fell silent. Dawn came; a white crane flapped slowly across the jonquil sky. Basket was awake. "Let us go now," he said. "It is today."

Two Indians entered the swamp, their movements noisy. Before they reached the Negro they stopped, because he began to sing. They could see him, naked and mud-caked, sitting on a log, singing. They squatted silently a short distance away, until he finished. He was chanting something in his own language, his face lifted to the rising sun. His voice was clear, full, with a quality wild and sad. "Let him have time," the Indians said, squatting, patient, waiting. He ceased and they approached. He looked back and up at them through the cracked mud mask. His eyes were bloodshot, his lips cracked upon his square short teeth. The mask of mud appeared to be loose on his face, as if he might have lost flesh since he put it there; he held his left arm close to his breast. From the elbow down it was caked and shapeless with black mud. They could smell him, a rank smell. He watched them quietly until one touched him on the arm. "Come," the Indian said. "You ran well. Do not be ashamed."

VI

As they neared the plantation in the tainted bright morning, the Negro's eyes began to roll a little, like those of a horse. The smoke from the cooking pit blew low along the earth and upon the squatting and waiting guests about the yard and upon the steamboat deck, in their bright, stiff, harsh finery; the women, the children, the old men. They had sent couriers along the bottom, and another on ahead, and Issetibbeha's body had already been removed to where the grave waited, along with the horse and the dog, though they could still smell him in death about the house where he had lived in life. The guests were beginning to move toward the grave when the bearers of Moketubbe's litter mounted the slope.

The Negro was the tallest there, his high, close, mud-caked head looming above them all. He was breathing hard, as though the desperate effort of the six suspended and desperate days had capitulated upon him at once; although they walked slowly, his naked scarred chest rose and fell above the close-clutched left arm. He looked this way and that continuously, as if he were not seeing, as though sight never quite caught up with the looking. His mouth was open a little upon his big white teeth; he began to pant. The already moving guests halted, pausing, looking back, some with pieces of meat in their hands, as the Negro looked about at their faces with his wild, restrained, unceasing eyes.

"Will you eat first?" Basket said. He had to say it twice.

"Yes," the Negro said. "That's it. I want to eat."

The throng had begun to press back toward the center; the word passed to the outermost: "He will eat first."

They reached the steamboat. "Sit down," Basket said. The Negro sat on the edge of the deck. He was still panting, his chest rising and falling, his head ceaseless with its white eyeballs, turning from side to side. It was as if the inability to see came from within, from hopelessness, not from absence of vision. They brought food and watched quietly as he tried to eat it. He put the food into his mouth and chewed it, but chewing, the half-masticated matter began to emerge from the corners of his mouth and to drool down his chin, onto his chest, and after a while he stopped chewing and sat there, naked, covered with dried mud, the plate on his knees, and his mouth filled with a mass of chewed food, open, his eyes wide and unceasing, panting and panting. They watched him, patient, implacable, waiting.

"Come," Basket said at last.

"It's water I want," the Negro said. "I want water."

The well was a little way down the slope toward the quarters. The slope lay dappled with the shadows of noon, of that peaceful hour when, Issetibbeha napping in his chair and waiting for the noon meal and the long afternoon to sleep in, the Negro, the body servant, would be free. He would sit in the kitchen door then, talking with the women that prepared the food. Beyond the kitchen the lane between the quarters would be quiet, peaceful, with the women talking to one another across the lane and the smoke of the dinner fires blowing upon the pickaninnies like ebony toys in the dust.

"Come," Basket said.

The Negro walked among them, taller than any. The guests were moving on toward where Issetibbeha and the horse and the dog waited. The Negro walked with his high ceaseless head, his panting chest. "Come," Basket said. "You wanted water."

"Yes," the Negro said. "Yes." He looked back at the house, then down to the quarters, where today no fire burned, no face showed in any door, no pickaninny in the dust, panting. "It struck me here, raking me across this arm; once, twice, three times. I said, 'Olé, Grandfather.' "

"Come now," Basket said. The Negro was still going through the motion of walking, his knee action high, his head high, as though he were on a treadmill. His eyeballs had a wild, restrained glare, like those of a horse. "You wanted water," Basket said. "Here it is."

There was a gourd in the well. They dipped it full and gave it to the Negro, and they watched him try to drink. His eyes had not ceased rolling as he tilted the gourd slowly against his caked face. They could watch his throat working and the bright water cascading from either side of the gourd, down his chin and breast. Then the water stopped. "Come," Basket said.

"Wait," the Negro said. He dipped the gourd again and tilted it against his face, beneath his ceaseless eyes. Again they watched his throat working and the unswallowed water sheathing broken and myriad down his chin, channeling his caked chest. They waited, patient, grave, decorous, implacable; clansman and guest and kin. Then the water ceased, though still the empty gourd tilted higher and higher, and still his black throat aped the vain motion of his frustrated swallowing. A piece of water-loosened mud carried away from his chest and broke at his muddy feet, and in the empty gourd they could hear his breath: ah-ah-ah.

"Come," Basket said, taking the gourd from the Negro and hanging it back in the well.

From *These 13* (1931)

THAT EVENING SUN [1]

Monday is no different from any other weekday in Jefferson now. The streets are paved now, and the telephone and electric companies are cutting down more and more of the shade trees—the water oaks, the maples and locusts and elms—to make room for iron poles bearing clusters of bloated and ghostly and bloodless grapes, and we have a city laundry which makes the rounds on Monday morning, gathering the bundles of clothes into bright-colored, specially made motorcars: the soiled wearing of a whole week now flees apparitionlike behind alert and irritable electric horns, with a long diminishing noise of rubber and asphalt like tearing silk, and even the Negro women who still take in white people's washing after the old custom, fetch and deliver it in automobiles.

But fifteen years ago, on Monday morning the quiet, dusty, shady streets would be full of Negro women with, balanced on their steady, turbaned heads, bundles of clothes tied up in sheets, almost as large as cotton bales, carried so without touch of hand between the kitchen door of the white house and the blackened washpot beside a cabin door in Negro Hollow.

Nancy would set her bundle on the top of her head, then upon the bundle in turn she would set the black straw sailor hat which she wore winter and summer. She was tall, with a high, sad face sunken a little where her teeth were missing. Sometimes we would go a part of the way down the lane and across the pasture with her, to watch the balanced bundle and the hat that never bobbed nor wavered, even when she walked down into the ditch and up the other side and stooped through the fence. She would go down on her hands and knees and crawl through the gap, her head rigid, uptilted, the bundle steady as a rock or a balloon, and rise to her feet again and go on.

Sometimes the husbands of the washing women would fetch and deliver the clothes, but Jesus never did that for Nancy, even before Father told him to stay away from our house, even when Dilsey was sick and Nancy would come to cook for us.

1. The title is taken from "St. Louis Blues," by W. C. Handy (1873–1958), where a woman sings of her unfaithful lover: "I hate to see de ev'nin' sun go down, / Hate to see de ev'nin' sun go down. / 'Cause my baby, he done lef' dis town."

The narrator of "That Evening Sun" is Quentin Compson, who also tells parts of *The Sound and the Fury* (1929) and *Absalom, Absalom!* (1936). The time of the story is approximately 1902, eight years before the events in Quentin's life reported in the two novels. Most of the characters in "That Evening Sun" are familiar from *The Sound and the Fury:* Jason Compson Sr., Quentin's genteel but weak father; his second son, Jason Jr.; Candace (Caddy), his only daughter; and Dilsey, the patient and enduring Negro who cooks for the Compsons.

And then about half the time we'd have to go down the lane to Nancy's cabin and tell her to come on and cook breakfast. We would stop at the ditch, because Father told us to not have anything to do with Jesus—he was a short black man, with a razor scar down his face—and we would throw rocks at Nancy's house until she came to the door, leaning her head around it without any clothes on.

"What yawl mean, chunking my house?" Nancy said. "What you little devils mean?"

"Father says for you to come on and get breakfast," Caddy said. "Father says it's over a half an hour now, and you've got to come this minute."

"I ain't studying no breakfast," Nancy said. "I going to get my sleep out."

"I bet you're drunk," Jason said. "Father says you're drunk. Are you drunk, Nancy?"

"Who says I is?" Nancy said. "I got to get my sleep out. I ain't studying no breakfast."

So after a while we quit chunking the cabin and went back home. When she finally came, it was too late for me to go to school. So we thought it was whiskey until that day they arrested her again and they were taking her to jail and they passed Mr. Stovall. He was the cashier in the bank and a deacon in the Baptist church, and Nancy began to say:

"When you going to pay me, white man? When you going to pay me, white man? It's been three times now since you paid me a cent—" Mr. Stovall knocked her down, but she kept on saying, "When you going to pay me, white man? It's been three times now since—" until Mr. Stovall kicked her in the mouth with his heel and the marshal caught Mr. Stovall back, and Nancy lying in the street, laughing. She turned her head and spat out some blood and teeth and said, "It's been three times now since he paid me a cent."

That was how she lost her teeth, and all that day they told about Nancy and Mr. Stovall, and all that night the ones that passed the jail could hear Nancy singing and yelling. They could see her hands holding to the window bars, and a lot of them stopped along the fence, listening to her and to the jailer trying to make her stop. She didn't shut up until almost daylight, when the jailer began to hear a bumping and scraping upstairs and he went up there and found Nancy hanging from the window bar. He said that it was cocaine and not whiskey, because no nigger would try to commit suicide unless he was full of cocaine, because a nigger full of co-caine wasn't a nigger any longer.

The jailer cut her down and revived her; then he beat her, whipped her. She had hung herself with her dress. She had fixed it all right, but when they arrested her she didn't have on anything except a dress and so she didn't have anything to tie her hands with and she couldn't make her hands let go of the window ledge. So the jailer heard the noise and ran up there and found Nancy hanging from the window, stark naked, her belly already swelling out a little, like a little balloon.

When Dilsey was sick in her cabin and Nancy was cooking for us, we could see her apron swelling out; that was before Father told Jesus to stay away from the house. Jesus was in the kitchen, sitting behind the stove, with his razor scar on his black face like a piece of dirty string. He said it was a watermelon that Nancy had under her dress.

"It never come off of your vine, though," Nancy said.

"Off of what vine?" Caddy said.

"I can cut down the vine it did come off of," Jesus said.

"What makes you want to talk like that before these chillen?" Nancy said. "Whyn't you go on to work? You done et. You want Mr. Jason to catch you hanging around his kitchen, talking that way before these chillen?"

"Talking what way?" Caddy said, "What vine?"

"I can't hang around white man's kitchen," Jesus said. "But white man can hang around mine. White man can come in my house, but I can't stop him. When white man want to come in my house, I ain't got no house. I can't stop him, but he can't kick me outen it. He can't do that."

Dilsey was still sick in her cabin. Father told Jesus to stay off our place. Dilsey was still sick. It was a long time. We were in the library after supper.

"Isn't Nancy through in the kitchen yet?" Mother said. "It seems to me that she has had plenty of time to have finished the dishes."

"Let Quentin go and see," Father said. "Go and see if Nancy is through, Quentin. Tell her she can go on home."

I went to the kitchen. Nancy was through. The dishes were put away and the fire was out. Nancy was sitting in a chair, close to the cold stove. She looked at me.

"Mother wants to know if you are through," I said.

"Yes," Nancy said. She looked at me. "I done finished." She looked at me.

"What is it?" I said. "What is it?"

"I ain't nothing but a nigger," Nancy said. "It ain't none of my fault."

She looked at me, sitting in the chair before the cold stove, the sailor hat on her head. I went back to the library. It was the cold stove and all, when you think of a kitchen being warm and busy and cheerful. And with a cold stove and the dishes all put away, and nobody wanting to eat at that hour.

"Is she through?" Mother said.

"Yessum," I said.

"What is she doing?" Mother said.

"She's not doing anything. She's through."

"I'll go and see," Father said.

"Maybe she's waiting for Jesus to come and take her home," Caddy said.

"Jesus is gone," I said. Nancy told us how one morning she woke up and Jesus was gone.

"He quit me," Nancy said. "Done gone to Memphis, I reckon. Dodging them city *po*-lice for a while, I reckon."

"And a good riddance," Father said. "I hope he stays there."

"Nancy's scaired of the dark," Jason said.

"So are you," Caddy said.

"I'm not," Jason said.

"Scairy cat," Caddy said.

"I'm not," Jason said.

"You, Candace!" Mother said. Father came back.

"I am going to walk down the lane with Nancy," he said. "She says that Jesus is back."

"Has she seen him?" Mother said.

"No. Some Negro sent her word that he was back in town. I won't be long."

"You'll leave me alone, to take Nancy home?" Mother said. "Is her safety more precious to you than mine?"

"I won't be long," Father said.

"You'll leave these children unprotected, with that Negro about?"

"I'm going too," Caddy said. "Let me go, Father."

"What would he do with them, if he were unfortunate enough to have them?" Father said.

"I want to go, too," Jason said.

"Jason!" Mother said. She was speaking to Father. You could tell that by the way she said the name. Like she believed that all day Father had been trying to think of doing the thing she wouldn't like the most, and that she knew all the time that after a while he would think of it. I stayed quiet, because Father and I both knew that Mother would want him to make me stay with her if she just thought of it in time. So Father didn't look at me. I was the oldest. I was nine and Caddy was seven and Jason was five.

"Nonsense," Father said. "We won't be long."

Nancy had her hat on. We came to the lane. "Jesus always been good to me," Nancy said. "Whenever he had two dollars, one of them was mine." We walked in the lane. "If I can just get through the lane," Nancy said, "I be all right then."

The lane was always dark. "This is where Jason got scaired on Hallowe'en," Caddy said.

"I didn't," Jason said.

"Can't Aunt Rachel do anything with him?" Father said. Aunt Rachel was old. She lived in a cabin beyond Nancy's, by herself. She had white hair and she smoked a pipe in the door, all day long; she didn't work any more. They said she was Jesus' mother. Sometimes she said she was and sometimes she said she wasn't any kin to Jesus.

"Yes you did," Caddy said. "You were scairder than Frony. You were scairder than T.P. even. Scairder than niggers."

"Can't nobody do nothing with him," Nancy said. "He say I done woke up the devil in him and ain't but one thing going to lay it down again."

"Well, he's gone now," Father said. "There's nothing for you to be afraid of now. And if you'd just let white men alone."

"Let what white men alone?" Caddy said. "How let them alone?"

"He ain't gone nowhere," Nancy said. "I can feel him. I can feel him now, in this lane. He hearing us talk, every word, hid somewhere, waiting. I ain't seen him, and I ain't going to see him again but once more, with that razor in his mouth. That razor on that string down his back, inside his shirt. And then I ain't going to be even surprised."

"I wasn't scaired," Jason said.

"If you'd behave yourself, you'd have kept out of this," Father said. "But it's all right now. He's probably in Saint Louis now. Probably got another wife by now and forgot all about you."

"If he has, I better not find out about it," Nancy said. "I'd stand there right over them, and every time he wropped her, I'd cut that arm off. I'd cut his head off and I'd slit her belly and I'd shove—"

"Hush," Father said.

"Slit whose belly, Nancy?" Caddy said.

"I wasn't scaired," Jason said. "I'd walk right down this lane by myself."

"Yah," Caddy said. "You wouldn't dare to put your foot down in it if we were not here too."

II

Dilsey was still sick, so we took Nancy home every night until Mother said, "How much longer is this going on? I to be left alone in this big house while you take home a frightened Negro?"

We fixed a pallet in the kitchen for Nancy. One night we waked up, hearing the sound. It was not singing and it was not crying, coming up the dark stairs. There was a light in Mother's room and we heard Father going down the hall, down the back stairs, and Caddy and I went into the hall. The floor was cold. Our toes curled away from it while we listened to the sound. It was like singing and it wasn't like singing, like the sounds that Negroes make.

Then it stopped and we heard Father going down the back stairs, and we went to the head of the stairs. Then the sound began again, in the stairway, not loud, and we could see Nancy's eyes halfway up the stairs, against the wall. They looked like cat's eyes do, like a big cat against the wall, watching us. When we came down the steps to where she was, she quit making the sound again, and we stood there until Father came back up from the kitchen, with his pistol in his hand. He went back down with Nancy and they came back with Nancy's pallet.

We spread the pallet in our room. After the light in Mother's room went off, we could see Nancy's eyes again. "Nancy," Caddy whispered, "are you asleep, Nancy?"

Nancy whispered something. It was oh or no, I don't know which. Like nobody had made it, like it came from nowhere and went nowhere, until it was like Nancy was not there at all; that I had looked so hard at her eyes on the stairs that they had got printed on my eyeballs, like the sun does when you have closed your eyes and there is no sun. "Jesus," Nancy whispered. "Jesus."

"Was it Jesus?" Caddy said. "Did he try to come into the kitchen?"

"Jesus," Nancy said. Like this: Jeeeeeeeeeeeeeeeesus, until the sound went out, like a match or a candle does.

"It's the other Jesus she means," I said.

"Can you see us, Nancy?" Caddy whispered. "Can you see our eyes too?"

"I ain't nothing but a nigger," Nancy said. "God knows. God knows."

"What did you see down there in the kitchen?" Caddy whispered. "What tried to get in?"

"God knows," Nancy said. We could see her eyes. "God knows."

Dilsey got well. She cooked dinner. "You'd better stay in bed a day or two longer," Father said.

"What for?" Dilsey said. "If I had been a day later, this place would be to rack and ruin. Get on out of here now, and let me get my kitchen straight again."

Dilsey cooked supper too. And that night, just before dark, Nancy came into the kitchen.

"How do you know he's back?" Dilsey said. "You ain't seen him."

"Jesus is a nigger," Jason said.

"I can feel him," Nancy said. "I can feel him laying yonder in the ditch."

"Tonight?" Dilsey said. "Is he there tonight?"

"Dilsey's a nigger too," Jason said.

"You try to eat something," Dilsey said.

"I don't want nothing," Nancy said.

"I ain't a nigger," Jason said.

"Drink some coffee," Dilsey said. She poured a cup of coffee for Nancy. "Do you know he's out there tonight? How come you know it's tonight?"

"I know," Nancy said. "He's there, waiting. I know. I done lived with him too long. I know what he is fixing to do fore he know it himself."

"Drink some coffee," Dilsey said. Nancy held the cup to her mouth and blew into the cup. Her mouth pursed out like a spreading adder's, like a rubber mouth, like she had blown all the color out of her lips with blowing the coffee.

"I ain't a nigger," Jason said. "Are you a nigger, Nancy?"

"I hellborn, child," Nancy said. "I won't be nothing soon. I going back where I come from soon."

III

She began to drink the coffee. While she was drinking, holding the cup in both hands, she began to make the sound again. She made the sound into the cup and the coffee sploshed out onto her hands and her dress. Her eyes looked at us and she sat there, her elbows on her knees, holding the cup in both hands, looking at us across the wet cup, making the sound.

"Look at Nancy," Jason said. "Nancy can't cook for us now. Dilsey's got well now."

"You hush up," Dilsey said. Nancy held the cup in both hands, looking at us, making the sound, like there were two of them: one looking at us and the other making the sound. "Whyn't you let Mr. Jason telefoam the marshal?" Dilsey said. Nancy stopped then holding the cup in her long brown hands. She tried to drink some coffee again, but it sploshed out of the cup, onto her hands and her dress, and she put the cup down. Jason watched her.

"I can't swallow it," Nancy said. "I swallows but it won't go down me."

"You go down to the cabin," Dilsey said. "Frony will fix you a pallet and I'll be there soon."

"Won't no nigger stop him," Nancy said.

"I ain't a nigger," Jason said. "Am I, Dilsey?"

"I reckon not," Dilsey said. She looked at Nancy. "I don't reckon so. What you going to do, then?"

Nancy looked at us. Her eyes went fast, like she was afraid there wasn't time to look, without hardly moving at all. She looked at us, at all three of us at one time. "You member that night I stayed in yawls' room?" she said. She told about how we waked up early the next morning, and played. We had to play quiet, on her pallet, until Father woke up and it was time to get breakfast. "Go and ask your maw to let me stay here tonight," Nancy said. "I won't need no pallet. We can play some more."

Caddy asked Mother. Jason went too. "I can't have Negroes sleeping in the bedrooms," Mother said. Jason cried. He cried until Mother said he couldn't have any dessert for three days if he didn't stop. Then Jason said he would stop if Dilsey would make a chocolate cake. Father was there.

"Why don't you do something about it?" Mother said. "What do we have officers for?"

"Why is Nancy afraid of Jesus?" Caddy said. "Are you afraid of Father, Mother?"

"What could the officers do?" Father said. "If Nancy hasn't seen him, how could the officers find him?"

"Then why is she afraid?" Mother said.

"She says he is there. She says she knows he is there tonight."

"Yet we pay taxes," Mother said. "I must wait here alone in this big house while you take a Negro woman home."

"You know that I am not lying outside with a razor," Father said.

"I'll stop if Dilsey will make a chocolate cake," Jason said. Mother told us to go out and Father said he didn't know if Jason would get a chocolate cake or not, but he knew what Jason was going to get in about a minute. We went back to the kitchen and told Nancy.

"Father said for you to go home and lock the door, and you'll be all right," Caddy said. "All right from what, Nancy? Is Jesus mad at you?" Nancy was holding the coffee cup in her hands again, her elbows on her knees and her hands holding the cup between her knees. She was looking into the cup. "What have you done that made Jesus mad?" Caddy said. Nancy let the cup go. It didn't break on the floor, but the coffee spilled out, and Nancy sat there with her hands still making the shape of the cup. She began to make the sound again, not loud. Not singing and not unsinging. We watched her.

"Here," Dilsey said. "You quit that, now. You get aholt of yourself. You wait here. I going to get Versh to walk home with you." Dilsey went out.

We looked at Nancy. Her shoulders kept shaking, but she quit making the sound. We stood and watched her.

"What's Jesus going to do to you?" Caddy said. "He went away."

Nancy looked at us. "We had fun that night I stayed in yawls' room, didn't we?"

"I didn't," Jason said. "I didn't have any fun."

"You were asleep in Mother's room," Caddy said. "You were not there."

"Let's go down to my house and have some more fun," Nancy said.

"Mother won't let us," I said. "It's too late now."

"Don't bother her," Nancy said. "We can tell her in the morning. She won't mind."

"She wouldn't let us," I said.

"Don't ask her now," Nancy said. "Don't bother her now."

"She didn't say we couldn't go," Caddy said.

"We didn't ask," I said.

"If you go, I'll tell," Jason said.

"We'll have fun," Nancy said. "They won't mind, just to my house. I been working for yawl a long time. They won't mind."

"I'm not afraid to go," Caddy said. "Jason is the one that's afraid. He'll tell."

"I'm not," Jason said.

"Yes, you are," Caddy said. "You'll tell."

"I won't tell," Jason said. "I'm not afraid."

"Jason ain't afraid to go with me," Nancy said. "Is you, Jason?"

"Jason is going to tell," Caddy said. The lane was dark. We passed the pasture gate. "I bet if something was to jump out from behind that gate, Jason would holler."

"I wouldn't," Jason said. We walked down the lane. Nancy was talking loud.

"What are you talking so loud for, Nancy?" Caddy said.

"Who; me?" Nancy said. "Listen at Quentin and Caddy and Jason saying I'm talking loud."

"You talk like there was five of us here," Caddy said. "You talk like Father was here too."

"Who; me talking loud, Mr. Jason?" Nancy said.

"Nancy called Jason 'Mister,' " Caddy said.

"Listen how Caddy and Quentin and Jason talk," Nancy said.

"We're not talking loud," Caddy said. "You're the one that's talking like Father—"

"Hush," Nancy said; "hush, Mr. Jason."

"Nancy called Jason 'Mister' aguh—"

"Hush," Nancy said. She was talking loud when we crossed the ditch and stooped through the fence where she used to stoop through with the clothes on her head. Then we came to her house.

We were going fast then. She opened the door. The smell of the house was like the lamp and the smell of Nancy was like the wick, like they were waiting for one another to begin to smell. She lit the lamp and closed the door and put the bar up. Then she quit talking loud, looking at us.

"What're we going to do?" Caddy said.

"What do yawl want to do?" Nancy said.

"You said we would have some fun," Caddy said.

There was something about Nancy's house; something you could smell besides Nancy and the house. Jason smelled it, even. "I don't want to stay here," he said. "I want to go home."

"Go home, then," Caddy said.

"I don't want to go by myself," Jason said.

"We're going to have some fun," Nancy said.

"How?" Caddy said.

Nancy stood by the door. She was looking at us, only it was like she had emptied her eyes, like she had quit using them. "What do you want to do?" she said.

"Tell us a story," Caddy said. "Can you tell a story?"

"Yes," Nancy said.

"Tell it," Caddy said. We looked at Nancy. "You don't know any stories."

"Yes," Nancy said. "Yes I do."

She came and sat in a chair before the hearth. There was a little fire there. Nancy built it up, when it was already hot inside. She built a good blaze. She told a story. She talked like her eyes looked, like her eyes watching us and her voice talking to us did not belong to her. Like she was living somewhere else, waiting somewhere else. She was outside the cabin. Her voice was inside and the shape of her, the Nancy that could stoop under a barbed wire fence with a bundle of clothes balanced on her head as though without weight, like a balloon, was there. But that was all. "And so this here queen come walking up to the ditch, where that bad man was hiding. She was walking up to the ditch, and she say, 'If I can just get past this here ditch,' was what she say . . ."

"What ditch?" Caddy said. "A ditch like that one out there? Why did a queen want to go into a ditch?"

"To get to her house," Nancy said. She looked at us. "She had to cross the ditch to get into her house quick and bar the door."

"Why did she want to go home and bar the door?" Caddy said.

IV

Nancy looked at us. She quit talking. She looked at us. Jason's legs stuck straight out of his pants where he sat on Nancy's lap. "I don't think that's a good story," he said. "I want to go home."

"Maybe we had better," Caddy said. She got up from the floor. "I bet they are looking for us right now." She went toward the door.

"No," Nancy said. "Don't open it." She got up quick and passed Caddy. She didn't touch the door, the wooden bar.

"Why not?" Caddy said.

"Come back to the lamp," Nancy said. "We'll have fun. You don't have to go."

"We ought to go," Caddy said. "Unless we have a lot of fun." She and Nancy came back to the fire, the lamp.

"I want to go home," Jason said. "I'm going to tell."

"I know another story," Nancy said. She stood close to the lamp. She looked at Caddy, like when your eyes look up at a stick balanced on your nose. She had to look down to see Caddy, but her eyes looked like that, like when you are balancing a stick.

"I won't listen to it," Jason said. "I'll bang on the floor."

"It's a good one," Nancy said. "It's better than the other one."

"What's it about?" Caddy said. Nancy was standing by the lamp. Her hand was on the lamp, against the light, long and brown.

"Your hand is on that hot globe," Caddy said. "Don't it feel hot to your hand?"

Nancy looked at her hand on the lamp chimney. She took her hand away, slow. She stood there, looking at Caddy, wringing her long hand as though it were tied to her wrist with a string.

"Let's do something else," Caddy said.

"I want to go home," Jason said.

"I got some popcorn," Nancy said. She looked at Caddy and then at Jason and then at me and then at Caddy again. "I got some popcorn."

"I don't like popcorn," Jason said. "I'd rather have candy."

Nancy looked at Jason. "You can hold the popper." She was still wringing her hand; it was long and limp and brown.

"All right," Jason said. "I'll stay a while if I can do that. Caddy can't hold it. I'll want to go home again if Caddy holds the popper."

Nancy built up the fire. "Look at Nancy putting her hands in the fire," Caddy said. "What's the matter with you, Nancy?"

"I got popcorn," Nancy said. "I got some." She took the popper from under the bed. It was broken. Jason began to cry.

"Now we can't have any popcorn," he said.

"We ought to go home, anyway," Caddy said. "Come on, Quentin."

"Wait," Nancy said; "wait. I can fix it. Don't you want to help me fix it?"

"I don't think I want any," Caddy said. "It's too late now."

"You help me, Jason," Nancy said. "Don't you want to help me?"

"No," Jason said. "I want to go home."

"Hush," Nancy said; "hush. Watch. Watch me. I can fix it so Jason can hold it and pop the corn." She got a piece of wire and fixed the popper.

"It won't hold good," Caddy said.

"Yes it will," Nancy said. "Yawl watch. Yawl help me shell some corn."

The popcorn was under the bed too. We shelled it into the popper and Nancy helped Jason hold the popper over the fire.

"It's not popping," Jason said. "I want to go home."

"You wait," Nancy said. "It'll begin to pop. We'll have fun then."

She was sitting close to the fire. The lamp was turned up so high it was beginning to smoke. "Why don't you turn it down some?" I said.

"It's all right," Nancy said. "I'll clean it. Yawl wait. The popcorn will start in a minute."

"I don't believe it's going to start," Caddy said. "We ought to start home, anyway. They'll be worried."

"No," Nancy said. "It's going to pop. Dilsey will tell um yawl with me. I been working for yawl long time. They won't mind if yawl at my house. You wait, now. It'll start popping any minute now."

Then Jason got some smoke in his eyes and he began to cry. He dropped the popper into the fire. Nancy got a wet rag and wiped Jason's face, but he didn't stop crying.

"Hush," she said. "Hush." But he didn't hush. Caddy took the popper out of the fire.

"It's burned up," she said. "You'll have to get some more popcorn, Nancy."

"Did you put all of it in?" Nancy said.

"Yes," Caddy said. Nancy looked at Caddy. Then she took the popper and opened it and poured the cinders into her apron and began to sort the grains, her hands long and brown, and we watching her.

"Haven't you got any more?" Caddy said.

"Yes," Nancy said; "yes. Look. This here ain't burnt. All we need to do is—"

"I want to go home," Jason said. "I'm going to tell."

"Hush," Caddy said. We all listened. Nancy's head was already turned toward the barred door, her eyes filled with red lamplight. "Somebody is coming," Caddy said.

Then Nancy began to make that sound again, not loud, sitting there above the fire, her long hands dangling between her knees; all of a sudden water began to come out on her face in big drops, running down her face, carrying in each one a little turning ball of firelight like a spark until it dropped off her chin. "She's not crying," I said.

"I ain't crying," Nancy said. Her eyes were closed. "I ain't crying. Who is it?"

"I don't know," Caddy said. She went to the door and looked out. "We've got to go now," she said. "Here comes Father."

"I'm going to tell," Jason said. "Yawl made me come."

The water still ran down Nancy's face. She turned in her chair. "Listen. Tell him. Tell him we going to have fun. Tell him I take good care of yawl until in the morning. Tell him to let me come home with yawl and sleep on the floor. Tell him I won't need no pallet. We'll have fun. You member last time how we had so much fun?"

"I didn't have fun," Jason said. "You hurt me. You put smoke in my eyes. I'm going to tell."

v

Father came in. He looked at us. Nancy did not get up.

"Tell him," she said.

"Caddy made us come down here," Jason said. "I didn't want to."

Father came to the fire. Nancy looked up at him. "Can't you go to Aunt Rachel's and stay?" he said. Nancy looked up at Father, her hands between her knees. "He's not here," Father said. "I would have seen him. There's not a soul in sight."

"He in the ditch," Nancy said. "He waiting in the ditch yonder."

"Nonsense," Father said. He looked at Nancy. "Do you know he's there?"

"I got the sign," Nancy said.

"What sign?"

"I got it. It was on the table when I come in. It was a hogbone, with blood meat still on it, laying by the lamp. He's out there. When yawl walk out that door, I gone."

"Gone where, Nancy?" Caddy said.

"I'm not a tattletale," Jason said.

"Nonsense," Father said.

"He out there," Nancy said. "He looking through that window this minute, waiting for yawl to go. Then I gone."

"Nonsense," Father said. "Lock up your house and we'll take you on to Aunt Rachel's."

"'Twon't do no good," Nancy said. She didn't look at Father now, but he looked down at her, at her long, limp, moving hands. "Putting it off won't do no good."

"Then what do you want to do?" Father said.

"I don't know," Nancy said. "I can't do nothing. Just put it off. And that don't do no good. I reckon it belong to me. I reckon what I going to get ain't no more than mine."

"Get what?" Caddy said. "What's yours?"

"Nothing," Father said. "You all must get to bed."

"Caddy made me come," Jason said.

"Go on to Aunt Rachel's," Father said.

"It won't do no good," Nancy said. She sat before the fire, her elbows on her knees, her long hands between her knees. "When even your own kitchen wouldn't do no good. When even if I was sleeping on the floor in the room with your chillen, and the next morning there I am, and blood—"

"Hush," Father said. "Lock the door and put out the lamp and go to bed."

"I scaired of the dark," Nancy said. "I scaired for it to happen in the dark."

"You mean you're going to sit right here with the lamp lighted?" Father said. Then Nancy began to make the sound again, sitting before the fire, her long hands between her knees. "Ah, damnation," Father said. "Come along, chillen. It's past bedtime."

"When yawl go home, I gone," Nancy said. She talked quieter now, and her face looked quiet, like her hands. "Anyway, I got my coffin money saved up with Mr. Lovelady." Mr. Lovelady was a short, dirty man who collected the Negro insurance, coming around to the cabins or the kitchens every Saturday morning, to collect fifteen cents. He and his wife lived at the hotel. One morning his wife committed suicide. They had a child, a little girl. He and the child went away. After a week or two he came back alone. We would see him going along the lanes and the back streets on Saturday mornings.

"Nonsense," Father said. "You'll be the first thing I'll see in the kitchen tomorrow morning."

"You'll see what you'll see, I reckon," Nancy said. "But it will take the Lord to say what that will be."

VI

We left her sitting before the fire.

"Come and put the bar up," Father said. But she didn't move. She didn't look at us again, sitting quietly there between the lamp and the fire. From some distance down the lane we could look back and see her through the open door.

"What, Father?" Caddy said. "What's going to happen?"

"Nothing," Father said. Jason was on Father's back, so Jason was the tallest of all of us. We went down into the ditch. I looked at it, quiet. I couldn't see much where the moonlight and the shadows tangled.

"If Jesus *is* hid here, he can see us, can't he?" Caddy said.

"He's not there," Father said. "He went away a long time ago."

"You made me come," Jason said, high; against the sky it looked like Father had two heads, a little one and a big one. "I didn't want to."

We went up out of the ditch. We could still see Nancy's house and the open door, but we couldn't see Nancy now, sitting before the fire with the door open, because she was tired. "I just done got tired," she said. "I just a nigger. It ain't no fault of mine."

But we could hear her, because she began just after we came up out of the ditch, the sound that was not singing and not unsinging. "Who will do our washing now, Father?" I said.

"I'm not a nigger," Jason said, high and close above Father's head.

"You're worse," Caddy said, "you are a tattletale. If something was to jump out, you'd be scairder than a nigger."

"I wouldn't," Jason said.

"You'd cry," Caddy said.

"Caddy," Father said.

"I wouldn't!" Jason said.

"Scairy cat," Caddy said.

"Candace!" Father said.

From *These 13* (1931)

·Eudora Welty·

PETRIFIED MAN

"Reach in my purse and git me a cigarette without no powder in it if you kin, Mrs Fletcher, honey," said Leota to her ten o'clock shampoo-and-set customer. "I don't like no perfumed cigarettes."

Mrs Fletcher gladly reached over to the lavender shelf under the lavender-framed mirror, shook a hair net loose from the clasp of the patent-leather bag, and slapped her hand down quickly on a powder puff which burst out when the purse was opened.

"Why, look at the peanuts, Leota!" said Mrs Fletcher in her marveling voice.

"Honey, them goobers has been in my purse a week if they's been in it a day. Mrs Pike bought them peanuts."

"Who's Mrs Pike?" asked Mrs Fletcher, settling back. Hidden in this den of curling fluid and henna packs, separated by a lavender swing door from the other customers, who were being gratified in other booths, she could give her curiosity its freedom. She looked expectantly at the black part in Leota's yellow curls as she bent to light the cigarette.

"Mrs Pike is this lady from New Orleans," said Leota, puffing, and pressing into Mrs Fletcher's scalp with strong red-nailed fingers. "A friend, not a customer. You see, like maybe I told you last time, me and Fred and Sal and Joe all had us a fuss, so Sal and Joe up and moved out, so we didn't do a thing but rent out their room. So we rented it to Mrs Pike. And Mr Pike." She flicked an ash into the basket of dirty towels. "Mrs Pike is a very decided blonde. *She* bought me the peanuts."

"She must be cute," said Mrs Fletcher.

"Honey, 'cute' ain't the word for what she is. I'm tellin' you, Mrs

Pike is attractive. She has her a good time. She's got a sharp eye out, Mrs Pike has."

She dashed the comb through the air, and paused dramatically as a cloud of Mrs. Fletcher's hennaed hair floated out of the lavender teeth like a small storm cloud.

"Hair fallin'."

"Aw, Leota."

"Uh-huh, commencin' to fall out," said Leota, combing again, and letting fall another cloud.

"Is it any dandruff in it?" Mrs Fletcher was frowning, her hair-line eyebrows diving down toward her nose, and her wrinkled, beady-lashed eyelids batting with concentration.

"Nope." She combed again. "Just fallin' out."

"Bet it was that last perm'nent you gave me that did it," Mrs Fletcher said cruelly. "Remember you cooked me fourteen minutes."

"You had fourteen minutes comin' to you," said Leota with finality.

"Bound to be somethin'," persisted Mrs Fletcher. "Dandruff, dandruff. I couldn't of caught a thing like that from Mr Fletcher, could I?"

"Well," Leota answered at last, "you know what I heard in here yestiddy, one of Thelma's ladies was settin' over yonder in Thelma's booth gittin' a machineless, and I don't mean to insist or insinuate or anything, Mrs Fletcher, but Thelma's lady just happ'med to throw out—I forgotten what she was talkin' about at the time—that you was p-r-e-g., and lots of times that'll make your hair do awful funny, fall out and God knows what all. It just ain't our fault, is the way I look at it."

There was a pause. The women stared at each other in the mirror.

"Who was it?" demanded Mrs Fletcher.

"Honey, I really couldn't say," said Leota. "Not that you look it."

"Where's Thelma? I'll get it out of her," said Mrs Fletcher.

"Now, honey, I wouldn't go and git mad over a little thing like that," Leota said, combing hastily, as though to hold Mrs Fletcher down by the hair. "I'm sure it was somebody didn't mean no harm in the world. How far gone are you?"

"Just wait," said Mrs Fletcher, and shrieked for Thelma, who came in and took a drag from Leota's cigarette.

"Thelma, honey, throw your mind back to yestiddy if you kin," said Leota, drenching Mrs Fletcher's hair with a thick fluid and catching the overflow in a cold wet towel at her neck.

"Well, I got my lady half wound for a spiral," said Thelma doubtfully.

"This won't take but a minute," said Leota. "Who is it you got in there, old Horse Face? Just cast your mind back and try to remember who your lady was yestiddy who happ'm to mention that my customer was pregnant, that's all. She's dead to know."

Thelma drooped her blood-red lips and looked over Mrs Fletcher's head into the mirror. "Why, honey, I ain't got the faintest," she breathed. "I really don't recollect the faintest. But I'm sure she meant no harm. I declare, I forgot my hair finally got combed and thought it was a stranger behind me."

"Was it that Mrs Hutchinson?" Mrs Fletcher was tensely polite.

"Mrs Hutchinson? Oh, Mrs Hutchinson." Thelma batted her eyes. "Naw, precious, she come on Thursday and didn't ev'm mention your name. I doubt if she ev'm knows you're on the way."

"Thelma!" cried Leota staunchly.

"All I know is, whoever it is 'll be sorry some day. Why, I just barely knew it myself!" cried Mrs Fletcher. "Just let her wait!"

"Why? What 're you gonna do to her?"

It was a child's voice, and the women looked down. A little boy was making tents with aluminum wave pinchers on the floor under the sink.

"Billy Boy, hon, mustn't bother nice ladies," Leota smiled. She slapped him brightly and behind her back waved Thelma out of the booth. "Ain't Billy Boy a sight? Only three years old and already just nuts about the beauty-parlor business."

"I never saw him here before," said Mrs Fletcher, still unmollified.

"He ain't been here before, that's how come," said Leota. "He belongs to Mrs Pike. She got her a job but it was Fay's Millinery. He oughtn't to try on those ladies' hats, they come down over his eyes like I don't know what. They just git to look ridiculous, that's what, an' of course he's gonna put 'em on: hats. They tole Mrs. Pike they didn't appreciate him hangin' around there. Here, he couldn't hurt a thing."

"Well! I don't like children that much," said Mrs Fletcher.

"Well!" said Leota moodily.

"Well! I'm almost tempted not to have this one," said Mrs Fletcher. "That Mrs Hutchinson! Just looks straight through you when she sees you on the street and then spits at you behind your back."

"Mr Fletcher would beat you on the head if you didn't have it now," said Leota reasonably. "After going this far."

Mrs Fletcher sat up straight. "Mr Fletcher can't do a thing with me."

"He can't!" Leota winked at herself in the mirror.

"No siree, he can't. If he so much as raises his voice against me, he knows good and well I'll have one of my sick headaches, and then I'm just not fit to live with. And if I really look that pregnant already——"

"Well, now, honey, I just want you to know—I habm't told any of my ladies and I ain't goin' to tell 'em—even that you're losin' your hair. You just get you one of those Stork-a-Lure dresses and stop worryin'. What people don't know don't hurt nobody, as Mrs Pike says."

"Did you tell Mrs Pike?" asked Mrs Fletcher sulkily.

"Well, Mrs Fletcher, look, you ain't ever goin' to lay eyes on Mrs Pike or her lay eyes on you, so what diffunce does it make in the long run?"

"I knew it!" Mrs Fletcher deliberately nodded her head so as to destroy a ringlet Leota was working on behind her ear. "Mrs Pike!"

Leota sighed. "I reckon I might as well tell you. It wasn't any more Thelma's lady tole me you was pregnant than a bat."

"Not Mrs Hutchinson?"

"Naw, Lord! It was Mrs Pike."

"Mrs Pike!" Mrs Fletcher could only sputter and let curling fluid roll into her ear. "How could Mrs Pike possible know I was pregnant or otherwise, when she doesn't even know me? The nerve of some people!"

"Well, here's how it was. Remember Sunday?"

"Yes," said Mrs Fletcher.

"Sunday, Mrs Pike an' me was all by ourself. Mr Pike and Fred had gone over to Eagle Lake, sayin' they was goin' to catch 'em some fish, but they didn't, a course. So we was settin' in Mrs Pike's car, is a 1939 Dodge——"

"1939, eh," said Mrs Fletcher.

"—An' we was gettin' us a Jax beer apiece—that's the beer that Mrs Pike says is made right in N.O., so she won't drink no other kind. So I seen you drive up to the drugstore an' run in for just a secont, leavin' I reckon Mr Fletcher in the car, an' come runnin' out with looked like a perscription. So I says to Mrs Pike, just to be makin' talk, 'Right yonder's Mrs Fletcher, and I reckon that's Mr Fletcher—she's one of my regular customers,' I says."

"I had on a figured print," said Mrs Fletcher tentatively.

"You sure did," agreed Leota. "So Mrs Pike, she give you a good look—she's very observant, a good judge of character, cute as a minute, you know—and she says, 'I bet you another Jax that lady's three months on the way.'"

"What gall!" said Mrs Fletcher. "Mrs Pike!"

"Mrs Pike ain't goin' to bite you," said Leota. "Mrs Pike is a lovely girl, you'd be crazy about her, Mrs Fletcher. But she can't sit still a minute. We went to the travelin' freak show yestiddy after work. I got through early—nine o'clock. In the vacant store next door? What, you ain't been?"

"No, I despise freaks," declared Mrs Fletcher.

"Aw. Well, honey, talkin' about bein' pregnant an' all, you ought to see those twins in a bottle, you really owe it to yourself."

"What twins?" asked Mrs Fletcher out of the side of her mouth.

"Well, honey, they got these two twins in a bottle, see? Born joined plumb together—dead a course." Leota dropped her voice into a soft lyrical hum. "They was about this long—pardon—must of been full time, all right, wouldn't you say?—an' they had these two heads an' two faces an' four arms an' four legs, all kind of joined *here*. See, this face looked this-a-way, and the other face looked that-a-way, over their shoulder, see. Kinda pathetic."

"Glah!" said Mrs Fletcher disapprovingly.

"Well, ugly? Honey, I mean to tell you—their parents was first cousins and all like that. Billy Boy, git me a fresh towel from off Tenny's stack—this 'n's wringin' wet—an' quit ticklin' my ankles with that curler. I declare! He don't miss nothin'.."

"Me and Mr Fletcher aren't one speck of kin, or he could never of had me," said Mrs Fletcher placidly.

"Of course not!" protested Leota. "Neither is me an' Fred, not that we know of. Well, honey, what Mrs Pike liked was the pygmies. They've got these pygmies down there, too, an' Mrs Pike was just wild about 'em. You know, the tee-niniest men in the universe? Well honey, they can just rest back on their little bohunkus an' roll around an' you can't hardly tell if they're sittin' or standin'. That 'll give you some idea. They're about forty-two years old. Just suppose it was your husband!"

"Well, Mr Fletcher is five foot nine and one half," said Mrs Fletcher quickly.

"Fred's five foot ten," said Leota, "but I tell him he's still a shrimp, account of I'm so tall." She made a deep wave over Mrs Fletcher's other temple with the comb. "Well, these pygmies are a kind of a dark brown, Mrs Fletcher. Not bad lookin' for what they are, you know."

"I wouldn't care for them," said Mrs Fletcher. "What does that Mrs Pike see in them?"

"Aw, I don't know," said Leota. "She's just cute, that's all. But they got this man, this petrified man, that ever'thing ever since he was nine years old, when it goes through his digestion, see, somehow Mrs Pike says it goes to his joints and has been turning to stone."

"How awful!" said Mrs Fletcher.

"He's forty-two too. That looks like a bad age."

"Who said so, that Mrs Pike? I bet she's forty-two," said Mrs Fletcher.

"Naw," said Leota, "Mrs Pike's thirty-three, born in January, an Aquarian. He could move his head—like this. A course his head and mind ain't a joint, so to speak, and I guess his stomach ain't, either—not yet anyways. But see—his food, he eats it, and it goes down, see, and then he disgests it"—Leota rose on her toes for an instant—"and it goes out to his joints and before you can say 'Jack Robinson,' it's stone—pure stone. He's turning to stone. How'd you like to be married to a guy like that? All he can do, he can move his head just a quarter of an inch. A course he *looks* just *terrible.*"

"I should think he would," said Mrs Fletcher frostily. "Mr Fletcher takes bending exercises every night of the world. I make him."

"All Fred does is lay around the house like a rug. I wouldn't be surprised if he woke up some day and couldn't move. The petrified man just sat there moving his quarter of an inch though," said Leota reminiscently.

"Did Mrs Pike like the petrified man?" asked Mrs Fletcher.

"Not as much as she did the others," said Leota deprecatingly. "And then she likes a man to be a good dresser, and all that."

"Is Mr Pike a good dresser?" asked Mrs Fletcher skeptically.

"Oh, well, yeah," said Leota, "but he's twelve- fourteen years older 'n her. She ast Lady Evangeline about him."

"Who's Lady Evangeline?" asked Mrs Fletcher.

"Well, it's this mind reader they got in the freak show," said Leota. "Was real good. Lady Evangeline is her name, and if I had another dollar I wouldn't do a thing but have my other palm read. She had what Mrs Pike said was the 'sixth mind' but she had the worst manicure I ever saw on a living person."

"What did she tell Mrs Pike?" asked Mrs Fletcher.

"She told her Mr Pike was as true to her as he could be and besides, would come into some money."

"Humph!" said Mrs Fletcher. "What does he do?"

"I can't tell," said Leota, "because he don't work. Lady Evangeline didn't tell me near enough about my nature or anything. And I would like to go back and find out some more about this boy. Used to go with this boy got married to this girl. Oh, shoot, that was about three and a half years ago, when you was still goin' to the Robert E. Lee Beauty Shop in Jackson. He married her for her money. Another fortune teller tole me that at the time. So I'm not in love with him any more, anyway, besides being married to Fred, but Mrs Pike thought, just for the hell of it, see, to ask Lady Evangeline was he happy."

"Does Mrs Pike know everything about you already?" asked Mrs Fletcher unbelievingly. "Mercy!"

"Oh yeah, I tole her ever'thing about ever'thing, from now on back to I don't know when—to when I first started goin' out," said Leota. "So I ast Lady Evangeline for one of my questions, was he happily married, and she says, just like she was glad I ask her, 'Honey,' she says, 'naw, he idn't. You write down this day, March 8, 1941,' she says, 'and mock it down: three years from today him and her won't be occupyin' the same bed.' There it is, up on the wall with them other dates—see, Mrs Fletcher? And she says, 'Child, you ought to be glad you didn't git him, because he's so mercenary.' So I'm glad I married Fred. He sure ain't mercenary, money don't mean a thing to him. But I sure would like to go back and have my other palm read."

"Did Mrs Pike believe in what the fortune teller said?" asked Mrs Fletcher in a superior tone of voice.

"Lord, yes, she's from New Orleans. Ever'body in New Orleans believes ever'thing spooky. One of 'em in New Orleans before it was raided says to Mrs Pike one summer she was goin' to go from state to state and meet some gray-headed men, and, sure enough, she says she went on a beautician convention up to Chicago. . . ."

"Oh!" said Mrs Fletcher. "Oh, is Mrs Pike a beautician too?"

"Sure she is," protested Leota. "She's a beautician. I'm goin' to git her in here if I can. Before she married. But it don't leave you. She says sure enough, there was three men who was a very large part of making her trip what it was, and they all three had gray in their hair and they went in six states. Got Christmas cards from 'em. Billy Boy, go see if Thelma's got any dry cotton. Look how Mrs Fletcher's a-drippin'."

"Where did Mrs Pike meet Mr Pike?" asked Mrs Fletcher primly.

"On another train," said Leota.

"I met Mr Fletcher, or rather he met me, in a rental library," said Mrs Fletcher with dignity, as she watched the net come down over her head.

"Honey, me an' Fred, we met in a rumble seat eight months ago and we was practically on what you might call the way to the altar inside of a half an hour," said Leota in a guttural voice, and bit a bobby pin open. "Course it don't last. Mrs Pike says nothin' like that ever lasts."

"Mr Fletcher and myself are as much in love as the day we married," said Mrs Fletcher belligerently as Leota stuffed cotton into her ears.

"Mrs Pike says it don't last," repeated Leota in a louder voice. "Now go git under the dryer. You can turn yourself on, can't you? I'll be back to comb you out. Durin' lunch I promised to give Mrs Pike a facial. You know—free. Her bein' in the business, so to speak."

"I bet she needs one," said Mrs Fletcher, letting the swing door fly back against Leota. "Oh, pardon me."

A week later, on time for her appointment, Mrs Fletcher sank heavily into Leota's chair after first removing a drugstore rental book, called *Life Is Like That,* from the seat. She stared in a discouraged way into the mirror.

"You can tell it when I'm sitting down, all right," she said.

Leota seemed preoccupied and stood shaking out a lavender cloth. She began to pin it around Mrs Fletcher's neck in silence.

"I said you sure can tell it when I'm sitting straight on and coming at you this way," Mrs Fletcher said.

"Why, honey, naw you can't," said Leota gloomily. "Why, I'd never know. If somebody was to come up to me on the street and say, 'Mrs Fletcher is pregnant!' I'd say, 'Heck, she don't look it to me.'"

"If a certain party hadn't found it out and spread it around, it wouldn't be too late even now," said Mrs Fletcher frostily, but Leota was almost choking her with the cloth, pinning it so tight, and she couldn't speak clearly. She paddled her hands in the air until Leota wearily loosened her.

"Listen, honey, you're just a virgin compared to Mrs Montjoy," Leota was going on, still absent-minded. She bent Mrs Fletcher back in the chair and, sighing, tossed liquid from a teacup onto her head and dug both hands into her scalp. "You know Mrs Montjoy— her husband's that premature-gray-headed fella?"

"She's in the Trojan Garden Club, is all I know," said Mrs Fletcher.

"Well, honey," said Leota, but in a weary voice, "she come in here not the week before and not the day before she had her baby— she come in here the very selfsame day, I mean to tell you. Child, we was all plumb scared to death. There she was! Come for her shampoo an' set. Why, Mrs Fletcher, in a hour an' twenty minutes she was layin' up there in the Babtist Hospital with a seb'm-pound son. It was that close a shave. I declare, if I hadn't been so tired I would of drank up a bottle of gin that night."

"What gall," said Mrs Fletcher. "I never knew her at all well."

"See, her husband was waitin' outside in the car, and her bags was all packed an' in the back seat, an' she was all ready, 'cept she wanted her shampoo an' set. An' havin' one pain right after another. Her husband kep' comin' in here, scared-like, but couldn't do nothin' with her a course. She yelled bloody murder, too, but she always yelled her head off when I give her a perm'nent."

"She must of been crazy," said Mrs Fletcher. "How did she look?"

"Shoot!" said Leota.

"Well, I can guess," said Mrs Fletcher. "Awful."

"Just wanted to look pretty while she was havin' her baby, is all," said Leota airily. "Course, we was glad to give the lady what she was after—that's our motto—but I bet a hour later she wasn't payin' no mind to them little end curls. I bet she wasn't thinkin' about she ought to have on a net. It wouldn't of done her no good if she had."

"No, I don't suppose it would," said Mrs Fletcher.

"Yeah man! She was a-yellin'. Just like when I give her her perm'nent."

"Her husband ought to could make her behave. Don't it seem that way to you?" asked Mrs Fletcher. "He ought to put his foot down."

"Ha," said Leota. "A lot he could do. Maybe some women is soft."

"Oh, you mistake me, I don't mean for her to get soft—far from it! Women have to stand up for themselves, or there's just no telling. But now you take me—I ask Mr Fletcher's advice now and then, and he appreciates it, especially on something important, like is it time for a permanent—not that I've told him about the baby. He says, 'Why dear, go ahead!' Just ask their *advice*."

"Huh! If I ever ast Fred's advice we'd be floatin' down the Yazoo River on a houseboat or somethin' by this time," said Leota. "I'm sick of Fred. I tole him to go over to Vicksburg."

"Is he going?" demanded Mrs Fletcher.

"Sure. See, the fortune teller—I went back and had my other palm read, since we've got to rent the room agin—said my lover was goin' to work in Vicksburg, so I don't know who she could mean, unless she meant Fred. And Fred ain't workin' here—that much is so."

"Is he going to work in Vicksburg?" asked Mrs Fletcher. "And——"

"Sure, Lady Evangeline said so. Said the future is going to be brighter than the present. He don't want to go, but I ain't gonna put up with nothin' like that. Lays around the house an' bulls—did bull—with that good-for-nothin' Mr Pike. He says if he goes who'll cook, but I says I never get to eat anyway—not meals. Billy Boy, take Mrs Grover that *Screen Secrets* and leg it."

Mrs Fletcher heard stamping feet go out the door.

"Is that that Mrs Pike's little boy here again?" she asked, sitting up gingerly.

"Yeah, that's still him." Leota stuck out her tongue.

Mrs. Fletcher could hardly believe her eyes. "Well! How's Mrs Pike, your attractive new friend with the sharp eyes who spreads it around town that perfect strangers are pregnant?" she asked in a sweetened tone.

"Oh, Mizziz Pike." Leota combed Mrs Fletcher's hair with heavy strokes.

"You act like you're tired," said Mrs Fletcher.

"Tired? Feel like it's four o'clock in the afternoon already," said Leota. "I ain't told you the awful luck we had, me and Fred? It's the worst thing you ever heard of. Maybe *you* think Mrs Pike's got sharp eyes. Shoot, there's a limit! Well, you know, we rented out our room to this Mr and Mrs Pike from New Orleans when Sal an' Joe Fentress got mad at us 'cause they drank up some home-brew we had in the closet—Sal an' Joe did. So, a week ago Sat'day Mr and Mrs Pike moved in. Well, I kinda fixed up the room, you know—put a sofa pillow on the couch and picked some ragged robbins and put in a vase, but they never did say they appreciated it. Anyway, then I put some old magazines on the table."

"I think that was lovely," said Mrs Fletcher.

"Wait. So, come night 'fore last, Fred and this Mr Pike, who Fred just took up with, was back from they said they was fishin', bein' as neither one of 'em has got a job to his name, and we was all settin' around in their room. So Mrs Pike was settin' there, readin' a old *Startling G-Man Tales* that was mine, mind you, I'd bought it myself, and all of a sudden she jumps!—into the air—you'd 'a' thought she'd set on a spider—an' says, 'Canfield'—ain't that silly, that's Mr Pike—'Canfield, my God A'mighty,' she says, 'honey,' she says, 'we're rich, and you won't have to work.' Not that he turned one hand anyway. Well, me and Fred rushes over to her, and Mr Pike, too, and there she sets, pointin' her finger at a photo in my copy of *Startling G-Man*. 'See that man?' yells Mrs Pike. 'Remember him, Canfield?' 'Never forget a face,' says Mr Pike. 'It's Mr Petrie, that we stayed with him in the apartment next to ours in Toulouse Street in N.O. for six weeks. Mr Petrie.' 'Well,' says Mrs Pike, like she can't hold out one secont longer, 'Mr Petrie is wanted for five hundred dollars cash, for rapin' four women in California, and I know where he is.'"

"Mercy!" said Mrs Fletcher. "Where was he?"

At some time Leota had washed her hair and now she yanked her up by the back locks and sat her up.

"Know where he was?"

"I certainly don't," Mrs Fletcher said. Her scalp hurt all over.

Leota flung a towel around the top of her customer's head. "Nowhere else but in that freak show! I saw him just as plain as Mrs Pike. *He* was the petrified man!"

"Who would ever have thought that!" cried Mrs Fletcher sympathetically.

"So Mr Pike says, 'Well whatta you know about that,' an' he looks real hard at the photo and whistles. And she starts dancin' and singin' about their good luck. She meant our bad luck! I made a point of tellin' that fortune teller the next time I saw her. I said,

'Listen, that magazine was layin' around the house for a month, and there was five hundred dollars in it for somebody. An' there was the freak show runnin' night an' day, not two steps away from my own beauty parlor, with Mr Petrie just settin' there waitin'. An' it had to be Mr and Mrs Pike, almost perfect strangers.' "

"What gall," said Mrs Fletcher. She was only sitting there, wrapped in a turban, but she did not mind.

"Fortune tellers don't care. And Mrs Pike, she goes around actin' like she thinks she was Mrs God," said Leota. "So they're goin' to leave tomorrow, Mr and Mrs Pike. And in the meantime I got to keep that mean, bad little ole kid here, gettin' under my feet ever' minute of the day an' talkin' back too."

"Have they gotten the five hundred dollars' reward already?" asked Mrs Fletcher.

"Well," said Leota, "at first Mr Pike didn't want to do anything about it. Can you feature that? Said he kinda liked that ole bird and said he was real nice to 'em, lent 'em money or somethin'. But Mrs Pike simply tole him he could just go to hell, and I can see her point. She says, 'You ain't worked a lick in six months, and here I make five hundred dollars in two seconts, and what thanks do I get for it? You go to hell, Canfield,' she says. So," Leota went on in a despondent voice, "they called up the cops and they caught the ole bird, all right, right there in the freak show where I saw him with my own eyes, thinkin' he was petrified. He's the one. Did it under his real name—Mr Petrie. Four women in California, all in the month of August. So Mrs Pike gits five hundred dollars. And my magazine, and right next door to my beauty parlor. I cried all night, but Fred said it wasn't a bit of use and to go to sleep, because the whole thing was just a sort of coincidence—you know: can't do nothin' about it. He says it put him clean out of the notion of goin' to Vicksburg for a few days till we rent out the room again—no tellin' who we'll git this time."

"But can you imagine anybody knowing this old man, that's raped four women?" persisted Mrs Fletcher, and she shuddered audibly. "Did Mrs Pike *speak* to him when she met him in the freak show?"

Leota had begun to comb Mrs Fletcher's hair. "I says to her, I says, 'I didn't notice you fallin' on his neck when he was the petrified man—don't tell me you didn't recognize your fine friend?' And she says, 'I didn't recognize him with that white powder all over his face. He just looked familiar,' Mrs Pike says, 'and lots of people look familiar.' But she says that ole petrified man did put her in mind of somebody. She wondered who it was! Kep' her awake, which man she'd ever knew it reminded her of. So when she seen the photo, it all come to her. Like a flash. Mr Petrie. The way he'd turn his head and look at her when she took him in his breakfast."

"Took him in his breakfast!" shrieked Mrs Fletcher. "Listen— don't tell me. I'd 'a' felt something."

"Four women. I guess those women didn't have the faintest notion at the time they'd be worth a hundred an' twenty-five bucks apiece someday to Mrs Pike. We ast her how old the fella was then, an' she says he musta had one foot in the grave, at least. Can you beat it?"

"Not really petrified at all, of course," said Mrs Fletcher meditatively. She drew herself up. "I'd 'a' felt something," she said proudly.

"Shoot! I did feel somethin'," said Leota. "I tole Fred when I got home I felt so funny. I said, 'Fred, that ole petrified man sure did leave me with a funny feelin'.' He says, 'Funny-haha or funny-peculiar?' and I says, 'Funny-peculiar.'" She pointed her comb into the air emphatically.

"I'll bet you did," said Mrs Fletcher.

They both heard a crackling noise.

Leota screamed, "Billy Boy! What you doin' in my purse?"

"Aw, I'm just eatin' these ole stale peanuts up," said Billy Boy.

"You come here to me!" screamed Leota, recklessly flinging down the comb, which scattered a whole ash tray full of bobby pins and knocked down a row of Coca-Cola bottles. "This is the last straw!"

"I caught him! I caught him!" giggled Mrs Fletcher. "I'll hold him on my lap. You bad, bad boy, you! I guess I better learn how to spank little old bad boys," she said.

Leota's eleven o'clock customer pushed open the swing door upon Leota paddling him heartily with the brush, while he gave angry but belittling screams which penetrated beyond the booth and filled the whole curious beauty parlor. From everywhere ladies began to gather round to watch the paddling. Billy Boy kicked both Leota and Mrs Fletcher as hard as he could, Mrs Fletcher with her new fixed smile.

"There, my little man!" gasped Leota. "You won't be able to set down for a week if I knew what I was doin'."

Billy Boy stomped through the group of wild-haired ladies and went out the door, but flung back the words, "If you're so smart, why ain't you rich?"

From *A Curtain of Green* (1941)

·Robert Penn Warren·

BLACKBERRY WINTER

It was getting into June and past eight o'clock in the morning, but there was a fire—even if it wasn't a big fire, just a fire of chunks—on the hearth of the big stone fireplace in the living room. I was standing on the hearth, almost into the chimney, hunched over the fire, working my bare toes slowly on the warm stone. I relished the heat which made the skin of my bare legs warp and creep and tingle, even as I called to my mother, who was somewhere back in the dining room or kitchen, and said: "But it's June, I don't have to put them on!"

"You put them on if you are going out," she called.

I tried to assess the degree of authority and conviction in the tone, but at that distance it was hard to decide. I tried to analyze the tone, and then I thought what a fool I had been to start out the back door and let her see that I was barefoot. If I had gone out the front door or the side door she would never have known, not till dinner time anyway, and by then the day would have been half gone and I would have been all over the farm to see what the storm had done and down to the creek to see the flood. But it had never crossed my mind that they would try to stop you from going barefoot in June, no matter if there had been a gully-washer and a cold spell.

Nobody had ever tried to stop me in June as long as I could remember, and when you are nine years old, what you remember seems forever; for you remember everything and everything is important and stands big and full and fills up Time and is so solid that you can walk around and around it like a tree and look at it. You are aware that time passes, that there is a movement in time, but that is not what Time is. Time is not a movement, a flowing, a wind then, but is, rather, a kind of climate in which things are, and when a thing happens it begins to live and keeps on living and stands solid in Time like the tree that you can walk around. And if there is a movement, the movement is not Time itself, any more than a breeze is climate, and all the breeze does is to shake a little the leaves on the tree which is alive and solid. When you are nine, you know that there are things that you don't know, but you know that when you know something you know it. You know how a thing has been and you know that you can go barefoot in June. You do not understand that voice from back in the kitchen which says that you cannot go barefoot outdoors and run to see what has happened and rub your feet over the wet shivery grass and make the perfect mark of your foot in the smooth, creamy, red mud and then muse upon it as though you had suddenly come upon that single mark on the glistening auroral beach of the world. You have never seen a beach, but you have read the book and how the footprint was there.

The voice had said what it had said, and I looked savagely at the black stockings and the strong, scuffed brown shoes which I had brought from my closet as far as the hearth rug. I called once more, "But it's June," and waited.

"It's June," the voice replied from far away, "but it's blackberry winter."

I had lifted my head to reply to that, to make one more test of what was in that tone, when I happened to see the man.

The fireplace in the living room was at the end; for the stone chimney was built, as in so many of the farmhouses in Tennessee, at the end of a gable, and there was a window on each side of the chimney. Out of the window on the north side of the fireplace I could see the man. When I saw the man I did not call out what I had intended, but, engrossed by the strangeness of the sight, watched him, still far off, come along the path by the edge of the woods.

What was strange was that there should be a man there at all. That path went along the yard fence, between the fence and the woods which came right down to the yard, and then on back past the chicken runs and on by the woods until it was lost to sight where the woods bulged out and cut off the back field. There the path disappeared into the woods. It led on back, I knew, through the woods and to the swamp, skirted the swamp where the big trees gave way to sycamores and water oaks and willows and tangled cane, and then led on to the river. Nobody ever went back there except people who wanted to gig frogs in the swamp or to fish in the river or to hunt in the woods, and those people, if they didn't have a standing permission from my father, always stopped to ask permission to cross the farm. But the man whom I now saw wasn't, I could tell even at that distance, a sportsman. And what would a sportsman have been doing down there after a storm? Besides, he was coming from the river, and nobody had gone down there that morning. I knew that for a fact, because if anybody had passed, certainly if a stranger had passed, the dogs would have made a racket and would have been out on him. But this man was coming up from the river and had come up through the woods. I suddenly had a vision of him moving up the grassy path in the woods, in the green twilight under the big trees, not making any sound on the path, while now and then, like drops off the eaves, a big drop of water would fall from a leaf or bough and strike a stiff oak leaf lower down with a small, hollow sound like a drop of water hitting tin. That sound, in the silence of the woods, would be very significant.

When you are a boy and stand in the stillness of woods, which can be so still that your heart almost stops beating and makes you want to stand there in the green twilight until you feel your very feet sinking into and clutching the earth like roots and your body breathing slow through its pores like the leaves—when you stand there and wait for the next drop to drop with its small, flat sound to a lower leaf, that sound seems to measure out something, to put an end to something, to begin something, and you cannot wait for it to happen and are afraid it will not happen, and then when it has happened, you are waiting again, almost afraid.

But the man whom I saw coming through the woods in my mind's eye did not pause and wait, growing into the ground and breathing with the enormous, soundless breathing of the leaves. Instead, I saw him moving in the green twilight inside my head as he was moving at that very moment along the path by the edge of the woods, coming toward the house. He was moving steadily, but not fast, with his shoulders hunched a little and his head thrust forward, like a man who has come a long way and has a long way to go. I shut my eyes for a couple of seconds, thinking that when I opened them he would not be there at all. There was no place for him to have come from, and there was no reason for him to come where he was coming, toward our house. But I opened my eyes, and there he was, and he was coming steadily along the side of the woods. He was not yet even with the back chicken yard.

"Mama," I called.

"You put them on," the voice said.

"There's a man coming," I called, "out back."

She did not reply to that, and I guessed that she had gone to the kitchen window to look. She would be looking at the man and wondering who he was and what he wanted, the way you always do in the country, and if I went back there now she would not notice right off whether or not I was barefoot. So I went back to the kitchen.

She was standing by the window. "I don't recognize him," she said, not looking around at me.

"Where could he be coming from?" I asked.

"I don't know," she said.

"What would he be doing down at the river? At night? In the storm?"

She studied the figure out the window, then said, "Oh, I reckon maybe he cut across from the Dunbar place."

That was, I realized, a perfectly rational explanation. He had not been down at the river in the storm, at night. He had come over this morning. You could cut across from the Dunbar place if you didn't mind breaking through a lot of elder and sassafras and blackberry bushes which had about taken over the old cross path, which nobody ever used any more. That satisfied me for a moment, but only for a moment. "Mamma," I asked, "what would he be doing over at the Dunbar place last night?"

Then she looked at me, and I knew I had made a mistake, for she was looking at my bare feet. "You haven't got your shoes on," she said.

But I was saved by the dogs. That instant there was a bark which I recognized as Sam, the collie, and then a heavier, churning kind of bark which was Bully, and I saw a streak of white as Bully tore round the corner of the back porch and headed out for the man. Bully was a big, bone-white bull dog, the kind of dog that they used to call a farm bull dog but that you don't see any more, heavy chested and heavy headed, but with pretty long legs. He could take a fence as light as a hound. He had just cleared the white paling fence toward the woods when my mother ran out to the back porch and began calling, "Here you, Bully! Here you!"

Bully stopped in the path, waiting for the man, but he gave a few more of those deep, gargling, savage barks that reminded you of something down a stone-lined well. The red clay mud, I saw, was splashed up over his white chest and looked exciting, like blood.

The man, however, had not stopped walking even when Bully took the fence and started at him. He had kept right on coming. All he had done was to switch a little paper parcel which he carried from the right hand to the left, and then reach into his pants pocket to get something. Then I saw the glitter and knew that he had a knife in his hand, probably the kind of mean knife just made for devilment and nothing else, with a blade as long as the blade of a frog-sticker, which will snap out ready when you press a button in the handle. That knife must have had a button in the handle, or else how could he have had the blade out glittering so quick and with just one hand?

Pulling his knife against the dogs was a funny thing to do, for Bully was a big, powerful brute and fast, and Sam was all right. If those dogs had meant business, they might have knocked him down and ripped him before he got a stroke in. He ought to have picked up a heavy stick, something to take a swipe at them with and something which they could see and respect when they came at him. But he apparently did not know much about dogs. He just held the knife blade close against the right leg, low down, and kept on moving down the path.

Then my mother had called, and Bully had stopped. So the man let the blade of the knife snap back into the handle, and dropped it into his pocket, and kept on coming. Many women would have been afraid with the strange man who they knew had that knife in his pocket. That is, if they were alone in the house with nobody but a nine-year-old boy. And my mother was alone, for my father had gone off, and Dellie, the cook, was down at her cabin because she wasn't feeling well. But my mother wasn't afraid. She wasn't a big woman, but she was clear and brisk about everything she did and looked everybody and everything right in the eye from her own blue eyes in her tanned face. She had been the first woman in the county to ride a horse astride (that was back when she was a girl and long before I was born), and I have seen her snatch up a pump gun and go out and knock a chicken hawk out of the air like a busted skeet when he came over her chicken yard. She was a steady and self-reliant woman, and when I think of her now after all the years she has been dead, I think of her brown hands, not big, but somewhat square for a woman's hands, with square-cut nails. They looked, as a matter of fact, more like a young boy's hands than a grown woman's. But back then it never crossed my mind that she would ever be dead.

She stood on the back porch and watched the man enter the back gate, where the dogs (Bully had leaped back into the yard) were dancing and muttering and giving sidelong glances back to my mother to see if she meant what she had said. The man walked right by the dogs, almost brushing them, and didn't pay them any attention. I could see now that he wore old khaki pants, and a dark wool coat with stripes in it, and a gray felt hat. He had on a gray shirt with blue stripes in it, and no tie. But I could see a tie, blue and reddish, sticking in his side coat-pocket. Everything was wrong about what he wore. He ought to have been wearing blue jeans or overalls, and a straw hat or an old black felt hat, and the coat, granting that he might have been wearing a wool coat and not a jumper, ought not to have had those stripes. Those clothes, despite the fact that that they were old enough and dirty enough for any tramp, didn't belong there in our back yard, coming down the path, in Middle Tennessee, miles away from any big town, and even a mile off the pike.

When he got almost to the steps, without having said anything, my mother, very matter-of-factly, said, "Good morning."

"Good morning," he said, and stopped and looked her over. He did not take off his hat, and under the brim you could see the perfectly unmemorable face, which wasn't old and wasn't young, or thick or thin. It was grayish and covered with about three days of stubble. The eyes were a kind of nondescript, muddy hazel, or something like that, rather bloodshot. His teeth, when he opened his mouth, showed yellow and uneven. A couple of them had been knocked out. You knew that they had been knocked out, because there was a scar, not very old, there on the lower lip just beneath the gap.

"Are you hunting work?" my mother asked him.

"Yes," he said—not "yes, mam"—and still did not take off his hat.

"I don't know about my husband, for he isn't here," she said, and didn't mind a bit telling the tramp, or whoever he was, with the mean knife in his pocket, that no man was around, "but I can give you a few things to do. The storm has drowned a lot of my chicks. Three coops of them. You can gather them up and bury them. Bury them deep so the dogs won't get at them. In the woods. And fix the coops the wind blew over. And down yonder beyond that pen by the edge of the woods are some drowned poults. They got out and I couldn't get them in. Even after it started to rain hard: Poults haven't got any sense."

"What are them things—poults?" he demanded, and spat on the brick walk. He rubbed his foot over the spot, and I saw that he wore a black, pointed-toe low shoe, all cracked and broken. It was a crazy kind of shoe to be wearing in the country.

"Oh, they're young turkeys," my mother was saying. "And they haven't got any sense. I oughtn't to try to raise them around here with so many chickens, anyway. They don't thrive near chickens, even in separate pens. And I won't give up my chickens." Then she stopped herself and resumed briskly on the note of business. "When you finish that, you can fix my flower beds. A lot of trash and mud and gravel has washed down. Maybe you can save some of my flowers if you are careful."

"Flowers," the man said, in a low, impersonal voice which seemed to have a wealth of meaning, but a meaning which I could not fathom. As I think back on it, it probably was not pure contempt. Rather, it was a kind of impersonal and distant marveling that he should be on the verge of grubbing in a flower bed. He said the word, and then looked off across the yard.

"Yes, flowers," my mother replied with some asperity, as though she would have nothing said or implied against flowers. "And they were very fine this year." Then she stopped and looked at the man. "Are you hungry?" she demanded.

"Yeah," he said.

"I'll fix you something," she said, "before you get started." She turned to me. "Show him where he can wash up," she commanded, and went into the house.

I took the man to the end of the porch where a pump was and where a couple of wash pans sat on a low shelf for people to use before they went into the house. I stood there while he laid down his little parcel wrapped in newspaper and took off his hat and looked around for a nail to hang it on. He poured the water and plunged his hands into it. They were big hands, and strong looking, but they did not have the creases and the earth-color of the hands of men who work outdoors. But they were dirty, with black dirt ground into the skin and under the nails. After he had washed his hands, he poured another basin of water and washed his face. He dried his face, and with the towel still dangling in his grasp, stepped over to the mirror on the house wall. He rubbed one hand over the stubble on his face. Then he carefully inspected his face, turning first one side and then the other, and stepped back and settled his striped coat down on his shoulders. He had the movements of a man who has just dressed up to go to church or a party— the way he settled his coat and smoothed it and scanned himself in the mirror.

Then he caught my glance on him. He glared at me for an instant out of the bloodshot eyes, then demanded in a low, harsh voice, "What you looking at?"

"Nothing," I managed to say, and stepped back a step from him.

He flung the towel down, crumpled, on the shelf, and went toward the kitchen door and entered without knocking.

My mother said something to him which I could not catch. I started to go in again, then thought about my bare feet, and decided to go back of the chicken yard, where the man would have to come to pick up the dead chicks. I hung around behind the chicken house until he came out.

He moved across the chicken yard with a fastidious, not quite finicking motion, looking down at the curdled mud flecked with bits of chicken-droppings. The mud curled up over the soles of his black shoes. I stood back from him some six feet and watched him pick up the first of the drowned chicks. He held it up by one foot and inspected it.

There is nothing deader looking than a drowned chick. The feet curl in that feeble, empty way which back when I was a boy, even if I was a country boy who did not mind hog-killing or frog-gigging, made me feel hollow in the stomach. Instead of looking plump and fluffy, the body is stringy and limp with the fluff plastered to it, and the neck is long and loose like a little string of rag. And the eyes have that bluish membrane over them which makes you think of a very old man who is sick about to die.

The man stood there and inspected the chick. Then he looked all around as though he didn't know what to do with it.

"There's a great big old basket in the shed," I said, and pointed to the shed attached to the chicken house.

He inspected me as though he had just discovered my presence, and moved toward the shed.

"There's a spade there, too," I added.

He got the basket and began to pick up the other chicks, picking each one up slowly by a foot and then flinging it into the basket with a nasty, snapping motion. Now and then he would look at me out of the bloodshot eyes. Every time he seemed on the verge of saying something, but he did not. Perhaps he was building up to say something to me, but I did not wait that long. His way of looking at me made me so uncomfortable that I left the chicken yard.

Besides, I had just remembered that the creek was in flood, over the bridge, and that people were down there watching it. So I cut across the farm toward the creek. When I got to the big tobacco field I saw that it had not suffered much. The land lay right and not many tobacco plants had washed out of the ground. But I knew that a lot of tobacco round the country had been washed right out. My father had said so at breakfast.

My father was down at the bridge. When I came out of the gap in the osage hedge into the road, I saw him sitting on his mare over the heads of the other men who were standing around, admiring the flood. The creek was big here, even in low water; for only a couple of miles away it ran into the river, and when a real flood came, the red water got over the pike where it dipped down to the bridge, which was an iron bridge, and high over the floor and even the side railings of the bridge. Only the upper iron work would show, with the water boiling and frothing red and white around it. That creek rose so fast and so heavy because a few miles back it came down out of the hills, where the gorges filled up with water in no time when a rain came. The creek ran in a deep bed with limestone bluffs along both sides until it got within three quarters of a mile of the bridge, and when it came out from between those bluffs in flood it was boiling and hissing and steaming like water from a fire hose.

Whenever there was a flood, people from half the county would come down to see the sight. After a gully-washer there would not be any work to do anyway. If it didn't ruin your crop, you couldn't plow and you felt like taking a holiday to celebrate. If it did ruin your crop, there wasn't anything to do except to try to take your mind off the mortgage, if you were rich enough to have a mortgage, and if you couldn't afford a mortgage you needed something to take your mind off how hungry you would be by Christmas. So people would come down to the bridge and look at the flood. It made something different from the run of days.

There would not be much talking after the first few minutes of trying to guess how high the water was this time. The men and kids just stood around, or sat their horses or mules, as the case might be, or stood up in the wagon beds. They looked at the strangeness of the flood for an hour or two, and then somebody would say that he had better be getting on home to dinner and would start walking down the gray, puddled limestone pike, or would touch heel to his mount and start off. Everybody always knew what it would be like when he got down to the bridge, but people always came. It was like church or a funeral. They always came, that is, if it was summer and the flood unexpected. Nobody ever came down in winter to see high water.

When I came out of the gap in the bodock hedge, I saw the crowd, perhaps fifteen or twenty men and a lot of kids, and saw my father sitting his mare, Nellie Gray. He was a tall, limber man and carried himself well. I was always proud to see him sit a horse, he was so quiet and straight, and when I stepped through the gap of the hedge that morning, the first thing that happened was, I remember, the warm feeling I always had when I saw him up on a horse, just sitting. I did not go toward him, but skirted the crowd on the far side, to get a look at the creek. For one thing, I was not sure what he would say about the fact that I was barefoot. But the first thing I knew, I heard his voice calling, "Seth!"

I went toward him, moving apologetically past the men, who bent their large, red or thin, sallow faces above me. I knew some of the men, and knew their names, but because those I knew were there in a crowd, mixed with the strange faces, they seemed foreign to me, and not friendly. I did not look up at my father until I was almost within touching distance of his heel. Then I looked up and tried to read his face, to see if he was angry about my being barefoot. Before I could decide anything from that impassive, high-boned face, he had leaned over and reached a hand to me. "Grab on," he commanded.

I grabbed on and gave a little jump, and he said, "Up-see-daisy!" and whisked me, light as a feather, up to the pommel of his McClellan saddle.

"You can see better up here," he said, slid back on the cantle a little to make me more comfortable, and then, looking over my head at the swollen, tumbling water, seemed to forget all about me. But his right hand was laid on my side, just above my thigh, to steady me.

I was sitting there as quiet as I could, feeling the faint stir of my father's chest against my shoulders as it rose and fell with his breath, when I saw the cow. At first, looking up the creek, I thought it was just another big piece of driftwood steaming down the creek in the ruck of water, but all at once a pretty good-size boy who had climbed part way up a telephone pole by the pike so that he could see better yelled out, "Golly-damn, look at that-air cow!"

Everybody looked. It was a cow all right, but it might just as well have been driftwood; for it was dead as a chunk, rolling and roiling down the creek, appearing and disappearing, feet up or head up, it didn't matter which.

The cow started up the talk again. Somebody wondered whether it would hit one of the clear places under the top girder of the bridge and get through or whether it would get tangled in the drift and trash that had piled against the upright girders and braces. Somebody remembered how about ten years before so much drift-wood had piled up on the bridge that it was knocked off its foundations. Then the cow hit. It hit the edge of the drift against one of the girders, and hung there. For a few seconds it seemed as though it might tear loose, but then we saw that it was really caught. It bobbed and heaved on its side there in a slow, grinding, uneasy fashion. It had a yoke around its neck, the kind made out of a forked limb to keep a jumper behind fence.

"She shore jumped one fence," one of the men said.

And another: "Well, she done jumped her last one, fer a fack."

Then they began to wonder about whose cow it might be. They decided it must belong to Milt Alley. They said that he had a cow that was a jumper, and kept her in a fenced-in piece of ground up the creek. I had never seen Milt Alley, but I knew who he was. He was a squatter and lived up the hills a way, on a shirt-tail patch of set-on-edge land, in a cabin. He was pore white trash. He had lots of children. I had seen the children at school, when they came. They were thin-faced, with straight, sticky-looking, dough-colored hair, and they smelled something like old sour buttermilk, not be-cause they drank so much buttermilk but because that is the sort of smell which children out of those cabins tend to have. The big Alley boy drew dirty pictures and showed them to the little boys at school.

That was Milt Alley's cow. It looked like the kind of cow he would have, a scrawny, old, sway-backed cow, with a yoke around her neck. I wondered if Milt Alley had another cow.

"Poppa," I said, "do you think Milt Alley has got another cow?"

"You say 'Mr. Alley,' " my father said quietly.

"Do you think he has?"

"No telling," my father said.

Then a big gangly boy, about fifteen, who was sitting on a scraggly little old mule with a piece of croker sack thrown across the saw-tooth spine, and who had been staring at the cow, suddenly said to nobody in particular, "Reckin anybody ever et drownt cow?"

He was the kind of boy who might just as well as not have been the son of Milt Alley, with his faded and patched overalls ragged at the bottom of the pants and the mud-stiff brogans hanging off his skinny, bare ankles at the level of the mule's belly. He had said what he did, and then looked embarrassed and sullen when all the eyes swung at him. He hadn't meant to say it, I am pretty sure now. He would have been too proud to say it, just as Milt Alley would have been too proud. He had just been thinking out loud, and the words had popped out.

There was an old man standing there on the pike, an old man with a white beard. "Son," he said to the embarrassed and sullen boy on the mule, "you live long enough and you'll find a man will eat anything when the time comes."

"Time gonna come fer some folks this year," another man said.

"Son," the old man said, "in my time I et things a man don't like to think on. I was a sojer and I rode with Gin'l Forrest,[1] and them things we et when the time come. I tell you. I et meat what got up and run when you taken out yore knife to cut a slice to put on the fire. You had to knock it down with a carbene butt, it was so active. That-air meat would jump like a bullfrog, it was so full of skippers."

But nobody was listening to the old man. The boy on the mule turned his sullen sharp face from him, dug a heel into the side of the mule and went off up the pike with a motion which made you think that any second you would hear mule bones clashing inside that lank and scrofulous hide.

"Cy Dundee's boy," a man said, and nodded toward the figure going up the pike on the mule.

"Reckin Cy Dundee's young-uns seen times they'd settle fer drownt cow," another man said.

The old man with the beard peered at them both from his weak, slow eyes, first at one and then at the other. "Live long enough," he said, "and a man will settle for what he kin git."

Then there was silence again, with the people looking at the red, foam-flecked water.

My father lifted the bridle rein in his left hand, and the mare

1. Nathan Bedford Forrest (1821–77), Confederate general in the Civil War. Forrest's strategy was based on mobility, and his troops lived off the land.

turned and walked around the group and up the pike. We rode on up to our big gate, where my father dismounted to open it and let me myself ride Nellie Gray through. When he got to the lane that led off from the drive about two hundred yards from our house, my father said, "Grab on." I grabbed on, and he let me down to the ground. "I'm going to ride down and look at my corn," he said. "You go on." He took the lane, and I stood there on the drive and watched him ride off. He was wearing cowhide boots and an old hunting coat, and I thought that that made him look very military, like a picture. That and the way he rode.

I did not go to the house. Instead, I went by the vegetable garden and crossed behind the stables, and headed down for Dellie's cabin. I wanted to go down and play with Jebb, who was Dellie's little boy about two years older than I was. Besides, I was cold. I shivered as I walked, and I had gooseflesh. The mud which crawled up between my toes with every step I took was like ice. Dellie would have a fire, but she wouldn't make me put on shoes and stockings.

Dellie's cabin was of logs, with one side, because it was on a slope, set on limestone chunks, with a little porch attached to it, and had a little white-washed fence around it and a gate with plow-points on a wire to clink when somebody came in, and had two big white oaks in the yard and some flowers and a nice privy in the back with some honeysuckle growing over it. Dellie and Old Jebb, who was Jebb's father and who lived with Dellie and had lived with her for twenty-five years even if they never had got married, were careful to keep everything nice around their cabin. They had the name all over the community for being clean and clever Negroes. Dellie and Jebb were what they used to call "white-folks' niggers." There was a big difference between their cabin and the other two cabins farther down where the other tenants lived. My father kept the other cabins weatherproof, but he couldn't undertake to go down and pick up after the litter they strewed. They didn't take the trouble to have a vegetable patch like Dellie and Jebb or to make preserves from wild plum, and jelly from crab apple the way Dellie did. They were shiftless, and my father was always threatening to get shed of them. But he never did. When they finally left, they just up and left on their own, for no reason, to go and be shiftless somewhere else. Then some more came. But meanwhile they lived down there, Matt Rawson and his family, and Sid Turner and his, and I played with their children all over the farm when they weren't working. But when I wasn't around they were mean sometimes to Little Jebb. That was because the other tenants down there were jealous of Dellie and Jebb.

I was so cold that I ran the last fifty yards to Dellie's gate. As soon as I had entered the yard, I saw that the storm had been hard on Dellie's flowers. The yard was, as I have said, on a slight slope, and the water running across had gutted the flower beds and washed out all the good black woods-earth which Dellie had brought in. What little grass there was in the yard was plastered sparsely down on the ground, the way the drainage water had left it. It reminded me of the way the fluff was plastered down on the skin of the drowned chicks that the strange man had been picking up, up in my mother's chicken yard.

I took a few steps up the path to the cabin, and then I saw that the drainage water had washed a lot of trash and filth out from under Dellie's house. Up toward the porch, the ground was not clean any more. Old pieces of rag, two or three rusted cans, pieces of rotten rope, some hunks of old dog dung, broken glass, old paper, and all sorts of things like that had washed out from under Dellie's house to foul her clean yard. It looked just as bad as the yards of the other cabins, or worse. It was worse, as a matter of fact, because it was a surprise. I had never thought of all that filth being under Dellie's house. It was not anything against Dellie that the stuff had been under the cabin. Trash will get under any house. But I did not think of that when I saw the foulness which had washed out on the ground which Dellie sometimes used to sweep with a twig broom to make nice and clean.

I picked my way past the filth, being careful not to get my bare feet on it, and mounted to Dellie's door. When I knocked, I heard her voice telling me to come in.

It was dark inside the cabin, after the daylight, but I could make out Dellie piled up in bed under a quilt, and Little Jebb crouched by the hearth, where a low fire simmered. "Howdy," I said to Dellie, "how you feeling?"

Her big eyes, the whites surprising and glaring in the black face, fixed on me as I stood there, but she did not reply. It did not look like Dellie, or act like Dellie, who would grumble and bustle around our kitchen, talking to herself, scolding me or Little Jebb, clanking pans, making all sorts of unnecessary noises and mutterings like an old-fashioned black steam thrasher engine when it has got up an extra head of steam and keeps popping the governor and rumbling and shaking on its wheels. But now Dellie just lay up there on the bed, under the patch-work quilt, and turned the black face, which I scarcely recognized, and the glaring white eyes to me.

"How you feeling?" I repeated.

"I'se sick," the voice said croakingly out of the strange black face which was not attached to Dellie's big, squat body, but stuck out from under a pile of tangled bedclothes. Then the voice added: "Mighty sick."

"I'm sorry," I managed to say.

The eyes remained fixed on me for a moment, then they left me and the head rolled back on the pillow. "Sorry," the voice said, in a flat way which wasn't question or statement of anything. It was just the empty word put into the air with no meaning or expression, to float off like a feather or a puff of smoke, while the big eyes, with the whites like the peeled white of hard-boiled eggs, stared at the ceiling.

"Dellie," I said after a minute, "there's a tramp up at the house. He's got a knife."

She was not listening. She closed her eyes.

I tiptoed over to the hearth where Jebb was and crouched beside him. We began to talk in low voices. I was asking him to get out his train and play train. Old Jebb had put spool wheels on three cigar boxes and put wire links between the boxes to make a train for Jebb. The box that was the locomotive had the top closed and a length of broom stick for a smoke stack. Jebb didn't want to get the train out, but I told him I would go home if he didn't. So he got out the train, and the colored rocks, and fossils of crinoid stems, and other junk he used for the load, and we began to push it around, talking the way we thought trainmen talked, making a chuck-chuck-ing sound under the breath for the noise of the locomotive and now and then uttering low, cautious toots for the whistle. We got so interested in playing train that the toots got louder. Then, before he thought, Jebb gave a good, loud *toot-toot*, blowing for a crossing.

"Come here," the voice said from the bed.

Jebb got up slow from his hands and knees, giving me a sudden, naked, inimical look.

"Come here!" the voice said.

Jebb went to the bed. Dellie propped herself weakly up on one arm, muttering, "Come closer."

Jebb stood closer.

"Last thing I do, I'm gonna do it," Dellie said. "Done tole you to be quiet."

Then she slapped him. It was an awful slap, more awful for the kind of weakness which it came from and brought to focus. I had seen her slap Jebb before, but the slapping had always been the kind of easy slap you would expect from a good-natured, grumbling Negro woman like Dellie. But this was different. It was awful. It was so awful that Jebb didn't make a sound. The tears just popped out and ran down his face, and his breath came sharp, like gasps.

Dellie fell back. "Cain't even be sick," she said to the ceiling. "Git sick and they won't even let you lay. They tromp all over you. Cain't even be sick." Then she closed her eyes.

I went out of the room. I almost ran getting to the door, and I did run across the porch and down the steps and across the yard, not caring whether or not I stepped on the filth which had washed out from under the cabin. I ran almost all the way home. Then I thought about my mother catching me with the bare feet. So I went down to the stables.

I heard a noise in the crib, and opened the door. There was Big Jebb, sitting on an old nail keg, shelling corn into a bushel basket. I went in, pulling the door shut behind me, and crouched on the floor near him. I crouched there for a couple of minutes before either of us spoke, and watched him shelling the corn.

He had very big hands, knotted and grayish at the joints, with calloused palms which seemed to be streaked with rust with the rust coming up between the fingers to show from the back. His hands were so strong and tough that he could take a big ear of corn and rip the grains right off the cob with the palm of his hand, all in one motion, like a machine. "Work long as me," he would say, "and the good Lawd'll give you a hand lak cass-ion won't nuthin' hurt." And his hands did look like cast iron, old cast iron streaked with rust.

He was an old man, up in his seventies, thirty years or more older than Dellie, but he was strong as a bull. He was a squat sort of man, heavy in the shoulders, with remarkably long arms, the kind of build they say the river natives have on the Congo from paddling so much in their boats. He had a round bullet-head, set on powerful shoulders. His skin was very black, and the thin hair on his head was now grizzled like tufts of old cotton batting. He had small eyes and a flat nose, not big, and the kindest and wisest old face in the world, the blunt, sad, wise face of an old animal peering tolerantly out on the goings-on of the merely human creatures before him. He was a good man, and I loved him next to my mother and father. I crouched there on the floor of the crib and watched him shell corn with the rusty cast-iron hands, while he looked down at me out of the little eyes set in the blunt face.

"Dellie says she's mighty sick," I said.

"Yeah," he said.

"What's she sick from?"

"Woman-mizry," he said.

"What's woman-mizry?"

"Hit comes on 'em," he said. "Hit just comes on 'em when the time comes."

"What is it?"

"Hit is the change," he said. "Hit is the change of life and time."

"What changes?"

"You too young to know."

"Tell me."

"Time come and you find out everything."

I knew that there was no use in asking him any more. When I asked him things and he said that, I always knew that he would not tell me. So I continued to crouch there and watch him. Now that I had sat there a little while, I was cold again.

"What you shiver fer?" he asked me.

"I'm cold. I'm cold because it's blackberry winter," I said.

"Maybe 'tis and maybe 'tain't," he said.

"My mother says it is."

"Ain't sayen Miss Sallie doan know and ain't sayen she do. But folks doan know everything."

"Why isn't it blackberry winter?"

"Too late fer blackberry winter. Blackberries done bloomed."

"She said it was."

"Blackberry winter just a leetle cold spell. Hit come and then hit go away, and hit is growed summer of a sudden lak a gunshot. Ain't no tellen hit will go way this time."

"It's June," I said.

"June," he replied with great contempt. "That what folks say. What June mean? Maybe hit is come cold to stay."

"Why?"

"Cause this-here old yearth is tahrd. Hit is tahrd and ain't gonna perduce. Lawd let hit come rain one time forty days and forty nights, 'cause He was tahrd of sinful folks. Maybe this-here old yearth say to the Lawd, Lawd, I done plum tahrd, Lawd, lemme rest. And Lawd say, Yearth, you done yore best, you give 'em cawn and you give 'em taters, and all they think on is they gut, and, Yearth, you kin take a rest."

"What will happen?"

"Folks will eat up everything. The yearth won't perduce no more. Folks cut down all the trees and burn 'em 'cause they cold, and the yearth won't grow no more. I been tellen 'em. I been tellen folks. Sayen, maybe this year, hit is the time. But they doan listen to me, how the yearth is tahrd. Maybe this year they find out."

"Will everything die?"

"Everything and everbody, hit will be so."

"This year?"

"Ain't no tellen. Maybe this year."

"My mother said it is blackberry winter," I said confidently, and got up.

"Ain't sayen nuthin' agin Miss Sallie," he said.

I went to the door of the crib. I was really cold now. Running, I had got up a sweat and now I was worse.

I hung on the door, looking at Jebb, who was shelling corn again.

"There's a tramp came to the house," I said. I had almost forgotten the tramp.

"Yeah."

"He came by the back way. What was he doing down there in the storm?"

"They comes and they goes," he said, "and ain't no tellen."

"He had a mean knife."

"The good ones and the bad ones, they comes and they goes. Storm or sun, light or dark. They is folks and they comes and they goes lak folks."

I hung on the door, shivering.

He studied me a moment, then said, "You git on to the house. You ketch yore death. Then what yore mammy say?"

I hesitated.

"You git," he said.

When I came to the back yard, I saw that my father was standing by the back porch and the tramp was walking toward him. They began talking before I reached them, but I got there just as my father was saying, "I'm sorry, but I haven't got any work. I got all the hands on the place I need now. I won't need any extra until wheat thrashing."

The stranger made no reply, just looked at my father.

My father took out his leather coin purse, and got out a half-dollar. He held it toward the man. "This is for half a day," he said.

The man looked at the coin, and then at my father, making no motion to take the money. But that was the right amount. A dollar a day was what you paid them back in 1910. And the man hadn't even worked half a day.

Then the man reached out and took the coin. He dropped it into the right side pocket of his coat. Then he said, very slowly and without feeling: "I didn't want to work on your —— farm."

He used the word which they would have frailed me to death for using.

I looked at my father's face and it was streaked white under the sunburn. Then he said, "Get off this place. Get off this place or I won't be responsible."

The man dropped his right hand into his pants pocket. It was the pocket where he kept the knife. I was just about to yell to my father about the knife when the hand came back out with nothing in it. The man gave a kind of twisted grin, showing where the teeth had been knocked out above the new scar. I thought that instant how maybe he had tried before to pull a knife on somebody else and had got his teeth knocked out.

So now he just gave that twisted, sickish grin out of the unmemorable, grayish face, and then spat on the brick path. The glob landed just about six inches from the toe of my father's right boot. My father looked down at it, and so did I. I thought that if the glob had hit my father's boot something would have happened. I looked down and saw the bright glob, and on one side of it my father's strong cowhide boots, with the brass eyelets and the leather thongs, heavy boots splashed with good red mud and set solid on the bricks, and on the other side the pointed-toe, broken, black shoes, on which the mud looked so sad and out of place. Then I saw one of the black shoes move a little, just a twitch first, then a real step backward.

The man moved in a quarter circle to the end of the porch, with my father's steady gaze upon him all the while. At the end of the porch, the man reached up to the shelf where the wash pans were to get his little newspaper-wrapped parcel. Then he disappeared around the corner of the house and my father mounted the porch and went into the kitchen without a word.

I followed around the house to see what the man would do. I wasn't afraid of him now, no matter if he did have the knife. When I got around in front, I saw him going out the yard gate and starting up the drive toward the pike. So I ran to catch up with him. He was sixty yards or so up the drive before I caught up.

I did not walk right up even with him at first, but trailed him, the way a kid will, about seven or eight feet behind, now and then running two or three steps in order to hold my place against his longer stride. When I first came up behind him, he turned to give me a look, just a meaningless look, and then fixed his eyes up the drive and kept on walking.

When we had got around the bend in the drive which cut the house from sight, and were going along by the edge of the woods, I decided to come up even with him. I ran a few steps, and was by his side, or almost, but some feet off to the right. I walked along in this position for a while, and he never noticed me. I walked along until we got within sight of the big gate that let on the pike.

Then I said: "Where did you come from?"

He looked at me then with a look which seemed almost surprised that I was there. Then he said, "It ain't none of yore business."

We went on another fifty feet.

Then I said, "Where are you going?"

He stopped, studied me dispassionately for a moment, then suddenly took a step toward me and leaned his face down at me. The lips jerked back, but not in any grin, to show where the teeth were knocked out and to make the scar on the lower lip come white with the tension.

He said: "Stop following me. You don't stop following me and I cut yore throat, you little son-of-a-bitch."

Then he went on to the gate, and up the pike.

That was thirty-five years ago. Since that time my father and mother have died. I was still a boy, but a big boy, when my father got cut on the blade of a mowing machine and died of lockjaw. My mother sold the place and went to town to live with her sister. But she never took hold after my father's death and she died within three years, right in middle life. My aunt always said, "Sallie just died of a broken heart, she was so devoted." Dellie is dead, too, but she died, I heard, quite a long time after we sold the farm.

As for Little Jebb, he grew up to be a mean and ficey Negro. He killed another Negro in a fight and got sent to the penitentiary, where he is yet, the last I heard tell. He probably grew up to be mean and ficey from just being picked on so much by the children of the other tenants, who were jealous of Jebb and Dellie for being thrifty and clever and being white-folks' niggers.

Old Jebb lived forever. I saw him ten years ago and he was about a hundred then, and not looking much different. He was living in town then, on relief—that was back in the Depression—when I went to see him. He said to me: "Too strong to die. When I was a young feller just comen on and seen how things wuz, I prayed the Lawd. I said, O, Lawd, gimme strength and meke me strong fer to do and to in-dure. The Lawd hearkened to my prayer. He give me strength. I was in-duren proud fer being strong and me much man. The Lawd give me my prayer and my strength. But now He done gone off and fergot me and left me alone with my strength. A man doan know what to pray fer, and him mortal."

Jebb is probably living yet, as far as I know.

That is what has happened since the morning when the tramp leaned his face down at me and showed his teeth and said: "Stop following me. You don't stop following me and I cut yore throat, you little son-of-a-bitch." That was what he said, for me not to follow him. But I did follow him, all the years.

From *The Circus in the Attic and Other Stories* (1947)

·Richard Wright·

THE MAN WHO WAS
ALMOST A MAN

Dave struck out across the fields, looking homeward through paling light. Whut's the use talkin wid em niggers in the field? Anyhow, his mother was putting supper on the table. Them niggers can't understan nothing. One of these days he was going to get a gun and practice shooting, then they couldn't talk to him as though he were a little boy. He slowed, looking at the ground. Shucks, Ah ain scareda them even ef they are biggern me! Aw, Ah know what Ahma do. Ahm going by ol Joe's sto n git that Sears Roebuck catlog n look at them guns. Mebbe Ma will lemme buy one when she gits mah pay from ol man Hawkins. Ahma beg her t gimme some money. Ahm ol ernough to hava gun. Ahm seventeen. Almost a man. He strode, feeling his long loose-jointed limbs. Shucks, a man oughta hava little gun aftah he done worked hard all day.

He came in sight of Joe's store. A yellow lantern glowed on the front porch. He mounted steps and went through the screen door, hearing it bang behind him. There was a strong smell of coal oil and mackerel fish. He felt very confident until he saw fat Joe walk in through the rear door, then his courage began to ooze.

"Howdy, Dave! Whutcha want?"

"How yuh, Mistah Joe? Aw, Ah don wanna buy nothing. Ah jus wanted t see ef yuhd lemme look at tha catlog erwhile."

"Sure! You wanna see it here?"

"Nawsuh. Ah wans t take it home wid me. Ah'll bring it back termorrow when Ah come in from the fiels."

"You plannin on buying something?"

"Yessuh."

"Your ma lettin you have your own money now?"

"Shucks. Mistah Joe, Ahm gittin t be a man like anybody else!"

Joe laughed and wiped his greasy white face with a red bandanna.

"Whut you plannin on buyin?"

Dave looked at the floor, scratched his head, scratched his thigh, and smiled. Then he looked up shyly.

"Ah'll tell yuh, Mistah Joe, ef yuh promise yuh won't tell."

"I promise."

"Waal, Ahma buy a gun."

"A gun? Whut you want with a gun?"

"Ah wanna keep it."

"You ain't nothing but a boy. You don't need a gun."

"Aw, lemme have the catlog, Mistah Joe. Ah'll bring it back."

Joe walked through the rear door. Dave was elated. He looked around at barrels of sugar and flour. He heard Joe coming back. He craned his neck to see if he was bringing the book. Yeah, he's got it. Gawddog, he's got it!

"Here, but be sure you bring it back. It's the only one I got."

"Sho, Mistah Joe."

"Say, if you wanna buy a gun, why don't you buy one from me? I gotta gun to sell."

"Will it shoot?"

"Sure it'll shoot."

"Whut kind is it?"

"Oh, it's kinda old . . . a left-hand Wheeler. A pistol. A big one."

"Is it got bullets in it?"

"It's loaded."

"Kin Ah see it?"

"Where's your money?"

"Whut yuh wan fer it?"

"I'll let you have it for two dollars."

"Just two dollahs? Shucks, Ah could buy tha when Ah git mah pay."

"I'll have it here when you want it."

"Awright, suh. Ah be in fer it."

He went through the door, hearing it slam again behind him. Ahma git some money from Ma n buy me a gun! Only two dollahs! He tucked the thick catalogue under his arm and hurried.

"Where yuh been, boy?" His mother held a steaming dish of black-eyed peas.

"Aw, Ma, Ah jus stopped down the road t talk wid the boys."

"Yuh know bettah t keep suppah waitin."

He sat down, resting the catalogue on the edge of the table.

"Yuh git up from there and git to the well n wash yosef! Ah ain feedin no hogs in mah house!"

She grabbed his shoulder and pushed him. He stumbled out of the room, then came back to get the catalogue.

"Whut this?"

"Aw, Ma, it's jusa catlog."

"Who yuh git it from?"

"From Joe, down at the sto."

"Waal, thas good. We kin use it in the outhouse."

"Naw, Ma." He grabbed for it. "Gimme ma catlog, Ma."

She held onto it and glared at him.

"Quit hollerin at me! Whut's wrong wid yuh? Yuh crazy?"

"But Ma, please. It ain mine! It's Joe's! He tol me t bring it back t im termorrow."

She gave up the book. He stumbled down the back steps, hugging the thick book under his arm. When he had splashed water on his face and hands, he groped back to the kitchen and fumbled in a corner for the towel. He bumped into a chair; it clattered to the floor. The catalogue sprawled at his feet. When he had dried his eyes he snatched up the book and held it again under his arm. His mother stood watching him.

"Now, ef yuh gonna act a fool over that ol book, Ah'll take it n burn it up."

"Naw, Ma, please."

"Waal, set down n be still!"

He sat down and drew the oil lamp close. He thumbed page after page, unaware of the food his mother set on the table. His father came in. Then his small brother.

"Whutcha got there, Dave?" his father asked.

"Jusa catlog," he answered, not looking up.

"Yeah, here they is!" His eyes glowed at blue-and-black revolvers. He glanced up, feeling sudden guilt. His father was watching him. He eased the book under the table and rested it on his knees. After the blessing was asked, he ate. He scooped up peas and swallowed fat meat without chewing. Buttermilk helped to wash it down. He did not want to mention money before his father. He would do much better by cornering his mother when she was alone. He looked at his father uneasily out of the edge of his eye.

"Boy, how come yuh don quit foolin wid tha book n eat yo suppah?"

"Yessuh."

"How you n old man Hawkins gitten erlong?"

"Suh?"

"Can't yuh hear? Why don yuh lissen? Ah ast yu how wuz yuh n ol man Hawkins gittin erlong?"

"Oh, swell, Pa. Ah plows mo lan than anybody over there."

"Waal, yuh oughta keep yo mind on whut yuh doin."

"Yessuh."

He poured his plate full of molasses and sopped it up slowly with a chunk of cornbread. When his father and brother had left the kitchen, he still sat and looked again at the guns in the catalogue, longing to muster courage enough to present his case to his mother. Lawd, ef Ah only had tha pretty one! He could almost feel the slickness of the weapon with his fingers. If he had a gun like that he would polish it and keep it shining so it would never rust. N Ah'd keep it loaded, by Gawd!

"Ma?" His voice was hesitant.

"Hunh?"

"Ol man Hawkins give yuh mah money yit?"

"Yeah, but ain no usa yuh thinking bout throwin nona it erway. Ahme keepin tha money sos yuh kin have cloes t go to school this winter."

He rose and went to her side with the open catalogue in his palms. She was washing dishes, her head bent low over a pan. Shyly he raised the book. When he spoke, his voice was husky, faint.

"Ma, Gawd knows Ah wans one of these."

"One of whut?" she asked, not raising her eyes.

"One of these," he said again, not daring even to point. She glanced up at the page, then at him with wide eyes.

"Nigger, is yuh gone plumb crazy?"

"Aw, Ma—"

"Git outta here! Don yuh talk t me about no gun! Yuh a fool!"

"Ma, Ah kin buy one fer two dollahs."

"Not ef Ah knows it, yuh ain!"

"But yuh promised me one—"

"Ah don care whut Ah promised! Yuh ain nothing but a boy yit!"

"Ma, ef yuh lemme buy one Ah'll *never* ast yuh fer nothing no mo."

"Ah tol yuh t git outta here! Yuh ain gonna toucha penny of tha money fer no gun! Thas how come Ah has Mistah Hawkins t pay yo wages t me, cause Ah knows yuh ain got no sense."

"But, Ma, we needa gun. Pa ain got no gun. We needa gun in the house. Yuh kin never tell whut might happen."

"Now don yuh try to maka fool outta me, boy! Ef we did hava gun, yuh wouldn't have it!"

He laid the catalogue down and slipped his arm around her waist.

"Aw, Ma, Ah done worked hard alla summer n ain ast yuh fer nothin, is Ah, now?"

"Thas whut yuh spose t do!"

"But Ma, Ah wans a gun. Yuh kin lemme have two dollahs outta mah money. Plese, Ma, I kin give it to Pa . . . Please, Ma! Ah loves yuh, Ma."

When she spoke her voice came soft and low.

"Whut yu wan wida gun, Dave? Yuh don need no gun. Yuh'll git in trouble. N ef yo pa jus thought Ah let yuh have money t buy a gun he'd hava fit."

"Ah'll hide it, Ma. It ain but two dollahs."

"Lawd, chil, whut's wrong wid yuh?"

"Ain nothin wrong, Ma. Ahm almos a man now. Ah wans a gun."

"Who gonna sell yuh a gun?"

"Ol Joe at the sto."

"N it don cos but two dollahs?"

"Thas all, Ma. Jus two dollahs. Please, Ma."

She was stacking the plates away; her hands moved slowly, reflectively. Dave kept an anxious silence. Finally, she turned to him.

"Ah'll let yuh git tha gun ef yuh promise me one thing."

"Whut's tha, Ma?"

"Yuh bring it straight back t me, yuh hear? It be fer Pa."

"Yessum! Lemme go now, Ma."

She stooped, turned slightly to one side, raised the hem of her dress, rolled down the top of her stocking, and came up with a slender wad of bills.

"Here," she said. "Lawd knows yuh don need no gun. But yer pa does. Yuh bring it right back t me, yuh hear? Ahma put it up. Now ef yuh don, Ahma have yuh pa lick yuh so hard yuh won fergit it."

"Yessum."

He took the money, ran down the steps, and across the yard.

"Dave! Yuuuuuh Daaaaave!"

He heard, but he was not going to stop now. "Naw, Lawd!"

The first movement he made the following morning was to reach under his pillow for the gun. In the gray light of dawn he held it loosely, feeling a sense of power. Could kill a man with a gun like this. Kill anybody, black or white. And if he were holding his gun in his hand, nobody could run over him; they would have to respect him. It was a big gun, with a long barrel and a heavy handle. He raised and lowered it in his hand, marveling at its weight.

He had not come straight home with it as his mother had asked; instead he had stayed out in the fields, holding the weapon in his hand, aiming it now and then at some imaginary foe. But he had not fired it; he had been afraid that his father might hear. Also he was not sure he knew how to fire it.

To avoid surrendering the pistol he had not come into the house until he knew that they were all asleep. When his mother had tiptoed to his bedside late that night and demanded the gun, he had first played possum; then he had told her that the gun was hidden out-doors, that he would bring it to her in the morning. Now he lay turning it slowly in his hands. He broke it, took out the cartridges, felt them, and then put them back.

He slid out of bed, got a long strip of old flannel from a trunk, wrapped the gun in it, and tied it to his naked thigh while it was still loaded. He did not go in to breakfast. Even though it was not yet daylight, he started for Jim Hawkins' plantation. Just as the sun was rising he reached the barns where the mules and plows were kept.

"Hey! That you, Dave?"

He turned. Jim Hawkins stood eying him suspiciously.

"What're yuh doing here so early?"

"Ah didn't know Ah wuz gittin up so early, Mistah Hawkins. Ah wuz fixin t hitch up ol Jenny n take her t the fiels."

"Good. Since you're so early, how about plowing that stretch down by the woods?"

"Suits me, Mistah Hawkins."

"O.K. Go to it!"

He hitched Jenny to a plow and started across the fields. Hot dog! This was just what he wanted. If he could get down by the woods, he could shoot his gun and nobody would hear. He walked behind the plow, hearing the traces creaking, feeling the gun tied tight to his thigh.

When he reached the woods, he plowed two whole rows before he decided to take out the gun. Finally, he stopped, looked in all directions, then untied the gun and held it in his hand. He turned to the mule and smiled.

"Know whut this is, Jenny? Naw, yuh wouldn know! Yuhs jusa ol mule! Anyhow, this is a gun, n it kin shoot, by Gawd!"

He held the gun at arm's length. Whut t hell, Ahma shoot this thing! He looked at Jenny again.

"Lissen here, Jenny! When Ah pull this ol trigger, Ah don wan yuh t run n acka fool now!"

Jenny stood with head down, her short ears pricked straight. Dave walked off about twenty feet, held the gun far out from him at arm's length, and turned his head. Hell, he told himself, Ah ain afraid. The gun felt loose in his fingers; he waved it wildly for a moment. Then he shut his eyes and tightened his forefinger. Bloom! A report half deafened him and he thought his right hand was torn from his arm. He heard Jenny whinnying and galloping over the field, and he found himself on his knees, squeezing his fingers hard between his legs. His hand was numb; he jammed it into his mouth, trying to warm it, trying to stop the pain. The gun lay at his feet. He did not quite know what had happened. He stood up and stared at the gun as though it were a living thing. He gritted his teeth and kicked the gun. Yuh almos broke mah arm! He turned to look for Jenny; she was far over the fields, tossing her head and kicking wildly.

"Hol on there, ol mule!"

When he caught up with her she stood trembling, walling her big white eyes at him. The plow was far away; the traces had broken. Then Dave stopped short, looking, not believing. Jenny was bleeding. Her left side was red and wet with blood. He went closer. Lawd, have mercy! Wondah did Ah shoot this mule? He grabbed for Jenny's mane. She flinched, snorted, whirled, tossing her head.

"Hol on now! Hol on."

Then he saw the hole in Jenny's side, right between the ribs. It was round, wet, red. A crimson stream streaked down the front leg, flowing fast. Good Gawd! Ah wuzn't shootin at tha mule. He felt panic. He knew he had to stop that blood, or Jenny would bleed to death. He had never seen so much blood in all his life. He chased the mule for half a mile, trying to catch her. Finally she stopped, breathing hard, stumpy tail half arched. He caught her mane and led her back to where the plow and gun lay. Then he stooped and grabbed handfuls of damp black earth and tried to plug the bullet hole. Jenny shuddered, whinnied, and broke from him.

"Hol on! Hol on now!"

He tried to plug it again, but blood came anyhow. His fingers were hot and sticky. He rubbed dirt into his palms, trying to dry them. Then again he attempted to plug the bullet hole, but Jenny shied away, kicking her heels high. He stood helpless. He had to do something. He ran at Jenny; she dodged him. He watched a red stream of blood flow down Jenny's leg and form a bright pool at her feet.

"Jenny . . . Jenny," he called weakly.

His lips trembled. She's bleeding t death! He looked in the direction of home, wanting to go back, wanting to get help. But he saw the pistol lying in the damp black clay. He had a queer feeling that if he only did something, this would not be; Jenny would not be there bleeding to death.

When he went to her this time, she did not move. She stood with sleepy, dreamy eyes; and when he touched her she gave a low-pitched whinny and knelt to the ground, her front knees slopping in blood.

"Jenny . . . Jenny . . ." he whispered.

For a long time she held her neck erect; then her head sank, slowly. Her ribs swelled with a mighty heave and she went over.

Dave's stomach felt empty, very empty. He picked up the gun

and held it gingerly between his thumb and forefinger. He buried it at the foot of a tree. He took a stick and tried to cover the pool of blood with dirt—but what was the use? There was Jenny lying with her mouth open and her eyes walled and glassy. He could not tell Jim Hawkins he had shot his mule. But he had to tell something. Yeah, Ah'll tell em Jenny started gittin wil n fell on the joint of the plow. . . . But that would hardly happen to a mule. He walked across the field slowly, head down.

It was sunset. Two of Jim Hawkins' men were over near the edge of the woods digging a hole in which to bury Jenny. Dave was surrounded by a knot of people, all of whom were looking down at the dead mule.

"I don't see how in the world it happened," said Jim Hawkins for the tenth time.

The crowd parted and Dave's mother, father, and small brother pushed into the center.

"Where Dave?" his mother called.

"There he is," said Jim Hawkins.

His mother grabbed him.

"Whut happened, Dave? Whut yuh done?"

"Nothin."

"C mon, boy, talk," his father said.

Dave took a deep breath and told the story he knew nobody believed.

"Waal," he drawled. "Ah brung old Jenny down here sos Ah could do mah plowin. Ah plowed bout two rows, just like yuh see." He stopped and pointed at the long rows of upturned earth. "Then something musta been wrong wid ol Jenny. She wouldn ack right a-tall. She started snortin n kickin her heels. Ah tried t hol her, but she pulled erway, rearin n goin in. Then when the point of the plow was stickin up in the air, she swung erroun n twisted herself back on it . . . She stuck herself n started t bleed. N fo Ah could do anything, she wuz dead."

"Did you ever hear of anything like that in all your life?" asked Jim Hawkins.

There were white and black standing in the crowd. They murmured. Dave's mother came close to him and looked hard into his face. "Tell the truth, Dave," she said.

"Looks like a bullet hole to me," said one man.

"Dave, whut yuh do wid the gun?" his mother asked.

The crowd surged in, looking at him. He jammed his hands into his pockets, shook his head slowly from left to right, and backed away. His eyes were wide and painful.

"Did he hava gun?" asked Jim Hawkins.

"By Gawd, Ah tol yuh that wuz a gun wound," said a man, slapping his thigh.

His father caught his shoulders and shook him till his teeth rattled.

"Tell whut happened, yuh rascal! Tell whut . . ."

Dave looked at Jenny's stiff legs and began to cry.

"Whut yuh do wid tha gun?" his mother asked.

"Whut wuz he doin wida gun?" his father asked.

"Come on and tell the truth," said Hawkins. "Ain't nobody going to hurt you . . ."

His mother crowded close to him.

"Did yuh shoot tha mule, Dave?"

Dave cried, seeing blurred white and black faces.

"Ahh ddinn gggo tt sshooot hher . . . Ah ssswear ffo Gawd Ahh ddin. . . . Ah wuz a-tryin t sssee ef the old gggun would sshoot—"

"Where yuh git the gun from?" his father asked.

"Ah got it from Joe, at the sto."

"Where yuh git the money?"

"Ma give it t me."

"He kept worryin me, Bob. Ah had t. Ah tol im t bring the gun right back t me . . . It was fer yuh, the gun."

"But how yuh happen to shoot that mule?" asked Jim Hawkins.

"Ah wuzn shootin at the mule, Mistah Hawkins. The gun jumped when Ah pulled the trigger . . . N fo Ah knowed anythin Jenny was there a-bleedin."

Somebody in the crowd laughed. Jim Hawkins walked close to Dave and looked into his face.

"Well, looks like you have bought you a mule, Dave."

"Ah swear fo Gawd, Ah didn go t kill the mule, Mistah Hawkins!"

"But you killed her!"

All the crowd was laughing now. They stood on tiptoe and poked heads over one another's shoulders.

"Well, boy, looks like yuh done bought a dead mule! Hahaha!"

"Ain tha ershame."

"Hohohohoho."

Dave stood, head down, twisting his feet in the dirt.

"Well, you needn't worry about it, Bob," said Jim Hawkins to Dave's father. "Just let the boy keep on working and pay me two dollars a month."

"Whut yuh wan fer yo mule, Mistah Hawkins?"

Jim Hawkins screwed up his eyes.

"Fifty dollars."

"Whut yuh do wid tha gun?" Dave's father demanded. Dave said nothing.

"Yuh wan me t take a tree n beat yuh till yuh talk!"

"Nawsuh!"

"Whut yuh do wid it?"

"Ah throwed it erway."

"Where?"

"Ah . . . Ah throwed it in the creek."

"Waal, c mon home. N firs thing in the mawnin git to tha creek n fin tha gun."

"Yessuh."

"What yuh pay fer it?"

"Two dollahs."

"Take tha gun n git yo money back n carry it t Mistah Hawkins, yuh hear? N don fergit Ahma lam you black bottom good fer this! Now march yosef on home, suh!"

Dave turned and walked slowly. He heard people laughing. Dave glared, his eyes welling with tears. Hot anger bubbled in him. Then he swallowed and stumbled on.

That night Dave did not sleep. He was glad that he had gotten out of killing the mule so easily, but he was hurt. Something hot seemed to turn over inside him each time he remembered how they had laughed. He tossed on his bed, feeling his hard pillow. N Pa says he's gonna beat me . . . He remembered other beatings, and his back quivered. Naw, naw, Ah sho don wan im t beat me tha way no mo. Dam em all! Nobody ever gave him anything. All he did was work. They treat me like a mule, n then they beat me. He gritted his teeth. N Ma had t tell on me.

Well, if he had to, he would take old man Hawkins that two dollars. But that meant selling the gun. And he wanted to keep that gun. Fifty dollars for a dead mule.

He turned over, thinking how he had fired the gun. He had an itch to fire it again. Ef other men kin shoota gun, by Gawd, Ah kin! He was still, listening. Mebbe they all sleepin now. The house was still. He heard the soft breathing of his brother. Yes, now! He would go down and get that gun and see if he could fire it! He eased out of bed and slipped into overalls.

The moon was bright. He ran almost all the way to the edge of the woods. He stumbled over the ground, looking for the spot where he had buried the gun. Yeah, here it is. Like a hungry dog scratching for a bone, he pawed it up. He puffed his black cheeks and blew dirt from the trigger and barrel. He broke it and found four cartridges unshot. He looked around; the fields were filled with silence and moonlight. He clutched the gun stiff and hard in his fingers. But, as soon as he wanted to pull the trigger, he shut his eyes and turned his head. Naw, Ah can't shoot wid mah eyes closed n mah head turned. With effort he held his eyes open; then he squeezed. *Blooooom!* He was stiff, not breathing. The gun was still in his hands. Dammit, he'd done it. He fired again. *Blooooom!* He smiled. *Bloooom! Blooooom! Click, click.* There! It was empty. If anybody could shoot a gun, he could. He put the gun into his hip pocket and started across the fields.

When he reached the top of a ridge he stood straight and proud in the moonlight, looking at Jim Hawkins' big white house, feeling the gun sagging in his pocket. Lawd, ef Ah had just one mo bullet Ah'd taka shot at tha house. Ah'd like t scare ol man Hawkins jusa little . . . Jusa enough t let im know Dave Saunders is a man.

To his left the road curved, running to the tracks of the Illinois Central. He jerked his head, listening. From far off came a faint *hoooof-hoooof; hoooof-hoooof; hoooof-hoooof.* . . . He stood rigid. Two dollahs a mont. Les see now . . . Tha means it'll take bout two years. Shucks! Ah'll be dam!

He started down the road, toward the tracks. Yeah, here she comes! He stood beside the track and held himself stiffy. Here she comes, erroun the ben . . . C mon, yuh slow poke! C mon! He had his hand on his gun; something quivered in his stomach. Then the train thundered past, the gray and brown box cars rumbling and clinking. He gripped the gun tightly; then he jerked his hand out of his pocket. Ah betcha Bill wouldn't do it! Ah betcha . . . The cars slid past, steel grinding upon steel. Ahm ridin yuh ternight, so hep me Gawd! He was hot all over. He hesitated just a moment; then he grabbed, pulled atop of a car, and lay flat. He felt his pocket; the gun was still there. Ahead the long rails were glinting in the moonlight, stretching away, away to somewhere, somewhere where he could be a man . . .

From *Eight Men* (1961; first published as "Almos' A Man" in 1940)

·Saul Bellow·

LOOKING FOR MR. GREEN

Whatsoever thy hand findeth to do, do it with thy might. . . .[1]

Hard work? No, it wasn't really so hard. He wasn't used to walking and stair-climbing, but the physical difficulty of his new job was not what George Grebe felt most. He was delivering relief checks in the Negro district, and although he was a native Chicagoan this was not a part of the city he knew much about—it needed a depression to introduce him to it. No, it wasn't literally hard work, not as reckoned in foot-pounds, but yet he was beginning to feel the strain of it, to grow aware of its peculiar difficulty. He could find the streets and numbers, but the clients were not where they were supposed to be, and he felt like a hunter inexperienced in the camouflage of his game. It was an unfavorable day, too—fall, and cold, dark weather, windy. But, anyway, instead of shells in his deep trench-coat pocket he had the cardboard of checks, punctured for the spindles of the file, the holes reminding him of the holes in player-piano paper. And he didn't look much like a hunter, either; his was a city figure entirely, belted up in this Irish conspirator's coat. He was slender without being tall, stiff in the back, his legs looking shabby in a pair of old tweed pants gone through and fringy at the cuffs. With this stiffness, he kept his head forward, so that his face was red from the sharpness of the weather; and it was an indoors sort of face with gray eyes that persisted in some kind of thought and yet seemed to avoid definiteness of conclusion. He wore side-

1. Eccl. 9:10. "Whatsoever thy hand findeth to do, do *it* with thy might; for there is no work, nor device, nor knowledge, nor wisdom, in the grave, whither thou goest."

burns that surprised you somewhat by the tough curl of the blond hair and the effect of assertion in their length. He was not so mild as he looked, nor so youthful; and nevertheless there was no effort on his part to seem what he was not. He was an educated man; he was a bachelor; he was in some ways simple; without lushing, he liked a drink; his luck had not been good. Nothing was deliberately hidden.

He felt that his luck was better than usual today. When he had reported for work that morning he had expected to be shut up in the relief office at a clerk's job, for he had been hired downtown as a clerk, and he was glad to have, instead, the freedom of the streets and welcomed, at least at first, the vigor of the cold and even the blowing of the hard wind. But on the other hand he was not getting on with the distribution of the checks. It was true that it was a city job; nobody expected you to push too hard at a city job. His supervisor, that young Mr. Raynor, had practically told him that. Still, he wanted to do well at it. For one thing, when he knew how quickly he could deliver a batch of checks, he would know also how much time he could expect to clip for himself. And then, too, the clients would be waiting for their money. That was not the most important consideration, though it certainly mattered to him. No, but he wanted to do well, simply for doing-well's sake, to acquit himself decently of a job because he so rarely had a job to do that required just this sort of energy. Of this peculiar energy he now had a superabundance; once it had started to flow, it flowed all too heavily. And, for the time being anyway, he was balked. He could not find Mr. Green.

So he stood in his big-skirted trenchcoat with a large envelope in his hand and papers showing from his pocket, wondering why people should be so hard to locate who were too feeble or sick to come to the station to collect their own checks. But Raynor had told him that tracking them down was not easy at first and had offered him some advice on how to proceed. "If you can see the postman, he's your first man to ask, and your best bet. If you can't connect with him, try the stores and tradespeople around. Then the janitor and the neighbors. But you'll find the closer you come to your man the less people will tell you. They don't want to tell you anything."

"Because I'm a stranger."

"Because you're white. We ought to have a Negro doing this, but we don't at the moment, and of course you've got to eat, too, and this is public employment. Jobs have to be made. Oh, that holds for me too. Mind you, I'm not letting myself out. I've got three years of seniority on you, that's all. And a law degree. Otherwise, you might be back of the desk and I might be going out into the field this cold day. The same dough pays us both and for the same, exact, identical reason. What's my law degree got to do with it? But you have to pass out these checks, Mr. Grebe, and it'll help if you're stubborn, so I hope you are."

"Yes, I'm fairly stubborn."

Raynor sketched hard with an eraser in the old dirt of his desk, left-handed, and said, "Sure, what else can you answer to such a question. Anyhow, the trouble you're going to have is that they don't like to give information about anybody. They think you're a plain-clothes dick or an installment collector, or summons-server or something like that. Till you've been seen around the neighborhood for a few months and people know you're only from the relief."

It was dark, ground-freezing, pre-Thanksgiving weather; the wind played hob with the smoke, rushing it down, and Grebe missed his gloves, which he had left in Raynor's office. And no one would admit knowing Green. It was past three o'clock and the postman had made his last delivery. The nearest grocer, himself a Negro, had never heard the name Tulliver Green, or said he hadn't. Grebe was inclined to think that it was true, that he had in the end convinced the man that he wanted only to deliver a check. But he wasn't sure. He needed experience in interpreting looks and signs and, even more, the will not to be put off or denied and even the force to bully if need be. If the grocer did know, he had got rid of him easily. But since most of his trade was with reliefers, why should he prevent the delivery of a check? Maybe Green, or Mrs. Green, if there was a Mrs. Green, patronized another grocer. And was there a Mrs. Green? It was one of Grebe's great handicaps that he hadn't looked at any of the case records. Raynor should have let him read files for a few hours. But he apparently saw no need for that, probably considering the job unimportant. Why prepare systematically to deliver a few checks?

But now it was time to look for the janitor. Grebe took in the building in the wind and gloom of the late November day—trampled, frost-hardened lots on one side; on the other, an automobile junk yard and then the infinite work of Elevated frames,[2] weak-looking, gaping with rubbish fires; two sets of leaning brick porches three stories high and a flight of cement stairs to the cellar. Descending, he entered the underground passage, where he tried the doors until one opened and he found himself in the furnace room. There someone rose toward him and approached, scraping on the coal grit and bending under the canvas-jacketed pipes.

"Are you the janitor?"

"What do you want?"

2. Elevated urban railway (the "El").

"I'm looking for a man who's supposed to be living here. Green."

"What Green?"

"Oh, you maybe have more than one Green?" said Grebe with new, pleasant hope. "This is Tulliver Green."

"I don't think I c'n help you, mister. I don't know any."

"A crippled man."

The janitor stood bent before him. Could it be that he was crippled? Oh, God! what if he was. Grebe's gray eyes sought with excited difficulty to see. But no, he was only very short and stooped. A head awakened from meditation, a strong-haired beard, low, wide shoulders. A staleness of sweat and coal rose from his black shirt and the burlap sack he wore as an apron.

"Crippled how?"

Grebe thought and then answered with the light voice of unmixed candor, "I don't know. I've never seen him." This was damaging, but his only other choice was to make a lying guess, and he was not up to it. "I'm delivering checks for the relief to shut-in cases. If he weren't crippled he'd come to collect himself. That's why I said crippled. Bedridden, chair-ridden—is there anybody like that?"

This sort of frankness was one of Grebe's oldest talents, going back to childhood. But it gained him nothing here.

"No suh. I've got four buildin's same as this that I take care of. I don' know all the tenants, leave alone the tenants' tenants. The rooms turn over so fast, people movin' in and out every day. I can't tell you."

The janitor opened his grimy lips but Grebe did not hear him in the piping of the valves and the consuming pull of air to flame in the body of the furnace. He knew, however, what he had said.

"Well, all the same, thanks. Sorry I bothered you. I'll prowl around upstairs again and see if I can turn up someone who knows him."

Once more in the cold air and early darkness he made the short circle from the cellarway to the entrance crowded between the brickwork pillars and began to climb to the third floor. Pieces of plaster ground under his feet; strips of brass tape from which the carpeting had been torn away marked old boundaries at the sides. In the passage, the cold reached him worse than in the street; it touched him to the bone. The hall toilets ran like springs. He thought grimly as he heard the wind burning around the building with a sound like that of the furnace, that this was a great piece of constructed shelter. Then he struck a match in the gloom and searched for names and numbers among the writings and scribbles on the walls. He saw WHOODY-DOODY GO TO JESUS, and zigzags, caricatures, sexual scrawls, and curses. So the sealed rooms of pyramids were also decorated, and the caves of human dawn.

The information on his card was, TULLIVER GREEN—APT 3D. There were no names, however, and no numbers. His shoulders drawn up, tears of cold in his eyes, breathing vapor, he went the length of the corridor and told himself that if he had been lucky enough to have the temperament for it he would bang on one of the doors and bawl out "Tulliver Green!" until he got results. But it wasn't in him to make an uproar and he continued to burn matches, passing the light over the walls. At the rear, in a corner off the hall, he discovered a door he had not seen before and he thought it best to investigate. It sounded empty when he knocked, but a young Negress answered, hardly more than a girl. She opened only a bit, to guard the warmth of the room.

"Yes suh?"

"I'm from the district relief station on Prairie Avenue. I'm looking for a man named Tulliver Green to give him his check. Do you know him?"

No, she didn't; but he thought she had not understood anything of what he had said. She had a dream-bound, dream-blind face, very soft and black, shut off. She wore a man's jacket and pulled the ends together at her throat. Her hair was parted in three directions, at the sides and transversely, standing up at the front in a dull puff.

"Is there somebody around here who might know?"

"I jus' taken this room las' week."

He observed that she shivered, but even her shiver was somnambulistic and there was no sharp consciousness of cold in the big smooth eyes of her handsome face.

"All right, miss, thank you. Thanks," he said, and went to try another place.

Here he was admitted. He was grateful, for the room was warm. It was full of people, and they were silent as he entered—ten people, or a dozen, perhaps more, sitting on benches like a parliament. There was no light, properly speaking, but a tempered darkness that the window gave, and everyone seemed to him enormous, the men padded out in heavy work clothes and winter coats, and the women huge, too, in their sweaters, hats, and old furs. And, besides, bed and bedding, a black cooking range, a piano piled towering to the ceiling with papers, a dining-room table of the old style of prosperous Chicago. Among these people Grebe, with his cold-heightened fresh color and his smaller stature, entered like a schoolboy. Even though he was met with smiles and good will, he knew, before a single word was spoken, that all the currents ran against him and that he would make no headway. Nevertheless he began. "Does anybody here know how I can deliver a check to Mr. Tulliver Green?"

"Green?" It was the man that had let him in who answered. He was in short sleeves, in a checkered shirt, and had a queer, high head, profusely overgrown and long as a shako; [3] the veins entered it strongly from his forehead. "I never heard mention of him. Is this where he live?"

"This is the address they gave me at the station. He's a sick man, and he'll need his check. Can't anybody tell me where to find him?"

He stood his ground and waited for a reply, his crimson wool scarf wound about his neck and drooping outside his trenchcoat, pockets weighted with the block of checks and official forms. They must have realized that he was not a college boy employed afternoons by a bill collector, trying foxily to pass for a relief clerk, recognized that he was an older man who knew himself what need was, who had had more than an average seasoning in hardship. It was evident enough if you looked at the marks under his eyes and at the sides of his mouth.

"Anybody know this sick man?"

"No suh." On all sides he saw heads shaken and smiles of denial. No one knew. And maybe it was true, he considered, standing silent in the earthen, musky human gloom of the place as the rumble continued. But he could never really be sure.

"What's the matter with this man?" said shako-head.

"I've never seen him. All I can tell you is that he can't come in person for his money. It's my first day in this district."

"Maybe they given you the wrong number?"

"I don't believe so. But where else can I ask about him?" He felt that this persistence amused them deeply, and in a way he shared their amusement that he should stand up so tenaciously to them. Though smaller, though slight, he was his own man, he retracted nothing about himself, and he looked back at them, gray-eyed, with amusement and also with a sort of courage. On the bench some man spoke in his throat, the words impossible to catch, and a woman answered with a wild, shrieking laugh, which was quickly cut off.

"Well, so nobody will tell me?"

"Ain't nobody who knows."

"At least, if he lives here, he pays rent to someone. Who manages the building?"

"Greatham Company. That's on Thirty-ninth Street."

Grebe wrote it in his pad. But, in the street again, a sheet of wind-driven paper clinging to his leg while he deliberated what di-

3. Peaked military cap.

rection to take next, it seemed a feeble lead to follow. Probably this Green didn't rent a flat, but a room. Sometimes there were as many as twenty people in an apartment; the real-estate agent would know only the lessee. And not even the agent could tell you who the renters were. In some places the beds were even used in shifts, watchmen or jitney drivers or short-order cooks in night joints turning out after a day's sleep and surrendering their beds to a sister, a nephew, or perhaps a stranger, just off the bus. There were large numbers of newcomers in this terrific, blight-bitten portion of the city between Cottage Grove and Ashland, wandering from house to house and room to room. When you saw them, how could you know them? They didn't carry bundles on their backs or look picturesque. You only saw a man, a Negro, walking in the street or riding in the car, like everyone else, with his thumb closed on a transfer. And therefore how were you supposed to tell? Grebe thought the Greatham agent would only laugh at his question.

But how much it would have simplified the job to be able to say that Green was old, or blind, or comsumptive. An hour in the files, taking a few notes, and he needn't have been at such a disadvantage. When Raynor gave him the block of checks he asked, "How much should I know about these people?" Then Raynor had looked as though he were preparing to accuse him of trying to make the job more important than it was. He smiled, because by then they were on fine terms, but nevertheless he had been getting ready to say something like that when the confusion began in the station over Staika and her children.

Grebe had waited a long time for this job. It came to him through the pull of an old schoolmate in the Corporation Counsel's office, never a close friend, but suddenly sympathetic and interested—pleased to show, moreover, how well he had done, how strongly he was coming on even in these miserable times. Well, he was coming through strongly, along with the Democratic administration itself. Grebe had gone to see him in City Hall, and they had had a counter lunch or beers at least once a month for a year, and finally it had been possible to swing the job. He didn't mind being assigned the lowest clerical grade, nor even being a messenger, though Raynor thought he did.

This Raynor was an original sort of guy and Grebe had taken to him immediately. As was proper on the first day, Grebe had come early, but he waited long, for Raynor was late. At last he darted into his cubicle of an office as though he had just jumped from one of those hurtling huge red Indiana Avenue cars. His thin, rough face was wind-stung and he was grinning and saying something breathlessly to himself. In his hat, a small fedora, and his coat, the velvet collar a neat fit about his neck, and his silk muffler that set off the nervous twist of his chin, he swayed and turned himself in his swivel chair, feet leaving the ground; so that he pranced a little as he sat. Meanwhile he took Grebe's measure out of his eyes, eyes of an unusual vertical length and slightly sardonic. So the two men sat for a while, saying nothing, while the supervisor raised his hat from his miscombed hair and put it in his lap. His cold-darkened hands were not clean. A steel beam passed through the little makeshift room, from which machine belts once had hung. The building was an old factory.

"I'm younger than you; I hope you won't find it hard taking orders from me," said Raynor. "But I don't make them up, either. You're how old, about?"

"Thirty-five."

"And you thought you'd be inside doing paper work. But it so happens I have to send you out."

"I don't mind."

"And it's mostly a Negro load we have in this district."

"So I thought it would be."

"Fine. You'll get along. *C'est un bon boulot.*[4] Do you know French?"

"Some."

"I thought you'd be a university man."

"Have you been in France?" said Grebe.

"No, that's the French of the Berlitz School. I've been at it for more than a year, just as I'm sure people have been, all over the world, office boys in China and braves in Tanganyika. In fact, I damn well know it. Such is the attractive power of civilization. It's overrated, but what do you want? *Que voulez-vous?* [5] I get *Le Rire* [6] and all the spicy papers, just like in Tanganyika. It must be mystifying, out there. But my reason is that I'm aiming at the diplomatic service. I have a cousin who's a courier, and the way he describes it is awfully attractive. He rides in the *wagon-lits* [7] and reads books. While we— What did you do before?"

"I sold."

"Where?"

"Canned meat at Stop and Shop. In the basement."

"And before that?"

"Window shades, at Goldblatt's."

"Steady work?"

"No, Thursdays and Saturdays. I also sold shoes."

"You've been a shoe-dog too. Well. And prior to that? Here it is

4. "It's a good job."
5. "What do you want?"
6. French humorous journal.
7. Railway sleeping-cars.

in your folder." He opened the record. "Saint Olaf's College, instructor in classical languages. Fellow, University of Chicago, 1926–27. I've had Latin, too. Let's trade quotations—'*Dum spiro spero.*'"

" '*Da dextram misero.*' "

" '*Alea jacta est.*' "

" '*Excelsior.*' " [8]

Raynor shouted with laughter, and other workers came to look at him over the partition. Grebe also laughed, feeling pleased and easy. The luxury of fun on a nervous morning.

When they were done and no one was watching or listening, Raynor said rather seriously, "What made you study Latin in the first place? Was it for the priesthood?"

"No."

"Just for the hell of it? For the culture? Oh, the things people think they can pull!" He made his cry hilarious and tragic. "I ran my pants off so I could study for the bar, and I've passed the bar, so I get twelve dollars a week more than you as a bonus for having seen life straight and whole. I'll tell you, as a man of culture, that even though nothing looks to be real, and everything stands for something else, and that thing for another thing, and that thing for a still further one—there ain't any comparison between twenty-five and thirty-seven dollars a week, regardless of the last reality. Don't you think that was clear to your Greeks? They were a thoughtful people, but they didn't part with their slaves."

This was a great deal more than Grebe had looked for in his first interview with his supervisor. He was too shy to show all the astonishment he felt. He laughed a little, aroused, and brushed at the sunbeam that covered his head with its dust. "Do you think my mistake was so terrible?"

"Damn right it was terrible, and you know it now that you've had the whip of hard times laid on your back. You should have been preparing yourself for trouble. Your people must have been well off to send you to the university. Stop me, if I'm stepping on your toes. Did your mother pamper you? Did your father give in to you? Were you brought up tenderly, with permission to go and find out what were the last things that everything else stands for while everybody else labored in the fallen world of appearances?"

"Well, no, it wasn't exactly like that." Grebe smiled. *The fallen world of appearances!* no less. But now it was his turn to deliver a surprise. "We weren't rich. My father was the last genuine English butler in Chicago—"

"Are you kidding?"

8. Familiar Latin slogans: "While I breathe, I hope"; "Give your right hand to the wretched"; "The die is cast"; "Higher!"

"Why should I be?"

"In a livery?"

"In livery. Up on the Gold Coast." [9]

"And he wanted you to be educated like a gentleman?"

"He did not. He sent me to the Armour Institute to study chemical engineering. But when he died I changed schools."

He stopped himself, and considered how quickly Raynor had reached him. In no time he had your valise on the table and all your stuff unpacked. And afterward, in the streets, he was still reviewing how far he might have gone, and how much he might have been led to tell if they had not been interrupted by Mrs. Staika's great noise.

But just then a young woman, one of Raynor's workers, ran into the cubicle exclaiming, "Haven't you heard all the fuss?"

"We haven't heard anything."

"It's Staika, giving out with all her might. The reporters are coming. She said she phoned the papers, and you know she did."

"But what is she up to?" said Raynor.

"She brought her wash and she's ironing it here, with our current, because the relief won't pay her electric bill. She has her ironing board set up by the admitting desk, and her kids are with her, all six. They never are in school more than once a week. She's always dragging them around with her because of her reputation."

"I don't want to miss any of this," said Raynor, jumping up. Grebe, as he followed with the secretary, said, "Who is this Staika?"

"They call her the 'Blood Mother of Federal Street.' She's a professional donor at the hospitals. I think they pay ten dollars a pint. Of course it's no joke, but she makes a very big thing out of it and she and the kids are in the papers all the time."

A small crowd, staff and clients divided by a plywood barrier, stood in the narrow space of the entrance, and Staika was shouting in a gruff, mannish voice, plunging the iron on the board and slamming it on the metal rest.

"My father and mother came in a steerage, and I was born in our house, Robey by Huron. I'm no dirty immigrant. I'm a U.S. citizen. My husband is a gassed veteran from France with lungs weaker'n paper, that hardly can he go to the toilet by himself. These six children of mine, I have to buy the shoes for their feet with my own blood. Even a lousy little white Communion necktie, that's a couple of drops of blood; a little piece of mosquito veil for my Vadja so she won't be ashamed in church for the other girls, they take my blood for it by Goldblatt. That's how I keep goin'. A fine thing if I

9. Lake Shore Drive and Near North Side, one of Chicago's wealthiest sections.

had to depend on the relief. And there's plenty of people on the rolls—fakes! There's nothin' *they* can't get, that can go and wrap bacon at Swift and Armour any time. They're lookin' for them by the Yards. They never have to be out of work. Only they rather lay in their lousy beds and eat the public's money." She was not afraid, in a predominantly Negro station, to shout this way about Negroes.

Grebe and Raynor worked themselves forward to get a closer view of the woman. She was flaming with anger and with pleasure at herself, broad and huge, a golden-headed woman who wore a cotton cap laced with pink ribbon. She was barelegged and had on black gym shoes, her Hoover apron was open and her great breasts, not much restrained by a man's undershirt, hampered her arms as she worked at the kid's dress on the ironing board. And the children, silent and white, with a kind of locked obstinacy, in sheepskins and lumberjackets, stood behind her. She had captured the station, and the pleasure this gave her was enormous. Yet her grievances were true grievances. She was telling the truth. But she behaved like a liar. The look of her small eyes was hidden, and while she raged she also seemed to be spinning and planning.

"They send me out college case workers in silk pants to talk me out of what I got comin'. Are they better'n me? Who told them? Fire them. Let 'em go and get married, and then you won't have to cut electric from people's budget."

The chief supervisor, Mr. Ewing, couldn't silence her and he stood with folded arms at the head of his staff, bald, bald-headed, saying to his subordinates like the ex-school principal he was, "Pretty soon she'll be tired and go."

"No she won't," said Raynor to Grebe. "She'll get what she wants. She knows more about the relief even then Ewing. She's been on the rolls for years, and she always gets what she wants because she puts on a noisy show. Ewing knows it. He'll give in soon. He's only saving face. If he gets bad publicity, the Commissioner'll have him on the carpet, downtown. She's got him submerged; she'll submerge everybody in time, and that includes nations and governments."

Grebe replied with his characteristic smile, disagreeing completely. Who would take Staika's orders, and what changes could her yelling ever bring about?

No, what Grebe saw in her, the power that made people listen, was that her cry expressed the war of flesh and blood, perhaps turned a little crazy and certainly ugly, on this place and this condition. And at first, when he went out, the spirit of Staika somehow presided over the whole district for him, and it took color from her; he saw her color, in the spotty curb fires, and the fires under the El, the straight alley of flamy gloom. Later, too, when he went into a tavern for a shot of rye, the sweat of beer, association with West Side Polish streets, made him think of her again.

He wiped the corners of his mouth with his muffler, his handkerchief being inconvenient to reach for, and went out again to get on with the delivery of his checks. The air bit cold and hard and a few flakes of snow formed near him. A train struck by and left a quiver in the frames and a bristling icy hiss over the rails.

Crossing the street, he descended a flight of board steps into a basement grocery, setting off a little bell. It was a dark, long store and it caught you with its stinks of smoked meat, soap, dried peaches, and fish. There was a fire wrinkling and flapping in the little stove, and the proprietor was waiting, an Italian with a long, hollow face and stubborn bristles. He kept his hands warm under his apron.

No, he didn't know Green. You knew people but not names. The same man might not have the same name twice. The police didn't know, either, and mostly didn't care. When somebody was shot or knifed they took the body away and didn't look for the murderer. In the first place, nobody would tell them anything. So they made up a name for the coroner and called it quits. And in the second place, they didn't give a goddamn anyhow. But they couldn't get to the bottom of a thing even if they wanted to. Nobody would get to know even a tenth of what went on among these people. They stabbed and stole, they did every crime and abomination you ever heard of, men and men, women and women, parents and children, worse than the animals. They carried on their own way, and the horrors passed off like a smoke. There was never anything like it in the history of the whole world.

It was a long speech, deepening with every word in its fantasy and passion and becoming increasingly senseless and terrible: a swarm amassed by suggestion and invention, a huge, hugging, despairing knot, a human wheel of heads, legs, bellies, arms, rolling through his shop.

Grebe felt that he must interrupt him. He said sharply, "What are you talking about! All I asked was whether you knew this man."

"That isn't even the half of it. I been here six years. You probably don't want to believe this. But suppose it's true?"

"All the same," said Grebe, "there must be a way to find a person."

The Italian's close-spaced eyes had been queerly concentrated, as were his muscles, while he leaned across the counter trying to convince Grebe. Now he gave up the effort and sat down on his stool. "Oh—I suppose. Once in a while. But I been telling you, even the cops don't get anywhere."

"They're always after somebody. It's not the same thing."

"Well, keep trying if you want. I can't help you."

But he didn't keep trying. He had no more time to spend on Green. He slipped Green's check to the back of the block. The next name on the list was FIELD, WINSTON.

He found the back-yard bungalow without the least trouble; it shared a lot with another house, a few feet of yard between. Grebe knew these two-shack arrangements. They had been built in vast numbers in the days before the swamps were filled and the streets raised, and they were all the same—a boardwalk along the fence, well under street level, three or four ball-headed posts for clothes-lines, greening wood, dead shingles, and a long, long flight of stairs to the rear door.

A twelve-year-old boy let him into the kitchen, and there the old man was, sitting by the table in a wheel chair.

"Oh, it's d' Government man," he said to the boy when Grebe drew out his checks. "Go bring me my box of papers." He cleared a space on the table.

"Oh, you don't have to go to all that trouble," said Grebe. But Field laid out his papers: Social Security card, relief certification, letters from the state hospital in Manteno, and a naval discharge dated San Diego, 1920.

"That's plenty," Grebe said. "Just sign."

"You got to know who I am," the old man said. "You're from the Government. It's not your check, it's a Government check and you got no business to hand it over till everything is proved."

He loved the ceremony of it, and Grebe made no more objections. Field emptied his box and finished out the circle of cards and letters.

"There's everything I done and been. Just the death certificate and they can close book on me." He said this with a certain happy pride and magnificence. Still he did not sign; he merely held the little pen upright on the golden-green corduroy of his thigh. Grebe did not hurry him. He felt the old man's hunger for conversation.

"I got to get better coal," he said. "I send my little gran'son to the yard with my order and they fill his wagon with screening. The stove ain't made for it. It fall through the grate. The order says Franklin County egg-size coal."

"I'll report it and see what can be done."

"Nothing can be done, I expect. You know and I know. There ain't no little ways to make things better, and the only big thing is money. That's the only sunbeams, money. Nothing is black where it shines, and the only place you see black is where it ain't shining. What we colored have to have is our own rich. There ain't no other way."

Grebe sat, his reddened forehead bridged levelly by his close-cut

hair and his cheeks lowered in the wings of his collar—the caked
fire shone hard within the isinglass-and-iron frames but the room
was not comfortable—sat and listened while the old man unfolded
his scheme. This was to create one Negro millionaire a month by
subscription. One clever, good-hearted young fellow elected every
month would sign a contract to use the money to start a business
employing Negroes. This would be advertised by chain letters and
word of mouth, and every Negro wage earner would contribute a
dollar a month. Within five years there would be sixty millionaires.

"That'll fetch respect," he said with a throat-stopped sound that
came out like a foreign syllable. "You got to take and organize all
the money that gets thrown away on the policy wheel and horse
race. As long as they can take it away from you, they got no respect
for you. Money, that's d' sun of human kind!" Field was a Negro of
mixed blood, perhaps Cherokee, or Natchez; his skin was reddish.
And he sounded, speaking about a golden sun in this dark room,
and looked, shaggy and slab-headed, with the mingled blood of his
face and broad lips, the little pen still upright in his hand, like one
of the underground kings of mythology, old judge Minos [10] himself.

And now he accepted the check and signed. Not to soil the slip,
he held it down with his knuckles. The table budged and creaked,
the center of the gloomy, heathen midden [11] of the kitchen covered with bread, meat, and cans, and the scramble of papers.

"Don't you think my scheme'd work?"

"It's worth thinking about. Something ought to be done, I agree."

"It'll work if people will do it. That's all. That's the only thing,
any time. When they understand it in the same way, all of them."

"That's true," said Grebe, rising. His glance met the old man's.

"I know you got to go," he said. "Well, God bless you, boy, you
ain't been sly with me. I can tell it in a minute."

He went back through the buried yard. Someone nursed a candle
in a shed, where a man unloaded kindling wood from a sprawl-
wheeled baby buggy and two voices carried on a high conversation.
As he came up the sheltered passage he heard the hard boost of the
wind in the branches and against the house fronts, and then, reaching the sidewalk, he saw the needle-eye red of cable towers in the
open icy height hundreds of feet above the river and the factories—
those keen points. From here, his view was obstructed all the way
to the South Branch and its timber banks, and the cranes beside the
water. Rebuilt after the Great Fire, this part of the city was, not fifty
years later, in ruins again, factories boarded up, buildings deserted
or fallen, gaps of prairie between. But it wasn't desolation that this
made you feel, but rather a faltering of organization that set free a

10. Legendary king of Crete, who commissioned Daedalus to build the Labyrinth.
11. Refuse heap.

huge energy, an escaped, unattached, unregulated power from the giant raw place. Not only must people feel it but, it seemed to Grebe, they were compelled to match it. In their very bodies. He no less than others, he realized. Say that his parents had been servants in their time, whereas he was not supposed to be one. He thought that they had never done any service like this, which no one visible asked for, and probably flesh and blood could not even perform. Nor could anyone show why it should be performed; or see where the performance would lead. That did not mean that he wanted to be released from it, he realized with a grimly pensive face. On the contrary. He had something to do. To be compelled to feel this energy and yet have no task to do—that was horrible; that was suffering; he knew what that was. It was now quitting time. Six o'clock. He could go home if he liked, to his room, that is, to wash in hot water, to pour a drink, lie down on his quilt, read the paper, eat some liver paste on crackers before going out to dinner. But to think of this actually made him feel a little sick, as though he had swallowed hard air. He had six checks left, and he was determined to deliver at least one of these: Mr. Green's check.

So he started again. He had four or five dark blocks to go, past open lots, condemned houses, old foundations, closed schools, black churches, mounds, and he reflected that there must be many people alive who had once seen the neighborhood rebuilt and new. Now there was a second layer of ruins; centuries of history accomplished through human massing. Numbers had given the place forced growth; enormous numbers had also broken it down. Objects once so new, so concrete that it could have occurred to anyone they stood for other things, had crumbled. Therefore, reflected Grebe, the secret of them was out. It was that they stood for themselves by agreement, and were natural and not unnatural by agreement, and when the things themselves collapsed the agreement became visible. What was it, otherwise, that kept cities from looking peculiar? Rome, that was almost permanent, did not give rise to thoughts like these. And was it abidingly real? But in Chicago, where the cycles were so fast and the familiar died out, and again rose changed, and died again in thirty years, you saw the common agreement or covenant, and you were forced to think about appearances and realities. (He remembered Raynor and he smiled. Raynor was a clever boy.) Once you had grasped this, a great many things became intelligible. For instance, why Mr. Field should conceive such a scheme. Of course, if people were to agree to create a millionaire, a real millionaire would come into existence. And if you wanted to know how Mr. Field was inspired to think of this, why, he had within sight of his kitchen window the chart, the very bones of a successful scheme—the El with its blue and green confetti of signals. People consented to pay dimes and ride the crash-box cars, and so it was a success. Yet how absurd it looked; how little reality there was to start with. And yet Yerkes,[12] the great financier who built it, had known that he could get people to agree to do it. Viewed as itself, what a scheme of a scheme it seemed, how close to an appearance. Then why wonder at Mr. Field's idea? He had grasped a principle. And then Grebe remembered, too, that Mr. Yerkes had established the Yerkes Observatory and endowed it with millions. Now how did the notion come to him in his New York museum of a palace or his Aegean-bound yacht to give money to astronomers? Was he awed by the success of his bizarre enterprise and therefore ready to spend money to find out where in the universe being and seeming were identical? Yes, he wanted to know what abides; and whether flesh is Bible grass; [13] and he offered money to be burned in the fire of suns. Okay, then, Grebe thought further, these things exist because people consent to exist with them—we have got so far—and also there is a reality which doesn't depend on consent but within which consent is a game. But what about need, the need that keeps so many vast thousands in position? You tell me that, you *private* little gentleman and decent soul—he used these words against himself scornfully. Why is the consent given to misery? And why so painfully ugly? Because there is *something* that is dismal and permanently ugly? Here he sighed and gave it up, and thought it was enough for the present moment that he had a real check in his pocket for a Mr. Green who must be real beyond question. If only his neighbors didn't think they had to conceal him.

This time he stopped at the second floor. He struck a match and found a door. Presently a man answered his knock and Grebe had the check ready and showed it even before he began. "Does Tulliver Green live here? I'm from the relief."

The man narrowed the opening and spoke to someone at his back.

"Does he live here?"

"Uh-uh. No."

"Or anywhere in this building? He's a sick man and he can't come for his dough." He exhibited the check in the light, which was smoky—the air smelled of charred lard—and the man held off the brim of his cap to study it.

"Uh-uh. Never seen the name."

"There's nobody around here that uses crutches?"

12. Charles Tyson Yerkes (1837–1905), American financier who obtained a virtual monopoly of the surface and elevated railway service in Chicago. He gave to the University of Chicago the great telescope installed in the Yerkes Observatory at Lake Geneva, Wisconsin.
13. See Isa. 40:6. "All flesh *is* grass, and all the goodliness thereof *is* as the flower of the field."

He seemed to think, but it was Grebe's impression that he was simply waiting for a decent interval to pass.

"No, suh. Nobody I ever see."

"I've been looking for this man all afternoon"—Grebe spoke out with sudden force—"and I'm going to have to carry this check back to the station. It seems strange not to be able to find a person to *give* him something when you're looking for him for a good reason. I suppose if I had bad news for him I'd find him quick enough."

There was a responsive motion in the other man's face. "That's right, I reckon."

"It almost doesn't do any good to have a name if you can't be found by it. It doesn't stand for anything. He might as well not have any," he went on, smiling. It was as much of a concession as he could make to his desire to laugh.

"Well, now, there's a little old knot-back man I see once in a while. He might be the one you lookin' for. Downstairs."

"Where? Right side or left? Which door?"

"I don't know which. Thin-face little knot-back with a stick."

But no one answered at any of the doors on the first floor. He went to the end of the corridor, searching by matchlight, and found only a stairless exit to the yard, a drop of about six feet. But there was a bungalow near the alley, an old house like Mr. Field's. To jump was unsafe. He ran from the front door, through the underground passage and into the yard. The place was occupied. There was a light through the curtains, upstairs. The name on the ticket under the broken, scoop-shaped mailbox was Green! He exultantly rang the bell and pressed against the locked door. Then the lock clicked faintly and a long staircase opened before him. Someone was slowly coming down—a woman. He had the impression in the weak light that she was shaping her hair as she came, making herself presentable, for he saw her arms raised. But it was for support that they were raised; she was feeling her way downward, down the wall, stumbling. Next he wondered about the pressure of her feet on the treads; she did not seem to be wearing shoes. And it was a freezing stairway. His ring had got her out of bed, perhaps, and she had forgotten to put them on. And then he saw that she was not only shoeless but naked; she was entirely naked, climbing down while she talked to herself, a heavy woman, naked and drunk. She blundered into him. The contact of her breasts, though they touched only his coat, made him go back against the door with a blind shock. See what he had tracked down, in his hunting game!

The woman was saying to herself, furious with insult, "So I cain't ——k, huh? I'll show that son-of-a-bitch kin I, cain't I."

What should he do now? Grebe asked himself. Why, he should go. He should turn away and go. He couldn't talk to this woman. He couldn't keep her standing naked in the cold. But when he tried he found himself unable to turn away.

He said, "Is this where Mr. Green lives?"

But she was still talking to herself and did not hear him.

"Is this Mr. Green's house?"

At last she turned her furious drunken glance on him. "What do you want?"

Again her eyes wandered from him; there was a dot of blood in their enraged brilliance. He wondered why she didn't feel the cold.

"I'm from the relief."

"Awright, what?"

"I've got a check for Tulliver Green."

This time she heard him and put out her hand.

"No, no, for *Mr.* Green. He's got to sign," he said. How was he going to get Green's signature tonight!

"I'll take it. He cain't."

He desperately shook his head, thinking of Mr. Field's precautions about identification. "I can't let you have it. It's for him. Are you Mrs. Green?"

"Maybe I is, and maybe I ain't. Who want to know?"

"Is he upstairs?"

"Awright. Take it up yourself, you goddamn fool."

Sure, he was a goddamn fool. Of course he could not go up because Green would probably be drunk and naked, too. And perhaps he would appear on the landing soon. He looked eagerly upward. Under the light was a high narrow brown wall. Empty! It remained empty!

"Hell with you, then!" he heard her cry. To deliver a check for coal and clothes, he was keeping her in the cold. She did not feel it, but his face was burning with frost and self-ridicule. He backed away from her.

"I'll come tomorrow, tell him."

"Ah, hell with you. Don' never come. What you doin' here in the nighttime? Don' come back." She yelled so that he saw the breadth of her tongue. She stood astride in the long cold box of the hall and held on to the banister and the wall. The bungalow itself was shaped something like a box, a clumsy, high box pointing into the freezing air with its sharp, wintry lights.

"If you are Mrs. Green, I'll give you the check," he said, changing his mind.

"Give here, then." She took it, took the pen offered with it in her left hand, and tried to sign the receipt on the wall. He looked around, almost as though to see whether his madness was being observed, and came near believing that someone was standing on a mountain of used tires in the auto-junking shop next door.

"But are you Mrs. Green?" he now thought to ask. But she was already climbing the stairs with the check, and it was too late, if he had made an error, if he was now in trouble, to undo the thing. But he wasn't going to worry about it. Though she might not be Mrs. Green, he was convinced that Mr. Green was upstairs. Whoever she was, the woman stood for Green, whom he was not to see this time. Well, you silly bastard, he said to himself, so you think you found him. So what? Maybe you really did find him—what of it? But it was important that there was a real Mr. Green whom they could not keep him from reaching because he seemed to come as an emissary from hostile appearances. And though the self-ridicule was slow to diminish, and his face still blazed with it, he had, nevertheless, a feeling of elation, too. "For after all," he said, "he *could* be found!"

From *Mosby's Memoirs and Other Stories* (1968;
first published in 1951)

·Flannery O'Connor·

A GOOD MAN IS HARD TO FIND

The grandmother didn't want to go to Florida. She wanted to visit some of her connections in east Tennessee and she was seizing at every chance to change Bailey's mind. Bailey was the son she lived with, her only boy. He was sitting on the edge of his chair at the table, bent over the orange sports section of the *Journal*. "Now look here, Bailey," she said, "see here, read this," and she stood with one hand on her thin hip and the other rattling the newspaper at his bald head. "Here this fellow that calls himself The Misfit is aloose from the Federal Pen and headed toward Florida and you read what it says he did to these people. Just you read it. I wouldn't take my children in any direction with a criminal like that aloose in it. I couldn't answer to my conscience if I did."

Bailey didn't look up from his reading so she wheeled around then and faced the children's mother, a young woman in slacks, whose face was as broad and innocent as a cabbage and was tied around with a green headkerchief that had two points on the top like rabbit's ears. She was sitting on the sofa, feeding the baby his apricots out of a jar. "The children have been to Florida before," the old lady said. "You all ought to take them somewhere else for a change so they would see different parts of the world and be broad. They never have been to east Tennessee."

The children's mother didn't seem to hear her but the eight-year-old boy, John Wesley, a stocky child with glasses, said, "If you don't want to go to Florida, why dontcha stay at home?" He and the little girl, June Star, were reading the funny papers on the floor.

"She wouldn't stay at home to be queen for a day," June Star said without raising her yellow head.

"Yes, and what would you do if this fellow, The Misfit, caught you?" the grandmother asked.

"I'd smack his face," John Wesley said.

"She wouldn't stay at home for a million bucks," June Star said. "Afraid she'd miss something. She has to go everywhere we go."

"All right, Miss," the grandmother said. "Just remember that the next time you want me to curl your hair."

June Star said her hair was naturally curly.

The next morning the grandmother was the first one in the car, ready to go. She had her big black valise that looked like the head of a hippopotamus in one corner, and underneath it she was hiding a basket with Pitty Sing, the cat, in it. She didn't intend for the cat to be left alone in the house for three days because he would miss her too much and she was afraid he might brush against one of the gas burners and accidentally asphyxiate himself. Her son, Bailey, didn't like to arrive at a motel with a cat.

She sat in the middle of the back seat with John Wesley and June Star on either side of her. Bailey and the children's mother and the baby sat in front and they left Atlanta at eight forty-five with the mileage on the car at 55890. The grandmother wrote this down because she thought it would be interesting to say how many miles they had been when they got back. It took them twenty minutes to reach the outskirts of the city.

The old lady settled herself comfortably, removing her white cotton gloves and putting them up with her purse on the shelf in front of the back window. The children's mother still had on slacks and still had her head tied up in a green kerchief, but the grandmother had on a navy blue straw sailor hat with a bunch of white violets on the brim and a navy blue dress with a small white dot in the print. Her collars and cuffs were white organdy trimmed with lace and at her neckline she had pinned a purple spray of cloth violets containing a sachet. In case of an accident, anyone seeing her dead on the highway would know at once that she was a lady.

She said she thought it was going to be a good day for driving, neither too hot nor too cold, and she cautioned Bailey that the speed limit was fifty-five miles an hour and that the patrolmen hid themselves behind billboards and small clumps of trees and sped out after you before you had a chance to slow down. She pointed out interesting details of the scenery: Stone Mountain; the blue granite that in some places came up to both sides of the highway; the brilliant red clay banks slightly streaked with purple; and the various crops that made rows of green lace-work on the ground. The trees were full of silver-white sunlight and the meanest of them sparkled. The children were reading comic magazines and their mother had gone back to sleep.

"Let's go through Georgia fast so we won't have to look at it much," John Wesley said.

"If I were a little boy," said the grandmother, "I wouldn't talk about my native state that way. Tennessee has the mountains and Georgia has the hills."

"Tennessee is just a hillbilly dumping ground," John Wesley said, "and Georgia is a lousy state too."

"You said it," June Star said.

"In my time," said the grandmother, folding her thin veined fingers, "children were more respectful to their native states and their parents and everything else. People did right then. Oh look at the cute little pickaninny!" she said and pointed to a Negro child standing in the door of a shack. "Wouldn't that make a picture, now?" she asked and they all turned and looked at the little Negro out of the back window. He waved.

"He didn't have any britches on," June Star said.

"He probably didn't have any," the grandmother explained. "Little niggers in the country don't have things like we do. If I could paint, I'd paint that picture," she said.

The children exchanged comic books.

The grandmother offered to hold the baby and the children's mother passed him over the front seat to her. She set him on her knee and bounced him and told him about the things they were passing. She rolled her eyes and screwed up her mouth and stuck her leathery thin face into his smooth bland one. Occasionally he gave her a faraway smile. They passed a large cotton field with five or six graves fenced in the middle of it, like a small island. "Look at the graveyard!" the grandmother said, pointing it out. "That was the old family burying ground. That belonged to the plantation."

"Where's the plantation?" John Wesley asked.

"Gone With the Wind," [1] said the grandmother. "Ha. Ha."

When the children finished all the comic books they had brought, they opened the lunch and ate it. The grandmother ate a peanut butter sandwich and an olive and would not let the children throw the box and the paper napkins out the window. When there was nothing else to do they played a game by choosing a cloud and making the other two guess what shape it suggested. John Wesley took one the shape of a cow and June Star guessed a cow and John Wesley said, no, an automobile, and June Star said he didn't play fair, and they began to slap each other over the grandmother.

1. The immensely popular novel by Margaret Mitchell, published in 1936 and later made into a record-breaking film (1939). A romance of the Civil War and Reconstruction, *Gone With the Wind* tells of the struggle to maintain a Georgia plantation.

The grandmother said she would tell them a story if they would keep quiet. When she told a story, she rolled her eyes and waved her head and was very dramatic. She said once when she was a maiden lady she had been courted by a Mr. Edgar Atkins Teagarden from Jasper, Georgia. She said he was a very good-looking man and a gentleman and that he brought her a watermelon every Saturday afternoon with his initials cut in it, E. A. T. Well, one Saturday, she said, Mr. Teagarden brought the watermelon and there was nobody at home and he left it on the front porch and returned in his buggy to Jasper, but she never got the watermelon, she said, because a nigger boy ate it when he saw the initials, E. A. T.! This story tickled John Wesley's funny bone and he giggled and giggled but June Star didn't think it was any good. She said she wouldn't marry a man that just brought her a watermelon on Saturday. The grandmother said she would have done well to marry Mr. Teagarden because he was a gentleman and had bought Coca-Cola stock when it first came out and that he had died only a few years ago, a very wealthy man.

They stopped at The Tower for barbecued sandwiches. The Tower was a part stucco and part wood filling station and dance hall set in a clearing outside of Timothy. A fat man named Red Sammy Butts ran it and there were signs stuck here and there on the building and for miles up and down the highway saying, TRY RED SAMMY'S FAMOUS BARBECUE. NONE LIKE FAMOUS RED SAMMY'S! RED SAM! THE FAT BOY WITH THE HAPPY LAUGH. A VETERAN! RED SAMMY'S YOUR MAN!

Red Sammy was lying on the bare ground outside The Tower with his head under a truck while a gray monkey about a foot high, chained to a small chinaberry tree, chattered nearby. The monkey sprang back into the tree and got on the highest limb as soon as he saw the children jump out of the car and run toward him.

Inside, The Tower was a long dark room with a counter at one end and tables at the other and dancing space in the middle. They all sat down at a board table next to the nickelodeon and Red Sam's wife, a tall burnt-brown woman with hair and eyes lighter than her skin, came and took their order. The children's mother put a dime in the machine and played "The Tennessee Waltz," and the grandmother said that tune always made her want to dance. She asked Bailey if he would like to dance but he only glared at her. He didn't have a naturally sunny disposition like she did and trips made him nervous. The grandmother's brown eyes were very bright. She swayed her head from side to side and pretended she was dancing in her chair. June Star said play something she could tap to so the children's mother put in another dime and played a fast number and June Star stepped out onto the dance floor and did her tap routine.

"Ain't she cute?" Red Sam's wife said, leaning over the counter. "Would you like to come be my little girl?"

"No I certainly wouldn't," June Star said. "I wouldn't live in a broken-down place like this for a million bucks!" and she ran back to the table.

"Ain't she cute?" the woman repeated, stretching her mouth politely.

"Aren't you ashamed?" hissed the grandmother.

Red Sam came in and told his wife to quit lounging on the counter and hurry up with these people's order. His khaki trousers reached just to his hip bones and his stomach hung over them like a sack of meal swaying under his shirt. He came over and sat down at a table nearby and let out a combination sigh and yodel. "You can't win," he said. "You can't win," and he wiped his sweating red face off with a gray handkerchief. "These days you don't know who to trust," he said. "Ain't that the truth?"

"People are certainly not nice like they used to be," said the grandmother.

"Two fellers come in here last week," Red Sammy said, "driving a Chrysler. It was a old beat-up car but it was a good one and these boys looked all right to me. Said they worked at the mill and you know I let them fellers charge the gas they bought? Now why did I do that?"

"Because you're a good man!" the grandmother said at once.

"Yes'm, I suppose so," Red Sam said as if he were struck with this answer.

His wife brought the orders, carrying the five plates all at once without a tray, two in each hand and one balanced on her arm. "It isn't a soul in this green world of God's that you can trust," she said. "And I don't count nobody out of that, not nobody," she repeated, looking at Red Sammy.

"Did you read about that criminal, The Misfit, that's escaped?" asked the grandmother.

"I wouldn't be a bit surprised if he didn't attack this place right here," said the woman. "If he hears about it being here, I wouldn't be none surprised to see him. If he hears it's two cent in the cash register, I wouldn't be at all surprised if he . . ."

"That'll do," Red Sam said. "Go bring these people their Co'-Colas," and the woman went off to get the rest of the order.

"A good man is hard to find," Red Sammy said. "Everything is getting terrible. I remember the day you could go off and leave your screen door unlatched. Not no more."

He and the grandmother discussed better times. The old lady said that in her opinion Europe was entirely to blame for the way things were now. She said the way Europe acted you would think we were made of money and Red Sam said it was no use talking about it, she was exactly right. The children ran outside into the white sunlight and looked at the monkey in the lacy chinaberry tree. He was busy catching fleas on himself and biting each one carefully between his teeth as if it were a delicacy.

They drove off again into the hot afternoon. The grandmother took cat naps and woke up every few minutes with her own snoring. Outside of Toombsboro she woke up and recalled an old plantation that she had visited in this neighborhood once when she was a young lady. She said the house had six white columns across the front and that there was an avenue of oaks leading up to it and two little wooden trellis arbors on either side in front where you sat down with your suitor after a stroll in the garden. She recalled exactly which road to turn off to get to it. She knew that Bailey would not be willing to lose any time looking at an old house, but the more she talked about it, the more she wanted to see it once again and find out if the little twin arbors were still standing. "There was a secret panel in this house," she said craftily, not telling the truth but wishing that she were, "and the story went that all the family silver was hidden in it when Sherman [2] came through but it was never found . . ."

"Hey!" John Wesley said. "Let's go see it! We'll find it! We'll poke all the woodwork and find it! Who lives there? Where do you turn off at? Hey Pop, can't we turn off there?"

"We never have seen a house with a secret panel!" June Star shrieked. "Let's go to the house with the secret panel! Hey Pop, can't we go see the house with the secret panel!"

"It's not far from here, I know," the grandmother said. "It wouldn't take over twenty minutes."

Bailey was looking straight ahead. His jaw was as rigid as a horseshoe. "No," he said.

The children began to yell and scream that they wanted to see the house with the secret panel. John Wesley kicked the back of the front seat and June Star hung over her mother's shoulder and whined desperately into her ear that they never had any fun even on their vacation, that they could never do what THEY wanted to do. The baby began to scream and John Wesley kicked the back of the seat so hard that his father could feel the blows in his kidney.

"All right!" he shouted and drew the car to a stop at the side of the road. "Will you all shut up? Will you all just shut up for one second? If you don't shut up, we won't go anywhere."

"It would be very educational for them," the grandmother murmured.

"All right," Bailey said, "but get this: this is the only time we're

2. William Tecumseh Sherman (1820–91), Civil War general who led the Union forces in a crushing campaign against the South. His famous march through Georgia, from Atlanta to the sea, took place in December 1864.

going to stop for anything like this. This is the one and only time."

"The dirt road that you have to turn down is about a mile back," the grandmother directed. "I marked it when we passed."

"A dirt road," Bailey groaned.

After they had turned around and were headed toward the dirt road, the grandmother recalled other points about the house, the beautiful glass over the front doorway and the candle-lamp in the hall. John Wesley said that the secret panel was probably in the fireplace.

"You can't go inside this house," Bailey said. "You don't know who lives there."

"While you all talk to the people in front, I'll run around behind and get in a window," John Wesley suggested.

"We'll all stay in the car," his mother said.

They turned onto the dirt road and the car raced roughly along in a swirl of pink dust. The grandmother recalled the times when there were no paved roads and thirty miles was a day's journey. The dirt road was hilly and there were sudden washes in it and sharp curves on dangerous embankments. All at once they would be on a hill, looking down over the blue tops of trees for miles around, then the next minute, they would be in a red depression with the dust-coated trees looking down on them.

"This place had better turn up in a minute," Bailey said, "or I'm going to turn around."

The road looked as if no one had traveled on it in months.

"It's not much farther," the grandmother said and just as she said it, a horrible thought came to her. The thought was so embarrassing that she turned red in the face and her eyes dilated and her feet jumped up, upsetting her valise in the corner. The instant the valise moved, the newspaper top she had over the basket under it rose with a snarl and Pitty Sing, the cat, sprang onto Bailey's shoulder.

The children were thrown to the floor and their mother, clutching the baby, was thrown out the door onto the ground; the old lady was thrown into the front seat. The car turned over once and landed right-side-up in a gulch off the side of the road. Bailey remained in the driver's seat with the cat—gray-striped with a broad white face and an orange nose—clinging to his neck like a caterpillar.

As soon as the children saw they could move their arms and legs, they scrambled out of the car, shouting, "We've had an AC-CIDENT!" The grandmother was curled up under the dashboard, hoping she was injured so that Bailey's wrath would not come down on her all at once. The horrible thought she had had before the accident was that the house she had remembered so vividly was not in Georgia but in Tennessee.

Bailey removed the cat from his neck with both hands and flung it out the window against the side of a pine tree. Then he got out of the car and started looking for the children's mother. She was sitting against the side of the red gutted ditch, holding the screaming baby, but she only had a cut down her face and a broken shoulder. "We've had an ACCIDENT!" the children screamed in a frenzy of delight.

"But nobody's killed," June Star said with disappointment as the grandmother limped out of the car, her hat still pinned to her head but the broken front brim standing up at a jaunty angle and the violet spray hanging off the side. They all sat down in the ditch, except the children, to recover from the shock. They were all shaking.

"Maybe a car will come along," said the children's mother hoarsely.

"I believe I have an injured organ," said the grandmother, pressing her side, but no one answered her. Bailey's teeth were clattering. He had on a yellow sport shirt with bright blue parrots designed on it and his face was as yellow as the shirt. The grandmother decided that she would not mention that the house was in Tennessee.

The road was about ten feet above and they could see only the tops of the trees on the other side of it. Behind the ditch they were sitting in there were more woods, tall and dark and deep. In a few minutes they saw a car some distance away on top of a hill, coming slowly as if the occupants were watching them. The grandmother stood up and waved both arms dramatically to attract their attention. The car continued to come on slowly, disappeared around a bend and appeared again, moving even slower, on top of the hill they had gone over. It was a big black battered hearse-like automobile. There were three men in it.

It came to a stop just over them and for some minutes, the driver looked down with a steady expressionless gaze to where they were sitting, and didn't speak. Then he turned his head and muttered something to the other two and they got out. One was a fat boy in black trousers and a red sweat shirt with a silver stallion embossed on the front of it. He moved around on the right side of them and stood staring, his mouth partly open in a kind of loose grin. The other had on khaki pants and a blue striped coat and a gray hat pulled down very low, hiding most of his face. He came around slowly on the left side. Neither spoke.

The driver got out of the car and stood by the side of it, looking down at them. He was an older man than the other two. His hair was just beginning to gray and he wore silver-rimmed spectacles that gave him a scholarly look. He had a long creased face and didn't have on any shirt or undershirt. He had on blue jeans that were too tight for him and was holding a black hat and a gun. The two boys also had guns.

"We've had an ACCIDENT!" the children screamed.

The grandmother had the peculiar feeling that the bespectacled man was someone she knew. His face was as familiar to her as if she had known him all her life but she could not recall who he was. He moved away from the car and began to come down the embankment, placing his feet carefully so that he wouldn't slip. He had on tan and white shoes and no socks, and his ankles were red and thin. "Good afternoon," he said. "I see you all had you a little spill."

"We turned over twice!" said the grandmother.

"Oncet," he corrected. "We seen it happen. Try their car and see will it run, Hiram," he said quietly to the boy with the gray hat.

"What you got that gun for?" John Wesley asked. "Whatcha gonna do with that gun?"

"Lady," the man said to the children's mother, "would you mind calling them children to sit down by you? Children make me nervous. I want all you to sit down right together there where you're at."

"What are you telling US what to do for?" June Star asked.

Behind them the line of woods gaped like a dark open mouth. "Come here," said their mother.

"Look here now," Bailey began suddenly, "we're in a predicament! we're in . . ."

The grandmother shrieked. She scrambled to her feet and stood staring. "You're The Misfit!" she said. "I recognized you at once!"

"Yes'm," the man said, smiling slightly as if he were pleased in spite of himself to be known, "but it would have been better for all of you, lady, if you hadn't of reckernized me."

Bailey turned his head sharply and said something to his mother that shocked even the children. The old lady began to cry and The Misfit reddened.

"Lady," he said, "don't you get upset. Sometimes a man says things he don't mean. I don't reckon he meant to talk to you thataway."

"You wouldn't shoot a lady, would you?" the grandmother said and removed the clean handkerchief from her cuff and began to slap at her eyes with it.

The Misfit pointed the toe of his shoe into the ground and made a little hole and then covered it up again. "I would hate to have to," he said.

"Listen," the grandmother almost screamed, "I know you're a good man. You don't look a bit like you have common blood. I know you must come from nice people!"

"Yes mam," he said, "finest people in the world." When he smiled he showed a row of strong white teeth. "God never made a finer woman than my mother and my daddy's heart was pure gold," he said. The boy with the red sweat shirt had come around behind them and was standing with his gun at his hip. The Misfit squatted down on the ground. "Watch them children, Bobby Lee," he said. "You know they make me nervous." He looked at the six of them huddled together in front of him and he seemed to be embarrassed as if he couldn't think of anything to say. "Ain't a cloud in the sky," he remarked, looking up at it. "Don't see no sun but don't see no cloud neither."

"Yes, it's a beautiful day," said the grandmother. "Listen," she said, "you shouldn't call yourself The Misfit because I know you're a good man at heart. I can just look at you and tell."

"Hush!" Bailey yelled. "Hush! Everybody shut up and let me handle this!" He was squatting in the position of a runner about to sprint forward but he didn't move.

"I pre-chate that, lady," The Misfit said and drew a little circle in the ground with the butt of his gun.

"It'll take a half a hour to fix this here car," Hiram called, looking over the raised hood of it.

"Well, first you and Bobby Lee get him and that little boy to step over yonder with you," The Misfit said, pointing to Bailey and John Wesley. "The boys want to ask you something," he said to Bailey. "Would you mind stepping back in them woods there with them?"

"Listen," Bailey began, "we're in a terrible predicament! Nobody realizes what this is," and his voice cracked. His eyes were as blue and intense as the parrots on his shirt and he remained perfectly still.

The grandmother reached up to adjust her hat brim as if she were going to the woods with him but it came off in her hand. She stood staring at it and after a second she let it fall on the ground. Hiram pulled Bailey up by the arm as if he were assisting an old man. John Wesley caught hold of his father's hand and Bobby Lee followed. The went off toward the woods and just as they reached the dark edge, Bailey turned and supported himself against a gray naked pine trunk; he shouted, "I'll be back in a minute, Mamma, wait on me!"

"Come back this instant!" his mother shrilled but they all disappeared into the woods.

"Bailey Boy!" the grandmother called in a tragic voice but she found she was looking at The Misfit squatting on the ground in front of her. "I just know you're a good man," she said desperately. "You're not a bit common!"

"Nome, I ain't a good man," The Misfit said after a second as if he had considered her statement carefully, "but I ain't the worst in the world neither. My daddy said I was a different breed of dog from my brothers and sisters. 'You know,' Daddy said, 'it's some that can live their whole life out without asking about it and it's others has to know why it is, and this boy is one of the latters. He's going to be into everything!' " He put on his black hat and looked up suddenly and then away deep into the woods as if he were embarrassed again. "I'm sorry I don't have on a shirt before you ladies," he said, hunching his shoulders slightly. "We buried our clothes that we had on when we escaped and we're just making do until we can get better. We borrowed these from some folks we met," he explained.

"That's perfectly all right," the grandmother said. "Maybe Bailey has an extra shirt in his suitcase."

"I'll look and see terrectly," The Misfit said.

"Where are they taking him?" the children's mother screamed.

"Daddy was a card himself," The Misfit said. "You couldn't put anything over on him. He never got in trouble with the Authorities though. Just had the knack of handling them."

"You could be honest too if you'd only try," said the grandmother. "Think how wonderful it would be to settle down and live a comfortable life and not have to think about somebody chasing you all the time."

The Misfit kept scratching in the ground with the butt of his gun as if he were thinking about it. "Yes'm, somebody is always after you," he murmured.

The grandmother noticed how thin his shoulder blades were just behind his hat because she was standing up looking down on him. "Do you ever pray?" she asked.

He shook his head. All she saw was the black hat wiggle between his shoulder blades. "Nome," he said.

There was a pistol shot from the woods, followed closely by another. Then silence. The old lady's head jerked around. She could hear the wind move through the tree tops like a long satisfied insuck of breath. "Bailey Boy!" she called.

"I was a gospel singer for a while," The Misfit said. "I been most everything. Been in the arm service, both land and sea, at home and abroad, been twict married, been an undertaker, been with the railroads, plowed Mother Earth, been in a tornado, seen a man burnt alive oncet," and he looked up at the children's mother and the little girl who were sitting close together, their faces white and their eyes glassy; "I even seen a woman flogged," he said.

"Pray, pray," the grandmother began, "pray, pray . . ."

"I never was a bad boy that I remember of," The Misfit said in an almost dreamy voice, "but somewheres along the line I done something wrong and got sent to the penitentiary. I was buried alive," and he looked up and held her attention to him by a steady stare.

"That's when you should have started to pray," she said. "What did you do to get sent to the penitentiary that first time?"

"Turn to the right, it was a wall," The Misfit said, looking up again at the cloudless sky. "Turn to the left, it was a wall. Look up it was a ceiling, look down it was a floor. I forget what I done, lady. I set there and set there, trying to remember what it was I done and I ain't recalled it to this day. Oncet in a while, I would think it was coming to me, but it never come."

"Maybe they put you in by mistake," the old lady said vaguely.

"Nome," he said. "It wasn't no mistake. They had the papers on me."

"You must have stolen something," she said.

The Misfit sneered slightly. "Nobody had nothing I wanted," he said. "It was a head-doctor at the penitentiary said what I had done was kill my daddy but I known that for a lie. My daddy died in nineteen ought nineteen of the epidemic flu and I never had a thing to do with it. He was buried in the Mount Hopewell Baptist churchyard and you can go there and see for yourself."

"If you would pray," the old lady said, "Jesus would help you."

"That's right," The Misfit said.

"Well then, why don't you pray?" she asked trembling with delight suddenly.

"I don't want no hep," he said. "I'm doing all right by myself."

Bobby Lee and Hiram came ambling back from the woods. Bobby Lee was dragging a yellow shirt with bright blue parrots in it.

"Throw me that shirt, Bobby Lee," The Misfit said. The shirt came flying at him and landed on his shoulder and he put it on. The grandmother couldn't name what the shirt reminded her of. "No, lady," The Misfit said while he was buttoning it up, "I found out the crime don't matter. You can do one thing or you can do another, kill a man or take a tire off his car, because sooner or later you're going to forget what it was you done and just be punished for it."

The children's mother had begun to make heaving noises as if she couldn't get her breath. "Lady," he asked, "would you and that little girl like to step off yonder with Bobby Lee and Hiram and join your husband?"

"Yes, thank you," the mother said faintly. Her left arm dangled helplessly and she was holding the baby, who had gone to sleep, in the other. "Hep that lady up, Hiram," The Misfit said as she struggled to climb out of the ditch, "and Bobby Lee, you hold onto that little girl's hand."

"I don't want to hold hands with him," June Star said. "He reminds me of a pig."

The fat boy blushed and laughed and caught her by the arm and pulled her off into the woods after Hiram and her mother.

Alone with The Misfit, the grandmother found that she had lost her voice. There was not a cloud in the sky nor any sun. There was nothing around her but woods. She wanted to tell him that he must pray. She opened and closed her mouth several times before anything came out. Finally she found herself saying, "Jesus, Jesus," meaning, Jesus will help you, but the way she was saying it, it sounded as if she might be cursing.

"Yes'm," The Misfit said as if he agreed. "Jesus thown everything off balance. It was the same case with Him as with me except He hadn't committed any crime and they could prove I had committed one because they had the papers on me. Of course," he said, "they never shown me my papers. That's why I sign myself now. I said long ago, you get you a signature and sign everything you do and keep a copy of it. Then you'll know what you done and you can hold up the crime to the punishment and see do they match and in the end you'll have something to prove you ain't been treated right. I call myself The Misfit," he said, "because I can't make what all I done wrong fit what all I gone through in punishment."

There was a piercing scream from the woods, followed closely by a pistol report. "Does it seem right to you, lady, that one is punished a heap and another ain't punished at all?"

"Jesus!" the old lady cried. "You've got good blood! I know you wouldn't shoot a lady! I know you come from nice people! Pray! Jesus, you ought not to shoot a lady. I'll give you all the money I've got!"

"Lady," The Misfit said, looking beyond her far into the woods, "there never was a body that give the undertaker a tip."

There were two more pistol reports and the grandmother raised her head like a parched old turkey hen crying for water and called, "Bailey Boy, Bailey Boy!" as if her heart would break.

"Jesus was the only One that ever raised the dead," The Misfit continued, "and He shouldn't have done it. He thown everything off balance. If He did what He said, then it's nothing for you to do but throw away everything and follow Him, and if He didn't, then it's nothing for you to do but enjoy the few minutes you got left the best way you can—by killing somebody or burning down his house or doing some other meanness to him. No pleasure but meanness," he said and his voice had become almost a snarl.

"Maybe He didn't raise the dead," the old lady mumbled, not knowing what she was saying and feeling so dizzy that she sank down in the ditch with her legs twisted under her.

"I wasn't there so I can't say He didn't," The Misfit said. "I wisht I had of been there," he said, hitting the ground with his fist. "It ain't right I wasn't there because if I had of been there I would of known. Listen lady," he said in a high voice, "if I had of been there I would of known and I wouldn't be like I am now." His voice seemed about to crack and the grandmother's head cleared for an instant. She saw the man's face twisted close to her own as if he were going to cry and she murmured. "Why you're one of my babies. You're one of my own children!" She reached out and touched him on the shoulder. The Misfit sprang back as if a snake had bitten him and shot her three times through the chest. Then he put his gun down on the ground and took off his glasses and began to clean them.

Hiram and Bobby Lee returned from the woods and stood over the ditch, looking down at the grandmother who half sat and half lay in a puddle of blood with her legs crossed under her like a child's and her face smiling up at the cloudless sky.

Without his glasses, The Misfit's eyes were red-rimmed and pale and defenseless-looking. "Take her off and thow her where you thown the others," he said, picking up the cat that was rubbing itself against his leg.

"She was a talker, wasn't she?" Bobby Lee said, sliding down the ditch with a yodel.

"She would of been a good woman," The Misfit said, "if it had been somebody there to shoot her every minute of her life."

"Some fun!" Bobby Lee said.

"Shut up, Bobby Lee," The Misfit said. "It's no real pleasure in life."

From *A Good Man Is Hard To Find and Other Stories* (1955)

·Bernard Malamud·

THE MAGIC BARREL

Not long ago there lived in uptown New York, in a small, almost meager room, though crowded with books, Leo Finkle, a rabbinical student in the Yeshivah University. Finkle, after six years of study, was to be ordained in June and had been advised by an acquaintance that he might find it easier to win himself a congregation if he were married. Since he had no present prospects of marriage, after two tormented days of turning it over in his mind, he called in Pinye Salzman, a marriage broker whose two-line advertisement he had read in the *Forward*.[1]

The matchmaker appeared one night out of the dark fourth-floor hallway of the graystone rooming house where Finkle lived, grasping a black, strapped portfolio that had been worn thin with use. Salzman, who had been long in the business, was of slight but dignified build, wearing an old hat, and an overcoat too short and tight for him. He smelled frankly of fish, which he loved to eat, and although he was missing a few teeth, his presence was not displeasing, because of an amiable manner curiously contrasted with mournful eyes. His voice, his lips, his wisp of beard, his bony fingers were animated, but give him a moment of repose and his mild blue eyes revealed a depth of sadness, a characteristic that put Leo a little at ease although the situation, for him, was inherently tense.

He at once informed Salzman why he had asked him to come, explaining that his home was in Cleveland, and that but for his parents, who had married comparatively late in life, he was alone in

1. *Jewish Daily Forward,* influential Yiddish-language newspaper with a famous advice column (romantic and otherwise)—"Bintel Brief."

the world. He had for six years devoted himself almost entirely to his studies, as a result of which, understandably, he had found himself without time for a social life and the company of young women. Therefore he thought it the better part of trial and error—of embarrassing fumbling—to call in an experienced person to advise him on these matters. He remarked in passing that the function of the marriage broker was ancient and honorable, highly approved in the Jewish community, because it made practical the necessary without hindering joy. Moreover, his own parents had been brought together by a matchmaker. They had made, if not a financially profitable marriage—since neither had possessed any worldly goods to speak of—at least a successful one in the sense of their everlasting devotion to each other. Salzman listened in embarrassed surprise, sensing a sort of apology. Later, however, he experienced a glow of pride in his work, an emotion that had left him years ago, and he heartily approved of Finkle.

The two went to their business. Leo had led Salzman to the only clear place in the room, a table near a window that overlooked the lamp-lit city. He seated himself at the matchmaker's side but facing him, attempting by an act of will to suppress the unpleasant tickle in his throat. Salzman eagerly unstrapped his portfolio and removed a loose rubber band from a thin packet of much-handled cards. As he flipped through them, a gesture and sound that physically hurt Leo, the student pretended not to see and gazed steadfastly out the window. Although it was still February, winter was on its last legs, signs of which he had for the first time in years begun to notice. He now observed the round white moon, moving high in the sky through a cloud menagerie, and watched with half-open mouth as it penetrated a huge hen, and dropped out of her like an egg laying itself. Salzman, though pretending through eyeglasses he had just slipped on, to be engaged in scanning the writing on the cards, stole occasional glances at the young man's distinguished face, noting with pleasure the long, severe scholar's nose, brown eyes heavy with learning, sensitive yet ascetic lips, and a certain, almost hollow quality of the dark cheeks. He gazed around at shelves upon shelves of books and let out a soft, contented sigh.

When Leo's eyes fell upon the cards, he counted six spread out in Salzman's hand.

"So few?" he asked in disappointment.

"You wouldn't believe me how much cards I got in my office," Salzman replied. "The drawers are already filled to the top, so I keep them now in a barrel, but is every girl good for a new rabbi?"

Leo blushed at this, regretting all he had revealed of himself in a curriculum vitae he had sent to Salzman. He had thought it best to acquaint him with his strict standards and specifications, but in having done so, felt he had told the marriage broker more than was absolutely necessary.

He hesitantly inquired, "Do you keep photographs of your clients on file?"

"First comes family, amount of dowry, also what kind promises," Salzman replied, unbuttoning his tight coat and settling himself in the chair. "After comes pictures, rabbi."

"Call me Mr. Finkle. I'm not yet a rabbi."

Salzman said he would, but instead called him doctor, which he changed to rabbi when Leo was not listening too attentively.

Salzman adjusted his horn-rimmed spectacles, gently cleared his throat and read in an eager voice the contents of the top card:

"Sophie P. Twenty-four years. Widow one year. No children. Educated high school and two years college. Father promises eight thousand dollars. Has wonderful wholesale business. Also real estate. On the mother's side comes teachers, also one actor. Well known on Second Avenue."

Leo gazed up in surprise. "Did you say a widow?"

"A widow don't mean spoiled, rabbi. She lived with her husband maybe four months. He was a sick boy she made a mistake to marry him."

"Marrying a widow has never entered my mind."

"This is because you have no experience. A widow, especially if she is young and healthy like this girl, is a wonderful person to marry. She will be thankful to you the rest of her life. Believe me, if I was looking now for a bride, I would marry a widow."

Leo reflected, then shook his head.

Salzman hunched his shoulders in an almost imperceptible gesture of disappointment. He placed the card down on the wooden table and began to read another:

"Lily H. High school teacher. Regular. Not a substitute. Has savings and new Dodge car. Lived in Paris one year. Father is successful dentist thirty-five years. Interested in professional man. Well Americanized family. Wonderful opportunity."

"I knew her personally," said Salzman. "I wish you could see this girl. She is a doll. Also very intelligent. All day you could talk to her about books and theyater and what not. She also knows current events."

"I don't believe you mentioned her age?"

"Her age?" Salzman said, raising his brows. "Her age is thirty-two years."

Leo said after a while, "I'm afraid that seems a little too old."

Salzman let out a laugh. "So how old are you, rabbi?"

"Twenty-seven."

"So what is the difference, tell me, between twenty-seven and thirty-two? My own wife is seven years older than me. So what did I suffer?—Nothing. If Rothschild's daughter wants to marry you, would you say on account her age, no?"

"Yes," Leo said dryly.

Salzman shook off the no in the yes. "Five years don't mean a thing. I give you my word that when you will live with her for one week you will forget her age. What does it mean five years—that she lived more and knows more than somebody who is younger? On this girl, God bless her, years are not wasted. Each one that it comes makes better the bargain."

"What subject does she teach in high school?"

"Languages. If you heard the way she speaks French, you will think it is music. I am in the business twenty-five years, and I recommend her with my whole heart. Believe me, I know what I'm talking, rabbi."

"What's on the next card?" Leo said abruptly.

Salzman reluctantly turned up the third card:

"Ruth K. Nineteen years. Honor student. Father offers thirteen thousand cash to the right bridegroom. He is a medical doctor. Stomach specialist with marvelous practice. Brother in law owns own garment business. Particular people."

Salzman looked as if he had read his trump card.

"Did you say nineteen?" Leo asked with interest.

"On the dot."

"Is she attractive?" He blushed. "Pretty?"

Salzman kissed his finger tips. "A little doll. On this I give you my word. Let me call the father tonight and you will see what means pretty."

But Leo was troubled. "You're sure she's that young?"

"This I am positive. The father will show you the birth certificate."

"Are you positive there isn't something wrong with her?" Leo insisted.

"Who says there is wrong?"

"I don't understand why an American girl her age should go to a marriage broker."

A smile spread over Salzman's face.

"So for the same reason you went, she comes."

Leo flushed. "I am pressed for time."

Salzman, realizing he had been tactless, quickly explained. "The father came, not her. He wants she should have the best, so he looks around himself. When we will locate the right boy he will introduce him and encourage. This makes a better marriage than if a young girl without experience takes for herself. I don't have to tell you this."

"But don't you think this young girl believes in love?" Leo spoke uneasily.

Salzman was about to guffaw but caught himself and said soberly, "Love comes with the right person, not before."

Leo parted dry lips but did not speak. Noticing that Salzman had snatched a glance at the next card, he cleverly asked, "How is her health?"

"Perfect," Salzman said, breathing with difficulty. "Of course, she is a little lame on her right foot from an auto accident that it happened to her when she was twelve years, but nobody notices on account she is so brilliant and also beautiful."

Leo got up heavily and went to the window. He felt curiously bitter and upbraided himself for having called in the marriage broker. Finally, he shook his head.

"Why not?" Salzman persisted, the pitch of his voice rising.

"Because I detest stomach specialists."

"So what do you care what is his business? After you marry her do you need him? Who says he must come every Friday night in your house?"

Ashamed of the way the talk was going, Leo dismissed Salzman, who went home with heavy, melancholy eyes.

Though he had felt only relief at the marriage broker's departure, Leo was in low spirits the next day. He explained it as arising from Salzman's failure to produce a suitable bride for him. He did not care for his type of clientele. But when Leo found himself hesitating whether to seek out another matchmaker, one more polished than Pinye, he wondered if it could be—his protestations to the contrary, and although he honored his father and mother—that he did not, in essence, care for the matchmaking institution? This thought he quickly put out of mind yet found himself still upset. All day he ran around in the woods—missed an important appointment, forgot to give out his laundry, walked out of a Broadway cafeteria without paying and had to run back with the ticket in his hand; had even not recognized his landlady in the street when she passed with a friend and courteously called out, "A good evening to you, Doctor Finkle." By nightfall, however, he had regained sufficient calm to sink his nose into a book and there found peace from his thoughts.

Almost at once there came a knock on the door. Before Leo could say enter, Salzman, commercial cupid, was standing in the room. His face was gray and meager, his expression hungry, and he looked as if he would expire on his feet. Yet the marriage broker managed, by some trick of the muscles, to display a broad smile.

"So good evening. I am invited?"

Leo nodded, disturbed to see him again, yet unwilling to ask the man to leave.

Beaming still, Salzman laid his portfolio on the table. "Rabbi, I got for you tonight good news."

"I've asked you not to call me rabbi. I'm still a student."

"Your worries are finished. I have for you a first-class bride."

"Leave me in peace concerning this subject." Leo pretended lack of interest.

"The world will dance at your wedding."

"Please, Mr. Salzman, no more."

"But first must come back my strength," Salzman said weakly. He fumbled with the portfolio straps and took out of the leather case an oily paper bag, from which he extracted a hard, seeded roll and a small, smoked white fish. With a quick motion of his hand he stripped the fish out of its skin and began ravenously to chew. "All day in a rush," he muttered.

Leo watched him eat.

"A sliced tomato you have maybe?" Salzman hesitantly inquired.

"No."

The marriage broker shut his eyes and ate. When he had finished he carefully cleaned up the crumbs and rolled up the remains of the fish, in the paper bag. His spectacled eyes roamed the room until he discovered, amid some piles of books, a one-burner gas stove. Lifting his hat he humbly asked, "A glass of tea you got, rabbi?"

Conscience-stricken, Leo rose and brewed the tea. He served it with a chunk of lemon and two cubes of lump sugar, delighting Salzman.

After he had drunk his tea, Salzman's strength and good spirits were restored.

"So tell me, rabbi," he said amiably, "you considered some more the three clients I mentioned yesterday?"

"There was no need to consider."

"Why not?"

"None of them suits me."

"What then suits you?"

Leo let it pass because he could give only a confused answer.

Without waiting for a reply, Salzman asked, "You remember this girl I talked to you—the high school teacher?"

"Age thirty-two?"

But, surprisingly, Salzman's face lit in a smile. "Age twenty-nine."

Leo shot him a look. "Reduced from thirty-two?"

"A mistake," Salzman avowed. "I talked today with the dentist. He took me to his safety deposit box and showed me the birth certificate. She was twenty-nine years last August. They made her a party in the mountains where she went for her vacation. When her father spoke to me the first time I forgot to write the age and I told you thirty-two, but now I remember this was a different client, a widow."

"The same one you told me about? I thought she was twenty-four?"

"A different. Am I responsible that the world is filled with widows?"

"No, but I'm not interested in them, nor for that matter, in school teachers."

Salzman pulled his clasped hand to his breast. Looking at the ceiling he devoutly exclaimed, "Yiddishe kinder,[2] what can I say to somebody that he is not interested in high school teachers? So what then you are interested?"

Leo flushed but controlled himself.

"In what else will you be interested," Salzman went on, "if you not interested in this fine girl that she speaks four languages and has personally in the bank ten thousand dollars? Also her father guarantees further twelve thousand. Also she has a new car, wonderful clothes, talks on all subjects, and she will give you a first-class home and children. How near do we come in our life to paradise?"

"If she's so wonderful, why wasn't she married ten years ago?"

"Why?" said Salzman with a heavy laugh. "—Why? Because she is *partikiler*. This is why. She wants the *best*."

Leo was silent, amused at how he had entangled himself. But Salzman had aroused his interest in Lily H., and he began seriously to consider calling on her. When the marriage broker observed how intently Leo's mind was at work on the facts he had supplied, he felt certain they would soon come to an agreement.

Late Saturday afternoon, conscious of Salzman, Leo Finkle walked with Lily Hirschorn along Riverside Drive. He walked briskly and erectly, wearing with distinction the black fedora he had that morning taken with trepidation out of the dusty hat box on his closet shelf, and the heavy black Saturday coat he had thoroughly whisked clean. Leo also owned a walking stick, a present from a distant relative, but quickly put temptation aside and did not use it. Lily, petite and not unpretty, had on something signifying the approach of spring. She was au courant, animatedly, with all sorts of subjects, and he weighed her words and found her surprisingly sound—score another for Salzman, whom he uneasily

2. "Jewish children!"

sensed to be somewhere around, hiding perhaps high in a tree along the street, flashing the lady signals with a pocket mirror; or perhaps a cloven-hoofed Pan,[3] piping nuptial ditties as he danced his invisible way before them, strewing wild buds on the walk and purple grapes in their path, symbolizing fruit of a union, though there was of course still none.

Lily startled Leo by remarking, "I was thinking of Mr. Salzman, a curious figure, wouldn't you say?"

Not certain what to answer, he nodded.

She bravely went on, blushing, "I for one am grateful for his introducing us. Aren't you?"

He courteously replied, "I am."

"I mean," she said with a little laugh—and it was all in good taste, or at least gave the effect of being not in bad—"do you mind that we came together so?"

He was not displeased with her honesty, recognizing that she meant to set the relationship aright, and understanding that it took a certain amount of experience in life, and courage, to want to do it quite that way. One had to have some sort of past to make that kind of beginning.

He said that he did not mind. Salzman's function was traditional and honorable—valuable for what it might achieve, which, he pointed out, was frequently nothing.

Lily agreed with a sigh. They walked on for a while and she said after a long silence, again with a nervous laugh, "Would you mind if I asked you something a little bit personal? Frankly, I find the subject fascinating." Although Leo shrugged, she went on half embarrassedly, "How was it that you came to your calling? I mean was it a sudden passionate inspiration?"

Leo, after a time, slowly replied. "I was always interested in the Law."

"You saw revealed in it the presence of the Highest?"

He nodded and changed the subject. "I understand that you spent a little time in Paris, Miss Hirschorn?"

"Oh, did Mr. Salzman tell you, Rabbi Finkle?" Leo winced but she went on, "It was ages ago and almost forgotten. I remember I had to return for my sister's wedding."

And Lily would not be put off. "When," she asked in a trembly voice, "did you become enamored of God?"

He stared at her. Then it came to him that she was talking not about Leo Finkle, but of a total stranger, some mystical figure, perhaps even passionate prophet that Salzman had dreamed up for her—no relation to the living or dead. Leo trembled with rage and

3. Greek god of woods, fields, and flocks, having a human body with the legs, horns, and ears of a goat. He played the music of love and fertility on his pipes.

weakness. The trickster had obviously sold her a bill of goods, just as he had him, who'd expected to become acquainted with a young lady of twenty-nine, only to behold, the moment he laid eyes upon her strained and anxious face, a woman past thirty-five and aging rapidly. Only his self control had kept him this long in her presence.

"I am not," he said gravely, "a talented religious person," and in seeking words to go on, found himself possessed by shame and fear. "I think," he said in a strained manner, "that I came to God not because I loved Him, but because I did not."

This confession he spoke harshly because its unexpectedness shook him.

Lily wilted. Leo saw a profusion of loaves of bread go flying like ducks high over his head, not unlike the winged loaves by which he had counted himself to sleep last night. Mercifully, then, it snowed, which he would not put past Salzman's machinations.

He was infuriated with the marriage broker and swore he would throw him out of the room the minute he reappeared. But Salzman did not come that night, and when Leo's anger had subsided, an unaccountable despair grew in its place. At first he thought this was caused by his disappointment in Lily, but before long it became evident that he had involved himself with Salzman without a true knowledge of his own intent. He gradually realized—with an emptiness that seized him with six hands—that he had called in the broker to find him a bride because he was incapable of doing it himself. This terrifying insight he had derived as a result of his meeting and conversation with Lily Hirschorn. Her probing questions had somehow irritated him into revealing—to himself more than her—the true nature of his relationship to God, and from that it had come upon him, with shocking force, that apart from his parents, he had never loved anyone. Or perhaps it went the other way, that he did not love God so well as he might, because he had not loved man. It seemed to Leo that his whole life stood starkly revealed and he saw himself for the first time as he truly was— unloved and loveless. This bitter but somehow not fully unexpected revelation brought him to a point of panic, controlled only by extraordinary effort. He covered his face with his hands and cried.

The week that followed was the worst of his life. He did not eat and lost weight. His beard darkened and grew ragged. He stopped attending seminars and almost never opened a book. He seriously considered leaving the Yeshivah, although he was deeply troubled at the thought of the loss of all his years of study—saw them like pages torn from a book, strewn over the city—and at the devastating effect of this decision upon his parents. But he had lived without knowledge of himself, and never in the Five Books [4] and all the Commentaries—mea culpa [5]—had the truth been revealed to him. He did not know where to turn, and in all this desolating loneliness there was no *to whom*, although he often thought of Lily but not once could bring himself to go downstairs and make the call. He became touchy and irritable, especially with his landlady, who asked him all manner of personal questions; on the other hand, sensing his own disagreeableness, he waylaid her on the stairs and apologized abjectly, until mortified, she ran from him. Out of this, however, he drew the consolation that he was a Jew and that a Jew suffered. But gradually, as the long and terrible week drew to a close, he regained his composure and some idea of purpose in life: to go on as planned. Although he was imperfect, the ideal was not. As for his quest of a bride, the thought of continuing afflicted him with anxiety and heartburn, yet perhaps with this new knowledge of himself he would be more successful than in the past. Perhaps love would now come to him and a bride to that love. And for this sanctified seeking who needed a Salzman?

The marriage broker, a skeleton with haunted eyes, returned that very night. He looked, withal, the picture of frustrated expectancy—as if he had steadfastly waited the week at Miss Lily Hirschorn's side for a telephone call that never came.

Casually coughing, Salzman came immediately to the point: "So how did you like her?"

Leo's anger rose and he could not refrain from chiding the matchmaker: "Why did you lie to me, Salzman?"

Salzman's pale face went dead white, the world had snowed on him.

"Did you not state that she was twenty-nine?" Leo insisted.

"I give you my word—"

"She was thirty-five, if a day. *At least* thirty-five."

"Of this don't be too sure. Her father told me—"

"Never mind. The worst of it was that you lied to her."

"How did I lie to her, tell me?"

"You told her things about me that weren't true. You made me out to be more, consequently less than I am. She had in mind a totally different person, a sort of semi-mystical Wonder Rabbi."

"All I said, you was a religious man."

"I can imagine."

Salzman sighed. "This is my weakness that I have," he confessed. "My wife says to me I shouldn't be a salesman, but when I

4. The Torah, or five books of Moses (the Pentateuch): Genesis, Exodus, Leviticus, Numbers, Deuteronomy.
5. Latin, "through my own fault."

have two fine people that they would be wonderful to be married, I am so happy that I talk too much." He smiled wanly. "This is why Salzman is a poor man."

Leo's anger left him. "Well, Salzman, I'm afraid that's all."

The marriage broker fastened hungry eyes on him.

"You don't want any more a bride?"

"I do," said Leo, "but I have decided to seek her in a different way. I am no longer interested in an arranged marriage. To be frank, I now admit the necessity of premarital love. That is, I want to be in love with the one I marry."

"Love?" said Salzman, astounded. After a moment he remarked, "For us, our love is our life, not for the ladies. In the ghetto they—"

"I know, I know," said Leo. "I've thought of it often. Love, I have said to myself, should be a by-product of living and worship rather than its own end. Yet for myself I find it necessary to establish the level of my need and fulfill it."

Salzman shrugged but answered, "Listen, rabbi, if you want love, this I can find for you also. I have such beautiful clients that you will love them the minute your eyes will see them."

Leo smiled unhappily. "I'm afraid you don't understand."

But Salzman hastily unstrapped his portfolio and withdrew a manila packet from it.

"Pictures," he said, quickly laying the envelope on the table.

Leo called after him to take the pictures away, but as if on the wings of the wind, Salzman had disappeared.

March came. Leo had returned to his regular routine. Although he felt not quite himself yet—lacked energy—he was making plans for a more active social life. Of course it would cost something, but he was an expert in cutting corners; and when there were no corners left he would make circles rounder. All the while Salzman's pictures had lain on the table, gathering dust. Occasionally as Leo sat studying, or enjoying a cup of tea, his eyes fell on the manila envelope, but he never opened it.

The days went by and no social life to speak of developed with a member of the opposite sex—it was difficult, given the circumstances of his situation. One morning Leo toiled up the stairs to his room and stared out the window at the city. Although the day was bright his view of it was dark. For some time he watched the people in the street below hurrying along and then turned with a heavy heart to his little room. On the table was the packet. With a sudden relentless gesture he tore it open. For a half-hour he stood by the table in a state of excitement, examining the photographs of the ladies Salzman had included. Finally, with a deep sigh he put them down. There were six, of varying degrees of attractiveness, but look at them long enough and they all became Lily Hirschorn: all past their prime, all starved behind bright smiles, not a true personality in the lot. Life, despite their frantic yoohooings, had passed them by; they were pictures in a brief case that stank of fish. After a while, however, as Leo attempted to return the photographs into the envelope, he found in it another, a snapshot of the type taken by a machine for a quarter. He gazed at it a moment and let out a cry.

Her face deeply moved him. Why, he could at first not say. It gave him the impression of youth—spring flowers, yet age—a sense of having been used to the bone, wasted; this came from the eyes, which were hauntingly familiar, yet absolutely strange. He had a vivid impression that he had met her before, but try as he might he could not place her although he could almost recall her name, as if he had read it in her own handwriting. No, this couldn't be; he would have remembered her. It was not, he affirmed, that she had an extraordinary beauty—no, though her face was attractive enough; it was that *something* about her moved him. Feature for feature, even some of the ladies of the photographs could do better; but she leaped forth to his heart—had *lived,* or wanted to—more than just wanted, perhaps regretted how she had lived—had somehow deeply suffered: it could be seen in the depths of those reluctant eyes, and from the way the light enclosed and shone from her, and within her, opening realms of possibility: this was her own. Her he desired. His head ached and eyes narrowed with the intensity of his gazing, then as if an obscure fog had blown up in the mind, he experienced fear of her and was aware that he had received an impression, somehow, of evil. He shuddered, saying softly, it is thus with us all. Leo brewed some tea in a small pot and sat sipping it without sugar, to calm himself. But before he had finished drinking, again with excitement he examined the face and found it good: good for Leo Finkle. Only such a one could understand him and help him seek whatever he was seeking. She might, perhaps, love him. How she had happened to be among the discards in Salzman's barrel he could never guess, but he knew he must urgently go find her.

Leo rushed downstairs, grabbed up the Bronx telephone book, and searched for Salzman's home address. He was not listed, nor was his office. Neither was he in the Manhattan book. But Leo remembered having written down the address on a slip of paper after he had read Salzman's advertisement in the "personals" column of the *Forward.* He ran up to his room and tore through his papers, without luck. It was exasperating. Just when he needed the matchmaker he was nowhere to be found. Fortunately Leo remembered to look in his wallet. There on a card he found his name written and a Bronx address. No phone number was listed, the reason—

Leo now recalled—he had originally communicated with Salzman by letter. He got on his coat, put a hat on over his skull cap and hurried to the subway station. All the way to the far end of the Bronx he sat on the edge of his seat. He was more than once tempted to take out the picture and see if the girl's face was as he remembered it, but he refrained, allowing the snapshot to remain in his inside coat pocket, content to have her so close. When the train pulled into the station he was waiting at the door and bolted out. He quickly located the street Salzman had advertised.

The building he sought was less than a block from the subway, but it was not an office building, nor even a loft, nor a store in which one could rent office space. It was a very old tenement house. Leo found Salzman's name in pencil on a soiled tag under the bell and climbed three dark flights to his apartment. When he knocked, the door was opened by a thin, asthmatic, gray-haired woman, in felt slippers.

"Yes?" she said, expecting nothing. She listened without listening. He could have sworn he had seen her, too, before but knew it was an illusion.

"Salzman—does he live here? Pinye Salzman," he said, "the matchmaker?"

She stared at him a long minute. "Of course."

He felt embarrassed. "Is he in?"

"No." Her mouth, though left open, offered nothing more.

"The matter is urgent. Can you tell me where his office is?"

"In the air." She pointed upward.

"You mean he has no office?" Leo asked.

"In his socks."

He peered into the apartment. It was sunless and dingy, one large room divided by a half-open curtain, beyond which he could see a sagging metal bed. The near side of the room was crowded with rickety chairs, old bureaus, a three-legged table, racks of cooking utensils, and all the apparatus of a kitchen. But there was no sign of Salzman or his magic barrel, probably also a figment of the imagination. An odor of frying fish made Leo weak to the knees.

"Where is he?" he insisted. "I've got to see your husband."

At length she answered, "So who knows where he is? Every time he thinks a new thought he runs to a different place. Go home, he will find you."

"Tell him Leo Finkle."

She gave no sign she had heard.

He walked downstairs, depressed.

But Salzman, breathless, stood waiting at his door.

Leo was astounded and overjoyed. "How did you get here before me?"

"I rushed."

"Come inside."

They entered. Leo fixed tea, and a sardine sandwich for Salzman. As they were drinking he reached behind him for the packet of pictures and handed them to the marriage broker.

Salzman put down his glass and said expectantly, "You found somebody you like?"

"Not among these."

The marriage broker turned away.

"Here is the one I want." Leo held forth the snapshot.

Salzman slipped on his glasses and took the picture into his trembling hand. He turned ghastly and let out a groan.

"What's the matter?" cried Leo.

"Excuse me. Was an accident this picture. She isn't for you."

Salzman frantically shoved the manila packet into his portfolio. He thrust the snapshot into his pocket and fled down the stairs.

Leo, after momentary paralysis, gave chase and cornered the marriage broker in the vestibule. The landlady made hysterical outcries but neither of them listened.

"Give me back the picture, Salzman."

"No." The pain in his eyes was terrible.

"Tell me who she is then."

"This I can't tell you. Excuse me."

He made to depart, but Leo, forgetting himself, seized the matchmaker by his tight coat and shook him frenziedly.

"Please," sighed Salzman. *"Please."*

Leo ashamedly let him go. "Tell me who she is," he begged. "It's very important for me to know."

"She is not for you. She is a wild one—wild, without shame. This is not a bride for a rabbi."

"What do you mean wild?"

"Like an animal. Like a dog. For her to be poor was a sin. This is why to me she is dead now."

"In God's name, what do you mean?"

"Her I can't introduce to you," Salzman cried.

"Why are you so excited?"

"Why, he asks," Salzman said, bursting into tears. "This is my baby, my Stella, she should burn in hell."

Leo hurried up to bed and hid under the covers. Under the covers he thought his life through. Although he soon fell asleep he could not sleep her out of his mind. He woke, beating his breast.

Though he prayed to be rid of her, his prayers went unanswered. Through days of torment he endlessly struggled not to love her; fearing success, he escaped it. He then concluded to convert her to goodness, himself to God. The idea alternately nauseated and exalted him.

He perhaps did not know that he had come to a final decision until he encountered Salzman in a Broadway cafeteria. He was sitting alone at a rear table, sucking the bony remains of a fish. The marriage broker appeared haggard, and transparent to the point of vanishing.

Salzman looked up at first without recognizing him. Leo had grown a pointed beard and his eyes were weighted with wisdom.

"Salzman," he said, "love has at last come to my heart."

"Who can love from a picture?" mocked the marriage broker.

"It is not impossible."

"If you can love her, then you can love anybody. Let me show you some new clients that they just sent me their photographs. One is a little doll."

"Just her I want," Leo murmured.

"Don't be a fool, doctor. Don't bother with her."

"Put me in touch with her, Salzman," Leo said humbly. "Perhaps I can be of service."

Salzman had stopped eating and Leo understood with emotion that it was now arranged.

Leaving the cafeteria, he was, however, afflicted by a tormenting suspicion that Salzman had planned it all to happen this way.

Leo was informed by letter that she would meet him on a certain corner, and she was there one spring night, waiting under a street lamp. He appeared carrying a small bouquet of violets and rosebuds. Stella stood by the lamp post, smoking. She wore white with red shoes, which fitted his expectations, although in a troubled moment he had imagined the dress red, and only the shoes white. She waited uneasily and shyly. From afar he saw that her eyes—clearly her father's—were filled with desperate innocence. He pictured, in her, his own redemption. Violins and lit candles revolved in the sky. Leo ran forward with flowers outthrust.

Around the corner, Salzman, leaning against a wall, chanted prayers for the dead.

From *The Magic Barrel* (1958)

·Peter Taylor·

VENUS, CUPID, FOLLY AND TIME

Their house alone would not have made you think there was anything so awfully wrong with Mr. Dorset or his old-maid sister. But
certain things about the way both of them dressed had, for a long
time, annoyed and disturbed everyone. We used to see them
together at the grocery store, for instance, or even in one of the big
department stores downtown, wearing their bedroom slippers.
Looking more closely, we would sometimes see the cuff of a pajama
top or the hem of a hitched-up nightgown showing from underneath
their ordinary daytime clothes. Such slovenliness in one's neighbors is so unpleasant that even husbands and wives in West Vesey
Place, which was the street where the Dorsets lived, had got so
they didn't like to joke about it with each other. Were the Dorsets,
poor old things, losing their minds? If so, what was to be done
about it? Some neighbors got so they would not even admit to
themselves what they saw. And a child coming home with an ugly
report on the Dorsets was apt to be told that it was time he learned
to curb his imagination.

Mr. Dorset wore tweed caps and sleeveless sweaters. Usually he
had his sweater stuffed down inside his trousers with his shirt tails.
To the women and young girls in West Vesey Place this was extremely distasteful. It made them feel as though Mr. Dorset had just
come from the bathroom and had got his sweater inside his trousers
by mistake. There was, in fact, nothing about Mr. Dorset that was
not offensive to the women. Even the old touring car he drove was
regarded by most of them as a disgrace to the neighborhood. Parked
out in front of his house, as it usually was, it seemed a worse violation of West Vesey's zoning than the house itself. And worst of all
was seeing Mr. Dorset wash the car.

Mr. Dorset washed his own car! He washed it not back in the alley or in his driveway but out there in the street of West Vesey Place. This would usually be on the day of one of the parties which he and his sister liked to give for young people or on a day when they were going to make deliveries of the paper flowers or the homegrown figs which they sold to their friends. Mr. Dorset would appear in the street carrying two buckets of warm water and wearing a pair of skin-tight coveralls. The skin-tight coveralls, of khaki material but faded almost to flesh color, were still more offensive to the women and young girls than his way of wearing his sweaters. With sponges and chamois cloths and a large scrub brush (for use on the canvas top) the old fellow would fall to and scrub away, gently at first on the canvas top and more vigorously as he progressed to the hood and body, just as though the car were something alive. Neighbor children felt that he went after the headlights exactly as if he were scrubbing the poor car's ears. There was an element of brutality in the way he did it and yet an element of tenderness too. An old lady visiting in the neighborhood once said that it was like the cleansing of a sacrificial animal. I suppose it was some such feeling as this that made all women want to turn away their eyes whenever the spectacle of Mr. Dorset washing his car presented itself.

As for Mr. Dorset's sister, her behavior was in its way just as offensive as his. To the men and boys in the neighborhood it was she who seemed quite beyond the pale. She would come out on her front terrace at midday clad in a faded flannel bathrobe and with her dyed black hair all undone and hanging down her back like the hair of an Indian squaw. To us whose wives and mothers did not even come downstairs in their negligees, this was very unsettling. It was hard to excuse it even on the grounds that the Dorsets were too old and lonely and hard-pressed to care about appearances any more.

Moreover, there was a boy who had gone to Miss Dorset's house one morning in the early fall to collect for his paper route and saw this very Miss Louisa Dorset pushing a carpet sweeper about one of the downstairs rooms without a stitch of clothes on. He saw her through one of the little lancet windows that opened on the front loggia of the house, and he watched her for quite a long while. She was cleaning the house in preparation for a party they were giving for young people that night, and the boy said that when she finally got hot and tired she dropped down in an easy chair and crossed her spindly, blue-veined, old legs and sat there completely naked, with her legs crossed and shaking one scrawny little foot, just as unconcerned as if she didn't care that somebody was likely to walk in on her at any moment. After a little bit the boy saw her get up again and go and lean across a table to arrange some paper flowers in a vase. Fortunately he was a nice boy, though he lived only on the edge of the West Vesey Place neighborhood, and he went away without ringing the doorbell or collecting for his paper that week. But he could not resist telling his friends about what he had seen. He said it was a sight he would never forget! And she an old lady more than sixty years old who, had she not been so foolish and self-willed, might have had a house full of servants to push that carpet sweeper for her!

This foolish pair of old people had given up almost everything in life for each other's sake. And it was not at all necessary. When they were young they could have come into a decent inheritance, or now that they were old they might have been provided for by a host of rich relatives. It was only a matter of their being a little tolerant—or even civil—toward their kinspeople. But this was something that old Mr. Dorset and his sister could never consent to do. Almost all their lives they had spoken of their father's kin as "Mama's in-laws" and of their mother's kin as "Papa's in-laws." Their family name was Dorset, not on one side but on both sides. Their parents had been distant cousins. As a matter of fact, the Dorset family in the city of Chatham had once been so large and was so long established there that it would have been hard to estimate how distant the kinship might be. But still it was something that the old couple never liked to have mentioned. Most of their mother's close kin had, by the time I am speaking of, moved off to California, and most of their father's people lived somewhere up East. But Miss Dorset and her old bachelor brother found any contact, correspondence, even an exchange of Christmas cards with these in-laws intolerable. It was a case, so they said, of the in-laws respecting the value of the dollar above all else, whereas they, Miss Louisa and Mr. Alfred Dorset, placed importance on other things.

They lived in a dilapidated and curiously mutilated house on a street which, except for their own house, was the most splendid street in the entire city. Their house was one that you or I would have been ashamed to live in—even in the lean years of the early thirties. In order to reduce taxes the Dorsets had had the third story of the house torn away, leaving an ugly, flat-topped effect without any trim or ornamentation. Also, they had had the south wing pulled down and had sealed the scars not with matching brick but with a speckled stucco that looked raw and naked. All this the old couple did in violation of the strict zoning laws of West Vesey Place, and for doing so they would most certainly have been prosecuted except that they were the Dorsets and except that this was during the Depression when zoning laws weren't easy to enforce in a city like Chatham.

To the young people whom she and her brother entertained at their house once each year Miss Louisa Dorset liked to say: "We have given up everything for each other. Our only income is from our paper flowers and our figs." The old lady, though without showing any great skill or talent for it, made paper flowers. During the winter months, her brother took her in that fifteen-year-old touring car of theirs, with its steering wheel on the wrong side and with isinglass side curtains that were never taken down, to deliver these flowers to her customers. The flowers looked more like sprays of tinted potato chips than like any real flowers. Nobody could possibly have wanted to buy them except that she charged next to nothing for them and except that to people with children it seemed important to be on the Dorsets' list of worthwhile people. Nobody could really have wanted Mr. Dorset's figs either. He cultivated a dozen little bushes along the back wall of their house, covering them in the wintertime with some odd-looking boxes which he had had constructed for the purpose. The bushes were very productive, but the figs they produced were dried up little things without much taste. During the summer months he and his sister went about in their car, with the side curtains still up, delivering the figs to the same customers who bought the paper flowers. The money they made could hardly have paid for the gas it took to run the car. It was a great waste and it was very foolish of them.

And yet, despite everything, this foolish pair of old people, this same Miss Louisa and Mr. Alfred Dorset, had become social arbiters of a kind in our city. They had attained this position entirely through their fondness for giving an annual dancing party for young people. To *young* people—to *very* young people—the Dorsets' hearts went out. I don't mean to suggest that their hearts went out to orphans or to the children of the poor, for they were not foolish in that way. The guests at their little dancing parties were the thirteen- and fourteen-year-olds from families like the one they had long ago set themselves against, young people from the very houses to which, in season, they delivered their figs and their paper flowers. And when the night of one of their parties came round, it was in fact the custom for Mr. Alfred to go in the same old car and fetch all the invited guests to his house. His sister might explain to reluctant parents that this saved the children the embarrassment of being taken to their first dance by Mommy or Daddy. But the parents knew well enough that for twenty years the Dorsets had permitted no adult person, besides themselves, to put foot inside their house.

At those little dancing parties which the Dorsets gave, peculiar things went on—unsettling things to the boys and girls who had been fetched round in the old car. Sensible parents wished to keep their children away. Yet what could they do? For a Chatham girl to have to explain, a few years later, why she never went to a party at the Dorsets' was like having to explain why she had never been a debutante. For a boy it was like having to explain why he had not gone up East to school or even why his father hadn't belonged to the Chatham Racquet Club. If when you were thirteen or fourteen you got invited to the Dorsets' house, you went; it was the way of letting people know from the outset who you were. In a busy, modern city like Chatham you cannot afford to let people forget who you are—not for a moment, not at any age. Even the Dorsets knew that.

Many a little girl, after one of those evenings at the Dorsets', was heard to cry out in her sleep. When waked, or half waked, her only explanation might be: "It was just the fragrance from the paper flowers." Or: "I dreamed I could really smell the paper flowers." Many a boy was observed by his parents to seem "different" afterward. He became "secretive." The parents of the generation that had to attend those parties never pretended to understand what went on at the Dorsets' house. And even to those of us who were in that unlucky generation, it seemed we were half a lifetime learning what really took place during our one evening under the Dorsets' roof. Before our turn to go ever came round, we had for years been hearing about what it was like from older boys and girls. Afterward, we continued to hear about it from those who followed us. And, looking back on it, nothing about the one evening when you were actually there ever seemed quite so real as the glimpses and snatches which you got from those people before and after you—the second-hand impressions of the Dorsets' behavior, of things they said, of looks that passed between them.

Since Miss Dorset kept no servants, she always opened her own door. I suspect that for the guests at her parties the sight of her opening her door, in her astonishing attire, came as the most violent shock of the whole evening. On these occasions, she and her brother got themselves up as we had never seen them before and never would again. The old lady invariably wore a modish white evening gown, a garment perfectly fitted to her spare and scrawny figure and cut in such high fashion that it must necessarily have been new that year. And never to be worn but that one night! Her hair, long and thick and newly dyed for the occasion, would be swept upward and forward in a billowy mass which was topped by a corsage of yellow and coral paper flowers. Her cheeks and lips would be darkly rouged. On her long bony arms and her bare shoulders she would have applied some kind of suntan powder. Whatever else you had been led to expect of the evening, no one had ever warned you sufficiently about the radical change to be noted in her appearance—or in that of her brother, either. By the end of the party Miss Louisa might look as dowdy as ever, and Mr. Alfred a little worse than usual. But at the outset, when the party was assembling in their drawing room, even Mr. Alfred appeared resplendent in a nattily tailored tuxedo, with exactly the shirt, the collar, and the tie which fashion prescribed that year. His gray hair was nicely trimmed, his puffy old face freshly shaven. He was powdered with the same dark powder that his sister used. One felt even that his cheeks had been lightly touched with rouge.

A strange perfume pervaded the atmosphere of the house. The moment you set foot inside, this awful fragrance engulfed you. It was like a mixture of spicy incense and sweet attar of roses. And always, too, there was the profusion of paper flowers. The flowers were everywhere—on every cabinet and console, every inlaid table and carved chest, on every high, marble mantelpiece, on the bookshelves. In the entrance hall special tiers must have been set up to hold the flowers, because they were there in overpowering masses. They were in such abundance that it seemed hardly possible that Miss Dorset could have made them all. She must have spent weeks and weeks preparing them, even months, perhaps even the whole year between parties. When she went about delivering them to her customers, in the months following, they were apt to be somewhat faded and dusty; but on the night of the party, the colors of the flowers seemed even more impressive and more unlikely than their number. They were fuchsia, they were chartreuse, they were coral, aquamarine, brown, they were even black.

Everywhere in the Dorsets' house too were certain curious illuminations and lighting effects. The source of the light was usually hidden and its purpose was never obvious at once. The lighting was a subtler element than either the perfume or the paper flowers, and ultimately it was more disconcerting. A shaft of lavender light would catch a young visitor's eye and lead it, seemingly without purpose, in among the flowers. Then just beyond the point where the strength of the light would begin to diminish, the eye would discover something. In a small aperture in the mass of flowers, or sometimes in a larger grotto-like opening, there would be a piece of sculpture—in the hall a plaster replica of Rodin's "The Kiss," in the library an antique plaque of Leda and the Swan.[1] Or just above the

1. "The Kiss," an over-lifesized sculpture by Auguste Rodin (1840–1917), first exhibited in 1898. It shows a couple joined in passionate embrace, and represents the familiar Romantic theme of Paolo and Francesca (*cf.* Dante, *Inferno*, V), which was also the subject of Tchaikovsky's operatic fantasia "Francesca da Rimini." A powerful and sensuous statement of Romantic love, it became immensely popular and soon lost most of its force through bad reproductions.

flowers would be hung a picture, usually a black and white print but sometimes a reproduction in color. On the landing of the stairway leading down to the basement ballroom was the only picture that one was likely to learn the title of at the time. It was a tiny color print of Bronzino's "Venus, Cupid, Folly and Time." [2] This picture was not even framed. It was simply tacked on the wall, and it had obviously been torn—rather carelessly, perhaps hurriedly— from a book or magazine. The title and the name of the painter were printed in the white margin underneath.

About these works of art most of us had been warned by older boys and girls; and we stood in painful dread of that moment when Miss Dorset or her brother might catch us staring at any one of their pictures or sculptures. We had been warned, time and again, that during the course of the evening moments would come when she or he would reach out and touch the other's elbow and indicate, with a nod or just the trace of a smile, some guest whose glance had strayed among the flowers.

To some extent the dread which all of us felt that evening at the Dorsets' cast a shadow over the whole of our childhood. Yet for nearly twenty years the Dorsets continued to give their annual party. And even the most sensible of parents were not willing to keep their children away.

But a thing happened finally which could almost have been predicted. Young people, even in West Vesey Place, will not submit forever to the prudent counsel of their parents. Or some of them won't. There was a boy named Ned Meriwether and his sister Emily Meriwether, who lived with their parents in West Vesey Place just one block away from the Dorsets' house. In November, Ned and Emily were invited to the Dorsets' party, and because they dreaded it they decided to play a trick on everyone concerned—even on themselves, as it turned out . . . They got up a plan for smuggling an uninvited guest into the Dorsets' party.

The parents of this Emily and Ned sensed that their children were concealing something from them and suspected that the two were up to mischief of some kind. But they managed to deceive

In Greek mythology, Zeus took the form of a swan in order to seduce the mortal queen, Leda.

2. A famous allegorical painting by Agnolo Bronzino (1503–72), a Florentine Mannerist; it now hangs in the National Gallery, London. The work portrays Cupid embracing Venus, while Time and Folly look on. For a discussion of the painting's iconographical significance, see Erwin Panofsky, *Studies in Iconology* (1939, 1962), pp. 86–91. As Panofsky describes the painting, Cupid and Venus form an emblem of Luxury, "surrounded by personifications and symbols of treacherous pleasures and manifest evils; this group . . . is unveiled by Time and Truth."

themselves with the thought that it was only natural for young people—"mere children"—to be nervous about going to the Dorsets' house. And so instead of questioning them during the last hour before they left for the party, these sensible parents tried to do everything in their power to calm their two children. The boy and the girl, seeing this was the case, took advantage of it.

"You must not go down to the front door with us when we leave," the daughter insisted to her mother. And she persuaded both Mr. and Mrs. Meriwether that after she and her brother were dressed for the party they should all wait together in the upstairs sitting room until Mr. Dorset came to fetch the two young people in his car.

When, at eight o'clock, the lights of the automobile appeared in the street below, the brother and sister were still upstairs— watching from the bay window of the family sitting room. They kissed Mother and Daddy goodbye and then they flew down the stairs and across the wide, carpeted entrance hall to a certain dark recess where a boy named Tom Bascomb was hidden. This boy was the uninvited guest whom Ned and Emily were going to smuggle into the party. They had left the front door unlatched for Tom, and from the upstairs window just a few minutes ago they had watched him come across their front lawn. Now in the little recess of the hall there was a quick exchange of overcoats and hats between Ned Meriwether and Tom Bascomb; for it was a feature of the plan that Tom should attend the party as Ned and that Ned should go as the uninvited guest.

In the darkness of the recess, Ned fidgeted and dropped Tom Bascomb's coat on the floor. But the boy, Tom Bascomb, did not fidget. He stepped out into the light of the hall and began methodically getting into the overcoat which he would wear tonight. He was not a boy who lived in the West Vesey Place neighborhood (he was in fact the very boy who had once watched Miss Dorset cleaning house without any clothes on), and he did not share Emily's and Ned's nervous excitement about the evening. The sound of Mr. Dorset's footsteps outside did not disturb him. When both Ned and Emily stood frozen by that sound, he continued buttoning the unfamiliar coat and even amused himself by stretching forth one arm to observe how high the sleeve came on his wrist.

The doorbell rang, and from his dark corner Ned Meriwether whispered to his sister and to Tom: "Don't worry. I'll be at the Dorsets' in plenty of time."

Tom Bascomb only shrugged his shoulders at this reassurance. Presently when he looked at Emily's flushed face and saw her batting her eyes like a nervous monkey, a crooked smile played upon his lips. Then, at a sign from Emily, Tom followed her to the entrance door and permitted her to introduce him to old Mr. Dorset as her brother.

From the window of the upstairs sitting room the Meriwether parents watched Mr. Dorset and this boy and this girl walking across the lawn toward Mr. Dorset's peculiar-looking car. A light shone bravely and protectively from above the entrance of the house, and in its rays the parents were able to detect the strange angle at which Brother was carrying his head tonight and how his new fedora already seemed too small for him. They even noticed that he seemed a bit taller tonight.

"I hope it's all right," said the mother.

"What do you mean 'all right'?" the father asked petulantly.

"I mean—" the mother began, and then she hesitated. She did not want to mention that the boy out there did not look like their own Ned. It would have seemed to give away her feelings too much. "I mean that I wonder if I should have put Sister in that long dress at this age and let her wear my cape. I'm afraid the cape is really inappropriate. She's still young for that sort of thing."

"Oh," said the father, "I thought you meant something else."

"Whatever else did you think I meant, Edwin?" the mother said, suddenly breathless.

"I thought you meant the business we've discussed before," he said, although this was of course not what he had thought she meant. He had thought she meant that the boy out there did not look like their Ned. To him it had seemed even that the boy's step was different from Ned's. "The Dorsets' parties," he said, "are not very nice affairs to be sending your children to, Muriel. That's all I thought you meant."

"But we *can't* keep them away," the mother said defensively.

"Oh, it's just that they are growing up faster than we realize," said the father, glancing at his wife out of the corner of his eye.

By this time Mr. Dorset's car had pulled out of sight, and from downstairs Muriel Meriwether thought she heard another door closing. "What was that?" she said, putting one hand on her husband's.

"Don't be so jumpy," her husband said irritably, snatching away his hand. "It's the servants closing up in the kitchen."

Both of them knew that the servants had closed up in the kitchen long before this. Both of them had heard quite distinctly the sound of the side door closing as Ned went out. But they went on talking and deceiving themselves in this fashion during most of the evening.

Even before she opened the door to Mr. Dorset, little Emily Meriwether had known that there would be no difficulty about passing Tom Bascomb off as her brother. In the first place, she knew that without his spectacles Mr. Dorset could hardly see his hand before his face and knew that due to some silly pride he had he never put on his spectacles except when he was behind the wheel of his automobile. This much was common knowledge. In the second place, Emily knew from experience that neither he nor his sister ever made any real pretense of knowing one child in their general acquaintance from another. And so, standing in the doorway and speaking almost in a whisper, Emily had merely to introduce first herself and then her pretended brother to Mr. Dorset. After that the three of them walked in silence from her father's house to the waiting car.

Emily was wearing her mother's second-best evening wrap, a white lapin cape which, on Emily, swept the ground. As she walked between the boy and the man, the touch of the cape's soft silk lining on her bare arms and on her shoulders spoke to her silently of a strange girl she had seen in her looking glass upstairs tonight. And with her every step toward the car the skirt of her long taffeta gown whispered her own name to her: *Emily . . . Emily.* She heard it distinctly, and yet the name sounded unfamiliar. Once during this unreal walk from house to car she glanced at the mysterious boy, Tom Bascomb, longing to ask him—if only with her eyes—for some reassurance that she was really she. But Tom Bascomb was absorbed in his own irrelevant observations. With his head tilted back he was gazing upward at the nondescript winter sky where, among drifting clouds, a few pale stars were shedding their dull light alike on West Vesey Place and on the rest of the world. Emily drew her wrap tightly about her, and when presently Mr. Dorset held open the door to the back seat of his car she shut her eyes and plunged into the pitch blackness of the car's interior.

Tom Bascomb was a year older than Ned Meriwether and he was nearly two years older than Emily. He had been Ned's friend first. He and Ned had played baseball together on Saturdays before Emily ever set eyes on him. Yet according to Tom Bascomb himself, with whom several of us older boys talked just a few weeks after the night he went to the Dorsets', Emily always insisted that it was she who had known him first. On what she based this false claim Tom could not say. And on the two or three other occasions when we got Tom to talk about that night, he kept saying that he didn't understand what it was that had made Emily and Ned quarrel over which of them knew him first and knew him better.

We could have told him what it was, I think. But we didn't. It would have been too hard to say to him that at one time or another all of us in West Vesey had had our Tom Bascombs. Tom lived with his parents in an apartment house on a wide thoroughfare known as Division Boulevard, and his only real connection with West Vesey Place was that that street was included in his paper route. During the early morning hours he rode his bicycle along West Vesey and along other quiet streets like it, carefully aiming a neatly rolled paper at the dark loggia, at the colonnaded porch, or at the ornamented doorway of each of the palazzi and châteaux and manor houses that glowered at him in the dawn.[3] He was well thought of as a paper boy. If by mistake one of his papers went astray and lit on an upstairs balcony or on the roof of a porch, Tom would always take more careful aim and throw another. Even if the paper only went into the shrubbery, Tom got off his bicycle and fished it out. He wasn't the kind of boy to whom it would have occurred that the old fogies and the rich kids in West Vesey could very well get out and scramble for their own papers.

Actually, a party at the Dorsets' house was more a grand tour of the house than a real party. There was a half hour spent over very light refreshments (fruit Jello, English tea biscuits, lime punch). There was another half hour ostensibly given to general dancing in the basement ballroom (to the accompaniment of victrola music). But mainly there was the tour. As the party passed through the house, stopping sometimes to sit down in the principal rooms, the host and hostess provided entertainment in the form of an almost continuous dialogue between themselves. This dialogue was famous and was full of interest, being all about how much the Dorsets had given up for each other's sake and about how much higher the tone of Chatham society used to be than it was nowadays. They would invariably speak of their parents, who had died within a year of each other when Miss Louisa and Mr. Alfred were still in their teens; they even spoke of their wicked in-laws. When their parents died, the wicked in-laws had first tried to make them sell the house, then had tried to separate them and send them away to boarding schools, and had ended by trying to marry them off to "just anyone." Their two grandfathers had still been alive in those days and each had had a hand in the machinations, after the failure of which each grandfather had disinherited them. Mr. Alfred and Miss Louisa spoke also of how, a few years later, a procession of "young nobodies" had come of their own accord trying to steal the two of them away from each other. Both he and she would scowl at the very recollection of those "just anybodies" and those "nobodies," those "would-be suitors" who always turned out to be misguided fortune hunters and had to be driven away.

The Dorsets' dialogue usually began in the living room the moment Mr. Dorset returned with his last collection of guests. (He sometimes had to make five or six trips in the car.) There, as in other rooms afterward, they were likely to begin with a reference to

3. Styles inspired by classical European architecture.

the room itself or perhaps to some piece of furniture in the room. For instance, the extraordinary length of the drawing room—or reception room, as the Dorsets called it—would lead them to speak of an even longer room which they had had torn away from the house. "It grieved us, we wept," Miss Dorset would say, "to have Mama's French drawing room torn away from us."

"But we tore it away from ourselves," her brother would add, "as we tore away our in-laws—because we could not afford them." Both of them spoke in a fine declamatory style, but they frequently interrupted themselves with a sad little laugh which expressed something quite different from what they were saying and which seemed to serve them as an aside not meant for our ears.

"That was one of our greatest sacrifices," Miss Dorset would say, referring still to her mother's French drawing room.

And her brother would say: "But we knew the day had passed in Chatham for entertainments worthy of that room."

"It was the room which Mama and Papa loved best, but we gave it up because we knew, from our upbringing, which things to give up."

From this they might go on to anecdotes about their childhood. Sometimes their parents had left them for months or even a whole year at a time with only the housekeeper or with trusted servants to see after them. "You could trust servants then," they explained. And: "In those days parents could do that sort of thing, because in those days there was a responsible body of people within which your young people could always find proper companionship."

In the library, to which the party always moved from the drawing room, Mr. Dorset was fond of exhibiting snapshots of the house taken before the south wing was pulled down. As the pictures were passed around, the dialogue continued. It was often there that they told the story of how the in-laws had tried to force them to sell the house. "For the sake of economy!" Mr. Dorset would exclaim, adding an ironic "Ha ha!"

"As though money—" he would begin.

"As though money ever took the place," his sister would come in, "of living with your own kind."

"Or of being well born," said Mr. Dorset.

After the billiard room, where everyone who wanted it was permitted one turn with the only cue that there seemed to be in the house, and after the dining room, where it was promised refreshments would be served later, the guests would be taken down to the ballroom—purportedly for dancing. Instead of everyone's being urged to dance, however, once they were assembled in the ballroom, Miss Dorset would announce that she and her brother understood the timidity which young people felt about dancing and that all that she and he intended to do was to set the party a good example . . . It was only Miss Louisa and Mr. Alfred who danced. For perhaps thirty minutes, in a room without light excepting that from a few weak bulbs concealed among the flowers, the old couple danced; and they danced with such grace and there was such perfect harmony in all their movements that the guests stood about in stunned silence, as if hypnotized. The Dorsets waltzed, they two-stepped, they even fox-trotted, stopping only long enough between dances for Mr. Dorset, amid general applause, to change the victrola record.

But it was when their dance was ended that all the effects of the Dorsets' careful grooming that night would have vanished. And, alas, they made no effort to restore themselves. During the remainder of the evening Mr. Dorset went about with his bow tie hanging limply on his damp shirtfront, a gold collar button shining above it. A strand of gray hair, which normally covered his bald spot on top, now would have fallen on the wrong side of his part and hung like fringe about his ear. On his face and neck the thick layer of powder was streaked with perspiration. Miss Dorset was usually in an even more disheveled state, depending somewhat upon the fashion of her dress that year. But always her powder was streaked, her lipstick entirely gone, her hair falling down on all sides, and her corsage dangling somewhere about the nape of her neck. In this condition they led the party upstairs again, not stopping until they had reached the second floor of the house.

On the second floor we—the guests—were shown the rooms which the Dorsets' parents had once occupied (the Dorsets' own rooms were never shown). We saw, in glass museum cases along the hallway, the dresses and suits and hats and even the shoes which Miss Louisa and Mr. Alfred had worn to parties when they were very young. And now the dialogue, which had been left off while the Dorsets danced, was resumed. "Ah, the happy time," one of them would say, "was when we were *your* age!" And then, exhorting us to be happy and gay while we were still safe in the bosom of our own kind and before the world came crowding in on us with its ugly demands, the Dorsets would recall the happiness they had known when they were very young. This was their *pièce de résistance.*[4] With many a wink and blush and giggle and shake of the forefinger—and of course standing before the whole party—they each would remind the other of his or her naughty behavior in some old-fashioned parlor game or of certain silly little flirtations which they had long ago caught each other in.

They were on their way downstairs again now, and by the time

4. Outstanding accomplishment.

they had finished with this favorite subject they would be downstairs. They would be in the dark, flower-bedecked downstairs hall
and just before entering the dining room for the promised refreshments: the fruit Jello, the English tea biscuits, the lime punch.

And now for a moment Mr. Dorset bars the way to the dining
room and prevents his sister from opening the closed door. "Now,
my good friends," he says, "let us eat, drink, and be merry!"

"For the night is yet young," says his sister.

"Tonight you must be gay and carefree," Mr. Dorset enjoins.

"Because in this house we are all friends," Miss Dorset says. "We
are all young, we all love one another."

"And love can make us all young forever," her brother says.
"Remember!"

"Remember this evening always, sweet young people!"

"Remember!"

"Remember what our life is like here!"

And now Miss Dorset, with one hand on the knob of the great
door which she is about to throw open, leans a little toward the
guests and whispers hoarsely: "This is what it is like to be young
forever!"

Ned Meriwether was waiting behind a big japonica shrub near
the sidewalk when, about twenty minutes after he had last seen
Emily, the queer old touring car drew up in front of the Dorsets'
house. During the interval, the car had gone from the Meriwether
house to gather a number of other guests, and so it was not only
Emily and Tom who alighted on the sidewalk before the Dorsets'
house. The group was just large enough to make it easy for Ned to
slip out from his dark hiding place and join them without being noticed by Mr. Dorset. And now the group was escorted rather unceremoniously up to the door of the house, and Mr. Dorset departed to fetch more guests.

They were received at the door by Miss Dorset. Her eyesight was
no doubt better than her brother's, but still there was really no
danger of her detecting an uninvited guest. Those of us who had
gone to that house in the years just before Ned and Emily came
along could remember that, during a whole evening, when their
house was full of young people, the Dorsets made no introductions
and made no effort to distinguish which of their guests was which.
They did not even make a count of heads. Perhaps they did vaguely
recognize some of the faces, because sometimes when they had
come delivering figs or paper flowers to a house they had of necessity encountered a young child there, and always they smiled
sweetly at it, asked its age, and calculated on their old fingers how
many years must pass before the child would be eligible for an invi-

tation. Yet at those moments something in the way they had held up
their fingers and in the way they had gazed *at* the little face instead
of into it had revealed their lack of interest in the individual child.
And later, when the child was finally old enough to receive their invitation, he found it was still no different with the Dorsets. Even in
their own house it was evidently to the young people as a group
that the Dorsets' hearts went out; while they had the boys and girls
under their roof they herded them about like so many little thoroughbred calves. Even when Miss Dorset opened the front door
she did so exactly as though she were opening a gate. She pulled it
open very slowly, standing half behind it to keep out of harm's way.
And the children, all huddled together, surged in.

How meticulously this Ned and Emily Meriwether must have
laid their plans for that evening! And the whole business might
have come out all right if only they could have foreseen the effect
which one part of their plan—rather a last-minute embellishment of
it—would produce upon Ned himself. Barely ten minutes after they
entered the house, Ned was watching Tom as he took his seat on
the piano bench beside Emily. Ned probably watched Tom closely,
because certainly he knew what the next move was going to be.
The moment Miss Louisa Dorset's back was turned Tom Bascomb
slipped his arm gently about Emily's little waist and commenced
kissing her all over her pretty face. It was almost as if he were kissing away tears.

This spectacle on the piano bench, and others like it which followed, had been an inspiration of the last day or so before the party.
Or so Ned and Emily maintained afterward when defending themselves to their parents. But no matter when it was conceived, a part
of their plan it was, and Ned must have believed himself fully
prepared for it. Probably he expected to join in the round of giggling which it produced from the other guests. But now that the
time had come—it is easy to imagine—the boy Ned Meriwether
found himself not quite able to join in the fun. He watched with the
others, but he was not quite infected by their laughter. He stood a
little apart, and possibly he was hoping that Emily and Tom would
not notice his failure to appreciate the success of their comedy. He
was no doubt baffled by his own feelings, by the failure of his own
enthusiasm, and by a growing desire to withdraw himself from the
plot and from the party itself.

It is easy to imagine Ned's uneasiness and confusion that night.
And I believe the account which I have given of Emily's impressions and her delicate little sensations while on the way to the party
has a ring of truth about it, though actually the account was supplied by girls who knew her only slightly, who were not at the
party, who could not possibly have seen her afterward. It may, after

all, represent only what other girls imagined she would have felt. As for the account of how Mr. and Mrs. Meriwether spent the evening, it is their very own. And they did not hesitate to give it to anyone who would listen.

It was a long time, though, before many of us had a clear picture of the main events of the evening. We heard very soon that the parties for young people were to be no more, that there had been a wild scramble and chase through the Dorsets' house, and that it had ended by the Dorsets locking some boy—whether Ned or Tom was not easy to determine at first—in a queer sort of bathroom in which the plumbing had been disconnected, and even the fixtures removed, I believe. (Later I learned that there was nothing literally sinister about the bathroom itself. By having the pipes disconnected to this, and perhaps other bathrooms, the Dorsets had obtained further reductions in their taxes.) But a clear picture of the whole evening wasn't to be had—not without considerable searching. For one thing, the Meriwether parents immediately, within a week after the party, packed their son and daughter off to boarding schools. Accounts from the other children were contradictory and vague—perversely so, it seemed. Parents reported to each other that the little girls had nightmares which were worse even than those which their older sisters had had. And the boys were secretive and elusive, even with us older boys when we questioned them about what had gone on.

One sketchy account of events leading up to the chase, however, did go the rounds almost at once. Ned must have written it back to some older boy in a letter, because it contained information which no one but Ned could have had. The account went like this: When Mr. Dorset returned from his last roundup of guests, he came hurrying into the drawing room where the others were waiting and said in a voice trembling with excitement: "Now, let us all be seated, my young friends, and let us warm ourselves with some good talk."

At that moment everyone who was not already seated made a dash for a place on one of the divans or love seats or even in one of the broad window seats. (There were no individual chairs in the room.) Everyone made a dash, that is, except Ned. Ned did not move. He remained standing beside a little table rubbing his fingers over its polished surface. And from this moment he was clearly an object of suspicion in the eyes of his host and hostess. Soon the party moved from the drawing room to the library, but in whatever room they stopped Ned managed to isolate himself from the rest. He would sit or stand looking down at his hands until once again an explosion of giggles filled the room. Then he would look up just in time to see Tom Bascomb's cheek against Emily's or his arm about her waist.

For nearly two hours Ned didn't speak a word to anyone. He endured the Dorsets' dialogue, the paper flowers, the perfumed air, the works of art. Whenever a burst of giggling forced him to raise his eyes, he would look up at Tom and Emily and then turn his eyes away. Before looking down at his hands again, he would let his eyes travel slowly about the room until they came to rest on the figures of the two Dorsets. That, it seems, was how he happened to discover that the Dorsets understood, or thought they understood, what the giggles meant. In the great mirror mounted over the library mantel he saw them exchanging half-suppressed smiles. Their smiles lasted precisely as long as the giggling continued, and then, in the mirror, Ned saw their faces change and grow solemn when their eyes—their identical, tiny, dull, amber-colored eyes—focused upon himself.

From the library the party continued on the regular tour of the house. At last when they had been to the ballroom and watched the Dorsets dance, had been upstairs to gaze upon the faded party clothes in the museum cases, they descended into the downstairs hall and were just before being turned into the dining room. The guests had already heard the Dorsets teasing each other about the silly little flirtations and about their naughtiness in parlor games when they were young and had listened to their exhortations to be gay and happy and carefree. Then just when Miss Dorset leaned toward them and whispered, "This is what it is like to be young forever," there rose a chorus of laughter, breathless and shrill, yet loud and intensely penetrating.

Ned Meriwether, standing on the bottom step of the stairway, lifted his eyes and looked over the heads of the party to see Tom and Emily half hidden in a bower of paper flowers and caught directly in a ray of mauve light. The two had squeezed themselves into a little niche there and stood squarely in front of the Rodin statuary. Tom had one arm placed about Emily's shoulders and he was kissing her lightly first on the lobe of one ear and then on the tip of her nose. Emily stood as rigid and pale as the plaster sculpture behind her and with just the faintest smile on her lips. Ned looked at the two of them and then turned his glance at once on the Dorsets.

He found Miss Louisa and Mr. Alfred gazing quite openly at Tom and Emily and frankly grinning at the spectacle. It was more than Ned could endure. "Don't you *know?*" he wailed, as if in great physical pain. "Can't you *tell?* Can't you see who they *are?* They're *brother* and *sister!*"

From the other guests came one concerted gasp. And then an instant later, mistaking Ned's outcry to be something he had planned all along and probably intended—as they imagined—for the very cream of the jest, the whole company burst once again into laughter—not a chorus of laughter this time but a volley of loud guffaws from the boys, and from the girls a cacophony of separately articulated shrieks and trills.

None of the guests present that night could—or would—give a satisfactory account of what happened next. Everyone insisted that he had not even looked at the Dorsets, that he, or she, didn't know how Miss Louisa and Mr. Alfred reacted at first. Yet this was precisely what those of us who had gone there in the past *had* to know. And when finally we did manage to get an account of it, we knew that it was a very truthful and accurate one. Because we got it, of course, from Tom Bascomb.

Since Ned's outburst came after the dancing exhibition, the Dorsets were in their most disheveled state. Miss Louisa's hair was fallen half over her face, and that long, limp strand of Mr. Alfred's was dangling about his left ear. Like that, they stood at the doorway to the dining room grinning at Tom Bascomb's antics. And when Tom Bascomb, hearing Ned's wail, whirled about, the grins were still on the Dorsets' faces even though the guffaws and the shrieks of laughter were now silenced. Tom said that for several moments they continued to wear their grins like masks and that you couldn't really tell how they were taking it all until presently Miss Louisa's face, still wearing the grin, began turning all the queer colors of her paper flowers. Then the grin vanished from her lips and her mouth fell open and every bit of color went out of her face. She took a step backward and leaned against the doorjamb with her mouth still open and her eyes closed. If she hadn't been on her feet, Tom said he would have thought she was dead. Her brother didn't look at her, but his own grin had vanished just as hers did, and his face, all drawn and wrinkled, momentarily turned a dull copperish green.

Presently, though, he too went white, not white in faintness but in anger. His little brown eyes now shone like resin. And he took several steps toward Ned Meriwether. "What we know is that you are not one of us," he croaked. "We have perceived that from the beginning. We don't know how you got here or who you are. But the important question is, What are you doing here among these nice children?"

The question seemed to restore life to Miss Louisa. Her amber eyes popped wide open. She stepped away from the door and began pinning up her hair which had fallen down on her shoulders, and at the same time addressing the guests who were huddled together in the center of the hall. "Who is he, children? He is an intruder, that we know. If you know who he is, you must tell us."

"Who *am* I? Why, I am Tom Bascomb!" shouted Ned, still from the bottom step of the stairway. "I am Tom Bascomb, your paper boy!"

Then he turned and fled up the stairs toward the second floor. In a moment Mr. Dorset was after him.

To the real Tom Bascomb it had seemed that Ned honestly believed what he had been saying; and his own first impulse was to shout a denial. But being a level-headed boy and seeing how bad things were, Tom went instead to Miss Dorset and whispered to her that Tom Bascomb was a pretty tough guy and that she had better let *him* call the police for her. She told him where the telephone was in the side hall, and he started away.

But Miss Dorset changed her mind. She ran after Tom telling him not to call. Some of the guests mistook this for the beginning of another chase. Before the old lady could overtake Tom, however, Ned himself had appeared in the doorway toward which she and Tom were moving. He had come down the back stairway and he was calling out to Emily, "We're going *home*, Sis!"

A cheer went up from the whole party. Maybe it was this that caused Ned to lose his head, or maybe it was simply the sight of Miss Dorset rushing at him that did it. At any rate, the next moment he was running up the front stairs again, this time with Miss Dorset in pursuit.

When Tom returned from the telephone, all was quiet in the hall. The guests—everybody except Emily—had moved to the foot of the stairs and they were looking up and listening. From upstairs Tom could hear Ned saying, "All right. All right. All right." The old couple had him cornered.

Emily was still standing in the little niche among the flowers. And it is the image of Emily Meriwether standing among the paper flowers that tantalizes me whenever I think or hear someone speak of that evening. That, more than anything else, can make me wish that I had been there. I shall never cease to wonder what kind of thoughts were in her head to make her seem so oblivious to all that was going on while she stood there, and, for that matter, what had been in her mind all evening while she endured Tom Bascomb's caresses. When, in years since, I have had reason to wonder what some girl or woman is thinking—some Emily grown older—my mind nearly always returns to the image of that girl among the paper flowers. Tom said that when he returned from the telephone she looked very solemn and pale still but that her mind didn't seem to be on any of the present excitement. Immediately he went to her and said, "Your dad is on his way over, Emily." For it was the Meriwether parents he had telephoned, of course, and not the police.

It seemed to Tom that so far as he was concerned the party was

now over. There was nothing more he could do. Mr. Dorset was upstairs guarding the door to the strange little room in which Ned was
locked up. Miss Dorset was serving lime punch to the other guests
in the dining room, all the while listening with one ear for the arrival of the police whom Tom pretended he had called. When the
doorbell finally rang and Miss Dorset hurried to answer it, Tom
slipped quietly out through the pantry and through the kitchen and
left the house by the back door as the Meriwether parents entered
by the front.

There was no difficulty in getting Edwin and Muriel Meriwether,
the children's parents, to talk about what happened after they arrived that night. Both of them were sensible and clear-headed people, and they were not so conservative as some of our other neighbors in West Vesey. Being fond of gossip of any kind and fond of
reasonably funny stories on themselves, they told how their children had deceived them earlier in the evening and how they had
deceived themselves later. They tended to blame themselves more
than the children for what had happened. They tried to protect the
children from any harm or embarrassment that might result from it
by sending them off to boarding school. In their talk they never referred directly to Tom's reprehensible conduct or to the possible
motives that the children might have had for getting up their plan.
They tried to spare their children and they tried to spare Tom, but
unfortunately it didn't occur to them to try to spare the poor old
Dorsets.

When Miss Louisa opened the door, Mr. Meriwether said, "I'm
Edwin Meriwether, Miss Dorset. I've come for my son Ned."

"And for your daughter Emily, I hope," his wife whispered to
him.

"And for my daughter Emily."

Before Miss Dorset could answer him, Edwin Meriwether spied
Mr. Dorset descending the stairs. With his wife, Muriel, sticking
close to his side Edwin now strode over to the foot of the stairs.
"Mr. Dorset," he began, "my son Ned—"

From behind them, Edwin and Muriel now heard Miss Dorset
saying, "All the invited guests are gathered in the dining room."
From where they were standing the two parents could see into the
dining room. Suddenly they turned and hurried in there. Mr. Dorset and his sister of course followed them.

Muriel Meriwether went directly to Emily who was standing in a
group of girls. "Emily, where is your brother?"

Emily said nothing, but one of the boys answered: "I think
they've got him locked up upstairs somewhere."

"Oh, no!" said Miss Louisa, a hairpin in her mouth—for she was
still rather absent-mindedly working at her hair. "It is an intruder
that my brother has upstairs."

Mr. Dorset began speaking in a confidential tone to Edwin. "My dear neighbor," he said, "our paper boy saw fit to intrude himself upon our company tonight. But we recognized him as an outsider from the start."

Muriel Meriwether asked: "Where *is* the paper boy? Where is the paper boy, Emily?"

Again one of the boys volunteered: "He went out through the back door, Mrs. Meriwether."

The eyes of Mr. Alfred and Miss Louisa searched the room for Tom. Finally their eyes met and they smiled coyly. "*All* the children are being mischievous tonight," said Miss Louisa, and it was quite as though she had said, "all *we* children." Then, still smiling, she said, "Your tie has come undone, Brother. Mr. and Mrs. Meriwether will hardly know what to think."

Mr. Alfred fumbled for a moment with his tie but soon gave it up. Now with a bashful glance at the Meriwether parents, and giving a nod in the direction of the children, he actually said, "I'm afraid we've all decided to play a trick on Mr. and Mrs. Meriwether."

Miss Louisa said to Emily: "We've hidden our brother somewhere, haven't we?"

Emily's mother said firmly: "Emily, tell me where Ned is."

"He's upstairs, Mother," said Emily in a whisper.

Emily's father said: "I wish you to take me to the boy upstairs, Mr. Dorset."

The coy, bashful expressions vanished from the faces of the two Dorsets. Their eyes were little dark pools of incredulity, growing narrower by the second. And both of them were now trying to put their hair in order. "Why, *we* know nice children when we see them," Miss Louisa said peevishly. There was a pleading quality in her voice, too. "We knew from the beginning that that boy upstairs didn't belong amongst us," she said. "Dear neighbors, it isn't just the money, you know, that makes the difference." All at once she sounded like a little girl about to burst into tears.

"It isn't just the money?" Edwin Meriwether repeated.

"Miss Dorset," said Muriel with new gentleness in her tone, as though she had just recognized that it was a little girl she was talking to, "there has been some kind of mistake—a misunderstanding."

Mr. Alfred Dorset said: "Oh, we wouldn't make a mistake of that kind! People *are* different. It isn't something you can put your finger on, but it isn't the money."

"I don't know what you're talking about," Edwin said, exasperated. "But I'm going upstairs and find that boy." He left the room with Mr. Dorset following him with quick little steps—steps like those of a small boy trying to keep up with a man.

Miss Louisa now sat down in one of the high-backed dining

chairs which were lined up along the oak wainscot. She was trembling, and Muriel came and stood beside her. Neither of them spoke, and in almost no time Edwin Meriwether came downstairs again with Ned. Miss Louisa looked at Ned, and tears came into her eyes. "Where is my brother?" she asked accusingly, as though she thought possibly Ned and his father had locked Mr. Dorset in the bathroom.

"I believe he has retired," said Edwin. "He left us and disappeared into one of the rooms upstairs."

"Then I must go up to him," said Miss Louisa. For a moment she seemed unable to rise. At last she pushed herself up from the chair and walked from the room with the slow, steady gait of a somnambulist. Muriel Meriwether followed her into the hall and as she watched the old woman ascending the steps, leaning heavily on the rail, her impulse was to go and offer to assist her. But something made her turn back into the dining room. Perhaps she imagined that her daughter, Emily, might need her now.

The Dorsets did not reappear that night. After Miss Louisa went upstairs, Muriel promptly got on the telephone and called the parents of some of the other boys and girls. Within a quarter of an hour, half a dozen parents had assembled. It was the first time in many years that any adult had set foot inside the Dorset house. It was the first time that any parent had ever inhaled the perfumed air or seen the masses of paper flowers and the illuminations and the statuary. In the guise of holding consultations over whether or not they should put out the lights and lock up the house, the parents lingered much longer than was necessary before taking the young people home. Some of them even tasted the lime punch. But in the presence of their children they made no comment on what had happened and gave no indication of what their own impressions were—not even their impressions of the punch. At last it was decided that two of the men should see to putting out the lights everywhere on the first floor and down in the ballroom. They were a long time in finding the switches for the indirect lighting. In most cases, they simply resorted to unscrewing the bulbs. Meanwhile the children went to the large cloak closet behind the stairway and got their wraps. When Ned and Emily Meriwether rejoined their parents at the front door to leave the house, Ned was wearing his own overcoat and held his own fedora in his hand.

Miss Louisa and Mr. Alfred Dorset lived on for nearly ten years after that night, but they gave up selling their figs and paper flowers and of course they never entertained young people again. I often wonder if growing up in Chatham can ever have seemed quite the same since. Some of the terror must have gone out of it. Half the dread of coming of age must have vanished with the dread of the Dorsets' parties.

After that night, their old car would sometimes be observed creeping about town, but it was never parked in front of their house any more. It stood usually at the side entrance where the Dorsets could climb in and out of it without being seen. They began keeping a servant too—mainly to run their errands for them, I imagine. Sometimes it would be a man, sometimes a woman, never the same one for more than a few months at a time. Both of the Dorsets died during the Second World War while many of us who had gone to their parties were away from Chatham. But the story went round— and I am inclined to believe it—that after they were dead and the house was sold, Tom Bascomb's coat and hat were found still hanging in the cloak closet behind the stairs.

Tom himself was a pilot in the war and was a considerable hero. He was such a success and made such a name for himself that he never came back to Chatham to live. He found bigger opportunities elsewhere I suppose, and I don't suppose he ever felt the ties to Chatham that people with Ned's kind of upbringing do. Ned was in the war too, of course. He was in the navy and after the war he did return to Chatham to live, though actually it was not until then that he had spent much time here since his parents bundled him off to boarding school. Emily came home and made her debut just two or three years before the war, but she was already engaged to some boy in the East; she never comes back any more except to bring her children to see their grandparents for a few days during Christmas or at Easter.

I understand that Emily and Ned are pretty indifferent to each other's existence nowadays. I have been told this by Ned Meriwether's own wife. Ned's wife maintains that the night Ned and Emily went to the Dorsets' party marked the beginning of this indifference, that it marked the end of their childhood intimacy and the beginning of a shyness, a reserve, even an animosity between them that was destined to be a sorrow forever to the two sensible parents who had sat in the upstairs sitting room that night waiting until the telephone call came from Tom Bascomb.

Ned's wife is a girl he met while he was in the navy. She was a Wave,[5] and her background isn't the same as his. Apparently, she isn't too happy with life in what she refers to as "Chatham proper." She and Ned have recently moved out into a suburban development, which she doesn't like either and which she refers to as "greater Chatham." She asked me at a party one night how Chatham got its name (she was just making conversation and ap-

5. Member of the Women's Reserve of the U.S. Navy, formed during World War II (Women Accepted for Volunteer Emergency Service).

pealing to my interest in such things) and when I told her that it was named for the Earl of Chatham and pointed out that the city is located in Pitt County, she burst out laughing. "How very elegant," she said. "Why has nobody ever told me that before?" But what interests me most about Ned's wife is that after a few drinks she likes to talk about Ned and Emily and Tom Bascomb and the Dorsets. Tom Bascomb has become a kind of hero—and I don't mean a wartime hero—in her eyes, though of course not having grown up in Chatham she has never seen him in her life. But she is a clever girl, and there are times when she will say to me, "Tell me about Chatham. Tell me about the Dorsets." And I try to tell her. I tell her to remember that Chatham looks upon itself as a rather old city. I tell her to remember that it was one of the first English-speaking settlements west of the Alleghenies and that by the end of the American Revolution, when veterans began pouring westward over the Wilderness Road or down the Ohio River, Chatham was often referred to as a thriving village. Then she tells me that I am being dull, because it is hard for her to concentrate on any aspect of the story that doesn't center around Tom Bascomb and that night at the Dorsets'.

But I make her listen. Or at least one time I did. The Dorset family, I insisted on saying, was in Chatham even in those earliest times right after the Revolution, but they had come here under somewhat different circumstances from those of the other early settlers. How could that really matter, Ned's wife asked, after a hundred and fifty years? How could distinctions between the first settlers matter after the Irish had come to Chatham, after the Germans, after the Italians? Well, in West Vesey Place it could matter. It had to. If the distinction was false, it mattered all the more and it was all the more necessary to make it.

But let me interject here that Chatham is located in a state about whose history most Chatham citizens—not newcomers like Ned's wife, but old-timers—have little interest and less knowledge. Most of us, for instance, are never even quite sure whether during the 1860's our state did secede or didn't secede. As for the city itself, some of us hold that it is geographically Northern and culturally Southern. Others say the reverse is true. We are all apt to want to feel misplaced in Chatham, and so we are not content merely to say that it is a border city. How you stand on this important question is apt to depend entirely on whether your family is one of those with a good Southern name or one that had its origin in New England, because those are the two main categories of old society families in Chatham.

But truly—I told Ned's wife—the Dorset family was never in either of those categories. The first Dorset had come, with his family and his possessions and even a little capital, direct from a city in the English Midlands to Chatham. The Dorsets came not as pioneers, but paying their way all the way. They had not bothered to stop for a generation or two to put down roots in Pennsylvania or Virginia or Massachusetts. And this was the distinction which some people wished always to make. Apparently those early Dorsets had cared no more for putting down roots in the soil of the New World than they had cared for whatever they had left behind in the Old. They were an obscure mercantile family who came to invest in a new Western city. Within two generations the business—no, the industry!—which they established made them rich beyond any dreams they could have had in the beginning. For half a century they were looked upon, if any family ever was, as our first family.

And then the Dorsets left Chatham—practically all of them except the one old bachelor and the one old maid—left it just as they had come, not caring much about what they were leaving or where they were going. They were city people, and they were Americans. They knew that what they had in Chatham they could buy more of in other places. For them Chatham was an investment that had paid off. They went to live in Santa Barbara and Laguna Beach, in Newport and on Long Island. And the truth which it was so hard for the rest of us to admit was that, despite our families of Massachusetts and Virginia, we were all more like the Dorsets—those Dorsets who left Chatham—than we were *un*like them. Their spirit was just a little closer to being the very essence of Chatham than ours was. The obvious difference was that we had to stay on here and pretend that our life had a meaning which it did not. And if it was only by a sort of chance that Miss Louisa and Mr. Alfred played the role of social arbiters among the young people for a number of years, still no one could honestly question their divine right to do so.

"It may have been their right," Ned's wife said at this point, "but just think what might have happened."

"It's not a matter of what might have happened," I said. "It is a matter of what did happen. Otherwise, what have you and I been talking about?"

"Otherwise," she said with an irrepressible shudder, "I would not be forever getting you off in a corner at these parties to talk about my husband and my husband's sister and how it is they care so little for each other's company nowadays."

And I could think of nothing to say to that except that probably we had now pretty well covered our subject.

From Happy Families Are All Alike (1959)

John Updike·

A & P

In walks these three girls in nothing but bathing suits. I'm in the
third checkout slot, with my back to the door, so I don't see them
until they're over by the bread. The one that caught my eye first
was the one in the plaid green two-piece. She was a chunky kid,
with a good tan and a sweet broad soft-looking can with those two
crescents of white just under it, where the sun never seems to hit, at
the top of the backs of her legs. I stood there with my hand on a box
of HiHo crackers trying to remember if I rang it up or not. I ring it
up again and the customer starts giving me hell. She's one of these
cash-register-watchers, a witch about fifty with rouge on her cheek-
bones and no eyebrows, and I know it made her day to trip me up.
She'd been watching cash registers for fifty years and probably
never seen a mistake before.

By the time I got her feathers smoothed and her goodies into a
bag—she gives me a little snort in passing, if she'd been born at the
right time they would have burned her over in Salem—by the time
I get her on her way the girls had circled around the bread and
were coming back, without a pushcart, back my way along the
counters, in the aisle between the checkouts and the Special bins.
They didn't even have shoes on. There was this chunky one, with
the two-piece—it was bright green and the seams on the bra were
still sharp and her belly was still pretty pale so I guessed she just
got it (the suit)—there was this one, with one of those chubby
berry-faces, the lips all bunched together under her nose, this one,
and a tall one, with black hair that hadn't quite frizzed right, and
one of these sunburns right across under the eyes, and a chin that
was too long—you know, the kind of girl other girls think is very
"striking" and "attractive" but never quite makes it, as they very

well know, which is why they like her so much—and then the third
one, that wasn't quite so tall. She was the queen. She kind of led
them, the other two peeking around and making their shoulders
round. She didn't look around, not this queen, she just walked
straight on slowly, on these long white prima-donna legs. She came
down a little hard on her heels, as if she didn't walk in her bare feet
that much, putting down her heels and then letting the weight
move along to her toes as if she was testing the floor with every
step, putting a little deliberate extra action into it. You never know
for sure how girls' minds work (do you really think it's a mind in
there or just a little buzz like a bee in a glass jar?) but you got the
idea she had talked the other two into coming in here with her, and
now she was showing them how to do it, walk slow and hold yourself straight.

She had on a kind of dirty-pink—beige maybe, I don't know—
bathing suit with a little nubble all over it and, what got me, the
straps were down. They were off her shoulders looped loose around
the cool tops of her arms, and I guess as a result the suit had
slipped a little on her, so all around the top of the cloth there was
this shining rim. If it hadn't been there you wouldn't have known
there could have been anything whiter than those shoulders. With
the straps pushed off, there was nothing between the top of the suit
and the top of her head except just *her,* this clean bare plane of the
top of her chest down from the shoulder bones like a dented sheet
of metal tilted in the light. I mean, it was more than pretty.

She had sort of oaky hair that the sun and salt had bleached, done
up in a bun that was unravelling, and a kind of prim face. Walking
into the A & P with your straps down, I suppose it's the only kind of
face you *can* have. She held her head so high her neck, coming up
out of those white shoulders, looked kind of stretched, but I didn't
mind. The longer her neck was, the more of her there was.

She must have felt in the corner of her eye me and over my
shoulder Stokesie in the second slot watching, but she didn't tip.
Not this queen. She kept her eyes moving across the racks, and
stopped, and turned so slow it made my stomach rub the inside of
my apron, and buzzed to the other two, who kind of huddled
against her for relief, and then they all three of them went up the
cat-and-dog-food-breakfast-cereal-macaroni-rice-raisins-seasonings-
spreads-spaghetti-soft-drinks-crackers-and-cookies aisle. From the
third slot I look straight up this aisle to the meat counter, and I
watched them all the way. The fat one with the tan sort of fumbled
with the cookies, but on second thought she put the package back.
The sheep pushing their carts down the aisle—the girls were walking against the usual traffic (not that we have one-way signs or
anything)—were pretty hilarious. You could see them, when

Queenie's white shoulders dawned on them, kind of jerk, or hop, or hiccup, but their eyes snapped back to their own baskets and on they pushed. I bet you could set off dynamite in an A & P and the people would by and large keep reaching and checking oatmeal off their lists and muttering "Let me see, there was a third thing, began with A, asparagus, no, ah, yes, applesauce!" or whatever it is they do mutter. But there was no doubt, this jiggled them. A few house-slaves in pin curlers even looked around after pushing their carts past to make sure what they had seen was correct.

You know, it's one thing to have a girl in a bathing suit down on the beach, where what with the glare nobody can look at each other much anyway, and another thing in the cool of the A & P, under the fluorescent lights, against all those stacked packages, with her feet paddling along naked over our checkerboard green-and-cream rubber-tile floor.

"Oh Daddy," Stokesie said beside me. "I feel so faint."

"Darling," I said. "Hold me tight." Stokesie's married, with two babies chalked up on his fuselage already, but as far as I can tell that's the only difference. He's twenty-two, and I was nineteen this April.

"Is it done?" he asks, the responsible married man finding his voice. I forgot to say he thinks he's going to be manager some sunny day, maybe in 1990 when it's called the Great Alexandrov and Petrooshki Tea Company [1] or something.

What he meant was, our town is five miles from a beach, with a big summer colony out on the Point, but we're right in the middle of town, and the women generally put on a shirt or shorts or something before they get out of the car into the street. And anyway these are usually women with six children and varicose veins mapping their legs and nobody, including them, could care less. As I say, we're right in the middle of town, and if you stand at our front doors you can see two banks and the Congregational church and the newspaper store and three real-estate offices and about twenty-seven old freeloaders tearing up Central Street because the sewer broke again. It's not as if we're on the Cape; we're north of Boston and there's people in this town haven't seen the ocean for twenty years.

The girls had reached the meat counter and were asking McMahon something. He pointed, they pointed, and they shuffled out of sight behind a pyramid of Diet Delight peaches. All that was left for us to see was old McMahon patting his mouth and looking after them sizing up their joints. Poor kids, I began to feel sorry for them, they couldn't help it.

1. "A & P" is actually an abbreviation of Great Atlantic and Pacific Tea Company.

Now here comes the sad part of the story, at least my family says it's sad, but I don't think it's so sad myself. The store's pretty empty, it being Thursday afternoon, so there was nothing much to do except lean on the register and wait for the girls to show up again. The whole store was like a pinball machine and I didn't know which tunnel they'd come out of. After a while they come around out of the far aisle, around the light bulbs, records at discount of the Caribbean Six or Tony Martin Sings or some such gunk you wonder they waste the wax on, sixpacks of candy bars, and plastic toys done up in cellophane that fall apart when a kid looks at them anyway. Around they come, Queenie still leading the way, and holding a little gray jar in her hand. Slots Three through Seven are unmanned and I could see her wondering between Stokes and me, but Stokesie with his usual luck draws an old party in baggy gray pants who stumbles up with four giant cans of pineapple juice (what do these bums *do* with all that pineapple juice? I've often asked myself) so the girls come to me. Queenie puts down the jar and I take it into my fingers icy cold. Kingfish Fancy Herring Snacks in Pure Sour Cream; 49¢. Now her hands are empty, not a ring or a bracelet, bare as God made them, and I wonder where the money's coming from. Still with that prim look she lifts a folded dollar bill out of the hollow at the center of her nubbled pink top. The jar went heavy in my hand. Really, I thought that was so cute.

Then everybody's luck begins to run out. Lengel comes in from haggling with a truck full of cabbages on the lot and is about to scuttle into that door marked MANAGER behind which he hides all day when the girls touch his eye. Lengel's pretty dreary, teaches Sunday school and the rest, but he doesn't miss that much. He comes over and says, "Girls, this isn't the beach."

Queenie blushes, though maybe it's just a brush of sunburn I was noticing for the first time, now that she was so close. "My mother asked me to pick up a jar of herring snacks." Her voice kind of startled me, the way voices do when you see the people first, coming out so flat and dumb yet kind of tony, too, the way it ticked over "pick up" and "snacks." All of a sudden I slid right down her voice into her living room. Her father and the other men were standing around in ice-cream coats and bow ties and the women were in sandals picking up herring snacks on toothpicks off a big glass plate and they were all holding drinks the color of water with olives and sprigs of mint in them. When my parents have somebody over they get lemonade and if it's a real racy affair Schlitz in tall glasses with "They'll Do It Every Time" cartoons stencilled on.

"That's all right," Lengel said. "But this isn't the beach." His repeating this struck me as funny, as if it had just occurred to him, and he had been thinking all these years the A & P was a great big dune and he was the head lifeguard. He didn't like my smiling—as I say he doesn't miss much—but he concentrates on giving the girls that sad Sunday-school-superintendent stare.

Queenie's blush is no sunburn now, and the plump one in plaid, that I liked better from the back—a really sweet can—pipes up, "We weren't doing any shopping. We just came in for the one thing."

"That makes no difference," Lengel tells her, and I could see from the way his eyes went that he hadn't noticed she was wearing a two-piece before. "We want you decently dressed when you come in here."

"We *are* decent," Queenie says suddenly, her lower lip pushing, getting sore now that she remembers her place, a place from which the crowd that runs the A & P must look pretty crummy. Fancy Herring Snacks flashed in her very blue eyes.

"Girls, I don't want to argue with you. After this come in here with your shoulders covered. It's our policy." He turns his back. That's policy for you. Policy is what the kingpins want. What the others want is juvenile delinquency.

All this while, the customers had been showing up with their carts but, you know, sheep, seeing a scene, they had all bunched up on Stokesie, who shook open a paper bag as gently as peeling a peach, not wanting to miss a word. I could feel in the silence everybody getting nervous, most of all Lengel, who asks me, "Sammy, have you rung up their purchase?"

I thought and said "No" but it wasn't about that I was thinking. I go through the punches, 4, 9, GROC, TOT—it's more complicated than you think, and after you do it often enough, it begins to make a little song, that you hear words to, in my case "Hello (*bing*) there, you (*gung*) hap-py *pee*-pul (*splat*)!"—the *splat* being the drawer flying out. I uncrease the bill, tenderly as you may imagine, it just having come from between the two smoothest scoops of vanilla I had ever known were there, and pass a half and a penny into her narrow pink palm, and nestle the herrings in a bag and twist its neck and hand it over, all the time thinking.

The girls, and who'd blame them, are in a hurry to get out, so I say "I quit" to Lengel quick enough for them to hear, hoping they'll stop and watch me, their unsuspected hero. They keep right on going, into the electric eye; the door flies open and they flicker across the lot to their car, Queenie and Plaid and Big Tall Goony-Goony (not that as raw material she was so bad), leaving me with Lengel and a kink in his eyebrow.

"Did you say something, Sammy?"

"I said I quit."

"I thought you did."

"You didn't have to embarrass them."

"It was they who were embarrassing us."

I started to say something that came out "Fiddle-de-doo." It's a saying of my grandmother's, and I know she would have been pleased.

"I don't think you know what you're saying," Lengel said.

"I know you don't," I said. "But I do." I pull the bow at the back of my apron and start shrugging it off my shoulders. A couple customers that had been heading for my slot begin to knock against each other, like scared pigs in a chute.

Lengel sighs and begins to look very patient and old and gray. He's been a friend of my parents for years. "Sammy, you don't want to do this to your Mom and Dad," he tells me. It's true, I don't. But it seems to me that once you begin a gesture it's fatal not to go through with it. I fold the apron, "Sammy" stitched in red on the pocket, and put it on the counter, and drop the bow tie on top of it. The bow tie is theirs, if you've ever wondered. "You'll feel this for the rest of your life," Lengel says, and I know that's true, too, but remembering how he made that pretty girl blush makes me so scrunchy inside I punch the No Sale tab and the machine whirs "pee-pul" and the drawer splats out. One advantage to this scene taking place in summer, I can follow this up with a clean exit, there's no fumbling around getting your coat and galoshes, I just saunter into the electric eye in my white shirt that my mother ironed the night before, and the door heaves itself open, and outside the sunshine is skating around on the asphalt.

I looked around for my girls, but they're gone, of course. There wasn't anybody but some young married screaming with her children about some candy they didn't get by the door of a powder-blue Falcon station wagon. Looking back in the big windows, over the bags of peat moss and aluminum lawn furniture stacked on the pavement, I could see Lengel in my place in the slot, checking the sheep through. His face was dark gray and his back stiff, as if he'd just had an injection of iron, and my stomach kind of fell as I felt how hard the world was going to be to me hereafter.

From *Pigeon Feathers and Other Stories* (1962)

·THE SHORT STORY TODAY·

A brief glance at earlier essays on the future of the short story must discourage anyone from making dogmatic predictions about the direction the form will take. Criticism is based on the past, while the forms of art are shaped by future events, many of them adventitious and unpredictable. But one thing seems clear. In the experimental stories of Coover, Barthelme, Barth, and their contemporaries, there is a deliberate attempt to go beyond conventional notions of continuity and design, to make the story a record of modern life's discontinuities. This trend may not become the dominant one, and the satisfactions of the traditional well-made story are by no means exhausted. John Cheever's "The World of Apples," the most recent story in this collection, shows how a change in landscape can reinvigorate a conventional form. Cheever began his career as a scrupulous chronicler of middle-class suburban life, but in later stories such as "The World of Apples" Cheever, like Hawthorne, has transported his art to Italy, where a rich but dangerously seductive setting can expose the ambiguities of American life. In similar fashion, Joyce Carol Oates has often chosen the violent conventions of Gothic fiction, since she believes that Gothicism is "not a literary tradition so much as a fairly realistic assessment of modern life."

But in spite of these contemporary achievements within familiar conventions, the immediate future of the short story would seem to lie in the experimental direction mapped out by Barthelme and Barth. Fiction is always accusing itself of being merely fictitious, and the wild oscillations between fantasy and fact in Barthelme's "The Indian Uprising" reflect his conviction that the hallmarks of the well-made story—consistency of style, rationality of structure,

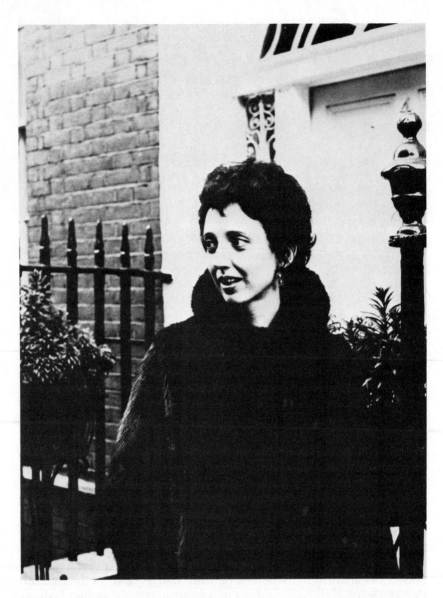

Joyce Carol Oates   (Fay Godwin, London)

and steadiness in viewpoint—cannot represent the illogic of our
lives. The danger, of course, is that all artistic control will collapse as traditional forms are jettisoned, but the example of John
Barth suggests quite the opposite. The subtitle of Barth's *Lost in
the Funhouse* (1968) is "Fiction for print, tape, live voice"; and
much of his writing—like that of Barthelme—may be seen as an
attempt to express the discontinuous nature of our technological
society, which is marked by sophisticated but essentially in-

John Barth   (Don Glena Photos)

human techniques of communication. In a world where print and tape are often sundered from the live voice, the funhouse itself becomes an image for the absurdities of the world around us, and the writer finds himself "lost in the funhouse." Unlike Barthelme, however, Barth wishes to regain the virtues of the "live voice." "Lost in the Funhouse" is, on one level, a story about the contemporary artist's paradoxical desire to go beyond the "action of conventional dramatic narrative" without losing that human "effect

John Cheever   (Jill Krementz)

of drama" which is the foundation of the storyteller's craft (notice
the discussion of "Freitag's Triangle" near the end of the story).
Barth is a master of parody and burlesque, and in his comic
treatments of the older story forms he is reaffirming the vitality of
narrative itself. Barth does not wish to destroy the story; instead,
he hopes to strike through outmoded conventions and recapture
the original energies of the oral tradition.

   Just as many modern novelists have disintegrated the well-made novel into its earliest components—legend, myth, the journal, "news"—and then reintegrated these into new forms, as in Joyce's *Ulysses,* so Barth has returned to the earliest examples of the story-teller's art for refreshment. As an undergraduate at Johns Hopkins University, he earned part of his tuition by shelving books in the Classics Library, which included the stacks of the Oriental Seminary; and his recollection of those hours tells us much about his narrative aims.

One was permitted to get lost for hours in that splendiferous labyrinth and intoxicate, engorge oneself with *story.* Especially I became enamored of the great tale-cycles and collections: Somadeva's *Ocean of Story* in ten huge volumes, Burton's *Thousand Nights and a Night* in twelve, the *Panchatantra,* the *Gesta Romanorum,* the *Novellini,* and the *Pent-Hept-*and *Decameron. . . .* Most of those spellbinding liars I have forgotten, but never Scheherazade. Though the tales she [Scheherazade] tells are not my favorites, she remains my favorite teller. . . . Like a parable of Kafka's or a great myth, the story of deflowered Scheherazade, yarning tirelessly through the dark hours to save her neck, corresponds to a number of things at once, and flashes meaning from all its facets. For me its rich dark circumstances, mixing the subtle and the coarse, the comic and the grim, the realistic and the fantastic, the apocalyptic and the hopeful, figure, among other things, both the estate of the fictioner in general and the particular endeavors and aspirations of this one, at least, who can wish nothing better than to spin like that vizier's excellent daughter, through what nights remain to him, tales within tales within tales, full-stored with 'description and discourse and rare traits and anecdotes and moral instances and reminiscences . . . proverbs and parables, chronicles and pleasantries, quips and jests, stories and . . . dialogues and histories and elegies and other verses . . .' until he and his scribblings are fetched low by the Destroyer of Delights.

Barth's fascination with the *Thousand Nights and a Night* brings us full circle, to Irving's preoccupation with folk narratives and Poe's admiration for Gothic intricacy, and reminds us that whatever form the short fiction may take in the future, it will never stray too far from its traditional origins in *story.*

·Joyce Carol Oates·

UPON THE SWEEPING FLOOD

One day in Eden County, in the remote marsh and swamplands to
the south, a man named Walter Stuart was stopped in the rain by a
sheriff's deputy along a country road. Stuart was in a hurry to get
home to his family—his wife and two daughters—after having endured a week at his father's old farm, arranging for his father's funeral, surrounded by aging relatives who had sucked at him for the
strength of his youth. He was a stern, quiet man of thirty-nine,
beginning now to lose some of the muscular hardness that had
always baffled others, masking as it did Stuart's remoteness, his refinement, his faith in discipline and order that seem to have
belonged, even in his youth, to a person already grown safely old.
He was a district vice-president for one of the gypsum mining
plants, a man to whom financial success and success in love had
come naturally, without fuss. When only a child he had shifted his
faith with little difficulty from the unreliable God of his family's
tradition to the things and emotions of this world, which he admired in his thoughtful, rather conservative way, and this faith had
given him access, as if by magic, to a communion with persons
vastly different from himself—with someone like the sheriff's deputy, for example, who approached him that day in the hard, cold
rain. "Is something wrong?" Stuart said. He rolled down the window and had nearly opened the door when the deputy, an old man
with gray eyebrows and a slack, sunburned face, began shouting
against the wind. "Just the weather, mister. You plan on going far?
How far are you going?"

"Two hundred miles," Stuart said. "What about the weather? Is it
a hurricane?"

"A hurricane—yes—a hurricane," the man said, bending to shout at Stuart's face. "You better go back to town and stay put. They're evacuating up there. We're not letting anyone through."

A long line of cars and pickup trucks, tarnished and gloomy in the rain, passed them on the other side of the road. "How bad is it?" said Stuart. "Do you need help?"

"Back at town, maybe, they need help," the man said. "They're putting up folks at the school house and the churches, and different families— The eye was spost to come by here, but last word we got it's veered further south. Just the same, though—"

"Yes, it's good to evacuate them," Stuart said. At the back window of an automobile passing them two children's faces peered out at the rain, white and blurred. "The last hurricane here—"

"Ah, God, leave off of that!" the old man said, so harshly that Stuart felt, inexplicably, hurt. "You better turn around now and get on back to town. You got money they can put you up somewheres good—not with these folks coming along here."

This was said without contempt, but Stuart flinched at its assumptions and, years afterward, he was to remember the old man's remark as the beginning of his adventure. The man's twisted face and unsteady, jumping eyes, his wind-snatched voice, would reappear to Stuart when he puzzled for reasons—but along with the deputy's face there would be the sad line of cars, the children's faces turned toward him, and, beyond them in his memory, the face of his dead father with skin wrinkled and precise as a withered apple.

"I'm going in to see if anybody needs help," Stuart said. He had the car going again before the deputy could even protest. "I know what I'm doing! I know what I'm doing!" Stuart said.

The car lunged forward into the rain, drowning out the deputy's outraged shouts. The slashing of rain against Stuart's faced excited him. Faces staring out of oncoming cars were pale and startled, and Stuart felt rising in him a strange compulsion to grin, to laugh madly at their alarm. . . . He passed cars for some time. Houses looked deserted, yards bare. Things had the look of haste about them, even trees—in haste to rid themselves of their leaves, to be stripped bare. Grass was twisted and wild. A ditch by the road was overflowing and at spots the churning, muddy water stretched across the red clay road. Stuart drove, splashing, through it. After a while his enthusiasm slowed, his foot eased up on the gas pedal. He had not passed any cars or trucks for some time.

The sky had darkened and the storm had increased. Stuart thought of turning back when he saw, a short distance ahead, someone standing in the road. A car approached from the opposite direction. Stuart slowed, bearing to the right. He came upon a farm—a small, run-down one with just a few barns and a small pasture in which a horse stood drooping in the rain. Behind the roofs of the buildings a shifting edge of foliage from the trees beyond curled in the wind, now dark, now silver. In a neat harsh line against the bottom of the buildings the wind had driven up dust and red clay. Rain streamed off roofs, plunged into fat, tilted rain barrels, and exploded back out of them. As Stuart watched, another figure appeared, running out of the house. Both persons—they looked like children—jumped about in the road, waving their arms. A spray of leaves was driven against them and against the muddy windshield of the car that approached and passed them. They turned: a girl and a boy, waving their fists in rage, their faces white and distorted. As the car sped past Stuart, water and mud splashed up in a vicious wave.

When Stuart stopped and opened the door the girl was already there, shouting, "Going the wrong way! Wrong way!" Her face was coarse, pimply about her forehead and chin. The boy pounded up behind her, straining for air. "Where the hell are you going, mister?" the girl cried. "The storm's coming from this way. Did you see that bastard, going right by us? Did you see him? If I see him when I get to town—" A wall of rain struck. The girl lunged forward and tried to push her way into the car; Stuart had to hold her back. "Where are your folks?" he shouted. "Let me in," cried the girl savagely. "We're getting out of here!" "Your folks," said Stuart. He had to cup his mouth to make her hear. "Your folks in there!" "There ain't nobody there— *Goddamn* you," she said, twisting about to slap her brother, who had been pushing at her from behind. She whirled upon Stuart again. "You letting us in, mister? You letting us in?" she screamed, raising her hands as if to claw him. But Stuart's size must have calmed her, for she shouted hoarsely and mechanically: "There ain't nobody in there. Our pa's been gone the last two days. *Last two days.* Gone into town *by himself.* Gone drunk somewhere. He ain't here. He left us here. LEFT US HERE!" Again she rushed at Stuart, and he leaned forward against the steering wheel to let her get in back. The boy was about to follow when something caught his eye back at the farm. "Get in," said Stuart. "Get in. Please. Get in." "My horse there," the boy muttered. "You little bastard! You get in here!" his sister screamed.

But once the boy got in, once the door was closed, Stuart knew that it was too late. Rain struck the car in solid walls and the road, when he could see it, had turned to mud. "Let's go! Let's go!" cried the girl, pounding on the back of the seat. "Turn it around! Go up on our drive and turn it around!" The engine and the wind roared together. "Turn it! Get it going!" cried the girl. There was a scuffle and someone fell against Stuart. "It ain't no good," the boy said. "Let me out." He lunged for the door and Stuart grabbed him. "I'm going back to the house," the boy cried, appealing to Stuart with his frightened eyes, and his sister, giving up suddenly, pushed him violently forward. "It's no use," Stuart said. "Goddamn fool," the girl screamed, "goddamn fool!"

The water was ankle deep as they ran to the house. The girl splashed ahead of Stuart, running with her head up and her eyes wide open in spite of the flying scud. When Stuart shouted to the boy, his voice was slammed back to him as if he were being mocked. "Where are you going? Go to the house! Go to the house!" The boy had turned and was running toward the pasture. His sister took no notice but ran to the house. "Come back, kid!" Stuart cried. Wind tore at him, pushing him back. "What are you—"

The horse was undersized, skinny and brown. It ran to the boy as if it wanted to run him down but the boy, stooping through the fence, avoided the frightened hoofs and grabbed the rope that dangled from the horse's halter. "That's it! That's it!" Stuart shouted as if the boy could hear. At the gate the boy stopped and looked around wildly, up to the sky—he might have been looking for someone who had just called him; then he shook the gate madly. Stuart reached the gate and opened it, pushing it back against the boy, who now turned to gape at him. "What? What are you doing here?" he said.

The thought crossed Stuart's mind that the child was insane. "Bring the horse through!" he said. "We don't have much time."

"What are you doing here?" the boy shouted. The horse's eyes rolled, its mane lifted and haloed about its head. Suddenly it lunged through the gate and jerked the boy off the ground. The boy ran in the air, his legs kicking. "Hang on and bring him around!" Stuart shouted. "Let me take hold!" He grabbed the boy instead of the rope. They stumbled together against the horse. It had stopped now and was looking intently at something just to the right of Stuart's head. The boy pulled himself along the rope, hand over hand, and Stuart held onto him by the strap of his overalls. "He's scairt of you!" the boy said. "He's scairt of you!" Stuart reached over and took hold of the rope above the boy's fingers and tugged gently at it. His face was about a foot away from the horse's. "Watch out for him," said the boy. The horse reared and broke free, throwing Stuart back against the boy. "Hey, hey," screamed the boy, as if mad. The horse turned in mid-air as if whirled about by the wind, and Stuart looked up through his fingers to see its hoofs and a vicious flicking of its tail, and the face of the boy being yanked past him and away with incredible speed. The boy fell heavily on his side in the mud, arms outstretched above him, hands still gripping the rope with wooden fists. But he scrambled to his feet at once and ran alongside the horse. He flung one arm up around its neck as

Stuart shouted, "Let him go! Forget about him!" Horse and boy pivoted together back toward the fence, slashing wildly at the earth, feet and hoofs together. The ground erupted beneath them. But the boy landed upright, still holding the rope, still with his arm about the horse's neck. "Let me help," Stuart said. "No," said the boy, "he's my horse, he knows me—" "Have you got him good?" Stuart shouted. "We got—we got each other here," the boy cried, his eyes shut tight.

Stuart went to the barn to open the door. While he struggled with it, the boy led the horse forward. When the door was open far enough, Stuart threw himself against it and slammed it around to the side of the barn. A cloud of hay and scud filled the air. Stuart stretched out his arms, as if pleading with the boy to hurry, and he murmured, "Come on. Please. Come on." The boy did not hear him or even glance at him: his own lips were moving as he caressed the horse's neck and head. The horse's muddy hoof had just begun to grope about the step before the door when something like an explosion came against the back of Stuart's head, slammed his back, and sent him sprawling out at the horse.

"Damn you! Damn you!" the boy screamed. Stuart saw nothing except rain. Then something struck him, his shoulder and hand, and his fingers were driven down into the mud. Something slammed beside him in the mud and he seized it—the horse's foreleg—and tried to pull himself up, insanely, lurching to his knees. The horse threw him backwards. It seemed to emerge out of the air before and above him, coming into sight as though out of a cloud. The boy he did not see at all—only the hoofs—and then the boy appeared, inexplicably, under the horse, peering intently at Stuart, his face struck completely blank. "Damn you!" Stuart heard, "he's my horse! My horse! I hope he kills you!" Stuart crawled back in the water, crab fashion, watching the horse form and dissolve, hearing its vicious tattoo against the barn. The door, swinging madly back and forth, parodied the horse's rage, seemed to challenge its frenzy; then the door was all Stuart heard, and he got to his feet, gasping, to see that the horse was out of sight.

The boy ran bent against the wind, out toward nowhere, and Stuart ran after him. "Come in the house, kid! Come on! Forget about it, kid!" He grabbed the boy's arm. The boy struck at him with his elbow. "He was my horse!" he cried.

In the kitchen of the house they pushed furniture against the door. Stuart had to stand between the boy and the girl to keep them from fighting. "Goddamn sniffling fool," said the girl. "So your goddamn horse run off for the night!" The boy crouched down on the floor, crying steadily. He was about thirteen: small for his age, with bony wrists and face. "We're all going to be blownt to hell, let alone your horse," the girl said. She sat with one big thigh and leg outstretched on the table, watching Stuart. He thought her perhaps eighteen. "Glad you come down to get us?" she said. "Where are you from, mister?" Stuart's revulsion surprised him; he had not supposed there was room in his stunned mind for emotion of this sort. If the girl noticed it she gave no sign, but only grinned at him. "I was—I was on my way home," he said. "My wife and daughters—" It occurred to him that he had forgotten about them entirely. He had not thought of them until now and, even now, no image came to his mind: no woman's face, no little girls' faces. Could he have imagined their lives, their love for him? For an instant he doubted everything. "Wife and daughters," said the girl, as if wondering whether to believe him. "Are they in this storm too?" "No—no," Stuart said. To get away from her he went to the window. He could no longer see the road. Something struck the house and he flinched away. "Them trees!" chortled the girl. "I knew it! Pa always said how he ought to cut them down, so close to the house like they are! I knew it! I knew it! And the old bastard off safe now where they can't get him!"

"Trees?" said Stuart slowly.

"Them trees! Old oak trees!" said the girl.

The boy, struck with fear, stopped crying suddenly. He crawled on the floor to a woodbox beside the big old iron stove and got in, patting the disorderly pile of wood as if he were blind. The girl ran to him and pushed him. "What are you doing?" Stuart cried in anguish. The girl took no notice of him. "What am I doing?" he said aloud. "What the hell am I doing here?" It seemed to him that the end would come in a minute or two, that the howling outside could get no louder, that the howling inside his mind could get no more intense, no more accusing. A goddamn fool! A goddamn fool! he thought. The deputy's face came to mind, and Stuart pictured himself groveling before the man, clutching at his knees, asking forgiveness and for time to be turned back. . . . Then he saw himself back at the old farm, the farm of his childhood, listening to tales of his father's agonizing sickness, the old peoples' heads craning around, seeing how he took it, their eyes charged with horror and delight. . . . "My wife and daughters," Stuart muttered.

The wind made a hollow, drumlike sound. It seemed to be tolling. The boy, crouching back in the woodbox, shouted: "I ain't scairt! I ain't scairt!" The girl gave a shriek. "Our chicken coop, I'll be gahdammed!" she cried. Try as he could, Stuart could see nothing out the window. "Come away from the window," Stuart said, pulling the girl's arm. She whirled upon him. "Watch yourself, mister," she said, "you want to go out to your gahdamn bastardly worthless car?" Her body was strong and big in her men's clothing; her shoulders looked muscular beneath the filthy shirt. Cords in her young neck stood out. Her hair had been cut short and was now wet, plastered about her blemished face. She grinned at Stuart as if she were about to poke him in the stomach, for fun. "I ain't scairt of what God can do!" the boy cried behind them.

When the water began to bubble up through the floor boards they decided to climb to the attic. "There's an ax!" Stuart exclaimed, but the boy got on his hands and knees and crawled to the corner where the ax was propped before Stuart could reach it. The boy cradled it in his arms. "What do you want with that?" Stuart said, and for an instant his heart was pierced with fear. "Let me take it. I'll take it." He grabbed it out of the boy's dazed fingers.

The attic was about half as large as the kitchen and the roof jutted down sharply on either side. Tree limbs rubbed and slammed against the roof on all sides. The three of them crouched on the middle beam, Stuart with the ax tight in his embrace, the boy pushing against him as if for warmth, and the girl kneeling, with her thighs straining her overalls. She watched the little paneless window at one end of the attic without much emotion or interest, like a large, wet turkey. The house trembled beneath them. "I'm going to the window," Stuart said, and was oddly relieved when the girl did not sneer at him. He crawled forward along the dirty beam, dragging the ax with him, and lay full length on the floor about a yard from the window. There was not much to see. At times the rain relaxed, and objects beneath in the water took shape: tree stumps, parts of buildings, junk whirling about in the water. The thumping on the roof was so loud at that end that he had to crawl backwards to the middle again. "I ain't scairt, nothing God can do!" the boy cried. "Listen to the sniveling baby," said the girl. "He thinks God pays him any mind! Hah!" Stuart crouched beside them, waiting for the boy to press against him again. "As if God gives a good damn about him," the girl said. Stuart looked at her. In the near dark her face did not seem so coarse; the set of her eyes was almost attractive. "You don't think God cares about you?" Stuart said slowly. "No, not specially," the girl said, shrugging her shoulders. "The hell with it. You seen the last one of these?" She tugged at Stuart's arm. "Mister? It was something to see. Me an' Jackie was little then—him just a baby. We drove a far ways north to get out of it. When we come back the roads was so thick with sightseers from the cities! They took all the dead ones floating in the water and put them in one place, part of a swamp they cleared out. The families and things—they were mostly fruit pickers—had to come by on rafts and rowboats to look and see could they find the ones they knew. That was there for a day. The bodies would turn round and round in the wash from the boats. Then the faces all got alike and they wouldn't let anyone come any more and put oil on them and set them afire. We stood on top of the car and watched all that day. I wasn't but nine them."

When the house began to shake, some time later, Stuart cried aloud: "This is it!" He stumbled to his feet, waving the ax. He turned around and around as if he were in a daze. "You goin' to chop somethin' with that?" the boy said, pulling at him. "Hey, no, that ain't yours to—it ain't yours to chop—" They struggled for the ax. The boy sobbed, "It ain't yours! It ain't yours!" and Stuart's rage at his own helplessness, at the folly of his being here, for an instant almost made him strike the boy with the ax. But the girl slapped him furiously. "Get away from him! I swear I'll kill you!" she screamed.

Something exploded beneath them. "That's the windows," the girl muttered, clinging to Stuart, "and how am I to clean it again! The old bastard will want it clean, and mud over everything!" Stuart pushed her away so that he could swing the ax. Pieces of soft, rotted wood exploded back onto his face. The boy screamed insanely as the boards gave way to a deluge of wind and water, and even Stuart wondered if he had made a mistake. The three of them fell beneath the onslaught and Stuart lost the ax, felt the handle slam against his leg. "You! You!" Stuart cried, pulling at the girl— for an instant, blinded by pain, he could not think who he was, what he was doing, whether he had any life beyond this moment. The big-faced, husky girl made no effort to hide her fear and cried, "wait, wait!" But he dragged her to the hole and tried to force her out. "My brother—" she gasped. She seized his wrists and tried to get away. "Get out there! There isn't any time!" Stuart muttered. The house seemed about to collapse at any moment. He was pushing her through the hole, against the shattered wood, when she suddenly flinched back against him and he saw that her cheek was cut and she was choking. He snatched her hands away from her mouth as if he wanted to see something secret: blood welled out between her lips. She coughed and spat blood onto him. "You're all right," he said, oddly pleased. "Now get out there and I'll get the kid. I'll take care of him." This time she managed to crawl through the hole, with Stuart pushing her from behind; when he turned to seize the boy, the boy clung to his neck, sobbing something about God. "God loves you!" Stuart yelled. "Loves the least of you! The least of you!" The girl pulled her brother up in her great arms and Stuart was free to climb through himself.

It was actually quite a while—perhaps an hour—before the battering of the trees and the wind pushed the house in. The roof fell slowly, and the section to which they clung was washed free. "We're going somewheres!" shouted the girl. "Look at the house! That gahdamn old shanty seen the last storm!"

The boy lay with his legs pushed in under Stuart's and had not spoken for some time. When the girl cried, "Look at that!" he tried to burrow in farther. Stuart wiped his eyes to see the wall of darkness dissolve. The rain took on another look—a smooth, piercing, metallic glint, like nails driving against their faces and bodies. There was no horizon. They could see nothing except the rushing water and a thickening mist that must have been rain, miles and miles of rain, slammed by the wind into one great wall that moved remorselessly upon them. "Hang on," Stuart said, gripping the girl. "Hang on to me."

Waves washed over the roof, pushing objects at them with soft, muted thuds—pieces of fence, boards, branches heavy with foliage. Stuart tried to ward them off with his feet. Water swirled around them, sucking at them, sucking the roof, until they were pushed against one of the farm buildings. Something crashed against the roof—another section of the house—and splintered, flying up against the girl. She was thrown backwards, away from Stuart, who lunged after her. They fell into the water while the boy screamed. The girl's arms threshed wildly against Stuart. The water was cold, and its aliveness, its sinister energy, surprised him more than the thought that he would drown—that he would never endure the night. Struggling with the girl, he forced her back to the roof, pushed her up. Bare, twisted nails raked his hands. "Gahdamn you, Jackie, you give a hand!" the girl said as Stuart crawled back up. He lay, exhausted, flat on his stomach and let the water and debris slosh over him.

His mind was calm beneath the surface buzzing. He liked to think that his mind was a clear, sane circle of quiet carefully preserved inside the chaos of the storm—that the three of them were safe within the sanctity of this circle, this was how man always conquered nature, how he subdued things greater than himself. But whenever he did speak to her it was in short grunts, in her own idiom: "This ain't so bad!" or "It'll let up pretty soon!" Now the girl held him in her arms as if he were a child, and he did not have the strength to pull away. Of his own free will he had given himself to the storm, or to the strange desire to save someone in it—but now he felt grateful for the girl, even for her brother, for they had saved him as much as he had saved them. Stuart thought of his wife at home, walking through the rooms, waiting for him; he thought of his daughters in their twin beds, two glasses of water on their bureau. . . . But these people knew nothing of him: in his experience now he did not belong to them. Perhaps he had misunderstood his role, his life? Perhaps he had blundered out of his way, drawn into the wrong life, surrendered to the wrong role. What had blinded him to the possibility of many lives, many masks, many arms that might so embrace him? A word not heard one day, a gesture misinterpreted, a leveling of someone's eyes in a certain unmistakable manner, which he had mistaken just the same! The consequences of such errors might trail insanely into the future, across miles of land, across worlds. He only now sensed the incompleteness of his former life. . . . "Look! Look!" the girl cried, jostling him out of his stupor. "Take a look at that, mister!"

He raised himself on one elbow. A streak of light broke out of the dark. Lanterns, he thought, a rescue party already. . . . But the rain dissolved the light; then it reappeared with a beauty that startled him. "What is it?" the boy screamed. "How come it's here?" They watched it filter through the rain, rays knifing through and showing, now, how buildings and trees crouched close about them. "It's the sun, the sun going down," the girl said. "The sun!" said Stuart, who had thought it was night. "The sun!" They stared at it until it disappeared.

The waves calmed sometime before dawn. By then the roof had lost its peak and water ran unchecked over it, in generous waves and then in thin waves, alternately, as the roof bobbed up and down. The three huddled together with their backs to the wind. Water came now in slow drifts. "It's just got to spread itself out far enough so's it will be even," said the girl, "then it'll go down." She spoke without sounding tired, only a little disgusted—as if things weren't working fast enough to suit her. "Soon as it goes down we'll start toward town and see if there ain't somebody coming out to get us in a boat," she said, chattily and comfortably, into Stuart's ear. Her manner astonished Stuart, who had been thinking all night of the humiliation and pain he had suffered. "Bet the old bastard will be glad to see us," she said, "even if he did go off like that. Well, he never knew a storm was coming. Me and him get along pretty well—he ain't so bad." She wiped her face; it was filthy with dirt and blood. "He'll buy you a drink, mister, for saving us how you did. That was something to have happen—a man just driving up to get us!" And she poked Stuart in the ribs.

The wind warmed as the sun rose. Rain turned to mist and back to rain again, still falling heavily, and now objects were clear about them. The roof had been shoved against the corner of the barn and a mound of dirt, and eddied there without much trouble. Right about them, in a kind of halo, a thick blanket of vegetation and filth bobbed. The fence had disappeared and the house had collapsed and been driven against a ridge of land. The barn itself had fallen in, but the stone support looked untouched, and it was against this they had been shoved. Stuart thought he could see his car—or something over there where the road used to be.

"I bet it ain't deep. Hell," said the girl, sticking her foot into the water. The boy leaned over the edge and scooped up some of the filth in his hands. "Lookit all the spiders," he said. He wiped his face slowly. "Leave them gahdamn spiders alone," said the girl. "You want me to shove them down your throat?" She slid to the edge and lowered her legs. "Yah, I touched bottom. It ain't bad." But then she began coughing and drew herself back. Her coughing made Stuart cough: his chest and throat were ravaged, shaken. He lay exhausted when the fit left him and realized, suddenly, that they were all sick—that something had happened to them. They had to get off the roof. Now, with the sun up, things did not look so bad: there was a ridge of trees a short distance away on a long, red clay hill. "We'll go over there," Stuart said. "Do you think you can make it?"

The boy played in the filth, without looking up, but the girl gnawed at her lip to show she was thinking. "I spose so," she said. "But him—I don't know about him."

"Your brother? What's wrong?"

"Turn around. Hey, stupid. Turn around." She prodded the boy, who jerked around, terrified, to stare at Stuart. His thin bony face gave way to a drooping mouth. "Gone loony, it looks like," the girl said with a touch of regret. "Oh, he had times like this before. It might go away."

Stuart was transfixed by the boy's stare. The realization of what had happened struck him like a blow, sickening his stomach. "We'll get him over there," he said, making his words sound good. "We can wait there for someone to come. Someone in a boat. He'll be better there."

"I spose so," said the girl vaguely.

Stuart carried the boy while the girl splashed eagerly ahead. The water was sometimes up to his thighs. "Hold on another minute," he pleaded. The boy stared out at the water as if he thought he were taken somewhere to be drowned. "Put your arms around my neck. Hold on," Stuart said. He shut his eyes and every time he looked up the girl was still a few yards ahead and the hill looked no closer. The boy breathed hollowly, coughing into Stuart's face. His own face and neck were covered with small red bites. Ahead, the girl walked with her shoulders lunged forward as if to hurry her there, her great thighs straining against the water, more than a match for it. As Stuart watched her, something was on the side of his face—in his ear—and with a scream he slapped at it, nearly dropping the boy. The girl whirled around. Stuart slapped at his face and must have knocked it off—probably a spider. The boy, upset by Stuart's outcry, began sucking in air faster and faster as if he were dying. "I'm all right, I'm all right," Stuart whispered, "just hold on another minute. . . ."

When he finally got to the hill the girl helped pull him up. He set the boy down with a grunt, trying to put the boy's legs under him so he could stand. But the boy sank to the ground and turned over and vomited into the water; his body shook as if he were having convulsions. Again the thought that the night had poisoned them, their own breaths had sucked germs into their bodies, struck Stuart with an irresistible force. "Let him lay down and rest," the girl said, pulling tentatively at the back of her brother's belt, as if she were thinking of dragging him farther up the slope. "We sure do thank you, mister," she said.

Stuart climbed to the crest of the hill. His heart pounded madly, blood pounded in his ears. What was going to happen? Was anything going to happen? How disappointing it looked—ridges of land showing through the water and the healthy sunlight pushing back the mist. Who would believe him when he told of the night, of the times when death seemed certain . . . ? Anger welled up in him already as he imagined the tolerant faces of his friends, his children's faces ready to turn to other amusements, other oddities. His wife would believe him; she would shudder, holding him, burying her small face in his neck. But what could she understand of his experience, having had no part in it? . . . Stuart cried out; he had nearly stepped on a tangle of snakes. Were they alive? He backed away in terror. The snakes gleamed wetly in the morning light, heads together as if conspiring. Four . . . five of them—they too had swum for this land, they too had survived the night, they had as much reason to be proud of themselves as Stuart.

He gagged and turned away. Down by the water line the boy lay flat on his stomach and the girl squatted nearby, wringing out her denim jacket. The water behind them caught the sunlight and gleamed mightily, putting them into silhouette. The girl's arms moved slowly, hard with muscle. The boy lay coughing gently. Watching them, Stuart was beset by a strange desire: he wanted to run at them, demand their gratitude, their love. Why should they not love him, when he had saved their lives? When he had lost what he was just the day before, turned now into a different person, a stranger even to himself? Stuart stooped and picked up a rock. A broad hot hand seemed to press against his chest. He threw the rock out into the water and said, "Hey!"

The girl glanced around but the boy did not move. Stuart sat down on the soggy ground and waited. After a while the girl looked away; she spread the jacket out to dry. Great banked clouds rose into the sky, reflected in the water—jagged and bent in the waves. Stuart waited as the sun took over the sky. Mist at the horizon glowed, thinned, gave way to solid shapes. Light did not strike cleanly across the land, but was marred by ridges of trees and parts of buildings, and around a corner at any time Stuart expected to see a rescuing party—in a rowboat or something.

"Hey, mister." He woke; he must have been dozing. The girl had called him. "Hey. Whyn't you come down here? There's all them snakes up there."

Stuart scrambled to his feet. When he stumbled downhill, embarrassed and frightened, the girl said chattily, "The sons of bitches are crawling all over here. He chast some away." The boy was on his feet and looking around with an important air. His coming alive startled Stuart—indeed, the coming alive of the day, of the world, evoked alarm in him. All things came back to what they were. The girl's alert eyes, the firm set of her mouth, had not changed—the sunlight had not changed, or the land, really; only Stuart had been changed. He wondered at it . . . and the girl must have seen something in his face that he himself did not yet know about, for her eyes narrowed, her throat gulped a big swallow, her arms moved slowly up to show her raw elbows. "We'll get rid of them," Stuart said, breaking the silence. "Him and me. We'll do it."

The boy was delighted. "I got a stick," he said, waving a thin whiplike branch. "There's some over here."

"We'll get them," Stuart said. But when he started to walk, a rock slipped loose and he fell back into the mud. He laughed aloud. The girl, squatting a few feet away, watched him silently. Stuart got to his feet, still laughing. "You know much about it, kid?" he said, cupping his hand on the boy's head.

"About what?" said the boy.

"Killing snakes," said Stuart.

"I spose—I spose you just kill them."

The boy hurried alongside Stuart. "I need a stick," Stuart said; they got him one from the water, about the size of an ax. "Go by that bush," Stuart said, "there might be some there."

The boy attacked the bush in a frenzy. He nearly fell into it. His enthusiasm somehow pleased Stuart, but there were no snakes in the bush. "Go down that way," Stuart ordered. He glanced back at the girl: she watched them. Stuart and the boy went on with their sticks held in mid-air. "God put them here to keep us awake," the boy said brightly. "See we don't forget about Him." Mud sucked at their feet. "Last year we couldn't fire the woods on account of it so dry. This year can't either on account of the water. We got to get the snakes like this."

Stuart hurried as if he had somewhere to go. The boy, matching his steps, went faster and faster, panting, waving his stick angrily in the air. The boy complained about snakes and, listening to him, fascinated by him, in that instant Stuart saw everything. He saw the conventional dawn that had mocked the night, had mocked his desire to help people in trouble; he saw, beyond that, his father's home emptied now even of ghosts. He realized that the God of these people had indeed arranged things, had breathed the order of chaos into forms, had animated them, had animated even Stuart himself forty years ago. The knowledge of this fact struck him about the same way as the nest of snakes had struck him—an image leaping right to the eye, pouncing upon the mind, joining itself with the perceiver. "Hey, hey!" cried the boy, who had found a snake: the snake crawled noisily and not very quickly up the slope, a brown-speckled snake. The boy ran clumsily after it. Stuart was astonished at the boy's stupidity, at his inability to see, now, that the snake had vanished. Still he ran along the slope, waving his stick, shouting, "I'll get you! I'll get you!" This must have been the sign Stuart was waiting for. When the boy turned, Stuart was right behind him. "It got away up there," the boy said. "We got to get it." When Stuart lifted his stick the boy fell back a step but went on in mechanical excitement, "It's up there, gotten hid in the weeds. It ain't me," he said, "it ain't me that—" Stuart's blow struck the boy on the side of the head, and the rotted limb shattered into soft wet pieces. The boy stumbled down toward the water. He was coughing when Stuart took hold of him and began shaking him madly, and he did nothing but cough, violently and with all his concentration, even when Stuart bent to grab a rock and brought it down on his head. Stuart let him fall into the water. He could hear him breathing and he could see, about the boy's lips, tiny flecks or bubbles of blood appearing and disappearing with his breath.

When the boy's eyes opened, Stuart fell upon him. They struggled savagely in the water. Again the boy went limp; Stuart stood, panting, and waited. Nothing happened for a minute or so. But then he saw something—the boy's fingers moving up through the water, soaring to the surface! "Will you quit it!" Stuart screamed. He was about to throw himself upon the boy again when the thought of the boy's life, bubbling out between his lips, moving his fingers, filled him with such outraged disgust that he backed away. He threw the rock out into the water and ran back, stumbling, to where the girl stood.

She had nothing to say: her jaw was hard, her mouth a narrow line, her thick nose oddly white against her dirty face. Only her eyes moved, and these were black, lustrous, at once demanding and terrified. She held a board in one hand. Stuart did not have time to think, but, as he lunged toward her, he could already see himself grappling with her in the mud, forcing her down, tearing her ugly clothing from her body— "Lookit!" she cried, the way a person might speak to a horse, cautious and coaxing, and pointed behind him. Stuart turned to see a white boat moving toward them, a half mile or so away. Immediately his hands dropped, his mouth opened in awe. The girl still pointed, breathing carefully, and Stuart, his mind shattered by the broken sunshine upon the water, turned to the boat, raised his hands, cried out, "Save me! Save me!" He had waded out a short distance by the time the men arrived.

From *Upon the Sweeping Flood and Other Stories* (1966)

·John Barth·

LOST IN THE FUNHOUSE

For whom is the funhouse fun? Perhaps for lovers. For Ambrose it is *a place of fear and confusion.* He has come to the seashore with his family for the holiday, *the occasion of their visit is Independence Day, the most important secular holiday of the United States of America.* A single straight underline is the manuscript mark for italic type, *which in turn* is the printed equivalent to oral emphasis of words and phrases as well as the customary type for titles of complete works, not to mention. Italics are also employed, in fiction stories especially, for "outside," intrusive, or artificial voices, such as radio announcements, the texts of telegrams and newspaper articles, et cetera. They should be used *sparingly.* If passages originally in roman type are italicized by someone repeating them, it's customary to acknowledge the fact. *Italics mine.*

Ambrose was "at that awkward age." His voice came out high-pitched as a child's if he let himself get carried away; to be on the safe side, therefore, he moved and spoke with *deliberate calm* and *adult gravity.* Talking soberly of unimportant or irrelevant matters and listening consciously to the sound of your own voice are useful habits for maintaining control in this difficult interval. *En route* to Ocean City he sat in the back seat of the family car with his brother Peter, age fifteen, and Magda G——, age fourteen, a pretty girl an exquisite young lady, who lived not far from them on B—— Street in the town of D——, Maryland. Initials, blanks, or both were often substituted for proper names in nineteenth-century fiction to enhance the illusion of reality. It is as if the author felt it necessary to delete the names for reasons of tact or legal liability. Interestingly, as with other aspects of realism, it is an *illusion* that is being enhanced, by purely artificial means. Is it likely, does it violate the principle of verisimilitude, that a thirteen-year-old boy could make such a sophisticated observation? A girl of fourteen is *the psychological coeval* of a boy of fifteen or sixteen; a thirteen-year-old boy, therefore, even one precocious in some other respects, might be three years *her emotional junior.*

Thrice a year—on Memorial, Independence, and Labor Days—the family visits Ocean City for the afternoon and evening. When Ambrose and Peter's father was their age, the excursion was made by train, as mentioned in the novel *The 42nd Parallel* by John Dos Passos.[1] Many families from the same neighborhood used to travel together, with dependent relatives and often with Negro servants; schoolfuls of children swarmed through the railway cars; everyone shared everyone else's Maryland fried chicken, Virginia ham, deviled eggs, potato salad, beaten biscuits, iced tea. Nowadays (that is, in 19—, the year of our story) the journey is made by automobile—more comfortably and quickly though without the extra fun though without the *camaraderie* of a general excursion. It's all part of the deterioration of American life, their father declares; Uncle Karl supposes that when the boys take *their* families to Ocean City for the holidays they'll fly in Autogiros. Their mother, sitting in the middle of the front seat like Magda in the second, only with her arms on the seat-back behind the men's shoulders, wouldn't want the good old days back again, the steaming trains and stuffy long dresses; on the other hand she can do without Autogiros, too, if she has to become a grandmother to fly in them.

Description of physical appearance and mannerisms is one of several standard methods of characterization used by writers of fiction. It is also important to "keep the senses operating"; when a detail from one of the five senses, say visual, is "crossed" with a detail from another, say auditory, the reader's imagination is oriented to the scene, perhaps unconsciously. This procedure may be compared to the way surveyors and navigators determine their positions by two or more compass bearings, a process known as triangulation. The brown hair on Ambrose's mother's forearms gleamed in the sun like. Though right-handed, she took her left arm from the seat-back to press the dashboard cigar lighter for Uncle Karl. When the glass bead in its handle glowed red, the lighter was ready for use. The smell of Uncle Karl's cigar smoke reminded one of. The fragrance of the ocean came strong to the picnic ground where they always stopped for lunch, two miles inland from Ocean City. Having to pause for a full hour almost within sound of the breakers was difficult for Peter and Ambrose when they were younger; even at their

1. *The 42nd Parallel* (1930), first volume in the trilogy *U.S.A.* by John Dos Passos (1896–1970).

present age it was not easy to keep their anticipation, *stimulated by the briny spume,* from turning into short temper. The Irish author James Joyce, in his unusual novel entitled *Ulysses,* now available in this country, uses the adjectives *snot-green* and *scrotum-tightening* to describe the sea.[2] Visual, auditory, tactile, olfactory, gustatory. Peter and Ambrose's father, while steering their black 1936 LaSalle sedan with one hand, could with the other remove the first cigarette from a white pack of Lucky Strikes and, more remarkably, light it with a match forefingered from its book and thumbed against the flint paper without being detached. The matchbook cover merely advertised U. S. War Bonds and Stamps. A fine metaphor, simile, or other figure of speech, in addition to its obvious "first-order" relevance to the thing it describes, will be seen upon reflection to have a second order of significance: it may be drawn from the *milieu* of the action, for example, or be particularly appropriate to the sensibility of the narrator, even hinting to the reader things of which the narrator is unaware; or it may cast further and subtler lights upon the thing it describes, sometimes ironically qualifying the more evident sense of the comparison.

To say that Ambrose's and Peter's mother was *pretty* is to accomplish nothing; the reader may acknowledge the proposition, but his imagination is not engaged. Besides, Magda was also pretty, yet in an altogether different way. Although she lived on B—— Street she had very good manners and did better than average in school. Her figure was very well developed for her age. Her right hand lay casually on the plush upholstery of the seat, very near Ambrose's left leg, on which his own hand rested. The space between their legs, between her right and his left leg, was out of the line of sight of anyone sitting on the other side of Magda, as well as anyone glancing into the rearview mirror. Uncle Karl's face resembled Peter's—rather, vice versa. Both had dark hair and eyes, short husky statures, deep voices. Magda's left hand was probably in a similar position on her left side. The boy's father is difficult to describe; no particular feature of his appearance or manner stood out. He wore glasses and was principal of a T—— County grade school. Uncle Karl was a masonry contractor.

Although Peter must have known as well as Ambrose that the latter, because of his position in the car, would be the first to see the electrical towers of the power plant at V——, the halfway point of their trip, he leaned forward and slightly toward the center of the car and pretended to be looking for them through the flat pinewoods and tuckahoe creeks along the highway. For as long as the boys could remember, "looking for the Towers" had been a feature

2. Joyce's *Ulysses,* published in Paris in 1922, was banned in the United States as "obscene" until a famous court decision of 1933 authorized its publication.

of the first half of their excursions to Ocean City, "looking for the standpipe" of the second. Though the game was childish, their mother preserved the tradition of rewarding the first to see the Towers with a candy-bar or piece of fruit. She insisted now that Magda play the game; the prize, she said, was "something hard to get nowadays." Ambrose decided not to join in; he sat far back in his seat. Magda, like Peter, leaned forward. Two sets of straps were discernible through the shoulders of her sun dress; the inside right one, a brassiere-strap, was fastened or shortened with a small safety pin. The right armpit of her dress, presumably the left as well, was damp with perspiration. The simple strategy for being first to espy the Towers, which Ambrose had understood by the age of four, was to sit on the right-hand side of the car. Whoever sat there, however, had also to put up with the worst of the sun, and so Ambrose, without mentioning the matter, chose sometimes the one and sometimes the other. Not impossibly Peter had never caught on to the trick, or thought that his brother hadn't simply because Ambrose on occasion preferred shade to a Baby Ruth or tangerine.

The shade-sun situation didn't apply to the front seat, owing to the windshield; if anything the driver got more sun, since the person on the passenger side not only was shaded below by the door and dashboard but might swing down his sunvisor all the way too.

"Is that them?" Magda asked. Ambrose's mother teased the boys for letting Magda win, insinuating that "somebody [had] a girl-friend." Peter and Ambrose's father reached a long thin arm across their mother to butt his cigarette in the dashboard ashtray, under the lighter. The prize this time for seeing the Towers first was a banana. Their mother bestowed it after chiding their father for wasting a half-smoked cigarette when everything was so scarce. Magda, to take the prize, moved her hand from so near Ambrose's that he could have touched it as though accidentally. She offered to share the prize, things like that were so hard to find; but everyone insisted it was hers alone. Ambrose's mother sang an iambic trimeter couplet from a popular song, femininely rhymed:

> "What's good is in the Army;
> What's left will never harm me." [3]

Uncle Karl tapped his cigar ash out the ventilator window; some particles were sucked by the slipstream back into the car through the rear window on the passenger side. Magda demonstrated her ability to hold a banana in one hand and peel it with her teeth. She still sat forward; Ambrose pushed his glasses back onto the bridge of his nose with his left hand, which he then negligently let fall to

3. From a popular song of World War II, "They're Either Too Young or Too Old."

the seat cushion immediately behind her. He even permitted the single hair, gold, on the second joint of his thumb to brush the fabric of her skirt. Should she have sat back at that instant, his hand would have been caught under her.

Plush upholstery prickles uncomfortably through gabardine slacks in the July sun. The function of the *beginning* of a story is to introduce the principal characters, establish their initial relationships, set the scene for the main action, expose the background of the situation if necessary, plant motifs and foreshadowings where appropriate, and initiate the first complication or whatever of the "rising action." Actually, if one imagines a story called "The Funhouse," or "Lost in the Funhouse," the details of the drive to Ocean City don't seem especially relevant. The *beginning* should recount the events between Ambrose's first sight of the funhouse early in the afternoon and his entering it with Magda and Peter in the evening. The *middle* would narrate all relevant events from the time he goes in to the time he loses his way; middles have the double and contradictory function of delaying the climax while at the same time preparing the reader for it and fetching him to it. Then the *ending* would tell what Ambrose does while he's lost, how he finally finds his way out, and what everybody makes of the experience. So far there's been no real dialogue, very little sensory detail, and nothing in the way of a *theme*. And a long time has gone by already without anything happening; it makes a person wonder. We haven't even reached Ocean City yet: we will never get out of the funhouse.

The more closely an author identifies with the narrator, literally or metaphorically, the less advisable it is, as a rule, to use the first-person narrative viewpoint. Once three years previously the young people *aforementioned* played Niggers and Masters in the backyard; when it was Ambrose's turn to be Master and theirs to be Niggers Peter had to go serve his evening papers; Ambrose was afraid to punish Magda alone, but she led him to the whitewashed Torture Chamber between the woodshed and the privy in the Slaves Quarters; there she knelt sweating among bamboo rakes and dusty Mason jars, pleadingly embraced his knees, and while bees droned in the lattice as if on an ordinary summer afternoon, purchased clemency at a surprising price set by herself. Doubtless she remembered nothing of this event; Ambrose on the other hand seemed unable to forget the least detail of his life. He even recalled how, standing beside himself with awed impersonality in the reeky heat, he'd stared the while at an empty cigar box in which Uncle Karl kept stone-cutting chisels: beneath the words *El Producto*, a laureled, loose-toga'd lady regarded the sea from a marble bench; beside her, forgotten or not yet turned to, was a five-stringed lyre. Her chin reposed on the back of her right hand; her left depended negligently from the bench-arm. The lower half of scene and lady was peeled away; the words EXAMINED BY—were inked there into the wood. Nowadays cigar boxes are made of pasteboard. Ambrose wondered what Magda would have done, Ambrose wondered what Magda would do when she sat back on his hand as he resolved she should. Be angry. Make a teasing joke of it. Give no sign at all. For a long time she leaned forward, playing cow-poker with Peter against Uncle Karl and Mother and watching for the first sign of Ocean City. At nearly the same instant, picnic ground and Ocean City standpipe hove into view; an Amoco filling station on their side of the road cost Mother and Uncle Karl fifty cows and the game; Magda bounced back, clapping her right hand on Mother's right arm; Ambrose moved clear "in the nick of time."

At this rate our hero, at this rate our protagonist will remain in the funhouse forever. Narrative ordinarily consists of alternating dramatization and summarization. One symptom of nervous tension, paradoxically, is repeated and violent yawning; neither Peter nor Magda nor Uncle Karl nor Mother reacted in this manner. Although they were no longer small children, Peter and Ambrose were each given a dollar to spend on boardwalk amusements in addition to what money of their own they'd brought along. Magda too, though she protested she had ample spending money. The boys' mother made a little scene out of distributing the bills; she pretended that her sons and Magda were small children and cautioned them not to spend the sum too quickly or in one place. Magda promised with a merry laugh and, having both hands free, took the bill with her left. Peter laughed also and pledged in a falsetto to be a good boy. His imitation of a child was not clever. The boys' father was tall and thin, balding, fair-complexioned. Assertions of that sort are not effective; the reader may acknowledge the proposition, but. We should be much farther along than we are; something has gone wrong; not much of this preliminary rambling seems relevant. Yet everyone begins in the same place; how is it that most go along without difficulty but a few lose their way?

"Stay out from under the boardwalk," Uncle Karl growled from the side of his mouth. The boys' mother pushed his shoulder *in mock annoyance*. They were all standing before Fat May the Laughing Lady who advertised the funhouse. Larger than life, Fat May mechanically shook, rocked on her heels, slapped her thighs while recorded laughter—uproarious, female—came amplified from a hidden loudspeaker. It chuckled, wheezed, wept; tried in vain to catch its breath; tittered, groaned, exploded raucous and anew. You couldn't hear it without laughing yourself, no matter how you felt. Father came back from talking to a Coast-Guardsman on duty and reported that the surf was spoiled with crude oil from tankers recently torpedoed offshore. Lumps of it, difficult to remove, made tarry tidelines on the beach and stuck on swimmers. Many bathed in the surf nevertheless and came out speckled; others paid to use a municipal pool and only sunbathed on the beach. We would do the latter. We would do the latter. We would do the latter.

Under the boardwalk, matchbook covers, grainy other things. What is the story's theme? Ambrose is ill. He perspires in the dark passages; candied apples-on-a-stick, delicious-looking, disappointing to eat. Funhouses need men's and ladies' rooms at intervals. Others perhaps have also vomited in corners and corridors; may even have had bowel movements liable to be stepped in in the dark. The word *fuck* suggests suction and/or and/or flatulence. Mother and Father; grandmothers and grandfathers on both sides; great-grandmothers and great-grandfathers on four sides, et cetera. Count a generation as thirty years: in approximately the year when Lord Baltimore was granted charter to the province of Maryland by Charles I, five hundred twelve women—English, Welsh, Bavarian, Swiss—of every class and character, received into themselves the penises the intromittent organs of five hundred twelve men, ditto, in every circumstance and posture, to conceive the five hundred twelve ancestors of the two hundred fifty-six ancestors of the et cetera et cetera et cetera et cetera et cetera et cetera et cetera et cetera of the author, of the narrator, of this story, *Lost in the Funhouse.* In alleyways, ditches, canopy beds, pinewoods, bridal suites, ship's cabins, coach-and-fours, coaches-and-four, sultry toolsheds; on the cold sand under boardwalks, littered with *El Producto* cigar butts, treasured with Lucky Strike cigarette stubs, Coca-Cola caps, gritty turds, cardboard lollipop sticks, matchbook covers warning that A Slip of the Lip Can Sink a Ship. The shluppish whisper, continuous as seawash round the globe, tidelike falls and rises with the circuit of dawn and dusk.

Magda's teeth. She *was* left-handed. Perspiration. They've gone all the way, through, Magda and Peter, they've been waiting for hours with Mother and Uncle Karl while Father searches for his lost son; they draw french-fried potatoes from a paper cup and shake their heads. They've named the children they'll one day have and bring to Ocean City on holidays. Can spermatozoa properly be thought of as male animalcules when there are no female spermatozoa? They grope through hot, dark windings, past Love's Tunnel's fearsome obstacles. Some perhaps lose their way.

Peter suggested then and there that they do the funhouse; he had been through it before, so had Magda, Ambrose hadn't and suggested, his voice cracking on account of Fat May's laughter, that they swim first. All were chuckling, couldn't help it; Ambrose's father, Ambrose's and Peter's father came up grinning like a lunatic with two boxes of syrup-coated popcorn, one for Mother, one for Magda; the men were to help themselves. Ambrose walked on Magda's right; being by nature left-handed, she carried the box in her left hand. Up front the situation was reversed.

"What are you limping for?" Magda inquired of Ambrose. He supposed in a husky tone that his foot had gone to sleep in the car. Her teeth flashed. "Pins and needles?" It was the honeysuckle on the lattice of the former privy that drew the bees. Imagine being stung there. How long is this going to take?

The adults decided to forgo the pool; but Uncle Karl insisted they change into swimsuits and do the beach. "He wants to watch the pretty girls," Peter teased, and ducked behind Magda from Uncle Karl's pretended wrath. "You've got all the pretty girls you need right here," Magda declared, and Mother said: "Now that's the gospel truth." Magda scolded Peter, who reached over her shoulder to sneak some popcorn. "Your brother and father aren't getting any." Uncle Karl wondered if they were going to have fireworks that night, what with the shortages. It wasn't the shortages, Mr. M—— replied; Ocean City had fireworks from pre-war. But it was too risky on account of the enemy submarines, some people thought.

"Don't seem like Fourth of July without fireworks," said Uncle Karl. The inverted tag in dialogue writing is still considered permissible with proper names or epithets, but sounds old-fashioned with personal pronouns. "We'll have 'em again soon enough," predicted the boys' father. Their mother declared she could do without fireworks: they reminded her too much of the real thing. Their father said all the more reason to shoot off a few now and again. Uncle Karl asked *rhetorically* who needed reminding, just look at people's hair and skin.

"The oil, yes," said Mrs. M——

Ambrose had a pain in his stomach and so didn't swim but enjoyed watching the others. He and his father burned red easily. Magda's figure was exceedingly well developed for her age. She too declined to swim, and got mad, and became angry when Peter attempted to drag her into the pool. She always swam, he insisted; what did she mean not swim? Why did a person come to Ocean City?

"Maybe I want to lay here with Ambrose," Magda teased.

Nobody likes a pedant.

"Aha," said Mother. Peter grabbed Magda by one ankle and ordered Ambrose to grab the other. She squealed and rolled over on the beach blanket. Ambrose pretended to help hold her back. Her tan was darker than even Mother's and Peter's. "Help out, Uncle

Karl!" Peter cried. Uncle Karl went to seize the other ankle. Inside the top of her swimsuit, however, you could see the line where the sunburn ended and, when she hunched her shoulders and squealed again, one nipple's auburn edge. Mother made them behave themselves. "*You* should certainly know," she said to Uncle Karl. Archly. "That when a lady says she doesn't feel like swimming, a gentleman doesn't ask questions." Uncle Karl said excuse *him;* Mother winked at Magda; Ambrose blushed; stupid Peter kept saying "Phooey on *feel like!*" and tugging at Magda's ankle; then even he got the point, and cannonballed with a holler into the pool.

"I swear," Magda said, in mock *in feigned* exasperation.

The diving would make a suitable literary symbol. To go off the high-board you had to wait in a line along the poolside and up the ladder. Fellows tickled girls and goosed one another and shouted to the ones at the top to hurry up, or razzed them for bellyfloppers. Once on the springboard some took a great while posing or clowning or deciding on a dive or getting up their nerve; others ran right off. Especially among the younger fellows the idea was to strike the funniest pose or do the craziest stunt as you fell, a thing that got harder to do as you kept on and kept on. But whether you hollered *Geronimo!* or *Sieg heil!*,[4] held your nose or "rode a bicycle," pretended to be shot or did a perfect jacknife or changed your mind halfway down and ended up with nothing, it was over in two seconds, after all that wait. Spring, pose, splash. Spring, neat-0, splash. Spring, aw fooey, splash.

The grown-ups had gone on; Ambrose wanted to converse with Magda; she was remarkably well developed for her age; it was said that that came from rubbing with a turkish towel, and there were other theories. Ambrose could think of nothing to say except how good a diver Peter was, who was showing off for her benefit. You could pretty well tell by looking at their bathing suits and arm muscles how far along the different fellows were. Ambrose was glad he hadn't gone in swimming, the cold water shrank you up so. Magda pretended to be uninterested in the diving; she probably weighed as much as he did. If you knew your way around in the funhouse like your own bedroom, you could wait until a girl came along and then slip away without ever getting caught, even if her boyfriend was right with her. She'd think *he* did it! It would be better to be the boyfriend, and act outraged, and tear the funhouse apart.

Not act; *be.*

"He's a master diver," Ambrose said. In feigned admiration. "You

4. "Geronimo" was the battle-cry of U.S. paratroopers in World War II (after the name of the Indian chief); "Sieg heil!" (hail to victory), the Nazi salute.

really have to slave away at it to get that good." What would it matter anyhow if he asked her right out whether she remembered, even teased her with it as Peter would have?

There's no point in going farther; this isn't getting anybody anywhere; they haven't even come to the funhouse yet. Ambrose is off the track, in some new or old part of the place that's not supposed to be used; he strayed into it by some one-in-a-million chance, like the time the roller-coaster car left the tracks in the nineteen-teens against all the laws of physics and sailed over the boardwalk in the dark. And they can't locate him because they don't know where to look. Even the designer and operator have forgotten this other part, that winds around on itself like a whelk shell. That winds around the right part like the snakes on Mercury's caduceus.[5] Some people, perhaps, don't "hit their stride" until their twenties, when the growing-up business is over and women appreciate other things besides wisecracks and teasing and strutting. Peter didn't have one-tenth the imagination *he* had, not one-tenth. Peter did this naming-their-children thing as a joke, making up names like Aloysius and Murgatroyd, but Ambrose knew *exactly* how it would feel to be married and have children of your own, and be a loving husband and father, and go comfortably to work in the mornings and to bed with your wife at night, and wake up with her there. With a breeze coming through the sash and birds and mockingbirds singing in the Chinese-cigar trees. His eyes watered, there aren't enough ways to say that. He would be quite famous in his line of work. Whether Magda was his wife or not, one evening when he was wise-lined and gray at the temples he'd smile gravely, at a fashionable dinner party, and remind her of his youthful passion. The time they went with his family to Ocean City; the *erotic fantasies* he used to have about her. How long ago it seemed, and childish! Yet tender, too, *n'est-ce pas?* [6] Would she have imagined that the world-famous whatever remembered how many strings were on the lyre on the bench beside the girl on the label of the cigar box he'd stared at in the toolshed at age ten while she, age eleven. Even then he had felt *wise beyond his years;* he'd stroked her hair and said in his deepest voice and correctest English, as to a dear child: "I shall never forget this moment."

But though he had breathed heavily, groaned as if ecstatic, what he'd really felt throughout was an odd detachment, as though someone else were Master. Strive as he might to be transported, he heard his mind take notes upon the scene: *This is what they call* passion. *I am experiencing it.* Many of the digger machines were

5. Winged staff carried by Hermes, with two serpents twined around it; today an emblem of the medical profession.
6. "Don't you agree?" An expression inviting assent.

out of order in the penny arcades and could not be repaired or replaced for the duration. Moreover the prizes, made now in USA, were less interesting than formerly, pasteboard items for the most part, and some of the machines wouldn't work on white pennies.[7] The gypsy fortune-teller machine might have provided a foreshadowing of the climax of this story if Ambrose had operated it. It was even dilapidateder than most: the silver coating was worn off the brown metal handles, the glass windows around the dummy were cracked and taped, her kerchiefs and silks long-faded. If a man lived by himself, he could take a department-store mannequin with flexible joints and modify her in certain ways. *However:* by the time he was that old he'd have a real woman. There was a machine that stamped your name around a white-metal coin with a star in the middle: A——. His son would be the second, and when the lad reached thirteen or so he would put a strong arm around his shoulder and tell him calmly: "It is perfectly normal. We have all been through it. It will not last forever." Nobody knew how to be what they were right. He'd smoke a pipe, teach his son how to fish and softcrab, assure him he needn't worry about himself. Magda would certainly give, Magda would certainly yield a great deal of milk, although guilty of occasional solecisms. It don't taste so bad. Suppose the lights came on now!

The day wore on. You think you're yourself, but there are other persons in you. Ambrose gets hard when Ambrose doesn't want to, *and obversely.* Ambrose watches them disagree; Ambrose watches him watch. In the funhouse mirror-room you can't see yourself go on forever, because no matter how you stand, your head gets in the way. Even if you had a glass periscope, the image of your eye would cover up the thing you really wanted to see. The police will come; there'll be a story in the papers. That must be where it happened. Unless he can find a surprise exit, an unofficial backdoor or escape hatch opening on an alley, say, and then stroll up to the family in front of the funhouse and ask where everybody's been; *he's* been out of the place for ages. That's just where it happened, in that last lighted room: Peter and Magda found the right exit; he found one that you weren't supposed to find and strayed off into the works somewhere. In a perfect funhouse you'd be able to go only one way, like the divers off the high-board; getting lost would be impossible; the doors and halls would work like minnow traps or the valves in veins.

On account of German U-boats, Ocean City was "browned out": streetlights were shaded on the seaward side; shop-windows and boardwalk amusement places were kept dim, not to silhouette

7. Wartime one-cent pieces made of white alloy rather than copper.

tankers and Liberty-ships for torpedoing. In a short story about
Ocean City, Maryland, during World War II, the author could make
use of the image of sailors on leave in the penny arcades and shooting galleries, sighting through the crosshairs of toy machine guns at
swastika'd subs, while out in the black Atlantic a U-boat skipper
squints through his periscope at real ships outlined by the glow of
penny arcades. After dinner the family strolled back to the amusement end of the boardwalk. The boys' father had burnt red as
always and was masked with Noxema, a minstrel in reverse. The
grown-ups stood at the end of the boardwalk where the Hurricane
of '33 had cut an inlet from the ocean to Assawoman Bay.

"Pronounced with a long *o*," Uncle Karl reminded Magda with a
wink. His shirt sleeves were rolled up; Mother punched his brown
biceps with the arrowed heart on it and said his mind was naughty.
Fat May's laugh came suddenly from the funhouse, as if she'd just
got the joke; the family laughed too at the coincidence. Ambrose
went under the boardwalk to search for out-of-town matchbook
covers with the aid of his pocket flashlight; he looked out from the
edge of the North American continent and wondered how far their
laughter carried over the water. Spies in rubber rafts; survivors in
lifeboats. If the joke had been beyond his understanding, he could
have said: *"The laughter was over his head."* And let the reader see
the serious wordplay on second reading.

He turned the flashlight on and then off at once even before the
woman whooped. He sprang away, heart athud, dropping the light.
What had the man grunted? Perspiration drenched and chilled him
by the time he scrambled up to the family. "See anything?" his father asked. His voice wouldn't come; he shrugged and violently
brushed sand from his pants legs.

"Let's ride the old flying horses!" Magda cried. I'll never be an
author. It's been forever already, everybody's gone home, Ocean
City's deserted, the ghost-crabs are tickling across the beach and
down the littered cold streets. And the empty halls of clapboard
hotels and abandoned funhouses. A tidal wave; an enemy air raid; a
monster-crab swelling like an island from the sea. *The inhabitants
fled in terror.* Magda clung to his trouser leg; he alone knew the
maze's secret. "He gave his life that we might live," said Uncle
Karl with a scowl of pain, as he. The fellow's hands had been tat-
tooed; the woman's legs, the woman's fat white legs had. *An astonishing coincidence.* He yearned to tell Peter. He wanted to
throw up for excitement. They hadn't even chased him. He wished
he were dead.

One possible ending would be to have Ambrose come across
another lost person in the dark. They'd match their wits together
against the funhouse, struggle like Ulysses past obstacle after ob-

stacle, help and encourage each other. Or a girl. By the time they found the exit they'd be closest friends, sweethearts if it were a girl; they'd know each other's inmost souls, be bound together *by the cement of shared adventure;* then they'd emerge into the light and it would turn out that his friend was a Negro. A blind girl. President Roosevelt's son. Ambrose's former archenemy.

Shortly after the mirror room he'd groped along a musty corridor, his heart already misgiving him at the absence of phosphorescent arrows and other signs. He'd found a crack of light—not a door, it turned out, but a seam between the plyboard wall panels—and squinting up to it, espied a small old man, *in appearance not unlike* the photographs at home of Ambrose's late grandfather, nodding upon a stool beneath a bare, speckled bulb. A crude panel of toggle- and knife-switches hung beside the open fuse box near his head; elsewhere in the little room were wooden levers and ropes belayed to boat cleats. At the time, Ambrose wasn't lost enough to rap or call; later he couldn't find that crack. Now it seemed to him that he'd possibly dozed off for a few minutes somewhere along the way; certainly he was exhausted from the afternoon's sunshine and the evening's problems; he couldn't be sure he hadn't dreamed part or all of the sight. Had an old black wall fan droned like bees and shimmied two flypaper streamers? Had the funhouse operator— gentle, somewhat sad and tired-appearing, in expression not unlike the photographs at home of Ambrose's late Uncle Konrad—murmured in his sleep? Is there really such a person as Ambrose, or is he a figment of the author's imagination? Was it Assawoman Bay or Sinepuxent? Are there other errors of fact in this fiction? Was there another sound besides the little slap slap of thigh on ham, like water sucking at the chine-boards of a skiff?

When you're lost, the smartest thing to do is stay put till you're found, hollering if necessary. But to holler guarantees humiliation as well as rescue; keeping silent permits some saving of face—you can act surprised at the fuss when your rescuers find you and swear you weren't lost, if they do. What's more you might find your own way yet, *however belatedly.*

"Don't tell me your foot's still asleep!" Magda exclaimed as the three young people walked from the inlet to the area set aside for ferris wheels, carrousels, and other carnival rides, they having decided in favor of the vast and ancient merry-go-round instead of the funhouse. What a sentence, everything was wrong from the outset. People don't know what to make of him, he doesn't know what to make of himself, he's only thirteen, *athletically and socially inept,* not astonishingly bright, but there are antennae; he has . . . some sort of receivers in his head; things speak to him, he understands more than he should, the world winks at him through its objects, grabs grinning at his coat. Everybody else is in on some secret he doesn't know; they've forgotten to tell him. Through simple *procrastination* his mother put off his baptism until this year. Everyone else had it done as a baby; he'd assumed the same of himself, as had his mother, so she claimed, until it was time for him to join Grace Methodist-Protestant and the oversight came out. He was mortified, but pitched sleepless through his private catechizing, intimidated by the ancient mysteries, a thirteen year old would never say that, resolved to experience conversion like St. Augustine. When the water touched his brow and Adam's sin left him, he contrived by a strain like defecation to bring tears into his eyes—but felt nothing. There was some simple, radical difference about him; he hoped it was genius, feared it was madness, devoted himself to amiability and inconspicuousness. Alone on the seawall near his house he was seized by the terrifying transports he'd thought to find in toolshed, in Communion-cup. The grass was alive! The town, the river, himself, were not imaginary; time roared in his ears like wind; the world was *going on!* This part ought to be dramatized. The Irish author James Joyce once wrote. Ambrose M—— is going to scream.

There is no *texture of rendered sensory detail*, for one thing. The faded distorting mirrors beside Fat May; the impossibility of choosing a mount when one had but a single ride on the great carrousel; the *vertigo attendant on his recognition* that Ocean City was worn out, the place of fathers and grandfathers, straw-boatered men and parasoled ladies survived by their amusements. Money spent, the three paused at Peter's insistence beside Fat May to watch the girls get their skirts blown up. The object was to tease Magda, who said: "I swear, Peter M——, you've got a one-track mind! Amby and me aren't *interested* in such things." In the tumbling-barrel, too, just inside the Devil's-mouth entrance to the funhouse, the girls were upended and their boyfriends and others could see up their dresses if they cared to. Which was the whole point, Ambrose realized. Of the entire funhouse! If you looked around, you noticed that almost all the people on the boardwalk were paired off into couples except the small children; in a way, that was the whole point of Ocean City! If you had X-ray eyes and could see everything going on at that instant under the boardwalk and in all the hotel rooms and cars and alleyways, you'd realize that all that normally *showed*, like restaurants and dance halls and clothing and test-your-strength machines, was merely preparation and intermission. Fat May screamed.

Because he watched the goings-on from the corner of his eye, it was Ambrose who spied the half-dollar on the boardwalk near the tumbling-barrel. Losers weepers. The first time he'd heard some people moving through a corridor not far away, just after he'd lost sight of the crack of light, he'd decided not to call to them, for fear they'd guess he was scared and poke fun; it sounded like roughnecks; he'd hoped they'd come by and he could follow in the dark without their knowing. Another time he'd heard just one person, unless he imagined it, bumping along as if on the other side of the plywood; perhaps Peter coming back for him, or Father, or Magda lost too. Or the owner and operator of the funhouse. He'd called out once, as though merrily: "Anybody know where the heck we are?" But the query was too stiff, his voice cracked, when the sounds stopped he was terrified: maybe it was a queer who waited for fellows to get lost, or a longhaired filthy monster that lived in some cranny of the funhouse. He stood rigid for hours it seemed like, scarcely respiring. His future was shockingly clear, in outline. He tried holding his breath to the point of unconsciousness. There ought to be a button you could push to end your life absolutely without pain; disappear in a flick, like turning out a light. He would push it instantly! He despised Uncle Karl. But he despised his father too, for not being what he was supposed to be. Perhaps his father hated *his* father, and so on, and his son would hate him, and so on. Instantly!

Naturally he didn't have nerve enough to ask Magda to go through the funhouse with him. With incredible nerve and to everyone's surprise he invited Magda, quietly and politely, to go through the funhouse with him. "I warn you, I've never been through it before," he added, *laughing easily;* "but I reckon we can manage somehow. The important thing to remember, after all, is that it's meant to be a *fun*house; that is, a place of amusement. If people really got lost or injured or too badly frightened in it, the owner'd go out of business. There'd even be lawsuits. No character in a work of fiction can make a speech this long without interruption or acknowledgment from the other characters."

Mother teased Uncle Karl: "Three's a crowd, I always heard." But actually Ambrose was relieved that Peter now had a quarter too. Nothing was what it looked like. Every instant, under the surface of the Atlantic Ocean, millions of living animals devoured one another. Pilots were falling in flames over Europe; women were being forcibly raped in the South Pacific. His father should have taken him aside and said: "There is a simple secret to getting through the funhouse, as simple as being first to see the Towers. Here it is. Peter does not know it; neither does your Uncle Karl. You and I are different. Not surprisingly, you've often wished you weren't. Don't think I haven't noticed how unhappy your childhood has been! But you'll understand, when I tell you, why it had to be kept secret until now. And you won't regret not being like your brother and your uncle. *On the contrary!*" If you knew all the stories behind all the people on the boardwalk, you'd see that *nothing* was what it looked like. Husbands and wives often hated each other; parents didn't necessarily love their children; et cetera. A child took things for granted because he had nothing to compare his life to and everybody acted as if things were as they should be. Therefore each saw himself as the hero of the story, when the truth might turn out to be that he's the villain, or the coward. And there wasn't one thing you could do about it!

Hunchbacks, fat ladies, fools—that no one chose what he was was unbearable. In the movies he'd meet a beautiful young girl in the funhouse; they'd have hairs-breadth escapes from real dangers; he'd do and say the right things; she also; in the end they'd be lovers; their dialogue lines would match up; he'd be perfectly at ease; she'd not only like him well enough, she'd think he was *marvelous;* she'd lie awake thinking about *him,* instead of vice versa— the way *his* face looked in different lights and how he stood and exactly what he'd said—and yet that would be only one small episode in his wonderful life, among many many others. Not a *turning point* at all. What had happened in the toolshed was nothing. He hated, he loathed his parents! One reason for not writing a lost-in-the-funhouse story is that either everybody's felt what Ambrose feels, in which case it goes without saying, or else no normal person feels such things, in which case Ambrose is a freak. "Is anything more tiresome, in fiction, than the problems of sensitive adolescents?" And it's all too long and rambling, as if the author. For all a person knows the first time through, the end could be just around any corner; perhaps, *not impossibly* it's been within reach any number of times. On the other hand he may be scarcely past the start, with everything yet to get through, an intolerable idea.

Fill in: His father's raised eyebrows when he announced his decision to do the funhouse with Magda. Ambrose understands now, but didn't then, that his father was wondering whether he knew what the funhouse was *for*—especially since he didn't object, as he should have, when Peter decided to come along too. The ticket-woman, witchlike, mortifying him when inadvertently he gave her his name-coin instead of the half-dollar, then unkindly calling Magda's attention to the birthmark on his temple: "Watch out for him, girlie, he's a marked man!" She wasn't even cruel, he understood, only vulgar and insensitive. Somewhere in the world there was a young woman with such splendid understanding that she'd see him entire, like a poem or story, and find his words so valuable after all that when he confessed his apprehensions she would explain why they were in fact the very things that made him precious to her . . . and to Western Civilization! There was no such girl, the simple truth being. Violent yawns as they approached the mouth. Whispered advice from an old-timer on a bench near the barrel: "Go crabwise and ye'll get an eyeful without upsetting!" Composure vanished at the first pitch: Peter hollered joyously, Magda tumbled, shrieked, clutched her skirt; Ambrose scrambled crabwise, tight-lipped with terror, was soon out, watched his dropped name-coin slide among the couples. Shamefaced he saw that to get through expeditiously was not the point; Peter feigned assistance in order to trip Magda up, shouted "I see Christmas!" when her legs went flying. The old man, his latest betrayer, cackled approval. A dim hall then of black-thread cobwebs and recorded gibber: he took Magda's elbow to steady her against revolving discs set in the slanted floor to throw your feet out from under, and explained to her in a calm, deep voice his theory that each phase of the funhouse was triggered either automatically, by a series of photoelectric devices, or else manually by operators stationed at peepholes. But he lost his voice thrice as the discs unbalanced him; Magda was anyhow squealing; but at one point she clutched him about the waist to keep from falling, and her right cheek pressed for a moment against his belt-buckle. Heroically he drew her up, it was his chance to clutch her close as if for support and say: "I love you." He even put an arm lightly about the small of her back before a sailor-and-girl pitched into them from behind, sorely treading his left big toe and knocking Magda asprawl with them. The sailor's girl was a string-haired hussy with a loud laugh and light blue drawers; Ambrose realized that he wouldn't have said "I love you" anyhow, and was smitten with self-contempt. How much better it would be to be that common sailor! A wiry little Seaman 3rd, the fellow squeezed a girl to each side and stumbled hilarious into the mirror room, closer to Magda in thirty seconds than Ambrose had got in thirteen years. She giggled at something the fellow said to Peter; she drew her hair from her eyes with a movement so womanly it struck Ambrose's heart; Peter's smacking her backside then seemed particularly coarse. But Magda made a pleased indignant face and cried, "All right for *you*, mister!" and pursued Peter into the maze without a backward glance. The sailor followed after, leisurely, drawing his girl against his hip; Ambrose understood not only that they were all so relieved to be rid of his burdensome company that they didn't even notice his absence, but that he himself shared their relief. Stepping from the treacherous passage at last into the mirror-maze, he saw once again, more clearly than ever, how readily he deceived himself into supposing he was a person. He even foresaw, wincing at his dreadful self-knowledge, that he would repeat the deception, at ever-rarer intervals, all his wretched life, so fearful were the alternatives. Fame, madness, suicide; perhaps all three. It's not believable that so young a boy could articulate that reflection, and in fiction the merely true must always yield to the plausible. Moreover, the symbolism is in places heavy-footed. Yet Ambrose M—— understood, as few adults do, that the famous loneliness of the great was no popular myth but a general truth—furthermore, that it was as much cause as effect.

All the preceding except the last few sentences is exposition that should've been done earlier or interspersed with the present action instead of lumped together. No reader would put up with so much with such *prolixity*. It's interesting that Ambrose's father, though presumably an intelligent man (as indicated by his role as grade-school principal), neither encouraged nor discouraged his sons at all in any way—as if he either didn't care about them or cared all right but didn't know how to act. If this fact should contribute to one of them's becoming a celebrated but wretchedly unhappy scientist, was it a good thing or not? He too might someday face the question; it would be useful to know whether it had tortured his father for years, for example, or never once crossed his mind.

In the maze two important things happened. First, our hero found a name-coin someone else had lost or discarded: *AMBROSE*, suggestive of the famous lightship and of his late grandfather's favorite dessert, which his mother used to prepare on special occasions out of coconut, oranges, grapes, and what else. Second, as he wondered at the endless replication of his image in the mirrors, second, as he *lost himself in the reflection* that the necessity for an observer makes perfect observation impossible, better make him eighteen at least, yet that would render other things unlikely, he heard Peter and Magda chuckling somewhere together in the maze. "Here!" "No, here!" they shouted to each other; Peter said, "Where's Amby?" Magda murmured. "Amb?" Peter called. In a pleased, friendly voice. He didn't reply. The truth was, his brother was a *happy-go-lucky youngster* who'd've been better off with a regular brother of his own, but who seldom complained of his lot and was generally cordial. Ambrose's throat ached; there aren't enough different ways to say that. He stood quietly while the two young people giggled and thumped through the glittering maze, hurrah'd their discovery of its exit, cried out in joyful alarm at what next beset them. Then he set his mouth and followed after, as he supposed, took a wrong turn, strayed into the pass *wherein he lingers yet*.

The action of conventional dramatic narrative may be represented by a diagram called Freitag's Triangle: [8]

8. Gustav Freytag (1816–95), German novelist and critic who analyzed the conventional divisions of dramatic plot in his *Technik des Dramas* (1863).

or more accurately by a variant of that diagram:

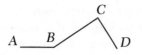

in which *AB* represents the exposition, *B* the introduction of conflict, *BC* the "rising action," complication, or development of the conflict, *C* the climax, or turn of the action, *CD* the dénouement, or resolution of the conflict. While there is no reason to regard this pattern as an absolute necessity, like many other conventions it became conventional because great numbers of people over many years learned by trial and error that it was effective; one ought not to forsake it, therefore, unless one wishes to forsake as well the effect of drama or has clear cause to feel that deliberate violation of the "normal" pattern can better can better effect that effect. This can't go on much longer; it can go on forever. He died telling stories to himself in the dark; years later, when that vast unsuspected area of the funhouse came to light, the first expedition found his skeleton in one of its labyrinthine corridors and mistook it for part of the entertainment. He died of starvation telling himself stories in the dark; but unbeknownst unbeknownst to him, an assistant operator of the funhouse, happening to overhear him, crouched just behind the plyboard partition and wrote down his every word. The operator's daughter, an exquisite young woman with a figure unusually well developed for her age, crouched just behind the partition and transcribed his every word. Though she had never laid eyes on him, she recognized that here was one of Western Culture's truly great imaginations, the eloquence of whose suffering would be an inspiration to unnumbered. And her heart was torn between her love for the misfortunate young man (yes, she loved him, though she had never laid though she knew him only—but how well!—through his words, and the deep, calm voice in which he spoke them) between her love et cetera and her womanly intuition that only in suffering and isolation could he give voice et cetera. Lone dark dying. Quietly she kissed the rough plyboard, and a tear fell upon the page. Where she had written in shorthand *Where she had written in shorthand* Where she had written in shorthand *Where she* et cetera. A long time ago we should haved passed the apex of Freitag's Triangle and made brief work of the *dénouement;*

the plot doesn't rise by meaningful steps but winds upon itself, digresses, retreats, hesitates, sighs, collapses, expires. The climax of the story must be its protagonist's discovery of a way to get through the funhouse. But he has found none, may have ceased to search.

What relevance does the war have to the story? Should there be fireworks outside or not?

Ambrose wandered, languished, dozed. Now and then he fell into his habit of rehearsing to himself the unadventurous story of his life, narrated from the third-person point of view, from his earliest memory parenthesis of maple leaves stirring in the summer breath of tidewater Maryland end of parenthesis to the present moment. Its principal events, on this telling, would appear to have been *A, B, C,* and *D.*

He imagined himself years hence, successful, married, at ease in the world, the trials of his adolescence far behind him. He has come to the seashore with his family for the holiday: how Ocean City has changed! But at one seldom at one ill-frequented end of the boardwalk a few derelict amusements survive from times gone by: the great carrousel from the turn of the century, with its monstrous griffins and mechanical concert band; the roller coaster rumored since 1916 to have been condemned; the mechanical shooting gallery in which only the image of our enemies changed. His own son laughs with Fat May and wants to know what a funhouse is; Ambrose hugs the sturdy lad close and smiles around his pipestem at his wife.

The family's going home. Mother sits between Father and Uncle Karl, who teases him good-naturedly who chuckles over the fact that the comrade with whom he'd fought his way shoulder to shoulder through the funhouse had turned out to be a blind Negro girl—to their mutual discomfort, as they'd opened their souls. But such are the walls of custom, which even. Whose arm is where? How must it feel. He dreams of a funhouse vaster by far than any yet constructed; but by then they may be out of fashion, like steamboats and excursion trains. Already quaint and seedy: the draperied ladies on the frieze of the carrousel are his father's father's moon-cheeked dreams; if he thinks of it more he will vomit his apple-on-a-stick.

He wonders: will he become a regular person? Something has gone wrong; his vaccination didn't take; at the Boy-Scout initiation campfire he only pretended to be deeply moved, as he pretends to this hour that it is not so bad after all in the funhouse, and that he has a little limp. How long will it last? He envisions a truly astonishing funhouse, incredibly complex yet utterly controlled from a great central switchboard like the console of a pipe organ. Nobody had enough imagination. He could design such a place himself, wiring and all, and he's only thirteen years old. He would be its operator: panel lights would show what was up in every cranny of its cunning of its multifarious vastness; a switch-flick would ease this fellow's way, complicate that's, to balance things out; if anyone seemed lost or frightened, all the operator had to do was.

He wishes he had never entered the funhouse. But he has. Then he wishes he were dead. But he's not. Therefore he will construct funhouses for others and be their secret operator—though he would rather be among the lovers for whom funhouses are designed.

From *Lost in the Funhouse: Fiction for print,*
tape, live voice (1968)

·Donald Barthelme·

THE INDIAN UPRISING

We defended the city as best we could. The arrows of the Comanches came in clouds. The war clubs of the Comanches clattered on the soft, yellow pavements. There were earthworks along the Boulevard Mark Clark [1] and the hedges had been laced with sparkling wire. People were trying to understand. I spoke to Sylvia. "Do you think this is a good life?" The table held apples, books, long-playing records. She looked up. "No."

Patrols of paras [2] and volunteers with armbands guarded the tall, flat buildings. We interrogated the captured Comanche. Two of us forced his head back while another poured water into his nostrils. His body jerked, he choked and wept. Not believing a hurried, careless, and exaggerated report of the number of casualties in the outer districts where trees, lamps, swans had been reduced to clear fields of fire we issued entrenching tools to those who seemed trustworthy and turned the heavy-weapons companies so that we could not be surprised from that direction. And I sat there getting drunker and drunker and more in love and more in love. We talked.

"Do you know Fauré's 'Dolly'?"

"Would that be Gabriel Fauré?" [3]

"It would."

"Then I know it," she said. "May I say that I play it at certain times, when I am sad, or happy, although it requires four hands."

1. The streets and boulevards in the story are named for famous military leaders of World War II such as Gen. Mark Clark, Adm. Chester W. Nimitz, Gen. George C. Marshall, Gen. Jonathan M. Wainwright, Gen. George S. Patton.
2. Paratroops.
3. French composer (1845–1924). His *Dolly Suite* (Op. 56) is a charming and sentimental tribute to childhood.

"How is that managed?"

"I accelerate," she said, "ignoring the time signature."

And when they shot the scene in the bed I wondered how you felt under the eyes of the cameramen, grips, juicers, men in the mixing booth: excited? stimulated? And when they shot the scene in the shower I sanded a hollow-core door working carefully against the illustrations in texts and whispered instructions from one who had already solved the problem. I had made after all other tables, one while living with Nancy, one while living with Alice, one while living with Eunice, one while living with Marianne.

Red men in waves like people scattering in a square startled by something tragic or a sudden, loud noise accumulated against the barricades we had made of window dummies, silk, thoughtfully planned job descriptions (including scales for the orderly progress of other colors), wine in demijohns, and robes. I analyzed the composition of the barricade nearest me and found two ashtrays, ceramic, one dark brown and one dark brown with an orange blur at the lip; a tin frying pan; two-litre bottles of red wine; three-quarter-litre bottles of Black & White, aquavit, cognac, vodka, gin, Fad #6 sherry; a hollow-core door in birch veneer on black wrought-iron legs; a blanket, red-orange with faint blue stripes; a red pillow and a blue pillow; a woven straw wastebasket; two glass jars for flowers; corkscrews and can openers; two plates and two cups, ceramic, dark brown; a yellow-and-purple poster; a Yugoslavian carved flute, wood, dark brown; and other items. I decided I knew nothing.

The hospitals dusted wounds with powders the worth of which was not quite established, other supplies having been exhausted early in the first day. I decided I knew nothing. Friends put me in touch with a Miss R., a teacher, unorthodox they said, excellent they said, successful with difficult cases, steel shutters on the windows made the house safe. I had just learned via an International Distress Coupon that Jane had been beaten up by a dwarf in a bar on Tenerife but Miss R. did not allow me to speak of it. "You know nothing," she said, "you feel nothing, you are locked in a most savage and terrible ignorance, I despise you, my boy, *mon cher*, my heart. You may attend but you must not attend now, you must attend later, a day or a week or an hour, you are making me ill. . . ." I nonevaluated these remarks as Korzybski [4] instructed. But it was difficult. Then they pulled back in a feint near the river and we rushed into that sector with a reinforced battalion hastily formed among the Zouaves [5] and cabdrivers. This unit was crushed in the

4. Alfred H. Korzybski (1879–1950), Polish-American scientist who developed a system called General Semantics.
5. Members of a French infantry unit composed formerly of Algerian recruits; they are noted for their colorful uniforms and precision drilling.

afternoon of a day that began with spoons and letters in hallways and under windows where men tasted the history of the heart, cone-shaped muscular organ that maintains *circulation of the blood.*

But it is you I want now, here in the middle of this Uprising, with the streets yellow and threatening, short, ugly lances with fur at the throat and inexplicable shell money lying in the grass. It is when I am with you that I am happiest, and it is for you that I am making this hollow-core door table with black wrought-iron legs. I held Sylvia by her bear-claw necklace. "Call off your braves," I said. "We have many years left to live." There was a sort of muck running in the gutters, yellowish, filthy stream suggesting excrement, or nervousness, a city that does not know what it has done to deserve baldness, errors, infidelity. "With luck you will survive until matins," Sylvia said. She ran off down the Rue Chester Nimitz, uttering shrill cries.

Then it was learned that they had infiltrated our ghetto and that the people of the ghetto instead of resisting had joined the smooth, well-coördinated attack with zipguns, telegrams, lockets, causing that portion of the line held by the I.R.A.[6] to swell and collapse. We sent more heroin into the ghetto, and hyacinths, ordering another hundred thousand of the pale, delicate flowers. On the map we considered the situation with its strung-out inhabitants and merely personal emotions. Our parts were blue and their parts were green. I showed the blue-and-green map to Sylvia. "Your parts are green," I said. "You gave me heroin first a year ago," [7] Sylvia said. She ran off down George C. Marshall Allée, uttering shrill cries. Miss R. pushed me into a large room painted white (jolting and dancing in the soft light, and I was excited! and there were people watching!) in which there were two chairs. I sat in one chair and Miss R. sat in the other. She wore a blue dress containing a red figure. There was nothing exceptional about her. I was disappointed by her plainness, by the bareness of the room, by the absence of books.

The girls of my quarter wore long blue mufflers that reached to their knees. Sometimes the girls hid Comanches in their rooms, the blue mufflers together in a room creating a great blue fog. Block opened the door. He was carrying weapons, flowers, loaves of bread. And he was friendly, kind, enthusiastic, so I related a little of the history of torture, reviewing the technical literature quoting the best modern sources, French, German, and American, and pointing out the flies which had gathered in anticipation of some new, cool color.

"What is the situation?" I asked.

6. Irish Republican Army, dedicated to the overthrow of British influence.
7. See T. S. Eliot's *The Waste Land*, 1. 35: "You gave me hyacinths first a year ago."

"The situation is liquid," he said. "We hold the south quarter and they hold the north quarter. The rest is silence." [8]

"And Kenneth?"

"That girl is not in love with Kenneth," Block said frankly. "She is in love with his coat. When she is not wearing it she is huddling under it. Once I caught it going down the stairs by itself. I looked inside. Sylvia."

Once I caught Kenneth's coat going down the stairs by itself but the coat was a trap and inside a Comanche who made a thrust with his short, ugly knife at my leg which buckled and tossed me over the balustrade through a window and into another situation. Not believing that your body brilliant as it was and your fat, liquid spirit distinguished and angry as it was were stable quantities to which one could return on wires more than once, twice, or another number of times I said: "See the table?"

In Skinny Wainwright Square the forces of green and blue swayed and struggled. The referees ran out on the field trailing chains. And then the blue part would be enlarged, the green diminished. Miss R. began to speak. "A former king of Spain, a Bonaparte, lived for a time in Bordentown, New Jersey. But that's no good." She paused. "The ardor aroused in men by the beauty of women can only be satisfied by God. That is *very* good (it is Valéry) [9] but it is not what I have to teach you, goat, muck, filth, heart of my heart." I showed the table to Nancy. "See the table?" She stuck out her tongue red as a cardinal's hat. "I made such a table once," Block said frankly. "People all over America have made such tables. I doubt very much whether one can enter an American home without finding at least one such table, or traces of its having been there, such as faded places in the carpet." And afterward in the garden the men of the 7th Cavalry played Gabrieli, Albinoni, Marcello, Vivaldi, Boccherini. I saw Sylvia. She wore a yellow ribbon, under a long blue muffler.[10] "Which side are you on," I cried, "after all?"

"The only form of discourse of which I approve," Miss R. said in her dry, tense voice, "is the litany. I believe our masters and teachers as well as plain citizens should confine themselves to what can safely be said. Thus when I hear the words *pewter, snake, tea, Fad #6 sherry, serviette, fenestration, crown, blue* coming from the mouth of some public official, or some raw youth, I am not disappointed. Vertical organization is also possible," Miss R. said, "as in

8. The last words of Hamlet's dying speech (*Hamlet* V.ii. 360).
9. Paul Valéry (1871–1945), French poet and aesthetician.
10. In contrast to the works of the classical composers ("Gabrieli . . . Boccherini"), "She Wore a Yellow Ribbon" is appropriate for the 7th Cavalry. It was the title song (based on an American folk ballad) of a 1949 Western starring John Wayne and directed by John Ford. The film tells of a U.S. Cavalry troop crossing Indian Territory in 1876, shortly after the Custer massacre.

pewter
snake
tea
Fad #6 sherry
serviette
fenestration
crown
blue.

I run to liquids and colors," she said, "but you, you may run to something else, my virgin, my darling, my thistle, my poppet, my own. Young people," Miss R. said, "run to more and more unpleasant combinations as they sense the nature of our society. Some people," Miss R. said, "run to conceits or wisdom but I hold to the hard, brown, nutlike word. I might point out that there is enough aesthetic excitement here to satisfy anyone but a damned fool." I sat in solemn silence.

Fire arrows lit my way to the post office in Patton Place where members of the Abraham Lincoln Brigade [11] offered their last, exhausted letters, postcards, calendars. I opened a letter but inside was a Comanche flint arrowhead played by Frank Wedekind in an elegant gold chain and congratulations. Your earring rattled against my spectacles when I leaned forward to touch the soft, ruined place where the hearing aid had been. "Pack it in! Pack it in!" I urged, but the men in charge of the Uprising refused to listen to reason or to understand that it was real and that our water supply had evaporated and that our credit was no longer what it had been, once.

We attached wires to the testicles of the captured Comanche. And I sat there getting drunker and drunker and more in love and more in love. When we threw the switch he spoke. His name, he said, was Gustave Aschenbach.[12] He was born at L——, a country town in the province of Silesia. He was the son of an upper official in the judicature, and his forebears had all been officers, judges, departmental functionaries. . . . And you can never touch a girl in the same way more than once, twice, or another number of times however much you may wish to hold, wrap, or otherwise fix her hand, or look, or some other quality, or incident, known to you previously. In Sweden the little Swedish children cheered when we managed nothing more remarkable than getting off a bus burdened with packages, bread and liver-paste and beer. We went to an old church and sat in the royal box. The organist was practicing. And then into

11. Unit of American volunteers that fought on the Republican side in the Spanish Civil War.
12. Gustave von Aschenbach, aging German writer in Thomas Mann's novella, *Death in Venice* (1912).

the graveyard next to the church. *Here lies Anna Pedersen, a good woman.* I threw a mushroom on the grave. The officer commanding the garbage dump reported by radio that the garbage had begun to move.

Jane! I heard via an International Distress Coupon that you were beaten up by a dwarf in a bar on Tenerife. That doesn't sound like you, Jane. Mostly you kick the dwarf in his little dwarf groin before he can get his teeth into your tasty and nice-looking leg, don't you, Jane? Your affair with Harold is reprehensible, you know that, don't you, Jane? Harold is married to Nancy. And there is Paula to think about (Harold's kid), and Billy (Harold's other kid). I think your values are peculiar, Jane! Strings of language extend in every direction to bind the world into a rushing, ribald whole.

And you can never return to felicities in the same way, the brilliant body, the distinguished spirit recapitulating moments that occur once, twice, or another number of times in rebellions, or water. The rolling consensus of the Comanche nation smashed our inner defenses on three sides. Block was firing a greasegun [13] from the upper floor of a building designed by Emery Roth & Sons. "See the table?" "Oh, pack it in with your bloody table!" The city officials were tied to trees. Dusky warriors padded with their forest tread into the mouth of the mayor. "Who do you want to be?" I asked Kenneth and he said he wanted to be Jean-Luc Godard [14] but later when time permitted conversations in large, lighted rooms, whispering galleries with black-and-white Spanish rugs and problematic sculpture on calm, red catafalques. The sickness of the quarrel lay thick in the bed. I touched your back, the white, raised scars.

We killed a great many in the south suddenly with helicopters and rockets but we found that those we had killed were children and more came from the north and from the east and from other places where there are children preparing to live. "Skin," Miss R. said softly in the white, yellow room. "This is the Clemency Committee. And would you remove your belt and shoelaces." I removed my belt and shoelaces and looked (rain shattering from a great height the prospects of silence and clear, neat rows of houses in the subdivisions) into their savage black eyes, paint, feathers, beads.

13. Automatic pistol or submachine gun.
14. French film director (1930–) noted for his technical improvisations.

From *Unspeakable Practices, Unnatural Acts* (1968)

·Robert Coover·

THE MAGIC POKER

I wander the island, inventing it. I make a sun for it, and trees—
pines and birch and dogwood and firs—and cause the water to lap
the pebbles of its abandoned shores. This, and more: I deposit
shadows and dampness, spin webs, and scatter ruins. Yes: ruins. A
mansion and guest cabins and boat houses and docks. Terraces, too,
and bath houses and even an observation tower. All gutted and
window-busted and autographed and shat upon. I impose a hot
midday silence, a profound and heavy stillness. But anything can
happen.

•

This small and secretive bay, here just below what was once the
caretaker's cabin and not far from the main boat house, probably
once possessed its own system of docks, built out to protect boats
from the big rocks along the shore. At least the refuse—the long
bony planks of gray lumber heaped up at one end of the bay—
would suggest that. But aside from the planks, the bay is now only a
bay, shallow, floored with rocks and cans and bottles. Schools of
silver fish, thin as fingernails, fog the bottom, and dragonflies dart
and hover over its placid surface. The harsh snarl of the boat
motor—for indeed a boat has been approaching, coming in off the
lake into this small bay—breaks off abruptly, as the boat carves a
long gentle arc through the bay, and slides, scraping bottom, toward
a shallow pebbly corner. There are two girls in the boat.

•

Bedded deep in the grass, near the path up to the first guest cabin,
lies a wrought-iron poker. It is long and slender with an intricately

worked handle, and it is orange with rust. It lies shadowed, not by trees, but by the grass that has grown up wildly around it. I put it there.

•

The caretaker's son, left behind when the island was deserted, crouches naked in the brambly fringe of the forest overlooking the bay. He watches, scratching himself, as the boat scrapes to a stop and the girls stand—then he scampers through the trees and bushes to the guest cabin.

•

The girl standing forward—fashionbook-trim in tight gold pants, ruffled blouse, silk neckscarf—hesitates, makes one false start, then jumps from the boat, her sandaled heel catching the water's edge. She utters a short irritable cry, hops up on a rock, stumbles, lands finally in dry weeds on the other side. She turns her heel up and frowns down over her shoulder at it. Tiny muscles in front of her ears tense and ripple. She brushes anxiously at a thick black fly in front of her face, and asks peevishly: "What do I do *now*, Karen?"

•

I arrange the guest cabin. I rot the porch and tatter the screen door and infest the walls. I tear out the light switches, gut the mattresses, smash the windows, and shit on the bathroom floor. I rust the pipes, kick in the papered walls, unhinge doors. Really, there's nothing to it. In fact, it's a pleasure.

•

Once, earlier in this age, a family with great wealth purchased this entire island, here up on the border, and built on it all these houses, these cabins and the mansion up there on the promontory, and the boat house, docks, bath houses, observation tower. They tamed the island some, seeded lawn grass, contrived their own sewage system with indoor appurtenances, generated electricity for the rooms inside and for the japanese lanterns and postlamps without, and they came up here from time to time in the summers. They used to maintain a caretaker on the island year round, housed him in the cabin by the boat house, but then the patriarch of the family died, and the rest had other things to do. They stopped coming to the island and forgot about caretaking.

•

The one in gold pants watches as the girl still in the boat switches the motor into neutral and upends it, picks up a yellowish-gray rope from the bottom, and tosses it ashore to her. She reaches for it straight-armed, then shies from it, letting it fall to the ground. She takes it up with two fingers and a thumb and holds it out in front of her. The other girl, Karen (she wears a light yellow dress with a beige cardigan over it), pushes a toolkit under a seat, gazes thoughtfully about the boat, then jumps out. Her canvas shoes splash in the water's edge, but she pays no notice. She takes the rope from the girl in gold pants, loops it around a birch near the shore, smiles warmly, and then, with a nod, leads the way up the path.

•

At the main house, the mansion, there is a kind of veranda or terrace, a balcony of sorts, high out on the promontory, offering a spectacular view of the lake with its wide interconnected expanses of blue and its many islands. Poised there now, gazing thoughtfully out on that view, is a tall slender man, dressed in slacks, white turtleneck shirt, and navy-blue jacket, smoking a pipe, leaning against the stone parapet. Has he heard a boat come to the island? He is unsure. The sound of the motor seemed to diminish, to grow more distant, before it stopped. Yet, on water, especially around islands, one can never trust what he hears.

•

Also this, then: the mansion with its many rooms, its debris, its fireplaces and wasps' nests, it musty basement, its grand hexagonal loggia [1] and bright red doors. Though the two girls will not come here for a while—first, they have the guest cabin to explore, the poker to find—I have been busy. In the loggia, I have placed a green piano. I have pulled out its wires, chipped and yellowed its ivory keys, and cracked its green paint. I am nothing if not thorough, a real stickler for detail. I have dismembered the piano's pedals and dropped an old boot in its body (this, too, I've designed: it is horizontal and harp-shaped). The broken wires hang like rusted hairs.

•

The caretaker's son watches for their approach through a shattered window of the guest cabin. He is stout and hairy, muscular, dark, with short bowed legs and a rounded spiny back. The hair on his head is long, and a thin young beard sprouts on his chin and upper lip. His genitals hang thick and heavy and his buttocks are shaggy. His small eyes dart to and fro: where are they?

•

1. Roofed but open gallery along the side of a building.

In the bay, the sun's light has been constant and oppressive; along the path, it is mottled and varied. Even in this variety, though, there is a kind of monotony, a determined patterning that wants a good wind. Through these patterns move the two girls, Karen long-striding with soft steps and expectant smile, the other girl hurrying behind, halting, hurrying again, slapping her arms, her legs, the back of her neck, cursing plaintively. Each time she passes between the two trees, the girl in pants stops, claws the space with her hands, runs through, but spiderwebs keep diving and tangling into her hair just the same.

•

Between two trees on the path, a large spider—black with a red heart on its abdomen—weaves an intricate web. The girl stops short, terrified. Nimbly, the shiny black creature works, as though spelling out some terrible message for her alone. How did Karen pass through here without brushing into it? The girl takes a step backward, holding her hands to her face. Which way around? To the left it is dark, to the right sunny: she chooses the sunny side and there, not far from the path, comes upon a wrought-iron poker, long and slender with an intricately worked handle. She bends low, her golden haunches gleaming over the grass: how beautiful it is! On a strange impulse, she kisses it—POOF! before her stands a tall slender man, handsome, dressed in dark slacks, white turtleneck shirt, and jacket, smoking a pipe. He smiles down at her. "Thank you," he says, and takes her hand.

•

Karen is some distance in front, almost out of sight, when the other girl discovers, bedded in the grass, a wrought-iron poker. Orange with rust, it is long and slender with an elaborate handle. She crouches to examine it, her haunches curving golden above the bluegreen grass, her long black hair drifting lightly down over her small shoulders and wafting in front of her fineboned face. "Oh!" she says softly. "How strange! How beautiful!" Squeamishly, she touches it, grips it, picks it up, turns it over. Not so rusty on the underside—but bugs! *millions* of them! She drops the thing, shudders, stands, wipes her hand several times on her pants, shudders again. A few steps away, she pauses, glances back, then around at everything about her, concentrating, memorizing the place probably. She hurries on up the path and sees her sister already at the first guest cabin.

•

The girl in gold pants? yes. The other one, Karen? also. In fact, they are sisters. I have brought two sisters to this invented island, and shall, in time, send them home again. I have dressed them and may well choose to undress them. I have given one three marriages, the other none at all, nor is that the end of my beneficence and cruelty. It might even be argued that I have invented their common parents. No, I have not. We have options that may, I admit, seem strangely limited to some . . .

•

She crouches, haunches flexing golden above the bluegreen grass, and kisses the strange poker, kisses its handle and its long rusted shaft. Nothing. Only a harsh unpleasant taste. I am a fool, she thinks, a silly romantic fool. Yet why else has she been diverted to this small meadow? She kisses the tip—POOF! "Thank you," he says, smiling down at her. He bows to kiss her cheek and take her hand.

•

The guest cabin is built of rough-hewn logs, hardly the fruit of necessity, given the funds at hand, but probably it was thought fashionable; proof of traffic with other cultures is adequately provided by its gabled roof and log columns. It is here, on the shaded porch, where Karen is standing, waiting for her sister. Karen waves when she sees her, ducking down there along the path; then she turns and enters the cabin through the broken front door.

•

He knows that one. He's been there before. He crouches inside the door, his hairy body tense. She enters, staring straight at him. He grunts. She smiles, backing away. "Karen!" His small eyes dart to the doorway, and he shrinks back into the shadows.

•

She kisses the rusted iron poker, kisses its ornate handle, its long rusted shaft, kisses the tip. Nothing happens. Only a rotten taste in her mouth. Something is wrong. "Karen!"

•

"Karen!" the girl in pants calls from outside the guest cabin. "Karen, I just found the most beautiful thing!" The second step of the porch is rotted away. She hops over it onto the porch, drags open the tattered screen door. "Karen, I—*oh, good God!* look what they've *done* to this house! Just *look!*" Karen, about to enter the kitchen, turns back, smiling, as her sister surveys the room: "The walls all smashed in, even the plugs in the wall and the light switches pulled out! Think of it, Karen! They even had electricity!

Out here on this island, so far from everything civilized! And, see, what beautiful paper they had on the walls! And now just look at it! It's so—oh! what a dreadful beautiful beastly thing all at once!"

•

But where is the caretaker's son? I don't know. He was here, shrinking into the shadows, when Karen's sister entered. Yet, though she catalogues the room's disrepair, there is no mention of the caretaker's son. This is awkward. Didn't I invent him myself, along with the girls and the man in the turtleneck shirt? Didn't I round his back and stunt his legs and cause the hair to hang between his buttocks? I don't know. The girls, yes, and the tall man in the shirt—to be sure, he's one of the first of my inventions. But the caretaker's son? To tell the truth, I sometimes wonder if it was not he who invented me . . .

•

The caretaker's son, genitals hanging hard and heavy, eyes aglitter, shrinks back into the shadows as the girl approaches, and then goes bounding silently into the empty rooms. Behind an unhinged door, he peeks stealthily at the declaiming girl in gold pants, then slips, almost instinctively, into the bathroom to hide. It was here, after all, where first they met.

•

Karen passes quietly through the house, as though familiar with it. In the kitchen, she picks up a chipped blue teakettle, peers inside. All rust. She thumps it, the sound is dull. She sets it on a bench in the sunlight. On all sides, there are broken things: rubble really. Windows gape, shards of glass in the edges pointing out the middle spaces. The mattresses on the floors have been slashed with knives. What little there is of wood is warped. The girl in the tight gold pants and silk neckscarf moves, chattering, in and out of rooms. She opens a white door, steps into a bathroom, steps quickly out again. "Judas God!" she gasps, clearly horrified. Karen turns, eyebrows raised in concern. "Don't go in there, Karen! *Don't go in there!*" She clutches one hand to her ruffled blouse. "About a hundred million people have gone to the *bath*room in there!" Exiting the bathroom behind her, a lone fly swims lazily past her elbow into the close warm air of the kitchen. It circles over a cracked table— the table bearing newspapers, shreds of wallpaper, tin cans, a stiff black washcloth—then settles on a counter near a rusted pipeless sink. It chafes its rear legs, walks past the blue teakettle's shadow into a band of pure sunlight stretched out along the counter, and sits there.

•

The tall man stands, one foot up on the stone parapet, gazing out on the blue sunlit lake, drawing meditatively on his pipe. He has been deeply moved by the desolation of this island. And yet, it is only the desolation of artifact, is it not, the ruin of man's civilized arrogance, nature reclaiming her own. Even the willful mutilations: a kind of instinctive response to the futile artifices of imposed order, after all. But such reasoning does not appease him. Leaning against his raised knee, staring out upon the vast wilderness, hoping indeed he has heard a boat come here, he puffs vigorously on his pipe and affirms reason, man, order. Are we merely blind brutes loosed in a system of mindless energy, impotent, misdirected, and insolent? "No," he says aloud, "we are not."

•

She peeks into the bathroom; yes, he is in there, crouching obscurely, shaggily, but eyes aglitter, behind the stool. She hears his urgent grunt and smiles. "Oh, Karen!" cries the other girl from the rear of the house. "It's so very sad!" Hastily, Karen steps out into the hallway, eases the bathroom door shut, her heart pounding.

•

"Oh, Karen, it's so very sad!" That's the girl in the gold pants again, of course. Now she is gazing out a window. At: high weeds and grass, crowding young birches, red rattan chair with the seat smashed out, backdrop of gray-trunked pines. She is thinking of her three wrecked marriages, her affairs, and her desolation of spirit. The broken rattan chair somehow communicates to her a sensation of real physical pain. Where have all the Princes gone? she wonders. "I mean, it's not the ones who stole the things, you know, the scavengers. I've seen people in Paris and Mexico and Algiers, lots of places, scooping rotten oranges and fishheads out of the heaped-up gutters and eating them, and I didn't blame them, I didn't dislike them, I felt *sorry* for them. I even felt sorry for them if they were just doing it to be stealing something, to get something for nothing, even if they weren't hungry or anything. But it isn't the people who look for things they want or need or even don't need and take them, it's the people who just *destroy*, destroy because— God! because they just *want* to destroy! Lust! That's all, Karen! See? Somebody just went around these rooms driving his fist in the walls because he had to hurt, it didn't matter who or what, or maybe he kicked them with his feet, and bashed the windows and ripped the curtains and then went to the *bath*room on it all! Oh my God! *Why?* Why would anybody want to *do* that?" The window in front of Karen (she has long since turned her back) is, but for one panel, still whole. In the expected panel, the rupture in the glass is now spanned by a spiderweb more intricate than a butterfly's wing, than a system of stars, its silver paths seeming to imitate or perhaps merely to extend the delicate tracery of the fractured glass still surrounding the hole. It is a new web, for nothing has entered it yet to alter its original construction. Karen's hand reaches toward it, but then withdraws. "Karen, let's get out of here!"

●

The girls have gone. The caretaker's son bounds about the guest cabin, holding himself with one hand, smashing walls and busting windows with the other, grunting happily as he goes. He leaps up onto the kitchen counter, watches the two girls from the window, as they wind their way up to the main mansion, then squats joyfully over the blue teakettle, depositing . . . a love letter, so to speak.

●

A love letter! Wait a minute, this is getting out of hand! What happened to that poker, I was doing much better with the poker, I had something going there, archetypal and even maybe beautiful, a blend of eros and wisdom, sex and sensibility, music and myth. But what am I going to do with shit in a rusty teakettle? No, no, there's nothing to be gained by burdening our fabrications with impieties. Enough that the skin of the world is littered with our contentious artifice, lepered with the stigmata of human aggression and despair, without suffering our songs to be flatted by savagery. Back to the poker.

●

"Thank you," he says, smiling down at her, her haunches gleaming golden over the shadowed grass. "But, tell me, how did you know to kiss it?" "Call it woman's intuition," she replies, laughing lightly, and rises with an appreciative glance. "But the neglected state that it was in, it must have tasted simply dreadful," he apologizes, and kisses her gently on the cheek. "What momentary bitterness I might have suffered," she responds, "has been more than indemnified by the sweetness of your disenchantment." "My disenchantment? Oh no, my dear, there *are* no disenchantments, merely progressions and styles of possession. To exist is to be spellbound." She collapses, marveling, at his feet.

●

Karen, alone on the path to the mansion, pauses. Where is her sister? Has something distracted her? Has she strayed? Perhaps she has gone on ahead. Well, it hardly matters, what can happen on a desolate island? they'll meet soon enough at the mansion. In fact,

Karen isn't even thinking about her sister, she's staring silently, entranced, at a small green snake, stretched across the path. Is it dozing? Or simply unafraid? Maybe it's never seen a real person before, doesn't know what people can do. It's possible: few people
come here now, and it looks like a very young snake. Slender,
wriggly, green, and shiny. No, probably it's asleep. Smiling, Karen
leaves the path, circling away from the snake so as not to disturb it.
To the right of the path is a small clearing and the sun is hot there;
to the left it is cool and shadowed in the gathering forest. Karen
moves that way, in under the trees, picking the flowers that grow
wildly here. Her cardigan catches on brambles and birch seedlings,
so she pulls it off, tosses it loosely over her shoulder, hooked on
one finger. She hears, not far away, a sound not unlike soft footfalls.
Curious, she wanders that way to see who or what it is.

•

The path up to the main house, the mansion, is not even mottled,
the sun does not reach back here at all, it is dark and damp-
smelling, an ambience of mushrooms and crickets and fingery rus-
tles and dead brown leaves never quite dry, or so it might seem to
the girl in gold pants, were she to come this way. Where is she? His
small eyes dart to and fro. Here, beside the path, trees have collapsed and rotted, seedlings and underbrush have sprung up, and
lichens have crept softly over all surfaces, alive and dead. Strange
creatures abide here.

•

"Call it woman's intuition," she says with a light laugh. He ap-
praises her fineboned features, her delicate hands, her soft maidenly breasts under the ruffled blouse, her firm haunches gleaming
golden over the shadowed grass. He pulls her gently to her feet,
kisses her cheek. "You are enchantingly beautiful, my dear!" he
whispers. "Wouldn't you like to lie with me here awhile?" "Of
course," she replies, and kisses his cheek in return, "but these
pants are an awful bother to remove, and my sister awaits us. Come!
Let us go up to the mansion!"

•

A small green snake lies motionless across the path. The girl approaching does not see it, sees only the insects flicking damply, the
girl in tight pants which are still golden here in the deep shadows.
Her hand flutters ceaselessly before her face, it was surely the bugs
that drove these people away from here finally, "Karen, is this the
right way?", and she very nearly walks right on the snake, which
has perhaps been dozing, but which now switches with a frantic

whip of its shiny green tail off into the damp leaves. The girl starts at the sudden whirring shush at her feet, spins around clutching her hands to her upper arms, expecting the worst, but though staring wide-eyed right at the sound, she can see nothing. Why did she ever let her sister talk her into coming here? *"Karen!"* She runs, ignoring the webs now, right through all the gnats and flies, on up the path, crying out her sister's name.

•

The caretaker's son, poised gingerly on a moss-covered rock, peeking through thick branches, watches the girl come up the path. Karen watches the caretaker's son. From the rear, his prominent feature is his back, broad and rounded, humped almost, where tufts of dark hair sprout randomly. His head is just a small hairy lump beyond the mound of heavy back. His arms are as long as his legs are short, and the elbows, like the knees, turn outward. Thick hair grows between his buttocks and down his thighs. Smiling, she picks up a pebble to toss at him, but then she hears her sister call her name.

•

Leaning against his raised knee, smoking his pipe, the tall man on the parapet stares out on the wilderness, contemplating the island's ruin. Trees have collapsed upon one another, and vast areas of the island, once cleared and no doubt the stage for garden parties famous for miles around, are now virtually impassable. Brambles and bunchberries grow wildly amid saxifrage and shinleaf, and everything in sight is mottled with moss. Lichens: the symbiotic union, he recalls, of fungi and algae. He smiles and at the same moment, as though it has been brought into being by his smile, hears a voice on the garden path. A girl. How charming, he's to have company, after all! At least two, for he heard the voice on the path behind the mansion, and below him, slipping surefootedly through the trees and bushes, moves another creature in a yellow dress, carrying a beige sweater over her shoulder. She looks a little simple, not his type really, but then dissimilar organisms can, at times, enjoy mutually advantageous partnerships, can they not? He knocks the ashes from his pipe and refills the bowl.

•

At times, I forget that this arrangement is my own invention. I begin to think of the island as somehow real, its objects solid and intractable, its condition of ruin not so much an aesthetic design as an historical denouement. I find myself peering into blue teakettles, batting at spiderwebs, and contemplating a greenish-gray

growth on the side of a stone parapet. I wonder if others might
wander here without my knowing it; I wonder if I might die and
the teakettle remain. "I have brought two sisters to this invented
island," I say. This is no extravagance. It is indeed I who burdens
them with curiosity and history, appetite and rhetoric. If they have
names and griefs, I have provided them. "In fact," I add, "without
me they'd have no cunts." This is not (I interrupt here to tell you
that I have done all that I shall do. I return here to bring you this
news, since this seemed as good a place as any. Though you have
more to face, and even more to suffer from me, this is in fact the last
thing I shall say to you. But can the end be in the middle? Yes, yes,
it always is . . .) meant to alarm, merely to make a truth manifest—yet *I* am myself somewhat alarmed. It is one thing to discover
the shag of hair between my buttocks, quite another to find myself
tugging the tight gold pants off Karen's sister. Or perhaps it is the
same thing, yet troubling in either case. Where does this illusion
come from, this sensation of "hardness" in a blue teakettle or an
iron poker, golden haunches or a green piano?

•

In the hexagonal loggia of the mansion stands a grand piano,
painted bright green, though chipped and cracked now with age
and abuse. One can easily imagine a child at such a piano, a piano
so glad and ready, perhaps two children, and the sun is shining—
no, rather, there is a storm on the lake, the sky is in a fury, all black
and pitching, the children are inside here out of the wind and
storm, the little girl on the right, the boy on the left, pushing at each
other a bit, staking out property lines on the keys, a grandmother, or
perhaps just a lady, yet why not a grandmother? sitting on a
window-bench gazing out on the frothy blue-black lake, and the
children are playing "Chopsticks," laughing, a little noisy surely,
and the grandmother, or lady, looks over from time to time, forms a
patient smile if they chance to glance up at her, then—well, but it's
only a supposition, who knows whether there were children or if
they cared a damn about a green piano even on a bad day, "Chopsticks" least of all? No, it's only a piece of fancy, the kind of fancy
that is passing through the mind of the girl in gold pants who now
reaches down, strikes a key. There is no sound, of course. The ivory
is chipped and yellowed, the pedals dismembered, the wires torn
out and hanging like rusted hairs. The girl wonders at her own
unkemptness, feels a lock loose on her forehead, but there are no
mirrors. Stolen or broken. She stares about her, nostalgically absorbed for some reason, at the elegantly timbered roof of the loggia,
at the enormous stone fireplace, at the old shoe in the doorway, the
wasps' nests over one broken-out window. She sighs, steps out on

the terrace, steep and proud over the lake. "It's a sad place," she says aloud.

•

The tall man in the navy-blue jacket stands, one foot up on the stone parapet, gazing out on the blue sunlit lake, drawing meditatively on his pipe, while being sketched by the girl in the tight gold pants. "I somehow expected to find you here," she says. "I've been waiting for you," replies the man. Her three-quarters view of him from the rear allows her to include only the tip of his nose in her sketch, the edge of his pipebowl, the collar of his white turtle-neck shirt. "I was afraid there might be others," she says. "Others?" "Yes. Children perhaps. Or somebody's grandmother. I saw so many names everywhere I went, on walls and doors and trees and even scratched into that green piano." She is carefully filling in on her sketch the dark contours of his navy-blue jacket. "No," he says, "whoever they were, they left here long ago." "It's a sad place," she says, "and all too much like my own life." He nods. "You mean, the losing struggle against inscrutable blind forces, young dreams brought to ruin?" "Yes, something like that," she says. "And getting kicked in and gutted and shat upon." "Mmm." He straightens. "Just a moment," she says, and he resumes his pose. The girl has accomplished a reasonable likeness of the tall man, except that his legs are stubby (perhaps she failed to center her drawing properly, and ran out of space at the bottom of the paper) and his buttocks are bare and shaggy.

•

"It's a sad place," he says, contemplating the vast wilderness. He turns to find her grinning and wiggling her ears at him. "Karen, you're mocking me!" he complains, laughing. She props one foot up on the stone parapet, leans against her leg, sticks an iron poker between her teeth, and scowls out upon the lake. "Come on! Stop it!" he laughs. She puffs on the iron poker, blowing imaginary smoke-rings, then turns it into a walking stick and hobbles about imitating an old granny chasing young children. Next, she puts the poker to her shoulder like a rifle and conducts an inspection of all the broken windows facing on the terrace, scowling or weeping broadly before each one. The man has slumped to the terrace floor, doubled up with laughter. Suddenly, Karen discovers an unbroken window. She leaps up and down, does a somersault, pirouettes, jumps up and clicks her heels together. She points at it, kisses it, points again. "Yes, yes!" the man laughs, "I see it, Karen!" She points to herself, then at the window, to herself again. "You? You're like the window, Karen?" he asks, puzzled, but still laughing. She nods her head vigorously, thrusts the iron poker into his hands. It is dirty and rusty and he feels clumsy with the thing. "I don't understand . . ." She grabs it out of his hands and—*crash!*—drives it through the window. "Oh no, Karen! No, no . . . !"

•

"It's a sad place." Karen has joined her sister on the terrace, the balcony, and they gaze out at the lake, two girls alone on a desolate island. "Sad and yet all too right for me, I suppose. Oh, I don't regret any of it, Karen. No, I was wrong, wrong as always, but I don't regret it. It'd be silly to be all pinched and morbid about it, wouldn't it, Karen?" The girl, of course, is talking about the failure of her third marriage. "Things are done and they are undone and then we get ready to do them again." Karen looks at her shyly, then turns her gentle gaze back out across the lake, blue with a river's muted blue under this afternoon sun. "The sun!" the girl in gold pants exclaims, though it is not clear why she thought of it. She tries to explain that she is like the sun somehow, or the sun is like her, but she becomes confused. Finally, she interrupts herself to blurt out: "Oh, Karen! *I'm so miserable!*" Karen looks up anxiously: there are no tears in her sister's eyes, but she is biting down painfully on her lower lip. Karen offers a smile, a little awkward, not quite understanding perhaps, and finally her sister, eyes closing a moment, then fluttering open, smiles wanly in return. A moment of grace settles between them, but Karen turns her back on it clumsily.

•

"No, Karen! Please! Stop!" The man, collapsed to the terrace floor, has tears of laughter running down his cheeks. Karen has found an old shoe and is now holding it up at arm's length, making broad silent motions with her upper torso and free arm as though declaiming upon the sadness of the shoe. She sets the shoe on the terrace floor and squats down over it, covering it with the skirt of her yellow dress. "No, Karen! No!" She leaps up, whacks her heels together in midair, picks up the shoe and peers inside. A broad smile spreads across her face, and she does a little dance, holding the shoe aloft. With a little curtsy, she presents the shoe to the man. "No! Please!" Warily, but still laughing, he looks inside. "What's this? Oh no! A flower! Karen, this is too much!" She runs into the mansion, returns carrying the green piano on her back. She drops it so hard, one leg breaks off. She finds an iron poker, props the piano up with it, sits down on an imaginary stool to play. She lifts her hands high over her head, then comes driving down with extravagant magisterial gestures. The piano, of course, has been completely disemboweled, so no sounds emerge, but up and down the broken keyboard Karen's stubby fingers fly, arriving at last, with a crescendo of violent flourishes, at a grand climactic coda, which she delivers with such force as to buckle the two remaining legs of the piano and send it all crashing to the terrace floor. "No, Karen! Oh my God!" Out of the wreckage, a wild goose springs, honking in holy terror, and goes flapping out over the lake. Karen carries the piano back inside, there's a splintering carash, and she returns wielding the poker. "Careful!" She holds the poker up with two hands and does a little dance, toes turned outward, hippety-hopping about the terrace. She stops abruptly over the man, thrusts the poker in front of his nose, then slowly brings it to her own lips and kisses it. She makes a wry face. "Oh, Karen! Whoo! Please! You're killing me!" She kisses the handle, the shaft, the tip. She wrinkles her nose and shudders, lifts her skirt and wipes her tongue with it. She scowls at the poker. She takes a firm grip on the poking end and bats the handle a couple times against the stone parapet as though testing it. "Oh, Karen! Oh!" Then she lifts it high over her head and brings it down with all her might—WHAM!—POOF! it is the caretaker's son, yowling with pain. She lets go and spins away from him, as he strikes out at her in distress and fury. She tumbles into a corner of the terrace and cowers there, whimpering, pale and terrified, as the caretaker's son, breathing heavily, back stooped and buttocks tensed, circles her, prepared to spring. Suddenly, she dashes for the parapet and leaps over, the caretaker's son bounding after, and off they go, scrambling frantically through the trees and brambles, leaving the tall man in the white turtleneck shirt alone and limp from laughter on the terrace.

•

There is a storm on the lake. Two children play "Chopsticks" on the green piano. Their grandmother stirs the embers in the fireplace with an iron poker, then returns to her seat on the window-bench. The children glance over at her and she smiles at them. Suddenly a strange naked creature comes bounding into the loggia, grinning idiotically. The children and their grandmother scream with terror and race from the room and on out of the mansion, running for their lives. The visitor leaps up on the piano bench and squats there, staring quizzically at the ivory keys. He reaches for one and it sounds a note—he jerks his hand back in fright. He reaches for another—a different note. He brings his fist down— BLAM! Aha! Again: BLAM! Excitedly, he leaps up and down on the piano bench, banging his fists on the piano keyboard. He hops up on the piano, finds wires inside, and pulls them out. TWANG! TWANG! He holds his genitals with one hand and rips out the wires with the other, grunting with delight. Then he spies the iron poker. He grabs it up, admires it, then bounds joyfully around the room, smashing windows and wrecking furniture. The girl in gold pants enters and takes the poker away from him. "Lust! That's all it is!" she scolds. She whacks him on the nates with the poker, and, yelping with pain and astonishment, he bounds away, leaping over the stone parapet, and slinks off through the brambly forest.

•

"Lust!" she says, "that's all it is!" Her sketch is nearly complete. "And they're not the worst ones. The worst ones are the ones who just let it happen. If they'd kept their caretaker here . . ." The man smiles. "There never was a caretaker," he explains. "Really? But I thought—!" "No," he says, "that's just a legend of the island." She seems taken aback by this new knowledge. "Then . . . then I don't understand . . ." He relights his pipe, wanders over to appraise her sketch. He laughs when he sees the shaggy buttocks. "Marvelous!" he exclaims, "but a poor likeness, I'm afraid! Look!" He lowers his dark slacks and shows her his hindend, smooth as marble and hairless as a movie starlet's. Her curiosity is caught, however, not by his barbered buttocks, but by the hair around his genitals: the tight neat curls fan out in both directions like the wings of an eagle, or a wild goose . . .

•

The two sisters return to the loggia, their visit nearly concluded, the one in gold pants still trying to explain about herself and the sun, about consuming herself with an outer fire, while harboring an icecold center within. Her gaze falls once more on the green piano. It is obvious she still has something more to say. But now as she declaims, she has less of an audience. Karen stands distractedly before the green piano. Haltingly, she lifts a finger, strikes a key. No note, only a dull thuck. Her sister reveals a new insight she has just obtained about it not being the people who steal or even those who wantonly destroy, but those who let it happen, who just don't give a proper damn. She provides instances. Once, Karen nods, but maybe only at something she has thought to herself. Her finger lifts, strikes. Thuck! Again. Thuck! Her whole arm drives the strong blunt finger. Thuck! Thuck! There is something genuinely beautiful about the girl in gold pants and silk neckscarf as she gestures and speaks. Her eyes are sorrowful and wise. Thuck! Karen strikes the key. Suddenly, her sister breaks off her message. "Oh, I'm sorry, Karen!" she says. She stares at the piano, then runs out of the room.

•

I am disappearing. You have no doubt noticed. Yes, and by some no doubt calculable formula of event and pagination. But before we drift apart to a distance beyond the reach of confessions (though I warn you: like Zeno's turtle,[2] I am with you always), listen: it's just as I feared, my invented island is really taking its place in world geography. Why, this island sounds very much like the old Dahlberg place on Jackfish Island up on Rainy Lake, people say, and I wonder: can it be happening? Someone tells me: I understand somebody bought the place recently and plans to fix it up, maybe put a resort there or something. On *my* island? Extraordinary!—and yet it seems possible. I look on a map: yes, there's Rainy Lake, there's Jackfish Island. Who invented this map? Well, I must have, surely. And the Dahlbergs, too, of course, and the people who told me about them. Yes, and perhaps tomorrow I will invent Chicago and Jesus Christ and the history of the moon. Just as I have invented you, dear reader, while lying here in the afternoon sun, bedded deeply in the bluegreen grass like an old iron poker . . .

•

There is a storm on the lake and the water is frothy and black. The wind howls around the corner of the stone parapet and the pine trees shake and creak. The two children playing "Chopsticks" on the green piano are arguing about the jurisdiction of the bench and keyboard. "Come over here," their grandmother says from her seat by the window, "and I'll tell you the story of 'The Magic Poker' . . ."

•

Once upon a time, a family of wealthy Minnesotans bought an island on Rainy Lake up on the Canadian border. They built a home on it and guest cabins and boat houses and an observation tower. They installed an electric generator and a sewage system with indoor toilets, maintained a caretaker, and constructed docks and bath houses. Did they name it Jackfish Island, or did it bear that name when they bought it? The legend does not say, nor should it. What it does say, however, is that when the family abandoned the island, they left behind an iron poker, which, years later, on a visit to the island, a beautiful young girl, not quite a princess perhaps, yet altogether equal to the occasion, kissed. And when she did so, something quite extraordinary happened . . .

•

2. Zeno of Elea, Greek philosopher of the 5th century B.C., formulated a number of paradoxes concerning the One and the Many. In the paradox of Achilles and the tortoise, Achilles will never catch up with the tortoise if it has a head start. For while Achilles is traveling the distance from his starting point to the starting point of the tortoise, the tortoise is advancing a certain distance, and while Achilles traverses this distance, the tortoise makes a certain advance, and so on *ad infinitum*.

Once upon a time there was an island visited by ruin and inhabited by strange woodland creatures. Some thought it had once had a caretaker who had either died or found another job elsewhere. Others said, no, there was never a caretaker, that was only a childish legend. Others believed there was indeed a caretaker and he lived there yet and was in fact responsible for the island's tragic condition. All this is neither here nor there. What is certainly beyond dispute is that no one who visited the island, whether searching for its legendary Magic Poker or avenging the loss of a loved one, ever came back. Only their names were left, inscribed hastily on walls and ceilings and carved on trees.

●

Once upon a time, two sisters visited a desolate island. They walked its paths with their proclivities and scruples, dreaming their dreams and sorrowing their sorrows. They scared a snake and probably a bird or two, broke a few windows (there were few left to break), and gazed meditatively out upon the lake from the terrace of the main house. They wrote their names above the stone fireplace in the hexagonal loggia and shat in the soundbox of an old green piano. One of them did anyway; the other one couldn't get her pants down. On the island, they found a beautiful iron poker, and when they went home, they took it with them.

●

The girl in gold pants hastens out of the big house and down the dark path where earlier the snake slept and past the gutted guest cabin and on down the mottled path toward the boat. To either side of her, flies and bees mumble indolently under the summer sun. A small speckled frog who will not live out the day squats staring on a stone, burps, hops into a darkness. A white moth drifts silently into the web of a spider, flutters there awhile before his execution. Suddenly, there on the path mottled with sunlight, the girl stops short, her breath coming in short gasps, looking around her. Wasn't this—? Yes, yes, it is the place! A smile begins to form. And in fact, there it is! She waits for Karen.

●

Once upon a time there was a beautiful young Princess in tight gold pants, so very tight in fact that no one could remove them from her. Knights came from far and wide, and they huffed and they puffed, and they grunted and they groaned, but the pants would not come down. One rash Knight even went so far as to jam the blade of his sword down the front of the gold pants, striving to pry them from

her, but he succeeded only in shattering his sword, much to his lifelong dismay and ignominy. The King at last delivered a Proclamation. "Whosoever shall succeed in pulling my daughter's pants
down," he declared, "shall have her for his bride!" Since this was
perhaps not the most tempting of trophies, the Princess having
been married off three times already in previous competitions, the
King added: "And moreover he shall have bestowed upon him the
Magic Poker, whose powers and prodigies are well-known in the
Kingdom!" "The Old Man's got his bloody cart before his horse,"
one Knight complained sourly to a companion upon hearing the
Proclamation. "If I had the bloody Poker, you could damn well bet
I'd have no trouble gettin' the bloody pants off her!" Now, it
chanced that this heedless remark was overheard by a peculiar little
gnome-like creature, huddling naked and unshaven in the brush
alongside the road, and no sooner had the words been uttered than
this strange fellow determined to steal the Magic Poker and win the
beauty for himself. Such an enterprise might well have seemed impossible for even the most dauntless of Knights, much less for so
hapless a creature as this poor naked brute with the shaggy loins,
but the truth, always stranger than fiction, was that his father had
once been the King's Official Caretaker, and the son had grown up
among the mysteries and secret chambers of the Court. Imagine the
entire Kingdom's astonishment, therefore, when, the very next day,
the Caretaker's son appeared, squat, naked, and hirsute, before the
King and with grunts and broad gestures made manifest his intention to quit the Princess of her pants and win the prizes for himself!
"Indeed!" cried her father. The King's laughter boomed throughout
the Palace, and all the Knights and Ladies joined in, creating the
jolliest of uproars. "Bring my daughter here at once!" the King
thundered, delighted by the droll spectacle. The Princess, amused,
but at the same time somewhat afrighted of the strange little man,
stepped timidly forward, her golden haunches gleaming in the
bright lights of the Palace. The Caretaker's son promptly drew forth
the Magic Poker, pointed it at the Princess, and—POOF!—the gold
pants dropped—plop!—to the Palace floor. "Oh's!" and "Ah's!"
of amazement and admiration rose up in excited chorus from the
crowd of nobles attending this most extraordinary moment.
Flushed, trembling, impatient, the Princess grasped the Magic
Poker and kissed it—POOF!—a handsome Knight in shining armor
of white and navy blue stood before her, smoking a pipe. He drew
his sword and slew the Caretaker's son. Then smiling at the
maiden standing in her puddle of gold pants, he sheathed his
sword, knocked the ashes from his pipe bowl, and knelt before the
King. "Your Majesty," he said, "I have slain the monster and res-

cued your daughter!" "Not at all," replied the King gloomily. "You have made her a widow. Kiss the fool, my dear!" "No, please!" the Knight begged. "Stop!"

•

"Look, Karen, look! See what I found! Do you think we can take it? It doesn't hurt, does it, I mean, what with everything else—? It's just beautiful and I can scour off the rust and—?" Karen glances at the poker in the grass, shrugs, smiles in assent, turns to stride on down the rise toward the boat, a small white edge of which can be glimpsed through the trees, below, at the end of the path. "Karen—? Could you please—?" Karen turns around, gazes quizzically at her sister, head tilted to one side—then laughs, a low grunting sound, something like a half-gargle, walks back and picks up the poker, brushes off the insects with her hand. Her sister, delighted, reaches for it, but Karen grunts again, keeps it, carries it down to their boat. There, she washes it clean in the lake water, scrubbing it with sand. She dries it on her dress. "Don't get your dress dirty, Karen! It's rusty anyway. We'll clean it when we get home." Karen holds it between them a moment before tossing it into the boat, and they both smile to see it. Wet still, it glistens, sparkling with flecks of rainbow-colored light in the sunshine.

•

The tall man stands poised before her, smoking his pipe, one hand in the pocket of his navy-blue jacket. Besides the jacket, he wears only a white turtleneck shirt. The girl in gold pants is kissing him. From the tip of his crown to the least of his toes. Nothing happens. Only a bitter wild goose taste in the mouth. Something is wrong. "Karen!" Karen laughs, a low grunting sound, then takes hold of the man and lifts her skirts. "No, Karen! Please!" he cries, laughing. "Stop!" POOF! From her skirts, Karen withdraws a wrought-iron poker, long and slender with an intricately worked handle. "It's beautiful, Karen!" her sister exclaims and reaches for it. Karen grunts again, holds it up between them a moment, and they both smile to see it. It glistens in the sunshine, a handsome souvenir of a beautiful day.

•

Soon the bay is still again, the silver fish and the dragonflies are returned, and only the slightest murmur near the shore by the old waterlogged lumber betrays the recent disquiet. The boat is already far out on the lake, its stern confronting us in retreat. The family who prepared this island does not know the girls have been here, nor would it astonish them to hear of it. As a matter of fact, with that touch of the divinity common to the rich, they have probably forgotten why they built all the things on this island in the first place, or whatever possessed them seriously to concern themselves, to squander good hours, over the selection of this or that object to decorate the newly made spaces or to do the things that had usually to be done, over the selection of this or that iron poker, for example. The boat is almost out of sight, so distant in fact, it's no longer possible to see its occupants or even to know how many there are—all just a blurred speck on the bright sheen laid on the lake by the lowering sun. The lake is calm. Here, a few shadows lengthen, a frog dies, a strange creature lies slain, a tanager sings.

From *Pricksongs & Descants* (1969)

· John Cheever ·

THE WORLD OF APPLES

Asa Bascomb, the old laureate,[1] wandered around his work house or study—he had never been able to settle on a name for a house where one wrote poetry—swatting hornets with a copy of *La Stampa* [2] and wondering why he had never been given the Nobel Prize. He had received nearly every other sign of renown. In a trunk in the corner there were medals, citations, wreaths, sheaves, ribbons, and badges. The stove that heated his study had been given to him by the Oslo P.E.N. Club,[3] his desk was a gift from the Kiev Writer's Union, and the study itself had been built by an international association of his admirers. The presidents of both Italy and the United States had wired their congratulations on the day he was presented with the key to the place. Why no Nobel Prize? Swat, swat. The study was a barny, raftered building with a large northern window that looked off to the Abruzzi.[4] He would sooner have had a much smaller place with smaller windows but he had not been consulted. There seemed to be some clash between the altitude of the mountains and the disciplines of verse. At the time of which I'm writing he was eighty-two years old and lived in a villa below the hill town of Monte Carbone, south of Rome.

He had strong, thick white hair that hung in a lock over his forehead. Two or more cowlicks at the crown were usually disorderly and erect. He wet them down with soap for formal receptions, but

1. One "crowned with laurel," an honored artist.
2. Respected daily newspaper published in Turin.
3. International literary association of poets, playwrights, editors, essayists, and novelists.
4. Region of central Italy, extending from the Apennines to the Adriatic.

they were never supine for more than an hour or two and were usually up in the air again by the time champagne was poured. It was very much a part of the impression he left. As one remembers a man for a long nose, a smile, birthmark, or scar, one remembered Bascomb for his unruly cowlicks. He was known vaguely as the Cézanne of poets.[5] There was some linear preciseness to his work that might be thought to resemble Cézanne but the vision that underlies Cézanne's paintings was not his. This mistaken comparison might have arisen because the title of his most popular work was *The World of Apples* — poetry in which his admirers found the pungency, diversity, color, and nostalgia of the apples of the northern New England he had not seen for forty years.

Why had he—provincial and famous for his simplicity—chosen to leave Vermont for Italy? Had it been the choice of his beloved Amelia, dead these ten years? She had made many of their decisions. Was he, the son of a farmer, so naïve that he thought living abroad might bring some color to his stern beginnings? Or had it been simply a practical matter, an evasion of the publicity that would, in his own country, have been an annoyance? Admirers found him in Monte Carbone, they came almost daily, but they came in modest numbers. He was photographed once or twice a year for *Match* or *Epoca* [6]—usually on his birthday— but he was in general able to lead a quieter life than would have been possible in the United States. Walking down Fifth Avenue on his last visit home he had been stopped by strangers and asked to autograph scraps of paper. On the streets of Rome no one knew or cared who he was and this was as he wanted it.

Monte Carbone was a Saracen town,[7] built on the summit of a loaf-shaped butte of sullen granite. At the top of the town were three pure and voluminous springs whose water fell in pools or conduits down the sides of the mountain. His villa was below the town and he had in his garden many fountains, fed by the springs on the summit. The noise of falling water was loud and unmusical—a clapping or clattering sound. The water was stinging cold, even in midsummer, and he kept his gin, wine, and vermouth in a pool on the terrace. He worked in his study in the mornings, took a siesta after lunch, and then climbed the stairs to the village.

The tufa and pepperoni and the bitter colors of the lichen that takes root in the walls and roofs are no part of the consciousness of an American, even if he had lived for years, as Bascomb had, sur-

5. Paul Cézanne (1839–1906), French painter of the post-Impressionist school, noted for his austere handling of spatial forms. Some of his most famous still lifes are of apples.
6. Popular illustrated magazines of France and Italy, respectively.
7. Town built by Muslim warriors who held Sicily and parts of southern Italy from the ninth to the eleventh centuries.

rounded by this bitterness.[8] The climb up the stairs winded him. He stopped again and again to catch his breath. Everyone spoke to him. *Salve, maestro, salve!* [9] When he saw the bricked-up transept of the twelfth-century church he always mumbled the date to himself as if he were explaining the beauties of the place to some companion. The beauties of the place were various and gloomy. He would always be a stranger there, but his strangeness seemed to him to be some metaphor involving time as if, climbing the strange stairs past the strange walls, he climbed through hours, months, years, and decades. In the piazza he had a glass of wine and got his mail. On any day he received more mail than the entire population of the village. There were letters from admirers, propositions to lecture, read, or simply show his face, and he seemed to be on the invitation list of every honorary society in the Western world excepting, of course, that society formed by the past winners of the Nobel Prize. His mail was kept in a sack, and if it was too heavy for him to carry, Antonio, the *postina's* son, would walk back with him to the villa. He worked over his mail until five or six. Two or three times a week some pilgrims would find their way to the villa and if he liked their looks he would give them a drink while he autographed their copy of *The World of Apples*. They almost never brought his other books, although he had published a dozen. Two or three evenings a week he played backgammon with Carbone, the local padrone. They both thought that the other cheated and neither of them would leave the board during a game, even if their bladders were killing them. He slept soundly.

Of the four poets with whom Bascomb was customarily grouped one had shot himself, one had drowned himself, one had hanged himself, and the fourth had died of delirium tremens. Bascomb had known them all, loved most of them, and had nursed two of them when they were ill, but the broad implication that he had, by choosing to write poetry, chosen to destroy himself was something he rebelled against vigorously. He knew the temptations of suicide as he knew the temptations of every other form of sinfulness and he carefully kept out of the villa all firearms, suitable lengths of rope, poisons, and sleeping pills. He had seen in Z—the closest of the four—some inalienable link between his prodigious imagination and his prodigious gifts for self-destruction, but Bascomb in his stubborn, countrified way was determined to break or ignore this link—to overthrow Marsyas and Orpheus.[10] Poetry was a lasting

8. Tufa (porous limestone) and peperino (volcanic rock) share the "bitter colors" of the lichen. Pepperoni is a highly seasoned sausage (Italian *peperone,* Cayenne pepper), but in this case the term is probably a variant of peperino.
9. "Hail, master, hail!"
10. Two mythical artists whose great gifts led to their destruction. The satyr Marsyas was so skillful a flutist that he challenged Apollo to a contest. Apollo won, and

glory and he was determined that the final act of a poet's life should not—as had been the case with Z—be played out in a dirty room with twenty-three empty gin bottles. Since he could not deny the connection between brilliance and tragedy he seemed determined to bludgeon it.

Bascomb believed, as Cocteau once said,[11] that the writing of poetry was the exploitation of a substrata of memory that was imperfectly understood. His work seemed to be an act of recollection. He did not, as he worked, charge his memory with any practical tasks but it was definitely his memory that was called into play—his memory of sensation, landscapes, faces, and the immense vocabulary of his own language. He could spend a month or longer on a short poem but discipline and industry were not the words to describe his work. He did not seem to choose his words at all but to recall them from the billions of sounds that he had heard since he first understood speech. Depending on his memory, then, as he did, to give his life usefulness he sometimes wondered if his memory were not failing. Talking with friends and admirers he took great pains not to repeat himself. Waking at two or three in the morning to hear the unmusical clatter of his fountains he would grill himself for an hour on names and dates. Who was Lord Cardigan's adversary at Balaklava? [12] It took a minute for the name of Lord Lucan to struggle up through the murk but it finally appeared. He conjugated the remote past of the verb *esse*, counted to fifty in Russian, recited poems by Donne, Eliot, Thomas, and Wordsworth, described the events of the Risorgimento [13] beginning with the riots in Milan in 1812 up through the coronation of Vittorio Emanuele, listed the ages of prehistory, the number of kilometers in a mile, the planets of the solar system, and the speed of light. There was a definite retard in the responsiveness of his memory but he remained adequate, he thought. The only impairment was anxiety. He had seen time destroy so much that he wondered if an old man's memory could have more strength and longevity than an oak; but the pin oak he had planted on the terrace thirty years ago was dying and he could still remember in detail the cut and color of the dress his

punished Marsyas by flaying him alive. Orpheus, son of one of the Muses, possessed the gift of music, and his lyre could charm the rocks and trees. But in the end he was torn limb from limb by a band of frenzied Maenads (female followers of Bacchus).
11. Jean Cocteau (1891–1963), French poet and aesthete.
12. Seaport on the Crimean coast, near Sebastopol, the scene during the Crimean war of the famous charge of the Light Brigade (September 26, 1854) celebrated in Tennyson's poem. Due to a misinterpretation of orders, Lord Lucan ordered the unnecessary charge, in which 247 out of 673 officers and men were either killed or wounded.
13. Italian for "resurrection," name given to the mid-nineteenth-century political movement for the union and liberation of Italy. Victor Emmanuel (King of Sicily), one of its leaders, was declared King of Italy in 1860.

beloved Amelia had been wearing when they first met. He taxed his memory to find its way through cities. He imagined walking from the railroad station in Indianapolis to the memorial fountain, from the Hotel Europe in Leningrad to the Winter Palace, from the Eden-Roma up through Trastevere to San Pietro in Montori. Frail, doubting his faculties, it was the solitariness of this inquisition that made it a struggle.

His memory seemed to wake him one night or morning, asking him to produce the first name of Lord Byron. He could not. He decided to disassociate himself momentarily from his memory and surprise it in possession of Lord Byron's name but when he returned, warily, to this receptacle it was still empty. Sidney? Percy? James? He got out of bed—it was cold—put on some shoes and an overcoat and climbed up the stairs through the garden to his study. He seized a copy of *Manfred* but the author was listed simply as Lord Byron. The same was true of *Childe Harold*. He finally discovered, in the encyclopedia, that his lordship was named George. He granted himself a partial excuse for this lapse of memory and returned to his warm bed. Like most old men he had begun a furtive glossary of food that seemed to put lead in his pencil. Fresh trout. Black olives. Young lamb roasted with thyme. Wild mushrooms, bear, venison, and rabbit. On the other side of the ledger were all frozen foods, cultivated greens, overcooked pasta, and canned soups.

In the spring a Scandinavian admirer wrote, asking if he might have the honor of taking Bascomb for a day's trip among the hill towns. Bascomb, who had no car of his own at the time, was delighted to accept. The Scandinavian was a pleasant young man and they set off happily for Monte Felici. In the fourteenth and fifteenth centuries the springs that supplied the town with water had gone dry and the population had moved halfway down the mountain. All that remained of the abandoned town on the summit were two churches or cathedrals of uncommon splendor. Bascomb loved these. They stood in fields of flowering weeds, their wall paintings still brilliant, their façades decorated with griffins, swans, and lions with the faces and parts of men and women, skewered dragons, winged serpents, and other marvels of metamorphoses. These vast and fanciful houses of God reminded Bascomb of the boundlessness of the human imagination and he felt lighthearted and enthusiastic. From Monte Felici they went on to San Georgio, where there were some painted tombs and a little Roman theater. They stopped in a grove below the town to have a picnic. Bascomb went into the woods to relieve himself and stumbled on a couple who were making love. They had not bothered to undress and the only flesh visible was the stranger's hairy backside. *Tanti, scusi,*[14] mumbled Bascomb and he retreated to another part of the forest but when he rejoined the Scandinavian he was uneasy. The struggling couple seemed to have dimmed his memories of the cathedrals. When he returned to his villa some nuns from a Roman convent were waiting for him to autograph their copies of *The World of Apples.* He did this and asked his housekeeper, Maria, to give them some wine. They paid him the usual compliments—he had created a universe that seemed to welcome man; he had divined the voice of moral beauty in a rain wind—but all that he could think of was the stranger's back. It seemed to have more zeal and meaning than his celebrated search for truth. It seemed to dominate all that he had seen that day—the castles, clouds, cathedrals, mountains, and fields of flowers. When the nuns left he looked up to the mountains to raise his spirits but the mountains looked then like the breasts of women. His mind had become unclean. He seemed to step aside from its recalcitrance and watch the course it took. In the distance he heard a train whistle and what would his wayward mind make of this? The excitements of travel, the *prix fixe* [15] in the dining car, the sort of wine they served on trains? It all seemed innocent enough until he caught his mind sneaking away from the dining car to the venereal [16] stalls of the Wagon-Lit [17] and thence into gross obscenity. He thought he knew what he needed and he spoke to Maria after dinner. She was always happy to accommodate him, although he always insisted that she take a bath. This, with the dishes, involved some delays but when she left him he definitely felt better but he definitely was not cured.

In the night his dreams were obscene and he woke several times trying to shake off this venereal pall or torpor. Things were no better in the light of morning. Obscenity—gross obscenity—seemed to be the only fact in life that possessed color and cheer. After breakfast he climbed up to his study and sat at his desk. The welcoming universe, the rain wind that sounded through the world of apples had vanished. Filth was his destiny, his best self, and he began with relish a long ballad called The Fart That Saved Athens. He finished the ballad that morning and burned it in the stove that had been given to him by the Oslo P.E.N. The ballad was, or had been until he burned it, an exhaustive and revolting exercise in scatology, and going down the stairs to his terrace he felt genuinely remorseful. He spent the afternoon writing a disgusting confession called The

14. "Excuse me!"
15. Menu at a set price.
16. Lascivious; under the influence of Venus.
17. Continental sleeping car.

Favorite of Tiberio.[18] Two admirers—a young married couple—came at five to praise him. They had met on a train, each of them carrying a copy of his *Apples*. They had fallen in love along the lines of the pure and ardent love he described. Thinking of his day's work, Bascomb hung his head.

On the next day he wrote The Confessions of a Public School Headmaster. He burned the manuscript at noon. As he came sadly down the stairs onto his terrace he found there fourteen students from the University of Rome who, as soon as he appeared, began to chant "The Orchards of Heaven"—the opening sonnet in *The World of Apples*. He shivered. His eyes filled with tears. He asked Maria to bring them some wine while he autographed their copies. They then lined up to shake his impure hand and returned to a bus in the field that had brought them out from Rome. He glanced at the mountains that had no cheering power—looked up at the meaningless blue sky. Where was the strength of decency? Had it any reality at all? Was the gross bestiality that obsessed him a sovereign truth? The most harrowing aspect of obscenity, he was to discover before the end of the week, was its boorishness. While he tackled his indecent projects with ardor he finished them with boredom and shame. The pornographer's course seems inflexible and he found himself repeating that tedious body of work that is circulated by the immature and the obsessed. He wrote The Confessions of a Lady's Maid, The Baseball Player's Honeymoon, and A Night in the Park. At the end of ten days he was at the bottom of the pornographer's barrel; he was writing dirty limericks. He wrote sixty of these and burned them. The next morning he took a bus to Rome.

He checked in at the Minerva where he always stayed and telephoned a long list of friends, but he knew that to arrive unannounced in a large city is to be friendless, and no one was home. He wandered around the streets and, stepping into a public toilet, found himself face to face with a male whore, displaying his wares. He stared at the man with the naïveté or the retard of someone very old. The man's face was idiotic—doped, drugged, and ugly—and yet, standing in his unsavory orisons, he seemed to old Bascomb angelic, armed with a flaming sword that might conquer banality and smash the glass of custom. He hurried away. It was getting dark and that hellish eruption of traffic noise that rings off the walls of Rome at dusk was rising to its climax. He wandered into an art gallery on the Via Sistina where the painter or photographer—he was both—seemed to be suffering from the same infection as Bascomb, only in a more acute form. Back in the streets he wondered if there was a

18. Italian form of Tiberius (42 B.C.–A.D. 37), Roman emperor. Although later scholars disagree, the historian Tacitus established Tiberius as the type of the blood-thirsty tyrant.

universality to this venereal dusk that had settled over his spirit. Had the world, as well as he, lost its way? He passed a concert hall where a program of songs was advertised and thinking that music might cleanse the thoughts of his heart he bought a ticket and went in. The concert was poorly attended. When the accompanist appeared, only a third of the seats were taken. Then the soprano came on, a splendid ash blonde in a crimson dress, and while she sang *Die Liebhaber der Brücken* old Bascomb began the disgusting and unfortunate habit of imagining that he was disrobing her. Hooks and eyes, he wondered? A zipper? While she sang *Die Feldspar* and went on to *Le temps des lilas et le temps des roses ne reviendra plus* he settled for a zipper and imagined unfastening her dress at the back and lifting it gently off her shoulders. He got her slip over her head while she sang *L'Amore Nascondere* and undid the hooks and eyes of her brassiere during *Les Rêves de Pierrot*.[19] His reverie was suspended when she stepped into the wings to gargle but as soon as she returned to the piano he got to work on her garter belt and all that it contained. When she took her bow at the intermission he applauded uproariously but not for her knowledge of music or the gifts of her voice. Then shame, limpid and pitiless as any passion, seemed to encompass him and he left the concert hall for the Minerva but his seizure was not over. He sat at his desk in the hotel and wrote a sonnet to the legendary Pope Joan. Technically it was an improvement over the limericks he had been writing but there was no moral improvement. In the morning he took the bus back to Monte Carbone and received some grateful admirers on his terrace. The next day he climbed to his study, wrote a few limericks and then took some Petronius and Juvenal [20] from the shelves to see what had been accomplished before him in this field of endeavor.

Here were candid and innocent accounts of sexual merriment. There was nowhere that sense of wickedness he experienced when he burned his work in the stove each afternoon. Was it simply that his world was that much older, its social responsibilities that much more grueling, and that lewdness was the only answer to an increase of anxiety? What was it that he had lost? It seemed then to be a sense of pride, an aureole of lightness and valor, a kind of crown. He seemed to hold the crown up to scrutiny and what did

19. Only one of these songs has been identified: "Le temps des lilas et le temps des roses" (words by Maurice Bouchot; melody by Ernest Chausson). The other song titles may be imaginary; most are cast in a form that violates either grammar or normal idiom. Rough translations would be: "The Lovers of Bridges," "The Feldspar," "The Time of Lilies and the Time of Roses Will Not Come Again," "The Hidden Love," and "The Dreams of Pierrot."

20. Petronius Arbiter, Roman courtier-writer of the first century A.D. and author of the *Satyricon*, was companion to the emperor Nero, and in charge of entertainment at the Imperial court. Decimus Junius Juvenalis (*c.* A.D. 60–140), Roman satirical poet, described contemporary society and its vices.

he find? Was it merely some ancient fear of Daddy's razor strap and Mummy's scowl, some childish subservience to the bullying world? He well knew his instincts to be rowdy, abundant, and indiscreet and had he allowed the world and all its tongues to impose upon him some structure of transparent values for the convenience of a conservative economy, an established church, and a bellicose army and navy? He seemed to hold the crown, hold it up into the light, it seemed made of light and what it seemed to mean was the genuine and tonic taste of exaltation and grief. The limericks he had just completed were innocent, factual, and merry. They were also obscene, but when had the facts of life become obscene and what were the realities of this virtue he so painfully stripped from himself each morning? They seemed to be the realities of anxiety and love: Amelia standing in the diagonal beam of light, the stormy night his son was born, the day his daughter married. One could disparage them as homely but they were the best he knew of life—anxiety and love—and worlds away from the limerick on his desk that began: "There was a young consul named Caesar / Who had an enormous fissure." He burned his limerick in the stove and went down the stairs.

The next day was the worst. He simply wrote F——k again and again covering six or seven sheets of paper. He put this into the stove at noon. At lunch Maria burned her finger, swore lengthily, and then said: "I should visit the sacred angel of Monte Giordano." "What is the sacred angel?" he asked. "The angel can cleanse the thoughts of a man's heart," said Maria. "He is in the old church at Monte Giordano. He is made of olive wood from the Mount of Olives and was carved by one of the saints himself. If you make a pilgrimage he will cleanse your thoughts." All Bascomb knew of pilgrimages was that you walked and for some reason carried a seashell. When Maria went up to take a siesta he looked among Amelia's relics and found a seashell. The angel would expect a present, he guessed, and from the box in his study he chose the gold medal the Soviet Government had given him on Lermontov's Jubilee.[21] He did not wake Maria or leave her a note. This seemed to be a conspicuous piece of senility. He had never before been, as the old often are, mischievously elusive, and he should have told Maria where he was going but he didn't. He started down through the vineyards to the main road at the bottom of the valley.

As he approached the river a little Fiat drew off the main road and parked among some trees. A man, his wife, and three carefully dressed daughters got out of the car and Bascomb stopped to watch them when he saw that the man carried a shotgun. What was he

---

21. Mikhail Y. Lermontov (1814–41), Russian poet and novelist.

going to do? Commit murder? Suicide? Was Bascomb about to see some human sacrifice? He sat down, concealed by the deep grass, and watched. The mother and the three girls were very excited. The father seemed to be enjoying complete sovereignty. They spoke a dialect and Bascomb understood almost nothing they said. The man took the shotgun from its case and put a single shell in the chamber. Then he arranged his wife and three daughters in a line and put their hands over their ears. They were squealing. When this was all arranged he stood with his back to them, aimed his gun at the sky, and fired. The three children applauded and exclaimed over the loudness of the noise and the bravery of their dear father. The father returned the gun to its case, they all got back into the Fiat and drove, Bascomb supposed, back to their apartment in Rome.

Bascomb stretched out in the grass and fell asleep. He dreamed that he was back in his own country. What he saw was an old Ford truck with four flat tires, standing in a field of buttercups. A child wearing a paper crown and a bath towel for a mantle hurried around the corner of a white house. An old man took a bone from a paper bag and handed it to a stray dog. Autumn leaves smoldered in a bathtub with lion's feet. Thunder woke him, distant, shaped, he thought, like a gourd. He got down to the main road where he was joined by a dog. The dog was trembling and he wondered if it was sick, rabid, dangerous, and then he saw that the dog was afraid of thunder. Each peal put the beast into a paroxysm of trembling and Bascomb stroked his head. He had never known an animal to be afraid of nature. Then the wind picked up the branches of the trees and he lifted his old nose to smell the rain, minutes before it fell. It was the smell of damp country churches, the spare rooms of old houses, earth closets, bathing suits put out to dry—so keen an odor of joy that he sniffed noisily. He did not, in spite of these transports, lose sight of his practical need for shelter. Beside the road was a little hut for bus travelers and he and the frightened dog stepped into this. The walls were covered with that sort of uncleanliness from which he hoped to flee and he stepped out again. Up the road was a farmhouse—one of those schizophrenic improvisations one sees so often in Italy. It seemed to have been bombed, spatch-cocked,[22] and put together, not at random but as a deliberate assault on logic. On one side there was a wooden lean-to where an old man sat. Bascomb asked him for the kindness of his shelter and the old man invited him in.

The old man seemed to be about Bascomb's age but he seemed to Bascomb enviably untroubled. His smile was gentle and his face

22. Split open. A spatch-cocked fowl is one that has been split open and grilled.

was clear. He had obviously never been harried by the wish to write a dirty limerick. He would never be forced to make a pilgrimage with a seashell in his pocket. He held a book in his lap—a stamp album—and the lean-to was filled with potted plants. He did not ask his soul to clap hands and sing,[23] and yet he seemed to have reached an organic peace of mind that Bascomb coveted. Should Bascomb have collected stamps and potted plants? Anyhow, it was too late. Then the rain came, thunder shook the earth, the dog whined and trembled, and Bascomb caressed him. The storm passed in a few minutes and Bascomb thanked his host and started up the road.

He had a nice stride for someone so old and he walked, like all the rest of us, in some memory of prowess—love or football, Amelia or a good dropkick—but after a mile or two he realized that he would not reach Monte Giordano until long after dark and when a car stopped and offered him a ride to the village he accepted it, hoping that this would not put a crimp in his cure. It was still light when he reached Monte Giordano. The village was about the same size as his own with the same tufa walls and bitter lichen. The old church stood in the center of the square but the door was locked. He asked for the priest and found him in a vineyard, burning prunings. He explained that he wanted to make an offering to the sainted angel and showed the priest his golden medal. The priest wanted to know if it was true gold and Bascomb then regretted his choice. Why hadn't he chosen the medal given him by the French Government or the medal from Oxford? The Russians had not hall-marked the gold and he had no way of proving its worth. Then the priest noticed that the citation was written in the Russian alphabet. Not only was it false gold; it was Communist gold and not a fitting present for the sacred angel. At that moment the clouds parted and a single ray of light came into the vineyard, lighting the medal. It was a sign. The priest drew a cross in the air and they started back to the church.

It was an old, small, poor country church. The angel was in a chapel on the left, which the priest lighted. The image, buried in jewelry, stood in an iron cage with a padlocked door. The priest opened this and Bascomb placed his Lermontov medal at the

23. From William Butler Yeats, "Sailing to Byzantium" (1927), st. 2:

> *An aged man is but a paltry thing,*
> *A tattered coat upon a stick, unless*
> *Soul clap its hands and sing, and louder sing*
> *For every tatter in its mortal dress . . .*

In the poem the timeless art-world of Byzantium is contrasted with the sensual world of change, "Whatever is begotten, born, and dies."

angel's feet. Then he got to his knees and said loudly: "God bless Walt Whitman. God Bless Hart Crane. God bless Dylan Thomas. God bless William Faulkner, Scott Fitzgerald, and especially Ernest Hemingway." The priest locked up the sacred relic and they left the church together. There was a café on the square where he got some supper and rented a bed. This was a strange engine of brass with brass angels at the four corners, but they seemed to possess some brassy blessedness since he dreamed of peace and woke in the middle of the night finding in himself that radiance he had known when he was younger. Something seemed to shine in his mind and limbs and lights and vitals and he fell asleep again and slept until morning.

On the next day, walking down from Monte Giordano to the main road, he heard the trumpeting of a waterfall. He went into the woods to find this. It was a natural fall, a shelf of rock and a curtain of green water, and it reminded him of a fall at the edge of the farm in Vermont where he had been raised. He had gone there one Sunday afternoon when he was a boy and sat on a hill above the pool. While he was there he saw an old man, with hair as thick and white as his was now, come through the woods. He had watched the old man unlace his shoes and undress himself with the haste of a lover. First he had wet his hands and arms and shoulders and then he had stepped into the torrent, bellowing with joy. He had then dried himself with his underpants, dressed, and gone back into the woods and it was not until he disappeared that Bascomb had realized that the old man was his father.

Now he did what his father had done—unlaced his shoes, tore at the buttons of his shirt and knowing that a mossy stone or the force of the water could be the end of him he stepped naked into the torrent, bellowing like his father. He could stand the cold for only a minute but when he stepped away from the water he seemed at last to be himself. He went on down to the main road where he was picked up by some mounted police, since Maria had sounded the alarm and the whole province was looking for the maestro. His return to Monte Carbone was triumphant and in the morning he began a long poem on the inalienable dignity of light and air that, while it would not get him the Nobel Prize, would grace the last months of his life.

From *The World of Apples* (1973)

·BIOGRAPHICAL AND BIBLIOGRAPHICAL NOTES·

SHERWOOD ANDERSON
(1876–1941)

Born and reared in Ohio, Sherwood Anderson knew at first hand the poverty and provinciality of small-town life. After brief service in the Army during the Spanish-American War, Anderson became a successful businessman and advertising writer, while in his private world he tried to write novels and short stories. Finally, in 1912, the tensions between his public and private lives led to a nervous breakdown, and Anderson abandoned his career and marriage to start afresh in Chicago. There he combined advertising writing with the composition of fiction, and the 1919 publication of *Winesburg, Ohio* brought him instant recognition. A series of sketches about the frustrations of provincial life, *Winesburg, Ohio* was followed by three other collections of stories: *The Triumph of the Egg* (1921), *Horses and Men* (1923), and *Death in the Woods* (1933).

Although Anderson also wrote several novels and plays, he is now remembered for his brief fictional sketches, and for the catalytic role he played in the careers of Ernest Hemingway and William Faulkner. One of the most fascinating aspects of Anderson's career was his constant attempt, in the later years, to construct a "fictional" yet truthful self-portrait: see *Sherwood Anderson's Memoirs* (1969), *A Story Teller's Story* (1968), and *Tar: A Midwest Childhood* (1969), all edited by Ray Lewis White.

Editions *Winesburg, Ohio* has been edited by Malcolm Cowley (1960). Other accessible collections are *The Portable Sherwood Anderson*, ed. Horace Gregory (1949), and *The Sherwood Anderson Reader*, ed. Paul Rosenfeld (1947).

BIOGRAPHY AND CRITICISM

David D. Anderson, *Sherwood Anderson* (1967).
Rex Burbank, *Sherwood Anderson* (1964).
Irving Howe, *Sherwood Anderson* (1951).
Howard Mumford Jones and Walter Rideout (eds.), *Letters of Sherwood Anderson* (1953).
Brom Weber, *Sherwood Anderson* (1964).
Ray L. White (ed.), *The Achievement of Sherwood Anderson: Essays in Criticism* (1966).

JOHN BARTH
(1930—)

John Simmons Barth was born in Cambridge, on the Eastern Shore of Maryland, and educated at Johns Hopkins University. His first interest was in music, but at Johns Hopkins he began writing short stories as a result of his "love affair" with Scheherazade and the *Thousand Nights and a Night*. His first novel, *The Floating Opera*, was published in 1956, followed by *The End of the Road* (1958), *The Sot-Weed Factor* (1960), and *Giles Goat-Boy: or The Revised New Syllabus* (1966). The talent for farce and parody brilliantly displayed in these novels informs Barth's collection of fictions "for print, tape, live voice," *Lost in the Funhouse* (1968).

CRITICISM

Gerhard Joseph, *John Barth* (1970).
Edgar H. Knapp, "Found in the Barthhouse: Novelist as Savior," *Modern Fiction Studies*, 14 (Winter 1968–69), 446–51.
Daniel Majdiak, "Barth and the Representation of Life," *Criticism*, 13 (1970), 51–67.
Robert Scholes, *The Fabulators* (1967).

DONALD BARTHELME
(1933—)

Born in Philadelphia and reared in Texas, Donald Barthelme has been a newspaper reporter and museum director, as well as managing editor of a review of art and literature, *Location*. He is the author of a novel, *Snow White* (1967), and four collections of stories: *Come Back, Dr. Caligari* (1964), *Unspeakable Practices, Unnatural Acts* (1968), *City Life* (1970), and *Sadness* (1972). His best works are marked by a surreal vision expressed through discontinuous forms, what Robert Scholes has called an "ethically controlled fantasy."

CRITICISM

William H. Gass, *Fiction and the Figures of Life* (1970).

SAUL BELLOW
(1915—)

Born in Quebec of Russian parents, Saul Bellow was brought up in Chicago and educated at the University of Chicago and Northwestern University. In the late 1930s he worked for a time on the WPA Writers Project, and after World War II he taught at a number of universities, including Minnesota, Princeton, and New York University. Since 1962 he has been a teaching member of the Committee on Social Thought at the University of Chicago.

Primarily a novelist, Bellow is noted for *Dangling Man* (1944), *The Victim* (1947), *The Adventures of Augie March* (1953), *Henderson the Rain King* (1959), *Herzog* (1964), and *Mr. Sammler's Planet* (1969). His collections of short fiction include *Seize the Day* (1956) and *Mosby's Memoirs and Other Stories* (1968).

CRITICISM

John Jacob Clayton, *Saul Bellow: In Defense of Man* (1968).
Robert Detweiler, *Saul Bellow* (1967).
Robert R. Dutton, *Saul Bellow* (1971).
Irving Malin (ed.), *Saul Bellow and His Critics* (1967).
Irving Malin, *Saul Bellow's Fiction* (1969).
Keith M. Opdahl, *The Novels of Saul Bellow* (1967).
Earl Rovit, *Saul Bellow* (1967).
Tony Tanner, *Saul Bellow* (1965).

JOHN CHEEVER
(1912—)

John Cheever was born in Quincy, Massachusetts, and educated at nearby Thayer Academy. He has published three novels, *The Wapshot Chronicle* (1957), *The Wapshot Scandal* (1964), and *Bullet Park* (1969), and has been a prolific writer of short fiction, many of his stories appearing in the *New Yorker*. While best known for his polished studies of suburban life, in recent years Cheever has widened the range of his art to include more exotic settings (as in "The World of Apples"). The short stories have appeared in five volumes: *The Way Some People Live* (1943), *The Enormous Radio and Other Stories* (1953), *The Housebreaker of Shady Hill* (1958), *Some People, Places, and Things That Will Not Appear in My Next Novel* (1961), *The Brigadier and the Golf Widow* (1964), and *The World of Apples* (1973).

CRITICISM

John W. Aldridge, *Time to Murder and Create: The Contemporary Novel in Crisis* (1966).
Ihab Hassan, *Radical Innocence: Studies in the Contemporary American Novel* (1961).

ROBERT COOVER
(1932—)

Born in Charles City, Iowa, Robert Coover graduated from the University of Indiana and received his M.A. from the University of Chicago. He has been writer-in-residence at several universities, including Wisconsin State, Washington University (St. Louis), and Princeton. His first novel, *The Origin of the Brunists*, received the William Faulkner Award for the best first novel of 1966; it was followed in 1968 by a second novel, *The Universal Baseball Association*, and in 1969 by *Pricksongs & Descants*, a collection of stories.

CRITICISM

R. H. W. Dillard, "The Wisdom of the Beast: The Fictions of Robert Coover," *Hollins Critic*, 7 (April 1970), 1-11.
Leo J. Hertzel, "An Interview with Robert Coover," *Critique: Studies in Modern Fiction*, 2 (1969), 25–29.

STEPHEN CRANE
(1871–1900)

Stephen Crane was born in Newark, New Jersey, the fourteenth and youngest child of a Methodist minister. His father died in 1880 and the family settled at last in Asbury Park, New Jersey, where one of Crane's brothers ran a news agency. Crane received his secondary education at private schools, and attended Lafayette College and Syracuse University in 1890–91. His first novel, *Maggie: A Girl of the Streets*, was written "in two days before Christmas" in 1891, but was not published until 1893. In 1892 Crane became a free-lance reporter in New York and during the remainder of his brief life he turned out a vast amount of newspaper copy, including reports on the Spanish-American War. Like Hemingway after him, Crane found inspiration for his fiction in the sharp, laconic style of the new journalism.

The Red Badge of Courage, Crane's classic novel of the Civil War, was written in 1894; and although Crane at that time had never "smelled even the powder of battle" he managed to endow the tale with powerful psychological realism. *The Open Boat and Other Tales of Adventure* followed in 1898. In 1899 Crane settled in England with his common-law wife, Cora Taylor, and soon established literary friendships with Joseph Conrad, H. G. Wells, Ford Madox Ford, and Henry James. He died of tuberculosis in 1900, at the age of twenty-nine.

Editions The definitive University of Virginia Edition of the *Works of Stephen Crane*, now under way, will eventually contain "every known piece of Crane's writing and journalism." *The Complete Short Stories and Sketches of Stephen Crane*, a single-volume edition compiled by Thomas A. Gullason, appeared in 1963. See also *The War Dispatches of Stephen Crane* (1964) and *The New York City Sketches of Stephen Crane and Related Pieces* (1966), edited by R. W. Stallman and E. R. Hagemann.

BIOGRAPHY

John Berryman, *Stephen Crane* (1950).
R. W. Stallman, *Stephen Crane: A Biography* (1968).
R. W. Stallman and Lillian Gilkes (eds.), *Stephen Crane: Letters* (1960).

CRITICISM

Maurice Bassan (ed.), *Stephen Crane: A Collection of Critical Essays* (1967).
Edwin H. Cady, *Stephen Crane* (1962).
Jean Cazemajou, *Stephen Crane* (1969).
Donald B. Gibson, *The Fiction of Stephen Crane* (1968).
Eric Solomon, *Stephen Crane: From Parody to Realism* (1966).

WILLIAM FAULKNER
(1897–1962)

William Faulkner was born in New Albany, Mississippi, but the family soon moved to nearby Oxford, the home of the University of Mississippi. Faulkner's ancestors had been active in Mississippi life for three generations, and his great-grandfather was the author of a popular romance of Southern manners, *The White Rose of Memphis*. In spite of this literary heritage William Faulkner was not interested in formal education, and left high school before graduation. After an abortive attempt to join the U.S. Army he enlisted in the Royal Canadian Flying Corps, but the war ended before he could see any action. After the Armistice he attended the University of Mississippi for a time, served as postmaster in Oxford, and then made his way to New Orleans, where he became a friend of Sherwood Anderson. After a walking tour in Europe he returned to Mississippi and settled in Oxford, which became his home for the greater part of his career. In 1950 he was awarded the Nobel Prize for literature.

Faulkner's early works, *Soldier's Pay* (1926) and *Mosquitoes* (1927), reflect his contact with the cosmopolitan literary world of the 1920s; but beginning with *Sartoris* (1929) and *The Sound and the Fury* (1929) Faulkner began to establish his mythical Southern world, Yoknapatawpha County, "William Faulkner, sole owner & proprietor." Between 1929 and 1942, in eight novels and four collections of stories, Faulkner mapped out the history and social dimensions of this legendary county, and most of his subsequent works were pendants to the created myth. In the saga of Yoknapatawpha County, from the early Indians and white settlers to the present-day Snopes clan, Faulkner found the local substance for a universal moral vision.

William Faulkner was essentially a teller of tales, and many of his novels had their origins in anecdotes or short stories. Even *The Sound and the Fury* and *Absalom, Absalom!* (1936), his most intricately constructed novels, began as a series of short vignettes: "That Evening Sun" was one of the stories of the Compson family that preceded the conception of the novel. The major collections of short fiction are *These 13* (1931), *Doctor Martino and Other Stories* (1934), *The Unvanquished* (1938, tales of the Civil War and Reconstruction), and *Go Down, Moses* (1942). *Go Down, Moses*, which contains "The Bear" as its centerpiece, is an integrated suite of stories tracing the impact of slavery and the past on contemporary Southern life.

Editions   Most of Faulkner's important short fiction is to be found in *The Unvanquished, Go Down, Moses,* and the *Collected Stories* of 1950. The *Big Woods* (1954) gathers together the hunting stories, including a shortened version of "The Bear." *The Portable Faulkner,* edited by Malcolm Cowley (1946), reprints many of the stories and fragments from the novels in historical order.

BIOGRAPHY

Joseph L. Blotner, *Faulkner: A Biography,* 2 vols. (1974).

CRITICISM

Cleanth Brooks, *William Faulkner: The Yoknapatawpha Country* (1963).

Lewis M. Dabney, *The Indians of Yoknapatawpha* (1974). Contains a chapter on "Red Leaves."

Elmo Howell, "William Faulkner's Chickasaw Legacy: A Note on 'Red Leaves,'" *Arizona Quarterly,* 26 (Winter 1970), 293–303.

Frederick J. Hoffman, *William Faulkner* (1961).

Frederick J. Hoffman and Olga Vickery (eds.), *William Faulkner: Three Decades of Criticism* (1960).

James B. Meriwether, "The Short Fiction of William Faulkner: A Bibliography," *Proof,* 1 (1971), 293–329.

Michael Millgate, *The Achievement of William Faulkner* (1966).

Norman H. Pearson, "Faulkner's Three 'Evening Suns,'" *Yale University Library Gazette,* 29 (1954), 61–70.

Edmond L. Volpe, *A Reader's Guide to William Faulkner* (1964).

Hyatt H. Waggoner, *William Faulkner: From Jefferson to the World* (1959).

F. SCOTT FITZGERALD
(1896–1940)

Francis Scott Key Fitzgerald was born in Minneapolis and educated at the Newman School, a private Roman Catholic institution, before entering Princeton in the Class of 1917. At Princeton he became a friend of Edmund Wilson and John Peale Bishop, and began to write fiction and poetry. Leaving Princeton without a degree, he was commissioned as an infantry lieutenant and met Zelda Sayre of Montgomery, Alabama; they were married in 1920. Fitzgerald's first novel, *This Side of Paradise* (originally *The Romantic Egoist*), was published in 1920, and he became instantly famous. His early stories established him as the spokesman for the "Jazz Age," and

Fitzgerald's life during the 1920s oscillated between New York and Europe. *The Great Gatsby* (1925), although not the popular success that Fitzgerald had hoped for, climaxed this phase of his career.

As the decade of the 1920s wore to a close, Fitzgerald's art succumbed to the pressure of the times. While he never lost his fine sense of style and social discriminations, he found it more and more difficult to write in the face of personal and economic disasters. These tensions are reflected in *Tender Is The Night* (1934), and in stories such as "Babylon Revisited." In the late 1930s, after his wife Zelda's breakdown and his own physical collapse, Fitzgerald moved to Hollywood; his last, unfinished work—*The Last Tycoon*—draws its background from these years. Fitzgerald died of a heart attack in 1940, after a long period of physical and psychological disintegration.

Editions Four volumes of stories were published during Fitzgerald's lifetime: *Flappers and Philosophers* (1921), *Tales of the Jazz Age* (1922), *All the Sad Young Men* (1926), and *Taps at Reveille* (1935). Some of the uncollected stories were printed in *The Stories of F. Scott Fitzgerald*, edited by Malcolm Cowley (1953). Arthur Mizener included fourteen uncollected stories in *Afternoon of an Author* (1957). There is no complete edition of Fitzgerald's stories, but most are available in paperback from Charles Scribner's Sons.

BIOGRAPHY

Sheilah Graham, *Beloved Infidel* (1958).
Nancy Milford, *Zelda* (1970).
Arthur Mizener, *The Far Side of Paradise* (1951, 1965).
Andrew Turnbull, *Scott Fitzgerald* (1962).
Andrew Turnbull (ed.), *The Letters of F. Scott Fitzgerald* (1963).

CRITICISM

Kenneth Eble, *F. Scott Fitzgerald* (1963).
John A. Higgins, *F. Scott Fitzgerald: A Study of the Stories* (1971).
Richard D. Lehan, *F. Scott Fitzgerald and the Craft of Fiction* (1966).
Sergio Perosa, *The Art of F. Scott Fitzgerald* (1965).
Robert Sklar, *F. Scott Fitzgerald: The Last Laocoon* (1967).
William White, "Two Versions of F. Scott Fitzgerald's 'Babylon Revisited,'" *Publications of the Bibliographical Society of America*, 60 (1966), 439–52.

HAMLIN GARLAND
(1860–1940)

Hamlin Garland was born in Wisconsin, but his family soon pioneered westward into Iowa and the Dakota Territory. His earliest memory was of his father's returning from the Civil War, with the "peculiar, measured, swinging stride" of the veteran. Brought up on the frontier, Garland made his way to Boston in 1884, where he educated himself after being rejected by Harvard University. He became a friend of William Dean Howells, and began to write of the "stern facts" of Western life, using the techniques of the new "realism" championed by Howells. *Crumbling Idols* (1894; reprinted 1952) lays down the theoretical basis for Garland's method, which he called "veritism."

Garland's most famous volume of short stories, *Main-Travelled Roads* (1891), was succeeded by *Prairie Folks* (1893) and *Wayside Courtships* (1897). His best work was published in the 1890s; during the rest of his long career he produced little fiction of lasting interest, although his autobiographical volumes have permanent value as records of the Populist heritage. *A Son of the Middle Border* (1917) provides the essential background for "The Return of a Private."

Editions   Donald Pizer is currently editing *The Works of Hamlin Garland. Main-Travelled Roads*, edited by Thomas A. Bledsoe, was reprinted in 1954.

BIOGRAPHY AND CRITICISM

Jean Holloway, *Hamlin Garland* (1960).
Robert Mane, *Hamlin Garland: L'Homme et l'oeuvre* (1968).
Donald Pizer, *Hamlin Garland's Early Work and Career* (1960).
Charles Child Walcutt, *American Literary Naturalism: A Divided Stream* (1956).

NATHANIEL HAWTHORNE
(1804–1864)

The son of a sea captain, Hawthorne was born in Salem, Massachusetts, and attended Bowdoin College from 1821 to 1825, graduating in the same class as Longfellow and Franklin Pierce. The years from 1825 to 1839 passed quietly in Salem, as Hawthorne gradually discovered the appropriate subjects and forms for his writing. His first novel, *Fanshawe* (1828), was a total failure, and it was not until the publication of *Twice-Told Tales* in 1837 that Hawthorne began to attract significant recognition. During the next five years Hawthorne worked for a time in the Boston Custom House, and spent a few months at the Brook Farm community. In 1842 he married Sophia Peabody, and from 1842 to 1846 they lived in the "Old Manse" at Concord, near Emerson and Thoreau. Another collection of tales, *Mosses from an Old Manse,* was published in 1846.

Hawthorne's years of slow and solitary artistic development ended with the publication of *The Scarlet Letter* in 1850. *The Scarlet Letter, The House of the Seven Gables* (1851), and *The Blithedale Romance* (1852) brought him fame, and in 1853 his friend President Pierce (for whom he had written a "campaign biography") appointed him U.S. Consul at Liverpool. Hawthorne served there for four years, and then traveled in Italy until 1860. His last great work, *The Marble Faun* (1860), was the product of this encounter with Italy. In 1860 Hawthorne returned to the United States, but his imaginative powers were failing, and he published little of note during his last years.

Editions   The Centenary Edition of the Works of Nathaniel Hawthorne (Ohio State University Press) has been under way since 1963. Other editions are the Riverside (12 vols., 1883) and the Old Manse (22 vols., 1900). Convenient collections are *Hawthorne's Short Stories,* edited by Newton Arvin (1946), and *Selected Tales and Sketches,* edited by Hyatt H. Waggoner (1950).

BIOGRAPHY

Randall Stewart, *Nathaniel Hawthorne* (1948).

CRITICISM

Newton Arvin, *Hawthorne* (1929).
Frederick C. Crews, *The Sins of the Fathers: Hawthorne's Psychological Themes* (1966).
Richard H. Fogle, *Hawthorne's Fiction: The Light and the Dark* (1964).
A. N. Kaul (ed.), *Hawthorne: A Collection of Critical Essays* (1966).
Harry Levin, *The Power of Blackness* (1958).
Terence Martin, *Nathaniel Hawthorne* (1965).
Mark Van Doren, *Nathaniel Hawthorne* (1949).
Edward Wagenknecht, *Nathaniel Hawthorne* (1961).
Hyatt H. Waggoner, *Hawthorne: A Critical Study* (1955).

ERNEST HEMINGWAY
(1898–1961)

Born and brought up in Oak Park, Illinois, a middle-class suburb of Chicago, Hemingway graduated from high school in 1917 and spent a brief period as a reporter for the Kansas City *Star*. When the United States entered World War I he volunteered for ambulance duty, and was severely wounded on the Italian front. After the war he became a foreign correspondent for the Toronto *Star*, but under the influence of Sherwood Anderson he soon settled in Paris as an expatriate writer. There he met Ezra Pound and Gertrude Stein, who exercised a major influence on the development of his austere early style. His first important volume of short stories, *In Our Time* (1925), was followed by *The Sun Also Rises* (1926), a novel of expatriate life which made him famous. Between 1923 and 1933 Hemingway wrote his most important work, including all his major short stories. *The Fifth Column and the First Forty-nine Stories* (1938) contains the stories of *In Our Time, Men Without Women* (1927), and *Winner Take Nothing* (1933), besides a few later stories and a play about the Spanish Civil War.

Hemingway's great novels of the 1920s—*The Sun Also Rises* and *A Farewell to Arms* (1929)—were followed in the 1930s by *To Have and Have Not* (1937) and *For Whom the Bell Tolls* (1940), while *Across the River and Into the Trees* (1950) and *The Old Man and the Sea* (1952) appeared during the period of international fame when Hemingway was awarded a Nobel Prize. Although Hemingway never wrote anything that did not bear his special stamp, many of the later works verge on parody of the early style, and he will be remembered longest for the short fictions of the 1920s and 1930s. In those spare and chiseled stories, where the traditions of journalistic economy and Flaubertian precision are fused into one, Hemingway forged a style for his time.

BIOGRAPHY

Carlos Baker, *Ernest Hemingway: A Life Story* (1969).

CRITICISM

Carlos Baker, *Hemingway: The Writer as Artist* (1972).
Carlos Baker (ed.), *Hemingway and His Critics: An International Anthology* (1961).
Sheridan Baker, *Ernest Hemingway* (1967).
Charles Fenton, *The Apprenticeship of Ernest Hemingway* (1954).

Leo Gurko, *Ernest Hemingway and the Pursuit of Heroism* (1968).
Robert P. Weeks (ed.), *Hemingway: A Collection of Critical Essays* (1962).
Philip Young, *Ernest Hemingway* (1952, 1966).

WILLIAM DEAN HOWELLS
(1837–1920)

Like Mark Twain, William Dean Howells was self-educated as a typesetter and a newspaper reporter. Son of a country printer and druggist in Ohio, he left Ohio in 1860 for Boston, where he met James Russell Lowell and other "Boston Brahmins." After writing Lincoln's "campaign biography" in 1860, Howells was named U.S. Consul in Venice. In 1866 he joined the *Atlantic Monthly* staff, and from 1871 to 1881 he was chief editor, introducing among others Henry James and Mark Twain. His best known novel, *The Rise of Silas Lapham,* appeared in 1884. In 1885 he moved to New York, and began his long association with *Harper's Magazine;* his most famous comments in defense of the new "realism" were published in *Criticism and Fiction* (1891). During his final years Howells was the acknowledged "elder statesman" of American letters.

Editions   Indiana University Press is currently publishing a *Selected Edition of W. D. Howells.* Howells's comments on the art of fiction are collected in *"Criticism and Fiction" and Other Essays,* edited by Clara M. Kirk and Rudolf Kirk (1959).

BIOGRAPHY

Edwin H. Cady, *The Road to Realism: The Early Years, 1837–1885* (1956), and *The Realist at War: The Mature Years, 1885–1920* (1958).
Henry Nash Smith and William M. Gibson (eds.), *Mark Twain—Howells Letters,* 2 vols. (1960).
Kenneth S. Lynn, *William Dean Howells: An American Life* (1971).

CRITICISM

Everett Carter, *Howells and the Age of Realism* (1954).
Kenneth E. Eble (ed.), *Howells: A Century of Criticism* (1962).
William M. Gibson, *William Dean Howells* (1967).
Clara M. Kirk and Rudolf Kirk, *William Dean Howells* (1962).
Kermit Vanderbilt, *The Achievement of William Dean Howells* (1968).

WASHINGTON IRVING
(1783–1859)

Washington Irving was born in New York City, the eleventh child of a Presbyterian merchant. As a young man he read law, but without great enthusiasm, and in 1804 he traveled abroad for his health, rambling through Italy, France, Holland, and England. In 1806 Irving was admitted to the New York bar, but his chief interests were literary: he helped edit *Salmagundi*, an American imitation of eighteenth-century English periodicals, and in 1809 published his burlesque *History of New York, by Diedrich Knickerbocker*. After a few years in the family hardware business Irving settled in England, where he met Walter Scott and completed work on *The Sketch-Book of Geoffrey Crayon, Gent*. When the *Sketch-Book* was published in 1819–20, Irving became a celebrity in England, with a popularity rivaling that of Scott and Byron. *Bracebridge Hall* (1822) reinforced his reputation, and in the same year he went to Germany to expand his long-standing interest in "the rich mine of German literature." *Tales of a Traveller* (1824) reflects this German influence in its Gothic stories.

During the years 1826–29 Irving made two journeys to Spain, living for a time in the Alhambra as American attaché. In addition to *The Conquest of Granada* (1829) and the volumes on Columbus, this period produced the stories and sketches later collected as *The Alhambra* (1832). Between 1829 and 1831 Irving served as secretary of the American Legation in London, and then returned to the United States after an absence of seventeen years. The works of the next five years—*A Tour on the Prairies, Astoria, The Adventures of Captain Bonneville*—reflect a determined attempt to assimilate the new forces in an expanding country. In 1836 Irving settled at "Sunnyside," a villa near Tarrytown, New York, and with the exception of his years as Minister to Spain (1842–45) he remained there until his death. His last great work was a five-volume *Life of Washington*.

Editions   The University of Wisconsin Press has begun publication of *The Complete Works of Washington Irving*. Until this project is completed, the reader must rely on the nineteenth-century editions, such as the Author's Uniform Revised Edition (21 vols., 1860–61). Useful collections are *Washington Irving: Representative Selections*, edited by Henry A. Pochmann (1934), and *Washington Irving: Selected Prose*, edited by Stanley T. Williams (1950).

BIOGRAPHY

Stanley T. Williams, *The Life of Washington Irving*, 2 vols. (1935).

CRITICISM

Van Wyck Brooks, *The World of Washington Irving* (1944).

William L. Hedges, *Washington Irving: An American Study, 1802–1832* (1965).

Terence Martin, "Rip, Ichabod, and the American Imagination," *American Literature*, 31 (May 1959), 137–49.

Philip Young, "Fallen from Time: The Mythic Rip Van Winkle," *Kenyon Review*, 22 (Autumn 1960), 547–73.

HENRY JAMES
(1843–1916)

Much of Henry James's life is summed up on the memorial tablet erected by his friends in Chelsea Old Church, London: "In memory of Henry James, Order of Merit, Novelist: born in New York, 1843; died in Chelsea, 1916: lover and interpreter of the fine amenities, of brave decisions and generous loyalties: a resident of this parish who renounced a cherished citizenship to give his allegiance to England in the first year of the Great War."

The son of a famous American philosopher-theologian, also named Henry, and the younger brother of an even more famous philosopher-psychologist, William, James received a cosmopolitan education in Europe and America. After a brief period at Harvard Law School (1862–63) he began to write reviews and stories for the American magazines, and in 1869 he undertook the first of a series of visits to Europe. In 1876 he settled in London, and between 1877 and 1881 produced the first of his masterly international fictions, including *Daisy Miller* (1878) and *The Portrait of a Lady* (1881). During the 1880s James wrote three major novels, *The Bostonians, The Princess Casamassima,* and *The Tragic Muse.* In the early 1890s he tried, unsuccessfully, to become a man of the theatre; but after the failure of his play *Guy Domville* in 1895 he turned his dramatic talents to the composition of even more subtle fictions. The three great novels of his later phase—*The Ambassadors, The Wings of the Dove,* and *The Golden Bowl*—were written between 1900 and 1904.

In 1904 James returned to America for the first time in more than twenty years, and recorded his impressions in the essays of *The American Scene* (1907). From 1907 to 1909 he worked continuously on the "New York Edition" of his stories and novels, which was issued with critical prefaces. The chief productions of his last years were the autobiographical volumes, *A Small Boy and Others, Notes of a Son and Brother,* and *The Middle Years.*

Editions   James's major works are readily available in the "New York Edition" of *The Novels and Tales of Henry James* (26 vols., 1907–9), which has recently been reissued. *The Novels and Stories of Henry James* (35 vols., London, 1921–23) contains the entire "New York Edition" (with James's original prefaces), and many additional novels and tales. *The Complete Tales of Henry James,* ed. Leon Edel (12 vols., 1962–65) is the definitive text of the stories, but there are many other useful collections and reprints. James was the most articulate of craftsmen, and two books are indispensable to the student of his technique: *The Notebooks of Henry James,* edited by F. O. Matthiessen and Kenneth Murdock (1947); and *The Art of the Novel,* edited by R. P. Blackmur (1934), which collects the critical prefaces to the "New York Edition." Another useful anthology is *The Art of Fiction and Other Essays,* edited by Morris Roberts (1948).

BIOGRAPHY

F. W. Dupee, *Henry James* (1951).
Leon Edel, *Henry James* (1953–72). Five volumes entitled *The Untried Years, The Conquest of London, The Middle Years, The Treacherous Years,* and *The Master.*
Leon Edel (ed.), *Selected Letters of Henry James* (1955).

CRITICISM

Joseph Warren Beach, *The Method of Henry James* (1918).
Leon Edel, *Henry James* (1960).
Laurence Holland, *The Expense of Vision* (1964).
Bruce R. McElderry, Jr., *Henry James* (1965).
Richard Poirier, *The Comic Sense of Henry James* (1960).
S. Gorley Putt, *Henry James: A Reader's Guide* (1966).
William T. Stafford (ed.), *James's "Daisy Miller": The Story, the Play, the Critics* (1963).

SARAH ORNE JEWETT
(1849–1909)

Born and reared in South Berwick, Maine, Sarah Orne Jewett became a faithful chronicler of life along the Maine coast. Her father was the village doctor, and from him she learned the art of compassionate observation. Between 1877 and 1901 she published three novels and ten collections of short stories. Her most famous work, *The Country of the Pointed Firs* (1896), is a series of related sketches informed by a sympathetic but unsentimental point of view. One of her favorite mottos was a sentence from Flaubert: "One should write of ordinary life as if one were writing history."

Editions   Kenneth S. Lynn is preparing a complete edition of *The Works of Sarah Orne Jewett*. Other collections are *Stories and Tales* (7 vols., 1910) and *The Best Stories of Sarah Orne Jewett*, edited by Willa Cather (1925; reissued as *The Country of the Pointed Firs and Other Stories*, 1954).

BIOGRAPHY AND CRITICISM

Richard Cary, *Sarah Orne Jewett* (1962).
Richard Cary (ed.), *Sarah Orne Jewett Letters* (1956, 1967).
John Eldridge Frost, *Sarah Orne Jewett* (1960).
F. O. Matthiessen, *Sarah Orne Jewett* (1929).
Margaret Thorp, *Sarah Orne Jewett* (1966).

BERNARD MALAMUD
(1914—)

Born in Brooklyn and educated at the City College of New York and Columbia University, Bernard Malamud is best known for his sensitive portrayals of Jewish life, in which realism is overlaid with an almost allegorical sense of fate and suffering. "The Jews are absolutely the very *stuff* of drama," Malamud once wrote, and this moral drama is the foundation of his stories. *The Magic Barrel*, his first collection (1958), was followed by *Idiots First* (1963), *Pictures of Fidelman* (1969), and *Rembrandt's Hat* (1973). Malamud has also written four novels: *The Natural* (1952), *The Assistant* (1957), *A*

New Life (1961), *The Fixer* (1966). *A Malamud Reader,* ed. Philip Rahv (1967), is a fine introduction to Malamud's fictional world.

CRITICISM

Leslie A. and Joyce W. Field (eds.), *Bernard Malamud and the Critics* (1970).

Ihab Hassan, *Radical Innocence: Studies in the Contemporary American Novel* (1961).

Sidney Richman, *Bernard Malamud* (1966).

Earl H. Rovit, "Bernard Malamud and the Jewish Literary Tradition," *Critique,* 3 (1960), 3–10.

Tony Tanner, "Bernard Malamud and the New Life," *Critical Quarterly,* 10 (1968), 151–68.

MARK TWAIN
(1835–1910)

Samuel Langhorne Clemens (Mark Twain) was born in Missouri, and apprenticed as a printer's helper at the age of thirteen. From 1853 to 1856 he was an itinerant newspaper reporter, and from 1857 to 1861 a riverboat pilot on the Mississippi. In 1861 he journeyed to the West Coast, where he worked as a printer and journalist. "The Celebrated Jumping Frog of Calaveras County," published in 1865, became the title story of his first collection of sketches (1867). *The Innocents Abroad* appeared in 1869, based on Twain's travels in Europe and Palestine during the previous year.

In 1870, the year of his marriage, Twain began the lifelong task of turning his early experiences into fiction. *The Adventures of Tom Sawyer* (1876) was followed by *Life on the Mississippi* (1883) and *Huckleberry Finn* (1884). In the 1890s, after publication of *A Connecticut Yankee in King Arthur's Court* (1889), Twain suffered a series of financial disasters, and these misfortunes, in combination with various personal sorrows, darkened his artistic vision at the time of his greatest popularity. His bitterest works, such as *The Mysterious Stranger* and "The Man That Corrupted Hadleyburg," date from these years.

Editions A complete edition of the works of Mark Twain is under way at the University of California Press. At present the definitive edition is *The Writings of Mark Twain*, edited by Albert B. Paine, 37 vols. (1922–25). *The Complete Short Stories of Mark*

Twain, edited by Charles Neider (1958), contains all the important sketches and stories.

BIOGRAPHY

Justin Kaplan, *Mr. Clemens and Mark Twain* (1966).
William M. Gibson and Henry Nash Smith (eds.), *The Correspondence of Samuel L. Clemens and William Dean Howells,* 2 vols. (1960).

CRITICISM

Gladys C. Bellamy, *Mark Twain as a Literary Artist* (1950).
Bernard De Voto, *Mark Twain's America* (1932).
Henry Nash Smith, *Mark Twain: The Development of a Writer* (1962).
Henry Nash Smith (ed.), *Mark Twain: A Collection of Critical Essays* (1963).

HERMAN MELVILLE
(1819–1891)

Herman Melville was a native New Yorker, the second son of a prosperous merchant. In 1830 financial difficulties forced Melville's father to remove the family to Albany, and two years later he died. As a youth Melville clerked in his brother's store, taught school, and tried his hand at writing. In 1841 he shipped on a whaling vessel for the South Pacific, and the next year jumped ship in the Marquesas Islands, where he "lived among the cannibals." By 1844 Melville had made his way back to Boston, and there he began work on *Typee,* a South Sea romance based in part on his recent experiences. *Typee* (1846) and its successor, *Omoo* (1847), gained Melville an appreciative audience, but his allegorical tale *Mardi* (1849) destroyed this popularity. In 1850 Melville met Nathaniel Hawthorne and formed a deep friendship; his great novel of the sea, *Moby-Dick* (1851), is dedicated to Hawthorne.

In the five years after the publication of *Moby-Dick* Melville wrote most of his tales and sketches, as well as the novels *Pierre* (1852) and *Israel Potter* (1855). *Piazza Tales,* containing "Bartleby," "Benito Cereno," "The Encantadas," and other stories, appeared in 1856. After *The Confidence Man* (1857) Melville turned much of his energy to poetry, and his years as customs inspector on the New York City docks (1866–86) were a time of relative obscurity. *Billy*

Budd, his last important story, was completed in the year of his death but not published until 1924.

Editions A definitive edition of *The Writings of Herman Melville* is now under way, sponsored by Northwestern University Press and the Newberry Library. *The Complete Stories of Herman Melville* was edited by Jay Leyda in 1949.

BIOGRAPHY

Leon Howard, *Herman Melville* (1951).
Jay Leyda, *The Melville Log: A Documentary Life of Herman Melville,* 2 vols. (1951).

BIOGRAPHY AND CRITICISM

Newton Arvin, *Herman Melville* (1950).
Warner Berthoff, *The Example of Melville* (1962).
Richard Chase, *Herman Melville* (1949).
Richard H. Fogle, *Melville's Shorter Tales* (1960).
Seymour L. Gross (ed.), *A Benito Cereno Handbook* (1965).
Harry Levin, *The Power of Blackness* (1958).
R. W. B. Lewis, *The American Adam* (1955).
Leo Marx, "Melville's Parable of the Walls," *Sewanee Review,* 41 (Autumn 1953), 602–27.
Mordecai Marcus, "Melville's Bartleby as a Psychological Double," *College English,* 23 (Feb. 1962), 365–68.
John P. Runden (ed.), *Melville's Benito Cereno: A Text for Guided Research* (1965).
Howard Vincent (ed.), *Bartleby the Scrivener* (1966).

JOYCE CAROL OATES
(1938—)

Joyce Carol Oates was born in Lockport, New York (near Buffalo), of Roman Catholic parents. She was educated at Syracuse University and the University of Wisconsin, and now teaches at the University of Windsor in Ontario (Canada). Her numerous publications include four volumes of short stories: *By the North Gate* (1963), *Upon the Sweeping Flood* (1966), *The Wheel of Love* (1970), and *Marriages and Infidelities* (1972). She has written several novels, including *Them,* which won the 1970 National Book Award. Her intense renderings of the horror and violence in everyday life have often been labeled "Gothic," and Oates herself has commented that "Gothicism, whatever it is, is not a literary tradition so much as a fairly realistic assessment of modern life."

BIBLIOGRAPHY AND CRITICISM

Lucienne P. McCormick, "A Bibliography of Works by and about Joyce Carol Oates," *American Literature*, 43 (1971), 124–32.

FLANNERY O'CONNOR
(1925–1964)

Mary Flannery O'Connor was born in Savannah, Georgia, of Roman Catholic parents, and was educated in parochial schools and at the Women's College of Georgia. In the early 1950s it was discovered that she had inherited the same incurable disease that had killed her father, and during the last ten years of her life she was a semi-invalid. Her first collection of stories, *A Good Man Is Hard To Find* (1955), was the only collection published during her lifetime. She also wrote two novellas, *Wise Blood* (1952) and *The Violent Bear It Away* (1960). The posthumous volume of short stories, *Everything That Rises Must Converge* (1965), contains a revealing and moving introduction by Robert Fitzgerald.

Editions   The Complete Stories (1971) prints thirty-one stories, twelve of them previously uncollected. *Mystery and Manners* (1969), edited by Robert and Sally Fitzgerald, contains her essays and lectures on the craft of fiction.

BIOGRAPHY AND CRITICISM

Robert Drake, *Flannery O'Connor* (1966).

Melvin J. Friedman and Lewis A. Lawson (eds.), *The Added Dimension: The Art and Mind of Flannery O'Connor* (1966).

Josephine Hendin, *The World of Flannery O'Connor* (1970).

Stanley Edgar Hyman, *Flannery O'Connor* (1966).

Carter W. Martin, *The True Country: Themes in the Fiction of Flannery O'Connor* (1969).

Sewanee Review, 76 (Spring 1968). An issue devoted to Flannery O'Connor.

EDGAR ALLAN POE
(1809–1849)

Edgar Allan Poe was born in Boston, the son of impoverished actors. Before the child was three years old his mother had died and his father had disappeared. He was informally adopted by John Allan, a Richmond merchant, and received most of his schooling in England. In 1826 Poe entered the University of Virginia, but left the following year when he and Mr. Allan quarreled over Poe's gambling debts. He then enlisted in the U.S. Army, and remained there for two years, meanwhile publishing his first books of verse: *Tamerlane and Other Poems* (1827) and *Al Aaraaf, Tamerlane, and Minor Poems* (1829). In 1830 John Allan secured Poe a West Point appointment, but the young poet disliked Academy life and deliberately provoked a discharge. Support from Allan was no longer possible, and for the remainder of his life Poe lived on the edge of poverty, supporting himself by literary journalism. In 1836 he secretly married his thirteen-year-old cousin, Virginia Clemm, and lived with her and her mother until Virginia's death eleven years later. *Tales of the Grotesque and Arabesque* appeared in 1839–40, and further *Tales* in 1845. The publication of "The Raven" in 1845 brought Poe temporary fame, but no release from physical and psychological suffering. He died obscurely in Baltimore in 1849.

All the circumstances of Poe's desperate life—his alcoholism, his aestheticism, his rejection by society, his bizarre artistic visions—make him the type of the *poète maudit*, and his greatest impact in the nineteenth century was upon the French and English symbolists, especially Baudelaire and Mallarmé. In our own century, however, as Poe's hypnotic influence has re-entered American literature by way of the French tradition, we have learned to view him not as a lonely and aberrant figure, but as a central artist in the development of American romanticism.

Editions Harvard University Press is currently publishing *The Collected Works of Edgar Allan Poe. The Complete Tales and Poems* was published by the Modern Library in 1938, and is still available.

BIOGRAPHY

William Bittner, *Poe: A Biography* (1962).
John W. Ostrom (ed.), *The Letters of Edgar Allan Poe*, 2 vols. (1948, 1966).
Arthur H. Quinn, *Edgar Allan Poe: A Critical Biography* (1941).
Edward Wagenknecht, *Edgar Allan Poe: The Man Behind the Legend* (1963).

CRITICISM

Edward H. Davidson, *Poe: A Critical Study* (1957).
Daniel Hoffman, *Poe Poe Poe Poe Poe Poe Poe* (1972).
William Howarth (ed.), *Twentieth Century Interpretations of Poe's Tales* (1971).
Harry Levin, *The Power of Blackness* (1958).
Robert Regan (ed.), *Poe: A Collection of Critical Essays* (1967).
Thomas Woodson (ed.), *Twentieth Century Interpretations of "The Fall of the House of Usher"* (1969).

PETER TAYLOR
(1919—)

A native of Tennessee, Peter Taylor attended Vanderbilt University and Southwestern at Memphis before graduating from Kenyon College in 1940. He has taught at a number of American universities, and in 1959 received the O. Henry Memorial Awards first prize for "Venus, Cupid, Folly and Time." His constant theme is the changing manners and morals of Southern life, which he treats with a fine sense of social nuance and personal relationships. Taylor's chosen form is short fiction, and parts of his only novel—*A Woman of Means* (1950)—appeared originally as short stories. He is the author of four volumes of stories: *A Long Fourth* (1948), *The Widows of Thornton* (1954), *Happy Families Are All Alike* (1959), and *Miss Leonora When Last Seen* (1963). *The Collected Stories of Peter Taylor* (1969) contains five new stories and fifteen reprinted from the earlier volumes.

CRITICISM

Morgan Blum, "Peter Taylor: Self-Limitation in Fiction," *Sewanee Review*, 70 (1962), 559–78.
Ashley Brown, "The Early Fiction of Peter Taylor," *Sewanee Review*, 70 (1962), 588–602.
Albert J. Griffith, *Peter Taylor* (1970).
William Peden, *The American Short Story* (1964).
Robert Penn Warren, Introduction to *A Long Fourth and Other Stories* (1948).

JOHN UPDIKE
(1932—)

John Updike was reared in Shillington, Pennsylvania, and educated at Harvard, where he was president of the *Lampoon*. After a year of study at the Ruskin School of Drawing and Fine Art at Oxford University (1954–55), Updike returned to the United States and joined the staff of the *New Yorker*. He contributed stories and wrote for the "Talk of the Town" section until 1957, when he left the staff of the *New Yorker* to devote full time to his own writing. His first collection of short stories, *The Same Door* (1959), was followed by *Pigeon Feathers* (1962), *The Music School* (1966), and *Museums and Women* (1972). Updike has been a prolific writer of verse and literary criticism, and has published a number of novels, including *The Poorhouse Fair* (1959), *Rabbit, Run* (1960), *The Centaur* (1963), *Of the Farm* (1965), *Couples* (1968), and *Rabbit Redux* (1971). A master of the well-made story based on ironic observation, Updike has been praised more often for his technical virtuosity than for the power of his subjects; yet his stories at their best are capable of lifting a trivial event to the level of complex significance.

CRITICISM

Rachael C. Burchard, *John Updike: Yea Sayings* (1971).

Robert Detweiler, *Four Spiritual Crises in Mid-Century American Fiction* (1963).

Robert Detweiler, *John Updike* (1972).

Alice and Kenneth Hamilton, *The Elements of John Updike* (1970).

Arthur Mizener, *The Sense of Life in the Modern Novel* (1964).

Richard H. Rupp, "John Updike: Style in Search of a Center," *Sewanee Review*, 75 (1967), 693–709.

Charles Thomas Samuels, *John Updike* (1969).

Larry E. Taylor, *Pastoral and Anti-pastoral Patterns in John Updike's Fiction* (1971).

ROBERT PENN WARREN
(1905—)

A Kentuckian by birth, Robert Penn Warren received his undergraduate education at Vanderbilt University, where he was associated with the *Fugitive* writers—among them Donald Davidson and John Crowe Ransom—who were seeking to establish a conservative rationale for Southern writing. After a Rhodes Scholarship at Oxford University, Warren returned to university teaching at Southwestern and Louisiana State, and for the next thirty-five years he was active as a teacher and scholar at a number of American universities.

Warren's first novel, *Night Rider* (1939), was followed by *At Heaven's Gate* (1943), *All the King's Men* (1946), *World Enough and Time* (1950), and *The Cave* (1959). Warren has also published several volumes of poetry, and his contributions to literary criticism have been substantial. In collaboration with Cleanth Brooks he authored *Understanding Poetry* (1938) and *Understanding Fiction* (1943), two textbooks which were decisive in introducing the methods of the New Criticism into American education. His early short stories were collected as *The Circus in the Attic* (1947).

Some of Warren's most sensitive literary criticism has been a response to William Faulkner, and his fiction may be viewed as an attempt to explore and extend the Southern world re-created in Faulkner's tales.

CRITICISM

Charles Bohner, *Robert Penn Warren* (1964).

Leonard Casper, *Robert Penn Warren: The Dark and Bloody Ground* (1960).

John L. Longley, Jr. (ed.), *Robert Penn Warren: A Collection of Critical Essays* (1965).

John L. Longley, Jr., *Robert Penn Warren* (1969).

Winston Weathers, "'Blackberry Winter' and the Use of Archetypes," *Studies in Short Fiction*, 1 (1963), 45–51.

Paul West, *Robert Penn Warren* (1964).

EUDORA WELTY
(1909—)

Except for the years 1927–31, when she was a student at the University of Wisconsin and the Columbia University School of Advertising, Eudora Welty has spent her entire life in her native state, drawing upon the history and contemporary culture of Jackson, Mississippi, as William Faulkner drew upon his native Oxford. She has published three novels, including the highly praised *Delta Wedding* (1946), a story of contemporary Southern life, and *The Ponder Heart* (1954), which was adapted for the stage. But her chief accomplishment has been in the shorter form; and with the publication of *A Curtain of Green* in 1941 she was recognized as a brilliant technician. *The Wide Net* (1943) and *A Curtain of Green* were reprinted in *Selected Stories* (1954), with a preface by Katherine Anne Porter. Later volumes are *The Golden Apples* (1949) and *The Bride of Innisfallen* (1955). Although Eudora Welty's fiction is essentially regional, it is redeemed from provinciality by her talent for fantasy and the grotesque.

No modern writer of short stories has been more articulate about his craft, and the reader should consult "How I Write" [*Virginia Quarterly Review*, 31 (Spring 1955), 240—51; reprinted in Cleanth Brooks and Robert Penn Warren, *Understanding Fiction*, 2nd ed. (1959)] and *Three Papers on Fiction* (1962).

BIOGRAPHY AND CRITICISM

Alfred Appel, Jr., *A Season of Dreams: The Fiction of Eudora Welty* (1965).

J. A. Bryant, Jr., *Eudora Welty* (1968).

Alun R. Jones, "The World of Love: The Fiction of Eudora Welty," in *The Creative Present*, ed. Nona Balakian and Charles Simmons (1963).

Louis D. Rubin, Jr., *The Faraway Country: Writers of the Modern South* (1963).

Ruth M. Vande Kieft, *Eudora Welty* (1962).

EDITH WHARTON
(1862–1937)

Born into the fashionable society of New York City during the Civil War era, Edith Wharton witnessed the gradual disintegration of that stable world as new standards of social and financial ostentation replaced the more decorous "European" values of her youth. Her disastrous marriage to a Boston banker at the age of twenty-three stifled her early interest in writing, and it was not until the end of the century that she was able to find her voice. *The House of Mirth* (1905), one of her best-known novels, was followed by *Ethan Frome* (1911), *The Custom of the Country* (1913), and *The Age of Innocence* (1920). Mrs. Wharton was a friend and admirer of Henry James, and like James she was fascinated by the plight of the free spirit in a world of intense social and economic pressures. She spent much of her early life in Europe, and in 1910 took up residence in France. Between 1899 and 1936 she produced eleven volumes of short stories. For her comments on the craft of fiction, see *The Writing of Fiction* (1925) and her discreet autobiography, *A Backward Glance* (1934).

Editions *The Collected Short Stories of Edith Wharton*, edited by R. W. B. Lewis, appeared in two volumes in 1968. Other useful collections are *The Best Short Stories of Edith Wharton*, edited by Wayne Andrews (1958), and *The Edith Wharton Reader*, edited by Louis Auchincloss (1965).

BIOGRAPHY AND CRITICISM

Louis Auchincloss, *Edith Wharton* (1961).
Millicent Bell, *Edith Wharton and Henry James: The Story of Their Friendship* (1965).
Irving Howe (ed.), *Edith Wharton: A Collection of Critical Essays* (1962).
Percy Lubbock, *Portrait of Edith Wharton* (1947).
Blake Nevius, *Edith Wharton: A Study of Her Fiction* (1953).

RICHARD WRIGHT
(1908–1960)

The story of Richard Wright's first seventeen years is told in his autobiographical novel, *Black Boy* (1945). Born into a Mississippi sharecropper family, he was abandoned by his father at age five and separated from his mother a few years later. After several years as an orphan he left Mississippi for Memphis and Chicago, where he lived on the edge of poverty. In 1934—in the depths of the Depression—Wright joined the Communist Party, and by the end of the 1930s he had established himself as a writer in New York. His first novel, *Native Son* (1940), was followed by *Twelve Million Black Voices* (a documentary text) in 1941. Wright left the Communist Party in 1944, and from 1946 until his death he was a resident of France. Four novellas were published in 1938 under the title *Uncle Tom's Children*, and in 1961 his stories were collected as *Eight Men*.

BIOGRAPHY

Constance Webb, *Richard Wright* (1968).
John A. Williams, *The Most Native of Sons* (1970).

CRITICISM

Robert A. Bone, *Richard Wright* (1969).
Russell C. Brignano, *Richard Wright: An Introduction to the Man and His Works* (1970).
Dan McCall, *The Example of Richard Wright* (1969).
Edward Margolies, *The Art of Richard Wright* (1969).

THE AMERICAN SHORT STORY
A General Bibliography

H. E. Bates, *The Modern Short Story: A Critical Survey* (1950).
Eugene Current-Garcia (with Walton R. Patrick), *What Is the Short Story?* (1961). Contains a collection of statements on critical theory, and a Selected Bibliography.
Edward J. O'Brien, *The Advance of the American Short Story* (1931).
Frank O'Connor, *The Lonely Voice: A Study of the Short Story* (1963).
Seán O'Faoláin, *The Short Story* (1948).
Fred L. Pattee, *The Development of the American Short Story* (1923; reprinted 1966). A thorough but outdated survey.
William Peden, *The American Short Story: Front Line in the National Defense of Literature* (1964). Covers the period 1940–63.
Danforth Ross, *The American Short Story*, University of Minnesota Pamphlets on American Literature (1961).
Studies in Short Fiction (Newberry, South Carolina, 1963—). A journal devoted to the history and form of the short story.
Jarvis Thurston *et al.*, *Short Fiction Criticism: A Checklist of Interpretations Since 1925 of Stories and Novelettes (American, British, Continental), 1800–1958* (1960).
Arthur Voss, *The American Short Story: A Critical Survey* (1973). The most useful recent survey, with detailed bibliography.
Warren S. Walker, *Twentieth-Century Short Story Explication: Interpretations, 1900–1966 Inclusive, of Short Fiction Since 1800* (1968; 1st edition, 1961). Supplement for 1967–69 available (1970).
Ray B. West, Jr., *The Short Story in America, 1900–1950* (1952).
Austin M. Wright, *The American Short Story in the Twenties* (1961).